The DREAM
of the
RED CHAMBER

The DREAM
of the
RED CHAMBER

Written by **Cao Xueqin**
Translated by **H. Bencraft Joly**
With a New Foreword by **John Minford**
and a New Introduction by **Edwin Lowe**

TUTTLE PUBLISHING
Tokyo • Rutland, Vermont • Singapore

ABOUT TUTTLE
"Books to Span the East and West"

Our core mission at Tuttle Publishing is to create books which bring people together one page at a time. Tuttle was founded in 1832 in the small New England town of Rutland, Vermont (USA). Our fundamental values remain as strong today as they were then—to publish best-in-class books informing the English-speaking world about the countries and peoples of Asia. The world has become a smaller place today and Asia's economic, cultural and political influence has expanded, yet the need for meaningful dialogue and information about this diverse region has never been greater. Since 1948, Tuttle has been a leader in publishing books on the cultures, arts, cuisines, languages and literatures of Asia. Our authors and photographers have won numerous awards and Tuttle has published thousands of books on subjects ranging from martial arts to paper crafts. We welcome you to explore the wealth of information available on Asia at **www.tuttlepublishing.com**.

Published by Tuttle Publishing, an imprint of Periplus Editions (HK) Ltd.

www.tuttlepublishing.com

Copyright © 2010 Periplus Editions (HK) Ltd.

Library of Congress Cataloging-in-Publication Data

Cao, Xueqin, ca. 1717-1763.
  [Hong lou meng. English]
  The dream of the red chamber / Cao Xueqin ; translated by H. Bencraft Joly ; with a foreword by John Minford and an introduction by Edwin Lowe. -- 1st ed.
    p. cm.
  ISBN 978-0-8048-4096-5 (pbk.)
1. China--Social life and customs--18th century--Fiction. 2. Families--China--Fiction. 3. Women--China--Fiction. 4. Domestic fiction. I. Joly, H. Bencraft. II. Title.
  PL2727.S2A26 2010
  895.1'348--dc22

2010005577

ISBN 978-0-8048-4096-5

Distributed by

North America, Latin America & Europe
Tuttle Publishing
364 Innovation Drive
North Clarendon, VT 05759-9436 U.S.A.
Tel: 1 (802) 773-8930
Fax: 1 (802) 773-6993
info@tuttlepublishing.com
www.tuttlepublishing.com

Japan
Tuttle Publishing
Yaekari Building, 3rd Floor
5-4-12 Osaki, Shinagawa-ku, Tokyo 141 0032
Tel: (81) 3 5437-0171
Fax: (81) 3 5437-0755
tuttle-sales@gol.com

Asia Pacific
Berkeley Books Pte. Ltd.
61 Tai Seng Avenue #02-12,
Singapore 534167
Tel: (65) 6280-1330; Fax: (65) 6280-6290
inquiries@periplus.com.sg
www.periplus.com

20 19 18 17 16
10 9 8 7 6 5 4 3 2
1608HX

Printed in China

Table of Contents

Foreword xi

Introduction.. xxiii

Preface... xxv

1. Zhen Shiyin, in a vision, apprehends perception and
   spirituality. Jia Yucun, in the (windy and dusty) world,
   cherishes fond thoughts of a beautiful maiden...................... 1

2. The spirit of Mrs. Jia Shiyin departs from the town of
   Yang Zhou. Leng Zixing dilates upon the Rong Guo Mansion... 21

3. Lin Ruhai appeals to his brother-in-law, Jia Zheng,
   recommending Yucun, his daughter's tutor,
   to his consideration. Dowager lady Jia sends to fetch her
   granddaughter, out of commiseration for her being a
   motherless child... 36

4. An ill-fated girl happens to meet an ill-fated young man.
   The Hulu Bonze adjudicates the Hulu case....................... 58

5. The spirit of Jia Baoyu visits the confines of the Great Void.
   The Monitory Vision Fairy expounds, in ballads, the Dream
   of the Red Chamber... 73

6. Jia Baoyu reaps his first experience in licentious love.
   Old goody Liu pays a visit to the Rong Guo Mansion. 96

7. Presentation of artificial flowers made in the Palace.
   Jia Lian disports himself with Xifeng. Baoyu meets
   Qin Zhong at a family party.................................... 113

8. By a strange coincidence, Jia Baoyu becomes acquainted
   with the golden clasp. In an unexpected meeting,
   Xue Baochai sees the jade of spiritual perception. 129

9. Jia Zheng gives good advice to his wayward son. Li Gui
   receives a reprimand. Jia Rui and Li Gui rebuke the obstinate
   youths! Mingyan causes trouble in the schoolroom. 144

10. Widow Jin, prompted by a desire to reap advantage, puts up temporarily with an insult. Dr. Zhang in discussing Mrs. Jin's illness minutely exhausts its origin....................................... 158

11. In honor of Jia Jing's birthday, a family banquet is spread in the Ning Mansion. At the sight of Xifeng, Jia Rui entertains feelings of licentious love... 170

12. Wang Xifeng maliciously lays a trap for Jia Rui, under pretence that his affection is reciprocated. Jia Tianxiang gazes at the face of the mirror of voluptuousness............... 183

13. Qin Keqing dies, and Jia Rong is invested with the rank of military officer to the Imperial Bodyguard. Wang Xifeng lends her help in the management of the Rong Guo Mansion........ 195

14. Lin Ruhai dies in the City of Yangzhou. Jia Baoyu meets the Prince of Beijing on the way... 209

15. Lady Feng, nee Wang, exercises her authority in the Iron Fence Temple. Qin Jingqing (Qin Zhong) amuses himself in the Mantou (Bread) nunnery....................................... 223

16. Jia Yuanchun is, on account of her talents, selected to enter the Feng Zao Palace. Qin Jingqing departs, in the prime of life, by the yellow spring road... 236

17. In the Daguan Garden, (Broad Vista,) the merits of Baoyu are put to the test, by his being told to write devices for scrolls and tablets. Yuanchun returns to the Rong Guo mansion, on a visit to her parents, and offers her congratulations to them on the feast of lanterns, on the fifteenth of the first moon............. 254

18. His Majesty shows magnanimous bounty. The Imperial consort Yuan pays a visit to her parents. The happiness of a family gathering. Baoyu displays his polished talents........ 279

19. In the vehemence of her feelings, Hua (Xiren) on a quiet evening admonishes Baoyu. While (the spell) of affection continues unbroken, Baoyu, on a still day, perceives the fragrance emitted from Daiyu's person. 299

20. Wang Xifeng with earnest words upbraids Mrs. Zhao's jealous notions. Lin Daiyu uses specious language to make sport of Shi Xiangyun's querulous tone of voice.................. 320

21. The eminent Xiren, with winsome ways, rails at Baoyu, with a view to exhortation. The beauteous Ping'er, with soft words, screens Jia Lian. 332

22. Upon hearing the text of the stanza, Baoyu comprehends the Buddhistic spells. While the enigmas for the lanterns are being devised, Jia Zheng is grieved by a prognostic. 347

23. Baoyu and Daiyu make use of some beautiful passages from the Record of the Western Side-building to bandy jokes. The excellent ballads sung in the Peony Pavilion touch the tender heart of Daiyu. 366

24. The drunken Jin Gang makes light of lucre and shows a preference for generosity. The foolish girl mislays her handkerchief and arouses mutual thoughts. 381

25. By a demoniacal art, a junior uncle and an elder brother's wife (Baoyu and lady Feng) come across five devils. The gem of Spiritual Perception meets, in a fit of torpor, the two perfect men. 399

26. On the Fengyao bridge, Xiao Hong makes known sentimental matters in equivocal language. In the Xiaoxiang lodge, Daiyu gives, while under the effects of the spring lassitude, expression to her secret feelings. 416

27. In the Dicui pavilion, Baochai diverts herself with the multi-colored butterflies. Over the mound, where the flowers had been interred, Daiyu bewails their withered bloom. 433

28. Jiang Yuhan lovingly presents a rubia-scented silk sash. Xue Baochai blushingly covers her musk-perfumed string of red beads. 448

29. A happy man enjoys a full measure of happiness, but still prays for happiness. A beloved girl is very much loved, but yet craves for more love. 473

30. Baochai avails herself of the excuse afforded her by a fan to administer a couple of raps. While Qiaoling traces, in an absent frame of mind, the outlines of the character Qiang, a looker-on appears on the scene. 493

31. Baoyu allows the girl Qingwen to tear his fan so as to afford her amusement. A wedding proves to be the result of the descent of a unicorn. 506

32. Xiren and Xiangyun tell their secret thoughts. Daiyu is infatuated with the living Baoyu. While trying to conceal her sense of shame and injury Jinchuan is driven by her impetuous feelings to seek death...................................... 522

33. A brother is prompted by ill-feeling to wag his tongue a bit. A depraved son receives heavy blows with a rattan cane. 535

34. Daiyu loves Baoyu with extreme affection; but, on account of this affection, her female cousin gets indignant. Xue Pan commits a grave mistake; but Baochai makes this mistake a pretext to tender advice to her brother.............................. 547

35. Bai Yuchuan tastes too the lotus-leaf soup. Huang Jinying skillfully plaits the plum-blossom-knotted nets.................. 564

36. While Xiren is busy embroidering mandarin ducks, Baoyu receives, in the Jiangyun Pavilion, an omen from a dream. Baoyu apprehends that there is a destiny in affections, when his feelings are aroused to a sense of the situation in the Pear Fragrance court... 582

37. In the Study of Autumnal Cheerfulness is accidentally formed the Cydonia Japonica Society. In the Hengwu Court, the chrysanthemum is, on a certain night, proposed as a subject for verses. 598

38. Lin Xiaoxiang carries the first prize in the poems on chrysanthemums. Xue Hengwu chaffs Baoyu by composing verses in the same style as his on the crabs. 621

39. The tongue of the village old dame finds as free vent as a river that has broken its banks. The affectionate cousin makes up his mind to sift to the very bottom the story told by old goody Liu... 640

40. The venerable lady Shi attends a second banquet in the garden of Broad Vista. Jin Yangyuan three times promulgates, by means of dominoes, the order to quote passages from old writers.. 655

41. Jia Baoyu tastes tea in the Longcui monastery. Old goody Liu gets drunk and falls asleep in the Yihong court.............. 678

42. The Princess of Hengwu dispels, with sweet words, some insane suspicions. The inmate of Xiaoxiang puts, with excellent repartee, the final touch to the jokes made about goody Liu... 693

43. Having time to amuse themselves, the Jia inmates raise, when least expected, funds to celebrate lady Feng's birthday. In his ceaseless affection for Jinchuan, Baoyu uses, for the occasion, a pinch of earth as incense and burns it. 710

44. By some inscrutable turn of affairs, lady Feng begins to feel the pangs of jealousy. Baoyu experiences joy, beyond all his expectations, when Ping'er (receives a slap from lady Feng and) has to adjust her hair. 727

45. Friends interchange words of friendship. Daiyu feels dull on a windy and rainy evening, and indites verses on wind and rain... 743

46. An improper man with difficulty keeps from improprieties. The maid, Yuanyang, vows to break off the marriage match... 761

47. An idiotic bully tries to be lewd and comes in for a sound thrashing. A cold-hearted fellow is prompted by a dread of trouble to betake himself to a strange place......................... 781

48. A sensual-minded man gets into such trouble through his sensuality that he entertains the idea of going abroad. An estimable and refined girl manages, after great exertion, to compose verses at a refined meeting............................. 797

49. White snow and red plum blossom in the crystal world. The pretty girl, fragrant with powder, cuts some meat and eats it.. 813

50. In the Luxue pavilion, they vie with each other in pairing verses on the scenery. In the Nuanxiang village, they compose, in beautiful style, riddles for the spring lanterns.... 829

51. The young maiden Xue Baoqin devises, in novel style, odes bearing on antiquities. A stupid doctor employs, in reckless manner, drugs of great strength....................................... 851

52. The beautiful Ping'er endeavors to conceal the loss of the bracelet, made of work as fine as the feelers of a shrimp. The brave Qingwen mends the down-cloak during her indisposition... 869

53. In the Ning Guo mansion, sacrifices are offered to their ancestors on the last night of the year. In the Rong Guo mansion, a banquet is given on the evening of the 15th of the first moon. 887

54. Dowager lady Jia does away with rotten old customs. Wang Xifeng imitates in jest (the dutiful son), by getting herself up in gaudy theatrical clothes............................. 907

55. The stupid secondary wife, dame Zhao, needlessly loses her temper and insults her own daughter, Tanchun. The perverse servant-girls are so full of malice that they look down contemptuously on their youthful mistresses..................... 927

56. The clever Tanchun increases their income and removes long standing abuses. The worthy Baochai preserves intact, by the display of a little intelligence, the great reputation enjoyed by the Jia family... 946

Foreword

The Story of the Stone (*Shitouji*, 石頭記), otherwise known as *A Dream of Red Mansions* or *The Dream of the Red Chamber* (*Hongloumeng*, 紅樓夢), is the greatest of all the traditional Chinese novels.[1] *Dream* inherits the proud tradition of vernacular fiction that had grown out of the storytellers' repertoire during the Ming dynasty (1368–1644)— such wonderful "blockbuster" sagas as *Water Margin* (*Shuihuzhuan*, 水滸傳) and *The Romance of the Three Kingdoms* (*Sanguo yanyi*, 三國演義), or the picaresque telling of the adventures of Monkey in *Journey to the West* (*Xiyouji*, 西遊記), rich in allegory and fantasy. Above all it is descended from the late-Ming novel of manners *Golden Lotus* (*Jinpingmei*, 金瓶梅), a Chinese *Liaisons Dangereuses*, in which dark and frequently comical human impulses, and elaborate sexual games, are played out against the vividly depicted daily life of a wealthy libertine. *Dream* builds on this grand story-telling tradition, but takes it in a wholly new direction. It transforms Chinese mainstream fiction for the first time into an eloquent and subtly crafted vehicle for introspective autobiography and psychological realism, for memory and self-reflection. At the same time it engages in a lyrical and riddling quest for meaning in human experience (the Tao), taking the reader on a witty excursion down the pathways of Zen enlightenment and holding up a searching mirror to the ambivalence of the worldling's "reality" and "illusion." It is superbly written and enormously long, well over one million words from beginning to end, with a gallery of over three hundred unforgettable characters from all walks of life.

The novel was begun in the mid-18th century by Cao Xueqin (曹雪芹, 1715?–1763), the empoverished grandson of Cao Yin (曹寅, 1658–1712), wealthy favorite of the great second emperor of the Manchu dynasty (and contemporary of Louis XIV), Kangxi (康熙, 1654–1723). The Cao family had known extraordinary wealth and privilege, belonging as they did to the elite inner circle of Bond-servants to the Imperial Household, attached to the Manchu Plain White Banner. This "honorary Manchu" family was later amalgamated into the ranks of the Chinese Banners, the organizational structure created for Han-Chinese families that had thrown in their lot with the invading Man-

---

1. I shall refer to the novel as *Dream* for the sake of simplicity.

chus. During the reign of Kangxi's successor, Yongzheng (雍正, reigned 1723–1736) the Cao family was disgraced and ruined, and Cao Xueqin himself lived most of his life in abject poverty in the rural outskirts of Peking, remembering and chronicling in fictional form the "golden days" of his youth, recreating his "dream," describing in loving detail the aristocratic *jeunesse dorée* that had surrounded his adolescence. He never lived to finish his great project. His incomplete *Dream*, which circulated for decades in hand-written and annotated copies, was later edited and brought to a conclusion by another Chinese Bannerman, Gao E (高鶚, ?1740–1815), who added to the eighty chapters left by Cao Xueqin an ending in forty chapters, most probably based on fragmentary manuscripts left behind by Cao.[2] This 120-chapter novel was printed and published for the first time in early 1792, complete with a series of fine woodblock illustrations, and it was this version that quickly became the standard one. It was reprinted again and again, with a growing number of commentaries, and went on to become enormously popular and influential in upper-class 19th-century Chinese households. As the saying went, if you were unable to drop references to this particular novel into your daily conversation, you were simply a nobody. It was loved for its extraordinarily vivid characterization, for its heightened Bannerman sensibility, for its encyclopedic recreation of a great culture in its last heyday (the book is an entertaining and exhaustive novelistic handbook on Chinese poetry, painting, medicine, furniture, food, tea, garden design and much more), and for its brilliantly authentic use of the 18th-century Peking vernacular, interlarded and embellished with choice morsels of the literary language.

This novel, more than any other work of traditional Chinese literature, captures what it meant and still means to be Chinese, to live a Chinese life, to feel Chinese. Ironically the fact that it was written and edited by Bannermen (technically "outsiders") only sharpened its vision of Chinese culture. It was and still is a work that is read and re-read constantly, a work that has fascinated, indeed obsessed, many prominent figures in Chinese public life, including Chairman Mao and his last wife, Jiang Qing. As one young reader from Peking recently observed to me, she reads it in winter to keep warm, and in summer to stay cool. It has occupied a central—and always controversial—space in Chinese cultural life ever since it was written. It has almost become a national fetish. Eminent scholars argue heatedly about the minutiae

---

2. This is a controversial issue, but recent evidence points more and more to the probability that Gao was working on an incomplete ending, and that he was a conscientious editor, not an unscrupulous forger.

of its complex problems of authorship and probe ever more deeply into its endless editorial variations. It has been rewritten, abridged, provided with numerous sequels, made into strip-cartoons, adapted countless times for stage and screen, ballet, opera, and cantata, and is currently being made into yet another enormously long (and fabulously extravagant) TV series (the previous series, made in the 1980s, having been a favorite for two decades).

It has also been translated into many languages: Mongolian, Russian, Vietnamese, Japanese, Korean, French, Russian, German. For several decades the English-language reader had to make do with two incomplete versions, one by the Chinese scholar from Columbia University, Wang Chi-chen (1899–1990), the other translated from the German of Franz Kuhn (1884–1961). In the 1970s and 1980s, two complete English translations finally appeared, one in Peking, *A Dream of Red Mansions*, in three volumes, from the state-owned Foreign Languages Press, done by the legendary couple Yang Xianyi and Gladys Yang as part of their penance after being released from solitary confinement in jail during the Cultural Revolution; one in London, *The Story of the Stone*, in five volumes, from Penguin Classics, done by David Hawkes and myself.[3] Partly because of the unique nature of the original work, and its charismatic status in China, these two translations have themselves become the subject of widespread debate, and at least one major conference has been held within China dedicated entirely to a discussion and comparisons of the two approaches used, and to the problems and challenges of translating this particular work.[4] In 2009, the newly appointed Ambassador to the court of St. James, Mme. Fu Ying, presented Queen Elizabeth II with a complete 5-volume set of the Penguin translation. It was a meaningful choice, not just of original, but of translation. In the course of 2010, one of Shanghai's largest publishing houses will bring out an elaborately edited bilingual edition of that same Penguin translation.

In this context, it is not surprising that attention is turning to some of the earlier attempts at turning this huge work into English. Recently

---

3. Both Yang Xianyi and David Hawkes sadly passed away during the course of 2009. For an account of the genesis of the Hawkes translation, see my essay in the forthcoming Reader's Guide edited by Tina Lu and Andrew Schoenbaum, to be published by the Modern Languages Association later in 2010. It is interesting to note that Hawkes, like the earlier 19th-century translators, first read his way through *Dream* as a graduate student in Peking in 1948, struggling through the text with a retired Manchu functionary.
4. The conference was held at Nankai University in Tianjin, in 2003. A book was published based on the proceedings: Liu Shicong ed., *Hongloumeng fanyi yanjiu lunwen ji* (Tianjin: Nankai University Press, 2004).

Ms. Amy Ko, a Hong Kong doctoral student conducting research into the career of the indefatigable Northumbrian missionary Robert Morrison (1781–1834), discovered in an attachment to a hitherto unpublished letter, dating from c. 1812, what must surely be the earliest translated extract from the novel. Morrison's English prose was stylish (he was a contemporary of Jane Austen), and his command of Chinese was comprehensive: he was at the time compiling his vast Chinese-English Dictionary in the Portuguese colony of Macao, supported by the wealthy East India Company, and simultaneously translating the Bible into Chinese. He was not a man to shy away from ambitious projects. His manuscript translation of the fourth chapter of *Dream* (the tale of the selling of the young abducted girl Yinglian, the murder of her young purchaser, and the antics of the corrupt mandarin Jia Yucun, who allows the wealthy playboy Xue Pan to escape unpunished) is both fluent and accurate. He offered it to his publisher in London for inclusion in a possible second volume of his anthology *Horae Sinicae*, as an item "which may afford some amusement." Morrison the missionary was more concerned with the social ills of Chinese society than he was with the literary qualities of the novel. The extract gives, as he himself wrote in the accompanying letter, "a lamentably faithful picture of the state of society in China. The checks to oppression are few. Anything may be bought—almost any crime be committed with impunity if the offending party can pay for it." But his extract never saw the light of day.

Some thirty years later, further extracts from the novel were translated by the Glaswegian Robert Thom (1807–1846), himself a member of the newly established British China Consular Service, posted to the Treaty Port of Ningpo in 1844. Twenty years later still a more substantial selection was offered by Edward Bowra (184–1874), member of a distinguished Belfast family, serving in the prestigious Imperial Customs Service.[5]

Thom's brief extract, taken from the sixth chapter of *Dream*, recounts the visit to the Rong-guo Mansion of Dame Lew, or goody Lew as Thom sometimes calls her—劉姥姥, Grannie Liu in the Penguin version. It is included in his little "Primer of Chinese," entitled *The Chinese Speaker, or extracts from works written in the Mandarin Language as spoken at Peking, compiled for the use of Students*, in Chinese 正音撮要. This book was printed complete with romanization and accompanying Chinese text at the Presbyterian Mission Press in Ningpo in 1846. Thom, who had previously published a Chinese-English

---

5. Sir Maurice Bowra, poet, literary critic, and Warden of Wadham College, Oxford, was his direct descendant.

vocabulary, was well known (and much criticized) in China-consular circles as someone who knew the Chinese language well (perhaps too well?) and enjoyed excellent and sympathetic relations (perhaps too sympathetic?) with the local Chinese. His little language primer had been hastily put together and brought out when he was already suffering from the "severe and long-continued illness" that had "shattered his constitution." He had planned a continuation, "should it please Almighty God to restore him to health and strength" after his planned return to Britain; but as he himself remarks in his note "To the Reader," "Man says, thus and thus; Heaven answers, not so! not so!" He even obligingly, and touchingly, provides us with the Chinese original of this saying: 人說如此如此，天說未然未然. His medical certificate preserved in the Foreign Office archives describes him as suffering from fever, diarrhea, dropsy, debilitation, and emaciation. The poor man never made it back to Britain, but died later that same year, aged 39, leaving behind a Chinese mistress and two children, a son and a daughter. His *Chinese Speaker* continued to be used for many years after his death by new entrants into the Consular Service.[6]

Edward Bowra's translation was a longer and more ambitious affair, comprising altogether eight chapters from the opening section of the novel.[7] He wrote it while serving as in Ningpo as 1st Class Clerk in the Customs, and acknowledges his debt to Thom at the end of the sixth chapter:

> The rendering of Lao-lao-ly as Goody, was suggested to the translator by Mr. R. Thom's translation of a part of this Chapter, published in the "Chinese Speaker" many years since.

Bowra had studied in Canton with the pioneer sinologist W. F. Mayers (1839-1878), who had published some translated extracts from the novel, and in a footnote to the fifth chapter he pays homage to his teacher:

> The Translator offers no apology to the reader of the CHINA MAGA-ZINE, for presenting them with the above translation of the verses from the pen of Mr. W. F. Mayers (NOTES AND QUERIES for December 1867), in place of an original one from himself. The accuracy of rendering, the grace and force of expression which characterize Mr. Mayers'

---

6. For Thom, see P. D. Coates, *The China Consuls* (Hong Kong, Oxford University Press, 1988), pp. 20-25. He must have served the Hong Kong novelist Timothy Mo as partial basis for one of the main characters in his brilliant novel *An Insular Possession*.

7. E. C. Bowra's story has been well told in Charles Drage's biography, *Servants of the Dragon Throne* (London: Peter Dawnay, 1966).

translations, would render any new attempt at translating what he has already done so well, as presumptuous as it would be certain of failure.[8]

Bowra's version was entitled *The Dream of the Red Chamber* (Hung Low Meng): *A Chinese novel literally translated.* It was carried in several instalments of the *China Magazine*, published by Noronha & Sons in Hong Kong, 1868-1870. He demonstrated great skill in translating into rhyming verse the many poetic passages that occur in the novel. He also captured with great sensitivity many of the innuendoes that have escaped other translators. A good example of this is to be found towards to the end of Chapter 5, where the Fairy explains to Baoyu the nature of the "gloomy river" ahead of him:

> "This," said the Fairy, "is the Ford of Bewilderment. It is a myriad fathoms deep and flows for a thousand miles. No boat plies on it, and there is nought but a wooden raft of which Father Wood is the Steersman, and Priest Ashes the Sculler..."[9]

Bowra adds an illuminating note:

> Wood and Ashes, the ferrymen at the Ford of Bewilderment, bear reference to the disregard for pleasure, recognition of the unreality of the material universe, and the deadness to emotion which are required of devout believers in Buddha. The Ford of Bewilderment (as for want of a better term the Translator has rendered it), like some of the terms in Bunyan's Pilgrim's Progress, e.g. *The Slough of Despond*, is an allegorical name. It refers in this case to the pleasures of the senses, which the Buddhist creed calls upon man to renounce. Unless the heart is dead like wood or ashes and absolutely unresponsive to all emotion, the temptations of the world will as in Pao Yü's case prove too strong and result in ultimate perdition.

In his translation and annotation of the well-known passage in Chapter 7, where the drunken household servant Big Jiao is making indiscrete remarks about the carryings-on in the Jia household (in particular the incestuous relationship between Jia Zhen and his daughter-in-law Qin Keqing), Bowra has no hesitation in spelling things out.

"Who could have expected that his descendants would have been such beasts? Fornication, beastliness, and incest every day; "Scraping of

---

8. Before moving to Ningpo, Bowra had served in Canton, where Mayers, a brilliant Chinese linguist, was the consular interpreter. According to his biographer, Bowra had a hand in Mayers' indispensable handbook, *The Chinese Reader's Manual*, first published in 1874 and still useful today.
9. Hawkes, p. 147, calls the ferrymen Numb and Dumb.

the ashes! Scraping of the ashes!" and philandering with brothers-in-law. I only know about it. It's best to wash our dirty linen at home." His note reads:

> "Scraping up the ashes" is a reference to a story (taken probably from some coarse Chinese Joe Miller), in which a man to avoid being discovered in incestuous intercourse with his son's wife, endeavors, on his son's unexpected approach, to hide himself in the ash-pan beneath the furnace. Discovered there, and asked as to his presence and business, he replied that he was "scraping up the ashes." So widely spread is this story, though apparently confined to oral tradition, that in place of the obvious phrase for "scraping up the ashes" (*Pa huei*) a circumlocution is now everywhere adopted, whenever, even in directions to servants, such a phrase is necessary.[10]

The Introduction (written either by Bowra himself or possibly by the magazine's editor, C. Langdon Davis) allows us to observe immediately that Bowra was the first translator to view his subject primarily as a work of literature, not as an object of missionary zeal and indignation, or as a tool for language acquisition. It is worth reproducing in full, as an early example of an open-minded, observant, sometimes humorous, European critique of Chinese fiction.

> There is nothing new under the sun, not even Novels. Considering how recent a growth they are in our own country, it may surprise some readers to find that for ages novels have delighted the multitudes of China. It is refreshing to find that a steady-going practical people like the Chinese, have been—say about since the Norman Conquest—solacing themselves with what a well meaning class of people at home denounce too indiscriminately as "pernicious trash." Before "Clarissa Harlowe" and "Sir Charles Grandison," before "Tom Jones" and his noisy adventures, before Addison prosed and Goldsmith rambled, before Sir John Falstaff fought and loved on the boards of the "Globe," before "Morte D'Arthur" was written, or Caxton's types were seen in the Abbey of Westminster, the Chinese were writing novels and reading them—were, for anything we know, subscribing to the vigorous circulating libraries which exist in their great cities to this day, and which, even in Mr. Mudie's latest fashion, bring the books to the doors of subscribers and call for them the next week.
>
> The readers of the MAGAZINE are about to be presented with a literal translation of a novel which holds perhaps the highest place amongst

---

10. *Joe Miller's Jests, or the Wits' Vade-Mecum* (1739) was a collection of contemporary and ancient coarse witticisms. Later editions were known as Joe Miller's Joke Book, and with time any time-worn jest came to be called "a Joe Miller."

Chinese Romances. An able pen has thus described it: "If it be lawful to avow a feeling approaching to enthusiasm for any Chinese production, 'The Hung Low Meng' or 'Dream of the Red Chamber,' is beyond possibility of cavil the work for which genuine admiration may be expressed. What, in English literature, the writings of Thackeray and Bulwer are in comparison with the wearisome and unskilful productions of previous generations, such is 'The Hung Low Meng', when compared with the works of fiction that have emanated from other Chinese authors. Human character in its complex variety of shades, the intricacies of family relations, the force of passion and the torture of disappointed yearnings after love are portrayed with a degree of skill and knowledge such as in truth suggests a resemblance with the two great master-spirits of English romance; whilst, as in Nature's own drama of existence, the reflections of storm and sunshine are closely interlaced, and the lighter thread of comedy runs side by side with the dark main strand of a story which opens with the omens of sorrow and is conducted to a tearful end. If, at the same time, a faint—a very faint—tinge of the supernatural is allowed to show itself in the conception of the tale, this is not only in full accord with the inclinations of the people for whom the work is written, but is also far less obtrusive than the similar element which pervades more than one of our own most celebrated fictions."

The reader will understand that if the text, especially in the introduction, be occasionally a little obscure, it is because the original is so. It is impossible to suppress a conviction, in reading any Chinese disquisitions that take a geomantic or mystical form, that the author himself did not quite see what he was driving at. When the boy said to Confucius "nine times nine are eighty-one, and this explains all things in heaven and earth" and went on to make further statements about dragons and other comprehensible subjects, thereby discomfiting "the master" not a little, he may have understood what he was talking about, or the master may have, but I am inclined to believe that as a matter of fact neither of them did.

Do not think that because a novel is Chinese it must necessarily be grotesque and clumsy. Carlyle, who had got hold of a translation of "Yuk Kiu Si" somewhere, admits that "the author is a man of real genius, but after the Dragon pattern." But he is no more after the Dragon pattern than George Eliot is after the conventional "Boule-dogue" pattern of perfide Albion. There is one scene in that same "Yuk Kiu Si," which for delicacy and sweetness is unequalled by anything I know, except the scenes in "As you like it," between Orlando and Rosalind in the forest of Arden. An orphan and friendless girl, comes disguised in a boy's dress to rescue the man she loves from a mercenary patron and from thankless drudgery. She gives him her bracelets and gold chain that he may go to Pekin and take his degree, and induces him to betroth himself to an imaginary sister of hers whom, in the person of his fair friend, he afterwards marries. Of course, all such scenes and some of the adventures you are about to read are improbable, still, even in the English world, we do not meet with romantic episodes in every-day life. Love—even love after the Dragon pattern—will be lord of all. And observe, lastly, that there are three things these simple people venerate—Authority, Learning, and Old Age—no fourth. Wealthy ignorance is the constant butt of Chinese romancers, and it is the poor bachelor of arts who always carries off the pretty girl. In a money-worshipping age, this is refreshing.[11]

In general, the Bowra translation is astonishingly good for its date. It is stylish, eloquent, and witty, and does not shy away from the inherent difficulties of the text. A single example of his talent at versification will have to suffice. This comes from chapter 5, and is the verse with which the Fairy Disenchantment opens her little song-and-dance performance, put on for the benefit of Jia Baoyu.

Guide to the Dream of the Red Chamber

When forth from out the formless void
    Creation first gave shape to earth,
Who was it gave to passion's seeds
    Their direful origin and birth.
The wooing breeze, the glowing moon,
    Their influence in one combined,
Propitious moments made, and there,
    Intensest passion's source we find.
Of hopes, resources, all bereft,
    In days of grief and sad distress,
    In hours of silent solitude
My simple thoughts I'd fain express;
And therefore now I would rehearse
This song of the Red Chamber's Dream,
Where mourning gold, despairing jade,
    Provide me with a fitting theme.

Bowra identified closely with the spirit of the original. If only it had been completed, his "Chinese novel" might have opened the eyes of a large English-speaking readership to the "real" China in a way that would have complemented perfectly the vast oeuvre of Confucian Classics James Legge had recently completed in Hong Kong. Sadly

---

11. The first chapter of Bowra's translation, and part of the Introduction, can be found at http://etext.lib.virginia.edu/chinese.

Bowra died a few years later in 1874, at the age of thirty-two, from an aneurism of the aorta, while on leave in England. His unexpected death brought to a sadly premature end what might have proved a highly significant contribution to the Victorian understanding of China.

Henry Bencraft Joly, the author of the 56-chapter extract now being re-issued in this elegant new guise, was born in 1857 in Smyrna (present-day Izmir, on the Ionian coast, then one of the principal cities of the Ottoman Empire), where his father Stephen Bencraft Joly (1832-1886) was British Vice-Consul. The Bencraft Joly family was an old and distinguished one. Henry himself married Clare Agnes Wilkins in Smyrna in 1886, and promptly entered the China Consular Service. After a stint of training in Peking, which included the study of the Chinese language using Sir Thomas Wade's primer, the *Tzu-erh chi*, he was posted as Vice-Consul to Macao. It was in Macao that he did his version of chapters 1-56 of *Dream*, publishing it in 1891. In my own copy of the first volume of this book, a previous owner has copied in by hand a short extract from the *China Journal*:

> Joly's chief object, I think, was to finish as much of this long novel speedily, knowing as he did that, with the advanced phthisis from which he suffered, his days could not be greatly prolonged.[12]

He was subsequently posted as Vice-Consul to the Chemulpo Consulate in Korea, and died there in 1898.

> He died of a chill caught in his unheated Chemulpo bedroom... [leaving] his widow and three young children almost entirely without provision.[13]

His grave, a tall stone column with inscriptions, can still be seen at the Yanghwajin Cemetery.[14] He was a mere 41 years old at his death, scarcely older than Robert Thom had been at his death in Ningpo, over fifty years earlier, or Bowra in 1874. It is altogether rather a melancholy tale. Three attempts had been made during the 19th century

---

12. *China Journal*, VI, 4, p. 175.

13. Coates, p. 300, citing Foreign Office papers. His widow later found work as teacher of the Korean Crown Prince, and his two sons joined the Chinese Customs Service.

14. Photographs and descriptions of it can be found on various Korean websites. For example: http://www.korea.net/news/news/NewsView.asp?serial_no=20090904004&part=114. "One of the more unusual grave markers is the tall stone column that marks the grave of British Consul to Seoul [stet] Henry Bencraft Joly (d. 1898). One side is carved entirely Chinese letters, while the other side once held Roman letters that have since fallen off, making reading the name or inscription very difficult. The column itself is very decorative, and topped with what appears to be a representation of an urn, although from behind it could be mistaken for an owl."

to translate *Dream*, and three times the lives of the translators were cut short prematurely.

As a fellow member of the China Coast consular community, Bencraft Joly would have known Herbert Giles, whose career as a consular official spanned the years 1867-1893. Giles writes in his Memoirs, under the year 1868, that as part of his training he read widely in Chinese literature:

> I tried to read through the famous and splendid novel known as *The Dream of the Red Chamber*, which should more correctly be *A Dream of (living in mansions with) Red Upper Storeys*, q.d. *A Dream of Wealth and Power*. For my failures in regards to the last-mentioned and ultimate success, see 1885.

Under the year 1885, he writes:

> In March I was elected President of the [North-China Branch of the Royal Asiatic] Society, and opened my year with a paper on the so-called *Dream if the Red Chamber*, which was later on reprinted in my *History of Chinese Literature*. It was a *précis*, not of the whole story, which runs to twenty-four 8vo volumes, but of the love-thread which runs through, and is the foundation of this wonderful work. As prematurely stated under 1868, I had made three attempts to read this work through, getting a little further at each attempt; but it was only in November of 1884, while taking my turn at night duty in a sick-room, that I managed to read it from beginning to end.

Giles' synopsis of *Dream* is excellent, and can still be recommended to readers of the novel.[15] It has always been my conviction that Giles would himself have attempted, some time in the late 1880s, at least a partial translation himself, had it not been for his awareness of Joly's ongoing work. Certainly there are many telltale traces of the novel in Giles' great Chinese-English Dictionary.

Bencraft Joly's incomplete translation has the merit of being quite a literal one. He himself writes with humility in his Preface that the work of translating the novel was suggested "not by any pretensions to range myself among the ranks of the body of sinologues, but by the perplexities and difficulties experienced by me as a student in Peking."

---

15. For Giles' synopsis, see http://www.wsu.edu/~dee/WORLD.HTM. The original appeared, as Giles states, in the *Journal of the North China Branch of the Royal Asiatic Society*, New Series 20, Shanghai, 1885. It was later expanded in his *History of Chinese Literature* (London: Heinemann, 1901). For the complete Memoirs, see Charles Aylmer, ed., 'The Memoirs of H. A. Giles', in *East Asian History* 13/14 (June/December 1997).

He admits that "shortcomings" will be discovered, "both in the prose, as well as among the doggerel and uncouth rhymes, in which the text has been more adhered to than rhythm."

It is indeed an extremely literal translation. The poem from chapter 5 so eloquently rendered into verse by Bowra, becomes in Joly's hands nothing more than a piece of somewhat stilted and awkward prose:

> When the Heavens were opened and earth was laid out, chaos prevailed. What was the germ of love? It arises entirely from the strength of licentious love.
>
> What day, by the will of heaven, I felt wounded at heart, and what time I was at leisure, I made an attempt to disburden my sad heart; and with this object in view I indited this Dream of the Red Chamber, on the subject of a disconsolate gold trinket and an unfortunate piece of jade.

One should not be too critical of Joly's refusal to deal with the mildly erotic layer of the novel. Although Bowra was an exception, Joly's contemporary Herbert Giles, in translating the *Strange Stories from a Chinese Studio* of Pu Songling, also bowlderized. They were both creatures of their time.[16]

Despite its shortcomings, this partial version certainly deserves a wider readership, as a brave early skirmish on the outer ramparts of this masterpiece. The re-issuing of Joly's work will undoubtedly provide a rich crop of fascinating raw material for the growing community of Translation Studies scholars.[17]

John Minford
2009

---

16. For a discussion of Giles and his bowlderized *Strange Stories*, see the essay by Tong Man and John Minford, "Whose Strange Stories? Pu Songling and Herbert Giles," in *East Asian History*, 17/18, 1999, pp. 1-48.

17. For a very brief account of the English fore-runners of the Penguin *Stone* (Thom, Bowra, Bencraft Joly, C. C. Wang, Kuhn, Bonsall, etc), see John Minford, 'The Slow Boat From China: The *Stone's* Journey to the West', in Elberfeld et al. eds., *Komparative Philosophie: Begegnungen zwischen östlichen und westlichen Denkwegen*, München, Wilhelm Fink Verlag, 1998, pp. 171-180. See also Connie Chan Oi-sum's fully documented account, 'The Story of the *Stone's* Journey to the West: a study in Chinese-English translation history', Hong Kong Polytechnic University, M. Phil thesis, 2001. The Rev. Bramwell Seaton Bonsall, a Wesleyan Methodist missionary to China from 1911 to 1926, in the 1950s completed a translation of the novel. This was later accepted for publication by The Asia Society of New York, but the project was abandoned when Penguin announced its proposed translation. The typescript of Bonsall's translation is held by the library of the University of Hong Kong, and can be found at: http://lib. hku.hk/bonsall/hongloumeng/index/.html.

Introduction

About Henry Bencraft Joly

This version of *Hong Lou Meng* by Cao Xueqin was first translated into English by H. Bencraft Joly as *The Dream of the Red Chamber* and published in two volumes in 1892 and 1893 in Hong Kong.

Henry Bencraft Joly was born in Symrna in modern Turkey in 1857. Joly married Clara Agnes Wilkins in Tianjian, China in 1886, and studied Chinese in Beijing while a member of Her Britannic Majesty's Consular Service, China. At the time of his translation of *Hong Lou Meng* around 1891, Joly was the British Vice Consul in Macau.

Joly's translation of *Hong Lou Meng* can only be described as meticulous. Unlike many early translations of Chinese literature, Joly did not use generalizations in translation to suit the level of Sinological knowledge of the average reader, at the expense of details in the original Chinese text. Neither did his use of the English language mask the intricacies of the use of language in the original Chinese.

Joly's critique of his own translation is largely directed at his treatment of the poetry contained within the text, in which he felt that the "text has been more adhered to than the rhythm." However, in spite of Joly's self criticisms and his temperance of a particularly vulgar sentence in the text to suit Victorian sensibilities, this translation remains eminently faithful to the original Chinese text.

Although an excellent work of translation, Joly's *The Dream of the Red Chamber* abruptly ends with Chapter 56, just short of half of the total of 120 chapters of the novel. The abrupt ending of Volume II suggests that Joly had every intention of completing the mammoth task of translating the *Hong Lou Meng*. This task, however, was never to be realised. Henry Bencraft Joly was appointed British Consul to Seoul, Korea at some point between commencing work on the first two volumes of *The Dream of the Red Chamber* in 1891 and his death in Chemulpo (modern day Incheon) in 1898 at the age of 41. Joly was buried in the Yanghwajin Foreigners' Cemetery, Seoul where his typically Victorian grave monument, with neatly incised Chinese characters can still be found.

About this edition

Given the meticulous detail of Henry Bencraft Joly's excellent translation, this revised edition of *The Dream of the Red Chamber* does not contain any significant revisions, beyond a few corrections of minor errors. Joly had used the then standard romanization system for Chinese, the Wade-Giles system, developed in part by his consular colleague, Herbert Giles. This edition has been revised using the Pinyin system, the official system of romanization of the People's Republic of China, which is recognised as the ISO international standard. In preparing this revision, several online sources of the Chinese text were used as a reference for each romanized Chinese word, and the conversion from Wade-Giles to Pinyin was based on the original Chinese text.

Henry Bencraft Joly's attention to detail and the faithfulness in his translation of *Hong Lou Meng* makes this revised edition of *The Dream of the Red Chamber* an excellent book for the student of modern Chinese. Students of Chinese will find *The Dream of the Red Chamber* especially useful in their further studies, due to the fact that *Hong Lou Meng* was primarily written in the vernacular form of Beijing dialect, which has since become the standard form of modern spoken and literary Chinese. Students of Chinese will find Joly's faithful translation useful when read in comparison with the original Chinese text, which is freely available online for any student.

Perhaps this translation of *The Dream of the Red Chamber* has become a greater epitaph for Henry Bencraft Joly than the English inscription on his grave monument, now almost completely lost to the ravages of time. With his life tragically cut short at the age of 41, the quality of Joly's translation of the first 56 chapters of *The Dream of the Red Chamber* suggests the premature loss of a potential giant in the field of Sinological studies. In describing his own work, Joly stated: "I shall feel satisfied with the result, if I succeed, even in the least degree, in affording a helping hand to present and future students of the Chinese language".

Henry Bencraft Joly can certainly rest assured.

Edwin H. Lowe
Macquarie University, Sydney
2009

Preface

This translation was suggested not by any pretensions to range myself among the ranks of the body of sinologues, but by the perplexities and difficulties experienced by me as a student in Peking, when, at the completion of the *Zi Er Ji*, I had to plunge in the maze of the *Hong Lou Meng*.

Shortcomings are, I feel sure, to be discovered, both in the prose, as well as among the doggerel and uncouth rhymes, in which the text has been more adhered to than rhythm; but I shall feel satisfied with the result, if I succeed, even in the least degree, in affording a helping hand to present and future students of the Chinese language.

H. Bencraft Joly
Her Britannic Majesty's Vice-Consulate, Macao
1st September, 1891.

CHAPTER 1

Zhen Shiyin, in a vision, apprehends perception and spirituality. Jia Yucun, in the (windy and dusty) world, cherishes fond thoughts of a beautiful maiden.

This is the opening section; this the first chapter. Subsequent to the visions of a dream which he had, on some previous occasion, experienced, the writer personally relates, he designedly concealed the true circumstances, and borrowed the attributes of perception and spirituality to relate this story of the Record of the Stone. With this purpose, he made use of such designations as Zhen Shiyin (truth under the garb of fiction) and the like. What are, however, the events recorded in this work? Who are the dramatis personae?

Wearied with the drudgery experienced of late in the world, the author speaking for himself, goes on to explain, with the lack of success which attended every single concern, I suddenly bethought myself of the womankind of past ages. Passing one by one under a minute scrutiny, I felt that in action and in lore, one and all were far above me; that in spite of the majesty of my manliness, I could not, in point of fact, compare with these characters of the gentle sex. And my shame forsooth then knew no bounds; while regret, on the other hand, was of no avail, as there was not even a remote possibility of a day of remedy.

On this very day it was that I became desirous to compile, in a connected form, for publication throughout the world, with a view to (universal) information, how that I bear inexorable and manifold retribution; inasmuch as what time, by the sustenance of the benevolence of Heaven, and the virtue of my ancestors, my apparel was rich and fine, and as what days my fare was savory and sumptuous, I disregarded the bounty of education and nurture of father and mother, and paid no heed to the virtue of precept and injunction of teachers and friends, with the result that I incurred the punishment, of failure recently in the least trifle, and the reckless waste of half my lifetime. There have been meanwhile, generation after generation, those in the inner chambers, the whole mass of whom could not, on any account, be, through my influence, allowed to fall into extinction, in order that I, unfilial as I have been, may have the means to screen my own shortcomings.

Hence it is that the thatched shed, with bamboo mat windows, the bed of tow and the stove of brick, which are at present my share, are not sufficient to deter me from carrying out the fixed purpose of my mind. And could I, furthermore, confront the morning breeze, the evening moon, the willows by the steps and the flowers in the courtyard, methinks these would moisten to a greater degree my mortal brush with ink; but though I lack culture and erudition, what harm is there, however, in employing fiction and unrecondite language to give utterance to the merits of these characters? And were I also able to induce the inmates of the inner chamber to understand and diffuse them, could I besides break the weariness of even so much as a single moment, or could I open the eyes of my contemporaries, will it not forsooth prove a boon?

This consideration has led to the usage of such names as Jia Yucun and other similar appellations.

More than any in these pages have been employed such words as dreams and visions; but these dreams constitute the main argument of this work, and combine, furthermore, the design of giving a word of warning to my readers.

Reader, can you suggest whence the story begins?

The narration may border on the limits of incoherency and triviality, but it possesses considerable zest. But to begin.

The Empress Nuwa, (the goddess of works,) in fashioning blocks of stones, for the repair of the heavens, prepared, at the Da Huang Hills and Wu Ji cave, 36,501 blocks of rough stone, each twelve zhang in height, and twenty-four zhang square. Of these stones, the Empress Wa only used 36,500; so that one single block remained over and above, without being turned to any account. This was cast down the Qing Keng peak. This stone, strange to say, after having undergone a process of refinement, attained a nature of efficiency, and could, by its innate powers, set itself into motion and was able to expand and to contract.

When it became aware that the whole number of blocks had been made use of to repair the heavens, that it alone had been destitute of the necessary properties and had been unfit to attain selection, it forthwith felt within itself vexation and shame, and day and night, it gave way to anguish and sorrow.

One day, while it lamented its lot, it suddenly caught sight, at a great distance, of a Buddhist bonze and of a Daoist priest coming towards that direction. Their appearance was uncommon, their easy manner remarkable. When they drew near this Qing Keng peak, they sat on the ground to rest, and began to converse. But on noticing the block newly-polished and brilliantly clear, which had moreover contracted in dimensions, and become no larger than the pendant of a fan, they were greatly filled with admiration. The Buddhist priest picked it up, and laid it in the palm of his hand.

"Your appearance," he said laughingly, "may well declare you to be a supernatural object, but as you lack any inherent quality it is necessary to inscribe a few characters on you, so that everyone who shall see you may at once recognise you to be a remarkable thing. And subsequently, when you will be taken into a country where honor and affluence will reign, into a family cultured in mind and of official status, in a land where flowers and trees shall flourish with luxuriance, in a town of refinement, renown and glory; when you once will have been there..."

The stone listened with intense delight.

"What characters may I ask," it consequently inquired, "will you inscribe? and what place will I be taken to? pray, pray explain to me in lucid terms." "You mustn't be inquisitive," the bonze replied, with a smile, "in days to come you'll certainly understand everything." Having concluded these words, he forthwith put the stone in his sleeve, and proceeded leisurely on his journey, in company with the Daoist priest. Whither, however, he took the stone, is not divulged. Nor can it be known how many centuries and ages elapsed, before a Daoist priest, Kong Kong by name, passed, during his researches after the eternal reason and his quest after immortality, by these Ta Huang Hills, Wu Ji cave, and Qing Keng Peak. Suddenly perceiving a large block of stone, on the surface of which the traces of characters giving, in a connected form, the various incidents of its fate, could be clearly deciphered, Kong Kong examined them from first to last. They, in fact, explained how that this block of worthless stone had originally been devoid of the properties essential for the repairs to the heavens, how it would be transmuted into human form and introduced by Mang Mang the High Lord, and Miao Miao, the Divine, into the world of mortals, and how it would be led over the other bank (across the San Sara). On the surface, the record of the spot where it would fall, the place of its birth, as well as various family trifles and trivial love affairs of young ladies, verses, odes, speeches, and enigmas was still complete; but the name of the dynasty and the year of the reign were obliterated, and could not be ascertained.

On the obverse, were also the following enigmatical verses:

Lacking in virtues meet the azure skies to mend,
In vain the mortal world full many a year I wend,

Of a former and after life these facts that be,
Who will for a tradition strange record for me?

Kong Kong, the Daoist, having pondered over these lines for a while, became aware that this stone had a history of some kind.

"Brother stone," he forthwith said, addressing the stone, "the concerns of past days recorded on you possess, according to your own account, a considerable amount of interest, and have been for this reason inscribed, with the intent of soliciting generations to hand them down as remarkable occurrences. But in my own opinion, they lack, in the first place, any data by means of which to establish the name of the Emperor and the year of his reign; and, in the second place, these constitute no record of any excellent policy, adopted by any high worthies or high loyal statesmen, in the government of the state, or in the rule of public morals. The contents simply treat of a certain number of maidens, of exceptional character; either of their love affairs or infatuations, or of their small deserts or insignificant talents; and were I to transcribe the whole collection of them, they would, nevertheless, not be estimated as a book of any exceptional worth."

"Sir Priest," the stone replied with assurance, "why are you so excessively dull? The dynasties recorded in the rustic histories, which have been written from age to age, have, I am fain to think, invariably assumed, under false pretences, the mere nomenclature of the Han and Tang dynasties. They differ from the events inscribed on my block, which do not borrow this customary practice, but, being based on my own experiences and natural feelings, present, on the contrary, a novel and unique character. Besides, in the pages of these rustic histories, either the aspersions upon sovereigns and statesmen, or the strictures upon individuals, their wives, and their daughters, or the deeds of licentiousness and violence are too numerous to be computed. Indeed, there is one more kind of loose literature, the wantonness and pollution in which work most easy havoc upon youth.

"As regards the works, in which the characters of scholars and beauties is delineated their allusions are again repeatedly of Wen Jun, their theme in every page of Zi Jian; a thousand volumes present no diversity; and a thousand characters are but a counterpart of each other. What is more, these works, throughout all their pages, cannot help bordering on extreme licence. The authors, however, had no other object in view than to give utterance to a few sentimental odes and elegant ballads of their own, and for this reason they have fictitiously invented the names and surnames of both men and women, and necessarily introduced, in addition, some low characters, who should, like a buffoon in a play, create some excitement in the plot.

"Still more loathsome is a kind of pedantic and profligate literature, perfectly devoid of all natural sentiment, full of self-contradictions; and, in fact, the contrast to those maidens in my work, whom I have, during half my lifetime, seen with my own eyes and heard with my own ears. And though I will not presume to estimate them as superior to the heroes and heroines in the works of former ages, yet the perusal of the motives and issues of their experiences, may likewise afford matter sufficient to banish dulness, and to break the spell of melancholy.

"As regards the several stanzas of doggerel verse, they may too evoke such laughter as to compel the reader to blurt out the rice, and to spurt out the wine.

"In these pages, the scenes depicting the anguish of separation, the bliss of reunion, and the fortunes of prosperity and of adversity are all, in every detail, true to human nature, and I have not taken upon myself to make the slightest addition, or alteration, which might lead to the perversion of the truth.

"My only object has been that men may, after a drinking bout, or after they wake from sleep or when in need of relaxation from the pressure of business, take up this light literature, and not only expunge the traces of antiquated books, and obtain a new kind of distraction, but that they may also lay by a long life as well as energy and strength; for it bears no point of similarity to those works, whose designs are false, whose course is immoral. Now, Sir Priest, what are your views on the subject?"

Kong Kong having pondered for a while over the words, to which he had listened intently, re-perused, throughout, this record of the stone; and funding that the general purport consisted of nought else than a treatise on love, and likewise of an accurate transcription of facts, without the least taint of profligacy injurious to the times, he thereupon copied the contents, from beginning to end, to the intent of charging the world to hand them down as a strange story.

Hence it was that Kong Kong, the Daoist, in consequence of his perception, (in his state of) abstraction, of passion, the generation, from this passion, of voluptuousness, the transmission of this voluptuousness into passion, and the apprehension, by means of passion, of its unreality, forthwith altered his name for that of "Qing Seng" (the Voluptuous Bonze), and changed the title of "the Memoir of a Stone" (Shitou Ji,) for that of "Qing Seng Lu," The Record of the Voluptuous Bonze; while Kong Meixi of Dong Lu gave it the name of "Feng Yue Bao

Jian," The Precious Mirror of Voluptuousness. In later years, owing to the devotion by Cao Xueqin in the Dao Hong study, of ten years to the perusal and revision of the work, the additions and modifications effected by him five times, the affix of an index, and the division into periods and chapters, the book was again entitled "Jinling Shi Er Chai," The Twelve Maidens of Jinling. A stanza was furthermore composed for the purpose. This then, and no other, is the origin of the Record of the Stone. The poet says appositely:

> Pages full of silly litter,
> Tears a handful sour and bitter,
> All a fool the author hold,
> But their zest who can unfold?

You have now understood the causes which brought about the Record of the Stone, but as you are not, as yet, aware what characters are depicted, and what circumstances are related on the surface of the block, reader, please lend an ear to the narrative on the stone, which runs as follows:

In old days, the land in the Southeast lay low. In this Southeast part of the world, was situated a walled town, Gusu by name. Within the walls a locality, called the Chang Men, was more than all others throughout the mortal world, the center, which held the second if not the first place for fashion and life. Beyond this Chang Men was a street called Shi Li Jie (Ten Li street); in this street a lane the Ren Qing lane (Humanity and Purity); and in this lane stood an old temple, which on account of its diminutive dimensions, was called by general consent, the Gourd temple. Next door to this temple lived the family of a district official, Zhen by surname, Fei by name and Shiyin by style. His wife, née Feng, possessed a worthy and virtuous disposition, and had a clear perception of moral propriety and good conduct. This family, though not in actual possession of excessive affluence and honors, was, nevertheless, in their district, conceded to be a clan of well-to-do standing. As this Zhen Shiyin was of a contented and unambitious frame of mind, and entertained no hankering after any official distinction, but day after day of his life took delight in gazing at flowers, planting bamboos, sipping his wine and conning poetical works, he was in fact, in the indulgence of these pursuits, as happy as a supernatural being.

One thing alone marred his happiness. He had lived over half a century and had, as yet, no male offspring around his knees. He had only one child, a daughter, whose infant name was Yinglian. She was just three years of age. On a long summer day, on which the heat had been intense, Shiyin sat leisurely in his library. Feeling his hand tired, he dropped the book he held, leant his head on a teapoy, and fell asleep.

Of a sudden, while in this state of unconsciousness, it seemed as if he had betaken himself on foot to some spot or other whither he could not discriminate. Unexpectedly he espied, in the opposite direction, two priests coming towards him: the one a Buddhist, the other a Daoist. As they advanced they kept up the conversation in which they were engaged. "Whither do you purpose taking the object you have brought away?" he heard the Daoist inquire. To this question the Buddhist replied with a smile: "Set your mind at ease," he said; "there's now in maturity a plot of a general character involving mundane pleasures, which will presently come to a denouement. The whole number of the votaries of voluptuousness have, as yet, not been quickened or entered the world, and I mean to avail myself of this occasion to introduce this object among their number, so as to give it a chance to go through the span of human existence." "The votaries of voluptuousness of these days will naturally have again to endure the ills of life during their course through the mortal world," the Daoist remarked; "but when, I wonder, will they spring into existence? and in what place will they descend?"

"The account of these circumstances," the bonze ventured to reply, "is enough to make you laugh! They amount to this: there existed in the west, on the bank of the Ling (spiritual) river, by the side of the San Sheng (thrice-born) stone, a blade of the Jiang Zhu (purple pearl) grass. At about the same time it was that the block of stone was, consequent upon its rejection by the goddess of works, also left to ramble and wander to its own gratification, and to roam about at pleasure to every and any place. One day it came within the precincts of the Jing Huan (Monitory Vision) Fairy; and this Fairy, cognizant of the fact that this stone had a history, detained it, therefore, to reside at the Chi Xia (purple clouds) palace, and apportioned to it the duties of attendant on Shen Ying, a fairy of the Chi Xia palace.

"This stone would, however, often stroll along the banks of the Ling river, and having at the sight of the blade of spiritual grass been filled with admiration, it, day by day, moistened its roots with sweet dew. This purple pearl grass, at the outset, tarried for months and years; but being at a later period imbued with the essence and luxuriance of heaven and earth, and having incessantly received the moisture and nurture of the sweet dew, divested itself, in course of time, of the form of a grass; assuming, in lieu, a human nature, which gradually became perfected into the person of a girl.

"Every day she was wont to wander beyond the confines of the Li Hen (divested animosities) heavens. When hungry she fed on the Pi Qing (hidden love) fruit—when thirsty she drank the Guan Zhou (discharged sorrows) water. Having, however, up to this time, not shewn her gratitude for the virtue of nurture lavished upon her, the result was but natural that she should resolve in her heart upon a constant and incessant purpose to make suitable acknowledgment.

"I have been," she would often commune within herself, "the recipient of the gracious bounty of rain and dew, but I possess no such water as was lavished upon me to repay it! But should it ever descend into the world in the form of a human being, I will also betake myself thither, along with it; and if I can only have the means of making restitution to it, with the tears of a whole lifetime, I may be able to make adequate return."

"This resolution it is that will evolve the descent into the world of so many pleasure-bound spirits of retribution and the experience of fantastic destinies; and this crimson pearl blade will also be among the number. The stone still lies in its original place, and why should not you and I take it along before the tribunal of the Monitory Vision Fairy, and place on its behalf its name on record, so that it should descend into the world, in company with these spirits of passion, and bring this plot to an issue?"

"It is indeed ridiculous," interposed the Daoist. "Never before have I heard even the very mention of restitution by means of tears! Why should not you and I avail ourselves of this opportunity to likewise go down into the world? and if successful in effecting the salvation of a few of them, will it not be a work meritorious and virtuous?"

"This proposal," remarked the Buddhist, "is quite in harmony with my own views. Come along then with me to the palace of the Monitory Vision Fairy, and let us deliver up this good-for-nothing object, and have done with it! And when the company of pleasure-bound spirits of wrath descend into human existence, you and I can then enter the world. Half of them have already fallen into the dusty universe, but the whole number of them have not, as yet, come together."

"Such being the case," the Daoist acquiesced, "I am ready to follow you, whenever you please to go."

But to return to Zhen Shiyin. Having heard everyone of these words distinctly, he could not refrain from forthwith stepping forward and paying homage. "My spiritual lords," he said, as he smiled, "accept my obeisance." The Buddhist and Daoist priests lost no time in responding to the compliment, and they exchanged the usual salutations. "My spiritual lords," Shiyin continued; "I have just heard the conversation that passed between you, on causes and effects, a conversation the like of which few mortals have forsooth listened to; but your younger brother is sluggish of intellect, and cannot lucidly fathom the import! Yet could this dullness and simplicity be graciously dispelled, your younger brother may, by listening minutely, with undefiled ear and careful attention, to a certain degree be aroused to a sense of understanding; and what is more, possibly find the means of escaping the anguish of sinking down into Hades."

The two spirits smiled, "The conversation," they added, "refers to the primordial scheme and cannot be divulged before the proper season; but, when the time comes, mind do not forget us two, and you will readily be able to escape from the fiery furnace."

Shiyin, after this reply, felt it difficult to make any further inquiries. "The primordial scheme," he however remarked smiling, "cannot, of course, be divulged; but what manner of thing, I wonder, is the good-for-nothing object you alluded to a short while back? May I not be allowed to judge for myself?"

"This object about which you ask," the Buddhist Bonze responded, "is intended, I may tell you, by fate to be just glanced at by you." With these words he produced it, and handed it over to Shiyin.

Shiyin received it. On scrutiny he found it, in fact, to be a beautiful gem, so lustrous and so clear that the traces of characters on the surface were distinctly visible. The characters inscribed consisted of the four "Tong Ling Bao Yu," Precious Gem of Spiritual Perception. On the obverse, were also several columns of minute words, which he was just in the act of looking at intently, when the Buddhist at once expostulated.

"We have already reached," he exclaimed, "the confines of vision." Snatching it violently out of his hands, he walked away with the Daoist, under a lofty stone portal, on the face of which appeared in large type the four characters: "Tai Xu Huan Jing," The Visionary limits of the Great Void. On each side was a scroll with the lines:

> When falsehood stands for truth, truth likewise becomes false,
> Where naught be made to aught, aught changes into naught.

Shiyin meant also to follow them on the other side, but, as he was about to make one step forward, he suddenly heard a crash, just as if the mountains had fallen into ruins, and the earth sunk into destruction. As Shiyin uttered a loud shout, he looked with strained eye; but all he could see was the fiery sun shining, with glowing rays, while the banana leaves drooped their heads. By that time, half of the circumstances connected with the dream he had had, had already slipped from his memory.

He also noticed a nurse coming towards him with Yinglian in her arms. To Shiyin's eyes his daughter appeared even more beautiful, such a bright gem, so precious, and so lovable. Forthwith stretching out his arms, he took her over, and, as he held her in his embrace, he coaxed her to play with him for a while; after which he brought her up to the street to see the great stir occasioned by the procession that was going past.

He was about to come in, when he caught sight of two priests, one a Daoist the other a Buddhist, coming hither from the opposite direction. The Buddhist had a head covered with mange, and went barefooted. The Daoist had a limping foot, and his hair was all dishevelled.

Like maniacs, they jostled along, chattering and laughing as they drew near.

As soon as they reached Shiyin's door, and they perceived him with Yinglian in his arms, the Bonze began to weep aloud.

Turning towards Shiyin, he said to him: "My good Sir, why need you carry in your embrace this living but luckless thing, which will involve father and mother in trouble?"

These words did not escape Shiyin's ear; but persuaded that they amounted to raving talk, he paid no heed whatever to the bonze.

"Part with her and give her to me," the Buddhist still went on to say.

Shiyin could not restrain his annoyance; and hastily pressing his daughter closer to him, he was intent upon going in, when the bonze pointed his hand at him, and burst out in a loud fit of laughter.

He then gave utterance to the four lines that follow:

> You indulge your tender daughter and are laughed at as inane;
> Vain you face the snow, oh mirror! for it will evanescent wane,
> When the festival of lanterns is gone by, guard 'gainst your doom,
> 'Tis what time the flames will kindle, and the fire will consume.

Shiyin understood distinctly the full import of what he heard; but his heart was still full of conjectures. He was about to inquire who and what they were, when he heard the Daoist remark, "You and I cannot speed together; let us now part company, and each of us will be then able to go after his own business. After the lapse of three ages, I shall be at the Beimang mount, waiting for you; and we can, after our reunion, betake ourselves to the Visionary Confines of the Great Void, there to cancel the name of the stone from the records."

"Excellent! first rate!" exclaimed the Bonze. And at the conclusion of these words, the two men parted, each going his own way, and no trace was again seen of them.

"These two men," Shiyin then pondered within his heart, "must have had many experiences, and I ought really to have made more inquiries of them; but at this juncture to indulge in regret is anyhow too late."

While Shiyin gave way to these foolish reflections, he suddenly noticed the arrival of a penniless scholar, Jia by surname, Hua by name, Shifei by style, and Yuchun by nickname, who had taken up his quarters in the Gourd temple next door. This Jia Yucun was originally a denizen of Huzhou, and was also of literary and official parentage, but as he was born of the youngest stock, and the possessions of his paternal and maternal ancestors were completely exhausted, and his parents and relatives were dead, he remained the sole and only survivor; and, as he found his residence in his native place of no avail, he therefore entered the capital in search of that reputation, which would enable him to put the family estate on a proper standing. He had arrived at this place since the year before last, and had, what is more, lived all along in very straitened circumstances. He had made the temple his temporary quarters, and earned a living by daily occupying himself in composing documents and writing letters for customers. Thus it was that Shiyin had been in constant relations with him.

As soon as Yucun perceived Shiyin, he lost no time in saluting him. "My worthy Sir," he observed with a forced smile; "how is it you are leaning against the door and looking out? Is there perchance any news astir in the streets, or in the public places?"

"None whatever," replied Shiyin, as he returned the smile. "Just a while back, my young daughter was in sobs, and I coaxed her out here to amuse her. I am just now without anything whatever to attend to, so that, dear brother Jia, you come just in the nick of time. Please walk into my mean abode, and let us endeavour, in each other's company, to while away this long summer day."

After he had made this remark, he bade a servant take his daughter in, while he, hand-in-hand with Yucun, walked into the library, where a young page served tea. They had hardly exchanged a few sentences, when one of the household came in, in flying haste, to announce that Mr. Yan had come to pay a visit.

Shiyin at once stood up. "Pray excuse my rudeness," he remarked apologetically, "but do sit down; I shall shortly rejoin you, and enjoy the pleasure of your society." "My dear Sir," answered Yucun, as he got up, also in a conceding way, "suit your own convenience. I've often had the honor of being your guest, and what will it matter if I wait a little?" While these apologies were yet being spoken, Shiyin had already walked out into the front parlor. During his absence, Yucun occupied himself in turning over the pages of some poetical work to dispel ennui, when suddenly he heard, outside the window, a woman's cough. Yucun hurriedly got up and looked out. He saw at a glance that it was a servant girl engaged in picking flowers. Her deportment was out of the common; her eyes so bright, her eyebrows so well defined. Though not a perfect beauty, she possessed nevertheless charms sufficient to arouse the feelings. Yucun unwittingly gazed at her with fixed eye. This waiting-maid, belonging to the Zhen family, had done picking flowers, and was on the point of going in, when she of a sudden raised her eyes and became aware of the presence of some person inside the window, whose head-gear consisted of a turban in tatters, while his clothes were the worse for wear. But in spite of his poverty, he was naturally endowed with a round waist, a broad back, a fat face, a square mouth; added to this, his eyebrows were swordlike, his eyes resembled stars, his nose was straight, his cheeks square.

This servant girl turned away in a hurry and made her escape.

"This man so burly and strong," she communed within herself, "yet at the same time got up in such poor attire, must, I expect, be no one else than the man, whose name is Jia Yucun or such like, time after time referred to by my master, and to whom he has repeatedly wished to give a helping hand, but has failed to find a favorable opportunity. And as related to our family there is no connexion or friend in such straits, I feel certain it cannot be any other person than he. Strange to say, my master has further remarked that this man will, for a certainty, not always continue in such a state of destitution."

As she indulged in this train of thought, she could not restrain herself from turning her head round once or twice.

When Yucun perceived that she had looked back, he readily interpreted it as a sign that in her heart her thoughts had been of him, and he was frantic with irrepressible joy.

"This girl," he mused, "is, no doubt, keen-eyed and eminently shrewd, and one in this world who has seen through me."

The servant youth, after a short time, came into the room; and when Yucun made inquiries and found out from him that the guests in the front parlor had been detained to dinner, he could not very well wait any longer, and promptly walked away down a side passage and out of a back door.

When the guests had taken their leave, Shiyin did not go back to rejoin Yucun, as he had come to know that he had already left.

In time the mid-autumn festivities drew near; and Shiyin, after the family banquet was over, had a separate table laid in the library, and crossed over, in the moonlight, as far as the temple and invited Yucun to come round.

The fact is that Yucun, ever since the day on which he had seen the girl of the Zhen family turn twice round to glance at him, flattered himself that she was friendly disposed towards him, and incessantly fostered fond thoughts of her in his heart. And on this day, which happened to be the mid-autumn feast, he could not, as he gazed at the moon, refrain from cherishing her remembrance. Hence it was that he gave vent to these pentameter verses:

> Alas! not yet divined my lifelong wish,
> And anguish ceaseless comes upon anguish
> I came, and sad at heart, my brow I frowned;
> She went, and oft her head to look turned round.
> Facing the breeze, her shadow she doth watch,
> Who's meet this moonlight night with her to match?
> The lustrous rays if they my wish but read
> Would soon alight upon her beauteous head!

Yucun having, after this recitation, recalled again to mind how that throughout his lifetime his literary attainments had had an adverse fate and not met with an opportunity (of reaping distinction), went on to rub his brow, and as he raised his eyes to the skies, he heaved a deep sigh and once more intoned a couplet aloud:

> The gem in the cask a high price it seeks,
> The pin in the case to take wing it waits.

As luck would have it, Shiyin was at the moment approaching, and upon hearing the lines, he said with a smile: "My dear Yucun, really your attainments are of no ordinary capacity."

Yucun lost no time in smiling and replying. "It would be presumption in my part to think so," he observed. "I was simply at random humming a few verses composed by former writers, and what reason is there to laud me to such an excessive degree? To what, my dear Sir, do I owe the pleasure of your visit?" he went on to inquire. "Tonight," replied Shiyin, "is the mid-autumn feast, generally known as the full-moon festival; and as I could not help thinking that living, as you my worthy brother are, as a mere stranger in this Buddhist temple, you could not but experience the feeling of loneliness. I have, for the express purpose, prepared a small entertainment, and will be pleased if you will come to my mean abode to have a glass of wine. But I wonder whether you will entertain favorably my modest invitation?" Yucun, after listening to the proposal, put forward no refusal of any sort; but remarked complacently: "Being the recipient of such marked attention, how can I presume to repel your generous consideration?"

As he gave expression to these words, he walked off there and then, in company with Shiyin, and came over once again into the court in front of the library. In a few minutes, tea was over.

The cups and dishes had been laid from an early hour, and needless to say the wines were luscious; the fare sumptuous.

The two friends took their seats. At first they leisurely replenished their glasses, and quietly sipped their wine; but as, little by little, they entered into conversation, their good cheer grew more genial, and unawares the glasses began to fly round, and the cups to be exchanged.

At this very hour, in every house of the neighborhood, sounded the fife and lute, while the inmates indulged in music and singing. Above head, the orb of the radiant moon shone with an all-pervading splendor, and with a steady lustrous light, while the two friends, as their exuberance increased, drained their cups dry so soon as they reached their lips.

Yucun, at this stage of the collation, was considerably under the influence of wine, and the vehemence of his high spirits was irrepressible. As he gazed at the moon, he fostered thoughts, to which he gave vent by the recital of a double couplet.

> Tis what time three meets five, Selene is a globe!
> Her pure rays fill the court, the jadelike rails enrobe!
> Lo! in the heavens her disk to view doth now arise,
> And in the earth below to gaze men lift their eyes.

"Excellent!" cried Shiyin with a loud voice, after he had heard these lines; "I have repeatedly maintained that it was impossible for you to remain long inferior to any, and now the verses you have recited are a prognostic of your rapid advancement. Already it is evident that, before long, you will extend your footsteps far above the clouds! I must congratulate you! I must congratulate you! Let me, with my own hands, pour a glass of wine to pay you my compliments."

Yucun drained the cup. "What I am about to say," he explained as he suddenly heaved a sigh, "is not the maudlin talk of a man under the effects of wine. As far as the subjects at present set in the examinations go, I could, perchance, also have well been able to enter the list, and to send in my name as a candidate; but I have, just now, no means whatever to make provision for luggage and for travelling expenses. The distance too to Shen Jing is a long one, and I could not depend upon the sale of papers or the composition of essays to find the means of getting there."

Shiyin gave him no time to conclude. "Why did you not speak about this sooner?" he interposed with haste. "I have long entertained this suspicion; but as, whenever I met you, this conversation was never broached, I did not presume to make myself officious. But if such be the state of affairs just now, I lack, I admit literary qualification, but on the two subjects of friendly spirit and pecuniary means, I have, nevertheless, some experience. Moreover, I rejoice that next year is just the season for the triennial examinations, and you should start for the capital with all despatch; and in the tripos next spring, you will, by carrying the prize, be able to do justice to the proficiency you can boast of. As regards the travelling expenses and the other items, the provision of everything necessary for you by my own self will again not render nugatory your mean acquaintance with me."

Forthwith, he directed a servant lad to go and pack up at once fifty taels of pure silver and two suits of winter clothes.

"The nineteenth," he continued, "is a propitious day, and you should lose no time in hiring a boat and starting on your journey westwards. And when, by your eminent talents, you shall have soared high to a lofty position, and we meet again next winter, will not the occasion be extremely felicitous?"

Yucun accepted the money and clothes with but scanty expression of gratitude. In fact, he paid no thought whatever to the gifts, but went on, again drinking his wine, as he chattered and laughed.

It was only when the third watch of that day had already struck that the two friends parted company; and Shiyin, after seeing Yucun off, retired to his room and slept, with one sleep all through, never waking until the sun was well up in the skies.

Remembering the occurrence of the previous night, he meant to write a couple of letters of recommendation for Yucun to take along with him to the capital, to enable him, after handing them over at the mansions of certain officials, to find some place as a temporary home. He accordingly despatched a servant to ask him to come round, but the man returned and reported that from what the bonze said, "Mr. Jia had started on his journey to the capital, at the fifth watch of that very morning, that he had also left a message with the bonze to deliver to you, Sir, to the effect that men of letters paid no heed to lucky or unlucky days, that the sole consideration with them was the nature of the matter in hand, and that he could find no time to come round in person and bid good-bye."

Shiyin after hearing this message had no alternative but to banish the subject from his thoughts.

In comfortable circumstances, time indeed goes by with easy stride. Soon drew near also the happy festival of the 15th of the 1st moon, and Shiyin told a servant Huo Qi to take Yinglian to see the sacrificial fires and flowery lanterns.

About the middle of the night, Huo Qi was hard pressed, and he forthwith set Yinglian down on the doorstep of a certain house. When he felt relieved, he came back to take her up, but failed to find anywhere any trace of Yinglian. In a terrible plight, Huo Qi prosecuted his search throughout half the night; but even by the dawn of day, he had not discovered any clue of her whereabouts. Huo Qi, lacking, on the other hand, the courage to go back and face his master, promptly made his escape to his native village.

Shiyin—in fact, the husband as well as the wife—seeing that their child had not come home during the whole night, readily concluded that some mishap must have befallen her. Hastily they despatched several servants to go in search of her, but one and all returned to report that there was neither vestige nor tidings of her.

This couple had only had this child, and this at the meridian of their life, so that her sudden disappearance plunged them in such great distress that day and night they mourned her loss to such a point as to well nigh pay no heed to their very lives.

A month in no time went by. Shiyin was the first to fall ill, and his wife, Dame Feng, likewise, by dint of fretting for her daughter, was also prostrated with sickness. The doctor was, day after day, sent for, and the oracle consulted by means of divination.

Little did any one think that on this day, being the 15th of the 3rd moon, while the sacrificial oblations were being prepared in the Hu Lu temple, a pan with oil would have caught fire, through the want of care on the part of the bonze, and that in a short time the flames would have consumed the paper pasted on the windows.

Among the natives of this district bamboo fences and wooden partitions were in general use, and these too proved a source of calamity so ordained by fate (to consummate this decree).

With promptness (the fire) extended to two buildings, then enveloped three, then dragged four (into ruin), and then spread to five houses, until the whole street was in a blaze, resembling the flames of a volcano. Though both the military and the people at once ran to the rescue, the fire had already assumed a serious hold, so that it was impossible for them to afford any effective assistance for its suppression.

It blazed away straight through the night, before it was extinguished, and consumed, there is in fact no saying how many dwelling houses. Anyhow, pitiful to relate, the Zhen house, situated as it was next door to the temple, was, at an early part of the evening, reduced to a heap of tiles and bricks; and nothing but the lives of that couple and several inmates of the family did not sustain any injuries.

Shiyin was in despair, but all he could do was to stamp his feet and heave deep sighs. After consulting with his wife, they betook themselves to a farm of theirs, where they took up their quarters temporarily. But as it happened that water had of late years been scarce, and no crops been reaped, robbers and thieves had sprung up like bees, and though the Government troops were bent upon their capture, it was anyhow difficult to settle down quietly on the farm. He therefore had no other resource than to convert, at a loss, the whole of his property into money, and to take his wife and two servant girls and come over for shelter to the house of his father-in-law.

His father-in-law, Feng Su, by name, was a native of Tayu Zhou. Although only a laborer, he was nevertheless in easy circumstances at home. When he on this occasion saw his son-in-law come to him in such distress, he forthwith felt at heart considerable displeasure. Fortunately Shiyin had still in his possession the money derived from the unprofitable realization of his property, so that he produced and handed it to his father-in-law, commissioning him to purchase, whenever a suitable opportunity presented itself, a house and land as a provision for food and raiment against days to come. This Feng Su, however, only expended the half of the sum, and pocketed the other half, merely acquiring for him some fallow land and a dilapidated house.

Shiyin being, on the other hand, a man of books and with no experience in matters connected with business and with sowing and reaping, subsisted, by hook and by crook, for about a year or two, when he became more impoverished.

In his presence, Feng Su would readily give vent to specious utterances, while, with others, and behind his back, he on the contrary expressed his indignation against his improvidence in his mode of living, and against his sole delight of eating and playing the lazy.

Shiyin, aware of the want of harmony with his father-in-law, could not help giving way, in his own heart, to feelings of regret and pain. In addition to this, the fright and vexation which he had undergone the year before, the anguish and suffering (he had had to endure), had already worked havoc (on his constitution); and being a man advanced in years, and assailed by the joint attack of poverty and disease, he at length gradually began to display symptoms of decline.

Strange coincidence, as he, on this day, came leaning on his staff and with considerable strain, as far as the street for a little relaxation, he suddenly caught sight, approaching from the off side, of a Daoist priest with a crippled foot; his maniac appearance so repulsive, his shoes of straw, his dress all in tatters, muttering several sentiments to this effect:

> All men spiritual life know to be good,
> But fame to disregard they ne'er succeed!
> From old till now the statesmen where are they?
> Waste lie their graves, a heap of grass, extinct.
> All men spiritual life know to be good,
> But to forget gold, silver, ill succeed!
> Through life they grudge their hoardings to be scant,
> And when plenty has come, their eyelids close.
> All men spiritual life hold to be good,
> Yet to forget wives, maids, they ne'er succeed!
> Who speak of grateful love while lives their lord,
> And dead their lord, another they pursue.
> All men spiritual life know to be good,
> But sons and grandsons to forget never succeed!
> From old till now of parents soft many,
> But filial sons and grandsons who have seen?

Shiyin upon hearing these words, hastily came up to the priest, "What were you so glibly holding forth?" he inquired. "All I could hear were a lot of hao liao (excellent, finality)."

"You may well have heard the two words 'hao liao,'" answered the Daoist with a smile, "but can you be said to have fathomed their meaning? You should know that all things in this world are excellent, when they have attained finality; when they have attained finality, they are excellent; but when they have not attained finality, they are not excellent; if they would be excellent, they should attain finality. My song is entitled Excellent-finality (hao liao)."

Shiyin was gifted with a natural perspicacity that enabled him, as soon as he heard these remarks, to grasp their spirit.

"Wait a while," he therefore said smilingly; "let me unravel this excellent finality song of yours; do you mind?"

"Please by all means go on with the interpretation," urged the Daoist; whereupon Shiyin proceeded in this strain:

Sordid rooms and vacant courts,
Replete in years gone by with beds where statesmen lay;
Parched grass and withered banian trees,
Where once were halls for song and dance!
Spiders' webs the carved pillars intertwine,
The green gauze now is also pasted on the straw windows!
What about the cosmetic fresh concocted or the powder just scented;
Why has the hair too on each temple become white like hoarfrost!
Yesterday the tumulus of yellow earth buried the bleached bones,
Tonight under the red silk curtain reclines the couple!
Gold fills the coffers, silver fills the boxes,
But in a twinkle, the beggars will all abuse you!
While you deplore that the life of others is not long,
You forget that you yourself are approaching death!
You educate your sons with all propriety,
But they may some day, 'tis hard to say become thieves;
Though you choose (your fare and home) the fatted beam,
You may, who can say, fall into some place of easy virtue!
Through your dislike of the gauze hat as mean,
You have come to be locked in a cangue;
Yesterday, poor fellow, you felt cold in a tattered coat,
Today, you despise the purple embroidered dress as long!
Confusion reigns far and wide! you have just sung your part, I come
   on the boards,
Instead of yours, you recognise another as your native land;
What utter perversion!
In one word, it comes to this we make wedding clothes for others!
(We sow for others to reap.)

The crazy limping Daoist clapped his hands. "Your interpretation is explicit," he remarked with a hearty laugh, "your interpretation is explicit!"

Shiyin promptly said nothing more than, "Walk on;" and seizing the stole from the Daoist's shoulder, he flung it over his own. He did not, however, return home, but leisurely walked away, in company with the eccentric priest.

The report of his disappearance was at once bruited abroad, and plunged the whole neighborhood in commotion; and converted into a piece of news, it was circulated from mouth to mouth.

Dame Feng, Shiyin's wife, upon hearing the tidings, had such a fit of weeping that she hung between life and death; but her only alternative was to consult with her father, and to despatch servants on all sides to institute inquiries. No news was however received of him, and she had nothing else to do but to practise resignation, and to remain dependent upon the support of her parents for her subsistence. She had fortunately still by her side, to wait upon her, two servant girls, who had been with her in days gone by; and the three of them, mistress as well as servants, occupied themselves day and night with needlework, to assist her father in his daily expenses.

This Feng Su had after all, in spite of his daily murmurings against his bad luck, no help but to submit to the inevitable.

On a certain day, the elder servant girl of the Zhen family was at the door purchasing thread, and while there, she of a sudden heard in the street shouts of runners clearing the way, and everyone explain that the new magistrate had come to take up his office.

The girl, as she peeped out from inside the door, perceived the lictors and policemen go by two by two; and when unexpectedly in a state chair, was carried past an official, in black hat and red coat, she was indeed quite taken aback.

"The face of this officer would seem familiar," she argued within herself; "just as if I had seen him somewhere or other ere this."

Shortly she entered the house, and banishing at once the occurrence from her mind, she did not give it a second thought. At night, however, while she was waiting to go to bed, she suddenly heard a sound like a rap at the door. A band of men boisterously cried out: "We are messengers, deputed by the worthy magistrate of this district, and come to summon one of you to an inquiry."

Feng Su upon hearing these words, fell into such a terrible consternation that his eyes stared wide and his mouth gaped.

What calamity was impending is not as yet ascertained, but, reader, listen to the explanation contained in the next chapter.

CHAPTER 2

The spirit of Mrs. Jia Shiyin departs from the town of Yang Zhou. Leng Zixing dilates upon the Rong Guo Mansion.

To continue, Feng Su, upon hearing the shouts of the public messengers, came out in a flurry and forcing a smile, he asked them to explain (their errand); but all these people did was to continue bawling out: "Be quick, and ask Mr. Zhen to come out."

"My surname is Feng," said Feng Su, as he promptly forced himself to smile; "It isn't Zhen at all. I had once a son-in-law whose surname was Zhen, but he has left home, it is now already a year or two back. Is it perchance about him that you are inquiring?"

To which the public servants remarked: "We know nothing about Zhen or Jia (true or false); but as he is your son-in-law, we'll take you at once along with us to make verbal answer to our master and have done with it."

And forthwith the whole bevy of public servants hustled Feng Su on, as they went on their way back; while everyone in the Feng family was seized with consternation, and could not imagine what it was all about.

It was no earlier than the second watch, when Feng Su returned home; and they, one and all, pressed him with questions as to what had happened.

"The fact is," he explained, "the newly-appointed Magistrate, whose surname is Jia, whose name is Hua, and who is a native of Huzhou, has been on intimate terms, in years gone by, with our son-in-law; that at the sight of the girl Jiaoxing, standing at the door, in the act of buying thread, he concluded that he must have shifted his quarters over here, and hence it was that his messengers came to fetch him. I gave him a clear account of the various circumstances (of his misfortunes), and the Magistrate was for a time much distressed and expressed his regret. He then went on to make inquiries about my grand-daughter, and I explained that she had been lost, while looking at the illuminations. 'No matter,' put in the Magistrate, 'I will by and by order my men to make search, and I feel certain that they will find her and bring her back.' Then ensued a short conversation, after which I was about to go, when he presented me with the sum of two taels."

The mistress of the Zhen family (Mrs. Zhen Shiyin) could not but feel very much affected by what she heard, and the whole evening she uttered not a word.

The next day, at an early hour, Yucun sent some of his men to bring over to Zhen's wife presents, consisting of two packets of silver, and four pieces of brocaded silk, as a token of gratitude, and to Feng Su also a confidential letter, requesting him to ask of Mrs. Zhen her maid Jiaoxing to become his second wife.

Feng Su was so intensely delighted that his eyebrows expanded, his eyes smiled, and he felt eager to toady to the Magistrate (by presenting the girl to him). He hastened to employ all his persuasive powers with his daughter (to further his purpose), and on the same evening he forthwith escorted Jiaoxing in a small chair to the Yamen.

The joy experienced by Yucun need not be dilated upon. He also presented Feng Su with a packet containing one hundred ounces of gold; and sent numerous valuable presents to Mrs. Zhen, enjoining her "to live cheerfully in the anticipation of finding out the whereabouts of her daughter."

It must be explained, however, that the maid Jiaoxing was the very person, who, a few years ago, had looked round at Yucun and who, by one simple, unpremeditated glance, evolved, in fact, this extraordinary destiny which was indeed an event beyond conception.

Who would ever have foreseen that fate and fortune would both have so favored her that she should, contrary to all anticipation, give birth to a son, after living with Yucun barely a year, that in addition to this, after the lapse of another half year, Yucun's wife should have contracted a sudden illness and departed this life, and that Yucun should have at once raised her to the rank of first wife. Her destiny is adequately expressed by the lines:

> Through but one single, casual look
> Soon an exalted place she took.

The fact is that after Yucun had been presented with the money by Shiyin, he promptly started on the 16th day for the capital, and at the triennial great tripos, his wishes were gratified to the full. Having successfully carried off his degree of graduate of the third rank, his name was put by selection on the list for provincial appointments. By this time, he had been raised to the rank of Magistrate in this district; but, in spite of the excellence and sufficiency of his accomplishments and abilities, he could not escape being ambitious and overbearing. He failed besides, confident as he was in his own merits, in respect toward his superiors, with the result that these officials looked upon him scornfully with the corner of the eye.

A year had hardly elapsed, when he was readily denounced in a memorial to the Throne by the High Provincial authorities, who represented that he was of a haughty disposition, that he had taken upon himself to introduce innovations in the rites and ceremonies, that overtly, while he endeavored to enjoy the reputation of probity and uprightness, he, secretly, combined the nature of the tiger and wolf; with the consequence that he had been the cause of much trouble in the district, and that he had made life intolerable for the people, &c. &c.

The Dragon countenance of the Emperor was considerably incensed. His Majesty lost no time in issuing commands, in reply to the Memorial, that he should be deprived of his official status.

On the arrival of the despatch from the Board, great was the joy felt by every officer, without exception, of the prefecture in which he had held office. Yucun, though at heart intensely mortified and incensed, betrayed not the least outward symptom of annoyance, but still preserved, as of old, a smiling and cheerful countenance.

He handed over charge of all official business and removed the savings which he had accumulated during the several years he had been in office, his family, and all his chattels to his original home; where, after having put everything in proper order, he himself traveled (carried the winds and sleeved the moon) far and wide, visiting every relic of note in the whole Empire.

As luck would have it, on a certain day while making a second journey through the Weiyang district, he heard the news that the Salt Commissioner appointed this year was Lin Ruhai. This Lin Ruhai's family name was Lin, his name Hai, and his style Ruhai. He had obtained the third place in the previous triennial examination, and had by this time, already risen to the rank of Director of the Court of Censors. He was a native of Gusu. He had been recently named by Imperial appointment a Censor attached to the Salt Inspectorate, and had arrived at his post only a short while back.

In fact, the ancestors of Lin Ruhai had, from years back, successively inherited the title of Marquis, which rank, by its present descent to Ruhai, had already been enjoyed by five generations. When first conferred, the hereditary right to the title had been limited to three generations; but of late years, by an act of magnanimous favor and generous beneficence, extraordinary bounty had been superadded; and on the arrival of the succession to the father of Ruhai, the right had been extended to another degree. It had now descended to Ruhai, who had, besides this title of nobility, begun his career as a successful graduate. But though his family had been through uninterrupted ages the recipient of imperial bounties, his kindred had all been anyhow men of culture.

The only misfortune had been that the several branches of the Lin family had not been prolific, so that the numbers of its members continued limited; and though there existed several households, they were all however to Ruhai no closer relatives than first cousins. Neither were there any connections of the same lineage, or of the same parentage.

Ruhai was at this date past forty; and had only had a son, who had died the previous year, in the third year of his age. Though he had several handmaids, he had not had the good fortune of having another son; but this was too a matter that could not be remedied.

By his wife, nee Jia, he had a daughter, to whom the infant name of Daiyu was given. She was, at this time, in her fifth year. Upon her the parents doated as much as if she were a brilliant pearl in the palm of their hand. Seeing that she was endowed with natural gifts of intelligence and good looks, they also felt solicitous to bestow upon her a certain knowledge of books, with no other purpose than that of satisfying, by this illusory way, their wishes of having a son to nurture and of dispelling the anguish felt by them, on account of the desolation and void in their family circle (round their knees).

But to proceed, Yucun, while sojourning at an inn, was unexpectedly laid up with a violent chill. Finding on his recovery, that his funds were not sufficient to pay his expenses, he was thinking of looking out for some house where he could find a resting place when he suddenly came across two friends acquainted with the new Salt Commissioner. Knowing that this official was desirous to find a tutor to instruct his daughter, they lost no time in recommending Yucun, who moved into the Yamen.

His female pupil was youthful in years and delicate in physique, so that her lessons were irregular. Besides herself, there were only two waiting girls, who remained in attendance during the hours of study, so that Yucun was spared considerable trouble and had a suitable opportunity to attend to the improvement of his health.

In a twinkle, another year and more slipped by, and when least expected, the mother of his ward, nee Jia, was carried away after a short illness. His pupil (during her mother's sickness) was dutiful in her attendance, and prepared the medicines for her use. (And after her death,) she went into the deepest mourning prescribed by the rites, and gave way to such excess of grief that, naturally delicate as she was, her old complaint, on this account, broke out anew.

Being unable for a considerable time to prosecute her studies, Yucun lived at leisure and had no duties to attend to. Whenever therefore the wind was genial and the sun mild, he was wont to stroll at random, after he had done with his meals.

On this particular day, he, by some accident, extended his walk beyond the suburbs, and desirous to contemplate the nature of the rustic scenery, he, with listless step, came up to a spot encircled by hills and streaming pools, by luxuriant clumps of trees and thick groves of bamboos. Nestling in the dense foliage stood a temple. The doors and courts were in ruins. The walls, inner and outer, in disrepair. An inscription on a tablet testified that this was the temple of Spiritual Perception. On the sides of the door was also a pair of old and dilapidated scrolls with the following enigmatical verses.

> Behind ample there is, yet to retract the hand, the mind heeds not, until.
> Before the mortal vision lies no path, when comes to turn the will.

"These two sentences," Yucun pondered after perusal, "although simple in language, are profound in signification. I have previous to this visited many a spacious temple, located on hills of note, but never have I beheld an inscription referring to anything of the kind. The meaning contained in these words must, I feel certain, owe their origin to the experiences of some person or other; but there's no saying. But why should I not go in and inquire for myself?"

Upon walking in, he at a glance caught sight of no one else, but of a very aged bonze, of unkempt appearance, cooking his rice. When Yucun perceived that he paid no notice, he went up to him and asked him one or two questions, but as the old priest was dull of hearing and a dotard, and as he had lost his teeth, and his tongue was blunt, he made most irrelevant replies.

Yucun lost all patience with him, and withdrew again from the compound with the intention of going as far as the village public house to have a drink or two, so as to enhance the enjoyment of the rustic scenery. With easy stride, he accordingly walked up to the place. Scarcely had he passed the threshold of the public house, when he perceived someone or other among the visitors who had been sitting sipping their wine on the divan, jump up and come up to greet him, with a face beaming with laughter.

"What a strange meeting! What a strange meeting!" he exclaimed aloud.

Yucun speedily looked at him, (and remembered) that this person had, in past days, carried on business in a curio establishment in the capital, and that his surname was Leng and his style Zixing.

A mutual friendship had existed between them during their sojourn, in days of yore, in the capital; and as Yucun had entertained the highest opinion of Leng Zixing, as being a man of action and of great abilities, while this Leng Zixing, on the other hand, borrowed of the reputation of refinement enjoyed by Yucun, the two had consequently all along lived in perfect harmony and companionship.

When did you get here?" Yucun eagerly inquired also smilingly. "I wasn't in the least aware of your arrival. This unexpected meeting is positively a strange piece of good fortune."

"I went home," Zixing replied, "about the close of last year, but now as I am again bound to the capital, I passed through here on my way to look up a friend of mine and talk some matters over. He had the kindness to press me to stay with him for a couple of days longer, and as I after all have no urgent business to attend to, I am tarrying a few days, but purpose starting about the middle of the moon. My friend is busy today, so I roamed listlessly as far as here, never dreaming of such a fortunate meeting."

While speaking, he made Yucun sit down at the same table, and ordered a fresh supply of wine and eatables; and as the two friends chatted of one thing and another, they slowly sipped their wine.

The conversation ran on what had occurred after the separation, and Yucun inquired, "Is there any news of any kind in the capital?"

"There's nothing new whatever," answered Zixing. "There is one thing however: in the family of one of your worthy kinsmen, of the same name as yourself, a trifling, but yet remarkable, occurrence has taken place."

"None of my kindred reside in the capital," rejoined Yucun with a smile. "To what can you be alluding?"

"How can it be that you people who have the same surname do not belong to one clan?" remarked Zixing, sarcastically.

"In whose family?" inquired Yucun.

"The Jia family," replied Zixing smiling, "whose quarters are in the Rong Guo Mansion, does not after all reflect discredit upon the lintel of your door, my venerable friend."

"What!" exclaimed Yucun, "did this affair take place in that family? Were we to begin reckoning, we would find the members of my clan to be anything but limited in number. Since the time of our ancestor

Jia Fu, who lived while the Eastern Han dynasty occupied the Throne, the branches of our family have been numerous and flourishing; they are now to be found in every single province, and who could, with any accuracy, ascertain their whereabouts? As regards the Rong Guo branch in particular, their names are in fact inscribed on the same register as our own, but rich and exalted as they are, we have never presumed to claim them as our relatives, so that we have become more and more estranged."

"Don't make any such assertions," Zixing remarked with a sigh, "the present two mansions of Rong and Ning have both alike also offered reverses, and they cannot come up to their state of days of yore."

"Up to this day, these two households of Ning and of Rong," Yucun suggested, "still maintain a very large retinue of people, and how can it be that they have met with reverses?"

"To explain this would be indeed a long story," said Leng Zixing. "Last year," continued Yucun, "I arrived at Jinling as I entertained a wish to visit the remains of interest of the six dynasties, and as I on that day entered the walled town of Shitou, I passed by the entrance of that old residence. On the east side of the street, stood the Ning Guo mansion; on the west the Rong Guo mansion; and these two, adjoining each other as they do, cover in fact well-nigh half of the whole length of the street. Outside the front gate everything was, it is true, lonely and deserted; but at a glance into the interior over the enclosing wall, I perceived that the halls, pavilions, two-storied structures, and porches presented still a majestic and lofty appearance. Even the flower garden, which extends over the whole area of the back grounds, with its trees and rockeries, also possessed to that day an air of luxuriance and freshness, which betrayed no signs of a ruined or decrepid establishment."

"You have had the good fortune of starting in life as a graduate," explained Zixing as he smiled, "and yet are not aware of the saying uttered by someone of old: that a centipede even when dead does not lie stiff. (These families) may, according to your version, not be up to the prosperity of former years, but, compared with the family of an ordinary official, their condition anyhow presents a difference. Of late the number of the inmates has, day by day, been on the increase; their affairs have become daily more numerous; of masters and servants, high and low, who live in ease and respectability very many there are; but of those who exercise any forethought, or make any provision, there is not even one. In their daily wants, their extravagances, and their expenditure, they are also unable to adapt themselves to circumstances and practice economy; (so that though) the present external framework may not have suffered any considerable collapse, their purses have anyhow begun to feel an exhausting process! But this is a mere trifle. There is another more serious matter. Would anyone ever believe that in such families of official status, in a clan of education and culture, the sons and grandsons of the present age would after all be each (succeeding) generation below the standard of the former?"

Yucun, having listened to these remarks, observed: "How ever can it be possible that families of such education and refinement can observe any system of training and nurture which is not excellent? Concerning the other branches, I am not in a position to say anything; but restricting myself to the two mansions of Rong and Ning, they are those in which, above all others, the education of their children is methodical."

"I was just now alluding to none other than these two establishments," Zixing observed with a sigh; "but let me tell you all. In days of yore, the duke of Ning Guo and the duke of Rong Guo were two uterine brothers. The Ning duke was the elder; he had four sons. After the death of the duke of Ning Guo, his eldest son, Jia Daihua, came into the title. He also had two sons; but the eldest, whose name was Fu, died at the age of eight or nine; and the only survivor, the second son, Jia Jing, inherited the title. His whole mind is at this time set upon Daoist doctrines; his sole delight is to burn the pill and refine the dual powers; while every other thought finds no place in his mind. Happily, he had, at an early age, left a son, Jia Zhen, behind in the lay world, and his father, engrossed as his whole heart was with the idea of attaining spiritual life, ceded the succession of the official title to him. His parent is, besides, not willing to return to the original family seat, but lives outside the walls of the capital, foolishly hobnobbing with all the Daoist priests. This Mr. Zhen had also a son Jia Rong, who is, at this period, just in his sixteenth year. Mr. Jing gives at present no attention to anything at all, so that Mr. Zhen naturally devotes no time to his studies, but being bent upon nought else but incessant high pleasure, he has subversed the order of things in the Ning Guo mansion, and yet no one can summon the courage to come and hold him in check. But I'll now tell you about the Rong mansion for your edification. The strange occurrence, to which I alluded just now, came about in this manner. After the demise of the Rong duke, the eldest son, Jia Daishan, inherited the rank. He took to himself as wife, the daughter of Marquis Shi, a noble family of Jinling, by whom he had two sons; the elder being Jia She, the younger Jia Zheng. This Daishan is now dead long ago; but his wife is still alive, and the elder son, Jia She, succeeded to the degree. He is a man of amiable and genial disposition, but he likewise gives no thought to the direction of any domestic concern. The second son

Jia Zheng displayed, from his early childhood, a great liking for books, and grew up to be correct and upright in character. His grandfather doated upon him, and would have had him start in life through the arena of public examinations, but, when least expected, Daishan, being on the point of death, bequeathed a petition, which was laid before the Emperor. His Majesty, out of regard for his former minister, issued immediate commands that the elder son should inherit the estate, and further inquired how many sons there were besides him, all of whom he at once expressed a wish to be introduced in his imperial presence. His Majesty, moreover, displayed exceptional favor, and conferred upon Mr. Zheng the brevet rank of second class Assistant Secretary (of a Board), and commanded him to enter the Board to acquire the necessary experience. He has already now been promoted to the office of second class Secretary. This Mr. Zheng's wife, nee Wang, first gave birth to a son called Jia Zhu, who became a Licentiate in his fourteenth year. At barely twenty, he married, but fell ill and died soon after the birth of a son. Her (Mrs. Cheng's) second child was a daughter, who came into the world, by a strange coincidence, on the first day of the year. She had an unexpected (pleasure) in the birth, the succeeding year, of another son, who, still more remarkable to say, had, at the time of his birth, a piece of variegated and crystal-like brilliant jade in his mouth, on which were yet visible the outlines of several characters. Now, tell me, was not this a novel and strange occurrence? eh?"

"Strange indeed!" exclaimed Yucun with a smile; "but I presume the coming experiences of this being will not be mean."

Zixing gave a faint smile. "One and all," he remarked, "entertain the same idea. Hence it is that his mother doats upon him like upon a precious jewel. On the day of his first birthday, Mr. Zheng readily entertained a wish to put the bent of his inclinations to the test, and placed before the child all kinds of things, without number, for him to grasp from. Contrary to every expectation, he scorned every other object, and, stretching forth his hand, he simply took hold of rouge, powder, and a few hair-pins, with which he began to play. Mr. Zheng experienced at once displeasure, as he maintained that this youth would, by and bye, grow up into a sybarite, devoted to wine and women, and for this reason it is, that he soon began to feel not much attachment for him. But his grandmother is the one who, in spite of everything, prizes him like the breath of her own life. The very mention of what happened is even strange! He is now grown up to be seven or eight years old, and, although exceptionally wilful, in intelligence and precocity, however, not one in a hundred could come up to him! And as for the utterances of this child, they are no less remarkable. The bones and flesh of woman, he argues, are made of water, while those of man of mud. 'Women to my eyes are pure and pleasing,' he says, 'while at the sight of man, I readily feel how corrupt, foul, and repelling they are!' Now tell me, are not these words ridiculous? There can be no doubt whatever that he will by and bye turn out to be a licentious roue."

Yucun, whose countenance suddenly assumed a stern air, promptly interrupted the conversation. "It doesn't quite follow," he suggested. "You people don't, I regret to say, understand the destiny of this child. The fact is that even the old Hanlin scholar Mr. Zheng was erroneously looked upon as a loose rake and dissolute debauchee! But unless a person, through much study of books and knowledge of letters, so increases (in lore) as to attain the talent of discerning the nature of things, and the vigour of mind to fathom the Daoist reason as well as to comprehend the first principle, he is not in a position to form any judgment."

Zixing upon perceiving the weighty import of what he propounded, "Please explain," he asked hastily, "the drift (of your argument)." To which Yucun responded: "Of the human beings created by the operation of heaven and earth, if we exclude those who are gifted with extreme benevolence and extreme viciousness, the rest, for the most part, present no striking diversity. If they be extremely benevolent, they fall in, at the time of their birth, with an era of propitious fortune; while those extremely vicious correspond, at the time of their existence, with an era of calamity. When those who coexist with propitious fortune come into life, the world is in order; when those who coexist with unpropitious fortune come into life, the world is in danger. Yao, Shun, Yu, Cheng Tang, Wen Wang, Wu Wang, Zhou Gong, Zhao Gong, Confucius, Mencius, Dong, Han Xin, Zhou Zi, Cheng Zi, Zhu Zi and Zhang Zi were ordained to see light in an auspicious era. Whereas Chi You, Gong Gong, Jie Wang, Zhou Wang, Shi Huang, Wang Mang, Cao Cao, Huan Wen, An Lushan, Qin Gui, and others were one and all destined to come into the world during a calamitous age. Those endowed with extreme benevolence set the world in order; those possessed of extreme maliciousness turn the world into disorder. Purity, intelligence, spirituality, and subtlety constitute the vital spirit of right which pervades heaven and earth, and the persons gifted with benevolence are its natural fruit. Malignity and perversity consritute the spirit of evil, which permeates heaven and earth, and malicious persons are affected by its influence. The days of perpetual happiness and eminent good fortune, and the era of perfect peace and tranquility, which now prevail, are the offspring of the pure, intelligent, divine, and subtle spirit which ascends above, to the very Emperor, and below reaches the rustic and uncultured classes. Everyone is without exception under its influence. The superfluity of the subtle spirit expands far and wide, and finding nowhere to betake itself to, becomes, in due course, transformed into dew, or gentle breeze; and, by a process of diffusion, it pervades the whole world.

"The spirit of malignity and perversity, unable to expand under the brilliant sky and transmuting sun, eventually coagulates, pervades and stops up the deep gutters and extensive caverns; and when of a sudden the wind agitates it or it be impelled by the clouds, and any slight disposition, on its part, supervenes to set itself in motion, or to break its bounds, and so little as even the minutest fraction does unexpectedly find an outlet, and happens to come across any spirit of perception and subtlety which may be at the time passing by, the spirit of right does not yield to the spirit of evil, and the spirit of evil is again envious of the spirit of right, so that the two do not harmonize. Just like wind, water, thunder, and lightning, which, when they meet in the bowels of the earth, must necessarily, as they are both to dissolve and are likewise unable to yield, clash and explode to the end that they may at length exhaust themselves. Hence it is that these spirits have also forcibly to diffuse themselves into the human race to find an outlet, so that they may then completely disperse, with the result that men and women are suddenly imbued with these spirits and spring into existence. At best, (these human beings) cannot be generated into philanthropists or perfect men; at worst, they cannot also embody extreme perversity or extreme wickedness. Yet placed among one million beings, the spirit of intelligence, refinement, perception, and subtlety will be above these one million beings; while, on the other hand, the perverse, depraved, and inhuman embodiment will likewise be below the million of men. Born in a noble and wealthy family, these men will be a salacious, lustful lot; born of literary, virtuous, or poor Parentage, they will turn out retired scholars or men of mark; though they may by some accident be born in a destitute and poverty-stricken home, they cannot possibly, in fact, ever sink so low as to become runners or menials, or contentedly brook to be of the common herd or to be driven and curbed like a horse in harness. They will become, for a certainty, either actors of note or courtesans of notoriety; as instanced in former years by Xu You, Tao Qian, Yuan Ji, Ji Kang, Liu Ling, the two families of Wang and Xie, Gu Hutou, Chen Houzhu, Tang Minghuang, Song Huizong, Liu Tingzhi, Wen Feiqing, Mi Nangong, Shi Manqing, Liu Qiqing, and Qin Shaoyou, and exemplified now-a-days by Ni Yunlin, Tang Bohu, Zhu Zhishan, and also by Li Guinian, Huang Fanchuo, Jing Xingmo, Zhuo Wenjun; and the women Hong Fu, Xie Tao, Cui Ying, Zhao Yun, and others; all of whom were and are of the same stamp, though placed in different scenes of action."

"From what you say," observed Zixing, "success makes (a man) a duke or a marquis; ruin, a thief!"

"Quite so; that's just my idea!" replied Yucun; "I've not as yet let you know that after my degradation from office, I spent the last couple of years in traveling for pleasure all over each province, and that I also myself came across two extraordinary youths. This is why, when a short while back you alluded to this Baoyu, I at once conjectured, with a good deal of certainty, that he must be a human being of the same stamp. There's no need for me to speak of any farther than the walled city of Jinling. This Mr. Zhen was, by imperial appointment, named Principal of the Government Public College of the Jinling province. Do you perhaps know him?"

"Who doesn't know him?" remarked Zixing. "This Zhen family is an old connection of the Jia family. These two families were on terms of great intimacy, and I myself likewise enjoyed the pleasure of their friendship for many a day."

"Last year, when at Jinling," Yucun continued with a smile, "someone recommended me as resident tutor to the school in the Zhen mansion; and when I moved into it I saw for myself the state of things. Who would ever think that that household was grand and luxurious to such a degree! But they are an affluent family, and withal full of propriety, so that a school like this was of course not one easy to obtain. The pupil, however, was, it is true, a young tyro, but far more troublesome to teach than a candidate for the examination of graduate of the second degree. Were I to enter into details, you would indeed have a laugh. 'I must needs,' he explained, 'have the company of two girls in my studies to enable me to read at all, and to keep likewise my brain clear. Otherwise, if left to myself, my head gets all in a muddle.' Time after time, he further expounded to his young attendants, how extremely honorable and extremely pure were the two words representing woman, that they are more valuable and precious than the auspicious animal, the felicitous bird, rare flowers, and uncommon plants. 'You may not' (he was wont to say), 'on any account heedlessly utter them, you set of foul mouths and filthy tongues! these two words are of the utmost import! Whenever you have occasion to allude to them, you must, before you can do so with impunity, take pure water and scented tea and rinse your mouths. In the event of any slip of the tongue, I shall at once have your teeth extracted, and your eyes gouged out.' His obstinacy and waywardness are, in every respect, out of the common. After he was allowed to leave school, and to return home, he became, at the sight of the young ladies, so tractable, gentle, sharp, and polite, transformed, in fact, like one of them. And though, for this reason, his father has punished him on more than one occasion, by giving him a sound thrashing, such as brought him to the verge of death, he cannot however change. Whenever he was being beaten, and could no more endure the pain, he was wont to promptly break forth in promiscuous loud shouts, 'Girls! girls!' The young ladies, who heard him from the inner chambers, subsequently made fun of him. 'Why,' they said, 'when you are being thrashed, and you are in pain, your only thought is to bawl out girls! Is it perchance that you expect us young ladies to go and intercede for you? How is that you have no sense of shame?' To their taunts he gave a most plausible explanation. 'Once,' he replied, 'when in the agony of pain, I gave vent to shouting girls, in the hope, perchance, I did not then know, of its being able to alleviate the soreness. After I had, with this purpose, given one cry, I really felt the pain considerably better; and now that I have obtained this secret spell, I have recourse, at once, when I am in the height of anguish, to shouts of girls, one shout after another. Now what do you say to this? Isn't this absurd, eh?"

The grandmother is so infatuated by her extreme tenderness for this youth, that, time after time, she has, on her grandson's account, found fault with the tutor, and called her son to task, with the result that I resigned my post and took my leave. A youth, with a disposition such as his, cannot assuredly either perpetuate intact the estate of his father and grandfather, or follow the injunctions of teacher or advice of friends. The pity is, however, that there are, in that family, several excellent female cousins, the like of all of whom it would be difficult to discover."

"Quite so!" remarked Zixing; "there are now three young ladies in the Jia family who are simply perfection itself. The eldest is a daughter of Mr. Zheng, Yuanchun by name, who, on account of her excellence, filial piety, talents, and virtue, has been selected as a governess in the palace. The second is the daughter of Mr. She's handmaid, and is called Yingchun; the third is Tanchun, the child of Mr. Zheng's handmaid; while the fourth is the uterine sister of Mr. Zhen of the Ning Mansion. Her name is Xichun. As dowager lady Shi is so fondly attached to her granddaughters, they come, for the most part, over to their grand-mother's place to prosecute their studies together, and each one of these girls is, I hear, without a fault."

"More admirable," observed Yucun, "is the regime (adhered to) in the Zhen family, where the names of the female children have all been selected from the list of male names, and are unlike all those out-of-the-way names, such as Spring Blossom, Scented Gem, and the like flowery terms in vogue in other families. But how is it that the Jia family have likewise fallen into this common practice?"

"Not so!" ventured Zixing. "It is simply because the eldest daughter was born on the first of the first moon, that the name of Yuanchun was given to her; while with the rest this character Chun (spring) was then followed. The names of the senior generation are, in like manner, adopted from those of their brothers; and there is at present an instance in support of this. The wife of your present worthy master, Mr. Lin, is the uterine sister of Mr. Jia. She and Mr. Jia Zheng, and she went, while at home, under the name of Jia Min. Should you question the truth of what I say, you are at liberty, on your return, to make minute inquiries and you'll be convinced."

Yucun clapped his hands and said smiling, "It's so, I know! for this female pupil of mine, whose name is Daiyu, invariably pronounces the character min as mi, whenever she comes across it in the course of her reading; while, in writing, when she comes to the character 'min,' she likewise reduces the strokes by one, sometimes by two. Often have I speculated in my mind (as to the cause), but the remarks I've heard you mention, convince me, without doubt, that it is no other reason (than that of reverence to her mother's name). Strange enough, this pupil of mine is unique in her speech and deportment, and in no way like any ordinary young lady. But considering that her mother was no commonplace woman herself, it is natural that she should have given birth to such a child. Besides, knowing, as I do now, that she is the granddaughter of the Rong family, it is no matter of surprise to me that she is what she is. Poor girl, her mother, after all, died in the course of the last month."

Zixing heaved a sigh. "Of three elderly sisters," he explained, "this one was the youngest, and she too is gone! Of the sisters of the senior generation not one even survives! But now we'll see what the husbands of this younger generation will be like by and bye!"

"Yes," replied Yucun. "But some while back you mentioned that Mr. Zheng has had a son, born with a piece of jade in his mouth, and that he has besides a tender-aged grandson left by his eldest son; but is it likely that this Mr. She has not, himself, as yet, had any male issue?"

"After Mr. Zheng had this son with the jade," Zixing added, "his handmaid gave birth to another son, who whether he be good or bad, I don't at all know. At all events, he has by his side two sons and a grandson, but what these will grow up to be by and bye, I cannot tell. As regards Mr. Jia She, he too has had two sons; the second of whom, Jia Lian, is by this time about twenty. He took to wife a relative of his, a niece of Mr. Zheng's wife, a Miss Wang, and has now been married for the last two years. This Mr. Lian has lately obtained by purchase the rank of sub-prefect. He too takes little pleasure in books, but as far as worldly affairs go, he is so versatile and glib of tongue, that he has recently taken up his quarters with his uncle Mr. Zheng, to whom he gives a helping hand in the management of domestic matters. Who would have thought it, however, ever since his marriage with his worthy wife, not a single person, whether high or low, has there been who has not looked up to her with regard: with the result that Mr. Lian himself has, in fact, had to take a back seat (lit. withdrew 35 li). In looks, she is also so extremely beautiful, in speech so extremely quick and fluent, in ingenuity so deep and astute, that even a man could, in no way, come up to her mark."

After hearing these remarks Yucun smiled. "You now perceive," he said, "that my argument is no fallacy, and that the several persons about whom you and I have just been talking are, we may presume, human beings, who, one and all, have been generated by the spirit of right, and the spirit of evil, and come to life by the same royal road; but of course there's no saying."

"Enough," cried Zixing, "of right and enough of evil; we've been doing nothing but settling other people's accounts; come now, have another glass, and you'll be the better for it!"

"While bent upon talking," Yucun explained, "I've had more glasses than is good for me."

"Speaking of irrelevant matters about other people," Zixing rejoined complacently, "is quite the thing to help us swallow our wine; so come now; what harm will happen, if we do have a few glasses more."

Yucun thereupon looked out of the window.

"The day is also far advanced," he remarked, "and if we don't take care, the gates will be closing; let us leisurely enter the city, and as we go along, there will be nothing to prevent us from continuing our chat."

Forthwith the two friends rose from their seats, settled and paid their wine bill, and were just going, when they unexpectedly heard someone from behind say with a loud voice:

"Accept my congratulations, Brother Yucun; I've now come, with the express purpose of giving you the welcome news!"

Yucun lost no time in turning his head round to look at the speaker. But reader, if you wish to learn who the man was, listen to the details given in the following chapter.

CHAPTER 3

Lin Ruhai appeals to his brother-in-law,
Jia Zheng, recommending Yucun,
his daughter's tutor, to his consideration.
Dowager lady Jia sends to fetch her
granddaughter, out of commiseration
for her being a motherless child.

But to proceed with our narrative, Yucun, on speedily turning round, perceived that the speaker was no other than a certain Zhang Rugui, an old colleague of his, who had been denounced and deprived of office, on account of some case or other; a native of that district, who had, since his degradation, resided in his family home.

Having lately come to hear the news that a memorial, presented in the capital, that the former officers (who had been cashiered) should be reinstated, had received the imperial consent, he had promptly done all he could, in every nook and corner, to obtain influence, and to find the means (of righting his position,) when he, unexpectedly, came across Yucun, to whom he therefore lost no time in offering his congratulations. The two friends exchanged the conventional salutations, and Zhang Rugui forthwith communicated the tidings to Yucun.

Yucun was delighted, but after he had made a few remarks, in a great hurry, each took his leave and sped on his own way homewards.

Leng Zixing, upon hearing this conversation, hastened at once to propose a plan, advising Yucun to request Lin Ruhai, in his turn, to appeal in the capital to Mr. Jia Zheng for support.

Yucun accepted the suggestion, and parted from his companion.

On his return to his quarters, he made all haste to lay his hand on the Metropolitan Gazette, and having ascertained that the news was authentic, he had on the next day a personal consultation with Ruhai.

"Providence and good fortune are both alike propitious!" exclaimed Ruhai. "After the death of my wife, my mother-in-law, whose residence is in the capital, was so very solicitous on my daughter's account, for having no one to depend upon, that she despatched, at an early period, boats with men and women servants to come and fetch her. But my child was at the time not quite over her illness, and that is why she has not yet started. I was, this very moment, cogitating to send my daughter to the capital. And in view of the obligation, under which I am to you for the instruction you have heretofore conferred upon her, remaining as yet unrequited, there is no reason why, when such an opportunity as this presents itself, I should not do my utmost to find means to make proper acknowledgment. I have already, in anticipation, given the matter my attention, and written a letter of recommendation to my brother-in-law, urging him to put everything right for you, in order that I may, to a certain extent, be able to give effect to my modest wishes. As for any outlay that may prove necessary, I have given proper explanation, in the letter to my brother-in-law, so that you, my brother, need not trouble yourself by giving way to much anxiety."

As Yucun bowed and expressed his appreciation in most profuse language: "Pray," he asked, "where does your honored brother-in-law reside? and what is his official capacity? But I fear I'm too coarse in my manner, and could not presume to obtrude myself in his presence."

Ruhai smiled. "And yet," he remarked, "this brother-in-law of mine is after all of one and the same family as your worthy self, for he is the grandson of the Duke Rong. My elder brother-in-law has now inherited the status of Captain-General of the first grade. His name is She, his style Enhou. My second brother-in-law's name is Zheng, his style is Cunzhou. His present post is that of a Second class Secretary in the Board of Works. He is modest and kindhearted, and has much in him of the habits of his grandfather; not one of that purse-proud and haughty kind of men. That is why I have written to him and made the request on your behalf. Were he different to what he really is, not only would he cast a slur upon your honest purpose, honorable brother, but I myself likewise would not have been as prompt in taking action."

When Yucun heard these remarks, he at length credited what had been told him by Zixing the day before, and he lost no time in again expressing his sense of gratitude to Lin Ruhai.

Ruhai resumed the conversation.

"I have fixed," (he explained,) "upon the second of next month, for my young daughter's departure for the capital, and, if you, brother mine, were to travel along with her, would it not be an advantage to herself, as well as to yourself?"

Yucun signified his acquiescence as he listened to his proposal-feeling in his inner self extremely elated.

Ruhai availed himself of the earliest opportunity to get ready the presents (for the capital) and all the requirements for the journey, which (when completed,) Yucun took over one by one. His pupil could not, at first, brook the idea, of a separation from her father, but the pressing wishes of her grandmother left her no course (but to comply).

"Your father," Ruhai furthermore argued with her, "is already fifty; and I entertain no wish to marry again; and then you are always ailing; besides, with your extreme youth, you have, above, no mother of your own to take care of you, and below, no sisters to attend to you. If you now go and have your maternal grandmother, as well as your mother's brothers and your cousins to depend upon, you will be doing the best thing to reduce the anxiety which I feel in my heart on your behalf. Why then should you not go?"

Daiyu, after listening to what her father had to say, parted from him in a flood of tears and followed her nurse and several old matrons from the Rong mansion on board her boat, and set out on her journey.

Yucun had a boat to himself, and with two youths to wait on him, he prosecuted his voyage in the wake of Daiyu.

By a certain day, they reached Jing Du; and Yucun, after first adjusting his hat and clothes, came, attended by a youth, to the door of the Rong mansion, and sent in a card, which showed his lineage.

Jia Zheng had, by this time, perused his brother-in-law's letter, and he speedily asked him to walk in. When they met, he found in Yucun an imposing manner and polite address.

This Jia Zheng had, in fact, a great penchant above all things for men of education, men courteous to the talented, respectful to the learned, ready to lend a helping hand to the needy and to succour the distressed, and was, to a great extent, like his grandfather. As it was besides a wish intimated by his brother-in-law, he therefore treated Yucun with a consideration still more unusual, and readily strained all his resources to assist him.

On the very day on which the memorial was submitted to the Throne, he obtained by his efforts, a reinstatement to office, and before the expiry of two months, Yucun was forthwith selected to fill the appointment of prefect of Yingtian in Jinling. Taking leave of Jia Zheng, he chose a propitious day, and proceeded to his post, where we will leave him without further notice for the present.

But to return to Daiyu. On the day on which she left the boat, and the moment she put her foot on shore, there were forthwith at her disposal chairs for her own use, and carts for the luggage, sent over from the Rong mansion.

Lin Daiyu had often heard her mother recount how different was her grandmother's house from that of other people's; and having seen for herself how above the common run were already the attendants of the three grades, (sent to wait upon her,) in attire, in their fare, in all their articles of use, "how much more," (she thought to herself) "now that I am going to her home, must I be careful at every step, and circumspect at every moment! Nor must I utter one word too many, nor make one step more than is proper, for fear lest I should be ridiculed by any of them!"

From the moment she got into the chair, and they had entered within the city walls, she found, as she looked around, through the gauze window, at the bustle in the streets and public places and at the immense concourse of people, everything naturally so unlike what she had seen elsewhere.

After they had also been a considerable time on the way, she suddenly caught sight, at the northern end of the street, of two huge squatting lions of marble and of three lofty gates with (knockers representing) the heads of animals. In front of these gates, sat, in a row about ten men in colored hats and fine attire. The main gate was not open. It was only through the side gates, on the east and west, that people went in and came out. Above the center gate was a tablet. On this tablet were inscribed in five large characters "The Ning Guo mansion erected by imperial command."

"This must be grandmother's eldest son's residence," reflected Daiyu.

Towards the east, again, at no great distance, were three more high gateways, likewise of the same kind as those she had just seen. This was the Rong Guo mansion.

They did not however go in by the main gate; but simply made their entrance through the east side door.

With the sedans on their shoulders, (the bearers) proceeded about the distance of the throw of an arrow, when upon turning a corner, they hastily put down the chairs. The matrons, who came behind, one and all also dismounted. (The bearers) were changed for four youths of seventeen or eighteen, with hats and clothes without a blemish, and while they carried the chair, the whole bevy of matrons followed on foot.

When they reached a creeper-laden gate, the sedan was put down, and all the youths stepped back and retired. The matrons came forward, raised the screen, and supported Daiyu to descend from the chair.

Lin Daiyu entered the door with the creepers, resting on the hand of a matron.

On both sides was a verandah, like two outstretched arms. An Entrance Hall stood in the center, in the middle of which was a door-screen of Da Li marble, set in an ebony frame. On the other side of this screen were three very small halls. At the back of these came at once an extensive courtyard, belonging to the main building.

In the front part were five parlors, the frieze of the ceiling of which was all carved, and the pillars ornamented. On either side, were covered avenues, resembling passages through a rock. In the side-rooms were suspended cages, full of parrots of every color, thrushes, and birds of every description.

On the terrace-steps, sat several waiting maids, dressed in red and green, and the whole company of them advanced, with beaming faces, to greet them, when they saw the party approach. "Her venerable ladyship," they said, "was at this very moment thinking of you, miss, and, by a strange coincidence, here you are."

Three or four of them forthwith vied with each other in raising the door curtain, while at the same time was heard someone announce: "Miss Lin has arrived."

No sooner had she entered the room, than she espied two servants supporting a venerable lady, with silver-white hair, coming forward to greet her. Convinced that this lady must be her grandmother, she was about to prostrate herself and pay her obeisance, when she was quickly clasped in the arms of her grandmother, who held her close against her bosom; and as she called her "my liver! my flesh!" (my love! my darling!) she began to sob aloud.

The bystanders too, at once, without one exception, melted into tears; and Daiyu herself found some difficulty in restraining her sobs. Little by little the whole party succeeded in consoling her, and Daiyu at length paid her obeisance to her grandmother. Her ladyship thereupon pointed them out one by one to Daiyu. "This," she said, "is the wife of your uncle, your mother's elder brother; this is the wife of your uncle, her second brother; and this is your eldest sister-in-law Zhu, the wife of your senior cousin Zhu."

Daiyu bowed to each one of them (with folded arms).

"Ask the young ladies in," dowager lady Jia went on to say; "tell them a guest from afar has just arrived, one who comes for the first time; and that they may not go to their lessons."

The servants with one voice signified their obedience, and two of them speedily went to carry out her orders.

Not long after three nurses and five or six waiting-maids were seen ushering in three young ladies. The first was somewhat plump in figure and of medium height; her cheeks had a congealed appearance, like a fresh lichee; her nose was glossy like goose fat. She was gracious, demure, and lovable to look at.

The second had sloping shoulders, and a slim waist. Tall and slender was she in stature, with a face like the egg of a goose. Her eyes so beautiful, with their well-curved eyebrows, possessed in their gaze a bewitching flash. At the very sight of her refined and elegant manners all idea of vulgarity was forgotten.

The third was below the medium size, and her mien was, as yet, childlike.

In their head ornaments, jewelry, and dress, the get-up of the three young ladies was identical.

Daiyu speedily rose to greet them and to exchange salutations. After they had made each other's acquaintance, they all took a seat, whereupon the servants brought the tea. Their conversation was confined to Daiyu's mother—how she had fallen ill, what doctors had attended her, what medicines had been given her, and how she had been buried and mourned; and dowager lady Jia was naturally again in great anguish.

"Of all my daughters," she remarked, "your mother was the one I loved best, and now in a twinkle, she has passed away, before me too, and I've not been able to so much as see her face. How can this not make my heart sore-stricken?"

And as she gave vent to these feelings, she took Daiyu's hand in hers, and again gave way to sobs; and it was only after the members of the family had quickly made use of much exhortation and coaxing, that they succeeded, little by little, in stopping her tears.

They all perceived that Daiyu, despite her youthful years and appearance, was lady-like in her deportment and address, and that though with her delicate figure and countenance, (she seemed as if) unable to bear the very weight of her clothes, she possessed, however, a certain captivating air. And as they readily noticed the symptoms of a weak constitution, they went on in consequence to make inquiries as to what medicines she ordinarily took, and how it was that her complaint had not been cured.

"I have," explained Daiyu, "been in this state ever since I was born; though I've taken medicines from the very time I was able to eat rice, up to the present, and have been treated by ever so many doctors of note, I've not derived any benefit. In the year when I was yet only three, I remember a mangy-headed bonze coming to our house, and saying that he would take me along, and make a nun of me; but my father and mother would, on no account, give their consent. 'As you cannot bear to part from her and to give her up,' he then remarked, 'her ailment will, I fear, never, throughout her life, be cured. If you wish to see her all right, it is only to be done by not letting her, from this day forward, on any account, listen to the sound of weeping, or see, with the exception of her parents, any relatives outside the family circle. Then alone will she be able to go through this existence in peace and in quiet.' No one heeded the nonsensical talk of this raving priest; but here am I, up to this very day, dosing myself with ginseng pills as a tonic."

"What a lucky coincidence!" interposed dowager lady Jia; "some of these pills are being compounded here, and I'll simply tell them to have an extra supply made; that's all."

Hardly had she finished these words, when a sound of laughter was heard from the back courtyard. "Here I am too late!" the voice said, "and not in time to receive the distant visitor!"

"Everyone of all these people," reflected Daiyu, "holds her peace and suppresses the very breath of her mouth; and who, I wonder, is this coming in this reckless and rude manner?"

While, as yet, preoccupied with these thoughts, she caught sight of a crowd of married women and waiting-maids enter from the back room, pressing round a regular beauty.

The attire of this person bore no similarity to that of the young ladies. In all her splendor and luster, she looked like a fairy or a goddess. In her coiffure, she had a band of gold filigree work, representing the eight precious things, inlaid with pearls; and wore pins, at the head of each of which were five phoenixes in a rampant position, with pendants of pearls. On her neck, she had a reddish gold necklet, like coiled dragons, with a fringe of tassels. On her person, she wore a tight-sleeved jacket, of dark red flowered satin, covered with hundreds of butterflies, embroidered in gold, interspersed with flowers. Over all, she had a variegated stiff-silk pelisse, lined with slate-blue ermine; while her nether garments consisted of a jupe of kingfisher-color foreign crepe, brocaded with flowers.

She had a pair of eyes, triangular in shape like those of the red phoenix, two eyebrows, curved upwards at each temple, like willow leaves. Her stature was elegant; her figure graceful; her powdered face like dawning spring, majestic, yet not haughty. Her carnation lips, long before they parted, betrayed a smile.

Daiyu eagerly rose and greeted her.

Old lady Jia then smiled. "You don't know her," she observed. "This is a cunning vixen, who has made quite a name in this establishment! In Nanjing, she went by the appellation of vixen, and if you simply call her Feng Vixen, it will do."

Daiyu was just at a loss how to address her, when all her cousins informed Daiyu, that this was her sister-in-law Lian.

Daiyu had not, it is true, made her acquaintance before, but she had heard her mother mention that her eldest maternal uncle Jia She's son, Jia Lian, had married the niece of Madame Wang, her second brother's wife, a girl who had, from her infancy, purposely been nurtured to supply the place of a son, and to whom the school name of Wang Xifeng had been given.

Daiyu lost no time in returning her smile and saluting her with all propriety, addressing her as my sister-in-law. This Xifeng laid hold of Daiyu's hand, and minutely scrutinised her, for a while, from head to foot; after which she led her back next to dowager lady Jia, where they both took a seat.

"If really there be a being of such beauty in the world," she consequently observed with a smile, "I may well consider as having set eyes upon it today! Besides, in the air of her whole person, she doesn't in fact look like your granddaughter-in-law, our worthy ancestor, but in every way like your ladyship's own kindred-granddaughter! It's no wonder then that your venerable ladyship should have, day after day, had her unforgotten, even for a second, in your lips and heart. It's a pity, however, that this cousin of mine should have such a hard lot! How did it happen that our aunt died at such an early period?"

As she uttered these words, she hastily took her handkerchief and wiped the tears from her eyes.

"I've only just recovered from a fit of crying," dowager lady Jia observed, as she smiled, "and have you again come to start me? Your cousin has only now arrived from a distant journey, and she is so delicate to boot! Besides, we have a few minutes back succeeded in coaxing her to restrain her sobs, so drop at once making any allusion to your former remarks!"

This Xifeng, upon hearing these words, lost no time in converting her sorrow into joy.

"Quite right," she remarked. "But at the sight of my cousin, my whole heart was absorbed in her, and I felt happy, and yet wounded at heart: but having disregarded my venerable ancestor's presence, I deserve to be beaten, I do indeed!"

And hastily taking once more Daiyu's hand in her own: "How old are you, cousin?" she inquired; "Have you been to school? What medicines are you taking? while you live here, you mustn't feel homesick; and if there's anything you would like to eat, or to play with, mind you come and tell me! or should the waiting maids or the matrons fail in their duties, don't forget also to report them to me."

Addressing at the same time the matrons, she went on to ask, "Have Miss Lin's luggage and effects been brought in? How many servants has she brought along with her? Go, as soon as you can, and sweep two lower rooms and ask them to go and rest."

As she spoke, tea and refreshments had already been served, and Xifeng herself handed round the cups and offered the fruits.

Upon hearing the question further put by her maternal aunt Secunda, "Whether the issue of the monthly allowances of money had been finished or not yet?" Xifeng replied: "The issue of the money has also been completed; but a few moments back, when I went along with several servants to the back upper-loft, in search of the satins, we looked for ever so long, but we saw nothing of the kind of satins alluded to by you, madame, yesterday; so may it not be that your memory misgives you?"

"Whether there be any or not, of that special kind, is of no consequence," observed Madame Wang. "You should take out," she therefore went on to add, "any two pieces which first come under your hand, for this cousin of yours to make herself dresses with; and in the evening, if I don't forget, I'll send someone to fetch them."

"I've in fact already made every provision," rejoined Xifeng; "knowing very well that my cousin would be arriving within these two days, I have had everything got ready for her. And when you, madame, go back, if you will pass an eye over everything, I shall be able to send them round."

Madame Wang gave a smile, nodded her head assentingly, but uttered not a word by way of reply.

The tea and fruit had by this time been cleared, and dowager lady Jia directed two old nurses to take Daiyu to go and see her two maternal uncles; whereupon Jia She's wife, Madame Xing, hastily stood up and with a smiling face suggested, "I'll take my niece over; for it will after all be considerably better if I go!"

"Quite so!" answered dowager lady Jia, smiling; "you can go home too, and there will be no need for you to come over again!"

Madame Xing expressed her assent, and forthwith led Daiyu to take leave of Madame Wang. The whole party escorted them as far as the door of the Entrance Hall, hung with creepers, where several youths had drawn a carriage, painted light blue, with a kingfisher-colored hood.

Madame Xing led Daiyu by the hand and they got up into their seats. The whole company of matrons put the curtain down, and then bade the youths raise the carriage; who dragged it along, until they came to an open space, where they at length put the mules into harness.

Going out again by the eastern side gate, they proceeded in an easterly direction, passed the main entrance of the Rong mansion, and entered a lofty doorway painted black. On the arrival in front of the ceremonial gate, they at once dismounted from the curricle, and Madame Xing, hand-in-hand with Daiyu, walked into the court.

"These grounds," surmised Daiyu to herself, "must have been originally converted from a piece partitioned from the garden of the Rong mansion."

Having entered three rows of ceremonial gates they actually caught sight of the main structure, with its vestibules and porches, all of which, though on a small scale, were full of artistic and unique beauty. They were nothing like the lofty, imposing, massive and luxurious style of architecture on the other side, yet the avenues and rockeries, in the various places in the court, were all in perfect taste.

When they reached the interior of the principal pavilion, a large concourse of handmaids and waiting maids, got up in gala dress, were already there to greet them. Madame Xing pressed Daiyu into a seat, while she bade someone go into the outer library and request Mr. Jia She to come over.

In a few minutes the servant returned. "Master," she explained, "says that he has not felt quite well for several days, that as the meeting with Miss Lin will affect both her as well as himself, he does not for the present feel equal to seeing each other, that he advises Miss Lin not to feel despondent or homesick; that she ought to feel quite at home with her venerable ladyship, (her grandmother,) as well as her maternal aunts; that her cousins are, it is true, blunt, but that if all the young ladies associated together in one place, they may also perchance dispel some dullness; that if ever (Miss Lin) has any grievance, she should at once speak out, and on no account feel a stranger; and everything will then be right."

Daiyu lost no time in respectfully standing up, resuming her seat after she had listened to every sentence of the message to her. After a while, she said goodbye, and though Madame Xing used every argument to induce her to stay for the repast and then leave, Daiyu smiled and said, "I shouldn't under ordinary circumstances refuse the invitation to dinner, which you, aunt, in your love kindly extend to me, but I have still to cross over and pay my respects to my maternal uncle Secundus; if I went too late, it would, I fear, be a lack of respect on my part; but I shall accept on another occasion. I hope therefore that you will, dear aunt, kindly excuse me."

"If such be the case," Madame Xing replied, "it's all right." And presently directing two nurses to take her niece over, in the carriage, in which they had come a while back, Daiyu thereupon took her leave; Madame Xing escorting her as far as the ceremonial gate, where she gave some further directions to all the company of servants. She followed the curricle with her eyes so long as it remained in sight, and at length retraced her footsteps.

Daiyu shortly entered the Rong Mansion, descended from the carriage, and preceded by all the nurses, she at once proceeded towards the east, turned a corner, passed through an Entrance Hall, running east and west, and walked in a southern direction, at the back of the Large Hall. On the inner side of a ceremonial gate, and at the upper end of a spacious court, stood a large main building, with five apartments, flanked on both sides by out-houses (stretching out) like the antlers on the head of deer; side-gates, resembling passages through a hill, establishing a thorough communication all round; (a main building) lofty, majestic, solid, and grand, and unlike those in the compound of dowager lady Jia.

Daiyu readily concluded that this at last was the main inner suite of apartments. A raised broad road led in a straight line to the large gate. Upon entering the Hall, and raising her head, she first of all perceived before her a large tablet with blue ground, upon which figured nine dragons of reddish gold. The inscription on this tablet consisted of three characters as large as a peck-measure, and declared that this was the Hall of Glorious Felicity.

At the end, was a row of characters of minute size, denoting the year, month and day, upon which His Majesty had been pleased to confer the tablet upon Jia Yuan, Duke of Rong Guo. Besides this tablet, were numberless costly articles bearing the autograph of the Emperor. On the large black ebony table, engraved with dragons, were placed three antique blue and green bronze tripods, about three feet in height. On the wall hung a large picture representing black dragons, such as were seen in waiting chambers of the Sui dynasty. On one side stood a gold cup of chased work, while on the other, a crystal casket. On the ground were placed, in two rows, sixteen chairs, made of hard-grained cedar.

There was also a pair of scrolls consisting of black-wood antithetical tablets, inlaid with the strokes of words in chased gold. Their burden was this:

On the platform shine resplendent pearls like sun or moon,
And the sheen of the Hall façade gleams like russet sky.

Below, was a row of small characters, denoting that the scroll had been written by the hand of Mu Shi, a fellow-countryman and old friend of the family, who, for his meritorious services, had the hereditary title of Prince of Dong An conferred upon him.

The fact is that Madame Wang was also not in the habit of sitting and resting, in this main apartment, but in three side-rooms on the east, so that the nurses at once led Daiyu through the door of the eastern wing.

On a stove-couch, near the window, was spread a foreign red carpet. On the side of honor, were laid deep red reclining-cushions, with dragons, with gold cash (for scales), and an oblong brown-colored sitting-cushion with gold-cash-spotted dragons. On the two sides, stood one of a pair of small teapoys of foreign lacquer of peach-blossom pattern. On the teapoy on the left, were spread out Wen Wang tripods, spoons, chopsticks and scent-bottles. On the teapoy on the right, were vases from the Ru Kiln, painted with girls of great beauty, in which were placed seasonable flowers; (on it were) also teacups, a tea service and the like articles.

On the floor on the west side of the room, were four chairs in a row, all of which were covered with antimacassars, embroidered with silverish-red flowers, while below, at the feet of these chairs, stood four footstools. On either side, was also one of a pair of high teapoys, and these teapoys were covered with teacups and flower vases.

The other nick-nacks need not be minutely described.

The old nurses pressed Daiyu to sit down on the stove-couch; but, on perceiving near the edge of the couch two embroidered cushions, placed one opposite the other, she thought of the gradation of seats, and did not therefore place herself on the couch, but on a chair on the eastern side of the room; whereupon the waiting maids, in attendance in these quarters, hastened to serve the tea.

While Daiyu was sipping her tea, she observed the headgear, dress, deportment and manners of the several waiting maids, which she really found so unlike what she had seen in other households. She had hardly finished her tea, when she noticed a waiting maid approach, dressed in a red satin jacket, and a waistcoat of blue satin with scollops.

"My lady requests Miss Lin to come over and sit with her," she remarked as she put on a smile.

The old nurses, upon hearing this message, speedily ushered Daiyu again out of this apartment, into the three-roomed small main building by the eastern porch.

On the stove-couch, situated at the principal part of the room, was placed, in a transverse position, a low couch-table, at the upper end of which were laid out, in a heap, books and a tea service. Against the partition-wall, on the east side, facing the west, was a reclining pillow, made of blue satin, neither old nor new.

Madame Wang, however, occupied the lower seat, on the west side, on which was likewise placed a rather shabby blue satin sitting-rug, with a back-cushion; and upon perceiving Daiyu come in she urged her at once to sit on the east side.

Daiyu concluded, in her mind, that this seat must certainly belong to Jia Zheng, and espying, next to the couch, a row of three chairs, covered with antimacassars, strewn with embroidered flowers, somewhat also the worse for use, Daiyu sat down on one of these chairs.

But as Madame Wang pressed her again and again to sit on the couch, Daiyu had at length to take a seat next to her.

"Your uncle," Madame Wang explained, "is gone to observe this day as a fast day, but you'll see him by and bye. There's, however, one thing I want to talk to you about. Your three female cousins are all, it is true, everything that is nice; and you will, when later on you come together for study, or to learn how to do needlework, or whenever, at any time, you romp and laugh together, find them all most obliging; but there's one thing that causes me very much concern. I have here one, who is the very root of retribution, the incarnation of all mischief, one who is a ne'er-do-well, a prince of malignant spirits in this family. He is gone today to pay his vows in the temple, and is not back yet, but you will see him in the evening, when you will readily be able to judge for yourself. One thing you must do, and that is, from this time forth, not to pay any notice to him. All these cousins of yours don't venture to bring any taint upon themselves by provoking him."

Daiyu had in days gone by heard her mother explain that she had a nephew, born into the world, holding a piece of jade in his mouth, who was perverse beyond measure, who took no pleasure in his books, and whose sole great delight was to play the giddy dog in the inner apartments; that her maternal grandmother, on the other hand, loved him so fondly that no one ever presumed to call him to account, so that when, in this instance, she heard Madame Wang's advice, she at once felt certain that it must be this very cousin.

"Isn't it to the cousin born with jade in his mouth, that you are alluding to, aunt?" she inquired as she returned her smile. "When I was at home, I remember my mother telling me more than once of this very cousin, who (she said) was a year older than I, and whose infant name was Baoyu. She added that his disposition was really wayward, but that he treats all his cousins with the utmost consideration. Besides, now that I have come here, I shall, of course, be always together with my female cousins, while the boys will have their own court, and separate quarters; and how ever will there be any cause of bringing any slur upon myself by provoking him?"

"You don't know the reasons (that prompt me to warn you)," replied Madame Wang laughingly. "He is so unlike all the rest, all because he has, since his youth up, been doated upon by our old lady! The fact is that he has been spoilt, through over-indulgence, by being always in the company of his female cousins! If his female cousins pay no heed to him, he is, at any rate, somewhat orderly, but the day his cousins say one word more to him than usual, much trouble forthwith arises, at the outburst of delight in his heart. That's why I enjoin upon you not to heed him. From his mouth, at one time, issue sugared words and mellifluous phrases; and at another, like the heavens devoid of the sun, he becomes a raving fool; so whatever you do, don't believe all he says."

Daiyu was assenting to every bit of advice as it was uttered, when unexpectedly she beheld a waiting-maid walk in. "Her venerable ladyship over there," she said, "has sent word about the evening meal."

Madame Wang hastily took Daiyu by the hand, and emerging by the door of the back-room, they went eastwards by the verandah at the back. Past the side gate, was a roadway, running north and south. On the southern side were a pavilion with three divisions and a Reception Hall with a colonnade. On the north, stood a large screen wall, painted white; behind it was a very small building, with a door of half the ordinary size.

"These are your cousin Feng's rooms," explained Madame Wang to Daiyu, as she pointed to them smiling. "You'll know in future your way to come and find her; and if you ever lack anything, mind you mention it to her, and she'll make it all right."

At the door of this court, were also several youths, who had recently had the tufts of their hair tied together, who all dropped their hands against their sides, and stood in a respectful posture. Madame Wang then led Daiyu by the hand through a corridor, running east and west, into what was dowager lady Jia's back-court. Forthwith they entered the door of the back suite of rooms, where stood, already in attendance, a large number of servants, who, when they saw Madame Wang arrive, set to work setting the tables and chairs in order.

Jia Zhu's wife, nee Li, served the eatables, while Xifeng placed the chopsticks, and Madame Wang brought the soup in. Dowager lady Jia was seated all alone on the divan, in the main part of the apartment, on the two sides of which stood four vacant chairs.

Xifeng at once drew Daiyu, meaning to make her sit in the foremost chair on the left side, but Daiyu steadily and concedingly declined.

"Your aunts and sisters-in-law, standing on the right and left," dowager lady Jia smilingly explained, "won't have their repast in here, and as you're a guest, it's but proper that you should take that seat."

Then alone it was that Daiyu asked for permission to sit down, seating herself on the chair.

Madame Wang likewise took a seat at old lady Jia's instance; and the three cousins, Yingchun and the others, having craved for leave to sit down, at length came forward, and Yingchun took the first chair on the right, Tanchun the second, and Xichun the second on the left. Waiting maids stood by holding in their hands, flips and finger-bowls and napkins, while Mrs. Li and lady Feng, the two of them, kept near the table advising them what to eat, and pressing them to help themselves.

In the outer apartments, the married women and waiting-maids in attendance, were, it is true, very numerous; but not even so much as the sound of the cawing of a crow could be heard.

The repast over, each one was presented by a waiting-maid, with tea in a small tea tray; but the Lin family had all along impressed upon the mind of their daughter that in order to show due regard to happiness, and to preserve good health, it was essential, after every meal, to wait a while, before drinking any tea, so that it should not do any harm to the intestines. When, therefore, Daiyu perceived how many habits there were in this establishment unlike those which prevailed in her home, she too had no alternative but to conform herself to a certain extent with them. Upon taking over the cup of tea, servants came once more and presented finger-bowls for them to rinse their mouths, and Daiyu also rinsed hers; and after they had all again finished washing their hands, tea was eventually served a second time, and this was, at length, the tea that was intended to be drunk.

"You can all go," observed dowager lady Jia, "and let us alone to have a chat."

Madame Wang rose as soon as she heard these words, and having made a few irrelevant remarks, she led the way and left the room along with the two ladies, Mrs. Li and lady Feng.

Dowager lady Jia, having inquired of Daiyu what books she was reading, "I have just begun reading the Four Books," Daiyu replied. "What books are my cousins reading?" Daiyu went on to ask.

"Books, you say!" exclaimed dowager lady Jia; "why all they know are a few characters, that's all."

The sentence was barely out of her lips, when a continuous sounding of footsteps was heard outside, and a waiting maid entered and announced that Baoyu was coming. Daiyu was speculating in her mind how it was that this Baoyu had turned out such a good-for-nothing fellow, when he happened to walk in.

He was, in fact, a young man of tender years, wearing on his head, to hold his hair together, a cap of gold of purplish tinge, inlaid with precious gems. Parallel with his eyebrows was attached a circlet, embroidered with gold, and representing two dragons snatching a pearl. He wore an archery-sleeved deep red jacket, with hundreds of butterflies worked in gold of two different shades, interspersed with flowers; and was girded with a sash of variegated silk, with clusters of designs, to which was attached long tassels; a kind of sash worn in the palace. Over all, he had a slate-blue fringed coat of Japanese brocaded satin, with eight bunches of flowers in relief; and wore a pair of light blue satin white-soled, half-dress court-shoes.

His face was like the full moon at mid-autumn; his complexion, like morning flowers in spring; the hair along his temples, as if chiselled with a knife; his eyebrows, as if pencilled with ink; his nose like a suspended gallbladder (a well-cut and shapely nose); his eyes like vernal waves; his angry look even resembled a smile; his glance, even when stern, was full of sentiment.

Round his neck he had a gold dragon necklace with a fringe; also a cord of variegated silk, to which was attached a piece of beautiful jade.

As soon as Daiyu became conscious of his presence, she was quite taken aback. "How very strange!" she was reflecting in her mind; "it would seem as if I had seen him somewhere or other, for his face appears extremely familiar to my eyes," when she noticed Baoyu face dowager lady Jia and make his obeisance. "Go and see your mother and then come back," remarked her venerable ladyship; and at once he turned round and quitted the room.

On his return, he had already changed his hat and suit. All round his head, he had a fringe of short hair, plaited into small queues, and bound with red silk. The queues were gathered up at the crown, and all the hair, which had been allowed to grow since his birth, was plaited into a thick queue, which looked as black and as glossy as lacquer. Between the crown of the head and the extremity of the queue, hung a string of four large pearls, with pendants of gold, representing the eight precious things. On his person, he wore a long silvery-red coat, more or less old, bestrewn with embroidery of flowers. He had still round his neck the necklet, precious gem, amulet of Recorded Name, philacteries, and other ornaments. Below were partly visible a fir-cone colored brocaded silk pair of trousers, socks spotted with black designs, with ornamented edges, and a pair of deep red, thick-soled shoes.

(Got up as he was now,) his face displayed a still whiter appearance, as if painted, and his eyes as if they were set off with carnation. As he rolled his eyes, they brimmed with love. When he gave utterance to speech, he seemed to smile. But the chief natural pleasing feature was mainly centered in the curve of his eyebrows. The ten thousand and one fond sentiments, fostered by him during the whole of his existence, were all amassed in the corner of his eyes.

His outward appearance may have been pleasing to the highest degree, but yet it was no easy matter to fathom what lay beneath it.

There are a couple of roundelays, composed by a later poet, (after the excellent rhythm of the Xijiang Yue), which depict Baoyu in a most adequate manner.

The roundelays run as follows:

> To gloom and passion prone, without a rhyme,
> Inane and madlike was he many a time,
> His outer self, forsooth, fine may have been,
> But one wild, howling waste his mind within:
> Addled his brain that nothing he could see;
> A dunce! to read essays so loth to be!
> Perverse in bearing, in temper wayward;
> For human censure he had no regard.
> When rich, wealth to enjoy he knew not how;
> When poor, to poverty he could not bow.
> Alas! what utter waste of lustrous grace!
> To state, to family what a disgrace!
> Of ne'er-do-wells below he was the prime,
> Unfilial like him none up to this time.
> Ye lads, pampered with sumptuous fare and dress,
> Beware! In this youth's footsteps do not press!

But to proceed with our story.

"You have gone and changed your clothes," observed dowager lady Jia, "before being introduced to the distant guest. Why don't you yet salute your cousin?"

Baoyu had long ago become aware of the presence of a most beautiful young lady, who, he readily concluded, must be no other than the daughter of his aunt Lin. He hastened to advance up to her, and make his bow; and after their introduction, he resumed his seat, whence he minutely scrutinised her features, (which he thought) so unlike those of all other girls.

Her two arched eyebrows, thick as clustered smoke, bore a certain not very pronounced frowning wrinkle. She had a pair of eyes, which possessed a cheerful, and yet one would say, a sad expression, overflowing with sentiment. Her face showed the prints of sorrow stamped on her two dimpled cheeks. She was beautiful, but her whole frame was the prey of a hereditary disease. The tears in her eyes glistened like small specks. Her balmy breath was so gentle. She was as demure as a lovely flower reflected in the water. Her gait resembled a frail willow, agitated by the wind. Her heart, compared with that of Bi Gan, had one more aperture of intelligence; while her ailment exceeded (in intensity) by three degrees the ailment of Xi Zi.

Baoyu, having concluded his scrutiny of her, put on a smile and said, "This cousin I have already seen in days gone by."

"There you are again with your nonsense," exclaimed lady Jia, sneeringly; "how could you have seen her before?"

"Though I may not have seen her, ere this," observed Baoyu with a smirk, "yet when I look at her face, it seems so familiar, and to my mind, it would appear as if we had been old acquaintances; just as if, in fact, we were now meeting after a long separation."

"That will do! that will do!" remarked dowager lady Jia; "such being the case, you will be the more intimate."

Baoyu, thereupon, went up to Daiyu, and taking a seat next to her, continued to look at her again with all intentness for a good long while.

"Have you read any books, cousin?" he asked.

"I haven't as yet," replied Daiyu, "read any books, as I have only been to school for a year; all I know are simply a few characters."

"What is your worthy name, cousin?" Baoyu went on to ask; whereupon Daiyu speedily told him her name.

"Your style?" inquired Baoyu; to which question Daiyu replied, "I have no style."

"I'll give you a style," suggested Baoyu smilingly; "won't the double style 'Pin Pin,' 'knitting brows,' do very well?"

"From what part of the standard books does that come?" Tanchun hastily interposed.

"It is stated in the Thorough Research into the state of Creation from remote ages to the present day," Baoyu went on to explain, "that, in the western quarter, there exists a stone, called Dai, (black,) which can be used, in lieu of ink, to blacken the eyebrows with. Besides the eyebrows of this cousin taper in a way, as if they were contracted, so that the selection of these two characters is most appropriate, isn't it?"

"This is just another plagiarism, I fear," observed Tanchun, with an ironic smirk.

"Exclusive of the Four Books," Baoyu remarked smilingly, "the majority of works are plagiarized; and is it only I, perchance, who plagiarize? Have you got any jade or not?" he went on to inquire, addressing Daiyu, (to the discomfiture) of all who could not make out what he meant.

"It's because he has a jade himself," Daiyu forthwith reasoned within her mind, that he asks me whether I have one or not. "No; I haven't one," she replied. "That jade of yours is besides a rare object, and how could everyone have one?"

As soon as Baoyu heard this remark, he at once burst out in a fit of his raving complaint, and unclasping the gem, he dashed it disdainfully on the floor. "Rare object, indeed!" he shouted, as he heaped invective on it; "it has no idea how to discriminate the excellent from the mean, among human beings; and do tell me, has it any perception or not? I too can do without this rubbish!"

All those, who stood below, were startled; and in a body they pressed forward, vying with each other as to who should pick up the gem.

Dowager lady Jia was so distressed that she clasped Baoyu in her embrace. "You child of wrath," she exclaimed. "When you get into a passion, it's easy enough for you to beat and abuse people; but what makes you fling away that stem of life?"

Baoyu's face was covered with the traces of tears. "All my cousins here, senior as well as junior," he rejoined, as he sobbed, "have no gem, and if it's only I to have one, there's no fun in it, I maintain! and now comes this angelic sort of cousin, and she too has none, so that it's clear enough that it is no profitable thing."

Dowager lady Jia hastened to coax him. "This cousin of yours," she explained, "would, under former circumstances, have come here with a jade; and it's because your aunt felt unable, as she lay on her deathbed, to reconcile herself to the separation from your cousin, that in the absence of any remedy, she forthwith took the gem belonging to her (daughter), along with her (in the grave); so that, in the first place, by the fulfilment of the rites of burying the living with the dead might be accomplished the filial piety of your cousin; and in the second place, that the spirit of your aunt might also, for the time being, use it to gratify the wish of gazing on your cousin. That's why she simply told you that she had no jade; for she couldn't very well have had any desire to give vent to self-praise. Now, how can you ever compare yourself with her? and don't you yet carefully and circumspectly put it on? Mind, your mother may come to know what you have done!"

As she uttered these words, she speedily took the jade over from the hand of the waiting-maid, and she herself fastened it on for him.

When Baoyu heard this explanation, he indulged in reflection, but could not even then advance any further arguments.

A nurse came at the moment and inquired about Daiyu's quarters, and dowager lady Jia at once added, "Shift Baoyu along with me, into the warm room of my suite of apartments, and put your mistress, Miss Lin, temporarily in the green gauze house; and when the rest of the winter is over, and repairs are taken in hand in spring in their rooms, an additional wing can be put up for her to take up her quarters in."

"My dear ancestor," ventured Baoyu; "the bed I occupy outside the green gauze house is very comfortable; and what need is there again for me to leave it and come and disturb your old ladyship's peace and quiet?"

"Well, all right," observed dowager lady Jia, after some consideration; "but let each one of you have a nurse, as well as a waiting-maid to attend on you; the other servants can remain in the outside rooms and keep night watch and be ready to answer any call."

At an early hour, besides, Xifeng had sent a servant round with a grey flowered curtain, embroidered coverlets and satin quilts and other such articles.

Daiyu had brought along with her only two servants; the one was her own nurse, dame Wang, and the other was a young waiting-maid of sixteen, whose name was called Xueyan. Dowager lady Jia, perceiving that Xueyan was too youthful and quite a child in her manner, while nurse Wang was, on the other hand, too aged, conjectured that Daiyu would, in all her wants, not have things as she liked, so she detached a waiting-maid, who was her own personal attendant, named Yingge and attached her to Daiyu's service. Just as had Yingchun and the other girls, each one of whom had besides the wet nurses of their youth, four other nurses to advise and direct them, and exclusive of two personal maids to look after their dress and toilette, four or five additional young maids to do the washing and sweeping of the rooms and the running about backwards and forwards on errands.

Nurse Wang, Yingge and other girls entered at once upon their attendance on Daiyu in the green gauze rooms, while Baoyu's wet-nurse, dame Li, together with an elderly waiting-maid, called Xiren, were on duty in the room with the large bed.

This Xiren had also been, originally, one of dowager lady Jia's servant-girls. Her name was in days gone by, Zhenzhu. As her venerable ladyship, in her tender love for Baoyu, had feared that Baoyu's servant girls were not equal to their duties, she readily handed her to Baoyu, as she had hitherto had experience of how sincere and considerate she was at heart.

Baoyu, knowing that her surname was at one time Hua, and having once seen in some verses of an ancient poet, the line "the fragrance of flowers wafts itself into man," lost no time in explaining the fact to dowager lady Jia, who at once changed her name into Xiren.

This Xiren had several simple traits. While in attendance upon dowager lady Jia, in her heart and her eyes there was no one but her venerable ladyship, and her alone; and now in her attendance upon Baoyu, her heart and her eyes were again full of Baoyu, and him alone. But as Baoyu was of a perverse temperament and did not heed her repeated injunctions, she felt at heart exceedingly grieved.

At night, after nurse Li had fallen asleep, seeing that in the inner chambers, Daiyu, Yingge and the others had not as yet retired to rest, she disrobed herself, and with gentle step walked in.

"How is it, miss," she inquired smiling, "that you have not turned in as yet?"

Daiyu at once put on a smile. "Sit down, sister," she rejoined, pressing her to take a seat. Xiren sat on the edge of the bed.

"Miss Lin," interposed Yingge smirkingly, "has been here in an awful state of mind! She has cried so to herself, that her eyes were flooded, as soon as she dried her tears. 'It's only today that I've come,' she said, 'and I've already been the cause of the outbreak of your young master's failing. Now had he broken that jade, as he hurled it on the ground, wouldn't it have been my fault? Hence it was that she was so wounded at heart, that I had all the trouble in the world, before I could appease her."

"Desist at once, Miss! Don't go on like this," Xiren advised her; "there will, I fear, in the future, happen things far more strange and ridiculous than this; and if you allow yourself to be wounded and affected to such a degree by a conduct such as his, you will, I apprehend, suffer endless wounds and anguish; so be quick and dispel this oversensitive nature!"

"What you sisters advise me," replied Daiyu, "I shall bear in mind, and it will be all right."

They had another chat, which lasted for some time, before they at length retired to rest for the night.

The next day, (she and her cousins) got up at an early hour and went over to pay their respects to dowager lady Jia, after which upon coming to Madame Wang's apartments, they happened to find Madame Wang and Xifeng together, opening the letters which had arrived from Jinling. There were also in the room two married women, who had been sent from Madame Wang's elder brother's wife's house to deliver a message.

Daiyu was, it is true, not aware of what was up, but Tanchun and the others knew that they were discussing the son of her mother's sister, married in the Xue family, in the city of Jinling, a cousin of theirs, Xue Pan, who relying upon his wealth and influence had, by assaulting a man, committed homicide, and who was now to be tried in the court of the Yingtian Prefecture.

Her maternal uncle, Wang Ziteng, had now, on the receipt of the tidings, despatched messengers to bring over the news to the Jia family. But the next chapter will explain what was the ultimate issue of the wish entertained in this mansion to send for the Xue family to come to the capital.

CHAPTER 4

An ill-fated girl happens to meet an ill-fated young man. The Hulu Bonze adjudicates the Hulu case.

Daiyu, for we shall now return to our story, having come, along with her cousin to Madame Wang's apartments, found Madame Wang discussing certain domestic occurrences with the messengers, who had arrived from her elder brother's wife's home, and conversing also about the case of homicide, in which the family of her mother's sister had become involved, and other such relevant topics. Perceiving how pressing and perplexing were the matters in which Madame Wang was engaged, the young ladies promptly left her apartments, and came over to the rooms of their widow sister-in-law, Mrs. Li.

This Mrs. Li had originally been the spouse of Jia Zhu. Although Zhu had died at an early age, he had the good fortune of leaving behind him a son, to whom the name of Jia Lan was given. He was, at this period, just in his fifth year, and had already entered school, and applied himself to books.

This Mrs. Li was also the daughter of an official of note in Jinling. Her father's name was Li Shouzhong, who had, at one time, been Imperial Libationer. Among his kindred, men as well as women had all devoted themselves to poetry and letters; but ever since Li Shouzhong continued the line of succession, he readily asserted that the absence of literary attainments in his daughter was indeed a virtue, so that it soon came about that she did not apply herself in real earnest to learning; with the result that all she studied were some parts of the "Four Books for women," and the "Memoirs of excellent women," that all she read did not extend beyond a limited number of characters, and that all she committed to memory were the examples of these few worthy female characters of dynasties of yore; while she attached special importance to spinning and female handiwork. To this reason is to be assigned the name selected for her, of Li Wan (Li, the weaver), and the style of Gongcai (Palace Sempstress).

Hence it was that, though this Li Wan still continued, after the loss of her mate, while she was as yet in the spring of her life, to live amidst affluence and luxury, she nevertheless resembled in every respect a block of rotten wood or dead ashes. She had no inclination whatsoever to inquire after anything or to listen to anything; while her sole and exclusive thought was to wait upon her relatives and educate her son; and, in addition to this, to teach her young sisters-in-law to do needlework and to read aloud.

Daiyu was, it is true, at this period living as a guest in the Jia mansion, where she certainly had the several young ladies to associate with her, but, outside her aged father, (she thought) there was really no need for her to extend affection to any of the rest.

But we will now speak of Jia Yucun. Having obtained the appointment of Prefect of Yingtian, he had no sooner arrived at his post than a charge of manslaughter was laid before his court. This had arisen from some rivalry between two parties in the purchase of a slave-girl, either of whom would not yield his right; with the result that a serious assault occurred, which ended in homicide.

Yucun had, with all promptitude, the servants of the plaintiffs brought before him, and subjected them to an examination.

"The victim of the assault," the plaintiffs deposed, "was your servants' master. Having on a certain day, purchased a servant-girl, she unexpectedly turned out to be a girl who had been carried away and sold by a kidnapper. This kidnapper had, first of all, got hold of our family's money, and our master had given out that he would on the third day, which was a propitious day, take her over into the house, but this kidnapper stealthily sold her over again to the Xue family. When we came to know of this, we went in search of the seller to lay hold of him, and bring back the girl by force. But the Xue party has been all along the bully of Jinling, full of confidence in his wealth, full of presumption on account of his prestige; and his arrogant menials in a body seized our master and beat him to death. The murderous master and his crew have all long ago made good their escape, leaving no trace behind them, while there only remain several parties not concerned in the affair. Your servants have for a whole year lodged complaints, but there has been no one to do our cause justice, and we therefore implore your Lordship to have the bloodstained criminals arrested, and thus conduce to the maintenance of humanity and benevolence; and the living, as well as the dead, will feel boundless gratitude for this heavenly bounty."

When Yucun heard their appeal, he flew into a fiery rage. "What!" he exclaimed. "How could a case of such gravity have taken place as the murder of a man, and the culprits have been allowed to run away scot-free, without being arrested? Issue warrants, and despatch constables to at once lay hold of the relatives of the bloodstained criminals and bring them to be examined by means of torture."

Thereupon he espied a Retainer, who was standing by the judgment-table, and winked at him, signifying that he should not issue the warrants. Yucun gave way to secret suspicion, and felt compelled to desist.

Withdrawing from the Court-room, he retired into a private chamber, from whence he dismissed his followers, only keeping this single Retainer to wait upon him.

The Retainer speedily advanced and paid his obeisance. "Your worship," he said smiling, "has persistently been rising in official honors, and increasing in wealth so that, in the course of about eight or nine years, you have forgotten me."

"Your face is, however, extremely familiar," observed Yucun, "but I cannot, for the moment, recall who you are."

"Honorable people forget many things," remarked the Retainer, as he smiled. "What! Have you even forgotten the place where you started in life? and do you not remember what occurred, in years gone by, in the Hulu Temple?"

Yucun was filled with extreme astonishment; and past events then began to dawn upon him.

The fact is that this Retainer had been at one time a young priest in the Hulu temple; but as, after its destruction by fire, he had no place to rest his frame, he remembered how light and easy was, after all, this kind of occupation, and being unable to reconcile himself to the solitude and quiet of a temple, he accordingly availed himself of his years, which were as yet few, to let his hair grow, and become a retainer.

Yucun had had no idea that it was he. Hastily taking his hand in his, he smilingly observed, "You are, indeed, an old acquaintance!" and then pressed him to take a seat, so as to have a chat with more ease, but the Retainer would not presume to sit down.

"Friendships," Yucun remarked, putting on a smiling expression, "contracted in poor circumstances should not be forgotten! This is a private room; so that if you sat down, what would it matter?"

The Retainer thereupon craved permission to take a seat, and sat down gingerly, all awry.

"Why did you, a short while back," Yucun inquired, "not allow me to issue the warrants?"

"Your illustrious office," replied the Retainer, "has brought your worship here, and is it likely you have not transcribed some philactery of your post in this province!"

"What is an office-philactery?" asked Yucun with alacrity.

"Now-a-days," explained the Retainer, "those who become local officers provide themselves invariably with a secret list, in which are entered the names and surnames of the most influential and affluent gentry of note in the province. This is in vogue in every province. Should inadvertently, at any moment, one give umbrage to persons of this status, why, not only office, but I fear even one's life, it would be difficult to preserve. That's why these lists are called office-philacteries. This Xue family, just a while back spoken of, how could your worship presume to provoke? This case in question affords no difficulties whatever in the way of a settlement; but the prefects, who have held office before you, have all, by doing violence to the feelings and good name of these people, come to the end they did."

As he uttered these words, he produced, from inside a purse which he had handy, a transcribed office-philactery, which he handed over to Yucun; who upon perusal, found it full of trite and unpolished expressions of public opinion, with regard to the leading clans and notable official families in that particular district. They ran as follows:

The "Jia" family is not "jia," a myth; white jade form the Halls; gold compose their horses! The "A Fang" Palace is three hundred li in extent, but is no fit residence for a "Shi" of Jinling. The eastern seas lack white jade beds, and the "Long Wang," king of the Dragons, has come to ask for one of the Jinling Wang, (Mr. Wang of Jinling.) In a plenteous year, snow, (Xue,) is very plentiful; their pearls and gems are like sand, their gold like iron.

Scarcely had Yucun done reading, when suddenly was heard the announcement, communicated by the beating of a gong, that Mr. Wang had come to pay his respects.

Yucun hastily adjusted his official clothes and hat, and went out of the room to greet and receive the visitor. Returning after a short while he proceeded to question the Retainer (about what he had been perusing.)

"These four families," explained the Retainer, "are all interlaced by ties of relationship, so that if you offend one, you offend all; if you honor one, you honor all. For support and protection, they all have those to take care of their interests! Now this Xue, who is charged with homicide, is indeed the Xue implied by 'in a plenteous year, (Xue,) snow, is very plentiful.' In fact, not only has he these three families to rely upon, but his (father's) old friends, and his own relatives and friends are both to be found in the capital, as well as abroad in the provinces; and they are, what is more, not few in number. Who is it then that your Worship purposes having arrested?"

When Yucun had heard these remarks, he forthwith put on a smile and inquired of the Retainer, "If what you say be true, how is then this lawsuit to be settled? Are you also perchance well aware of the place of retreat of this homicide?"

"I don't deceive your Worship," the Retainer ventured smiling, "when I say that not only do I know the hiding-place of this homicide, but that I also am acquainted with the man who kidnapped and sold the girl; I likewise knew full well the poor devil and buyer, now deceased. But wait, and I'll tell your worship all, with full details. This person, who succumbed to the assault, was the son of a minor gentry. His name was Feng Yuan. His father and mother are both deceased, and he has likewise no brothers. He looked after some scanty property in order to eke out a living. His age was eighteen or nineteen; and he had a strong penchant for men's, and not much for women's society. But this was too the retribution (for sins committed) in a previous existence! for coming, by a strange coincidence, in the way of this kidnapper, who was selling the maid, he straightway at a glance fell in love with this girl, and made up his mind to purchase her and make her his second wife; entering an oath not to associate with any male friends, nor even to marry another girl. And so much in earnest was he in this matter that he had to wait until after the third day before she could enter his household (so as to make the necessary preparations for the marriage). But who would have foreseen the issue? This kidnapper quietly disposed of her again by sale to the Xue family; his intention being to pocket the price-money from both parties, and effect his escape. Contrary to his calculations, he couldn't after all run away in time, and the two buyers laid hold of him and beat him, till he was half dead; but neither of them would take his coin back, each insisting upon the possession of the girl. But do you think that young gentleman, Mr. Xue, would yield his claim to her person? Why, he at once summoned his servants and bade them have recourse to force; and, taking this young man Feng, they assailed him till they made mincemeat of him. He was then carried back to his home, where he finally died after the expiry of three days. This young Mr. Xue had previously chosen a day, on which he meant to set out for the capital, and though he had beaten the young man Feng to death, and carried off the girl, he nevertheless behaved in the manner of a man who had had no concern in the affair. And all he gave his mind to was to take his family and go along on his way; but not in any wise in order to evade (the consequences) of this (occurrence). This case of homicide, (he looked upon) as a most trivial and insignificant matter, which, (he thought), his brother and servants, who were on the spot, would be enough to settle. But, however, enough of this person. Now does your worship know who this girl is who was sold?"

"How could I possibly know?" answered Yucun.

"And yet," remarked the Retainer, as he laughed coldly, "this is a person to whom you are indebted for great obligations; for she is no one else than the daughter of Mr. Chen, who lived next door to the Hulu temple. Her infant name is 'Yinglian.'"

"What! is it really she?" exclaimed Yucun full of surprise. "I heard that she had been kidnapped, ever since she was five years old; but has she only been sold recently?"

"Kidnappers of this kind," continued the Retainer, "only abduct infant girls, whom they bring up till they reach the age of twelve or thirteen, when they take them into strange districts and dispose of them through their agents. In days gone by, we used daily to coax this girl, Yinglian, to romp with us, so that we got to be exceedingly friendly. Hence it is that though, with the lapse of seven or eight years, her mien has assumed a more surpassingly lovely appearance, her general features have, on the other hand, undergone no change; and this is why I can recognise her. Besides, in the center of her two eyebrows, she had a spot, of the size of a grain of rice, of carnation color, which she has had ever since she was born into the world. This kidnapper, it also happened, rented my house to live in; and on a certain day, on which the kidnapper was not at home, I even set her a few questions. She said, that the kidnapper had so beaten her, that she felt intimidated, and couldn't on any account, venture to speak out; simply averring that the kidnapper was her own father, and that, as he had no funds to repay his debts, he had consequently disposed of her by sale! I tried time after time to induce her to answer me, but she again gave way to tears and added no more than: 'I don't really remember anything of my youth.' Of this, anyhow, there can be no doubt; on a certain day the young man Feng and the kidnapper met, said the money was paid down; but as the kidnapper happened to be intoxicated, Yinglian exclaimed, as she sighed: 'My punishment has this day been consummated!' Later on again, when she heard that young Feng would, after three days, have her taken over to his house, she once more underwent a change and put on such a sorrowful look that, unable to brook the sight of it, I waited till the kidnapper went out, when I again told my wife to go and cheer her by representing to her that this Mr. Feng's fixed purpose to wait for a propitious day, on which to come and take her over, was ample proof that he would not look upon her as a servant-girl. 'Furthermore,' (explained my wife to her), 'he is a sort of person exceedingly given to fast habits, and has at home ample means to live upon, so that if, besides, with his extreme aversion to women, he actually purchases you now, at a fancy price, you should be able to guess the issue, without any explanation. You have to bear suspense only for two or three days, and what need is there to be sorrowful and dejected?' After these assurances, she became somewhat composed, flattering herself that she would from henceforth have a home of her own.

"But who would believe that the world is but full of disappointments! On the succeeding day, it came about that the kidnapper again sold her to the Xue family! Had he disposed of her to any other party, no harm would anyhow have resulted; but this young gentleman Xue, who is nicknamed by all, 'the Foolish and overbearing Prince,' is the most perverse and passionate being in the whole world. What is more, he throws money away as if it were dust. The day on which he gave the thrashing with blows like falling leaves and flowing water, he dragged (lit. pull alive, drag dead) Yinglian away more dead than alive, by sheer force, and no one, even up to this date, is aware whether she be among the dead or the living. This young Feng had a spell of empty happiness; for (not only) was his wish not fulfilled, but on the contrary he spent money and lost his life; and was not this a lamentable case?"

When Yucun heard this account he also heaved a sigh. "This was indeed," he observed, "a retribution in store for them! Their encounter was likewise not accidental; for had it been, how was it that this Feng Yuan took a fancy to Yinglian?

"This Yinglian had, during all these years, to endure much harsh treatment from the hands of the kidnapper, and had, at length, obtained the means of escape; and being besides full of warm feeling, had he actually made her his wife, and had they come together, the event would certainly have been happy; but, as luck would have it, there occurred again this contretemps.

"This Xue is, it is true, more laden with riches and honors than Feng was, but when we bear in mind what kind of man he is he certainly, with his large bevy of handmaids, and his licentious and inordinate habits, cannot ever be held equal to Feng Yuan, who had set his heart upon one person! This may appositely be termed a fantastic sentimental destiny, which, by a strange coincidence, befell a couple consisting of an ill-fated young fellow and girl! But why discuss third parties? The only thing now is how to decide this case, so as to put things right."

"Your worship," remarked the Retainer smiling, "displayed, in years gone by, such great intelligence and decision, and how is it that today you, on the contrary, become a person without any resources! Your servant has heard that the promotion of your worship to fill up this office is due to the exertions of the Jia and Wang families; and as this Xue Pan is a relative of the Jia mansion, why doesn't your worship take your craft along with the stream, and bring, by the performance of a kindness, this case to an issue, so that you may again in days to come, be able to go and face the two Dukes Jia and Wang?"

"What you suggest," replied Yucun, "is, of course, right enough; but this case involves a human life, and honored as I have been, by His Majesty the Emperor, by a restoration to office, and selection to an appointment, how can I at the very moment, when I may strain all my energies to show my gratitude, by reason of a private consideration, set the laws at nought? This is a thing which I really haven't the courage to do."

"What your worship says is naturally right and proper," remarked the Retainer at these words, smiling sarcastically, "but at the present stage of the world, such things cannot be done. Haven't you heard the saying of a man of old to the effect that great men take action suitable to the times. 'He who presses,' he adds, 'towards what is auspicious and avoids what is inauspicious is a perfect man.' From what your worship says, not only you couldn't, by any display of zeal, repay your obligation to His Majesty, but, what is more, your own life you will find it difficult to preserve. There are still three more considerations necessary to insure a safe settlement."

Yucun drooped his head for a considerable time.

"What is there in your idea to be done?" he at length inquired.

"Your servant," responded the Retainer, "has already devised a most excellent plan. It's this: Tomorrow, when your Lordship sits in court, you should, merely for form's sake, make much ado, by despatching letters and issuing warrants for the arrest of the culprits. The murderer will naturally not be forthcoming; and as the plaintiffs will be strong in their displeasure, you will of course have some members of the clan of the Xue family, together with a few servants and others, taken into custody, and examined under torture, when your servant will be behind the scenes to bring matters to a settlement, by bidding them report that the victim had succumbed to a sudden ailment, and by urging the whole number of the kindred, as well as the headmen of the place, to hand in a declaration to that effect. Your Worship can aver that you understand perfectly how to write charms in dust, and conjure the spirit; having had an altar, covered with dust, placed in the court, you should bid the military and people to come and look on to their heart's content. Your Worship can give out that the divining spirit has declared: 'that the deceased, Feng Yuan, and Xue Pan had been enemies in a former life, that having now met in the narrow road, their

destinies were consummated; that Xue Pan has, by this time, contracted some indescribable disease and perished from the effects of the per-
secution of the spirit of Feng.' That as the calamity had originated
entirely from the action of the kidnapper, exclusive of dealing with the
kidnapper according to law, the rest need not be interfered with, and
so on. Your servant will be in the background to speak to the kidnapper and urge him to make a full confession; and when people find that
the response of the divining spirit harmonizes with the statements of
the kidnapper, they will, as a matter of course, entertain no suspicion.

"The Xue family have plenty of money, so that if your Worship adjudicates that they should pay five hundred, they can afford it, or one
thousand will also be within their means; and this sum can be handed
to the Feng family to meet the outlay of burning incense and burial expenses. The Feng family are, besides, people of not much consequence,
and (the fuss made by them) being simply for money, they too will,
when they have got the cash in hand, have nothing more to say. But
may it please your worship to consider carefully this plan and see what
you think of it?"

"It isn't a safe course! It isn't a safe course!" Yucun observed as he
smiled. "Let me further think and deliberate; and possibly by succeeding in suppressing public criticism, the matter might also be settled."

These two closed their consultation by a fixed determination, and
the next day, when he sat in judgment, he marked off a whole company
of the plaintiffs as well as of the accused, as were mentioned by name,
and had them brought before him. Yucun examined them with additional minuteness, and discovered in point of fact, that the inmates of
the Feng family were extremely few, that they merely relied upon this
charge with the idea of obtaining some compensation for joss-sticks
and burials; and that the Xue family, presuming on their prestige and
confident of patronage, had been obstinate in the refusal to make any
mutual concession, with the result that confusion had supervened, and
that no decision had been arrived at.

Following readily the bent of his feelings, Yucun disregarded the
laws, and adjudicated this suit in a random way; and as the Feng family came in for a considerable sum, with which to meet the expense for
incense and the funeral, they had, after all, not very much to say (in
the way of objections).

With all despatch, Yucun wrote and forwarded two letters, one to Jia
Zheng, and the other to Wang Ziteng, at that time commander-in-chief
of a Metropolitan Division, simply informing them: that the case, in
which their worthy nephew was concerned, had come to a close, and
that there was no need for them to give way to any extreme solicitude.

This case had been settled through the exclusive action of the young priest of the Hulu temple, now an official Retainer; and Yucun, apprehending, on the other hand, lest he might in the presence of others, divulge the circumstances connected with the days gone by, when he was in a state of penury, naturally felt very unhappy in his mind. But at a later period, he succeeded, by ultimately finding in him some shortcoming, and deporting him to a far-away place, in setting his fears at rest.

But we will put Yucun on one side, and refer to the young man Xue, who purchased Yinglian, and assaulted Feng Yuan to death.

He too was a native of Jinling and belonged to a family literary during successive generations; but this young Xue had recently, when of tender age, lost his father, and his widowed mother out of pity for his being the only male issue and a fatherless child, could not help doating on him and indulging him to such a degree, that when he, in course of time, grew up to years of manhood, he was good for nothing.

In their home, furthermore, was the wealth of a millionaire, and they were, at this time, in receipt of an income from His Majesty's privy purse, for the purvey of various articles.

This young Xue went at school under the name of Pan. His style was Wenqi. His natural habits were extravagant; his language haughty and supercilious. He had, of course, also been to school, but all he knew was a limited number of characters, and those not well. The whole day long, his sole delight was in cock-fighting and horse-racing, rambling over hills and doing the sights.

Though a Purveyor, by Imperial appointment, he had not the least idea of anything relating to matters of business or of the world. All he was good for was: to take advantage of the friendships enjoyed by his grandfather in days of old, to present himself at the Board of Revenue to perfunctorily sign his name, and to draw the allowance and rations; while the rest of his affairs he, needless to say, left his partners and old servants of the family to manage for him.

His widowed mother, a Miss Wang, was the youngest sister of Wang Ziteng, whose present office was that of Commander-in-Chief of a Metropolitan Division; and was, with Madame Wang, the spouse of Jia Zheng, of the Rong Guo Mansion, sisters born of one mother. She was, in this year, more or less forty years of age and had only one son: this Xue Pan.

She also had a daughter, who was two years younger than Xue Pan, and whose infant name was Baochai. She was beautiful in appearance, and elegant and refined in deportment. In days gone by, when her father lived, he was extremely fond of this girl, and had her read books and study characters, so that, as compared with her brother, she was actually a hundred times his superior. Having become aware, ever since her father's death, that her brother could not appease the anguish of her mother's heart, she at once dispelled all thoughts of books, and gave her sole mind to needlework, to the menage and other such concerns, so as to be able to participate in her mother's sorrow, and to bear the fatigue in lieu of her.

As of late the Emperor on the Throne held learning and propriety in high esteem. His Majesty called together and singled out talent and ability, upon which he deigned to display exceptional grace and favor. Besides the number called forth from private life and chosen as Imperial secondary wives, the daughters of families of hereditary official status and renown were without exception, reported by name to the authorities, and communicated to the Board, in anticipation of the selection for maids in waiting to the Imperial Princesses and daughters of Imperial Princes in their studies, and for filling up the offices of persons of eminence, to urge them to become excellent.

Ever since the death of Xue Pan's father, the various assistants, managers, and partners, and other employees in the respective provinces, perceiving how youthful Xue Pan was in years, and how much he lacked worldly experience, readily availed themselves of the time to begin swindling and defrauding. The business, carried on in various different places in the capital, gradually also began to fall off and to show a deficit.

Xue Pan had all along heard that the capital was the one place for gaieties, and was just entertaining the idea of going on a visit, when he eagerly jumped at the opportunity (that presented itself,) first of all to escort his sister, who was going to wait for the selection, in the second place to see his relatives, and in the third to enter personally the capital, (professedly) to settle up long-standing accounts, and to make arrangements for new outlays, but, in reality, with the sole purpose of seeing the life and splendor of the metropolis.

He therefore, had, at an early period, got ready his baggage and small luggage, as well as the presents for relatives and friends, things of every description of local production, presents in acknowledgment of favors received, and other such effects, and he was about to choose a day to start on his journey when unexpectedly he came in the way of the kidnapper who offered Yinglian for sale. As soon as Xue Pan saw how *distinguée* Yinglian was in her appearance, he formed the resolution of buying her; and when he encountered Feng Yuan, come with the object of depriving him of her, he in the assurance of superiority, called his sturdy menials together, who set upon Feng Yuan and beat him to death. Forthwith collecting all the affairs of the household, and entrusting them one by one to the charge of some members of the clan and several elderly servants of the family, he promptly took his mother, sister, and others and after all started on his distant journey, while the charge of homicide he, however, treated as child's play, flattering himself that if he spent a few filthy pieces of money, there was no doubt as to its settlement.

He had been on his journey how many days he had not reckoned, when, on a certain day, as they were about to enter the capital, he furthermore heard that his maternal uncle, Wang Ziteng, had been raised to the rank of Supreme Governor of nine provinces, and had been honored with an Imperial command to leave the capital and inspect the frontiers.

Xue Pan was at heart secretly elated. "I was just lamenting," he thought, "that on my visit to the capital, I would have my maternal uncle to exercise control over me, and that I wouldn't be able to gambol and frisk to my heart's content, but now that he is leaving the capital, on promotion, it's evident that Heaven accomplishes man's wishes."

As he consequently held consultation with his mother; "Though we have," he argued, "several houses of our own in the capital, yet for these last ten years or so, there has been no one to live in them, and the people charged with the looking after them must unavoidably have stealthily rented them to someone or other. It's therefore needful to let servants go ahead to sweep and get the place in proper order, before we can very well go ourselves."

"What need is there to go to such trouble?" retorted his mother; "the main object of our present visit to the capital is first of all to pay our respects to our relatives and friends; and it is, either at your elder uncle's, my brother's place, or at your other uncle's, my sister's husband's home, both of which families' houses are extremely spacious, that we can put up provisionally, and by and bye, at our ease, we can send servants to make our house tidy. Now won't this be a considerable saving of trouble?"

"My uncle, your brother," suggested Xue Pan, "has just been raised to an appointment in an outside province, so that, of course, in his house, things must be topsy-turvey, on account of his departure; and should we betake ourselves, like a hive of bees and a long trail, to him for shelter; won't we appear very inconsiderate?"

"Your uncle," remarked his mother, "is, it is true, going on promotion, but there's besides the house of your aunt, my sister. What is more, during these last few years from both your uncle's and aunt's have, time after time, been sent messages, and letters forwarded, asking us to come over; and now that we've come, is it likely, though your uncle is busy with his preparations to start on his journey, that your aunt of the Jia family won't do all she can to press us to stay? Besides, were we to have our house got ready in a scramble, won't it make people think it strange? I however know your idea very well that were we kept to stay at your uncle's and aunt's, you won't escape being under strict restraint, unlike what would be the case were we to live in our own house, as you would be free then to act as you please! Such being the case, go, on your own account, and choose some place to take up your quarters in, while I myself, who have been separated from your aunt and cousins for these several years, would however like to stay with them for a few days; and I'll go along with your sister and look up your aunt at her home. What do you say; will this suit you or not?"

Xue Pan, upon hearing his mother speak in this strain, knew well enough that he could not bring her round from her determination; and he had no help but to issue the necessary directions to the servants to make straight for the Rong Guo mansion. Madame Wang had by this time already come to know that in the lawsuit, in which Xue Pan was concerned, Jia Yucun had fortunately intervened and lent his good offices, and was at length more composed in her mind. But when she again saw that her eldest brother had been advanced to a post on the frontier, she was just deploring that, deprived of the intercourse of the relatives of her mother's family, how doubly lonely she would feel; when, after the lapse of a few days, someone of the household brought the unexpected announcement that "our lady, your sister, has, with the young gentleman, the young lady and her whole household, entered the capital and have dismounted from their vehicles outside the main entrance." This news so delighted Madame Wang that she rushed out, with a few attendants, to greet them in the large Entrance Hall, and brought Mrs. Xue and the others into her house.

The two sisters were now reunited, at an advanced period of their lives, so that mixed feelings of sorrow and joy thronged together, but on these it is, of course, needless to dilate.

After conversing for a time on what had occurred, subsequent to their separation, Madame Wang took them to pay their obeisance to dowager lady Jia. They then handed over the various kinds of presents and indigenous articles, and after the whole family had been introduced, a banquet was also spread to greet the guests.

Xue Pan, having paid his respects to Jia Zheng and Jia Lian, was likewise taken to see Jia She, Jia Zhen, and the other members.

Jia Zheng sent a messenger to tell Madame Wang that "'aunt' Xue had already seen many springs and autumns, while their nephew was of tender age, with no experience, so that there was every fear, were he to live outside, that something would again take place. In the Southeast corner of our compound," (he sent word,) "there are in the Pear Fragrance Court, over ten apartments, all of which are vacant and lying idle; and were we to tell the servants to sweep them, and invite 'aunt' Xue and the young gentleman and lady to take up their quarters there, it would be an extremely wise thing."

Madame Wang had in fact been entertaining the wish to keep them to live with them, when dowager lady Jia also sent someone to say that, "Mrs. Xue should be asked to put up in the mansion in order that a greater friendliness should exist between them all."

Mrs. Xue herself had all along been desirous to live in one place with her relatives, so as to be able to keep a certain check over her son, fearing that, if they lived in a separate house outside, the natural bent of his habits would run riot, and that some calamity would be brought on; and she therefore, there and then, expressed her sense of appreciation, and accepted the invitation. She further privately told Madame Wang in clear terms, that every kind of daily expense and general contribution would have to be entirely avoided and withdrawn as that would be the only thing to justify her to make any protracted stay. And Madame Wang aware that she had, in her home, no difficulty in this line, promptly in fact complied with her wishes.

From this date it was that "aunt" Xue and her children took up their quarters in the Pear Fragrance Court.

This Court of Pear Fragrance had, we must explain, been at one time used as a place for the quiet retirement of the Duke Rong in his advanced years. It was on a small scale, but ingeniously laid out. There were, at least, over ten structures. The front halls and the back houses were all in perfect style. There was a separate door giving on to the street, and the people of the household of Xue Pan used this door to go in and out. At the southwest quarter, there was also a side door, which communicated with a narrow roadway. Beyond this narrow road, was the eastern court of Madame Wang's principal apartment; so that every day, either after her repast, or in the evening, Mrs. Xue would readily come over and converse, on one thing and another, with dowager lady Jia, or have a chat with Madame Wang; while Baochai came together, day after day, with Daiyu, Yingchun, her sisters, and the other girls, either to read, to play chess, or to do needlework, and the pleasure which they derived was indeed perfect.

Xue Pan however had all along from the first instance, been loath to live in the Jia mansion, as he dreaded that with the discipline enforced by his uncle, he would not be able to be his own master; but his mother had made up her mind so positively to remain there, and what was more, everyone in the Jia mansion was most pressing in their efforts to keep them, that there was no alternative for him but to take up his quarters temporarily there, while he at the same time directed servants to go and sweep the apartments of their own house, with a view that they should move into them when they were ready.

But, contrary to expectation, after they had been in their quarters for not over a month, Xue Pan came to be on intimate relations with all the young men among the kindred of the Jia mansion, the half of whom were extravagant in their habits, so that great was, of course, his delight to frequent them. Today, they would come together to drink wine; the next day to look at flowers. They even assembled to gamble, to dissipate and to go everywhere and anywhere; leading, with all their enticements, Xue Pan so far astray, that he became far worse, by a hundred times, than he was hitherto.

Although it must be conceded that Jia Zheng was in the education of his children quite correct, and in the control of his family quite systematic, yet in the first place, the clan was so large and the members so numerous, that he was unable to attend to the entire supervision; and, in the second place, the head of the family, at this period, was Jia Zhen, who, as the eldest grandchild of the Ning mansion, had likewise now come into the inheritance of the official status, with the result that all matters connected with the clan devolved upon his sole and exclusive control. In the third place, public as well as private concerns were manifold and complex, and being a man of negligent disposition, he estimated ordinary affairs of so little consequence that any respite from his official duties he devoted to no more than the study of books and the playing of chess.

Furthermore, this Pear Fragrance Court was separated by two rows of buildings from his quarters and was also provided with a separate door opening into the street, so that, being able at their own heart's desire to go out and to come in, these several young fellows could well indulge their caprices, and gratify the bent of their minds.

Hence it was that Xue Pan, in course of time gradually extinguished from his memory every idea of shifting their quarters.

But what transpired, on subsequent days, the following chapter will explain.

CHAPTER 5

The spirit of Jia Baoyu visits the confines of the Great Void. The Monitory Vision Fairy expounds, in ballads, the Dream of the Red Chamber.

Having in the fourth Chapter explained, to some degree, the circumstances attending the settlement of the mother and children of the Xue family in the Rong mansion, and other incidental matters, we will now revert to Lin Daiyu.

Ever since her arrival in the Rong mansion, dowager lady Jia showed her the highest sympathy and affection, so that in everything connected with sleeping, eating, rising, and accommodation she was on the same footing as Baoyu; with the result that Yingchun, Xichun, and Tanchun, her three granddaughters, had after all to take a back seat. In fact, the intimate and close friendliness and love which sprung up between the two persons Baoyu and Daiyu, was, in the same degree, of an exceptional kind, as compared with those existing between the others. By daylight they were wont to walk together, and to sit together. At night, they would desist together, and rest together. Really it was a case of harmony in language and concord in ideas, of the consistency of varnish or of glue, (a close friendship), when at this unexpected juncture there came this girl, Xue Baochai, who, though not very much older in years (than the others), was, nevertheless, in manner so correct, and in features so beautiful that the consensus of opinion was that Daiyu herself could not come up to her standard.

What is more, in her ways Baochai was so full of good tact, so considerate and accommodating, so unlike Daiyu, who was supercilious, self-confident, and without any regard for the world below, that the natural consequence was that she soon completely won the hearts of the lower classes. Even the whole number of waiting-maids would also for the most part, play and joke with Baochai. Hence it was that Daiyu fostered, in her heart, considerable feelings of resentment, but of this however Baochai had not the least inkling.

Baoyu was, likewise, in the prime of his boyhood, and was, besides, as far as the bent of his natural disposition was concerned, in every respect absurd and perverse; regarding his cousins, whether male or female, one and all with one common sentiment, and without any distinction whatever between the degrees of distant or close relationship. Sitting and sleeping, as he now was under the same roof with Daiyu in dowager lady Jia's suite of rooms, he naturally became comparatively more friendly with her than with his other cousins; and this friendliness led to greater intimacy and this intimacy once established, rendered unavoidable the occurrence of the blight of harmony from unforeseen slight pretexts.

These two had had on this very day, for some unknown reason, words between them more or less unfriendly, and Daiyu was again sitting all alone in her room, giving way to tears. Baoyu was once more within himself quite conscience-smitten for his ungraceful remarks, and coming forward, he humbly made advances, until, at length, Daiyu little by little came round.

As the plum blossom, in the eastern part of the garden of the Ning mansion, was in full bloom, Jia Zhen's spouse, Mrs. You, made preparations for a collation, (purposing) to send invitations to dowager lady Jia, mesdames Xing and Wang, and the other members of the family, to come and admire the flowers; and when the day arrived the first thing she did was to take Jia Rong and his wife, the two of them, and come and ask them round in person. Dowager lady Jia and the other inmates crossed over after their early meal; and they at once promenaded the Huifang (Concentrated Fragrance) Garden. First tea was served, and next wine; but the entertainment was no more than a family banquet of the kindred of the two mansions of Ning and Rong, so that there was a total lack of any novel or original recreation that could be put on record.

After a little time, Baoyu felt tired and languid and inclined for his midday siesta. "Take good care," dowager lady Jia enjoined some of them, "and stay with him, while he rests for a while, when he can come back;" whereupon Jia Rong's wife, Mrs. Qin, smiled and said with eagerness: "We got ready in here a room for uncle Bao, so let your venerable ladyship set your mind at ease. Just hand him over to my charge, and he will be quite safe. Mothers and sisters," she continued, addressing herself to Baoyu's nurses and waiting maids, "invite uncle Bao to follow me in here."

Dowager lady Jia had always been aware of the fact that Mrs. Qin was a most trustworthy person, naturally courteous and scrupulous, and in every action likewise so benign and gentle; indeed the most estimable among the whole number of her great-grandsons' wives, so that when she saw her about to go and attend to Baoyu, she felt that, for a certainty, everything would be well.

Mrs. Qin, there and then, led away a company of attendants, and came into the rooms inside the drawing room. Baoyu, upon raising his head, and catching sight of a picture hung on the upper wall, representing a human figure, in perfect style, the subject of which was a portrait of Ran Li, speedily felt his heart sink within him.

There was also a pair of scrolls, the text of which was:

A thorough insight into worldly matters arises from knowledge;
A clear perception of human nature emanates from literary lore.

On perusal of these two sentences, albeit the room was sumptuous and beautifully laid out, he would on no account remain in it. "Let us go at once," he hastened to observe, "let us go at once."

Mrs. Qin upon hearing his objections smiled. "If this," she said, "is really not nice, where are you going? if you won't remain here, well then come into my room."

Baoyu nodded his head and gave a faint grin.

"Where do you find the propriety," a nurse thereupon interposed, "of an uncle going to sleep in the room of a nephew's wife?"

"Ai ya!" exclaimed Mrs. Qin laughing, "I don't mind whether he gets angry or not (at what I say); but how old can he be as to reverentially shun all these things? Why my brother was with me here last month; didn't you see him? he's, true enough, of the same age as uncle Bao, but were the two of them to stand side by side, I suspect that he would be much higher in stature."

"How is it," asked Baoyu, "that I didn't see him? Bring him along and let me have a look at him!"

"He's separated," they all ventured as they laughed, "by a distance of twenty or thirty li, and how can he be brought along? but you'll see him some day."

As they were talking, they reached the interior of Mrs. Qin's apartments. As soon as they got in, a very faint puff of sweet fragrance was wafted into their nostrils. Baoyu readily felt his eyes itch and his bones grow weak. "What a fine smell!" he exclaimed several consecutive times.

Upon entering the apartments, and gazing at the partition wall, he saw a picture the handiwork of Tang Bohu, consisting of Begonias drooping in the spring time; on either side of which was one of a pair of scrolls, written by Qin Taixu, a Literary Chancellor of the Song era, running as follows:

> A gentle chill doth circumscribe the dreaming man, because the
> spring is cold.
> The fragrant whiff, which wafts itself into man's nose, is the per-
> fume of wine!

On the table was a mirror, one which had been placed, in days of
yore, in the Mirror Palace of the Empress Regnant Wu Zetian. On one
side stood a gold platter, in which Fei Yan, who lived in the Zhao state,
used to stand and dance. In this platter, was laid a quince, which An
Lushan had flung at the Empress Tai Zhen, inflicting a wound on her
breast. In the upper part of the room, stood a divan ornamented with
gems, on which the Emperor's daughter, Shou Chang, was wont to
sleep, in the Han Chang Palace Hanging, were curtains embroidered
with strings of pearls, by Tong Chang, the Imperial Princess.

"It's nice in here, it's nice in here," exclaimed Baoyu with a chuckle.

"This room of mine," observed Mrs. Qin smilingly, "is I think, good
enough for even spirits to live in!" and, as she uttered these words, she
with her own hands, opened a gauze coverlet, which had been washed
by Xi Zi, and removed a bridal pillow, which had been held in the
arms of Hong Niang. Instantly, the nurses attended to Baoyu, until he
had laid down comfortably; when they quietly dispersed, leaving only
the four waiting maids: Xiren, Meiren, Qingwen, and Sheyue to keep
him company.

"Mind be careful, as you sit under the eaves," Mrs. Qin recommended the young waiting maids, "that the cats do not start a fight!"

Baoyu then closed his eyes, and, little by little, became drowsy, and
fell asleep.

It seemed to him just as if Mrs. Qin was walking ahead of him.
Forthwith, with listless and unsettled step, he followed Mrs. Qin to
some spot or other, where he saw carnation-like railings, jade-like
steps, verdant trees and limpid pools—a spot where actually no trace
of any human being could be met with, where of the shifting mundane
dust little had penetrated.

Baoyu felt, in his dream, quite delighted. "This place," he mused, "is
pleasant, and I may as well spend my whole lifetime in here! though I
may have to lose my home, I'm quite ready for the sacrifice, for it's far
better being here than being flogged, day after day, by father, mother,
and teacher."

While he pondered in this erratic strain, he suddenly heard the voice
of some human being at the back of the rocks, giving vent to this song:

Like scattering clouds doth fleet a vernal dream;
The transient flowers pass like a running stream;
Maidens and youths bear this, ye all, in mind;
In useless grief what profit will ye find?

Baoyu perceived that the voice was that of a girl. The song was barely at an end, when he soon espied in the opposite direction, a beautiful girl advancing with majestic and elastic step; a girl quite unlike any ordinary mortal being. There is this poem, which gives an adequate description of her:

Lo she just quits the willow bank; and sudden now she issues from the flower-bedecked house;

As onward alone she speeds, she startles the birds perched in the trees, by the pavilion; to which as she draws nigh, her shadow flits by the verandah!

Her fairy clothes now flutter in the wind! a fragrant perfume like unto musk or olea is wafted in the air; Her apparel lotus-like is sudden wont to move; and the jingle of her ornaments strikes the ear.

Her dimpled cheeks resemble, as they smile, a vernal peach; her kingfisher coiffure is like a cumulus of clouds; her lips part cherry-like; her pomegranate-like teeth conceal a fragrant breath.

Her slender waist, so beauteous to look at, is like the skipping snow wafted by a gust of wind; the sheen of her pearls and kingfisher trinkets abounds with splendor, green as the feathers of a duck, and yellow as the plumes of a goose;

Now she issues to view, and now is hidden among the flowers; beautiful she is when displeased, beautiful when in high spirits; with lissome step, she treads along the pond, as if she soars on wings or sways in the air.

Her eyebrows are crescent moons, and knit under her smiles; she speaks, and yet she seems no word to utter; her lotus-like feet with ease pursue their course; she stops, and yet she seems still to be in motion; the charms of her figure all vie with ice in purity, and in splendor with precious gems; Lovely is her brilliant attire, so full of grandeur and refined grace.

Loveable her countenance, as if moulded from some fragrant substance, or carved from white jade; elegant is her person, like a phoenix, dignified like a dragon soaring high.

What is her chastity like? Like a white plum in spring with snow nestling in its broken skin; Her purity? Like autumn orchids bedecked with dewdrops.

Her modesty? Like a fir-tree growing in a barren plain; Her comeliness? Like russet clouds reflected in a limpid pool.

Her gracefulness? Like a dragon in motion wriggling in a stream; Her refinement? Like the rays of the moon shooting onto a cool river.

Sure is she to put Xi Zi to shame! Bound to put Wang Qiang to the blush! What a remarkable person! Where was she born? And whence does she come?

One thing is true that in Fairy-land there is no second like her! That in the Purple Courts of Heaven there is no one fit to be her peer!

Forsooth, who can it be, so surpassingly beautiful!

Baoyu, upon realising that she was a fairy, was much elated; and with eagerness advanced and made a bow.

"My divine sister," he ventured, as he put on a smile. "I don't know whence you come, and whither you are going. Nor have I any idea what this place is, but I make bold to entreat that you would take my hand and lead me on."

"My abode," replied the Fairy, "is above the Heavens of Divested Animosities, and in the ocean of Discharged Sorrows. I'm the Fairy of Monitory Vision, of the cave of Drooping Fragrance, in the mount of Emitted Spring, within the confines of the Great Void. I preside over the voluptuous affections and sensual debts among the mortal race, and supervise in the dusty world, the envies of women and the lusts of man. It's because I've recently come to hear that the retribution for voluptuousness extends up to this place, that I betake myself here in order to find suitable opportunities of disseminating mutual affections. My encounter with you now is also not a matter of accident! This spot is not distant from my confines. I have nothing much there besides a cup of the tender buds of tea plucked by my own hands, and a pitcher of luscious wine, fermented by me as well as several sprite-like singing and dancing maidens of great proficiency, and twelve ballads of spiritual song, recently completed, on the Dream of the Red Chamber; but won't you come along with me for a stroll?"

Baoyu, at this proposal, felt elated to such an extraordinary degree that he could skip from joy, and there and then discarding from his mind all idea of where Mrs. Qin was, he readily followed the Fairy.

They reached some spot, where there was a stone tablet, put up in a horizontal position, on which were visible the four large characters: "The confines of the Great Void," on either side of which was one of a pair of scrolls, with the two antithetical sentences:

> When falsehood stands for truth, truth likewise becomes false;
> When naught be made to aught, aught changes into naught!

Past the Portal stood the door of a Palace, and horizontally, above this door, were the four large characters: "The Sea of Retribution, the Heaven of Love." There were also a pair of scrolls, with the inscription in large characters:

> Passion, alas! thick as the earth, and lofty as the skies, from ages-
>   past to the present hath held incessant sway;
> How pitiful your lot! ye lustful men and women envious, that your
>   voluptuous debts should be so hard to pay!

Baoyu, after perusal, communed with his own heart. "Is it really so!" he thought, "but I wonder what implies the passion from old till now, and what are the voluptuous debts! Henceforward, I must enlighten myself!"

Baoyu was bent upon this train of thoughts when he unwittingly attracted several evil spirits into his heart, and with speedy step he followed in the track of the fairy, and entered two rows of doors when he perceived that the Lateral Halls were, on both sides, full of tablets and scrolls, the number of which he could not in one moment ascertain. He however discriminated in numerous places the inscriptions: The Board of lustful love; the Board of contracted grudges; The Board of matutinal sobs; the Board of nocturnal tears; the Board of vernal affections; and the Board of autumnal anguish.

After he had perused these inscriptions, he felt impelled to turn round and address the Fairy. "May I venture to trouble my Fairy," he said, "to take me along for a turn into the interior of each of these boards? May I be allowed, I wonder, to do so?"

"Inside each of these boards," explained the Fairy, "are accumulated the registers with the records of all women of the whole world; of those who have passed away, as well as of those who have not as yet come into it, and you, with your mortal eyes and human body, could not possibly be allowed to know anything in anticipation."

But would Baoyu, upon hearing these words, submit to this decree? He went on to implore her permission again and again, until the Fairy casting her eye upon the tablet of the board in front of her observed, "Well, all right! you may go into this board and reap some transient pleasure."

Baoyu was indescribably joyous, and, as he raised his head, he perceived that the text on the tablet consisted of the three characters: the Board of ill-fated lives; and that on each side was a scroll with the inscription:

> Upon one's self are mainly brought regrets in spring and autumn gloom;
> A face, flowerlike may be and moonlike too; but beauty all for whom?

Upon perusal of the scroll Baoyu was, at once, the more stirred with admiration; and, as he crossed the door, and reached the interior, the only things that struck his eye were about ten large presses, the whole number of which were sealed with paper slips; on everyone of these slips, he perceived that there were phrases peculiar to each province.

Baoyu was in his mind merely bent upon discerning, from the rest, the slip referring to his own native village, when he espied, on the other side, a slip with the large characters: "the Principal Record of the Twelve Maidens of Jinling."

"What is the meaning," therefore inquired Baoyu, "of the Principal Record of the twelve maidens of Jinling?"

"As this is the record," explained the Fairy, "of the most excellent and prominent girls in your honorable province, it is, for this reason, called the Principal Record."

"I've often heard people say," observed Baoyu, "that Jinling is of vast extent; and how can there only be twelve maidens in it! why, at present, in our own family alone, there are more or less several hundreds of young girls!"

The Fairy gave a faint smile. "Through there be," she rejoined, "so large a number of girls in your honorable province, those only of any note have been selected and entered in this record. The two presses, on the two sides, contain those who are second best; while, for all who remain, as they are of the ordinary run, there are, consequently, no registers to make any entry of them in."

Baoyu upon looking at the press below, perceived the inscription: "Secondary Record of the twelve girls of Jinling;" while again in another press was inscribed: "Supplementary Secondary Record of the twelve girls of Jinling." Forthwith stretching out his hand, Baoyu opened first the doors of the press, containing the "Supplementary Secondary

Record," extracted a volume of the registers, and opened it. When he came to examine it, he saw on the front page a representation of something, which, though bearing no resemblance to a human being, presented, at the same time, no similitude to scenery; consisting simply of huge blotches made with ink. The whole paper was full of nothing else but black clouds and turbid mists, after which appeared the traces of a few characters, explaining that:

> A cloudless moon is rare forsooth to see,
> And pretty clouds so soon scatter and flee!
> Thy heart is deeper than the heavens are high,
> Thy frame consists of base ignominy!
> Thy looks and clever mind resentment will provoke,
> And thine untimely death vile slander will evoke!
> A loving noble youth in vain for love will yearn.

After reading these lines, Baoyu looked below, where was pictured a bouquet of fresh flowers and a bed covered with tattered matting. There were also several distiches running as follows:

> Thy self-esteem for kindly gentleness is but a fancy vain!
> Thy charms that they can match the olea or orchid, but thoughts
>   inane!
> While an actor will, envious lot, with fortune's smiles be born,
> A youth of noble birth will, strange to say, be luckless and forlorn.

Baoyu perused these sentences, but could not unfold their meaning, so, at once discarding this press, he went over and opened the door of the press of the "Secondary Records" and took out a book, in which, on examination, he found a representation of a twig of olea fragrans. Below, was a pond, the water of which was parched up and the mud dry, the lotus flowers decayed, and even the roots dead. At the back were these lines:

> The lotus root and flower but one fragrance will give;
> How deep alas! the wounds of thy life's span will be;
> What time a desolate tree in two places will live,
> Back to its native home the fragrant ghost will flee!

Baoyu read these lines, but failed to understand what they meant. He then went and fetched the "Principal Record," and set to looking it over. He saw on the first page a picture of two rotten trees, while on these trees was suspended a jade girdle. There was also a heap of snow, and under this snow was a golden hair-pin. There were in addition these four lines in verse:

> Bitter thy cup will be, e'en were the virtue thine to stop the loom,
> Thine though the gift the willow fluff to sing, pity who will thy
>   doom?
> High in the trees doth hang the girdle of white jade.
> And lo! among the snow the golden pin is laid!

To Baoyu the meaning was again, though he read the lines over, quite unintelligible. He was about to make inquiries, but he felt convinced that the Fairy would be loath to divulge the decrees of Heaven; and though intent upon discarding the book, he could not however tear himself away from it. Forthwith, therefore, he prosecuted a further perusal of what came next, when he caught sight of a picture of a bow. On this bow hung a citron. There was also this ode:

> Full twenty years right and wrong to expound will be thy fate!
> What place pomegranate blossoms come in bloom will face the
>   Palace Gate!
> The third portion of spring, of the first spring in beauty short will
>   fall!
> When tiger meets with hare thou wilt return to sleep perennial.

Further on, was also a sketch of two persons flying a kite; a broad expanse of sea, and a large vessel; while in this vessel was a girl, who screened her face bedewed with tears. These four lines were likewise visible:

> Pure and bright will be thy gifts, thy purpose very high;
> But born thou wilt be late in life and luck be passed by;
> At the tomb feast thou wilt repine tearful along the stream,
> East winds may blow, but home miles off will be, even in dream.

After this followed a picture of several streaks of fleeting clouds, and of a creek whose waters were exhausted, with the text:

> Riches and honors too what benefit are they?
> In swaddling clothes thou'lt be when parents pass away;
> The rays will slant, quick as the twinkle of an eye;
> The Xiang stream will recede, the Chu clouds onward fly!

Then came a picture of a beautiful gem, which had fallen into the mire, with the verse:

> Thine aim is chastity, but chaste thou wilt not be;
> Abstraction is thy faith, but void thou may'st not see;
> Thy precious, gemlike self will, pitiful to say,
> Into the mundane mire collapse at length some day.

A rough sketch followed of a savage wolf, in pursuit of a beautiful girl, trying to pounce upon her as he wished to devour her. This was the burden of the distich:

> Thy mate is like a savage wolf prowling among the hills;
> His wish once gratified a haughty spirit his heart fills!
> Though fair thy form like flowers or willows in the golden moon,
> Upon the yellow beam to hang will shortly be its doom.

Below, was an old temple, in the interior of which was a beautiful person, just in the act of reading the religious manuals, as she sat all alone; with this inscription:

> In light esteem thou hold'st the charms of the three springs for
>   their short-liv'd fate;
> Thine attire of past years to lay aside thou chang'st, a Daoist dress
>   to don;
> How sad, alas! of a reputed house and noble kindred the scion,
> Alone, behold! she sleeps under a glimmering light, an old idol for
>   mate.

Next in order came a hill of ice, on which stood a hen-phoenix, while under it was this motto:

> When time ends, sure coincidence, the phoenix doth alight;
> The talents of this human form all know and living see,
> For first to yield she kens, then to control, and third genial to be;
> But sad to say, things in Jinling are in more sorry plight.

This was succeeded by a representation of a desolate village, and a dreary inn. A pretty girl sat in there, spinning thread. These were the sentiments affixed below:

> When riches will have flown will honors then avail?

When ruin breaks your home, e'en relatives will fail!
But sudden through the aid extended to Dame Liu,
A friend in need fortune will make to rise for you.

Following these verses, was drawn a pot of orchids, by the side of which, was a beautiful maiden in a phoenix-crown and cloudy mantle (bridal dress); and to this picture was appended this device:

What time spring wanes, then fades the bloom of peach as well as
   plum!
Whoever can like a pot of the olea be winsome!
With ice thy purity will vie, vain their envy will be!
In vain a laughing-stock people will try to make of thee.

At the end of this poetical device, came the representation of a lofty edifice, on which was a beauteous girl, suspending herself on a beam to commit suicide; with this verse:

Love high as heav'n, love ocean-wide, thy lovely form will don;
What time love will encounter love, license must rise wanton;
Why hold that all impiety in Rong doth find its spring,
The source of trouble, verily, is centred most in Ning.

Baoyu was still bent upon prosecuting his perusal, when the Fairy perceiving that his intellect was eminent and bright, and his natural talents quick-witted, and apprehending lest the decrees of heaven should be divulged, hastily closed the Book of Record, and addressed herself to Baoyu. "Come along with me," she said smiling, "and see some wonderful scenery. What's the need of staying here and beating this gourd of ennui?"

In a dazed state, Baoyu listlessly discarded the record, and again followed in the footsteps of the Fairy. On their arrival at the back, he saw carnation portieres, and embroidered curtains, ornamented pillars, and carved eaves. But no words can adequately give an idea of the vermilion apartments glistening with splendor, of the floors garnished with gold, of the snow reflecting lustrous windows, of the palatial mansions made of gems. He also saw fairyland flowers, beautiful and fragrant, and extraordinary vegetation, full of perfume. The spot was indeed elysian.

He again heard the Fairy observe with a smiling face: "Come out all of you at once and greet the honored guest!"

These words were scarcely completed, when he espied fairies walk out of the mansion, all of whom were, with their dangling lotus sleeves, and their fluttering feather habiliments, as comely as spring flowers, and as winsome as the autumn moon. As soon as they caught sight of Baoyu, they all, with one voice, resentfully reproached the Monitory Vision Fairy. "Ignorant as to who the honored guest could be," they argued, "we hastened to come out to offer our greetings simply because you, elder sister, had told us that, on this day, and at this very time, there would be sure to come on a visit, the spirit of the younger sister of Jiang Zhu. That's the reason why we've been waiting for ever so long; and now why do you, in lieu of her, introduce this vile object to contaminate the confines of pure and spotless maidens?"

As soon as Baoyu heard these remarks, he was forthwith plunged in such a state of consternation that he would have retired, but he found it impossible to do so. In fact, he felt the consciousness of the foulness and corruption of his own nature quite intolerable. The Monitory Vision Fairy promptly took Baoyu's hand in her own, and turning towards her younger sisters, smiled and explained: "You, and all of you, are not aware of the why and wherefore. Today I did mean to have gone to the Rong mansion to fetch Jiang Zhu, but as I went by the Ning mansion, I unexpectedly came across the ghosts of the two dukes of Rong and Ning, who addressed me in this wise: 'Our family has, since the dynasty established itself on the Throne, enjoyed merit and fame, which pervaded many ages, and riches and honors transmitted from generation to generation. One hundred years have already elapsed, but this good fortune has now waned, and this propitious luck is exhausted; so much so that they could not be retrieved! Our sons and grandsons may be many, but there is no one among them who has the means to continue the family estate, with the exception of our kindred grandson, Baoyu alone, who, though perverse in disposition and wayward by nature, is nevertheless intelligent and quick-witted and qualified in a measure to give effect to our hopes. But alas! the good fortune of our family is entirely decayed, so that we fear there is no person to incite him to enter the right way! Fortunately you worthy fairy come at an unexpected moment, and we venture to trust that you will, above all things, warn him against the foolish indulgence of inordinate desire, lascivious affections and other such things, in the hope that he may, at your instigation, be able to escape the snares of those girls who will allure him with their blandishments, and to enter on the right track; and we two brothers will be ever grateful.'

"On language such as this being addressed to me, my feelings of commiseration naturally burst forth; and I brought him here, and bade him, first of all, carefully peruse the records of the whole lives of the maidens in his family, belonging to the three grades, the upper, middle, and lower, but as he has not yet fathomed the import, I have consequently led him into this place to experience the vision of drinking, eating, singing, and licentious love, in the hope, there is no saying, of his at length attaining that perception."

Having concluded these remarks, she led Baoyu by the hand into the apartment, where he felt a whiff of subtle fragrance, but what it was that reached his nostrils he could not tell.

To Baoyu's eager and incessant inquiries, the Fairy made reply with a sardonic smile. "This perfume," she said, "is not to be found in the world, and how could you discern what it is? This is made of the essence of the first sprouts of rare herbs, growing on all hills of fame and places of superior excellence, admixed with the oil of every species of splendid shrubs in precious groves, and is called the marrow of Conglomerated Fragrance."

At these words Baoyu was, of course, full of no other feeling than wonder.

The whole party advanced and took their seats, and a young maidservant presented tea, which Baoyu found of pure aroma, of excellent flavor and of no ordinary kind. "What is the name of this tea?" he therefore asked; upon which the Fairy explained. "This tea," she added, "originates from the Hills of Emitted Spring and the Valley of Drooping Fragrance, and is, besides, brewed in the night dew, found on spiritual plants and divine leaves. The name of this tea is 'one thousand red in one hole.'"

At these words Baoyu nodded his head, and extolled its qualities. Espying in the room lutes, with jasper mountings, and tripods, inlaid with gems, antique paintings, and new poetical works, which were to be seen everywhere, he felt more than ever in a high state of delight. Below the windows, were also shreds of velvet sputtered about and a toilet case stained with the traces of time and smudged with cosmetic; while on the partition wall was likewise suspended a pair of scrolls, with the inscription:

A lonesome, small, ethereal, beauteous nook!
What help is there, but Heaven's will to brook?

Baoyu having completed his inspection felt full of admiration, and proceeded to ascertain the names and surnames of the Fairies. One was called the Fairy of Lustful Dreams; another "the High Ruler of Propagated Passion;" the name of one was "the Golden Maiden of

Perpetuated Sorrow;" of another the "Intelligent Maiden of Transmitted Hatred." (In fact,) the respective Daoist appellations were not of one and the same kind.

In a short while, young maid-servants came in and laid the table, put the chairs in their places, and spread out wines and eatables. There were actually crystal tankards overflowing with luscious wines, and amber glasses full to the brim with pearly strong liquors. But still less need is there to give any further details about the sumptuousness of the refreshments.

Baoyu found it difficult, on account of the unusual purity of the bouquet of the wine, to again restrain himself from making inquiries about it.

"This wine," observed the Monitory Dream Fairy, "is made of the twigs of hundreds of flowers, and the juice of ten thousands of trees, with the addition of musk composed of unicorn marrow, and yeast prepared with phoenix milk. Hence the name of 'Ten thousand Beauties in one Cup' was given to it."

Baoyu sang its incessant praise, and, while he sipped his wine, twelve dancing girls came forward, and requested to be told what songs they were to sing.

"Take," suggested the Fairy, "the newly-composed Twelve Sections of the Dream of the Red Chamber, and sing them."

The singing girls signified their obedience, and forthwith they lightly clapped the castagnettes and gently thrummed the virginals. These were the words which they were heard to sing:

> At the time of the opening of the heavens and the laying out of the
> earth chaos prevailed.

They had just sung this one line when the Fairy exclaimed: "This ballad is unlike the ballads written in the dusty world whose purport is to hand down remarkable events, in which the distinction of scholars, girls, old men and women, and fools is essential, and in which are furthermore introduced the lyrics of the Southern and Northern Palaces. These fairy songs consist either of elegaic effusions on some person or impressions of some occurrence or other, and are impromptu songs readily set to the music of wind or string instruments, so that any one who is not cognisant of their gist cannot appreciate the beauties contained in them. So you are not likely, I fear, to understand this lyric with any clearness; and unless you first peruse the text and then listen to the ballad, you will, instead of pleasure, feel as if you were chewing wax (devoid of any zest)."

After these remarks, she turned her head round, and directed a young maid-servant to fetch the text of the Dream of the Red Chamber, which she handed to Baoyu, who took it over; and as he followed the words with his eyes, with his ears he listened to the strains of this song:

Preface of the Bream of the Red Chamber: "When the Heavens were opened and earth was laid out chaos prevailed! What was the germ of love? It arises entirely from the strength of licentious love.

"What day, by the will of heaven, I felt wounded at heart, and what time I was at leisure, I made an attempt to disburden my sad heart; and with this object in view I indited this Dream of the Red Chamber, on the subject of a disconsolate gold trinket and an unfortunate piece of jade.

"Waste of a whole Lifetime. All maintain that the match between gold and jade will be happy. All I can think of is the solemn oath contracted in days gone by by the plant and stone! Vain will I gaze upon the snow, Xue, [Baochai], pure as crystal and lustrous like a gem of the eminent priest living among the hills! Never will I forget the noiseless Fairy Grove, Lin [Daiyu], beyond the confines of the mortal world! Alas! now only have I come to believe that human happiness is incomplete; and that a couple may be bound by the ties of wedlock for life, but that after all their hearts are not easy to lull into contentment.

"Vain knitting of the brows. The one is a spirit flower of Fairyland; the other is a beautiful jade without a blemish. Do you maintain that their union will not be remarkable? Why how then is it that he has come to meet her again in this existence? If the union will you say, be strange, how is it then that their love affair will be but empty words? The one in her loneliness will give way to useless sighs. The other in vain will yearn and crave. The one will be like the reflection of the moon in water; the other like a flower reflected in a mirror. Consider, how many drops of tears can there be in the eyes? and how could they continue to drop from autumn to winter and from spring to flow till summer time?"

But to come to Baoyu, after he had heard these ballads, so diffuse and vague, he failed to see any point of beauty in them; but the plaintive melody of the sound was nevertheless sufficient to drive away his spirit and exhilarate his soul. Hence it was that he did not make any inquiries about the arguments, and that he did not ask about the matter treated, but simply making these ballads the means for the time being of dispelling melancholy, he therefore went on with the perusal of what came below.

"Despicable Spirit of Death! You will be rejoicing that glory is at its height when hateful death will come once again, and with eyes wide with horror, you will discard all things, and dimly and softly the fragrant spirit will waste and dissolve! You will yearn for native home, but distant will be the way, and lofty the mountains. Hence it is that you will betake yourself in search of father and mother, while they lie under the influence of a dream, and hold discourse with them. 'Your child,' you will say, 'has already trodden the path of death! Oh my parents, it behoves you to speedily retrace your steps and make good your escape!'

"Separated from Relatives. You will speed on a journey of three thousand li at the mercy of wind and rain, and tear yourself from all your family ties and your native home! Your fears will be lest anguish should do any harm to your parents in their failing years! 'Father and mother,' you will bid them, 'do not think with any anxiety of your child. From ages past poverty as well as success have both had a fixed destiny; and is it likely that separation and reunion are not subject to predestination? Though we may now be far apart in two different places, we must each of us try and preserve good cheer. Your abject child has, it is true, gone from home, but abstain from distressing yourselves on her account!'

"Sorrow in the midst of Joy. While wrapped as yet in swaddling clothes, father and mother, both alas! will depart, and dwell though you will in that mass of gauze, who is there who will know how to spoil you with any fond attention? Born you will be fortunately with ample moral courage, and high-minded and boundless resources, for your parents will not have, in the least, their child's secret feelings at heart! You will be like a moon appearing to view when the rain holds up, shedding its rays upon the Jade Hall; or a gentle breeze (wafting its breath upon it). Wedded to a husband, fairy-like fair and accomplished, you will enjoy a happiness enduring as the earth and perennial as the Heavens! and you will be the means of snapping asunder the bitter fate of your youth! But, after all, the clouds will scatter in Gao Tang and the waters of the Xiang river will get parched! This is the inevitable destiny of dissolution and continuance which prevails in the mortal world, and what need is there to indulge in useless grief?

"Intolerable to the world. Your figure will be as winsome as an olea fragrans; your talents as ample as those of a Fairy! You will by nature be so haughty that of the whole human race few will be like you! You will look upon a meat diet as one of dirt, and treat splendor as coarse and loathsome! And yet you will not be aware that your high notions will bring upon you the excessive hatred of man! You will be very eager in your desire after chastity, but the human race will despise you! Alas, you will wax old in that antique temple hall under a faint light, where you will waste ungrateful for beauty, looks, and freshness! But after all you will still be worldly, corrupt, and unmindful of your vows; just like a spotless white jade you will be whose fate is to fall into the mire! And what need will there be for the grandson of a prince or the son of a duke to deplore that his will not be the good fortune (of winning your affections)?

"The Voluptuary. You will resemble a wolf in the mountains! a savage beast devoid of all human feeling! Regardless in every way of the obligations of days gone by, your sole pleasure will be in the indulgence of haughtiness, extravagance, licentiousness and dissolute habits! You will be inordinate in your conjugal affections, and look down upon the beautiful charms of the child of a marquis, as if they were cat-tail rush or willow; trampling upon the honorable daughter of a ducal mansion, as if she were one of the common herd. Pitiful to say, the fragrant spirit and beauteous ghost will in a year softly and gently pass away!

"The Perception that all things are transient like flowers. You will look lightly upon the three springs and regard the blush of the peach and the green of the willow as of no avail. You will beat out the fire of splendor, and treat solitary retirement as genial! What is it that you say about the delicate peaches in the heavens (marriage) being excellent, and the petals of the almond in the clouds being plentiful (children)? Let him who has after all seen one of them, (really a mortal being) go safely through the autumn, (wade safely through old age), behold the people in the white poplar village groan and sigh; and the spirits under the green maple whine and moan! Still more wide in expanse than even the heavens is the dead vegetation which covers the graves! The moral is this, that the burden of man is poverty one day and affluence another; that bloom in spring, and decay in autumn, constitute the doom of vegetable life! In the same way, this calamity of birth and the visitation of death, who is able to escape? But I have heard it said that there grows in the western quarter a tree called the Po Suo (Patient Bearing) which bears the fruit of Immortal life!

"The bane of intelligence. Yours will be the power to estimate, in a thorough manner, the real motives of all things, as yours will be intelligence of an excessive degree; but instead (of reaping any benefit) you will cast the die of your own existence! The heart of your previous life is already reduced to atoms, and when you shall have died, your nature will have been intelligent to no purpose! Your home will be in easy circumstances; your family will enjoy comforts; but your connexions will, at length, fall a prey to death, and the inmates of your family scatter, each one of you speeding in a different direction, making room for others! In vain, you will have harassed your mind with cankering thoughts for half a lifetime; for it will be just as if you had gone through the confused mazes of a dream on the third watch! Sudden a crash (will be heard) like the fall of a spacious palace, and a dusky gloominess (will supervene) such as is caused by a lamp about to spend itself! Alas! a spell of happiness will be suddenly (dispelled by) adversity! Woe is man in the world! for his ultimate doom is difficult to determine!

"Leave behind a residue of happiness! Hand down an excess of happiness; hand down an excess of happiness! Unexpectedly you will come across a benefactor! Fortunate enough your mother, your own mother, will have laid by a store of virtue and secret meritorious actions! My advice to you, mankind, is to relieve the destitute and succor the distressed! Do not resemble those who will harp after lucre and show themselves unmindful of the ties of relationship: that wolflike maternal uncle of yours and that impostor of a brother! True it is that addition and subtraction, increase and decrease, (reward and punishment,) rest in the hands of Heaven above!

"Splendor at last. Loving affection in a mirror will be still more ephemeral than fame in a dream. That fine splendor will fleet how soon! Make no further allusion to embroidered curtain, to bridal coverlet; for though you may come to wear on your head a pearl-laden coronet, and, on your person, a jacket ornamented with phoenixes, yours will not nevertheless be the means to atone for the short life (of your husband)! Though the saying is that mankind should not have, in their old age, the burden of poverty to bear, yet it is also essential that a store of benevolent deeds should be laid up for the benefit of sons and grandsons! (Your son) may come to be dignified in appearance and wear on his head the official tassel, and on his chest may be suspended the gold seal resplendent in luster; he may be imposing in his majesty, and he may rise high in status and emoluments, but the dark and dreary way which leads to death is short! Are the generals and ministers who have been from ages of old still in the flesh, forsooth? They exist only in a futile name handed down to posterity to reverence!

"Death ensues when things propitious reign! Upon the ornamented beam will settle at the close of spring the fragrant dust! Your reckless indulgence of licentious love and your naturally moonlike face will soon be the source of the ruin of a family. The decadence of the family estate will emanate entirely from Jing; while the wane of the family affairs will be entirely attributable to the fault of Ning! Licentious love will be the main reason of the long-standing grudge.

"The flying birds each perch upon the trees! The family estates of those in official positions will fade! The gold and silver of the rich and honored will be scattered! those who will have conferred benefit will, even in death, find the means of escape! those devoid of human feelings will reap manifest retribution! Those indebted for a life will make, in due time, payment with their lives; those indebted for tears have already (gone) to exhaust their tears! Mutual injuries will be revenged in no light manner! Separation and reunion will both alike be determined by predestination! You wish to know why your life will be short; look into your previous existence! Verily, riches and honors, which will come with old age, will likewise be a question of chance! Those who will hold the world in light esteem will retire within the gate of abstraction; while those who will be allured by enticement will have forfeited their lives (The Jia family will fulfil its destiny) as surely as birds take to the trees after they have exhausted all they had to eat, and which as they drop down will pile up a hoary, vast, and lofty heap of dust, (leaving) indeed a void behind!"

When the maidens had finished the ballads, they went on to sing the "Supplementary Record;" but the Monitory Vision Fairy, perceiving the total absence of any interest in Baoyu, heaved a sigh. "You silly brat!" she exclaimed. "What! haven't you, even now, attained perception!"

"There's no need for you to go on singing," speedily observed Baoyu, as he interrupted the singing maidens; and feeling drowsy and dull, he pleaded being under the effects of wine, and begged to be allowed to lie down.

The Fairy then gave orders to clear away the remains of the feast, and escorted Baoyu to a suite of female apartments, where the splendor of such objects as were laid out was a thing which he had not hitherto seen. But what evoked in him wonder still more intense, was the sight, at an early period, of a girl seated in the room, who, in the freshness of her beauty and winsomeness of her charms, bore some resemblance to Baochai, while, in elegance and comeliness, on the other hand, to Daiyu.

While he was plunged in a state of perplexity, the Fairy suddenly remarked: "All those female apartments and ladies' chambers in so many wealthy and honorable families in the world are, without exception, polluted by voluptuous opulent puppets and by all that bevy of profligate girls. But still more despicable are those from old till now numberless dissolute roues, one and all of whom maintain that libidinous affections do not constitute lewdness; and who try, further, to prove that licentious love is not tantamount to lewdness. But all these arguments are mere apologies for their shortcomings, and a screen for their pollutions; for if libidinous affection be lewdness, still more does the perception of licentious love constitute lewdness. Hence it is that the indulgence of sensuality and the gratification of licentious affection originate entirely from a relish of lust, as well as from a hankering after licentious love. Lo you, who are the object of my love, are the most lewd being under the heavens from remote ages to the present time!"

Baoyu was quite dumbstruck by what he heard, and hastily smiling, he said by way of reply: "My Fairy labors under a misapprehension. Simply because of my reluctance to read my books my parents have, on repeated occasions, extended to me injunction and reprimand, and would I have the courage to go so far as to rashly plunge in lewd habits? Besides, I am still young in years, and have no notion what is implied by lewdness!"

"Not so!" exclaimed the Fairy; "lewdness, although one thing in principle is, as far as meaning goes, subject to different constructions; as is exemplified by those in the world whose heart is set upon lewdness. Some delight solely in faces and figures; others find insatiable pleasure in singing and dancing; some in dalliance and raillery; others in the incessant indulgence of their lusts; and these regret that all the beautiful maidens under the heavens cannot minister to their short-lived pleasure. These several kinds of persons are foul objects steeped skin and all in lewdness. The lustful love, for instance, which has sprung to life and taken root in your natural affections, I and such as myself extend to it the character of an abstract lewdness; but abstract lewdness can be grasped by the mind, but cannot be transmitted by the mouth; can be fathomed by the spirit, but cannot be divulged in words. As you now are imbued with this desire only in the abstract, you are certainly well fit to be a trustworthy friend in (Fairyland) inner apartments, but, on the path of the mortal world, you will inevitably be misconstrued and defamed; every mouth will ridicule you; every eye will look down upon you with contempt. After meeting recently your worthy ancestors, the two Dukes of Ning and Rong, who opened their hearts and made their wishes known to me with such fervor, (but I will not have you solely on account of the splendor of our inner apartments look down despisingly upon the path of the world), I consequently led you along, my son, and inebriated you with luscious wines, steeped you in spiritual tea, and admonished you with excellent songs, bringing also here a young sister of mine, whose infant name is Jianmei, and her style Keqing, to be given to you as your wedded wife. Tonight, the time will be propitious and suitable for the immediate consummation of the union, with the express object of letting you have a certain insight into the fact that if the condition of the abode of spirits within the confines of Fairyland be still so (imperfect), how much the more so should be the nature of the affections which prevail in the dusty world; with the intent that from this time forth you should positively break loose from bondage, perceive and amend your former disposition, devote your attention to the works of Confucius and Mencius, and set your steady purpose upon the principles of morality."

Having ended these remarks, she initiated him into the mysteries of licentious love, and, pushing Baoyu into the room, she closed the door, and took her departure all alone. Baoyu in a dazed state complied with the admonitions given him by the Fairy, and the natural result was, of course, a violent flirtation, the circumstances of which it would be impossible to recount.

When the next day came, he was by that time so attached to her by ties of tender love and their conversation was so gentle and full of charm that he could not brook to part from Keqing. Hand-in-hand, the two of them therefore, went out for a stroll, when they unexpectedly reached a place, where nothing else met their gaze than thorns and brambles, which covered the ground, and a wolf and a tiger walking side by side. Before them stretched the course of a black stream, which obstructed their progress; and over this stream there was, what is more, no bridge to enable one to cross it.

While they were exercising their minds with perplexity, they suddenly espied the Fairy coming from the back in pursuit of them. "Desist at once," she exclaimed, "from making any advance into the stream; it is urgent that you should, with all speed, turn your faces round!"

Baoyu lost no time in standing still. "What is this place?" he inquired.

"This is the Ford of Enticement," explained the Fairy. "Its depth is ten thousand zhang; its breadth is a thousand li; in its stream there are no boats or paddles by means of which to effect a passage. There is simply a raft, of which Mu Jushi directs the rudder, and which Hui Shizhe punts with the poles. They receive no compensation in the shape of gold or silver, but when they come across any one whose destiny it is to cross, they ferry him over. You now have by accident strolled as far as here, and had you fallen into the stream you would have rendered quite useless the advice and admonition which I previously gave you."

These words were scarcely concluded, when suddenly was heard from the midst of the Ford of Enticement, a sound like unto a peal of thunder, whereupon a whole crowd of goblins and sea-urchins laid hands upon Baoyu and dragged him down.

This so filled Baoyu with consternation that he fell into a perspiration as profuse as rain, and he simultaneously broke forth and shouted, "Rescue me, Keqing!"

These cries so terrified Xiren and the other waiting-maids, that they rushed forward, and taking Baoyu in their arms, "Don't be afraid, Baoyu," they said, "we are here."

But we must observe that Mrs. Qin was just inside the apartment in the act of recommending the young waiting-maids to be mindful that the cats and dogs did not start a fight, when she unawares heard Baoyu, in his dream, call her by her infant name. In a melancholy mood she therefore communed within herself, "As far as my infant name goes, there is, in this establishment, no one who has any idea what it is, and how is it that he has come to know it, and that he utters it in his dream?" And she was at this period unable to fathom the reason. But, reader, listen to the explanations given in the chapter which follows.

CHAPTER 6

Jia Baoyu reaps his first experience in licentious love. Old goody Liu pays a visit to the Rong Guo Mansion.

Mrs. Qin, to resume our narrative, upon hearing Baoyu call her in his dream by her infant name, was at heart very exercised, but she did not however feel at liberty to make any minute inquiry.

Baoyu was, at this time, in such a dazed state, as if he had lost something, and the servants promptly gave him a decoction of lungngan. After he had taken a few sips, he forthwith rose and tidied his clothes.

Xiren put out her hand to fasten the band of his garment, and as soon as she did so, and it came in contact with his person, it felt so icy cold to the touch, covered as it was all over with perspiration, that she speedily withdrew her hand in utter surprise.

"What's the matter with you?" she exclaimed.

A blush suffused Baoyu's face, and he took Xiren's hand in a tight grip. Xiren was a girl with all her wits about her; she was besides a couple of years older than Baoyu and had recently come to know something of the world, so that at the sight of his state, she to a great extent readily accounted for the reason in her heart. From modest shame, she unconsciously became purple in the face, and not venturing to ask another question she continued adjusting his clothes. This task accomplished, she followed him over to old lady Jia's apartments; and after a hurry-scurry meal, they came back to this side, and Xiren availed herself of the absence of the nurses and waiting-maids to hand Baoyu another garment to change.

"Please, dear Xiren, don't tell any one," entreated Baoyu, with concealed shame.

"What did you dream of?" inquired Xiren, smiling, as she tried to stifle her blushes, "and whence comes all this perspiration?"

"It's a long story," said Baoyu, "which only a few words will not suffice to explain."

He accordingly recounted minutely, for her benefit, the subject of his dream. When he came to where the Fairy had explained to him the mysteries of love, Xiren was overpowered with modesty and covered her face with her hands; and as she bent down, she gave way to a fit of laughter. Baoyu had always been fond of Xiren, on account of her gentleness, pretty looks and graceful and elegant manner, and he forthwith expounded to her all the mysteries he had been taught by the Fairy.

Xiren was, of course, well aware that dowager lady Jia had given her over to Baoyu, so that her present behavior was likewise no transgression. And subsequently she secretly attempted with Baoyu a violent flirtation, and lucky enough no one broke in upon them during their tête-à-tête. From this date, Baoyu treated Xiren with special regard, far more than he showed to the other girls, while Xiren herself was still more demonstrative in her attentions to Baoyu. But for a time we will make no further remark about them.

As regards the household of the Rong mansion, the inmates may, on adding up the total number, not have been found many; yet, counting the high as well as the low, there were three hundred persons and more. Their affairs may not have been very numerous, still there were, every day, ten and twenty matters to settle; in fact, the household resembled, in every way, raveled hemp, devoid even of a clue-end, which could be used as an introduction.

Just as we were considering what matter and what person it would be best to begin writing of, by a lucky coincidence suddenly from a distance of a thousand li, a person small and insignificant as a grain of mustard seed happened, on account of her distant relationship with the Rong family, to come on this very day to the Rong mansion on a visit. We shall therefore readily commence by speaking of this family, as it after all affords an excellent clue for a beginning.

The surname of this mean and humble family was in point of fact Wang. They were natives of this district. Their ancestor had filled a minor office in the capital, and had, in years gone by, been acquainted with lady Feng's grandfather, that is Madame Wang's father. Being covetous of the influence and affluence of the Wang family, he consequently joined ancestors with them, and was recognized by them as a nephew.

At that time, there were only Madame Wang's eldest brother, that is lady Feng's father, and Madame Wang herself, who knew anything of these distant relations, from the fact of having followed their parents to the capital. The rest of the family had one and all no idea about them.

This ancestor had, at this date, been dead long ago, leaving only one son called Wang Cheng. As the family estate was in a state of ruin, he once more moved outside the city walls and settled down in his native village. Wang Cheng also died soon after his father, leaving a son, known in his infancy as Gou'er, who married a Miss Liu, by whom he had a son called by the infant name of Ban'er, as well as a daughter, Qing'er. His family consisted of four, and he earned a living from farming.

As Gou'er was always busy with something or other during the day and his wife, dame Liu, on the other hand, drew the water, pounded the rice and attended to all the other domestic concerns, the brother and sister, Qing'er and Ban'er, the two of them, had no one to look after them. (Hence it was that) Gou'er brought over his mother-in-law, old goody Liu, to live with them.

This goody Liu was an old widow, with a good deal of experience. She had besides no son round her knees, so that she was dependent for her maintenance on a couple of acres of poor land, with the result that when her son-in-law received her in his home, she naturally was ever willing to exert heart and mind to help her daughter and her son-in-law to earn their living.

This year, the autumn had come to an end, winter had commenced, and the weather had begun to be quite cold. No provision had been made in the household for the winter months, and Gou'er was, inevitably, exceedingly exercised in his heart. Having had several cups of wine to dispel his distress, he sat at home and tried to seize upon every trifle to give vent to his displeasure. His wife had not the courage to force herself in his way, and hence goody Liu it was who encouraged him, as she could not bear to see the state of the domestic affairs.

"Don't pull me up for talking too much," she said; "but who of us country people isn't honest and open-hearted? As the size of the bowl we hold, so is the quantity of the rice we eat. In your young days, you were dependent on the support of your old father, so that eating and drinking became quite a habit with you; that's how, at the present time, your resources are quite uncertain; when you had money, you looked ahead, and didn't mind behind; and now that you have no money, you blindly fly into huffs. A fine fellow and a capital hero you have made! Living though we now be away from the capital, we are after all at the feet of the Emperor; this city of Chang'an is strewn all over with money, but the pity is that there's no one able to go and fetch it away; and it's no use your staying at home and kicking your feet about."

"All you, old lady, know," rejoined Gou'er, after he had heard what she had to say, "is to sit on the couch and talk trash! Is it likely you would have me go and play the robber?"

"Who tells you to become a robber?" asked goody Liu. "But it would be well, after all, that we should put our heads together and devise some means; for otherwise, is the money, pray, able of itself to run into our house?"

"Had there been a way," observed Gou'er, smiling sarcastically, "would I have waited up to this moment? I have besides no revenue collectors as relatives, or friends in official positions; and what way could we devise? 'But even had I any, they wouldn't be likely, I fear, to pay any heed to such as ourselves!"

"That, too, doesn't follow," remarked goody Liu; "the planning of affairs rests with man, but the accomplishment of them rests with Heaven. After we have laid our plans, we may, who can say, by relying on the sustenance of the gods, find some favorable occasion. Leave it to me, I'll try and devise some lucky chance for you people! In years gone by, you joined ancestors with the Wang family of Jinling, and twenty years back, they treated you with consideration; but of late, you've been so high and mighty, and not condescended to go and bow to them, that an estrangement has arisen. I remember how in years gone by, I and my daughter paid them a visit. The second daughter of the family was really so pleasant and knew so well how to treat people with kindness, and without in fact any high airs! She's at present the wife of Mr. Jia, the second son of the Rong Guo mansion; and I hear people say that now that she's advanced in years, she's still more considerate to the poor, regardful of the old, and very fond of preparing vegetable food for the bonzes and performing charitable deeds. The head of the Wang mansion has, it is true, been raised to some office on the frontier, but I hope that this lady Secunda will anyhow notice us. How is it then that you don't find your way as far as there; for she may possibly remember old times, and some good may, no one can say, come of it? I only wish that she would display some of her kind-heartedness, and pluck one hair from her person which would be, yea thicker than our waist."

"What you suggest, mother, is quite correct," interposed Mrs. Liu, Gou'er's wife, who stood by and took up the conversation, "but with such mouth and phiz as yours and mine, how could we present ourselves before her door? Why I fear that the man at her gate won't also like to go and announce us! and we'd better not go and have our mouths slapped in public!"

Gou'er, who would have thought it, prized highly both affluence and fame, so that when he heard these remarks, he forthwith began to feel at heart a little more at ease. When he furthermore heard what his wife had to say, he at once caught up the word as he smiled.

"Old mother," he rejoined; "since that be your idea, and what's more, you have in days gone by seen this lady on one occasion, why shouldn't you, old lady, start tomorrow on a visit to her and first ascertain how the wind blows!"

"Ai Ya!" exclaimed old Goody, "It may very well be said that the marquis' door is like the wide ocean!' what sort of thing am I? why the servants of that family wouldn't even recognise me! even were I to go, it would be on a wild goose chase."

"No matter about that," observed Gou'er; "I'll tell you a good way; you just take along with you, your grandson, little Ban'er, and go first and call upon Zhou Rui, who is attached to that household; and when once you've seen him, there will be some little chance. This Zhou Rui, at one time, was connected with my father in some affair or other, and we were on excellent terms with him."

"That I too know," replied goody Liu, "but the thing is that you've had no dealings with him for so long, that who knows how he's disposed towards us now? this would be hard to say. Besides, you're a man, and with a mouth and phiz like that of yours, you couldn't, on any account, go on this errand. My daughter is a young woman, and she too couldn't very well go and expose herself to public gaze. But by my sacrificing this old face of mine, and by going and knocking it (against the wall) there may, after all, be some benefit and all of us might reap profit."

That very same evening, they laid their plans, and the next morning before the break of day, old goody Liu speedily got up, and having performed her toilette, she gave a few useful hints to Ban'er; who, being a child of five or six years of age, was, when he heard that he was to be taken into the city, at once so delighted that there was nothing that he would not agree to.

Without further delay, goody Liu led off Ban'er, and entered the city, and reaching the Ning Rong street, she came to the main entrance of the Rong mansion, where, next to the marble lions, were to be seen a crowd of chairs and horses. Goody Liu could not however muster the courage to go by, but having shaken her clothes, and said a few more seasonable words to Ban'er, she subsequently squatted in front of the side gate, whence she could see a number of servants, swelling out their chests, pushing out their stomachs, gesticulating with their hands, and kicking their feet about, while they were seated at the main entrance chattering about one thing and another.

Goody Liu felt constrained to edge herself forward. "Gentlemen," she ventured, "may happiness betide you!"

The whole company of servants scrutinised her for a time. "Where do you come from?" they at length inquired.

"I've come to look up Mr. Zhou, an attendant of my lady's, remarked goody Liu, as she forced a smile; "which of you, gentlemen, shall I trouble to do me the favor of asking him to come out?"

The servants, after hearing what she had to say, paid, the whole number of them, no heed to her; and it was after the lapse of a considerable time that they suggested: "Go and wait at a distance, at the foot of that wall; and in a short while, the visitors, who are in their house, will be coming out."

Among the party of attendants was an old man, who interposed. "Don't baffle her object," he expostulated; "why make a fool of her?" and turning to goody Liu: "This Mr. Zhou," he said, "is gone south: his house is at the back row; his wife is anyhow at home; so go round this way, until you reach the door, at the back street, where, if you will ask about her, you will be on the right track."

Goody Liu, having expressed her thanks, forthwith went, leading Ban'er by the hand, round to the back door, where she saw several pedlars resting their burdens. There were also those who sold things to eat, and those who sold playthings and toys; and besides these, twenty or thirty boys bawled and shouted, making quite a noise.

Goody Liu readily caught hold of one of them. "I'd like to ask you just a word, my young friend," she observed; "there's a Mrs. Zhou here; is she at home?"

"Which Mrs. Zhou?" inquired the boy; "we here have three Mrs. Zhous; and there are also two young married ladies of the name of Zhou. What are the duties of the one you want, I wonder?"

"She's a waiting-woman of my lady," replied goody Liu.

"It's easy to get at her," added the boy; "just come along with me."

Leading the way for goody Liu into the backyard, they reached the wall of a court, when he pointed and said, "This is her house. Mother Zhou!" he went on to shout with alacrity; "there's an old lady who wants to see you."

Zhou Rui's wife was at home, and with all haste she came out to greet her visitor. "Who is it?" she asked.

Goody Liu advanced up to her. "How are you," she inquired, "Mrs. Zhou?"

Mrs. Zhou looked at her for some time before she at length smiled and replied, "Old goody Liu, are you well? How many years is it since we've seen each other; tell me, for I forget just now; but please come in and sit."

"You're a lady of rank," answered goody Liu smiling, as she walked along, "and do forget many things. How could you remember such as ourselves?"

With these words still in her mouth, they had entered the house, whereupon Mrs. Zhou ordered a hired waiting-maid to pour the tea. While they were having their tea she remarked, "How Ban'er has managed to grow!" and then went on to make inquiries on the subject of various matters, which had occurred after their separation.

"Today," she also asked of goody Liu, "were you simply passing by? or did you come with any express object?"

"I've come, the fact is, with an object!" promptly replied goody Liu; "(first of all) to see you, my dear sister-in-law; and, in the second place also, to inquire after my lady's health. If you could introduce me to see her for a while, it would be better; but if you can't, I must readily borrow your good offices, my sister-in-law, to convey my message."

Mr. Zhou Rui's wife, after listening to these words, at once became to a great extent aware of the object of her visit. Her husband had, however, in years gone by in his attempt to purchase some land, obtained considerably the support of Gou'er, so that when she, on this occasion, saw goody Liu in such a dilemma, she could not make up her mind to refuse her wish. Being in the second place keen upon making a display of her own respectability, she therefore said smilingly: "Old goody Liu, pray compose your mind! You've come from far off with a pure heart and honest purpose, and how can I ever not show you the way how to see this living Buddha? Properly speaking, when people come and guests arrive, and verbal messages have to be given, these matters are not any of my business, as we all here have each one kind of duties to carry out. My husband has the special charge of the rents of land coming in, during the two seasons of spring and autumn, and when at leisure, he takes the young gentlemen out of doors, and then his business is done. As for myself, I have to accompany my lady and young married ladies on anything connected with out-of-doors; but as you are a relative of my lady and have besides treated me as a high person and come to me for help, I'll, after all, break this custom and deliver your message. There's only one thing, however, and which you, old lady, don't know. We here are not what we were five years before. My lady now doesn't much worry herself about anything; and it's entirely lady Secunda who looks after the menage. But who do you presume is this lady Secunda? She's the niece of my lady, and the daughter of my master, the eldest maternal uncle of by-gone days. Her infant name was Fengge."

"Is it really she?" inquired promptly goody Liu, after this explanation. "Isn't it strange? what I said about her years back has come out quite correct; but from all you say, shall I today be able to see her?"

"That goes without saying," replied Zhou Rui's wife; "when any visitors come now-a-days, it's always lady Feng who does the honors and entertains them, and it's better today that you should see her for a while, for then you will not have walked all this way to no purpose."

"Amituo Fo!" exclaimed old goody Liu; "I leave it entirely to your convenience, sister-in-law."

"What's that you're saying?" observed Zhou Rui's wife. "The proverb says: 'Our convenience is the convenience of others.' All I have to do is to just utter one word, and what trouble will that be to me."

Saying this, she bade the young waiting maid go to the side pavilion, and quietly ascertain whether, in her old ladyship's apartment, table had been laid.

The young waiting-maid went on this errand, and during this while, the two of them continued a conversation on certain irrelevant matters.

"This lady Feng," observed goody Liu, "can this year be no older than twenty, and yet so talented as to manage such a household as this! the like of her is not easy to find!"

"Hai! my dear old goody," said Zhou Rui's wife, after listening to her, "it's not easy to explain; but this lady Feng, though young in years, is nevertheless, in the management of affairs, superior to any man. She has now excelled the others and developed the very features of a beautiful young woman. To say the least, she has ten thousand eyes in her heart, and were they willing to wager their mouths, why ten men gifted with eloquence couldn't even outdo her! But by and bye, when you've seen her, you'll know all about her! There's only this thing, she can't help being rather too severe in her treatment of those below her."

While yet she spake, the young waiting-maid returned. "In her venerable lady's apartment," she reported, "repast has been spread, and already finished; lady Secunda is in Madame Wang's chamber."

As soon as Zhou Rui's wife heard this news, she speedily got up and pressed goody Liu to be off at once. "This is," she urged, "just the hour for her meal, and as she is free we had better first go and wait for her; for were we to be even one step too late, a crowd of servants will come with their reports, and it will then be difficult to speak to her; and after her siesta, she'll have still less time to herself."

As she passed these remarks, they all descended the couch together. Goody Liu adjusted their dresses, and, having impressed a few more words of advice on Ban'er, they followed Zhou Rui's wife through winding passages to Jia Lian's house. They came in the first instance into the side pavilion, where Zhou Rui's wife placed old goody Liu to wait a little, while she herself went ahead, past the screen-wall and into the entrance of the court.

Hearing that lady Feng had not come out, she went in search of an elderly waiting-maid of lady Feng, Ping'er by name, who enjoyed her confidence, to whom Zhou Rui's wife first recounted from beginning to end the history of old goody Liu.

"She has come today," she went on to explain, "from a distance to pay her obeisance. In days gone by, our lady used often to meet her, so that, on this occasion, she can't but receive her; and this is why I've brought her in! I'll wait here for lady Feng to come down, and explain everything to her; and I trust she'll not call me to task for officious rudeness."

Ping'er, after hearing what she had to say, speedily devised the plan of asking them to walk in, and to sit there pending (lady Feng's arrival), when all would be right.

Zhou Rui's wife thereupon went out and led them in. When they ascended the steps of the main apartment, a young waiting-maid raised a red woolen portiere, and as soon as they entered the hall, they smelt a whiff of perfume as it came wafted into their faces: what the scent was they could not discriminate; but their persons felt as if they were among the clouds.

The articles of furniture and ornaments in the whole room were all so brilliant to the sight, and so vying in splendor that they made the head to swim and the eyes to blink, and old goody Liu did nothing else the while than nod her head, smack her lips, and invoke Buddha. Forthwith she was led to the eastern side into the suite of apartments, where was the bedroom of Jia Lian's eldest daughter. Ping'er, who was standing by the edge of the stove-couch, cast a couple of glances at old goody Liu, and felt constrained to inquire how she was, and to press her to have a seat.

Goody Liu, noticing that Ping'er was entirely robed in silks, that she had gold pins fixed in her hair, and silver ornaments in her coiffure, and that her countenance resembled a flower or the moon (in beauty), readily imagined her to be lady Feng, and was about to address her as my lady; but when she heard Mrs. Zhou speak to her as Miss Ping, and Ping'er promptly address Zhou Rui's wife as Mrs. Zhou, she eventually became aware that she could be no more than a waiting-maid of a certain respectability.

She at once pressed old goody Liu and Ban'er to take a seat on the stove-couch. Ping'er and Zhou Rui's wife sat face to face, on the edges of the couch. The waiting-maids brought the tea. After they had partaken of it, old goody Liu could hear nothing but a "lo tang, lo tang" noise, resembling very much the sound of a bolting frame winnowing flour, and she could not resist looking now to the East, and now to the West. Suddenly in the great Hall, she espied, suspended on a pillar, a box at the bottom of which hung something like the weight of a balance, which incessantly wagged to and fro.

"What can this thing be?" communed goody Liu in her heart, "What can be its use?" While she was aghast, she unexpectedly heard a sound of "tang" like the sound of a golden bell or copper cymbal, which gave her quite a start. In a twinkle of the eyes followed eight or nine consecutive strokes; and she was bent upon inquiring what it was, when she caught sight of several waiting-maids enter in a confused crowd. "Our lady has come down!" they announced.

Ping'er, together with Zhou Rui's wife, rose with all haste. "Old goody Liu," they urged, "do sit down and wait till it's time, when we'll come and ask you in."

Saying this, they went out to meet lady Feng.

Old goody Liu, with suppressed voice and ear intent, waited in perfect silence. She heard at a distance the voices of some people laughing, whereupon about ten or twenty women, with rustling clothes and petticoats, made their entrance, one by one, into the hall, and thence into the room on the other quarter. She also detected two or three women, with red-lacquered boxes in their hands, come over on this part and remain in waiting.

"Get the repast ready!" she heard someone from the offside say.

The servants gradually dispersed and went out; and there only remained in attendance a few of them to bring in the courses. For a long time, not so much as the caw of a crow could be heard, when she unexpectedly perceived two servants carry in a couch-table, and lay it on this side of the divan. Upon this table were placed bowls and plates, in proper order replete, as usual, with fish and meats; but of these only a few kinds were slightly touched.

As soon as Ban'er perceived (all these delicacies), he set up such a noise, and would have some meat to eat, but goody Liu administered to him such a slap, that he had to keep away.

Suddenly, she saw Mrs. Zhou approach, full of smiles, and as she waved her hand, she called her. Goody Liu understood her meaning, and at once pulling Ban'er off the couch, she proceeded to the center of the Hall; and after Mrs. Zhou had whispered to her again for a while, they came at length with slow step into the room on this side, where they saw on the outside of the door, suspended by brass hooks, a deep red flowered soft portiere. Below the window, on the southern side, was a stove-couch, and on this couch was spread a crimson carpet. Leaning against the wooden partition wall, on the east side, stood a chain-embroidered back-cushion and a reclining pillow. There was also spread a large watered satin sitting cushion with a gold embroidered center, and on the side stood cuspidores made of silver.

Lady Feng, when at home, usually wore on her head a front-piece of dark martin a la Zhao Jun, surrounded with tassels of strung pearls. She had on a robe of peach-red flowered satin, a short pelisse of slate-blue stiff silk, lined with squirrel, and a jupe of deep red foreign crepe, lined with ermine. Resplendent with pearl-powder and with cosmetics, she sat in there, stately and majestic, with a small brass poker in her hands, with which she was stirring the ashes of the hand-stove. Ping'er stood by the side of the couch, holding a very small lacquered tea-tray. In this tray was a small tea-cup with a cover. Lady Feng neither took any tea, nor did she raise her head, but was intent upon stirring the ashes of the hand-stove.

"How is it you haven't yet asked her to come in?" she slowly inquired; and as she spake, she turned herself round and was about to ask for some tea, when she perceived that Mrs. Zhou had already introduced the two persons and that they were standing in front of her.

She forthwith pretended to rise, but did not actually get up, and with a face radiant with smiles, she ascertained about their health, after which she went in to chide Zhou Rui's wife. "Why didn't you tell me they had come before?" she said.

Old goody Liu was already by this time prostrated on the ground, and after making several obeisances, "How are you, my lady?" she inquired.

"Dear Mrs. Zhou," lady Feng immediately observed, "do pull her up, and don't let her prostrate herself! I'm yet young in years and don't know her much; what's more, I've no idea what's the degree of the relationship between us, and I daren't speak directly to her."

"This is the old lady about whom I spoke a short while back," speedily explained Mrs. Zhou.

Lady Feng nodded her head assentingly.

By this time old goody Liu had taken a seat on the edge of the stove-couch. As for Ban'er, he had gone further, and taken refuge behind her back; and though she tried, by every means, to coax him to come forward and make a bow, he would not, for the life of him, consent.

"Relatives though we be," remarked lady Feng, as she smiled, "we haven't seen much of each other, so that our relations have been quite distant. But those who know how matters stand will assert that you all despise us, and won't often come to look us up; while those mean people, who don't know the truth, will imagine that we have no eyes to look at any one."

Old goody Liu promptly invoked Buddha. "We are at home in great straits," she pleaded, "and that's why it wasn't easy for us to manage to get away and come! Even supposing we had come as far as this, had we not given your ladyship a slap on the mouth, those gentlemen would also, in point of fact, have looked down upon us as a mean lot."

"Why, language such as this," exclaimed lady Feng smilingly, "cannot help making one's heart full of displeasure! We simply rely upon the reputation of our grandfather to maintain the status of a penniless official; that's all! Why, in whose household is there anything substantial? we are merely the denuded skeleton of what we were in days of old, and no more! As the proverb has it: The Emperor himself has three families of poverty-stricken relatives; and how much more such as you and I?"

Having passed these remarks, she inquired of Mrs. Zhou, "Have you let madame know, yes or no?"

"We are now waiting," replied Mrs. Zhou, "for my lady's orders."

"Go and have a look," said lady Feng; "but, should there be anyone there, or should she be busy, then don't make any mention; but wait until she's free, when you can tell her about it and see what she says."

Zhou Rui's wife, having expressed her compliance, went off on this errand. During her absence, lady Feng gave orders to some servants to take a few fruits and hand them to Ban'er to eat; and she was inquiring about one thing and another, when there came a large number of married women, who had the direction of affairs in the household, to make their several reports.

Ping'er announced their arrival to lady Feng, who said: "I'm now engaged in entertaining some guests, so let them come back again in the evening; but should there be anything pressing then bring it in and I'll settle it at once."

Ping'er left the room, but she returned in a short while. "I've asked them," she observed, "but as there's nothing of any urgency, I told them to disperse." Lady Feng nodded her head in token of approval, when she perceived Zhou Rui's wife come back. "Our lady," she reported, as she addressed lady Feng, "says that she has no leisure today, that if you, lady Secunda, will entertain them, it will come to the same thing; that she's much obliged for their kind attention in going to the trouble of coming; that if they have come simply on a stroll, then well and good, but that if they have aught to say, they should tell you, lady Secunda, which will be tantamount to their telling her."

"I've nothing to say," interposed old goody Liu. "I simply come to see our elder and our younger lady, which is a duty on my part, a relative as I am."

"Well, if there's nothing particular that you've got to say, all right," Mrs. Zhou forthwith added, "but if you do have anything, don't hesitate telling lady Secunda, and it will be just as if you had told our lady."

As she uttered these words, she winked at goody Liu. Goody Liu understood what she meant, but before she could give vent to a word, her face got scarlet, and though she would have liked not to make any mention of the object of her visit, she felt constrained to suppress her shame and to speak out.

"Properly speaking," she observed, "this being the first time I see you, my lady, I shouldn't mention what I've to say, but as I come here from far off to seek your assistance, my old friend, I have no help but to mention it."

She had barely spoken as much as this, when she heard the youths at the inner-door cry out: "The young gentleman from the Eastern Mansion has come."

Lady Feng promptly interrupted her. "Old goody Liu," she remarked, "you needn't add anything more." She, at the same time, inquired, "Where's your master, Mr. Rong?" when became audible the sound of footsteps along the way, and in walked a young man of seventeen or eighteen. His appearance was handsome, his person slender and graceful. He had on light furs, a girdle of value, costly clothes, and a beautiful cap.

At this stage, goody Liu did not know whether it was best to sit down or to stand up, neither could she find anywhere to hide herself.

"Pray sit down," urged lady Feng, with a laugh; "this is my nephew!" Old goody Liu then wriggled herself, now one way, and then another, on to the edge of the couch, where she took a seat.

"My father," Jia Rong smilingly ventured, "has sent me to ask a favor of you, aunt. On some previous occasion, our grand-aunt gave you, dear aunt, a stove-couch glass screen, and as tomorrow father has invited some guests of high standing, he wishes to borrow it to lay it out for a little show; after which he purposes sending it back again."

"You're late by a day," replied lady Feng. "It was only yesterday that I gave it to someone."

Jia Rong, upon hearing this, forthwith, with giggles and smiles, made, near the edge of the couch, a sort of genuflexion. "Aunt," he went on, "if you don't lend it, father will again say that I don't know how to speak, and I shall get another sound thrashing. You must have pity upon your nephew, aunt."

"I've never seen anything like this," observed lady Feng sneeringly; "the things belonging to the Wang family are all good, but where have you put all those things of yours? the only good way is that you shouldn't see anything of ours, for as soon as you catch sight of anything, you at once entertain a wish to carry it off."

"Pray, aunt," entreated Jia Rong with a smile, "do show me some compassion."

"Mind your skin!" lady Feng warned him, "if you do chip or spoil it in the least."

She then bade Ping'er take the keys of the door of the upstairs room and send for several trustworthy persons to carry it away.

Jia Rong was so elated that his eyebrows dilated and his eyes smiled. "I've brought myself," he added, with vehemence, "some men to take it away; I won't let them recklessly bump it about."

Saying this, he speedily got up and left the room.

Lady Feng suddenly bethought herself of something, and turning towards the window, she called out, "Rong Ge, come back." Several servants who stood outside caught up her words: "Mr. Rong," they cried, "you're requested to go back;" whereupon Jia Rong turned round and retraced his steps; and with hands drooping respectfully against his sides, he stood ready to listen to his aunt's wishes.

Lady Feng was however intent upon gently sipping her tea, and after a good long while of abstraction, she at last smiled: "Never mind," she remarked; "you can go. But come after you've had your evening meal, and I'll then tell you about it. Just now there are visitors here; and besides, I don't feel in the humor."

Jia Rong thereupon retired with gentle step.

Old goody Liu, by this time, felt more composed in body and heart. "I've today brought your nephew," she then explained, "not for anything else, but because his father and mother haven't at home so much as anything to eat; the weather besides is already cold, so that I had no help but to take your nephew along and come to you, old friend, for assistance!"

As she uttered these words, she again pushed Ban'er forward. "What did your father at home tell you to say?" she asked of him; "and what did he send us over here to do? Was it only to give our minds to eating fruit?"

Lady Feng had long ago understood what she meant to convey, and finding that she had no idea how to express herself in a decent manner, she readily interrupted her with a smile. "You needn't mention anything," she observed, "I'm well aware of how things stand;" and addressing herself to Mrs. Zhou, she inquired, "Has this old lady had breakfast, yes or no?"

Old goody Liu hurried to explain. "As soon as it was daylight," she proceeded, "we started with all speed on our way here, and had we even so much as time to have any breakfast?"

Lady Feng promptly gave orders to send for something to eat. In a short while Zhou Rui's wife had called for a table of viands for the guests, which was laid in the room on the eastern side, and then came to take goody Liu and Ban'er over to have their repast.

"My dear Mrs. Zhou," enjoined lady Feng, "give them all they want, as I can't attend to them myself;" which said, they hastily passed over into the room on the eastern side.

Lady Feng having again called Mrs. Zhou, asked her: "When you first informed madame about them, what did she say?" "Our Lady observed," replied Zhou Rui's wife, "that they don't really belong to the same family; that, in former years, their grandfather was an official at the same place as our old master; that hence it came that they joined ancestors; that these few years there hasn't been much intercourse (between their family and ours); that some years back, whenever they came on a visit, they were never permitted to go empty-handed, and that as their coming on this occasion to see us is also a kind attention on their part, they shouldn't be slighted. If they've anything to say," (our lady continued), "tell lady Secunda to do the necessary, and that will be right."

"Isn't it strange!" exclaimed lady Feng, as soon as she had heard the message; "since we are all one family, how is it I'm not familiar even with so much as their shadow?"

While she was uttering these words, old goody Liu had had her repast and come over, dragging Ban'er; and, licking her lips and smacking her mouth, she expressed her thanks.

Lady Feng smiled. "Do pray sit down," she said, "and listen to what I'm going to tell you. What you, old lady, meant a little while back to convey, I'm already as much as yourself well acquainted with! Relatives, as we are, we shouldn't in fact have waited until you came to the threshold of our doors, but ought, as is but right, to have attended to your needs. But the thing is that, of late, the household affairs are exceedingly numerous, and our lady, advanced in years as she is, couldn't at a moment, it may possibly be, bethink herself of you all! What's more, when I took over charge of the management of the menage, I myself didn't know of all these family connections! Besides, though to look at us from outside everything has a grand and splendid aspect, people aren't aware that large establishments have such great hardships, which, were we to recount to others, they would hardly like to credit as true. But since you've now come from a great distance, and this is the first occasion that you open your mouth to address me, how can I very well allow you to return to your home with empty hands!

By a lucky coincidence our lady gave, yesterday, to the waiting-maids, twenty taels to make clothes with, a sum which they haven't as yet touched, and if you don't despise it as too little, you may take it home as a first instalment, and employ it for your wants."

When old goody Liu heard the mention made by lady Feng of their hardships, she imagined that there was no hope; but upon hearing her again speak of giving her twenty taels, she was exceedingly delighted, so much so that her eyebrows dilated and her eyes gleamed with smiles.

"We too know," she smilingly remarked, "all about difficulties! but the proverb says, 'A camel dying of leanness is even bigger by much than a horse!' No matter what those distresses may be, were you yet to pluck one single hair from your body, my old friend, it would be stouter than our own waist."

Zhou Rui's wife stood by, and on hearing her make these coarse utterances, she did all she could to give her a hint by winking, and make her desist. Lady Feng laughed and paid no heed; but calling Ping'er, she bade her fetch the parcel of money, which had been given to them the previous day, and to also bring a string of cash; and when these had been placed before goody Liu's eyes: "This is," said lady Feng, "silver to the amount of twenty taels, which was for the time given to these young girls to make winter clothes with; but some other day, when you've nothing to do, come again on a stroll, in evidence of the good feeling which should exist between relatives. It's besides already late, and I don't wish to detain you longer and all for no purpose; but, on your return home, present my compliments to all those of yours to whom I should send them."

As she spake, she stood up. Old goody Liu gave utterance to a thousand and ten thousand expressions of gratitude, and taking the silver and cash, she followed Zhou Rui's wife on her way to the out-houses. "Well, mother dear," inquired Mrs. Zhou, "what did you think of my lady that you couldn't speak; and that whenever you opened your mouth it was all 'your nephew?' I'll make just one remark, and I don't mind if you do get angry. Had he even been your kindred nephew, you should in fact have been somewhat milder in your language; for that gentleman, Mr. Rong, is her kith and kin nephew, and whence has appeared such another nephew of hers (as Ban'er)?"

Old goody Liu smiled. "My dear sister-in-law," she replied, "as I gazed upon her, were my heart and eyes, pray, full of admiration or not? and how then could I speak as I should?"

As they were chatting, they reached Zhou Rui's house. They had been sitting for a while, when old goody Liu produced a piece of silver, which she was purposing to leave behind, to be given to the young servants in Zhou Rui's house to purchase fruit to eat; but how could Mrs. Zhou satiate her eye with such a small piece of silver? She was determined in her refusal to accept it, so that old goody Liu, after assuring her of her boundless gratitude, took her departure out of the back gate she had come in from.

Reader, you do not know what happened after old goody Liu left, but listen to the explanation which will be given in the next chapter.

CHAPTER 7

Presentation of artificial flowers made in the Palace. Jia Lian disports himself with Xifeng. Baoyu meets Qin Zhong at a family party.

To resume our narrative. Zhou Rui's wife having seen old goody Liu off, speedily came to report the visit to Madame Wang; but, contrary to her expectation, she did not find Madame Wang in the drawing-room; and it was after inquiring of the waiting-maids that she eventually learnt that she had just gone over to have a chat with "aunt" Xue. Mrs. Zhou, upon hearing this, hastily went out by the eastern corner door, and through the yard on the east, into the Pear Fragrance Court.

As soon as she reached the entrance, she caught sight of Madame Wang's waiting-maid, Jinchuan'er, playing about on the terrace steps, with a young girl, who had just let her hair grow. When they saw Zhou Rui's wife approach, they forthwith surmised that she must have some message to deliver, so they pursed up their lips and directed her to the inner-room. Zhou Rui's wife gently raised the curtain-screen, and upon entering discovered Madame Wang, in voluble conversation with "aunt" Xue, about family questions and people in general.

Mrs. Zhou did not venture to disturb them, and accordingly came into the inner room, where she found Xue Baochai in a house dress, with her hair simply twisted into a knot round the top of the head, sitting on the inner edge of the stove-couch, leaning on a small divan table, in the act of copying a pattern for embroidery, with the waiting-maid Ying'er. When she saw her enter, Baochai hastily put down her brush, and turning round with a face beaming with smiles, "Sister Zhou," she said, "take a seat."

Zhou Rui's wife likewise promptly returned the smile.

"How is my young lady?" she inquired, as she sat down on the edge of the couch. "I haven't seen you come over on the other side for two or three days! Has Mr. Baoyu perhaps given you offence?"

"What an idea!" exclaimed Baochai, with a smile. "It's simply that I've had for the last couple of days my old complaint again, and that I've in consequence kept quiet all this time, and looked after myself."

"Is that it?" asked Zhou Rui's wife; "but after all, what rooted kind of complaint are you subject to, miss? you should lose really no time in sending for a doctor to diagnose it, and give you something to make you all right. With your tender years, to have an organic ailment is indeed no trifle!"

Baochai laughed when she heard these remarks.

"Pray," she said, "don't allude to this again; for this ailment of mine I've seen, I can't tell you, how many doctors; taken no end of medicine and spent I don't know how much money; but the more we did so, not the least little bit of relief did I see. Lucky enough, we eventually came across a bald-pated bonze, whose speciality was the cure of nameless illnesses. We therefore sent for him to see me, and he said that I had brought this along with me from the womb as a sort of inflammatory virus, that luckily I had a constitution strong and hale so that it didn't matter; and that it would be of no avail if I took pills or any medicines. He then told me a prescription from abroad, and gave me also a packet of a certain powder as a preparative, with a peculiar smell and strange flavor. He advised me, whenever my complaint broke out, to take a pill, which would be sure to put me right again. And this has, after all, strange to say, done me a great deal of good."

"What kind of prescription is this one from abroad, I wonder," remarked Mrs. Zhou; "if you, miss, would only tell me, it would be worth our while bearing it in mind, and recommending it to others: and if ever we came across any one afflicted with this disease, we would also be doing a charitable deed."

"You'd better not ask for the prescription," rejoined Baochai smiling. "Why, its enough to wear one out with perplexity! the necessaries and ingredients are few, and all easy to get, but it would be difficult to find the lucky moment! You want twelve ounces of the pollen of the white peone, which flowers in spring, twelve ounces of the pollen of the white summer lily, twelve ounces of the pollen of the autumn hibiscus flower, and twelve ounces of the white plum in bloom in the winter. You take the four kinds of pollen, and put them in the sun, on the very day of the vernal equinox of the succeeding year to get dry, and then you mix them with the powder and pound them well together. You again want twelve mace of water, fallen on 'rain water' day."

"Good gracious!" exclaimed Mrs. Zhou promptly, as she laughed. "From all you say, why you want three years' time! and what if no rain falls on 'rain water' day! What would one then do?"

"Quite so!" Baochai remarked smilingly; "how can there be such an opportune rain on that very day! but to wait is also the best thing, there's nothing else to be done. Besides, you want twelve mace of dew, collected on 'White Dew' day, and twelve mace of the hoarfrost, gathered on 'Frost Descent' day, and twelve mace of snow, fallen on 'Slight Snow' day! You next take these four kinds of waters and mix them with the other ingredients, and make pills of the size of a longan. You keep them in an old porcelain jar, and bury them under the roots of some flowers; and when the ailment betrays itself, you produce it and take a pill, washing it down with two candareens of a yellow cedar decoction."

"Amituo Fo!" cried Mrs. Zhou, when she heard all this, bursting out laughing. "It's really enough to kill one! you might wait ten years and find no such lucky moments!"

"Fortunate for me, however," pursued Baochai, "in the course of a year or two, after the bonze had told me about this prescription, we got all the ingredients; and, after much trouble, we compounded a supply, which we have now brought along with us from the south to the north; and lies at present under the pear trees."

"Has this medicine any name or other of its own?" further inquired Mrs. Zhou.

"It has a name," replied Baochai; "the mangy-headed bonze also told it me; he called it 'cold fragrance' pill."

Zhou Rui's wife nodded her head, as she heard these words. "What do you feel like after all when this complaint manifests itself?" she went on to ask.

"Nothing much," replied Baochai; "I simply pant and cough a bit; but after I've taken a pill, I get over it, and it's all gone."

Mrs. Zhou was bent upon making some further remark, when Madame Wang was suddenly heard to inquire, "Who is in here?"

Mrs. Zhou went out hurriedly and answered; and forthwith told her all about old goody Liu's visit. Having waited for a while, and seeing that Madame Wang had nothing to say, she was on the point of retiring, when "aunt" Xue unexpectedly remarked smiling: "Wait a bit! I've something to give you to take along with you."

And as she spoke, she called for Xiangling. The sound of the screen-board against the sides of the door was heard, and in walked the waiting-maid, who had been playing with Jinchuan. "Did my lady call?" she asked.

"Bring that box of flowers," said Mrs. Xue.

Xiangling assented, and brought from the other side a small embroidered silk box.

"These," explained "aunt" Xue, "are a new kind of flowers, made in the palace. They consist of twelve twigs of flowers of piled gauze. I thought of them yesterday, and as they will, the pity is, only get old, if uselessly put away, why not give them to the girls to wear them in their hair! I meant to have sent them over yesterday, but I forgot all about them. You come today most opportunely, and if you will take them with you, I shall have got them off my hands. To the three young ladies in your family give two twigs each, and of the six that will remain give a couple to Miss Lin, and the other four to lady Feng."

"Better keep them and give them to your daughter Baochai to wear," observed Madame Wang, "and have done with it; why think of all the others?"

"You don't know, sister," replied "aunt" Xue, "what a crotchety thing Baochai is! she has no liking for flower or powder."

With these words on her lips, Zhou Rui's wife took the box and walked out of the door of the room. Perceiving that Jinchuan was still sunning herself outside, Zhou Rui's wife asked her: "Isn't this Xiangling, the waiting-maid that we've often heard of as having been purchased just before the departure of the Xue family for the capital, and on whose account there occurred some case of manslaughter or other?"

"Of course it's she," replied Jinchuan. But as they were talking, they saw Xiangling draw near smirkingly, and Zhou Rui's wife at once seized her by the hand, and after minutely scrutinizing her face for a time, she turned round to Jinchuan and smiled. "With these features she really resembles slightly the style of lady Rong of our Eastern Mansion."

"So I too maintain!" said Jinchuan.

Zhou Rui's wife then asked Xiangling, "At what age did you enter this family? and where are your father and mother at present?" and also inquired, "In what year of your teens are you? and of what place are you a native?"

But Xiangling, after listening to all these questions, simply nodded her head and replied, "I can't remember."

When Mrs. Zhou and Jinchuan heard these words, their spirits changed to grief, and for a while they felt affected and wounded at heart; but in a short time, Mrs. Zhou brought the flowers into the room at the back of Madame Wang's principal apartment.

The fact is that dowager lady Jia had explained that as her granddaughters were too numerous, it would not be convenient to crowd them together in one place, that Baoyu and Daiyu should only remain with her in this part to break her loneliness, but that Yingchun, Tanchun, and Xichun, the three of them, should move on this side in the three rooms within the antechamber, at the back of lady Wang's quarters; and that Li Wan should be told to be their attendant and to keep an eye over them.

Zhou Rui's wife, therefore, on this occasion came first to these rooms as they were on her way, but she only found a few waiting-maids assembled in the antechamber, waiting silently to obey a call.

Yingchun's waiting-maid, Siqi, together with Daishu, Tanchun's waiting-maid, just at this moment raised the curtain, and made their egress, each holding in her hand a tea-cup and saucer; and Zhou Rui's wife readily concluding that the young ladies were sitting together also walked into the inner room, where she only saw Yingchun and Tanchun seated near the window, in the act of playing chess. Mrs. Zhou presented the flowers and explained whence they came, and what they were.

The girls forthwith interrupted their game, and both with a curtsey, expressed their thanks, and directed the waiting-maids to put the flowers away.

Mrs. Zhou complied with their wishes (and handing over the flowers); "Miss Xichun," she remarked, "is not at home; and possibly she's over there with our old lady."

"She's in that room, isn't she?" inquired the waiting-maids.

Mrs. Zhou at these words readily came into the room on this side, where she found Xichun, in company with a certain Zhineng, a young nun of the "moon reflected on water" convent, talking and laughing together. On seeing Zhou Rui's wife enter, Xichun at once asked what she wanted, whereupon Zhou Rui's wife opened the box of flowers, and explained who had sent them.

"I was just telling Zhineng," remarked Xichun laughing, "that I also purpose shortly shaving my head and becoming a nun; and strange enough, here you again bring me flowers; but supposing I shave my head, where can I wear them?"

They were all very much amused for a time with this remark, and Xichun told her waiting-maid, Ju Hua, to come and take over the flowers.

"What time did you come over?" then inquired Mrs. Zhou of Zhineng. "Where is that bald-pated and crotchety superior of yours gone?"

"We came," explained Zhineng, "as soon as it was day; after calling upon Madame Wang, my superior went over to pay a visit in the mansion of Mr. Yü, and told me to wait for her here."

"Have you received," further asked Mrs. Zhou, "the monthly allowance for incense offering due on the fifteenth or not?"

"I can't say," replied Zhineng.

"Who's now in charge of the issue of the monthly allowances to the various temples?" interposed Xichun, addressing Mrs. Zhou, as soon as she heard what was said.

"It's Yu Xin," replied Zhou Rui's wife, "who's intrusted with the charge."

"That's how it is," observed Xichun with a chuckle; "soon after the arrival of the Superior, Yu Xin's wife came over and kept on whispering with her for some time; so I presume it must have been about this allowance."

Mrs. Zhou then went on to bandy a few words with Zhineng, after which she came over to lady Feng's apartments. Proceeding by a narrow passage, she passed under Li Wan's back windows, and went along the wall ornamented with creepers on the west. Going out of the western side gate, she entered lady Feng's court, and walked over into the Entrance Hall, where she only found the waiting-girl Feng'er, sitting on the doorsteps of lady Feng's apartments.

When she caught sight of Mrs. Zhou approaching, she at once waved her hand, bidding her go to the eastern room. Zhou Rui's wife understood her meaning, and hastily came on tiptoe to the chamber on the east, where she saw a nurse patting lady Feng's daughter to sleep.

Mrs. Zhou promptly asked the nurse in a low tone of voice: "Is the young lady asleep at this early hour? But if even she is I must wake her up."

The nurse nodded her head in assent, but as these inquiries were being made, a sound of laughter came from over the other side, in which lady Feng's voice could be detected; followed, shortly after, by the sound of a door opening, and out came Ping'er, with a large brass basin in her hands, which she told Feng'er to fill with water and take inside.

Ping'er forthwith entered the room on this side, and upon perceiving Zhou Rui's wife: "What have you come here again for, my old lady?" she readily inquired.

Zhou Rui's wife rose without any delay, and handed her the box. "I've come," said she, "to bring you a present of flowers."

Upon hearing this, Ping'er opened the box, and took out four sprigs, and, turning round, walked out of the room. In a short while she came from the inner room with two sprigs in her hand, and calling first of all Caiming, she bade her take the flowers over to the mansion on the other side and present them to "madame" Rong, after which she asked Mrs. Zhou to express her thanks on her return.

Zhou Rui's wife thereupon came over to dowager lady Jia's room on this side of the compound, and as she was going through the Entrance Hall, she casually came, face to face, with her daughter, got up in gala dress, just coming from the house of her mother-in-law.

"What are you running over here for at this time?" promptly inquired Mrs. Zhou.

"Have you been well of late, mother?" asked her daughter. "I've been waiting for ever so long at home, but you never come out! What's there so pressing that has prevented you from returning home? I waited till I was tired, and then went on all alone, and paid my respects to our venerable lady; I'm now, on my way to inquire about our lady Wang. What errand haven't you delivered as yet, ma; and what is it you're holding?"

"Ai! as luck would have it," rejoined Zhou Rui's wife smilingly, "old goody Liu came over today, so that besides my own hundred and one duties, I've had to run about here and there ever so long, and all for her! While attending to these, Mrs. Xue came across me, and asked me to take these flowers to the young ladies, and I've been at it up to this very moment, and haven't done yet! But coming at this time, you must surely have something or other that you want me to do for you! what's it?"

"Really ma, you're quick at guessing." exclaimed her daughter with a smile; "I'll tell you what it's all about. The day before yesterday, your son-in-law had a glass of wine too many, and began altercating with some person or other; and someone, I don't know why, spread some evil report, saying that his antecedents were not clear, and lodged a charge against him at the Yamen, pressing the authorities to deport him to his native place. That's why I've come over to consult with you, as to whom we should appeal to, to do us this favor of helping us out of our dilemma!"

"I knew at once," Mrs. Zhou remarked after listening, "that there was something wrong; but this is nothing hard to settle! Go home and wait for me and I'll come straightway, as soon as I've taken these flowers to Miss Lin; our Madame Wang and lady Secunda have both no leisure (to attend to you now,) so go back and wait for me! What's the use of so much hurry!"

Her daughter, upon hearing this, forthwith turned round to go back, when she added as she walked away, "Mind, mother, and make haste."

"All right," replied Zhou Rui's wife, "of course I will; you are young yet, and without experience, and that's why you are in this flurry."

As she spoke, she betook herself into Daiyu's apartments. Contrary to her expectation Daiyu was not at this time in her own room, but in Baoyu's; where they were amusing themselves in trying to solve the "nine strung rings" puzzle. On entering Mrs. Zhou put on a smile. "'Aunt' Xue," she explained, "has told me to bring these flowers and present them to you to wear in your hair."

"What flowers?" exclaimed Baoyu. "Bring them here and let me see them."

As he uttered these words, he readily stretched out his hands and took them over, and upon opening the box and looking in, he discovered, in fact, two twigs of a novel and artistic kind of artificial flowers, of piled gauze, made in the palace.

Daiyu merely cast a glance at them, as Baoyu held them. "Have these flowers," she inquired eagerly, "been sent to me alone, or have all the other girls got some too?"

"Each one of the young ladies has the same," replied Mrs. Zhou; "and these two twigs are intended for you, miss."

Daiyu forced a smile. "Oh! I see," she observed. "If all the others hadn't chosen, even these which remain over wouldn't have been given to me."

Zhou Rui's wife did not utter a word in reply.

"Sister Zhou, what took you over on the other side?" asked Baoyu.

"I was told that our Madame Wang was over there," explained Mrs. Zhou, "and as I went to give her a message, 'aunt' Xue seized the opportunity to ask me to bring over these flowers."

"What was cousin Baochai doing at home?" asked Baoyu. "How is it she's not even been over for these few days?"

"She's not quite well," remarked Mrs. Zhou.

When Baoyu heard this news, "Who'll go," he speedily ascertained of the waiting-maids, "and inquire after her? Tell her that cousin Lin and I have sent round to ask how our aunt and cousin are getting on! ask her what she's ailing from and what medicines she's taking, and explain to her that I know I ought to have gone over myself, but that on my coming back from school a short while back, I again got a slight chill; and that I'll go in person another day."

While Baoyu was yet speaking, Xixue volunteered to take the message, and went off at once; and Mrs. Zhou herself took her leave without another word.

Mrs. Zhou's son-in-law was, in fact, Leng Zixing, the intimate friend of Yucun. Having recently become involved with some party in a lawsuit, on account of the sale of some curios, he had expressly charged his wife to come and sue for the favor (of a helping hand). Zhou Rui's wife, relying upon her master's prestige, did not so much as take the affair to heart; and having waited till evening, she simply went over and requested lady Feng to befriend her, and the matter was forthwith ended.

When the lamps were lit, lady Feng came over, after having disrobed herself, to see Madame Wang. "I've already taken charge," she observed, "of the things sent round today by the Zhen family. As for the presents from us to them, we should avail ourselves of the return of the boats, by which the fresh delicacies for the new year were forwarded, to hand them to them to carry back."

Madame Wang nodded her head in token of approval.

"The birthday presents," continued lady Feng, "for lady Linan, the mother of the Earl of Linan, have already been got together, and whom will you depute to take them over?"

"See," suggested Madame Wang, "who has nothing to do; let four maids go and all will be right! why come again and ask me?"

"Our eldest sister-in-law Zhen," proceeded lady Feng, "came over to invite me to go tomorrow to their place for a little change. I don't think there will be anything for me to do tomorrow."

"Whether there be or not," replied Madame Wang, "it doesn't matter; you must go, for whenever she comes with an invitation, it includes us, who are your seniors, so that, of course, it isn't such a pleasant thing for you; but as she doesn't ask us this time, but only asks you, it's evident that she's anxious that you should have a little distraction, and you mustn't disappoint her good intention. Besides it's certainly right that you should go over for a change."

Lady Feng assented, and presently Li Wan, Yingchun and the other cousins, likewise paid each her evening salutation and retired to their respective rooms, where nothing of any notice transpired.

The next day lady Feng completed her toilette, and came over first to tell Madame Wang that she was off, and then went to say good-bye to dowager lady Jia; but when Baoyu heard where she was going, he also wished to go; and as lady Feng had no help but to give in, and to wait until he had changed his clothes, the sister and brother-in-law got into a carriage, and in a short while entered the Ning mansion.

Mrs. You, the wife of Jia Zhen, and Mrs. Qin, the wife of Mr. Jia Rong, the two sisters-in-law, had, along with a number of maids, waiting-girls, and other servants, come as far as the ceremonial gate to receive them, and Mrs. You, upon meeting lady Feng, for a while indulged, as was her wont, in humorous remarks, after which, leading Baoyu by the hand, they entered the drawing room and took their seats, Mrs. Qin handed tea round.

"What have you people invited me to come here for?" promptly asked lady Feng; "if you have anything to present me with, hand it to me at once, for I've other things to attend to."

Mrs. You and Mrs. Qin had barely any time to exchange any further remarks, when several matrons interposed, smilingly: "Had our lady not come today, there would have been no help for it, but having come, you can't have it all your own way."

While they were conversing about one thing and another, they caught sight of Jia Rong come in to pay his respects, which prompted Baoyu to inquire, "Isn't my elder brother at home today?"

"He's gone out of town today," replied Mrs. You, "to inquire after his grandfather. You'll find sitting here," she continued, "very dull, and why not go out and have a stroll?"

"A strange coincidence has taken place today," urged Mrs. Qin, with a smile; "some time back you, uncle Bao, expressed a wish to see my brother, and today he too happens to be here at home. I think he's in the library; but why not go and see for yourself, uncle Bao?"

Baoyu descended at once from the stove-couch, and was about to go, when Mrs. You bade the servants to mind and go with him. "Don't you let him get into trouble," she enjoined. "It's a far different thing when he comes over under the charge of his grandmother, when he's all right."

"If that be so," remarked lady Feng, "why not ask the young gentleman to come in, and then I too can see him. There isn't, I hope, any objection to my seeing him?"

"Never mind! never mind!" observed Mrs. You, smilingly; "it's as well that you shouldn't see him. This brother of mine is not, like the boys of our Jia family, accustomed to roughly banging and knocking about. Other people's children are brought up politely and properly, and not in this vixenish style of yours. Why, you'd ridicule him to death!"

"I won't laugh at him then, that's all," smiled lady Feng; "tell them to bring him in at once."

"He's shy," proceeded Mrs. Qin, "and has seen nothing much of the world, so that you are sure to be put out when you see him, sister."

"What an idea!" exclaimed lady Feng. "Were he even No Cha himself, I'd like to see him; so don't talk trash; if, after all, you don't bring him round at once, I'll give you a good slap on the mouth."

"I daren't be obstinate," answered Mrs. Qin smiling; "I'll bring him round!"

In a short while she did in fact lead in a young lad, who, compared with Baoyu, was somewhat more slight but, from all appearances, superior to Baoyu in eyes and eyebrows (good looks), which were so clear and well-defined, in white complexion and in ruddy lips, as well as graceful appearance and pleasing manners. He was however bashful and timid, like a girl.

In a shy and demure way, he made a bow to lady Feng and asked after her health.

Lady Feng was simply delighted with him. "You take a low seat next to him!" she ventured laughingly as she first pushed Baoyu back. Then readily stooping forward, she took this lad by the hand and asked him to take a seat next to her. Presently she inquired about his age, his studies and such matters, when she found that at school he went under the name of Qin Zhong.

The matrons and maids in attendance on lady Feng, perceiving that this was the first time their mistress met Qin Zhong, (and knowing) that she had not at hand the usual presents, forthwith ran over to the other side and told Ping'er about it.

Ping'er, aware of the close intimacy that existed between lady Feng and Mrs. Qin, speedily took upon herself to decide, and selecting a piece of silk, and two small gold medals, (bearing the wish that he should attain) the highest degree, the senior wranglership, she handed them to the servants who had come over, to take away.

Lady Feng, however, explained that her presents were too mean by far, but Mrs. Qin and the others expressed their appreciation of them; and in a short time the repast was over, and Mrs. You, lady Feng, and Mrs. Qin played at dominoes, but of this no details need be given; while both Baoyu and Qin Zhong sat down, got up, and talked, as they pleased.

Since he had first glanced at Qin Zhong, and seen what kind of person he was, he felt at heart as if he had lost something, and after being plunged in a dazed state for a time, he began again to give way to foolish thoughts in his mind.

"There are then such beings as he in the world!" he reflected. "I now see there are! I'm however no better than a wallowing pig or a mangy cow! Despicable destiny! why was I ever born in this household of a marquis and in the mansion of a duke? Had I seen the light in the home of some penniless scholar, or poverty-stricken official, I could long ago have enjoyed the communion of his friendship, and I would not have lived my whole existence in vain! Though more honorable than he, it is indeed evident that silk and satins only serve to swathe this rotten trunk of mine, and choice wines and rich meats only to gorge the filthy drain and miry sewer of this body of mine! Wealth! and splendor! ye are no more than contaminated with pollution by me!"

Ever since Qin Zhong had noticed Baoyu's unusual appearance, his sedate deportment, and what is more, his hat ornamented with gold, and his dress full of embroidery, attended by beautiful maids and handsome youths, he did not indeed think it a matter of surprise that everyone was fond of him.

"Born as I have had the misfortune to be," he went on to commune within himself, "in an honest, though poor family, how can I presume to enjoy his companionship! This is verily a proof of what a barrier poverty and wealth set between man and man. What a serious misfortune is this too in this mortal world!"

In wild and inane ideas of the same strain, indulged these two youths!

Baoyu by and by further asked of him what books he was reading, and Qin Zhong, in answer to these inquiries, told him the truth. A few more questions and answers followed; and after about ten remarks, a greater intimacy sprang up between them.

Tea and fruits were shortly served, and while they were having their tea, Baoyu suggested, "We two don't take any wine, and why shouldn't we have our fruit served on the small couch inside, and go and sit there, and thus save you all the trouble?"

The two of them thereupon came into the inner apartment to have their tea; and Mrs. Qin attended to the laying out of fruit and wines for lady Feng, and hurriedly entered the room and hinted to Baoyu: "Dear uncle Bao, your nephew is young, and should he happen to say anything disrespectful, do please overlook it, for my sake, for though shy, he's naturally of a perverse and willful disposition, and is rather given to having his own way."

"Off with you!" cried Baoyu laughing; "I know it all." Mrs. Qin then went on to give a bit of advice to her brother, and at length came to keep lady Feng company. Presently lady Feng and Mrs. You sent another servant to tell Baoyu that there was outside of everything they might wish to eat and that they should mind and go and ask for it; and Baoyu simply signified that they would; but his mind was not set upon drinking or eating; all he did was to keep making inquiries of Qin Zhong about recent family concerns.

Qin Zhong went on to explain that his tutor had last year relinquished his post, that his father was advanced in years and afflicted with disease, and had multifarious public duties to preoccupy his mind, so that he had as yet had no time to make arrangements for another tutor, and that all he did was no more than to keep up his old tasks; that as regards study, it was likewise necessary to have the company of one or two intimate friends, as then only, by dint of a frequent exchange of ideas and opinions, one could arrive at progress; and Baoyu gave him no time to complete, but eagerly urged, "Quite so! But in our household, we have a family school, and those of our kindred who have no means sufficient to engage the services of a tutor are at liberty to come over for the sake of study, and the sons and brothers of our relatives are likewise free to join the class. As my own tutor went home last year, I am now also wasting my time doing nothing; my father's intention was that I too should have gone over to this school, so that I might at least temporarily keep up what I have already read, pending the arrival of my tutor next year, when I could again very well resume my studies alone at home. But my grandmother raised objections; maintaining first of all, that the boys who attend the family classes being so numerous, she feared we would be sure to be up to mischief, which wouldn't be at all proper; and that, in the second place, as I had been ill for some time, the matter should be dropped, for the present. But as, from what you say, your worthy father is very much exercised on this score, you should, on your return, tell him all about it, and come over to our school. I'll also be there as your schoolmate; and as you and I will reap mutual benefit from each other's companionship, won't it be nice!"

"When my father was at home the other day," Qin Zhong smiled and said, "he alluded to the question of a tutor, and explained that the free schools were an excellent institution. He even meant to have come and talked matters over with his son-in-law's father about my introduction, but with the urgent concerns here, he didn't think it right for him to come about this small thing, and make any trouble. But if you really believe that I might be of use to you, in either grinding the ink, or washing the slab, why shouldn't you at once make the needful arrangements, so that neither you nor I may idle our time? And as we shall be able to come together often and talk matters over, and set at the same time our parents' minds at ease, and to enjoy the pleasure of friendship, won't it be a profitable thing!"

"Compose your mind!" suggested Baoyu. "We can by and by first of all, tell your brother-in-law, and your sister, as well as sister-in-law Secunda Lian; and on your return home today, lose no time in explaining all to your worthy father, and when I get back, I'll speak to my grandmother; and I can't see why our wishes shouldn't speedily be accomplished."

By the time they had arrived at this conclusion, the day was far advanced, and the lights were about to be lit; and they came out and watched them once more for a time as they played at dominoes. When they came to settle their accounts Mrs. Qin and Mrs. You were again the losers and had to bear the expense of a theatrical and dinner party; and while deciding that they should enjoy this treat the day after the morrow, they also had the evening repast.

Darkness having set in, Mrs. You gave orders that two youths should accompany Mr. Qin home. The matrons went out to deliver the directions, and after a somewhat long interval, Qin Zhong said goodbye and was about to start on his way.

"Whom have you told to escort him?" asked Mrs. You.

"Jiao Da," replied the matrons, "has been told to go, but it happens that he's under the effects of drink and making free use again of abusive language."

Mrs. You and Mrs. Chin remonstrated. "What's the use," they said, "of asking him? that mean fellow shouldn't be chosen, but you will go again and provoke him."

"People always maintain," added lady Feng, "that you are far too lenient. But fancy allowing servants in this household to go on in this way; why, what will be the end of it?"

"You don't mean to tell me," observed Mrs. You, "that you don't know this Jiao Da? Why, even the gentlemen one and all pay no heed to his doings! your eldest brother, Jia Zheng, he too doesn't notice him. It's all because when he was young he followed our ancestor in three or four wars, and because on one occasion, by extracting our senior from the heap of slain and carrying him on his back, he saved his life. He himself suffered hunger and stole food for his master to eat; they had no water for two days; and when he did get half a bowl, he gave it to his master, while he himself had sewage water. He now simply presumes upon the sentimental obligations imposed by these services. When the seniors of the family still lived, they all looked upon him with exceptional regard; but who at present ventures to interfere with him? He is also advanced in years, and doesn't care about any decent manners; his sole delight is wine; and when he gets drunk, there isn't a single person whom he won't abuse. I've again and again told the stewards not to henceforward ask Jiao Da to do any work whatever, but to treat him as dead and gone; and here he's sent again today."

"How can I not know all about this Jiao Da?" remarked lady Feng; "but the secret of all this trouble is, that you won't take any decisive step. Why not pack him off to some distant farm, and have done with him?" And as she spoke, "Is our carriage ready?" she went on to inquire.

"All ready and waiting," interposed the married women.

Lady Feng also got up, said good-bye, and hand in hand with Baoyu, they walked out of the room, escorted by Mrs. You and the party, as far as the entrance of the Main Hall, where they saw the lamps shedding a brilliant light and the attendants all waiting on the platforms. Jiao Da, however, availing himself of Jia Zhen's absence from home, and elated by wine, began to abuse the head steward Lai Erh for his injustice.

"You bully of the weak and coward with the strong," he cried, "when there's any pleasant charge, you send the other servants, but when it's a question of seeing anyone home in the dark, then you ask me, you disorderly clown! a nice way you act the steward, indeed! Do you forget that if Mr. Jiao Da chose to raise one leg, it would be a good deal higher than your head! Remember please, that twenty years ago, Mr.

Jiao Da wouldn't even so much as look at anyone, no matter who it was; not to mention a pack of hybrid creatures like yourselves!"

While he went on cursing and railing with all his might, Jia Rong appeared, walking by lady Feng's carriage. All the servants having tried to hush him and not succeeding, Jia Rong became exasperated; and forthwith blew up for a time. "Let someone bind him up," he cried, "and tomorrow, when he's over the wine, I'll call him to task, and we'll see if he won't seek death."

Jiao Da showed no consideration for Jia Rong. On the contrary, he shouted with more vigor. Going up to Jia Rong: "Brother Rong," he said, "don't put on the airs of a master with Jiao Da. Not to speak of a man such as you, why even your father and grandfather wouldn't presume to display such side with Jiao Da. Were it not for Jiao Da, and him alone, where would your office, honors, riches, and dignity be? Your ancestor, whom I brought back from the jaws of death, heaped up all this estate, but up to this very day have I received no thanks for the services I rendered! on the contrary, you come here and play the master; don't say a word more, and things may come right; but if you do, I'll plunge the blade of a knife white in you and extract it red."

Lady Feng, from inside the carriage, remarked to Jia Rong: "Don't you yet pack off this insolent fellow! Why, if you keep him in your house, won't he be a source of mischief? Besides, were relatives and friends to hear about these things, won't they have a laugh at our expense, that a household like ours should be so devoid of all propriety?"

Jia Rong assented. The whole band of servants finding that Jiao Da was getting too insolent had no help but to come up and throw him over, and binding him up, they dragged him towards the stables. Jiao Da abused even Jia Zhen with still more vehemence, and shouted in a boisterous manner. "I want to go," he cried, "to the family Ancestral Temple and mourn my old master. Who would have ever imagined that he would leave behind such vile creatures of descendants as you all, day after day indulging in obscene and incestuous practices, 'in scraping of the ashes' and in philandering with brothers-in-law. I know all about your doings; the best thing is to hide one's stump of an arm in one's sleeve!" (wash one's dirty clothes at home).

The servants who stood by, upon hearing this wild talk, were quite at their wits' end, and they at once seized him, tied him up, and filled his mouth to the fullest extent with mud mixed with some horse refuse.

Lady Feng and Jia Rong heard all he said from a distance, but pretended not to hear; but Baoyu, seated in the carriage as he was, also caught this extravagant talk and inquired of lady Feng: "Sister, did you hear him say something about 'scraping of the ashes?' What's it?"

"Don't talk such rubbish!" hastily shouted lady Feng; "it was the maudlin talk of a drunkard! A nice boy you are! not to speak of your listening, but you must also inquire! wait and I'll tell your mother and we'll see if she doesn't seriously take you to task."

Baoyu was in such a state of fright that he speedily entreated her to forgive him. "My dear sister," he craved, "I won't venture again to say anything of the kind"

"My dear brother, if that be so, it's all right!" rejoined lady Feng reassuringly; "on our return we'll speak to her venerable ladyship and ask her to send someone to arrange matters in the family school, and invite Qin Zhong to come to school for his studies."

While yet this conversation was going on, they arrived at the Rong Mansion.

Reader, do you wish to know what follows? If you do, the next chapter will unfold it.

CHAPTER 8

By a strange coincidence, Jia Baoyu
becomes acquainted with the golden clasp.
In an unexpected meeting, Xue Baochai
sees the jade of spiritual perception.

Baoyu and lady Feng, we will now explain, paid, on their return home, their respects to all the inmates, and Baoyu availed himself of the first occasion to tell dowager lady Jia of his wish that Qin Zhong should come over to the family school. "The presence for himself of a friend as schoolmate would," he argued, "be fitly excellent to stir him to zeal," and he went on to speak in terms of high praise of Qin Zhong, his character and his manners, which most of all made people esteem him.

Lady Feng besides stood by him and backed his request. "In a day or two," she added, "Qin Zhong will be coming to pay his obeisance to your venerable ladyship."

This bit of news greatly rejoiced the heart of dowager lady Jia, and lady Feng likewise did not let the opportunity slip, without inviting the old lady to attend the theatrical performance to come off the day after the morrow. Dowager lady Jia was, it is true, well on in years, but was, nevertheless, very fond of enjoyment, so that when the day arrived and Mrs. You came over to invite her round, she forthwith took Madame Wang, Lin Daiyu, Baoyu, and others along and went to the play.

It was about noon, when dowager lady Jia returned to her apartments for her siesta; and Madame Wang, who was habitually partial to a quiet life, also took her departure after she had seen the old lady retire. Lady Feng subsequently took the seat of honor; and the party enjoyed themselves immensely till the evening, when they broke up.

But to return to Baoyu. Having accompanied his grandmother Jia back home, and waited till her ladyship was in her midday sleep, he had in fact an inclination to return to the performance, but he was afraid lest he should be a burden to Mrs. Qin and the rest and lest they should not feel at ease. Remembering therefore that Baochai had been at home unwell for the last few days, and that he had not been to see her, he was anxious to go and look her up, but he dreaded that if he went by the side gate, at the back of the drawing-room, he would be prevented by something or other, and fearing, what would be making matters worse, lest he should come across his father, he consequently thought it better to go on his way by a detour. The nurses and waiting-maids thereupon came to help him to change his clothes; but they saw him not change, but go out again by the second door. These nurses and maids could not help following him out; but they were still under the impression that he was going over to the other mansion to see the theatricals. Contrary to their speculations, upon reaching the entrance hall, he forthwith went to the east, then turned to the north, and walking round by the rear of the hall, he happened to come face to face with two of the family companions, Mr. Zhan Guang, and Mr. Dan Pingren. As soon as they caught sight of Baoyu, they both readily drew up to him, and as they smiled, the one put his arm round his waist, while the other grasped him by the hand.

"Oh divine brother!" they both exclaimed, "this we call dreaming a pleasant dream, for it's no easy thing to come across you!"

While continuing their remarks they paid their salutations, and inquired after his health; and it was only after they had chatted for ever so long, that they went on their way. The nurse called out to them and stopped them, "Have you two gentlemen," she said, "come out from seeing master?"

They both nodded assent. "Your master," they explained, "is in the Meng Po Zhai small library having his siesta; so that you can go through there with no fear."

As they uttered these words, they walked away.

This remark also evoked a smile from Baoyu, but without further delay he turned a corner, went towards the north, and came into the Pear Fragrance Court, where, as luck would have it, he met the head manager of the Household Treasury, Wu Xindeng, who, in company with the head of the granary, Dailiang, and several other head stewards, seven persons in all, was issuing out of the Account Room.

On seeing Baoyu approaching, they, in a body, stood still, and hung down their arms against their sides. One of them alone, a certain butler, called Qianhua, promptly came forward, as he had not seen Baoyu for many a day, and bending on one knee, paid his respects to Baoyu. Baoyu at once gave a smile and pulled him up.

"The day before yesterday," smiled all the bystanders, "we were somewhere together and saw some characters written by you, master Secundus, in the composite style. The writing is certainly better than it was before! When will you give us a few sheets to stick on the wall?"

"Where did you see them?" inquired Baoyu, with a grin.

"They are to be found in more than one place," they replied, "and everyone praises them very much, and what's more, asks us for a few."

"They are not worth having," observed Baoyu smilingly; "but if you do want any, tell my young servants and it will be all right."

As he said these words, he moved onwards. The whole party waited till he had gone by, before they separated, each one to go his own way.

But we need not dilate upon matters of no moment, but return to Baoyu.

On coming to the Pear Fragrance Court, he entered, first, into "aunt" Xue's room, where he found her getting some needlework ready to give to the waiting-maids to work at. Baoyu forthwith paid his respects to her, and "aunt" Xue, taking him by the hand, drew him towards her and clasped him in her embrace.

"With this cold weather," she smilingly urged, "it's too kind of you, my dear child, to think of coming to see me; come along on the stove-couch at once! Bring some tea," she continued, addressing the servants, "and make it as hot as it can be!"

"Isn't Xue Pan at home?" Baoyu having inquired: "He's like a horse without a halter," Mrs. Xue remarked with a sigh; "he's daily running here and there and everywhere, and nothing can induce him to stay at home one single day."

"Is sister (Baochai) all right again?" asked Baoyu. "Yes," replied Mrs. Xue, "she's well again. It was very kind of you two days ago to again think of her, and send round to inquire after her. She's now in there, and you can go and see her. It's warmer there than it's here; go and sit with her inside, and, as soon as I've put everything away, I'll come and join you and have a chat."

Baoyu, upon hearing this, jumped down with alacrity from the stove-couch, and walked up to the door of the inner room, where he saw hanging a portiere somewhat the worse for use, made of red silk. Baoyu raised the portiere and making one step towards the interior, he found Baochai seated on the couch, busy over some needlework. On the top of her head was gathered, and made into a knot, her chevelure, black as lacquer, and glossy like pomade. She wore a honey-colored wadded robe, a rose-brown short-sleeved jacket, lined with the fur of the squirrel of two colors: the "gold and silver;" and a jupe of leek-yellow silk. Her whole costume was neither too new, neither too old, and displayed no sign of extravagance.

Her lips, though not rouged, were naturally red; her eyebrows, though not pencilled, were yet blue-black; her face resembled a silver basin, and her eyes, juicy plums. She was sparing in her words, chary in her talk, so much so that people said that she posed as a simpleton. She was quiet in the acquittal of her duties and scrupulous as to the proper season for everything. "I practise simplicity," she would say of herself.

"How are you? are you quite well again, sister?" inquired Baoyu, as he gazed at her; whereupon Baochai raised her head, and perceiving Baoyu walk in, she got up at once and replied with a smile, "I'm all right again; many thanks for your kindness in thinking of me."

While uttering this, she pressed him to take a seat on the stove-couch, and as he sat down on the very edge of the couch, she told Ying'er to bring tea and asked likewise after dowager lady Jia and lady Feng. "And are all the rest of the young ladies quite well?" she inquired.

Saying this she scrutinised Baoyu, who she saw had a head-dress of purplish-gold twisted threads, studded with precious stones. His forehead was bound with a gold circlet, representing two dragons, clasping a pearl. On his person he wore a light yellow, archery-sleeved jacket, ornamented with rampant dragons, and lined with fur from the ribs of the silver fox; and was clasped with a dark sash, embroidered with different-colored butterflies and birds. Round his neck was hung an amulet, consisting of a clasp of longevity, a talisman of recorded name, and, in addition to these, the precious jade which he had had in his mouth at the time of his birth.

"I've daily heard everyone speak of this jade," said Baochai with a smile, "but haven't, after all, had an opportunity of looking at it closely, but anyhow today I must see it."

As she spoke, she drew near. Baoyu himself approached, and taking it from his neck, he placed it in Baochai's hand. Baochai held it in her palm. It appeared to her very much like the egg of a bird, resplendent as it was like a bright russet cloud; shiny and smooth like variegated curd, and covered with a net for the sake of protection.

Readers, you should know that this was the very block of useless stone which had been on the Da Huang Hills, and which had dropped into the Qing Keng cave, in a state of metamorphosis. A later writer expresses his feelings in a satirical way as follows:

> Nu Wa's fusion of stones was e'er a myth inane,
> But from this myth hath sprung fiction still more insane!
> Lost is the subtle life, divine, and real!—gone!
> Assumed, mean subterfuge! foul bags of skin and bone!
> Fortune, when once adverse, how true! gold glows no more!
> In evil days, alas! the jade's splendor is o'er!
> Bones, white and bleached, in nameless hill-like mounds are flung,
> Bones once of youths renowned and maidens fair and young.

The rejected stone has in fact already given a record of the circumstances of its transformation, and the inscription in seal characters, engraved upon it by the bald-headed bonze, and below will now be also appended a faithful representation of it; but its real size is so very diminutive, as to allow of its being held by a child in his mouth while yet unborn, that were it to have been drawn in its exact proportions, the characters would, it is feared, have been so insignificant in size, that the beholder would have had to waste much of his eyesight, and it would besides have been no pleasant thing.

While therefore its shape has been adhered to, its size has unavoidably been slightly enlarged, to admit of the reader being able, conveniently, to peruse the inscription, even by very lamplight, and though he may be under the influence of wine.

These explanations have been given to obviate any such sneering remarks as: "What could be, pray, the size of the mouth of a child in his mother's womb, and how could it grasp such a large and clumsy thing?"

On the face of the jade was written:

Precious Gem of Spiritual Perception.
If thou wilt lose me not and never forget me,
Eternal life and constant luck will be with thee!

On the reverse was written:

To exorcise evil spirits and the accessory visitations;
To cure predestined sickness;
To prognosticate weal and woe.

Baochai having looked at the amulet, twisted it again to the face, and scrutinising it closely, read aloud:

If thou wilt lose me not and never forget me,
Eternal life and constant luck will be with thee!

She perused these lines twice, and, turning round, she asked Ying'er laughingly: "Why don't you go and pour the tea? why are you standing here like an idiot!"

"These two lines which I've heard," smiled Ying'er, "would appear to pair with the two lines on your necklet, miss!"

"What!" eagerly observed Baoyu with a grin, when he caught these words, "are there really eight characters too on your necklet, cousin? do let me too see it."

"Don't listen to what she says," remarked Baochai, "there are no characters on it."

"My dear cousin," pleaded Baoyu entreatingly, "how is it you've seen mine?"

Baochai was brought quite at bay by this remark of his, and she consequently added, "There are also two propitious phrases engraved on this charm, and that's why I wear it every day. Otherwise, what pleasure would there be in carrying a clumsy thing."

As she spoke, she unfastened the button, and produced from inside her crimson robe, a crystal-like locket, set with pearls and gems, and with a brilliant golden fringe. Baoyu promptly received it from her, and upon minute examination, found that there were in fact four characters on each side; the eight characters on both sides forming two sentences of good omen. The similitude of the locket is likewise then given below. On the face of the locket is written:

"Part not from me and cast me not away;"

And on the reverse:

"And youth, perennial freshness will display!"

Baoyu examined the charm, and having also read the inscription twice over aloud, and then twice again to himself, he said as he smiled, "Dear cousin, these eight characters of yours form together with mine an antithetical verse."

"They were presented to her," ventured Ying'er, "by a mangy-pated bonze, who explained that they should be engraved on a golden trinket...."

Baochai left her no time to finish what she wished to say, but speedily called her to task for not going to bring the tea, and then inquired of Baoyu where he had come from.

Baoyu had, by this time, drawn quite close to Baochai, and perceived whiff after whiff of some perfume or other, of what kind he could not tell. "What perfume have you used, my cousin," he forthwith asked, "to fumigate your dresses with? I really don't remember smelling any perfumery of the kind before."

"I'm very averse," replied Baochai blandly, "to the odor of fumigation; good clothes become impregnated with the smell of smoke."

"In that case," observed Baoyu, "what scent is it?"

"Yes, I remember," Baochai answered, after some reflection; "it's the scent of the 'cold fragrance' pills which I took this morning."

"What are these 'cold fragrance' pills," remarked Baoyu smiling, "that they have such a fine smell? Give me, cousin, a pill to try."

"Here you are with your nonsense again," Baochai rejoined laughingly; "is a pill a thing to be taken recklessly?"

She had scarcely finished speaking, when she heard suddenly someone outside say, "Miss Lin is come; " and shortly Lin Daiyu walked in in a jaunty manner.

"Oh, I come at a wrong moment!" she exclaimed forthwith, smirking significantly when she caught sight of Baoyu.

Baoyu and the rest lost no time in rising and offering her a seat, whereupon Baochai added with a smile, "How can you say such things?"

"Had I known sooner," continued Daiyu, "that he was here, I would have kept away."

"I can't fathom this meaning of yours," protested Baochai.

"If one comes," Daiyu urged smiling, "then all come, and when one doesn't come, then no one comes. Now were he to come today, and I to come tomorrow, wouldn't there be, by a division of this kind, always someone with you every day? and in this way, you wouldn't feel too lonely, nor too crowded. How is it, cousin, that you didn't understand what I meant to imply?"

"Is it snowing?" inquired Baoyu, upon noticing that she wore a cloak made of crimson camlet, buttoning in front.

"It has been snowing for some time," ventured the matrons, who were standing below. "Fetch my wrapper!" Baoyu remarked, and Daiyu readily laughed. "Am I not right? I come, and, of course, he must go at once."

"Did I ever mention that I was going?" questioned Baoyu; "I only wish it brought to have it ready when I want it."

"It's a snowy day," consequently remarked Baoyu's nurse, dame Li, "and we must also look to the time, but you had better remain here and amuse yourself with your cousin. Your aunt has, in there, got ready tea and fruits. I'll tell the waiting-maid to go and fetch your wrapper and the boys to return home." Baoyu assented, and nurse Li left the room and told the boys that they were at liberty to go.

By this time Mrs. Xue had prepared tea and several kinds of nice things and kept them all to partake of those delicacies. Baoyu, having spoken highly of some goose feet and ducks' tongues he had tasted some days before, at his eldest sister-in-law's, Mrs. You's, "aunt" Xue promptly produced several dishes of the same kind, made by herself, and gave them to Baoyu to try. "With a little wine," added Baoyu with a smile, "they would be first rate."

Mrs. Xue thereupon bade the servants fetch some wine of the best quality; but dame Li came forward and remonstrated. "My lady," she said, "never mind the wine."

Baoyu smilingly pleaded: "My nurse, I'll take just one cup and no more."

"It's no use," nurse Li replied, "were your grandmother and mother present, I wouldn't care if you drank a whole jar. I remember the day when I turned my eyes away but for a moment, and some ignorant fool or other, merely with the view of pandering for your favor, gave you only a drop of wine to drink, and how this brought reproaches upon me for a couple of days. You don't know, my lady, you have no idea of his disposition! it's really dreadful; and when he has had a little wine he shows far more temper. On days when her venerable ladyship is in high spirits, she allows him to have his own way about drinking, but he's not allowed to have wine on any and every day; and why should I have to suffer inside and all for nothing at all?"

"You antiquated thing!" replied Mrs. Xue laughing, "set your mind at ease, and go and drink your own wine! I won't let him have too much, and should even the old lady say anything, let the fault be mine."

Saying this, she asked a waiting-maid to take nurse Li along with her and give her also a glass of wine so as to keep out the cold air.

When nurse Li heard these words, she had no alternative but to go for a time with all the others and have some wine to drink.

"The wine need not be warmed: I prefer it cold!" Baoyu went on to suggest meanwhile.

"That won't do," remonstrated Mrs. Xue; "cold wine will make your hand tremble when you write."

"You have," interposed Baochai smiling, "the good fortune, cousin Baoyu, of having daily opportunities of acquiring a knowledge of every kind of subject, and yet don't you know that the properties of wine are mostly heating? If you drink wine warm, its effects soon dispel, but if you drink it cold, it at once congeals in you; and as upon your intestines devolves the warming of it, how can you not derive any harm? and won't you yet from this time change this habit of yours? leave off at once drinking that cold wine."

Baoyu finding that the words he had heard contained a good deal of sense, speedily put down the cold wine, and having asked them to warm it, he at length drank it.

Daiyu was bent upon cracking melon seeds, saying nothing but simply pursing up her lips and smiling, when, strange coincidence,

Xueyan, Daiyu's waiting-maid, walked in and handed her mistress a small hand-stove.

"Who told you to bring it?" ascertained Daiyu grinningly. "I'm sorry to have given whoever it is the trouble; I'm obliged to her. But did she ever imagine that I would freeze to death?"

"Zijuan was afraid," replied Xueyan, "that you would, miss, feel cold, and she asked me to bring it over."

Daiyu took it over and held it in her lap. "How is it," she smiled, "that you listen to what she tells you, but that you treat what I say, day after day, as so much wind blowing past your ears! How is it that you at once do what she bids you, with even greater alacrity than you would an imperial edict?"

When Baoyu heard this, he felt sure in his mind that Daiyu was availing herself of this opportunity to make fun of him, but he made no remark, merely laughing to himself and paying no further notice. Baochai, again, knew full well that this habit was a weak point with Daiyu, so she too did not go out of her way to heed what she said.

"You've always been delicate and unable to stand the cold," interposed "aunt" Xue, "and is it not a kind attention on their part to have thought of you?"

"You don't know, aunt, how it really stands," responded Daiyu smilingly; "fortunately enough, it was sent to me here at your quarters; for had it been in anyone else's house, wouldn't it have been a slight upon them? Is it forsooth nice to think that people haven't so much as a hand-stove, and that one has fussily to be sent over from home? People won't say that the waiting-maids are too officious, but will imagine that I'm in the habit of behaving in this offensive fashion."

"You're far too punctilious," remarked Mrs. Xue, "as to entertain such notions! No such ideas as these crossed my mind just now."

While they were conversing, Baoyu had taken so much as three cups of wine, and nurse Li came forward again to prevent him from having any more. Baoyu was just then in a state of exultation and excitement, (a state) enhanced by the conversation and laughter of his cousins, so that was he ready to agree to having no more! But he was constrained in a humble spirit to entreat for permission. "My dear nurse," he implored, "I'll just take two more cups and then have no more."

"You'd better be careful," added nurse Li, "your father is at home today, and see that you're ready to be examined in your lessons."

When Baoyu heard this mention, his spirits at once sank within him, and gently putting the wine aside, he dropped his head upon his breast.

Daiyu promptly remonstrated. "You've thrown cold water," she said, "over the spirits of the whole company; why, if uncle should ask to see you, well, say that aunt Xue detained you. This old nurse of yours has been drinking, and again makes us the means of clearing her muddled head!"

While saying this, she gave Baoyu a big nudge with the intent of stirring up his spirits, adding, as she addressed him in a low tone of voice: "Don't let us heed that old thing, but mind our own enjoyment."

Dame Li also knew very well Daiyu's disposition, and therefore remarked: "Now, Miss Lin, don't you urge him on; you should after all, give him good advice, as he may, I think, listen to a good deal of what you say to him."

"Why should I urge him on?" rejoined Lin Daiyu, with a sarcastic smile, "nor will I trouble myself to give him advice. You, old lady, are far too scrupulous! Old lady Jia has also time after time given him wine, and if he now takes a cup or two more here, at his aunt's, lady Xue's house, there's no harm that I can see. Is it perhaps, who knows, that aunt is a stranger in this establishment, and that we have in fact no right to come over here to see her?"

Nurse Li was both vexed and amused by the words she had just heard. "Really," she observed, "every remark this girl Lin utters is sharper than a razor! I didn't say anything much!"

Baochai too could not suppress a smile, and as she pinched Daiyu's cheek, she exclaimed, "Oh the tongue of this frowning girl! one can neither resent what it says, nor yet listen to it with any gratification!"

"Don't be afraid!" Mrs. Xue went on to say, "don't be afraid; my son, you've come to see me, and although I've nothing good to give you, you mustn't, through fright, let the trifle you've taken lie heavy on your stomach, and thus make me uneasy; but just drink at your pleasure, and as much as you like, and let the blame fall on my shoulders. What's more, you can stay to dinner with me, and then go home; or if you do get tipsy, you can sleep with me, that's all."

She thereupon told the servants to heat some more wine. "I'll come," she continued, "and keep you company while you have two or three cups, after which we'll have something to eat!"

It was only after these assurances that Baoyu's spirits began at length, once more to revive, and dame Li then directed the waiting-maids what to do. "You remain here," she enjoined, "and mind, be diligent while I go home and change; when I'll come back again. Don't allow him," she also whispered to "aunt" Xue, "to have all his own way and drink too much."

Having said this, she betook herself back to her quarters; and during this while, though there were two or three nurses in attendance, they did not concern themselves with what was going on. As soon as they saw that nurse Li had left, they likewise all quietly slipped out, at the first opportunity they found, while there remained but two waiting-maids, who were only too glad to curry favor with Baoyu. But fortunately "aunt" Xue, by much coaxing and persuading, only let him have a few cups, and the wine being then promptly cleared away, pickled bamboo shoots and chicken-skin soup were prepared, of which Baoyu drank with relish several bowls full, eating besides more than half a bowl of finest rice congee.

By this time, Xue Baochai and Lin Daiyu had also finished their repast; and when Baoyu had drunk a few cups of strong tea, Mrs. Xue felt more easy in her mind. Xueyan and the others, three or four of them in all, had also had their meal, and came in to wait upon them.

"Are you now going or not?" inquired Daiyu of Baoyu.

Baoyu looked askance with his drowsy eyes. "If you want to go," he observed, "I'll go with you."

Daiyu hearing this, speedily rose. "We've been here nearly the whole day," she said, "and ought to be going back."

As she spoke the two of them bade good-bye, and the waiting-maids at once presented a hood to each of them.

Baoyu readily lowered his head slightly and told a waiting-maid to put it on. The girl promptly took the hood, made of deep red cloth, and shaking it out of its folds, she put it on Baoyu's head.

"That will do," hastily exclaimed Baoyu. "You stupid thing! gently a bit; is it likely you've never seen anyone put one on before? let me do it myself."

"Come over here, and I'll put it on for you," suggested Daiyu, as she stood on the edge of the couch. Baoyu eagerly approached her, and Daiyu carefully kept the cap, to which his hair was bound, fast down, and taking the hood she rested its edge on the circlet round his forehead. She then raised the ball of crimson velvet, which was as large as a walnut, and put it in such a way that, as it waved tremulously, it should appear outside the hood. These arrangements completed she cast a look for a while at what she had done. "That's right now," she added, "throw your wrapper over you!"

When Baoyu caught these words, he eventually took the wrapper and threw it over his shoulders.

"None of your nurses," hurriedly interposed aunt Xue, "are yet come, so you had better wait a while."

"Why should we wait for them?" observed Baoyu. "We have the waiting-maids to escort us, and surely they should be enough."

Mrs. Xue finding it difficult to set her mind at ease deputed two married women to accompany the two cousins; and after they had both expressed (to these women) their regret at having troubled them, they came straightway to dowager lady Jia's suite of apartments.

Her venerable ladyship had not, as yet, had her evening repast. Hearing that they had been at Mrs. Xue's, she was extremely pleased; but noticing that Baoyu had had some wine, she gave orders that he should be taken to his room, and put to bed, and not be allowed to come out again.

"Do take good care of him," she therefore enjoined the servants, and when suddenly she bethought herself of Baoyu's attendants, "How is it," she at once inquired of them all, "that I don't see nurse Li here?"

They did not venture to tell her the truth, that she had gone home, but simply explained that she had come in a few moments back, and that they thought she must have again gone out on some business or other.

"She's better off than your venerable ladyship," remarked Baoyu, turning round and swaying from side to side. "Why then ask after her? Were I rid of her, I believe I might live a little longer."

While uttering these words, he reached the door of his bedroom, where he saw brush and ink laid out on the writing table.

"That's nice," exclaimed Qingwen, as she came to meet him with a smile on her face, "you tell me to prepare the ink for you, but though when you get up, you were full of the idea of writing, you only wrote three characters, when you discarded the brush, and ran away, fooling me, by making me wait the whole day! Come now at once and exhaust all this ink before you're let off."

Baoyu then remembered what had taken place in the morning. "Where are the three characters I wrote?" he consequently inquired, smiling.

"Why this man is tipsy," remarked Qingwen sneeringly. "As you were going to the other mansion, you told me to stick them over the door. I was afraid lest any one else should spoil them, as they were being pasted, so I climbed up a high ladder and was ever so long in putting them up myself; my hands are even now numb with cold."

"Oh I forgot all about it," replied Baoyu grinning, "if your hands are cold, come and I'll rub them warm for you."

Promptly stretching out his hand, he took those of Qingwen in his, and the two of them looked at the three characters, which he recently had written, and which were pasted above the door. In a short while, Daiyu came.

"My dear cousin," Baoyu said to her smilingly, "tell me without any prevarication which of the three characters is the best written?"

Daiyu raised her head and perceived the three characters: Red, Rue, Hall. "They're all well done," she rejoined, with a smirk, "How is it you've written them so well? By and bye you must also write a tablet for me."

"Are you again making fun of me?" asked Baoyu smiling; "what about sister Xiren?" he went on to inquire.

Qingwen pouted her lips, pointing towards the stove-couch in the inner room, and, on looking in, Baoyu espied Xiren fast asleep in her daily costume.

"Well," Baoyu observed laughing, "there's no harm in it, but its rather early to sleep. When I was having my early meal, on the other side," he proceeded, speaking to Qingwen, "there was a small dish of dumplings, with bean curd outside; and as I thought you would like to have some, I asked Mrs. You for them, telling her that I would keep them, and eat them in the evening; I told someone to bring them over, but have you perchance seen them?"

"Be quick and drop that subject," suggested Qingwen; "as soon as they were brought over, I at once knew they were intended for me; as I had just finished my meal, I put them by in there, but when nurse Li came she saw them. 'Baoyu,' she said, 'is not likely to eat them, so I'll take them and give them to my grandson.' And forthwith she bade someone take them over to her home."

While she was speaking, Xixue brought in tea, and Baoyu pressed his cousin Lin to have a cup.

"Miss Lin has gone long ago," observed all of them, as they burst out laughing, "and do you offer her tea?"

Baoyu drank about half a cup, when he also suddenly bethought himself of some tea, which had been brewed in the morning. "This morning," he therefore inquired of Xixue, "when you made a cup of maple-dew tea, I told you that that kind of tea requires brewing three or four times before its color appears; and how is that you now again bring me this tea?"

"I did really put it by," answered Xixue, "but nurse Li came and drank it, and then went off."

Baoyu upon hearing this, dashed the cup he held in his hand on the ground, and as it broke into small fragments, with a crash it spattered Xixue's petticoat all over.

"Of whose family is she the mistress?" inquired Baoyu of Xixue, as he jumped up, "that you all pay such deference to her. I just simply had a little of her milk, when I was a brat, and that's all; and now she has got into the way of thinking herself more high and mighty than even the heads of the family! She should be packed off, and then we shall all have peace and quiet."

Saying this, he was bent upon going, there and then, to tell dowager lady Jia to have his nurse driven away.

Xiren was really not asleep, but simply feigning, with the idea, when Baoyu came, to startle him in play. At first, when she heard him speak of writing, and inquire after the dumplings, she did not think it necessary to get up, but when he flung the tea-cup on the floor, and got into a temper, she promptly jumped up and tried to appease him, and to prevent him by coaxing from carrying out his threat.

A waiting-maid sent by dowager lady Jia came in, meanwhile, to ask what was the matter.

"I had just gone to pour tea," replied Xiren, without the least hesitation, "and I slipped on the snow and fell, while the cup dropped from my hand and broke. Your decision to send her away is good," she went on to advise Baoyu, "and we are all willing to go also; and why not avail yourself of this opportunity to dismiss us in a body? It will be for our good, and you too on the other hand, needn't perplex yourself about not getting better people to come and wait on you!"

When Baoyu heard this taunt, he had at length not a word to say, and supported by Xiren and the other attendants on to the couch, they divested him of his clothes. But they failed to understand the drift of what Baoyu kept on still muttering, and all they could make out was an endless string of words; but his eyes grew heavier and drowsier, and they forthwith waited upon him until he went to sleep; when Xiren unclasped the jade of spiritual perception, and rolling it up in a handkerchief, she lay it under the mattress, with the idea that when he put it on the next day it should not chill his neck.

Baoyu fell sound asleep the moment he lay his head on the pillow. By this time nurse Li and the others had come in, but when they heard that Baoyu was tipsy, they too did not venture to approach, but gently made inquiries as to whether he was asleep or not. On hearing that he was, they took their departure with their minds more at ease.

The next morning the moment Baoyu awoke, someone came in to tell him that young Mr. Rong, living in the mansion on the other side, had brought Qin Zhong to pay him a visit.

Baoyu speedily went out to greet them and to take them over to pay their respects to dowager lady Jia. Her venerable ladyship upon perceiving that Qin Zhong, with his handsome countenance, and his refined manners, would be a fit companion for Baoyu in his studies, felt extremely delighted at heart; and having readily detained him to tea, and kept him to dinner, she went further and directed a servant to escort him to see Madame Wong and the rest of the family.

With the fond regard of the whole household for Mrs Qin they were, when they saw what a kind of person Qin Zhong was, so enchanted with him, that at the time of his departure, they all had presents to give him; even dowager lady Jia herself presented him with a purse and a golden image of the God of Learning, with a view that it should incite him to study and harmony.

"Your house," she further advised him, "is far off, and when it's cold or hot, it would be inconvenient for you to come all that way, so you had better come and live over here with me. You'll then be always with your cousin Baoyu, and you won't be together, in your studies, with those fellow-pupils of yours who have no idea what progress means.

Qin Zhong made a suitable answer to each one of her remarks, and on his return home he told everything to his father.

His father, Qin Ye, held at present the post of Secretary in the Peking Field Force, and was well-nigh seventy. His Wife had died at an early period, and as she left no issue, he adopted a son and a daughter from a foundling asylum.

But who would have thought it, the boy also died, and there only remained the girl, known as Ke'er in her infacy, who when she grew up, was beautiful in face and graceful in manners, and who by reason of some relationship with the Jia family, was consequently united by the ties of marriage (to one of the household).

Qin Ye was in his fiftieth year when he at length got this son. As his tutor had the previous year left to go south, he remained at home keeping up his former lessons; and (his father) had been just thinking of talking over the matter with his relatives of the Jia family, and sending his son to the private school, when, as luck would have it, this opportunity of meeting Baoyu presented itself.

Knowing besides that the family school was under the direction of the venerable scholar Jia Dairu, and hoping that by joining his class, (his son) might advance in knowledge and by these means reap reputation, he was therefore intensely gratified. The only drawbacks were that his official emoluments were scanty, and that both the eyes of everyone in the other establishment were set upon riches and honors, so that he could not contribute anything short of the amount (given by others); but his son's welfare throughout life was a serious consideration, and he, needless to say, had to scrape together from the East and to collect from the West; and making a parcel, with all deference, of twenty-four taels for an introduction present, he came along with Qin Zhong to Dairu's house to pay their respects. But he had to wait subsequently until Baoyu could fix on an auspicious date on which they could together enter the school.

As for what happened after they came to school, the next chapter will divulge.

CHAPTER 9

Jia Zheng gives good advice to his wayward son. Li Gui receives a reprimand. Jia Rui and Li Gui rebuke the obstinate youths! Mingyan causes trouble in the schoolroom.

But to return to our story, Mr. Qin, the father, and Qin Zhong, his son, only waited until the receipt, by the hands of a servant, of a letter from the Jia family about the date on which they were to go to school. Indeed, Baoyu was only too impatient that he and Qin Zhong should come together, and, without loss of time, he fixed upon two days later as the day upon which they were definitely to begin their studies, and he despatched a servant with a letter to this effect.

On the day appointed, as soon as it was daylight, Baoyu turned out of bed. Xiren had already by that time got books, brushes, and all writing necessaries in perfect readiness, and was sitting on the edge of the bed in a moping mood; but as soon as she saw Baoyu approach, she was constrained to wait upon him in his toilette and ablutions.

Baoyu, noticing how despondent she was, made it a point to address her. "My dear sister," he said, "how is it you aren't again yourself? Is it likely that you bear me a grudge for being about to go to school, because when I leave you, you'll all feel dull?"

Xiren smiled. "What an idea!" she replied. "Study is a most excellent thing, and without it a whole lifetime is a mere waste, and what good comes in the long run? There's only one thing, which is simply that when engaged in reading your books, you should set your mind on your books; and that you should think of home when not engaged in reading. Whatever you do, don't romp together with them, for were you to meet our master, your father, it will be no joke. Although it's asserted that a scholar must strain every nerve to excel, yet it's preferable that the tasks should be somewhat fewer, as, in the first place, when one eats too much, one cannot digest it; and, in the second place, good health must also be carefully attended to. This is my view on the subject, and you should at all times consider it in practice."

While Xiren gave utterance to a sentence, Baoyu nodded his head in sign of approval of that sentence. Xiren then went on to speak. "I've also packed up," she continued, "your long pelisse, and handed it to the pages to take it over; so mind, when it's cold in the school-room, please remember to put on this extra clothing, for it's not like home, where you have people to look after you. The foot-stove and hand-stove, I've also sent over; and urge that pack of lazy-bones to attend to their work, for if you say nothing, they will be so engrossed in their frolics, that they'll be loath to move, and let you, all for nothing, take a chill and ruin your constitution."

"Compose your mind," replied Baoyu; "when I go out, I know well enough how to attend to everything my own self. But you people shouldn't remain in this room, and mope yourselves to death; and it would be well if you would often go over to cousin Lin's for a romp."

While saying this, he had completed his toilette, and Xiren pressed him to go and wish good morning to dowager lady Jia, Jia Zheng, Madame Wang, and the other members of the family.

Baoyu, after having gone on to give a few orders to Qingwen and Sheyue, at length left his apartments, and coming over, paid his obeisance to dowager lady Jia. Her venerable Ladyship had likewise, as a matter of course, a few recommendations to make to him, which ended, he next went and greeted Madame Wang; and leaving again her quarters, he came into the library to wish Jia Zheng good morning.

As it happened, Jia Zheng had on this day returned home at an early hour, and was, at this moment, in the library, engaged in a friendly chat with a few gentlemen, who were family companions. Suddenly perceiving Baoyu come in to pay his respects, and report that he was about to go to school, Jia Zheng gave a sardonic smile. "If you do again," he remarked, "make allusions to the words going to school, you'll make even me blush to death with shame! My advice to you is that you should after all go your own way and play; that's the best thing for you; and mind you don't pollute with dirt this floor by standing here, and soil this door of mine by leaning against it!"

The family companions stood up and smilingly expostulated: "Venerable Sir," they pleaded, "why need you be so down upon him? Our worthy brother is this day going to school, and may in two or three years be able to display his abilities and establish his reputation. He will, beyond doubt, not behave like a child, as he did in years gone past. But as the time for breakfast is also drawing nigh, you should, worthy brother, go at once."

When these words had been spoken, two among them, who were advanced in years, readily took Baoyu by the hand, and led him out of the library.

"Who are in attendance upon Baoyu?" Jia Zheng having inquired, he heard a suitable reply, "We, Sir!" given from outside; and three or four sturdy fellows entered at an early period and fell on one knee, and bowed and paid their obeisance.

When Jia Zheng came to scrutinise who they were, and he recognised Li Gui, the son of Baoyu's nurse, he addressed himself to him. "You people," he said, "remain waiting upon him the whole day long at school, but what books has he after all read? Books indeed! why, he has read and filled his brains with a lot of trashy words and nonsensical phrases, and learnt some ingenious way of waywardness. Wait till I have a little leisure, and I'll set to work, first and foremost, and flay your skin off, and then settle accounts with that good-for-nothing!"

This threat so terrified Li Gui that he hastily fell on both his knees, pulled off his hat, knocked his head on the ground, and gave vent to repeated assenting utterances: "Oh, quite so, Sir! Our elder brother Mr. Bao has," he continued, "already read up to the third book of the *Book of Odes*, up to where there's something or other like: 'You, you, the deer bleat; the lotus leaves and duckweed.' Your servant wouldn't presume to tell a lie!"

As he said this, the whole company burst out into a boisterous fit of laughter, and Jia Zheng himself could not also contain his countenance and had to laugh. "Were he even," he observed, "to read thirty books of the *Book of Odes*, it would be as much an imposition upon people and no more, as (when the thief) who, in order to steal the bell, stops up his own ears! You go and present my compliments to the gentleman in the schoolroom, and tell him, from my part, that the whole lot of *Odes* and old writings are of no use, as they are subjects for empty show; and that he should, above all things, take the Four Books, and explain them to him, from first to last, and make him know them all thoroughly by heart—that this is the most important thing!"

Li Gui signified his obedience with all promptitude, and perceiving that Jia Zheng had nothing more to say, he retired out of the room.

During this while, Baoyu had been standing all alone outside in the court, waiting quietly with suppressed voice, and when they came out he at once walked away in their company.

Li Gui and his companions observed as they shook their clothes, "Did you, worthy brother, hear what he said that he would first of all flay our skins off! People's servants acquire some respectability from the master whom they serve, but we poor fellows fruitlessly wait upon you, and are beaten and blown up in the bargain. It would be well if we were, from henceforward, to be treated with a certain amount of regard."

Baoyu smiled, "Dear Brother," he added, "don't feel aggrieved; I'll invite you to come round tomorrow!"

"My young ancestor," replied Li Gui, "who presumes to look forward to an invitation? all I entreat you is to listen to one or two words I have to say, that's all."

As they talked they came over once more to dowager lady Jia's on this side.

Qin Zhong had already arrived, and the old lady was first having a chat with him. Forthwith the two of them exchanged salutations, and took leave of her ladyship; but Baoyu, suddenly remembering that he had not said good-bye to Daiyu, promptly betook himself again to Daiyu's quarters to do so.

Daiyu was, at this time, below the window, facing the mirror, and adjusting her toilette. Upon hearing Baoyu mention that he was on his way to school, she smiled and remarked, "That's right! you're now going to school and you'll be sure to reach the lunar palace and pluck the olea fragrans; but I can't go along with you."

"My dear cousin," rejoined Baoyu, "wait for me to come out from school, before you have your evening meal; wait also until I come to prepare the cosmetic of rouge."

After a protracted chat, he at length tore himself away and took his departure.

"How is it," interposed Daiyu, as she once again called out to him and stopped him, "that you don't go and bid farewell to your cousin Baochai?"

Baoyu smiled, and saying not a word by way of reply he straightway walked to school, accompanied by Qin Zhong.

This public school, which it must be noticed was also not far from his quarters, had been originally instituted by the founder of the establishment, with the idea that should there be among the young fellows of his clan any who had not the means to engage a tutor, they should readily be able to enter this class for the prosecution of their studies; that all those of the family who held official position should all give (the institution) pecuniary assistance, with a view to meet the expenses necessary for allowances to the students; and that they were to select men advanced in years and possessed of virtue to act as tutors of the family school.

The two of them, Qin Zhong and Baoyu, had now entered the class, and after they and the whole number of their schoolmates had made each other's acquaintance, their studies were commenced. Ever since this time, these two were wont to come together, go together, get up together, and sit together, till they became more intimate and close. Besides, dowager lady Jia got very fond of Qin Zhong, and would again and again keep him to stay with them for three and five days at a time, treating him as if he were one of her own great-grandsons. Perceiving that in Qin Zhong's home there was not much in the way of sufficiency, she also helped him in clothes and other necessaries; and scarcely had one or two months elapsed before Qin Zhong got on friendly terms with everyone in the Rong mansion.

Baoyu was, however, a human being who could not practise contentment and observe propriety; and as his sole delight was to have every caprice gratified, he naturally developed a craving disposition. "We two, you and I, are," he was also wont secretly to tell Qin Zhong, "of the same age, and fellow-scholars besides, so that there's no need in the future to pay any regard to our relationship of uncle and nephew; and we should treat each other as brothers or friends, that's all."

Qin Zhong at first (explained that) he could not be so presumptuous; but as Baoyu would not listen to any such thing, but went on to address him as brother and to call him by his style Qingqing, he had likewise himself no help, but to begin calling him, at random, anything and anyhow.

There were, it is true, a large number of pupils in this school, but these consisted of the sons and younger brothers of that same clan, and of several sons and nephews of family connections. The proverb appositely describes that there are nine species of dragons, and that each species differs; and it goes of course without saying that in a large number of human beings there were dragons and snakes, confusedly admixed, and that creatures of a low standing were included.

Ever since the arrival of the two young fellows, Qin Zhong and Baoyu, both of whom were in appearance as handsome as budding flowers, and they, on the one hand, saw how modest and genial Qin Zhong was, how he blushed before he uttered a word, how he was timid and demure like a girl, and on the other hand, how that Baoyu was naturally proficient in abasing and demeaning himself, how he was so affable and good-natured, considerate in his temperament and so full of conversation, and how that these two were, in consequence, on such terms of intimate friendship, it was, in fact, no matter of surprise that the whole company of fellow-students began to foster envious thoughts, that they, behind their backs, passed on their account, this one disparaging remark and that one another, and that they insinuated slanderous lies against them, which extended inside as well as outside the school-room.

Indeed, after Xue Pan had come over to take up his quarters in Madame Wang's suite of apartments, he shortly came to hear of the existence of a family school, and that this school was mainly attended by young fellows of tender years, and inordinate ideas were suddenly aroused in him. While he therefore fictitiously gave out that he went to school, [he was as irregular in his attendance as the fisherman] who catches fish for three days, and suns his nets for the next two; simply presenting his school-fee gift to Jia Dairu and making not the least progress in his studies; his sole dream being to knit a number of familiar friendships. Who would have thought it, there were in this school young pupils, who, in their greed to obtain money, clothes, and eatables from Xue Pan, allowed themselves to be cajoled by him, and played tricks upon; but on this topic, it is likewise superfluous to dilate at any length.

There were also two lovable young scholars, relatives of what branch of the family is not known, and whose real surnames and names have also not been ascertained, who, by reason of their good and winsome looks, were, by the pupils in the whole class, given two nicknames, to one that of "Xianglian," Fragrant Love, and to the other "Yuai," Precious Affection. But although everyone entertained feelings of secret admiration for them, and had the wish to take liberties with the young fellows, they lived, nevertheless, one and all, in such terror of Xue Pan's imperious influence, that they had not the courage to come forward and interfere with them.

As soon as Qin Zhong and Baoyu had, at this time, come to school, and they had made the acquaintance of these two fellow-pupils, they too could not help becoming attached to them and admiring them, but as they also came to know that they were great friends of Xue Pan, they did not, in consequence, venture to treat them lightly, or to be unseemly in their behaviour towards them. Xianglian and Yuai both kept to themselves the same feelings, which they fostered for Qin Zhong and Baoyu, and to this reason is to be assigned the fact that though these four persons nurtured fond thoughts in their hearts there was however no visible sign of them. Day after day, each one of them would, during school hours, sit in four distinct places: but their eight eyes were secretly linked together; and, while indulging either in innuendoes or in double entendres, their hearts, in spite of the distance between them, reflected the whole number of their thoughts.

But though their outward attempts were devoted to evade the detection of other people's eyes, it happened again that, while least expected, several sly lads discovered the real state of affairs, with the result that the whole school stealthily frowned their eyebrows at them, winked their eyes at them, or coughed at them, or raised their voices at them; and these proceedings were, in fact, not restricted to one single day.

As luck would have it, on this day Dairui was, on account of business, compelled to go home; and having left them as a task no more than a heptameter line for an antithetical couplet, explaining that they should find a sentence to rhyme, and that the following day when he came back, he would set them their lessons, he went on to hand the affairs connected with the class to his elder grandson, Jia Rui, whom he asked to take charge.

Wonderful to say Xue Pan had of late not frequented school very often, not even so much as to answer the roll, so that Qin Zhong availed himself of his absence to ogle and smirk with Xianglian; and these two pretending that they had to go out, came into the back court for a chat.

"Does your worthy father at home mind your having any friends?" Qin Zhong was the first to ask. But this sentence was scarcely ended, when they heard a sound of coughing coming from behind. Both were taken much aback, and, speedily turning their heads round to see, they found that it was a fellow-scholar of theirs, called Jin Rong.

Xianglian was naturally of somewhat hasty temperament, so that with shame and anger mutually impelling each other, he inquired of him, "What's there to cough at? Is it likely you wouldn't have us speak to each other?"

"I don't mind your speaking," Jin Rong observed laughing; "but would you perchance not have me cough? I'll tell you what, however; if you have anything to say, why not utter it in intelligible language? Were you allowed to go on in this mysterious manner, what strange doings would you be up to? But I have sure enough found you out, so what's the need of still prevaricating? But if you will, first of all, let me partake of a share in your little game, you and I can hold our tongue and utter not a word. If not, why the whole school will begin to turn the matter over."

At these words, Qin Zhong and Xianglian were so exasperated that their blood rushed up to their faces. "What have you found out?" they hastily asked.

"What I have now detected," replied Jin Rong smiling, "is the plain truth!" and saying this he went on to clap his hands and to call out with a loud voice as he laughed: "They have moulded some nice well-baked cakes, won't you fellows come and buy one to eat!" (These two have been up to larks, won't you come and have some fun!)

Both Qin Zhong and Xianglian felt resentful as well as fuming with rage, and with hurried step they went in, in search of Jia Rui, to whom they reported Jin Rong, explaining that Jin Rong had insulted them both, without any rhyme or reason.

The fact is that this Jia Rui was, in an extraordinary degree, a man with an eye to the main chance, and devoid of any sense of propriety. His wont was at school to take advantage of public matters to serve his private interest, and to bring pressure upon his pupils with the intent that they should regale him. While subsequently he also lent his countenance to Xue Pan, scheming to get some money or eatables out of him, he left him entirely free to indulge in disorderly behavior; and not only did he not go out of his way to hold him in check, but, on the contrary, he encouraged him, infamous though he was already, to become a bully, so as to curry favor with him.

But this Xue Pan was, by nature, gifted with a fickle disposition; today, he would incline to the east, and tomorrow to the west, so that having recently obtained new friends, he put Xianglian and Yuai aside. Jin Rong too was at one time an intimate friend of his, but ever since he had acquired the friendship of the two lads, Xianglian and Yuai, he forthwith deposed Jin Rong. Of late, he had already come to look down upon even Xianglian and Yuai, with the result that Jia Rui as well was deprived of those who could lend him support, or stand by him; but he bore Xue Pan no grudge, for wearying with old friends, as soon as he found new ones, but felt angry that Xianglian and Yuai had not put in a word on his behalf with Xue Pan. Jia Rui, Jin Rong and, in fact, the whole crowd of them were, for this reason, just harboring a jealous grudge against these two, so that when he saw Qin Zhong and Xianglian come on this occasion and lodge a complaint against Jin Rong, Jia Rui readily felt displeasure creep into his heart; and, although he did not venture to call Qin Zhong to account, he nevertheless made an example of Xianglian. And instead (of taking his part), he called him a busybody and denounced him in much abusive language, with the result that Xianglian did not, contrariwise, profit in any way, but brought displeasure upon himself. Even Qin Zhong grumbled against the treatment, as each of them resumed their places.

Jin Rong became still more haughty, and wagging his head and smacking his lips, he gave vent to many more abusive epithets; but as it happened that they also reached Yuai's ears, the two of them, though seated apart, began an altercation in a loud tone of voice.

Jin Rong, with obstinate pertinacity, clung to his version. "Just a short while back," he said, "I actually came upon them, as they were indulging in demonstrations of intimate friendship in the back court. These two had resolved to be one in close friendship, and were eloquent in their protestations, mindful only in persistently talking their trash, but they were not aware of the presence of another person."

But his language had, contrary to all expectations, given, from the very first, umbrage to another person, and who do you, (gentle reader,) imagine this person to have been?

This person was, in fact, one whose name was Jia Se; a grandson likewise of a main branch of the Ning mansion. His parents had died at an early period, and he had, ever since his youth, lived with Jia Zhen. He had at this time grown to be sixteen years of age, and was, as compared with Jia Rong, still more handsome and good looking. These two cousins were united by ties of the closest intimacy, and were always together, whether they went out or stayed at home.

The inmates of the Ning mansion were many in number, and their opinions of a mixed kind; and that whole bevy of servants, devoid as they were of all sense of right, solely excelled in the practice of inventing stories to backbite their masters; and this is how some mean person or other again, who it was is not known, insinuated slanderous and opprobrious reports (against Jia Se). Jia Zhen had, presumably, also come to hear some unfavorable criticisms (on his account), and having, of course, to save himself from odium and suspicion, he had, at this juncture, after all, to apportion him separate quarters, and to bid Jia Se move outside the Ning mansion, where he went and established a home of his own to live in.

This Jia Se was handsome as far as external appearances went, and intelligent withal in his inward natural gifts, but, though he nominally came to school, it was simply however as a mere blind; for he treated, as he had ever done, as legitimate occupations, such things as cock fighting, dog-racing, and visiting places of easy virtue. And as, above, he had Jia Zhen to spoil him by over-indulgence; and below, there was Jia Rong to stand by him, who of the clan could consequently presume to run counter to him?

Seeing that he was on the closest terms of friendship with Jia Rong, how could he reconcile himself to the harsh treatment which he now saw Qin Zhong receive from some persons? Being now bent upon pushing himself forward to revenge the injustice, he was, for the time, giving himself up to communing with his own heart. "Jin Rong, Jia Rui, and the rest are," he pondered, "friends of uncle Xue, but I too am on friendly terms with him, and he with me, and if I do come forward and they tell old Xue, won't we impair the harmony which exists between us? and if I don't concern myself, such idle tales make, when spoken, everyone feel uncomfortable; and why shouldn't I now devise some means to hold them in check, so as to stop their mouths, and prevent any loss of face!"

Having concluded this train of thought, he also pretended that he had to go out, and, walking as far as the back, he, with low voice, called to his side Mingyan, the page attending upon Baoyu in his studies, and in one way and another, he made use of several remarks to egg him on.

This Mingyan was the smartest of Baoyu's attendants, but he was also young in years and lacked experience, so that he lent a patient ear to what Jia Se had to say about the way Chin Rong had insulted Qin Zhong. "Even your own master, Baoyu," (Jia Se added), "is involved, and if you don't let him know a bit of your mind, he will next time be still more arrogant."

This Mingyan was always ready, even with no valid excuse, to be insolent and overbearing to people, so that after hearing the news and being furthermore instigated by Jia Se, he speedily rushed into the schoolroom and cried out "Jin Rong;" nor did he address him as Mr. Jin, but merely shouted "What kind of fellow is this called Jin?"

Jia Se presently shuffled his feet, while he designedly adjusted his dress and looked at the rays of the sun. "It's time," he observed and walking forthwith, first up to Jia Rui, he explained to him that he had something to attend to and would like to get away a little early; and as Jia Rui did not venture to stop him, he had no alternative but to let him have his way and go.

During this while, Mingyan had entered the room and promptly seizing Jin Rong in a grip: "What we do, whether proper or improper," he said, "doesn't concern you! It's enough anyway that we don't defile your father! A fine brat you are indeed, to come out and meddle with your Mr. Ming!"

These words plunged the scholars of the whole class in such consternation that they all wistfully and absently looked at him.

"Mingyan," hastily shouted out Jia Rui, "you're not to kick up a rumpus."

Jin Rong was so full of anger that his face was quite yellow. "What a subversion of propriety! a slave and a menial to venture to behave in this manner! I'll just simply speak to your master," he exclaimed as he readily pushed his hands off and was about to go and lay hold of Baoyu to beat him.

Qin Zhong was on the point of turning round to leave the room, when with a sound of whiff which reached him from behind, he at once caught sight of a square inkslab come flying that way. Who had thrown it he could not say, but it struck the desk where Jia Lan and Jia Jun were seated.

These two, Jia Lan and Jia Jun, were also the great-grandsons of a close branch of the Rong mansion. This Jia Jun had been left fatherless at an early age, and his mother doated upon him in an unusual manner, and it was because at school he was on most friendly terms with Jia Lan, that these two sat together at the same desk. Who would have believed that Jia Jun would, in spite of being young in years, have had an extremely strong mind, and that he would be mostly up to mischief without the least fear of anyone? He watched with listless eye from his seat Jun Rong's friends stealthily assist Jun Rong, as they flung an ink-slab to strike Mingyan, but when, as luck would have it, it hit the wrong mark, and fell just in front of him, smashing to atoms the porcelain inkslab and water bottle, and smudging his whole book with ink, Jia Jun was, of course, much incensed, and hastily gave way to abuse. "You consummate pugnacious criminal rowdies! why, doesn't this amount to all of you taking a share in the fight!" And as he uttered this abuse, he too forthwith seized an inkslab, which he was bent upon flinging.

Jia Lan was one who always tried to avoid trouble, so that he lost no time in pressing down the inkslab, while with all the words his mouth could express, he tried to pacify him, adding "My dear brother, it's no business of yours and mine."

Jia Jun could not repress his resentment; and perceiving that the inkslab was held down, he at once laid hold of a box containing books, which he flung in this direction; but being, after all, short of stature, and weak of strength, he was unable to send it anywhere near the mark; so that it dropped instead when it got as far as the desk belonging to Baoyu and Qin Zhong, while a dreadful crash became audible as it fell smash on the table. The books, papers, brushes, inkslabs, and other writing materials were all scattered over the whole table; and Baoyu's cup besides containing tea was itself broken to pieces and the tea spilt.

Jia Jun forthwith jumped forward with the intent of assailing the person who had flung the inkslab at the very moment that Jin Rong took hold of a long bamboo pole which was near by; but as the space was limited, and the pupils many, how could he very well brandish a long stick? Mingyan at an early period received a whack, and he shouted wildly, "Don't you fellows yet come to start a fight."

Baoyu had, besides, along with him several pages, one of whom was called Saohong, another Chuyao, another Moyu. These three were naturally up to every mischief, so that with one voice, bawling boisterously, "You children of doubtful mothers, have you taken up arms?" Moyu promptly took up the bar of a door; while Sao Hung and Chuyao both laid hold of horsewhips, and they all rushed forward like a hive of bees.

Jia Rui was driven to a state of exasperation; now he kept this one in check, and the next moment he reasoned with another, but who would listen to his words? They followed the bent of their inclinations and stirred up a serious disturbance.

Of the whole company of wayward young fellows, some there were who gave sly blows for fun's sake; others there were who were not gifted with much pluck and hid themselves on one side; there were those too who stood on the tables, clapping their hands and laughing immoderately, shouting out: "Go at it."

The row was, at this stage, like water bubbling over in a cauldron, when several elderly servants, like Li Gui and others, who stood outside, heard the uproar commence inside, and one and all came in with all haste and united in their efforts to pacify them. Upon asking "What's the matter?" the whole bevy of voices shouted out different versions; this one giving this account, while another again another story. But Li Gui temporized by rebuking Mingyan and others, four in all, and packing them off.

Qin Zhong's head had, at an early period, come into contact with Jin Rong's pole and had had the skin grazed off. Baoyu was in the act of rubbing it for him, with the overlap of his coat, but realizing that the whole lot of them had been hushed up, he forthwith bade Li Gui collect his books.

"Bring my horse round," he cried; "I'm going to tell Mr. Jia Dairu that we have been insulted. I won't venture to tell him anything else, but (tell him I will) that having come with all propriety and made our report to Mr. Jia Rui, Mr. Jia Rui instead (of helping us) threw the fault upon our shoulders. That while he heard people abuse us, he went so far as to instigate them to beat us; that Mingyan seeing others insult us, did naturally take our part; but that they, instead (of desisting,) combined together and struck Mingyan and even broke open Qin Zhong's head. And that how is it possible for us to continue our studies in here?"

"My dear sir," replied Li Gui coaxingly, "don't be so impatient! As Mr. Jia Dairu has had something to attend to and gone home, were you now, for a trifle like this, to go and disturb that aged gentleman, it will make us, indeed, appear as if we had no sense of propriety: my idea is that wherever a thing takes place, there should it be settled; and what's the need of going and troubling an old man like him. This is all you, Mr. Jia Rui, who is to blame; for in the absence of Mr. Jia Dairu, you, sir, are the head in this school, and everyone looks to you to take action. Had all the pupils been at fault, those who deserved a beating should have been beaten, and those who merited punishment should have been punished! and why did you wait until things came to such a pass, and didn't even exercise any check?"

"I blew them up," pleaded Jia Rui, "but not one of them would listen."

"I'll speak out, whether you, worthy sir, resent what I'm going to say or not," ventured Li Gui. "It's you, sir, who all along have after all had considerable blame attached to your name; that's why all these young men wouldn't hear you! Now if this affair is bruited, until it reaches Mr. Jia Dairu's ears, why even you, sir, will not be able to escape condemnation; and why don't you at once make up your mind to disentangle the ravelled mess and dispel all trouble and have done with it!"

"Disentangle what?" inquired Baoyu; "I shall certainly go and make my report."

"If Jin Rong stays here," interposed Qin Zhong sobbing, "I mean to go back home."

"Why that?" asked Baoyu. "Is it likely that others can safely come and that you and I can't? I feel it my bounden duty to tell everyone everything at home so as to expel Jin Rong. This Jin Rong," he went on to inquire as he turned towards Li Gui, "is the relative or friend of what branch of the family?"

Li Gui gave way to reflection and then said by way of reply: "There's no need whatever for you to raise this question; for were you to go and report the matter to the branch of the family to which he belongs, the harmony which should exist between cousins will be still more impaired."

"He's the nephew of Mrs. Huang, of the Eastern mansion," interposed Mingyan from outside the window. "What a determined and self-confident fellow he must be to even come and bully us; Mrs. Huang is his paternal aunt! That mother of yours is only good for tossing about like a millstone, for kneeling before our lady Lian, and begging for something to pawn. I've no eye for such a specimen of mistress."

"What!" speedily shouted Li Gui, "does this son of a dog happen to know of the existence of all these gnawing maggots?" (these disparaging facts).

Baoyu gave a sardonic smile. "I was wondering whose relative he was," he remarked; "is he really sister-in-law Huang's nephew? well, I'll go at once and speak to her."

As he uttered these words, his purpose was to start there and then, and he called Mingyan in, to come and pack up his books. Mingyan walked in and put the books away. "Master," he went on to suggest, in an exultant manner, "there's no need for you to go yourself to see her; I'll go to her house and tell her that our old lady has something to ask of her. I can hire a carriage to bring her over, and then, in the presence of her venerable ladyship, she can be spoken to; and won't this way save a lot of trouble?"

"Do you want to die?" speedily shouted Li Gui; "mind, when you go back, whether right or wrong, I'll first give you a good bumping, and then go and report you to our master and mistress, and just tell them that it's you, and only you, who instigated Mr. Baoyu! I've succeeded, after ever so much trouble, in coaxing them, and mending matters to a certain extent, and now you come again to continue a new plan. It's you who stirred up this row in the school-room; and not to speak of your finding, as would have been the proper course, some way of suppressing it, there you are instead still jumping into the fire."

Mingyan, at this juncture, could not muster the courage to utter a sound. By this time Jia Rui had also apprehended that if the row came to be beyond clearing up, he himself would likewise not be clear of blame, so that circumstances compelled him to pocket his grievances and to come and entreat Qin Zhong as well as to make apologies to Baoyu. These two young fellows would not at first listen to his advances, but Baoyu at length explained that he would not go and report the occurrence, provided only Jin Rong admitted his being in the wrong. Jin Rong refused, at the outset, to agree to this, but he ultimately could find no way out of it, as Jia Rui himself urged him to make some temporizing apology.

Li Gui and the others felt compelled to tender Jin Rong some good advice: "It's you," they said, "who have given rise to the disturbance, and if you don't act in this manner, how will the matter ever be brought to an end?" so that Jin Rong found it difficult to persist in his obstinacy, and was constrained to make a bow to Qin Zhong.

Baoyu was, however, not yet satisfied, but would insist upon his knocking his head on the ground, and Jia Rui, whose sole aim was to temporarily smother the affair, quietly again urged Jin Rong, adding that the proverb has it: "That if you keep down the anger of a minute, you will for a whole lifetime feel no remorse."

Whether Jin Rong complied or not to his advice is not known, but the following chapter will explain.

CHAPTER 10

Widow Jin, prompted by a desire to reap advantage, puts up temporarily with an insult. Dr. Zhang in discussing Mrs. Jin's illness minutely exhausts its origin.

We will now resume our story. As the persons against Jin Rong were so many and their pressure so great, and as, what was more, Jia Rui urged him to make amends, he had to knock his head on the ground before Qin Zhong. Baoyu then gave up his clamorous remonstrances and the whole crowd dispersed from school.

Jin Rong himself returned home all alone, but the more he pondered on the occurrence, the more incensed he felt. "Qin Zhong," he argued, "is simply Jia Rong's young brother-in-law, and is no son or grandson of the Jia family, and he too joins the class and prosecutes his studies on no other footing than that of mine; but it's because he relies upon Baoyu's friendship for him that he has no eye for anyone. This being the case, he should be somewhat proper in his behavior, and there would be then not a word to say about it! He has besides all along been very mystical with Baoyu, imagining that we are all blind, and have no eyes to see what's up! Here he goes again today and mixes with people in illicit intrigues; and it's all because they happened to obtrude themselves before my very eyes that this rumpus has broken out; but of what need I fear?"

His mother, née Hu, hearing him mutter; "Why meddle again," she explained, "in things that don't concern you? I had endless trouble in getting to speak to your paternal aunt; and your aunt had, on the other hand, a thousand and one ways and means to devise, before she could appeal to lady Secunda, of the Western mansion; and then only it was that you got this place to study in. Had we not others to depend upon for your studies, would we have in our house the means sufficient to engage a teacher? Besides, in other people's school, tea and eatables are all ready and found; and these two years that you've been there for your lessons, we've likewise effected at home a great saving in what would otherwise have been necessary for your eating and use. Something has been, it's true, economized; but you have further a liking for spick and span clothes. Besides, it's only through your being there to study, that you've come to know Mr. Xue! that Mr. Xue, who has even in one year given us so much pecuniary assistance as seventy and eighty taels! And now you would go and raise a row in this school-room! why, if we were bent upon finding such another place, I tell you plainly, and once for all, that we would find it more difficult than if we tried to scale the heavens! Now do quietly play for a while, and then go to sleep, and you'll be ever so much better for it then."

Jin Rong thereupon stifled his anger and held his tongue; and, after a short while, he in fact went to sleep of his own accord.

The next day he again went to school, and no further comment need be made about it; but we will go on to explain that a young lady related to her had at one time been given in marriage to a descendant (of the eldest branch) of the Jia family, (whose names were written) with the jade radical, Jia Huang by name; but how could the whole number of members of the clan equal in affluence and power the two mansions of Ning and Rong? This fact goes, as a matter of course, without saying. The Jia Huang couple enjoyed some small income; but they also went, on frequent occasions, to the mansions of Ning and Rong to pay their respects; and they knew likewise so well how to adulate lady Feng and Mrs. You, that lady Feng and Mrs. You would often grant them that assistance and support which afforded them the means of meeting their daily expenses.

It just occurred on this occasion that the weather was clear and fine, and that there happened, on the other hand, to be nothing to attend to at home, so forthwith taking along with her a matron, (Mrs. Jia Huang) got into a carriage and came over to see widow Jin and her nephew. While engaged in a chat, Jin Rong's mother accidentally broached the subject of the affair, which had transpired in the school-room of the Jia mansion on the previous day, and she gave, for the benefit of her young sister-in-law, a detailed account of the whole occurrence from beginning to end.

This Mrs. Huang would not have had her temper ruffled had she not come to hear what had happened; but having heard about it, anger sprung from the very depths of her heart. "This fellow, Qin Zhong," she exclaimed, "is a relative of the Jia family, but is it likely that Rong'er isn't, in like manner, a relative of the Jia family; and when relatives are many, there's no need to put on airs! Besides, does his conduct consist, for the most part, of anything that would make one get any face? In fact, Baoyu himself shouldn't do injury to himself by condescending to look at him. But, as things have come to this pass, give me time and

I'll go to the Eastern mansion and see our lady Cheng and then have a chat with Qin Zhong's sister, and ask her to decide who's right and who's wrong!"

Jin Rong's mother upon hearing these words was terribly distressed. "It's all through my hasty tongue," she observed with vehemence, "that I've told you all, sister-in-law: but please, sister, give up at once the idea of going over to say anything about it! Don't trouble yourself as to who is in the right, and who is in the wrong; for were any unpleasantness to come out of it, how could we here stand on our legs? and were we not to stand on our legs, not only would we never be able to engage a tutor, but the result will be, on the contrary, that for his own person will be superadded many an expense for eatables and necessaries."

"What do I care about how many?" replied Mrs. Huang; "wait till I've spoken about it, and we'll see what will be the result." Nor would she accede to her sister-in-law's entreaties, but bidding, at the same time, the matron look after the carriage, she got into it, and came over to the Ning Mansion.

On her arrival at the Ning Mansion, she entered by the eastern side gate, and dismounting from the carriage, she went in to call on Mrs. You, the spouse of Jia Zhen, with whom she had not the courage to put on any high airs; but gently and quietly she made inquiries after her health, and after passing some irrelevant remarks, she ascertained: "How is it I don't see lady Rong today?"

"I don't know," replied Mrs. You, "what's the matter with her these last few days; but she hasn't been herself for two months and more; and the doctor who was asked to see her declares that it is nothing connected with any happy event. A couple of days back, she felt, as soon as the afternoon came, both to move, and both even to utter a word; while the brightness of her eyes was all dimmed; and I told her, 'You needn't stick to etiquette, for there's no use for you to come in the forenoon and evening, as required by conventionalities; but what you must do is, to look after your own health. Should any relative come over, there's also myself to receive them; and should any of the senior generation think your absence strange, I'll explain things for you, if you'll let me.'

"I also advised brother Rong on the subject: 'You shouldn't,' I said, 'allow anyone to trouble her; nor let her be put out of temper, but let her quietly attend to her health, and she'll get all right. Should she fancy anything to eat, just come over here and fetch it; for, in the event of anything happening to her, were you to try and find another such a wife to wed, with such a face and such a disposition, why, I fear, were you even to seek with a lantern in hand, there would really be no place where you could discover her. And with such a temperament and deportment as hers, which of our relatives and which of our elders don't love her?' That's why my heart has been very distressed these two days! As luck would have it early this morning her brother turned up to see her, but who would have fancied him to be such a child, and so ignorant of what is proper and not proper to do? He saw well enough that his sister was not well; and what's more all these matters shouldn't have been recounted to her; for even supposing he had received the gravest offences imaginable, it behoved him anyhow not to have broached the subject to her! Yesterday, one would scarcely believe it, a fight occurred in the school-room, and some pupil or other who attends that class, somehow insulted him; besides, in this business, there were a good many indecent and improper utterances, but all these he went and told his sister! Now, sister-in-law, you are well aware that though (our son Rong's) wife talks and laughs when she sees people, that she is nevertheless imaginative and withal too sensitive, so that no matter what she hears, she's for the most part bound to brood over it for three days and five nights, before she loses sight of it, and it's from this excessive sensitiveness that this complaint of hers arises. Today, when she heard that someone had insulted her brother, she felt both vexed and angry; vexed that those fox-like, cur-like friends of his had moved right and wrong, and intrigued with this one and deluded that one; angry that her brother had, by not learning anything profitable, and not having his mind set upon study, been the means of bringing about a row at school; and on account of this affair, she was so upset that she did not even have her early meal. I went over a short while back and consoled her for a time, and likewise gave her brother a few words of advice; and after having packed off that brother of hers to the mansion on the other side, in search of Baoyu, and having stood by and seen her have half a bowl of birds' nests soup, I at length came over. Now, sister-in-law, tell me, is my heart sore or not? Besides, as there's nowadays no good doctor, the mere thought of her complaint makes my heart feel as if it were actually pricked with needles! But do you and yours, perchance, know of any good practitioner?"

Mrs. Jin had, while listening to these words, been, at an early period, so filled with concern that she cast away to distant lands the reckless rage she had been in recently while at her sister-in-law's house, when she had determined to go and discuss matters over with Mrs. Qin. Upon hearing Mrs. You inquire of her about a good doctor, she lost no time in saying by way of reply: "Neither have we heard of anyone speak of a good doctor; but from the account I've just heard of Mrs. Qin's illness, it may still, there's no saying, be some felicitous ailment; so, sister-in-law, don't let any one treat her recklessly, for were she to be treated for the wrong thing, the result may be dreadful!"

"Quite so!" replied Mrs. You.

But while they were talking, Jia Zhen came in from out of doors, and upon catching sight of Mrs. Jin; "Isn't this Mrs. Huang?" he inquired of Mrs. You; whereupon Mrs. Jin came forward and paid her respects to Jia Zhen.

"Invite this lady to have her repast here before she goes," observed Jia Zhen to Mrs. You; and as he uttered these words he forthwith walked into the room on the off side.

The object of Mrs. Jin's present visit had originally been to talk to Mrs. Qin about the insult which her brother had received from the hands of Qin Zhong, but when she heard that Mrs. Qin was ill, she did not have the courage to even so much as make mention of the object of her errand. Besides, as Jia Zhen and Mrs. You had given her a most cordial reception, her resentment was transformed into pleasure, so that after a while spent in a further chat about one thing and another, she at length returned to her home.

It was only after the departure of Mrs. Jin that Jia Zhen came over and took a seat. "What did she have to say for herself during this visit today?" he asked of Mrs. You.

"She said nothing much," replied Mrs. You. "When she first entered the room, her face bore somewhat of an angry look, but, after a lengthy chat and as soon as mention of our son's wife's illness was made, this angered look after all gradually abated. You also asked me to keep her for the repast, but, having heard that our son's wife was so ill she could not very well stay, so that all she did was to sit down, and after making a few more irrelevant remarks, she took her departure. But she had no request to make. To return however now to the illness of Rong's wife, it's urgent that you should find somewhere a good doctor to diagnose it for her; and whatever you do, you should lose no time. The whole body of doctors who at present go in and out of our household, are they worth having? Each one of them listens to what the patient has to say of the ailment, and then, adding a string of flowery sentences, out he comes with a long rigmarole; but they are exceedingly diligent in paying us visits; and in one day, three or four of them are here at least four and five times in rotation! They come and feel her pulse, they hold consultation together, and write their prescriptions, but, though she has taken their medicines, she has seen no improvement; on the contrary, she's compelled to change her clothes three and five times each day, and to sit up to see the doctor; a thing which, in fact, does the patient no good."

"This child too is somewhat simple," observed Jia Zhen; "for what need has she to be taking off her clothes, and changing them for others? And were she again to catch a chill, she would add something more to her illness; and won't it be dreadful! The clothes may be no matter how fine, but what is their worth, after all? The health of our child is what is important to look to! and were she even to wear out a suit of new clothes a day, what would that too amount to? I was about to tell you that a short while back, Feng Ziying came to see me, and, perceiving that I had somewhat of a worried look, he asked me what was up; and I told him that our son's wife was not well at all, that as we couldn't get any good doctor, we couldn't determine with any certainty, whether she was in an interesting condition, or whether she was suffering from some disease; that as we could neither tell whether there was any danger or not, my heart was, for this reason, really very much distressed. Feng Ziying then explained that he knew a young doctor who had made a study of his profession, Zhang by surname, and Youshi by name, whose learning was profound to a degree; who was besides most proficient in the principles of medicine, and had the knack of discriminating whether a patient would live or die; that this year he had come to the capital to purchase an official rank for his son, and that he was now living with him in his house. In view of these circumstances, not knowing but that if, perchance, the case of our daughter-in-law were placed in his hands, he couldn't avert the danger, I readily despatched a servant, with a card of mine, to invite him to come; but the hour today being rather late, he probably won't be round, but I believe he's sure to be here tomorrow. Besides, Feng Ziying was also on his return home, to personally entreat him on my behalf, so that he's bound, when he has asked him, to come and see her. Let's therefore wait till Dr. Zhang has been here and seen her, when we can talk matters over!"

Mrs. You was very much cheered when she heard what was said. "The day after tomorrow," she felt obliged to add, "is again our senior's, Mr. Jia Jing's birthday, and how are we to celebrate it after all?"

"I've just been over to our Senior's and paid my respects," replied Jia Zhen, "and further invited the old gentleman to come home, and receive the congratulations of the whole family.

"'I'm accustomed,' our Senior explained, 'to peace and quiet, and have no wish to go over to that worldly place of yours; for you people are certain to have published that it's my birthday, and to entertain the design to ask me to go round to receive the bows of the whole lot of you. But won't it be better if you were to give the "Record of Meritorious Acts," which I annotated some time ago, to someone to copy out clean for me, and have it printed? Compared with asking me to come, and uselessly receive the obeisances of you all, this will be yea even a hundred times more profitable! In the event of the whole family wishing to pay me a visit on any of the two days, tomorrow or the day after tomorrow, if you were to stay at home and entertain them in proper style, that will be all that is wanted; nor will there be any need to send me anything! Even you needn't come two days from this; and should you not feel contented at heart, well, you had better bow your head before me today before you go. But if you do come again the day after tomorrow, with a lot of people to disturb me, I shall certainly be angry with you.' After what he said, I will not venture to go and see him two days hence; but you had better send for Lai Sheng, and bid him get ready a banquet to continue for a couple of days."

Mrs. You, having asked Jia Rong to come round, told him to direct Lai Sheng to make the usual necessary preparations for a banquet to last for a couple of days, with due regard to a profuse and sumptuous style.

"You go by-and-by," (she advised him), "in person to the Western Mansion and invite dowager lady Jia, mesdames Xing and Wang, and your sister-in-law Secunda lady Lian to come over for a stroll. Your father has also heard of a good doctor, and having already sent someone to ask him round, I think that by tomorrow he's sure to come; and you had better tell him, in a minute manner, the serious symptoms of her ailment during these few days."

Jia Rong having signified his obedience to each of her recommendations, and taken his leave, was just in time to meet the youth coming back from Feng Ziying's house, whither he had gone a short while back to invite the doctor round.

"Your slave," he consequently reported, "has just been with a card of master's to Mr. Feng's house and asked the doctor to come. 'The gentleman here,' replied the doctor, 'has just told me about it; but today, I've had to call on people the whole day, and I've only this moment come home; and I feel now my strength (so worn out), that I couldn't really stand any exertion. In fact were I even to get as far as the mansion, I shouldn't be in a fit state to diagnose the pulses! I must therefore have a night's rest, but, tomorrow for certain, I shall come to the mansion. My medical knowledge,' he went on to observe, 'is very shallow, and I don't deserve the honor of such eminent recommendation; but as Mr. Feng has already thus spoken of me in your mansion, I can't but present myself. It will be all right if in anticipation you deliver this message for me to your honorable master; but as for your worthy master's card, I cannot really presume to keep it.' It was again at his instance that I've brought it back; but, Sir, please mention this result for me (to master)."

Jia Rong turned back again, and entering the house delivered the message to Jia Zhen and Mrs. You; whereupon he walked out, and, calling Lai Sheng before him, he transmitted to him the orders to prepare the banquet for a couple of days.

After Lai Sheng had listened to the directions, he went off, of course, to get ready the customary preparations; but upon these we shall not dilate, but confine ourselves to the next day.

At noon, a servant on duty at the gate announced that the Doctor Zhang, who had been sent for, had come, and Jia Zhen conducted him along the Court into the large reception Hall, where they sat down; and after they had partaken of tea, he broached the subject.

"Yesterday," he explained, "the estimable Mr. Feng did me the honor to speak to me of your character and proficiency, venerable doctor, as well as of your thorough knowledge of medicine, and I, your mean brother, was filled with an immeasurable sense of admiration!"

"Your Junior," remonstrated Dr. Zhang, "is a coarse, despicable, and mean scholar and my knowledge is shallow and vile! but as worthy Mr. Feng did me the honor yesterday of telling me that your family, sir, had condescended to look upon me, a low scholar, and to favor me too with an invitation, could I presume not to obey your commands? But as I cannot boast of the least particle of real learning, I feel overburdened with shame!"

"Why need you be so modest?" observed Jia Zhen; "Doctor, do please walk in at once to see our son's wife, for I look up, with full reliance, to your lofty intelligence to dispel my solicitude!"

Jia Rong forthwith walked in with him. When they reached the inner apartment, and he caught sight of Mrs. Qin, he turned round and asked Jia Rong, "This is your honorable spouse, isn't it?"

"Yes, it is," assented Jia Rong; "but please, Doctor, take a seat, and let me tell you the symptoms of my humble wife's ailment, before her pulse be felt. Will this do?"

"My mean idea is," remarked the Doctor, "that it would, after all, be better that I should begin by feeling her pulse, before I ask you to inform me what the source of the ailment is. This is the first visit I pay to your honorable mansion; besides, I possess no knowledge of anything; but as our worthy Mr. Feng would insist upon my coming over to see you, I had in consequence no alternative but to come. After I have now made a diagnosis, you can judge whether what I say is right or not, before you explain to me the phases of the complaint during the last few days, and we can deliberate together upon some prescription; as to the suitableness or unsuitableness of which your honorable father will then have to decide, and what is necessary will have been done."

"Doctor," rejoined Jia Rong, "you are indeed eminently clear sighted; all I regret at present is that we have met so late! But please, Doctor, diagnose the state of the pulse, so as to find out whether there be hope of a cure or not; if a cure can be effected, it will be the means of allaying the solicitude of my father and mother."

The married women attached to that menage forthwith presented a pillow; and as it was being put down for Mrs. Qin to rest her arm on, they raised the lower part of her sleeve so as to leave her wrist exposed. The Doctor thereupon put out his hand and pressed it on the pulse of the right hand. Regulating his breath (to the pulsation) so as to be able to count the beatings, he with due care and minuteness felt the action for a considerable time, when, substituting the left hand, he again went through the same operation.

"Let us go and sit outside," he suggested, after he had concluded feeling her pulses. Jia Rong readily adjourned, in company with the Doctor, to the outer apartment, where they seated themselves on the stove-couch. A matron having served tea; "Please take a cup of tea, doctor," Jia Rong observed. When tea was over, "Judging," he inquired, "Doctor, from the present action of the pulses, is there any remedy or not?"

"The action of the pulse, under the forefinger, on the left hand of your honorable spouse," proceeded the Doctor, "is deep and agitated; the left hand pulse, under the second finger, is deep and faint. The pulse, under the forefinger, of the right hand, is gentle and lacks vitality. The right hand pulse, under my second finger, is superficial, and has lost all energy. The deep and agitated beating of the forepulse of the left hand arises from the febrile state, due to the weak action of the heart. The deep and delicate condition of the second part of the pulse of the left wrist, emanates from the sluggishness of the liver, and the scarcity of the blood in that organ. The action of the forefinger pulse, of the right wrist, is faint and lacks strength, as the breathing of the lungs is too weak. The second finger pulse of the right wrist is superficial and devoid of vigor, as the spleen must be affected injuriously by the liver. The weak action of the heart, and its febrile state, should be the natural causes which conduce to the present irregularity in the catamenia, and insomnia at night; the poverty of blood in the liver, and the sluggish condition of that organ must necessarily produce pain in the ribs; while the overdue of the catamenia, the cardiac fever, and debility of the respiration of the lungs, should occasion frequent giddiness in the head, and swimming of the eyes, the certain recurrence of perspiration between the periods of 3 to 5 and 5 to 7, and the sensation of being seated on board ship. The obstruction of the spleen by the liver should naturally create distaste for liquid or food, debility of the vital energies and prostration of the four limbs. From my diagnosis of these pulses, there should exist these various symptoms, before (the pulses and the symptoms can be said) to harmonize. But should perchance (any doctor maintain) that this state of the pulses imports a felicitous event, your servant will not presume to give an ear to such an opinion!"

A matron, who was attached as a personal attendant (to Mrs. Qin,) and who happened to be standing by interposed: "How could it be otherwise?" she ventured. "In real truth, Doctor, you speak like a supernatural being, and there's verily no need for us to say anything! We have now, ready at hand, in our household, a good number of medical gentlemen, who are in attendance upon her, but none of these are proficient enough to speak in this positive manner. Some there are who say that it's a genital complaint; others maintain that it's an organic disease. This doctor explains that there is no danger: while another, again, holds that there's fear of a crisis either before or after the winter solstice; but there is, in one word, nothing certain said by them. May it please you, sir, now to favor us with your clear directions."

"This complaint of your lady's," observed the Doctor, "has certainly been neglected by the whole number of doctors; for had a treatment with certain medicines been initiated at the time of the first occurrence of her habitual sickness, I cannot but opine that, by this time, a perfect cure would have been effected. But seeing that the organic complaint has now been, through neglect, allowed to reach this phase, this calamity was, in truth, inevitable. My ideas are that this illness stands, as yet, a certain chance of recovery, (three chances out of ten); but we will see how she gets on, after she has had these medicines of mine. Should they prove productive of sleep at night, then there will be added furthermore two more chances in the grip of our hands. From my diagnosis, your lady is a person, gifted with a preeminently excellent, and intelligent disposition; but an excessive degree of intelligence is the cause of frequent contrarieties; and frequent contrarieties give origin to an excessive amount of anxious cares. This illness arises from the injury done, by worrying and fretting, to the spleen, and from the inordinate vigor of the liver; hence it is that the relief cannot come at the proper time and season. Has not your lady, may I ask, heretofore at the period of the catamenia, suffered, if indeed not from anaemia, then necessarily from plethora? Am I right in assuming this or not?"

"To be sure she did," replied the matron; "but she has never been subject to anaemia, but to a plethora, varying from either two to three days, and extending, with much irregularity, to even ten days."

"Quite so!" observed the Doctor, after hearing what she had to say, "and this is the source of this organic illness! Had it in past days been treated with such medicine as could strengthen the heart, and improve the respiration, would it have reached this stage? This has now overtly made itself manifest in an ailment originating from the paucity of water and the vigor of fire; but let me make use of some medicines, and we'll see how she gets on!"

There and then he set to work and wrote a prescription, which he handed to Jia Rong, the purpose of which was: Decoction for the improvement of respiration, the betterment of the blood, and the restoration of the spleen. Ginseng, *Atractylodes Lancea*; Yunnan root; Prepared Di root; *Aralia edulis*; Peony roots; *Levisticum* from Sichuan; *Sophora tormentosa*; *Cyperus rotundus*, prepared with rice; Gentian, soaked in vinegar; Huai Shan Yao root; Real "O" glue; *Carydalis Ambigua*; and dried liquorice. Seven Fujian lotus seeds, (the cores of which should be extracted,) and two large *zizyphi* to be used as a preparative.

"What exalted intelligence!" Jia Rong, after perusing it, exclaimed. "But I would also ask you, Doctor, to be good enough to tell me whether this illness will, in the long run, endanger her life or not?"

The Doctor smiled. "You, sir, who are endowed with most eminent intelligence (are certain to know) that when a human illness has reached this phase, it is not a derangement of a day or of a single night; but after these medicines have been taken, we shall also have to watch the effect of the treatment! My humble opinion is that, as far as the winter of this year goes, there is no fear; in fact, after the spring equinox, I entertain hopes of a complete cure."

Jia Rong was likewise a person with all his wits about him, so that he did not press any further minute questions.

Jia Rong forthwith escorted the Doctor and saw him off, and taking the prescription and the diagnosis, he handed them both to Jia Zhen for his perusal, and in like manner recounted to Jia Zhen and Mrs. You all that had been said on the subject.

"The other doctors have hitherto not expressed any opinions as positive as this one has done," observed Mrs. You, addressing herself to Jia Zhen, "so that the medicines to be used are, I think, surely the right ones!"

"He really isn't a man," rejoined Jia Zhen, "accustomed to give much of his time to the practice of medicine, in order to earn rice for his support: and it's Feng Ziying, who is so friendly with us, who is mainly to be thanked for succeeding, after ever so much trouble, in inducing him to come. But now that we have this man, the illness of our son's wife may, there is no saying, stand a chance of being cured. But on that prescription of his there is ginseng mentioned, so you had better make use of that catty of good quality which was bought the other day."

Jia Rong listened until the conversation came to a close, after which he left the room, and bade a servant go and buy the medicines, in order that they should be prepared and administered to Mrs. Qin.

What was the state of Mrs. Qin's illness, after she partook of these medicines, we do not know; but, reader, listen to the explanation given in the chapter which follows.

CHAPTER 11

In honor of Jia Jing's birthday, a family banquet is spread in the Ning Mansion. At the sight of Xifeng, Jia Rui entertains feelings of licentious love.

We will now explain, in continuation of our story, that on the day of Jia Jing's birthday, Jia Zhen began by getting ready luscious delicacies and rare fruits, which he packed in sixteen spacious present boxes, and bade Jia Rong take them, along with the servants belonging to the household, over to Jia Jing.

Turning round towards Jia Rong: "Mind," he said, "that you observe whether your grandfather be agreeable or not, before you set to work and pay your obeisance! 'My father,' tell him, 'has complied with your directions, venerable senior, and not presumed to come over; but he has at home ushered the whole company of the members of the family (into your apartments), where they all paid their homage facing the side of honor.'"

After Jia Rong had listened to these injunctions, he speedily led off the family domestics, and took his departure. During this interval, one by one arrived the guests. First came Jia Lian and Jia Se, who went to see whether the seats in the various places (were sufficient). "Is there to be any entertainment or not?" they also inquired.

"Our master," replied the servants, "had, at one time, intended to invite the venerable Mr. Jia Jing to come and spend this day at home, and hadn't for this reason presumed to get up any entertainment. But when the other day he came to hear that the old gentleman was not coming, he at once gave us orders to go in search of a troupe of young actors, as well as a band of musicians, and all these people are now engaged making their preparations on the stage in the garden."

Next came, in a group, mesdames Xing and Wang, lady Feng and Baoyu, followed immediately after by Jia Zhen and Mrs. You; Mrs. You's mother having already arrived and being in there in advance of her. Salutations were exchanged between the whole company, and they pressed one another to take a seat. Jia Zhen and Mrs. You both handed the tea round.

"Our venerable lady," they explained, as they smiled, "is a worthy senior; while our father is, on the other hand, only her nephew; so that on a birthday of a man of his age, we should really not have had the audacity to invite her ladyship; but as the weather, at this time, is cool, and the chrysanthemums, in the whole garden, are in luxuriant blossom, we have requested our venerable ancestor to come for a little distraction, and to see the whole number of her children and grand-children amuse themselves. This was the object we had in view, but, contrary to our expectations, our worthy senior has not again conferred upon us the luster of her countenance."

Lady Feng did not wait until Madame Wang could open her mouth, but took the initiative to reply. "Our venerable lady," she urged, "had, even so late as yesterday, said that she meant to come; but, in the evening, upon seeing brother Bao eating peaches, the mouth of the old lady once again began to water, and after partaking of a little more than the half of one, she had, about the fifth watch, to get out of bed two consecutive times, with the result that all the forenoon today, she felt her body considerably worn out. She therefore bade me inform our worthy senior that it was utterly impossible for her to come today; adding however that, if there were any delicacies, she fancied a few kinds, but that they should be very tender."

When Jia Zhen heard these words, he smiled. "Our dowager lady," he replied, "is, I argued, so fond of amusement that, if she doesn't come today, there must, for a certainty, be some valid reason; and that's exactly what happens to be the case."

"The other day I heard your eldest sister explain," interposed Madame Wang, "that Jia Rong's wife was anything but well; but what's after all the matter with her?"

"She has," observed Mrs. You, "contracted this illness verily in a strange manner! Last moon at the time of the mid-autumn festival, she was still well enough to be able to enjoy herself, during half the night, in company with our dowager lady and Madame Wang. On her return, she continued in good health, until after the twentieth, when she began to feel more and more languid every day, and loath, likewise, to eat anything; and this has been going on for well-nigh half a month and more; she hasn't besides been anything like her old self for two months."

"May she not," remarked Madame Xing, taking up the thread of the conversation, "be ailing for some happy event?"

But while she was uttering these words, someone from outside announced: "Our senior master, second master, and all the gentlemen of the family have come, and are standing in the Reception Hall!" Whereupon Jia Zhen and Jia Lian quitted the apartment with hurried step; and during this while, Mrs. You reiterated how that some time ago a doctor had also expressed the opinion that she was ailing for a happy event, but that the previous day, had come a doctor, recommended by Feng Ziying—a doctor, who had from his youth up made medicine his study, and was very proficient in the treatment of diseases—who asserted, after he had seen her, that it was no felicitous ailment, but that it was some grave complaint. "It was only yesterday," (she explained,) "that he wrote his prescription; and all she has had is but one dose, and already today the giddiness in the head is considerably better; as regards the other symptoms they have as yet shown no marked improvement."

"I maintain," remarked lady Feng, "that, were she not quite unfit to stand the exertion, would she in fact, on a day like this, be unwilling to strain every nerve and come round."

"You saw her," observed Mrs. You, "on the third in here; how that she bore up with a violent effort for ever so long, but it was all because of the friendship that exists between you two, that she still longed for your society, and couldn't brook the idea of tearing herself away."

When lady Feng heard these words, her eyes got quite red, and after a time she at length exclaimed: "In the Heavens of a sudden come wind and rain; while with man, in a day and in a night, woe and weal survene! But with her tender years, if for a complaint like this she were to run any risk, what pleasure is there for any human being to be born and to sojourn in the world?"

She was just speaking, when Jia Rong walked into the apartment; and after paying his respects to Madame Xing, Madame Wang, and lady Feng, he then observed to Mrs. You: "I have just taken over the eatables to our venerable ancestor; and, at the same time, I told him that my father was at home waiting upon the senior, and entertaining the junior gentlemen of the whole family, and that in compliance with grandfather's orders, he did not presume to go over. The old gentleman was much delighted by what he heard me say, and having signified that that was all in order, bade me tell father and you, mother, to do all you can in your attendance upon the senior gentlemen and ladies, enjoining me to entertain, with all propriety, my uncles, aunts, and my cousins. He also went on to urge me to press the men to cut, with all despatch, the blocks for the *Record of Meritorious Deeds*, and to print ten thousand copies for distribution. All these messages I have duly delivered to my father, but I must now be quick and go out, so as to send the eatables for the elder as well as for the younger gentlemen of the entire household."

"Brother Rong'er," exclaimed lady Feng, "wait a moment. How is your wife getting on? how is she, after all, today?"

"Not well," replied Jia Rong. "But were you, aunt, on your return to go in and see her, you will find out for yourself."

Jia Rong forthwith left the room. During this interval, Mrs. You addressed herself to mesdames Xing and Wang; "My ladies," she asked, "will you have your repast in here, or will you go into the garden for it? There are now in the garden some young actors engaged in making their preparations?"

"It's better in here," Madame Wang remarked, as she turned towards Madame Xing.

Mrs. You thereupon issued directions to the married women and matrons to be quick in serving the eatables. The servants, in waiting outside the door, with one voice signified their obedience; and each of them went off to fetch what fell to her share. In a short while, the courses were all laid out, and Mrs. You pressed mesdames Xing and Wang, as well as her mother, into the upper seats; while she, together with lady Feng and Baoyu, sat at a side table.

"We've come," observed mesdames Xing and Wang, "with the original idea of paying our congratulations to our venerable senior on the occasion of his birthday; and isn't this as if we had come for our own birthdays?"

"The old gentleman," answered lady Feng, "is a man fond of a quiet life; and as he has already consummated a process of purification, he may well be looked upon as a supernatural being, so that the purpose to which your ladyships have given expression may be considered as manifest to his spirit, upon the very advent of the intention."

As this sentence was uttered the whole company in the room burst out laughing. Mrs. You's mother, mesdames Xing and Wang, and lady Feng having one and all partaken of the banquet, rinsed their mouths and washed their hands, which over, they expressed a wish to go into the garden.

Jia Rong entered the room. "The senior gentlemen," he said to Mrs. You, "as well as all my uncles and cousins, have finished their repast; but the elder gentleman Mr. Jia She, who excused himself on the score of having at home something to attend to, and Mr. Secundus (Jia Zheng), who is not partial to theatrical performances and is always afraid that people will be too boisterous in their entertainments, have both of them taken their departure. The rest of the family gentlemen have been taken over by uncle Secundus Mr. Lian, and Mr. Se, to the other side to listen to the play. A few moments back Prince Nanan, Prince Dongping, Prince Xining, Prince Beijing, these four Princes, with Niu, Duke of Zhengguo, and five other dukes, six in all, and Shi, Marquis of Zhongjing, and other seven, in all eight marquises, sent their messengers with their cards and presents. I have already told father all about it; but before I did so, the presents were put away in the counting room, the lists of presents were all entered in the book, and the 'received with thanks' cards were handed to the respective messengers of the various mansions; the men themselves were also tipped in the customary manner, and all of them were kept to have something to eat before they went on their way. But, mother, you should invite the two ladies, your mother and my aunt, to go over and sit in the garden."

"Just so!" observed Mrs. You, "but we've only now finished our repast, and were about to go over."

"I wish to tell you, madame," interposed lady Feng, "that I shall go first and see brother Rong's wife and then come and join you."

"All right," replied Madame Wang; "we should all have been fain to have paid her a visit, did we not fear lest she should look upon our disturbing her with displeasure, but just tell her that we would like to know how she is getting on!"

"My dear sister," remarked Mrs. You, "as our son's wife has a ready ear for all you say, do go and cheer her up, (and if you do so,) it will besides set my own mind at ease; but be quick and come as soon as you can into the garden."

Baoyu being likewise desirous to go along with lady Feng to see lady Jin, Madame Wang remarked, "Go and see her just for a while, and then come over at once into the garden; (for remember) she is your nephew's wife, (and you couldn't sit in there long)."

Mrs. You forthwith invited mesdames Wang and Xing, as well as her own mother, to adjourn to the other side, and they all in a body walked into the garden of Concentrated Fragrance; while lady Feng and Baoyu betook themselves, in company with Jia Rong, over to this side.

Having entered the door, they with quiet step walked as far as the entrance of the inner chamber. Mrs. Qin, upon catching sight of them, was bent upon getting up; but "Be quick," remonstrated lady Feng, "and give up all idea of standing up; for take care your head will feel dizzy."

Lady Feng hastened to make a few hurried steps forward and to grasp Mrs. Qin's hand in hers. "My dear girl!" she exclaimed; "How is it that during the few days I've not seen you, you have grown so thin?"

Readily she then took a seat on the rug, on which Mrs. Qin was seated, while Baoyu, after inquiring too about her health, sat in the chair on the opposite side.

"Bring the tea in at once," called out Jia Rong, "for aunt and uncle Secundus have not had any tea in the drawing room."

Mrs. Qin took lady Feng's hand in her own and forced a smile. "This is all due to my lack of good fortune; for in such a family as this, my father and mother-in-law treat me just as if I were a daughter of their own flesh and blood! Besides, your nephew, (my husband,) may, it is true, my dear aunt, be young in years, but he is full of regard for me, as I have regard for him, and we have had so far no misunderstanding between us! In fact, among the senior generation, as well as that of the same age as myself, in the whole clan, putting you aside, aunt, about whom no mention need be made, there is not one who has not ever had anything but love for me, and not one who has not ever shown me anything but kindness! But since I've fallen ill with this complaint, all my energy has even every bit of it been taken out of me, so that I've been unable to show to my father and mother-in-law any mark of filial attention, yea so much as for one single day and to you, my dear aunt, with all this affection of yours for me, I have every wish to be dutiful to the utmost degree, but, in my present state, I'm really not equal to it; my own idea is, that it isn't likely that I shall last through this year."

Baoyu kept, while (she spoke,) his eyes fixed intently upon a picture on the opposite side, representing some begonias drooping in the spring time, and upon a pair of scrolls, with this inscription written by Qin Taixu:

A gentle chill doth circumscribe the dreaming man because the spring is cold.
The fragrant whiff which wafts itself into man's nose, is the perfume of wine!

And he could not help recalling to mind his experiences at the time when he had fallen asleep in this apartment, and had, in his dream, visited the confines of the Great Void. He was just plunged in a state of abstraction, when he heard Mrs. Qin give utterance to these sentiments, which pierced his heart as if they were ten thousand arrows, (with the result that) tears unwittingly trickled from his eyes.

Lady Feng perceiving him in tears felt it extremely painful within herself to bear the sight; but she was on pins and needles lest the patient should detect their frame of mind, and feel, instead (of benefit), still more sore at heart, which would not, after all, be quite the purpose of her visit; which was to afford her distraction and consolation. "Baoyu," she therefore exclaimed, "you are like an old woman! Ill, as she is, simply makes her speak in this wise, and how ever could things come to such a pass! Besides, she is young in years, so that after a short indisposition, her illness will get all right! Don't," she said as she turned towards Mrs. Qin, "give way to silly thoughts and idle ideas! for by so doing won't you yourself be aggravating your ailment?"

"All that her sickness in fact needs," observed Jia Rong, "is that she should be able to take something to eat, and then there will be nothing to fear."

"Brother Bao," urged lady Feng, "your mother told you to go over, as soon as you could, so that don't stay here, and go on in the way you're doing, for you after all incite this lady also to feel uneasy at heart. Besides, your mother over there is solicitous on your account. You had better go ahead with your uncle Bao," she consequently continued, addressing herself to Jia Rong, "while I sit here a little longer."

When Jia Rong heard this remark, he promptly crossed over with Baoyu into the garden of Concentrated Fragrance, while lady Feng went on both to cheer her up for a time, and to impart to her, in an undertone, a good deal of confidential advice.

Mrs. You had despatched servants, on two or three occasions, to hurry lady Feng, before she said to Mrs. Qin: "Do all you can to take good care of yourself, and I'll come and see you again. You're bound to get over this illness; and now, in fact, that you've come across that renowned doctor, you have really nothing more to fear."

"He might," observed Mrs. Qin as she smiled, "even be a supernatural being and succeed in healing my disease, but he won't be able to remedy my destiny; for, my dear aunt, I feel sure that with this complaint of mine, I can do no more than drag on from day to day."

"If you encourage such ideas," remonstrated lady Feng, "how can this illness ever get all right? What you absolutely need is to cast away all these notions, and then you'll improve. I hear moreover that the doctor asserts that if no cure be effected, the fear is of a change for the worse in spring, and not till then. Did you and I moreover belong to a family that hadn't the means to afford any ginseng, it would be difficult to say how we could manage to get it; but were your father and mother-in-law to hear that it's good for your recovery, why not to speak of two mace of ginseng a day, but even two catties will be also within their means! So mind you do take every care of your health.' I'm now off on my way into the garden."

"Excuse me, my dear aunt," added Mrs. Qin, "that I can't go with you; but when you have nothing to do, I entreat you do come over and see me! and you and I can sit and have a long chat."

After lady Feng had heard these words, her eyes unwillingly got quite red again. "When I'm at leisure I shall, of course," she rejoined, "come often to see you;" and forthwith leading off the matrons and married women, who had come over with her, as well as the women and matrons of the Ning mansion, she passed through the inner part of the house, and entered, by a circuitous way, the side gate of the park, when she perceived yellow flowers covering the ground; white willows flanking the slopes; diminutive bridges spanning streams, resembling the Ruo Ye; zigzag pathways (looking as if) they led to the steps of Heaven; limpid springs dripping from among the rocks; flowers hanging from hedges emitting their fragrance, as they were flapped by the winds; red leaves on the tree tops swaying to and fro; groves picture-like, half stripped of foliage; the western breeze coming with sudden gusts, and the wail of the oriole still audible; the warm sun shining with genial rays, and the cicada also adding its chirp; structures, visible to the gaze at a distance in the southeast, soaring high on various sites and resting against the hills; three halls, visible near by on the northwest, stretching in one connected line, on the bank of the stream; strains of music filling the pavilion, imbued with an unwonted subtle charm; and maidens in fine attire penetrating the groves, lending an additional spell to the scene.

Lady Feng, while engaged in contemplating the beauties of the spot, advanced onwards step by step. She was plunged in a state of ecstasy, when suddenly, from the rear of the artificial rockery, egressed a person, who approached her and facing her said, "My respects to you, sister-in-law."

Lady Feng was so startled by this unexpected appearance that she drew back. "Isn't this Mr. Rui?" she ventured.

"What! sister-in-law," exclaimed Jia Rui, "don't you recognise even me?"

"It isn't that I didn't recognise you," explained lady Feng, "but at the sudden sight of you, I couldn't conceive that it would possibly be you, sir, in this place!"

"This was in fact bound to be," replied Jia Rui; "for there's some subtle sympathy between me and you, sister-in-law. Here I just stealthily leave the entertainment, in order to revel for a while in this solitary place when, against every expectation, I come across you, sister-in-law; and isn't this a subtle sympathy?"

As he spoke, he kept his gaze fixed on lady Feng, who being an intelligent person, could not but arrive, at the sight of his manner, at the whole truth in her surmises. "It isn't to be wondered at," she consequently observed, as she smiled hypocritically, "that your eldest brother should make frequent allusion to your qualities! for after seeing you on this occasion, and hearing you utter these few remarks, I have readily discovered what an intelligent and genial person you are! I am just now on my way to join the ladies on the other side, and have no leisure to converse with you; but wait until I've nothing to attend to, when we can meet again."

"I meant to have gone over to your place and paid my respects to you, sister-in-law," pleaded Jia Rui, "but I was afraid lest a person of tender years like yourself mightn't lightly receive any visitors!"

Lady Feng gave another sardonic smile. "Relatives," she continued, "of one family, as we are, what need is there to say anything of tender years?"

After Jia Rui had heard these words, he felt his heart swell within him with such secret joy that he was urged to reflect: "I have at length today, when least I expected it, obtained this remarkable encounter with her!"

But as the display of his passion became still more repulsive, lady Feng urged him to go. "Be off at once," she remarked, "and join the entertainment; for mind, if they find you out, they will mulct you in so many glasses of wine!"

By the time this suggestion had reached Jia Rui's ears, half of his body had become stiff like a log of wood; and as he betook himself away, with loathful step, he turned his head round to cast glances at her. Lady Feng purposely slackened her pace; and when she perceived that he had gone a certain distance, she gave way to reflection. "This is indeed," she thought, "knowing a person, as far as face goes, and not as heart! Can there be another such a beast as he! If he really continues to behave in this manner, I shall soon enough compass his death, with my own hands, and he'll then know what stuff I'm made of."

Lady Feng, at this juncture moved onward, and after turning round a chain of hillocks, she caught sight of two or three matrons coming along with all speed. As soon as they espied lady Feng they put on a smile. "Our mistress," they said, "perceiving that your ladyship was not forthcoming, has been in a great state of anxiety, and bade your servants come again to request you to come over.

"Is your mistress," observed lady Feng, "so like a quick-footed demon?"

While lady Feng advanced leisurely, she inquired, "How many plays have been recited?" to which question one of the matrons replied, "They have gone through eight or nine." But while engaged in conversation, they had already reached the back door of the Tower of Celestial Fragrance, where she caught sight of Baoyu playing with a company of waiting-maids and pages. "Brother Bao," lady Feng exclaimed, "don't be up to too much mischief!" "The ladies are all sitting upstairs," interposed one of the maids. "Please, my lady, this is the way up."

At these words lady Feng slackened her pace, raised her dress, and walked up the stairs, where Mrs. You was already at the top of the landing waiting for her.

"You two," remarked Mrs. You, smiling, "are so friendly, that having met you couldn't possibly tear yourself away to come. You had better tomorrow move over there and take up your quarters with her and have done; but sit down and let me, first of all, present you a glass of wine."

Lady Feng speedily drew near mesdames Xing and Wang, and begged permission to take a seat; while Mrs. You brought the programme, and pressed lady Feng to mark some plays.

"The senior ladies occupy the seats of honor," remonstrated lady Feng, "and how can I presume to choose?"

"We, and our relative by marriage, have selected several plays," explained mesdames Xing and Wang, "and it's for you now to choose some good ones for us to listen to."

Standing up, lady Feng signified her obedience; and taking over the programme, and perusing it from top to bottom, she marked off one entitled, the "Return of the Spirit," and another called "Thrumming and Singing;" after which she handed back the programme, observing, "When they have done with the 'Ennoblement of two Officers,' which they are singing just at present, it will be time enough to sing these two."

"Of course it will," retorted Madame Wang, "but they should get it over as soon as they can, so as to allow your elder brother and your sister-in-law to have rest; besides, their hearts are not at ease."

"You senior ladies don't come often," expostulated Mrs. You, "and you and I will derive more enjoyment were we to stay a little longer; it's as yet early in the day!"

Lady Feng stood up and looked downstairs. "Where have all the gentlemen gone to?" she inquired.

"The gentlemen have just gone over to the Pavilion of Plenteous Effulgence," replied a matron, who stood by; "they have taken along with them ten musicians and gone in there to drink their wine."

"It wasn't convenient for them," remarked lady Feng, "to be over here; but who knows what they have again gone to do behind our backs?"

"Could everyone," interposed Mrs. You, "resemble you, a person of such propriety!"

While they indulged in chatting and laughing, the plays they had chosen were all finished; whereupon the tables were cleared of the wines, and the repast was served. The meal over, the whole company adjourned into the garden, and came and sat in the drawing-room. After tea, they at length gave orders to get ready the carriages, and they took their leave of Mrs. You's mother. Mrs. You, attended by all the secondary wives, servants, and married women, escorted them out, while Jia Zhen, along with the whole bevy of young men, stood by the vehicles, waiting in a group for their arrival.

After saluting mesdames Xing and Wang, "Aunts," they said, "you must come over again tomorrow for a stroll."

"We must be excused," observed Madame Wang, "we've sat here the whole day today, and are, after all, feeling quite tired; besides, we shall need to have some rest tomorrow."

Both of them thereupon got into their carriages and took their departure, while Jia Rui still kept a fixed gaze upon lady Feng; and it was after Jia Zhen had gone in that Li Gui led round the horse, and that Baoyu mounted and went off, following in the track of mesdames Xing and Wang.

Jia Zhen and the whole number of brothers and nephews belonging to the family had, during this interval, partaken of their meal, and the whole party at length broke up. But in like manner, all the inmates of the clan and the guests spent on the morrow another festive day, but we need not advert to it with any minuteness.

After this occasion, lady Feng came in person and paid frequent visits to Mrs. Qin; but as there were some days on which her ailment was considerably better, and others on which it was considerably worse, Jia Zhen, Mrs. You, and Jia Rong were in an awful state of anxiety.

Jia Rui, it must moreover be noticed, came over, on several instances, on a visit to the Rong mansion; but it invariably happened that he found that lady Feng had gone over to the Ning mansion.

This was just the thirtieth of the eleventh moon, the day on which the winter solstice fell; and the few days preceding that season, dowager lady Jia, Madame Wang, and lady Feng did not let one day go by without sending someone to inquire about Mrs. Qin; and as the servants, on their return, repeatedly reported that, during the last few days, neither had her ailment aggravated, nor had it undergone any marked improvement, Madame Wang explained to dowager lady Jia, that as a complaint of this nature had reached this kind of season without getting any worse, there was some hope of recovery.

"Of course there is!" observed the old lady; "what a dear child she is! should anything happen to her, won't it be enough to make people die from grief!" and as she spake she felt for a time quite sore at heart. "You and she," continuing, she said to lady Feng, "have been friends for ever so long; tomorrow is the glorious first (and you can't go), but after tomorrow you should pay her a visit and minutely scrutinise her appearance: and should you find her any better, come and tell me on your return! Whatever things that dear child has all along a fancy for, do send her round a few even as often as you can by someone or other!"

Lady Feng assented to each of her recommendations; and when the second arrived, she came, after breakfast, to the Ning mansion to see how Mrs. Qin was getting on; and though she found her none the worse, the flesh all over her face and person had however become emaciated and parched up. She readily sat with Mrs. Qin for a long while, and after they had chatted on one thing and another, she again reiterated the assurances that this illness involved no danger, and distracted her for ever so long.

"Whether I get well or not," observed Mrs. Qin, "we'll know in spring; now winter is just over, and I'm anyhow no worse, so that possibly I may get all right; and yet there's no saying; but, my dear sister-in-law, do press our old lady to compose her mind! yesterday, her ladyship sent me some potato dumplings, with minced dates in them, and though I had two, they seem after all to be very easily digested!"

"I'll send you round some more tomorrow," lady Feng suggested; "I'm now going to look up your mother-in-law, and will then hurry back to give my report to our dowager lady."

"Please, sister-in-law," Mrs. Qin said, "present my best respects to her venerable ladyship, as well as to Madame Wang."

Lady Feng signified that she would comply with her wishes, and, forthwith leaving the apartment, she came over and sat in Mrs. You's suite of rooms.

"How do you, who don't see our son's wife very often, happen to find her?" inquired Mrs. You.

Lady Feng drooped her head for some time. "There's no help," she ventured, "for this illness! but you should likewise make every subsequent preparation, for it would also be well if you could scour it away."

"I've done so much as to secretly give orders," replied Mrs. You, "to get things ready; but for that thing (the coffin), there's no good timber to be found, so that it will have to be looked after by and by."

Lady Feng swallowed hastily a cup of tea, and after a short chat, "I must be hurrying back," she remarked, "to deliver my message to our dowager lady!"

"You should," urged Mrs. You, "be sparse in what you tell her lady ship so as not to frighten an old person like her!"

"I know well enough what to say," replied lady Feng.

Without any further delay, lady Feng then sped back. On her arrival at home she looked up the old lady. "Brother Rong's wife," she explained, "presents her compliments, and pays obeisance to your venerable ladyship; she says that she's much better, and entreats you, her worthy senior, to set your mind at ease! That as soon as she's a little better she will come and prostrate herself before your ladyship."

"How do you find her?" inquired dowager lady Jia.

"For the present there's nothing to fear," continued lady Feng; "for her mien is still good."

After the old lady had heard these words, she was plunged for a long while in deep reflection; and as she turned towards lady Feng, "Go and divest yourself of your toilette," she said, "and have some rest."

Lady Feng in consequence signified her obedience, and walked away, returning home after paying Madame Wang a visit. Ping'er helped lady Feng to put on the house costume, which she had warmed by the fire, and lady Feng eventually took a seat and asked "whether there was anything doing at home?"

Ping'er then brought the tea, and after going over to hand the cup: "There's nothing doing," she replied; "as regards the interest on the three hundred taels, Wang'er's wife has brought it in, and I've put it away. Besides this, Mr. Rui sent round to inquire if your ladyship was at home or not, as he meant to come and pay his respects and to have a chat."

"Heng!" exclaimed lady Feng at these words. "Why should this beast compass his own death? we'll see when he comes what is to be done."

"Why is this Mr. Rui so bent upon coming?" Ping'er having inquired, lady Feng readily gave her an account of how she had met him in the course of the ninth moon in the Ning mansion, and of what had been said by him.

"What a mangy frog to be bent upon eating the flesh of a heavenly goose!" ejaculated Ping'er. "A stupid and disorderly fellow with no conception of relationship, to harbor such a thought! but we'll make him find an unnatural death!"

"Wait till he comes," added lady Feng, "when I feel certain I shall find some way."

What happened, however, when Jia Rui came has not, as yet, been ascertained, but listen, reader, to the explanation given in the next chapter.

CHAPTER 12

Wang Xifeng maliciously lays a trap for Jia Rui, under pretence that his affection is reciprocated. Jia Tianxiang gazes at the face of the mirror of voluptuousness.

Lady Feng, it must be noticed in continuation of our narrative, was just engaged in talking with Ping'er, when they heard someone announce that Mr. Rui had come, lady Feng gave orders that he should be invited to step in, and Jia Rui perceiving that he had been asked to walk in was at heart elated at the prospect of seeing her.

With a face beaming with smiles, lady Feng inquired again and again how he was; and, with simulated tenderness she further pressed him to take a seat and urged him to have a cup of tea.

Jia Rui noticed how still more voluptuous lady Feng looked in her present costume, and, as his eyes burnt with love, "How is it," he inquired, "that my elder brother Secundus is not yet back?"

"What the reason is I cannot tell," lady Feng said by way of reply.

"May it not be," Jia Rui smilingly insinuated, "that some fair damsel has got hold of him on the way, and that he cannot brook to tear himself from her to come home?"

"That makes it plain that there are those among men who fall in love with any girl they cast their eyes on," hinted lady Feng.

"Your remarks are, sister-in-law, incorrect, for I'm none of this kind!" Jia Rui explained smirkingly.

"How many like you can there be!" rejoined lady Feng with a sarcastic smile; "in ten, not one even could be picked out!"

When Jia Rui heard these words, he felt in such high glee that he rubbed his ears and smoothed his cheeks. "My sister-in-law," he continued, "you must of course be extremely lonely day after day"

"Indeed I am," observed lady Feng, "and I only wish someone would come and have a chat with me to break my dull monotony."

"I daily have ample leisure," Jia Rui ventured with a simper, "and wouldn't it be well if I came every day to dispel your dulness, sister-in-law?"

"You are simply fooling me," exclaimed lady Feng laughing. "It isn't likely you would wish to come over here to me?"

"If in your presence, sister-in-law, I utter a single word of false-hood, may the thunder from heaven blast me!" protested Jia Rui. "It's only because I had all along heard people say that you were a dreadful person, and that you cannot condone even the slightest shortcoming committed in your presence, that I was induced to keep back by fear; but after seeing you, on this occasion, so chatty, so full of fun and most considerate to others, how can I not come? were it to be the cause of my death, I would be even willing to come!"

"You're really a clever person," lady Feng observed sarcastically. "And oh so much superior to both Jia Rong and his brother! Hand-some as their presence was to look at, I imagined their minds to be full of intelligence, but who would have thought that they would, after all, be a couple of stupid worms, without the least notion of human affection!"

The words which Jia Rui heard, fell in so much the more with his own sentiments, that he could not restrain himself from again pressing forward nearer to her; and as with eyes strained to give intentness to his view, he gazed at lady Feng's purse: "What rings have you got on?" he went on to ask.

"You should be a little more deferential," remonstrated lady Feng in a low tone of voice, "so as not to let the waiting-maids detect us."

Jia Rui withdrew backward with as much alacrity as if he had re-ceived an Imperial decree or a mandate from Buddha.

"You ought to be going!" lady Feng suggested, as she gave him a smile.

"Do let me stay a while longer," entreated Jia Rui, "you are indeed ruthless, my sister-in-law."

But with gentle voice did lady Feng again expostulate. "In broad daylight," she said, "with people coming and going, it is not really con-venient that you should abide in here; so you had better go, and when it's dark and the watch is set, you can come over, and quietly wait for me in the corridor on the Eastern side!"

At these words, Jia Rui felt as if he had received some jewel or pre-cious thing. "Don't make fun of me!" he remarked with vehemence. "The only thing is that crowds of people are ever passing from there, and how will it be possible for me to evade detection?"

"Set your mind at ease!" lady Feng advised; "I shall dismiss on leave all the youths on duty at night; and when the doors, on both sides, are closed, there will be no one else to come in!"

Jia Rui was delighted beyond measure by the assurance, and with impetuous haste, he took his leave and went off; convinced at heart of the gratification of his wishes. He continued, up to the time of dusk, a prey to keen expectation; and, when indeed darkness fell, he felt his way into the Rong mansion, availing himself of the moment, when the doors were being closed, to slip into the corridor, where everything was actually pitch dark, and not a soul to be seen going backwards or forwards.

The door leading over to dowager lady Jia's apartments had already been put under key, and there was but one gate, the one on the east, which had not as yet been locked. Jia Rui lent his ear, and listened for ever so long, but he saw no one appear. Suddenly, however, was heard a sound like "lo deng," and the east gate was also bolted; but though Jia Rui was in a great state of impatience, he none the less did not venture to utter a sound. All that necessity compelled him to do was to issue, with quiet steps, from his corner, and to try the gates by pushing; but they were closed as firmly as if they had been made fast with iron bolts; and much though he may, at this juncture, have wished to find his way out, escape was, in fact, out of the question; on the south and north was one continuous dead wall, which, even had he wished to scale, there was nothing which he could clutch and pull himself up by.

This room, besides, was one the interior (of which was exposed) to the wind, which entered through (the fissure) of the door; and was perfectly empty and bare; and the weather being, at this time, that of December, and the night too very long, the northerly wind, with its biting gusts, was sufficient to penetrate the flesh and to cleave the bones, so that the whole night long he had a narrow escape from being frozen to death; and he was yearning, with intolerable anxiety for the break of day, when he espied an old matron go first and open the door on the east side, and then come in and knock at the western gate.

Jia Rui seeing that she had turned her face away, bolted out, like a streak of smoke, as he hugged his shoulders with his hands (from intense cold). As luck would have it, the hour was as yet early, so that the inmates of the house had not all got out of bed; and making his escape from the postern door, he straightaway betook himself home, running back the whole way.

Jia Rui's parents had, it must be explained, departed life at an early period, and he had no one else, besides his grandfather Dairu, to take charge of his support and education. This Dairu had, all along, exercised a very strict control, and would not allow Jia Rui to even make one step too many, in the apprehension that he might gad about out of doors drinking and gambling, to the neglect of his studies.

Seeing, on this unexpected occasion, that he had not come home the whole night, he simply felt positive, in his own mind, that he was certain to have run about, if not drinking, at least gambling, and dissipating in houses of the demi-monde up to the small hours; but he never even gave so much as a thought to the possibility of a public scandal, as that in which he was involved. The consequence was that during the whole length of the night he boiled with wrath.

Jia Rui himself, on the other hand, was (in such a state of trepidation) that he could wipe the perspiration (off his face) by handfuls; and he felt constrained on his return home, to have recourse to deceitful excuses, simply explaining that he had been at his eldest maternal uncle's house, and that when it got dark, they kept him to spend the night there.

"Hitherto," remonstrated Dairu, "when about to go out of doors, you never ventured to go, on your own hook, without first telling me about it, and how is it that yesterday you surreptitiously left the house? for this offence alone you deserve a beating, and how much more for the lie imposed upon me."

Into such a violent fit of anger did he consequently fly that laying hands on him, he pulled him over and administered to him thirty or forty blows with a cane. Nor would he allow him to have anything to eat, but bade him remain on his knees in the court reading essays; impressing on his mind that he would not let him off, before he had made up for the last ten days' lessons.

Jia Rui had in the first instance, frozen the whole night, and, in the next place, came in for a flogging. With a stomach, besides, gnawed by the pangs of hunger, he had to kneel in a place exposed to drafts reading the while literary compositions, so that the hardships he had to endure were of manifold kinds.

Jia Rui's infamous intentions had at this junction undergone no change; but far from his thoughts being even then any idea that lady Feng was humbugging him, he seized, after the lapse of a couple of days, the first leisure moments to come again in search of that lady.

Lady Feng pretended to bear him a grudge for his breach of faith, and Jia Rui was so distressed that he tried by vows and oaths (to establish his innocence). Lady Feng perceiving that he had, of his own accord, fallen into the meshes of the net laid for him, could not but devise another plot to give him a lesson and make him know what was right and mend his ways.

With this purpose, she gave him another assignation. "Don't go over there," she said, "tonight, but wait for me in the empty rooms giving on to a small passage at the back of these apartments of mine. But whatever you do, mind don't be reckless."

"Are you in real earnest?" Jia Rui inquired.

"Why, who wants to play with you?" replied lady Feng; "if you don't believe what I say, well then don't come!"

"I'll come, I'll come, yea I'll come, were I even to die!" protested Jia Rui.

"You should first at this very moment get away!" lady Feng having suggested, Jia Rui, who felt sanguine that when evening came, success would for a certainty crown his visit, took at once his departure in anticipation (of his pleasure).

During this interval lady Feng hastily set to work to dispose of her resources, and to add to her stratagems, and she laid a trap for her victim; while Jia Rui, on the other hand, was until the shades of darkness fell, a prey to incessant expectation.

As luck would have it a relative of his happened to likewise come on that very night to their house and to only leave after he had dinner with them, and at an hour of the day when the lamps had already been lit; but he had still to wait until his grandfather had retired to rest before he could, at length with precipitate step, betake himself into the Rong mansion.

Straightway he came into the rooms in the narrow passage, and waited with as much trepidation as if he had been an ant in a hot pan. He however waited and waited, but he saw no one arrive; he listened but not even the sound of a voice reached his ear. His heart was full of intense fear, and he could not restrain giving way to surmises and suspicion. "May it not be," he thought, "that she is not coming again; and that I may have once more to freeze for another whole night?"

While indulging in these erratic reflections, he discerned someone coming, looking like a black apparition, who Jia Rui readily concluded, in his mind, must be lady Feng; so that, unmindful of distinguishing black from white, he as soon as that person arrived in front of him, speedily clasped her in his embrace, like a ravenous tiger pouncing upon its prey, or a cat clawing a rat, and cried: "My darling sister, you have made me wait till I'm ready to die."

As he uttered these words, he dragged the comer, in his arms, on to the couch in the room; and while indulging in kisses and protestations of warm love, he began to cry out random epithets of endearment.

Not a sound, however, came from the lips of the other person; and Jia Rui had in the fullness of his passion, exceeded the bounds of timid love and was in the act of becoming still more affectionate in his protestations, when a sudden flash of a light struck his eye, by the rays of which he espied Jia Se with a candle in hand, casting the light round the place, "Who's in this room?" he exclaimed.

"Uncle Rui," he heard someone on the couch explain, laughing, "was trying to take liberties with me!"

Jia Rui at one glance became aware that it was no other than Jia Rong; and a sense of shame at once so overpowered him that he could find nowhere to hide himself; nor did he know how best to extricate himself from the dilemma. Turning himself round, he made an attempt to make good his escape, when Jia Se with one grip clutched him in his hold.

"Don't run away," he said; "sister-in-law Lian has already reported your conduct to Madame Wang; and explained that you had tried to make her carry on an improper flirtation with you; that she had temporized by having recourse to a scheme to escape your importunities, and that she had imposed upon you in such a way as to make you wait for her in this place. Our lady was so terribly incensed, that she wellnigh succumbed; and hence it is that she bade me come and catch you! Be quick now and follow me, and let us go and see her."

After Jia Rui had heard these words, his very soul could not be contained within his body.

"My dear nephew," he entreated, "do tell her that it wasn't I; and I'll show you my gratitude tomorrow in a substantial manner."

"Letting you off," rejoined Jia Se, "is no difficult thing; but how much, I wonder, are you likely to give? Besides, what you now utter with your lips, there will be no proof to establish; so you had better write a promissory note."

"How could I put what happened in black and white on paper?" observed Jia Rui.

"There's no difficulty about that either!" replied Jia Se; "just write an account of a debt due, for losses in gambling, to someone outside; number of taels, from the head of the house; and that will be all that is required."

"This is in fact, easy enough!" Jia Rui having added by way of answer; Jia Se turned round and left the room; and returning with paper and brushes, which had been got ready beforehand for the purpose, he bade Jia Rui write. The two of them (Jia Rong and Jia Se) tried, the one to do a good turn, and the other to be perverse in his insistence; but (Jia Rui) put down no more than fifty taels, and appended his signature.

Jia Se pocketed the note, and endeavored subsequently to induce Jia Rong to come away; but Jia Rong was, at the outset, obdurate and unwilling to give in, and kept on repeating; "Tomorrow, I'll tell the members of our clan to look into your nice conduct!"

These words plunged Jia Rui in such a state of dismay, that he even went so far as to knock his head on the ground; but, as Jia Se was trying to get unfair advantage of him though he had at first done him a good turn, he had to write another promissory note for fifty taels, before the matter was dropped.

Taking up again the thread of the conversation, Jia Se remarked, "Now when I let you go, I'm quite ready to bear the blame! But the gate at our old lady's over there is already bolted, and Mr. Jia Zheng is just now engaged in the Hall, looking at the things which have arrived from Nanjing, so that it would certainly be difficult for you to pass through that way. The only safe course at present is by the back gate; but if you do go by there, and perchance meet anyone, even I will be in for a mess; so you might as well wait until I go first and have a peep, when I'll come and fetch you! You couldn't anyhow conceal yourself in this room; for in a short time they'll be coming to stow the things away, and you had better let me find a safe place for you."

These words ended, he took hold of Jia Rui, and, extinguishing again the lantern, he brought him out into the court, feeling his way up to the bottom of the steps of the large terrace. "It's safe enough in this nest," he observed, "but just squat down quietly and don't utter a sound; wait until I come back before you venture out."

Having concluded this remark, the two of them (Jia Se and Jia Rong) walked away; while Jia Rui was, all this time, out of his senses, and felt constrained to remain squatting at the bottom of the terrace stairs. He was about to consider what course was open for him to adopt, when he heard a noise just over his head; and, with a splash, the contents of a bucket, consisting entirely of filthy water, was emptied straight down over him from above, drenching, as luck would have it, his whole person and head.

Jia Rui could not suppress an exclamation. "Ai ya!" he cried, but he hastily stopped his mouth with his hands, and did not venture to give vent to another sound. His whole head and face were a mass of filth, and his body felt icy cold. But as he shivered and shook, he espied Jia Se come running. "Get off," he shouted, "with all speed! off with you at once!"

As soon as Jia Rui returned to life again, he bolted with hasty strides, out of the back gate, and ran the whole way home. The night had already reached the third watch, so that he had to knock at the door for it to be opened.

"What's the matter?" inquired the servants, when they saw him in this sorry plight; (an inquiry) which placed him in the necessity of making some false excuse. "The night was dark," he explained, "and my foot slipped and I fell into a gutter."

Saying this, he betook himself speedily to his own apartment; and it was only after he had changed his clothes and performed his ablutions, that he began to realise that lady Feng had made a fool of him. He consequently gave way to a fit of wrath; but upon recalling to mind the charms of lady Feng's face, he felt again extremely aggrieved that he could not there and then clasp her in his embrace, and as he indulged in these wild thoughts and fanciful ideas, he could not the whole night long close his eyes.

From this time forward his mind was, it is true, still with lady Feng, but he did not have the courage to put his foot into the Rong mansion; and with Jia Rong and Jia Se both coming time and again to ask him for the money, he was likewise full of fears lest his grandfather should come to know everything.

His passion for lady Feng was, in fact, already a burden hard to bear, and when, moreover, the troubles of debts were superadded to his tasks, which were also during the whole day arduous, he, a young man of about twenty, as yet unmarried, and a prey to constant cravings for lady Feng, which were difficult to gratify, could not avoid giving way, to a great extent, to such evil habits as exhausted his energies. His lot had, what is more, been on two occasions to be frozen, angered, and to endure much hardship, so that with the attacks received time and again from all sides, he unconsciously soon contracted an organic disease. In his heart inflammation set in; his mouth lost the sense of taste; his feet got as soft as cotton from weakness; his eyes stung as if there were vinegar in them. At night, he burnt with fever. During the day, he was repeatedly under the effects of lassitude. Perspiration was profuse, while with his expectorations of phlegm, he brought up blood. The whole number of these several ailments came upon him, before the expiry of a year, (with the result that) in course of time, he had not the strength to bear himself up. Of a sudden, he would fall down, and with his eyes, albeit closed, his spirit would be still plunged in confused dreams, while his mouth would be full of nonsense and he would be subject to strange starts.

Every kind of doctor was asked to come in, and every treatment had recourse to; and, though of such medicines as cinnamon, aconitum seeds, turtle shell, ophiopogon, Yuzhu herb, and the like, he took several tens of catties, he nevertheless experienced no change for the better; so that by the time the twelfth moon drew once again to an end, and spring returned, this illness had become still more serious.

Dairu was very much concerned, and invited doctors from all parts to attend to him, but none of them could do him any good. And as later on, he had to take nothing else but decoctions of pure ginseng, Dairu could not of course afford it. Having no other help but to come over to the Rong mansion, and make requisition for some, Madame Wang asked lady Feng to weigh two taels of it and give it to him. "The other day," rejoined lady Feng, "not long ago, when we concocted some medicine for our dowager lady, you told us, madame, to keep the pieces that were whole, to present to the spouse of General Yang to make physic with, and as it happens it was only yesterday that I sent someone round with them."

"If there's none over here in our place," suggested Madame Wang, "just send a servant to your mother-in-law's, on the other side, to inquire whether they have any. Or it may possibly be that your elder brother-in-law Zhen, over there, might have a little. If so, put all you get together, and give it to them; and when he shall have taken it, and got well and you shall have saved the life of a human being, it will really be to the benefit of you all."

Lady Feng acquiesced; but without directing a single person to institute any search, she simply took some refuse twigs, and making up a few mace, she despatched them with the meager message that they had been sent by Madame Wang, and that there was, in fact, nomore; subsequently reporting to Madame Wang that she had asked for and obtained all there was and that she had collected as much as two taels, and forwarded it to them.

Jia Rui was, meanwhile, very anxious to recover his health, so that there was no medicine that he would not take, but the outlay of money was of no avail, for he derived no benefit.

On a certain day and at an unexpected moment, a lame Daoist priest came to beg for alms, and he averred that he had the special gift of healing diseases arising from grievances received, and as Jia Rui happened, from inside, to hear what he said, he forthwith shouted out: "Go at once, and bid that divine come in and save my life!" while he reverentially knocked his head on the pillow.

The whole bevy of servants felt constrained to usher the Daoist in; and Jia Rui, taking hold of him with a dash, "My Buddha!" he repeatedly cried out, "save my life!"

The Daoist heaved a sigh. "This ailment of yours," he remarked, "is not one that could be healed with any medicine; I have a precious thing here which I'll give you, and if you gaze at it every day, your life can be saved!"

When he had done talking, he produced from his pouch a look-ing-glass which could reflect a person's face on the front and back as well. On the upper part of the back were engraved the four characters: "Precious Mirror of Voluptuousness." Handing it over to Jia Rui: "This object," he proceeded, "emanates from the primordial confines of the Great Void and has been wrought by the Monitory Dream Fairy in the Palace of Unreality and Spirituality, with the sole intent of healing the illnesses which originate from evil thoughts and improper designs. Possessing, as it does, the virtue of relieving mankind and preserving life, I have consequently brought it along with me into the world, but I only give it to those intelligent preeminent and refined princely men to set their eyes on. On no account must you look at the front side; and you should only gaze at the back of it; this is urgent, this is expedient! After three days, I shall come and fetch it away; by which time, I'm sure, it will have made him all right."

These words finished, he walked away with leisurely step, and though all tried to detain him, they could not succeed.

Jia Rui received the mirror. "This Daoist," he thought, "would seem to speak sensibly, and why should I not look at it and try its effect?" At the conclusion of these thoughts, he took up the Mirror of Volup-tuousness, and cast his eyes on the obverse side; but upon perceiv-ing nought else than a skeleton standing in it, Jia Rui sustained such a fright that he lost no time in covering it with his hands and in abusing the Daoist. "You good-for-nothing!" he exclaimed, "why should you frighten me so? but I'll go further and look at the front and see what it's like."

While he reflected in this manner, he readily looked into the face of the mirror, wherein he caught sight of lady Feng standing, nodding her head and beckoning to him. With one gush of joy, Jia Rui felt himself, in a vague and mysterious manner, transported into the mirror, where he held an affectionate tête-à-tête with lady Feng. Lady Feng escorted him out again. On his return to bed, he gave vent to an exclamation of "Ai yah!" and opening his eyes, he turned the glass over once more; but still, as hitherto, stood the skeleton in the back part.

Jia Rui had, it is true, experienced all the pleasant sensations of a tête-à-tête, but his heart nevertheless did not feel gratified; so that he again turned the front round, and gazed at lady Feng, as she still waved her hand and beckoned to him to go. Once more entering the mirror, he went on in the same way for three or four times, until this occasion, when just as he was about to issue from the mirror, he espied two per-sons come up to him, who made him fast with chains round the neck, and hauled him away. Jia Rui shouted. "Let me take the mirror and I'll come along." But only this remark could he utter, for it was forthwith beyond his power to say one word more. The servants, who stood by in attendance, saw him at first still holding the glass in his hand and looking in, and then, when it fell from his grasp, open his eyes again to pick it up, but when at length the mirror dropped, and he at once ceased to move, they in a body came forward to ascertain what had happened to him. He had already breathed his last. The lower part of his body was icy-cold; his clothes moist from profuse perspiration. With all promptitude they changed him there and then, and carried him to another bed.

Dairu and his wife wept bitterly for him, to the utter disregard of their own lives, while in violent terms they abused the Daoist priest. "What kind of magical mirror is it?" they asked. "If we don't destroy this glass, it will do harm to not a few men in the world!"

Having forthwith given directions to bring fire and burn it, a voice was heard in the air to say, "Who told you to look into the face of it? You yourselves have mistaken what is false for what is true, and why burn this glass of mine?"

Suddenly the mirror was seen to fly away into the air; and when Dairu went out of doors to see, he found no one else than the limping Daoist, shouting, "Who is he who wishes to destroy the Mirror of Voluptuousness?" While uttering these words, he snatched the glass, and, as all eyes were fixed upon him, he moved away lissomely, as if swayed by the wind.

Dairu at once made preparations for the funeral and went everywhere to give notice that on the third day the obsequies would commence, that on the seventh the procession would start to escort the coffin to the Iron Fence Temple, and that on the subsequent day, it would be taken to his original home.

Not much time elapsed before all the members of the Jia family came, in a body, to express their condolences. Jia She, of the Rong Mansion, presented twenty taels, and Jia Zheng also gave twenty taels. Of the Ning Mansion, Jia Zhen likewise contributed twenty taels. The remainder of the members of the clan, of whom some were poor and some rich, and not equally well off, gave either one or two taels, or three or four, some more, some less. Among strangers, there were also contributions, respectively presented by the families of his fellow-scholars, amounting, likewise, collectively to twenty or thirty taels.

The private means of Dairu were, it is true, precarious, but with the monetary assistance he obtained, he anyhow performed the funeral rites with all splendor and eclat.

But who would have thought it, at the close of winter of this year, Lin Ruhai contracted a serious illness, and forwarded a letter, by someone, with the express purpose of fetching Lin Daiyu back. These tidings, when they reached dowager lady Jia, naturally added to the grief and distress (she already suffered), but she felt compelled to make speedy preparations for Daiyu's departure. Baoyu too was intensely cut up, but he had no alternative but to defer to the affection of father and daughter; nor could he very well place any hindrance in the way.

Old lady Jia, in due course, made up her mind that she would like Jia Lian to accompany her, and she also asked him to bring her back again along with him. But no minute particulars need be given of the manifold local presents and of the preparations, which were, of course, everything that could be wished for in excellence and perfectness. Forthwith the day for starting was selected, and Jia Lian, along with Lin Daiyu, said good-bye to all the members of the family, and, followed by their attendants, they went on board their boats, and set out on their journey for Yangzhou.

But, reader, should you have any wish to know fuller details, listen to the account given in the subsequent Chapter.

CHAPTER 13

Qin Keqing dies, and Jia Rong is invested with the rank of military officer to the Imperial Bodyguard. Wang Xifeng lends her help in the management of the Rong Guo Mansion.

Lady Feng, it must be added, in prosecuting our narrative, was ever since Jia Lian's departure to accompany Daiyu to Yang Zhou, really very dejected at heart; and every day, when evening came, she would, after simply indulging in a chat and a laugh with Ping'er, turn in, in a heedless frame of mind, for the night.

In the course of the night of this day, she had been sitting with Ping'er by lamp-light clasping the hand-stove; and weary of doing her work of embroidery, she had at an early hour, given orders to warm the embroidered quilt, and both had gone to bed; and as she was bending her fingers, counting the progress of the journey, and when they should be arriving, unexpectedly, the third watch struck.

Ping'er had already fallen fast asleep; and lady Feng was feeling at length her sleepy eyes slightly dose, when she faintly discerned Mrs. Qin walk in from outside.

"My dear sister-in-law," she said as she smiled, "sleep in peace; I'm on my way back today, and won't even you accompany me just one stage? But as you and I have been great friends all along, I cannot part from you, sister-in-law, and have therefore come to take my leave of you. There is, besides, a wish of mine, which isn't yet accomplished; and if I don't impart it to you, it isn't likely that telling any one else will be of any use."

Lady Feng could not make out the sense of the words she heard. "What wish is it you have?" she inquired, "do tell me, and it will be safe enough with me."

"You are, my dear sister-in-law, a heroine among women," observed Mrs. Qin, "so much so that those famous men, with sashes and official hats, cannot excel you; how is it that you're not aware of even a couple of lines of common adages, of that trite saying, 'when the moon is full, it begins to wane; when the waters are high, they must overflow?' and of that other which says that 'if you ascend high, heavy must be your fall.' Our family has now enjoyed splendor and prosperity for already well-nigh a century, but a day comes when at the height of good fortune, calamity arises; and if the proverb that 'when the tree falls, the monkeys scatter,' be fulfilled, will not futile have been the reputation of culture and old standing of a whole generation?"

Lady Feng at these words felt her heart heavy, and overpowered by intense awe and veneration.

"The fears you express are well founded," she urgently remarked, "but what plan is there adequate to preserve it from future injury?"

"My dear sister-in-law," rejoined Mrs. Qin with a sardonic smile, "you're very simple indeed! When woe has reached its climax, weal supervenes. Prosperity and adversity, from days of yore up to the present time, now pass away, and now again revive, and how can (prosperity) be perpetuated by any human exertion? But if now, we could in the time of good fortune, make provision against any worldly concerns, which might arise at any season of future adversity, we might in fact prolong and preserve it. Everything, for instance, is at present well-regulated; but there are two matters which are not on a sure footing, and if such and such suitable action could be adopted with regard to these concerns, it will, in subsequent days, be found easy to perpetuate the family welfare in its entity."

"What matters are these?" inquired lady Feng.

"Though at the graves of our ancestors," explained Mrs. Qin, "sacrifices and oblations be offered at the four seasons, there's nevertheless no fixed source of income. In the second place, the family school is, it is true, in existence; but it has no definite grants-in-aid. According to my views, now that the times are prosperous, there's, as a matter of course, no lack of offerings and contributions; but by and bye, when reverses set in, whence will these two outlays be met from? Would it not be as well, and my ideas are positive on this score, to avail ourselves of the present time, when riches and honors still reign, to establish in the immediate vicinity of our ancestral tombs, a large number of farms, cottages, and estates, in order to enable the expenditure for offerings and grants to entirely emanate from this source? And if the household school were also established on this principle, the old and young in the whole clan can, after they have, by common consent, determined upon rules, exercise in days to come control in the order of the branches, over the affairs connected with the landed property, revenue, ancestral worship, and school maintenance for the year (of their respective term.) Under this rotatory system, there will likewise be no animosities; neither will there be any mortgages, or sales, or any of these numerous malpractices; and should anyone happen to incur blame, his personal effects can be confiscated by Government. But the properties, from which will be derived the funds for ancestral worship, even the officials should not be able to appropriate, so that when reverses do supervene, the sons and grandsons of the family may be able to return to their homes, and prosecute their studies, or go in for farming. Thus, while they will have something to fall back upon, the ancestral worship will, in like manner, be continued in perpetuity. But, if the present affluence and splendor be looked upon as bound to go on without intermission, and with no thought for the day to come, no enduring plan be after all devised, presently, in a little while, there will, once again, transpire a felicitous occurrence of exceptional kind, which, in point of fact, will resemble the splendor of oil scorched on a violent fire, or fresh flowers decorated with brocades. You should bear in mind that it will also be nothing more real than a transient pageant, nothing but a short-lived pleasure! Whatever you do, don't forget the proverb, that 'there's no banquet, however sumptuous, from which the guests do not disperse;' and unless you do, at an early date, take precautions against later evils, regret will, I apprehend, be of no avail."

"What felicitous occurrence will take place?" lady Feng inquired with alacrity.

"The decrees of Heaven cannot be divulged; but as I have been very friendly with you, sister-in-law, for so long, I will present you, before I take my leave, with two lines, which it behoves you to keep in mind," rejoined Mrs. Qin, as she consequently proceeded to recite what follows:

> The three springs, when over, all radiance will wane;
> The inmates to seek each a home will be fain.

Lady Feng was bent upon making further inquiries, when she heard a messenger at the second gate strike the "cloudy board" four consecutive blows. It was indeed the announcement of a death; and it woke up lady Feng with a start. A servant reported that lady Rong of the eastern mansion was no more.

Lady Feng was so taken aback that a cold perspiration broke out all over her person, and she fell for a while into vacant abstraction. But she had to change her costume, with all possible haste, and to come over to Madame Wang's apartments.

By this time, all the members of the family were aware of the tidings, and there was not one of them who did not feel disconsolate; one and all of them were much wounded at heart. The elder generation bethought themselves of the dutiful submission which she had all along displayed; those of the same age as herself reflected upon the friendship and intimacy which had ever existed with her; those younger than her remembered her past benevolence. Even the servants of the household, whether old or young, looked back upon her qualities of sympathy with the poor, pity of the destitute, affection for the old, and consideration for the young; and not one of them all was there who did not mourn her loss, and give way to intense grief.

But these irrelevant details need not be dilated upon; suffice it to confine ourselves to Baoyu.

Consequent upon Lin Daiyu's return home, he was left to his own self and felt very lonely. Neither would he go and disport himself with others; but with the daily return of dusk, he was wont to retire quietly to sleep.

On this day, while he was yet under the influence of a dream, he heard the announcement of Mrs. Qin's death, and turning himself round quickly he crept out of bed, when he felt as if his heart had been stabbed with a sword. With a sudden retch, he straightway expectorated a mouthful of blood, which so frightened Xiren and the rest that they rushed forward and supported him.

"What is the matter?" they inquired, and they meant also to go and let dowager lady Jia know, so as to send for a doctor, but Baoyu dissuaded them.

"There's no need of any flurry; it's nothing at all," he said, "it's simply that the fire of grief has attacked the heart, and that the blood did not circulate through the arteries."

As he spoke, he speedily raised himself up, and, after asking for his clothes and changing, he came over to see dowager lady Jia. His wish was to go at once to the other side; and Xiren, though feeling uneasy at heart, seeing the state of mind he was in, did not again hinder him, as she felt constrained to let him please himself.

When old lady Jia saw that he was bent upon going: "The breath is just gone out of the body," she consequently remonstrated, "and that side is still sullied. In the second place it's now dark, and the wind is high; so you had better wait until tomorrow morning, when you will be in ample time."

Baoyu would not agree to this, and dowager lady Jia gave orders to get the carriage ready, and to depute a few more attendants and followers to go with him. Under this escort he went forward and straightway arrived in front of the Ning mansion, where they saw the main entrance wide open, the lamps on the two sides giving out a light as bright as day, and people coming and going in confused and large numbers; while the sound of weeping inside was sufficient to shake the mountains and to move the hills.

Baoyu dismounted from the carriage; and with hurried step, walked into the apartment, where the coffin was laid. He gave vent to bitter tears for a few minutes, and subsequently paid his salutations to Mrs. You. Mrs. You, as it happened, had just had a relapse of her old complaint of pains in the stomach and was lying on her bed.

He eventually came out again from her chamber to salute Jia Zhen, just at the very moment that Jia Dairu, Jia Daixiu, Jia Chi, Jia Xiao, Jia Dun, Jia She, Jia Zheng, Jia Cong, Jia Pin, Jia Xing, Jia Guang, Jia Shen, Jia Qiong, Jia Lin, Jia Se, Jia Chang, Jia Ling, Jia Yun, Jia Qin, Jia Zhen, Jia Ping, Jia Zao, Jia Heng, Jia Fen, Jia Fang, Jia Lan, Jia Jun, Jia Zhi, and the other relatives of the families had likewise arrived in a body.

Jia Zhen wept so bitterly that he was like a man of tears. "Of the whole family, whether young or old, distant relatives or close mends," he was just explaining to Jia Dairu and the rest, "who did not know that this girl was a hundred times better than even our son? but now that her spirit has retired, it's evident that this elder branch of the family will be cut off and that there will be no survivor."

While he gave vent to these words, he again burst into tears, and the whole company of relatives set to work at once to pacify him. "She has already departed this life," they argued, "and tears are also of no avail, besides the pressing thing now is to consult as to what kind of arrangements are to be made."

Jia Zhen clapped his hands. "What arrangements are to be made!" he exclaimed; "nothing is to be done, but what is within my means."

As they conversed, they perceived Qin Ye and Qin Zhong, as well as several relations of Mrs. You, arrive, together with Mrs. You's sisters; and Jia Zhen forthwith bade Jia Qiong, Jia Shen, Jia Lin, and Jia Se, the four of them, to go and entertain the guests; while he, at the same time, issued directions to go and ask the Astrologer of the Imperial Observatory to come and choose the days for the ceremonies.

(This Astrologer) decided that the coffin should remain in the house for seven times seven days, that is forty-nine days; that after the third day, the mourning rites should be begun and the formal cards should be distributed; that all that was to be done during these forty-nine days was to invite one hundred and eight Buddhist bonzes to perform, in the main Hall, the High Confession Mass, in order to ford the souls of departed relatives across the abyss of suffering, and afterwards to transmute the spirit (of Mrs. Qin); that, in addition, an altar should be erected in the Tower of Heavenly Fragrance, where nine times nine virtuous Daoist priests should, for nineteen days, offer up prayers for absolution from punishment, and purification from retribution. That after these services, the tablet should be moved into the Garden of Concentrated Fragrance, and that in the presence of the tablet, fifteen additional eminent bonzes and fifteen renowned Daoist Priests should confront the altar and perform meritorious deeds every seven days.

The news of the death of the wife of his eldest grandson reached Jia Jing; but as he himself felt sure that, at no distant date, he would ascend to the regions above, he was loath to return again to his home, and so expose himself to the contamination of the world, as to completely waste the meritorious excellence acquired in past days. For this reason, he paid no heed to the event, but allowed Jia Zhen a free hand to accomplish the necessary preparations.

Jia Zhen, to whom we again revert, was fond of display and extravagance, so that he found, on inspection of coffins, those few made of pine-wood unsuitable to his taste; when, strange coincidence, Xue Pan came to pay his visit of condolence, and perceiving that Jia Zhen was in quest of a good coffin: "In our establishment," he readily suggested, "we have a lot of timber of some kind or other called Qiang wood, which comes from the Tie Wang Mount, in Huanghai; and which made into coffins will not rot, not for ten thousand years. This lot was, in fact, brought down, some years back, by my late father; and had at one time been required by His Highness Yizhong, a Prince of the royal blood; but as he became guilty of some mismanagement, it was, in consequence, not used, and is still lying stored up in our establishment; and another thing besides is that there's no one with the means to purchase it. But if you do want it, you should come and have a look at it."

Jia Zhen, upon hearing this, was extremely delighted, and gave orders that the planks should be there and then brought over. When the whole family came to inspect them, they found those for the sides and the bottom to be all eight inches thick, the grain like betel-nut, the smell like sandal-wood or musk, while, when tapped with the hand, the sound emitted was like that of precious stones; so that one and all agreed in praising the timber for its remarkable quality.

"What is their price?" Jia Zhen inquired with a smile.

"Even with one thousand taels in hand," explained Xue Pan laughingly, "I feel sure you wouldn't find any place where you could buy the like. Why ask about price? if you just give the workmen a few taels for their labor, it will be quite sufficient."

Jia Zhen, at these words, lost no time in giving expression to profuse assurances of gratitude, and was forthwith issuing directions that the timber should be split, sawn, and made up, when Jia Zheng proffered his advice. "Such articles shouldn't," he said, "be, in my idea, enjoyed by persons of the common run; it would be quite ample if the body were placed in a coffin made of pine of the best quality."

But Jia Zhen would not listen to any suggestion.

Suddenly he further heard that Mrs. Qin's waiting-maid, Ruizhu by name, had, after she had become alive to the fact that her mistress had died, knocked her head against a post, and likewise succumbed to the blows. This unusual occurrence the whole clan extolled in high terms; and Jia Zhen promptly directed that, with regard to ceremonies, she should be treated as a granddaughter, and that the body should, after it had been placed in the coffin, be also deposited in the Hall of Attained Immortality, in the Garden of Concentrated Fragrance.

There was likewise a young waiting-maid, called Baozhu, who, as Mrs. Qin left no issue, was willing to become an adopted child, and begged to be allowed to undertake the charge of dashing the mourning bowl, and accompanying the coffin; which pleased Jia Zhen so much that he speedily transmitted orders that from that time forth Baozhu should be addressed by all as "young miss."

Baozhu, after the rites of an unmarried daughter, mourned before the coffin to such an unwonted degree, as if bent upon snapping her own life; while the members of the entire clan, as well as the inmates of the Mansions, each and all, readily observed, in their conduct, the established mourning usages, without of course any transgression or confusion.

"Jia Rong," pondered Jia Zhen, "has no higher status than that of graduate by purchase, and were this designation written on the funeral streamer, it will not be imposing, and, in point of fact, the retinue will likewise be small." He therefore was exceedingly unhappy, in his own mind, when, as luck would have it, on this day, which was the fourth day of the first seven, Daiquan, a eunuch of the Palace of High Renown, whose office was that of Palace Overseer, first prepared sacrificial presents, which he sent round by messengers, and next came himself in an official chair, preceded by criers beating the gong, to offer sacrificial oblations.

Jia Zhen promptly received him, and pressed him into a seat; and when they adjourned into the Hall of the Loitering Bees, tea was presented.

Jia Zhen had already arrived at a fixed purpose, so that he seized an opportunity to tell him of his wish to purchase an office for Jia Rong's advancement.

Daiquan understood the purport of his remark. "It is, I presume," he added smilingly, "that the funeral rites should be a little more sumptuous."

"My worthy sir," eagerly rejoined Jia Zhen, "your surmise on that score is perfectly correct."

"The question," explained Daiquan, "comes up at an opportune moment; for there is just at present a good vacancy. Of the three hundred officers who at present constitute the Imperial Body Guard, there are two wanting. Yesterday marquis Xiangyang's third brother came to appeal to me with one thousand five hundred taels of ready money, which he brought over to my house. You know the friendship of old standing which exists between him and me, so that, placing other considerations aside, I without a second thought, assented for his father's sake. But there still remains another vacancy, which, who would have thought it, fat general Feng, of Yongxing, asked to purchase for his son; but I have had no time to give him an answer. Besides, as our child wants to purchase it, you had better at once write a statement of his antecedents."

jia Zhen lost no time in bidding someone write the statement on red paper, which Daiquan found, on perusal, to record that Jia Rong was a graduate, by purchase, of the District of Jiangning, of the Jiangling Prefecture, in Jiangnan; that Jia Daihua, his great grandfather, had been Commander-in-Chief of the Metropolitan Camp, and an hereditary general of the first class, with the prefix of Spiritual Majesty; that his grandfather Jia Jing was a metropolitan graduate of the tripos in the Ping Zhen year; and that his father Jia Zhen had inherited a rank of nobility of the third degree, and was a general, with the prefix of Majestic Intrepidity.

Daiquan, after perusal, turned his hand behind him and passed (the statement) to a constant attendant of his, to put away: "Go back," he enjoined him, "and give it to His Excellency Mr. Zhao, at the head of the Board of Revenue, and tell him that I present him my compliments, and would like him to draw up a warrant for subaltern of the Imperial Bodyguard of the fifth grade, and to also issue a commission; that he should take the particulars from this statement and fill them up; and that tomorrow I'll come and have the money weighed and sent over."

The young attendant signified his obedience, and Daiquan thereupon took his leave. Jia Zhen did all he could to detain him, but with no success; so that he had no alternative but to escort him as far as the entrance of the mansion. As he was about to mount into his chair, Jia Zhen inquired, "As regards the money, shall I go and pay it into the Board, or am I to send it to the Board of Eunuchs?"

"If you were to go and pay it at the Board," observed Daiquan; "you are sure to suffer loss; so that it would be better if you just weighed exactly one thousand taels and sent them over to my place; for then an end will be put to all trouble."

Jia Zhen was incessant in his expression of gratitude. "When the period of mourning has expired," he consequently added, "I shall lead in person, my despicable eldest son to your mansion, to pay our obeisance, and express our thanks."

They then parted company, but close upon this were heard again the voices of runners. It was, in fact, the spouse of Shiding, the marquis of Zhongjing, who was just arriving. Shi Xiangyun, mesdames Wang, and Xing, lady Feng and the rest came out at once, to greet her, and lead her into the Main Building; when they further saw the sacrificial presents of the three families, of the marquis of Jinxiang, the marquis of Chuaning, and the earl of Shoushan, likewise spread out in front of the tablet.

In a short while, these three noblemen descended from their chairs, and Jia Zhen received them in the Large Hall. In like manner all the relatives and friends arrived in such quick succession, one coming, another going, that it is impossible to remember even so much as their number. One thing need be said that during these forty-nine days the street on which the Ning Guo mansion stood, was covered with a sheet of white, formed by the people, coming and going; and thronged with clusters of flowers, as the officials came and went.

At the instance of Jia Zhen, Jia Rong, the next day donned his gala dress and went over for his papers; and on his return the articles in use in front of the coffin, as well as those belonging to the cortege and other such things, were all regulated by the rules prescribed for an official status of the fifth degree; while, on the tablet and notice alike the inscription consisted of: Spirit of lady Qin, (by marriage) of the Jia mansion, and by patent a lady of the fifth rank (of the titles of honor).

The main entrance of the Garden of Concentrated Fragrance, adjoining the street, was opened wide; and on both sides were raised sheds for the musicians, and two companies of players, dressed in blue, discoursed music at the proper times; while one pair after another of the paraphernalia was drawn out so straight as if cut by a knife or slit by an axe. There were also two large carmine boards, carved with gilt inscriptions, erected outside the gate; the designations in bold characters on the upper sides being: Guard of the Imperial Antechamber, charged with the protection of the Inner Palace and Roads, in the Red Prohibited City.

On the opposite side, facing each other, rose, high above the ground, two altars for the services of the Buddhist and Daoist priests, while a placard bore the inscription in bold type: "Funeral Obsequies of lady

Qin, (by marriage) of the Jia mansion, by patent a lady of the fifth rank, consort of the eldest grandson of the hereditary duke of Ning Guo, and guard of the Imperial Antechamber, charged with the protection of the Inner Palace and Roads in the Red Prohibited City. We, Wan Xu, by Heaven's commands charged with the perennial preservation of perfect peace in the Kingdom of the Four Continents, as well as of the lands contained therein, Head Controller of the School of Void and Asceticism, and Superior in Chief (of the Buddhist hierarchy); and Ye Sheng, Principal Controller, since the creation, of the Disciples of Perfect Excellence and Superior in Chief (of the Daoist priesthood), and others, having in a reverent spirit purified ourselves by abstinence, now raise our eyes up to Heaven, prostrate ourselves humbly before Buddha, and devoutly pray all the Jia Lan's, Jie Di's, Gong Cao's, and other divinities to extend their sacred bounties, and from afar to display their spiritual majesty, during the forty-nine days (of the funeral rites), for the deliverance from judgment and the absolution from retribution (of the spirit of lady Qin), so that it may enjoy a peaceful and safe passage, whether by sea or by land;" and other such prayers to this effect, which are in fact not worth the trouble of putting on record.

Jia Zhen had, it is true, all his wishes gratified; but, as his wife was laid up in the inner chambers, with a relapse of her old complaint, and was not in a fit state to undertake the direction of the ceremonies, he was very much distressed lest, when the high officials (and their wives) came and went, there should occur any breach of the prescribed conventionalities, which he was afraid would evoke ridicule. Hence it was that he felt in low spirits; but while he was plunged in solicitude Baoyu, who happened to be close by, readily inquired, "Everything may be safely looked upon as being satisfactorily settled, and why need you, elder brother, still be so full of concern?"

Jia Zhen forthwith explained to him how it was that in the ladies' apartments there was no one (to do the honors), but Baoyu at these words smiled: "What difficulty is there about it?" he remarked; "I'll recommend someone to take temporary charge of the direction of things for you during the month, and I can guarantee that everything will be properly carried out."

"Who is it?" Jia Zhen was quick to ask; but as Baoyu perceived that there were still too many relatives and friends seated around, he did not feel as if he could very well speak out; so that he went up to Jia Zhen and whispered a couple of remarks in his ear.

Jia Zhen's joy knew no bounds when he heard this suggestion. "Everything will indeed be properly carried out," he added laughingly; "but I must now be going at once."

With these words, he drew Baoyu along, and taking leave of the whole number of visitors, they forthwith came into the drawing rooms.

This day was luckily not a grand occasion, so that few relatives and friends had come. In the inner apartments there were only a small number of ladies of close kinship. Mesdames Xing and Wang, and lady Feng, and the women of the whole household, were entertaining the guests, when they heard a servant announce that Mr. Jia Zhen had come. (This announcement) took the whole body of ladies and young ladies so much by surprise, that, with a rushing sound, they tried to hide in the back rooms; but they were not quick enough (to effect their escape).

Lady Feng alone composedly stood up. Jia Zhen was himself at this time rather unwell, and being also very much cut up, he entered the room shuffling along, propping himself up with a staff.

"You are not well?" therefore remarked Madame Xing and the others, "and you've had besides so much to attend to during these consecutive days, that what you require is rest to get all right; and why do you again come over?"

Jia Zhen was, as he leant on his staff, straining every nerve to bend his body so as to fall on his knees and pay his respects to them, and express his sense of obligation for the trouble they had taken, when Madame Xing and the other ladies hastily called Baoyu to raise him up, bidding a servant move a chair for him to sit on. Jia Zhen would not take a seat; but making an effort to return a smile, "Your nephew," he urged, "has come over, as there's a favor that I want to ask of my two aunts as well as of my eldest cousin."

"What is it?" promptly inquired Madame Xing and the rest.

"My aunts," Jia Zhen replied with all haste, "you surely are aware that your grandson's wife is now no more; your nephew's wife is also laid up unwell, and, as I see that things in the inner apartments are really not what they should properly be, I would trouble my worthy eldest cousin to undertake in here the direction of affairs for a month; and if she does, my mind will be set at ease."

Madame Xing smiled. "Is it really about this that you've come?" she asked; "your eldest cousin is at present staying with your aunt Secunda, and all you have to do is to speak to her and it will be all right."

"How ever could a mere child like her," speedily remonstrated Madame Wang, "carry out all these matters? and shouldn't she manage things properly, she will, on the contrary, make people laugh, so it would therefore be better that you should trouble someone else."

"What your ideas are, aunt," rejoined Jia Zhen smiling, "your nephew has guessed; you're afraid lest my eldest cousin should have to bear fatigue and annoyance; for as to what you say, that she cannot manage things, why my eldest cousin has, from her youth up, ever been in her romping and playing so firm and decided; and now that she has entered the married estate, and has the run of affairs in that mansion, she must have reaped so much the more experience, and have become quite an old hand! I've been thinking these last few days that outside my eldest cousin, there's no one else who could come to my help; and, aunt, if you don't do it for the face of your nephew and your nephew's wife, do it, at least, for the affection you bore to her who is no more."

While he uttered these words tears trickled down his face. The fears that Madame Wang inwardly entertained were that lady Feng had no experience in funeral matters, and she apprehended, that if she was not equal to managing them, she would incur the ridicule of others; but when she now heard Jia Zhen make the appeal in such a disconsolate mood, she relented considerably in her resolution. But as she turned her eyes towards lady Feng (to ascertain her wishes), she saw that she was plunged in abstraction.

Lady Feng had all along found the greatest zest in taking the initiative in everything, with the idea of making a display of her abilities, so that when she perceived how earnest Jia Zhen was in his entreaties, she had, at an early period, made up her mind to give a favorable reply. Seeing besides Madame Wang show signs of relenting, she readily turned round and said to her, "My elder cousin has made his appeal in such a solicitous way that your ladyship should give your consent and have done with it."

"Do you think you are equal to the task?" inquired Madame Wang in a whisper.

"What's there that I couldn't be equal to?" replied lady Feng; "for urgent matters outside, my cousin may be said to have already made full provision; and all there is to be done is to keep an eye over things inside. But should there occur anything that I don't know, I can ask you, madame, and it will be right."

Madame Wang perceiving the reasonableness of what she heard her say, uttered not a word, and when Jia Zhen saw that lady Feng had assented; "How much you do attend to I don't mind," he observed, forcing another smile, "but I must, in any case, entreat you, cousin, to assume the onerous charge. As a first step I'll pay my obeisance to you in here, and when everything has been finished, I shall then come over into that mansion to express my thanks."

With these words still on his lips, he made a low bow, but lady Feng had scarcely had time to return the compliment, before Jia Zhen had directed a servant to fetch the warrant of the Ning mansion, which he bade Baoyu hand over to lady Feng.

"Cousin," he added, "take whatever steps you think best; and if you want anything, all you have to do is to simply send for it with this, and there will even be no use to consult me. The only thing I must ask you is, not to be too careful in order to save me expense, for the main consideration is that things should be handsomely done. In the second place, it will be well if you were also to treat servants here in the same way as in the other mansion, and not be too scrupulous in the fear that anyone might take offence. Outside these two concerns, there's nothing else to disturb my mind."

Lady Feng did not venture to take over the warrant at once, but merely turned round to ascertain what were Madame Wang's wishes.

"In view of the reason brother Zhen advances," Madame Wang rejoined, "you had better assume the charge at once and finish with it; don't, however, act on your own ideas; but when there's aught to be done, be careful and send someone to consult your cousin's wife, ever so little though it be on the subject."

Baoyu had already taken over the warrant from Jia Zhen's grasp, and forcibly handed it to lady Feng, "Will you, cousin," he went on to question, "take up your quarters here or will you come every day? should you cross over, day after day, it will be ever so much more fatiguing for you, so that I shall speedily have a separate court got ready for you in here, where you, cousin, can put up for these several days and be more comfortable."

"There's no need," replied lady Feng smiling; "for on that side they can't do without me; and it will be better if I were to come daily."

"Do as you like," Jia Zhen observed; and after subsequently passing a few more irrelevant remarks, he at length left the room.

After a time, the lady relatives dispersed, and Madame Wang seized the opportunity to inquire of lady Feng, "What do you purpose doing today?"

"You had better, please madame, go back," urged lady Feng, "for I must first of all find out some clue before I can go home."

Madame Wang, upon hearing these words, returned to her quarters, in advance, in company with Madame Xing, where we will leave them.

Lady Feng meanwhile came into a colonnade, which enclosed a suite of three apartments, and taking a seat, she gave way to reflection. "The first consideration," she communed within herself, "is that the household is made up of mixed elements, and things might be lost; the second is that the preparations are under no particular control, with the result that, when the time comes, the servants might shirk their duties; the third is that the necessary expenditure being great, there will be reckless disbursements and counterfeit receipts; the fourth, that with the absence of any distinction in the matter of duties, whether large or small, hardship and ease will be unequally shared; and the fifth, that the servants being arrogant, through leniency, those with any self-respect will not brook control, while those devoid of 'face' will not be able to improve their ways."

These five were, in point of fact, usages in vogue in the Ning mansion. But as you are unable, reader, to ascertain here how lady Feng set things right, listen to the explanations given in the following chapter.

CHAPTER 14

Lin Ruhai dies in the City of Yangzhou. Jia Baoyu meets the Prince of Beijing on the way.

When Lai Sheng, be it noticed in continuing our story, the major-domo in the Ning Guo mansion, came to hear that from inside an invitation had been extended to lady Feng to act as deputy, he summoned together his co-workers and other servants. "Lady Secunda, of the western mansion," he harangued them, "has now been asked to take over the control of internal affairs; and should she come we must, when we apply for anything, or have anything to say, be circumspect in our service; we should all every day come early and leave late; and it's better that we should exert ourselves during this one month and take rest after it's over. We mustn't throw away our old 'face,' for she's well known to be an impetuous thing, with a soured face and a hard heart, who, when angry, knows no distinction of persons."

The whole company unanimously admitted that he was right; and one of their number too observed smilingly, "It's but right that for the inner apartments, we should, in fact, get her to come and put things in proper order, as everything is very much what it should not be."

But while he uttered these words, they saw Lai Wang's wife coming, with an indent in hand, to fetch paper for the supplications and prayers, the amount of which was mentioned on the order; and they one and all hastened to press her into a seat, and to help her to a cup of tea; while a servant was told to fetch the quantity of paper required. (When it was brought,) Lai Wang carried it in his arms and came, the whole way with his wife, as far as the ceremonial gate; when he, at length, delivered it over to her and she clasped it, and walked into the room all alone.

Lady Feng issued prompt directions to Caiming to prepare a register; and sending, there and then, for Lai Sheng's wife, she asked her to submit, for her perusal, the roll with the servants' names. She furthermore fixed upon an early hour of the following day to convene the domestics and their wives in the mansion, in order that they should receive their orders; but, after cursorily glancing over the number of entries in the list, and making a few inquiries of Lai Sheng's wife, she soon got into her curricle, and went home.

On the next day, at six and two quarters, she speedily came over. The matrons and married women of the Ning Guo mansion assembled together, as soon as they heard of her arrival; but, perceiving lady Feng, assisted by Lai Sheng's wife, engaged in apportioning the duties of each servant, they could not presume to intrude, but remained outside the window listening to what was going on.

"As I've been asked to take over the charge," they heard lady Feng explain to Lai Sheng's wife, "I'm, needless to say, sure to incur the displeasure of you all, for I can't compare with your mistress, who has such a sweet temper, and allows you to have your own way. But saying nothing more of those ways, which prevailed hitherto among your people in this mansion, you must now do as I tell you; for on the slightest disregard of my orders, I shall, with no discrimination between those who may be respectable and those who may not be, clearly and distinctly call all alike to account."

Having concluded these remarks, she went on to order Caiming to read the roll; and, as their names were uttered, one by one was called in, and passed under inspection. After this inspection, which was got over in a short time, she continued giving further directions. "These twenty," she said "should be divided into two companies; ten in each company, whose sole daily duties should be to attend inside to the guests, coming and going, and to serve tea for them; while with any other matters, they needn't have anything to do. These other twenty should also be divided into two companies, whose exclusive duties will be, day after day, to look after the tea and eatables of the relatives of our family; and these too will have no business to concern themselves with outside matters. These forty will again be divided into two companies, who will have nothing else to look to than to remain in front of the coffin and offer incense, renew the oil, hang up the streamers, watch the coffin, offer sacrifices of rice, and oblations of tea, and mourn with the mourners; and neither need they mind anything outside these duties. These four servants will be specially attached to the inner tearooms to look after cups, saucers, and the tea articles generally; and in the event of the loss of any single thing, the four of them will have to make it good between them. These other four servants will have the sole charge of the articles required for eatables and wine; and should any get mislaid compensation will have likewise to be made by them. These eight servants will only have to attend to taking over the sacrificial offerings; while these eight will have nothing more to see to beyond keeping an eye over the lamps, oil, candles, and paper wanted everywhere. I'll have a whole supply served out and handed to you eight to by and by apportion to the various places, in quantities which I will determine. These thirty servants are each day, by rotation, to keep watch everywhere during the night, looking after the gates and windows, taking care of the fires and candles, and sweeping the grounds; while the servants, who remain, are to be divided for duty in the houses and rooms, each one having charge of a particular spot. And beginning from the tables, chairs, and curios in each place, up to the very cuspidors and brooms, yea even to each blade of grass or sprout of herb, which may be there, the servants looking after this part will be called upon to make good anything that may be either mislaid or damaged. You, Lai Sheng's wife, will every day have to exercise general supervision and inspection; and should there be those who be lazy, any who may gamble, drink, fight, or wrangle, come at once and report the matter to me; and you mustn't show any leniency, for if I come to find it out, I shall have no regard to the good old name of three or four generations, which you may enjoy. You now all have your fixed duties, so that whatever batch of you after this acts contrary to these orders, I shall simply have something to say to that batch and to no one else. The servants, who have all along been in my service, carry watches on their persons, and things, whether large or small, are invariably done at a fixed time. But, in any case, you also have clocks in your master's rooms, so that at 6:30, I shall come and read the roll, and at ten you'll have breakfast. Whenever there is any indent of any permits to be made or any report to be submitted, it should be done at 11:30 A.M. and no later. At 7 P.M., after the evening paper has been burnt, I shall come to each place in person to hold an inspection; and on my return, the servants on watch for the night will hand over the keys. The next day, I shall again come over at 6:30 in the morning; and needless to say we must all do the best we can for these few days; and when the work has been finished your master is sure to recompense you."

When she had done speaking, she went on to give orders that tea, oil, candles, feather dusters, brooms, and other necessaries should he issued, according to the fixed quantities. She also had furniture, such as table-covers, antimacassars, cushions, rugs, cuspidors, stools, and the like brought over and distributed; while, at the same time, she took up the brush and made a note of the names of the persons in charge of the various departments, and of the articles taken over by the respective servants, in entries remarkable for the utmost perspicacity.

The whole body of servants received their charge and left; but they all had work to go and attend to; not as in former times, when they were at liberty to select for themselves what was convenient to do, while the arduous work, which remained over, no one could be found to take in hand. Neither was it possible for them in the various establishments to any longer avail themselves of the confusion to carelessly mislay things. In fact, visitors came and guests left, but everything after all went off quietly, unlike the disorderly way which prevailed hitherto, when there was no clue to the ravel; and all such abuses as indolence, and losses, and the like were completely eradicated.

Lady Feng, on her part, (perceiving) the weight her influence had in enjoining the observance of her directions, was in her heart exceedingly delighted. But as she saw, that Jia Zhen was, in consequence of Mrs. You's indisposition, even so much the more grieved as to take very little to drink or to eat, she daily, with her own hands, prepared, in the other mansion, every kind of fine congee and luscious small dishes, which she sent over, in order that he might be tempted to eat.

And Jia Lian had likewise given additional directions that every day the finest delicacies should be taken into the ante-chamber, for the exclusive use of lady Feng.

Lady Feng was not one to shirk exertion and fatigue, so that, day after day, she came over at the proper time, called the roll, and managed business, sitting all alone in the ante-chamber, and not congregating with the whole bevy of sisters-in-law. Indeed, even when relatives or visitors came or went, she did not go to receive them, or see them off.

This day was the thirty-fifth day, the very day of the fifth seven, and the whole company of bonzes had just (commenced the services) for unclosing the earth, and breaking Hell open; for sending a light to show the way to the departed spirit; for its being admitted to an audience by the king of Hell; for arresting all the malicious devils, as well as for soliciting the soul-saving Buddha to open the golden bridge and to lead the way with streamers. The Daoist priests were engaged in reverently reading the prayers; in worshipping the Three Pure Ones, and in prostrating themselves before the Gemmy Lord. The disciples of abstraction were burning incense, in order to release the hungered spirits, and were reading the water regrets manual. There was also a company of twelve nuns of tender years, got up in embroidered dresses, and wearing red shoes, who stood before the coffin, silently reading all the incantations for the reception of the spirit (from the lower regions,) with the result that the utmost bustle and stir prevailed.

Lady Feng, well aware that not a few guests would call on this day, was quick to get out of bed at four sharp, to dress her hair and perform her ablutions. After having completed every arrangement for the day, she changed her costume, washed her hands, and swallowed a couple of mouthfuls of milk. By the time she had rinsed her mouth, it was exactly 6:30; and Lai Wang's wife, at the head of a company of servants, had been waiting a good long while, when lady Feng appeared in front of the Entrance Hall, mounted her carriage and betook herself, preceded by a pair of transparent horn lanterns, on which were written, in large type, the three characters, Rong Guo mansion, to the main entrance gate of the Ning Household. The door lanterns shed brilliant rays from where they were suspended; while on either side the lanterns, of uniform colors, propped upright, emitted a lustrous light as bright as day.

The servants of the family, got up in their mourning clothes, covered the ground far and wide like a white sheet. They stood drawn in two rows, and requested that the carriage should drive up to the main entrance. The youths retired, and all the married women came forward, and raising the curtain of the carriage, lady Feng alighted; and as with one arm she supported herself on Feng'er, two married women, with lanterns in their hands, lighted the way. Pressed round by the servants, lady Feng made her entry. The married women of the Ning mansion advanced to greet her, and to pay their respects; and this over, lady Feng, with graceful bearing, entered the Garden of Concentrated Fragrance. Ascending the Spirit Hall, where the tablet was laid, the tears, as soon as she caught sight of the coffin, trickled down her eyes like pearls whose string had snapped; while the youths in the court, and their number was not small, stood in a reverent posture, with their arms against their sides, waiting to burn the paper. Lady Feng uttered one remark, by way of command: "Offer the tea and burn the paper!" when the sound of two blows on the gong was heard and the whole band struck up together. A servant had at an early period placed a large armchair in front of the tablet, and lady Feng sat down, and gave way to loud lamentations. Promptly all those, who stood inside or outside, whether high or low, male or female, took up the note, and kept on wailing and weeping until Jia Zhen and Mrs. You, after a time, sent a message to advise her to withhold her tears; when at length lady Feng desisted.

Lai Wang's wife served the tea; and when she had finished rinsing her mouth, lady Feng got up; and, taking leave of all the members of the clan, she walked all alone into the ante-chamber, where she ascertained, in the order of their names, the number of the servants of every denomination in there. They were all found to be present, with the exception of one, who had failed to appear, whose duties consisted in receiving and escorting the relatives and visitors. Orders were promptly given to summon him, and the man appeared in a dreadful fright. "What!" exclaimed lady Feng, as she forced a smile, "is it you who have been remiss? Is it because you're more respectable than they that you don't choose to listen to my words?"

"Your servant," he pleaded, "has come at an early hour every day; and it's only today that I come late by one step; and I entreat your ladyship to forgive this my first offence."

While yet he spoke, she perceived the wife of Wang Xing, of the Rong Guo mansion, come forward and pop her head in to see what was going on; but lady Feng did not let this man go, but went on to inquire of Wang Xing's wife what she had come for.

Wang Xing's wife drew near. "I've come," she explained, "to get an order, so as to obtain some thread to make tassels for the carriages and chairs." Saying this, she produced the permit and handed it up, whereupon lady Feng directed Caiming to read the contents aloud. "For two large, sedan chairs," he said, "four small sedan chairs, and four carriages, are needed in all so many large and small tassels, each tassel requiring so many catties of beads and thread."

Lady Feng finding, after she had heard what was read, that the numbers (and quantities) corresponded, forthwith bade Caiming make the proper entry; and when the order from the Rong Guo mansion had been fetched, and thrown at her, Wang Xing's wife took her departure.

Lady Feng was on the very point of saying something, when she espied four managers of the Rong Guo mansion walk in; all of whom wanted permits to indent for stores. Having asked them to read out the list of what they required, she ascertained that they wanted four kinds of articles in all. Drawing attention to two items: "These entries," she remarked, "are wrong; and you had better go again and make out the account clearly, and then come and fetch a permit."

With these words, she flung down the requisitions, and the two men went their way in lower spirits than when they had come.

Lady Feng then caught sight of the wife of Zhang Cai standing by, and asked her what was her business, whereupon Zhang Cai's wife promptly produced an indent. "The covers of the carriages and sedan chairs," she reported, "have just been completed, and I've come to fetch the amount due to the tailors for wages."

Lady Feng, upon hearing her explanation, took over the indent, and directed Caiming to enter the items in the book. After Wang Xing had handed over the money, and obtained the receipt of the accountant, duly signed, which tallied with the payment, he subsequently walked away in company with Zhang Cai's wife. Lady Feng simultaneously proceeded to give orders that another indent should be read, which was for money to purchase paper with to paste on the windows of Baoyu's outer school-room, the repairs to which had been brought to completion, and as soon as lady Feng heard the nature of the application, she there and then gave directions that the permit should be taken over and an entry made, and that the money should be issued after Zhang Cai's wife had delivered everything clearly.

"If tomorrow he were to come late," lady Feng then remarked, "and if the day after, I were to come late; why by and by there'll be no one here at all! I should have liked to have let you off, but if I be lenient with you on this first instance, it will be hard for me, on the occurrence of another offence, to exercise any control over the rest. It's much better therefore that I should settle accounts with you."

The moment she uttered these words, she put on a serious look, and gave orders that he should be taken out and administered twenty blows with the bamboo. When the servants perceived that lady Feng was in an angry mood, they did not venture to dilly-dally, but dragged him out, and gave him the full number of blows; which done, they came in to report that the punishment had been inflicted.

Lady Feng likewise threw down the Ning Mansion order and exclaimed, addressing herself to Lai Sheng: "Cut him a month's wages and rice! and tell them all to disperse, and have done with it!"

All the servants at length withdrew to attend to their respective duties, while the man too, who had been flogged, walked away, as he did all he could to conceal his shame and stifle his tears. About this time arrived and went, in an incessant stream, servants from both the Rong and Ning mansions, bent upon applying for permits and returning permits, and with one by one again did lady Feng settle accounts. And, as in due course, the inmates of the Ning mansion came to know how terrible lady Feng was, each and all were ever since so wary and dutiful that they did not venture to be lazy.

But without going into further details on this subject, we shall now return to Baoyu. Seeing that there were a lot of people about and fearing lest Qin Zhong might receive some offence, he lost no time in coming along with him to sit over at lady Feng's. Lady Feng was just having her repast, and upon seeing them arrive: "Your legs are long enough, and couldn't you have come somewhat quicker!" she laughingly observed.

"We've had our rice, thanks," replied Baoyu.

"Have you had it," inquired lady Feng, "outside here, or over on the other side?"

"Would we eat anything with all that riff-raff?" exclaimed Baoyu; "we've really had it over there; in fact, I now come after having had mine with dowager lady Jia."

As he uttered these words, they took their seats. Lady Feng had just finished her meal, when a married woman from the Ning mansion came to get an order to obtain an advance of money to purchase incense and lanterns with.

"I calculated," observed lady Feng, "that you would come today to make requisition, but I was under the impression that you had forgotten; had you really done so you would certainly have had to get them on your own account, and I would have been the one to benefit."

"Didn't I forget? I did," rejoined the married woman as she smiled; "and it's only a few minutes back that it came to my mind; had I been one second later I wouldn't have been in time to get the things."

These words ended, she took over the order and went off. Entries had, at the time to be made in the books, and orders to be issued, and Qin Zhong was induced to interpose with a smirk, "In both these mansions of yours, such orders are alike in use; but were any outsider stealthily to counterfeit one and to abscond, after getting the money, what could ever be done?"

"In what you say," replied lady Feng, "you take no account of the laws of the land."

"How is it that from our house, no one comes to get any orders or to obtain anything?" Baoyu having inquired: "At the time they come to fetch them," rejoined lady Feng, "you're still dreaming; but let me ask you one thing, when will you two at last begin your evening course of studies?"

"Oh, I wish we were able to begin our studies this very day," Baoyu added; "that would be the best thing, but they're very slow in putting the school-room in order, so that there's no help for it!"

Lady Feng laughed. "Had you asked me," she remarked, "I can assure you it would have been ready quick enough."

"You too would have been of no use," observed Baoyu, "for it will certainly be ready by the time they ought to finish it in."

"But in order that they should do the work," suggested lady Feng, "it's also necessary that they should have the material, they can't do without them; and if I don't give them any permits, it will be difficult to obtain them."

Baoyu at these words readily drew near to lady Feng, and there and then applied for the permits. "My dear sister," he added, "do give them the permits to enable them to obtain the material and effect the repairs."

"I feel quite sore from fatigue," ventured lady Feng, "and how can I stand your rubbing against me? but compose your mind. They have this very day got the paper, and gone to paste it; and would they, for whatever they need, have still waited until they had been sent for? they are not such fools after all!"

Baoyu would not believe it, and lady Feng at once called Caiming to look up the list, which she handed for Baoyu's inspection; but while they were arguing a servant came in to announce that Zhao'er, who had gone to Suzhou, had returned, and lady Feng all in a flurry directed that he should be asked to walk in. Zhao'er bent one knee and paid his obeisance.

"Why have you come back?" lady Feng readily inquired.

"Mr. Secundus (Jia Lian)," he reported, "sent me back to tell you that Mr. Lin (our dowager lady's) son-in-law, died on the third of the ninth moon; that Master Secundus is taking Miss Lin along with him to escort the coffin of Mr. Lin as far as Suzhou; and that they hope to be back some time about the end of the year. Master despatched me to come and announce the news, to bring his compliments, and to crave our old lady's instructions as well as to see how you are getting on in my lady's home. He also bade me take back to him a few long fur pelisses."

"Have you seen anyone else besides me?" lady Feng inquired.

"I've seen everyone," rejoined Zhao'er; and withdrew hastily at the conclusion of this remark, out of the apartment, while lady Feng turned towards Baoyu with a smile and said, "Your cousin Lin can now live in our house forever."

"Poor thing!" exclaimed Baoyu. "I presume that during all these days she has wept who knows how much;" and saying this he wrinkled his brow and heaved a deep sigh.

Lady Feng saw Zhao'er on his return, but as she could not very well, in the presence of third persons, make minute inquiries after Jia Lian, she had to continue a prey to inward solicitude till it was time to go home, for, not having got through what she had to do, she was compelled to wait patiently until she went back in the evening, when she again sent word for Zhao'er to come in, and asked him with all minuteness whether the journey had been pleasant throughout, and for full particulars. That very night, she got in readiness the long pelisses, which she herself, with the assistance of Ping'er, packed up in a bundle; and after careful thought as to what things he would require, she put them in the same bundle and committed them to Zhao'er's care. She went on to solicitously impress upon Zhao'er to be careful in his attendance abroad. "Don't provoke your master to wrath," she said, "and from time to time do advise him not to drink too much wine; and don't entice him to make the acquaintance of any low people; for if you do, when you come back I will cut your leg off."

The preparations were hurriedly and confusedly completed; and it was already the fourth watch of the night when she went to sleep. But soon again the day dawned, and after hastily performing her toilette and ablutions, she came over to the Ning Mansion.

As Jia Zhen realized that the day for escorting the body away was drawing nigh, he in person went out in a curricle, along with geomancers, to the Temple of the Iron Fence to inspect a suitable place for depositing the coffin. He also, point by point, enjoined the resident managing-bonze, Sekong, to mind and get ready brand-new articles of decoration and furniture, and to invite a considerable number of bonzes of note to be at hand to lend their services for the reception of the coffin.

Sekong lost no time in getting ready the evening meal, but Jia Zhen had, in fact, no wish for any tea or rice; and, as the day was far advanced and he was not in time to enter the city, he had, after all, to rest during that night as best he could in a "chaste" room in the temple. The next morning, as soon as it was day, he hastened to come into the city and to make every preparation for the funeral. He likewise deputed messengers to proceed ahead to the Temple of the Iron Fence to give, that very night, additional decorative touches to the place where the coffin was to be deposited, and to get ready tea and all the other necessaries, for the use of the persons who would be present at the reception of the coffin.

Lady Feng, seeing that the day was not far distant, also apportioned duties and made provision for everything beforehand with circumspect care; while at the same time she chose in the Rong mansion, such carriages, sedan chairs, and retinue as were to accompany the cortege, in attendance upon Madame Wang, and gave her mind furthermore to finding a place where she herself could put up in at the time of the funeral. About this very time, it happened that the consort of the Duke Shanguo departed this life, and that mesdames Wang and Xing had likewise to go and offer sacrifices, and to follow the burial procession; that the birthday occurred of the consort of Prince Xi'an; that presents had to be forwarded on the occasion of this anniversary; and that the consort of the Duke of Zhenguo gave birth to a first child, a son, and congratulatory gifts had, in like manner, to be provided. Besides, her uterine brother Wang Ren was about to return south, with all his family, and she had too to write her home letters, to send her reverent compliments to her father and mother, as well as to get the things ready that were to be taken along. There was also Yingchun, who had contracted some illness, and the doctor had every day to be sent for, and medicines to be administered, the notes of the doctor to be looked after, consisting of the bulletins of the diagnosis and the prescriptions, with the result that the various things that had to be attended to by lady Feng were so manifold that it would, indeed, be difficult to give an exhaustive idea of them.

In addition to all this, the day for taking the coffin away was close at hand, so that lady Feng was so hard pressed for time that she had even no desire for any tea to drink or anything to eat, and that she could not sit or rest in peace. As soon as she put her foot into the Ning mansion, the inmates of the Rong mansion would follow close upon her heels; and the moment she got back into the Rong mansion, the servants again of the Ning mansion would follow her about. In spite however of this great pressure, lady Feng, whose natural disposition had ever been to try and excel, was urged to strain the least of her energies, as her sole dread was lest she should incur unfavorable criticism from anyone; and so excellent were the plans she devised, that everyone in the clan, whether high or low, readily conceded her unlimited praise.

On the night of this day, the body had to be watched, and in the inner suite of apartments two companies of young players as well as jugglers entertained the relatives, friends, and other visitors during the whole of the night. Mrs. You was still laid up in the inside room, so that the whole task of attending to and entertaining the company devolved upon lady Feng alone, who had to look after everything; for though there were, in the whole clan, many sisters-in-law, some there were too bashful to speak, others too timid to stand on their feet; while there were also those who were not accustomed to meeting company; and those likewise who were afraid of people of high estate and shy of officials. Of every kind there were, but the whole number of them could not come up to lady Feng's standard, whose deportment was correct and whose speech was according to rule. Hence it was that she did not even so much as heed any of that large company, but gave directions and issued orders, adopting any course of action which she fancied, just as if there were no bystander.

The whole night, the lanterns emitted a bright light and the fires brilliant rays; while guests were escorted on their way out and officials greeted on their way in; but of this hundredfold bustle and stir nothing need, of course, be said.

The next morning at the dawn of day, and at a propitious moment, sixty-four persons, dressed all alike in blue, carried the coffin, preceded by a streamer with the record in large characters: "Coffin of lady Qin, a lady of the fifth degree, (by marriage) of the Jia mansion, deceased at middle age, consort of the grandson of the Ning Guo Duke with the first rank title of honor, (whose status is) a guard of the Imperial ante-chamber, charged with the protection of the Inner Palace and Roads in the Red Prohibited City."

The various paraphernalia and ornaments were all brand-new, hurriedly made for the present occasion, and the uniform lustrous brilliancy they shed was sufficient to dazzle the eyes.

Baozhu, of course, observed the rites prescribed for unmarried daughters, and dashed the bowl and walked by the coffin, as she gave way to most bitter lamentations.

At that time, among the officials who escorted the funeral procession, were Niu Jizong, the grandson of the Zhenguo duke, who had now inherited the status of earl of the first degree; Liu Fang, the grandson of Liu Biao, duke of Liguo, who had recently inherited the rank of viscount of the first class; Chen Ruiwen, a grandson of Chen Yi, duke of Liguo, who held the hereditary rank of general of the third degree, with the prefix of majestic authority; Ma Shang, the grandson of Ma Kui, duke of Zhiguo, by inheritance general of the third rank with the prefix of majesty afar; Hou Xiaokang, an hereditary viscount of the first degree, grandson of the duke of Xiuguo, Hou Xiaoming by name; while the death of the consort of the duke of Shanguo had obliged his grandson Shi Guangzhu to go into mourning so that he could not be present. These were the six families which had, along with the two households of Rong and Ning, been, at one time, designated the eight dukes.

Among the rest, there were besides the grandson of the Prince of Nan'an; the grandson of the Prince of Xi'an; Shi Ding, marquis of Zhongjing; Jiang Zining, an hereditary baron of the second grade, grandson of the earl of Pingyuan; Xie Jing, an hereditary baron of the second order and Captain of the Metropolitan camp, grandson of the marquis of Dingchang: Qi Jianhui, an hereditary baron of the second rank, a grandson of the marquis of Xiangyang; Qiu Liang, in command of the Five Cities, grandson of the marquis of Jingtian. The remainder were Wei Chi, the son of the earl of Jinxiang; Feng Ziying, the son of a general, whose prefix was supernatural martial spirit; Chen Yejun, Wei Ruolan, and others, grandsons and sons of princes who could not be enumerated.

In the way of ladies, there were also in all about ten large official sedan chairs full of them, thirty or forty private chairs, and including the official and non-official chairs, and carriages containing inmates of the household, there must have been over a hundred and ten; so that with the various kinds of paraphernalia, articles of decoration, and hundreds of nick-nacks, which preceded, the vast expanse of the cortege covered a continuous line extending over three or four li.

They had not been very long on their way, when they reached variegated sheds soaring high by the roadside, in which banquets were spread, feasts laid out, and music discoursed in unison. These were the viatory sacrificial offerings contributed by the respective families. The first shed contained the sacrificial donations of the mansion of the Prince of Dongping; the second shed those of the Prince of Nan'an; the third those of the Prince of Xining; and the fourth those of the Prince of Beijing.

Indeed of these four Princes, the reputation enjoyed in former days by the Prince of Beijing had been the most exalted, and to this day his sons and grandsons still succeeded to the inheritance of the princely dignity. The present incumbent of the Princedom of Beijing, Shui Rong, had not as yet come of age, but he was gifted with a presence of exceptional beauty, and with a disposition condescending and genial. At the demise, recently, of the consort of the eldest grandson of the mansion of Ning Guo, he, in consideration of the friendship which had formerly existed between the two grandfathers, by virtue of which they had been inseparable, both in adversity as well as in prosperity, treating each other as if they had not been of different surnames, was consequently induced to pay no regard to princely dignity or to his importance, but having like the others paid, on the previous day, his condolences and presented sacrificial offerings, he had further now raised a shed wherein to offer libations. Having directed everyone of his subordinate officers to remain in this spot in attendance, he himself went at the fifth watch to court, and when he acquitted himself of his public duties he forthwith changed his attire for a mourning costume, and came along, in an official sedan chair, preceded by gongs and umbrellas. Upon reaching the front of the shed, the chair was deposited on the ground, and as his subordinate officers pressed on either side and waited upon him, neither the military nor the populace, which composed the mass of people, ventured to make any commotion. In a short while, the long procession of the Ning mansion became visible, spreading far and wide, covering in its course from the north, the whole ground like a silver mountain. At an early hour, the forerunners, messengers, and other attendants on the staff of the Ning mansion apprised Jia Zhen (of the presence of the sheds), and Jia Zhen with all alacrity gave orders that the foremost part of the cortege should halt. Attended by Jia She and Jia Zhen, the three of them came with hurried step to greet (the Prince of Beijing), whom they saluted with due ceremony. Shui Rong, who was seated in his sedan chair, made a bow and returned their salutations with a smile, proceeding to address them and to treat them, as he had done hitherto, as old friends, without any airs of self-importance.

"My daughter's funeral has," observed Jia Zhen, "put your Highness to the trouble of coming, an honor which we, though noble by birth, do not deserve."

Shui Rong smiled. "With the terms of friendship," he added, "which have existed for so many generations (between our families), is there any need for such apologies?"

Turning his head round there and then, he gave directions to the senior officer of his household to preside at the sacrifices and to offer libations in his stead; and Jia She and the others stood together on one side and made obeisance in return, and then came in person again and gave expression to their gratitude for his bounty.

Shui Rong was most affable and complaisant. "Which is the gentleman," he inquired of Jia Zhen, "who was born with a piece of jade in his mouth? I've long had a wish to have the pleasure of seeing him, and as he's sure to be on the spot on an occasion like this, why shouldn't you invite him to come round?"

Jia Zhen speedily drew back, and bidding Baoyu change his mourning clothes, he led him forward and presented him.

Baoyu had all along heard that Shui Rong was a worthy Prince, perfect in ability as well as in appearance, pleasant and courteous, not bound down by any official custom or state rite, so that he had repeatedly felt a keen desire to meet him. With the sharp control, however, which his father exercised over him, he had not been able to gratify his wish. But on this occasion, he saw on the contrary that he came to call him, and it was but natural that he should be delighted. Whilst advancing, he scrutinised Shui Rong with the corner of his eye, who, seated as he was in the sedan chair, presented an imposing sight.

But, reader, what occurred on his approach is not yet known, but listen to the next chapter, which will divulge it.

CHAPTER 15

Lady Feng, nee Wang, exercises her authority in the Iron Fence Temple. Qin Jingqing (Qin Zhong) amuses himself in the Mantou (Bread) nunnery.

But we shall now resume our story. When Baoyu raised his eyes, he noticed that Shui Rong, Prince of Beijing, wore on his head a princely cap with pure white tassels and silvery feathers, that he was appareled in a white ceremonial robe, (with a pattern representing) the tooth-like ripple of a river and the waters of the sea, embroidered with five-clawed dragons; and that he was girded with a red leather belt, inlaid with white jade. That his face was like a beauteous gem; that his eyes were like sparkling stars; and that he was, in very truth, a human being full of graceful charms.

Baoyu hastily pressed forward and made a reverent obeisance, and Shui Rong lost no time in extending his arms from inside the sedan-chair, and embracing him. At a glance, he saw that Baoyu had on his head a silver cap, to which the hair was attached, that he had, round his forehead, a flap on which were embroidered a couple of dragons issuing from the sea, that he wore a white archery-sleeved robe, orna-mented with dragons, and that his waist was encircled by a silver belt, inlaid with pearls; that his face resembled vernal flowers and that his eyes were like drops of lacquer.

Shui Rong smiled. "Your name is," he said, "no trumped-up story; for you, verily, resemble a precious gem; but where's the valuable trin-ket you had in your mouth?" he inquired.

As soon as Baoyu heard this inquiry, he hastened to produce the jade from inside his clothes and to hand it over to Shui Rong. Shui Rong minutely examined it; and having also read the motto on it, he consequently ascertained whether it was really efficacious or not.

It's true that it's said to be," Baoyu promptly explained, "but it hasn't yet been put to the test."

Shui Rong extolled it with unbounded praise, and, as he did so, he set the variegated tassels in proper order, and, with his own hands, attached it on to Baoyu's neck. Taking also his hand in his, he inquired of Baoyu what was his age? and what books he was reading at present, to each of which questions Baoyu gave suitable answer.

Shui Rong perceiving the perspicacity of his speech and the propriety of his utterances, simultaneously turned towards Jia Zhen and observed with a smile on his face: "Your worthy son is, in very truth, like the young of a dragon or like the nestling of a phoenix! and this isn't an idle compliment which I, a despicable prince, utter in your venerable presence! But how much more glorious will be, in the future, the voice of the young phoenix than that of the old phoenix, it isn't easy to ascertain."

Jia Zhen forced a smile: "My cur-like son," he replied, "cannot presume to such bountiful praise and golden commendation; but if, by the virtue of your Highness' excess of happiness, he does indeed realize your words, he will be a source of joy to us all!"

"There's one thing, however," continued Shui Rong; "with the excellent abilities which your worthy scion possesses, he's sure, I presume, to be extremely loved by her dowager ladyship, (his grandmother), and by all classes. But for young men of our age it's a great drawback to be doated upon, for with over-fondness, we cannot help utterly frustrating the benefits of education. When I, a despicable prince, was young, I walked in this very track, and I presume that your honorable son cannot likewise but do the same. By remaining at home, your worthy scion will find it difficult to devote his attention to study; and he will not reap any harm, were he to come, at frequent intervals, to my humble home; for though my deserts be small, I nevertheless enjoy the great honor of the acquaintance of all the scholars of note in the Empire, so that, whenever any of them visit the capital, not one of them is there who does not lower his blue eyes upon me. Hence it is that in my mean abode, eminent worthies rendezvous; and were your esteemed son to come, as often as he can, and converse with them and meet them, his knowledge would, in that case, have every opportunity of making daily strides towards improvement."

Jia Zhen speedily bent his body and expressed his acquiescence, by way of reply; whereupon Shui Rong went further, and taking off from his wrist a chaplet of pearls, he presented it to Baoyu.

"This is the first time we meet," he observed. "Our meeting was so unexpected that I have no suitable congratulatory present to offer you. This was conferred upon me by His Majesty, and is a string of chaplet-pearls, scented with Ling Ling, which will serve as a temporary token of respectful congratulations."

Baoyu hastened to receive it from his hands, and turning round, he reverently presented it to Jia Zhen. Jia Zhen and Baoyu jointly returned thanks; and forthwith Jia She, Jia Zhen, and the rest came forward in a body, and requested the Prince to turn his chair homewards.

"The departed," expostulated Shui Rong, "has already ascended the spiritual regions, and is no more a mortal being in this dusty world exposed to vicissitude like you and I. Although a mean prince like me has been the recipient of the favor of the Emperor, and has undeservedly been called to the princely inheritance, how could I presume to go before the spiritual hearse and return home?"

Jia She and the others, perceiving how persistent he was in his refusal had no course but to take their leave, express their sense of gratitude and to rejoin the cortege. They issued orders to their servants to stop the band, and to hush the music, and making the procession go by, they at length left the way clear for Shui Rong to prosecute his way.

But we will now leave him and resume our account of the funeral of the Ning mansion. All along its course the road was plunged in unusual commotion. As soon as they reached the city gates Jia She, Jia Zheng, Jia Zhen, and the others again received donations from all their fellow officers and subordinates, in sacrificial sheds erected by their respective families, and after they returned thanks to one after another, they eventually issued from the city walls, and proceeded eventually along the highway, in the direction of the Temple of the Iron Fence.

Jia Zhen, at this time, went, together with Jia Rong, up to all their seniors, and pressed them to get into their sedan chairs, and to ride their horses; and Jia She and all of the same age as himself were consequently induced to mount into their respective carriages or chairs. Jia Zhen and those of the same generation were likewise about to ride their horses, when lady Feng, through her solicitude on Baoyu's account, gave way to fears lest now that they had reached the open country, he should do as he pleased, and not listen to the words of any of the household, and lest Jia Zhen should not be able to keep him in check; and, as she dreaded that he might go astray, she felt compelled to bid a youth call him to her; and Baoyu had no help but to appear before her curricle.

"My dear brother," lady Feng remarked smiling, "you are a respectable person, and like a girl in your ways, and shouldn't imitate those monkeys on horseback! do get down and let both you and I sit together in this carriage; and won't that be nice?"

At these words, Baoyu readily dismounted and climbed up into the carriage occupied by lady Feng; and they both talked and laughed, as they continued their way.

But not a long time elapsed before two men, on horseback, were seen approaching from the opposite direction. Coming straight up to lady Feng's vehicle they dismounted, and said, as they leaned on the sides of her carriage, "There's a halting place here, and will it not please your ladyship to have a rest and change?"

Lady Feng directed them to ask the two ladies Xing and Wang what they would like to do, and the two men explained: "These ladies have signified that they had no desire to rest, and they wish your ladyship to suit your convenience."

Lady Feng speedily issued orders that they should have a rest, before they prosecuted their way, and the servant youth led the harnessed horses through the crowd of people and came towards the north, while Baoyu, from inside the carriage, urgently asked that Mr. Qin should be requested to come.

Qin Zhong was at this moment on horseback following in the track of his father's carriage, when unexpectedly he caught sight of Baoyu's page, come at a running pace and invite him to have some refreshment. Qin Zhong perceived from a distance that the horse, which Baoyu had been riding, walked behind lady Feng's vehicle, as it went towards the north, with its saddle and bridles all piled up, and readily concluding that Baoyu must be in the same carriage with that lady, he too turned his horse and came over in haste and entered, in their company, the door of a farm-house.

This dwelling of the farmer's did not contain many rooms so that the women and girls had nowhere to get out of the way; and when the village lasses and country women perceived the bearing and costumes of lady Feng, Baoyu, and Qin Zhong, they were inclined to suspect that celestial beings had descended into the world.

Lady Feng entered a thatched house, and, in the first place, asked Baoyu and the rest to go out and play. Baoyu took the hint, and, along with Qin Zhong, he led off the servant boys and went to romp all over the place.

The various articles in use among the farmers they had not seen before, with the result that after Baoyu had inspected them, he thought them all very strange; but he could neither make out their names nor their uses. But among the servant boys, there were those who knew, and they explained to them, one after another, what they were called, as well as what they were for. As Baoyu, after this explanation, nodded his head; "It isn't strange," he said, "that an old writer has this line in his poetical works, 'Who can realise that the food in a bowl is, grain by grain, all the fruit of labor.' This is indeed so!" As he spoke, they had come into another house; and at the sight of a spinning wheel on a stove-bed, they thought it still more strange and wonderful, but the servant boys again told them that it was used for spinning the yarn to weave cloth with, and Baoyu speedily jumping on to the stove-bed, set to work turning the wheel for the sake of fun, when a village lass of about seventeen or eighteen years of age came forward, and asked them not to meddle with it and spoil it.

The servant boys promptly stopped her interference; but Baoyu himself desisted, as he added: "It's because I hadn't seen one before that I came to try it for fun."

"You people can't do it," rejoined the lass, "let me turn it for you to see."

Qin Zhong secretly pulled Baoyu and remarked, "It's great fun in this village!" but Baoyu gave him a nudge and observed, "If you talk nonsense again, I'll beat you." Watching intently, as he uttered these words, the village girl who started reeling the thread, and presented, in very truth, a pretty sight. But suddenly an old woman from the other side gave a shout. "My girl Secunda, come over at once;" and the lass discarded the spinning-wheel and hastily went on her way.

Baoyu was the while feeling disappointed and unhappy, when he espied a servant, whom lady Feng had sent, come and call them both in. Lady Feng had washed her hands and changed her costume; and asked him whether he would change or not, and Baoyu, having replied "No! it doesn't matter after all if I don't change," the female attendants served tea, cakes, and fruits and also poured the scented tea. Lady Feng and the others drank their tea, and waiting until they had put the various articles by, and made all the preparations, they promptly started to get into their carriages. Outside, Wang'er had got ready tips and gave them to the people of the farm, and the farm women and all the inmates went up to them to express their gratitude; but when Baoyu came to look carefully, he failed to see anything of the lass who had reeled the thread. But they had not gone far before they caught sight of this girl Secunda coming along with a small child in her arms, who, they concluded, was her young brother, laughing and chatting, in company with a few young girls.

Baoyu could not suppress the voice of love, but being seated in the carriage, he was compelled to satisfy himself by following her with his eyes. Soon however the vehicle sped on as rapidly as a cloud impelled by the wind, so that when he turned his head round, there was already no vestige to be seen of her; but, while they were bandying words, they had unexpectedly overtaken the great concourse of the cortege.

Likewise, at an early stage men were stationed ahead, with Buddhist drums and gold cymbals, with streamers, and jeweled coverings; and the whole company of bonzes, belonging to the Iron Fence Temple, had already been drawn out in a line by the sides of the road. In a short while, they reached the interior of the temple, where additional sacrifices were offered and Buddhistic services performed; and where altars had again been erected to burn incense on. The coffin was deposited in a side room of the inner court; and Baozhu got ready a bedroom in which she could keep her watch.

In the outer apartments, Jia Zhen did the honors among the whole party of relatives and friends, some of whom asked to be allowed to stay for their meals, while others at this stage took their leave. And after they had one by one returned thanks, the dukes, marquises, earls, viscounts, and barons, each in respective batches, (got up to go,) and they kept on leaving from between 1 and 3 P.M. before they had finally all dispersed.

In the inner chambers, the ladies were solely entertained and attended to by lady Feng. First to make a move were the consorts of officials; and noon had also come, by the time the whole party of them had taken their departure. Those that remained were simply a few relatives of the same clan and others like them, who eventually left after the completion of the three days' rationalistic liturgies.

The two ladies Xing and Wang, well aware at this time that lady Feng could on no account return home, desired to enter the city at once; and Madame Wang wanted to take Baoyu home; but Baoyu, who had, on an unexpected occasion, come out into the country, entertained, of course, no wish to go back; and he would agree to nothing else than to stay behind with lady Feng, so that Madame Wang had no alternative but to hand him over to her charge and to start.

This Temple of the Iron Fence had, in fact, been erected in days gone by, at the expense of the two dukes Ning and Rong; and there still remained up to these days, acres of land, from which were derived the funds for incense and lights for such occasions, on which the coffins of any members, old or young, (who died) in the capital, had to be deposited in this temple; and the inner and outer houses, in this compound were all kept in readiness and good order, for the accommodation of those who formed part of the cortège.

At this time, as it happened, the descendants mustered an immense crowd, and among them were poor and rich of various degrees, or with likes and dislikes diametrically opposed. There were those, who, being in straitened circumstances at home, and easily contented, readily took up their quarters in the temple. And there were those with money and position, and with extravagant ideas, who maintained that the accommodation in the temple was not suitable, and, of course, went in search of additional quarters, either in country houses, or in convents, where they could have their meals and retire, after the ceremonies were over.

On the occasion of Mrs. Qin's funeral, all the members of the clan put up temporarily in the Iron Fence Temple; lady Feng alone looked down upon it as inconvenient, and consequently despatched a servant to go and tell Jingxu, a nun in the Bread Convent, to empty two rooms for her to go and live in.

This Bread Convent had at one time been styled the Shuiyue nunnery (water moon); but as good bread was made in that temple, it gave rise to this nickname.

This convent was not very distant from the Temple of the Iron Fence, so that as soon as the bonzes brought their functions to a close, and the sacrifice of evening was offered, Jia Zhen asked Jia Rong to request lady Feng to retire to rest; and as lady Feng perceived that there still remained several sisters-in-law to keep company to the female relatives, she readily, of her own accord, took leave of the whole party, and, along with Baoyu and Qin Zhong, came to the Water Moon Convent.

Qin Ye, it must be noticed, was advanced in years and a victim to many ailments, so that he was unable to remain in the temple long, and he bade Qin Zhong tarry until the coffin had been set in its resting place, with the result that Qin Zhong came along, at the same time as lady Feng and Baoyu, to the Water Moon Convent, where Jingxu appeared, together with two neophytes, Zhishan and Zhineng, to receive them. After they had exchanged greetings, lady Feng and the others entered the "chaste" apartments to change their clothes and wash their hands; and when they had done, as she perceived how much taller in stature Zhineng had grown and how much handsomer were her features, she felt prompted to inquire, "How is it that your prioress and yourselves haven't been all these days as far as our place?"

"It's because during these days we haven't had any time which we could call our own," explained Jingxu. "Owing to the birth of a son in Mr. Hu's mansion, dame Hu sent over about ten taels and asked that we should invite several head-nuns to read during three days the service for the churching of women, with the result that we've been so very busy and had so little leisure, that we couldn't come over to pay our respects to your ladyship."

But leaving aside the old nun, who kept lady Feng company, we will now return to the two lads Baoyu and Qin Zhong. They were up to their pranks in the main building of the convent, when seeing Zhineng come over: "Here's Neng'er," Baoyu exclaimed with a smile.

"Why notice a creature like her?" remarked Qin Zhong; to which Baoyu rejoined laughingly: "Don't be sly! why then did you the other day, when you were in the old lady's rooms, and there was not a soul present, hold her in your arms? and do you want to fool me now?"

"There was nothing of the kind," observed Qin Zhong smiling.

"Whether there was or not," replied Baoyu, "doesn't concern me; but if you will stop her and tell her to pour a cup of tea and bring it to me to drink, I'll then keep hands off."

"This is indeed very strange!" Qin Zhong answered laughing; "do you fear that if you told her to pour you one, that she wouldn't; and what need is there that I should tell her?"

"If I ask her," Baoyu observed, "to pour it, she wouldn't be as ready as she would were you to tell her about it."

Qin Zhong had no help but to speak. "Neng'er!" he said, "bring a cup of tea."

This Neng'er had, since her youth, been in and out of the Rong mansion, so that there was no one that she did not know; and she had also, time after time, romped and laughed with Baoyu and Qin Zhong. Being now grown up she gradually came to know the import of love, and she readily took a fancy to Qin Zhong, who was an amorous being. Qin Zhong too returned her affection, on account of her good looks; and, although he and she had not had any very affectionate tête-à-têtes, they had, however, long ago come to understand each other's feelings and wishes.

Zhineng walked away and returned after having poured the tea.

"Give it to me," Qin Zhong cried out smirkingly; while Baoyu likewise shouted: "Give it to me."

Zhineng compressed her lips and sneeringly rejoined, "Are you going to have a fight even over a cup of tea? Is it forsooth likely that there's honey in my hand?"

Baoyu was the first to grasp and take over the cup, but while drinking it, he was about to make some inquiry, when he caught sight of Zhishan, who came and called Zhineng away to go and lay the plates with fruit on the table. Not much time elapsed before she came round to request the two lads to go and have tea and refreshments; but would they eat such things as were laid before them? They simply sat for a while and came out again and resumed their play.

Lady Feng too stayed for a few moments, and then returned, with the old nun as her escort, into the "unsullied" rooms to lie down. By this time, all the matrons and married women discovered that there was nothing else to be done, and they dispersed in succession, retiring each to rest. There only remained in attendance several young girls who enjoyed her confidence, and the old nun speedily availed herself of the opportunity to speak. "I've got something," she said, "about which I mean to go to your mansion to beg of Madame Wang; but I'll first request you, my lady, to tell me how to set to work."

"What's it?" ascertained lady Feng.

"Amito Fo!" exclaimed the old nun, "It's this: in days gone by, I first lived in the Chang'an district. When I became a nun and entered the monastery of Excellent Merit, there lived, at that time, a subscriber, Zhang by surname, a very wealthy man. He had a daughter, whose infant name was Jinge; the whole family came in the course of that year to the convent I was in, to offer incense, and as luck would have it they met Li Yanei, a brother of a secondary wife of the Prefect of the Chang'an Prefecture. This Li Yanei fell in love at first sight with her, and would wed Jinge as his wife. He sent go-betweens to ask her in marriage, but, contrary to his expectations, Jinge had already received the engagement presents of the son of the ex-Major of the Chang'an Prefecture. The Zhang family, on the other hand, were afraid that if they withdrew from the match, the Major would not give up his claim, and they therefore replied that she was already promised to another. But, who would have thought it, this Mr. Li was seriously bent upon marrying the young lady. But while the Zhang family were at a loss what plan to devise, and both parties were in a dilemma, the family of the Major came unexpectedly to hear of the news; and without even looking thoroughly into the matter, they there and then had recourse to insult and abuse. 'Is a girl,' they insinuated, 'to be promised to the sons of several families!' And obstinately refusing to allow the restitution of the betrothal presents, they at once had recourse to litigation and brought an action (against the girl's people). That family was at their wits' end, and had no alternative but to find someone to go to the capital to obtain means of assistance; and, losing all patience, they insisted upon the return of the presents. I believe that the present commander of the troops at Chang'an, Mr. Yun, is on friendly terms with your honorable family, and could one solicit Madame Wang to put in a word with Mr. Jia Zheng to send a letter and ask Mr. Yun to speak to that Major, I have no fear that he will not agree. Should (your ladyship) be willing to take action, the Zhang family are even ready to present all they have, though it may entail the ruin of their estate."

"This affair is, it's true, of no great moment," lady Feng replied smiling, after hearing this appeal; "but the only thing is that Madame Wang does no longer attend to matters of this nature."

"If madame doesn't heed them," suggested the old nun, "you, my lady, can safely assume the direction."

"I'm neither in need of any money to spend," added lady Feng with a smirk, "nor do I undertake such matters!"

These words did not escape Jingxu's ear; they scattered to the winds her vain hopes. After a minute or so she heaved a sigh.

"What you say may be true enough," she remarked; "but the Zhang family are also aware that I mean to come and make my appeal to your mansion; and were you now not to manage this affair, the Zhang family having no idea that the lack of time prevents any steps being taken and that no importance is attached to their presents, it will appear, on the contrary, as if there were not even this little particle of skill in your household."

At these words lady Feng felt at once inspirited. "You've known of old," she added, "that I've never had any faith in anything concerning retribution in the Court of Judgment in the unseen or in hell; and that whatever I say that I shall do, that I do; tell them therefore to bring three thousand taels; and I shall then remedy this grievance of theirs."

The old nun upon hearing this remark was so exceedingly delighted, that she precipitately exclaimed, "They've got it, they've got it! there will be no difficulty about it."

"I'm not," lady Feng went on to add, "like those people, who afford help and render assistance with an eye to money; these three thousand taels will be exclusively devoted for the traveling expenses of those youths, who will be sent to deliver messages and for them to make a few cash for their trouble; but as for me I don't want even so much as a cash. In fact I'm able at this very moment to produce as much as thirty thousand taels."

The old nun assented with alacrity, and said by way of reply, "If that be so, my lady, do display your charitable bounty at once tomorrow and bring things to an end."

"Just see," remarked lady Feng, "how hard pressed I am; which place can do without me? but since I've given you my word, I shall, needless to say, speedily bring the matter to a close."

"A small trifle like this," hinted the old nun, "would, if placed in the hands of anyone else, flurry her to such an extent that she would be quite at a loss what to do; but in your hands, my lady, even if much more were superadded, it wouldn't require as much exertion as a wave of your hand. But the proverb well says: 'that those who are able have much to do;' for Madame Wang, seeing that your ladyship manages all concerns, whether large or small, properly, has still more shoved the burden of everything on your shoulders, my lady; but you should, it's but right, also take good care of your precious health."

This string of flattery pleased lady Feng more and more, so that heedless of fatigue she went on to chat with still greater zest.

But, thing unthought of, Qin Zhong availed himself of the darkness, as well as of the absence of anyone about, to come in quest of Zhineng. As soon as he reached the room at the back, he espied Zhineng all alone inside washing the tea cups; and Qin Zhong forthwith seized her in his arms and implanted kisses on her cheek. Zhineng got in a dreadful state, and stamping her feet, cried, "What are you up to?" and she was just on the point of shouting out, when Qin Zhong rejoined: "My dear girl! I'm nearly dead from impatience, and if you don't again today accept my advances, I shall this very moment die on this spot."

"What you're bent upon," added Zhineng, "can't be effected; not unless you wait until I've left this den and parted company from these people, when it will be safe enough."

"This is of course easy enough!" remonstrated Qin Zhong; "but the distant water cannot extinguish the close fire!"

As he spoke, with one puff, he put out the light, plunging the whole room in pitch darkness; and seizing Zhineng, he pushed her on to the stove-couch and started a violent love affair. Zhineng could not, though she strained every nerve, escape his importunities; nor could she very well shout, so that she felt compelled to humor him; but while he was in the midst of his ecstatic joy, they perceived a person walk in, who pressed both of them down, without uttering even so much as a sound, and plunged them both in such a fright that their very souls flew away and their spirits wandered from their bodies; and it was after the third party had burst out laughing with a spurting sound that they eventually became aware that it was Baoyu; when, springing to his feet impetuously, Qin Zhong exclaimed full of resentment, "What's this that you're up to!"

"If you get your monkey up," retorted Baoyu, "why, then let you and I start bawling out;" which so abashed Zhineng that she availed herself of the gloomy light to make her escape; while Baoyu had dragged Qin Zhong out of the room and asked, "Now then, do you still want to play the bully!"

"My dear fellow," pleaded Qin Zhong smilingly, "whatever you do don't shout out and let everyone know; and all you want, I'll agree to."

"We needn't argue just now," Baoyu observed with a grin; "wait a while, and when all have gone to sleep, we can minutely settle accounts together."

Soon it was time to ease their clothes, and go to bed; and lady Feng occupied the inner room; Qin Zhong and Baoyu the outer; while the whole ground was covered with matrons of the household, who had spread their bedding, and sat watching. As lady Feng entertained fears that the jade of Spiritual Perception might be lost, she waited until Baoyu fell asleep, when having directed a servant to bring it to her, she placed it under the side of her own pillow.

What accounts Baoyu settled with Qin Zhong cannot be ascertained; and as in the absence of any positive proof what is known is based upon surmises, we shall not venture to place it on record.

Nothing worth noticing occurred the whole night; but the next day, as soon as the morning dawned, dowager lady Jia and Madame Wang promptly despatched servants to come and see how Baoyu was getting on; and to tell him likewise to put on two pieces of extra clothing, and that if there was nothing to be done it would be better for him to go back.

But was it likely that Baoyu would be willing to go back? Besides Qin Zhong, in his inordinate passion for Zhineng, instigated Baoyu to entreat lady Feng to remain another day. Lady Feng pondered in her own mind that, although the most important matters connected with the funeral ceremonies had been settled satisfactorily, there were still a few minor details, for which no provision had been made, so that could she avail herself of this excuse to remain another day would she not win from Jia Zhen a greater degree of approbation, in the second place, would she not be able further to bring Jingxu's business to an issue, and, in the third place, to humor Baoyu's wish? In view of these three advantages, which would accrue, "All that I had to do, I have done," she readily signified to Baoyu, "and if you be bent upon running about in here, you'll unavoidably place me in still greater trouble; so that we must for certain start homewards tomorrow."

"My dear cousin, my own dear cousin," urgently entreated Baoyu, when he heard these words, "let's stay only this one day, and tomorrow we can go back without fail."

They actually spent another night there, and lady Feng availed herself of their stay to give directions that the case which had been entrusted to her the previous day by the old nun should be secretly communicated to Lai Wang'er. Lai Wang's mind grasped the import of all that was said to him, and, having entered the city with all despatch, he went in search of the gentleman, who acted as secretary (in Mr. Yun's office,) pretending that he had been directed by Mr. Jia Lian to come and ask him to write a letter and to send it that very night to the Chang'an magistrate. The distance amounted to no more than one hundred li, so that in the space of two days everything was brought to a satisfactory settlement. The general, whose name was Yun Guang, had been for a long time under obligations to the Jia family, so that he naturally could not refuse his co-operation in such small trifles.

When he had handed his reply, Wang'er started on his way back; where we shall leave him and return to lady Feng.

Having spent another day, she on the morrow took leave of the old nun, whom she advised to come to the mansion after the expiry of three days to fetch a reply.

Qin Zhong and Zhineng could not, by any means, brook the separation, and they secretly agreed to a clandestine assignation; but to these details we need not allude with any minuteness; sufficient to say that they had no alternative but to bear the anguish and to part.

Lady Feng crossed over again to the temple of the Iron Fence and ascertained how things were progressing. But as Baozhu was obstinate in her refusal to return home, Jia Zhen found himself under the necessity of selecting a few servants to act as her companions. But the reader must listen to what is said in the next chapter by way of explanation.

CHAPTER 16

Jia Yuanchun is, on account of her talents, selected to enter the Feng Zao Palace. Qin Jingqing departs, in the prime of life, by the yellow spring road.

But we must now return to the two lads, Qin Zhong and Baoyu. After they had passed, along with lady Feng from the Temple of the Iron Fence, whither she had gone to see how things were getting on, they entered the city in their carriages. On their arrival at home, they paid their obeisance to dowager lady Jia, Madame Wang, and the other members of the family, whence they returned to their own quarters, where nothing worth mentioning transpired during the night.

On the next day, Baoyu perceiving that the repairs to the outer school-room had been completed, settled with Qin Zhong that they should have evening classes. But as it happened that Qin Zhong, who was naturally of an extremely delicate physique, caught somewhat of a chill in the country and clandestinely indulged, besides, in an intimacy with Zhineng, which unavoidably made him fail to take good care of himself, he was, shortly after his return, troubled with a cough and a feverish cold, with nausea for drink and food, and fell into such an extremely poor state of health that he simply kept indoors and nursed himself, and was not in a fit condition to go to school. Baoyu's spirits were readily damped, but as there was likewise no remedy he had no other course than to wait until his complete recovery, before he could make any arrangements.

Lady Feng had meanwhile received a reply from Yun Guang, in which he informed her that everything had been satisfactorily settled, and the old nun apprised the Zhang family that the major had actually suppressed his indignation, hushed his complaints, and taken back the presents of the previous engagement. But who would have ever anticipated that a father and mother, whose hearts were set upon position and their ambition upon wealth, could have brought up a daughter so conscious of propriety and so full of feeling as to seize the first opportunity, after she had heard that she had been withdrawn from her former intended, and been promised to the Li family, to stealthily devise a way to commit suicide, by means of a handkerchief. The son of the Major, upon learning that Jinge had strangled herself, there and then jumped into the river and drowned himself, as he too was a being full of love. The Zhang and Li families were, sad to relate, very much cut up, and, in very truth, two lives and money had been sacrificed all to no use.

Lady Feng, however, during this while, quietly enjoyed the three thousand taels, and Madame Wang did not have even so much as the faintest idea of the whole matter. But ever since this occasion, lady Feng's audacity acquired more and more strength; and the actions of this kind, which she, in after days, performed, defy enumeration.

One day, the very day on which Jia Zheng's birthday fell, while the members of the two households of Ning and Rong were assembled together offering their congratulations, and unusual bustle and stir prevailed, a gatekeeper came in, at quite an unexpected moment, to announce that Mr. Xia, Metropolitan Head Eunuch of the six palaces, had come with the special purpose of presenting an edict from his Majesty; a bit of news which plunged Jia She, Jia Zheng, and the whole company into great consternation, as they could not make out what was up. Speedily interrupting the theatrical performance, they had the banquet cleared, and the altar laid out with incense, and opening the center gate they fell on their knees to receive the edict.

Soon they caught sight of the head eunuch, Xia Shouzhong, advancing on horseback, and besides himself, a considerable retinue of eunuchs. The eunuch Xia did not, in fact, carry any mandate or present any decree; but straightway advancing as far as the main hall, he dismounted, and, with a face beaming with smiles, he walked into the Hall and took his stand on the southern side.

"I have had the honor," he said, "of receiving a special order to at once summon Jia Zheng to present himself at Court and be admitted in His Majesty's presence in the Lin Jing Hall."

When he had delivered this message, he did not so much as take any tea, but forthwith mounted his horse and took his leave.

Jia Zheng and the others could not even conceive what omen this summons implied, but he had no alternative but to change his clothes with all haste and to present himself at Court, while dowager lady Jia and the inmates of the whole household were, in their hearts, a prey to such perplexity and uncertainty that they incessantly despatched messengers on flying steeds to go and bring the news.

After the expiry of four hours, they suddenly perceived Lai Da and three or four other butlers run in, quite out of breath, through the ceremonial gate and report the glad tidings. "We have received," they added, "our master's commands, to hurriedly request her venerable ladyship to take Madame Wang and the other ladies into the Palace, to return thanks for His Majesty's bounty;" and other words to the same purport.

Dowager lady Jia was, at this time, standing, with agitated heart, under the verandah of the Large Hall waiting for tidings, whilst the two ladies, mesdames Xing and Wang, Mrs. You, Li Wan, lady Feng, Yingchun and her sisters, even up to Mrs. Xue and the rest, were congregated in one place ascertaining what was the news. Old lady Jia likewise called Lai Da in and minutely questioned him as to what had happened. "Your servants," replied Lai Da, "simply stood waiting outside the Lin Jing gate, so that we were in total ignorance of what was going on inside, when presently the Eunuch Xia came out and imparted to us the glad tidings; telling us that the eldest of the young ladies in our household had been raised, by His Majesty, to be an overseer in the Feng Zao Palace, and that he had, in addition, conferred upon her the rank of worthy and virtuous secondary consort. By and by, Mr. Jia Zheng came out and also told us the same thing. Master is now gone back again to the Eastern Palace, whither he requests your venerable ladyship to go at once and offer thanks for the Imperial favor."

When old lady Jia and the other members of the family heard these tidings they were at length reassured in their minds, and so elated were they all in one moment that joy was visible in their very faces. Without loss of time, they commenced to don the gala dresses suitable to their rank; which done, old lady Jia led the way for the two ladies, mesdames Xing and Wang, as well as for Mrs. You; and their official chairs, four of them in all, entered the palace like a trail of fish; while Jia She and Jia Zhen, who had likewise changed their clothes for their court dress, took Jia Se and Jia Rong along and proceeded in attendance upon dowager lady Jia.

Indeed, of the two households of Ning and Rong, there was not one, whether high or low, woman or man, who was not in a high state of exultation, with the exception of Baoyu, who behaved just as if the news had not reached his ears; and can you, reader, guess why? The fact is that Zhineng, of the Water Moon Convent, had recently entered the city in a surreptitious manner in search of Qin Zhong; but, contrary to expectation, her visit came to be known by Qin Ye, who drove Zhineng away and laid hold of Qin Zhong and gave him a flogging. But this outburst of temper of his brought about a relapse of his old complaint, with the result that in three or five days, he, sad to say, succumbed. Qin Zhong had himself ever been in a delicate state of health and had besides received a caning before he had got over his sickness, so that when he now saw his aged father pass away from the consequences of a fit of anger, he felt, at this stage, so full of penitence and distress that the symptoms of his illness were again considerably aggravated. Hence it was that Baoyu was downcast and unhappy at heart, and that nothing could, in spite of the promotion of Yuanchun by Imperial favor, dispel the depression of his spirits.

Dowager lady Jia and the rest in due course offered thanks and returned home, the relatives and friends came to present their congratulations, great stir and excitement prevailed during these few days in the two mansions of Ning and Rong, and everyone was in high glee; but he alone looked upon everything as if it were nothing; taking not the least interest in anything; and as this reason led the whole family to sneer at him, the result was that he got more and more doltish.

Luckily, however, Jia Lian and Daiyu were on their way back, and had despatched messengers, in advance, to announce the news that they would be able to reach home the following day, so that when Baoyu heard the tidings, he was at length somewhat cheered. And when he came to institute minute inquiries, he eventually found out "that Jia Yucun was also coming to the capital to have an audience with His Majesty, that it was entirely because Wang Ziteng had repeatedly laid before the Throne memorials recommending him that he was coming on this occasion to wait in the metropolis for a vacancy which he could fill up; that as he was a kinsman of Jia Lian's, acknowledging the same ancestors as he did, and he stood, on the other hand, with Daiyu, in the relationship of tutor and pupil, he was in consequence following the same road and coming as their companion; that Lin Ruhai had already been buried in the ancestral vault, and that every requirement had been attended to with propriety; that Jia Lian, on this voyage to the capital, would, had he progressed by the ordinary stages, have been over a month before he could reach home, but that when he came to hear the good news about Yuanchun, he pressed on day and night to enter the capital; and that the whole journey had been throughout, in every respect, both pleasant and propitious."

But Baoyu merely ascertained whether Daiyu was all right, and did not even so much as trouble his mind with the rest of what he heard; and he remained on the tiptoe of expectation, till noon of the morrow; when, in point of fact, it was announced that Mr. Lian, together with Miss Lin, had made their entrance into the mansion. When they came face to face, grief and joy vied with each other; and they could not help having a good cry for a while; after which followed again expressions of sympathy and congratulations; while Baoyu pondered within himself that Daiyu had become still more surpassingly handsome.

Daiyu had also brought along with her a good number of books, and she promptly gave orders that the sleeping rooms should be swept, and that the various nicknacks should be put in their proper places. She further produced a certain quantity of paper, brushes, and other such things, and distributed them among Baochai, Yingchun, Baoyu, and the rest; and Baoyu also brought out, with extreme care, the string of Lingling scented beads, which had been given to him by the Prince of Beijing, and handed them, in his turn, to Daiyu as a present.

"What foul man has taken hold of them?" exclaimed Daiyu. "I don't want any such things;" and as she forthwith dashed them down, and would not accept them, Baoyu was under the necessity of taking them back. But for the time being we will not allude to them, but devote our attention to Jia Lian.

Having, after his arrival home, paid his salutations to all the inmates, he retired to his own quarters at the very moment that lady Feng had multifarious duties to attend to, and had not even a minute to spare; but, considering that Jia Lian had returned from a distant journey, she could not do otherwise than put by what she had to do, and to greet him and wait on him.

"Imperial uncle," she said, in a jocose manner, when she realized that there was no outsider present in the room, "I congratulate you! What fatigue and hardship you, Imperial uncle, have had to bear throughout the whole journey, your humble servant heard yesterday, when the courier sent ahead came and announced that Your Highness would this day reach this mansion. I have merely got ready a glass of mean wine for you to wipe down the dust with, but I wonder, whether Your Highness will deign to bestow upon it the luster of your countenance, and accept it."

Jia Lian smiled. "How dare I presume to such an honor," he added by way of rejoinder; "I'm unworthy of such attention! Many thanks, many thanks."

Ping'er and the whole company of waiting-maids simultaneously paid their obeisance to him, and this ceremony concluded, they presented tea. Jia Lian thereupon made inquiries about the various matters, which had transpired in their home after his departure, and went on to thank lady Feng for all the trouble she had taken in the management of them.

"How could I control all these manifold matters," remarked lady Feng; "my experience is so shallow, my speech so dull and my mind so simple, that if anyone showed me a club, I would mistake it for a pin. Besides, I'm so tender-hearted that were anyone to utter a couple of glib remarks, I couldn't help feeling my heart give way to compassion and sympathy. I've had, in addition, no experience in any weighty questions; my pluck is likewise so very small that when Madame Wang has felt in the least displeased, I have not been able to close my eyes and sleep. Urgently did I more than once resign the charge, but her ladyship wouldn't again agree to it; maintaining, on the contrary, that my object was to be at ease, and that I was not willing to reap experience. Leaving aside that she doesn't know that I take things so much to heart, that I can scoop the perspiration in handfuls, that I daren't utter one word more than is proper, nor venture to recklessly take one step more than I ought to, you know very well which of the women servants, in charge of the menage in our household, is easy to manage! If ever I make the slightest mistake, they laugh at me and poke fun at me; and if I incline a little one way, they show their displeasure by innuendoes; they sit by and look on, they use every means to do harm, they stir up trouble, they stand by on safe ground and look on and don't give a helping hand to lift anyone they have thrown over, and they are, one and all of them, old hands in such tricks. I'm moreover young in years and not able to keep people in check, so that they naturally don't show any regard for me! What is still more ridiculous is that after the death of Rong'er's wife in that mansion, brother Zhen, time and again, begged Madame Wang, on his very knees, to do him the favor to ask me to lend him a hand for several days. I repeatedly signified my refusal, but her ladyship gave her consent in order to oblige him, so that I had no help but to carry out her wish; putting, as is my wont, everything topsy-turvey, and making matters worse than they were; with the result that brother Zhen up to this day bears me a grudge and regrets having asked for my assistance. When you see him tomorrow, do what you can to excuse me by him. 'Young as she is,' tell him, 'and without experience of the world, who ever could have instigated Mr. Jia Zheng to make such a mistake as to choose her.'"

While they were still chatting, they heard people talking in the outer apartments, and lady Feng speedily inquired who it was. Ping'er entered the room to reply. "Lady Xue," she said, "has sent sister Xiangling over to ask me something; but I've already given her my answer and sent her back."

"Quite so," interposed Jia Lian with a smile. "A short while ago I went to look up Mrs. Xue and came face to face with a young girl, whose features were supremely perfect, and as I suspected that, in our household, there was no such person, I asked in the course of conversation, Mrs. Xue about her, and found out eventually that this was the young waiting-maid they had purchased on their way to the capital, Xiangling by name, and that she had after all become an inmate of the household of that big fool Xue. Since she's had her hair dressed as a married woman she does look so much more pre-eminently beautiful! But that big fool Xue has really brought contamination upon her."

"Ai!" exclaimed lady Feng, "here you are back from a trip to Suzhou and Hangzhou, where you should have seen something of the world! and have you still an eye as envious and a heart so covetous? Well, if you wish to bestow your love on her, there's no difficulty worth speaking of. I'll take Ping'er over and exchange her for her; what do you say to that? that old brother Xue is also one of those men, who, while eating what there is in the bowl, keeps an eye on what there is in the pan! For the last year or so, as he couldn't get Xiangling to be his, he made ever so many distressing appeals to Mrs. Xue; and Mrs. Xue while esteeming Xiangling's looks, though fine, as after all a small matter, (thought) her deportment and conduct so far unlike those of other girls, so gentle and so demure that almost the very daughters of masters and mistresses couldn't attain her standard, that she therefore went to the trouble of spreading a banquet, and of inviting guests, and in open court, and in the legitimate course, she gave her to him for a secondary wife. But half a month had scarcely elapsed before he looked upon her also as a good-for-nothing person as he did upon a large number of them! I can't however help feeling pity for her in my heart."

Scarcely had she time to conclude what she had to say when a youth, on duty at the second gate, transmitted the announcement that Mr. Jia Zheng was in the Library waiting for Mr. Secundus. At these words, Jia Lian speedily adjusted his clothes, and left the apartment; and during his absence, lady Feng inquired of Ping'er what Mrs. Xue wanted a few minutes back, that she sent Xiangling round in such a hurry.

"What Xiangling ever came?" replied Ping'er. "I simply made use of her name to tell a lie for the occasion. Tell me, my lady, (what's come to) Wang'er's wife? why she's got so bad that there's even no common sense left in her!" Saying this she again drew near lady Feng's side, and in a soft tone of voice, she continued: "That interest of yours, my lady, she doesn't send later, nor does she send it sooner; but she must send it round the very moment when master Secundus is at home! But as luck would have it, I was in the hall, so that I came across her; otherwise, she would have walked in and told your ladyship, and Mr. Secundus would naturally have come to know about it! And our master would, with that frame of mind of his, have fished it out and spent it, had the money even been at the bottom of a pan full of oil! and were he to have heard that my lady had private means, would he not have been still more reckless in spending? Hence it was that, losing no time in taking the money over, I had to tell her a few words which, who would have thought, happened to be overheard by your ladyship; that's why, in the presence of master Secundus, I simply explained that Xiangling had come!"

These words evoked a smile from lady Feng. "Mrs. Xue, I thought to myself," she observed, "knows very well that your Mr. Secundus has come, and yet, regardless of propriety, she, instead (of keeping her at home), sends someone over from her inner rooms! and it was you after all, you vixen, playing these pranks!"

As she uttered this remark, Jia Lian walked in, and lady Feng issued orders to serve the wine and the eatables, and husband and wife took their seats opposite to each other; but notwithstanding that lady Feng was very partial to drink, she nevertheless did not have the courage to indulge her weakness, but merely partook of some to keep him company. Jia Lian's nurse, dame Zhao, entered the room, and Jia Lian and lady Feng promptly pressed her to have a glass of wine, and bade her sit on the stove-couch, but dame Zhao was obstinate in her refusal. Ping'er and the other waiting-maids had at an early hour placed a square stool next to the edge of the couch, where was likewise a small footstool, and on this footstool dame Zhao took a seat, whereupon Jia Lian chose two dishes of delicacies from the table, which he handed her to place on the square stool for her own use.

"Dame Zhao," lady Feng remarked, "couldn't very well bite through that, for mind it might make her teeth drop! This morning," she therefore asked of Ping'er, "I suggested that that shoulder of pork stewed with ham was so tender as to be quite the thing to be given to dame Zhao to eat; and how is it you haven't taken it over to her? But go at once and tell them to warm it and bring it in! Dame Zhao," she went on, "just you taste this Huiquan wine brought by your foster-son."

"I'll drink it," replied dame Zhao, "but you, my lady, must also have a cup: what's there to fear? the one thing to guard against is any excess, that's all! But I've now come over, not for any wine or eatables; on the contrary, there's a serious matter, which I would ask your ladyship to impress on your mind, and to show me some regard, for this master of ours is only good to utter fine words, but when the time (to act) does come, he forgets all about us! As I have had the good fortune to nurse him in his infancy and to bring him up to this age, 'I too have grown old in years,' I said to him, 'and all that belong to me are those two sons, and do look upon them with some particular favor!' With any one else I shouldn't have ventured to open my mouth, but him I anyway entreated time and again on several occasions. His assent was of course well and good, but up to this very moment he still withholds his help. Now besides from the heavens has dropped such a mighty piece of good luck; and in what place will there be no need of servants? that's why I come to tell you, my lady, as is but right, for were I to depend upon our master, I fear I shall even die of starvation."

Lady Feng laughed. "You'd better," she suggested, "put those two elder foster-brothers of his both under my charge! But you've nursed that foster-son from his babyhood, and don't you yet know that disposition of his, how that he takes his skin and flesh and sticks it, (not on the body of a relative), but, on the contrary, on that of an outsider and stranger? (to Jia Lian.) Which of those foster-brothers whom you have now discarded, isn't clearly better than others? and were you to have shown them some favor and consideration, who would have ventured to have said 'don't?' Instead of that, you confer benefits upon thorough strangers, and all to no purpose whatever! But these words of mine are also incorrect, eh? for those whom we regard as strangers you, contrariwise, will treat just as if they were relatives!"

At these words everyone present in the room burst out laughing; even nurse Zhao could not repress herself; and as she invoked Buddha, "In very truth," she exclaimed, "in this room has sprung up a kind-hearted person! as regards relatives and strangers, such foolish distinctions aren't drawn by our master; and it's simply because he's full of pity and is tenderhearted that he can't put off anyone who gives vent to a few words of entreaty, and nothing else!"

"That's quite it!" rejoined lady Feng smiling sarcastically, "to those whom he looks upon as relatives, he's kindhearted, but with me and his mother he's as hard as steel."

"What you say, my lady, is very considerate," remarked nurse Zhao, "and I'm really so full of delight that I'll have another glass of good wine! and, if from this time forward, your ladyship will act as you think best, I'll have then nothing to be sorry for!"

Jia Lian did not at this juncture feel quite at his ease, but he could do no more than feign a smile. "You people," he said, "should leave off talking nonsense, and bring the eatables at once and let us have our meal, as I have still to go on the other side and see Mr. Jia Zhen, to consult with him about business."

"To be sure you have," ventured lady Feng, "and you shouldn't neglect your legitimate affairs; but what did Mr. Jia Zhen tell you when he sent for you just a while back?"

"It was about the visit (of Yuanchun) to her parents," Jia Lian explained.

"Has after all permission for the visit been granted?" lady Feng inquired with alacrity.

"Though not quite granted," Jia Lian replied joyously, "it's nevertheless more or less an accomplished fact."

"This is indeed evidence of the great bounty of the present Emperor!" lady Feng observed smirkingly; "one doesn't hear in books, or see in plays, written from time to time, any mention of such an instance, even so far back as the days of old!"

Dame Zhao took up again the thread of the conversation. "Indeed it's so!" she interposed; "But I'm in very truth quite stupid from old age, for I've heard everyone, high and low, clamoring during these few days, something or other about 'Xingqin' or no 'Xingqin,' but I didn't really pay any heed to it; and now again, here's something more about this 'Xingqin,' but what's it all about, I wonder?"

"The Emperor at present on the Throne," explained Jia Lian, "takes into consideration the feelings of his people. In the whole world, there is (in his opinion), no more essential thing than filial piety; maintaining that the feelings of father, mother, son, and daughter are indiscriminately subject to one principle, without any distinction between honorable and mean. The present Emperor himself day and night waits upon their majesties his Father and the Empress Dowager, and yet cannot, in the least degree, carry out to the full his ideal of filial piety. The secondary consorts, meritorious persons, and other inmates of the Palace, he remembered, had entered within its precincts many years back, casting aside fathers and mothers, so how could they not help thinking of them? Besides, the fathers and mothers, who remain at home must long for their daughter of whom they cannot get even so much as a glimpse, and if, through this solicitude, they were to contract any illness, the harmony of heaven would also be seriously impaired, so for this reason, he memorialized the Emperor, his father, and the Empress Dowager that every month, on the recurrence of the second and sixth days, permission should be accorded to the relatives of the Imperial consorts to enter the palace and make application to see their daughters. The Emperor, his father, and Empress Dowager were, forthwith, much delighted by this representation, and eulogised, in high terms, the piety and generosity of the present Emperor, his regard for the will of heaven and his research into the nature of things. Both their sacred Majesties consequently also issued a decree to the effect: that the entrance of the relatives of the Imperial consorts into the Palace could not but interfere with the dignity of the state, and the rules of conventional rites, but that as the mothers and daughters could not gratify the wishes of their hearts, their Majesties would, after all, show a high proof of expedient grace, and issue a special command that: 'exclusive of the generous bounty, by virtue of which the worthy relations of the imperial consorts could enter the palace on the second and sixth days, any family, having extensive accommodation and separate courts suitable for the cantonment of the imperial bodyguard, could, without any detriment, make application to the Inner Palace, for the entrance of the Imperial chair into the private residences, to the end that the personal feelings of relations might be gratified, and that they should collectively enjoy the bliss of a family reunion.' After the issue of this decree, who did not leap from grateful joy! The father of the honorable secondary consort Zhou has now already initiated works, in his residence, for the repairs to the separate courts necessary for the visiting party. Wu Tianyu too, the father of Wu the distinguished consort, has likewise gone outside the city walls in search of a suitable plot of ground; and don't these amount to well-nigh accomplished facts?"

"Amituo Fo!" exclaimed dame Zhao. "Is it really so? but from what you say, our family will also be making preparations for the reception of the eldest young lady!"

"That goes without saying," added Jia Lian, "otherwise, for what purpose could we be in such a stir just now?"

"It's of course so!" interposed lady Feng smiling "and I shall now have an opportunity of seeing something great of the world. My misfortune is that I'm young by several years; for had I been born twenty or thirty years sooner, all these old people wouldn't really be now treating me contemptuously for not having seen the world. To begin with, the Emperor Taizu, in years gone by, imitated the old policy of Shun, and went on a tour, giving rise to more stir than any book could have ever produced; but I happen to be devoid of that good fortune which could have enabled me to come in time."

"Ai ya, ya!" ejaculated dame Zhao, "such a thing is rarely met with in a thousand years! I was old enough at that time to remember the occurrence! Our Jia family was then at Gusu, Yangzhou and all along that line, superintending the construction of ocean vessels, and the repairs to the seaboard. This was the only time in which preparations were made for the reception of the Emperor, and money was lavished in quantities as great as the billowing waters of the sea!"

This subject once introduced, lady Feng took up the thread of the conversation with vehemence. "Our Wang family," she said, "did also make preparations on one occasion. At that time my grandfather was in sole charge of all matters connected with tribute from various states, as well as with general levees, so that whenever any foreigners arrived, they all came to our house to be entertained, while the whole of the goods, brought by foreign vessels from the two Guang provinces, from Fujian, Yunnan, and Zhejiang, were the property of our family."

"Who isn't aware of these facts?" ventured dame Zhao; "there is up to this day a saying that, 'in the eastern sea, there was a white jade bed required, and the dragon prince came to request Mr. Wang of Jinling (to give it to him)!' This saying relates to your family, my lady, and remains even now in vogue. The Zhen family of Jiangnan has recently held, oh such a fine old standing! it alone has entertained the Emperor on four occasions! Had we not seen these things with our own eyes, were we to tell no matter whom, they wouldn't surely ever believe them! Not to speak of the money, which was as plentiful as mud, all things, whether they were to be found in the world or not, were they not heaped up like hills, and collected like the waters of the sea? But with the four characters representing sin and pity they didn't however trouble their minds."

"I've often heard," continued lady Feng, "my eldest uncle say that things were in such a state, and how couldn't I believe? but what surprises me is how it ever happened that this family attained such opulence and honor!"

"I'll tell your ladyship and all in one sentence," replied nurse Zhao. "Why they simply took the Emperor's money and spent it for the Emperor's person, that's all! for what family has such a lot of money as to indulge in this useless extravagance?"

While they were engaged in this conversation, a servant came a second time, at the instance of Madame Wang, to see whether lady Feng had finished her meal or not; and lady Feng forthwith concluding that there must be something waiting for her to attend to, hurriedly rushed through her repast. She had just rinsed her mouth and was about to start when the youths, on duty at the second gate, also reported that the two gentlemen, Mr. Jia Rong and Mr. Jia Se, belonging to the Eastern mansion, had arrived.

Jia Lian had, at length, rinsed his mouth; but while Ping'er presented a basin for him to wash his hands, he perceived the two young men walk in, and readily inquired of them what they had to say.

Lady Feng was, on account (of their arrival), likewise compelled to stay, and she heard Jia Rong take the lead and observe: "My father has sent me to tell you, uncle, that the gentlemen have already decided that the whole extent of ground, starting from the east side, borrowing (for the occasion) the flower garden of the Eastern mansion, straight up to the northwest, had been measured and found to amount in all to three and a half li; that it will be suitable for the erection of extra accommodation for the visiting party; that they have already commissioned an architect to draw a plan, which will be ready by tomorrow; that as you, uncle, have just returned home, and must unavoidably feel fatigued, you need not go over to our house, but that if you have anything to say you should please come tomorrow morning, as early as you can, and consult verbally with him."

"Thank uncle warmly," Jia Lian rejoined smilingly, "for the trouble he has taken in thinking of me; I shall, in that case, comply with his wishes and not go over. This plan is certainly the proper one, for while trouble will thus be saved, the erection of the quarters will likewise be an easy matter; for had a distinct plot to be selected and to be purchased, it would involve far greater difficulties. What's more, things wouldn't, after all, be what they properly should be. When you get back, tell your father that this decision is the right one, and that should the gentlemen have any further wish to introduce any change in their proposals, it will rest entirely with my uncle to prevent them, as it's on no account advisable to go and cast one's choice on some other plot; that tomorrow as soon as it's daylight, I'll come and pay my respects to uncle, when we can enter into further details in our deliberations!"

Jia Rong hastily signified his assent by several yes's, and Jia Se also came forward to deliver his message. "The mission to Gusu," he explained, "to find tutors, to purchase servant girls, and to obtain musical instruments, and theatrical properties and the like, my uncle has confided to me; and as I'm to take along with me the two sons of a couple of majordomos, and two companions of the family, besides, Dan Pinren and Bu Guxiu, he has, for this reason, enjoined me to come and see you, uncle."

Upon hearing this, Jia Lian scrutinised Jia Se. "What!" he asked, "are you able to undertake these commissions? These matters are, it's true, of no great moment; but there's something more hidden in them!"

Jia Se smiled. "The best thing I can do," he remarked, "will be to execute them in my novice sort of way, that's all."

Jia Rong was standing next to lady Feng, out of the light of the lamp, and stealthily pulled the lapel of her dress. Lady Feng understood the hint, and putting on a smiling expression, "You are too full of fears!" she interposed. "Is it likely that our uncle Zhen doesn't, after all, know better than we do what men to employ, that you again give way to apprehensions that he isn't up to the mark! but who are those who are, in every respect, up to the mark? These young fellows have grown up already to this age, and if they haven't eaten any pork, they have nevertheless seen a pig run. If Mr. Zhen has deputed him to go, he is simply meant to sit under the general's standard; and do you imagine, forsooth, that he has, in real earnest, told him to go and bargain about the purchase money, and to interview the brokers himself? My own idea is that (the choice) is a very good one."

"Of course it is!" observed Jia Lian; "but it isn't that I entertain any wish to be factious; my only object is to devise some plan or other for him. Whence will," he therefore went on to ask, "the money required for this purpose come from?"

"A little while ago the deliberations reached this point," rejoined Jia Se; "and Mr. Lai suggested that there was no necessity at all to take any funds from the capital, as the Zhen family, in Jiangnan, had still in their possession 50,000 taels of our money. That he would tomorrow write a letter of advice and a draft for us to take along, and that we should, first of all, obtain cash to the amount of 30,000 taels, and let the balance of 20,000 taels remain over, for the purchase of painted lanterns, and colored candles, as well as for the outlay for every kind of portieres, banners, curtains, and streamers."

Jia Lian nodded his head. "This plan is first-rate!" he added.

"Since that be so," observed lady Feng, as she addressed herself to Jia Se, "I've two able and reliable men; and if you would take them with you, to attend to these matters, won't it be to your convenience?"

Jia Se forced a smile. "I was just on the point," he rejoined, "of asking you, aunt, for the loan of two men, so that this suggestion is a strange coincidence."

As he went on to ascertain what were their names, lady Feng inquired what they were of nurse Zhao. But nurse Zhao had, by this time, become quite dazed from listening to the conversation, and Ping'er had to give her a push, as she smiled, before she returned to consciousness. "The one," she hastened to reply, "is called Zhao Tianliang and the other Zhao Tiandong."

"Whatever you do," suggested lady Feng, "don't forget them; but now I'm off to look after my duties."

With these words, she left the room, and Jia Rong promptly followed her out, and with gentle voice he said to her: "Of whatever you want, aunt, issue orders that a list be drawn up, and I'll give it to my brother to take with him, and he'll carry out your commissions according to the list."

"Don't talk nonsense!" replied lady Feng laughing; "I've found no place, as yet, where I could put away all my own things; and do the stealthy practices of you people take my fancy?"

As she uttered these words she straightway went her way.

Jia Se, at this time, likewise, asked Jia Lian: "If you want anything (in the way of curtains,) I can conveniently have them woven for you, along with the rest, and bring them as a present to you."

"Don't be in such high glee!" Jia Lian urged with a grin, "you've but recently been learning how to do business, and have you come first and foremost to excel in tricks of this kind? If I require anything, I'll of course write and tell you, but we needn't talk about it."

Having finished speaking, he dismissed the two young men; and, in quick succession, servants came to make their business reports, not limited to three and five companies, but as Jia Lian felt exhausted, he forthwith sent word to those on duty at the second gate not to allow anyone at all to communicate any reports, and that the whole crowd should wait till the next day, when he would give his mind to what had to be done.

Lady Feng did not come to retire to rest till the third watch; but nothing need be said about the whole night.

The next morning, at an early hour, Jia Lian got up and called on Jia She and Jia Zheng; after which, he came over to the Ning Guo mansion; when, in company with the old major-domos and other servants, as well as with several old family friends and companions, he inspected the grounds of the two mansions, and drew plans of the palatial buildings (for the accommodation of the Imperial consort and her escort) on her visit to her parents; deliberating at the same time, on the subject of the works and workmen.

From this day the masons and workmen of every trade were collected to the full number; and the articles of gold, silver, copper, and pewter, as well as the earth, timber, tiles, and bricks, were brought over, and carried in, in incessant supplies. In the first place, orders were issued to the workmen to demolish the wall and towers of the garden of Concentrated Fragrance, and extend a passage to connect in a straight line with the large court in the east of the Rong mansion; for the whole extent of servants' quarters on the eastern side of the Rong mansion had previously been pulled down.

The two residences of Ning and Rong were, in these days, it is true, divided by a small street, which served as a boundary line, and there was no communication between them, but this narrow passage was also private property, and not in any way a government street, so that they could easily be connected, and as in the garden of Concentrated Fragrance, there was already a stream of running water, which had been introduced through the corner of the northern wall, there was no further need now of going to the trouble of bringing in another. Although the rockeries and trees were not sufficient, the place where Jia She lived, was an old garden of the Rong mansion, so that the bamboos, trees, and rockeries in that compound, as well as the arbors, railings, and other such things could all be very well removed to the front; and by these means, these two grounds, situated as they were besides so very near to each other, could, by being thrown into one, conduce to the saving of considerable capital and labor; for, in spite of some deficiency, what had to be supplied did not amount to much. And it devolved entirely upon a certain old Hu, a man of note, styled Shan Ziye, to deliberate upon one thing after another, and to initiate its construction.

Jia Zheng was not up to these ordinary matters, so that it fell to Jia She, Jia Zhen, Jia Lian, Lai Da, Lai Sheng, Lin Zhixiao, Wu Xindeng, Zhan Guang, and several others to allot the sites, to set things in order, (and to look after) the heaping up of rockeries, the digging of ponds, the construction of two-storied buildings, the erection of halls, the plantation of bamboos and the cultivation of flowers, everything connected with the improvement of the scenery devolving, on the other hand, upon Shan Ziye to make provision for, and after leaving Court, he would devote such leisure moments as he had to merely going everywhere to give a look at the most important spots, and to consult with Jia She and the others; after which he troubled his mind no more with anything. And as Jia She did nothing else than stay at home and lie off, whenever any matter turned up, trifling though it may have been as a grain of mustard seed or a bean, Jia Zhen and his associates had either to go and report it in person or to write a memorandum of it. Or if he had anything to say, he sent for Jia Lian, Lai Da, and others to come and receive his instructions. Jia Rong had the sole direction of the manufacture of the articles in gold and silver; and as for Jia Se, he had already set out on his journey to Gusu. Jia Zhen, Lai Da, and the rest had also to call out the roll with the names of the workmen, to superintend the works, and other duties relative thereto, which could not be recorded by one brush alone; sufficient to say that a great bustle and stir prevailed, but to this subject we shall not refer for a time, but allude to Baoyu.

As of late there were in the household concerns of this magnitude to attend to, Jia Zheng did not come to examine him in his lessons, so that he was, of course, in high spirits, but, as unfortunately Qin Zhong's complaint became, day by day, more serious, he was at the same time really so very distressed at heart on his account, that enjoyment was for him out of the question.

On this day, he got up as soon as it was dawn, and having just combed his hair and washed his face and hands, he was bent upon going to ask dowager lady Jia to allow him to pay a visit to Qin Zhong, when he suddenly espied Mingyan peep round the curtain-wall at the second gate, and then withdraw his head. Baoyu promptly walked out and inquired what he was up to.

"Mr. Qin Zhong," observed Mingyan, "is not well at all."

Baoyu at these words was quite taken aback. "It was only yesterday," he hastily added, "that I saw him, and he was still bright and cheery; and how is it that he's anything but well now?"

"I myself can't explain," replied Mingyan; "but just a few minutes ago an old man belonging to his family came over with the express purpose of giving me the tidings."

Upon hearing this news, Baoyu there and then turned round and told dowager lady Jia; and the old lady issued directions to depute some trustworthy persons to accompany him. "Let him go," (she said), "and satisfy his feelings towards his fellow-scholar; but as soon as he has done, he must come back; and don't let him tarry too long."

Baoyu with hurried step left the room and came and changed his clothes. But as on his arrival outside, the carriage had not as yet been got ready, he fell into such a state of excitement, that he went round and round all over the hall in quite an erratic manner. In a short while, after pressure had been brought to bear, the carriage arrived, and speedily mounting the vehicle, he drove up to the door of Qin Zhong's house, followed by Li Gui, Mingyan, and the other servants. Everything was quiet. Not a soul was about. Like a hive of bees they flocked into the house, to the astonishment of two distant aunts, and of several male cousins of Qin Zhong, all of whom had no time to effect their retreat.

Qin Zhong had, by this time, had two or three fainting fits. As soon as Baoyu realized the situation, he felt unable to repress himself from bursting forth aloud. Li Gui promptly reasoned with him. "You shouldn't go on in this way," he urged, "you shouldn't. It's because Mr. Qin is so weak that lying flat on the stove-couch narurally made his bones feel uncomfortable; and that's why he has temporarily been removed down here to ease him a little. But if you, sir, go on in this way, will you not, instead of doing him any good, aggravate his illness?"

At these words, Baoyu accordingly restrained himself, and held his tongue; and drawing near, he gazed at Qin Zhong's face, which was as white as wax, while with closed eyes, he gasped for breath, rolling about on his pillow.

"Brother Jing," speedily exclaimed Baoyu, "Baoyu is here!" But though he shouted out two or three consecutive times, Qin Zhong did not heed him.

"Baoyu has come!" Baoyu went on again to cry. But Qin Zhong's spirit had already departed from his body, leaving behind only a faint breath of superfluous air in his lungs.

He had just caught sight of a number of recording devils, holding a warrant and carrying chains, coming to seize him, but Qin Zhong's soul would on no account go along with them; and remembering how that there was in his home no one to assume the direction of domestic affairs, and feeling concerned that Zhineng had as yet no home, he consequently used hundreds of arguments in his entreaties to the recording devils; but alas! these devils would, none of them, show him any favor. On the contrary, they heaped invectives upon Qin Zhong.

"You're fortunate enough to be a man of letters," they insinuated, "and don't you know the common saying that: 'if the Prince of Hell call upon you to die at the third watch, who can presume to retain you, a human being, up to the fifth watch?' In our abode, in the unseen, high as well as low, have all alike a face made of iron, and heed not selfish motives; unlike the mortal world, where favoritism and partiality prevail. There exist therefore many difficulties in the way (to our yielding to your wishes)."

While this fuss was going on, Qin Zhong's spirit suddenly grasped the four words, "Baoyu has come," and without loss of time, it went on again to make further urgent appeals. "Gentlemen, spiritual deputies," it exclaimed; "show me a little mercy and allow me to return to make just one remark to an intimate friend of mine, and I'll be back again."

"What intimate friend is this again?" the devils observed with one voice.

"I'm not deceiving you, gentlemen," rejoined Qin Zhong; "it's the grandson of the duke of Rong Guo, whose infant name is Baoyu."

The Decider of life was, at first, upon hearing these words, so seized with dismay that he vehemently abused the devils sent on the errand.

"I told you," he shouted, "to let him go back for a turn; but you would by no means comply with my words! and now do you wait until he has summoned a man of glorious fortune and prosperous standing to at last desist?"

When the company of devils perceived the manner of the Decider of life, they were all likewise so seized with consternation that they bustled with hand and feet; while with hearts also full of resentment: "You, sir," they replied, "were at one time such a terror, formidable as lightning; and are you not forsooth able to listen with equanimity to the two sounds of 'Baoyu?' our humble idea is that mortal as he is, and immortal as we are, it wouldn't be to our credit if we feared him!"

But whether Qin Zhong, after all, died or survived, the next chapter will explain.

CHAPTER 17

In the Daguan Garden, (Broad Vista,) the merits of Baoyu are put to the test, by his being told to write devices for scrolls and tablets. Yuanchun returns to the Rong Guo mansion, on a visit to her parents, and offers her congratulations to them on the feast of lanterns, on the fifteenth of the first moon.

Qin Zhong, to resume our story, departed this life, and Baoyu went on so unceasingly in his bitter lamentations, that Li Gui and the other servants had, for ever so long, an arduous task in trying to comfort him before he desisted; but on his return home he was still exceedingly disconsolate.

Dowager lady Jia afforded monetary assistance to the amount of several tens of taels; and exclusive of this, she had sacrificial presents likewise got ready. Baoyu went and paid a visit of condolence to the family, and after seven days the funeral and burial took place, but there are no particulars about them which could be put on record.

Baoyu, however, continued to mourn (his friend) from day to day, and was incessant in his remembrance of him, but there was likewise no help for it. Neither is it known after how many days he got over his grief.

On this day, Jia Zhen and the others came to tell Jia Zheng that the works in the garden had all been reported as completed, and that Mr. Jia She had already inspected them. "It only remains," (they said), "for you, sir, to see them; and should there possibly be anything which is not proper, steps will be at once taken to effect the alterations, so that the tablets and scrolls may conveniently be written."

After Jia Zheng had listened to these words, he pondered for a while. "These tablets and scrolls," he remarked, "present however a difficult task. According to the rites, we should, in order to obviate any shortcoming, request the Imperial consort to deign and compose them; but if the honorable consort does not gaze upon the scenery with her own eyes, it will also be difficult for her to conceive its nature and indite upon it! And were we to wait until the arrival of her highness, to request her to honor the grounds with a visit, before she composes the inscriptions, such a wide landscape, with so many pavilions and arbors, will, without one character in the way of a motto, albeit it may abound with flowers, willows, rockeries, and streams, nevertheless in no way be able to show off its points of beauty to advantage."

The whole party of family companions, who stood by, smiled. "Your views, remarkable sir," they ventured, "are excellent; but we have now a proposal to make. Tablets and scrolls for every locality cannot, on any account, be dispensed with, but they could not likewise, by any means, be determined upon for good! Were now, for the time being, two, three, or four characters fixed upon, harmonizing with the scenery, to carry out, for form's sake, the idea, and were they provisionally utilized as mottoes for the lanterns, tablets, and scrolls, and hung up, pending the arrival of her highness, and her visit through the grounds, when she could be requested to decide upon the devices, would not two exigencies be met with satisfactorily?"

"Your views are perfectly correct," observed Jia Zheng, after he had heard their suggestion; "and we should go today and have a look at the place so as then to set to work to write the inscriptions; which, if suitable, can readily be used; and, if unsuitable, Yucun can then be sent for, and asked to compose fresh ones."

The whole company smiled. "If you, sir, were to compose them today," they ventured, "they are sure to be excellent; and what need will there be again to wait for Yucun!"

"You people are not aware," Jia Zheng added with a smiling countenance, "that I've been, even in my young days, very mediocre in the composition of stanzas on flowers, birds, rockeries, and streams; and that now that I'm well up in years and have moreover the fatigue and trouble of my official duties, I've become in literary compositions like these, which require a light heart and gladsome mood, still more inapt. Were I even to succeed in composing any, they will unavoidably be so doltish and forced that they would contrariwise be instrumental in making the flowers, trees, garden, and pavilions, through their demerits, lose in beauty, and present instead no pleasing feature."

"This wouldn't anyhow matter," remonstrated all the family companions, "for after perusing them we can all decide upon them together, each one of us recommending those he thinks best; which if excellent can be kept, and if faulty can be discarded; and there's nothing unfeasible about this!"

"This proposal is most apposite," rejoined Jia Zheng. "What's more, the weather is, I rejoice, fine today; so let's all go in a company and have a look."

Saying this, he stood up and went forward, at the head of the whole party; while Jia Zhen betook himself in advance into the garden to let everyone know of their coming. As luck would have it, Baoyu—for he had been these last few days thinking of Qin Zhong and so ceaselessly sad and wounded at heart, that dowager lady Jia had frequently directed the servants to take him into the new garden to play—made his entrance just at this very time, and suddenly became aware of the arrival of Jia Zhen, who said to him with a smile, "Don't you yet run away as fast as you can? Mr. Jia Zheng will be coming in a while."

At these words, Baoyu led off his nurse and the youths, and rushed at once out of the garden, like a streak of smoke; but as he turned a corner, he came face to face with Jia Zheng, who was advancing towards that direction, at the head of all the visitors; and as he had no time to get out of the way, the only course open to him was to stand on one side.

Jia Zheng had, of late, heard the tutor extol him by saying that he displayed special ability in rhyming antithetical lines, and that although he did not like to read his books, he nevertheless possessed some depraved talents, and hence it was that he was induced at this moment to promptly bid him follow him into the garden, with the intent of putting him to the test.

Baoyu could not make out what his object was, but he was compelled to follow. As soon as they reached the garden gate, and he caught sight of Jia Zhen, standing on one side, along with several managers: "See that the garden gate is closed for a time," Jia Zheng exclaimed, "for we'll first see the outside and then go in."

Jia Zhen directed a servant to close the gate, and Jia Zheng first looked straight ahead of him towards the gate and espied on the same side as the main entrance a suite of five apartments. Above, the cylindrical tiles resembled the backs of mud eels. The doors, railings, windows, and frames were all finely carved with designs of the new fashion, and were painted neither in vermilion nor in white colors. The whole extent of the walls was of polished bricks of uniform color; while below, the white marble on the terrace and steps was engraved with western foreign designs; and when he came to look to the right and to the left, everything was white as snow. At the foot of the whitewashed walls, tiger-skin pebbles were, without regard to pattern, promiscuously inserted in the earth in such a way as of their own selves to form streaks. Nothing fell in with the custom of gaudiness and display so much in vogue, so that he naturally felt full of delight; and, when he forthwith asked that the gate should be thrown open, all that met their eyes was a long stretch of verdant hills, which shut in the view in front of them.

"What a fine hill, what a pretty hill!" exclaimed all the companions with one voice.

"Were it not for this one hill," Jia Zheng explained, "whatever scenery is contained in it would clearly strike the eye, as soon as one entered into the garden, and what pleasure would that have been?"

"Quite so," rejoined all of them. "But without large hills and ravines in one's breast (liberal capacities), how could one attain such imagination!"

After the conclusion of this remark, they cast a glance ahead of them, and perceived white rugged rocks looking, either like goblins, or resembling savage beasts, lying either crossways, or in horizontal or upright positions; on the surface of which grew moss and lichen with mottled hues, or parasitic plants, which screened off the light; while, slightly visible, wound, among the rocks, a narrow pathway like the intestines of a sheep.

"If we were now to go and stroll along by this narrow path," Jia Zheng suggested, "and to come out from over there on our return, we shall have been able to see the whole grounds."

Having finished speaking, he asked Jia Zhen to lead the way; and he himself, leaning on Baoyu, walked into the gorge with leisurely step. Raising his head, he suddenly beheld on the hill a block of stone, as white as the surface of a looking-glass, in a site which was, in very deed, suitable to be left for an inscription, as it was bound to meet the eye.

"Gentlemen," Jia Zheng observed, as he turned his head round and smiled, "please look at this spot. What name will it be fit to give it?"

When the company heard his remark, some maintained that the two words "Heaped verdure" should be written; and others upheld that the device should be "Embroidered Hill." Others again suggested: "Vying with the Xiang Lu;" and others recommended "the small Zhong Nan." And various kinds of names were proposed, which did not fall short of several tens.

All the visitors had been, it must be explained, aware at an early period of the fact that Jia Zheng meant to put Baoyu's ability to the test, and for this reason they merely proposed a few combinations in common use. But of this intention, Baoyu himself was likewise cognizant.

After listening to the suggestions, Jia Zheng forthwith turned his head round and bade Baoyu think of some motto.

"I've often heard," Baoyu replied, "that writers of old opine that it's better to quote an old saying than to compose a new one; and that an old engraving excels in every respect an engraving of the present day. What's more, this place doesn't constitute the main hill or the chief feature of the scenery, and is really no site where any inscription should be put, as it no more than constitutes the first step in the inspection of the landscape. Won't it be well to employ the exact text of an old writer consisting of 'a tortuous path leading to a secluded (nook).' This line of past days would, if inscribed, be, in fact, liberal to boot."

After listening to the proposed line, they all sang its praise. "First-rate! excellent!" they cried, "the natural talents of your second son, dear friend, are lofty; his mental capacity is astute; he is unlike ourselves, who have read books but are simple fools."

"You shouldn't," urged Jia Zheng smilingly, "heap upon him excessive praise; he's young in years, and merely knows one thing which he turns to the use of ten purposes; you should laugh at him, that's all; but we can by and by choose some device."

As he spoke, he entered the cave, where he perceived beautiful trees with thick foliage, quaint flowers in lustrous bloom, while a line of limpid stream emanated out of a deep recess among the flowers and trees, and oozed down through the crevice of the rock. Progressing several steps further in, they gradually faced the northern side, where a stretch of level ground extended far and wide, on each side of which soared lofty buildings, intruding themselves into the skies, whose carved rafters and engraved balustrades nestled entirely among the depressions of the hills and the tops of the trees. They lowered their eyes and looked, and beheld a pure stream flowing like jade, stone steps traversing the clouds, a balustrade of white marble encircling the pond in its embrace, and a stone bridge with three archways, the animals upon which had faces disgorging water from their mouths. A pavilion stood on the bridge, and in this pavilion Jia Zhen and the whole party went and sat.

"Gentlemen," he inquired, "what shall we write about this?"

"In the record," they all replied, "of the 'Drunken Old Man's Pavilion,' written in days of old by Ouyang, appears this line: 'There is a pavilion pinioned-like,' so let us call this 'the pinioned-like pavilion,' and finish."

"Pinioned-like," observed Jia Zheng smiling, "is indeed excellent; but this pavilion is constructed over the water, and there should, after all, be some allusion to the water in the designation. My humble opinion is that of the line in Ouyang's work, '(the water) drips from between the two peaks,' we should only make use of that single word 'drips.'"

"First-rate!" rejoined one of the visitors, "capital! but what would really be appropriate are the two characters 'dripping jadelike.'"

Jia Zhen pulled at his moustache, as he gave way to reflection; after which, he asked Baoyu to also propose one himself.

"What you, sir, suggested a while back," replied Baoyu, "will do very well; but if we were now to sift the matter thoroughly, the use of the single word 'drip' by Ouyang, in his composition about the Niang spring, would appear quite apposite; while the application, also on this occasion, to this spring, of the character 'drip' would be found not quite suitable. Moreover, seeing that this place is intended as a separate residence (for the Imperial consort), on her visit to her parents, it is likewise imperative that we should comply with all the principles of etiquette, so that were words of this kind to be used, they would besides be coarse and inappropriate; and may it please you to fix upon something else more recondite and abstruse."

"What do you, gentlemen, think of this argument?" Jia Zheng remarked sneeringly. "A little while ago, when the whole company devised something original, you observed that it would be better to quote an old device; and now that we have quoted an old motto, you again maintain that it's coarse and inappropriate! But you had better give us one of yours."

"If two characters like 'dripping jadelike' are to be used," Baoyu explained, "it would be better then to employ the two words 'Penetrating Fragrance,' which would be unique and excellent, wouldn't they?"

Jia Zheng pulled his moustache, nodded his head and did not utter a word; whereupon the whole party hastily pressed forward with one voice to eulogize Baoyu's acquirements as extraordinary.

"The selection of two characters for the tablet is an easy matter," suggested Jia Zheng, "but now go on and compose a pair of antithetical phrases with seven words in each."

Baoyu cast a glance round the four quarters, when an idea came into his head, and he went on to recite:

> The willows, which enclose the shore, the green borrow from three
>   bamboos;
> On banks apart, the flowers asunder grow, yet one perfume they
>   give.

Upon hearing these lines, Jia Zheng gave a faint smile, as he nodded his head, whilst the whole party went on again to be effusive in their praise. But forthwith they issued from the pavilions, and crossed the pond, contemplating with close attention each elevation, each stone, each flower, or each tree. And as suddenly they raised their heads, they caught sight, in front of them, of a line of white wall, of numbers of columns, and beautiful cottages, where flourished hundreds and thousands of verdant bamboos, which screened off the rays of the sun.

What a lovely place!" they one and all exclaimed.

Speedily the whole company penetrated inside, perceiving, as soon as they had entered the gate, a zigzag arcade, below the steps of which was a raised pathway, laid promiscuously with stones, and on the furthest part stood a diminutive cottage with three rooms, two with doors leading into them and one without. Everything in the interior, in the shape of beds, teapoys, chairs, and tables, were made to harmonize with the space available. Leading out of the inner room of the cottage was a small door from which, as they egressed, they found a back-court with lofty pear trees in blossom and banana trees, as well as two very small retiring back-courts. At the foot of the wall, unexpectedly became visible an aperture where was a spring, for which a channel had been opened scarcely a foot or so wide, to enable it to run inside the wall. Winding round the steps, it skirted the buildings until it reached the front court, where it coiled and curved, flowing out under the bamboos.

"This spot," observed Jia Zheng full of smiles, "is indeed pleasant! and could one, on a moonlight night, sit under the window and study, one would not spend a whole lifetime in vain!"

As he said this, he quickly cast a glance at Baoyu, and so terrified did Baoyu feel that he hastily drooped his head. The whole company lost no time in choosing some irrelevant talk to turn the conversation, and two of the visitors prosecuted their remarks by adding that on the tablet, in this spot, four characters should be inscribed.

"Which four characters?" Jia Zheng inquired, laughingly.

"The bequeathed aspect of the river Qi!" suggested one of them.

"It's commonplace," observed Jia Zheng.

Another person recommended "the remaining vestiges of the Sui Garden."

"This too is commonplace!" replied Jia Zheng.

"Let brother Baoyu again propound one!" interposed Jia Zhen, who stood by.

"Before he composes any himself," Jia Zheng continued, "his wont is to first discuss the pros and cons of those of others; so it's evident that he's an impudent fellow!"

"He's most reasonable in his arguments," all the visitors protested, "and why should he be called to task?"

"Don't humor him so much!" Jia Zheng expostulated. "I'll put up for today," he however felt constrained to tell Baoyu, "with your haughty manner, and your rubbishy speech, so that after you have, to begin with, given us your opinion, you may next compose a device. But tell me, are there any that will do among the mottoes suggested just now by all the gentlemen?"

"They all seem to me unsuitable!" Baoyu did not hesitate to say by way of reply to this question.

Jia Zheng gave a sardonic smile. "How all unsuitable?" he exclaimed.

"This," continued Baoyu, "is the first spot which her highness will honor on her way, and there should be inscribed, so that it should be appropriate, something commending her sacred majesty. But if a tablet with four characters has to be used, there are likewise devices ready at hand, written by poets of old; and what need is there to compose any more?"

"Are forsooth the devices 'the river Qi and the Sui Garden' not those of old authors?" insinuated Jia Zheng.

"They are too stiff," replied Baoyu. "Would not the four characters: 'a phoenix comes with dignified air,' be better?"

With clamorous unanimity the whole party shouted: "Excellent!" and Jia Zheng nodding his head; "You beast, you beast.'" he ejaculated, "it may well be said about you that you see through a thin tube and have no more judgment than an insect! Compose another stanza," he consequently bade him; and Baoyu recited:

> In the precious tripod kettle, tea is brewed, but green is still the smoke!
> O'er is the game of chess by the still window, but the fingers are yet cold.

Jia Zheng shook his head. "Neither does this seem to me good!" he said; and having concluded this remark he was leading the company out, when just as he was about to proceed, he suddenly bethought himself of something.

"The several courts and buildings and the teapoys, sideboards, tables and chairs," he added, "may be said to be provided for. But there are still all those curtains, screens, and portieres, as well as the furniture, nicknacks, and curios; and have they too all been matched to suit the requirements of each place?"

"Of the things that have to be placed about," Jia Zhen explained, a good number have, at an early period, been added, and of course when the time comes everything will be suitably arranged. As for the curtains, screens, and portieres, which have to be hung up, I heard yesterday brother Lian say that they are not as yet complete, that when the works were first taken in hand, the plan of each place was drawn, the measurements accurately calculated and someone despatched to attend to the things, and that he thought that yesterday half of them were bound to come in.

Jia Zheng, upon hearing this explanation, readily remembered that with all these concerns Jia Zhen had nothing to do; so that he speedily sent someone to go and call Jia Lian.

Having arrived in a short while, "How many sorts of things are there in all?" Jia Zheng inquired of him. "Of these how many kinds have by this time been got ready? and how many more are short?"

At this question, Jia Lian hastily produced, from the flaps of his boot, a paper pocket-book, containing a list, which he kept inside the tops of his boot. After perusing it and reperusing it, he made suitable reply. "Of the hundred and twenty curtains," he proceeded, "of stiff spotted silks, embroidered with dragons in relief, and of the curtains large and small, of every kind of damask silk, eighty were got yesterday, so that there still remain forty of them to come. The two portieres were both received yesterday; and besides these, there are the two hundred red woollen portieres, two hundred portieres of Xiang Fei bamboo; two hundred door-screens of rattan, with gold streaks, and of red lacquered bamboo; two hundred portieres of black lacquered rattan; two hundred door-screens of variegated thread-netting with clusters of flowers. Of each of these kinds, half have come in, but the whole lot of them will be complete no later than autumn. Antimacassars, table-cloths, flounces for the beds, and cushions for the stools, there are a thousand two hundred of each but these likewise are ready and at hand."

As he spoke, they proceeded outwards, but suddenly they perceived a hill extending obliquely in such a way as to intercept the passage; and as they wound round the curve of the hill faintly came to view a line of yellow mud walls, the whole length of which was covered with paddy stalks for the sake of protection, and there were several hundreds of apricot trees in bloom, which presented the appearance of being fire, spurted from the mouth, or russet clouds, rising in the air. Inside this enclosure, stood several thatched cottages. Outside grew, on the other hand, mulberry trees, elms, mallows, and silkworm oaks, whose tender shoots and new twigs, of every hue, were allowed to bend and to intertwine in such a way as to form two rows of green fence. Beyond this fence and below the white mound, was a well, by the side of which stood a well-sweep, windlass, and such like articles; the ground further down being divided into parcels, and apportioned into fields, which, with the fine vegetables and cabbages in flower, presented, at the first glance, the aspect of being illimitable.

"This is," Jia Zheng observed chuckling, "the place really imbued with a certain amount of the right principle; and laid out, though it has been by human labor, yet when it strikes my eye, it so moves my heart, that it cannot help arousing in me the wish to return to my native place and become a farmer. But let us enter and rest a while."

As he concluded these words, they were on the point of walking in, when they unexpectedly discerned a stone, outside the trellis gate, by the roadside, which had also been left as a place on which to inscribe a motto.

"Were a tablet," argued the whole company smilingly, "put up high in a spot like this, to be filled up by and by, the rustic aspect of a farm would in that case be completely done away with; and it will be better, yea far better to erect this slab on the ground, as it will further make manifest many points of beauty. But unless a motto could be composed of the same excellence as that in Fan Shihu's song on farms, it will not be adequate to express its charms!"

"Gentlemen," observed Jia Zheng, "please suggest something."

"A short while back," replied the whole company, "your son, venerable brother, remarked that devising a new motto was not equal to quoting an old one, and as sites of this kind have been already exhausted by writers of days of old, wouldn't it be as well that we should straightway call it the 'apricot blossom village?' and this will do splendidly."

When Jia Zheng heard this remark, he smiled and said, addressing himself to Jia Zhen: "This just reminds me that although this place is perfect in every respect, there's still one thing wanting in the shape of a wine board; and you had better then have one made tomorrow on the very same pattern as those used outside in villages; and it needn't be anything gaudy, but hung above the top of a tree by means of bamboos."

Jia Zhen assented. "There's no necessity," he went on to explain, "to keep any other birds in here, but only to rear a few geese, ducks, fowls, and such like; as in that case they will be in perfect keeping with the place."

"A splendid idea!" Jia Zheng rejoined, along with all the party.

"'Apricot blossom village' is really first-rate," continued Jia Zheng as he again addressed himself to the company; "but the only thing is that it encroaches on the real designation of the village; and it will be as well to wait (until her highness comes), when we can request her to give it a name."

"Certainly!" answered the visitors with one voice; "but now as far as a name goes, for mere form, let us all consider what expressions will be suitable to employ."

Baoyu did not however give them time to think; nor did he wait for Jia Zheng's permission, but suggested there and then: "In old poetical works there's this passage: 'At the top of the red apricot tree hangs the flag of an inn,' and wouldn't it be advisable, on this occasion, to temporarily adopt the four words: 'the sign on the apricot tree is visible?'"

"'Is visible' is excellent," suggested the whole number of them, "and what's more it secretly accords with the meaning implied by 'apricot blossom village.'"

"Were the two words 'apricot blossom' used for the name of the village, they would be too commonplace and unsuitable;" added Baoyu with a sardonic grin, "but there's another passage in the works of a poet of the Tang era: 'By the wooden gate near the water the cornflower emits its fragrance;' and why not make use of the motto 'corn fragrance village,' which will be excellent?"

When the company heard his proposal, they, with still greater vigor, unanimously combined in crying out "Capital!" as they clapped their hands.

Jia Zheng, with one shout, interrupted their cries, "You ignorant child of wrath!" he ejaculated; "how many old writers can you know, and how many stanzas of ancient poetical works can you remember, that you will have the boldness to show off in the presence of all these experienced gentlemen? (In allowing you to give vent to) all the nonsense you uttered my object was no other than to see whether your brain was clear or muddled; and all for fun's sake, that's all; and lo, you've taken things in real earnest!"

Saying this, he led the company into the interior of the hall with the mallows. The windows were pasted with paper, and the bedsteads made of wood, and all appearance of finery had been expunged, and Jia Zheng's heart was naturally much gratified; but nevertheless, scowling angrily at Baoyu, "What do you think of this place?" he asked.

When the party heard this question, they all hastened to stealthily give a nudge to Baoyu, with the express purpose of inducing him to say it was nice; but Baoyu gave no ear to what they all urged. "It's by far below the spot," he readily replied, "designated 'a phoenix comes with dignified air.'"

"You ignorant stupid thing!" exclaimed Jia Zheng at these words; "what you simply fancy as exquisite, with that despicable reliance of yours upon luxury and display, are two-storied buildings and painted pillars! But how can you know anything about this aspect so pure and unobtrusive, and this is all because of that failing of not studying your books!"

"Sir," hastily answered Baoyu, "your injunctions are certainly correct; but men of old have often made allusion to 'natural;' and what is, I wonder, the import of these two characters?"

The company had perceived what a perverse mind Baoyu possessed, and they one and all were much surprised that he should be so silly beyond the possibility of any change; and when now they heard the question he asked, about the two characters representing "natural," they, with one accord, speedily remarked, "Everything else you understand, and how is it that on the contrary you don't know what 'natural' implies? The word 'natural' means effected by heaven itself and not made by human labor."

"Well, just so," rejoined Baoyu; "but the farm, which is laid out in this locality, is distinctly the handiwork of human labor; in the distance, there are no neighboring hamlets; near it, adjoin no wastes; though it bears a hill, the hill is destitute of streaks; though it be close to water, this water has no spring; above, there is no pagoda nestling in a temple; below, there is no bridge leading to a market; it rises abrupt and solitary, and presents no grand sight! The palm would seem to be carried by the former spot, which is imbued with the natural principle, and possesses the charms of nature; for, though bamboos have been planted in it, and streams introduced, they nevertheless do no violence to the works executed. 'A natural landscape,' says, an ancient author in four words; and why? Simply because he apprehended that what was not land, would, by forcible ways, be converted into land; and that what was no hill would, by unnatural means, be raised into a hill. And ingenious though these works might be in a hundred and one ways, they cannot, after all, be in harmony...."

But he had no time to conclude, as Jia Zheng flew into a rage. "Drive him off," he shouted; (but as Baoyu) was on the point of going out, he again cried out: "Come back! make up," he added, "another couplet, and if it isn't clear, I'll for all this give you a slap on your mouth."

Baoyu had no alternative but to recite as follows:

A spot in which the "Ge" fiber to bleach, as the fresh tide doth swell the waters green!

A beauteous halo and a fragrant smell the man encompass who the cress did pluck!

Jia Zheng, after this recital, nodded his head. "This is still worse!" he remarked, but as he reproved him, he led the company outside, and winding past the mound, they penetrated among flowers, and wending their steps by the willows, they touched the rocks and lingered by the stream. Passing under the trellis with yellow roses, they went into the shed with white roses; they crossed by the pavilion with peonies, and walked through the garden, where the white peony grew; and entering the court with the cinnamon roses, they reached the island of bananas. As they meandered and zigzagged, suddenly they heard the rustling sound of the water, as it came out from a stone cave, from the top of which grew parasitic plants drooping downwards, while at its bottom floated the fallen flowers.

"What a fine sight!" they all exclaimed; "what beautiful scenery!"

"Gentlemen," observed Jia Zheng, "what name do you propose for this place?"

"There's no further need for deliberation," the company rejoined; "for this is just the very spot fit for the three words 'Wu Ling Spring.'"

"This too is matter-of-fact!" Jia Zheng objected laughingly, "and likewise antiquated."

"If that won't do," the party smiled, "well then what about the four characters implying 'An old cottage of a man of the Qin dynasty?'"

"This is still more exceedingly plain!" interposed Baoyu. "'The old cottage of a man of the Qin dynasty' is meant to imply a retreat from revolution, and how will it suit this place? Wouldn't the four characters be better denoting 'an isthmus with smart weed, and a stream with flowers?'"

When Jia Zheng heard these words, he exclaimed: "You're talking still more stuff and nonsense?" and forthwith entering the grotto, Jia Zheng went on to ask of Jia Zhen, "Are there any boats or not?"

"There are to be," replied Jia Zhen, "four boats in all from which to pick the lotus, and one boat for sitting in; but they haven't now as yet been completed."

"What a pity!" Jia Zheng answered smilingly, "that we cannot go in."

"But we could also get into it by the tortuous path up the hill," Jia Zhen ventured; and after finishing this remark, he walked ahead to show the way, and the whole party went over, holding on to the creepers, and supporting themselves by the trees, when they saw a still larger quantity of fallen leaves on the surface of the water, and the stream itself, still more limpid, gently and idly meandering along on its circuitous course. By the bank of the pond were two rows of weeping willows, which, intermingling with peach and apricot trees, screened the heavens from view, and kept off the rays of the sun from this spot, which was in real truth devoid of even a grain of dust.

Suddenly, they espied in the shade of the willows, an arched wooden bridge also reveal itself to the eye, with bannisters of vermilion color. They crossed the bridge, and lo, all the paths lay open before them; but their gaze was readily attracted by a brick cottage spotless and cool-looking; whose walls were constructed of polished bricks, of uniform color; (whose roof was laid) with speckless tiles; and whose enclosing walls were painted; while the minor slopes, which branched off from the main hill, all passed along under the walls on to the other side.

"This house, in a site like this, is perfectly destitute of any charm!" added Jia Zheng.

And as they entered the door, abruptly appeared facing them a large boulder studded with holes and soaring high in the skies, which was surrounded on all four sides by rocks of every description, and completely, in fact, hid from view the rooms situated in the compound. But of flowers or trees, there was not even one about; and all that was visible were a few strange kinds of vegetation; some being of the creeper genus, others parasitic plants, either hanging from the apex of the hill, or inserting themselves into the base of the rocks; drooping down even from the eaves of the house, entwining the pillars, and closing round the stone steps. Or like green bands, they waved and flapped; or like gold thread, they coiled and bent, either with seeds resembling cinnabar, or with blossoms like golden olea; whose fragrance and aroma could not be equalled by those emitted by flowers of ordinary species.

"This is pleasant!" Jia Zheng could not refrain from saying; "the only thing is that I don't know very much about flowers."

"What are here are lianas and *ficus pumila*!" some of the company observed.

"How ever can the liana and the ficus have such unusual scent?" questioned Jia Zheng.

"Indeed they aren't!" interposed Baoyu. "Among all these flowers, there are also ficus and liana, but those scented ones are iris, *ligularia*, and 'Wu' flowers; that kind consist, for the most part, of 'Zhi' flowers and orchids; while this mostly of gold-colored dolichos. That species is the hypericum plant, this the 'Yu Lu' creeper. The red ones are, of course, the purple rue; the green ones consist for certain, of the green 'Zhi' plant; and, to the best of my belief, these various plants are mentioned in the 'Li Sao' and 'Wen Xuan.' These rare plants are, some of them called something or other like 'Huo Na' and 'Jiang Hui;' others again are designated something like 'Lun Zu' and 'Zi Jiang;' while others there are whose names sound like 'Shi Fan,' 'Shui Song,' and 'Fu Liu,' which together with other species are to be found in the 'Treatise about the Wu city' by Zuo Daizhong. There are also those which go under the appellation of 'Lu Ti,' or something like that; while there are others that are called something or other like 'Dan Jiao,' 'Mi Wu,' and 'Feng Lian;' reference to which is made in the 'Treatise on the Shu city.' But so many years have now elapsed, and the times have so changed (since these treatises were written), that people, being unable to discriminate (the real names) may consequently have had to appropriate in every case such names as suited the external aspect, so that they may, it is quite possible, have gradually come to be called by wrong designations."

But he had no time to conclude; for Jia Zheng interrupted him. "Who has ever asked you about it?" he shouted; which plunged Baoyu into such a fright, that he drew back, and did not venture to utter another word.

Jia Zheng perceiving that on both sides alike were covered passages resembling outstretched arms, forthwith continued his steps and entered the covered way, when he caught sight, at the upper end, of a five-roomed building, without spot or blemish, with folding blinds extending in a connected line, and with corridors on all four sides; (a building) which with its windows so green, and its painted walls, excelled, in spotless elegance, the other buildings they had seen before, to which it presented such a contrast.

Jia Zheng heaved a sigh. "If one were able," he observed, "to boil his tea and thrum his lyre in here, there wouldn't even be any need for him to burn any more incense. But the execution of this structure is so beyond conception that you must, gentlemen, compose something nice and original to embellish the tablet with, so as not to render such a place of no effect!"

"There's nothing so really pat," suggested the company smiling; "as 'the orchid-smell-laden breeze' and 'the dew-bedecked epidendrum!'"

"These are indeed the only four characters," rejoined Jia Zheng, "that could be suitably used; but what's to be said as far as the scroll goes?"

"I've thought of a couplet," interposed one of the party, "which you'll all have to criticize, and put into ship-shape; its burden is this:

> "The musk-like epidendrum smell enshrouds the court, where shines the sun with oblique beams;
> The iris fragrance is wafted over the isle illumined by the moon's clear rays."

"As far as excellence is concerned, it's excellent," observed the whole party, "but the two words representing 'with oblique beams' are not felicitous."

And as someone quoted the line from an old poem:

> The angelica fills the court with tears, what time the sun doth slant.

"Lugubrious, lugubrious!" expostulated the company with one voice.

Another person then interposed. "I also have a couplet, whose merits you, gentlemen, can weigh; it runs as follows:

"Along the three pathways doth float the Yuhui scented breeze!
The radiant moon in the whole hall shines on the gold orchid!"

Jia Zheng tugged at his moustache and gave way to meditation. He was just about also to suggest a stanza, when, upon suddenly raising his head, he espied Baoyu standing by his side, too timid to give vent to a single sound.

"How is it," he purposely exclaimed, "that when you should speak, you contrariwise don't? Is it likely that you expect someone to request you to confer upon us the favor of your instruction?"

"In this place," Baoyu rejoined at these words, "there are no such things as orchids, musk, resplendent moon, or islands; and were one to begin quoting such specimens of allusions, to scenery, two hundred couplets could be readily given without, even then, having been able to exhaust the supply!"

"Who presses your head down," Jia Zheng urged, "and uses force that you must come out with all these remarks?"

"Well, in that case," added Baoyu, "there are no fitter words to put on the tablet than the four representing: 'The fragrance pure of the *ligularia* and iris.' While the device on the scroll might be:

"Sung is the nutmeg song, but beauteous still is the sonnet!
Near the Tu Mei to sleep, makes e'en a dream with fragrance full!"

"This is," laughed Jia Zheng sneeringly, "an imitation of the line:

"A book when it is made of plaintain leaves, the writing green is
also bound to be!

"So that there's nothing remarkable about it."

"Li Bai, in his work on the Phoenix Terrace," protested the whole party, "copied, in every point, the Huang He Lou. But what's essential is a faultless imitation. Now were we to begin to criticize minutely the couplet just cited, we would indeed find it to be, as compared with the line 'A book when it is made of plaintain leaves,' still more elegant and of wider application!"

"What an idea?" observed Jia Zheng derisively.

But as he spoke, the whole party walked out; but they had not gone very far before they caught sight of a majestic summer house, towering high peak-like, and of a structure rising loftily with story upon story; and completely locked in as they were on every side they were as beautiful as the Jade palace. Far and wide, road upon road coiled and wound; while the green pines swept the eaves, the jady epidendrum encompassed the steps, the animals' faces glistened like gold, and the dragons' heads shone resplendent in their variegated hues.

"This is the Main Hall," remarked Jia Zheng; "the only word against it is that there's a little too much finery."

"It should be so," rejoined one and all, "so as to be what it's intended to be! The imperial consort has, it is true, an exalted preference for economy and frugality, but her present honorable position requires the observance of such courtesies, so that (finery) is no fault."

As they made these remarks and advanced on their way the while, they perceived, just in front of them, an archway project to view, constructed of jadelike stone; at the top of which the coils of large dragons and the scales of small dragons were executed in perforated style.

"What's the device to be for this spot?" inquired Jia Zheng.

"It should be 'fairy land,'" suggested all of them, "so as to be apposite!"

Jia Zheng nodded his head and said nothing. But as soon as Baoyu caught sight of this spot something was suddenly aroused in his heart and he began to ponder within himself. "This place really resembles something that I've seen somewhere or other." But he could not at the moment recall to mind what year, moon, or day this had happened.

Jia Zheng bade him again propose a motto; but Baoyu was bent upon thinking over the details of the scenery he had seen on a former occasion, and gave no thought whatever to this place, so that the whole company were at a loss what construction to give to his silence, and came simply to the conclusion that, after the bullying he had had to put up with for ever so long, his spirits had completely vanished, his talents become exhausted and his speech impoverished; and that if he were harassed and pressed, he might perchance, as the result of anxiety, contract some ailment or other, which would of course not be a suitable issue, and they lost no time in combining together to dissuade Jia Zheng.

"Never mind," they said, "tomorrow will do to compose some device; let's drop it now."

Jia Zheng himself was inwardly afraid lest dowager lady Jia should be anxious, so that he hastily remarked as he forced a smile. "You beast, there are, after all, also occasions on which you are no good! but never mind! I'll give you one day to do it in, and if by tomorrow you haven't been able to compose anything, I shall certainly not let you off. This is the first and foremost place and you must exercise due care in what you write."

Saying this, he sallied out, at the head of the company, and cast another glance at the scenery.

Indeed from the time they had entered the gate up to this stage, they had just gone over five or six tenths of the whole ground, when it happened again that a servant came and reported that someone had arrived from Mr. Yucun's to deliver a message. "These several places (which remain)," Jia Zheng observed with a smile, "we have no time to pass under inspection; but we might as well nevertheless go out at least by that way, as we shall be able, to a certain degree, to have a look at the general aspect."

With these words, he showed the way for the family companions until they reached a large bridge, with water entering under it, looking like a curtain made of crystal. This bridge, the fact is, was the dam, which communicated with the river outside, and from which the stream was introduced into the grounds.

"What's the name of this water-gate?" Jia Zheng inquired.

"This is," replied Baoyu, "the main stream of the Qinfang river, and is therefore called the Qinfang water-gate."

"Nonsense!" exclaimed Jia Zheng. "The two words Qinfang must on no account be used!"

And as they speedily advanced on their way, they either came across elegant halls, or thatched cottages; walls made of piled-up stone, or gates fashioned of twisted plants; either a secluded nunnery or Buddhist fane, at the foot of some hill; or some unsullied houses, hidden in a grove, tenanted by rationalistic priestesses; either extensive corridors and winding grottoes; or square buildings, and circular pavilions. But Jia Zheng had not the energy to enter any of these places, for as he had not had any rest for ever so long, his legs felt shaky and his feet weak.

Suddenly they also discerned ahead of them a court disclose itself to view.

"When we get there," Jia Zheng suggested, "we must have a little rest." Straightway as he uttered the remark, he led them in, and winding round the jade-green peach-trees, covered with blossom, they passed through the bamboo fence and flower-laden hedge, which were twisted in such a way as to form a circular, cave-like gateway, when unexpectedly appeared before their eyes an enclosure with whitewashed walls, in which verdant willows drooped in every direction.

Jia Zheng entered the gateway in company with the whole party. Along the whole length of both sides extended covered passages, connected with each other; while in the court were laid out several rockeries. In one quarter were planted a number of banana trees; on the opposite stood a plant of begonia from Xifu. Its appearance was like an open umbrella. The gossamer hanging (from its branches) resembled golden threads. The corollas (seemed) to spurt out cinnabar.

"What a beautiful flower! what a beautiful flower!" ejaculated the whole party with one voice; "begonias are verily to be found; but never before have we seen anything the like of this in beauty."

"This is called the maiden begonia and is, in fact, a foreign species," Jia Zheng observed. "There's a homely tradition that it is because it emanates from the maiden kingdom that its flowers are most prolific; but this is likewise erratic talk and devoid of common sense."

"They are, after all," rejoined the whole company, "so unlike others (we have seen), that what's said about the maiden kingdom is, we are inclined to believe, possibly a fact."

"I presume," interposed Baoyu, "that some clever bard or poet, (perceiving) that this flower was red like cosmetic, delicate as if propped up in sickness, and that it closely resembled the nature of a young lady, gave it, consequently, the name of maiden! People in the world will propagate idle tales, all of which are unavoidably treated as gospel!"

"We receive (with thanks) your instructions; what excellent explanation!" they all remarked unanimously, and as they expressed these words, the whole company took their seats on the sofas under the colonnade.

"Let's think of some original text or other for a motto," Jia Zheng having suggested, one of the companions opined that the two characters: "Banana and stork" would be felicitous; while another one was of the idea that what would be faultless would be: "Collected splendor and waving elegance!"

"'Collected splendor and waving elegance' is excellent," Jia Zheng observed addressing himself to the party; and Baoyu himself, while also extolling it as beautiful, went on to say: "There's only one thing however to be regretted!"

"What about regret?" the company inquired.

"In this place," Baoyu explained, "are set out both bananas as well as begonias, with the intent of secretly combining in them the two properties of red and green; and if mention of one of them be made, and the other be omitted, (the device) won't be good enough for selection."

"What would you then suggest?" Jia Zheng asked.

"I would submit the four words, 'the red (flowers) are fragrant, the green (banana leaves) like jade,' which would render complete the beauties of both (the begonias and bananas)."

"It isn't good! it isn't good!" Jia Zheng remonstrated as he shook his head; and while passing this remark, he conducted the party into the house, where they noticed that the internal arrangements effected differed from those in other places, as no partitions could, in fact, be discerned. Indeed, the four sides were all alike covered with boards carved hollow with fretwork, (in designs consisting) either of rolling clouds and hundreds of bats; or of the three friends of the cold season of the year, (fir, bamboo, and almond); of scenery and human beings, or of birds or flowers; either of clusters of decoration, or of relics of olden times; either of ten thousand characters of happiness or of ten thousand characters of longevity. The various kinds of designs had been all carved by renowned hands, in variegated colors, inlaid with gold, and studded with precious gems; while on shelf upon shelf were either arranged collections of books, or tripods were laid out; either brushes and inkslabs were distributed about, or vases with flowers set out, or figured pots were placed about; the designs of the shelves being either round or square; or similar to sunflowers or banana leaves; or like links, half overlapping each other. And in very truth they resembled bouquets of flowers or clusters of tapestry, with all their fretwork so transparent. Suddenly (the eye was struck) by variegated gauzes pasted (on the wood-work), actually forming small windows; and of a sudden by fine thin silks lightly overshadowing (the fretwork) just as if there were, after all, secret doors. The whole walls were in addition traced, with no regard to symmetry, with outlines of the shapes of curios and nick-nacks in imitation of lutes, double-edged swords, hanging bottles and the like, the whole number of which, though (apparently) suspended on the walls, were all however on a same level with the surface of the partition walls.

"What fine ingenuity!" they all exclaimed extollingly; "what a labor they must have been to carry out!"

Jia Zheng had actually stepped in; but scarcely had they reached the second stage, before the whole party readily lost sight of the way by which they had come in. They glanced on the left, and there stood a door, through which they could go. They cast their eyes on the right, and there was a window which suddenly impeded their progress. They went forward, but there again they were obstructed by a bookcase. They turned their heads round, and there too stood windows pasted with transparent gauze and available doorways: but the moment they came face to face with the door, they unexpectedly perceived that a whole company of people had likewise walked in, just in front of them, whose appearance resembled their own in every respect. But it was only a mirror. And when they rounded the mirror, they detected a still larger number of doors.

"Sir," Jia Zhen remarked with a grin; "if you'll follow me out through this door, we'll forthwith get into the back-court; and once out of the back-court, we shall be, at all events, nearer than we were before."

Taking the lead, he conducted Jia Zheng and the whole party round two gauze mosquito houses, when they verily espied a door through which they made their exit, into a court, replete with stands of cinnamon roses. Passing round the flower-laden hedge, the only thing that spread before their view was a pure stream impeding their advance. The whole company was lost in admiration. "Where does this water again issue from?" they cried.

Jia Zhen pointed to a spot at a distance. "Starting originally," he explained, "from that water-gate, it runs as far as the mouth of that cave, when from among the hills on the northeast side, it is introduced into that village, where again a diverging channel has been opened and it is made to flow in a southwesterly direction; the whole volume of water then runs to this spot, where collecting once more in one place, it issues, on its outward course, from beneath that wall."

"It's most ingenious!" they one and all exclaimed, after they had listened to him; but, as they uttered these words, they unawares realized that a lofty hill obstructed any further progress. The whole party felt very hazy about the right road. But "Come along after me," Jia Zhen smilingly urged, as he at once went ahead and showed the way, whereupon the company followed in his steps, and as soon as they turned round the foot of the hill, a level place and broad road lay before them; and wide before their faces appeared the main entrance.

"This is charming! this is delightful!" the party unanimously exclaimed, "what wits must have been ransacked, and ingenuity attained, so as to bring things to this extreme degree of excellence!"

Forthwith the party egressed from the garden, and Baoyu's heart anxiously longed for the society of the young ladies in the inner quarters, but as he did not hear Jia Zheng bid him go, he had no help but to follow him into the library. But suddenly Jia Zheng bethought himself of him. "What," he said, "you haven't gone yet! the old lady will I fear be anxious on your account; and is it pray that you haven't as yet had enough walking?"

Baoyu at length withdrew out of the library. On his arrival in the court, a page, who had been in attendance on Jia Zheng, at once pressed forward, and took hold of him fast in his arms. "You've been lucky enough," he said, "today to have been in master's good graces! just a while back when our old mistress despatched servants to come on several occasions and ask after you, we replied that master was pleased with you; for had we given any other answer, her ladyship would have sent to fetch you to go in, and you wouldn't have had an opportunity of displaying your talents. Everyone admits that the several stanzas you recently composed were superior to those of the whole company put together; but you must, after the good luck you've had today, give us a tip!"

"I'll give each one of you a tiao," Baoyu rejoined smirkingly.

"Who of us hasn't seen a tiao?" they all exclaimed, "let's have that purse of yours, and have done with it!"

Saying this, one by one advanced and proceeded to unloosen the purse, and to unclasp the fan-case; and allowing Baoyu no time to make any remonstrance, they stripped him of every ornament in the way of appendage which he carried about on his person. "Whatever we do let's escort him home!" they shouted, and one after another hustled round him and accompanied him as far as dowager lady Jia's door.

Her ladyship was at this moment awaiting his arrival, so that when she saw him walk in, and she found out that (Jia Zheng) had not bullied him, she felt, of course, extremely delighted. But not a long interval elapsed before Xiren came to serve the tea; and when she perceived that on his person not one of the ornaments remained, she consequently smiled and inquired: "Have all the things that you had on you been again taken away by these barefaced rascals?"

As soon as Lin Daiyu heard this remark, she crossed over to him and saw at a glance that not one single trinket was, in fact, left. "Have you also given them," she felt constrained to ask, "the purse that I gave you? Well, by and by, when you again covet anything of mine, I shan't let you have it."

After uttering these words, she returned into her apartment in high dudgeon, and taking the scented bag, which Baoyu had asked her to make for him, and which she had not as yet finished, she picked up a pair of scissors, and instantly cut it to pieces.

Baoyu noticing that she had lost her temper, came after her with hurried step, but the bag had already been cut with the scissors; and as Baoyu observed how extremely fine and artistic this scented bag was, in spite of its unfinished state, he verily deplored that it should have been rent to pieces for no rhyme or reason. Promptly therefore unbuttoning his coat, he produced from inside the lapel the purse, which had been fastened there. "Look at this!" he remarked as he handed it to Daiyu; "what kind of thing is this! have I given away to any one what was yours?" Lin Daiyu, upon seeing how much he prized it as to wear it within his clothes, became alive to the fact that it was done with intent, as he feared lest anyone should take it away; and as this conviction made her sorry that she had been so impetuous as to have cut the scented bag, she lowered her head and uttered not a word.

"There was really no need for you to have cut it," Baoyu observed; "but as I know that you're loath to give me anything, what do you say to my returning even this purse?"

With these words, he threw the purse in her lap and walked off; which vexed Daiyu so much the more that, after giving way to tears, she took up the purse in her hands to also destroy it with the scissors, when Baoyu precipitately turned round and snatched it from her grasp.

"My dear cousin," he smilingly pleaded, "do spare it!" and as Daiyu dashed down the scissors and wiped her tears: "You needn't," she urged, "be kind to me at one moment, and unkind at another; if you wish to have a tiff, why then let's part company!" But as she spoke, she lost control over her temper, and, jumping on her bed, she lay with her face turned towards the inside, and set to work drying her eyes.

Baoyu could not refrain from approaching her. "My dear cousin, my own cousin," he added, "I confess my fault!"

"Go and find Baoyu!" dowager lady Jia thereupon gave a shout from where she was in the front apartment, and all the attendants explained that he was in Miss Lin's room.

"All right, that will do! that will do!" her ladyship rejoined, when she heard this reply; "let the two cousins play together; his father kept him a short while back under check, for ever so long, so let him have some distraction. But the only thing is that you mustn't allow them to have any quarrels." To which the servants in a body expressed their obedience.

Daiyu, unable to put up with Baoyu's importunity, felt compelled to rise. "Your object seems to be," she remarked, "not to let me have any rest. If it is, I'll run away from you." Saying which, she there and then was making her way out, when Baoyu protested with a face full of smiles: "Wherever you go, I'll follow!" and as he, at the same time, took the purse and began to fasten it on him, Daiyu stretched out her hand, and snatching it away, "You say you don't want it," she observed, "and now you put it on again! I'm really much ashamed on your account!" And these words were still on her lips when with a sound of "chi", she burst out laughing.

"My dear cousin," Baoyu added, "tomorrow do work another scented bag for me!"

"That too will rest upon my good pleasure," Daiyu rejoined.

As they conversed, they both left the room together and walked into Madame Wang's suite of apartments, where, as luck would have it, Baochai was also seated.

Unusual commotion prevailed, at this time, over at Madame Wang's, for the fact is that Jia Se had already come back from Gusu, where he had selected twelve young girls, and settled about an instructor, as well as about the theatrical properties and the other necessaries. And as Mrs. Xue had by this date moved her quarters into a separate place on the northeast side, and taken up her abode in a secluded and quiet house, (Madame Wang) had had repairs of a distinct character executed in the Pear Fragrance Court, and then issued directions that the instructor should train the young actresses in this place; and casting her choice upon all the women, who had, in days of old, received a training in singing, and who were now old matrons with white hair, she bade them have an eye over them and keep them in order. Which done, she enjoined Jia Se to assume the chief control of all matters connected with the daily and monthly income and outlay, as well as of the accounts of all articles in use of every kind and size.

Lin Zhixiao also came to report: "that the twelve young nuns and Daoist girls, who had been purchased after proper selection, had all arrived, and that the twenty newly-made Daoist coats had also been received. That there was besides a maiden, who though devoted to asceticism, kept her chevelure unshaved; that she was originally a denizen of Suchow, of a family whose ancestors were also people of letters and official status; that as from her youth up she had been stricken with much sickness, (her parents) had purchased a good number of substitutes (to enter the convent), but all with no relief to her, until at last this girl herself entered the gate of abstraction when she at once recovered. That hence it was that she grew her hair, while she devoted herself to an ascetic life; that she was this year eighteen years of age, and that the name given to her was Miaoyu; that her father and mother were, at this time, already dead; that she had only by her side, two old nurses and a young servant girl to wait upon her; that she was most proficient in literature, and exceedingly well versed in the classics and canons; and that she was likewise very attractive as far as looks went; that having heard that in the city of Chang'an, there were vestiges of Guanyin and relics of the canons inscribed on leaves, she followed, last year, her teacher (to the capital). She now lives," he said, "in the Mao Ni nunnery, outside the western gate; her teacher was a great expert in prophetic divination, but she died in the winter of last year, and her dying words were that as it was not suitable for (Miaoyu) to return to her native place, she should await here, as something in the way of a denouement was certain to turn up; and this is the reason why she hasn't as yet borne the coffin back to her home!"

"If such be the case," Madame Wang readily suggested, "why shouldn't we bring her here?"

"If we are to ask her," Lin Zhixiao's wife replied, "she'll say that a marquis' family and a duke's household are sure, in their honorable position, to be overbearing to people; and I had rather not go."

As she's the daughter of an official family," Madame Wang continued, "she's bound to be inclined to be somewhat proud; but what harm is there to our sending her a written invitation to ask her to come!"

Lin Zhixiao's wife assented; and leaving the room, she made the secretary write an invitation and then went to ask Miaoyu. The next day servants were despatched, and carriages and sedan chairs were got ready to go and bring her over.

What subsequently transpired is not as yet known, but, reader, listen to the account given in the following chapter.

CHAPTER 18

His Majesty shows magnanimous bounty.
The Imperial consort Yuan pays a visit to her
parents. The happiness of a family gathering.
Baoyu displays his polished talents.

But let us resume our story. A servant came, at this moment, to report that for the works in course of execution, they were waiting for gauze and damask silk to paste on various articles, and that they requested lady Feng to go and open the depot for them to take the gauze and silk, while another servant also came to ask lady Feng to open the treasury for them to receive the gold and silver ware. And as Madame Wang, the waiting-maids, and the other domestics of the upper rooms had all no leisure, Baochai suggested: "Don't let us remain in here and be in the way of their doing what there is to be done, and of going where they have to go," and saying this, she betook herself, escorted by Baoyu and the rest, into Yingchun's rooms.

Madame Wang continued day after day in a great state of flurry and confusion, straight up to within the tenth moon, by which time every arrangement had been completed, and the overseers had all handed in a clear statement of their accounts. The curios and writing materials, wherever needed, had all already been laid out and everything got ready, and the birds (and animals), from the stork, the deer, and rabbits to the chickens, geese, and the like, had all been purchased and handed over to be reared in the various localities in the garden; and over at Jia Se's, had also been learnt twenty miscellaneous plays, while a company of young nuns and Daoist priestesses had likewise the whole number of them, mastered the intonation of Buddhist classics and incantations.

Jia Zheng after this, at length, was slightly composed in mind, and cheerful at heart; and having further invited dowager lady Jia and other inmates to go into the garden, he deliberated with them on, and made arrangements for, every detail in such a befitting manner that not the least trifle remained for which suitable provision had not been made; and Jia Zheng eventually mustered courage to indite a memorial, and on the very day on which the memorial was presented, a decree was received fixing upon the fifteenth day of the first moon of the ensuing year, the very day of the Shang Yuan festival, for the honorable consorts to visit their homes.

Upon the receipt of this decree, with which the Jia family was honored, they had still less leisure, both by day as well as by night; so much so that they could not even properly observe the new year festivities. But in a twinkle of the eye, the festival of the full moon of the first moon drew near; and beginning from the eighth day of the first moon, eunuchs issued from the palace and inspected beforehand the various localities, the apartments in which the Imperial consort was to change her costume; the place where she would spend her leisure moments; the spot where she would receive the conventionalities; the premises where the banquets would be spread; the quarters where she would retire for rest.

There were also eunuchs who came to assume the patrol of the grounds and the direction of the defenses; and they brought along with them a good many minor eunuchs, whose duty it was to look after the safety of the various localities, to screen the place with enclosing curtains, to instruct the inmates and officials of the Jia mansion whither to go out and whence to come in from, what side the viands should be brought in from, where to report matters, and in the observance of every kind of etiquette; and for outside the mansion, there were, on the other hand, officers from the Board of Works, and a superintendent of the Police, of the "Five Cities," in charge of the sweeping of the streets and roads, and the clearing away of loungers. While Jia She and the others superintended the workmen in such things as the manufacture of flowered lanterns and fireworks.

The fourteenth day arrived and everything was in order; but on this night, one and all whether high or low, did not get a wink of sleep; and when the fifteenth came, everyone, at the fifth watch, beginning from dowager lady Jia and those who enjoyed any official status, appeared in full gala dress, according to their respective ranks. In the garden, the curtains were, by this time, flapping like dragons, the portieres flying about like phoenixes with variegated plumage. Gold and silver glistened with splendor. Pearls and precious gems shed out their brilliant luster. The tripod censers burnt the Baihe incense. In the vases were placed evergreens. Silence and stillness prevailed, and not a man ventured so much as to cough.

Jia She and the other men were standing outside the door giving on to the street on the west; and old lady Jia and the other ladies were outside the main entrance of the Rong mansion at the head of the street, while at the mouth of the lane were placed screens to rigorously obstruct the public gaze. They were unable to bear the fatigue of any further waiting when, at an unexpected moment, a eunuch arrived on horseback, and Jia Zheng went up to meet him, and ascertained what tidings he was the bearer of.

"It's as yet far too early," rejoined the eunuch, "for at one o'clock (her highness) will have her evening repast, and at two she has to betake herself to the Palace of Precious Perception to worship Buddha. At five, she will enter the Palace of Great Splendor to partake of a banquet, and to see the lanterns, after which, she will request His Majesty's permission; so that, I'm afraid, it won't be earlier than seven before they set out."

Lady Feng's ear caught what was said. "If such be the case," she interposed, "may it please your venerable ladyship, and you, my lady, to return for a while to your apartments, and wait; and if you come when it's time you'll be here none too late."

Dowager lady Jia and the other ladies immediately left for a time and suited their own convenience, and as everything in the garden devolved upon lady Feng to supervise, she ordered the butlers to take the eunuchs and give them something to eat and drink; and at the same time, she sent word that candles should be brought in and that the lanterns in the various places should be lit.

But unexpectedly was heard from outside the continuous patter of horses running, whereupon about ten eunuchs hurried in gasping and out of breath. They clapped their hands, and the several eunuchs (who had come before), understanding the signal, and knowing that the party had arrived, stood in their respective positions; while Jia She, at the head of all the men of the clan, remained at the western street door, and dowager lady Jia, at the head of the female relatives of the family, waited outside the principal entrance to do the honors.

For a long interval, everything was plunged in silence and quiet; when suddenly two eunuchs on horseback were espied advancing with leisurely step. Reaching the western street gate, they dismounted, and, driving their horses beyond the screens, they forthwith took their stand facing the west. After another long interval, a second couple arrived, and went likewise through the same proceedings. In a short time, drew near about ten couples, when, at length, were heard the gentle strains of music, and couple by couple advanced with banners, dragons, with fans made with phoenix feathers, and palace flabella of pheasant plumes; and those besides who carried gold-washed censers burning imperial incense. Next in order was brought past a state umbrella of golden yellow, with crooked handle and embroidered with seven phoenixes; after which quickly followed the crown, robe, girdle, and shoes.

There were likewise eunuchs who took a part in the procession, holding scented handkerchiefs and embroidered towels, cups for rinsing the mouth, dusters, and other such objects; and company after company went past, when, at the rear, approached with stately step eight eunuchs carrying an imperial sedan chair, of golden yellow, with a gold knob and embroidered with phoenixes.

Old lady Jia and the other members of the family hastily fell on their knees, but a eunuch came over at once to raise her ladyship and the rest; and the imperial chair was thereupon carried through the main entrance, the ceremonial gate and into a court on the eastern side, at the door of which stood a eunuch, who prostrated himself and invited (her highness) to dismount and change her costume.

Having forthwith carried her inside the gate, the eunuchs dispersed; and only the maids-of-honor and ladies-in-waiting ushered Yuanchun out of the chair, when what mainly attracted her eye in the park was the brilliant luster of the flowered lamps of every color, all of which were made of gauze or damask, and were beautiful in texture, and out of the common run; while on the upper side was a flat lantern with the inscription in four characters, "Regarded (by His Majesty's) benevolence and permeated by his benefits."

Yuanchun entered the apartment and effected the necessary changes in her toilette; after which, she again egressed, and, mounting her chair, she made her entry into the garden, when she perceived the smoke of incense whirling and twirling, and the reflection of the flowers confusing the eyes. Far and wide, the rays of light, shed by the lanterns, intermingled their brilliancy, while, from time to time, fine strains of music sounded with clamorous din. But it would be impossible to express adequately the perfect harmony in the aspect of this scene, and the grandeur of affluence and splendor.

The Imperial consort of the Jia family, we must now observe, upon catching sight, from the interior of her chair, of the picture presented within as well as without the confines of this garden, shook her head and heaved a sigh. "What lavish extravagance! What excessive waste!" she soliloquized.

But of a sudden was again seen a eunuch who, on his knees, invited her to get into a boat; and the Jia consort descended from the chair and stepped into the craft, when the expanse of a limpid stream met her gaze, whose grandeur resembled that of the dragon in its listless course. The stone bannisters, on each side, were one mass of air-tight lanterns, of every color, made of crystal or glass, which threw out a light like the luster of silver or the brightness of snow.

The willow, almond, and the whole lot of trees, on the upper side, were, it is true, without blossom and leaves; but pongee and damask silks, paper and lustring had been employed, together with rice-paper, to make flowers of which had been affixed on the branches. Upon each tree were suspended thousands of lanterns; and what is more, the lotus and aquatic plants, the ducks and water fowl in the pond had all, in like manner, been devised out of conches and clams, plumes and feathers. The various lanterns, above and below, vied in refulgence. In real truth, it was a crystal region, a world of pearls and precious stones. On board the boat were also every kind of lanterns representing such designs as are used on flower-pots, pearl-laden portieres, embroidered curtains, oars of cinnamon wood, and paddles of magnolia, which need not of course be minutely described.

They entered a landing with a stone curb; and on this landing was erected a flat lantern upon which were plainly visible the four characters the "Persicary beach and flower-laden bank." But, reader, you have heard how that these four characters "the persicary beach and the flower-laden bank," the motto "a phoenix comes with dignified air," and the rest owe one and all their origin to the unexpected test to which Jia Zheng submitted, on a previous occasion, Baoyu's literary abilities; but how did it come about that they were actually adopted?

You must remember that the Jia family had been, generation after generation, given to the study of letters, so that it was only natural that there should be among them one or two renowned writers of verses; for how could they ever resemble the families of such upstarts, who only employ puerile expressions as a makeshift to get through what they have to do? But the why and the wherefore must be sought in the past. The consort, belonging to the Jia mansion, had, before she entered the palace, been, from her infancy, also brought up by dowager lady Jia; and when Baoyu was subsequently added to the family, she was the eldest sister and Baoyu the youngest child. The Jia consort, bearing in mind how that she had, when her mother was verging on old age, at length obtained this younger brother, she for this reason doated upon him with single love; and as they were besides companions in their attendance upon old lady Jia, they were inseparable for even a moment. Before Baoyu had entered school, and when three or four years of age, he had already received oral instruction from the Imperial spouse Jia from the contents of several books and had committed to memory several thousands of characters, for though they were only sister and brother, they were like mother and child. And after she had entered the Palace, she was wont time and again to have letters taken out to her father and her cousins, urgently recommending them to be careful with his bringing up, that if they were not strict, he could not possibly become good for anything, and that if they were immoderately severe, there was the danger of something unpropitious befalling him, with the result, moreover, that his grandmother would be stricken with sorrow; and this solicitude on his account was never for an instant lost sight of by her.

Hence it was that Jia Zheng having, a few days back, heard his teacher extol him for his extreme abilities, he forthwith put him to the test on the occasion of their ramble through the garden. And though (his compositions) were not in the bold style of a writer of note, yet they were productions of their own family, and would, moreover, be instrumental, when the Jia consort had her notice attracted by them, and come to know that they were devised by her beloved brother, in also not rendering nugatory the anxious interest which she had ever entertained on his behalf, and he, therefore, purposely adopted what had been suggested by Baoyu; while for those places, for which on that day no devices had been completed, a good number were again subsequently composed to make up what was wanted.

After the Jia consort had, for we shall now return to her, perused the four characters, she gave a smile. "The two words 'flower-laden bank,'" she said, "are really felicitous, so what use was there for 'persicary beach?'"

When the eunuch in waiting heard this observation, he promptly jumped off the craft on to the bank, and at a flying pace hurried to communicate it to Jia Zheng, and Jia Zheng instantly effected the necessary alteration.

By this time the craft had reached the inner bank, and leaving the boat, and mounting into her sedan chair, she in due course contemplated the magnificent Jade-like Palace; the Hall of cinnamon wood, lofty and sublime; and the marble portals with the four characters in bold style: the "Precious confines of heavenly spirits," which the Jia consort gave directions should be changed for the four words denoting: "additional Hall (for the imperial consort) on a visit to her parents." And forthwith making her entrance into the traveling lodge her gaze was attracted by torches burning in the court encompassing the heavens, fragments of incense strewn on the ground, fire-like trees and gem-like flowers, gold-like windows and jade-like bannisters. But it would be difficult to give a full account of the curtains, which rolled up (as fine as a) shrimp's moustache; of the carpets of other skins spread on the floor; of the tripods exhaling the fragrant aroma of the brain of the musk deer; of the screens in a row resembling fans made of pheasant tails. Indeed, the gold-like doors and the windows like jade were suggestive of the abode of spirits; while the halls made of cinnamon wood and the palace of magnolia timber, of the very homes of the Imperial secondary consorts.

"Why is it," the Jia consort inquired, "that there is no tablet in this Hall?"

The eunuch in waiting fell on his knees. "This is the main Hall," he reverently replied, "and the officials, outside the palace, did not presume to take upon themselves to suggest any motto."

The Jia consort shook her head and said not a word; whereupon the eunuch, who acted as master of ceremonies, requested Her Majesty to ascend the throne and receive homage. The band stationed on the two flights of steps struck up a tune, while two eunuchs ushered Jia She, Jia Zheng, and the other members on to the moon-like stage, where they arranged themselves in order and ascended into the hall, but when the ladies-in-waiting transmitted her commands that the homage could be dispensed with, they at once retraced their footsteps.

(The master of the ceremonies), in like manner led forward the dowager lady of the Rong Guo mansion, as well as the female relatives, from the steps on the east side, on to the moon-like stage; where they were placed according to their ranks. But the maids-of-honor again commanded that they should dispense with the ceremony, so they likewise promptly withdrew.

After tea had been thrice presented, the Jia consort descended the Throne, and the music ceased. She retired into a side room to change her costume, and the private chairs were then got ready for her visit to her parents. Issuing from the garden, she came into the main quarters belonging to dowager lady Jia, where she was bent upon observing the domestic conventionalities, when her venerable ladyship, and the other members of the family, prostrated themselves in a body before her, and made her desist. Tears dropped down from the eyes of the Jia consort as (she and her relatives) mutually came forward, and greeted each other, and as with one hand she grasped old lady Jia, and with the other she held Madame Wang, the three had plenty in their hearts which they were fain to speak about; but, unable as each one of them was to give utterance to their feelings, all they did was to sob and to weep, as they kept face to face to each other; while Madame Xing, widow Li Wan, Wang Xifeng, and the three sisters: Yingchun, Tanchun, and Xichun, stood aside in a body shedding tears and saying not a word.

After a long time, the Jia consort restrained her anguish, and forcing a smile, she set to work to reassure old lady Jia and Madame Wang.

"Having in days gone by," she urged, "been sent to that place where no human being can be seen, I have today after extreme difficulty returned home; and now that you ladies and I have been reunited, instead of chatting or laughing we contrariwise give way to incessant tears! But shortly, I shall be gone, and who knows when we shall be able again to even see each other!"

When she came to this sentence, they could not help bursting into another fit of crying; and Madame Xing hastened to come forward, and to console dowager lady Jia and the rest. But when the Jia consort resumed her seat, and one by one came again, in turn, to exchange salutations, they could not once more help weeping and sobbing for a time.

Next in order, were the managers and servants of the eastern and western mansions to perform their obeisance in the outer pavilion; and after the married women and waiting-maids had concluded their homage, the Jia consort heaved a sigh. "How many relatives," she observed, "there are all of whom, alas! I may not see."

"There are here now," Madame Wang rejoined with due respect, "kindred with outside family names, such as Mrs. Xue, nee Wang, Baochai, and Daiyu waiting for your commands; but as they are distant relatives, and without official status, they do not venture to arrogate to themselves the right of entering into your presence." But the Jia consort issued directions that they should be invited to come that they should see each other; and in a short while, Mrs. Xue and the other relatives walked in, but as they were on the point of performing the rites, prescribed by the state, she bade them relinquish the observance so that they came forward, and each, in turn, alluded to what had transpired during the long separation.

Baoqin also and a few other waiting-maids, whom the Jia consort had originally taken along with her into the palace, knocked their heads before dowager lady Jia, but her ladyship lost no time in raising them up, and in bidding them go into a separate suite of rooms to be entertained; and as for the retainers, eunuchs as well as maids-of-honor, ladies-in-waiting and every attendant, there were needless to say, those in the two places, the Ning mansion and Jia She's residence, to wait upon them; there only remained three or four young eunuchs to answer the summons.

The mother and daughter and her cousins conversed for some time on what had happened during the protracted separation, as well as on domestic affairs and their private feelings, when Jia Zheng likewise advanced as far as the other side of the portiere, and inquired after her health, and the Jia consort from inside performed the homage and other conventionalities (due to her parent).

"The families of farmers," she further went on to say to her father, "feed on salted cabbage, and clothe in cotton material; but they readily enjoy the happiness of the relationships established by heaven! We, however, relatives though we now be of one bone and flesh, are, with all our affluence and honors, living apart from each other, and deriving no happiness whatsoever!"

Jia Zheng, on his part endeavored, to restrain his tears. "I belonged," he rejoined, "to a rustic and poor family; and among that whole number of pigeons and pheasants, how could I have imagined that I would have obtained the blessing of a hidden phoenix! Of late all for the sake of your honorable self, His Majesty, above, confers upon us his heavenly benefits; while we, below, show forth the virtue of our ancestors! And it is mainly because the vital principle of the hills, streams, sun, and moon, and the remote virtue of our ancestors have been implanted in you alone that this good fortune has attained me Zheng and my wife! Moreover, the present emperor, bearing in mind the great bounty shewn by heaven and earth in promoting a ceaseless succession, has vouchsafed a more generous act of grace than has ever been displayed from old days to the present. And although we may besmear our liver and brain in the mire, how could we show our gratitude, even to so slight a degree as one ten-thousandth part. But all I can do is, in the daytime, to practise diligence, vigilance at night, and loyalty in my official duties. My humble wish is that His Majesty, my master, may live ten thousand years and see thousands of autumns, so as to promote the welfare of all mankind in the world! And you, worthy Imperial consort, must, on no account, be mindful of me Zheng and my wife, decrepid as we are in years. What I would solicit more than anything is that you should be more careful of yourself, and that you should be diligent and reverential in your service to His Majesty, with the intent that you may not prove ungrateful of his affectionate regard and bountiful grace."

The Jia consort, on the other hand, enjoined "that much as it was expedient to display zeal, in the management of state matters, it behoved him, when he had any leisure, to take good care of himself, and that he should not, whatever he did, give way to solicitude on her behalf." And Jia Zheng then went on to say "that the various inscriptions in the park over the pavilions, terraces, halls, and residences had been all composed by Baoyu, and, that in the event of there being one or two that could claim her attention, he would be happy if it would please her to at once favor him with its name." Whereupon the Imperial consort Yuan, when she heard that Baoyu could compose verses, forthwith exclaimed with a smile: "He has in very truth made progress!"

After Jia Zheng had retired out of the hall, the Jia consort made it a point to ask: "How is it that I do not see Baoyu?" and dowager lady Jia explained: "An outside male relative as he is, and without official rank, he does not venture to appear before you of his own accord."

"Bring him in!" the Imperial consort directed; whereupon a young eunuch ushered Baoyu in. After he had first complied with the state ceremonies, she bade him draw near to her, and taking his hand, she held it in her lap, and, as she went on to caress his head and neck, she smiled and said: "He's grown considerably taller than he was before;" but she had barely concluded this remark, when her tears ran down as profuse as rain. Mrs. You, lady Feng, and the rest pressed forward. "The banquet is quite ready," they announced, "and your highness is requested to favor the place with your presence."

The Imperial consort Yuan stood up and asking Baoyu to lead the way, she followed in his steps, along with the whole party, and betook herself on foot as far as the entrance of the garden gate, whence she at once espied, in the luster shed by the lanterns, every kind of decorations. Entering the garden, they first passed the spots with the device "a phoenix comes with dignified air," "the red (flowers are) fragrant and the green (banana leaves) like jade!" "the sign on the apricot tree is visible," "the fragrance pure of the ligularia and iris," and other places; and ascending the towers they walked up the halls, forded the streams, and wound round the hills; contemplating as they turned their gaze from side to side, each place arranged in a different style, and each kind of article laid out in unique designs. The Jia consort expressed her admiration in most profuse eulogiums, and then went on to advise them: "that it was not expedient to indulge in future in such excessive extravagance and that all these arrangements were over and above what should have been done."

Presently they reached the main pavilion, where she commanded that they could dispense with the rites and take their seats. A sumptuous banquet was laid out, at which dowager lady Jia and the other ladies occupied the lower seats and entertained each other, while Mrs. You, widow Li Wan, lady Feng, and the rest presented the soup and handed the cups. The Imperial consort Yuan subsequently directed that the brushes and inkslabs should be brought, and with her own hands she opened the silken paper. She chose the places she liked, and conferred upon them a name; and devising a general designation for the garden, she called it the Daguan garden (Broad vista), while for the tablet of the main pavilion the device she composed ran as follows: "Be mindful of the grace and remember the equity (of His Majesty);" with this inscription on the antithetical scrolls:

Mercy excessive Heaven and earth display,
And it men young and old hail gratefully;
From old till now they pour their bounties great
Those rich gifts which Cathay and all states permeate.

Changing also the text: "A phoenix comes with dignified air for the Xiaoxiang Lodge."

"The red (flowers are) fragrant and the green (banana leaves) like jade," she altered into "Happy red and joyful green;" bestowing upon the place the appellation of the I Hung court (joyful red). The spot where "the fragrance pure of the ligularia and iris," was inscribed, she called "the ligularia and the 'Wu' weed court;" and where was "the sign in the apricot tree is visible," she designated "the cottage in the hills where dolichos is bleached." The main tower she called the Broad Vista Tower. The lofty tower facing the east, she designated "the variegated and flowery Hall;" bestowing on the line of buildings, facing the west, the appellation of "the Hall of Occult Fragrance;" and besides these figured such further names as: "the Hall of peppery wind," "the Arbor of lotus fragrance," "the Islet of purple caltrop," "the Bank of golden lotus," and the like. There were also tablets with four characters such as: "the peach blossom and the vernal rain;" "the autumnal wind prunes the Eloecocca," "the artemisia leaves and the night snow," and other similar names which could not all be placed on record. She furthermore directed that such tablets as were already put up, should not be dismounted, and she forthwith took the lead and composed an heptameter stanza, the burden of which was:

Hills it enclasps, embraces streams, with skill it is laid out:
What task the grounds to raise! the works to start and bring about!
Of scenery in heaven and amongst men store has been made;
The name Broad Vista o'er the fragrant park should be engraved.

When she had finished writing, she observed smilingly, as she addressed herself to all the young ladies: "I have all along lacked the quality of sharpness and never besides been good at verses; as you, sisters, and all of you have ever been aware; but, on a night like this I've been fain to do my best, with the object of escaping censure, and of not reflecting injustice on this scenery and nothing more. But some other day when I've got time, be it ever so little, I shall deem it my duty to make up what remains by inditing a record of the Broad Vista Garden, as well as a song on my visit to my parents and other such literary productions in memory of the events of this day. You sisters and others must, each of you, in like manner compose a stanza on the motto on each tablet, expressing your sentiments, as you please, without being restrained by any regard for my meager ability. Knowing as I do besides that Baoyu is, indeed, able to write verses, I feel the more delighted! But among his compositions, those I like the best are those in the two places, 'the Xiaoxiang Lodge,' and 'the court of Heng and Wu;' and next those of 'the Joyful red court,' and 'the cottage in the hills, where the dolichos is bleached.' As for grand sites like these four, there should be found some out-of-the-way expressions to insert in the verses so that they should be felicitous. The antithetical lines composed by you, (Baoyu), on a former occasion are excellent, it is true; but you should now further indite for each place, a pentameter stanza, so that by allowing me to test you in my presence, you may not show yourself ungrateful for the trouble I have taken in teaching you from your youth up."

Baoyu had no help but to assent, and descending from the hall, he went off all alone to give himself up to reflection.

Of the three Yingchun, Tanchun, and Xichun, Tanchun must be considered to have also been above the standard of her sisters, but she, in her own estimation, imagined it, in fact, difficult to compete with Xue Baochai and Lin Daiyu. With no alternative however than that of doing her best, she followed the example of all the rest with the sole purpose of warding off criticism. And Li Wan too succeeded, after much exertion, in putting together a stanza.

The consort of the Jia family perused in due order the verses written by the young ladies, the text of which is given below.

The lines written by Yingchun on the tablet of "Boundless spirits and blissful heart" were:

> A park laid out with scenery surpassing fine and rare!
> Submissive to thy will, on boundless bliss bashful I write!
> Who could believe that yonder scenes in this world found a share!
> Will not thy heart be charmed on thy visit by the sight?

These are the verses by Tanchun on the tablet of "All nature vies in splendor":

> Of aspect lofty and sublime is raised a park of fame!
> Honored with thy bequest, my shallow lore fills me with shame.
> No words could e'er amply exhaust the beauteous skill,
> For lo! in very truth glory and splendor all things fill!

Thus runs Xichun's stanza on the tablet of the "Conception of literary compositions":

> The hillocks and the streams crosswise beyond a thousand li extend!
> The towers and terraces 'midst the five-colored clouds lofty ascend!
> In the resplendent radiance of both sun and moon the park it lies!
> The skill these scenes to raise the skill e'en essays to conceive outvies!

The lines composed by Li Wan on the tablet "grace and elegance," consisted of:

> The comely streams and hillocks clear, in double folds, embrace;
> E'en Fairyland, forsooth, transcend they do in elegance and grace!
> The "Fragrant Plant" the theme is of the ballad fan, green-made.
> Like drooping plum-bloom flap the lapel red and the Xiang gown.
> From prosperous times must have been handed down those pearls and jade.
> What bliss! the fairy on the jasper terrace will come down!
> When to our prayers she yields, this glorious park to contemplate,
> No mortal must e'er be allowed these grounds to penetrate.

The ode by Xue Baochai on the tablet of "Concentrated splendor and accumulated auspiciousness" was:

> Raised on the west of the Imperial city, lo! the park stored with fragrant smell,
> Shrouded by Phoebe's radiant rays and clouds of good omen, in wondrous glory lies!
> The willows tall with joy exult that the parrots their nests have shifted from the dell.
> The bamboo groves, when laid, for the phoenix with dignity to come, were meant to rise.
> The very eve before the Empress' stroll, elegant texts were ready and affixed.
> If even she her parents comes to see, how filial piety supreme must be!
> When I behold her beauteous charms and talents supernatural, with awe transfixed,
> One word, to utter more how can I troth ever presume, when shame overpowers me.

The distich by Lin Daiyu on the tablet of "Spiritual stream outside the world," ran thus:

Th' imperial visit doth enhance joy and delight.
This fairy land from mortal scenes what diff'rent sight!
The comely grace it borrows of both hill and stream;
And to the landscape it doth add a charm supreme.
The fumes of Jin Gu wine everything permeate;
The flowers the inmate of the Jade Hall fascinate.
The Imperial favor to receive how blessed our lot!
For oft the palace carriage will pass through this spot.

The Jia consort having concluded the perusal of the verses, and extolled them for a time: "After all," she went on to say with a smile, "those composed by my two cousins, Xue Baochai and Lin Daiyu, differ in excellence from those of all the rest; and neither I, stupid as I am, nor my sisters can attain their standard."

Lin Daiyu had, in point of fact, made up her mind to display, on this evening, her extraordinary abilities to their best advantage, and to put down everyone else, but contrary to her expectations the Jia consort had expressed her desire that no more than a single stanza should be written on each tablet, so that unable, after all, to disregard her directions by writing anything in excess, she had no help but to compose a pentameter stanza, in an offhand way, merely with the intent of complying with her wishes.

Baoyu had by this time not completed his task. He had just finished two stanzas on the Xiaoxiang Lodge and the Hengwu garden, and was just then engaged in composing a verse on the "Happy red Court." In his draft figured a line: "The (leaves) of jade-like green in spring are yet rolled up," which Baochai stealthily observed as she turned her eyes from side to side; and availing herself of the very first moment, when none of the company could notice her, she gave him a nudge. "As her highness," she remarked, "doesn't relish the four characters, representing the red (flowers are) fragrant, and the green (banana leaves) like jade, she changed them, just a while back, for 'the joyful red and gladsome green;' and if you deliberately now again employ these two words 'jade-like green,' won't it look as if you were bent upon being at variance with her? Besides, very many are the old books, in which the banana leaves form the theme, so you had better think of another line and substitute it and have done with it!"

When Baoyu heard the suggestion made by Baochai, he speedily replied, as he wiped off the perspiration: "I can't at all just at present call to mind any passage from the contents of some old book."

"Just simply take," proposed Baochai smilingly, "the character jade in jade-like green and change it into the character wax, that's all."

"Does 'green wax,'" Baoyu inquired, "come out from anywhere?"

Baochai gently smacked her lips and nodded her head as she laughed. "I fear," she said, "that if, on an occasion like tonight, you show no more brains than this, by and by when you have to give any answers in the golden hall, to the questions (of the examiner), you will, really, forget (the very first four names) of Zhao, Qian, Sun, and Li (out of the hundred)! What, have you so much as forgotten the first line of the poem by Han Yu, of the T'ang dynasty, on the Banana leaf:

"Cold is the candle and without a flame, the green wax dry?"

On hearing these words, Baoyu's mind suddenly became enlightened. "What a fool I am!" he added with a simper; "I couldn't for the moment even remember the lines, ready-made though they were and staring at me in my very eyes! Sister, you really can be styled my teacher, little though you may have taught me, and I'll henceforward address you by no other name than 'teacher,' and not call you 'sister' any more!"

"Don't you yet hurry to go on," Baochai again observed in a gentle tone of voice sneeringly, "but keep on calling me elder sister and younger sister? Who's your sister? that one over there in a yellow coat is your sister!"

But apprehending, as she bandied these jokes, lest she might be wasting his time, she felt constrained to promptly move away; whereupon Baoyu continued the ode he had been working at, and brought it to a close, writing in all three stanzas.

Daiyu had not had so far an opportunity of making a display of her ability, and was feeling at heart in a very dejected mood; but when she perceived that Baoyu was having intense trouble in conceiving what he had to write, and she found, upon walking up to the side of the table, that he had only one stanza short, that on "the sign on the apricot tree is visible," she consequently bade him copy out clean the first three odes, while she herself composed a stanza, which she noted down on a slip of paper, rumpled up into a ball, and threw just in front of Baoyu.

As soon as Baoyu opened it and glanced at it, he realised that it was a hundred times better than his own three stanzas, and transcribing it without loss of time, in a bold writing, he handed up his compositions.

On perusal, the Jia Consort read what follows.

On: "A phoenix comes with dignified air":

The bamboos just now don that jade-like grace,
Which worthy makes them the pheasant to face;
Each culm so tender as if to droop fain,
Each one so verdant, in aspect so cool,
The curb protects, from the steps wards the pool.
The pervious screens the tripod smell restrain.
The shadow will be strewn, mind do not shake
And (Xue) from her now long fine dream (awake)!

On "the pure fragrance of the Ligularia and Iris Florentina":

Hengs and Wus the still park permeate;
The luos and pis their sweet perfume enhance;
And supple charms the third spring flowers ornate;
Softly is wafted one streak of fragrance!
A light mist doth becloud the tortuous way!
With moist the clothes bedews, that verdure cold!
The pond who ever sinuous could hold?
Dreams long and subtle, dream the household Xue.

On "the happy red and joyful green":

Stillness pervades the deep pavilion on a lengthy day.
The green and red, together matched, transcendent grace display.
Unfurled do still remain in spring the green and waxlike leaves.
No sleep yet seeks the red-clad maid, though night's hours be far-
   spent,
But o'er the rails lo, she reclines, dangling her ruddy sleeves;
Against the stone she leans shrouded by taintless scent,
And stands the quarter facing whence doth blow the eastern
   wind!
Her lord and master must look up to her with feelings kind.

On "the sign on the apricot tree is visible":

The apricot tree sign to drink wayfarers doth invite;
A farm located on a hill, lo! yonder strikes the sight!
And water caltrops, golden lotus, geese, as well as flows,
And mulberry and elm trees which afford rest to swallows.
That wide extent of spring leeks with verdure covers the ground;
And o'er ten li the paddy blossom fragrance doth abound.

In days of plenty there's a lack of dearth and of distress,
And what need then is there to plough and weave with such brisk-
ness?

When the Jia consort had done with the perusal, excessive joy filled
her heart. "He has indeed made progress!" she exclaimed, and went
on to point at the verses on "the sign on the apricot tree," as being
the crowning piece of the four stanzas. In due course, she with her
own hands changed the motto "a cottage in the hills where dolichos
is bleached" into "the paddy-scented village;" and bidding also Tanchun to take the several tens of stanzas written then, and to transcribe
them separately on ornamented silk paper, she commanded a eunuch
to send them to the outer quarters. And when Jia Zheng and the other
men perused them, one and all sung their incessant praise, while Jia
Zheng, on his part, sent in some complimentary message, with regard
to her return home on a visit.

Yuanchun went further and gave orders that luscious wines, a ham,
and other such presents should be conferred upon Baoyu, as well as
upon Jia Lan. This Jia Lan was as yet at this time a perfect youth without any knowledge of things in general, so that all that he could do was
to follow the example of his mother, and imitate his uncle in performing the conventional rites.

At the very moment that Jia Se felt unable, along with a company of
actresses, to bear the ordeal of waiting on the ground floor of the two-
storied building, he caught sight of a eunuch come running at a flying
pace. "The composition of verses is over," he said, "so quick give me the
programme;" whereupon Jia Se hastened to present the programme as
well as a roll of the names of the twelve girls. And not a long interval
elapsed before four plays were chosen; No. 1 being the Imperial Banquet; No. 2 Begging (the weaver goddess) for skill in needlework; No.
3 The spiritual match; and No. 4 the Parting spirit. Jia Se speedily lent
a hand in the getting up, and the preparations for the performance,
and each of the girls sang with a voice sufficient to split the stones and
danced in the manner of heavenly spirits; and though their exterior
was that of the characters in which they were dressed up for the play,
their acting nevertheless represented, in a perfect manner, both sorrow
as well as joy. As soon as the performance was brought to a close, a
eunuch walked in holding a golden salver containing cakes, sweets, and
the like, and inquired who was Ling Guan; and Jia Se readily concluding that these articles were presents bestowed upon Ling Guan, made
haste to take them over, as he bade Ling Guan prostrate herself.

"The honorable consort," the eunuch further added, "directs that Ling Guan, who is the best actress of the lot, should sing two more songs; any two will do, she does not mind what they are."

Jia Se at once expressed his obedience, and felt constrained to urge Ling Guan to sing the two ballads entitled "The walk through the garden" and "Frightened out of a dream." But Ling Guan asserted that these two ballads had not originally been intended for her own role; and being firm in her refusal to accede and insisting upon rendering the two songs "The Mutual Promise" and "The Mutual Abuse," Jia Se found it hard to bring her round, and had no help but to let her have her own way. The Jia consort was so extremely enchanted with her that she gave directions that she should not be treated harshly, and that this girl should receive a careful training, while besides the fixed number of presents, she gave her two rolls of palace silk, two purses, gold and silver ingots, and presents in the way of eatables.

Subsequently, when the banquet had been cleared, and she once more prosecuted her visit through those places to which she had not been, she quite accidentally espied the Buddhist Temple encircled by hills, and promptly rinsing her hands, she walked in and burnt incense and worshipped Buddha. She also composed the device for a tablet, "a humane boat on the (world's) bitter sea," and went likewise so far as to show special acts of additional grace to a company of ascetic nuns and Daoist priestesses.

A eunuch came in a short while and reverently fell on his knees. "The presents are all in readiness," he reported, "and may it please you to inspect them and to distribute them, in compliance with custom;" and presented to her a list, which the Jia consort perused from the very top throughout without raising any objection, and readily commanding that action should be taken according to the list, a eunuch descended and issued the gifts one after another. The presents for dowager lady Jia consisted, it may be added, of two scepters, one of gold, the other of jade, with "may your wishes be fulfilled" inscribed on them; a staff made of lign-aloes; a string of chaplet beads of Jia'nan fragrant wood; four rolls of imperial satins with words "Affluence and honors" and "Perennial Spring" (woven in them); four rolls of imperial silk with Perennial Happiness and Longevity; two shoes of purple gold bullion, representing a brush, an ingot, and "as you like;" and ten silver ingots with the device "Felicitous Blessings." While the two shares for Madame Xing and Madame Wang were only short of hers by the scepters and staffs, four things in all. Jia She, Jia Zheng, and the others had each apportioned to him a work newly written by the Emperor, two boxes of superior ink, and gold and silver cups, two pairs of each; their other gifts being identical with those above. Baochai, Daiyu, all the sisters and the rest were assigned each a copy of a new book, a fine slab, and two pair of gold and silver ornaments of a novel kind and original shape; Baoyu likewise receiving the same presents. Jia Lan's gifts consisted of two necklets, one of gold, the other of silver, and of two pair of gold ingots. Mrs. You, widow Li Wan, lady Feng, and the others had each of them, four ingots of gold and silver; and, in the way of keepsakes, four pieces of silk. There were, in addition, presents consisting of twenty-four pieces of silk and a thousand strings of good cash to be allotted to the nurses, and waiting-maids, in the apartments of dowager lady Jia, Madame Wang and of the respective sisters; while Jia Zhen, Jia Lian, Jia Huan, Jia Rong, and the rest had, everyone, for presents, a piece of silk, and a pair of gold and silver ingots.

As regards the other gifts, there were a hundred rolls of various colored silks, a thousand ounces of pure silver, and several bottles of imperial wine, intended to be bestowed upon all the men-servants of the mansions, on the East and the West, as well as upon those who had been in the garden overseeing works, arranging the decorations, and in waiting to answer calls, and upon those who looked after the theaters and managed the lanterns. There being, besides, five hundred strings of pure cash for the cooks, waiters, jugglers, and hundreds of actors and every kind of domestic.

The whole party had finished giving expression to their thanks for her bounty, when the managers and eunuchs respectfully announced: "It is already a quarter to three, and may it please your Majesty to turn back your Imperial chariot;" whereupon, much against her will, the Jia consort's eyes brimmed over, and she once more gave vent to tears. Forcing herself however again to put on a smile, she clasped old lady Jia's and Madame Wang's hands, and could not bring herself to let them go; while she repeatedly impressed upon their minds that there was no need to give way to any solicitude, and that they should take good care of their healths; that the grace of the present emperor was so vast, that once a month he would grant permission for them to enter the palace and pay her a visit. "It is easy enough for us to see each other," (she said,) "and why should we indulge in any excess of grief? But when his majesty in his heavenly generosity allows me another time to return home, you shouldn't go in for such pomp and extravagance."

Dowager lady Jia and the other inmates had already cried to such an extent that sobs choked their throats and they could with difficulty give utterance to speech. But though the Jia consort could not reconcile herself to the separation, the usages in vogue in the Imperial household could not be disregarded or infringed, so that she had no alternative but to stifle the anguish of her heart, to mount her chariot, and take her departure.

The whole family experienced meanwhile a hard task before they succeeded in consoling the old lady and Madame Wang and in supporting them away out of the garden. But as what follows is not ascertained, the next chapter will disclose it.

CHAPTER 19

In the vehemence of her feelings, Hua (Xiren) on a quiet evening admonishes Baoyu. While (the spell) of affection continues unbroken, Baoyu, on a still day, perceives the fragrance emitted from Daiyu's person.

The Jia consort, we must now go on to explain, returned to the Palace, and the next day, on her appearance in the presence of His Majesty, she thanked him for his bounty and gave him furthermore an account of her experiences on her visit home. His Majesty's dragon countenance was much elated, and he also issued from the privy store colored satins, gold and silver and such like articles to be presented to Jia Zheng and the other officials in the various households of her relatives. But dispensing with minute details about them, we will now revert to the two mansions of Rong and Ning.

With the extreme strain on mind and body for successive days, the strength of one and all was, in point of fact, worn out and their respective energies exhausted. And it was besides after they had been putting by the various decorations and articles of use for two or three days, that they, at length, got through the work.

Lady Feng was the one who had most to do, and whose responsibilities were greatest. The others could possibly steal a few leisure moments and retire to rest, while she was the sole person who could not slip away. In the second place, naturally anxious as she was to excel and not to fall in people's estimation, she put up with the strain just as if she were like one of those who had nothing to attend to. But the one who had the least to do and had the most leisure was Baoyu.

As luck would have it on this day, at an early hour, Xiren's mother came again in person and told dowager lady Jia that she would take Xiren home to drink a cup of tea brewed in the new year and that she would return in the evening. For this reason Baoyu was only in the company of all the waiting-maids, throwing dice, playing at chess and amusing himself. But while he was in the room playing with them with a total absence of zest, he unawares perceived a few waiting-maids arrive, who informed him that their senior master Mr. Zhen, of the Eastern Mansion, had come to invite him to go and see a theatrical performance, and the fireworks, which were to be let off.

Upon hearing these words, Baoyu speedily asked them to change his clothes; but just as he was ready to start, presents of cream, steamed with sugar, arrived again when least expected from the Jia Consort, and Baoyu recollecting with what relish Xiren had partaken of this dish on the last occasion forthwith bid them keep it for her; while he went himself and told dowager lady Jia that he was going over to see the play.

The plays sung over at Jia Zhen's consisted, who would have thought it, of "Dinglang recognises his father," and "Huang Boyang deploys the spirits for battle," and in addition to these, "Sun Xingzhe causes great commotion in the heavenly palace;" "Jiang Taikong kills the general and deifies him," and other such like. Soon appeared the spirits and devils in a confused crowd on the stage, and suddenly also became visible the whole band of sprites and goblins, among which were some waving streamers, as they went past in a procession, invoking Buddha and burning incense. The sound of the gongs and drums and of shouts and cries were audible at a distance beyond the lane; and in the whole street, one and all extolled the performance as exceptionally grand, and that the like could never have been had in the house of any other family.

Baoyu, noticing that the commotion and bustle had reached a stage so unbearable to his taste, speedily betook himself, after merely sitting for a little while, to other places in search of relaxation and fun. First of all, he entered the inner rooms, and after spending some time in chatting and laughing with Mrs. You, the waiting-maids, and secondary wives, he eventually took his departure out of the second gate; and as Mrs. You and her companions were still under the impression that he was going out again to see the play, they let him speed on his way, without so much as keeping an eye over him.

Jia Zhen, Jia Lian, Xue Pan, and the others were bent upon guessing enigmas, enforcing the penalties, and enjoying themselves in a hundred and one ways, so that even allowing that they had for a moment noticed that he was not occupying his seat, they must merely have imagined that he had gone inside and not, in fact, worried their minds about him. And as for the pages, who had come along with Baoyu, those who were a little advanced in years, knowing very well that Baoyu would, on an occasion like the present, be sure not to be going before dusk, stealthily therefore took advantage of his absence, those, who could, to gamble for money, and others to go to the houses of relatives and friends to drink of the new year tea, so that what with gambling and drinking the whole bevy surreptitiously dispersed, waiting for dusk before they came back; while those who were younger, had all crept into the green rooms to watch the excitement; with the result that Baoyu perceiving not one of them about bethought himself of a small reading room, which existed in previous days on this side, in which was suspended a picture of a beauty so artistically executed as to look life-like. "On such a bustling day as this," he reasoned, "it's pretty certain, I fancy, that there will be no one in there; and that beautiful person must surely too feel lonely, so that it's only right that I should go and console her a bit." With these thoughts, he hastily betook himself towards the side-house yonder, and as soon as he came up to the window, he heard the sound of groans in the room. Baoyu was really quite startled. "What!" (he thought), "can that beautiful girl, possibly, have come to life!" and screwing up his courage, he licked a hole in the paper of the window and peeped in. It was not she, however, who had come to life, but Mingyan holding down a girl and likewise indulging in what the Monitory Dream Fairy had taught him.

"Dreadful!" exclaimed Baoyu, aloud, unable to repress himself, and, stamping one of his feet, he walked into the door to the terror of both of them, who parting company, shivered with fear, like clothes that are being shaken. Mingyan perceiving that it was Baoyu promptly fell on his knees and piteously implored for pardon.

"What! in broad daylight! what do you mean by it? Were your master Mr. Zhen to hear of it, would you die or live?" asked Baoyu, as he simultaneously cast a glance at the servant-girl, who although not a beauty was anyhow so spick and span, and possessed besides a few charms sufficient to touch the heart. From shame, her face was red and her ears purple, while she lowered her head and uttered not a syllable.

Baoyu stamped his foot. "What!" he shouted, "don't you yet bundle yourself away!"

This simple remark suggested the idea to the girl's mind who ran off, as if she had wings to fly with; but as Baoyu went also so far as to go in pursuit of her, calling out: "Don't be afraid, I'm not one to tell anyone," Mingyan was so exasperated that he cried, as he went after them, "My worthy ancestor, this is distinctly telling people about it."

"How old is that servant girl?" Baoyu having asked; "She's, I expect, no more than sixteen or seventeen," Mingyan rejoined.

"Well, if you haven't gone so far as to even ascertain her age," Baoyu observed, "you're sure to know still less about other things; and it makes it plain enough that her acquaintance with you is all vain and futile! What a pity! what a pity!"

He then went on to inquire what her name was; and "Were I," continued Mingyan smiling, "to tell you about her name it would involve a long yarn; it's indeed a novel and strange story! She relates that while her mother was nursing her, she dreamt a dream and obtained in this dream possession of a piece of brocaded silk, on which were designs, in variegated colors, representing opulence and honor, and a continuous line of the character Wan; and that this reason accounts for the name of Wan'er, which was given her."

"This is really strange!" Baoyu exclaimed with a grin, after lending an ear to what he had to say; "and she is bound, I think, by and by to have a good deal of good fortune!"

These words uttered, he plunged in deep thought for a while, and Mingyan having felt constrained to inquire: "Why aren't you, Mr. Secundus, watching a theatrical performance of this excellent kind?" "I had been looking on for ever so long," Baoyu replied, "until I got quite weary; and had just come out for a stroll, when I happened to meet you two. But what's to be done now?"

Mingyan gave a faint smile. "As there's no one here to know anything about it," he added, "I'll stealthily take you, Mr. Secundus, for a walk outside the city walls; and we'll come back shortly, before they've got wind of it."

"That won't do," Baoyu demurred, "we must be careful, or else some beggar might kidnap us away; besides, were they to come to hear of it, there'll be again a dreadful row; and isn't it better that we should go to some nearer place, from which we could, after all, return at once?"

"As for some nearer place," Mingyan observed; "to whose house can we go? It's really no easy matter!"

"My idea is," Baoyu suggested with a smirk, "that we should simply go, and find sister Hua, and see what she's up to at home."

"Yes! Yes!" Mingyan replied laughingly; "the fact is I had forgotten all about her home; but should it reach their ears," he continued, "they'll say that it was I who led you, Mr. Secundus, astray, and they'll beat me!"

"I'm here for you!" Baoyu having assured him, Mingyan at these words led the horses round, and the two of them speedily made their exit by the back gate. Luckily Xiren's house was not far off. It was no further than half a li's distance, so that in a twinkle they had already reached the front of the door, and Mingyan was the first to walk in and to call for Xiren's eldest brother Hua Zifang.

Xiren's mother had, on this occasion, united in her home Xiren, several of her sister's daughters, as well as a few of her nieces, and they were engaged in partaking of fruits and tea, when they heard someone outside call out, "Brother Hua." Hua Zifang lost no time in rushing out; and upon looking and finding that it was the two of them, the master and his servant, he was so taken by surprise that his fears could not be set at rest. Promptly, he clasped Baoyu in his arms and dismounted him, and coming into the court, he shouted out at the top of his voice: "Mr. Bao has come." The other persons heard the announcement of his arrival, with equanimity, but when it reached Xiren's ears, she truly felt at such a loss to fathom the object of his visit that issuing hastily out of the room, she came to meet Baoyu, and as she laid hold of him: "Why did you come?" she asked.

"I felt awfully dull," Baoyu rejoined with a smile, "and came to see what you were up to."

Xiren at these words banished, at last, all anxiety from her mind. "You're again up to your larks," she observed, "but what's the aim of your visit? Who else has come along with him?" she at the same time went on to question Mingyan.

"All the others know nothing about it!" explained Mingyan exultingly; "only we two do, that's all."

When Xiren heard this remark, she gave way afresh to solicitous fears: "This is dreadful!" she added; "for were you to come across any one from the house, or to meet master; or were, in the streets, people to press against you, or horses to collide with you, as to make (his horse) shy, and he were to fall, would that too be a joke? The gall of both of you is larger than a peck measure; but it's all you, Mingyan, who has incited him, and when I go back, I'll surely tell the nurses to beat you."

Mingyan pouted his mouth. "Mr. Secundus," he pleaded, "abused me and beat me, as he bade me bring him here, and now he shoves the blame on my shoulders! 'Don't let us go,' I suggested; 'but if you do insist, well then let us go and have done.'"

Hua Zifang promptly interceded. "Let things alone," he said; "now that they're already here, there's no need whatever of much ado. The only thing is that our mean house with its thatched roof is both so crammed and so filthy that how could you, sir, sit in it!"

Xiren's mother also came out at an early period to receive him, and Xiren pulled Baoyu in. Once inside the room, Baoyu perceived three or five girls, who, as soon as they caught sight of him approaching, all lowered their heads, and felt so bashful that their faces were suffused with blushes. But as both Hua Zifang and his mother were afraid that Baoyu would catch cold, they pressed him to take a seat on the stove-bed, and hastened to serve a fresh supply of refreshments, and to at once bring him a cup of good tea.

"You needn't be flurrying all for nothing," Xiren smilingly interposed; "I, naturally, should know; and there's no use of even laying out any fruits, as I daren't recklessly give him anything to eat."

Saying this, she simultaneously took her own cushion and laid it on a stool, and after Baoyu took a seat on it, she placed the footstove she had been using, under his feet; and producing, from a satchet, two peach-blossom-scented small cakes, she opened her own hand-stove and threw them into the fire; which done, she covered it well again and placed it in Baoyu's lap. And eventually, she filled her own tea-cup with tea and presented it to Baoyu, while, during this time, her mother and sister had been fussing about, laying out in fine array a tableful of every kind of eatables.

Xiren noticed that there were absolutely no things that he could eat, but she felt urged to say with a smile: "Since you've come, it isn't right that you should go empty away; and you must, whether the things be good or bad, taste a little, so that it may look like a visit to my house!"

As she said this, she forthwith took several seeds of the fir-cone, and cracking off the thin skin, she placed them in a handkerchief and presented them to Baoyu. But Baoyu, espying that Xiren's two eyes were slightly red, and that the powder was shiny and moist, quietly therefore inquired of Xiren, "Why do you cry for no rhyme or reason?"

"Why should I cry?" Xiren laughed; "something just got into my eyes and I rubbed them." By these means she readily managed to evade detection; but seeing that Baoyu wore a deep red archery-sleeved pelisse, ornamented with gold dragons, and lined with fur from foxes' ribs and a grey sable fur surtout with a fringe round the border. "What! have you," she asked, "put on again your new clothes for? specially to come here? and didn't they inquire of you where you were going?"

"I had changed," Baoyu explained with a grin, "as Mr. Zhen had invited me to go over and look at the play."

"Well, sit a while and then go back;" Xiren continued as she nodded her head; "for this isn't the place for you to come to!"

"You'd better be going home now," Baoyu suggested smirkingly; "where I've again kept something good for you."

"Gently," smiled Xiren, "for were you to let them hear, what figure would we cut?" And with these, words, she put out her hand and unclasping from Baoyu's neck the jade of Spiritual Perception, she faced her cousins and remarked exultingly. "Here! see for yourselves; look at this and learn! When I repeatedly talked about it, you all thought it extraordinary, and were anxious to have a glance at it; today, you may gaze on it with all your might, for whatever precious thing you may by and by come to see will really never excel such an object as this!"

When she had finished speaking, she handed it over to them, and after they had passed it round for inspection, she again fastened it properly on Baoyu's neck, and also bade her brother go and hire a small carriage, or engage a small chair, and escort Baoyu back home.

"If I see him back," Hua Zifang remarked, "there would be no harm, were he even to ride his horse!"

"It isn't because of harm," Xiren replied; "but because he may come across someone from the house."

Hua Zifang promptly went and bespoke a small chair; and when it came to the door, the whole party could not very well detain him, and they of course had to see Baoyu out of the house; while Xiren, on the other hand, snatched a few fruits and gave them to Mingyan; and as she at the same time pressed in his hand several cash to buy crackers with to let off, she enjoined him not to tell anyone as he himself would likewise incur blame.

As she uttered these words, she straightway escorted Baoyu as far as outside the door, from whence having seen him mount into the sedan chair, she dropped the curtain; whereupon Mingyan and her brother, the two of them, led the horses and followed behind in his wake. Upon reaching the street where the Ning mansion was situated, Mingyan told the chair to halt, and said to Hua Zifang, "It's advisable that I should again go, with Mr. Secundus, into the Eastern mansion, to show ourselves before we can safely betake ourselves home; for if we don't, people will suspect!"

Hua Zifang, upon hearing that there was good reason in what he said, promptly clasped Baoyu out of the chair and put him on the horse, whereupon after Baoyu smilingly remarked: "Excuse me for the trouble I've surely put you to," they forthwith entered again by the back gate; but putting aside all details, we will now confine ourselves to Baoyu.

After he had walked out of the door, the several waiting-maids in his apartments played and laughed with greater zest and with less restraint. Some there were who played at chess, others who threw the dice or had a game of cards; and they covered the whole floor with the shells of melon-seeds they were cracking, when dame Li, his nurse, happened to come in, propping herself on a staff, to pay her respects and to see Baoyu, and perceiving that Baoyu was not at home and that the servant-girls were only bent upon romping, she felt intensely disgusted. "Since I've left this place," she therefore exclaimed with a sigh, "and don't often come here, you've become more and more unmannerly; while the other nurse does still less than ever venture to expostulate with you; Baoyu is like a candlestick eighty feet high, shedding light on others, and throwing none upon himself! All he knows is to look down upon people as being filthy; and yet this is his room and he allows you to put it topsy-turvey, and to become more and more unmindful of decorum!"

These servant-girls were well aware that Baoyu was not particular in these respects, and that in the next place nurse Li, having pleaded old age, resigned her place and gone home, had nowadays no control over them, so that they simply gave their minds to romping and joking, and paid no heed whatever to her. Nurse Li however still kept on asking about Baoyu, "How much rice he now ate at one meal? and at what time he went to sleep?" to which questions, the servant-girls replied quite at random; some there being too who observed: "What a dreadful despicable old thing she is!"

"In this covered bowl," she continued to inquire, "is cream, and why not give it to me to eat?" and having concluded these words, she took it up and there and then began eating it.

"Be quick, and leave it alone!" a servant-girl expostulated, "that, he said, was kept in order to be given to Xiren; and on his return, when he again gets into a huff, you, old lady, must, on your own motion, confess to having eaten it, and not involve us in anyway as to have to bear his resentment."

Nurse Li, at these words, felt both angry and ashamed. "I can't believe," she forthwith remarked, "that he has become so bad at heart! Not to speak of the milk I've had, I have, in fact every right to even something more expensive than this; for is it likely that he holds Xiren dearer than myself? It can't forsooth be that he doesn't bear in mind how that I've brought him up to be a big man, and how that he has eaten my blood transformed into milk and grown up to this age! and will be because I'm now having a bowl of milk of his be angry on that score! I shall, yes, eat it, and we'll see what he'll do! I don't know what you people think of Xiren, but she was a lowbred girl, whom I've with my own hands raised up! and what fine object indeed was she!"

As she spoke, she flew into a temper, and taking the cream she drank the whole of it.

"They don't know how to speak properly!" another servant-girl interposed sarcastically, "and it's no wonder that you, old lady, should get angry! Baoyu still sends you, venerable dame, presents as a proof of his gratitude, and is it possible that he will feel displeased for such a thing like this?"

"You girls shouldn't also pretend to be artful flatterers to cajole me!" nurse Li added; "do you imagine that I'm not aware of the dismissal, the other day, of Xixue, on account of a cup of tea? and as it's clear enough that I've incurred blame, I'll come by and by and receive it!"

Having said this, she went off in a dudgeon, but not a long interval elapsed before Baoyu returned, and gave orders to go and fetch Xiren; and perceiving Qingwen reclining on the bed perfectly still: "I presume she's ill," Baoyu felt constrained to inquire, "or if she isn't ill, she must have lost at cards."

"Not so!" observed Qiuwen; "she had been a winner, but dame Li came in quite casually and muddled her so that she lost; and angry at this she rushed off to sleep."

"Don't place yourselves," Baoyu smiled, "on the same footing as nurse Li, and if you were to let her alone, everything will be all right."

These words were still on his lips when Xiren arrived. After the mutual salutations, Xiren went on to ask of Baoyu: "Where did you have your repast? and what time did you come back?" and to present likewise, on behalf of her mother and sister, her compliments to all the girls, who were her companions. In a short while, she changed her costume and divested herself of her fineries, and Baoyu bade them fetch the cream.

"Nurse Li has eaten it," the servant-girls rejoined, and as Baoyu was on the point of making some remark Xiren hastened to interfere, laughing the while; "Is it really this that you had kept for me? many thanks for the trouble; the other day, when I had some, I found it very toothsome, but after I had partaken of it, I got a pain in the stomach, and was so much upset, that it was only after I had brought it all up that I felt all right. So it's as well that she has had it, for, had it been kept here, it would have been wasted all for no use. What I fancy are dry chestnuts; and while you clean a few for me, I'll go and lay the bed!"

Baoyu upon hearing these words credited them as true, so that he discarded all thought of the cream and fetched the chestnuts, which he, with his own hands, selected and pealed. Perceiving at the same time that none of the party were present in the room, he put on a smile and inquired of Xiren: "Who were those persons dressed in red to day?"

"They're my two cousins on my mother's side," Xiren explained, and hearing this, Baoyu sang their praise as he heaved a couple of sighs.

"What are you sighing for?" Xiren remarked. "I know the secret reasons of your heart; it's I fancy because she isn't fit to wear red!"

"It isn't that," Baoyu protested smilingly, "it isn't that; if such a person as that isn't good enough to be dressed in red, who would forsooth presume to wear it? It's because I find her so really lovely! and if we could, after all, manage to get her into our family, how nice it would be then!"

Xiren gave a sardonic smile. "That it's my own fate to be a slave doesn't matter, but is it likely that the destiny of even my very relatives could be to become one and all of them bond servants? But you should certainly set your choice upon some really beautiful girl, for she would in that case be good enough to enter your house."

"Here you are again with your touchiness!" Baoyu eagerly exclaimed smiling, "if I said that she should come to our house, does it necessarily imply that she should be a servant? and wouldn't it do were I to mention that she should come as a relative!"

"That too couldn't exalt her to be a fit match for you!" rejoined Xiren; but Baoyu being loath to continue the conversation, simply busied himself with cleaning the chestnuts.

"How is it you utter not a word?" Xiren laughed; "I expect it's because I just offended you by my inconsiderate talk! But if by and by you have your purpose fixed on it, just spend a few ounces of silver to purchase them with, and bring them in and have done!"

"How would you have one make any reply?" Baoyu smilingly rejoined; "all I did was to extol her charms; for she's really fit to have been born in a deep hall and spacious court as this; and it isn't for such foul things as myself and others to contrariwise spend our days in this place!"

"Though deprived of this good fortune," Xiren explained, "she's nevertheless also petted and indulged and the jewel of my maternal uncle and my aunt! She's now seventeen years of age, and everything in the way of trousseau has been got ready, and she's to get married next year."

Upon hearing the two words "get married," he could not repress himself from again ejaculating: "Hai hai!" but while he was in an unhappy frame of mind, he once more heard Xiren remark as she heaved a sigh: "Ever since I've come here, we cousins haven't all these years been able to get to live together, and now that I'm about to return home, they, on the other hand, will all be gone!"

Baoyu, realising that there lurked in this remark some meaning or other, was suddenly so taken aback that dropping the chestnuts, he inquired: "How is it that you now want to go back?"

"I was present today," Xiren explained, "when mother and brother held consultation together, and they bade me be patient for another year, and that next year they'll come up and redeem me out of service!"

Baoyu, at these words, felt the more distressed. "Why do they want to redeem you?" he consequently asked.

"This is a strange question!" Xiren retorted, "for I can't really be treated as if I were the issue born in this homestead of yours! All the members of my family are elsewhere, and there's only myself in this place, so that how could I end my days here?"

"If I don't let you go, it will verily be difficult for you to get away!" Baoyu replied.

"There has never been such a principle of action!" urged Xiren; even in the Imperial palace itself, there's a fixed rule, by which possibly every certain number of years a selection (of those who have to go takes place), and every certain number of years a new batch enters; and there's no such practice as that of keeping people forever; not to speak of your own home."

Baoyu realised, after reflection, that she, in point of fact, was right, and he went on to observe: "Should the old lady not give you your release, it will be impossible for you to get off."

"Why shouldn't she release me?" Xiren questioned. "Am I really so very extraordinary a person as to have perchance made such an impression upon her venerable ladyship and my lady that they will be positive in not letting me go? They may, in all likelihood, give my family some more ounces of silver to keep me here; that possibly may come about. But, in truth, I'm also a person of the most ordinary run, and there are many more superior to me, yea very many! Ever since my youth up, I've been in her old ladyship's service; first by waiting upon Miss Shi for several years, and recently by being in attendance upon you for another term of years; and now that our people will come to redeem me, I should, as a matter of right, be told to go. My idea is that even the very redemption money won't be accepted, and that they will display such grace as to let me go at once. And, as for being told that I can't be allowed to go as I'm so diligent in my service to you, that's a thing that can on no account come about! My faithful attendance is an obligation of my duties, and is no exceptional service! and when I'm gone you'll again have some other faithful attendant, and it isn't likely that when I'm no more here, you'll find it impracticable to obtain one!"

After Baoyu had listened to these various arguments, which proved the reasonableness of her going and the unreasonableness of any detention, he felt his heart more than ever a prey to distress. "In spite of all you say," he therefore continued, "the sole desire of my heart is to detain you; and I have no doubt but that the old lady will speak to your mother about it; and if she were to give your mother ample money, she'll, of course, not feel as if she could very well with any decency take you home!"

"My mother won't naturally have the audacity to be headstrong!" Xiren ventured, "not to speak besides of the nice things, which may be told her and the lots of money she may, in addition, be given; but were she even not to be paid any compliments, and not so much as a single cash given her, she won't, if you set your mind upon keeping me here, presume not to comply with your wishes, were it also against my inclination. One thing however; our family would never rely upon prestige, and trust upon honorability to do anything so domineering as this! for this isn't like anything else, which, because you take a fancy to it, a hundred percent profit can be added, and it obtained for you! This action can be well taken if the seller doesn't suffer loss! But in the present instance, were they to keep me back for no rhyme or reason, it would also be of no benefit to yourself; on the contrary, they would be instrumental in keeping us blood relatives far apart; a thing the like of which, I feel positive that dowager lady Jia and my lady will never do!"

After lending an ear to this argument, Baoyu cogitated within himself for a while. "From what you say," he then observed, "when you say you'll go, it means that you'll go for certain!"

"Yes, that I'll go for certain," Xiren rejoined.

"Who would have anticipated," Baoyu, after these words, mused in his own heart, "that a person like her would have shown such little sense of gratitude, and such a lack of respect! Had I," he then remarked aloud with a sigh, "been aware, at an early date, that your whole wish would have been to go, I wouldn't, in that case, have brought you over! But when you're away, I shall remain alone, a solitary spirit!"

As he spoke, he lost control over his temper, and, getting into bed, he went to sleep.

The fact is that when Xiren had been at home, and she heard her mother and brother express their intention of redeeming her back, she there and then observed that were she even at the point of death, she would not return home. "When in past days," she had argued, "you had no rice to eat, there remained myself, who was still worth several taels; and hadn't I urged you to sell me, wouldn't I have seen both father and mother die of starvation under my very eyes? and you've now had the good fortune of selling me into this place, where I'm fed and clothed just like a mistress, and where I'm not beaten by day, nor abused by night! Besides, though now father be no more, you two have anyhow by putting things straight again, so adjusted the family estate that it has resumed its primitive condition. And were you, in fact, still in straitened circumstances, and you could by redeeming me back, make again some more money, that would be well and good; but the truth is that there's no such need, and what would be the use for you to redeem me at such a time as this? You should temporarily treat me as dead and gone, and shouldn't again recall any idea of redeeming me!"

Having in consequence indulged in a loud fit of crying, her mother and brother resolved, when they perceived her in this determined frame of mind, that for a fact there was no need for her to come out of service. What is more they had sold her under contract until death, in the distinct reliance that the Jia family, charitable and generous a family as it was, would, possibly, after no more than a few entreaties, make them a present of her person as well as the purchase money. In the second place, never had they in the Jia mansion ill-used any of those below; there being always plenty of grace and little of imperiousness. Besides, the servant-girls, who acted as personal attendants in the apartments of the old as well as of the young, were treated so far unlike the whole body of domestics in the household that the daughters even of an ordinary and penniless parentage could not have been so looked up to. And these considerations induced both the mother as well as her son to at once dispel the intention and not to redeem her, and when Baoyu had subsequently paid them an unexpected visit, and the two of them (Baoyu and Xiren) were seen to be also on such terms, the mother and her son obtained a clearer insight into their relations, and still one more burden (which had pressed on their mind) fell to the ground, and as besides this was a contingency, which they had never reckoned upon, they both composed their hearts, and did not again entertain any idea of ransoming her.

It must be noticed moreover that Xiren had ever since her youth not been blind to the fact that Baoyu had an extraordinary temperament, that he was self-willed and perverse, far even in excess of all young lads, and that he had, in addition, a good many peculiarities and many unspeakable defects. And as of late he had placed such reliance in the fond love of his grandmother that his father and mother even could not exercise any extreme control over him, he had become so much the more remiss, dissolute, selfish, and unconcerned, not taking the least pleasure in what was proper, that she felt convinced, whenever she entertained the idea of tendering him advice, that he would not listen to her. On this day, by a strange coincidence, came about the discussion respecting her ransom, and she designedly made use, in the first instance, of deception with a view to ascertain his feelings, to suppress his temper, and to be able subsequently to extend to him some words of admonition; and when she perceived that Baoyu had now silently gone to sleep, she knew that his feelings could not brook the idea of her return and that his temper had already subsided. She had never had, as far as she was concerned, any desire of eating chestnuts, but as she feared lest, on account of the cream, some trouble might arise, which might again lead to the same results as when Xixue drank the tea, she consequently made use of the pretence that she fancied chestnuts, in order to put off Baoyu from alluding (to the cream) and to bring the matter speedily to an end. But telling forthwith the young waiting-maids to take the chestnuts away and eat them, she herself came and pushed Baoyu; but at the sight of Baoyu with the traces of tears on his face, she at once put on a smiling expression and said: "What's there in this to wound your heart? If you positively do wish to keep me, I shall, of course, not go away!"

Baoyu noticed that these words contained some hidden purpose, and readily observed: "Do go on and tell me what else I can do to succeed in keeping you here, for of my own self I find it indeed difficult to say how!"

"Of our friendliness all along," Xiren smilingly rejoined, "there's naturally no need to speak; but, if you have this day made up your mind to retain me here, it isn't through this friendship that you'll succeed in doing so. But I'll go on and mention three distinct conditions, and, if you really do accede to my wishes, you'll then have shown an earnest desire to keep me here, and I won't go, were even a sword to be laid on my neck!"

"Do tell me what these conditions are," Baoyu pressed her with alacrity, as he smiled, "and I'll assent to one and all. My dear sister, my own dear sister, not to speak of two or three, but even two or three hundred of them I'm quite ready to accept. All I entreat you is that you and all of you should combine to watch over me and take care of me, until some day when I shall be transformed into flying ashes; but flying ashes are, after all, not opportune, as they have form and substance and they likewise possess sense, but until I've been metamorphosed into a streak of subtle smoke. And when the wind shall have with one puff dispelled me, all of you then will be unable to attend to me, just as much as I myself won't be able to heed you. You will, when that time comes, let me go where I please, as I'll let you speed where you choose to go!"

These words so harassed Xiren that she hastened to put her hand over his mouth. "Speak decently," she said; "I was on account of this just about to admonish you, and now here you are uttering all this still more loathsome trash."

"I won't utter these words again," Baoyu eagerly added.

"This is the first fault that you must change," Xiren replied.

"I'll amend," Baoyu observed, "and if I say anything of the kind again you can wring my mouth; but what else is there?"

"The second thing is this," Xiren explained; "whether you really like to study or whether you only pretend to like study is immaterial; but you should, when you are in the presence of master, or in the presence of anyone else, not do nothing else than find fault with people and make fun of them, but behave just as if you were genuinely fond of study, so that you shouldn't besides provoke your father so much to anger, and that he should before others have also a chance of saying something! 'In my family,' he reflects within himself, 'generation after generation has been fond of books, but ever since I've had you, you haven't accomplished my expectations, and not only is it that you don't care about reading books,'—and this has already filled his heart with anger and vexation—'but both before my face and behind my back, you utter all that stuff and nonsense, and give those persons, who have, through their knowledge of letters, attained high offices, the nickname of the "the salaried worms." You also uphold that there's no work exclusive (of the book where appears) "fathom spotless virtue;" and that all other books consist of foolish compilations, which owe their origin to former authors, who, unable themselves to expound the writings of Confucius, readily struck a new line and invented original notions.' Now with words like these, how can one wonder if master loses all patience, and if he does from time to time give you a thrashing! and what do you make other people think of you?"

"I won't say these things again," Baoyu laughingly protested, "these are the reckless and silly absurdities of a time when I was young and had no idea of the height of the heavens and the thickness of the earth; but I'll now no more repeat them. What else is there besides?"

"It isn't right that you should sneer at the bonzes and vilify the Daoist priests, nor mix cosmetics or prepare rouge," Xiren continued; "but there's still another thing more important, you shouldn't again indulge the bad habits of licking the cosmetic, applied by people on their lips, nor be fond of (girls dressed) in red!"

"I'll change in all this," Baoyu added by way of rejoinder; "I'll change in all this; and if there's anything more be quick and tell me."

"There's nothing more," Xiren observed; "but you must in everything exercise a little more diligence, and not indulge your caprices and allow your wishes to run riot, and you'll be all right. And should you comply to all these things in real earnest, you couldn't carry me out, even in a chair with eight bearers."

"Well, if you do stay in here long enough," Baoyu remarked with a smile, "there's no fear as to your not having an eight-bearer-chair to sit in!"

Xiren gave a sardonic grin. "I don't care much about it," she replied; "and were I even to have such good fortune, I couldn't enjoy such a right. But allowing I could sit in one, there would be no pleasure in it!"

While these two were chatting, they saw Qiuwen walk in. "It's the third watch of the night," she observed, "and you should go to sleep.

Just a few moments back your grandmother lady Jia and our lady sent a nurse to ask about you, and I replied that you were asleep."

Baoyu bade her fetch a watch, and upon looking at the time, he found indeed that the hand was pointing at ten; whereupon rinsing his mouth again and loosening his clothes, he retired to rest, where we will leave him without any further comment.

The next day, Xiren got up as soon as it was dawn, feeling her body heavy, her head sore, her eyes swollen, and her limbs burning like fire. She managed however at first to keep up, an effort though it was, but as subsequently she was unable to endure the strain, and all she felt disposed to do was to recline, she therefore lay down in her clothes on the stove-couch. Baoyu hastened to tell dowager lady Jia, and the doctor was sent for, who, upon feeling her pulse and diagnosing her complaint, declared that there was nothing else the matter with her than a chill, which she had suddenly contracted, that after she had taken a dose or two of medicine, it would be dispelled, and that she would be quite well. After he had written the prescription and taken his departure, someone was despatched to fetch the medicines, which when brought were properly decocted. As soon as she had swallowed a dose, Baoyu bade her cover herself with her bed-clothes so as to bring on perspiration; while he himself came into Daiyu's room to look her up. Daiyu was at this time quite alone, reclining on her bed having a midday siesta, and the waiting-maids having all gone out to attend to whatever they pleased, the whole room was plunged in stillness and silence. Baoyu raised the embroidered soft thread portiere and walked in; and upon espying Daiyu in the room fast asleep, he hurriedly approached her and pushing her: "Dear cousin," he said, "you've just had your meal, and are you asleep already?" and he kept on calling "Daiyu" till he woke her out of her sleep.

Perceiving that it was Baoyu, "You had better go for a stroll," Daiyu urged, "for the day before yesterday I was disturbed the whole night, and up to this day I haven't had rest enough to get over the fatigue. My whole body feels languid and sore."

"This languor and soreness," Baoyu rejoined, "are of no consequence; but if you go on sleeping you'll be feeling very ill; so I'll try and distract you, and when we've dispelled this lassitude, you'll be all right."

Daiyu closed her eyes. "I don't feel any lassitude," she explained, "all I want is a little rest; and you had better go elsewhere and come back after romping about for a while."

"Where can I go?" Baoyu asked as he pushed her. "I'm quite sick and tired of seeing the others."

At these words, Daiyu burst out laughing with a sound of "chi." "Well! since you wish to remain here," she added, "go over there and sit down quietly, and let's have a chat."

"I'll also recline," Baoyu suggested.

"Well, then, recline!" Daiyu assented.

"There's no pillow," observed Baoyu, "so let us lie on the same pillow."

"What nonsense!" Daiyu urged, "aren't those pillows outside? get one and lie on it."

Baoyu walked into the outer apartment, and having looked about him, he returned and remarked with a smile: "I don't want those, they may be, for aught I know, some dirty old hag's."

Daiyu at this remark opened her eyes wide, and as she raised herself up: "You're really," she exclaimed laughingly, "the evil star of my existence! here, please recline on this pillow!" and as she uttered these words, she pushed her own pillow towards Baoyu, and, getting up she went and fetched another of her own, upon which she lay her head in such a way that both of them then reclined opposite to each other. But Daiyu, upon turning up her eyes and looking, espied on Baoyu's cheek on the left side of his face, a spot of blood about the size of a button, and speedily bending her body, she drew near to him, and rubbing it with her hand, she scrutinised it closely. "Whose nail," she went on to inquire, "has scratched this open?"

Baoyu with his body still reclining withdrew from her reach, and as he did so, he answered with a smile: "It isn't a scratch; it must, I presume, be simply a drop, which bespattered my cheek when I was just now mixing and clarifying the cosmetic paste for them."

Saying this, he tried to get at his handkerchief to wipe it off; but Daiyu used her own and rubbed it clean for him, while she observed: "Do you still give your mind to such things? attend to them you may; but must you carry about you a placard (to make it public)? Though uncle mayn't see it, were others to notice it, they would treat it as a strange occurrence and a novel bit of news, and go and tell him to curry favor, and when it has reached uncle's ear, we shall all again not come out clean, and provoke him to anger."

Baoyu did not in the least heed what she said, being intent upon smelling a subtle scent which, in point of fact, emanated from Daiyu's sleeve, and when inhaled inebriated the soul and paralyzed the ones. With a snatch, Baoyu laid hold of Daiyu's sleeve meaning to see what object was concealed in it; but Daiyu smilingly expostulated: "At such a time as this," she said, "who keeps scents about one?"

"Well, in that case," Baoyu rejoined with a smirking face, "where does this scent come from?"

"I myself don't know," Daiyu replied; "I presume it must be, there's no saying, some scent in the press which has impregnated the clothes."

"It doesn't follow," Baoyu added, as he shook his head; "the fumes of this smell are very peculiar, and don't resemble the perfume of scent-bottles, scent-balls, or scented satchets!"

"Is it likely that I have, like others, Buddhistic disciples," Daiyu asked laughing ironically, "or worthies to give me novel kinds of scents? But supposing there is about me some peculiar scent, I haven't, at all events, any older or younger brothers to get the flowers, buds, dew, and snow, and concoct any for me; all I have are those common scents, that's all."

"Whenever I utter any single remark," Baoyu urged with a grin, "you at once bring up all these insinuations; but unless I deal with you severely, you'll never know what stuff I'm made of; but from henceforth I'll no more show you any grace!"

As he spoke, he turned himself over, and raising himself, he puffed a couple of breaths into both his hands, and hastily stretching them out, he tickled Daiyu promiscuously under her armpits, and along both sides. Daiyu had never been able to stand tickling, so that when Baoyu put out his two hands and tickled her violently, she forthwith giggled to such an extent that she could scarcely gasp for breath. "If you still go on teasing me," she shouted, "I'll get angry with you!"

Baoyu then kept his hands off, and as he laughed, "Tell me," he asked, "will you again come out with all those words or not?"

"I daren't do it again," Daiyu smiled and adjusted her hair; adding with another laugh: "I may have peculiar scents, but have you any 'warm' scents?"

Baoyu at this question, could not for a time unfold its meaning: "What 'warm' scent?'" he therefore asked.

Daiyu nodded her head and smiled deridingly. "How stupid! what a fool!" she sighed; "you have jade, and another person has gold to match with you, and if someone has 'cold' scent, haven't you any 'warm' scent as a set-off?"

Baoyu at this stage alone understood the import of her remark.

"A short while back you craved for mercy," Baoyu observed smilingly, "and here you are now going on talking worse than ever;" and as he spoke he again put out his hands.

"Dear cousin," Daiyu speedily implored with a smirk, "I won't venture to do it again."

"As for letting you off," Baoyu remarked laughing, "I'll readily let you off, but do allow me to take your sleeve and smell it!" and while uttering these words, he hastily pulled the sleeve, and pressing it against his face, kept on smelling it incessantly, whereupon Daiyu drew her hand away and urged: "You must be going now!"

"Though you may wish me to go, I can't," Baoyu smiled, "so let us now lie down with all propriety and have a chat," laying himself down again, as he spoke, while Daiyu likewise reclined, and covered her face with her handkerchief. Baoyu in a rambling way gave vent to a lot of nonsense, which Daiyu did not heed, and Baoyu went on to inquire: "How old she was when she came to the capital? what sights and antiquities she saw on the journey? what relics and curiosities there were at Yangzhou? what were the local customs and the habits of the people?"

Daiyu made no reply; and Baoyu fearing lest she should go to sleep, and get ill, readily set to work to beguile her to keep awake. "Ai yah!" he exclaimed, "at Yangzhou, where your official residence is, has occurred a remarkable affair; have you heard about it?"

Daiyu perceiving that he spoke in earnest, that his words were correct and his face serious, imagined that what he referred to was a true story, and she therefore inquired what it was?

Baoyu upon hearing her ask this question, forthwith suppressed a laugh, and, with a glib tongue, he began to spin a yarn. "At Yangzhou," he said, "there's a hill called the Dai hill; and on this hill stands a cave called the Linzi."

"This must all be lies," Daiyu answered sneeringly, "as I've never before heard of such a hill."

"Under the heavens many are the hills and rivers," Baoyu rejoined, "and how could you know them all? Wait until I've done speaking, when you will be free to express your opinion!"

"Go on then," Daiyu suggested, whereupon Baoyu prosecuted his raillery. "In this Linzi cave," he said, "there was once upon a time a whole swarm of rat-elves. In some year or other and on the seventh day of the twelfth moon, an old rat ascended the throne to discuss matters. 'Tomorrow,' he argued, 'is the eighth of the twelfth moon, and men in the world will all be cooking the congee of the eighth of the twelfth moon. We have now in our cave a short supply of fruits of all kinds, and it would be well that we should seize this opportunity to steal a few and bring them over.' Drawing a mandatory arrow, he handed it to a small rat, full of aptitude, to go forward on a tour of inspection. The young rat on his return reported that he had already concluded his search and inquiries in every place and corner, and that in the temple at the bottom of the hill alone was the largest stock of fruits and rice. 'How many kinds of rice are there?' the old rat ascertained, 'and how many species of fruits?' 'Rice and beans,' the young rat rejoined, 'how many barns-full there are, I can't remember; but in the way of fruits there are five kinds: 1st, red dates; 2nd, chestnuts; 3rd, ground nuts; 4th, water caltrops, and 5th, scented taros.' At this report the old rat was so much elated that he promptly detailed rats to go forth; and as he drew the mandatory arrow, and inquired who would go and steal the rice, a rat readily received the order and went off to rob the rice. Drawing another mandatory arrow, he asked who would go and abstract the beans, when once more a rat took over the arrow and started to steal the beans; and one by one subsequently received each an arrow and started on his errand. There only remained the scented taros, so that picking again a mandatory arrow, he ascertained who would go and carry away the taros: whereupon a very puny and very delicate rat was heard to assent. 'I would like,' he said, 'to go and steal the scented taros.' The old rat and all the swarm of rats, upon noticing his state, feared that he would not be sufficiently expert, and apprehending at the same time that he was too weakly and too devoid of energy, they one and all would not allow him to proceed. 'Though I be young in years and though my frame be delicate,' the wee rat expostulated, 'my devices are unlimited, my talk is glib, and my designs deep and farseeing; and I feel convinced that, on this errand, I shall be more ingenious in pilfering than any of them.' 'How could you be more ingenious than they?' the whole company of rats asked. 'I won't,' explained the young rat, 'follow their example, and go straight to work and steal, but by simply shaking my body, and transforming myself, I shall metamorphose myself into a taro, and roll myself among the heap of taros, so that people will not be able to detect me, and to hear me; whereupon I shall stealthily, by means of the magic art of dividing my body into many, begin the removal, and little by little transfer the whole lot away, and will not this be far more ingenious than any direct pilfering or forcible abstraction?' After the whole swarm of rats had listened to what he had to say, they, with one voice, exclaimed: 'Excellent it is indeed, but what is this art of metamorphosis we wonder? Go forth you may, but first transform yourself and let us see you.' At these words the young rat laughed. 'This isn't a hard task!' he observed, 'wait till I transform myself.'

"Having done speaking, he shook his body and shouted out 'transform,' when he was converted into a young girl, most beauteous and with a most lovely face.

"'You've transformed yourself into the wrong thing,' all the rats promptly added deridingly; 'you said that you were to become a fruit, and how is it that you've turned into a young lady?'

"The young rat in its original form rejoined with a sneering smile: 'You all lack, I maintain, experience of the world; what you simply are aware of is that this fruit is the scented taro, but have no idea that the young daughter of Mr. Lin, of the salt tax, is, in real truth, a genuine scented taro.'"

Daiyu having listened to this story, turned herself round and raising herself, she observed laughing, while she pushed Baoyu: "I'll take that mouth of yours and pull it to pieces! Now I see that you've been imposing upon me."

With these words on her lips, she readily gave him a pinch, and Baoyu hastened to plead for mercy. "My dear cousin," he said, "spare me; I won't presume to do it again; and it's when I came to perceive this perfume of yours, that I suddenly bethought myself of this old story."

'You freely indulge in abusing people,' Daiyu added with a smile, "and then go on to say that it's an old story."

But hardly had she concluded this remark before they caught sight of Baochai walk in. "Who has been telling old stories?" she asked with a beaming face; "do let me also hear them."

Daiyu pressed her at once into a seat. "Just see for yourself who else besides is here!" she smiled; "he goes in for profuse abuses and then maintains that it's an old story!"

"Is it indeed cousin Baoyu?" Baochai remarked. "Well, one can't feel surprised at his doing it; for many have ever been the stories stored up in his brain. The only pity is that when he should make use of old stories, he invariably forgets them! Today, he can easily enough recall them to mind, but in the stanza of the other night on the banana leaves, when he should have remembered them, he couldn't after all recollect what really stared him in the face! and while everyone else seemed so cool, he was in such a flurry that he actually perspired! And yet, at this moment, he happens once again to have a memory!"

At these words, Daiyu laughed. "Amituo Fo!" she exclaimed. "You are indeed my very good cousin! But you've also (to Baoyu) come across your match. And this makes it clear that requital and retribution never fail or err."

She had just reached this part of her sentence, when in Baoyu's rooms was heard a continuous sound of wrangling; but as what transpired is not yet known, the ensuing chapter will explain.

CHAPTER 20

Wang Xifeng with earnest words upbraids Mrs. Zhao's jealous notions. Lin Daiyu uses specious language to make sport of Shi Xiangyun's querulous tone of voice.

But to continue, Baoyu was in Daiyu's apartments relating about the rat-elves, when Baochai entered unannounced, and began to gibe Baoyu, with trenchant irony: how that on the fifteenth of the first moon, he had shown ignorance of the allusion to the green wax; and the three of them then indulged in that room in mutual poignant satire, for the sake of fun. Baoyu had been giving way to solicitude lest Daiyu should, by being bent upon napping soon after her meal, be shortly getting an indigestion, or lest sleep should, at night, be completely dispelled, as neither of these things were conducive to the preservation of good health, when luckily Baochai walked in, and they chatted and laughed together; and when Lin Daiyu at length lost all inclination to dose, he himself then felt composed in his mind. But suddenly they heard clamoring begin in his room, and after they had all lent an ear and listened, Lin Daiyu was the first to smile and make a remark. "It's your nurse having a row with Xiren!" she said. "Xiren treats her well enough, but that nurse of yours would also like to keep her well under her thumb; she's indeed an old dotard;" and Baoyu was anxious to go over at once, but Baochai laid hold of him and kept him back, suggesting: "It's as well that you shouldn't wrangle with your nurse, for she's quite stupid from old age; and it's but fair, on the contrary, that you should bear with her a little."

"I know all about that!" Baoyu rejoined. But having concluded this remark, he walked into his room, where he discovered nurse Li, leaning on her staff, standing in the center of the floor, abusing Xiren, saying: "You young wench! how utterly unmindful you are of your origin! It's I who've raised you up, and yet, when I came just now, you put on high airs and mighty side, and remained reclining on the stove-couch! You saw me well enough, but you paid not the least heed to me! Your whole heart is set upon acting like a wily enchantress to befool Baoyu;

and you so impose upon Baoyu that he doesn't notice me, but merely lends an ear to what you people have to say! You're no more than a low girl bought for a few taels and brought in here; and will it ever do that you should be up to your mischievous tricks in this room? But whether you like it or not, I'll drag you out from this, and give you to some mean fellow, and we'll see whether you will still behave like a very imp, and cajole people or not?"

Xiren was, at first, under the simple impression that the nurse was wrath for no other reason than because she remained lying down, and she felt constrained to explain that "she was unwell, that she had just succeeded in perspiring, and that having had her head covered, she hadn't really perceived the old lady;" but when she came subsequently to hear her mention that she imposed upon Baoyu, and also go so far as to add that she would be given to some mean fellow, she unavoidably experienced both a sense of shame and injury, and found it impossible to restrain herself from beginning to cry.

Baoyu had, it is true, caught all that had been said, but unable with any propriety to take notice of it, he thought it his duty to explain matters for her. "She's ill," he observed, "and is taking medicines; and if you don't believe it," he went on, "well then ask the rest of the servant-girls."

Nurse Li at these words flew into a more violent dudgeon. "Your sole delight is to screen that lot of sly foxes!" she remarked, "and do you pay any notice to me? No, none at all! and whom would you like me to go and ask; who's it that doesn't back you? and who hasn't been dismounted from her horse by Xiren? I know all about it; but I'll go with you and explain all these matters to our old mistress and my lady; for I've nursed you till I've brought you to this age, and now that you don't feed on milk, you thrust me on one side, and avail yourself of the servant-girls, in your wish to browbeat me."

As she uttered this remark, she too gave way to tears, but by this time, Daiyu and Baochai had also come over, and they set to work to reassure her. "You, old lady," they urged, "should bear with them a little, and everything will be right!" And when nurse Li saw these two arrive, she hastened to lay bare her grievances to them; and taking up the question of the dismissal in days gone by, of Xixue, for having drunk some tea, of the cream eaten on the previous day, and other similar matters, she spun a long, interminable yarn.

By a strange coincidence lady Feng was at this moment in the upper rooms, where she had been making up the account of losses and winnings, and upon hearing at the back a continuous sound of shouting and bustling, she readily concluded that nurse Li's old complaint was breaking forth, and that she was finding fault with Baoyu's servants. But she had, as luck would have it, lost money in gambling on this occasion, so that she was ready to visit her resentment upon others. With hurried step, she forthwith came over, and laying hold of nurse Li, "Nurse," she said smiling, "don't lose your temper, on a great festival like this, and after our venerable lady has just gone through a day in excellent spirits! You're an old dame, and should, when others get up a row, still do what is right and keep them in proper order; and aren't you, instead of that, aware what good manners imply, that you will start vociferating in this place, and make our dowager lady full of displeasure? Tell me who's not good, and I'll beat her for you; but be quick and come along with me over to my quarters, where a pheasant which they have roasted is scalding hot, and let us go and have a glass of wine!" And as she spoke, she dragged her along and went on her way. "Feng'er," she also called, "hold the staff for your old lady Li, and the handkerchief to wipe her tears with!" While nurse Li walked along with lady Feng, her feet scarcely touched the ground, as she kept on saying: "I don't really attach any value to this decrepid existence of mine! and I had rather disregard good manners, have a row and lose face, as it's better, it seems to me, than to put up with the temper of that wench!"

Behind followed Baochai and Daiyu, and at the sight of the way in which lady Feng dealt with her, they both clapped their hands, and exclaimed, laughing, "What piece of luck that this gust of wind has come, and dragged away this old matron!" while Baoyu nodded his head to and fro and soliloquised with a sigh: "One can neither know whence originates this score; for she will choose the weak one to maltreat; nor can one see what girl has given her offence that she has come to be put in her black books!"

Scarcely had he ended this remark, before Qingwen, who stood by, put in her word. "Who's gone mad again?" she interposed, "and what good would come by hurting her feelings? But did even anyone happen to hurt her, she would have pluck enough to bear the brunt, and wouldn't act so improperly as to involve others!"

Xiren wept, and as she did so, she drew Baoyu towards her: "All through my having aggrieved an old nurse," she urged, "you've now again given umbrage, entirely on my account, to this crowd of people; and isn't this still enough for me to bear but must you also go and drag in third parties?"

When Baoyu realised that to this sickness of hers, had also been superadded all these annoyances, he promptly stifled his resentment, suppressed his voice, and consoled her so far as to induce her to lie down again to perspire. And when he further noticed how scalding like soup and burning like fire she was, he himself watched by her, and reclining by her side, he tried to cheer her, saying: "All you must do is to take good care of your ailment; and don't give your mind to those trifling matters, and get angry."

"Were I," Xiren smiled sardonically, "to lose my temper over such concerns, would I be able to stand one moment longer in this room? The only thing is that if she goes on, day after day, doing nothing else than clamor in this manner, how can she let people get along? But you rashly go and hurt people's feelings for our sakes; but they'll bear it in mind, and when they find an opportunity, they'll come out with what's easy enough to say, but what's not pleasant to hear, and how will we all feel then?"

While her mouth gave utterance to these words, she could not stop her tears from running; but fearful, on the other hand, lest Baoyu should be annoyed, she felt compelled to again strain every nerve to repress them. But in a short while, the old matrons employed for all sorts of duties, brought in some mixture of two drugs; and, as Baoyu noticed that she was just on the point of perspiring, he did not allow her to get up, but readily taking it up to her, she immediately swallowed it, with her head still on her pillow; whereupon he gave speedy directions to the young servant-maids to lay her stove-couch in order.

"Whether you mean to have anything to eat or not," Xiren advised, "you should after all sit for a time with our old mistress and our lady, and have a romp with the young ladies; after which you can come back again; while I, by quietly keeping lying down, will also feel the better."

When Baoyu heard this suggestion, he had no help but to accede, and, after she had divested herself of her hair-pins and earrings, and he saw her lie down, he betook himself into the drawing-rooms, where he had his repast with old lady Jia. But the meal over, her ladyship felt still disposed to play at cards with the nurses, who had looked after the household for many years; and Baoyu, bethinking himself of Xiren, hastened to return to his apartments; where seeing that Xiren was drowsily falling asleep, he himself would have wished to go to bed, but the hour was yet early. And as about this time Qingwen, Qixian, Qiuwen, Bihen had all, in their desire of getting some excitement, started in search of Yuanyang, Hupo, and their companions, to have a romp with them, and he espied Sheyue alone in the outer room, having a game of dominoes by lamp-light, Baoyu inquired full of smiles: "How is it you don't go with them?"

"I've no money," Sheyue replied.

"Under the bed," continued Baoyu, "is heaped up all that money, and isn't it enough yet for you to lose from?"

"Had we all gone to play," Sheyue added, "to whom would the charge of this apartment have been handed over? That other one is sick again, and the whole room is above, one mass of lamps, and below, full of fire; and all those old matrons, ancient as the heavens, should, after all their exertions in waiting upon you from morning to night, be also allowed some rest; while the young servant girls, on the other hand, have likewise been on duty the whole day long, and shouldn't they even at this hour be left to go and have some distraction? and that's why I am in here on watch."

When Baoyu heard these words, which demonstrated distinctly that she was another Xiren, he consequently put on a smile and remarked: "I'll sit in here, so you had better set your mind at ease and go!"

"Since you remain in here, there's less need for me to go," resumed Sheyue, "for we two can chat and play and laugh; and won't that be nice?"

"What can we two do? it will be awfully dull! but never mind," Baoyu rejoined; "this morning you said that your head itched, and now that you have nothing to do, I may as well comb it for you."

"Yes! do so!" readily assented Sheyue, upon catching what he suggested; and while still speaking, she brought over the dressing-case containing a set of small drawers and looking-glass, and taking off her ornaments, she dishevelled her hair; whereupon Baoyu picked up the fine comb and passed it repeatedly through her hair; but he had only combed it three or five times, when he perceived Qingwen hurriedly walk in to fetch some money. As soon as she caught sight of them both: "You haven't as yet drunk from the marriage cup," she said with a smile full of irony, "and have you already put up your hair?"

"Now that you've come, let me also comb yours for you," Baoyu continued.

"I'm not blessed with such excessive good fortune!" Qingwen retorted, and as she uttered these words, she took the money, and forthwith dashing the portiere after her, she quitted the room.

Baoyu stood at the back of Sheyue, and Sheyue sat opposite the glass, so that the two of them faced each other in it, and Baoyu readily observed as he gazed in the glass, "In the whole number of rooms she's the only one who has a glib tongue!"

Sheyue at these words hastily waved her hand towards the inside of the glass, and Baoyu understood the hint; and suddenly a sound of "hu" was heard from the portiere, and Qingwen ran in once again.

"How have I got a glib tongue?" she inquired; "it would be well for us to explain ourselves."

"Go after your business, and have done," Sheyue interposed laughingly; "what's the use of your coming and asking questions of people?"

"Will you also screen him?" Qingwen smiled significantly; "I know all about your secret doings, but wait until I've got back my capital, and we'll then talk matters over!"

With this remark still on her lips, she straightway quitted the room, and during this while, Baoyu having finished combing her hair, asked Sheyue to quietly wait upon him, while he went to sleep, as he would not like to disturb Xiren.

Of the whole night there is nothing to record. But the next day, when he got up at early dawn, Xiren had already perspired, during the night, so that she felt considerably lighter and better; but limiting her diet to a little rice soup, she remained quiet and nursed herself, and Baoyu was so relieved in mind that he came, after his meal, over on this side to his aunt Xue's on a saunter. The season was the course of the first moon, and the school was shut up for the new year holidays; while in the inner chambers the girls had put by their needlework, and were all having a time of leisure, and hence it was that when Jia Huan too came over in search of distraction, he discovered Baochai, Xiangling, Ying'er, the three of them, in the act of recreating themselves by playing at chess. Jia Huan, at the sight of them, also wished to join in their games; and Baochai, who had always looked upon him with, in fact, the same eye as she did Baoyu, and with no different sentiment of any kind, pressed him to come up, upon hearing that he was on this occasion desirous to play; and, when he had seated himself together with them, they began to gamble, staking each time a pile of ten cash. The first time, he was the winner, and he felt supremely elated at heart, but as it happened that he subsequently lost in several consecutive games he soon became a prey to considerable distress. But in due course came the game in which it was his turn to cast the dice, and, if in throwing, he got seven spots, he stood to win, but he was likewise bound to be a winner were he to turn up six; and when Ying'er had turned up three spots and lost, he consequently took up the dice, and dashing them with spite, one of them settled at five; and, as the other reeled wildly about, Ying'er clapped her hands, and kept on shouting, "one spot;" while Jia Huan at once gazed with fixed eye and cried at random: "It's six, it's seven, it's eight!" But the dice, as it happened, turned up at one spot, and Jia Huan was so exasperated that putting out his hand, he speedily made a snatch at the dice, and eventually was about to lay hold of the money, arguing that it was six spot. But Ying'er expostulated, "It was distinctly an ace," she said. And as Baochai noticed how distressed Jia Huan was, she forthwith cast a glance at Ying'er and observed: "The older you get, the less manners you have! Is it likely that gentlemen will cheat you? and don't you yet put down the money?"

Ying'er felt her whole heart much aggrieved, but as she heard Baochai make these remarks, she did not presume to utter a sound, and as she was under the necessity of laying down the cash, she muttered to herself: "This one calls himself a gentleman, and yet cheats us of these few cash, for which I myself even have no eye! The other day when I played with Mr. Baoyu, he lost ever so many, and yet he did not distress himself! and what remained of the cash were besides snatched away by a few servant-girls, but all he did was to smile, that's all!"

Baochai did not allow her time to complete what she had to say, but there and then called her to account and made her desist; whereupon Jia Huan exclaimed: "How can I compare with Baoyu; you all fear him, and keep on good terms with him, while you all look down upon me for not being the child of my lady." And as he uttered these words, he at once gave way to tears.

"My dear cousin," Baochai hastened to advise him, "leave off at once language of this kind, for people will laugh at you;" and then went on to scold Ying'er, when Baoyu just happened to come in. Perceiving him in this plight, "What is the matter?" he asked; but Jia Huan had not the courage to say anything.

Baochai was well aware of the custom, which prevailed in their family, that younger brothers lived in respect of the elder brothers, but she was not however cognisant of the fact that Baoyu would not that anyone should entertain any fear of him. His idea being that elder as well as younger brothers had, all alike, father and mother to admonish them, and that there was no need for any of that officiousness, which, instead of doing good gave, on the contrary, rise to estrangement. "Besides," (he reasoned,) "I'm the offspring of the primary wife, while he's the son of the secondary wife, and, if by treating him as leniently as I have done, there are still those to talk about me, behind my back, how could I exercise any control over him?" But besides these, there were other still more foolish notions, which he fostered in his mind; but what foolish notions they were can you, reader, guess? As a result of his growing up, from his early youth, among a crowd of girls, of whom, in the way of sister, there was Yuanchun, of cousins, from his paternal uncle's side, there were Yingchun, and Xichun, and of relatives also there were Shi Xiangyun, Lin Daiyu, Xue Baochai, and the rest, he, in due course, resolved in his mind that the divine and unsullied virtue of Heaven and earth was only implanted in womankind, and that men were no more than feculent dregs and foul dirt. And for this reason it was that men were without discrimination, considered by him as so many filthy objects, which might or might not exist; while the relationships of father, paternal uncles, and brothers, he did not however presume to disregard, as these were among the injunctions bequeathed by the holy men, and he felt bound to listen to a few of their precepts. But to the above causes must be assigned the fact that, among his brothers, he did no more than accomplish the general purport of the principle of human affections; bearing in mind no thought whatever that he himself was a human being of the male sex, and that it was his duty to be an example to his younger brothers. And this is why Jia Huan and the others entertained no respect for him, though in their veneration for dowager lady Jia, they yielded to him to a certain degree.

Baochai harbored fears lest, on this occasion, Baoyu should call him to book, and put him out of face, and she there and then lost no time in taking Jia Huan's part with a view to screening him.

"In this felicitous first moon what are you blubbering for?" Baoyu inquired, "if this place isn't nice, why then go somewhere else to play. But from reading books, day after day, you've studied so much that you've become quite a dunce. If this thing, for instance, isn't good, that must, of course, be good, so then discard this and take up that, but is it likely that by sticking to this thing and crying for a while that it will become good? You came originally with the idea of reaping some fun, and you've instead provoked yourself to displeasure, and isn't it better then that you should be off at once."

Jia Huan upon hearing these words could not but come back to his quarters; and Mrs. Zhao noticing the frame of mind in which he was felt constrained to inquire: "Where is it that you've been looked down upon by being made to fill up a hole, and being trodden under foot?"

"I was playing with cousin Baochai," Jia Huan readily replied, "when Ying'er insulted me, and deprived me of my money, and brother Baoyu drove me away."

"Cui!" exclaimed Mrs. Zhao, "who bade you (presume so high) as to get up into that lofty tray? You low and barefaced thing! What place is there that you can't go to and play; and who told you to run over there and bring upon yourself all this shame?"

As she spoke, lady Feng was, by a strange coincidence, passing outside under the window; so that every word reached her ear, and she speedily asked from outside the window: "What are you up to in this happy first moon? These brothers are, really, but mere children, and will you just for a slight mistake, go on preaching to him! what's the use of coming out with all you've said? Let him go wherever he pleases; for there are still our lady and Mr. Jia Zheng to keep him in order. But you go and sputter him with your gigantic mouth; he's at present a master, and if there be anything wrong about him, there are, after all, those to rate him; and what business is that of yours? Brother Huan, come out with you, and follow me and let us go and enjoy ourselves."

Jia Huan had ever been in greater fear and trembling of lady Feng, than of Madame Wang, so that when her summons reached his ear, he hurriedly went out, while Mrs. Zhao, on the other hand, did not venture to breathe a single word.

"You too," resumed lady Feng, addressing Jia Huan; "are a thing devoid of all natural spirit! I've often told you that if you want to eat, drink, play, or laugh, you were quite free to go and play with whatever female cousin, male cousin, or sister-in-law you choose to disport yourself with; but you won't listen to my words. On the contrary, you let all these persons teach you to be depraved in your heart, perverse in your mind, to be sly, artful, and domineering; and you've, besides, no respect for your own self, but will go with that low-bred lot! and your perverse purpose is to begrudge people's preferences! But what you've lost are simply a few cash, and do you behave in this manner? How much did you lose?" she proceeded to ask Jia Huan; and Jia Huan, upon hearing this question, felt constrained to obey, by saying something in the way of a reply. "I've lost," he explained, "some hundred or two hundred cash."

"You have," rejoined lady Feng, "the good fortune of being a gentleman, and do you make such a fuss for the loss of a hundred or two hundred cash!" and turning her head round, "Feng'er," she added, "go and fetch a thousand cash; and as the girls are all playing at the back, take him along to go and play. And if again by and by, you're so mean and deceitful, I shall, first of all, beat you, and then tell someone to report it at school, and won't your skin be flayed for you? All because of this want of respect of yours, your elder cousin is so angry with you that his teeth itch; and were it not that I prevent him, he would hit you with his foot in the stomach and kick all your intestines out! Get away," she then cried; whereupon Jia Huan obediently followed Feng'er, and taking the money he went all by himself to play with Yingchun and the rest; where we shall leave him without another word.

But to return to Baoyu. He was just amusing himself and laughing with Baochai, when at an unexpected moment, he heard someone announce that Miss Shi had come. At these words, Baoyu rose, and was at once going off when "Wait," shouted Baochai with a smile, "and we'll go over together and see her."

Saying this, she descended from the stove-couch, and came, in company with Baoyu, to dowager lady Jia's on this side, where they saw Shi Xingyun laughing aloud, and talking immoderately; and upon catching sight of them both, she promptly inquired after their healths, and exchanged salutations.

Lin Daiyu just happened to be standing by, and having set the question to Baoyu "Where do you come from?" "I come from cousin Baochai's rooms," Baoyu readily replied.

Daiyu gave a sardonic smile. "What I maintain is this," she rejoined, "that lucky enough for you, you were detained over there; otherwise, you would long ago have, at once, come flying in here!"

"Am I only free to play with you?" Baoyu inquired, "and to dispel your ennui! I simply went over to her place for a run, and that quite casually, and will you insinuate all these things?"

"Your words are quite devoid of sense," Daiyu added; "whether you go or not what's that to me? neither did I tell you to give me any distraction; you're quite at liberty from this time forth not to pay any notice to me!"

Saying this, she flew into a high dudgeon and rushed back into her room; but Baoyu promptly followed in her footsteps: "Here you are again in a huff," he urged, "and all for no reason! Had I even passed any remark that I shouldn't, you should anyhow have still sat in there, and chatted and laughed with the others for a while; instead of that, you come again to sit and mope all alone!"

"Are you my keeper?" Daiyu expostulated.

"I couldn't, of course," Baoyu smiled, "presume to exercise any influence over you; but the only thing is that you are doing your own health harm!"

"If I do ruin my health," Daiyu rejoined, "and I die, it's my own lookout! what's that to do with you?"

"What's the good," protested Baoyu, "of talking in this happy first moon of dying and of living?"

"I will say die," insisted Daiyu, "die now, at this very moment! but you're afraid of death; and you may live a long life of a hundred years, but what good will that be!"

"If all we do is to go on nagging in this way," Baoyu remarked smiling, "will I anymore be afraid to die? on the contrary, it would be better to die, and be free!"

"Quite so!" continued Daiyu with alacrity, "if we go on nagging in this way, it would be better for me to die, and that you should be free of me!"

"I speak of my own self dying," Baoyu added, "so don't misunderstand my words and accuse people wrongly."

While he was as yet speaking, Baochai entered the room: "Cousin Shi is waiting for you," she said; and with these words, she hastily pushed Baoyu on, and they walked away.

Daiyu, meanwhile, became more and more a prey to resentment; and disconsolate as she felt, she shed tears in front of the window. But not time enough had transpired to allow two cups of tea to be drunk, before Baoyu came back again. At the sight of him, Daiyu sobbed still more fervently and incessantly, and Baoyu realizing the state she was in, and knowing well enough how arduous a task it would be to bring her round, began to join together a hundred, yea a thousand kinds of soft phrases and tender words to console her. But at an unforeseen moment, and before he could himself open his mouth, he heard Daiyu anticipate him.

"What have you come back again for?" she asked. "Let me die or live, as I please, and have done! You've really got at present someone to play with you, one who, compared with me, is able to read and able to compose, able to write, to speak, as well as to joke, one too who for fear lest you should have ruffled your temper dragged you away, and what do you return here for now?"

Baoyu, after listening to all she had to say, hastened to come up to her. "Is it likely," he observed in a low tone of voice, "that an intelligent person like you isn't so much as aware that near relatives can't be separated by a distant relative, and a remote friend set aside an old friend! I'm stupid, there's no gainsaying, but I do anyhow understand what these two sentiments imply. You and I are, in the first place, cousins on my father's sister's side; while sister Baochai and I are two cousins on mother's sides, so that, according to the degrees of relationship, she's more distant than yourself. In the second place, you came here first, and we two have our meals at one table and sleep in one bed, having ever since our youth grown up together; while she has only recently come, and how could I ever distance you on her account?"

"Cui!" Daiyu exclaimed. "Will I forsooth ever make you distance her! who and what kind of person have I become to do such a thing? What (I said) was prompted by my own motives."

"I too," Baoyu urged, "made those remarks prompted by my own heart's motives, and do you mean to say that your heart can only read the feelings of your own heart, and has no idea whatsoever of my own?"

Daiyu at these words, lowered her head and said not a word. But after a long interval, "You only know," she continued, "how to feel bitter against people for their action in censuring you: but you don't, after all, know that you yourself provoke people to such a degree, that it's hard for them to put up with it! Take for instance the weather of today as an example. It's distinctly very cold, today, and yet, how is it that you are so contrary as to go and divest yourself of the pelisse with the bluish breast-fur overlapping the cloth?"

"Why say I didn't wear it?" Baoyu smilingly observed. "I did, but seeing you get angry I felt suddenly in such a terrible blaze, that I at once took it off!"

Daiyu heaved a sigh. "You'll by and by catch a cold," she remarked, "and then you'll again have to starve, and vociferate for something to eat!"

While these two were having this colloquy, Xiangyun was seen to walk in! "You two, Ai cousin and cousin Lin," she ventured jokingly, "are together playing every day, and though I've managed to come after ever so much trouble, you pay no heed to me at all!"

"It's invariably the rule," Daiyu retorted smilingly, "that those who have a defect in their speech will insist upon talking; she can't even come out correctly with 'er' (secundus) cousin, and keeps on calling him 'Ai' cousin, 'Ai' cousin! And by and by when you play 'Wei Qi' you're sure also to shout out yao, ai, (instead of er), san; (one, two, three)."

Baoyu laughed. "If you imitate her," he interposed, "and get into that habit, you'll also begin to bite your tongue when you talk."

"She won't make even the slightest allowance for anyone," Xingyun rejoined; "her sole idea being to pick out others' faults. You may readily be superior to any mortal being, but you shouldn't, after all, offend against what's right and make fun of every person you come across! But I'll point out someone, and if you venture to jeer her, I'll at once submit to you."

"Who is it?" Daiyu vehemently inquired.

"If you do have the courage," Xiangyun answered, "to pick out cousin Baochai's faults, you then may well be held to be first-rate!"

Daiyu after hearing these words, gave a sarcastic smile. "I was wondering," she observed, "who it was. Is it indeed she? How could I ever presume to pick out hers?"

Baoyu allowed her no time to finish, but hastened to say something to interrupt the conversation.

"I couldn't, of course, during the whole of this my lifetime," Xiangyun laughed, "attain your standard! but my earnest wish is that by and by should be found for you, cousin Lin, a husband, who bites his tongue when he speaks, so that you should every minute and second listen to 'ai-ya-os!' Amituo Fo, won't then your reward be manifest to my eyes!"

As she made this remark, they all burst out laughing heartily, and Xiangyun speedily turned herself round and ran away.

But reader, do you want to know the sequel? Well, then listen to the explanation given in the next chapter.

CHAPTER 21

The eminent Xiren, with winsome ways, rails at Baoyu, with a view to exhortation. The beauteous Ping'er, with soft words, screens Jia Lian.

But to resume our story, when Shi Xiangyun ran out of the room, she was all in a flutter lest Lin Daiyu should catch her up; but Baoyu, who came after her, readily shouted out, "You'll trip and fall. How ever could she come up to you?"

Lin Daiyu went in pursuit of her as far as the entrance, when she was impeded from making further progress by Baoyu, who stretched his arms out against the posts of the door.

"Were I to spare Yun'er, I couldn't live!" Lin Daiyu exclaimed, as she tugged at his arms. But Xiangyun, perceiving that Baoyu obstructed the door, and surmising that Daiyu could not come out, speedily stood still. "My dear cousin," she smilingly pleaded, "do let me off this time!"

But it just happened that Baochai, who was coming along, was at the back of Xiangyun, and with a face also beaming with smiles: "I advise you both," she said, "to leave off out of respect for cousin Baoyu, and have done."

"I don't agree to that," Daiyu rejoined; "are you people, pray, all of one mind to do nothing but make fun of me?"

"Who ventures to make fun of you?" Baoyu observed advisingly; "and hadn't you made sport of her, would she have presumed to have said anything about you?"

While this quartet were finding it an arduous task to understand one another, a servant came to invite them to have their repast, and they eventually crossed over to the front side, and as it was already time for the lamps to be lit, Madame Wang, widow Li Wan, lady Feng, Yingchun, Tanchun, Xichun, and the other cousins, adjourned in a body to dowager lady Jia's apartments on this side, where the whole company spent a while in a chat on irrelevant topics, after which they each returned to their rooms and retired to bed. Xiangyun, as of old, betook herself to Daiyu's quarters to rest, and Baoyu escorted them both into their apartment, and it was after the hour had already past the second watch, and Xiren had come and pressed him several times, that he at length returned to his own bedroom and went to sleep. The next morning, as soon as it was daylight, he threw his clothes over him, put on his low shoes and came over into Daiyu's room, where he however saw nothing of the two girls Zijuan and Cuilu, as there was no one else here in there besides his two cousins, still reclining under the coverlets. Daiyu was closely wrapped in a quilt of almond-red silk, and lying quietly, with closed eyes fast asleep; while Shi Xiangyun, with her handful of shiny hair draggling along the edge of the pillow, was covered only up to the chest, and outside the coverlet rested her curved snow-white arm, with the gold bracelets, which she had on.

At the sight of her, Baoyu heaved a sigh. "Even when asleep," he soliloquized, "she can't be quiet! but by and by, when the wind will have blown on her, she'll again shout that her shoulder is sore!" With these words, he gently covered her, but Lin Daiyu had already awoke out of her sleep, and becoming aware that there was someone about, she promptly concluded that it must, for a certainty, be Baoyu, and turning herself accordingly round, and discovering at a glance that the truth was not beyond her conjectures, she observed: "What have you run over to do at this early hour?" to which question Baoyu replied: "Do you call this early? but get up and see for yourself!"

"First quit the room," Daiyu suggested, "and let us get up!"

Baoyu thereupon made his exit into the ante-chamber, and Daiyu jumped out of bed, and awoke Xiangyun. When both of them had put on their clothes, Baoyu re-entered and took a seat by the side of the toilet table; whence he beheld Zijuan and Xueyan walk in and wait upon them, as they dressed their hair and performed their ablutions. Xiangyun had done washing her face, and Cuilu at once took the remaining water and was about to throw it away, when Baoyu interposed, saying: "Wait, I'll avail myself of this opportunity to wash too and finish with it, and thus save myself the trouble of having again to go over!" Speaking the while, he hastily came forward, and bending his waist, he washed his face twice with two handfuls of water, and when Zijuan went over to give him the scented soap, Baoyu added: "In this basin, there's a good deal of it and there's no need of rubbing any more!" He then washed his face with two more handfuls, and forthwith asked for a towel, and Cuilu exclaimed: "What! have you still got this failing? when will you turn a new leaf?" But Baoyu paid not so much as any heed to her, and there and then called for some salt, with which he rubbed his teeth, and rinsed his mouth. When he had done, he perceived that Xiangyun had already finished combing her hair, and speedily coming up to her, he put on a smile, and said: "My dear cousin, comb my hair for me!"

"This can't be done!" Xiangyun objected.

"My dear cousin," Baoyu continued smirkingly, "how is it that you combed it for me in former times?"

"I've forgotten now how to comb it!" Xiangyun replied.

"I'm not, after all, going out of doors," Baoyu observed, "nor will I wear a hat or frontlet, so that all that need be done is to plait a few queues, that's all!" Saying this, he went on to appeal to her in a thousand and one endearing terms, so that Xiangyun had no alternative, but to draw his head nearer to her and to comb one queue after another, and as when he stayed at home he wore no hat, nor had, in fact, any tufted horns, she merely took the short surrounding hair from all four sides, and twisting it into small tufts, she collected it together over the hair on the crown of the head, and plaited a large queue, binding it fast with red ribbon; while from the root of the hair to the end of the queue, were four pearls in a row, below which, in the way of a tip, was suspended a golden pendant.

"Of these pearls there are only three," Xiangyun remarked as she went on plaiting; "this isn't one like them; I remember these were all of one kind, and how is it that there's one short?"

"I've lost one," Baoyu rejoined.

"It must have dropped," Xiangyun added, "when you went out of doors, and been picked up by someone when you were off your guard; and he's now, instead of you, the richer for it."

"One can neither tell whether it has been really lost," Daiyu, who stood by, interposed, smiling the while sarcastically; "nor could one say whether it hasn't been given away to someone to be mounted in some trinket or other and worn!"

Baoyu made no reply; but set to work, seeing that the two sides of the dressing table were all full of toilet boxes and other such articles, taking up those that came under his hand and examining them. Grasping unawares a box of cosmetic, which was within his reach, he would have liked to have brought it to his lips, but he feared again lest Xiangyun should chide him. While he was hesitating whether to do so or not, Xiangyun, from behind, stretched forth her arm and gave him a smack, which sent the cosmetic flying from his hand, as she cried out: "You good-for-nothing! when will you mend those weaknesses of yours!" But hardly had she had time to complete this remark, when she caught sight of Xiren walk in, who upon perceiving this state of things, became aware that he was already combed and washed, and she felt constrained to go back and attend to her own coiffure and ablutions.

But suddenly, she saw Baochai come in and inquire: "Where's cousin Baoyu gone?"

"Do you mean to say," Xiren insinuated with a sardonic smile, "that your cousin Baoyu has leisure to stay at home?"

When Baochai heard these words, she inwardly comprehended her meaning, and when she further heard Xiren remark with a sigh: "Cousins may well be on intimate terms, but they should also observe some sort of propriety; and they shouldn't night and day romp together; and no matter how people may tender advice it's all like so much wind blowing past the ears." Baochai began, at these remarks, to cogitate within her mind: "May I not, possibly, have been mistaken in my estimation of this girl; for to listen to her words, she would really seem to have a certain amount of savoir faire!"

Baochai thereupon took a seat on the stove-couch, and quietly, in the course of their conversation on one thing and another, she managed to ascertain her age, her native village, and other such particulars, and then setting her mind diligently to put, on the sly, her conversation and mental capacity to the test, she discovered how deeply worthy she was to be respected and loved. But in a while Baoyu arrived, and Baochai at once quitted the apartment.

"How is it," Baoyu at once inquired, "that cousin Baochai was chatting along with you so lustily, and that as soon as she saw me enter, she promptly ran away?"

Xiren did not make any reply to his first question, and it was only when he had repeated it that Xiren remarked: "Do you ask me? How can I know what goes on between you two?"

When Baoyu heard these words, and he noticed that the look on her face was so unlike that of former days, he lost no time in putting on a smile and asking: "Why is it that you too are angry in real earnest?"

"How could I presume to get angry!" Xiren rejoined smiling indifferently; "but you mustn't, from this day forth, put your foot into this room! and as you have anyhow people to wait on you, you shouldn't come again to make use of my services, for I mean to go and attend to our old mistress, as in days of old."

With this remark still on her lips, she lay herself down on the stove-couch and closed her eyes. When Baoyu perceived the state of mind she was in, he felt deeply surprised and could not refrain from coming forward and trying to cheer her up. But Xiren kept her eyes closed and paid no heed to him, so that Baoyu was quite at a loss how to act. But espying Sheyue enter the room, he said with alacrity: "What's up with your sister?"

"Do I know?" answered Sheyue, "examine your own self and you'll readily know!"

After these words had been heard by Baoyu, he gazed vacantly for some time, feeling the while very unhappy; but raising himself impetuously: "Well!" he exclaimed, "if you don't notice me, all right, I too will go to sleep," and as he spoke he got up, and, descending from the couch, he betook himself to his own bed and went to sleep. Xiren noticing that he had not budged for ever so long, and that he faintly snored, presumed that he must have fallen fast asleep, so she speedily rose to her feet, and, taking a wrapper, came over and covered him. But a sound of "hu" reached her ear, as Baoyu promptly threw it off and once again closed his eyes and feigned sleep. Xiren distinctly grasped his idea and, forthwith nodding her head, she smiled coldly. "You really needn't lose your temper! but from this time forth, I'll become mute, and not say one word to you; and what if I do?"

Baoyu could not restrain himself from rising. "What have I been up to again," he asked, "that you're once more at me with your advice? As far as your advice goes, it's all well and good; but just now without one word of counsel, you paid no heed to me when I came in, but, flying into a huff, you went to sleep. Nor could I make out what it was all about, and now here you are again maintaining that I'm angry. But when did I hear you, pray, give me a word of advice of any kind?"

"Doesn't your mind yet see for itself?" Xiren replied; "and do you still expect me to tell you?"

While they were disputing, dowager lady Jia sent a servant to call him to his repast, and he thereupon crossed over to the front; but after he had hurriedly swallowed a few bowls of rice, he returned to his own apartment, where he discovered Xiren reclining on the outer stove-couch, while Sheyue was playing with the dominoes by her side. Baoyu had been ever aware of the intimacy which existed between Sheyue and Xiren, so that paying not the slightest notice to even Sheyue, he raised the soft portiere and straightway walked all alone into the inner apartment. Sheyue felt constrained to follow him in, but Baoyu at once pushed her out, saying: "I don't venture to disturb you two;" so that Sheyue had no alternative but to leave the room with a smiling countenance, and to bid two young waiting-maids go in. Baoyu took hold of a book and read for a considerable time in a reclining position; but upon raising his head to ask for some tea, he caught sight of a couple of waiting-maids, standing below; the one of whom, slightly older than the other, was exceedingly winsome.

"What's your name?" Baoyu eagerly inquired.

"I'm called Huixiang, (orchid fragrance)," that waiting-maid rejoined simperingly.

"Who gave you this name?" Baoyu went on to ask.

"I went originally under the name of Yunxiang (Gum Sandarac)," added Huixiang, "but Miss Hua it was who changed it."

"You should really be called Huiqi, (latent fragrance), that would be proper; and why such stuff as Huixiang, (orchid fragrance)?"

How many sisters have you got?" he further went on to ask of her.

"Four," replied Huixiang.

"Which of them are you?" Baoyu asked.

"The fourth," answered Huixiang.

"By and by you must be called Si'er, (fourth child)," Baoyu suggested, "for there's no need for any such nonsense as Huixiang (orchid fragrance) or Lanqi (*epidendrum* perfume.) Which single girl deserves to be compared to all these flowers, without profaning pretty names and fine surnames!"

As he uttered these words, he bade her give him some tea, which he drank; while Xiren and Sheyue, who were in the outer apartment, had been listening for a long time and laughing with compressed lips.

Baoyu did not, on this day, so much as put his foot outside the door of his room, but sat all alone sad and dejected, simply taking up his books, in order to dispel his melancholy fit, or diverting himself with his writing materials; while he did not even avail himself of the services of any of the family servants, but simply bade Si'er answer his calls.

This Si'er was, who would have thought it, a girl gifted with matchless artfulness, and perceiving that Baoyu had requisitioned her services, she speedily began to devise extreme ways and means to inveigle him. When evening came, and dinner was over, Baoyu's eyes were scorching hot and his ears burning from the effects of two cups of wine that he had taken. Had it been in past days, he would have now had Xiren and her companions with him, and with all their good cheer and laughter, he would have been enjoying himself. But here was he, on this occasion, dull and forlorn, a solitary being, gazing at the lamp with an absolute lack of pleasure. By and by he felt a certain wish to go after them, but dreading that if they carried their point, they would, in the future, come and tender advice still more immoderate, and that, were he to put on the airs of a superior to intimidate them, he would appear to be too deeply devoid of all feeling, he therefore, needless to say, thwarted the wish of his heart, and treated them just as if they were dead. And as anyway he was constrained also to live, alone though he was, he readily looked upon them, for the time being as departed, and did not worry his mind in the least on their account. On the contrary, he was able to feel happy and contented with his own society. Hence it was that bidding Si'er trim the candles and brew the tea, he himself perused for a time the "Nanhuajing," and upon reaching the precept: "On thieves," given on some additional pages, the burden of which was: "Therefore by exterminating intuitive wisdom, and by discarding knowledge, highway robbers will cease to exist, and by taking off the jade and by putting away the pearls, pilferers will not spring to existence; by burning the slips and by breaking up the seals, by smashing the measures, and snapping the scales, the result will be that the people will not wrangle; by abrogating, to the utmost degree, wise rules under the heavens, the people will, at length, be able to take part in deliberation. By putting to confusion the musical scale, and destroying fifes and lutes, by deafening the ears of the blind Kuang, then, at last, will the human race in the world constrain his sense of hearing. By extinguishing literary compositions, by dispersing the five colors and by sticking the eyes of Lizhu, then, at length, mankind under the whole sky, will restrain the perception of his eyes. By destroying and eliminating the hooks and lines, by discarding the compasses and squares, and by amputating Gongzhui's fingers, the human race will ultimately succeed in constraining his ingenuity,"—his high spirits, on perusal of this passage, were so exultant that taking advantage of the exuberance caused by the wine, he picked up his brush, for he could not repress himself, and continued the text in this wise: "By burning the flower, (Hua Xiren) and dispersing the musk, (Sheyue), the consequence will be that the inmates of the inner chambers will, eventually, keep advice to themselves. By obliterating Baochai's supernatural beauty, by reducing to ashes Daiyu's spiritual perception, and by destroying and extinguishing my affectionate preferences, the beautiful in the inner chambers as well as the plain will then, at length, be put on the same footing. And as they will keep advice to themselves, there will be no fear of any disagreement. By obliterating her supernatural beauty, I shall then have no incentive for any violent affection; by dissolving her spiritual perception, I will have no feelings with which to foster the memory of her talents. The hairpin, jade, flower, and musk (Baochai, Daiyu, Xiren, and Sheyue) do each and all spread out their snares and dig mines, and thus succeed in inveigling and entrapping everyone in the world."

At the conclusion of this annex, he flung the brush away, and lay himself down to sleep. His head had barely reached the pillow before he at once fell fast asleep, remaining the whole night long perfectly unconscious of everything straight up to the break of day, when upon waking and turning himself round, he, at a glance, caught sight of no one else than Xiren, sleeping in her clothes over the coverlet.

Baoyu had already banished from his mind every thought of what had transpired the previous day, so that forthwith giving Xiren a push: "Get up!" he said, "and be careful where you sleep, as you may catch cold."

The fact is that Xiren was aware that he was, without regard to day or night, ever up to mischief with his female cousins; but presuming that if she earnestly called him to account, he would not mend his ways, she had, for this reason, had recourse to tender language to exhort him, in the hope that, in a short while, he would come round again to his better self. But against all her expectations Baoyu had, after the lapse of a whole day and night, not changed the least in his manner, and as she really was in her heart quite at a loss what to do, she failed to find throughout the whole night any proper sleep. But when on this day, she unexpectedly perceived Baoyu in this mood, she flattered herself that he had made up his mind to effect a change, and readily thought it best not to notice him. Baoyu, seeing that she made no reply, forthwith stretched out his hand and undid her jacket; but he had just unclasped the button, when his arm was pushed away by Xiren, who again made it fast herself.

Baoyu was so much at his wit's ends that he had no alternative but to take her hand and smilingly ask: "What's the matter with you, after all, that I've had to ask you something time after time?"

Xiren opened her eyes wide. "There's nothing really the matter with me!" she observed; "but as you're awake, you surely had better be going over into the opposite room to comb your hair and wash; for if you dilly-dally any longer, you won't be in time."

"Where shall I go over to?" Baoyu inquired.

Xiren gave a sarcastic grin. "Do you ask me?" she rejoined; "do I know? you're at perfect liberty to go over wherever you like; from this day forth you and I must part company so as to avoid fighting like cocks or brawling like geese, to the amusement of third parties. Indeed, when you get surfeited on that side, you come over to this, where there are, after all, such girls as Fours and Fives (Si'er and Wu'er) to dance attendance upon you. But such kind of things as ourselves uselessly defile fine names and fine surnames."

"Do you still remember this today!" Baoyu asked with a smirk.

"Hundred years hence I shall still bear it in mind," Xiren protested; "I'm not like you, who treat my words as so much wind blowing by the side of your ears, that what I've said at night, you've forgotten early in the morning."

Baoyu perceiving what a seductive though angry air pervaded her face found it difficult to repress his feelings, and speedily taking up, from the side of the pillow, a hair-pin made of jade, he dashed it down breaking it into two exclaiming: "If I again don't listen to your words, may I fare like this hair-pin."

Xiren immediately picked up the hair-pin, as she remarked: "What's up with you at this early hour of the morning? Whether you listen or not is of no consequence; and is it worth while that you should behave as you do?"

"How can you know," Baoyu answered, "the anguish in my heart!"

"Do you also know what anguish means?" Xiren observed laughing; "if you do, then you can judge what the state of my heart is! But be quick and get up, and wash your face and be off!"

As she spoke, they both got out of bed and performed their toilette; but after Baoyu had gone to the drawing rooms, and at a moment least expected by anyone, Daiyu walked into his apartment. Noticing that Baoyu was not in, she was fumbling with the books on the table and examining them, when, as luck would have it, she turned up the Zhuangzi of the previous day. Upon perusing the passage tagged on by Baoyu, she could not help feeling both incensed and amused. Nor could she restrain herself from taking up the brush and appending a stanza to this effect:

> Who is that man, who of his brush, without good rhyme, made use,
> A toilsome task to do into the Zhuangzi text to steal,
> Who for the knowledge he doth lack no sense of shame doth feel,
> But language vile and foul employs third parties to abuse?

At the conclusion of what she had to write, she too came into the drawing room; but after paying her respects to dowager lady Jia, she walked over to Madame Wang's quarters.

Contrary to everybody's expectations, lady Feng's daughter, Da Jie'er, had fallen ill, and a great fuss was just going on as the doctor had been sent for to diagnose her ailment.

"My congratulations to you, ladies," the doctor explained; "this young lady has fever, as she has small-pox; indeed it's no other complaint!"

As soon as Madame Wang and lady Feng heard the tidings, they lost no time in sending round to ascertain whether she was getting on all right or not, and the doctor replied: "The symptoms are, it is true, serious, but favorable; but though after all importing no danger, it's necessary to get ready the silkworms and pigs' tails."

When lady Feng received this report, she, there and then, hastened to make the necessary preparations, and while she had the rooms swept and oblations offered to the goddess of small-pox, she, at the same time, transmitted orders to her household to avoid viands fried or roasted in fat, or other such heating things; and also bade Ping'er get ready the bedding and clothes for Jia Lian in a separate room, and taking pieces of deep red cotton material, she distributed them to the nurses, waiting-maids and all the servants, who were in close attendance, to cut out clothes for themselves. And having had likewise some apartments outside swept clean, she detained two doctors to alternately deliberate on the treatment, feel the pulse, and administer the medicines; and for twelve days, they were not at liberty to return to their homes; while Jia Lian had no help but to move his quarters temporarily into the outer library, and lady Feng and Ping'er remained both in daily attendance upon Madame Wang in her devotions to the goddess.

Jia Lian, now that he was separated from lady Feng, soon felt disposed to look round for a flame. He had only slept alone for a couple of nights, but these nights had been so intensely intolerable that he had no option than to choose, for the time being, from among the young pages, those who were of handsome appearance, and bring them over to relieve his monotony. In the Rong Guo mansion, there was, it happened, a cook, a most useless, good-for-nothing drunkard, whose name was Duoguan, in whom people recognised an infirm and a useless husband so that they all dubbed him with the name of Duo Hunchong, the stupid worm Duo. As the wife given to him in marriage by his father and mother was this year just twenty, and possessed further several traits of beauty, and was also naturally of a flighty and frivolous disposition, she had an extreme penchant for violent flirtations. But Duo Hunchong, on the other hand, did not concern himself (with her deportment), and as long as he had wine, meat, and money he paid no heed whatever to anything. And for this reason it was that all the men in the two mansions of Ning and Rong had been successful in their attentions; and as this woman was exceptionally fascinating and incomparably giddy, she was generally known by all by the name Duo Gu Niang'er (Miss To).

Jia Lian, now that he had his quarters outside, chafed under the pangs of irksome ennui, yet he too, in days gone by, had set his eyes upon this woman, and had for long, watered in the mouth with admiration; but as, inside, he feared his winsome wife, and outside, he dreaded his beloved lads, he had not made any advances. But this Duo Gu Niang'er had likewise a liking for Jia Lian, and was full of resentment at the absence of a favorable opportunity; but she had recently come to hear that Jia Lian had shifted his quarters into the outer library, and her wont was, even in the absence of any legitimate purpose, to go over three and four times to entice him on; but though Jia Lian was, in every respect, like a rat smitten with hunger, he could not dispense with holding consultation with the young friends who enjoyed his confidence; and as he struck a bargain with them for a large amount of money and silks, how could they ever not have come to terms (with him to speak on his behalf)? Besides, they were all old friends of this woman, so that, as soon as they conveyed the proposal, she willingly accepted it. When night came Duo Hunchong was lying on the couch in a state of drunkenness, and at the second watch, when everyone was quiet, Jia Lian at once slipped in, and they had their assignation. As soon as he gazed upon her face, he lost control over his senses, and without even one word of ordinary greeting or commonplace remark, they forthwith, fervently indulged in a most endearing tête-à-tête.

This woman possessed, who could have thought it, a strange natural charm; for, as soon as any one of her lovers came within any close distance of her, he speedily could not but notice that her very tendons and bones mollified, paralyzed-like from feeling, so that his was the sensation of basking in a soft bower of love. What is more, her demonstrative ways and free-and-easy talk put even those of a born coquette to shame, with the result that while Jia Lian, at this time, longed to become heart and soul one with her, the woman designedly indulged in immodest innuendoes.

"Your daughter is at home," she insinuated in her recumbent position, "ill with the small-pox, and prayers are being offered to the goddess; and your duty too should be to abstain from love affairs for a couple of days, but on the contrary, by flirting with me, you've contaminated yourself! but, you'd better be off at once from me here!"

"You're my goddess!" gaspingly protested Jia Lian, as he gave way to demonstrativeness; "what do I care about any other goddess!"

The woman began to be still more indelicate in her manner, so that Jia Lian could not refrain himself from making a full exhibition of his warm sentiments. When their tête-à-tête had come to a close, they both went on again to vow by the mountains and swear by the seas, and though they found it difficult to part company and hard to tear themselves away, they, in due course, became, after this occasion, mutual sworn friends. But by a certain day the virus in Da Jie's system had become exhausted, and the spots subsided, and at the expiry of twelve days the goddess was removed, and the whole household offered sacrifices to heaven, worshipped the ancestors, paid their vows, burnt incense, exchanged congratulations, and distributed presents. And these formalities observed, Jia Lian once more moved back into his own bedroom and was reunited with lady Feng. The proverb is indeed true which says: "That a new marriage is not equal to a long separation," for there ensued between them demonstrations of loving affection still more numerous than heretofore, to which we need not, of course, refer with any minuteness.

The next day, at an early hour, after lady Feng had gone into the upper rooms, Ping'er set to work to put in order the clothes and bedding, which had been brought from outside, when, contrary to her expectation, a tress of hair fell out from inside the pillow-case, as she was intent upon shaking it. Ping'er understood its import, and taking at once the hair, she concealed it in her sleeve, and there and then came over into the room on this side, where she produced the hair, and smirkingly asked Jia Lian, "What's this?"

Jia Lian, at the sight of it, lost no time in making a snatch with the idea of depriving her of it; and when Ping'er speedily endeavored to run away, she was clutched by Jia Lian, who put her down on the stove-couch, and came up to take it from her hand.

"You heartless fellow!" Ping'er laughingly exclaimed, "I conceal this, with every good purpose, from her knowledge, and come to ask you about it, and you, on the contrary, fly into a rage! But wait till she comes back, and I'll tell her, and we'll see what will happen."

At these words, Jia Lian hastily forced a smile. "Dear girl!" he entreated, "give it to me, and I won't venture again to fly into a passion."

But hardly was this remark finished, when they heard the voice of lady Feng penetrate into the room. As soon as it reached the ear of Jia Lian, he was at a loss whether it was better to let her go or to snatch it away, and kept on shouting, "My dear girl! don't let her know."

Ping'er at once rose to her feet; but lady Feng had already entered the room; and she went on to bid Ping'er be quick and open a box and find a pattern for Madame Wang. Ping'er expressed her obedience with alacrity; but while in search of it, lady Feng caught sight of Jia Lian; and suddenly remembering something, she hastened to ask Ping'er about it.

"The other day," she observed, "some things were taken out, and have you brought them all in or not?"

"I have!" Ping'er assented.

"Is there anything short or not?" lady Feng inquired.

"I've carefully looked at them," Ping'er added, "and haven't found even one single thing short."

"Is there anything in excess?" lady Feng went on to ascertain.

Ping'er laughed. "It's enough," she rejoined, "that there's nothing short; and how could there really turn out to be anything over and above?"

"That this half month," lady Feng continued still smiling, "things have gone on immaculately it would be hard to vouch; for some ini-mate friend there may have been, who possibly has left something behind, in the shape of a ring, handkerchief, or other such object, there's no saying for certain!"

While these words were being spoken, Jia Lian's face turned perfectly sallow, and, as he stood behind lady Feng, he was intent upon gazing at Ping'er, making signs to her (that he was going) to cut her throat as a chicken is killed, (threatening her not to utter a sound) and entreating her to screen him; but Ping'er pretended not to notice him, and consequently observed smiling: "How is it that my ideas should coincide with those of yours, my lady; and as I suspected that there may have been something of the kind, I carefully searched all over, but I didn't find even so much as the slightest thing wrong; and if you don't believe me, my lady, you can search for your own self."

"You fool!" lady Feng laughed, "had he any things of the sort, would he be likely to let you and I discover them!"

With these words still on her lips, she took the patterns and went her way; whereupon Ping'er pointed at her nose, and shook her head to and fro. "In this matter," she smiled, "how much you should be grateful to me!" A remark which so delighted Jia Lian that his eyebrows distended, and his eyes smiled, and running over, he clasped her in his embrace, and called her promiscuously: "My darling, my pet, my own treasure!"

"This," observed Ping'er, with the tress in her hand, "will be my source of power, during all my lifetime! if you treat me kindly, then well and good! but if you behave unkindly, then we'll at once produce this thing!"

"Do put it away, please," Jia Lian entreated smirkingly, "and don't, on an any account, let her know about it!" and as he uttered these words, he noticed that she was off her guard, and, with a snatch, readily grabbed it adding laughingly: "In your hands, it would be a source of woe, so that it's better that I should burn it, and have done with it!" Saying this he simultaneously shoved it down the sides of his boot, while Ping'er shouted as she set her teeth close: "You wicked man! you cross the river and then demolish the bridge! but do you imagine that I'll by and by again tell lies on your behalf!"

Jia Lian perceiving how heart-stirring her seductive charms were, forthwith clasped her in his arms, and begged her to be his; but Ping'er snatched her hands out of his grasp and ran away out of the room; which so exasperated Jia Lian that as he bent his body, he exclaimed, full of indignation: "What a dreadful niggardly young wench! she actually sets her mind to stir up people's affections with her wanton blandishments, and then, after all, she runs away!"

"If I be wanton, it's my own look-out;" Ping'er answered, from outside the window, with a grin, "and who told you to arouse your affections? Do you forsooth mean to imply that my wish is to become your tool? And did she come to know about it would she again ever forgive me?"

"You needn't dread her!" Jia Lian urged; "wait till my monkey is up, and I'll take this jealous woman, and beat her to atoms; and she'll then know what stuff I'm made of. She watches me just as she would watch a thief! and she's only to hobnob with men, and I'm not to say a word to any girl! and if I do say aught to a girl, or get anywhere near one, she must at once give way to suspicion. But with no regard to younger brothers or nephews, to young and old, she prattles and giggles with them, and doesn't entertain any fear that I may be jealous; but henceforward I too won't allow her to set eyes upon any man."

"If she be jealous, there's every reason," Ping'er answered, "but for you to be jealous on her account isn't right. Her conduct is really straightforward, and her deportment upright, but your conduct is actuated by an evil heart, so much so that even I don't feel my heart at ease, not to say anything of her."

"You two," continued Jia Lian, "have a mouth full of malicious breath! Everything the couple of you do is invariably proper, while whatever I do is all from an evil heart! But some time or other I shall bring you both to your end with my own hands!"

This sentence was scarcely at an end, when lady Feng walked into the court. "If you're bent upon chatting," she urgently inquired, upon seeing Ping'er outside the window, "why don't you go into the room? and what do you mean, instead, by running out, and speaking with the window between?"

Jia Lian from inside took up the string of the conversation. "You should ask her," he said. "It would verily seem as if there were a tiger in the room to eat her up."

"There's not a single person in the room," Ping'er rejoined, "and what shall I stay and do with him?"

"It's just the proper thing that there should be no one else! Isn't it?" lady Feng remarked grinning sarcastically.

"Do these words allude to me?" Ping'er hastily asked, as soon as she had heard what she said.

Lady Feng forthwith laughed. "If they don't allude to you," she continued, "to whom do they?"

"Don't press me to come out with some nice things!" Ping'er insinuated, and, as she spoke, she did not even raise the portiere (for lady Feng to enter), but straightway betook herself to the opposite side.

Lady Feng lifted the portiere with her own hands, and walked into the room. "That girl Ping'er," she exclaimed, "has gone mad, and if this hussey does in real earnest wish to try and get the upper hand of me, it would be well for you to mind your skin."

Jia Lian listened to her, as he kept reclining on the couch. "I never in the least knew," he ventured, clapping his hands and laughing, "that Ping'er was so dreadful; and I must, after all, from henceforth look up to her with respect!"

"It's all through your humoring her," lady Feng rejoined; "so I'll simply settle scores with you and finish with it."

"Cui!" ejaculated Jia Lian at these words, "because you two can't agree, must you again make a scapegoat of me! Well then, I'll get out of the way of both of you!"

"I'll see where you'll go and hide," lady Feng observed.

"I've got somewhere to go!" Jia Lian added; and with these words, he was about to go, when lady Feng urged: "Don't be off! I have something to tell you."

What it is, is not yet known, but, reader, listen to the account given in the next chapter.

CHAPTER 22

Upon hearing the text of the stanza, Baoyu comprehends the Buddhistic spells. While the enigmas for the lanterns are being devised, Jia Zheng is grieved by a prognostic.

Jia Lian, for we must now prosecute our story, upon hearing lady Feng observe that she had something to consult about with him, felt constrained to halt and to inquire what it was about.

"On the 21st," lady Feng explained, "is cousin Xue's birthday, and what do you, after all, purpose doing?"

"Do I know what to do?" exclaimed Jia Lian; "you have made, time and again, arrangements for ever so many birthdays of grown-up people, and do you, really, find yourself on this occasion without any resources?"

"Birthdays of grown-up people are subject to prescribed rules," lady Feng expostulated; "but her present birthday is neither one of an adult nor that of an infant, and that's why I would like to deliberate with you!"

Jia Lian upon hearing this remark, lowered his head and gave himself to protracted reflection. "You're indeed grown dull!" he cried; "why you've a precedent ready at hand to suit your case! Cousin Lin's birthday affords a precedent, and what you did in former years for cousin Lin, you can in this instance likewise do for cousin Xue, and it will be all right."

At these words lady Feng gave a sarcastic smile. "Do you, pray, mean to insinuate," she added, "that I'm not aware of even this! I too had previously come, after some thought, to this conclusion; but old lady Jia explained, in my hearing yesterday, that having made inquiries about all their ages and their birthdays, she learnt that cousin Xue would this year be fifteen, and that though this was not the birthday, which made her of age, she could anyhow well be regarded as being on the dawn of the year, in which she would gather up her hair, so that our dowager lady enjoined that her anniversary should, as a matter of course, be celebrated, unlike that of cousin Lin."

"Well, in that case," Jia Lian suggested, "you had better make a few additions to what was done for cousin Lin!"

"That's what I too am thinking of," lady Feng replied, "and that's why I'm asking your views; for were I, on my own hook, to add anything you would again feel hurt for my not have explained things to you."

"That will do, that will do!" Jia Lian rejoined laughing, "none of these sham attentions for me! So long as you don't pry into my doings it will be enough; and will I go so far as to bear you a grudge?"

With these words still in his mouth, he forthwith went off. But leaving him alone we shall now return to Shi Xiangyun. After a stay of a couple of days, her intention was to go back, but dowager lady Jia said: "Wait until after you have seen the theatrical performance, then you can return home."

At this proposal, Shi Xiangyun felt constrained to remain, but she, at the same time, despatched a servant to her home to fetch two pieces of needlework, which she had in former days worked with her own hands, for a birthday present for Baochai.

Contrary to all expectations old lady Jia had, since the arrival of Baochai, taken quite a fancy to her, for her sedateness and good nature, and as this happened to be the first birthday which she was about to celebrate (in the family) she herself readily contributed twenty taels which, after sending for lady Feng, she handed over to her, to make arrangements for a banquet and performance.

"A venerable senior like yourself," lady Feng thereupon smiled and ventured, with a view to enhancing her good cheer, "is at liberty to celebrate the birthday of a child in any way agreeable to you, without any one presuming to raise any objection; but what's the use again of giving a banquet? But since it be your good pleasure and your purpose to have it celebrated with eclat, you could, needless to say, your own self have spent several taels from the private funds in that old treasury of yours! But you now produce those twenty taels, spoiled by damp and mold, to play the hostess with, with the view indeed of compelling us to supply what's wanted! But hadn't you really been able to contribute any more, no one would have a word to say; but the gold and silver, round as well as flat, have with their heavy weight pressed down the bottom of the box! and your sole object is to harass us and to extort from us. But raise your eyes and look about you; who isn't your venerable ladyship's son and daughter? and is it likely, pray, that in the future there will only be cousin Baoyu to carry you, our old lady, on his head, up the Wutai Shan? You may keep all these things for him alone! but though we mayn't at present, deserve that anything should be spent upon us, you shouldn't go so far as to place us in any perplexities (by compelling us to subscribe). And is this now enough for wines, and enough for the theatricals?"

As she bandied these words, everyone in the whole room burst out laughing, and even dowager lady Jia broke out in laughter while she observed: "Do you listen to that mouth? I myself am looked upon as having the gift of the gab, but why is it that I can't talk in such a wise as to put down this monkey? Your mother-in-law herself doesn't dare to be so overbearing in her speech; and here you are jabber, jabber with me!"

"My mother-in-law," explained lady Feng, "is also as fond of Baoyu as you are, so much so that I haven't anywhere I could go and give vent to my grievances; and instead of (showing me some regard) you say that I'm overbearing in my speech!"

With these words, she again enticed dowager lady Jia to laugh for a while. The old lady continued in the highest of spirits, and, when evening came, and they all appeared in her presence to pay their obeisance, her ladyship made it a point, while the whole company of ladies and young ladies were engaged in chatting, to ascertain of Baochai what play she liked to hear, and what things she fancied to eat.

Baochai was well aware that dowager lady Jia, well up in years though she was, delighted in sensational performances, and was partial to sweet and tender viands, so that she readily deferred, in every respect, to those things, which were to the taste of her ladyship, and enumerated a whole number of them, which made the old lady become the more exuberant. And the next day, she was the first to send over clothes, nicknacks, and such presents, while Madame Wang and lady Feng, Daiyu and the other girls, as well as the whole number of inmates had all presents for her, regulated by their degree of relationship, to which we need not allude in detail.

When the 21st arrived, a stage of an ordinary kind, small but yet handy, was improvised in dowager lady Jia's inner court, and a troupe of young actors, who had newly made their debut, was retained for the nonce, among whom were both those who could sing tunes, slow as well as fast. In the drawing rooms of the old lady were then laid out several tables for a family banquet and entertainment, at which there was not a single outside guest; and with the exception of Mrs. Xue, Shi Xiangyun, and Baochai, who were visitors, the rest were all inmates of her household.

On this day, Baoyu failed, at any early hour, to see anything of Lin Daiyu, and coming at once to her rooms in search of her, he discovered her reclining on the stove-couch. "Get up," Baoyu pressed her with a smile, "and come and have breakfast, for the plays will commence shortly; but whichever plays you would like to listen to, do tell me so that I may be able to choose them."

Daiyu smiled sarcastically. "In that case," she rejoined, "you had better specially engage a troupe and select those I like sung for my benefit; for on this occasion you can't be so impertinent as to make use of their expense to ask me what I like!"

"What's there impossible about this?" Baoyu answered smiling; "well, tomorrow I'll readily do as you wish, and ask them too to make use of what is yours and mine."

As he passed this remark, he pulled her up, and taking her hand in his own, they walked out of the room and came and had breakfast. When the time arrived to make a selection of the plays, dowager lady Jia of her own motion first asked Baochai to mark off those she liked; and though for a time Baochai declined, yielding the choice to others, she had no alternative but to decide, fixing upon a play called, "the Record of the Western Tour," a play of which the old lady was herself very fond. Next in order, she bade lady Feng choose, and lady Feng, had, after all, in spite of Madame Wang ranking before her in precedence, to consider old lady Jia's request, and not to presume to show obstinacy by any disobedience. But as she knew well enough that her ladyship had a penchant for what was exciting, and that she was still more partial to jests, jokes, epigrams, and buffoonery, she therefore hastened to precede (Madame Wang) and to choose a play, which was in fact no other than "Liu'er pawns his clothes."

Dowager lady Jia was, of course, still more elated. And after this she speedily went on to ask Daiyu to choose. Daiyu likewise concedingly yielded her turn in favor of Madame Wang and the other seniors, to make their selections before her, but the old lady expostulated. "Today," she said, "is primarily an occasion, on which I've brought all of you here for your special recreation; and we had better look after our own selves and not heed them! For have I, do you imagine, gone to the trouble of having a performance and laying a feast for their special benefit? they're already reaping benefit enough by being in here, listening to the plays and partaking of the banquet, when they have no right to either; and are they to be pressed further to make a choice of plays?"

At these words, the whole company had a hearty laugh; after which, Daiyu, at length, marked off a play; next in order following Baoyu, Shi Xiangyun, Yingchun, Tanchun, Xichun, widow Li Wan, and the rest, each and all of whom made a choice of plays, which were sung in the costumes necessary for each. When the time came to take their places at the banquet, dowager lady Jia bade Baochai make another selection, and Baochai cast her choice upon the play: "Lu Zhishen, in a fit of drunkenness stirs up a disturbance up the Wutai Mountain;" whereupon Baoyu interposed, with the remark: "All you fancy is to choose plays of this kind;" to which Baochai rejoined, "You've listened to plays all these years to no avail! How could you know the beauties of this play? the stage effect is grand, but what is still better are the apt and elegant passages in it."

"I've always had a dread of such sensational plays as these!" Baoyu retorted.

"If you call this play sensational," Baochai smilingly expostulated, well then you may fitly be looked upon as being no connoisseur of plays. But come over and I'll tell you. This play constitutes one of a set of books, entitled the 'Beidian Jiangchun,' which, as far as harmony, musical rests and closes, and tune go, is, it goes without saying, perfect; but there's among the elegant compositions a ballad entitled 'the Parasitic Plant,' written in a most excellent style; but now could you know anything about it?"

Baoyu, upon hearing her speak of such points of beauty, hastily drew near to her. "My dear cousin," he entreated, "recite it and let me hear it!" Whereupon Baochai went on as follows:

My manly tears I will not wipe away,
But from this place, the scholar's home, I'll stray.
The bonze for mercy I shall thank; under the lotus altar shave my
    pate;
With Yuan to be the luck I lack; soon in a twinkle we shall separate,
And needy and forlorn I'll come and go, with none to care about
    my fate.
Thither shall I a suppliant be for a fog wrapper and rain hat; my
    warrant I shall roll,
And listless with straw shoes and broken bowl, wherever to convert my fate may be, I'll stroll.

As soon as Baoyu had listened to her recital, he was so full of enthusiasm, that, clapping his knees with his hands, and shaking his head, he gave vent to incessant praise; after which he went on to extol Baochai, saying: "There's no book that you don't know."

"Be quiet, and listen to the play," Lin Daiyu urged; "they haven't yet sung about the mountain gate, and you already pretend to be mad!"

At these words, Xiangyun also laughed. But, in due course, the whole party watched the performance until evening, when they broke up. Dowager lady Jia was so very much taken with the young actor, who played the role of a lady, as well as with the one who acted the buffoon, that she gave orders that they should be brought in; and, as she looked at them closely, she felt so much the more interest in them, that she went on to inquire what their ages were. And when the would-be lady (replied) that he was just eleven, while the would-be buffoon (explained) that he was just nine, the whole company gave vent for a time to expressions of sympathy with their lot; while dowager lady Jia bade servants bring a fresh supply of meats and fruits for both of them, and also gave them, besides their wages, two tiaos as a present.

"This lad," lady Feng observed smiling, "is when dressed up (as a girl), a living likeness of a certain person; did you notice it just now?"

Baochai was also aware of the fact, but she simply nodded her head assentingly and did not say who it was. Baoyu likewise expressed his assent by shaking his head, but he too did not presume to speak out. Shi Xiangyun, however, readily took up the conversation. "He resembles," she interposed, "cousin Lin's face!" When this remark reached Baoyu's ear, he hastened to cast an angry scowl at Xiangyun, and to make her a sign; while the whole party, upon hearing what had been said, indulged in careful and minute scrutiny of (the lad); and as they all began to laugh: "The resemblance is indeed striking!" they exclaimed.

After a while, they parted; and when evening came Xiangyun directed Cuilu to pack up her clothes.

"What's the hurry?" Cuilu asked. "There will be ample time to pack up, on the day on which we go!"

"We'll go tomorrow," Xiangyun rejoined; "for what's the use of remaining here any longer—to look at people's mouths and faces?"

Baoyu, at these words, lost no time in pressing forward.

"My dear cousin," he urged; "you're wrong in bearing me a grudge! My cousin Lin is a girl so very touchy, that though everyone else distinctly knew (of the resemblance), they wouldn't speak out; and all because they were afraid that she would get angry; but unexpectedly out you came with it, at a moment when off your guard; and how ever couldn't she but feel hurt? and it's because I was in dread that you would give offence to people that I then winked at you; and now here you are angry with me; but isn't that being ungrateful to me? Had it been any one else, would I have cared whether she had given offence to even ten; that would have been none of my business!"

Xiangyun waved her hand: "Don't," she added, "come and tell me these flowery words and this specious talk, for I really can't come up to your cousin Lin. If others poke fun at her, they all do so with impunity, while if I say anything, I at once incur blame. The fact is I shouldn't have spoken of her, undeserving as I am; and as she's the daughter of a master, while I'm a slave, a mere servant girl, I've heaped insult upon her!"

"And yet," pleaded Baoyu, full of perplexity, "I had done it for your sake; and through this, I've come in for reproach. But if it were with an evil heart I did so, may I at once become ashes, and be trampled upon by ten thousands of people!"

"In this felicitous first month," Xiangyun remonstrated, "you shouldn't talk so much reckless nonsense! All these worthless despicable oaths, disjointed words, and corrupt language, go and tell for the benefit of those mean sort of people, who in everything take pleasure in irritating others, and who keep you under their thumb! But mind don't drive me to spit contemptuously at you."

As she gave utterance to these words, she betook herself in the inner room of dowager lady Jia's suite of apartments, where she lay down in high dudgeon, and, as Baoyu was so heavy at heart, he could not help coming again in search of Daiyu; but strange to say, as soon as he put his foot inside the doorway, he was speedily hustled out of it by Daiyu, who shut the door in his face.

Baoyu was once more unable to fathom her motives, and as he stood outside the window, he kept on calling out: "My dear cousin," in a low tone of voice; but Daiyu paid not the slightest notice to him so that Baoyu became so melancholy that he drooped his head, and was plunged in silence. And though Xiren had, at an early hour, come to know the circumstances, she could not very well at this juncture tender any advice.

Baoyu remained standing in such a vacant mood that Daiyu imagined that he had gone back; but when she came to open the door she caught sight of Baoyu still waiting in there; and as Daiyu did not feel justified to again close the door, Baoyu consequently followed her in.

"Everything has," he observed, "a why and a wherefore; which, when spoken out, don't even give people pain; but you will rush into a rage, and all without any rhyme! but to what really does it owe its rise?"

"It's well enough, after all, for you to ask me," Daiyu rejoined with an indifferent smile, "but I myself don't know why! But am I here to afford you people amusement that you will compare me to an actress, and make the whole lot have a laugh at me?"

"I never did liken you to anything," Baoyu protested, "neither did I ever laugh at you! and why then will you get angry with me?"

"Was it necessary that you should have done so much as made the comparison," Daiyu urged, "and was there any need of even any laughter from you? why, though you mayn't have likened me to anything, or had a laugh at my expense, you were, yea more dreadful than those who did compare me (to a singing girl) and ridiculed me!"

Baoyu could not find anything with which to refute the argument he had just heard, and Daiyu went on to say. "This offence can, anyhow, be condoned; but, what is more, why did you also wink at Yun'er? What was this idea which you had resolved in your mind? wasn't it perhaps that if she played with me, she would be demeaning herself, and making herself cheap? She's the daughter of a duke or a marquis, and we forsooth the mean progeny of a poor plebeian family; so that, had she diverted herself with me, wouldn't she have exposed herself to being depreciated, had I, perchance, said anything in retaliation? This was your idea wasn't it? But though your purpose was, to be sure, honest enough, that girl wouldn't, however, receive any favors from you, but got angry with you just as much as I did; and though she made me also a tool to do you a good turn, she, on the contrary, asserts that I'm mean by nature and take pleasure in irritating people in everything! and you again were afraid lest she should have hurt my feelings, but, had I had a row with her, what would that have been to you? and had she given me any offence, what concern would that too have been of yours?"

When Baoyu heard these words, he at once became alive to the fact that she too had lent an ear to the private conversation he had had a short while back with Xiangyun: "All because of my, fears," he carefully mused within himself, "lest these two should have a misunderstanding, I was induced to come between them, and act as a mediator; but I myself have, contrary to my hopes, incurred blame and abuse on both sides! This just accords with what I read the other day in the 'Nanhua Jing.' 'The ingenious toil, the wise are full of care; the good-for-nothing seek for nothing, they feed on vegetables, and roam where they list; they wander purposeless like a boat not made fast!' 'The mountain trees,' the text goes on to say, 'lead to their own devastation; the spring (conduces) to its own plunder; and so on.' And the more he therefore indulged in reflection, the more depressed he felt. "Now there are only these few girls," he proceeded to ponder minutely, "and yet, I'm unable to treat them in such a way as to promote perfect harmony; and what will I forsooth do by and by (when there will be more to deal with)!"

When he had reached this point in his cogitations, (he decided) that it was really of no avail to agree with her, so that turning round, he was making his way all alone into his apartments; but Lin Daiyu, upon noticing that he had left her side, readily concluded that reflection had marred his spirits and that he had so thoroughly lost his temper as to be going without even giving vent to a single word, and she could not restrain herself from feeling inwardly more and more irritated. "After you've gone this time," she hastily exclaimed, "don't come again, even for a whole lifetime; and I won't have you either so much as speak to me!"

Baoyu paid no heed to her, but came back to his rooms, and laying himself down on his bed, he kept on muttering in a state of chagrin;

and though Xiren knew full well the reasons of his dejection, she found it difficult to summon up courage to say anything to him at the moment, and she had no alternative but to try and distract him by means of irrelevant matters. "The theatricals which you've seen today," she consequently observed smiling, "will again lead to performances for several days, and Miss Baochai will, I'm sure, give a return feast."

"Whether she gives a return feast or not," Baoyu rejoined with an apathetic smirk, "is no concern of mine!"

When Xiren perceived the tone, so unlike that of other days, with which these words were pronounced: "What's this that you're saying?" she therefore remarked as she gave another smile. "In this pleasant and propitious first moon, when all the ladies and young ladies are in high glee, how is it that you're again in a mood of this sort?"

"Whether the ladies and my cousins be in high spirits or not," Baoyu replied forcing a grin, "is also perfectly immaterial to me."

"They are all," Xiren added, smilingly, "pleasant and agreeable, and were you also a little pleasant and agreeable, wouldn't it conduce to the enjoyment of the whole company?"

"What about the whole company, and they and I?" Baoyu urged. "They all have their mutual friendships; while I, poor fellow, all forlorn, have none to care a rap for me."

His remarks had reached this clause, when inadvertently the tears trickled down; and Xiren realising the state of mind he was in, did not venture to say anything further. But as soon as Baoyu had reflected minutely over the sense and import of this sentence, he could not refrain from bursting forth into a loud fit of crying, and, turning himself round, he stood up, and, drawing near the table, he took up the brush, and eagerly composed these enigmatical lines:

> If thou wert me to test, and I were thee to test,
> Our hearts were we to test, and our minds to test,
> When naught more there remains for us to test
> That will yea very well be called a test,
> And when there's naught to put, we could say, to the test,
> We will a place set up on which our feet to rest.

After he had finished writing, he again gave way to fears that though he himself could unfold their meaning, others, who came to peruse these lines, would not be able to fathom them, and he also went on consequently to indite another stanza, in imitation of the "Parasitic Plant," which he inscribed at the close of the enigma; and when he had read it over a second time, he felt his heart so free of all concern that forthwith he got into his bed, and went to sleep.

But, who would have thought it, Daiyu, upon seeing Baoyu take his departure in such an abrupt manner, designedly made use of the excuse that she was bent upon finding Xiren, to come round and see what he was up to.

"He's gone to sleep long ago!" Xiren replied.

At these words, Daiyu felt inclined to betake herself back at once; but Xiren smiled and said: "Please stop, miss. Here's a slip of paper, and see what there is on it!" and speedily taking what Baoyu had written a short while back, she handed it over to Daiyu to examine. Daiyu, on perusal, discovered that Baoyu had composed it, at the spur of the moment, when under the influence of resentment; and she could not help thinking it both a matter of ridicule as well as of regret; but she hastily explained to Xiren: "This is written for fun, and there's nothing of any consequence in it! and having concluded this remark, she readily took it along with her to her room, where she conned it over in company with Xiangyun; handing it also the next day to Baochai to peruse. The burden of what Baochai read was:

> In what was no concern of mine, I should to thee have paid no heed,
> For while I humor this, that one to please I don't succeed!
> Act as thy wish may be! go, come whene'er thou list; 'tis naught to me.
> Sorrow or joy, without limit or bound, to indulge thou art free!
> What is this hazy notion about relatives distant or close?
> For what purpose have I for all these days racked my heart with woes?
> Even at this time when I look back and think, my mind no pleasure knows.

After having finished its perusal, she went on to glance at the Buddhistic stanza, and smiling: "This being," she soliloquised; "has awakened to a sense of perception; and all through my fault, for it's that ballad of mine yesterday which has incited this! But the subtle devices in all these rationalistic books have a most easy tendency to unsettle the natural disposition, and if tomorrow he does actually get up, and talk a lot of insane trash, won't his having fostered this idea owe its origin to that ballad of mine; and shan't I have become the prime of all guilty people?"

Saying this, she promptly tore the paper, and, delivering the pieces to the servant girls, she bade them go at once and burn them.

"You shouldn't have torn it!" Daiyu remonstrated laughingly. "But wait and I'll ask him about it! so come along all of you, and I vouch I'll make him abandon that idiotic frame of mind and that depraved language."

The three of them crossed over, in point of fact, into Baoyu's room, and Daiyu was the first to smile and observe. "Baoyu, may I ask you something? What is most valuable is a precious thing; and what is most firm is jade, but what value do you possess and what firmness is innate in you?"

But as Baoyu could not, say anything by way of reply, two of them remarked sneeringly: "With all this doltish bluntness of his will he after all absorb himself in abstraction?" While Xiangyun also clapped her hands and laughed, "Cousin Bao has been discomfited."

"The latter part of that apothegm of yours," Daiyu continued, "says: 'We would then find some place on which our feet to rest.'

"Which is certainly good; but in my view, its excellence is not as yet complete! and I should still tag on two lines at its close;" as she proceeded to recite:

"If we do not set up some place on which our feet to rest,
For peace and freedom then it will be best."

"There should, in very truth, be this adjunct to make it thoroughly explicit!" Baochai added. "In days of yore, the sixth founder of the Southern sect, Huineng, came, when he went first in search of his patron, in the Shaozhou district; and upon hearing that the fifth founder, Hongren, was at Huangmei, he readily entered his service in the capacity of Buddhist cook; and when the fifth founder, prompted by a wish to select a Buddhistic successor, bade his neophytes and all the bonzes to each compose an enigmatical stanza, the one who occupied the upper seat, Shenxiu, recited:

"A Puti tree the body is, the heart so like a stand of mirror bright,
On which must needs, by constant careful rubbing, not be left dust to alight!

"And Huineng, who was at this time in the cook-house pounding rice, overheard this enigma. 'Excellent, it is excellent,' he ventured, 'but as far as completeness goes it isn't complete;' and having bethought himself of an apothegm: 'The Puti, (an expression for Buddha or intelligence),' he proceeded, 'is really no tree; and the resplendent mirror, (Buddhistic term for heart), is likewise no stand; and as, in fact, they do not constitute any tangible objects, how could they be contaminated by particles of dust?' Whereupon the fifth founder at once took his robe and clap-dish and handed them to him. Well, the text now of this enigma presents too this identical idea, for the simple fact is that those lines full of subtleties of a short while back are not, as yet, perfected or brought to an issue, and do you forsooth readily give up the task in this manner?"

"He hasn't been able to make any reply," Daiyu rejoined sneeringly, and must therefore be held to be discomfited; but were he even to make suitable answer now, there would be nothing out of the common about it! Anyhow, from this time forth you mustn't talk about Buddhistic spells, for what even we two know and are able to do you don't as yet know and can't do; and do you go and concern yourself with abstraction?"

Baoyu had, in his own mind, been under the impression that he had attained perception, but when he was unawares and all of a sudden subjected to this question by Daiyu, he soon found it beyond his power to give any ready answer. And when Baochai furthermore came out with a religious disquisition, by way of illustration, and this on subject, in all of which he had hitherto not seen them display any ability, he communed within himself: "If with their knowledge, which is indeed in advance of that of mine, they haven't, as yet, attained perception, what need is there for me now to bring upon myself labor and vexation?"

"Who has, pray," he hastily inquired smilingly, after arriving at the end of his reflections, "indulged in Buddhistic mysteries? what I did amounts to nothing more than nonsensical trash, written, at the spur of the moment, and nothing else."

At the close of this remark all four came to be again on the same terms as of old; but suddenly a servant announced that the Empress (Yuanchun) had despatched a messenger to bring over a lantern-conundrum with the directions that they should all go and guess it, and that after they had found it out, they should each also devise one and send it in. At these words, the four of them left the room with hasty step, and adjourned into dowager lady Jia's drawing room, where they discovered a young eunuch, holding a four-cornered, flat-topped lantern, of white gauze, which had been specially fabricated for lantern riddles. On the front side, there was already a conundrum, and the whole company were vying with each other in looking at it and making wild guesses; when the young eunuch went on to transmit his orders, saying: "Young ladies, you should not speak out when you are guessing; but each one of you should secretly write down the solutions for me to wrap them up, and take them all in together to await her Majesty's personal inspection as to whether they be correct or not."

Upon listening to these words, Baochai drew near, and perceived at a glance, that it consisted of a stanza of four lines, with seven characters in each; but though there was no novelty or remarkable feature about it, she felt constrained to outwardly give utterance to words of praise. "It's hard to guess!" she simply added, while she pretended to be plunged in thought, for the fact is that as soon as she had cast her eye upon it, she had at once solved it. Baoyu, Daiyu, Xiangyun, and Tanchun, had all four also hit upon the answer, and each had secretly put it in writing; and Jia Huan, Jia Lan, and the others were at the same time sent for, and everyone of them set to work to exert the energies of his mind, and, when they arrived at a guess, they noted it down on paper; after which every individual member of the family made a choice of some object, and composed a riddle, which was transcribed in a large round hand, and affixed on the lantern. This done, the eunuch took his departure, and when evening drew near, he came out and delivered the commands of the imperial consort. "The conundrum," he said, "written by Her Highness, the other day, has been solved by everyone, with the exception of Miss Secunda and master Tertius, who made a wrong guess. Those composed by you, young ladies, have likewise all been guessed; but Her Majesty does not know whether her solutions are right or not." While speaking, he again produced the riddles, which had been written by them, among which were those which had been solved, as well as those which had not been solved; and the eunuch, in like manner, took the presents, conferred by the imperial consort, and handed them over to those who had guessed right. To each person was assigned a bamboo vase, inscribed with verses, which had been manufactured for palace use, as well as articles of bamboo for tea; with the exception of Yingchun and Jia Huan, who were the only two persons who did not receive any. But as Yingchun looked upon the whole thing as a joke and a trifle, she did not trouble her mind on that score, but Jia Huan at once felt very disconsolate.

"This one devised by Mr. Tertius," the eunuch was further heard to say, "is not properly done; and as Her Majesty herself has been unable to guess it she commanded me to bring it back, and ask Mr. Tertius what it is about."

After the party had listened to these words, they all pressed forward to see what had been written. The burden of it was this:

The elder brother has horns only eight;
The second brother has horns only two;
The elder brother on the bed doth sit;
Inside the room the second likes to squat.

After perusal of these lines, they broke out, with one voice, into a loud fit of laughter; and Jia Huan had to explain to the eunuch that the one was a pillow, and the other the head of an animal. Having committed the explanation to memory and accepted a cup of tea, the eunuch took his departure; and old lady Jia, noticing in what buoyant spirits Yuanchun was, felt herself so much the more elated, that issuing forthwith directions to devise, with every despatch, a small but ingenious lantern of fine texture in the shape of a screen, and put it in the Hall, she bade each of her grandchildren secretly compose a conundrum, copy it out clean, and affix it on the frame of the lantern; and she had subsequently scented tea and fine fruits, as well as every kind of nicknacks, got ready, as prizes for those who guessed right.

And when Jia Zheng came from court and found the old lady in such high glee he also came over in the evening, as the season was furthermore holiday time, to avail himself of her good cheer to reap some enjoyment. In the upper part of the room seated themselves, at one table dowager lady Jia, Jia Zheng, and Baoyu; Madame Wang, Baochai, Daiyu, Xiangyun sat round another table, and Yingchun, Tanchun, and Xichun the three of them, occupied a separate table, and both these tables were laid in the lower part, while below, all over the floor, stood matrons and waiting-maids for Li Gongcai and Xifeng were both seated in the inner section of the Hall, at another table.

Jia Zheng failed to see Jia Lan, and he therefore inquired: "How is it I don't see brother Lan," whereupon the female servants, standing below, hastily entered the inner room and made inquiries of widow Li. "He says," Mrs. Li stood up and rejoined with a smile, "that as your master didn't go just then to ask him round, he has no wish to come!" and when a matron delivered the reply to Jia Zheng; the whole company exclaimed much amused: "How obstinate and perverse his natural disposition is!" But Jia Zheng lost no time in sending Jia Huan, together with two matrons, to fetch Jia Lan; and, on his arrival, dowager lady Jia bade him sit by her side, and, taking a handful of fruits, she gave them to him to eat; after which the party chatted, laughed, and enjoyed themselves.

Ordinarily, there was no one but Baoyu to say much or talk at any length, but on this day, with Jia Zheng present, his remarks were limited to assents. And as to the rest, Xiangyun had, though a young girl, and of delicate physique, nevertheless ever been very fond of talking and discussing; but, on this instance, Jia Zheng was at the feast, so that she also held her tongue and restrained her words. As for Daiyu she was naturally peevish and listless, and not very much inclined to indulge in conversation; while Baochai, who had never been reckless in her words or frivolous in her deportment, likewise behaved on the present occasion in her usual dignified manner. Hence it was that this banquet, although a family party, given for the sake of relaxation, assumed contrariwise an appearance of restraint, and as old lady Jia was herself too well aware that it was to be ascribed to the presence of Jia Zheng alone, she therefore, after the wine had gone round three times, forthwith hurried off Jia Zheng to retire to rest.

No less cognisant was Jia Zheng himself that the old lady's motives in packing him off were to afford a favorable opportunity to the young ladies and young men to enjoy themselves, and that is why, forcing a smile, he observed: "Having today heard that your venerable ladyship had got up in here a large assortment of excellent riddles, on the occasion of the spring festival of lanterns, I too consequently prepared prizes, as well as a banquet, and came with the express purpose of joining the company; and why don't you in some way confer a fraction of the fond love, which you cherish for your grandsons and granddaughters, upon me also, your son?"

"When you're here," old lady Jia replied smilingly, "they won't venture to chat or laugh; and unless you go, you'll really fill me with intense dejection! But if you feel inclined to guess conundrums, well, I'll tell you one for you to solve; but if you don't guess right, mind, you'll be mulcted!"

"Of course I'll submit to the penalty," Jia Zheng rejoined eagerly, as he laughed, "but if I do guess right, I must in like manner receive a reward!"

"This goes without saying!" dowager lady Jia added; whereupon she went on to recite: "the monkey's body gently rests on the tree top!

"This refers," she said, "to the name of a fruit."

Jia Zheng was already aware that it was a lichee, but he designedly made a few guesses at random, and was fined several things; but he subsequently gave, at length, the right answer, and also obained a present from her ladyship.

In due course he too set forth this conundrum for old lady Jia to guess:

> Correct its body is in appearance,
> Both firm and solid is it in substance;
> To words, it is true, it cannot give vent,
> But spoken to, it always does assent.

When he had done reciting it, he communicated the answer in an undertone to Baoyu; and Baoyu fathoming what his intention was, gently too told his grandmother Jia, and her ladyship finding, after some reflection, that there was really no mistake about it, readily remarked that it was an inkslab.

"After all," Jia Zheng smiled; "Your venerable ladyship it is who can hit the right answer with one guess!" and turning his head round, "Be quick," he cried, "and bring the prizes and present them!" whereupon the married women and waiting-maids below assented with one voice, and they simultaneously handed up the large trays and small boxes.

Old lady Jia passed the things, one by one, under inspection; and finding that they consisted of various kinds of articles, novel and ingenious, of use and of ornament, in vogue during the lantern festival, her heart was so deeply elated that with alacrity she shouted, "Pour a glass of wine for your master!"

Baoyu took hold of the decanter, while Yingchun presented the cup of wine.

"Look on that screen!" continued dowager lady Jia, "all those riddles have been written by the young ladies; so go and guess them for my benefit!"

Jia Zheng signified his obedience, and rising and walking up to the front of the screen, he noticed the first riddle, which was one composed by the Imperial consort Yuan, in this strain:

> The pluck of devils to repress in influence it abounds,
> Like bound silk is its frame, and like thunder its breath resounds.
> But one report rattles, and men are lo! in fear and dread;
> Transformed to ashes 'tis what time to see you turn the head.

"Is this a cracker?" Jia Zheng inquired.

"It is," Baoyu assented.

Jia Zheng then went on to peruse that of Yingchun's, which referred to an article of use:

> Exhaustless is the principle of heavenly calculations and of human skill;

Skill may exist, but without proper practice the result to find hard
    yet will be!
Whence cometh all this mixed confusion on a day so still?
Simply it is because the figures Yin and Yang do not agree.

"It's an abacus," Jia Zheng observed.

"Quite so!" replied Yingchun smiling; after which they also conned
the one below, by Tanchun, which ran thus and had something to do
with an object:

This is the time when 'neath the stairs the pages their heads raise!
The term of "pure brightness" is the meetest time this thing to make!
The vagrant silk it snaps, and slack, without tension it strays!
The East wind don't begrudge because its farewell it did take!

"It would seem," Jia Zheng suggested, "as if that must be a kite!"

"It is," answered Tanchun; whereupon Jia Zheng read the one below,
which was written by Daiyu to this effect and bore upon some thing:

After the audience, his two sleeves who brings with fumes replete?
Both by the lute and in the quilt, it lacks luck to abide!
The dawn it marks; reports from cock and man renders effete!
At midnight, maids no trouble have a new one to provide!
The head, it glows during the day, as well as in the night!
Its heart, it burns from day to day and 'gain from year to year!
Time swiftly flies and mete it is that we should hold it dear!
Changes might come, but it defies wind, rain, days dark or bright!

Isn't this a scented stick to show the watch?" Jia Zheng inquired.

"Yes!" assented Baoyu, speaking on Daiyu's behalf; and Jia Zheng
thereupon prosecuted the perusal of a conundrum, which ran as follows, and referred to an object:

With the South, it sits face to face,
And the North, the while, it doth face;
If the figure be sad, it also is sad,
If the figure be glad, it likewise is glad!

"Splendid! splendid!" exclaimed Jia Zheng, "my guess is that it's a
looking-glass. It's excellently done!"

Baoyu smiled. "It is a looking glass!" he rejoined.

"This is, however, anonymous; whose work is it?" Jia Zheng went on to ask, and dowager lady Jia interposed: "This, I fancy, must have been composed by Baoyu," and Jia Zheng then said not a word, but continued reading the following conundrum, which was that devised by Baochai, on some article or other:

Eyes though it has; eyeballs it has none, and empty 'tis inside!
The lotus flowers out of the water peep, and they with gladness meet,
But when dryandra leaves begin to drop, they then part and divide,
For a fond pair they are, but, united, winter they cannot greet.

When Jia Zheng finished scanning it, he gave way to reflection. "This object," he pondered, "must surely be limited in use! But for persons of tender years to indulge in all this kind of language, would seem to be still less propitious; for they cannot, in my views, be any of them the sort of people to enjoy happiness and longevity!" When his reflections reached this point, he felt the more dejected, and plainly betrayed a sad appearance, and all he did was to droop his head and to plunge in a brown study.

But upon perceiving the frame of mind in which Jia Zheng was, dowager lady Jia arrived at the conclusion that he must be fatigued; and fearing, on the other hand, that if she detained him, the whole party of young ladies would lack the spirit to enjoy themselves, she there and then faced Jia Zheng and suggested: "There's no need really for you to remain here any longer, and you had better retire to rest; and let us sit a while longer; after which, we too will break up!"

As soon as Jia Zheng caught this hint, he speedily assented several consecutive yes's; and when he had further done his best to induce old lady Jia to have a cup of wine, he eventually withdrew out of the Hall. On his return to his bedroom, he could do nothing else than give way to cogitation, and, as he turned this and turned that over in his mind, he got still more sad and pained.

"Amuse yourselves now!" readily exclaimed dowager lady Jia, during this while, after seeing Jia Zheng off; but this remark was barely finished, when she caught sight of Baoyu run up to the lantern screen, and give vent, as he gesticulated with his hands and kicked his feet about, to any criticisms that first came to his lips. "In this," he remarked, "this line isn't happy; and that one, hasn't been suitably solved!" while he behaved just like a monkey, whose fetters had been let loose.

"Were the whole party after all," hastily ventured Daiyu, "to sit down, as we did a short while back and chat and laugh; wouldn't that be more in accordance with good manners?"

Lady Feng thereupon egressed from the room in the inner end and interposed her remarks. "Such a being as you are," she said, "shouldn't surely be allowed by Mr. Jia Zheng, an inch or a step from his side, and then you'll be all right. But just then it slipped my memory, for why didn't I, when your father was present, instigate him to bid you compose a rhythmical enigma; and you would, I have no doubt, have been up to this moment in a state of perspiration!"

At these words, Baoyu lost all patience, and laying hold of lady Feng, he hustled her about for a few moments.

But old lady Jia went on for some time to bandy words with Li Gongcai, with the whole company of young ladies and the rest, so that she, in fact, felt considerably tired and worn out; and when she heard that the fourth watch had already drawn nigh, she consequently issued directions that the eatables should be cleared away and given to the crowd of servants, and suggested, as she readily rose to her feet, "Let us go and rest! for the next day is also a feast, and we must get up at an early hour; and tomorrow evening we can enjoy ourselves again!" whereupon the whole company dispersed.

But now, reader, listen to the sequel given in the chapter which follows.

CHAPTER 23

Baoyu and Daiyu make use of some beautiful passages from the Record of the Western Side-building to bandy jokes. The excellent ballads sung in the Peony Pavilion touch the tender heart of Daiyu.

Soon after the day on which Jia Yuanchun honored the garden of Broad Vista with a visit, and her return to the Palace, so our story goes, she forthwith desired that Tanchun should make a careful copy, in consecutive order, of the verses, which had been composed and read out on that occasion, in order that she herself should assign them their rank, and adjudge the good and bad. And she also directed that an inscription should be engraved on a stone, in the Broad Vista park, to serve in future years as a record of the pleasant and felicitous event; and Jia Zheng, therefore, gave orders to servants to go far and wide, and select skilful artificers and renowned workmen, to polish the stone and engrave the characters in the garden of Broad Vista; while Jia Zhen put himself at the head of Jia Rong, Jia Ping, and others to superintend the work. And as Jia Se had, on the other hand, the control of Wenguan and the rest of the singing girls, twelve in all, as well as of their costumes and other properties, he had no leisure to attend to anything else, and consequently once again sent for Jia Chang and Jia Ling to come and act as overseers.

On a certain day, the works were taken in hand for rubbing the stones smooth with wax, for carving the inscription, and tracing it with vermilion, but without entering into details on these matters too minutely, we will return to the two places, the Yuhuang temple and the Damo monastery. The company of twelve young bonzes and twelve young Daoist priests had now moved out of the Garden of Broad Vista, and Jia Zheng was meditating upon distributing them to various temples to live apart, when unexpectedly Jia Qin's mother, nee Zhou—who resided in the back street, and had been at the time contemplating to pay a visit to Jia Zheng on this side so as to obtain some charge, be it either large or small, for her son to look after, that he too should be put in the way of turning up some money to meet his expenses with—came, as luck would have it, to hear that some work was in hand in this mansion, and lost no time in driving over in a curricle and making her appeal to lady Feng. And as lady Feng remembered that she had all along not presumed on her position to put on airs, she willingly acceded to her request, and after calling to memory some suitable remarks, she at once went to make her report to Madame Wang: "These young bonzes and Daoist priests," she said, "can by no means be sent over to other places; for were the Imperial consort to come out at an unexpected moment, they would then be required to perform services; and in the event of their being scattered, there will, when the time comes to requisition their help, again be difficulties in the way; and my idea is that it would be better to send them all to the family temple, the Iron Fence Temple; and every month all there will be to do will be to depute someone to take over a few taels for them to buy firewood and rice with, that's all, and when there's even a sound of their being required uttered, someone can at once go and tell them just one word 'come,' and they will come without the least trouble!"

Madame Wang gave a patient ear to this proposal, and, in due course, consulted with Jia Zheng.

"You've really," smiled Jia Zheng at these words, "reminded me how I should act! Yes, let this be done!" And there and then he sent for Jia Lian.

Jia Lian was, at the time, having his meal with lady Feng, but as soon as he heard that he was wanted, he put by his rice and was just walking off, when lady Feng clutched him and pulled him back. "Wait a while," she observed with a smirk, "and listen to what I've got to tell you! if it's about anything else, I've nothing to do with it; but if it be about the young bonzes and young Daoists, you must, in this particular matter, please comply with this suggestion of mine," after which she went on in this way and that way to put him up to a whole lot of hints.

"I know nothing about it," Jia Lian rejoined smilingly, "and as you have the knack you yourself had better go and tell him!"

But as soon as lady Feng heard this remark, she stiffened her head and threw down the chopsticks; and, with an expression on her cheeks, which looked like a smile and yet not a smile, she glanced angrily at Jia Lian. "Are you speaking in earnest," she inquired, "or are you only jesting?"

"Yun'er, the son of our fifth sister-in-law of the western porch, has come and appealed to me two or three times, asking for something to look after," Jia Lian laughed, "and I assented and bade him wait; and now, after a great deal of trouble, this job has turned up; and there you are once again snatching it away!"

"Compose your mind," lady Feng observed grinning, "for the Imperial Consort has hinted that directions should be given for the planting, in the northeast corner of the park, of a further plentiful supply of pine and cedar trees, and that orders should also be issued for the addition, round the base of the tower, of a large number of flowers and plants and such like; and when this job turns up, I can safely tell you that Yun'er will be called to assume control of these works."

"Well if that be really so," Jia Lian rejoined, "it will after all do! But there's only one thing; all I was up to last night was simply to have some fun with you, but you obstinately and perversely wouldn't."

Lady Feng, upon hearing these words, burst out laughing with a sound of "chi," and spurting disdainfully at Jia Lian, she lowered her head and went on at once with her meal; during which time Jia Lian speedily walked away laughing the while, and betook himself to the front, where he saw Jia Zheng. It was, indeed, about the young bonzes, and Jia Lian readily carried out lady Feng's suggestion. "As from all appearances," he continued, "Qin'er has, actually, so vastly improved, this job should, after all, be entrusted to his care and management; and provided that in observance with the inside custom Qin'er were each day told to receive the advances, things will go on all right." And as Jia Zheng had never had much attention to give to such matters of detail, he, as soon as he heard what Jia Lian had to say, immediately signified his approval and assent. And Jia Lian, on his return to his quarters, communicated the issue to lady Feng; whereupon lady Feng at once sent someone to go and notify dame Zhou.

Jia Qin came, in due course, to pay a visit to Jia Lian and his wife, and was incessant in his expressions of gratitude; and lady Feng bestowed upon him a further favor by giving him, as a first instalment, an advance of the funds necessary for three months' outlay, for which she bade him write a receipt; while Jia Lian filled up a cheque and signed it; and a counter-order was simultaneously issued, and he came out into the treasury where the sum specified for three months' supplies, amounting to three hundred taels, was paid out in pure ingots.

Jia Qin took the first piece of silver that came under his hand, and gave it to the men in charge of the scales, with which he told them to have a cup of tea, and bidding, shortly after, a boy-servant take the money to his home, he held consultation with his mother; after which, he hired a donkey for himself to ride on, and also bespoke several carriages, and came to the back gate of the Rong Guo mansion; where having called out the twenty young priests, they got into the carriages, and sped straightway beyond the city walls, to the Temple of the Iron Fence, where nothing of any note transpired at the time.

But we will now notice Jia Yuanchun, within the precincts of the Palace. When she had arranged the verses composed in the park of Broad Vista in their order of merit, she suddenly recollected that the sights in the garden were sure, ever since her visit through them, to be diligently and respectfully kept locked up by her father and mother; and that by not allowing anyone to go in was not an injustice done to this garden? "Besides," (she pondered), "in that household, there are at present several young ladies, capable of composing odes, and able to write poetry, and why should not permission be extended to them to go and take their quarters in it; in order too that those winsome persons might not be deprived of good cheer, and that the flowers and willows may not lack anyone to admire them!"

But remembering likewise that Baoyu had from his infancy grown up among that crowd of female cousins, and was such a contrast to the rest of his male cousins that were he not allowed to move into it, he would, she also apprehended, be made to feel forlorn; and dreading lest his grandmother and his mother should be displeased at heart, she thought it imperative that he too should be permitted to take up his quarters inside, so that things should be put on a satisfactory footing; and directing the eunuch Hsia Chung to go to the Rong mansion and deliver her commands, she expressed the wish that Baochai and the other girls should live in the garden and that it should not be kept closed, and urged that Baoyu should also shift into it, at his own pleasure, for the prosecution of his studies. And Jia Zheng and Madame Wang, upon receiving her commands, hastened, after the departure of Xia Shouzhong, to explain them to dowager lady Jia, and to despatch servants into the garden to tidy every place, to dust, to sweep, and to lay out the portieres and bed-curtains. The tidings were heard by the rest even with perfect equanimity, but Baoyu was immoderately delighted; and he was engaged in deliberation with dowager lady Jia as to this necessary and to that requirement, when suddenly they descried a waiting-maid arrive, who announced: "Master wishes to see Baoyu."

Baoyu gazed vacantly for a while. His spirits simultaneously were swept away; his countenance changed color; and clinging to old lady Jia, he readily wriggled her about, just as one would twist the sugar (to make sweetmeats with), and could not, for the very death of him, summon up courage to go; so that her ladyship had no alternative but to try and reassure him. "My precious darling" she urged, "just you go, and I'll stand by you! He won't venture to be hard upon you; and besides, you've devised these excellent literary compositions; and I presume as Her Majesty has desired that you should move into the garden, his object is to give you a few words of advice; simply because he fears that you might be up to pranks in those grounds. But to all he tells you, whatever you do, mind you acquiesce and it will be all right!"

And as she tried to compose him, she at the same time called two old nurses and enjoined them to take Baoyu over with due care, "And don't let his father," she added, "frighten him!"

The old nurses expressed their obedience, and Baoyu felt constrained to walk ahead; and with one step scarcely progressing three inches, he leisurely came over to this side. Strange coincidence Jia Zheng was in Madame Wang's apartments consulting with her upon some matter or other, and Jinchuan, Caiyun, Caixia, Xiuluan, Xiufeng, and the whole number of waiting-maids were all standing outside under the verandah. As soon as they caught sight of Baoyu, they puckered up their mouths and laughed at him; while Jinchuan grasped Baoyu with one hand, and remarked in a low tone of voice: "On these lips of mine has just been rubbed cosmetic, soaked with perfume, and are you now inclined to lick it or not?" whereupon Caiyun pushed off Jinchuan with one shove, as she interposed laughingly, "A person's heart is at this moment in low spirits and do you still go on cracking jokes at him? But avail yourself of this opportunity when master is in good cheer to make haste and get in!"

Baoyu had no help but to sidle against the door and walk in. Jia Zheng and Madame Wang were, in fact, both in the inner rooms, and dame Zhou raised the portiere. Baoyu stepped in gingerly and perceived Jia Zheng and Madame Wang sitting opposite to each other, on the stove-couch, engaged in conversation; while below on a row of chairs sat Yingchun, Tanchun, Xichun, and Jia Huan; but though all four of them were seated in there only Tanchun, Xichun, and Jia Huan rose to their feet as soon as they saw him make his appearance in the room; and when Jia Zheng raised his eyes and noticed Baoyu standing in front of him, with a gait full of ease and with those winsome looks of his, so captivating, he once again realized what a mean being Jia Huan was, and how coarse his deportment. But suddenly he also bethought himself of Jia Zhu, and as he reflected too that Madame Wang had only this son of her own flesh and blood, upon whom she ever doated as upon a gem, and that his own beard had already begun to get hoary, the consequence was that he unwittingly stifled, well nigh entirely, the feeling of hatred and dislike, which, during the few recent years he had ordinarily fostered towards Baoyu. And after a long pause, "Her Majesty," he observed, "bade you day after day ramble about outside to disport yourself, with the result that you gradually became remiss and lazy; but now her desire is that we should keep you under strict control, and that in prosecuting your studies in the company of your cousins in the garden, you should carefully exert your brains to learn; so that if you don't again attend to your duties, and mind your regular tasks, you had better be on your guard!" Baoyu assented several consecutive yes's; whereupon Madame Wang drew him by her side and made him sit down, and while his three cousins resumed the seats they previously occupied: "Have you finished all the pills you had been taking a short while back?" Madame Wang inquired, as she rubbed Baoyu's neck.

"There's still one pill remaining," Baoyu explained by way of reply.

"You had better," Madame Wang added, "fetch ten more pills tomorrow morning; and every day about bedtime tell Xiren to give them to you; and when you've had one you can go to sleep!"

"Ever since you, mother, bade me take them," Baoyu rejoined, "Xiren has daily sent me one, when I was about to turn in."

"Who's this called Xiren?" Jia Zhen thereupon ascertained.

"She's a waiting-maid!" Madame Wang answered.

"A servant girl," Jia Zheng remonstrated, "can be called by whatever name one chooses; anything is good enough; but who's it who has started this kind of pretentious name!"

Madame Wang noticed that Jia Zheng was not in a happy frame of mind, so that she forthwith tried to screen matters for Baoyu, by saying: "It's our old lady who has originated it!"

"How can it possibly be," Jia Zheng exclaimed, "that her ladyship knows anything about such kind of language? It must, for a certainty, be Baoyu!"

Baoyu perceiving that he could not conceal the truth from him, was under the necessity of standing up and of explaining; "As I have all along read verses, I remembered the line written by an old poet:

"What time the smell of flowers wafts itself into man, one knows the day is warm.

"And as this waiting-maid's surname was Hua (flower), I readily gave her the name, on the strength of this sentiment."

"When you get back," Madame Wang speedily suggested addressing Baoyu, "change it and have done; and you, sir, needn't lose your temper over such a trivial matter!"

"It doesn't really matter in the least," Jia Zheng continued; "so that there's no necessity of changing it; but it's evident that Baoyu doesn't apply his mind to legitimate pursuits, but mainly devotes his energies to such voluptuous expressions and wanton verses!" And as he finished these words, he abruptly shouted out: "You brute-like child of retribution! Don't you yet get out of this?"

"Get away, off with you!" Madame Wang in like manner hastened to urge; "our dowager lady is waiting, I fear, for you to have her repast!"

Baoyu assented, and, with gentle step, he withdrew out of the room, laughing at Jinchuan, as he put out his tongue; and leading off the two nurses, he went off on his way like a streak of smoke. But no sooner had he reached the door of the corridor than he espied Xiren standing leaning against the side; who perceiving Baoyu come back safe and sound heaped smile upon smile, and asked: "What did he want you for?"

"There was nothing much," Baoyu explained, "he simply feared that I would, when I get into the garden, be up to mischief, and he gave me all sorts of advice;" and, as while he explained matters, they came into the presence of lady Jia, he gave her a clear account, from first to last, of what had transpired. But when he saw that Lin Daiyu was at the moment in the room, Baoyu speedily inquired of her: "Which place do you think best to live in?"

Daiyu had just been cogitating on this subject, so that when she unexpectedly heard Baoyu's inquiry, she forthwith rejoined with a smile: "My own idea is that the Xiao Xiang Guan is best; for I'm fond of those clusters of bamboos, which hide from view the tortuous balustrade and make the place more secluded and peaceful than any other!"

Baoyu at these words clapped his hands and smiled. "That just meets with my own views!" he remarked; "I too would like you to go and live in there; and as I am to stay in the Yihongyuan, we two will be, in the first place, near each other; and next, both in quiet and secluded spots."

While the two of them were conversing, a servant came, sent over by Jia Zheng, to report to dowager lady Jia that: "The 22nd of the second moon was a propitious day for Baoyu and the young ladies to shift their quarters into the garden; that during these few days, servants should be sent in to put things in their proper places and to clean; that Xue Baochai should put up in the Hengwu court; that Lin Daiyu was to live in the Xiaoxiang lodge; that Jia Yingchun should move into the Chuojin two-storied building; that Tanchun should put up in the Qiushuang library; that Xichun should take up her quarters in the Liaofeng house; that widow Li should live in the Daoxiang village, and that Baoyu was to live in the Yihong court. That at every place two old nurses should be added and four servant-girls; that exclusive of the nurse and personal waiting-maid of each, there should, in addition, be servants, whose special duties should be to put things straight and to sweep the place; and that on the 22nd, they should all, in a body, move into the garden."

When this season drew near, the interior of the grounds, with the flowers waving like embroidered sashes, and the willows fanned by the fragrant breeze, was no more as desolate and silent as it had been in previous days; but without indulging in any further irrelevant details, we shall now go back to Baoyu.

Ever since he shifted his quarters into the park, his heart was full of joy, and his mind of contentment, fostering none of those extraordinary ideas, whose tendency could be to give birth to longings and hankerings. Day after day, he simply indulged, in the company of his female cousins and the waiting-maids, in either reading his books, or writing characters, or in thrumming the lute, playing chess, drawing pictures, and scanning verses, even in drawing patterns of argus pheasants, in embroidering phoenixes, contesting with them in searching for strange plants, and gathering flowers, in humming poetry with gentle tone, singing ballads with soft voice, dissecting characters, and in playing at mora, so that, being free to go everywhere and anywhere, he was of course completely happy. From his brush emanate four ballads on the times of the four seasons, which, although they could not be looked upon as first-rate, afford anyhow a correct idea of his sentiments, and a true account of the scenery.

The ballad on the spring night runs as follows:

> The silken curtains, thin as russet silk, at random are spread out.
> The croak of frogs from the adjoining lane but faintly strikes the ear.
> The pillow a slight chill pervades, for rain outside the window falls.
> The landscape, which now meets the eye, is like that seen in dreams by man.
> In plenteous streams the candles' tears do drop, but for whom do they weep?
> Each particle of grief felt by the flowers is due to anger against me. It's all because the maids have by indulgence indolent been made. The cover over me I'll pull, as I am loath to laugh and talk for long.

This is the description of the aspect of nature on a summer night:

> The beauteous girl, weary of needlework, quiet is plunged in a long dream.
> The parrot in the golden cage doth shout that it is time the tea to brew.
> The lustrous windows with the musky moon like open palace mirrors look;
> The room abounds with fumes of sandalwood and all kinds of imperial scents.

From the cups made of amber is poured out the slippery dew from the lotus.

The banisters of glass, the cool zephyr enjoy flapped by the willow trees.

In the stream-spanning kiosk, the curtains everywhere all at one time do wave.

In the vermilion tower the blinds the maidens roll, for they have made the night's toilette.

The landscape of an autumnal evening is thus depicted:

In the interior of the Jiangyun house are hushed all clamorous din and noise.

The sheen, which from Selene flows, pervades the windows of carnation gauze.

The moss-locked, streaked rocks shelter afford to the cranes, plunged in sleep.

The dew, blown on the long tree by the well, doth wet the roosting rooks.

Wrapped in a quilt, the maid comes the gold phoenix coverlet to spread.

The girl, who on the rails did lean, on her return drops the kingfisher flowers!

This quiet night his eyes in sleep he cannot close, as he doth long for wine.

The smoke is stifled, and the fire restirred, when tea is ordered to be brewed.

The picture of a winter night is in this strain:

The sleep of the plum trees, the dream of the bamboos the third watch have already reached.

Under the embroidered quilt and the kingfisher coverlet one can't sleep for the cold.

The shadow of fir trees pervades the court, but cranes are all that meet the eye.

Both far and wide the pear blossom covers the ground, but yet the hawk cannot be heard.

The wish, verses to write, fostered by the damsel with the green sleeves, has waxed cold.

The master, with the gold sable pelisse, cannot endure much wine.
But yet he doth rejoice that his attendant knows the way to brew
the tea.
The newly-fallen snow is swept what time for tea the water must
be boiled.

But putting aside Baoyu, as he leisurely was occupied in scanning
some verses, we will now allude to all these ballads. There lived, at that
time, a class of people, whose wont was to servilely court the influential
and wealthy, and who, upon perceiving that the verses were composed
by a young lad of the Rong Guo mansion, of only twelve or thirteen
years of age, had copies made, and taking them outside sang their praise
far and wide. There were besides another sort of light-headed young
men, whose heart was so set upon licentious and seductive lines, that
they even inscribed them on fans and screen-walls, and time and again
kept on humming them and extolling them. And to the above reasons
must therefore be ascribed the fact that persons came in search of stanzas and in quest of manuscripts, to apply for sketches, and to beg for
poetical compositions, to the increasing satisfaction of Baoyu, who day
after day, when at home, devoted his time and attention to these ex-
traneous matters. But who would have anticipated that he could ever
in his quiet seclusion have become a prey to a spirit of restlessness? Of
a sudden, one day he began to feel discontent, finding fault with this
and turning up his nose at that; and going in and coming out he was
simply full of ennui. And as all the girls in the garden were just in the
prime of youth, and at a time of life when, artless and unaffected, they
sat and reclined without regard to retirement, and disported themselves
and joked without heed, how could they ever have come to read the
secrets which at this time occupied a place in the heart of Baoyu? But
so unhappy was Baoyu within himself that he soon felt loath to stay in
the garden, and took to gadding about outside like an evil spirit; but
he behaved also the while in an idiotic manner.

Mingyan, upon seeing him go on in this way, felt prompted, with
the idea of affording his mind some distraction, to think of this and
to devise that expedient; but everything had been indulged in with
surfeit by Baoyu, and there was only this resource, (that suggested itself
to him,) of which Baoyu had not as yet had any experience. Bringing
his reflections to a close, he forthwith came over to a bookshop, and
selecting novels, both of old and of the present age, traditions intended
for outside circulation on Feiyan, Hede, Wu Zetian, and Yang Guifei, as
well as books of light literature consisting of strange legends, he purchased a good number of them with the express purpose of enticing

Baoyu to read them. As soon as Baoyu caught sight of them, he felt as if he had obtained some gem or jewel. "But you mustn't," Mingyan went on to enjoin him, "take them into the garden; for if anyone were to come to know anything about them, I shall then suffer more than I can bear; and you should, when you go along, hide them in your clothes!"

But would Baoyu agree to not introducing them into the garden? So after much wavering, he picked out only several volumes of those whose style was more refined, and took them in, and threw them over the top of his bed for him to peruse when no one was present; while those coarse and very indecent ones, he concealed in a bundle in the outer library.

On one day, which happened to be the middle decade of the third moon, Baoyu, after breakfast, took a book, the "Huizhen Ji," in his hand and walked as far as the bridge of the Qinfang lock. Seating himself on a block of rock, that lay under the peach trees in that quarter, he opened the "Huizhen Ji" and began to read it carefully from the beginning. But just as he came to the passage: "the falling red (flowers) have formed a heap," he felt a gust of wind blow through the trees, bringing down a whole bushel of peach blossoms; and, as they fell, his whole person, the entire surface of the book as well as a large extent of ground were simply bestrewn with petals of the blossoms. Baoyu was bent upon shaking them down; but as he feared lest they should be trodden under foot, he felt constrained to carry the petals in his coat and walk to the bank of the pond and throw them into the stream. The petals floated on the surface of the water, and, after whirling and swaying here and there, they at length ran out by the Qinfang lock. But, on his return under the tree, he found the ground again one mass of petals, and Baoyu was just hesitating what to do, when he heard someone behind his back inquire, "What are you up to here?" and as soon as Baoyu turned his head round, he discovered that it was Lin Daiyu, who had come over carrying on her shoulder a hoe for raking flowers, that on this hoe was suspended a gauze-bag, and that in her hand she held a broom.

"That's right, well done!" Baoyu remarked smiling; "come and sweep these flowers, and throw them into the water yonder. I've just thrown a lot in there myself!"

"It isn't right," Lin Daiyu rejoined, "to throw them into the water. The water, which you see, is clean enough here, but as soon as it finds its way out, where are situated other people's grounds, what isn't there in it? so that you would be misusing these flowers just as much as if you left them here! But in that corner, I have dug a hole for flowers, and I'll now sweep these and put them into this gauze-bag and bury them in there; and, in course of many days, they will also become converted into earth, and won't this be a clean way (of disposing of them)?"

Baoyu, after listening to these words, felt inexpressibly delighted. "Wait!" he smiled, "until I put down my book, and I'll help you to clear them up!"

"What's the book?" Daiyu inquired.

Baoyu at this question was so taken aback that he had no time to conceal it. "It's," he replied hastily, "the Zhong Yong and the Da Xue!"

"Are you going again to play the fool with me? Be quick and give it to me to see; and this will be ever so much better a way!"

"Cousin," Baoyu replied, "as far as you yourself are concerned I don't mind you, but after you've seen it, please don't tell anyone else. It's really written in beautiful style; and were you to once begin reading it, why even for your very rice you wouldn't have a thought?"

As he spoke, he handed it to her; and Daiyu deposited all the flowers on the ground, took over the book, and read it from the very first page; and the more she perused it, she got so much the more fascinated by it, that in no time she had finished reading sixteen whole chapters. But aroused as she was to a state of rapture by the diction, what remained even of the fascination was enough to overpower her senses; and though she had finished reading, she nevertheless continued in a state of abstraction, and still kept on gently recalling the text to mind, and humming it to herself.

"Cousin, tell me is it nice or not?" Baoyu grinned.

"It is indeed full of zest!" Lin Daiyu replied exultingly.

"I'm that very sad and very sickly person," Baoyu explained laughing, "while you are that beauty who could subvert the empire and overthrow the city."

Lin Daiyu became, at these words, unconsciously crimson all over her cheeks, even up to her very ears; and raising, at the same moment, her two eyebrows, which seemed to knit and yet not to knit, and opening wide those eyes, which seemed to stare and yet not to stare, while her peach-like cheeks bore an angry look and on her thin-skinned face lurked displeasure, she pointed at Baoyu and exclaimed: "You do deserve death, for the rubbish you talk! without any provocation you bring up these licentious expressions and wanton ballads to give vent to all this insolent rot, in order to insult me; but I'll go and tell uncle and aunt."

As soon as she pronounced the two words "insult me," her eyeballs at once were suffused with purple, and turning herself round she there and then walked away; which filled Baoyu with so much distress that he jumped forward to impede her progress, as he pleaded: "My dear cousin, I earnestly entreat you to spare me this time! I've indeed said what I shouldn't; but if I had any intention to insult you, I'll throw myself tomorrow into the pond, and let the scabby-headed turtle eat me up, so that I become transformed into a large tortoise. And when you shall have by and by become the consort of an officer of the first degree, and you shall have fallen ill from old age and returned to the west, I'll come to your tomb and bear your stone tablet forever on my back!"

As he uttered these words, Lin Daiyu burst out laughing with a sound of "pu chi," and rubbing her eyes, she sneeringly remarked: "I too can come out with this same tune; but will you now still go on talking nonsense? Pshaw! you're, in very truth, like a spear-head, (which looks) like silver, (but is really soft as) wax!"

"Go on, go on!" Baoyu smiled after this remark; "and what you've said, I too will go and tell!"

"You maintain," Lin Daiyu rejoined sarcastically, "that after glancing at anything you're able to recite it; and do you mean to say that I can't even do so much as take in ten lines with one gaze?"

Baoyu smiled and put his book away, urging: "Let's do what's right and proper, and at once take the flowers and bury them; and don't let us allude to these things!"

Forthwith the two of them gathered the fallen blossoms; but no sooner had they interred them properly than they espied Xiren coming, who went on to observe: "Where haven't I looked for you? What! have you found your way as far as this! But our senior master, Mr. Jia She, over there isn't well; and the young ladies have all gone over to pay their respects, and our old lady has asked that you should be sent over; so go back at once and change your clothes!"

When Baoyu heard what she said, he hastily picked up his books, and saying good bye to Daiyu, he came along with Xiren, back into his room, where we will leave him to effect the necessary change in his costume. But during this while, Lin Daiyu was, after having seen Baoyu walk away, and heard that all her cousins were likewise not in their rooms, wending her way back alone, in a dull and dejected mood, towards her apartment, when upon reaching the outside corner of the wall of the Pear Fragrance court, she caught, issuing from inside the walls, the harmonious strains of the fife and the melodious modulations of voices singing. Lin Daiyu readily knew that it was the twelve singing-girls rehearsing a play; and though she did not give her mind to go and listen, yet a couple of lines were of a sudden blown into her ears, and with such clearness, that even one word did not escape. Their burden was this:

These troth are beauteous purple and fine carmine flowers, which
   in this way all round do bloom,
And all together lie ensconced along the broken well, and the dilapidated wall!

But the moment Lin Daiyu heard these lines, she was, in fact, so
intensely affected and agitated that she at once halted and lending an
ear listened attentively to what they went on to sing, which ran thus:

A glorious day this is, and pretty scene, but sad I feel at heart!
Contentment and pleasure are to be found in whose family courts?

After overhearing these two lines, she unconsciously nodded her
head, and sighed, and mused in her own mind. "Really," she thought,
"there is fine diction even in plays! but unfortunately what men in this
world simply know is to see a play, and they don't seem to be able to
enjoy the beauties contained in them."

At the conclusion of this train of thought, she experienced again a
sting of regret, (as she fancied) she should not have given way to such
idle thoughts and missed attending to the ballads; but when she once
more came to listen, the song, by some coincidence, went on thus:

It's all because thy loveliness is like a flower and like the comely
   spring,
That years roll swiftly by just like a running stream.

When this couplet struck Daiyu's ear, her heart felt suddenly a prey
to excitement and her soul to emotion; and upon further hearing the
words:

Alone you sit in the secluded inner rooms to self-compassion giving way.

and other such lines, she became still more as if inebriated, and like
as if out of her head, and unable to stand on her feet, she speedily
stooped her body, and, taking a seat on a block of stone, she minutely
pondered over the rich beauty of the eight characters:

It's all because thy loveliness is like a flower and like the comely
   spring,
That years roll swiftly by just like a running stream.

Of a sudden, she likewise bethought herself of the line:

Water flows away and flowers decay, for both no feelings have.

which she had read some days back in a poem of an ancient writer, and also of the passage:

When on the running stream the flowers do fall, spring then is past and gone;

and of:

Heaven (differs from) the human race,

which also appeared in that work; and besides these, the lines, which she had a short while back read in the "Xixiang Ji":

The flowers, lo, fall, and on their course the waters red do flow!
Petty misfortunes of ten thousand kinds (my heart assail!)

both simultaneously flashed through her memory; and, collating them all together, she meditated on them minutely, until suddenly her heart was stricken with pain and her soul fleeted away, while from her eyes trickled down drops of tears. But while nothing could dispel her present state of mind, she unexpectedly realized that someone from behind gave her a tap; and, turning her head round to look, she found that it was a young girl; but who it was, the next chapter will make known.

CHAPTER 24

The drunken Jin Gang makes light of lucre and shows a preference for generosity. The foolish girl mislays her handkerchief and arouses mutual thoughts.

But to return to our narrative, Lin Daiyu's sentimental reflections were the while reeling and ravelling in an intricate maze, when unexpectedly someone from behind gave her a tap, saying: "What are you up to all alone here?" which took Lin Daiyu so much by surprise that she gave a start, and turning her head round to look and noticing that it was Xiangling and no one else; "You stupid girl!" Lin Daiyu replied, "you've given me such a fright! But where do you come from at this time?"

Xiangling giggled and smirked. "I've come," she added, "in search of our young lady, but I can't find her anywhere. But your Zijuan is also looking after you; and she says that lady Secunda has sent a present to you of some tea. But you had better go back home and sit down."

As she spoke, she took Daiyu by the hand, and they came along back to the Xiaoxiang Guan; where lady Feng had indeed sent her two small catties of a new season tea, of superior quality. But Lin Daiyu sat down, in company with Xiangling, and began to converse on the merits of this tapestry and the fineness of that embroidery; and after they had also had a game at chess, and read a few sentences out of a book, Xiangling took her departure. But we need not speak of either of them, but return now to Baoyu. Having been found, and brought back home, by Xiren, he discovered Yuanyang reclining on the bed, in the act of examining Xiren's needlework; but when she perceived Baoyu arrive, she forthwith remarked: "Where have you been? her venerable ladyship is waiting for you to tell you to go over and pay your obeisance to our Senior master, and don't you still make haste to go and change your clothes and be off!"

Xiren at once walked into the room to fetch his clothes, and Baoyu sat on the edge of the bed, and pushed his shoes off with his toes; and, while waiting for his boots to put them on, he turned round and perceiving that Yuanyang, who was clad in a light red silk jacket and a green satin waistcoat, and girdled with a white crepe sash, had her face turned the other way, and her head lowered giving her attention to the criticism of the needlework, while round her neck she wore a collar with embroidery, Baoyu readily pressed his face against the nape of her neck, and as he sniffed the perfume about it, he did not stay his hand from stroking her neck, which in whiteness and smoothness was not below that of Xiren; and as he approached her, "My dear girl," he said smiling and with a drivelling face, "do let me lick the cosmetic off your mouth!" clinging to her person, as he uttered these words, like twisted sweetmeat.

"Xiren!" cried Yuanyang at once, "come out and see! You've been with him a whole lifetime, and don't you give him any advice; but let him still behave in this fashion!" Whereupon, Xiren walked out, clasping the clothes, and turning to Baoyu, she observed, "I advise you in this way and it's no good, I advise you in that way and you don't mend; and what do you mean to do after all? But if you again behave like this, it will then, in fact, be impossible for me to live any longer in this place!"

As she tendered these words of counsel, she urged him to put his clothes on, and, after he had changed, he betook himself, along with Yuanyang, to the front part of the mansion, and bade good-bye to dowager lady Jia; after which he went outside, where the attendants and horses were all in readiness; but when he was about to mount his steed, he perceived Jia Lian back from his visit and in the act of dismounting; and as the two of them stood face to face, and mutually exchanged some inquiries, they saw someone come round from the side, and say: "My respects to you, uncle Baoyu!"

When Baoyu came to look at him, he noticed that this person had an oblong face, that his body was tall and lanky, that his age was only eighteen or nineteen, and that he possessed, in real truth, an air of refinement and elegance; but though his features were, after all, exceedingly familiar, he could not recall to mind to what branch of the family he belonged, and what his name was.

What are you staring vacantly for?" Jia Lian inquired laughing.

"Don't you even recognise him? He's Yun'er, the son of our fifth sister-in-law, who lives in the back court!"

"Of course!" Baoyu assented complacently. "How is it that I had forgotten just now!" And having gone on to ask how his mother was, and what work he had to do at present; "I've come in search of uncle Secundus, to tell him something," Jia Yun replied, as he pointed at Jia Lian.

"You've really improved vastly from what you were before," added Baoyu smiling; "you verily look just is if you were my son!"

"How very barefaced!" Jia Lian exclaimed as he burst out laughing; "here's a person four or five years your senior to be made your son!"

"How far are you in your teens this year?" Baoyu inquired with a smile.

"Eighteen!" Jia Yun rejoined.

This Jia Yun was, in real deed, sharp and quick-witted; and when he heard Baoyu remark that he looked like his son, he readily gave a sarcastic smile and observed, "The proverb is true which says, 'the grandfather is rocked in the cradle while the grandson leans on a staff.' But though old enough in years, I'm nevertheless like a mountain, which, in spite of its height, cannot screen the sun from view. Besides, since my father's death, I've had no one to look after me, and were you, uncle Bao, not to disdain your doltish nephew, and to acknowledge me as your son, it would be your nephew's good fortune!"

"Have you heard what he said?" Jia Lian interposed cynically. "But to acknowledge him as a son is no easy question to settle!" and with these words, he walked in; whereupon Baoyu smilingly said: "Tomorrow when you have nothing to do, just come and look me up; but don't go and play any devilish pranks with them! I've just now no leisure, so come tomorrow, into the library, where I'll have a chat with you for a whole day, and take you into the garden for some fun!"

With this remark still on his lips, he laid hold of the saddle and mounted his horse; and, followed by the whole bevy of pages, he crossed over to Jia She's on this side; where having discovered that Jia She had nothing more the matter with him than a chill which he had suddenly contracted, he commenced by delivering dowager lady Jia's message, and next paid his own obeisance. Jia She, at first, stood up and made suitable answer to her venerable ladyship's inquiries, and then calling a servant, "Take the gentleman," he said, "into my lady's apartment to sit down."

Baoyu withdrew out of the room, and came by the back to the upper apartment; and as soon as Madame Xing caught sight of him, she, before everything else, rose to her feet and asked after old lady Jia's health; after which, Baoyu made his own salutation, and Madame Xing drew him on to the stove-couch, where she induced him to take a seat, and eventually inquired after the other inmates, and also gave orders to serve the tea. But scarcely had they had tea, before they perceived Jia Cong come in to pay his respects to Baoyu.

"Where could one find such a living monkey as this!" Madame Xing remarked; "is that nurse of yours dead and gone that she doesn't even keep you clean and tidy, and that she lets you go about with those eyebrows of yours so black and that mouth so filthy! you scarcely look like the child of a great family of scholars."

While she spoke, she perceived both Jia Huan and Jia Lan, one of whom was a young uncle and the other his nephew, also advance and present their compliments, and Madame Xing bade the two of them sit down on the chairs. But when Jia Huan noticed that Baoyu sat on the same rug with Madame Xing, and that her ladyship was further caressing and petting him in every possible manner, he soon felt so very unhappy at heart, that, after sitting for a short time, he forthwith made a sign to Jia Lan that he would like to go; and as Jia Lan could not but humor him, they both got up together to take their leave. But when Baoyu perceived them rise, he too felt a wish to go back along with them, but Madame Xing remarked smilingly, "You had better sit a while as I've something more to tell you," so that Baoyu had no alternative but to stay. "When you get back," Madame Xing added, addressing the other two, "present, each one of you, my regards to your respective mothers. The young ladies, your cousins, are all here making such a row that my head is dazed, so that I won't today keep you to have your repast here." To which Jia Huan and Jia Lan assented and quickly walked out.

If it be really the case that all my cousins have come over," Baoyu ventured with a smirk, "how is it that I don't see them?"

"After sitting here for a while," Madame Xing explained, "they all went at the back; but in what rooms they have gone, I don't know."

"My senior aunt, you said you had something to tell me," Baoyu observed; "what's it, I wonder?"

"What can there possibly be to tell you?" Madame Xing laughed; "it was simply to make you wait and have your repast with the young ladies and then go; but there's also a fine plaything that I'll give you to take back to amuse yourself with."

These two, the aunt and her nephew, were going on with their colloquy when, much to their surprise, it was time for dinner and the young ladies were all invited to come. The tables and chairs were put in their places, and the cups and plates were arranged in proper order; and, after the mother, her daughter, and the cousins had finished their meal, Baoyu bade good-bye to Jia She and returned home in company with all the young ladies; and when they had said good-night to dowager lady Jia, Madame Wang, and the others, they each went back into their rooms and retired to rest; where we shall leave them without any further comment and speak of Jia Yun's visit to the mansion. As soon as he saw Jia Lian, he inquired what business it was that had turned up, and Jia Lian consequently explained: "The other day something did actually present itself, but as it happened that your aunt had again and again entreated me, I gave it to Jia Qin; as she promised me that there would be by and by in the garden several other spots where flowers and trees would be planted; and that when this job did occur, she would, for a certainty, give it to you and finish!"

Jia Yun, upon hearing these words, suggested after a short pause; "If that be so, there's nothing for me to do than to wait; but, uncle, you too mustn't make any allusion beforehand in the presence of aunt to my having come today to make any inquiries; for there will really be ample time to speak to her when the job turns up!"

"Why should I allude to it?" Jia Lian rejoined. "Have I forsooth got all this leisure to talk of irrelevant matters! But tomorrow, besides, I've got to go as far as Xing Yi for a turn, and it's absolutely necessary that I should hurriedly come back the very same day; so off with you now and go and wait; and the day after tomorrow, after the watch has been set, come and ask for news; but mind at any earlier hour, I shan't have any leisure!" With these words, he hastily went at the back to change his clothes. And from the time Jia Yun put his foot out of the door of the Rong Guo mansion, he was, the whole way homeward, plunged in deep thought; but having bethought himself of some expedient, he straightway wended his steps towards the house of his maternal uncle, Bu Shiren. This Bu Shiren, it must be explained, kept, at the present date, a shop for the sale of spices. He had just returned home from his shop, and as soon as he noticed Jia Yun, he inquired of him what business brought him there.

"There's something," Jia Yun replied, "in which I would like to crave your assistance, uncle; I'm in need of some baroos camphor and musk, so please, uncle, give me on credit four ounces of each kind, and on the festival of the eighth moon, I'll bring you the amount in full."

Bu Shiren gave a sardonic smile. "Don't," he said, "again allude to any such thing as selling on tick! Some time back a partner in our establishment got several ounces of goods for his relatives on credit, and up to this date the bill hasn't as yet been settled; the result being that we've all had to make the amount good, so that we've entered into an agreement that we should no more allow any one to obtain on tick anything on behalf of either relative or friend, and that whoever acted contrary to this resolution should be, at once, fined twenty taels, with which to stand a treat. Besides, the stock of these articles is now short, and were you also to come, with ready money to this our mean shop to buy any, we wouldn't even have as much to give you. The best way therefore is for you to go elsewhere. This is one side of the question; for on the other, you can't have anything above-board in view; and were you to obtain what you want as a loan you would again go and play the giddy dog! But you'll simply say that on every occasion your uncle sees you, he avails himself of it to find fault with you, but a young fellow like you doesn't know what's good and what is bad; and you should, besides, make up your mind to earn a few cash, wherewith to clothe and feed yourself, so that, when I see you, I too may rejoice!"

"What you, uncle, say," Jia Yun rejoined smiling, "is perfectly right; the only thing is that at the time of my father's death, I was likewise so young in years that I couldn't understand anything; but later on, I heard my mother explain how that for everything, it was lucky that you, after all, my uncles, went over to our house and devised the ways and means, and managed the funeral; and is it likely you, uncle, aren't aware of these things? Besides, have I forsooth had a single acre of land or a couple of houses, the value of which I've run through as soon as it came into my hands? An ingenious wife cannot make boiled rice without raw rice; and what would you have me do? It's your good fortune however that you've got to deal with one such as I am, for had it been anyone else barefaced and shameless, he would have come, twice every three days, to worry you, uncle, by asking for two pints of rice and two of beans, and you then, uncle, would have had no help for it."

"My dear child," Bu Shiren exclaimed, "had I anything that I could call my own, your uncle as I am, wouldn't I feel bound to do something for you? I've day after day mentioned to your aunt that the misfortune was that you had no resources. But should you ever succeed in making up your mind, you should go into that mighty household of yours, and when the gentlemen aren't looking, forthwith pocket your pride and hobnob with those managers, or possibly with the butlers, as you may, even through them, be able to get some charge or other! The other day, when I was out of town, I came across that old Quartus of the third branch of the family, astride of a tall donkey, at the head of four or five carriages, in which were about forty to fifty bonzes and Daoist priests on their way to the family fane, and that man can't lack brains, for such a charge to have fallen to his share!"

Jia Yun, upon hearing these words, indulged in a long and revolting rigmarole, and then got up to take his leave.

"What are you in such a hurry for?" Bu Shiren remarked. "Have your meal and then go!"

But this remark was scarcely ended when they heard his wife say: "Are you again in the clouds? When I heard that there was no rice, I bought half a catty of dry rice paste, and brought it here for you to eat; and do you pray now still put on the airs of a well-to-do, and keep your nephew to feel the pangs of hunger?"

"Well, then, buy half a catty more, and add to what there is, that's all," Bu Shiren continued; whereupon her mother explained to her daughter, Yin Jie, "Go over to Mrs. Wang's opposite, and ask her if she has any cash, to lend us twenty or thirty of them; and tomorrow, when they're brought over, we'll repay her."

But while the husband and wife were carrying on this conversation, Jia Yun had, at an early period, repeated several times: "There's no need to go to this trouble," and off he went, leaving no trace or shadow behind. But without passing any further remarks on the husband and wife of the Bu family, we will now confine ourselves to Jia Yun. Having gone in high dudgeon out of the door of his uncle's house, he started straight on his way back home; but while distressed in mind, and preoccupied with his thoughts, he paced on with drooping head, he unexpectedly came into collision with a drunken fellow, who gripped Jia Yun, and began to abuse him, crying: "Are your eyes gone blind, that you come bang against me?"

The tone of voice, when it reached Jia Yun's ears, sounded like that of someone with whom he was intimate; and, on careful scrutiny, he found, in fact, that it was his next-door neighbour, Ni'er. This Ni'er was a dissolute knave, whose only idea was to give out money at heavy rates of interest and to have his meals in the gambling dens. His sole delight was to drink and to fight.

He was, at this very moment, coming back home from the house of a creditor, whom he had dunned, and was already far gone with drink, so that when, at an unforeseen moment, Jia Yun ran against him, he meant there and then to start a scuffle with him.

"Old Er!" Jia Yun shouted, "stay your hand; it's I who have hustled against you."

As soon as Ni'er heard the tone of his voice, he opened wide his drunken eyes and gave him a look; and realising that it was Jia Yun, he hastened to loosen his grasp and to remark with a smile, as he staggered about, "Is it you indeed, master Jia Secundus? where were you off to now?"

I couldn't tell you!" Jia Yun rejoined; "I've again brought displeasure upon me, and all through no fault of mine."

Never mind!" urged Ni'er, "if you're in any trouble you just tell me, and I'll give vent to your spite for you; for in these three streets, and six lanes, no matter who may give offence to any neighbors of mine, of me, Ni'er, the drunken Jin Gang, I'll wager that I compel that man's family to disperse, and his home to break up!"

"Old Ni, don't lose your temper," Jia Yun protested, "but listen and let me tell you what happened!" After which, he went on to tell Ni'er the whole affair with Bu Shiren. As soon as Ni'er heard him, he got into a frightful rage; "Were he not," he shouted, "a relative of yours, master Secundus, I would readily give him a bit of my mind! Really resentment will stifle my breath! but never mind! you needn't however distress yourself. I've got here a few taels ready at hand, which, if you require, don't scruple to take; and from such good neighbors as you are, I won't ask any interest upon this money."

With this remark still on his lips, he produced from his pouch a bundle of silver.

"Ni'er has, it is true, ever been a rogue," Jia Yun reflected in his own mind, "but as he is regulated in his dealings by a due regard to persons, he enjoys, to a great degree, the reputation of generosity; and were I today not to accept this favor of his, he'll, I fear, be put to shame; and it won't contrariwise be nice on my part! and isn't it better that I should make use of his money, and by and by I can repay him double, and things will be all right!"

"Old Er," he therefore observed aloud with a smile, "you're really a fine fellow, and as you've shown me such eminent consideration, how can I presume not to accept your offer! On my return home, I'll write the customary I. O. U., and send it to you, and all will be in order."

Ni'er gave a broad grin. "It's only fifteen taels and three mace," he answered, "and if you insist upon writing an I. O. U., I won't then lend it to you!"

Jia Yun at these words, took over the money, smiling the while. "I'll readily," he retorted, "comply with your wishes and have done; for what's the use of exasperating you!"

"Well then that will be all right!" Ni'er laughed; "but the day is getting dark; and I shan't ask you to have a cup of tea or stand you a drink, for I've some small things more to settle. As for me, I'm going over there, but you, after all, should please wend your way homewards; and I shall also request you to take a message for me to my people. Tell them to close the doors and turn in, as I'm not returning home; and that in the event of anything occurring, to bid our daughter come over tomorrow, as soon as it is daylight, to short-legged Wang's house, the horse-dealer's, in search of me!" And as he uttered this remark he walked away, stumbling and hobbling along. But we will leave him without further notice and allude to Jia Yun.

He had, at quite an unexpected juncture, met this piece of luck, so that his heart was, of course, delighted to the utmost degree. "This Ni'er," he mused, "is really a good enough sort of fellow, but what I dread is that he may have been open-handed in his fit of drunkenness, and that he mayn't, by and by, ask for his money to be paid twice over; and what will I do then? Never mind," he suddenly went on to ponder, "when that job has become an accomplished fact, I shall even have the means to pay him back double the original amount."

Prompted by this resolution, he came over to a money-shop, and when he had the silver weighed, and no discrepancy was discovered in the weight, he was still more elated at heart; and on his way back, he first and foremost delivered Ni'er's message to his wife, and then returned to his own home, where he found his mother seated all alone on a stove-couch spinning thread. As soon as she saw him enter, she inquired where he had been the whole day long, in reply to which Jia Yun, fearing lest his parent should be angry, forthwith made no allusion to what transpired with Bu Shiren, but simply explained that he had been in the western mansion, waiting for his uncle Secundus, Lien. This over, he asked his mother whether she had had her meal or not, and his parent said by way of reply: "I've had it, but I've kept something for you in there," and calling to the servant-maid, she bade her bring it round, and set it before him to eat. But as it was already dark, when the lamps had to be lit, Jia Yun, after partaking of his meal, got ready and turned in.

Nothing of any notice transpired the whole night; but the next day, as soon it was dawn, he got up, washed his face, and came to the main street, outside the south gate, and purchasing some musk from a perfumery shop, he, with rapid stride, entered the Rong Guo mansion; and having, as a result of his inquiries, found out that Jia Lian had gone out of doors, Jia Yun readily betook himself to the back, in front of the door of Jia Lian's court, where he saw several servant-lads, with immense brooms in their hands, engaged in that place in sweeping the court. But as he suddenly caught sight of Zhou Rui's wife appear outside the door, and call out to the young boys; "Don't sweep now, our lady is coming out," Jia Yun eagerly walked up to her and inquired, with a face beaming with smiles: "Where's aunt Secunda going to?"

To this inquiry, Zhou Rui's wife explained: "Our old lady has sent for her, and I expect, it must be for her to cut some piece of cloth or other." But while she yet spoke, they perceived a whole bevy of people, pressing round lady Feng, as she egressed from the apartment.

Jia Yun was perfectly aware that lady Feng took pleasure in flattery, and delighted in display, so that hastily dropping his arms, he with all reverence, thrust himself forward and paid his respects to her. But lady Feng did not even so much as turn to look at him with straight eyes; but continued, as hitherto, her way onwards, simply confining herself to ascertaining whether his mother was all right, and adding: "How is it that she doesn't come to our house for a stroll?"

"The thing is," Jia Yun replied, "that she's not well: she, however, often thinks fondly of you, aunt, and longs to see you; but as for coming round, she's quite unable to do so."

"You have, indeed, the knack of telling lies!" lady Feng laughed with irony; "for hadn't I alluded to her, she would never have thought of me!"

"Isn't your nephew afraid," Jia Yun protested smilingly, "of being blasted by lightning to have the audacity of telling lies in the presence of an elder! Even so late as yesterday evening, she alluded to you, aunt! 'Though naturally,' she said, 'of a weak constitution, you had, however, plenty to attend to! that it's thanks to your supremely eminent energies,' aunt, 'that you're, after all, able to manage everything in such a perfect manner; and that had you ever made the slightest slip, there would have long ago crept up, goodness knows, what troubles!'"

As soon as lady Feng heard these words, her whole face beamed with smiles, and she unconsciously halted her steps, while she proceeded to ask: "How is it that, both your mother and yourself, tattle about me behind my back, without rhyme or reason?"

"There's a reason for it," Jia Yun observed, "which is simply this. I've an excellent friend with considerable money of his own at home, who recently kept a perfumery shop; but as he obtained, by purchase, the rank of deputy sub-prefect, he was, the other day, selected for a post in Yunnan, in some prefecture or other unknown to me; whither he has gone together with his family. He even closed this shop of his, and forthwith collecting all his wares, he gave away, what he could give away, and what he had to sell at a discount, was sold at a loss; while such valuable articles, as these, were all presented to relatives or friends; and that's why it is that I came in for some baroos camphor and musk. But I at the time, deliberated with my mother that to sell them below their price would be a pity, and that if we wished to give them as a present to any one, there was no one good enough to use such perfumes. But remembering how you, aunt, had all along in years gone by, even to this day, to spend large bundles of silver, in purchasing such articles, and how, not to speak of this year with an Imperial consort in the Palace, what's even required for this dragon boat festival, will also necessitate the addition of hundred times as much as the quantity of previous years, I therefore present them to you, aunt, as a token of my esteem!"

With these words still on his lips, he simultaneously produced an ornamented box, which he handed over to her. And as lady Feng was, at this time, making preparations for presents for the occasion of the dragon boat festival, for which perfumes were obligatory, she, with all promptitude, directed Feng'er: "Receive Mr. Yun's present and take it home and hand it over to Ping'er. To one," she consequently added, "who seems to me so full of discrimination, it isn't a wonder that your uncle is repeatedly alluding, and that he speaks highly of you; how that you talk with all intelligence and that you have experience stored up in your mind."

Jia Yun upon hearing this propitious language, hastily drew near one step, and designedly asked: "Does uncle really often refer to me?

The moment lady Feng caught this question, she was at once inclined to tell him all about the charge to be entrusted to him, but on second thought, she again felt apprehensive lest she should be looked lightly upon by him, by simply insinuating that she had promptly and needlessly promised him something to do, so soon as she got a little scented ware; and this consideration urged her to once more restrain her tongue, so that she never made the slightest reference even to so much as one word about his having been chosen to look after the works of planting the flowers and trees. And after confining herself to making the first few irrelevant remarks which came to her lips, she hastily betook herself into dowager lady Jia's apartments.

Jia Yun himself did not feel as if he could very well advert to the subject, with the result that he had no alternative but to retrace his steps homewards. But as when he had seen Baoyu the previous day, he had asked him to go into the outer library and wait for him, he therefore finished his meal and then once again entered the mansion and came over into the Qixian study, situated outside the ceremonial gate, over at old lady Jia's part of the compound, where he discovered the two lads Mingyan, whose name had been changed into Beiming, and Chuyao playing at chess, and just arguing about the capture of a castle; and besides them, Yinquan, Saohua, Tiaoyun, Banhe, these four or five of them, up to larks, stealing the young birds from the nests under the eaves of the house.

As soon as Jia Yun entered the court, he stamped his foot and shouted, "The monkeys are up to mischief! Here I am, I've come;" and when the company of servant-boys perceived him, they one and all promptly dispersed; while Jia Yun walked into the library, and seating himself at once in a chair, he inquired, "Has your master Secundus, Mr. Bao, come down?"

"He hasn't been down here at all today," Beiming replied, "but if you, Mr. Secundus, have anything to tell him, I'll go and see what he's up to for you."

Saying this he there and then left the room; and Jia Yun meanwhile gave himself to the inspection of the pictures and nicknacks. But some considerable time elapsed, and yet he did not see him arrive; and noticing besides that the other lads had all gone to romp, he was just plunged in a state of despondency, when he heard outside the door a voice cry out, with winning tone, and tender accents: "My elder brother!"

Jia Yun looked out, and saw that it was a servant-maid of fifteen or sixteen, who was indeed extremely winsome and spruce. As soon however as the maid caught a glimpse of Jia Yun, she speedily turned herself round and withdrew out of sight. But, as luck would have it, it happened that Beiming was coming along, and seeing the servant-maid in front of the door, he observed: "Welcome, welcome! I was quite at a loss how to get any news of Baoyu." And as Jia Yun discerned Beiming, he hastily too, ran out in pursuit of him, and ascertained what was up; whereupon Beiming returned for answer: "I waited a whole day long, and not a single soul came over; but this girl is attached to master Secundus' (Mr. Bao's) rooms!" and, "My dear girl," he consequently went on to say, "go in and take a message. Say that Mr. Secundus, who lives under the portico, has come!"

The servant-maid, upon hearing these words, knew at once that he was a young gentleman belonging to the family in which she served, and she did not skulk out of sight, as she had done in the first instance; but with a gaze sufficient to kill, she fixed her two eyes upon Jia Yun, when she heard Jia Yun interpose: "What about over the portico and under the portico; you just tell him that Yun'er is come, that's all."

After a while this girl gave a sarcastic smile. "My idea is," she ventured, "that you, master Secundus, should really, if it so please you, go back, and come again tomorrow; and tonight, if I find time, I'll just put in a word with him!"

"What's this that you're driving at?" Beiming then shouted.

And the maid rejoined: "He's not even had a siesta today, so that he'll have his dinner at an early hour, and won't come down again in the evening; and is it likely that you would have master Secundus wait here and suffer hunger? and isn't it better that he should return home? The right thing is that he should come tomorrow; for were even by and by someone to turn up, who could take a message, that person would simply acquiesce with the lips, but would he be willing to deliver the message in for you?"

Jia Yun, upon finding how concise and yet how well expressed this girl's remarks had been, was bent upon inquiring what her name was; but as she was a maid employed in Baoyu's apartments, he did not therefore feel justified in asking the question, and he had no other course but to add, "What you say is quite right, I'll come tomorrow!" and as he spoke, he there and then was making his way outside, when

Beiming remarked: "I'll go and pour a cup of tea; and master Secundus, have your tea and then go."

Jia Yun turned his head round, as he kept on his way, and said by way of rejoinder: "I won't have any tea; for I've besides something more to attend to!" and while with his lips he uttered these words, he, with his eyes, stared at the servant-girl, who was still standing in there.

Jia Yun wended his steps straightway home; and the next day he came to the front entrance, where, by a strange coincidence, he met lady Feng on her way to the opposite side to pay her respects. She had just mounted her carriage, but perceiving Jia Yun arrive, she eagerly bade a servant stop him, and, with the window between them, she smiled and observed: "Yun'er, you're indeed bold in playing your pranks with me! I thought it strange that you should give me presents; but the fact is you had a favor to ask of me; and your uncle told me even yesterday that you had appealed to him!"

Jia Yun smiled. "Of my appeal to uncle, you needn't, aunt, make any mention; for I'm at this moment full of regret at having made it. Had I known, at an early hour, that things would have come to this pass, I would, from the very first, have made my request to you, aunt; and by this time everything would have been settled long ago! But who would have anticipated that uncle was, after all, a man of no worth!"

"Strange enough," lady Feng remarked sneeringly, "when you found that you didn't succeed in that quarter, you came again yesterday in search of me!"

"Aunt, you do my filial heart an injustice," Jia Yun protested; "I never had such a thought; had I entertained any such idea, wouldn't I, aunt, have made my appeal to you yesterday? But as you are now aware of everything, I'll really put uncle on one side, and prefer my request to you; for circumstances compel me to entreat you, aunt, to be so good as to show me some little consideration!"

Lady Feng laughed sardonically. "You people will choose the long road to follow and put me also in a dilemma! Had you told me just one word at an early hour, what couldn't have been brought about? an affair of state indeed to be delayed up to this moment! In the garden, there are to be more trees planted and flowers laid down, and I couldn't think of any person that I could have recommended, and had you spoken before this, wouldn't the whole question have been settled soon enough?"

"Well, in that case, aunt," ventured Jia Yun with a smile, "you had better depute me tomorrow, and have done!"

"This job," continued lady Feng after a pause, "is not, my impression is, very profitable; and if you were to wait till the first moon of next year, when the fireworks, lanterns, and candles will have to be purveyed, I'll depute you as soon as those extensive commissions turn up."

"My dear aunt," pleaded Jia Yun, "first appoint me to this one, and if I do really manage this satisfactorily, you can then commission me with that other!"

"You know in truth how to draw a long thread," lady Feng observed laughing. "But hadn't it been that your uncle had spoken to me on your account, I wouldn't have concerned myself about you. But as I shall cross over here soon after the repast, you had better come at 11 A.M., and fetch the money, for you to enter into the garden the day after tomorrow, and have the flowers planted!"

As she said this, she gave orders to drive the "scented" carriage, and went on her way by the quickest cut; while Jia Yun, who was irrepressibly delighted, betook himself into the Qixian study, and inquired after Baoyu. But, who would have thought it, Baoyu had, at an early hour, gone to the mansion of the Prince of Beijing, so that Jia Yun had to sit in a listless mood till noon; and when he found out that lady Feng had returned, he speedily wrote an acknowledgment and came to receive the warrant. On his arrival outside the court, he commissioned a servant to announce him, and Caiming thereupon walked out, and merely asking for the receipt, went in, and, after filling in the amount, the year and moon, he handed it over to Jia Yun together with the warrant. Jia Yun received them from him, and as the entry consisted of two hundred taels, his heart was full of exultant joy; and turning round, he hurried to the treasury, where after he had taken over the amount in silver, he returned home and laid the case before his mother, and needless to say, that both the parent and her son were in high spirits. The next day, at the fifth watch, Jia Yun first came in search of Ni'er, to whom he repaid the money, and then taking fifty taels along with him, he sped outside the western gate to the house of Fang Chun, a gardener, to purchase trees, where we will leave him without saying anything more about him.

We will now resume our story with Baoyu. The day on which he encountered Jia Yun, he asked him to come in on the morrow and have a chat with him, but this invitation was practically the mere formal talk of a rich and well-to-do young man, and was not likely to be so much as borne in mind; and so it was that it readily slipped from his memory. On the evening of the day, however, on which he returned home from the mansion of the Prince of Beijing, he came, after paying his salutations to dowager lady Jia, Madame Wang, and the other inmates, back into the garden; but upon divesting himself of all his fineries, he was just about to have his bath, when, as Xiren had, at the invitation of Xue Baochai, crossed over to tie a few knotted buttons, as Qiuwen and Bihen had both gone to hurry the servants to bring the water, as Tanyun had likewise been taken home, on account of her mother's illness, and Sheyue, on the other hand, was at present ailing in her quarters, while the several waiting-maids, who were in there besides to attend to the dirty work, and answer the calls, had, surmising that he would not requisition their services, one and all gone out in search of their friends and in quest of their companions, it occurred, contrary to their calculations, that Baoyu remained this whole length of time quite alone in his apartments; and as it so happened that Baoyu wanted tea to drink, he had to call two or three times before he at last saw three old matrons walk in. But at the sight of them, Baoyu hastily waved his hand and exclaimed: "No matter, no matter; I don't want you," whereupon the matrons had no help but to withdraw out of the rooms; and as Baoyu perceived that there were no waiting-maids at hand, he had to come down and take a cup and go up to the teapot to pour the tea; when he heard someone from behind him observe: "Master Secundus, beware, you'll scorch your hand; wait until I come to pour it!" And as she spoke, she walked up to him, and took the cup from his grasp, to the intense surprise, in fact, of Baoyu, who inquired: "Where were you that you have suddenly come to give me a start?"

The waiting-maid smiled as she handed him the tea. "I was in the back court," she replied, "and just came in from the back door of the inner rooms; and is it likely that you didn't, sir, hear the sound of my footsteps?"

Baoyu drank his tea, and as he simultaneously passed the servant-girl under a minute inspection, he found that though she wore several articles of clothing the worse for wear, she was, nevertheless, with that head of beautiful hair, as black as the plumage of a raven, done up in curls, her face so oblong, her figure so slim and elegant, indeed, supremely beautiful, sweet, and spruce, and Baoyu eagerly inquired: "Are you also a girl attached to this room of mine?"

"I am," rejoined that waiting-maid.

"But since you belong to this room, how is it I don't know you?" Baoyu added.

When the maid heard these words, she forced a laugh. "There are even many," she explained, "that are strangers to you; and is it only myself? I've never, before this, served tea, or handed water, or brought in anything; nor have I attended to a single duty in your presence, so how could you know me?"

"But why don't you attend to any of those duties that would bring you to my notice?" Baoyu questioned.

"I too," answered the maid, "find it as difficult to answer such a question. There's however one thing that I must report to you, master Secundus. Yesterday, some Mr. Yun'er or other came to see you; but as I thought you, sir, had no leisure, I speedily bade Beiming tell him to come early today. But you unexpectedly went over again to the mansion of the Prince of Beijing."

When she had spoken as far as this, she caught sight of Qiuwen and Bihen enter the court, giggling and laughing; the two of them carrying between them a bucket of water; and while raising their skirts with one hand, they hobbled along, as the water spurted and splashed. The waiting-maid hastily came out to meet them so as to relieve them of their burden, but Qiuwen and Bihen were in the act of standing face to face and finding fault with each other; one saying, "You've wetted my clothes," the other adding, "You've trod on my shoes," and upon, all of a sudden, espying someone walk out to receive the water, and discovering, when they came to see, that it was actually no one else than Xiao Hong, they were at once both so taken aback that, putting down the bucket, they hurried into the room; and when they looked about and saw that there was no other person inside besides Baoyu they were at once displeased. But as they were meanwhile compelled to get ready the articles necessary for his bath, they waited until Baoyu was about to divest himself of his clothes, when the couple of them speedily pulled the door to behind them, as they went out, and walked as far as the room on the opposite side, in search of Xiao Hong; of whom they inquired: "What were you doing in his room a short while back?"

"When was I ever in the room?" Xiao Hong replied; "simply because I lost sight of my handkerchief, I went to the back to try and find it, when unexpectedly Mr. Secundus, who wanted tea, called for you sisters; and as there wasn't even one of you there, I walked in and poured a cup for him, and just at that very moment you sisters came back."

"You barefaced, low-bred thing!" cried Qiuwen, turning towards her and spurting in her face. "It was our bounden duty to tell you to go and hurry them for the water, but you simply maintained that you were busy and made us go instead, in order to afford you an opportunity of performing these wily tricks! and isn't this raising yourself up li by li? But don't we forsooth, even so much as come up to you? and you just take that looking-glass and see for yourself, whether you be fit to serve tea and to hand water or not?"

"Tomorrow," continued Bihen, "I'll tell them that whenever there's anything to do connected with his wanting tea, or asking for water, or with fetching things for him, not one of us should budge, and that she alone should be allowed to go, and have done!"

"If this be your suggestion," remarked Qiuwen, "wouldn't it be still better that we should all disperse, and let her reign supreme in this room!"

But while the two of them were up to this trouble, one saying one thing, and another, another, they caught sight of two old nurses walk in to deliver a message from lady Feng; who explained: "Tomorrow, someone will bring in gardeners to plant trees, and she bids you keep under more rigorous restraint, and not sun your clothes and petticoats anywhere and everywhere; nor air them about heedlessly; that the artificial hill will, all along, be entirely shut in by screening curtains, and that you mustn't be running about at random."

"I wonder," interposed Qiuwen with alacrity, "who it is that will bring the workmen tomorrow, and supervise the works?"

"Someone or other called Mr. Yun, living at the back portico," the old woman observed.

But Qiuwen and Bihen were neither of them acquainted with him, and they went on promiscuously asking further questions on his account, but Xiao Hong knew distinctly in her mind who it was, and was well aware that it was the person whom she had seen, the previous day, in the outer library.

The surname of this Xiao Hong had, in fact, been originally Lin, while her infant name had been Hongyu; but as the word Yu improperly corresponded with the names of Baoyu and Daiyu, she was, in due course, simply called Xiao Hong. She was indeed an hereditary servant of the mansion; and her father had latterly taken over the charge of all matters connected with the farms and farmhouses in every locality. This Hongyu came, at the age of sixteen, into the mansion, to enter into service, and was attached to the Hong Yuan, where in point of fact she found both a quiet and pleasant home; and when contrary to all expectation, the young ladies as well as Baoyu, were subsequently permitted to move their quarters into the garden of Broad Vista, it so happened that this place was, moreover, fixed upon by Baoyu. This Xiao Hong was, it is true, a girl without any experience, but as she could, to a certain degree, boast of a pretty face, and as, in her own heart, she recklessly fostered the idea of exalting herself to a higher standard, she was ever ready to thrust herself in Baoyu's way, with a view to showing herself off. But attached to Baoyu's personal service were a lot of servants, all of whom were glib and specious, so that how could she ever find an opportunity of thrusting herself forward? But contrary to her anticipations, there turned up, eventually on this day, some faint glimmer of hope, but as she again came in for a spell of spiteful abuse from Qiuwen and her companion, her expectations were soon considerably frustrated, and she was just plunged in a melancholy mood, when suddenly she heard the old nurse begin the conversation about Jia Yun, which unconsciously so affected her heart that she hastily returned, quite disconsolate, into her room, and lay herself down on her bed, giving herself quietly to reflection. But while she was racking and torturing her brain and at a moment when she was at a loss what decision to grasp, her ear unexpectedly caught, emanating from outside the window, a faint voice say: Xiao Hong, I've picked up your pocket handkerchief in here!" and as soon as Xiao Hong heard these words, she walked out with hurried step and found that it was no one else than Jia Yun in person; and as Xiao Hong unwillingly felt her powdered face suffused with brushes: "Where did you pick it up, Mr. Secundus?" she asked.

"Come over," Jia Yun smiled, "and I'll tell you!" And as he uttered these words, he came up and drew her to him; but Xiao Hong twisted herself round and ran away; but was however tripped over by the step of the door.

Now, reader, do you want to know the sequel? If so the next chapter will explain.

CHAPTER 25

By a demoniacal art, a junior uncle and an
elder brother's wife (Baoyu and lady Feng)
come across five devils. The gem of Spiritual
Perception meets, in a fit of torpor,
the two perfect men.

Xiao Hong, the story continues, was much unsettled in her mind. Her
thoughts rolled on in one connected string. But suddenly she became
drowsy, and falling asleep, she encountered Jia Yun, who tried to carry
out his intention to drag her near him. She twisted herself round, and
endeavored to run away; but was tripped over by the doorstep. This
gave her such a start that she woke up. Then, at length, she realized
that it was only a dream. But so restlessly did she, in consequence of
this fright, keep on rolling and tossing that she could not close her eyes
during the whole night. As soon as the light of the next day dawned,
she got up. Several waiting-maids came at once to tell her to go and
sweep the floor of the rooms, and to bring water to wash the face with.
Xiao Hong did not even wait to arrange her hair or perform her ablutions; but, turning towards the looking-glass, she pinned her chevelure
up anyhow; and, rinsing her hands, and, tying a sash round her waist,
she repaired directly to sweep the apartments.

Who would have thought it, Baoyu also had set his heart upon her
the moment he caught sight of her the previous day. Yet he feared, in
the first place, that if he mentioned her by name and called her over
into his service, Xiren and the other girls might feel the pangs of jealousy. He did not, either in the second place, have any idea what her
disposition was like. The consequence was that he felt downcast; so
much so that when he got up at an early hour, he did not even comb
his hair or wash, but simply remained seated, and brooded in a state of
abstraction. After a while, he lowered the window. Through the gauze
frame, from which he could distinctly discern what was going on outside, he espied several servant-girls, engaged in sweeping the court. All
of them were rouged and powdered; they had flowers inserted in their

hair, and were grandly got up. But the only one of whom he failed to get a glimpse, was the girl he had met the day before.

Baoyu speedily walked out of the door with slipshod shoes. Under the pretence of admiring the flowers, he glanced, now towards the east; now towards the west. But upon raising his head, he descried, in the southwest corner, someone or other leaning by the side of the railing under the covered passage. A crab-apple tree, however, obstructed the view and he could not see distinctly who it was, so advancing a step further in, he stared with intent gaze. It was, in point of fact, the waiting-maid of the day before, tarrying about plunged in a reverie. His wish was to go forward and meet her, but he did not, on the other hand, see how he could very well do so. Just as he was cogitating within himself, he, of a sudden, perceived Bihen come and ask him to go and wash his face. This reminder placed him under the necessity of betaking himself into his room. But we will leave him there, without further details, so as to return to Xiao Hong.

She was communing with her own thoughts. But unawares perceiving Xiren wave her hand and call her by name, she had to walk up to her.

"Our watering-pot is spoilt," Xiren smiled and said, "so go to Miss Lin's over there and find one for us to use."

Xiao Hong hastened on her way towards the Xiaoxiang Guan.

When she got as far as the Cuiyan bridge, she saw, on raising her head and looking round, the mounds and lofty places entirely shut in by screens, and she bethought herself that laborers were that day to plant trees in that particular locality.

At a great distance off, a band of men were, in very deed, engaged in digging up the soil, while Jia Yun was seated on a boulder on the hill, superintending the works. The time came for Xiao Hong to pass by, but she could not muster the courage to do so. Nevertheless she had no other course than to quietly proceed to the Xiaoxiang Guan. Then getting the watering-pot, she sped on her way back again. But being in low spirits, she retired alone into her room and lay herself down. One and all, however, simply maintained that she was out of sorts, so they did not pay any heed to her.

A day went by. On the morrow fell, in fact, the anniversary of the birth of Wang Ziteng's spouse, and someone was despatched from his residence to come and invite dowager lady Jia and Madame Wang. Madame Wang found out however that dowager lady Jia would not avail herself of the invitation, and neither would she go. So Mrs. Xue went along with lady Feng, and the three sisters of the Jia family, and Baochai and Baoyu, and only returned home late in the evening.

Madame Wang was sitting in Mrs. Xue's apartments, whither she had just crossed, when she perceived Jia Huan come back from school, and she bade him transcribe incantations out of the Jin Gang Canon and intonate them. Jia Huan accordingly came and seated himself on the stove-couch, occupied by Madame Wang, and, directing a servant to light the candles, he started copying in an ostentatious and dashing manner. Now he called Caixia to pour a cup of tea for him. Now he asked Yuchuan to take the scissors and cut the snuff of the wick. "Jinchuan!" he next cried, "you're in the way of the rays of the lamp."

The servant-girls had all along entertained an antipathy for him, and not one of them therefore worried her mind about what he said. Caixia was the only one who still got on well with him, so pouring a cup of tea, she handed it to him. But she felt prompted to whisper to him: "Keep quiet a bit! what's the use of making people dislike you?"

"I know myself how matters stand," Jia Huan rejoined, as he cast a steady glance at her; "so don't you try and befool me! Now that you are on intimate terms with Baoyu, you don't pay much heed to me. I've also seen through it myself."

Caixia set her teeth together, and gave him a fillip on the head. "You heartless fellow!" she cried. "You're like the dog that bit Lu Dongbin. You have no idea of what's right and what's wrong!"

While these two nagged away, they noticed lady Feng and Madame Wang cross together over to them. Madame Wang at once assailed him with questions. She asked him how many ladies had been present on that day, whether the play had been good or bad, and what the banquet had been like.

But a brief interval over, Baoyu too appeared on the scene. After saluting Madame Wang, he also made a few remarks, with all decorum; and then bidding a servant remove his frontlet, divest him of his long gown, and pull off his boots, he rushed head foremost, into his mother's lap.

Madame Wang caressed and patted him. But while Baoyu clung to his mother's neck, he spoke to her of one thing and then another.

"My child," said Madame Wang, "you've again had too much to drink; your face is scalding hot, and if you still keep on rubbing and scraping it, why, you'll by and bye stir up the fumes of wine! Don't you yet go and lie down quietly over there for a little!"

Chiding him the while, she directed a servant to fetch a pillow. Baoyu therefore lay himself down at the back of Madame Wang, and called Caixia to come and stroke him.

Baoyu then began to bandy words with Caixia. But perceiving that Caixia was reserved, and, that instead of paying him any attention, she kept her eyes fixed upon Jia Huan, Baoyu eagerly took her hand. "My dear girl!" he said; "do also heed me a little; " and as he gave utterance to this appeal, he kept her hand clasped in his.

Caixia, however, drew her hand away and would not let him hold it. "If you go on in this way," she vehemently exclaimed, "I'll shout out at once."

These two were in the act of wrangling, when verily Jia Huan overheard what was going on. He had, in fact, all along hated Baoyu; so when on this occasion, he espied him up to his larks with Caixia, he could much less than ever stifle feelings of resentment in his heart. After some reflection, therefore, an idea suggested itself to his mind, and pretending that it was by a slip of the hand, he shoved the candle, overflowing with tallow, into Baoyu's face.

"Ai ya!" Baoyu was heard to exclaim. Everyone in the whole room was plunged in consternation. With precipitate haste, the lanterns, standing on the floor, were moved over; and, with the first ray of light, they discovered that Baoyu's face was one mass of tallow.

Madame Wang gave way to anger as well as anxiety. At one time, she issued directions to the servants to rub and wash Baoyu clean. At another, she heaped abuse upon Jia Huan.

Lady Feng jumped on to the stone-couch by leaps and bounds. But while intent upon removing the stuff from Baoyu's face, she simultaneously ejaculated: "Master Tertius, are you still such a trickster! I'll tell you what, you'll never turn to any good account! Yet dame Zhao should ever correct and admonish him."

This single remark suggested the idea to Madame Wang, and she lost no time in sending for Mrs. Zhao to come round.

"You bring up," she berated her, "such a black-hearted offspring like this, and don't you, after all, advise and reprove him? Time and again I paid no notice whatever to what happened, and you and he have become more audacious, and have gone from worse to worse!"

Mrs. Zhao had no alternative but to suppress every sense of injury, silence all grumblings, and go herself and lend a hand to the others in tidying Baoyu. She then perceived that a whole row of blisters had risen on the left side of Baoyu's face, but that fortunately no injury had been done to his eyes.

When Madame Wang's attention was drawn to them she felt her heart sore. It fell a prey to fears also lest when dowager lady Jia made any inquiries about them she should find it difficult to give her any satisfactory reply. And so distressed did she get that she gave Mrs. Zhao another scolding. But while she tried to comfort Baoyu, she, at the same time, fetched some powder for counteracting the effects of the virus, and applied it on his face.

"It's rather sore," said Baoyu, "but it's nothing to speak of. Tomorrow when my old grandmother asks about it, I can simply explain that I scalded it myself; that will be quite enough to tell her."

"If you say that you scalded it yourself," lady Feng observed, "why, she'll also call people to task for not looking out; and a fit of rage will, beyond doubt, be the outcome of it all."

Madame Wang then ordered the servants to take care and escort Baoyu back to his room. On their arrival, Xiren and his other attendants saw him, and they were all in a great state of flurry.

As for Lin Daiyu, when she found that Baoyu had gone out of doors, she continued the whole day a prey to ennui. In the evening, she deputed messengers two and three times to go and inquire about him. But when she came to know that he had been scalded, she hurried in person to come and see him. She then discovered Baoyu all alone, holding a glass and scanning his features in it; while the left side of his face was plastered all over with some medicine.

Lin Daiyu imagined that the burn was of an extremely serious nature, and she hastened to approach him with a view to examine it. Baoyu, however, screened his face, and, waving his hand, bade her leave the room; for knowing her usual knack for tidiness he did not feel inclined to let her get a glimpse of his face. Daiyu then gave up the attempt, and confined herself to asking him: "whether it was very painful?"

"It isn't very sore," replied Baoyu, "if I look after it for a day or two, it will get all right."

But after another short stay, Lin Daiyu repaired back to her quarters.

The next day Baoyu saw dowager lady Jia. But in spite of his confession that he himself was responsible for the scalding of his face, his grandmother could not refrain from reading another lecture to the servants who had been in attendance.

A day after, Ma, a Daoist matron, whose name was recorded as Baoyu's godmother, came on a visit to the mansion. Upon perceiving Baoyu, she was very much taken aback, and asked all about the circumstances of the accident. When he explained that he had been scalded, she forthwith shook her head and heaved a sigh; then while making with her fingers a few passes over Baoyu's face, she went on to mutter incantations for several minutes. "I can guarantee that he'll get all right," she added, "for this is simply a sad and fleeting accident!"

Turning towards dowager lady Jia: "Venerable ancestor," she observed, "Venerable Buddha! how could you ever be aware of the existence of the portentous passage in that Buddhistic classic, 'to the effect that a son of every person, who holds the dignity of prince, duke, or high functionary, has no sooner come into the world and reached a certain age than numerous evil spirits at once secretly haunt him, and pinch him, when they find an opportunity; or dig their nails into him; or knock his bowl of rice down, during meal-time; or give him a shove and send him over, while he is quietly seated.' So this is the reason why the majority of the sons and grandsons of those distinguished families do not grow up to attain manhood."

Dowager lady Jia, upon hearing her speak in this wise, eagerly asked: "Is there any Buddhistic spell, by means of which to check their influence or not?"

"This is an easy job!" rejoined the Daoist matron Ma, "all one need do is to perform several meritorious deeds on his account so as to counteract the consequences of retribution and everything will then be put right. That canon further explains: 'that in the western part of the world there is a mighty Buddha, whose glory illumines all things, and whose special charge is to cast his luster on the evil spirits in dark places; that if any benevolent man or virtuous woman offers him oblations with sincerity of heart, he is able to so successfully perpetuate the peace and quiet of their sons and grandsons that these will no more meet with any calamities arising from being possessed by malevolent demons.'"

"But what, I wonder," inquired dowager lady Jia, "could be offered to this god?"

"Nothing of any great value," answered the Daoist matron, Ma. "Exclusive of offerings of scented candles, several catties of scented oil can be added, each day, to keep the lantern of the Great Sea alight. This 'Great Sea' lantern is the visible embodiment and Buddhistic representation of this divinity, so day and night we don't venture to let it go out!"

"For a whole day and a whole night," asked dowager lady Jia, "how much oil is needed, so that I too should accomplish a good action?"

"There is really no limit as to quantity. It rests upon the goodwill of the donor," Ma, the Daoist matron, put in by way of reply. "In my quarters, for instance, I have several lanterns, the gifts of the consorts of princes and the spouses of high officials living in various localities. The consort of the mansion of the Prince of Nan'an has been prompted in her beneficence by a liberal spirit; she allows each day forty-eight catties of oil, and a catty of wick; so that her 'Great Sea' lamp is only a trifle smaller than a water-jar. The spouse of the marquis of Jintian comes next, with no more than twenty catties a day. Besides these, there are several other families; some giving ten catties; some eight catties;

some three; some five; subject to no fixed rule; and of course I feel bound to keep the lanterns alight on their behalf."

Dowager lady Jia nodded her head and gave way to reflection.

"There's still another thing," continued the Daoist matron, Ma. "If it be on account of father or mother or seniors, any excessive donation would not matter. But were you, venerable ancestor, to bestow too much in your offering for Baoyu, our young master won't, I fear, be equal to the gift; and instead of being benefited, his happiness will be snapped. If you therefore want to make a liberal gift seven catties will do; if a small one, then five catties will even be sufficient."

"Well, in that case," responded dowager lady Jia, "let us fix upon five catties a day, and every month come and receive payment of the whole lump sum!"

"Amituo Fo!" exclaimed Ma, the Daoist matron, "Oh merciful, and mighty Pusa!"

Dowager lady Jia then called the servants and impressed on their minds that whenever Baoyu went out of doors in the future, they should give several strings of cash to the pages to bestow on charity among the bonzes and Daoist priests, and the poor and needy they might meet on the way.

These directions concluded, the Daoist matron trudged into the various quarters, and paid her respects, and then strolled leisurely about. Presently, she entered Mrs. Zhao's apartments. After the two ladies had exchanged salutations, Mrs. Zhao bade a young servant-girl hand her guest a cup of tea. While Mrs. Zhao busied herself pasting shoes, Ma, the Daoist matron, espied, piled up in a heap on the stove-couch, sundry pieces of silks and satins. "It just happens," she consequently remarked, "that I have no facings for shoes, so my lady do give me a few odd cuttings of silk and satin, of no matter what color, to make myself a pair of shoes with."

Mrs. Zhao heaved a sigh. "Look," she said, "whether there be still among them any pieces good for anything. But anything that's worth anything doesn't find its way in here. If you don't despise what's worthless, you're at liberty to select any two pieces and to take them away, and have done."

The Daoist matron, Ma, chose with alacrity several pieces and shoved them in her breast.

"The other day," Mrs. Zhao went on to inquire, "I sent a servant over with five hundred cash; have you presented any offerings before the god of medicine or not?"

"I've offered them long ago for you," the Daoist matron Ma rejoined.

"Amintuo Fo!" ejaculated Mrs. Zhao with a sigh, "were I a little better off, I'd also come often and offer gifts; but though my will be boundless, my means are insufficient!"

"Don't trouble your mind on this score," suggested Ma, the Daoist matron. "By and bye, when Mr. Huan has grown up into a man and obtained some official post or other, will there be then any fear of your not being able to afford such offerings as you might like to make?"

At these words Mrs. Zhao gave a smile. "Enough, enough!" she cried. "Don't again refer to such contingencies! the present is a fair criterion. For up to whom in this house can my son and I come? Baoyu is still a mere child; but he is such that he wins people's love. Those big people may be partial to him, and love him a good deal, I've nothing to say to it; but I can't eat humble pie to this sort of mistress!"

While uttering this remark, she stretched out her two fingers.

Ma, the Daoist matron, understood the meaning she desired to convey. "It's your lady Secunda Lian, eh?" she forthwith asked.

Mrs. Zhao was filled with trepidation. Hastily waving her hand, she got to her feet, raised the portiere, and peeped outside. Perceiving that there was no one about, she at length retraced her footsteps. "Dreadful!" she then said to the Daoist matron. "Dreadful! But speaking of this sort of mistress, I'm not so much as a human being, if she doesn't manage to shift over into her mother's home the whole of this family estate."

"Need you tell me this!" Ma, the Daoist matron, at these words, remarked with a view to ascertain what she implied. "Haven't I, forsooth, discovered it all for myself? Yet it's fortunate that you don't trouble your minds about her; for it's far better that you should let her have her own way."

"My dear woman," rejoined Mrs. Zhao, "Not let her have her own way! why, is it likely that anyone would have the courage to tell her anything?"

"I don't mean to utter any words that may bring upon me retribution," added Ma, the Daoist matron, "but you people haven't got the wits. But it's no matter of surprise. Yet if you daren't openly do anything, why, you could stealthily have devised some plan. And do you still tarry up to this day?"

Mrs. Zhao realised that there lurked something in her insinuation, and she felt an inward secret joy. "What plan could I stealthily devise?" she asked. "I've got the will right enough, but I'm not a person gifted with this sort of gumption. So were you to impart to me some way or other, I would reward you most liberally."

When the Daoist matron, Ma, heard this, she drew near to her. "Amituo Fo! desist at once from asking me!" she designedly exclaimed. "How can I know anything about such matters, contrary as they are to what is right?"

"There you are again!" Mrs. Zhao replied. "You're one ever most ready to succour those in distress, and to help those in danger, and is it likely that you'll quietly look on, while someone comes and compasses my death as well as that of my son? Are you, pray, fearful lest I shouldn't give you any reward?"

Ma, the Daoist matron, greeted this remark with a smile. "You're right enough in what you say," she ventured, "of my being unable to bear the sight of yourself and son receiving insult from a third party; but as for your mention of rewards, why, what's there of yours that I still covet?"

This answer slightly reassured Mrs. Zhao's mind. "How is it," she speedily urged, "that an intelligent person like you should have become so dense? If, indeed, the spell prove efficacious, and we exterminate them both, is there any apprehension that this family estate won't be ours? and when that time comes, won't you get all you may wish?"

At this disclosure, Ma, the Daoist matron, lowered her head for a long time. "When everything," she observed, "shall have been settled satisfactorily, and when there'll be, what's more, no proof at all, will you still pay any heed to me?"

"What's there hard about this?" remarked Mrs. Zhao. "I've saved several taels from my own pin-money, and have besides a good number of clothes and head-ornaments. So you can first take several of these away with you. And I'll further write an I.O.U., and entrust it to you, and when that time does come, I'll pay you in full."

"That will do!" answered the Daoist matron, Ma.

Mrs. Zhao thereupon dismissed even a young servant-girl, who happened to be in the room, and hastily opening a trunk, she produced several articles of clothing and jewelry, as well as a few odd pieces of silver from her own pocket-money. Then also writing a promissory note for fifty taels, she surrendered the lot to Ma, the Daoist matron. "Take these," she said, "in advance for presents in your temple."

At the sight of the various articles and of the promissory note, the Daoist matron became at once unmindful of what was right and what was wrong; and while her mouth was full of assent, she stretched out her arm, and first and foremost laid hold of the hard cash, and next clutched the I.O.U. Turning then towards Mrs. Zhao, she asked for a sheet of paper; and taking up a pair of scissors, she cut out two human beings and gave them to Mrs. Zhao, enjoining her to write on the upper part of them the respective ages of the two persons in question. Looking further for a sheet of blue paper, she cut out five blue-faced devils, which she bade her place together side by side with the paper men, and taking a pin she made them fast. "When I get home," she remarked, "I'll have recourse to some art, which will, beyond doubt, prove efficacious."

When she however had done speaking, she suddenly saw Madame Wang's waiting-maid make her appearance inside the room. "What! my dame, are you in here!" the girl exclaimed. "Why, our lady is waiting for you!"

The two dames then parted company.

But passing them over, we will now allude to Lin Daiyu. As Baoyu had scalded his face, and did not go out of doors very much, she often came to have a chat with him. On this particular day she took up, after her meal, some book or other and read a couple of pages out of it. Next, she busied herself a little with needlework, in company with Zijuan. She felt however thoroughly dejected and out of sorts. So she strolled out of doors along with her. But catching sight of the newly sprouted bamboo shoots, in front of the pavilion, they involuntarily stepped out of the entrance of the court, and penetrated into the garden. They cast their eyes on all four quarters; but not a soul was visible. When they became conscious of the splendor of the flowers and the chatter of the birds, they, with listless step, turned their course towards the I Hung court. There they found several servant-girls baling out water; while a bevy of them stood under the verandah, watching the thrushes having their bath. They heard also the sound of laughter in the rooms.

The fact is that Li Gongcai, lady Feng, and Baochai were assembled inside. As soon as they saw them walk in, they with one voice shouted, smiling: "Now, are not these two more!"

"We are a full company today," laughed Daiyu, "but who has issued the cards and invited us here?"

"The other day," interposed lady Feng, "I sent servants with a present of two caddies of tea for you, Miss Lin; was it, after all, good?"

"I had just forgotten all about it," Daiyu rejoined, "many thanks for your kind attention!

"I tasted it," observed Baoyu. "I did not think it anything good. But I don't know how others, who've had any of it, find it."

"Its flavor," said Daiyu, "is good; the only thing is, it has no color."

"It's tribute tea from the Laos Kingdom," continued lady Feng. "When I tried it, I didn't either find it anything very fine. It's not up to what we ordinarily drink."

"To my taste, it's all right," put in Daiyu. "But what your palates are like, I can't make out."

"As you say it's good," suggested Baoyu, "you're quite at liberty to take all I have for your use."

"I've got a great deal more of it over there," lady Feng remarked.

"I'll tell a servant-girl to go and fetch it," Daiyu replied.

"No need," lady Feng went on. "I'll send it over with someone. I also have a favor to ask of you tomorrow, so I may as well tell the servant to bring it along at the same time."

When Lin Daiyu heard these words, she put on a smile. "You just mark this," she observed. "I've had today a little tea from her place, and she at once begins making a tool of me!"

"Since you've had some of our tea," lady Feng laughed, "how is it that you have not yet become a wife in our household?"

The whole party burst out laughing aloud. So much so, that they found it difficult to repress themselves. But Daiyu's face was suffused with blushes. She turned her head the other way, and uttered not a word.

"Our sister-in-law Secunda's jibes are first-rate!" Baochai chimed in with a laugh.

"What jibes!" exclaimed Daiyu; "they're purely and simply the prattle of a mean mouth and vile tongue! They're enough to evoke people's displeasure!"

Saying this, she went on to sputter in disgust.

"Were you," insinuated lady Feng, "to become a wife in my family, what is there that you would lack?" Pointing then at Baoyu, "Look here!" she cried, "Is not this human being worthy of you? Is not his station in life good enough for you? Are not our stock and estate sufficient for you? and in what slight degree can he make you lose caste?"

Daiyu rose to her feet, and retired immediately. But Baochai shouted out: "Here's Pin'er in a huff! Don't you yet come back? when you've gone, there will really be no fun!"

While calling out to her, she jumped up to pull her back. As soon, however, as she reached the door of the room, she beheld Mrs. Zhao, accompanied by Mrs. Zhou; both coming to look up Baoyu. Baoyu and his companions got up in a body and pressed them into a seat. Lady Feng was the sole person who did not heed them.

But just as Baochai was about to open her lips, she perceived a servant-girl, attached to Madame Wang's apartments, appear on the scene. "Your maternal uncle's wife has come," she said, "and she requests you, ladies and young ladies, to come out and see her."

Li Gongcai hurriedly walked away in company with lady Feng. The two dames, Mrs. Zhao and Mrs. Zhou, in like manner took their leave and quitted the room.

"As for me, I can't go out," Baoyu shouted. "But whatever you do, pray, don't ask aunt to come in here. Cousin Lin," he went on to say, "do stay on a while; I've got something to tell you."

Lady Feng overheard him. Turning her head towards Lin Daiyu, "There's someone," she cried; "who wants to speak to you." And forthwith laying hold of Lin Daiyu, she pushed her back and then trudged away, along with Li Gongcai.

During this time, Baoyu clasped Daiyu's hand in his. He did nothing than smile. Not a word did he utter. Daiyu naturally, therefore, got crimson in the face, and struggled to escape his importunities.

"Ai-ya!" exclaimed Baoyu. "How my head is sore!"

"It should be!" rejoined Daiyu. "Amituo Fo."

Baoyu then gave vent to a loud shout. His body bounced three or four feet high from the ground. His mouth was full of confused shrieks. But all he said was rambling talk.

Daiyu and the servant-girls were full of consternation, and, with all possible haste, they ran and apprised Madame Wang and dowager lady Jia.

Wang Ziteng's wife was, at this time, also with them, so they all came in a body to see him. Baoyu behaved more and more as if determined to clutch a sword or seize a spear to put an end to his existence. He raged in a manner sufficient to subvert the heavens and upset the earth.

As soon as dowager lady Jia and Madame Wang caught sight of him, they were struck with terror. They trembled wildly like a piece of clothing that is being shaken. Uttering a shout of: "My son," and another of: "My flesh," they burst out into a loud fit of crying. Presently, all the inmates were seized with fright. Even Jia She, Madame Xing, Jia Zheng, Jia Zhen, Jia Lian, Jia Rong, Jia Yun, Jia Ping, Mrs. Xue, Xue Pan, Zhou Rui's wife, and the various members of the household, whether high or low, and the servant-girls and married women too, rushed into the garden to see what was up.

The confusion that prevailed was, at the moment, like entangled flax. Everyone was at a loss what to do, when they espied lady Feng dash into the garden, a glistening sword in hand, and try to cut down everything that came in her way, ogle vacantly whomsoever struck her gaze, and make forthwith an attempt to despatch them. A greater panic than ever broke out among the whole assemblage. But placing herself at the head of a handful of sturdy female servants, Zhou Rui's wife precipitated herself forward, and clasping her tight, they succeeded in snatching the sword from her grip, and carrying her back into her room.

Ping'er, Feng'er, and the other girls began to weep. They invoked the heavens and appealed to the earth. Even Jia Zheng was distressed at heart. One and all at this stage started shouting, some, one thing; some, another. Some suggested exorcists. Some cried out for the posture-makers to attract the devils. Others recommended that Zhang, the Daoist priest, of the Yuhuang temple, should catch the evil spirits. A thorough turmoil reigned supreme for a long time. The gods were implored. Prayers were offered. Every kind of remedy was tried, but no benefit whatever became visible.

After sunset, the spouse of Wang Ziteng said good-bye and took her departure. On the ensuing day, Wang Ziteng himself also came to make inquiries. Following closely upon him, arrived, in a body, messengers from the young marquis Shi, Madame Xing's young brother, and their various relatives to ascertain for themselves how (lady Feng and Baoyu) were progressing. Some brought charm-water. Some recommended bonzes and Daoist priests. Others spoke highly of doctors. But that young fellow and his elder brother's wife fell into such greater and greater stupor that they lost all consciousness. Their bodies were hot like fire. As they lay prostrate on their beds, they talked deliriously. With the fall of the shades of night their condition aggravated. So much so that the matrons and servant-girls did not venture to volunteer their attendance. They had, therefore, to be both moved into Madame Wang's quarters, where servants were told off to take their turn and watch them.

Dowager lady Jia, Madame Wang, Madame Xing, and Mrs. Xue did not budge an inch or a step from their side. They sat round them, and did nothing but cry. Jia She and Jia Zheng too were a prey, at this juncture, to misgivings lest weeping should upset dowager lady Jia. Day and night oil was burnt and fires were, mindless of expense, kept alight. The bustle and confusion was such that no one, either master or servant, got any rest.

Jia She also sped on every side in search of Buddhist and Daoist priests. But Jia Zheng had witnessed how little relief these things could afford, and he felt constrained to dissuade Jia She from his endeavors. "The destiny," he argued, "of our son and daughter is entirely dependent upon the will of Heaven, and no human strength can prevail. The malady of these two persons would not be healed, even were every kind of treatment tried, and as I feel confident that it is the design of heaven that things should be as they are, all we can do is to allow it to carry out its purpose."

Jia She, however, paid no notice to his remonstrances and continued as hitherto to fuss in every imaginable way. In no time three days elapsed. Lady Feng and Baoyu were still confined to their beds. Their very breaths had grown fainter. The whole household, therefore, unanimously arrived at the conclusion that there was no hope, and with all despatch they made every necessary preparation for the subsequent requirements of both their relatives.

Dowager lady Jia, Madame Wang, Jia Lian, Ping'er, Xiren, and the others indulged in tears with keener and keener anguish. They hung between life and death. Mrs. Zhao alone was the one who assumed an outward sham air of distress, while in her heart she felt her wishes gratified.

The fourth day arrived. At an early hour Baoyu suddenly opened his eyes and addressed himself to his grandmother Jia. "From this day forward," he said, "I may no longer abide in your house, so you had better send me off at once!"

These words made dowager lady Jia feel as if her very heart had been wrenched out of her. Mrs. Zhao, who stood by, exhorted her. "You shouldn't, venerable lady," she said, "indulge in excessive grief. This young man has been long ago of no good; so wouldn't it be as well to dress him up and let him go back a moment sooner from this world. You'll also be thus sparing him considerable suffering. But, if you persist, in not reconciling yourself to the separation and this breath of his is not cut off, he will lie there and suffer without any respite...."

Her arguments were scarcely ended, when she was spat upon by dowager lady Jia. "You rotten-tongued, good-for-nothing hag!" she cried abusively. "What makes you fancy him of no good! You wish him dead and gone; but what benefit will you then derive? Don't give way to any dreams; for, if he does die, I'll just exact your lives from you! It's all because you've been continuously at him, inciting and urging him to read and write, that his spirit has become so intimidated that, at the sight of his father, he behaves just like a rat trying to get out of the way of a cat! And is not all this the result of the bullying of such a mean herd of women as yourselves! Could you now drive him to death, your wishes would immediately be fulfilled; but which of you will I let off?"

Now she shed tears; now she gave vent to abuse.

Jia Zheng, who stood by, heard these invectives; and they so enhanced his exasperation that he promptly shouted out and made Mrs. Zhao withdraw. He then exerted himself for a time to console (his senior) by using kindly accents. But suddenly someone came to announce that the two coffins had been completed. This announcement pierced, like a dagger, dowager lady Jia to the heart; and while weeping with despair more intense, she broke forth in violent upbraidings.

"Who is it," she inquired; "who gave orders to make the coffins? Bring at once the coffin-makers and beat them to death!"

A stir ensued sufficient to convulse the heavens and to subvert the earth. But at an unforeseen moment resounded in the air the gentle rapping of a 'wooden fish' bell. A voice recited the sentence: "Ave! Buddha able to unravel retribution and dispel grievances! Should any human being lie in sickness, and his family be solicitous on his account; or should anyone have met with evil spirits and come across any baleful evils, we have the means to effect a cure."

Dowager lady Jia and Madame Wang at once directed servants to go out into the street and find out who it was. It turned out to be, in fact, a mangy-headed bonze and a hobbling Daoist priest. What was the appearance of the bonze?

His nose like a suspended gall; his two eyebrows so long,
His eyes, resembling radiant stars, possessed a precious glow,
His coat in tatters and his shoes of straw, without a home;
Rolling in filth, and, a worse fate, his head one mass of boils.

And the Daoist priest, what was he like?

With one leg perched high he comes, with one leg low;
His whole frame drenching wet, bespattered all with mud.
If you perchance meet him, and ask him where's his home,
"In fairyland, west of the 'Weak Water,' he'll say."

Jia Zheng ordered the servants to invite them to walk in. "On what hill," he asked those two persons, "do you cultivate the principles of reason?

"Worthy official!" the bonze smiled, "you must not ask too many questions! It's because we've learnt that there are inmates of your honorable mansion in a poor state of health that we come with the express design of working a cure."

"There are," explained Jia Zheng, "two of our members, who have been possessed of evil spirits. But, is there, I wonder, any remedy by means of which they could be healed?"

"In your family," laughingly observed the Daoist priest, "you have ready at hand a precious thing, the like of which is rare to find in the world. It possesses the virtue of alleviating the ailment, so why need you inquire about remedies?"

Jia Zheng's mind was forthwith aroused. "It's true," he consequently rejoined, "that my son brought along with him, at the time of his birth, a piece of jade, on the surface of which was inscribed that it had the virtue of dispelling evil influences, but we haven't seen any efficacy in it."

"There is, worthy officer," said the bonze, "something in it which you do not understand. That precious jade was, in its primitive state, efficacious, but consequent upon its having been polluted by music, lewdness, property, and gain it has lost its spiritual properties. But produce now that valuable thing and wait till I have taken it into my hands and pronounced incantations over it, when it will become as full of efficacy as of old!"

Jia Zheng accordingly unclasped the piece of jade from Baoyu's neck, and handed it to the two divines. The Buddhist priest held it with reverence in the palm of his hand and heaving a deep sigh, "Since our parting," he cried, "at the foot of the Qing Keng peak, about thirteen years have elapsed. How time flies in the mortal world! Thine earthly destiny has not yet been determined. Alas, alas! how admirable were the qualities thou did'st possess in those days!

"By Heaven unrestrained, without constraint from Earth,
No joys lived in thy heart, but sorrows none as well;
Yet when perception, through refinement, thou did'st reach,
Thou went'st among mankind to trouble to give rise.
How sad the lot which thou of late hast had to hear!
Powder prints and rouge stains thy precious luster dim.
House bars both day and night encage thee like a duck.
Deep wilt thou sleep, but from thy dream at length thou'lt wake,
Thy debt of vengeance, once discharged, thou wilt depart."

At the conclusion of this recital, he again rubbed the stone for a while, and gave vent to some nonsensical utterances, after which he surrendered it to Jia Zheng. "This object," he said, "has already resumed its efficacy; but you shouldn't do anything to desecrate it. Hang it on the post of the door in his bedroom, and with the exception of his own relatives, you must not let any outside female pollute it. After the expiry of thirty-three days, he will, I can guarantee, be all right."

Jia Zheng then gave orders to present tea; but the two priests had already walked away. He had, however, no alternative but to comply with their injunctions, and lady Feng and Baoyu, in point of fact, got better from day to day. Little by little they returned to their senses and experienced hunger. Dowager lady Jia and Madame Wang, at length, felt composed in their minds. All the cousins heard the news outside.

Daiyu, previous to anything else, muttered a Prayer to Buddha; while Baochai laughed and said not a word.

"Sister Bao," inquired Xichun, "what are you laughing for?"

"I laugh," replied Baochai, "because the 'Thus-Come' Joss has more to do than any human being. He's got to see to the conversion of all mankind, and to take care of the ailments to which all flesh is heir; for he restores everyone of them at once to health; and he has as well to control people's marriages so as to bring them about through his aid; and what do you say, has he ample to do or not? Now, isn't this enough to make one laugh, eh?"

Lin Daiyu blushed. "Cui!" she exclaimed; "none of you are good people. Instead of following the example of worthy persons, you try to rival the mean mouth of that hussey Feng."

As she uttered these words, she raised the portiere and made her exit.

But, reader, do you want to know any further circumstances? If so, the next chapter will explain them to you.

CHAPTER 26

On the Fengyao bridge, Xiao Hong makes known sentimental matters in equivocal language. In the Xiaoxiang lodge, Daiyu gives, while under the effects of the spring lassitude, expression to her secret feelings.

After thirty days' careful nursing, Baoyu, we will now notice, not only got strong and hale in body, but the scars even on his face completely healed up; so he was able to shift his quarters again into the garden of Broad Vista.

But we will banish this topic as it does not deserve any additional explanations. Let us now turn our attention elsewhere. During the time that Baoyu was of late laid up in bed, Jia Yun along with the young pages of the household sat up on watch to keep an eye over him, and both day and night, they tarried on this side of the mansion. But Xiao Hong as well as all the other waiting-maids remained in the same part to nurse Baoyu, so (Jia Yun) and she saw a good deal of each other on several occasions, and gradually an intimacy sprung up between them.

Xiao Hong observed that Jia Yun held in his hand a handkerchief very much like the one she herself had dropped some time ago and was bent upon asking him for it, but she did, on the other hand, not think she could do so with propriety. The unexpected visit of the bonze and Daoist priest rendered, however, superfluous the services of the various male attendants, and Jia Yun had therefore to go again and oversee the men planting the trees. Now she had a mind to drop the whole question, but she could not reconcile herself to it; and now she longed to go and ask him about it, but fears rose in her mind lest people should entertain any suspicions as to the relations that existed between them. But just as she faltered, quite irresolute, and her heart was thoroughly unsettled, she unawares heard someone outside inquire: "Sister, are you in the room or not?"

Xiao Hong, upon catching this question, looked out through a hole in the window; and perceiving at a glance that it was no one else than a young servant-girl, attached to the same court as herself, Jiahui by name, she consequently said by way of reply: "Yes, I am; come in!"

When these words reached her ear, Jiahui ran in, and taking at once a seat on the bed, she observed with a smile: "How lucky I've been! I was a little time back in the court washing a few things, when Baoyu cried out that some tea should be sent over to Miss Lin, and sister Hua handed it to me to go on the errand. By a strange coincidence our old lady had presented some money to Miss Lin and she was engaged at the moment in distributing it among their servant-girls. As soon therefore as she saw me get there, Miss Lin forthwith grasped two handfuls of cash and gave them to me; how many there are I don't know, but do keep them for me!"

Speedily then opening her handkerchief, she emptied the cash. Xiao Hong counted them for her by fives and tens at a time. She was beginning to put them away, when Jiahui remarked: "How are you, after all, feeling of late in your mind? I'll tell you what; you should really go and stay at home for a couple of days. And were you to ask a doctor round and to have a few doses of medicine you'll get all right at once!"

"What are you talking about?" Xiao Hong replied. "What shall I go home for, when there's neither rhyme nor reason for it!"

"Miss Lin, I remember, is naturally of a weak physique, and has constantly to take medicines," Jiahui added, "so were you to ask her for some and bring them over and take them, it would come to the same thing."

"Nonsense!" rejoined Xiao Hong, "are medicines also to be recklessly taken?"

"You can't go on forever like this," continued Jiahui; "you're besides loath to eat and loath to drink, and what will you be like in the long run?"

"What's there to fear?" observed Xiao Hong; "won't it anyhow be better to die a little earlier? It would be a riddance!"

"Why do you deliberately come out with all this talk?" Jiahui demurred.

"How could you ever know anything of the secrets of my heart?" Xiao Hong inquired.

Jiahui nodded her head and gave way to reflection. "I don't think it strange on your part," she said after a time; "for it is really difficult to abide in this place! Yesterday, for instance, our dowager lady remarked that the servants in attendance had had, during all the days that Baoyu was ill, a good deal to put up with, and that now that he has recovered, incense should be burnt everywhere, and the vows fulfilled; and she expressed a wish that those in his service should, one and all, be rewarded according to their grade. I and several others can be safely looked upon as young in years, and unworthy to presume so high; so I don't feel in any way aggrieved; but how is it that one like you couldn't be included in the number? My heart is much annoyed at it! Had there been any fear that Xiren would have got ten times more, I could not even then have felt sore against her, for she really deserves it! I'll just tell you an honest truth; who else is there like her? Not to speak of the diligence and carefulness she has displayed all along, even had she not been so diligent and careful, she couldn't have been set aside! But what is provoking is that that lot, like Qingwen and Qixian, should have been included in the upper class. Yet it's because everyone places such reliance on the fine reputation of their father and mother that they exalt them. Now, do tell me, is this sufficient to anger one or not?"

"It won't do to be angry with them!" Xiao Hong observed. "The proverb says: 'You may erect a shed a thousand li long, but there is no entertainment from which the guests will not disperse!' And who is it that will tarry here for a whole lifetime? In another three years or five years every single one of us will have gone her own way; and who will, when that time comes, worry her mind about anyone else?"

These allusions had the unexpected effect of touching Jiahui to the heart; and in spite of herself the very balls of her eyes got red. But so uneasy did she feel at crying for no reason that she had to exert herself to force a smile. "What you say is true," she ventured. And yet, Baoyu even yesterday explained how the rooms should be arranged by and bye; and how the clothes should be made, just as if he was bound to hang on to dear life for several hundreds of years."

Xiao Hong, at these words, gave a couple of sardonic smiles. But when about to pass some remark, she perceived a youthful servant-girl, who had not as yet let her hair grow, walk in, holding in her hands several patterns and two sheets of paper. "You are asked," she said, "to trace these two designs!"

As she spoke, she threw them at Xiao Hong, and twisting herself round, she immediately scampered away.

"Whose are they, after all?" Xiao Hong inquired, addressing herself outside. "Couldn't you wait even so much as to conclude what you had to say, but flew off at once? Who is steaming bread and waiting for you? Or are you afraid, forsooth, lest it should get cold?"

"They belong to sister Qi," the young servant-girl merely returned for answer from outside the window; and raising her feet high, she ran tramp-tramp on her way back again.

Xiao Hong lost control over her temper, and snatching the designs, she flung them on one side. She then rummaged in a drawer for a brush, but finding, after a prolonged search, that they were all blunt; "Where did I," she thereupon ejaculated, "put that brand-new brush the other day? How is it I can't remember where it is?"

While she soliloquised, she became wrapt in thought. After some reflection she, at length, gave a smile. "Of course!" she exclaimed, "the other evening Ying'er took it away." And turning towards Jiahui, "Fetch it for me," she shouted.

"Sister Hua," Jiahui rejoined, "is waiting for me to get a box for her, so you had better go for it yourself!"

"What!" remarked Xiao Hong, "she's waiting for you, and are you still squatting here chatting leisurely? Hadn't it been that I asked you to go and fetch it, she too wouldn't have been waiting for you; you most perverse vixen!"

With these words on her lips, she herself walked out of the room, and leaving the Yihong court, she straightway proceeded in the direction of Baochai's court. As soon, however, as she reached the Qinfang pavilion, she saw dame Li, Baoyu's nurse, appear in view from the opposite side; so Xiao Hong halted and putting on a smile, "Nurse Li," she asked, "where are you, old dame, bound for? How is it you're coming this way?"

Nurse Li stopped short, and clapped her hands. "Tell me," she said, "has he deliberately again gone and fallen in love with that Mr. something or other like Yun (cloud), or Yu (rain)? They now insist upon my bringing him inside, but if they get wind of it by and bye in the upper rooms, it won't again be a nice thing."

"Are you, old lady," replied Xiao Hong smiling, "taking things in such real earnest that you readily believe them and want to go and ask him in here?"

"What can I do?" rejoined nurse Li.

"Why, that fellow," added Xiao Hong laughingly, "will, if he has any idea of decency, do the right thing and not come."

"Besides, he's not a fool!" pleaded nurse Li; "so why shouldn't he come in?"

"Well, if he is to come," answered Xiao Hong, "it will devolve upon you, worthy dame, to lead him along with you; for were you by and bye to let him penetrate inside all alone and knock recklessly about, why, it won't do at all."

"Have I got all that leisure," retorted nurse Li, "to trudge along with him? I'll simply tell him to come; and later on I can despatch a young servant-girl or some old woman to bring him in, and have done."

Saying this, she continued her way, leaning on her staff.

After listening to her rejoinder, Xiao Hong stood still; and plunging in abstraction, she did not go and fetch the brush. But presently, she caught sight of a servant-girl running that way. Espying Xiao Hong lingering in that spot, "Sister Hong," she cried, "what are you doing in here?"

Xiao Hong raised her head, and recognised a young waiting-maid called Zhui'er. "Where are you off too?" Xiao Hong asked.

"I've been told to bring in master Secundus, Mr. Yun," Zhui'er replied. After which answer, she there and then departed with all speed.

Xiao Hong reached, meanwhile, the Fengyao bridge. As soon as she approached the gateway, she perceived Zhui'er coming along with Jia Yun from the opposite direction. While advancing Jia Yun ogled Xiao Hong; and Xiao Hong too, though pretending to be addressing herself to Zhui'er, cast a glance at Jia Yun; and their four eyes, as luck would have it, met. Xiao Hong involuntarily blushed all over; and turning herself round, she walked off towards the Hengwu court. But we will leave her there without further remarks.

During this time, Jia Yun followed Zhui'er, by a circuitous way, into the Yihong court. Zhui'er entered first and made the necessary announcement. Then subsequently she ushered in Jia Yun. When Jia Yun scrutinised the surroundings, he perceived, here and there in the court, several blocks of rockery, among which were planted banana-trees. On the opposite side were two storks preening their feathers under the fir trees. Under the covered passage were suspended, in a row, cages of every description, containing all sorts of fairy-like, rare birds. In the upper part were five diminutive anterooms, uniformly carved with, unique designs; and above the framework of the door was hung a tablet with the inscription in four huge characters "Yi Hong Kuai Lu," the happy red and joyful green.

"I thought it strange," Jia Yun argued mentally, "that it should be called the Yihong court; but these are, in fact, the four characters inscribed on the tablet!"

But while he was communing within himself, he heard someone laugh and then exclaim from the inner side of the gauze window: "Come in at once! How is it that I've forgotten you these two or three months?"

As soon as Jia Yun recognized Baoyu's voice, he entered the room with hurried step. On raising his head, his eye was attracted by the brilliant splendor emitted by gold and jade and by the dazzling luster of the elegant arrangements. He failed, however, to detect where Baoyu was ensconced. The moment he turned his head round, he espied, on the left side, a large cheval-glass; behind which appeared to view, standing side by side, two servant-girls of fifteen or sixteen years of age. "Master Secundus," they ventured, "please take a seat in the inner room."

Jia Yun could not even muster courage to look at them straight in the face; but promptly assenting, he walked into a green gauze mosquito-to-house, where he saw a small lacquered bed, hung with curtains of a deep red color, with clusters of flowers embroidered in gold. Baoyu, wearing a house-dress and slipshod shoes, was reclining on the bed, a book in hand. The moment he perceived Jia Yun walk in, he discarded his book, and forthwith smiled and raised himself up. Jia Yun hurriedly pressed forward and paid his salutation. Baoyu then offered him a seat; but he simply chose a chair in the lower part of the apartment.

"Ever since the moon in which I came across you," Baoyu observed smilingly, "and told you to come into the library, I've had, who would have thought it, endless things to continuously attend to, so that I forgot all about you."

"It's I, indeed, who lacked good fortune!" rejoined Jia Yun, with a laugh; "particularly so, as it again happened that you, uncle, fell ill. But are you quite right once more?"

"All right!" answered Baoyu. "I heard that you've been put to much trouble and inconvenience on a good number of days!"

"Had I even had any trouble to bear," added Jia Yun, "it would have been my duty to bear it. But your complete recovery, uncle, is really a blessing to our whole family."

As he spoke, he discerned a couple of servant-maids come to help him to a cup of tea. But while conversing with Baoyu, Jia Yun was intent upon scrutinising the girl with slim figure and oval face, and clad in a silvery-red jacket, a blue satin waistcoat, and a white silk petticoat with narrow pleats.

At the time of Baoyu's illness, Jia Yun had spent a couple of days in the inner apartments, so that he remembered half of the inmates of note, and the moment he set eyes upon this servant-girl he knew that it was Xiren; and that she was in Baoyu's rooms on a different standing to the rest. Now therefore that she brought the tea in herself and that Baoyu was, besides, sitting by, he rose to his feet with alacrity and put on a smile. "Sister," he said, "how is it that you are pouring tea for me? I came here to pay uncle a visit; what's more I'm no stranger, so let me pour it with my own hands!"

"Just you sit down and finish!" Baoyu interposed; "will you also behave in this fashion with servant-girls?"

"In spite of what you say;" remarked Jia Yun smiling, "they are young ladies attached to your rooms, uncle, and how could I presume to be disorderly in my conduct?"

So saying, he took a seat and drank his tea. Baoyu then talked to him about trivial and irrelevant matters; and afterwards went on to tell him in whose household the actresses were best, and whose gardens were pretty. He further mentioned to him in whose quarters the servant-girls were handsome, whose banquets were sumptuous, as well as in whose home were to be found strange things, and what family possessed remarkable objects. Jia Yun was constrained to humor him in his conversation; but after a chat, which lasted for some time, he noticed that Baoyu was somewhat listless, and he promptly stood up and took his leave. And Baoyu too did not use much pressure to detain him. "Tomorrow, if you have nothing to do, do come over!" he merely observed; after which, he again bade the young waiting-maid, Zhui'er, see him out.

Having left the Yihong court, Jia Yun cast a glance all round; and, realizing that there was no one about, he slackened his pace at once, and while proceeding leisurely, he conversed, in a friendly way, with Zhui'er on one thing and another. First and foremost he inquired of her what was her age; and her name. "Of what standing are your father and mother?" he said, "How many years have you been in uncle Bao's apartments? How much money do you get a month? In all how many girls are there in uncle Bao's rooms?"

As Zhui'er heard the questions set to her, she readily made suitable reply to each.

"The one, who was a while back talking to you," continued Jia Yun, "is called Xiao Hong, isn't she?"

"Yes, her name is Xiao Hong!" replied Zhui'er smiling; "but why do you ask about her?"

"She inquired of you just now about some handkerchief or other," answered Jia Yun; "well, I've picked one up."

Zhui'er greeted this response with a smile. "Many are the times," she said; "that she has asked me whether I had seen her handkerchief; but have I got all that leisure to worry my mind about such things? She spoke to me about it again today; and she suggested that I should find it for her, and that she would also recompense me. This she told me when we were just now at the entrance of the Hengwu court, and you too, Mr. Secundus, overheard her, so that I'm not lying. But, dear Mr. Secundus, since you've picked it up, give it to me. Do! And I'll see what she will give me as a reward."

The truth is that Jia Yun had, the previous moon when he had come into the garden to attend to the planting of trees, picked up a handkerchief, which he conjectured must have been dropped by some inmate of those grounds; but as he was not aware whose it was, he did not consequently presume to act with indiscretion. But on this occasion, he overheard Xiao Hong make inquiries of Zhui'er on the subject; and concluding that it must belong to her, he felt immeasurably delighted. Seeing, besides, how importunate Zhui'er was, he at once devised a plan within himself, and vehemently producing from his sleeve a handkerchief of his own, he observed, as he turned towards Zhui'er with a smile: "As for giving it to you, I'll do so; but in the event of your obtaining any present from her, you mustn't impose upon me."

Zhui'er assented to his proposal most profusely; and, taking the handkerchief, she saw Jia Yun out and then came back in search of Xiao Hong. But we will leave her there for the present.

We will now return to Baoyu. After dismissing Jia Yun, he lay in such complete listlessness on the bed that he betrayed every sign of being half asleep. Xiren walked up to him, and seated herself on the edge of the bed, and pushing him, "What are you about to go to sleep again," she said. "Would it not do your languid spirits good if you went out for a bit of a stroll?"

Upon hearing her voice, Baoyu grasped her hand in his. "I would like to go out," he smiled, "but I can't reconcile myself to the separation from you!

"Get up at once!" laughed Xiren. And as she uttered these words, she pulled Baoyu up.

"Where can I go?" exclaimed Baoyu. "I'm quite surfeited with everything."

"Once out you'll be all right," Xiren answered, "but if you simply give way to this languor, you'll be more than ever sick of everything at heart."

Baoyu could not do otherwise, dull and out of sorts though he was, than accede to her importunities. Strolling leisurely out of the door of the room, he amused himself a little with the birds suspended under the verandah; then he wended his steps outside the court, and followed the course of the Qinfang stream; but after admiring the golden fish for a time, he espied, on the opposite hillock, two young deer come rushing down as swift as an arrow. What they were up to Baoyu could not discern; but while abandoning himself to melancholy, he caught sight of Jia Lan, following behind, with a small bow in his hand, and hurrying down hill in pursuit of them.

As soon as he realised that Baoyu stood ahead of him, he speedily halted. "Uncle Secundus," he smiled, "are you at home? I imagined you had gone out of doors!"

"You are up to mischief again, eh?" Baoyu rejoined. "They've done nothing to you, and why shoot at them with your arrows?"

"I had no studies to attend to just now, so, being free with nothing to do," Jia Lan replied laughingly, "I was practicing riding and archery."

"Shut up!" exclaimed Baoyu. "When are you not engaged in practicing?"

Saying this, he continued his way and straightway reached the entrance of a court. Here the bamboo foliage was thick, and the breeze sighed gently. This was the Xiaoxiang lodge. Baoyu listlessly rambled in. He saw a bamboo portiere hanging down to the ground. Stillness prevailed. Not a human voice fell on the ear. He advanced as far as the window. Noticing that a whiff of subtle scent stole softly through the green gauze casement, Baoyu applied his face closely against the frame to peep in, but suddenly he caught the faint sound of a deep sigh and the words: "Day after day my feelings slumber drowsily!" Upon overhearing this exclamation, Baoyu unconsciously began to feel a prey to inward longings; but casting a second glance, he saw Daiyu stretching herself on the bed.

"Why is it," smiled Baoyu, from outside the window, "that your feelings day after day slumber drowsily?" So saying, he raised the portiere and stepped in.

The consciousness that she had not been reticent about her feelings made Daiyu unwittingly flush scarlet. Taking hold of her sleeve, she screened her face; and, turning her body round towards the inside, she pretended to be fast asleep. Baoyu drew near her. He was about to pull her round when he saw Daiyu's nurse enter the apartment, followed by two matrons.

"Is Miss asleep?" they said. "If so, we'll ask her over, when she wakes up."

As these words were being spoken, Daiyu eagerly twisted herself round and sat up. "Who's asleep?" she laughed.

"We thought you were fast asleep, Miss," smiled the two or three matrons as soon as they perceived Daiyu get up. This greeting over, they called Zijuan. "Your young mistress," they said, "has awoke; come in and wait on her!"

While calling her, they quitted the room in a body. Daiyu remained seated on the bed. Raising her arms, she adjusted her hair, and smilingly she observed to Baoyu, "When people are asleep, what do you walk in for?"

At the sight of her half-closed star-like eyes and of her fragrant cheeks, suffused with a crimson blush, Baoyu's feelings were of a sudden awakened; so, bending his body, he took a seat on a chair, and asked with a smile: "What were you saying a short while back?"

"I wasn't saying anything," Daiyu replied.

What a lie you're trying to ram down my throat!" laughed Baoyu. "I heard all."

But in the middle of their colloquy, they saw Zijuan enter. Baoyu then put on a smiling face. "Zijuan!" he cried, "pour me a cup of your good tea!"

"Where's the good tea to be had?" Zijuan answered. "If you want good tea, you'd better wait till Xiren comes."

"Don't heed him!" interposed Daiyu. "Just go first and draw me some water."

"He's a visitor," remonstrated Zijuan, "and, of course, I should first pour him a cup of tea, and then go and draw the water."

With this answer, she started to serve the tea.

"My dear girl," Baoyu exclaimed laughingly, "If I could only share the same bridal curtain with your lovable young mistress, would I ever be able (to treat you as a servant) by making you fold the covers and make the beds."

Lin Daiyu at once drooped her head. "What are you saying?" she remonstrated.

"What, did I say anything?" smiled Baoyu.

Daiyu burst into tears. "You've recently," she observed, "got into a new way. Whatever slang you happen to hear outside you come and tell me. And whenever you read any improper book, you poke your fun at me. What! have I become a laughing-stock for gentlemen!"

As she began to cry, she jumped down from bed, and promptly left the room. Baoyu was at a loss how to act. So agitated was he that he hastily ran up to her, "My dear cousin," he pleaded, "I do deserve death; but don't go and tell any one! If again I venture to utter such kind of language, may blisters grow on my mouth and may my tongue waste away!"

But while appealing to her feelings, he saw Xiren approach him. "Go back at once," she cried, "and put on your clothes as master wants to see you."

At the very mention of his father, Baoyu felt suddenly as if struck by lightning. Regardless of everything and anything, he rushed, as fast as possible, back to his room, and changing his clothes, he came out into the garden. Here he discovered Beiming, standing at the second gateway, waiting for him.

"Do you perchance know what he wants me for?" Baoyu inquired.

"Master, hurry out at once!" Beiming replied. "You must, of course, go and see him. When you get there, you are sure to find out what it's all about."

This said, he urged Baoyu on, and together they turned past the large pavilion. Baoyu was, however, still laboring under suspicion, when he heard, from the corner of the wall, a loud outburst of laughter. Upon turning his head round, he caught sight of Xue Pan jump out, clapping his hands. "Hadn't I said that my uncle wanted you?" he laughed. "Would you ever have rushed out with such alacrity?"

Beiming also laughed, and fell on his knees. But Baoyu remained for a long time under the spell of utter astonishment, before he, at length, realised that it was Xue Pan who had inveigled him to come out.

Xue Pan hastily made a salutation and a curtsey, and confessed his fault. He next gave way to entreaties, saying: "Don't punish the young servant, for it is simply I who begged him go."

Baoyu too had then no other alternative but to smile. "I don't mind your playing your larks on me; but why," he inquired, "did you mention my father? Were I to go and tell my aunt, your mother, to see to the rights and the wrongs of the case, how would you like it?"

"My dear cousin," remarked Xue Pan vehemently, "the primary idea I had in view was to ask you to come out a moment sooner and I forgot to respectfully shun the expression. But by and bye, when you wish to chaff me, just you likewise allude to my father, and we'll thus be square."

"Ai-ya!" exclaimed Baoyu. "You do more than ever deserve death!! "Then turning again towards Beiming, "You ruffian!" he said, "what are you still kneeling for?"

Beiming began to bump his head on the ground with vehemence.

"Had it been for anything else," Xue Pan chimed in, "I wouldn't have made bold to disturb you; but it's simply in connection with my birthday which is tomorrow, the third day of the fifth moon.

"Cheng Rixing, who is in that curio shop of ours, unexpectedly brought along, goodness knows where he fished them from, fresh lotus so thick and so long, so mealy and so crisp; melons of this size; and a Siamese porpoise, that long and that big, smoked with cedar, such as is sent as tribute from the kingdom of Siam. Are not these four presents, pray, rare delicacies? The porpoise is not only expensive, but difficult to get, and that kind of lotus and melon must have cost him no end of trouble to grow! I lost no time in presenting some to my mother, and at once sent some to your old grandmother, and my aunt. But a good many of them still remain now; and were I to eat them all alone, it would, I fear, be more than I deserve; so I concluded, after thinking right and left, that there was, besides myself, only you good enough to partake of some. That is why I specially invite you to taste them. But, as luck would have it, a young singing-boy has also come, so what do you say to you and I having a jolly day of it?"

As they talked, they walked; and, as they walked, they reached the interior of the library. Here they discovered a whole assemblage consisting of Dan Guang, Cheng Rixing, Hu Silai, Dan Pingren, and others, and the singing-boy as well. As soon as these saw Baoyu walk in, some paid their respects to him; others inquired how he was; and after the interchange of salutations, tea was drunk. Xue Pan then gave orders to serve the wine. Scarcely were the words out of his mouth than the servant-lads bustled and fussed for a long while laying the table. When at last the necessary arrangements had been completed, the company took their seats.

Baoyu verily found the melons and lotus of an exceptional description. "My birthday presents have not as yet been sent round," he felt impelled to say, a smile on his lips, "and here I come, ahead of them, to trespass on your hospitality."

"Just so!" retorted Xue Pan, "but when you come tomorrow to congratulate me we'll consider what novel kind of present you can give me."

"I've got nothing that I can give you," rejoined Baoyu. "As far as money, clothes, eatables, and other such articles go, they are not really mine: all I can call my own are such pages of characters that I may write, or pictures that I may draw."

"Your reference to pictures," added Xue Pan smiling, "reminds me of a book I saw yesterday, containing immodest drawings; they were, truly, beautifully done. On the front page there figured also a whole lot of characters. But I didn't carefully look at them; I simply noticed the name of the person, who had executed them. It was, in fact, something or other like Geng Huang. The pictures were, actually, exceedingly good!"

This allusion made Baoyu exercise his mind with innumerable conjectures.

"Of pictures drawn from past years to the present, I have," he said, "seen a good many, but I've never come across any Geng Huang."

After considerable thought, he could not repress himself from bursting out laughing. Then asking a servant to fetch him a brush, he wrote a couple of words on the palm of his hand. This done, he went on to inquire of Xue Pan: "Did you see correctly that it read Geng Huang?"

"How could I not have seen correctly?" ejaculated Xue Pan.

Baoyu thereupon unclenched his hand and allowed him to peruse, what was written in it. "Were they possibly these two characters?" he remarked. "These are, in point of fact, not very dissimilar from what Geng Huang look like?"

On scrutinizing them, the company noticed the two words Tang Yin, and they all laughed. "They must, we fancy, have been these two characters!" they cried. "Your eyes, Sir, may, there's no saying, have suddenly grown dim!"

Xue Pan felt utterly abashed. "Who could have said," he smiled, whether they were Tang Yin or Guo Yin, (candied silver or fruit silver)."

As he cracked this joke, however, a young page came and announced that Mr. Feng had arrived. Baoyu concluded that the new comer must be Feng Ziying, the son of Feng Tang, general with the prefix of Shen Wu.

"Ask him in at once," Xue Pan and his companions shouted with one voice.

But barely were these words out of their mouths, than they realized that Feng Ziying had already stepped in, talking and laughing as he approached.

The company speedily rose from table and offered him a seat.

"That's right!" smiled Feng Ziying. "You don't go out of doors, but remain at home and go in for high fun!"

Both Baoyu and Xue Pan put on a smile. "We haven't," they remarked, "seen you for ever so long. Is your venerable father strong and hale?"

"My father," rejoined Ziying, "is, thanks to you, strong and hale; but my mother recently contracted a sudden chill and has been unwell for a couple of days."

Xue Pan discerned on his face a slight bluish wound. "With whom have you again been boxing," he laughingly inquired, "that you've hung up this sign board?"

"Since the occasion," laughed Feng Ziying, "on which I wounded lieutenant-colonel Chou's son, I've borne the lesson in mind, and never lost my temper. So how is it you say that I've again been boxing? This thing on my face was caused, when I was out shooting the other day on the Tiewang hills, by a flap from the wing of the falcon."

"When was that?" asked Baoyu.

"I started," explained Ziying, "on the 28th of the third moon and came back only the day before yesterday."

"It isn't to be wondered at then," observed Baoyu, "that when I went the other day, on the third and fourth, to a banquet at friend Shen's house, I didn't see you there. Yet I meant to have inquired about you; but I don't know how it slipped from my memory. Did you go alone, or did your venerable father accompany you?"

"Of course, my father went," Ziying replied, "so I had no help but to go. For is it likely, forsooth, that I've gone mad from lack of anything to do! Don't we, a goodly number as we are, derive enough pleasure from our wine-bouts and plays that I should go in quest of such kind of fatiguing recreation! But in this instance a great piece of good fortune turned up in evil fortune!"

Xue Pan and his companions noticed that he had finished his tea. "Come along," they one and all proposed, "and join the banquet; you can then quietly recount to us all your experiences."

At this suggestion Feng Ziying there and then rose to his feet. "According to etiquette," he said. "I should join you in drinking a few cups; but today I have still a very urgent matter to see my father about on my return so that I truly cannot accept your invitation."

Xue Pan, Baoyu, and the other young fellows would on no account listen to his excuses. They pulled him vigorously about and would not let him go.

"This is, indeed, strange!" laughed Feng Ziying. "When have you and I had, during all these years, to have recourse to such proceedings! I really am unable to comply with your wishes. But if you do insist upon making me have a drink, well, then bring a large cup and I'll take two cups full and finish."

After this rejoinder, the party could not but give in. Xue Pan took hold of the kettle, while Baoyu grasped the cup, and they poured two large cups full. Feng Ziying stood up and quaffed them with one draught.

"But do, after all," urged Baoyu, "finish this thing about a piece of good fortune in the midst of misfortune before you go."

"To tell you this today," smiled Feng Ziying, "will be no great fun. But for this purpose I intend standing a special entertainment, and inviting you all to come and have a long chat; and, in the second place, I've also got a favor to ask of you."

Saying this, he pushed his way and was going off at once, when Xue Pan interposed. "What you've said," he observed, "has put us more than ever on pins and needles. We cannot brook any delay. Who knows when you will ask us round; so better tell us, and thus avoid keeping people in suspense!"

"The latest," rejoined Feng Ziying, "in ten days; the earliest in eight." With this answer he went out of the door, mounted his horse, and took his departure.

The party resumed their seats at table. They had another bout, and then eventually dispersed.

Baoyu returned into the garden in time to find Xiren thinking with solicitude that he had gone to see Jia Zheng and wondering whether it foreboded good or evil. As soon as she perceived Baoyu come back in a drunken state, she felt urged to inquire the reason of it all. Baoyu told her one by one the particulars of what happened.

"People," added Xiren, "wait for you with lacerated heart and anxious mind, and there you go and make merry; yet you could very well, after all, have sent someone with a message."

"Didn't I purpose sending a message?" exclaimed Baoyu. "Of course, I did! But I failed to do so, as on the arrival of friend Feng, I got so mixed up that the intention vanished entirely from my mind."

While excusing himself, he saw Baochai enter the apartment. "Have you tasted any of our new things?" she asked, a smile curling her lips.

"Cousin," laughed Baoyu, "you must have certainly tasted what you've got in your house long before us."

Baochai shook her head and smiled. "Yesterday," she said, "my brother did actually make it a point to ask me to have some; but I had none; I told him to keep them and send them to others, so confident am I that with my mean lot and scanty blessings I little deserve to touch such dainties."

As she spoke, a servant-girl poured her a cup of tea and brought it to her. While she sipped it, she carried on a conversation on irrelevant matters; which we need not notice, but turn our attention to Lin Daiyu.

The instant she heard that Jia Zheng had sent for Baoyu, and that he had not come back during the whole day, she felt very distressed on his account. After supper, the news of Baoyu's return reached her, and she keenly longed to see him and ask him what was up.

Step by step she trudged along, when espying Baochai going into Baoyu's garden, she herself followed close in her track. But on their arrival at the Qinfang bridge, she caught sight of the various kinds of water-fowl, bathing together in the pond, and although unable to discriminate the numerous species, her gaze became so transfixed by their respective variegated and bright plumage and by their exceptional beauty, that she halted. And it was after she had spent some considerable time in admiring them that she repaired at last to the Yihong court. The gate was already closed. Daiyu, however, lost no time in knocking. But Qingwen and Bihen had, who would have thought it, been having a tiff, and were in a captious mood, so upon unawares seeing Baochai step on the scene, Qingwen at once visited her resentment upon Baochai. She was just standing in the court giving vent to her wrongs, shouting: "You're always running over and seating yourself here, whether you've got good reason for doing so or not; and there's no sleep for us at the third watch, the middle of the night though it be," when, all of a sudden, she heard someone else calling at the door. Qingwen was the more moved to anger. Without even asking who it was, she rapidly bawled out: "They've all gone to sleep; you'd better come tomorrow."

Lin Daiyu was well aware of the natural peculiarities of the waiting-maids, and of their habit of playing practical jokes upon each other, so fearing that the girl in the inner room had failed to recognise her voice, and had refused to open under the misconception that it was some other servant-girl, she gave a second shout in a higher pitch. "It's I!" she cried, "don't you yet open the gate?"

Qingwen, as it happened, did not still distinguish her voice; and in an irritable strain, she rejoined: "It's no matter who you may be; Mr. Secundus has given orders that no one at all should be allowed to come in."

As these words reached Lin Daiyu's ear, she unwittingly was overcome with indignation at being left standing outside. But when on the point of raising her voice to ask her one or two things, and to start a quarrel with her; "albeit," she again argued mentally, "I can call this my aunt's house, and it should be just as if it were my own, it's, after all, a strange place, and now that my father and mother are both dead, and that I am left with no one to rely upon, I have for the present to depend upon her family for a home. Were I now therefore to give way to a regular fit of anger with her, I'll really get no good out of it."

While indulging in reflection, tears trickled from her eyes. But just as she was feeling unable to retrace her steps, and unable to remain standing any longer, and quite at a loss what to do, she overheard the sound of jocular language inside, and listening carefully, she discovered that it was, indeed, Baoyu and Baochai. Lin Daiyu waxed more wroth. After much thought and cogitation, the incidents of the morning flashed unawares through her memory. "It must, in fact," she mused, "be because Baoyu is angry with me for having explained to him the true reasons. But why did I ever go and tell you? You should, however, have made inquiries before you lost your temper to such an extent with me as to refuse to let me in today; but is it likely that we shall not by and bye meet face to face again?"

The more she gave way to thought, the more she felt wounded and agitated; and without heeding the moss, laden with cold dew, the path covered with vegetation, and the chilly blasts of wind, she lingered all alone, under the shadow of the bushes at the corner of the wall, so thoroughly sad and dejected that she broke forth into sobs.

Lin Daiyu was, indeed, endowed with exceptional beauty and with charms rarely met with in the world. As soon therefore as she suddenly melted into tears, and the birds and rooks roosting on the neighboring willow boughs and branches of shrubs caught the sound of her plaintive tones, they one and all fell into a most terrific flutter, and, taking to their wings, they flew away to distant recesses, so little were they able to listen with equanimity to such accents. But the spirits of the flowers were, at the time, silent and devoid of feeling, the birds

were plunged in dreams and in a state of stupor, so why did they start?
A stanza appositely assigns the reason:

> Pin'er's mental talents and looks must in the world be rare.
> Alone, clasped in a subtle smell, she quits her maiden room.
> The sound of but one single sob scarcely dies away,
> And drooping flowers cover the ground and birds fly in dismay.

Lin Daiyu was sobbing in her solitude, when a creaking noise struck her ear and the door of the court was flung open. Who came out, is not yet ascertained; but, reader, should you wish to know, the next chapter will explain.

CHAPTER 27

In the Dicui pavilion, Baochai diverts herself with the multi-colored butterflies. Over the mound, where the flowers had been interred, Daiyu bewails their withered bloom.

Lin Daiyu, we must explain in taking up the thread of our narrative, was disconsolately bathed in tears, when her ear was suddenly attracted by the creak of the court gate, and her eyes by the appearance of Baochai beyond the threshold. Baoyu, Xiren, and a whole posse of inmates then walked out. She felt inclined to go up to Baoyu and ask him a question; but dreading that if she made any inquiries in the presence of such a company, Baoyu would be put to the blush and placed in an awkward position, she slipped aside and allowed Baochai to prosecute her way. And it was only after Baoyu and the rest of the party had entered and closed the gate behind them that she at last issued from her retreat. Then fixing her gaze steadfastly on the gateway, she dropped a few tears. But inwardly conscious of their utter futility she retraced her footsteps and wended her way back into her apartment. And with heavy heart and despondent spirits, she divested herself of the remainder of her habiliments.

Zijuan and Xueyan were well aware, from the experience they had reaped in past days, that Lin Daiyu was, in the absence of anything to occupy her mind, prone to sit and mope, and that if she did not frown her eyebrows, she anyway heaved deep sighs; but they were quite at a loss to divine why she was, with no rhyme or reason, ever so ready to indulge, to herself, in inexhaustible gushes or tears. At first, there were such as still endeavored to afford her solace; or who, suspecting lest she brooded over the memory of her father and mother, felt homesick, or aggrieved, through some offence given her, tried by every persuasion to console and cheer her; but, as contrary to all expectations, she subsequently persisted time and again in this dull mood, through each succeeding month and year, people got accustomed to her eccentricities and did not extend to her the least sympathy. Hence it was that no one (on this occasion) troubled her mind about her, but letting her sit and sulk to her heart's content, they one and all turned in and went to sleep.

Lin Daiyu leaned against the railing of the bed, clasping her knees with both hands, her eyes suffused with tears. She looked, in very truth, like a carved wooden image or one fashioned of mud. There she sat straight up to the second watch, even later, when she eventually fell asleep.

The whole night nothing remarkable transpired. The morrow was the 26th day of the fourth moon. Indeed on this day, at 1 P.M., commenced the season of the 'Sprouting seeds,' and, according to an old custom, on the day on which this feast of 'Sprouting seeds' fell, everyone had to lay all kinds of offerings and sacrificial viands on the altar of the god of flowers. Soon after the expiry of this season of 'Sprouting seeds' follows summertide, and as plants in general then wither and the god of flowers resigns his throne, it is compulsory to feast him at some entertainment, previous to his departure.

In the ladies' apartments this custom was observed with still more rigor; and, for this reason, the various inmates of the park of Broad Vista had, without a single exception, got up at an early hour. The young people either twisted flowers and willow twigs in such a way as to represent chairs and horses, or made tufted banners with damask, brocaded gauze and silk, and bound them with variegated threads. These articles of decoration were alike attached on every tree and plant; and throughout the whole expanse of the park, embroidered sashes waved to and fro, and ornamented branches nodded their heads about. In addition to this, the members of the family were clad in such fineries that they put the peach tree to shame, made the almond yield the palm, the swallow envious, and the hawk to blush. We could not therefore exhaustively describe them within our limited space of time.

Baochai, Yingchun, Tanchun, Xichun, Li Wan, lady Feng, and other girls, as well as Da Jie'er, Xiangling, and the waiting-maids were, one and all, we will now notice, in the garden enjoying themselves; the only person who could not be seen was Lin Daiyu.

"How is it," consequently inquired Yingchun, "that I don't see cousin Liu? What a lazy girl! Is she forsooth fast asleep even at this late hour of the day?"

"Wait all of you here," rejoined Baochai, "and I'll go and shake her up and bring her."

With these words, she speedily left her companions and repaired straightway into the Xiaoxiang lodge.

While she was going on her errand, she met Wenguan and the rest of the girls, twelve in all, on their way to seek the party. Drawing near, they inquired after her health. After exchanging a few commonplace remarks, Baochai turned round and pointing, said: "you will find them all in there; you had better go and join them. As for me, I'm going to fetch Miss Lin, but I'll be back soon."

Saying this, she followed the winding path, and came to the Xiao-xiang lodge. Upon suddenly raising her eyes, she saw Baoyu walk in. Baochai immediately halted, and, lowering her head, she gave way to meditation for a time. "Baoyu and Lin Daiyu," she reflected, "have grown up together from their very infancy. But cousins, though they be, there are many instances in which they cannot evade suspicion, for they joke without heeding propriety; and at one time they are friends and at another at daggers drawn. Daiyu has, moreover, always been full of envy; and has ever displayed a peevish disposition, so were I to follow him in at this juncture, why, Baoyu would, in the first place, not feel at ease, and, in the second, Daiyu would give way to jealousy. Better therefore for me to turn back."

At the close of this train of thought, she retraced her steps. But just as she was starting to join her other cousins, she unexpectedly descried, ahead of her, a pair of jade-colored butterflies, of the size of a circular fan. Now they soared high, now they made a swoop down, in their flight against the breeze; much to her amusement.

Baochai felt a wish to catch them for mere fun's sake, so producing a fan from inside her sleeve, she descended on to the turfed ground to flap them with it. The two butterflies suddenly were seen to rise; suddenly to drop: sometimes to come; at others to go. Just as they were on the point of flying across the stream to the other side, the enticement proved too much for Baochai, and she pursued them on tiptoe straight up to the Dicui pavilion, nestling on the bank of the pond; while fragrant perspiration dripped drop by drop, and her sweet breath panted gently. But Baochai abandoned the idea of catching them, and was about to beat a retreat, when all at once she overheard, in the pavilion, the chatter of people engaged in conversation.

This pavilion had, it must be added, a verandah and zig-zag balustrades running all round. It was erected over the water, in the center of a pond, and had on the four sides window-frames of carved woodwork, stuck with paper. So when Baochai caught, from without the pavilion, the sound of voices, she at once stood still and lent an attentive ear to what was being said.

"Look at this handkerchief," she overheard. "If it's really the one you've lost, well then keep it; but if it isn't you must return it to Mr. Yun."

"To be sure it is my own," another party observed, "bring it along and give it to me."

"What reward will you give me?" she further heard. "Is it likely that I've searched all for nothing!"

"I've long ago promised to recompense you, and of course I won't play you false," someone again rejoined.

"I found it and brought it round," also reached her ear, "and you naturally will recompense me; but won't you give anything to the person who picked it up?"

"Don't talk nonsense," the other party added, "he belongs to a family of gentlemen, and anything of ours he may pick up it's his bounden duty to restore to us. What reward could you have me give him?"

"If you don't reward him," she heard someone continue, "what will I be able to tell him? Besides, he enjoined me time after time that if there was to be no recompense, I was not to give it to you."

A short pause ensued. "Never mind!" then came out again to her, "take this thing of mine and present it to him and have done! But do you mean to let the cat out of the bag with anyone else? You should take some oath."

"If I tell anyone," she likewise overheard, "may an ulcer grow on my mouth, and may I, in course of time, die an unnatural death!"

"Ai-ya!" was the reply she heard; "our minds are merely bent upon talking, but someone might come and quietly listen from outside; wouldn't it be as well to push all the Venetians open? Anyone seeing us in here will then imagine that we are simply chatting about nonsense. Besides, should they approach, we shall be able to observe them, and at once stop our conversation!"

Baochai listened to these words from outside, with a heart full of astonishment. "How can one wonder," she argued mentally, "if all those lewd and dishonest people, who have lived from olden times to the present, have devised such thorough artifices! But were they now to open and see me here, won't they feel ashamed. Moreover, the voice in which those remarks were uttered resembles very much that of Hong'er, attached to Baoyu's rooms, who has all along shown a sharp eye and a shrewd mind. She's an artful and perverse thing of the first class! And as I have now overheard her peccadilloes, and a person in despair rebels as sure as a dog in distress jumps over the wall, not only will trouble arise, but I too shall derive no benefit. It would be better at present therefore for me to lose no time in retiring. But as I fear I mayn't be in time to get out of the way, the only alternative for me is to make use of some art like that of the cicada, which can divest itself of its *exuviae*."

She had scarcely brought her reflections to a close before a sound of "ke-zhi" reached her ears. Baochai purposely hastened to tread with heavy step. "Pin'er, I see where you're hiding!" she cried out laugh-ingly; and as she shouted, she pretended to be running ahead in pur-suit of her.

As soon as Xiao Hong and Zhui'er pushed the windows open from in-side the pavilion, they heard Baochai screaming, while rushing forward; and both fell into a state of trepidation from the fright they sustained.

Baochai turned round and faced them. "Where have you been hid-ing Miss Lin?" she smiled.

"Who has seen anything of Miss Lin," retorted Zhui'er.

"I was just now," proceeded Baochai, "on that side of the pool, and discerned Miss Lin squatting down over there and playing with the wa-ter. I meant to have gently given her a start, but scarcely had I walked up to her, when she saw me, and, with a detour towards the East, she at once vanished from sight. So mayn't she be concealing herself in there?"

As she spoke, she designedly stepped in and searched about for her. This over, she betook herself away, adding: "she's certain to have got again into that cave in the hill, and come across a snake, which must have bitten her and put an end to her."

So saying, she distanced them, feeling again very much amused. "I have managed," she thought, "to ward off this piece of business, but I wonder what those two think about it."

Xiao Hong, who would have anticipated, readily credited as gospel the remarks she heard Baochai make. But allowing just time enough to Baochai to have got to a certain distance, she instantly drew Zhui'er to her. "Dreadful!" she observed, "Miss Lin was squatting in here and must for a certainty have overheard what we said before she left."

Albeit Zhui'er listened to her words, she kept her own counsel for a long time. "What's to be done?" Xiao Hong consequently exclaimed.

"Even supposing she did overhear what we said," rejoined Zhui'er by way of answer, "why should she meddle in what does not concern her? Everyone should mind her own business."

"Had it been Miss Bao, it would not have mattered," remarked Xiao Hong, "but Miss Lin delights in telling mean things of people and is, besides, so petty-minded. Should she have heard and anything per-chance comes to light, what will we do?"

During their colloquy, they noticed Wenguan, Xiangling, Siqi, Shi-shu, and the other girls enter the pavilion, so they were compelled to drop the conversation and to play and laugh with them. They then espied lady Feng standing on the top of the hillock, waving her hand, beckoning to Xiao Hong. Hurriedly therefore leaving the company, she ran up to lady Feng and with smile heaped upon smile, "my lady," she inquired, "what is it that you want?"

Lady Feng scrutinized her for a time. Observing how spruce and pretty she was in looks, and how genial in her speech, she felt prompted to give her a smile. "My own waiting-maid," she said, "hasn't followed me in here today; and as I've just this moment bethought myself of something and would like to send someone on an errand, I wonder whether you're fit to undertake the charge and deliver a message faithfully."

"Don't hesitate in entrusting me with any message you may have to send," replied Xiao Hong with a laugh. "I'll readily go and deliver it. Should I not do so faithfully, and blunder in fulfilling your business, my lady, you may visit me with any punishment your ladyship may please, and I'll have nothing to say."

"What young lady's servant are you," smiled lady Feng? "Tell me, so that when she comes back, after I've sent you out, and looks for you, I may be able to tell her about you."

"I'm attached to our Master Secundus, Mr. Bao's rooms," answered Xiao Hong.

"Ai-ya!" ejaculated lady Feng, as soon as she heard these words. "Are you really in Baoyu's rooms! How strange! Yet it comes to the same thing. Well, if he asks for you, I'll tell him where you are. Go now to our house and tell your sister Ping that she'll find on the table in the outer apartment and under the stand with the plate from the Ru kiln, a bundle of silver; that it contains the one hundred and twenty taels for the embroiderers' wages; and that when Zhang Cai's wife comes, the money should be handed to her to take away, after having been weighed in her presence and been given to her to tally. Another thing too I want. In the inner apartment and at the head of the bed you'll find a small purse, bring it along to me."

Xiao Hong listened to her orders and then started to carry them out. On her return, in a short while, she discovered that lady Feng was not on the hillock. But perceiving Siqi egress from the cave and stand still to tie her petticoat, she walked up to her. "Sister, do you know where our lady Secunda is gone to?" she asked.

"I didn't notice," rejoined Siqi.

At this reply, Xiao Hong turned round and cast a glance on all four quarters. Seeing Tanchun and Baochai standing by the bank of the pond on the opposite side and looking at the fish, Xiao Hong advanced up to them. "Young ladies," she said, straining a smile, "do you perchance have any idea where our lady Secunda is gone to now?"

"Go into your senior lady's court and look for her!" Tanchun answered.

Hearing this, Xiao Hong was proceeding immediately towards the Daoxiang village, when she caught sight, just ahead of her, of Qingwen,

Qixian, Bihen, Qiuwen, Sheyue, Shishu, Ruhua, Ying'er, and some other girls coming towards her in a group.

The moment Qingwen saw Xiao Hong, she called out to her. "Are you gone clean off your head?" she exclaimed. "You don't water the flowers, nor feed the birds or prepare the tea stove, but gad about outside!"

"Yesterday," replied Xiao Hong, "Mr. Secundus told me that there was no need for me to water the flowers today; that it was enough if they were watered every other day. As for the birds, you're still in the arms of Morpheus, sister, when I give them their food."

"And what about the tea-stove?" interposed Bihen.

"Today," retorted Xiao Hong, "is not my turn on duty, so don't ask me whether there be any tea or not!"

"Do you listen to that mouth of hers!" cried Qixian, "but don't you girls speak to her; let her stroll about and have done!"

"You'd better all go and ask whether I've been gadding about or not," continued Xiao Hong. "Our lady Secunda has just bidden me go and deliver a message, and fetch something."

Saying this, she raised the purse and let them see it; and they, finding they could hit upon nothing more to taunt her with, trudged along onwards.

Qingwen smiled a sarcastic smile. "How funny!" she cried. "Lo, she climbs up a high branch and doesn't condescend to look at any one of us! All she told her must have been just some word or two, who knows! But is it likely that our lady has the least notion of her name or surname that she rides such a high horse, and behaves in this manner! What credit is it in having been sent on a trifling errand like this! Will we, by and bye, pray, hear anything more about you? If you've got any gumption, you'd better skedaddle out of this garden this very day. For, mind, it's only if you manage to hold your lofty perch for any length of time that you can be thought something of!"

As she derided her, she continued on her way.

During this while, Xiao Hong listened to her, but as she did not find it a suitable moment to retaliate, she felt constrained to suppress her resentment and go in search of lady Feng.

On her arrival at widow Li's quarters, she, in point of fact, discovered lady Feng seated inside with her having a chat. Xiao Hong approached her and made her report. "Sister Ping says," she observed, "that as soon as your ladyship left the house, she put the money by, and that when Zhang Cai's wife went in a little time to fetch it, she had it weighed in her presence, after which she gave it to her to take away."

With these words, she produced the purse and presented it to her. "Sister Ping bade me come and tell your ladyship," she added, continuing, "that Wang'er came just now to crave your orders, as to who are the parties from whom he has to go and (collect interest on money due) and sister Ping explained to him what your wishes were and sent him off."

"How could she tell him where I wanted him to go?" Lady Feng laughed.

"Sister Ping says," Xiao Hong proceeded, "that our lady presents her compliments to your ladyship (widow Li) here-(*To lady Feng*) that our master Secundus has in fact not come home, and that albeit a delay of (a day) or two will take place (in the collection of the money), your ladyship should, she begs, set your mind at ease. *(To Li Wan)* That when lady Quinta is somewhat better, our lady will let lady Quinta know and come along with her to see your ladyship. *(To lady Feng)* That lady Quinta sent a servant the day before yesterday to come over and say that our lady, your worthy maternal aunt, had despatched a letter to inquire after your ladyship's health; that she also wished to ask you, my lady, her worthy niece in here, for a couple of 'long-life-great-efficacy-full-of-every-virtue' pills; and that if you have any, they should, when our lady bids a servant come over, be simply given her to bring to our lady here, and that any one bound tomorrow for that side could then deliver them on her way to her ladyship, your aunt yonder, to take along with her."

"Ai-yo-yo!" exclaimed widow Li, before the close of the message. "It's impossible for me to make out what you're driving at! What a heap of ladyships and misters!"

"It's not to be wondered at that you can't make them out," interposed lady Feng laughing. "Why, her remarks refer to four or five distinct families."

While speaking, she again faced Xiao Hong. "My dear girl," she smiled, "what a trouble you've been put to! But you speak decently, and unlike the others who keep on buzz-buzz-buzz, like mosquitoes! You're not aware, sister-in-law, that I actually dread uttering a word to any of the girls outside the few servant-girls and matrons in my own immediate service; for they invariably spin out, what could be condensed in a single phrase, into a long interminable yarn, and they munch and chew their words; and sticking to a peculiar drawl, they groan and moan; so much so that they exasperate me till I fly into a regular rage. Yet how are they to know that our Ping'er too was once like them. But when I asked her: 'must you forsooth imitate the humming of a mosquito, in order to be accounted a handsome girl?' and spoke to her, on several occasions, she at length improved considerably."

"What a good thing it would be," laughed Li Gongcai, "if they could all be as smart as you are."

"This girl is first-rate!" rejoined lady Feng, "she just now delivered two messages. They didn't, I admit, amount to much, yet to listen to her, she spoke to the point."

"Tomorrow," she continued, addressing herself to Xiao Hong smilingly, "come and wait on me, and I'll acknowledge you as my daughter; and the moment you come under my control, you'll readily improve."

At this news, Xiao Hong spurted out laughing aloud.

"What are you laughing for?" Lady Feng inquired. "You must say to yourself that I am young in years and that how much older can I be than yourself to become your mother; but are you under the influence of a spring dream? Go and ask all those people older than yourself. They would be only too ready to call me mother. But snapping my fingers at them, I today exalt you."

"I wasn't laughing about that," Xiao Hong answered with a smiling face. "I was amused by the mistake your ladyship made about our generations. Why, my mother claims to be your daughter, my lady, and are you now going to recognize me too as your daughter?"

"Who's your mother?" Lady Feng exclaimed.

"Don't you actually know her?" put in Li Gongcai with a smile. "She's Lin Zhixiao's child."

This disclosure greatly surprised lady Feng. "What!" she consequently cried, "is she really his daughter?"

"Why Lin Zhixiao and his wife," she resumed smilingly, "couldn't either of them utter a sound if even they were pricked with an awl. I've always maintained that they're a well-suited couple; as the one is as deaf as a post, and the other as dumb as a mute. But who would ever have expected them to have such a clever girl! By how much are you in your teens?"

"I'm seventeen," replied Xiao Hong.

"What is your name?" she went on to ask.

"My name was once Hongyu." Xiao Hong rejoined. "But as it was a duplicate of that of Master Secundus, Mr. Baoyu, I'm now simply called Xiao Hong."

Upon hearing this explanation, lady Feng raised her eyebrows into a frown, and turning her head round: "It's most disgusting!" she remarked, "Those bearing the name Yu would seem to be very cheap; for your name is Yu, and so is also mine Yu. Sister-in-law," she then observed; "I never let you know anything about it, but I mentioned to her mother that Lai Da's wife has at present her hands quite full, and that she hasn't either any notion as to who is who in this mansion. 'You had better,' (I said), 'carefully select a couple of girls for my service.' She assented unreservedly, but she put it off and never chose any. On the contrary, she sent this girl to some other place. But is it likely that she wouldn't have been well off with me?"

"Here you are again full of suspicion!" Li Wan laughed. "She came in here long before you ever breathed a word to her! So how could you bear a grudge against her mother?"

"Well, in that case," added lady Feng, "I'll speak to Baoyu tomorrow, and induce him to find another one, and to allow this girl to come along with me. I wonder, however, whether she herself is willing or not?"

"Whether willing or not," interposed Xiao Hong smiling, "such as we couldn't really presume to raise our voices and object. We should feel it our privilege to serve such a one as your ladyship, and learn a little how to discriminate when people raise or drop their eyebrows and eyes (with pleasure or displeasure), and reap as well some experience in such matters as go out or come in, whether high or low, great and small."

But during her reply, she perceived Madame Wang's waiting-maid come and invite lady Feng to go over. Lady Feng bade good-bye at once to Li Gongcai and took her departure.

Xiao Hong then returned into the Yihong court, where we will leave her and devote our attention for the present to Lin Daiyu.

As she had had but little sleep in the night, she got up the next day at a late hour. When she heard that all her cousins were collected in the park, giving a farewell entertainment for the god of flowers, she hastened, for fear people should laugh at her for being lazy, to comb her hair, perform her ablutions, and go out and join them. As soon as she reached the interior of the court, she caught sight of Baoyu, entering the door, who speedily greeted her with a smile. "My dear cousin," he said, "did you lodge a complaint against me yesterday? I've been on pins and needles the whole night long."

Daiyu forthwith turned her head away. "Put the room in order," she shouted to Zijuan, "and lower one of the gauze window-frames. And when you've seen the swallows come back, drop the curtain; keep it down then by placing the lion on it, and after you have burnt the incense, mind you cover the censer."

So saying she stepped outside.

Baoyu perceiving her manner, concluded again that it must be on account of the incident of the previous noon, but how could he have had any idea about what had happened in the evening? He kept on still bowing and curtseying; but Lin Daiyu did not even so much as look at him straight in the face, but egressing alone out of the door of the court, she proceeded there and then in search of the other girls.

Baoyu fell into a despondent mood and gave way to conjectures.

"Judging," he reflected, "from this behavior of hers, it would seem as if it could not be for what transpired yesterday. Yesterday too I came back late in the evening, and, what's more, I didn't see her, so that there was no occasion on which I could have given her offence."

As he indulged in these reflections, he involuntarily followed in her footsteps to try and catch her up, when he descried Baochai and Tanchun on the opposite side watching the frolics of the storks.

As soon as they saw Daiyu approach, the trio stood together and started a friendly chat. But noticing Baoyu also come up, Tanchun smiled. "Brother Bao," she said, "are you all right. It's just three days that I haven't seen anything of you?"

"Are you, sister, quite well?" Baoyu rejoined, a smile on his lips. "The other day, I asked news of you of our senior sister-in-law."

"Brother Bao," Tanchun remarked, "come over here; I want to tell you something."

The moment Baoyu heard this, he quickly went with her. Distancing Baochai and Daiyu, the two of them came under a pomegranate tree. "Has father sent for you these last few days?" Tanchun then asked.

"He hasn't," Baoyu answered laughingly by way of reply.

"Yesterday," proceeded Tanchun, "I heard vaguely something or other about father sending for you to go out."

"I presume," Baoyu smiled, "that someone must have heard wrong, for he never sent for me."

"I've again managed to save during the last few months," added Tanchun with another smile, "fully ten tiaos, so take them and bring me, when at any time you stroll out of doors, either some fine writings or some ingenious knicknack."

"Much as I have roamed inside and outside the city walls," answered Baoyu, "and seen grand establishments and large temples, I've never come across anything novel or pretty. One simply sees articles made of gold, jade, copper, and porcelain, as well as such curios for which we could find no place here. Besides these, there are satins, eatables, and wearing apparel."

"Who cares for such baubles!" exclaimed Tanchun. "How could they come up to what you purchased the last time; that wee basket, made of willow twigs, that scent-box, scooped out of a root of real bamboo, that portable stove fashioned of glutinous clay; these things were, oh, so very nice! I was as fond of them as I don't know what; but, who'd have thought it, they fell in love with them and bundled them all off, just as if they were precious things."

"Is it things of this kind that you really want?" laughed Baoyu. "Why, these are worth nothing! Were you to take a hundred cash and give them to the servant-boys, they could, I'm sure, bring two cart-loads of them."

"What do the servant-boys know?" Tanchun replied. "Those you chose for me were plain yet not commonplace. Neither were they of coarse make. So were you to procure me as many as you can get of them, I'll work you a pair of slippers like those I gave you last time, and spend twice as much trouble over them as I did over that pair you have. Now, what do you say to this bargain?"

"Your reference to this," smiled Baoyu, "reminds me of an old incident. One day I had them on, and by a strange coincidence, I met father, whose fancy they did not take, and he inquired who had worked them. But how could I muster up courage to allude to the three words: my sister Tertia, so I answered that my maternal aunt had given them to me on the recent occasion of my birthday. When father heard that they had been given to me by my aunt, he could not very well say anything. But after a while, 'why uselessly waste,' he observed, 'human labor, and throw away silks to make things of this sort!' On my return, I told Xiren about it. 'Never mind,' said Xiren; but Mrs. Zhao got angry. 'Her own brother,' she murmured indignantly, 'wears slipshod shoes and socks in holes, and there's no one to look after him, and does she go and work all these things!'"

Tanchun, hearing this, immediately lowered her face. "Now tell me, aren't these words utter rot!" she shouted. "What am I that I have to make shoes? And is it likely that Huan Erh hasn't his own share of things! Clothes are clothes, and shoes and socks are shoes and socks; and how is it that any grudges arise in the room of a mere servant-girl and old matron? For whose benefit does she come out with all these things! I simply work a pair or part of a pair when I am at leisure, with time on my hands. And I can give them to any brother, elder or younger, I fancy; and who has a right to interfere with me? This is just another bit of blind anger!"

After listening to her, Baoyu nodded his head and smiled. "Yet," he said, "you don't know what her motives may be. It's but natural that she should also cherish some expectations."

This apology incensed Tanchun more than ever, and twisting her head round, "Even you have grown dull!" she cried. "She does, of course, indulge in expectations, but they are actuated by some underhand and paltry notion! She may go on giving way to these ideas, but I, for my part, will only care for Mr. Jia Zheng and Madame Wang. I won't care a rap for any one else. In fact, I'll be nice with such of my sisters and brothers, as are nice to me; and won't even draw any distinction between those born of primary wives and those of secondary ones. Properly speaking, I shouldn't say these things about her, but she's narrow-minded to a degree, and unlike what she should be. There's besides another ridiculous thing. This took place the last time I gave you the money to get me those trifles. Well, two days after that, she saw me, and she began again to represent that she had no money and that she was hard up. Nevertheless, I did not worry my brain with her goings on. But as it happened, the servant-girls subsequently quitted the room, and she at once started finding fault with me. 'Why,' she asked, 'do I give you my savings to spend and don't, after all, let Huan'er have them and enjoy them?' When I heard these reproaches, I felt both inclined to laugh, and also disposed to lose my temper; but I there and then skedaddled out of her quarters, and went over to our Madame Wang."

As she was recounting this incident, "Well," she overheard Baochai sarcastically observe from the opposite direction, "have you done spinning your yarns? If you have, come along! It's quite evident that you are brother and sister, for here you leave everyone else and go and discuss your own private matters. Couldn't we too listen to a single sentence of what you have to say?"

While she taunted them, Tanchun and Baoyu eventually drew near her with smiling faces.

Baoyu, however, failed to see Lin Daiyu and he concluded that she had dodged out of the way and gone elsewhere. "It would be better," he muttered, after some thought, "that I should let two days elapse, and give her temper time to evaporate before I go to her. " But as he drooped his head, his eye was attracted by a heap of touch-me-nots, pomegranate blossom, and various kinds of fallen flowers, which covered the ground thick as tapestry, and he heaved a sigh. "It's because," he pondered, "she's angry that she did not remove these flowers; but I'll take them over to the place, and by and bye ask her about them."

As he argued to himself, he heard Baochai bid them go out. "I'll join you in a moment," Baoyu replied; and waiting till his two cousins had gone some distance, he bundled the flowers into his coat, and ascending the hill, he crossed the stream, penetrated into the arbor, passed through the avenues with flowers and wended his way straight for the spot, where he had, on a previous occasion, interred the peach-blossoms with the assistance of Lin Daiyu. But scarcely had he reached the mound containing the flowers, and before he had, as yet, rounded the brow of the hill, than he caught, emanating from the off side, the sound of someone sobbing, who while giving way to invective, wept in a most heart-rending way.

"I wonder," soliloquised Baoyu, "whose servant-girl this is, who has been so aggrieved as to run over here to have a good cry!"

While speculating within himself, he halted. He then heard, mingled with wails:

Flowers wither and decay; and flowers do fleet; they fly all o'er the skies;
Their bloom wanes; their smell dies; but who is there with them to sympathize?
While vagrant gossamer soft doth on fluttering spring-bowers bind its coils,
And drooping catkins lightly strike and cling on the embroidered screens,
A maiden in the inner rooms, I sore deplore the close of spring.
Such ceaseless sorrow fills my breast, that solace nowhere can I find.
Past the embroidered screen I issue forth, taking with me a hoe,
And on the faded flowers to tread I needs must, as I come and go.
The willow fibers and elm seeds have each a fragrance of their own.
What care I, peach blossoms may fall, pear flowers away be blown;
Yet peach and pear will, when next year returns, burst out again in bloom,
But can it e'er be told who will next year dwell in the inner room?
What time the third moon comes, the scented nests have been already built.
And on the beams the swallows perch, excessive spiritless and staid;
Next year, when the flowers bud, they may, it's true, have ample to feed on:
But they know not that when I'm gone beams will be vacant and nests fall!
In a whole year, which doth consist of three hundred and sixty days,
Winds sharp as swords and frost like unto spears each other rigorous press,
So that how long can last their beauty bright; their fresh charm how long stays?
Sudden they droop and fly; and whither they have flown, 'tis hard to guess.
Flowers, while in bloom, easy the eye attract; but, when they wither, hard they are to find.
Now by the footsteps, I bury the flowers, but sorrow will slay me.
Alone I stand, and as I clutch the hoe, silent tears trickle down,
And drip on the bare twigs, leaving behind them the traces of blood.

The goatsucker hath sung his song, the shades lower of eventide,
So with the lotus hoe I return home and shut the double doors.
Upon the wall the green lamp sheds its rays just as I go to sleep,
The cover is yet cold; against the window patters the bleak rain.
How strange! Why can it ever be that I feel so wounded at heart!
Partly, because spring I regret; partly, because with spring I'm vexed!
Regret for spring, because it sudden comes; vexed, for it sudden goes.
For without warning, lo! it comes; and without asking it doth fleet.
Yesterday night, outside the hall sorrowful songs burst from my mouth,
For I found out that flowers decay, and that birds also pass away.
The soul of flowers, and the spirit of birds are both hard to restrain.
Birds, to themselves when left, in silence plunge; and flowers, alone, they blush.
Oh! would that on my sides a pair of wings could grow,
That to the end of heaven I may fly in the wake of flowers!
Yea to the very end of heaven,
Where I could find a fragrant grave!
For better, is it not, that an embroidered bag should hold my well-shaped bones,
And that a heap of stainless earth should in its folds my winsome charms enshroud.
For spotless once my frame did come, and spotless again it will go!
Far better than that I, like filthy mire, should sink into some drain!
Ye flowers are now faded and gone, and, lo, I come to bury you.
But as for me, what day I shall see death is not as yet divined!
Here I am fain these flowers to inter; but humankind will laugh me as a fool.
Who knows, who will, in years to come, commit me to my grave!
Mark, and you'll find the close of spring, and the gradual decay of flowers,
Resemble faithfully the time of death of maidens ripe in years!
In a twinkle, spring time draws to a close, and maidens wax in age.
Flowers fade and maidens die; and of either nought any more is known.

After listening to these effusions, Baoyu unconsciously threw himself down in a wandering frame of mind.

But, reader, do you feel any interest in him? If you do, the subsequent chapter contains further details about him.

CHAPTER 28

Jiang Yuhan lovingly presents a rubia-scented silk sash. Xue Baochai blushingly covers her musk-perfumed string of red beads.

Lin Daiyu, the story goes, dwelt, after Qingwen's refusal, the previous night, to open the door, under the impression that the blame lay with Baoyu. The following day, which by another remarkable coincidence, happened to correspond with the season when the god of flowers had to be feasted, her total ignorance of the true circumstances, and her resentment, as yet unspent, aroused again in her despondent thoughts, suggested by the decline of spring time. She consequently gathered a quantity of faded flowers and fallen petals, and went and interred them. Unable to check the emotion, caused by the decay of the flowers, she spontaneously recited, after giving way to several loud lamentations, those verses which Baoyu, she little thought, overheard from his position on the mound. At first, he did no more than nod his head and heave sighs, full of feeling. But when subsequently his ear caught:

> "Here I am fain these flowers to inter, but humankind will laugh
>   me as a fool;
> Who knows who will, in years to come, commit me to my grave!
> In a twinkle springtime draws to an end, and maidens wax in age.
> Flowers fade and maidens die; and of either naught any more is
>   known."

he unconsciously was so overpowered with grief that he threw himself on the mound, bestrewing the whole ground with the fallen flowers he carried in his coat, close to his chest. "When Daiyu's flowerlike charms and moon-like beauty," he reflected, "by and bye likewise reach a time when they will vanish beyond any hope of recovery, won't my heart be lacerated and my feelings be mangled! And extending, since Daiyu must at length some day revert to a state when it will be difficult to find her, this reasoning to other persons, like Baochai, Xiangling, Xiren, and the other girls, they too are equally liable to attain a state beyond the reach of human search. But when Baochai and all the rest have ultimately reached that stage when no trace will be visible of them, where shall I myself be then? And when my own human form will have vanished and gone, whither I know not yet, to what person, I wonder, will this place, this garden, and these plants, revert?"

From one to a second, and from a second to a third, he thus pursued his reflections, backwards and forwards, until he really did not know how he could best, at this time and at such a juncture, dispel his fit of anguish. His state is adequately described by:

> The shadow of a flower cannot err from the flower itself to the left or the right.
> The song of birds can only penetrate into the ear from the east or the west.

Lin Daiyu was herself a prey to emotion and agitation, when unawares sorrowful accents also struck her ear, from the direction of the mound. "Everyone," she cogitated, "laughs at me for laboring under a foolish mania, but is there likely another fool besides myself?" She then raised her head, and, casting a glance about her, she discovered that it was Baoyu. "Cui!" eagerly cried Daiyu, "I was wondering who it was; but is it truly this ruthless-hearted and short-lived fellow!"

But the moment the two words "short-lived" dropped from her mouth, she sealed her lips; and, heaving a deep sigh, she turned herself round and hurriedly walked off.

Baoyu, meanwhile, remained for a time a prey to melancholy. But perceiving that Daiyu had retired, he at once realized that she must have caught sight of him and got out of his way; and, as his own company afforded him no pleasure, he shook the dust off his clothes, rose to his feet, and descending the hill he started for the I Hung court by the path by which he had come. But he espied Daiyu walking in advance of him, and with rapid stride he overtook her. "Stop a little!" he cried. "I know you don't care a rap for me; but I'll just make one single remark, and from this day forward we'll part company."

Daiyu looked round. Observing that it was Baoyu, she was about to ignore him; hearing him however mention that he had only one thing to say, "Please tell me what it is," she forthwith rejoined.

Baoyu smiled at her. "If I pass two remarks will you listen to me; yes or no?" he asked.

At these words, Daiyu twisted herself round and beat a retreat. Baoyu however followed behind.

"Since this is what we've come to now," he sighed, "what was the use of what existed between us in days gone by?"

As soon as Daiyu heard his exclamation, she stopped short impulsively. Turning her face towards him, "what about days gone by," she remarked, "and what about now?"

"Ai!" ejaculated Baoyu, "when you got here in days gone by, wasn't I your playmate in all your romps and in all your fun? My heart may have been set upon anything, but if you wanted it you could take it away at once. I may have been fond of any eatable, but if I came to learn that you too fancied it, I there and then put away what could be put away, in a clean place, to wait, Miss, for your return. We had our meals at one table; we slept in one and the same bed; whatever the servant-girls could not remember, I reminded them of, for fear lest your temper, Miss, should get ruffled. I flattered myself that cousins, who have grown up together from their infancy, as you and I have, would have continued, through intimacy or friendship, either would have done, in peace and harmony until the end, so as to make it palpable that we are above the rest. But, contrary to all my expectations, now that you, Miss, have developed in body as well as in mind, you don't take the least heed of me. You lay hold instead of some cousin Pao or cousin Feng or other from here, there, and everywhere and give them a place in your affections; while on the contrary you disregard me for three days at a stretch and decline to see anything of me for four! I have besides no brother or sister of the same mother as myself. It's true there are a couple of them, but these, are you not forsooth aware, are by another mother! You and I are only children, so I ventured to hope that you would have reciprocated my feelings. But, who'd have thought it, I've simply thrown away this heart of mine, and here I am with plenty of woes to bear, but with nowhere to go and utter them!"

While expressing these sentiments, tears, unexpectedly, trickled from his eyes.

When Lin Daiyu caught, with her ears, his protestations, and noticed with her eyes his state of mind, she unconsciously experienced an inward pang, and, much against her will, tears too besprinkled her cheeks; so, drooping her head, she kept silent.

Her manner did not escape Baoyu's notice. "I myself am aware," he speedily resumed, "that I'm worth nothing now; but, however imperfect I may be, I could on no account presume to become guilty of any shortcoming with you cousin. Were I to ever commit the slightest fault, your task should be either to tender me advice and warn me not to do it again, or to blow me up a little, or give me a few whacks; and all this reproof I wouldn't take amiss. But no one would have ever anticipated that you wouldn't bother your head in the least about me, and that you would be the means of driving me to my wits' ends, and so much out of my mind and off my head, as to be quite at a loss how to act for the best. In fact, were death to come upon me, I would be a spirit driven to my grave by grievances. However much exalted bonzes and eminent Daoist priests might do penance, they wouldn't succeed in releasing my soul from suffering; for it would still be needful for you to clearly explain the facts, so that I might at last be able to come to life."

After lending him a patient ear, Daiyu suddenly banished from her memory all recollection of the occurrences of the previous night. "Well, in that case," she said, "why did you not let a servant-girl open the door when I came over?"

This question took Baoyu by surprise. "What prompts you to say this?" he exclaimed. "If I have done anything of the kind, may I die at once."

"Cui!" cried Daiyu, "it's not right that you should recklessly broach the subject of living or dying at this early morn! If you say yea, it's yea; and nay, it's nay; what use is there to utter such oaths!"

"I didn't really see you come over," protested Baoyu. "Cousin Baochai it was, who came and sat for a while and then left."

After some reflection, Lin Daiyu smiled. "Yes," she observed, "your servant-girls must, I fancy, have been too lazy to budge, grumpy and in a cross-grained mood; this is probable enough."

"This is, I feel sure, the reason," answered Baoyu, "so when I go back, I'll find out who it was, call them to task, and put things right."

"Those girls of yours;" continued Daiyu, "should be given a lesson, but properly speaking it isn't for me to mention anything about it. Their present insult to me is a mere trifle; but were tomorrow some Miss Bao (precious) or some Miss Bei (jewel) or other to come, and were she to be subjected to insult, won't it be a grave matter?"

While she taunted him, she pressed her lips, and laughed sarcastically.

Baoyu heard her remarks and felt both disposed to gnash his teeth with rage, and to treat them as a joke; but in the midst of their colloquy, they perceived a waiting-maid approach and invite them to have their meal.

Presently, the whole body of inmates crossed over to the front.

"Miss," inquired Madame Wang at the sight of Daiyu, "have you taken any of Dr. Wang's medicines? Do you feel any better?"

"I simply feel so-so," replied Lin Daiyu, "but grandmother Jia recommended me to go on taking Dr. Wang's medicines."

"Mother," Baoyu interposed, "you've no idea that cousin Lin's is an internal derangement; it's because she was born with a delicate physique that she can't stand the slightest cold. All she need do is to take a couple of doses of some decoction to dispel the chill; yet it's preferable that she should have medicine in pills."

"The other day," said Madame Wang, "the doctor mentioned the name of some pills, but I've forgotten what it is."

"I know something about pills," put in Baoyu; "he merely told her to take some pills or other called 'ginseng as-a-restorative-of-the-system.'"

"That isn't it," Madame Wang demurred.

"The 'Eight-precious-wholesome-to-mother' pills," Baoyu proceeded, "or the 'Left-*angelica*' or 'Right-*angelica*;' if these also aren't the ones, they must be the 'Eight-flavor *Rehmannia glutinosa*' pills."

"None of these," rejoined Madame Wang, "for I remember well that there were the two words 'jin gang' (guardians in Buddhistic temples)."

"I've never before," observed Baoyu, clapping his hands, "heard of the existence of jin gang pills; but in the event of there being any jin gang pills, there must, for a certainty, be such a thing as Pusa (Buddha) powder."

At this joke, everyone in the whole room burst out laughing. Baochai compressed her lips and gave a smile. "It must, I'm inclined to think," she suggested, "be the 'lord-of-heaven-strengthen-the-heart' pills!"

"Yes, that's the name," Madame Wang laughed, "why, now, I too have become muddle-headed."

"You're not muddle-headed, mother," said Baoyu, "it's the mention of jin gangs and Buddhas which confused you."

"Stuff and nonsense!" ejaculated Madame Wang. "What you want again is your father to whip you!"

"My father," Baoyu laughed, "wouldn't whip me for a thing like this."

"Well, this being their name," resumed Madame Wang, "you had better tell someone tomorrow to buy you a few."

"All these drugs," expostulated Baoyu, "are of no earthly use. Were you, mother, to give me three hundred and sixty taels, I'll concoct a supply of pills for my cousin, which I can certify will make her feel quite herself again before she has finished a single supply."

"What trash!" cried Madame Wang. "What kind of medicine is there so costly!"

"It's a positive fact," smiled Baoyu. "This prescription of mine is unlike all others. Besides, the very names of those drugs are quaint, and couldn't be enumerated in a moment; suffice it to mention the placenta of the first child; three hundred and sixty ginseng roots, shaped like human beings and studded with leaves; four fat tortoises; full-grown polygonum multiflorum; the core of the Pachyma cocos, found on the roots of a fir tree of a thousand years old; and other such species of medicines. They're not, I admit, out-of-the-way things; but they are the most excellent among that whole crowd of medicines; and were I to begin to give you a list of them, why, they'd take you all quite aback. The year before last, I at length let Xue Pan have this recipe, after he had made ever so many entreaties during one or two years. When, however, he got the prescription, he had to search for another two or three years and to spend over and above a thousand taels before he succeeded in having it prepared. If you don't believe me, mother, you are at liberty to ask cousin Baochai about it."

At the mention of her name, Baochai laughingly waved her hand. "I know nothing about it," she observed. "Nor have I heard anything about it, so don't tell your mother to ask me any questions."

"Really," said Madame Wang smiling, "Baochai is a good girl; she does not tell lies."

Baoyu was standing in the center of the room. Upon hearing these words, he turned round sharply and clapped his hands. "What I stated just now," he explained, "was the truth; yet you maintain that it was all lies."

As he defended himself, he casually looked round, and caught sight of Lin Daiyu at the back of Baochai laughing with tight-set lips, and applying her fingers to her face to put him to shame.

But lady Feng, who had been in the inner rooms overseeing the servants laying the table, came out at once, as soon as she overheard the conversation. "Brother Bao tells no lies," she smilingly chimed in, "this is really a fact. Some time ago cousin Xue Pan came over in person and asked me for pearls, and when I inquired of him what he wanted them for, he explained that they were intended to compound some medicine with; adding, in an aggrieved way, that it would have been better hadn't he taken it in hand for he never had any idea that it would involve such a lot of trouble! When I questioned him what the medicine was, he returned for answer that it was a prescription of brother Bao's; and he mentioned ever so many ingredients, which I don't even remember. 'Under other circumstances,' he went on to say, 'I would have purchased a few pearls, but what are absolutely wanted are such pearls as have been worn on the head; and that's why I come to ask you, cousin, for some. If, cousin, you've got no broken ornaments at hand, in the shape of flowers, why, those that you have on your head will do as well; and by and bye I'll choose a few good ones and give them to you, to wear.' I had no other course therefore than to snap a couple of twigs from some flowers I have, made of pearls, and to let him take them away. One also requires a piece of deep red gauze, three feet in length of the best quality; and the pearls must be triturated to powder in a mortar."

After each sentence expressed by lady Feng, Baoyu muttered an invocation to Buddha. "The thing is as clear as sunlight now," he remarked.

The moment lady Feng had done speaking, Baoyu put in his word. "Mother," he added, "you should know that this is a mere makeshift, for really, according to the letter of the prescription, these pearls and precious stones should, properly speaking, consist of such as had been obtained from, some old grave and been worn as head-ornaments by some wealthy and honorable person of bygone days. But how could one go now on this account and dig up graves, and open tombs! Hence it is that such as are simply in use among living persons can equally well be substituted."

"Amituo Fo!" exclaimed Madame Wang, after listening to him throughout. "That will never do, and what an arduous job to uselessly saddle one's self with; for even though there be interred in some graves people who've been dead for several hundreds of years, it wouldn't be a propitious thing were their corpses turned topsy-turvey now and the bones abstracted; just for the sake of preparing some medicine or other."

Baoyu thereupon addressed himself to Daiyu. "Have you heard what was said or not?" he asked. "And is there, pray, any likelihood that cousin Secunda would also follow in my lead and tell lies?"

While saying this, his eyes were, albeit his face was turned towards Lin Daiyu, fixed upon Baochai.

Lin Daiyu pulled Madame Wang. "You just listen to him, aunt," she observed. "All because cousin Baochai would not accommodate him by lying, he appeals to me."

"Baoyu has a great knack," Madame Wang said, "of dealing contemptuously with you, his cousin."

"Mother," Baoyu smilingly protested, "you are not aware how the case stands. When cousin Baochai lived at home, she knew nothing whatever about my elder cousin Xue Pan's affairs, and how much less now that she has taken up her quarters inside the garden? She, of course, knows less than ever about them! Yet, cousin Lin just now stealthily treated my statements as lies, and put me to the blush."

These words were still on his lips, when they perceived a waiting-maid, from dowager lady Jia's apartments, come in quest of Baoyu and Lin Daiyu to go and have their meal. Lin Daiyu, however, did not even call Baoyu, but forthwith rising to her feet, she went along, dragging the waiting-maid by the hand.

"Let's wait for master Secundus, Mr. Bao, to go along with us," demurred the girl.

"He doesn't want anything to eat," Lin Daiyu replied; "he won't come with us, so I'll go ahead. " So saying she promptly left the room.

"I'll have my repast with my mother today," Baoyu said.

"Not at all," Madame Wang remarked, "not at all. I'm going to fast today, so it's only right and proper that you should go and have your own."

"I'll also fast with you then," Baoyu retorted.

As he spoke, he called out to the servant to go back, and rushing up to the table, he took a seat.

Madame Wang faced Baochai and her companions. "You, girls," she observed, "had better have your meal, and let him have his own way!"

It's only right that you should go," Baochai smiled. "Whether you have anything to eat or not, you should go over for a while to keep company to cousin Lin, as she will be quite distressed and out of spirits."

"Who cares about her!" Baoyu rejoined, "she'll get all right again after a time."

Shortly, they finished their repast. But Baoyu apprehended, in the first place, that his grandmother Jia, would be solicitous on his account, and longed, in the second, to be with Lin Daiyu, so he hurriedly asked for some tea to rinse his mouth with.

"Cousin Secundus," Tanchun and Xichun interposed with an ironic laugh, "what's the use of the hurry-scurry you're in the whole day long! Even when you're having your meals, or your tea, you're in this sort of fussy helter-skelter!"

"Make him hurry up and have his tea," Baochai chimed in smiling, "so that he may go and look up his cousin Lin. He'll be up to all kinds of mischief if you keep him here!"

Baoyu drank his tea. Then hastily leaving the apartment, he proceeded straightway towards the eastern court. As luck would have it, the moment he got near lady Feng's court, he descried lady Feng standing at the gateway. While standing on the step, and picking her teeth with an ear-cleaner, she superintended about ten young servant-boys removing the flower-pots from place to place. As soon as she caught sight of Baoyu approaching, she put on a smiling face. "You come quite opportunely," she said; "walk in, walk in, and write a few characters for me."

Baoyu had no option but to follow her in. When they reached the interior of her rooms, lady Feng gave orders to a servant to fetch a brush, inkslab, and paper.

"Forty rolls of deep red ornamented satin," she began, addressing herself to Baoyu, "forty rolls of satin with dragons; a hundred rolls of gauzes of every color, of the finest quality; four gold necklaces...."

"What's this?" Baoyu shouted, "it is neither a bill; nor is it a list of presents, and in what style shall I write it?"

Lady Feng remonstrated with him. "Just you go on writing," she said, "for, in fact, as long as I can make out what it means, it's all that is needed."

Baoyu at this response felt constrained to proceed with the writing. This over lady Feng put the paper by. As she did so, "I've still something more to tell you," she smilingly pursued, "but I wonder whether you will accede to it or not. There is in your rooms a servant-maid, Xiao Hong by name, whom I would like to bring over into my service, and I'll select several girls tomorrow to wait on you; will this do?"

"The servants in my quarters," answered Baoyu, "muster a large crowd, so that, cousin, you are at perfect liberty to send for any one of them, who might take your fancy; what's the need therefore of asking me about it?"

"If that be so," continued lady Feng laughingly, "I'll tell someone at once to go and bring her over."

"Yes, she can go and fetch her," acquiesced Baoyu.

While replying, he made an attempt to take his leave. "Come back," shouted lady Feng, "I've got something more to tell you."

"Our venerable senior has sent for me," Baoyu rejoined; "if you have anything to tell me you must wait till my return."

After this explanation, he there and then came over to his grandmother Jia's on this side, where he found that they had already got through their meal.

"Have you had anything nice to eat with your mother?" old lady Jia asked.

"There was really nothing nice," Baoyu smiled. "Yet I managed to have a bowl of rice more than usual."

"Where's cousin Lin?" he then inquired.

"She's in the inner rooms," answered his grandmother.

Baoyu stepped in. He caught sight of a waiting-maid, standing below, blowing into an iron, and two servant-girls seated on the stove-couch making a chalk line. Daiyu with stooping head was cutting out something or other with a pair of scissors she held in her hand.

Baoyu advanced further in. "O! what's this that you are up to!" he smiled. "You have just had your rice and do you bob your head down in this way! Why, in a short while you'll be having a headache again!"

Daiyu, however, did not heed him in the least, but busied herself cutting out what she had to do.

"The corner of that piece of satin is not yet right," a servant-girl put in. "You had better iron it again!"

Daiyu threw down the scissors. "Why worry yourself about it?" she said; "it will get quite right after a time."

But while Baoyu was listening to what was being said, and was inwardly feeling in low spirits, he became aware that Baochai, Tanchun, and the other girls had also arrived. After a short chat with dowager lady Jia, Baochai likewise entered the apartment to find out what her cousin Lin was up to. The moment she espied Lin Daiyu engaged in cutting out something: "You have," she cried, "attained more skill than ever; for there you can even cut out clothes!"

"This too," laughed Daiyu sarcastically, "is a mere falsehood, to hoodwink people with, nothing more."

"I'll tell you a joke," replied Baochai smiling, "when I just now said that I did not know anything about that medicine, cousin Baoyu felt displeased." "Who cares!" shouted Lin Daiyu. "He'll get all right shortly."

"Our worthy grandmother wishes to play at dominoes," Baoyu thereupon interposed directing his remarks to Baochai; "and there's no one there at present to have a game with her; so you'd better go and play with her."

"Have I come over now to play dominoes!" promptly smiled Baochai when she heard his suggestion. With this remark, she nevertheless at once quitted the room.

"It would be well for you to go," urged Lin Daiyu, "for there's a tiger in here; and, look out, he might eat you up."

As she spoke, she went on with her cutting.

Baoyu perceived how loath she was to give him any of her attention, and he had no alternative but to force a smile and to observe: "You should also go for a stroll! It will be time enough by and bye to continue your cutting."

But Daiyu would pay no heed whatever to him. Baoyu addressed himself therefore to the servant-girls. "Who has taught her how to cut out these things?" he asked.

"What does it matter who taught me how to cut?" Daiyu vehemently exclaimed, when she realised that he was speaking to the maids. "It's no business of yours, Mr. Secundus."

Baoyu was then about to say something in his defense when he saw a servant come in and report that there was someone outside who wished to see him. At this announcement, Baoyu betook himself with alacrity out of the room.

"Amituo Fo!" observed Daiyu, turning outwards, "it wouldn't matter to you if you found me dead on your return!"

On his arrival outside, Baoyu discovered Beiming. "You are invited," he said, "to go to Mr. Feng's house."

Upon hearing this message, Baoyu knew well enough that it was about the project mooted the previous day, and accordingly he told him to go and ask for his clothes, while he himself wended his steps into the library.

Beiming came forthwith to the second gate and waited for someone to appear. Seeing an old woman walk out, Beiming went up to her. "Our Master Secundus, Mr. Bao," he told her, "is in the study waiting for his outdoor clothes; so do go in, worthy dame, and deliver the message."

"It would be better," replied the old woman, "if you did not echo your mother's absurdities! Our Master Secundus, Mr. Bao, now lives in the garden, and all the servants, who attend on him, stay in the garden; and do you again come and bring the message here?"

At these words, Beiming smiled. "You're quite right," he rejoined, "in reproving me, for I've become quite idiotic."

So saying, he repaired with quick step to the second gate on the east side, where, by a lucky hit, the young servant-boys on duty, were kicking marbles on the raised road. Beiming explained to them the object of his coming. A young boy thereupon ran in. After a long interval, he, at length, made his appearance, holding, enfolded in his arms, a bundle of clothes, which he handed to Beiming, who then returned to the library. Baoyu effected a change in his costume, and giving directions to saddle his horse, he only took along with him the four servant-boys, Beiming, Chuyao, Shuangrui, and Shuangshou, and started on his way. He reached Feng Ziying's doorway by a short cut. A servant announced his arrival, and Feng Ziying came out and ushered him in. Here he discovered Xue Pan, who had already been waiting a long time, and several singing-boys besides; as well as Jiang Yuhan, who played female roles, and Yun'er, a courtesan in the Jinxiang court. The whole company exchanged salutations. They next had tea. "What you said the other day," smiled Baoyu, raising his cup, "about good fortune coming out of evil fortune has preyed so much upon my mind, both by day and night, that the moment I received your summons I hurried to come immediately."

"My worthy cousins," rejoined Feng Ziying smiling. "You're all far too credulous! It's a mere hoax that I made use of the other day. For so much did I fear that you would be sure to refuse if I openly asked you to a drinking bout, that I thought it fit to say what I did. But your attendance today, so soon after my invitation, makes it clear, little though one would have thought it, that you've all taken it as pure gospel truth."

This admission evoked laughter from the whole company. The wines were afterwards placed on the table, and they took the seats consistent with their grades. Feng Ziying first and foremost called the singing-boys and offered them a drink. Next he told Yun'er to also approach and have a cup of wine.

By the time, however, that Xue Pan had had his third cup, he of a sudden lost control over his feelings, and clasping Yun'er's hand in his: "Do sing me," he smiled, "that novel ballad of your own composition; and I'll drink a whole jar full. Eh, will you?"

This appeal compelled Yun'er to take up the guitar. She then sang:

> Lovers have I two.
> To set aside either I cannot bear.
> When my heart longs for thee to come,
> It also yearns for him.
> Both are in form handsome and fair.
> Their beauty to describe it would be hard.
> Just think, last night, when at a silent hour, we met in secret, by the trellis
> frame laden with roses white,
> One to his feelings stealthily was giving vent,
> When lo, the other caught us in the act,
> And laying hands on us; there we three stood like litigants before the bar.
> And I had, verily, no word in answer for myself to give.

At the close of her song, she laughed. "Well now," she cried, "down with that whole jar!"

"Why, it isn't worth a jarful," smiled Xue Pan at these words. "Favor us with some other good song!"

"Listen to what I have to suggest," Baoyu interposed, a smile on his lips. "If you go on drinking in this reckless manner, we will easily get drunk and there will be no fun in it. I'll take the lead and swallow a large cupful and put in force a new penalty; and anyone of you who doesn't comply with it, will be mulcted in ten large cupfuls, in quick succession!"

Speedily rising from the banquet, he poured the wine for the company. Feng Ziying and the rest meanwhile exclaimed with one voice: "Quite right! quite right!"

Baoyu then lifted a large cup and drained it with one draught. "We will now," he proposed, "dilate on the four characters, 'sad, wounded, glad, and joyful.' But while discoursing about young ladies, we'll have to illustrate the four states as well. At the end of this recitation, we'll have to drink the 'door cup' over the wine, to sing an original and seasonable ballad, while over the heel taps, to make allusion to some object on the table, and devise something with some old poetical lines or ancient scrolls, from the Four Books or the Five Classics, or with some set phrases."

Xue Pan gave him no time to finish. He was the first to stand up and prevent him from proceeding. "I won't join you, so don't count me; this is, in fact, done in order to play tricks upon me."

Yun'er, however, also rose to her feet and shoved him down into his seat.

"What are you in such a funk for?" she laughed. "You're fortunate enough to be able to drink wine daily, and can't you, forsooth, even come up to me? Yet I mean to recite, by and bye, my own share. If you say what's right, well and good; if you don't, you will simply have to swallow several cups of wine as a forfeit, and is it likely you'll die from drunkenness? Are you, pray, going now to disregard this rule and to drink, instead, ten large cups; besides going down to pour the wine?"

One and all clapped in applause. "Well said!" they shouted.

After this, Xue Pan had no way out of it and felt compelled to resume his seat.

They then heard Baoyu recite:

> A girl is sad,
> When her springtime of life is far advanced and she still occupies a vacant inner room.
> A girl feels wounded in her heart,
> When she regrets having allowed her better half to go abroad and win a marquisdom.
> A girl is glad,
> When looking in the mirror, at the time of her morning toilette, she finds her color fair.
> A girl is joyful,
> What time she sits on the frame of a gallows-swing, clad in a thin spring gown.

Having listened to him, "Capital!" one and all cried out in a chorus. Xue Pan alone raised his face, shook his head, and remarked: "It isn't good, he must be fined."

"Why should he be fined?" demurred the party.

"Because," retorted Xue Pan, "what he says is entirely unintelligible to me. So how can he not be fined?"

Yun'er gave him a pinch. "Just you quietly think of yours," she laughed; "for if by and bye you are not ready you'll also have to bear a fine."

In due course Baoyu took up the guitar. He was heard to sing:

> "When mutual thoughts arise, tears, blood-stained, endless drop, like lentiles sown broadcast.
> In spring, in ceaseless bloom nourish willows and flowers around the painted tower.
> Inside the gauze-lattice peaceful sleep flies, when, after dark, come wind and rain.
> Both newborn sorrows and long-standing griefs cannot from memory ever die!
> E'en jade-fine rice, and gold-like drinks they make hard to go down; they choke the throat.
> The lass has not the heart to desist gazing in the glass at her wan face.
> Nothing can from that knitted brow of hers those frowns dispel;
> For hard she finds it patient to abide till the clepsydra will have run its course.
> Alas! how fitly like the faint outline of a green hill which nought can screen;
> Or like a green-tinged stream, which ever ceaseless floweth onward far and wide!"

When the song drew to an end, his companions with one voice cried out:

"Excellent!"

Xue Pan was the only one to find fault. "There's no meter in them," he said.

Baoyu quaffed the "opening cup," then seizing a pear, he added:

> "While the rain strikes the pear-blossom I firmly close the door,"

and thus accomplished the requirements of the rule.

Feng Ziying's turn came next.

> "A maid is glad," he commenced:

> "When at her first confinement she gives birth to twins, both sons.
> A maid is joyful,
> When on the sly she to the garden creeps crickets to catch.

A maid is sad,
When her husband some sickness gets and lies in a bad state.
A maiden is wounded at heart,
When a fierce wind blows down the tower, where she makes her
   toilette."

Concluding this recitation, he raised the cup and sang:

"Thou art what one could aptly call a man.
But thou'rt endowed with somewhat too much heart!
How queer thou art, cross-grained and impish shrewd!
A spirit too, thou couldst not be more shrewd.
If all I say thou dost not think is true,
In secret just a minute search pursue;
For then thou'lt know if I love thee or not."

His song over, he drank the "opening cup" and then observed:

"The cock crows when the moon's rays shine upon the thatched
   inn."

After his observance of the rule followed Yun'er's turn.

"A girl is sad," Yun'er began,

"When she tries to divine on whom she will depend towards the
   end of life.

"My dear child!" laughingly exclaimed Xue Pan, "your worthy Mr.
Xue still lives, and why do you give way to fears?"
"Don't confuse her!" remonstrated everyone of the party, "don't
muddle her!"

"A maiden is wounded at heart," Yun'er proceeded:

"When her mother beats and scolds her and never for an instant
   doth desist."

"It was only the other day," interposed Xue Pan, "that I saw your
mother and that I told her that I would not have her beat you."
"If you still go on babbling," put in the company with one consent,
"you'll be fined ten cups."

Xue Pan promptly administered himself a slap on the mouth. "How you lack the faculty of hearing!" he exclaimed. "You are not to say a word more!"

"A girl is glad," Yun'er then resumed:
"When her lover cannot brook to leave her and return home.
A maiden is joyful,
When hushing the pan-pipe and double pipe, a stringed instru-
ment she thrums."

At the end of her effusion, she at once began to sing:

"T'is the third day of the third moon, the nutmegs bloom;
A maggot, lo, works hard to pierce into a flower;
But though it ceaseless bores it cannot penetrate.
So crouching on the buds, it swing-like rocks itself.
My precious pet, my own dear little darling,
If I don't choose to open how can you steal in?"

Finishing her song, she drank the "opening cup," after which she added: "the delicate peach-blossom," and thus complied with the exigencies of the rule.
Next came Xue Pan. "Is it for me to speak now?" Xue Pan asked.

"A maiden is sad..."

But a long time elapsed after these words were uttered and yet noth-
ing further was heard.
"Sad for what?" Feng Ziying laughingly asked. "Go on and tell us at once!"
Xue Pan was much perplexed. His eyes rolled about like a bell.

"A girl is sad..."

he hastily repeated. But here again he coughed twice before he proceeded.

"A girl is sad," he said:

"When she marries a spouse who is a libertine."

This sentence so tickled the fancy of the company that they burst out into a loud fit of laughter.

"What amuses you so?" shouted Xue Pan, "is it likely that what I say is not correct? If a girl marries a man, who chooses to forget all virtue, how can she not feel sore at heart?"

But so heartily did they all laugh that their bodies were bent in two. "What you say is quite right," they eagerly replied. "So proceed at once with the rest."

Xue Pan thereupon stared with vacant gaze.

"A girl is grieved..." he added.

But after these few words he once more could find nothing to say. "What is she grieved about?" they asked.

> "When a huge monkey finds its way into the inner room," Xue Pan
> retorted.

This reply set everyone laughing. "He must be mulcted," they cried. "He must be mulcted. The first one could anyhow be overlooked; but this line is more unintelligible."

As they said this, they were about to pour the wine, when Baoyu smilingly interfered. "The rhyme is all right," he observed.

"The master of the rules," Xue Pan remarked, "approves it in every way, so what are you people fussing about?"

Hearing this, the company eventually let the matter drop.

"The two lines, that follow, are still more difficult," suggested Yun'er with a smile, "so you had better let me recite for you."

"Fiddlesticks!" exclaimed Xue Pan, "do you really fancy that I have no good ones! Just you listen to what I shall say.

> "A girl is glad,
> When in the bridal room she lies, with flowery candles burning,
> and she is loth to rise at morn."

This sentiment filled one and all with amazement. "How supremely excellent this line is!" they ejaculated.

> "A girl is joyful," Xue Pan resumed,

> "During the consummation of wedlock."

Upon catching this remark, the party turned their heads away, and shouted: "Dreadful! Dreadful! But quick sing your song and have done."

Forthwith Xue Pan sang:

"A mosquito buzzes heng, heng, heng!"

Everyone was taken by surprise. "What kind of song is this?" they inquired.

But Xue Pan went on singing:

"Two flies buzz weng, weng, weng."

"Enough," shouted his companions, "that will do, that will do!"

"Do you want to hear it or not?" asked Xue Pan, "this is a new kind of song, called the 'Heng, heng air,' but if you people are not disposed to listen, let me off also from saying what I have to say over the heel-taps and I won't then sing."

"We'll let you off! We'll let you off," answered one and all, "so don't be hindering others."

"A maiden is sad," Jiang Yuhan at once began,

"When her husband leaves home and never does return.
A maiden is disconsolate,
When she has no money to go and buy some *olea frangrans* oil.
A maiden is glad,
When the wick of the lantern forms two heads like twin flowers
   on one stem.
A maiden is joyful,
When true conjugal peace prevails between her and her mate."

His recital over, he went on to sing:

"How I love thee with those seductive charms of thine, heaven born!
In truth thou'rt like a living fairy from the azure skies!
The spring of life we now enjoy; we are yet young in years.
Our union is, indeed, a happy match!
But, lo! the milky way doth at its zenith soar;
Hark to the drums which beat around in the watch towers;
So raise the silver lamp and let us soft under the nuptial curtain
   steal."

Finishing the song, he drank the "opening cup." "I know," he smiled, "few poetical quotations bearing on this sort of thing. By a stroke of good fortune, however, I yesterday conned a pair of antithetical scrolls; of these I can only remember just one line, but lucky enough for me the object it refers to figures as well on this festive board."

This said he forthwith drained the wine, and, picking up a bud of a diminutive variety of *olea fragrans,* he recited:

"When the perfume of flowers wafts (xi ren) itself into a man, he knows the day is warm."

The company unanimously conceded that the rule had been adhered to. But Xue Pan once again jumped up. "It's awful, awful!" he bawled out boisterously; "he should be fined, he should be made to pay a forfeit; there's no precious article whatever on this table; how is it then that you introduce precious things?"

"There was nothing about precious things!" Jiang Yuhan vehemently explained.

"What! are you still prevaricating?" Xue Pan cried, "Well, repeat it again!"

Jiang Yuhan had no other course but to recite the line a second time. "Now is not Xiren a precious thing?" Xue Pan asked. "If she isn't, what is she? And if you don't believe me, you ask him about it," pointing, at the conclusion of this remark, at Baoyu.

Baoyu felt very uncomfortable. Rising to his feet, "Cousin," he observed, "you should be fined heavily."

"I should be! I should be!" Xue Pan shouted, and saying this, he took up the wine and poured it down his throat with one gulp.

Feng Ziying, Jiang Yuhan, and their companions thereupon asked him to explain the allusion. Yun'er readily told them, and Jiang Yuhan hastily got up and pleaded guilty.

"Ignorance," the party said with one consent, "does not amount to guilt."

But presently Baoyu quitted the banquet to go and satisfy a natural want and Jiang Yuhan followed him out. The two young fellows halted under the eaves of the verandah, and Jiang Yuhan then recommenced to make ample apologies. Baoyu, however, was so attracted by his handsome and genial appearance, that he took quite a violent fancy to him; and squeezing his hand in a firm grip. "If you have nothing to do," he urged, "do let us go over to our place. I've got something more to ask you. It's this, there's in your worthy company someone called Qiguan, with a reputation extending at present throughout the world; but, unfortunately, I alone have not had the good luck of seeing him even once."

"This is really," rejoined Jiang Yuhan with a smile, "my own infant name."

This disclosure at once made Baoyu quite exuberant, and stamping his feet he smiled. "How lucky! I'm in luck's way!" he exclaimed. "In very truth your reputation is no idle report. But today is our first meeting, and what shall I do?"

After some thought, he produced a fan from his sleeve, and, unloosening one of the jade pendants, he handed it to Qiguan. "This is a mere trifle," he said. "It does not deserve your acceptance, yet it will be a small souvenir of our acquaintance today."

Qiguan received it with a smile. "I do not deserve," he replied, "such a present. How am I worthy of such an honor! But never mind, I've also got about me here a strange thing, which I put on this morning; it is brand new yet, and will, I hope, suffice to prove to you a little of the feeling of esteem which I entertain for you."

With these protestations, he raised his garment, and, untying a deep red sash, with which his nether clothes were fastened, he presented it to Baoyu. "This sash," he remarked, "is an article brought as tribute from the Queen of the Xixiang Kingdom. If you attach this round you in summer, your person will emit a fragrant perfume, and it will not perspire. It was given to me yesterday by the Prince of Beijing, and it is only today that I put it on. To anyone else, I would certainly not be willing to present it. But, Mr. Secundus, please do unfasten the one you have on and give it to me to bind round me."

This proposal extremely delighted Baoyu. With precipitate haste, he accepted his gift, and, undoing the dark brown sash he wore, he surrendered it to Qiguan. But both had just had time to adjust their respective sashes when they heard a loud voice say: "Oh! I've caught you!" And they perceived Xue Pan come out by leaps and bounds. Clutching the two young fellows, "What do you," he exclaimed, "leave your wine for and withdraw from the banquet. Be quick and produce those things, and let me see them!"

"There's nothing to see!" rejoined the two young fellows with one voice.

Xue Pan, however, would by no means fall in with their views. And it was only Feng Ziying, who made his appearance on the scene, who succeeded in dissuading him. So resuming their seats, they drank until dark, when the company broke up.

Baoyu, on his return into the garden, loosened his clothes, and had tea. But Xiren noticed that the pendant had disappeared from his fan and she inquired of him what had become of it.

"I must have lost it this very moment," Baoyu replied.

At bedtime, however, descrying a deep red sash, with spots like specks of blood, attached round his waist, Xiren guessed more or less the truth of what must have transpired. "As you have such a nice sash to fasten your trousers with," Xiren consequently said, "you'd better return that one of mine."

This reminder made the fact dawn upon Baoyu that the sash had originally been the property of Xiren, and that he should by rights not have parted with it; but however much he felt his conscience smitten by remorse, he failed to see how he could very well disclose the truth to her. He could therefore only put on a smiling expression and add, "I'll give you another one instead."

Xiren was prompted by his rejoinder to nod her head and sigh. "I felt sure; " she observed; "that you'd go again and do these things! Yet you shouldn't take my belongings and bestow them on that lowbred sort of people. Can it be that no consideration finds a place in your heart?"

She then felt disposed to tender him a few more words of admonition, but dreading, on the other hand, lest she should, by irritating him, bring the fumes of the wine to his head, she thought it best to also retire to bed.

Nothing worth noticing occurred during that night. The next day, when she woke up at the break of day, she heard Baoyu call out laughingly: "Robbers have been here in the night; are you not aware of it? Just you look at my trousers."

Xiren lowered her head and looked. She saw at a glance that the sash, which Baoyu had worn the previous day, was bound round her own waist, and she at once realised that Baoyu must have effected the change during the night; but promptly unbinding it, "I don't care for such things!" she cried, "quick, take it away!"

At the sight of her manner, Baoyu had to coax her with gentle terms. This so disarmed Xiren, that she felt under the necessity of putting on the sash; but, subsequently when Baoyu stepped out of the apartment, she at last pulled it off, and, throwing it away in an empty box, she found one of hers and fastened it round her waist.

Baoyu, however, did not in the least notice what she did, but inquired whether anything had happened the day before.

"Lady Secunda," Xiren explained, "dispatched someone and fetched Xiao Hong away. Her wish was to have waited for your return; but as

I thought that it was of no consequence, I took upon myself to decide, and sent her off."

"That's all right!" rejoined Baoyu. "I knew all about it, there was no need for her to wait."

"Yesterday," resumed Xiren, "the Imperial Consort deputed the Eunuch Hsia to bring a hundred and twenty ounces of silver and to convey her commands that from the first to the third, there should be offered, in the Jingxu temple, thanksgiving services to last for three days and that theatrical performances should be given, and oblations presented; and to tell our senior master, Mr. Jia Zhen, to take all the gentlemen, and go and burn incense and worship Buddha. Besides this, she also sent presents for the dragon festival."

Continuing, she bade a young servant-maid produce the presents, which had been received the previous day. Then he saw two palace fans of the best quality, two strings of musk-scented beads, two rolls of silk, as fine as the phoenix tail, and a superior mat worked with hibiscus. At the sight of these things, Baoyu was filled with immeasurable pleasure, and he asked whether the articles brought to all the others were similar to his.

"The only things in excess of yours that our venerable mistress has," Xiren explained, "consist of a scented jade scepter and a pillow made of agate. Those of your worthy father and mother, our master and mistress, and of your aunt exceed yours by a scented scepter of jade. Yours are the same as Miss Bao's. Miss Lin's are like those of Misses Secunda, Tertia and Quarta, who received nothing beyond a fan and several pearls and none of all the other things. As for our senior lady, Mrs. Jia Zhu, and lady Secunda, these two got each two rolls of gauze, two rolls of silk, two scented bags, and two sticks of medicine."

After listening to her enumeration, "What's the reason of this?" he smiled. "How is it that Miss Lin's are not the same as mine, but that Miss Bao's instead are like my own? May not the message have been wrongly delivered?"

"When they were brought out of the palace yesterday," Xiren rejoined, "they were already divided in respective shares, and slips were also placed on them, so that how could any mistake have been made? Yours were among those for our dowager lady's apartments. When I went and fetched them, her venerable ladyship said that I should tell you to go there tomorrow at the fifth watch to return thanks.

"Of course, it's my duty to go over," Baoyu cried at these words, but forthwith calling Zijuan: "Take these to your Miss Lin," he told her, "and say that I got them yesterday, and that she is at liberty to keep out of them any that take her fancy."

Zijuan expressed her obedience and took the things away. After a short time she returned. "Miss Lin says," she explained, "that she also got some yesterday, and that you, Master Secundus, should keep yours."

Hearing this reply, Baoyu quickly directed a servant to put them away. But when he had washed his face and stepped out of doors, bent upon going to his grandmother's on the other side, in order to pay his obeisance, he caught sight of Lin Daiyu coming along towards him, from the opposite direction. Baoyu hurriedly walked up to her, "I told you," he smiled, "to select those you liked from my things; how is it you didn't choose any?"

Lin Daiyu had long before banished from her recollection the incident of the previous day, which had made her angry with Baoyu, and was only exercised about the occurrence of this present occasion. "I'm not gifted with such extreme good fortune," she consequently answered, "as to be able to accept them. I can't compete with Miss Bao, in connection with whom something or other about gold or about jade is mentioned. We are simply beings connected with the vegetable kingdom."

The allusion to the two words "gold and jade," aroused, of a sudden, much emotion in the heart of Baoyu. "If beyond what people say about gold or jade," he protested, "the idea of any such things ever crosses my mind, may the heavens annihilate me, and may the earth extinguish me, and may I for ten thousand generations never assume human form!"

These protestations convinced Lin Daiyu that suspicion had been aroused in him. With all promptitude, she smiled and observed, "They're all to no use! Why utter such oaths, when there's no rhyme or reason! Who cares about any gold or any jade of yours!"

"It would be difficult for me to tell you, to your face, all the secrets of my heart," Baoyu resumed, "but by and bye you'll surely come to know all about them! After the three—my old grandmother, my father, and my mother—you, my cousin, hold the fourth place; and, if there be a fifth, I'm ready to swear another oath."

"You needn't swear any more," Lin Daiyu replied, "I'm well aware that I, your younger cousin, have a place in your heart; but the thing is that at the sight of your elder cousin, you at once forget all about your younger cousin."

"This comes again from over-suspicion!" ejaculated Baoyu; "for I'm not at all disposed that way."

"Well," resumed Lin Daiyu, "why did you yesterday appeal to me when that hussey Baochai would not help you by telling a story? Had it been I, who had been guilty of any such thing, I don't know what you wouldn't have done again."

But during their tête-a-tête, they espied Baochai approach from the opposite direction, so readily they beat a retreat. Baochai had distinctly caught sight of them, but pretending she had not seen them, she trudged on her way, with lowered head, and repaired into Madame Wang's apartments. After a short stay, she came to this side to pay dowager lady Jia a visit. With her she also found Baoyu.

Baochai ever made it a point to hold Baoyu aloof as her mother had in days gone by mentioned to Madame Wang and her other relatives that the gold locket had been the gift of a bonze, that she had to wait until such time as some suitor with jade turned up before she could be given in marriage, and other similar confidences. But on discovery the previous day that Yuanchun's presents to her alone resembled those of Baoyu, she began to feel all the more embarrassed. Luckily, however, Baoyu was so entangled in Lin Daiyu's meshes and so absorbed in heart and mind with fond thoughts of his Lin Daiyu that he did not pay the least attention to this circumstance. But she unawares now heard Baoyu remark with a smile: "Cousin Bao, let me see that string of scented beads of yours!"

By a strange coincidence, Baochai wore the string of beads round her left wrist so she had no alternative, when Baoyu asked her for it, than to take it off. Baochai, however, was naturally inclined to embonpoint, and it proved therefore no easy matter for her to get the beads off; and while Baoyu stood by watching her snow-white arm, feelings of admiration were quickly stirred up in his heart. "Were this arm attached to Miss Lin's person," he secretly pondered, "I might, possibly have been able to caress it! But it is, as it happens, part and parcel of her body; how I really do deplore this lack of good fortune."

Suddenly he bethought himself of the secret of gold and jade, and he again scanned Baochai's appearance. At the sight of her countenance, resembling a silver bowl, her eyes limpid like water and almond-like in shape, her lips crimson, though not rouged, her eyebrows jet-black, though not pencilled, also of that fascination and grace which presented such a contrast to Lin Daiyu's style of beauty, he could not refrain from falling into such a stupid reverie, that though Baochai had got the string of beads off her wrist, and was handing them to him, he forgot all about them and made no effort to take them. Baochai realized that he was plunged in abstraction, and conscious of the awkward position in which she was placed, she put down the string of beads, and turning round was on the point of betaking herself away, when she perceived Lin Daiyu, standing on the doorstep, laughing significantly while biting a handkerchief she held in her mouth. "You can't resist," Baochai said, "a single puff of wind; and why do you stand there and expose yourself to the very teeth of it?"

"Wasn't I inside the room?" rejoined Lin Daiyu, with a cynical smile. "But I came out to have a look as I heard a shriek in the heavens; it turned out, in fact, to be a stupid wild goose!"

"A stupid wild goose!" repeated Baochai. "Where is it, let me also see it!"

"As soon as I got out," answered Lin Daiyu, "it flew away with a 'te-er' sort of noise."

While replying, she threw the handkerchief, she was holding, straight into Baoyu's face. Baoyu was quite taken by surprise. He was hit on the eye. "Ai-yah!" he exclaimed.

But, reader, do you want to hear the sequel? In that case, listen to the circumstances, which will be disclosed in the next chapter.

CHAPTER 29

A happy man enjoys a full measure of happiness, but still prays for happiness. A beloved girl is very much loved, but yet craves for more love.

Baoyu, so our story runs, was gazing vacantly, when Daiyu, at a moment least expected, flung her handkerchief at him, which just hit him on the eyes, and frightened him out of his wits. "Who was it?" he cried.

Lin Daiyu nodded her head and smiled. "I would not venture to do such a thing," she said, "it was a mere slip of my hand. As cousin Baochai wished to see the silly wild goose, I was pointing it out to her, when the handkerchief inadvertently flew out of my grip."

Baoyu kept on rubbing his eyes. The idea suggested itself to him to make some remonstrance, but he could not again very well open his lips.

Presently, lady Feng arrived. She then alluded, in the course of conversation, to the thanksgiving service, which was to be offered on the first, in the Jingxu temple, and invited Baochai, Baoyu, Daiyu, and the other inmates with them to be present at the theatricals.

"Never mind," smiled Baochai, "it's too hot; besides, what plays haven't I seen? I don't mean to come."

"It's cool enough over at their place," answered lady Feng. "There are also two-storied buildings on either side; so we must all go! I'll send servants a few days before to drive all that herd of Daoist priests out, to sweep the upper stories, hang up curtains, and to keep out every single loafer from the interior of the temple; so it will be all right like that. I've already told our Madame Wang that if you people don't go, I mean to go all alone, as I've been again in very low spirits these last few days, and as when theatricals come off at home, it's out of the question for me to look on with any peace and quiet."

When dowager lady Jia heard what she said, she smiled. "Well, in that case," she remarked, "I'll go along with you."

Lady Feng, at these words, gave a smile. "Venerable ancestor," she replied, "were you also to go, it would be ever so much better; yet I won't feel quite at my ease!"

"Tomorrow," dowager lady Jia continued, "I can stay in the two-storied building, situated on the principal site, while you can go to the one on the side. You can then likewise dispense with coming over to where I shall be to stand on any ceremonies. Will this suit you or not?"

"This is indeed," lady Feng smiled, "a proof of your regard for me, my worthy senior."

Old lady Jia at this stage faced Baochai. "You too should go," she said, "so should your mother; for if you remain the whole day long at home, you will again sleep your head off."

Baochai felt constrained to signify her assent. Dowager lady Jia then also despatched domestics to invite Mrs. Xue; and, on their way, they notified Madame Wang that she was to take the young ladies along with her. But Madame Wang felt, in the first place, in a poor state of health, and was, in the second, engaged in making preparations for the reception of any arrivals from Yuanchun, so that she, at an early hour, sent word that it was impossible for her to leave the house. Yet when she received old lady Jia's behest, she smiled and exclaimed: "Are her spirits still so buoyant!" and transmitted the message into the garden that any, who had any wish to avail themselves of the opportunity, were at liberty to go on the first, with their venerable senior as their chaperone. As soon as these tidings were spread abroad, everyone else was indifferent as to whether they went or not; but of those girls who, day after day, never put their foot outside the doorstep, which of them was not keen upon going, the moment they heard the permission conceded to them? Even if any of their respective mistresses were too lazy to move, they employed every expedient to induce them to go. Hence it was that Li Gongcai and the other inmates signified their unanimous intention to be present. Dowager lady Jia, at this, grew more exultant than ever, and she issued immediate directions for servants to go and sweep and put things in proper order. But to all these preparations, there is no necessity of making detailed reference; sufficient to relate that on the first day of the moon, carriages stood in a thick maze, and men and horses in close concourse, at the entrance of the Rong Guo mansion.

When the servants, the various managers, and other domestics came to learn that the Imperial Consort was to perform good deeds and that dowager lady Jia was to go in person and offer incense, they arranged, as it happened that the first of the moon, which was the principal day of the ceremonies, was, in addition, the season of the dragon boat festival, all the necessary articles in perfect readiness and with unusual splendor. Shortly, old lady Jia and the other inmates started on their way. The old lady sat in an official chair, carried by eight bearers: widow Li, lady Feng and Mrs. Xue, each in a four-bearer chair. Baochai and Daiyu mounted together a curricle with green cover and pearl tassels, bearing the eight precious things. The three sisters, Yingchun, Tanchun, and Xichun got in a carriage with red wheels and ornamented hood. Next in order, followed dowager lady Jia's waiting-maids, Yuanyang, Yingwu, Hupo, Zhenzhu; Lin Daiyu's waiting-maids Zijuan, Xueyan, and Chunqian; Baochai's waiting-maids Ying'er and Wen Xing; Yingchun's servant-girls Siqi and Xiujie; Tanchun's waiting-maids Shishu and Cuimo; Xichun's servant-girls Rhua and Caiping; and Mrs. Xue's waiting-maids Tongxi, and Tonggui. Besides these, were joined to their retinue: Xiangling and Xiangling's servant-girl Zhen'er; Mrs. Li's waiting-maids Suyun and Biyue; lady Feng's servant-girls Ping'er, Feng'er, and Xiao Hong, as well as Madame Wang's two waiting-maids Jinchuan and Caiyun. Along with lady Feng, came a nurse carrying Da Jie'er. She drove in a separate carriage, together with a couple of servant-girls. Added also to the number of the suite were matrons and nurses, attached to the various establishments, and the wives of the servants of the household, who were in attendance out of doors. Their carriages, forming one black solid mass, therefore, crammed the whole extent of the street.

Dowager lady Jia and other members of the party had already proceeded a considerable distance in their chairs, and yet the inmates at the gate had not finished mounting their vehicles. This one shouted: "I won't sit with you." That one cried: "You've crushed our mistress' bundle." In the carriages yonder, one screamed: "You've pulled my flowers off." Another one nearer exclaimed: "You've broken my fan." And they chatted and chatted, and talked and laughed with such incessant volubility, that Zhou Rui's wife had to go backward and forward calling them to task. "Girls," she said, "this is the street. The on-lookers will laugh at you!" But it was only after she had expostulated with them several times that any sign of improvement became at last visible.

The van of the procession had long ago reached the entrance of the Jingxu Temple. Baoyu rode on horseback. He preceded the chair occupied by his grandmother Jia. The throngs that filled the streets ranged themselves on either side.

On their arrival at the temple, the sound of bells and the rattle of drums struck their ear. Forthwith appeared the head-bonze Zhang, a stick of incense in hand; his cloak thrown over his shoulders. He took his stand by the wayside at the head of a company of Daoist priests to present his greetings. The moment dowager lady Jia reached, in her chair, the interior of the main gate, she descried the lares and penates, the lord presiding over that particular district, and the clay images of the various gods, and she at once gave orders to halt. Jia Zhen advanced to receive her, acting as leader to the male members of the family. Lady Feng was well aware that Yuanyang and the other attendants were at the back and could not overtake their old mistress, so she herself alighted from her chair to volunteer her services. She was about to hastily press forward and support her, when, by a strange accident, a young Daoist neophyte, of twelve or thirteen years of age, who held a case containing scissors, with which he had been snuffing the candles burning in the various places, just seized the opportunity to run out and hide himself, when he unawares rushed, head foremost, into lady Feng's arms. Lady Feng speedily raised her hand and gave him such a slap on the face that she made the young fellow reel over and perform a somersault. "You boorish young bastard!" she shouted, "where are you running to?"

The young Daoist did not even give a thought to picking up the scissors, but crawling up on to his feet again, he tried to scamper outside. But just at that very moment Baochai and the rest of the young ladies were dismounting from their vehicles, and the matrons and women-servants were closing them in so thoroughly on all sides that not a puff of wind or a drop of rain could penetrate, and when they perceived a Daoist neophyte come rushing headlong out of the place, they, with one voice, exclaimed: "Catch him, catch him! Beat him, beat him!"

Old lady Jia overheard their cries. She asked with alacrity what the fuss was all about. Jia Zhen immediately stepped outside to make inquiries. Lady Feng then advanced and, propping up her old senior, she went on to explain to her that a young Daoist priest, whose duties were to snuff the candles, had not previously retired out of the compound, and that he was now endeavoring to recklessly force his way out."

"Be quick and bring the lad here," shouted dowager lady Jia, as soon as she heard her explanation, "but, mind, don't frighten him. Children of mean families invariably get into the way of being spoilt by over-indulgence. However could he have set eyes before upon such display as this! Were you to frighten him, he will really be much to be pitied; and won't his father and mother be exceedingly cut up?"

As she spoke, she asked Jia Zhen to go and do his best to bring him round. Jia Zhen felt under the necessity of going, and he managed to drag the lad into her presence. With the scissors still clasped in his hand, the lad fell on his knees, and trembled violently.

Dowager lady Jia bade Jia Zhen raise him up. "There's nothing to fear!" she said reassuringly. Then she asked him how old he was.

The boy, however, could on no account give vent to speech.

"Poor boy!" once more exclaimed the old lady. And continuing: "Brother Zhen," she added, addressing herself to Jia Zhen, "take him away, and give him a few cash to buy himself fruit with; and do impress upon everyone that they are not to bully him."

Jia Zhen signified his assent and led him off.

During this time, old lady Jia, taking along with her the whole family party, paid her devotions in story after story, and visited every place.

The young pages, who stood outside, watched their old mistress and the other inmates enter the second row of gates. But of a sudden they espied Jia Zhen wend his way outwards, leading a young Daoist priest, and calling the servants to come, say; "Take him and give him several hundreds of cash and abstain from ill-treating him." At these orders, the domestics approached with hurried step and led him off.

Jia Zhen then inquired from the terrace-steps where the majordomo was. At this inquiry, the pages standing below, called out in chorus, "Majordomo!"

Lin Zhixiao ran over at once, while adjusting his hat with one hand, and appeared in the presence of Jia Zhen.

"Albeit this is a spacious place," Jia Zhen began, "we muster a good concourse today, so you'd better bring into this court those servants, who'll be of any use to you, and send over into that one those who won't. And choose a few from among those young pages to remain on duty, at the second gate and at the two side entrances, so as to ask for things and deliver messages. Do you understand me, yes or no? The young ladies and ladies have all come out of town today, and not a single outsider must be permitted to put his foot in here."

"I understand," replied Lin Zhixiao, hurriedly signifying his obedience. Next he uttered several yes's.

"Now," proceeded Jia Zhen; "you can go on your way. But how is it, I don't see anything of Rong'er?" he went on to ask.

This question was barely out of his lips, when he caught sight of Rong'er running out of the belfry. "Look at him," shouted Jia Zhen. "Look at him! I don't feel hot in here, and yet he must go in search of a cool place. Spit at him!" he cried to the family servants.

The young pages were fully aware that Jia Zhen's ordinary disposition was such that he could not brook contradiction, and one of the lads speedily came forward and sputtered in Jia Rong's face. But Jia Zhen still kept his gaze fixed on him, so the young page had to inquire of Jia Rong: "Master doesn't feel hot here, and how is it that you, Sir, have been the first to go and get cool?"

Jia Rong however dropped his arms, and did not venture to utter a single sound. Jia Yun, Jia Ping, Jia Qin, and the other young people overheard what was going on and not only were they scared out of their wits, but even Jia Lian, Jia Pin, Jia Qiong, and their companions were stricken with intense fright and one by one they quietly slipped down along the foot of the wall.

"What are you standing there for?" Jia Zhen shouted to Jia Rong. "Don't you yet get on your horse and gallop home and tell your mother that our venerable senior is here with all the young ladies, and bid them come at once and wait upon them?"

As soon as Jia Rong heard these words, he ran out with hurried stride and called out repeatedly for his horse. Now he felt resentment, arguing within himself: "Who knows what he has been up to the whole morning, that he now finds fault with me!" Now he went on to abuse the young servants, crying: "Are your hands made fast, that you can't lead the horse round?" And he felt inclined to bid a servant-boy go on the errand, but fearing again lest he should subsequently be found out, and be at a loss how to account for his conduct he felt compelled to proceed in person; so mounting his steed, he started on his way.

But to return to Jia Zhen. Just as he was about to take himself inside, he noticed the Daoist Zhang, who stood next to him, force a smile. "I'm not properly speaking," he remarked, "on the same footing as the others and should be in attendance inside, but as on account of the intense heat, the young ladies have come out of doors, I couldn't presume to take upon myself to intrude and ask what your orders, Sir, are. But the dowager lady may possibly inquire about me, or may like to visit any part of the temple, so I shall wait in here.

Jia Zhen was fully cognisant that this Daoist priest, Zhang, had, it is true, in past days, stood as a substitute for the Duke of the Rong Guo mansion, but that the former Emperor had, with his own lips, conferred upon him the appellation of the "Immortal being of the Great Unreal," that he held at present the seal of "Daoist Superior," that the reigning Emperor had raised him to the rank of the "Pure man," that the princes, now-a-days, dukes, and high officials styled him the "Supernatural being," and he did not therefore venture to treat him with any disrespect. In the second place, (he knew that) he had paid frequent visits to the mansions, and that he had made the acquaintance of the ladies and young ladies, so when he heard his present remark he smilingly rejoined. "Do you again make use of such language amongst ourselves? One word more, and I'll take that beard of yours, and outroot it! Don't you yet come along with me inside?"

"Hah, hah," laughed the Daoist Zhang aloud, as he followed Jia Zhen in. Jia Zhen approached dowager lady Jia. Bending his body he strained a laugh. "Grandfather Zhang," he said, "has come in to pay his respects."

"Raise him up!" old lady Jia vehemently called out.

Jia Zhen lost no time in pulling him to his feet and bringing him over.

The Daoist Zhang first indulged in loud laughter. "Oh Buddha of unlimited years!" he then observed. "Have you kept all right and in good health, throughout, venerable Senior? Have all the ladies and young ladies continued well? I haven't been for some time to your mansion to pay my obeisance, but you, my dowager lady, have improved more and more."

"Venerable Immortal Being!" smiled old lady Jia, "how are you; quite well?"

"Thanks to the ten thousand blessings he has enjoyed from your hands," rejoined Zhang the Daoist, "your servant too continues pretty strong and hale. In every other respect, I've, after all, been all right; but I have felt much concern about Mr. Baoyu. Has he been all right all the time? The other day, on the 26th of the fourth moon, I celebrated the birthday of the 'Heaven-Pervading-Mighty-King;' few people came and everything went off right and proper. I told them to invite Mr. Bao to come for a stroll; but how was it they said that he wasn't at home?"

"It was indeed true that he was away from home," remarked dowager lady Jia. As she spoke, she turned her head round and called Baoyu.

Baoyu had, as it happened, just returned from outside where he had been to make himself comfortable, and with speedy step, he came forward. "My respects to you, grandfather Zhang," he said.

The Daoist Zhang eagerly clasped him in his arms and inquired how he was getting on. Turning towards old lady Jia, "Mr. Bao," he observed, "has grown fatter than ever."

"Outwardly, his looks," replied dowager lady Jia, "may be all right, but, inwardly, he is weak. In addition to this, his father presses him so much to study that he has again and again managed, all through this bullying, to make his child fall sick."

"The other day," continued Zhang the Daoist, "I went to several places on a visit, and saw characters written by Mr. Bao and verses composed by him, all of which were exceedingly good; so how is it that his worthy father still feels displeased with him, and maintains that Mr. Bao is not very fond of his books? According to my humble idea, he knows quite enough. As I consider Mr. Bao's face, his bearing, his speech, and his deportment," he proceeded, heaving a sigh, "what a striking resemblance I find in him to the former duke of the Rong mansion!" As he uttered these words, tears rolled down his cheeks.

At these words, old lady Jia herself found it hard to control her feelings. Her face became covered with the traces of tears. "Quite so," she assented, "I've had ever so many sons and grandsons, and not one of them betrayed the slightest resemblance to his grandfather; and this Baoyu turns out to be the very image of him!"

"What the former duke of Rong Guo was like in appearance," Zhang, the Daoist went on to remark, addressing himself to Jia Zhen, "you gentlemen, and your generation, were, of course, needless to say, not in time to see for yourselves; but I fancy that even our Senior master and our Master Secundus have but a faint recollection of it."

This said, he burst into another loud fit of laughter. "The other day," he resumed, "I was at someone's house and there I met a young girl, who is this year in her fifteenth year, and verily gifted with a beautiful face, and I bethought myself that Mr. Bao must also have a wife found for him. As far as looks, intelligence, and mental talents, extraction and family standing go, this maiden is a suitable match for him. But as I didn't know what your venerable ladyship would have to say about it, your servant did not presume to act recklessly, but waited until I could ascertain your wishes before I took upon myself to open my mouth with the parties concerned."

"Some time ago," responded dowager lady Jia, "a bonze explained that it was ordained by destiny that this child shouldn't be married at an early age, and that we should put things off until he grew somewhat in years before anything was settled. But mark my words now. Pay no regard as to whether she be of wealthy and honorable stock or not, the essential thing is to find one whose looks make her a fit match for him and then come at once and tell me. For even admitting that the girl is poor, all I shall have to do will be to bestow on her a few ounces of silver; but fine looks and a sweet temperament are not easy things to come across."

When she had done speaking, lady Feng was heard to smilingly interpose: "Grandfather Zhang, aren't you going to change the talisman of 'Recorded Name' of our daughter? The other day, lucky enough for you, you had again the great cheek to send someone to ask me for some satin of gosling-yellow color. I gave it to you, for had I not, I was afraid lest your old face should have been made to feel uneasy."

"Hah, hah," roared the Daoist Zhang, "just see how my eyes must have grown dim! I didn't notice that you, my lady, were in here; nor did I express one word of thanks to you! The talisman of 'Recorded Name' is ready long ago. I meant to have sent it over the day before yesterday, but the unforeseen visit of the Empress to perform meritorious deeds upset my equilibrium, and made me quite forget it. But it's still placed before the gods, and if you will wait I'll go and fetch it."

Saying this, he rushed into the main hall. Presently, he returned with a tea-tray in hand, on which was spread a deep red satin cover, brocaded with dragons. In this, he presented the charm. Da Jie'er's nurse took it from him.

But just as the Daoist was on the point of taking Da Jie'er in his embrace, lady Feng remarked with a smile: "It would have been sufficient if you'd carried it in your hand! And why use a tray to lay it on?"

"My hands aren't clean," replied the Daoist Zhang, "so how could I very well have taken hold of it? A tray therefore made things much cleaner!"

"When you produced that tray just now," laughed lady Feng, "you gave me quite a start; I didn't imagine that it was for the purpose of bringing the charm in. It really looked as if you were disposed to beg donations of us."

This observation sent the whole company into a violent fit of laughter. Even Jia Zhen could not suppress a smile.

"What a monkey!" dowager lady Jia exclaimed, turning her head round. "What a monkey you are! Aren't you afraid of going down to that Hell, where tongues are cut off?"

"I've got nothing to do with any men whatever," rejoined lady Feng laughing, "and why does he time and again tell me that it's my bounden duty to lay up a store of meritorious deeds; and that if I'm remiss, my life will be short?"

Zhang, the Daoist, indulged in further laughter. "I brought out," he explained, "the tray so as to kill two birds with one stone. It wasn't, however, to beg for donations. On the contrary, it was in order to put in it the jade, which I meant to ask Mr. Bao to take off, so as to carry it outside and let all those Daoist friends of mine, who come from far away, as well as my neophytes and the young apprentices, see what it's like."

"Well, since that be the case," added old lady Jia, "why do you, at your age, try your strength by running about the whole day long? Take him at once along and let them see it! But were you to have called him in there, wouldn't it have saved a lot of trouble?"

"Your venerable ladyship," resumed Zhang, the Daoist, "isn't aware that though I be, to look at, a man of eighty, I, after all, continue, thanks to your protection, my dowager lady, quite hale and strong. In the second place, there are crowds of people in the outer rooms; and the smells are not agreeable. Besides it's a very hot day and Mr. Bao couldn't stand the heat as he is not accustomed to it. So were he to catch any disease from the filthy odors, it would be a grave thing!"

After these forebodings old lady Jia accordingly desired Baoyu to unclasp the jade of Spiritual Perception, and to deposit it in the tray.

The Daoist Zhang, carefully ensconced it in the folds of the wrapper, embroidered with dragons, and left the room, supporting the tray with both his hands.

During this while, dowager lady Jia and the other inmates devoted more of their time in visiting the various places. But just as they were on the point of going up the two-storied building, they heard Jia Zhen shout: "Grandfather Zhang has brought back the jade."

As he spoke, the Daoist Zhang was seen advancing up to them, the tray in hand. "The whole company," he smiled, "were much obliged to me. They think Mr. Bao's jade really lovely! None of them have, however, any suitable gifts to bestow. These are religious articles, used by each of them in propagating the doctrines of Reason, but they're all only too ready to give them as congratulatory presents. If, Mr. Bao, you don't fancy them for anything else, just keep them to play with or to give away to others."

Dowager lady Jia, at these words, looked into the tray. She discovered that its contents consisted of gold signets, and jade rings, or scepters, implying: "may you have your wishes accomplished in everything," or "may you enjoy peace and health from year to year;" that the various articles were strung with pearls or inlaid with precious stones, worked in jade or mounted in gold; and that they were in all from thirty to fifty.

"What nonsense you're talking!" she then exclaimed. "Those people are all divines, and where could they have rummaged up these things? But what need is there for any such presents? He may, on no account, accept them."

"These are intended as a small token of their esteem," responded Zhang, the Daoist, smiling, "your servant cannot therefore venture to interfere with them. If your venerable ladyship will not keep them, won't you make it patent to them that I'm treated contemptuously, and unlike what one should be, who has joined the order through your household?"

Only when old lady Jia heard these arguments did she direct a servant to receive the presents.

"Venerable senior," Baoyu smilingly chimed in. "After the reasons advanced by grandfather Zhang, we cannot possibly refuse them. But albeit I feel disposed to keep these things, they are of no avail to me; so would it not be well were a servant told to carry the tray and to follow me out of doors, that I may distribute them to the poor?

"You are perfectly right in what you say!" smiled dowager lady Jia.

The Daoist Zhang, however, went on speedily to use various arguments to dissuade him. "Mr. Bao," he observed, "your intention is, it is true, to perform charitable acts; but though you may aver that these things are of little value, you'll nevertheless find among them several articles you might turn to some account. Were you to let the beggars have them, why they will, first of all, be none the better for them; and, next, it will contrariwise be tantamount to throwing them away! If you want to distribute anything among the poor, why don't you dole out cash to them?"

"Put them by!" promptly shouted Baoyu, after this rejoinder, "and when evening comes, take a few cash and distribute them."

These directions given, Zhang, the Daoist, retired out of the place.

Dowager lady Jia and her companions thereupon walked upstairs and sat in the main part of the building. Lady Feng and her friends adjourned into the eastern part, while the waiting-maids and servants remained in the western portion, and took their turns in waiting on their mistresses.

Before long, Jia Zhen came back. "The plays," he announced, "have been chosen by means of slips picked out before the god. The first one on the list is the 'Record of the White Snake.'"

"Of what kind of old story does 'the Record of the White Snake,' treat?" old lady Jia inquired.

"The story about Han Gaozu," replied Jia Zhen, "killing a snake and then ascending the throne. The second play is, 'the Bed covered with ivory tablets.'"

"Has this been assigned the second place?" asked dowager lady Jia. "Yet never mind; for as the gods will it thus, there is no help than not to demur. But what about the third play?" she went on to inquire.

"The 'Nan Ke Dream' is the third," Jia Zhen answered.

This response elicited no comment from dowager lady Jia. Jia Zhen therefore withdrew downstairs, and betook himself outside to make arrangements for the offerings to the gods, for the paper money and eatables that had to be burnt, and for the theatricals about to begin. So we will leave him without any further allusion, and take up our narrative with Baoyu.

Seating himself upstairs next to old lady Jia, he called to a servant-girl to fetch the tray of presents given to him a short while back, and putting on his own trinket of jade, he fumbled about with the things for a bit, and picking up one by one, he handed them to his grandmother to admire. But old lady Jia espied among them a unicorn, made of purplish gold, with kingfisher feathers inserted, and eagerly extending her arm, she took it up. "This object," she smiled, "seems to me to resemble very much one I've seen worn also by the young lady of some household or other of ours."

"Senior cousin, Shi Xiangyun," chimed in Baochai, a smile playing on her lips, "has one, but it's a trifle smaller than this."

"Is it indeed Yun'er who has it?" exclaimed old lady Jia.

"Now that she lives in our house," remarked Baoyu, "how is it that even I haven't seen anything of it?"

"Cousin Baochai," rejoined Tanchun laughingly, "has the power of observation; no matter what she sees, she remembers."

Lin Daiyu gave a sardonic smile. "As far as other matters are concerned," she insinuated, "her observation isn't worth speaking of; where she's extra-observant is in articles people may wear about their persons."

Baochai, upon catching this sneering remark, at once turned her head round, and pretended she had not heard. But as soon as Baoyu learnt that Shi Xiangyun possessed a similar trinket, he speedily picked up the unicorn, and hid it in his breast, indulging, at the same time, in further reflection. Yet, fearing lest people might have noticed that he kept back that particular thing the moment he discovered that Shi Xiangyun had one identical with it, he fixed his eyes intently upon all around while clutching it. He found however that not one of them was paying any heed to his movements except Lin Daiyu, who, while gazing at him was, nodding her head, as if with the idea of expressing her admiration. Baoyu, therefore, at once felt inwardly ill at ease, and pulling out his hand, he observed, addressing himself to Daiyu with an assumed smile, "This is really a fine thing to play with; I'll keep it for you, and when we get back home, I'll pass a ribbon through it for you to wear." "I don't care about it," said Lin Daiyu, giving her head a sudden twist.

"Well," continued Baoyu laughingly, "if you don't like it, I can't do otherwise than keep it myself."

Saying this, he once again thrust it away. But just as he was about to open his lips to make some other observation, he saw Mrs. You, the spouse of Jia Zhen, arrive along with the second wife recently married by Jia Rong, that is, his mother and her daughter-in-law, to pay their obeisance to dowager lady Jia.

"What do you people rush over here for again?" old lady Jia inquired.

"I came here for a turn, simply because I had nothing to do."

But no sooner was this inquiry concluded than they heard a messenger announce: "that someone had come from the house of general Feng."

The family of Feng Ziying had, it must be explained, come to learn the news that the inmates of the Jia mansion were offering a thanksgiving service in the temple, and, without loss of time, they got together presents of pigs, sheep, candles, tea, and eatables and sent them over.

The moment lady Feng heard about it she hastily crossed to the main part of the two-storied building. "Ai-ya," she ejaculated, clapping her hands and laughing. "I never expected anything of the sort; we merely said that we ladies were coming for a leisurely stroll and people imagined that we were spreading a sumptuous altar with lenten viands and came to bring us offerings! But it's all our old lady's fault for bruiting it about! Why, we haven't even got any slips of paper with tips ready."

She had just finished speaking, when she perceived two matrons, who acted as housekeepers in the Feng family, walk upstairs. But before the Feng servants could take their leave, presents likewise arrived, in quick succession, from Zhao, the Vice-President of the Board. In due course, one lot of visitors followed another. For as everyone got wind of the fact that the Jia family was having thanksgiving services, and that the ladies were in the temple, distant and close relatives, friends, old friends, and acquaintances all came to present their contributions. So much so, that dowager lady Jia began at this juncture to feel sorry that she had ever let the cat out of the bag. "This is no regular fasting," she said, "we simply have come for a little change; and we should not have put anyone to any inconvenience!" Although therefore she was to have remained present all day at the theatrical performance, she promptly returned home soon after noon, and the next day she felt very loath to go out of doors again.

"By striking the wall, we've also stirred up dust," lady Feng argued. "Why we've already put those people to the trouble so we should only be too glad today to have another outing."

But as when dowager lady Jia interviewed the Daoist Zhang, the previous day, he made allusion to Baoyu and canvassed his engagement, Baoyu experienced, little as one would have thought it, much secret displeasure during the whole of that day, and on his return home he flew into a rage and abused Zhang the rationalistic priest, for harboring designs to try and settle a match for him. At every breath and at every word he resolved that henceforward he would not set eyes again upon the Daoist Zhang. But no one but himself had any idea of the reason that actuated him to absent himself. In the next place, Lin Daiyu began also, on her return the day before, to ail from a touch of the sun, so their grandmother was induced by these two considerations to remain firm in her decision not to go. When lady Feng, however, found that she would not join them, she herself took charge of the family party and set out on the excursion.

But without descending to particulars, let us advert to Baoyu. Seeing that Lin Daiyu had fallen ill, he was so full of solicitude on her account that he even had little thought for any of his meals, and not long elapsed before he came to inquire how she was.

Daiyu, on her part, gave way to fear lest anything should happen to him, (and she tried to re-assure him). "Just go and look at the plays," she therefore replied, "what's the use of boxing yourself up at home?"

Baoyu was, however, not in a very happy frame of mind on account of the reference to his marriage made by Zhang, the Daoist, the day before, so when he heard Lin Daiyu's utterances: "If others don't understand me;" he mused, "it's anyhow excusable; but has she too begun to make fun of me?" His heart smarted in consequence under the sting of a mortification a hundred times keener than he had experienced up to that occasion. Had he been with anyone else, it would have been utterly impossible for her to have brought into play feelings of such resentment, but as it was no other than Daiyu who spoke the words, the impression produced upon him was indeed different from that left in days gone by, when others employed similar language. Unable to curb his feelings, he instantaneously lowered his face. "My friendship with you has been of no avail" he rejoined. "But, never mind, patience!"

This insinuation induced Lin Daiyu to smile a couple of sarcastic smiles. "Yes, your friendship with me has been of no avail," she repeated; "for how can I compare with those whose manifold qualities make them fit matches for you?"

As soon as this sneer fell on Baoyu's ear he drew near to her. "Are you by telling me this," he asked straight to her face, "deliberately bent upon invoking imprecations upon me that I should be annihilated by heaven and extinguished by earth?"

Lin Daiyu could not for a time fathom the import of his remarks. "It was," Baoyu then resumed, "on account of this very conversation that I yesterday swore several oaths, and now would you really make me repeat another one? But were the heavens to annihilate me and the earth to extinguish me, what benefit would you derive?"

This rejoinder reminded Daiyu of the drift of their conversation on the previous day. And as indeed she had on this occasion framed in words those sentiments, which should not have dropped from her lips, she experienced both annoyance and shame, and she tremulously observed: "If I entertain any deliberate intention to bring any harm upon you, may I too be destroyed by heaven and exterminated by earth! But what's the use of all this! I know very well that the allusion to marriage made yesterday by Zhang the Daoist, fills you with dread lest he might interfere with your choice. You are inwardly so irate that you come and treat me as your malignant influence."

Baoyu, the fact is, had ever since his youth developed a peculiar kind of mean and silly propensity. Having moreover from tender infancy grown up side by side with Daiyu, their hearts and their feelings were in perfect harmony. More, he had recently come to know to a great extent what was what, and had also filled his head with the contents of a number of corrupt books and licentious stories. Of all the eminent and beautiful girls that he had met too in the families of either distant or close relatives or of friends, not one could reach the standard of Lin Daiyu. Hence it was that he commenced, from an early period of his life, to foster sentiments of love for her; but as he could not very well give utterance to them, he felt time and again sometimes elated, sometimes vexed, and wont to exhaust every means to secretly subject her heart to a test.

Lin Daiyu happened, on the other hand, to possess in like manner a somewhat silly disposition; and she too frequently had recourse to feigned sentiments to feel her way. And as she began to conceal her true feelings and inclinations and to simply dissimulate, and he to conceal his true sentiments and wishes and to dissemble, the two unrealities thus blending together constituted eventually one reality. But it was hardly to be expected that trifles would not be the cause of tiffs between them. Thus it was that in Baoyu's mind at this time prevailed the reflection: "that were others unable to read my feelings, it would anyhow be excusable; but is it likely that you cannot realize that in my heart and in my eyes there is no one else besides yourself. But as you were not able to do anything to dispel my annoyance, but made use, instead, of the language you did to laugh at me, and to gag my mouth, it's evident that though you hold, at every second and at every moment, a place in my heart, I don't, in fact, occupy a place in yours." Such was the construction attached to her conduct by Baoyu, yet he did not have the courage to tax her with it.

"If, really, I hold a place in your heart," Lin Daiyu again reflected, "why do you, albeit what's said about gold and jade being a fit match, attach more importance to this perverse report and think nothing of what I say? Did you, when I so often broach the subject of this gold and jade, behave as if you, verily, had never heard anything about it, I would then have seen that you treat me with preference and that you don't harbor the least particle of a secret design. But how is it that the moment I allude to the topic of gold and jade, you at once lose all patience? This is proof enough that you are continuously pondering over that gold and jade, and that as soon as you hear me speak to you about them, you apprehend that I shall once more give way to conjectures, and intentionally pretend to be quite out of temper, with the deliberate idea of cajoling me!"

These two cousins had, to all appearances, once been of one and the same mind, but the many issues, which had sprung up between them, brought about a contrary result and made them of two distinct minds.

"I don't care what you do, everything is well," Baoyu further argued, "so long as you act up to your feelings; and if you do, I shall be ever only too willing to even suffer immediate death for your sake. Whether you know this or not, doesn't matter; it's all the same. Yet were you to just do as my heart would have you, you'll afford me a clear proof that you and I are united by close ties and that you are no stranger to me!"

"Just you mind your own business," Lin Daiyu on her side cogitated. "If you will treat me well, I'll treat you well. And what need is there to put an end to yourself for my sake? Are you not aware that if you kill yourself, I'll also kill myself? But this demonstrates that you don't wish me to be near to you, and that you really want that I should be distant to you."

It will thus be seen that the desire, by which they were both actuated, to strive and draw each other close and ever closer became contrariwise transformed into a wish to become more distant. But as it is no easy task to frame into words the manifold secret thoughts entertained by either, we will now confine ourselves to a consideration of their external manner.

The three words "a fine match," which Baoyu heard again Lin Daiyu pronounce proved so revolting to him that his heart got full of disgust and he was unable to give utterance to a single syllable. Losing all control over his temper, he snatched from his neck the jade of Spiritual Perception and, clenching his teeth, he spitefully dashed it down on the floor. "What rubbishy trash!" he cried. "I'll smash you to atoms and put an end to the whole question!"

The jade, however, happened to be of extraordinary hardness, and did not, after all, sustain the slightest injury from this single fall. When Baoyu realised that it had not broken, he forthwith turned himself round to get the trinket with the idea of carrying out his design of smashing it, but Daiyu divined his intention, and soon started crying. "What's the use of all this!" she demurred, "and why, pray, do you batter that dumb thing about? Instead of smashing it, wouldn't it be better for you to come and smash me!"

But in the middle of their dispute, Zijuan, Xueyan, and the other maids promptly interfered and quieted them. Subsequently, however, they saw how deliberately bent Baoyu was upon breaking the jade, and they vehemently rushed up to him to snatch it from his hands.

But they failed in their endeavors, and perceiving that he was getting more troublesome than he had ever been before, they had no alternative but to go and call Xiren. Xiren lost no time in running over and succeeded, at length, in getting hold of the trinket.

"I'm smashing what belongs to me," remarked Baoyu with a cynical smile, "and what has that to do with you people?"

Xiren noticed that his face had grown quite sallow from anger, that his eyes had assumed a totally unusual expression, and that he had never hitherto had such a fit of ill-temper and she hastened to take his hand in hers and to smilingly expostulate with him. "If you've had a tiff with your cousin," she said, "it isn't worth while flinging this down! Had you broken it, how would her heart and face have been able to bear the mortification?"

Lin Daiyu shed tears and listened the while to her remonstrances. Yet these words, which so corresponded with her own feelings, made it clear to her that Baoyu could not even compare with Xiren and wounded her heart so much more to the quick that she began to weep aloud. But the moment she got so vexed she found it hard to keep down the potion of boletus and the decoction, for counteracting the effects of the sun, she had taken only a few minutes back, and with a retch she brought everything up. Zijuan immediately pressed to her side and used her handkerchief to stop her mouth with. But mouthful succeeded mouthful, and in no time the handkerchief was soaked through and through.

Xueyan then approached in a hurry and tapped her on the back.

"You may, of course, give way to displeasure," Zijuan argued; "but you should, after all, take good care of yourself Miss. You had just taken the medicines and felt the better for them; and here you now begin vomitting again; and all because you've had a few words with our master Secundus. But should your complaint break out afresh how will Mr. Bao bear the blow?"

The moment Baoyu caught this advice, which accorded so thoroughly with his own ideas, he found how little Daiyu could hold her own with Zijuan. And perceiving how flushed Daiyu's face was, how her temples were swollen, how, while sobbing, she panted; and how, while crying, she was suffused with perspiration, and betrayed signs of extreme weakness, he began, at the sight of her condition, to reproach himself. "I shouldn't," he reflected, "have bandied words with her; for now that she's got into this frame of mind, I mayn't even suffer in her stead!"

The self-reproaches, however, which gnawed his heart made it impossible for him to refrain from tears, much as he fought against them.

Xiren saw them both crying, and while attending to Baoyu, she too unavoidably experienced much soreness of heart. She nevertheless went on rubbing Baoyu's hands, which were icy cold. She felt inclined to advise Baoyu not to weep, but fearing again lest, in the first place, Baoyu might be inwardly aggrieved, and nervous, in the next, lest she should not be dealing rightly by Daiyu, she thought it advisable that they should all have a good cry, as they might then be able to leave off. She herself therefore also melted into tears. As for Zijuan, at one time, she cleaned the expectorated medicine; at another, she took up a fan and gently fanned Daiyu. But at the sight of the trio plunged in perfect silence, and of one and all sobbing for reasons of their own, grief, much though she did to struggle against it, mastered her feelings too, and producing a handkerchief, she dried the tears that came to her eyes. So there stood four inmates, face to face, uttering not a word and indulging in weeping.

Shortly, Xiren made a supreme effort, and smilingly said to Baoyu: "If you don't care for anything else, you should at least have shown some regard for those tassels, strung on the jade, and not have wrangled with Miss Lin."

Daiyu heard these words, and, mindless of her indisposition, she rushed over, and snatching the trinket, she picked up a pair of scissors, lying close at hand, bent upon cutting the tassels. Xiren and Zijuan were on the point of wresting it from her, but she had already managed to mangle them into several pieces.

I have," sobbed Daiyu, "wasted my energies on them for nothing; for he doesn't prize them. He's certain to find others to string some more fine tassels for him."

Xiren promptly took the jade. "Is it worth while going on in this way!" she cried. "But this is all my fault for having blabbered just now what should have been left unsaid."

"Cut it, if you like!" chimed in Baoyu, addressing himself to Daiyu. "I will on no account wear it, so it doesn't matter a rap."

But while all they minded inside was to create this commotion, they little dreamt that the old matrons had descried Daiyu weep bitterly and vomit copiously, and Baoyu again dash his jade on the ground, and that not knowing how far the excitement might not go, and whether they themselves might not become involved, they had repaired in a body to the front, and reported the occurrence to dowager lady Jia and Madame Wang, their object being to try and avoid being themselves implicated in the matter. Their old mistress and Madame Wang, seeing them make so much of the occurrence as to rush with precipitate haste to bring it to their notice, could not in the least imagine what great disaster might not have befallen them, and without loss of time they betook themselves together into the garden and came to see what the two cousins were up to.

Xiren felt irritated and harbored resentment against Zijuan, unable to conceive what business she had to go and disturb their old mistress and Madame Wang. But Zijuan, on the other hand, presumed that it was Xiren, who had gone and reported the matter to them, and she too cherished angry feelings towards Xiren.

Dowager lady Jia and Madame Wang walked into the apartment. They found Baoyu on one side saying not a word. Lin Daiyu on the other uttering not a sound. "What's up again?" they asked. But throwing the whole blame upon the shoulders of Xiren and Zijuan, "why is it," they inquired, "that you were not diligent in your attendance on them. They now start a quarrel, and don't you exert yourselves in the least to restrain them?"

Therefore with obloquy and hard words they rated the two girls for a time in such a way that neither of them could put in a word by way of reply, but felt compelled to listen patiently. And it was only after dowager lady Jia had taken Baoyu away with her that things quieted down again.

One day passed. Then came the third of the moon. This was Xue Pan's birthday, so in their house a banquet was spread and preparations made for a performance; and to these the various inmates of the Jia mansion went. But as Baoyu had so hurt Daiyu's feelings, the two cousins saw nothing whatever of each other, and conscience-stricken, despondent, and unhappy as he was at this time could he have had any inclination to be present at the plays? Hence it was that he refused to go on the pretext of indisposition.

Lin Daiyu had got, a couple of days back, but a slight touch of the sun and naturally there was nothing much the matter with her. When the news however reached her that he did not intend to join the party, "If with his weakness for wine and for theatricals," she pondered within herself, "he now chooses to stay away, instead of going, why, that quarrel with me yesterday must be at the bottom of it all. If this isn't the reason, well then it must be that he has no wish to attend, as he sees that I'm not going either. But I should on no account have cut the tassels from that jade, for I feel sure he won't wear it again. I shall therefore have to string some more on to it, before he puts it on."

On this account the keenest remorse gnawed her heart.

Dowager lady Jia saw well enough that they were both under the influence of temper. "We should avail ourselves of this occasion," she said to herself, "to go over and look at the plays, and as soon as the two young people come face to face, everything will be squared." Contrary to her expectations neither of them would volunteer to go. This so exasperated their old grandmother that she felt vexed with them. "In what part of my previous existence could an old sufferer like myself," she exclaimed, "have incurred such retribution that my destiny is to come across these two troublesome new-fledged foes! Why, not a single day goes by without their being instrumental in worrying my mind! The proverb is indeed correct which says: 'that people who are not enemies are not brought together!' But shortly my eyes shall be closed, this breath of mine shall be snapped, and those two enemies will be free to cause trouble even up to the very skies; for as my eyes will then loose their power of vision, and my heart will be void of concern, it will really be nothing to me. But I couldn't very well stifle this breath of life of mine!" While inwardly a prey to resentment, she also melted into tears.

These words were brought to the ears of Baoyu and Daiyu. Neither of them had hitherto heard the adage: "people who are not enemies are not brought together," so when they suddenly got to know the line, it seemed as if they had apprehended abstraction. Both lowered their heads and meditated on the subtle sense of the saying. But unconsciously a stream of tears rolled down their cheeks. They could not, it is true, get a glimpse of each other; yet as the one was in the Xiaoxiang lodge, standing in the breeze, bedewed with tears, and the other in the Yihong court, facing the moon and heaving deep sighs, was it not, in fact, a case of two persons living in two distinct places, yet with feelings emanating from one and the same heart?

Xiren consequently tendered advice to Baoyu. "You're a million times to blame," she said, "it's you who are entirely at fault! For when some time ago the pages in the establishment, wrangled with their sisters, or when husband and wife fell out, and you came to hear anything about it, you blew up the lads, and called them fools for not having the heart to show some regard to girls; and now here you go and follow their lead. But tomorrow is the fifth day of the moon, a great festival, and will you two still continue like this, as if you were very enemies? If so, our venerable mistress will be the more angry, and she certainly will be driven sick! I advise you therefore to do what's right by suppressing your spite and confessing your fault, so that we should all be on the same terms as hitherto. You here will then be all right, and so will she over there."

Baoyu listened to what she had to say; but whether he fell in with her views or not is not yet ascertained; yet if you, reader, choose to know, we will explain in the next chapter.

CHAPTER 30

Baochai avails herself of the excuse afforded her by a fan to administer a couple of raps. While Qiaoling traces, in an absent frame of mind, the outlines of the character Qiang, a looker-on appears on the scene.

Lin Daiyu herself, for we will now resume our narrative, was also, ever since her tiff with Baoyu, full of self-condemnation, yet as she did not see why she should run after him, she continued, day and night, as despondent as she would have been had she lost some thing or other belonging to her.

Zijuan surmised her sentiments. "As regards what happened the other day," she advised her, "you were, after all, Miss, a little too hasty; for if others don't understand that temperament of Baoyu's, have you and I, surely, also no idea about it? Besides, haven't there been already one or two rows on account of that very jade?"

"Cui!" exclaimed Daiyu. "Have you come, on behalf of others, to find fault with me? But how ever was I hasty?"

"Why did you," smiled Zijuan, "take the scissors and cut that tassel when there was no good reason for it? So isn't Baoyu less to blame than yourself, Miss? I've always found his behaviour towards you, Miss, without a fault. It's all that touchy disposition of yours, which makes you so often perverse, that induces him to act as he does."

Lin Daiyu had every wish to make some suitable reply, when she heard someone calling at the door. Zijuan discerned the tone of voice. "This sounds like Baoyu's voice," she smiled. "I expect he's come to make his apologies."

"I won't have anyone open the door," Daiyu cried at these words.

"Here you are in the wrong again, Miss," Zijuan observed. "How will it ever do to let him get a sunstroke and come to some harm on a day like this, and under such a scorching sun?"

Saying this, she speedily walked out and opened the door. It was indeed Baoyu. While ushering him in, she gave him a smile. "I imagined," she said, "that you would never again put your foot inside our

door, Master Secundus. But here you are once more and quite unexpectedly!"

"You have by dint of talking," Baoyu laughed, "made much ado of
nothing; and why shouldn't I come, when there's no reason for me to
keep away? Were I even to die, my spirit too will come a hundred times
a day! But is cousin quite well?"

"She is," replied Zijuan, "physically all right; but, mentally, her resentment is not quite over."

"I understand," continued Baoyu with a smile. "But resentment, for
what?"

With this inquiry, he wended his steps inside the apartment. He then
caught sight of Lin Daiyu reclining on the bed in the act of crying. Daiyu had not in fact shed a tear, but hearing Baoyu break in upon her,
she could not help feeling upset. She found it impossible therefore to
prevent her tears from rolling down her cheeks.

Baoyu assumed a smiling expression and drew near the bed.

"Cousin, are you quite well again?" he inquired.

Daiyu simply went on drying her tears, and made no reply of any
kind.

Baoyu approached the bed, and sat on the edge of it. "I know," he
smiled, "that you're not vexed with me. But had I not come, third parties would have been allowed to notice my absence, and it would have
appeared to them as if we had had another quarrel. And had I to wait
until they came to reconcile us, would we not by that time become
perfect strangers? It would be better, supposing you wish to beat me
or blow me up, that you should please yourself and do so now; but
whatever you do, don't give me the cold shoulder!"

Continuing, he proceeded to call her "my dear cousin" for several
tens of times.

Daiyu had resolved not to pay any more heed to Baoyu. When she,
however, now heard Baoyu urge: "don't let us allow others to know
anything about our having had a quarrel, as it will look as if we had
become thorough strangers," it once more became evident to her, from
this single remark, that she was really dearer and nearer to him than
any of the other girls, so she could not refrain from saying sobbingly:
"You needn't have come to chaff me! I couldn't presume henceforward
to be on friendly terms with you, Master Secundus! You should treat
me as if I were gone!"

At these words, Baoyu gave way to laughter. "Where are you off to?"
he inquired.

"I'm going back home," answered Daiyu.

"I'll go along with you then," smiled Baoyu

"But if I die?" asked Daiyu.

"Well, if you die," rejoined Baoyu, "I'll become a bonze."

The moment Daiyu caught this reply, she hung down her head. "You must, I presume, be bent upon dying?" she cried. "But what stuff and nonsense is this you're talking? You've got so many beloved elder and younger cousins in your family, and how many bodies will you have to go and become bonzes, when by and bye they all pass away! But tomorrow I'll tell them about this to judge for themselves what your motives are!"

Baoyu was himself aware of the fact that this rejoinder had been recklessly spoken, and he was seized with regret. His face immediately became suffused with blushes. He lowered his head and had not the courage to utter one word more. Fortunately, however, there was no one present in the room.

Daiyu stared at him for ever so long with eyes fixed straight on him, but losing control over her temper, "Ai!" she shouted, "can't you speak?" Then when she perceived Baoyu reduced to such straits as to turn purple, she clenched her teeth and spitefully gave him, on the forehead, a fillip with her finger. "Heng!" she cried gnashing her teeth, "you, this!" But just as she had pronounced these two words, she heaved another sigh, and picking up her handkerchief, she wiped her tears.

Baoyu treasured at one time numberless tender things in his mind, which he meant to tell her, but feeling also, while he smarted under the sting of self-reproach (for the indiscretion he had committed), Daiyu gave him a rap, he was utterly powerless to open his lips, much though he may have liked to speak, so he kept on sighing and snivelling to himself. With all these things therefore to work upon his feelings, he unwillingly melted into tears. He tried to find his handkerchief to dry his face with, but unexpectedly discovering that he had again forgotten to bring one with him, he was about to make his coat-sleeve answer the purpose, when Daiyu, albeit her eyes were watery, noticed at a glance that he was going to use the brand new coat of gray colored gauze he wore, and while wiping her own, she turned herself round, and seized a silk kerchief thrown over the pillow, and thrust it into Baoyu's lap. But without saying a word, she screened her face and continued sobbing.

Baoyu saw the handkerchief she threw, and hastily snatching it, he wiped his tears. Then drawing nearer to her, he put out his hand and clasped her hand in his, and smilingly said to her: "You've completely lacerated my heart, and do you still cry? But let's go; I'll come along with you and see our venerable grandmother."

Daiyu thrust his hand aside. "Who wants to go hand in hand with you?" she cried. "Here we grow older day after day, but we're still so full of brazen-faced effrontery that we don't even know what right means?"

But scarcely had she concluded before she heard a voice say aloud: "They're all right!"

Baoyu and Daiyu were little prepared for this surprise, and they were startled out of their senses. Turning round to see who it was, they caught sight of lady Feng running in, laughing and shouting. "Our old lady," she said, "is over there, giving way to anger against heaven and earth. She would insist upon my coming to find out whether you were reconciled or not. 'There's no need for me to go and see,' I told her, 'they will before the expiry of three days, be friends again of their own accord.' Our venerable ancestor, however, called me to account, and maintained that I was lazy; so here I come! But my words have in very deed turned out true. I don't see why you two should always be wrangling! For three days you're on good terms and for two on bad. You become more and more like children. And here you are now hand in hand blubbering! But why did you again yesterday become like black-eyed fighting cocks? Don't you yet come with me to see your grandmother and make an old lady like her set her mind at ease a bit?" While reproaching them, she clutched Daiyu's hand and was trudging away, when Daiyu turned her head round and called out for her servant-girls. But not one of them was in attendance.

"What do you want them for again?" lady Feng asked. "I am here to wait on you!"

Still speaking, she pulled her along on their way, with Baoyu following in their footsteps. Then making their exit out of the garden gate, they entered dowager lady Jia's suite of rooms. "I said that it was super-fluous for anyone to trouble," lady Feng smiled, "as they were sure of themselves to become reconciled; but you, dear ancestor, so little be-lieved it that you insisted upon my going to act the part of mediator. Yet when I got there, with the intention of inducing them to make it up, I found them, though one did not expect it, in each other's com-pany, confessing their faults, and laughing and chatting. Just like a yel-low eagle clutching the feet of a kite were those two hanging on to each other. So where was the necessity for anyone to go?"

These words evoked laughter from everyone in the room. Baochai, however, was present at the time so Lin Daiyu did not retort, but went and ensconced herself in a seat near her grandmother.

When Baoyu noticed that no one had anything to say, he smilingly addressed himself to Baochai. "On cousin Xue Pan's birthday," he re-marked, "I happened again to be unwell, so not only did I not send him any presents, but I failed to go and knock my head before him. Yet cousin knows nothing about my having been ill, and it will seem to him that I had no wish to go, and that I brought forward excuses so as to avoid paying him a visit. If tomorrow you find any leisure, cousin, do therefore explain matters for me to him."

"This is too much punctiliousness!" smiled Baochai. "Even had you insisted upon going, we wouldn't have been so arrogant as to let you put yourself to the trouble, and how much less when you were not feeling well? You two are cousins and are always to be found together the whole day; if you encourage such ideas, some estrangement will, after all, arise between you."

"Cousin," continued Baoyu smilingly, "you know what to say; and so long as you're lenient with me all will be all right. But how is it," he went on to ask, "that you haven't gone over to see the theatricals?"

"I couldn't stand the heat" rejoined Baochai. "I looked on while two plays were being sung, but I found it so intensely hot, that I felt anxious to retire. But the visitors not having dispersed, I had to give as an excuse that I wasn't feeling up to the mark, and so came away at once."

Baoyu, at these words, could not but feel ill at ease. All he could do was to feign another smile. "It's no wonder," he observed, "that they compare you, cousin, to Yang Guifei; for she too was fat and afraid of hot weather."

Hearing this, Baochai involuntarily flew into a violent rage. Yet when about to call him to task, she found that it would not be nice for her to do so. After some reflection, the color rushed to her cheeks. Smiling ironically twice, "I may resemble," she said, "Yang Guifei, but there's not one of you young men, whether senior or junior, good enough to play the part of Yang Guozhong."

While they were bandying words, a servant-girl Dian'er, lost sight of her fan and laughingly remarked to Baochai: "It must be you, Miss Bao, who have put my fan away somewhere or other; dear mistress, do let me have it!"

"You'd better be mindful!" rejoined Baochai, shaking her finger at her. "With whom have I ever been up to jokes, that you come and suspect me? Have I hitherto laughed and smirked with you? There's that whole lot of girls, go and ask them about it!"

At this suggestion, Dian'er made her escape.

The consciousness then burst upon Baoyu, that he had again been inconsiderate in his speech, in the presence of so many persons, and he was overcome by a greater sense of shame than when, a short while back, he had been speaking with Lin Daiyu. Precipitately turning himself round, he went, therefore, and talked to the others as well.

The sight of Baoyu poking fun at Baochai gratified Daiyu immensely. She was just about to put in her word and also seize the opportunity of chaffing her, but as Dian'er unawares asked for her fan and Baochai added a few more remarks, she at once changed her purpose. "Cousin Baochai," she inquired, "what two plays did you hear?" Baochai caught the expression of gratification in Daiyu's countenance, and concluded that she had for a certainty heard the raillery recently indulged in by Baoyu and that it had fallen in with her own wishes; and hearing her also suddenly ask the question she did, she answered with a significant laugh: "What I saw was: 'Li Gui blows up Song Jiang and subsequently again tenders his apologies.'"

Baoyu smiled. "How is it," he said, "that with such wide knowledge of things new as well as old; and such general information as you possess, you aren't even up to the name of a play, and that you've come out with such a whole string of words. Why, the real name of the play is: 'Carrying a birch and begging for punishment.'"

"Is it truly called: 'Carrying a birch and begging for punishment?'" Baochai asked with laugh. "But you people know all things new and old so are able to understand the import of 'carrying a birch and begging for punishment.' As for me I've no idea whatever what 'carrying a birch and begging for punishment' implies."

One sentence was scarcely ended when Baoyu and Daiyu felt guilty in their consciences; and by the time they heard all she said, they were quite flushed from shame. Lady Feng did not, it is true, fathom the gist of what had been said, but at the sight of the expression betrayed on the faces of the three cousins, she readily got an inkling of it. "On this broiling hot day," she inquired laughing also; "who still eats raw ginger?"

None of the party could make out the import of her insinuation. "There's no one eating raw ginger," they said.

Lady Feng intentionally then brought her hands to her cheeks, and rubbing them, she remarked with an air of utter astonishment, "Since there's no one eating raw ginger, how is it that you are all so fiery in the face?"

Hearing this, Baoyu and Daiyu waxed more uncomfortable than ever. So much so, that Baochai, who meant to continue the conversation, did not think it nice to say anything more when she saw how utterly abashed Baoyu was and how changed his manner. Her only course was therefore to smile and hold her peace. And as the rest of the inmates had not the faintest notion of the drift of the remarks exchanged between the four of them, they consequently followed her lead and put on a smile.

In a short while, however, Baochai and lady Feng took their leave.

"You've also tried your strength with them," Daiyu said to Baoyu laughingly. "But they're far worse than I. Is everyone as simple in mind and dull of tongue as I am as to allow people to say whatever they like."

Baoyu was inwardly giving way to that unhappiness, which had been occasioned by Baochai's touchiness, so when he also saw Daiyu approach him and taunt him, displeasure keener than ever was aroused in him. A desire then asserted itself to speak out his mind to her, but dreading lest Daiyu should he in one of her sensitive moods, he, needless to say, stifled his anger and straightway left the apartment in a state of mental depression.

It happened to be the season of the greatest heat. Breakfast time too was already past, and masters as well as servants were, for the most part, under the influence of the lassitude felt on lengthy days. As Baoyu therefore strolled, from place to place, his hands behind his back he heard not so much as the caw of a crow. Issuing out of his grandmother's compound on the near side, he wended his steps westwards, and crossed the passage, on which lady Feng's quarters gave. As soon as he reached the entrance of her court, he perceived the door ajar. But aware of lady Feng's habit of taking, during the hot weather, a couple of hours' siesta at noon, he did not feel it a convenient moment to intrude. Walking accordingly through the corner door, he stepped into Madame Wang's apartment. Here he discovered several waiting-maids, dozing with their needlework clasped in their hands. Madame Wang was asleep on the cool couch in the inner rooms. Jinchuan'er was sitting next to her massaging her legs. But she too was quite drowsy, and her eyes were all awry. Baoyu drew up to her with gentle tread. The moment, however, that he unfastened the pendants from the earrings she wore, Jinchuan opened her eyes, and realized that it was no one than Baoyu.

"Are you feeling so worn out!" he smilingly remarked in a low tone of voice.

Jinchuan pursed up her lips and gave him a smile. Then waving her hand so as to bid him quit the room, she again closed her eyes.

Baoyu, at the sight of her, felt considerable affection for her and unable to tear himself away, so quietly stretching his head forward, and noticing that Madame Wang's eyes were shut, he extracted from a purse, suspended about his person, one of the "scented-snow-for-moistening-mouth pills," with which it was full, and placed it on Jinchuan'er's lips. Jinchuan'er, however, did not open her eyes, but simply held (the pill) in her mouth. Baoyu then approached her and took her hand in his. "I'll ask you of your mistress," he gently observed smiling, "and you and I will live together."

To this Jinchuan'er said not a word.

"If that won't do," Baoyu continued, "I'll wait for your mistress to wake and appeal to her at once."

Jinchuan'er distended her eyes wide, and pushed Baoyu off. "What's the hurry?" she laughed. "'A gold hair-pin may fall into the well; but if it's yours it will remain yours only.' Is it possible that you don't even see the spirit of this proverb? But I'll tell you a smart thing. Just you go into the small court, on the east side, and you'll find for yourself what Mr. Jia Huan and Caiyun are up to!"

"Let them be up to whatever they like," smiled Baoyu, "I shall simply stick to your side!"

But he then saw Madame Wang twist herself round, get up, and give a slap to Jinchuan'er on her mouth. "You mean wench!" she exclaimed, abusing her, while she pointed her finger at her, "it's you, and the like of you, who corrupt these fine young fellows with all the nice things you teach them!"

The moment Baoyu perceived Madame Wang rise, he bolted like a streak of smoke. Jinchuan'er, meanwhile, felt half of her face as hot as fire, yet she did not dare utter one word of complaint. The various waiting-maids soon came to hear that Madame Wang had awoke and they rushed in in a body.

"Go and tell your mother," Madame Wang thereupon said to Yu-chuan'er, "to fetch your elder sister away."

Jinchuan'er, at these words, speedily fell on her knees. With tears in her eyes: "I won't venture to do it again," she pleaded. "If you, Madame, wish to flog me, or to scold me do so at once, and as much as you like but don't send me away. You will thus accomplish an act of heavenly grace! I've been in attendance on your ladyship for about ten years, and if you now drive me away, will I be able to look at anyone in the face?"

Though Madame Wang was a generous, tender-hearted person, and had at no time raised her hand to give a single blow to any servant girl, she, however, when she accidentally discovered Jinchuan'er behave on this occasion in this barefaced manner, a manner which had all her life-time been most reprehensible to her, was so overcome by passion that she gave Jinchuan'er just one slap and spoke to her a few sharp words. And albeit Jinchuan'er indulged in solicitous entreaties, she would not on any account keep her in her service. At length, Jinchuan'er's mother, Dame Bao, was sent for to take her away. Jinchuan'er therefore had to conceal her disgrace, suppress her resentment, and quit the mansion.

But without any further reference to her, we will now take up our story with Baoyu. As soon as he saw Madame Wang awake, his spirits were crushed. All alone he hastily made his way into the Daguan garden. Here his attention was attracted by the ruddy sun, shining in the zenith, the shade of the trees extending far and wide, the song of the cicadas, filling the ear; and by a perfect stillness, not even broken by the echo of a human voice. But the instant he got near the trellis, with the cinnamon roses, the sound of sobs fell on his ear. Doubts and surmises crept into Baoyu's mind, so halting at once, he listened with intentness. Then actually he discerned someone on the off-side of the trellis. This was the fifth moon, the season when the flowers and foliage of the cinnamon roses were in full bloom. Furtively peeping through an aperture in the fence, Baoyu saw a young girl squatting under the flowers and digging the ground with a hair-pin she held in her hand. As she dug, she silently gave way to tears.

"Can it be possible," mused Baoyu, "that this girl too is stupid? Can she also be following Pin'er's example and come to inter flowers? Why if she's likewise really burying flowers," he afterwards went on to smilingly reflect, "this can aptly be termed: 'Dong Shi tries to imitate a frown.' But not only is what she does not original, but it is despicable to boot. You needn't," he meant to shout out to the girl, at the conclusion of this train of thought, "try and copy Miss Lin's example." But before the words had issued from his mouth, he luckily scrutinized her a second time, and found that the girl's features were quite unfamiliar to him, that she was no menial, and that she looked like one of the twelve singing maids, who were getting up the plays. He could not, however, make out what roles she filled: scholars, girls, old men, women, or buffoons. Baoyu quickly put out his tongue and stopped his mouth with his hand. "How fortunate," he inwardly soliloquized, "that I didn't make any reckless remark! It was all because of my inconsiderate talk on the last two occasions, that Pin'er got angry with me, and that Baochai felt hurt. And had I now given them offence also, I would have been in a still more awkward fix!"

While wrapt in these thoughts, he felt much annoyance at not being able to recognize who she was. But on further minute inspection, he noticed that this maiden, with contracted eyebrows, as beautiful as the hills in spring, frowning eyes as clear as the streams in autumn, a face, with transparent skin, and a slim waist, was elegant and beautiful and almost the very image of Lin Daiyu. Baoyu could not, from the very first, make up his mind to wrench himself away. But as he stood gazing at her in a doltish mood, he realised that, although she was tracing on the ground with the gold hair-pin, she was not digging a hole to bury flowers in, but was merely delineating characters on the surface of the soil. Baoyu's eyes followed the hair-pin from first to last, as it went up and as it came down. He watched each dash, each dot, and each hook.

He counted the strokes. They numbered eighteen. He himself then set to work and sketched with his finger on the palm of his hand, the lines, in their various directions, and in the order they had been traced a few minutes back, so as to endeavour to guess what the character was. On completing the sketch, he discovered, the moment he came to reflect, that it was the character "qiang," in the combination, "qiang wei," representing cinnamon roses.

"She too," pondered Baoyu, "must have been bent upon writing verses, or supplying some line or other, and at the sight now of the flowers, the idea must have suggested itself to her mind. Or it may very likely be that having spontaneously devised a couplet, she got suddenly elated and began, for fear it should slip from her memory, to trace it on the ground so as to tone the rhythm. Yet there's no saying. Let me see, however, what she's going to write next."

While cogitating, he looked once more. Lo, the girl was still tracing. But tracing up or tracing down, it was ever the character "qiang." When he gazed again, it was still the self-same qiang.

The one inside the fence fell, in fact, from an early stage, into a foolish mood, and no sooner was one "qiang" finished than she started with another; so that she had already written several tens of them. The one outside gazed and gazed, until he unwittingly also got into the same foolish mood. Intent with his eyes upon following the movements of the pin, in his mind, he communed thus with his own thoughts: "This girl must, for a certainty, have something to say, or some unspeakable momentous secret that she goes on like this. But if outwardly she behaves in this wise, who knows what anguish she mayn't suffer at heart? And yet, with a frame to all appearances so very delicate, how could she ever resist much inward anxiety! Woe is me that I'm unable to transfer some part of her burden onto my own shoulders!"

In midsummer, cloudy and bright weather are uncertain. A few specks of clouds suffice to bring about rain. Of a sudden, a cold blast swept by, and tossed about by the wind fell a shower of rain. Baoyu perceived that the water trickling down the girl's head saturated her gauze attire in no time. "It's pouring," Baoyu debated within himself, "and how can a frame like hers resist the brunt of such a squall." Unable therefore to restrain himself, he vehemently shouted: "Leave off writing! See, it's pouring; you're wet through!"

The girl caught these words, and was frightened out of her wits. Raising her head, she at once descried someone or other standing beyond the flowers and calling out to her: "Leave off writing. It's pouring!" But as Baoyu was, firstly, of handsome appearance, and as secondly the luxuriant abundance of flowers and foliage screened with their boughs, thick-laden with leaves, the upper and lower part of his person, just leaving half of his countenance exposed to view, the maiden simply jumped at the conclusion that he must be a servant-girl, and never for a moment dreamt that it might be Baoyu.

"Many thanks, sister, for recalling me to my senses," she consequently smiled. "Yet is there forsooth anything outside there to protect you from the rain?"

This single remark proved sufficient to recall Baoyu to himself. With an exclamation of "Ai-ya," he at length became conscious that his whole body was cold as ice. Then drooping his head, he realized that his own person too was drenched. "This will never do," he cried, and with one breath he had to run back into the Yihong court. His mind, however, continued much exercised about the girl as she had nothing to shelter her from the rain.

As the next day was the dragon-boat festival, Wenguan and the other singing girls, twelve in all, were given a holiday, so they came into the garden and amused themselves by roaming everywhere and anywhere. As luck would have it, the two girls Baoguan, who filled the role of young men, and Yuguan, who represented young women, were in the Yihong court enjoying themselves with Xiren, when rain set in and they were prevented from going back, so in a body they stopped up the drain to allow the water to accumulate in the yard. Then catching those that could be caught, and driving those that had to be driven, they laid hold of a few of the green-headed ducks, variegated marsh-birds, and colored mandarin-ducks, and tying their wings they let them loose in the court to disport themselves. Closing the court Xiren and her playmates stood together under the verandah and enjoyed the fun. Baoyu therefore found the entrance shut. He gave a rap at the door. But as everyone inside was bent upon laughing, they naturally did not catch the sound; and it was only after he had called and called, and made a noise by thumping at the door, that they at last heard. Imagining, however, that Baoyu could not be coming back at that hour, Xiren shouted laughing: "who's it now knocking at the door? There's no one to go and open."

"It's I," rejoined Baoyu.

"It's Miss Baochai's tone of voice," added Sheyue.

"Nonsense!" cried Qingwen. "What would Miss Baochai come over to do at such an hour?"

"Let me go," chimed in Xiren, "and see through the fissure in the door, and if we can open, we'll open; for we mustn't let her go back, wet through."

With these words, she came along the passage to the doorway. On looking out, she espied Baoyu dripping like a chicken drenched with rain.

Seeing him in this plight, Xiren felt solicitous as well as amused. With alacrity, she flung the door wide open, laughing so heartily that she was doubled in two. "How could I ever have known," she said, clapping her hands, "that you had returned, Sir! Yet how is it that you've run back in this heavy rain?"

Baoyu had, however, been feeling in no happy frame of mind. He had fully resolved within himself to administer a few kicks to the person who came to open the door, so as soon as it was unbarred, he did not try to make sure who it was, but under the presumption that it was one of the servant-girls, he raised his leg and gave her a kick on the side.

"Ai-ya!" ejaculated Xiren.

Baoyu nevertheless went on to abuse. "You mean things!" he shouted. "It's because I've always treated you so considerately that you don't respect me in the least! And you now go to the length of making a laughing-stock of me!"

As he spoke, he lowered his head. Then catching sight of Xiren, in tears, he realized that he had kicked the wrong person. "Hallo!" he said, promptly smiling, "is it you who've come? Where did I kick you?"

Xiren had never, previous to this, received even a harsh word from him. When therefore she on this occasion unexpectedly saw Baoyu gave her a kick in a fit of anger and, what made it worse, in the presence of so many people, shame, resentment, and bodily pain overpowered her and she did not, in fact, for a time know where to go and hide herself. She was then about to give rein to her displeasure, but the reflection that Baoyu could not have kicked her intentionally obliged her to suppress her indignation. "Instead of kicking," she remarked, "don't you yet go and change your clothes?"

Baoyu walked into the room. As he did so, he smiled. "Up to the age I've reached," he observed, "this is the first instance on which I've ever so thoroughly lost control over my temper as to strike anyone; and, contrary to all my thoughts, it's you that happened to come in my way?"

Xiren, while patiently enduring the pain, effected the necessary change in his attire. "I've been here from the very first," she simultaneously added, smilingly, "so in all things, whether large or small, good or bad, it has naturally fallen to my share to bear the brunt. But not to say another word about your assault on me, why, tomorrow you'll indulge your hand and start beating others!"

"I did not strike you intentionally just now," retorted Baoyu.

"Who ever said," rejoined Xiren, "that you did it intentionally! It has ever been the duty of that tribe of servant-girls to open and shut the doors, yet they've got into the way of being obstinate, and have long ago become such an abomination that people's teeth itch to revenge themselves on them. They don't know, besides, what fear means. So had you first assured yourself that it was they and given them a kick, a little intimidating would have done them good. But I'm at the bottom of the mischief that happened just now, for not calling those, upon whom it devolves, to come and open for you."

During the course of their conversation, the rain ceased, and Baoguan and Yuguan had been able to take their leave. Xiren, however, experienced such intense pain in her side, and felt such inward vexation, that at supper she could not put a morsel of anything in her mouth. When in the evening, the time came for her to have her bath, she discovered, on divesting herself of her clothes, a bluish bruise on her side of the size of a saucer and she was very much frightened. But as she could not very well say anything about it to anyone, she presently retired to rest. But twitches of pain made her involuntarily moan in her dreams and groan in her sleep.

Baoyu did, it is true, not hurt her with any malice, but when he saw Xiren so listless and restless, and suddenly heard her groan in the course of the night, he realized how severely he must have kicked her. So getting out of bed, he gently seized the lantern and came over to look at her. But as soon as he reached the side of her bed, he perceived Xiren expectorate, with a retch, a whole mouthful of phlegm. "Oh me!" she gasped, as she opened her eyes. The presence of Baoyu startled her out of her wits. "What are you up to?" she asked.

"You groaned in your dreams," answered Baoyu, "so I must have kicked you hard. Do let me see!"

"My head feels giddy," said Xiren. "My throat foul and sweet; throw the light on the floor!"

At these words, Baoyu actually raised the lantern. The moment he cast the light below, he discerned a quantity of fresh blood on the floor. Baoyu was seized with consternation. "Dreadful!" was all he could say. At the sight of the blood, Xiren's heart too partly waxed cold.

But, reader, the next chapter will reveal the sequel, if you really have any wish to know more about them.

CHAPTER 31

Baoyu allows the girl Qingwen to tear his fan so as to afford her amusement. A wedding proves to be the result of the descent of a unicorn.

But to proceed, when she saw on the floor the blood she had brought up, Xiren immediately grew partly cold. What she had often heard people mention in past days "that the lives of young people, who expectorate blood, are uncertain, and that although they may live long, they are, after all, mere wrecks," flashed through her mind. The remembrance of this saying at once completely scattered to the winds the wish, she had all along cherished, of striving for honor and of being able to boast of glory; and from her eyes unwittingly ran down streams of tears.

When Baoyu saw her crying, his heart was seized with anguish. "What's it that preys on your mind?" he consequently asked her.

Xiren strained every nerve to smile. "There's no rhyme or reason for anything," she replied, "so what can it be?"

Baoyu's intention was to there and then give orders to the servant to warm some white wine and to ask them for a few "Lidong" pills compounded with goat's blood, but Xiren clasped his hand tight. "My troubling you is of no matter," she smiled, "but were I to put ever so many people to inconvenience, they'll bear me a grudge for my impudence. Not a soul, it's clear enough, knows anything about it now, but were you to make such a bustle as to bring it to people's notice, you'll be in an awkward fix, and so will I. The proper thing, therefore, is for you to send a page tomorrow to request Dr. Wang to prepare some medicine for me. When I take this I shall be all right. And as neither any human being nor spirit will thus get wind of it won't it be better?"

Baoyu found her suggestion so full of reason that he thought himself obliged to abandon his purpose; so approaching the table, he poured a cup of tea, and came over and gave it to Xiren to rinse her mouth with. Aware, however, as Xiren was that Baoyu himself was not feeling at ease in his mind, she was on the point of bidding him not wait upon her; but convinced that he would once more be certain not to accede to her wishes, and that the others would, in the second place, have to be disturbed, she deemed it expedient to humor him. Leaning on the couch, she consequently allowed Baoyu to come and attend to her.

As soon as the fifth watch struck, Baoyu, unmindful of combing or washing, hastily put on his clothes and left the room; and sending for Wang Jiren, he personally questioned him with all minuteness about her ailment.

Wang Jiren asked how it had come about. "It's simply a bruise; nothing more," (he said), and forthwith he gave him the names of some pills and medicines, and told him how they were to be taken, and how they were to be applied.

Baoyu committed every detail to memory, and on his return into the garden, the treatment was, needless for us to explain, taken in hand in strict compliance with the directions.

This was the day of the dragon-boat festival. Cattail and artemisia were put over the doors. Tiger charms were suspended on every back. At noon, Madame Wang got a banquet ready, and to this midday feast, she invited the mother, daughter, and the rest of the members of the Xue household.

Baoyu noticed that Baochai was in such low spirits that she would not even speak to him, and concluded that the reason was to be sought in the incident of the previous day. Madame Wang seeing Baoyu in a sullen humor jumped at the surmise that it must be due to Jinchuan's affair of the day before; and so ill at ease did she feel that she heeded him less than ever. Lin Daiyu, detected Baoyu's apathy, and presumed that he was out of sorts for having given umbrage to Baochai, and her manner likewise assumed a listless air. Lady Feng had, in the course of the previous evening, been told by Madame Wang what had taken place between Baoyu and Jinchuan, and when she came to know that Madame Wang was in an unhappy frame of mind she herself did not venture to chat or laugh, but at once regulated her behaviour to suit Madame Wang's mood. So the lack of animation became more than ever perceptible; for the good cheer of Yingchun and her sisters was also damped by the sight of all of them down in the mouth. The natural consequence therefore was that they all left after a very short stay.

Lin Daiyu had a natural predilection for retirement. She did not care for social gatherings. Her notions, however, were not entirely devoid of reason. She maintained that people who gathered together must soon part; that when they came together, they were full of rejoicing, but did they not feel lonely when they broke up? That since this sense of loneliness gave rise to chagrin, it was consequently preferable not to have any gatherings. That flowers afforded an apt example. When they opened, they won people's admiration; but when they faded, they added to the feeling of vexation; so that better were it if they did not blossom at all! To this cause therefore must be assigned the fact that when other people were glad, she, on the contrary, felt unhappy.

Baoyu's disposition was such that he simply yearned for frequent gatherings, and looked forward with sorrow to the breaking up which must too soon come round. As for flowers, he wished them to bloom repeatedly and was haunted with the dread of their dying in a little time. Yet albeit manifold anguish fell to his share when banquets drew to a close and flowers began to fade, he had no alternative but to practice resignation.

On this account was it that, when the company cheerlessly broke up from the present feast, Lin Daiyu did not mind the separation; and that Baoyu experienced such melancholy and depression, that, on his return to his apartments, he gave way to deep groans and frequent sighs.

Qingwen, as it happened, came to the upper quarters to change her costume. In an unguarded moment, she let her fan slip out of her hand and drop on the ground. As it fell, the bones were snapped. "You stupid thing!" Baoyu exclaimed, sighing, "what a dunce! what next will you be up to by and bye? When, in a little time, you get married and have a home of your own, will you, forsooth, still go on in this happy-go-lucky careless sort of way?"

"Master Secundus," replied Qingwen with a sardonic smile, "your temper is of late dreadfully fiery, and time and again it leaks out on your very face! The other day you even beat Xiren and here you are again now finding fault with us! If you feel disposed to kick or strike us, you are at liberty, Sir, to do so at your pleasure; but for a fan to slip on the ground is an everyday occurrence! How many of those crystal jars and cornelian bowls were smashed the other time, I don't remember, and yet you were not seen to fly into a tantrum; and now, for a fan do you distress yourself so? What's the use of it? If you dislike us, well pack us off and select some good girls to serve you, and we will quietly go away. Won't this be better?"

This rejoinder so exasperated Baoyu that his whole frame trembled violently. "You needn't be in a hurry!" he then shouted. "There will be a day of parting by and bye."

Xiren was on the other side, and from an early period she listened to the conversation between them. Hurriedly crossing over, "what are you up to again?" she said to Baoyu, "why, there's nothing to put your monkey up! I'm perfectly right in my assertion that when I'm away for any length of time, something is sure to happen."

Qingwen heard these remarks. "Sister," she interposed smiling iron-ically, "since you've got the gift of the gab, you should have come at once; you would then have spared your master his fit of anger. It's you who have from bygone days up to the present waited upon master; we've never had anything to do with attending on him; and it's because you've served him so faithfully that he repaid you yesterday with a kick on the stomach. But who knows what punishment mayn't be in store for us, who aren't fit to wait upon him decently!"

At these insinuations, Xiren felt both incensed and ashamed. She was about to make some response but Baoyu had worked himself into such another passion as to get quite yellow in the face, and she was obliged to rein in her temper. Pushing Qingwen, "Dear sister," she cried, "you had better be off for a stroll! it's really we who are to blame!"

The very mention of the word "we" made it certain to Qingwen that she implied herself and Baoyu, and thus unawares more fuel was add-ed again to her jealous notions. Giving way to several loud smiles, full of irony: "I can't make out," she insinuated, "who you may mean. But don't make me blush on your account! Even those devilish pranks of yours can't hoodwink me! How and why is it that you've started styl-ing yourself as 'we?' Properly speaking, you haven't as yet so much as attained the designation of 'Miss!' You're simply no better than I am, and how is it then that you presume so high as to call yourself 'we?'"

Xiren's face grew purple from shame. "The fact is," she reflected, "that I've said more than I should."

"As one and all of you are ever bearing her malice," Baoyu simulta-neously observed, "I'll actually raise her tomorrow to a higher status!"

Xiren quickly snatched Baoyu's hand. "She's a stupid girl," she said, "what's the use of arguing with her? What's more, you've so far borne with them and overlooked ever so many other things more grievous than this; and what are you up to today?"

"If I'm really a stupid girl," repeated Qingwen, smiling sarcastically, "am I a fit person for you to hold converse with? Why, I'm purely and simply a slave-girl; that's all."

"Are you, after all," cried Xiren, at these words, "bickering with me, or with Master Secundus? If you bear me a grudge, you'd better then address your remarks to me alone; albeit it isn't right that you should kick up such a hullaballoo in the presence of Mr. Secundus. But if you have a spite against Mr. Secundus, you shouldn't be shouting so bois-terously as to make thousands of people know all about it! I came in, a few minutes back, merely for the purpose of setting matters right, and of urging you to make up your quarrels so that we should all be on the safe side; and here I have the unlucky fate of being set upon by you, Miss! Yet you neither seem to be angry with me, nor with Mr. Secundus! But armed cap-á-pie as you appear to be, what is your ultimate design? I won't utter another word, but let you have your say!"

While she spoke, she was hurriedly wending her way out.

"You needn't raise your dander." Baoyu remarked to Qingwen. "I've guessed the secret of your heart, so I'll go and tell mother that as you've also attained a certain age, she should send you away. Will this please you, yes or no?"

This allusion made Qingwen unwittingly feel again wounded at heart. She tried to conceal her tears. "Why should I go away?" she asked. "If even you be so prejudiced against me as to try and devise means to pack me off, you won't succeed."

"I never saw such brawling!" Baoyu exclaimed. "You're certainly bent upon going! I might as well therefore let mother know so as to bundle you off!"

While addressing her, he rose to his feet and was intent upon trudging off at once. Xiren lost no time in turning round and impeding his progress. "Where are you off to?" she cried.

"I'm going to tell mother," answered Baoyu.

"It's no use whatever!" Xiren smiled, "you may be in real earnest to go and tell her, but aren't you afraid of putting her to shame? If even she positively means to leave, you can very well wait until you two have got over this bad blood. And when everything is past and gone, it won't be any too late for you to explain, in the course of conversation, the whole case to our lady, your mother. But if you now go in hot haste and tell her, as if the matter were an urgent one, won't you be the means of making our mistress give way to suspicion?"

"My mother," demurred Baoyu, "is sure not to entertain any suspicions, as all I will explain to her is that she insists upon leaving."

"When did I ever insist upon going?" sobbed Qingwen. "You fly into a rage, and then you have recourse to threats to intimidate me. But you're at liberty to go and say anything you like; for as I'll knock my brains out against the wall, I won't get alive out of this door."

"This is, indeed, strange!" exclaimed Baoyu. "If you won't go, what's the good of all this fuss? I can't stand this bawling, so it will be a riddance if you would get out of the way!"

Saying this, he was resolved upon going to report the matter. Xiren found herself powerless to dissuade him. She had in consequence no other resource but to fall on her knees.

Bihen, Qiuwen, Sheyue, and the rest of the waiting-maids had realized what a serious aspect the dispute had assumed, and not a sound was to be heard to fall from their lips. They remained standing outside listening to what was going on. When they now overheard Xiren making solicitous entreaties on her knees, they rushed into the apartment in a body; and with one consent they prostrated themselves on the floor.

Baoyu at once pulled Xiren up. Then with a sigh, he took a seat on the bed. "Get up," he shouted to the body of girls, "and clear out! What would you have me do?" he asked, addressing himself to Xiren. "This heart of mine has been rent to pieces, and no one has any idea about it!"

While speaking, tears of a sudden rolled down his cheek. At the sight of Baoyu weeping, Xiren also melted into a fit of crying. Qingwen was standing by them, with watery eyes. She was on the point of reasoning with them, when espying Lin Daiyu step into the room, she speedily walked out.

"On a grand holiday like this," remonstrated Lin Daiyu smiling, "how is it that you're snivelling away, and all for nothing? Is it likely that high words have resulted all through that 'dumpling' contest?"

Baoyu and Lin Daiyu blurted out laughing.

"You don't tell me, cousin Secundus," Lin Daiyu put in, "but I know all about it, even though I have asked no questions."

Now she spoke, and now she patted Xiren on the shoulder. "My dear sister-in-law," she smiled, "just you tell me! It must surely be that you two have had a quarrel. Confide in me, your cousin, so that I might reconcile you."

"Miss Lin," rejoined Xiren, pushing her off, "what are you fussing about? I am simply one of our servant-girls; you're therefore rather erratic in your talk!"

"You say that you're only a servant-girl," smilingly replied Daiyu, "and yet I treat you like a sister-in-law."

"Why do you," Baoyu chimed in, "give her this abusive epithet? But however much she may make allowance for this, can she, when there are so many others who tell idle tales on her account, put up with your coming and telling her all you've said?"

"Miss Lin," smiled Xiren, "you're not aware of the purpose of my heart. Unless my breath fails and I die, I shall continue in his service."

"If you die," remarked Lin Daiyu smiling, "what will others do, I wonder? As for me, I shall be the first to die from crying."

"Were you to die," added Baoyu laughingly, "I shall become a bonze."

"You'd better be a little more sober-minded!" laughed Xiren. "What's the good of coming out with all these things?"

Lin Daiyu put out two of her fingers, and puckered up her lips. "Up to this," she laughed, "he's become a bonze twice. Henceforward, I'll try and remember how many times you make up your mind to become a Buddhist priest!"

This reminded Baoyu that she was referring to a remark he had made on a previous occasion, but smiling to himself, he allowed the matter to drop.

After a short interval, Lin Daiyu went away. A servant then came to announce that Mr. Xue wanted to see him, and Baoyu had to go. The purpose of this visit was in fact to invite him to a banquet, and as he could not very well put forward any excuse to refuse, he had to remain till the end of the feast before he was able to take his leave. The result was that, on his return, in the evening, he was to a great extent under the effect of wine. With bustling step, he wended his way into his own court. Here he perceived that the cool couch with a back to it, had already been placed in the yard, and that there was someone asleep on it. Prompted by the conviction that it must be Xiren, Baoyu seated himself on the edge of the couch. As he did so, he gave her a push, and inquired whether her sore place was any better. But thereupon he saw the occupant turn herself round, and exclaim: "What do you come again to irritate me for?"

Baoyu, at a glance, realised that it was not Xiren, but Qingwen. Baoyu then clutched her and compelled her to sit next to him. "Your disposition," he smiled, "has been more and more spoilt through indulgence. When you let the fan drop this morning, I simply made one or two remarks, and out you came with that long rigmarole. Had you gone for me it wouldn't have mattered; but you also dragged in Xiren, who only interfered with every good intention of inducing us to make it up again. But, ponder now, ought you to have done it; yes or no?" "With this intense heat," remonstrated Qingwen, "why do you pull me and toss me about? Should any people see you, what will they think? But this person of mine isn't meet to be seated in here."

"Since you yourself know that it isn't meet," replied Baoyu with a smile, "why then were you sleeping here?"

To this taunt Qingwen had nothing to say. But she spurted out into fresh laughter. "It was all right," she retorted, "during your absence; but the moment you come, it isn't meet for me to stay! Get up and let me go and have my bath. Xiren and Sheyue have both had theirs, so I'll call them here!"

"I've just had again a good deal of wine," remarked Baoyu, laughingly; "so a wash will be good for me. And since you've not had your bath, you had better bring the water and let's both have it together."

"No, no!" smiled Qingwen, waving her hand, "I cannot presume to put you to any trouble, Sir. I still remember how when Bihen used to look after your bath you occupied fully two or three hours. What you were up to during that time we never knew. We could not very well walk in. When you had however done washing, and we entered your room, we found the floor so covered with water that the legs of the bed were soaking and the matting itself a regular pool. Nor could we make out what kind of washing you'd been having; and for days afterwards we had a laugh over it. But I've neither any time to get the water ready; nor do I see the need for you to have a wash along with me. Besides, today it's chilly, and as you've had a bath only a little while back, you can very well just now dispense with one. But I'll draw a basin of water for you to wash your face, and to shampoo your head with. Not long ago, Yuanyang sent you a few fruits; they were put in that crystal bowl, so you'd better tell them to bring them to you to taste."

"Well, in that case." laughed Baoyu, "you needn't also have a bath. Just simply wash your hands, and bring the fruit and let's have some together."

"I'm so shaky," smiled Qingwen "that even fans slip out of my hands, and how could I fetch the fruit for you. Were I also to break the dish, it will be still more dreadful!"

"If you want to break it, break it!" smiled Baoyu. "These things are only intended for general use. You like this thing; I fancy that; our respective tastes are not identical. The original use of that fan, for instance, was to fan one's self with; but if you chose to break it for fun, you were quite at liberty to do so. The only thing is, when you get angry don't make it the means of giving vent to your temper! Just like those salvers. They are really meant for serving things in. But if you fancy that kind of sound, then deliberately smash them, that will be all right. But don't, when you are in high dudgeon avail yourself of them to air your resentment! That's what one would call having a fancy for a thing!"

Qingwen greeted his words with a smile.

"Since that be so," she said, "bring me your fan and let me tear it. What most takes my fancy is tearing!"

Upon hearing this Baoyu smilingly handed it to her. Qingwen, in point of fact, took it over, and with a crash she rent it in two. Close upon this, the sound of crash upon crash became audible.

Baoyu was standing next to her. "How nice the noise is!" he laughed. "Tear it again and make it sound a little more!"

But while he spoke, Sheyue was seen to walk in. "Don't," she smiled, "be up to so much mischief!" Baoyu, however, went up to her and snatching her fan also from her hand, he gave it to Qingwen. Qingwen took it and there and then likewise broke it in two. Both he and she then had a hearty laugh.

"What do you call this?" Sheyue expostulated. "Do you take my property and make it the means of distracting yourselves!"

"Open the fan-box," shouted Baoyu, "and choose one and take it away! What, are they such fine things!"

"In that case," ventured Sheyue, "fetch the fans and let her break as many as she can. Won't that be nice!"

"Go and bring them at once!" Baoyu laughed.

"I won't be up to any such tomfoolery!" Sheyue demurred. "She hasn't snapped her hands, so bid her go herself and fetch them!"

"I'm feeling tired," interposed Qingwen, as she laughingly leant on the bed. "I'll therefore tear some more tomorrow again."

"An old writer says," added Baoyu with a smile, "'that a thousand ounces of gold cannot purchase a single laugh!' What can a few fans cost?"

After moralizing, he went on to call Xiren. Xiren had just finished the necessary change in her dress so she stepped in; and a young servant-girl, Jiahui, crossed over and picked up the broken fans. Then they all sat and enjoyed the cool breeze. But we can well dispense with launching into any minute details.

On the morrow, noon found Madame Wang, Xue Baochai, Lin Daiyu, and the rest of the young ladies congregated in dowager lady Jia's suite of rooms. Someone then brought the news that: "Miss Shi had arrived." In a little time they perceived Shi Xiangyun make her appearance in the court, at the head of a bevy of waitingmaids and married women. Baochai, Daiyu, and her other cousins, quickly ran down the steps to meet her and exchange greetings. But with what fervor girls of tender years reunite some day after a separation of months need not, of course, be explained. Presently, she entered the apartments, paid her respects and inquired how they all were. But after this conventional interchange of salutations, old lady Jia pressed her to take off her outer garments as the weather was so close. Shi Xiangyun lost no time in rising to her feet and loosening her clothes. "I don't see why," Madame Wang thereupon smiled, "you wear all these things!"

"It's entirely at aunt Secunda's bidding," retorted Shi Xiangyun, "that I put them on. Why, would any one of her own accord wear so many things!"

"Aunt," interposed Baochai, who stood by, with a smile, "you're not aware that what most delights her in the matter of dress is to don other people's clothes! Yes, I remember how, during her stay here in the third and fourth moons of last year, she used to wear cousin Bao's pelisses. She even put on his shoes, and attached his frontlets as well round her head. At a casual glance, she looked the very image of cousin Bao;

what was superfluous was that pair of earrings of hers. As she stood at the back of that chair she so thoroughly took in our venerable ancestor that she kept on shouting: 'Baoyu, come over! Mind the tassels suspended on that lamp; for if you shake the dust off, it may get into your eyes!' But all she did was to laugh; she did not budge; and it was only after everyone found it hard to keep their countenance that our worthy senior also started laughing. 'You do look well in male habiliments!' she said to her."

"What about that!" cried Lin Daiyu, "why, she had scarcely been here with us a couple of days in the first moon of last year, when we sent and fetched her, that we had a fall of snow. You, venerable senior, and her maternal aunt had on that day, I remember so well, just returned from worshipping the images of our ancestors, and a brand-new deep red felt wrapper of yours, dear grandmother, had been lying over there, when suddenly it disappeared. But, lo, she it was who had put it on! Being, however, too large and too long for her, she took a couple of handkerchiefs, and fastened them round her waist. She was then trudging into the back court with the servant-girls to make snow men when she tripped and fell flat in front of the drain, and got covered all over with mud."

As she narrated this incident, everyone recalled the circumstances to mind, and had a good laugh.

"Dame Zhou," Baochai smilingly inquired of nurse Zhou, "is your young lady always as fond of pranks as ever or not?"

Nurse Zhou then also gave a laugh.

"Pranks are nothing," Yingchun smiled. "What I do detest is her fondness for tittle-tattle! I've never seen anyone who, even when asleep, goes on chatter-chatter; now laughing, and now talking, as she does. Nor can I make out where she gets all those idle yarns of hers."

"I think she's better of late," interposed Madame Wang. "The other day some party or other came and they met; so she's to have a mother-in-law very soon; and can she still be comporting herself like that!"

"Are you going to stay today," dowager lady Jia then asked, "or going back home?"

Nurse Zhou smiled. "Your venerable ladyship has not seen what an amount of clothes we've brought," she replied. "We mean, of course, to stay a couple of days."

"Is cousin Baoyu not at home?" inquired Xiangyun.

"There she's again! She doesn't think of others," remarked Baochai smiling significantly. "She only thinks of her cousin Baoyu. They're both so fond of larks! This proves that she hasn't yet got rid of that spirit of mischief."

"You're all now grown up," observed old lady Jia; "and you shouldn't allude to infant names."

But while she was chiding them, they noticed Baoyu arrive.

"Cousin Yun, have you come?" he smiled. "How is it that you wouldn't come the other day when someone was despatched to fetch you?"

"It's only a few minutes," Madame Wang said, "since our venerable senior called that one to task, and now here he comes and refers to names and surnames!"

"Your cousin Bao," ventured Lin Daiyu, "has something good, which he has been waiting to give you."

"What good thing is it?" asked Xiangyun.

"Do you believe what she says?" observed Baoyu laughingly. "But how many days is it that I have not seen you, and you've grown so much taller!"

"Is cousin Xiren all right?" inquired Xiangyun.

"She's all right," answered Baoyu. "Many thanks for your kind thought of her."

"I've brought something nice for her," resumed Xiangyun.

Saying this, she produced her handkerchief, tied into a knot.

"What's this something nice?" asked Baoyu. "Wouldn't it have been better if you'd brought her a couple of those rings with streaked stones of the kind you sent the other day?"

"Why, what's this?" exclaimed Xiangyun laughing, opening, as she spoke, the handkerchief.

On close scrutiny, they actually found four streaked rings, similar to those she had previously sent, tied up in the same packet.

"Look here!" Lin Daiyu smiled, "what a girl she is! Had you, when sending that fellow the other day to bring ours, given him these also to bring along with him, wouldn't it have saved trouble? Instead of that, here you fussily bring them yourself today! I presumed that it was something out of the way again; but is it really only these things? In very truth, you're a mere dunce!"

"It's you who behave like a dunce now!" Shi Xiangyun smiled.

"I'll speak out here and let everyone judge for themselves who is the dunce. The servant, deputed to bring the things to you, had no need to open his mouth and say anything; for, as soon as they were brought in, it was of course evident, at a glance, that they were to be presented to you young ladies. But had he been the bearer of these things for them, I would have been under the necessity of explaining to him which was intended for this servant-girl, and which for that. Had the messenger had his wits about him, well and good; but had he been at all stupid he wouldn't have been able to remember so much as the names of the girls! He would have made an awful mess of it, and talked a lot of nonsense. So instead of being of any use he would have even muddled, hickledy-pickledy, your things. Had a female servant been despatched, it would have been all right. But as it happened, a servant-boy was again sent the other day, so how could he have mentioned the names of the waiting-girls? And by my bringing them in person to give them to them, doesn't it make things clearer?"

As she said this, she put down the four rings. "One is for sister Xiren," she continued, "one is for sister Yuanyang. One for sister Jinchuan'er, and one for sister Ping'er. They are only for these four girls; but would the servant-boys too forsooth have remembered them so clearly!"

At these words, the whole company smiled. "How really clear!" they cried.

"This is what it is to be able to speak!" Baoyu put in. "She doesn't spare anyone!"

Hearing this, Lin Daiyu gave a sardonic smile. "If she didn't know how to use her tongue," she observed, "would she deserve to wear that unicorn of gold!"

While speaking, she rose and walked off.

Luckily, everyone did not hear what she said. Only Xue Baochai pursed up her lips and laughed. Baoyu, however, had overheard her remark, and he blamed himself for having once more talked in a heedless manner. Unawares his eye espied Baochai much amused, and he too could not suppress a smile. But at the sight of Baoyu in laughter, Baochai hastily rose to her feet and withdrew. She went in search of Daiyu, to have a chat and laugh with her.

"After you've had tea," old lady Jia thereupon said to Xiangyun, "you'd better rest a while and then go and see your sisters-in-law. Besides, it's cool in the garden, so you can walk about with your cousins."

Xiangyun expressed her assent, and, collecting the three rings, she wrapped them up, and went and lay down to rest. Presently, she got up with the idea of paying visits to lady Feng and her other relatives. Followed by a whole bevy of nurses and waiting-maids, she repaired into lady Feng's quarters on the off side. She bandied words with her for a while and then coming out she betook herself into the garden of Broad Vista, and called on Li Gongcai. But after a short visit, she turned her steps towards the Yihong court to look up Xiren. "You people needn't," she said, turning her head round, "come along with me! You may go and see your friends and relatives. It will be quite enough if you simply leave Cuilu to wait upon me."

Hearing her wishes, each went her own way in quest of aunts, or sisters-in-law. There only remained but Xiangyun and Cuilu.

"How is it," inquired Cuilu, "that these lotus flowers have not yet opened?"

"The proper season hasn't yet arrived," rejoined Shi Xiangyun.

"They too," continued Cuilu, "resemble those in our pond; they are double flowers."

"These here," remarked Xiangyun, "are not however up to ours."

"They have over there," observed Cuilu, "a pomegranate tree, with four or five branches joined one to another, just like one story raised above another story. What trouble it must have cost them to rear!"

"Flowers and plants," suggested Shi Xiangyun, "are precisely like the human race. With sufficient vitality, they grow up in a healthy condition."

"I can't credit these words," replied Cuilu, twisting her face round. "If you maintain that they are like human beings, how is it that I haven't seen any person, with one head growing over another.

This rejoinder evoked a smile from Xiangyun. "I tell you not to talk," she cried, "but you will insist upon talking! How do you expect people to be able to answer everything you say! All things, whether in heaven or on earth come into existence by the cooperation of the dual powers, the male and female. So all things, whether good or bad, novel or strange, and all those manifold changes and transformations arise entirely from the favorable or adverse influence exercised by the male and female powers. And though some things seldom seen by mankind might come to life, the principle at work is, after all, the same."

"In the face of these arguments," laughed Cuilu, "everything, from old till now, from the very creation itself, embodies a certain proportion of the Yin and Yang principles."

"You stupid thing!" exclaimed Xiangyun smiling, "the more you talk, the more stuff and nonsense falls from your lips! What about everything embodying a certain proportion of the principles Yin and Yang! Besides, the two words Yin and Yang are really one word; for when the Yang principle is exhausted, it becomes the Yin; and when the Yin is exhausted, it becomes Yang. And it isn't that, at the exhaustion of the Yin, another Yang comes into existence; and that, at the exhaustion of the Yang, a second Yin arises."

"This trash is sufficient to kill me!" ejaculated Cuilu. "What are the Yin and Yang? Why, they are without substance or form! But pray, Miss, tell me what sort of things these Yin and Yang can be!"

"The Yin and Yang," explained Xiangyun, "are no more than spirits, but anything affected by their influence at once assumes form. The heavens, for instance, are Yang, and the earth is Yin; water is Yin and fire is Yang; the sun is Yang and the moon Yin."

"Quite so! quite so!" cried out Cuilu, much amused by these explanations, "I've at length attained perception! It isn't strange then that people invariably call the sun 'Taiyang.' While astrologers keep on speaking of the moon as 'Taiyinxing,' or something like it. It must be on account of this principle."

"Amituo Fo!" laughed Xiangyun, "you have at last understood!"

"All these things possess the Yin and Yang; that's all right." Cuilu put in. "But is there any likelihood that all those mosquitoes, fleas, and worms, flowers, herbs, bricks, and tiles have, in like manner, anything to do with the Yin and Yang?"

"How don't they!" exclaimed Xiangyun. "For example, even the leaves of that tree are distinguished by Yin and Yang. The side, which looks up and faces the sun, is called Yang; while that in the shade and looking downwards, is called Yin."

"Is it really so!" ejaculated Cuilu, upon hearing this; while she smiled and nodded her head. "Now I know all about it! But which is Yang and which Yin in these fans we're holding."

"This side, the front, is Yang," answered Xiangyun; "and that, the reverse, is Yin."

Cuilu went on to nod her head, and to laugh. She felt inclined to apply her questions to several other things, but as she could not fix her mind upon anything in particular, she, all of a sudden, drooped her head. Catching sight of the pendant in gold, representing a unicorn, which Xiangyun had about her person, she forthwith made allusion to it. "This, Miss," she said smiling, "cannot likely also have any Yin and Yang!"

"The beasts of the field and the birds of the air," proceeded Xiangyun, "are, the cock birds, Yang, and the hen birds, Yin. The females of beasts are Yin; and the males, Yang; so how is there none?"

"Is this male, or is this female?" inquired Cuilu.

"Cui!" exclaimed Xiangyun, "what about male and female! Here you are with your nonsense again."

"Well, never mind about that," added Cuilu, "But how is it that all things have Yin and Yang, and that we human beings have no Yin and no Yang?"

Xiangyun then lowered her face. "You low-bred thing!" she exclaimed. "But it's better for us to proceed on our way, for the more questions you ask, the nicer they get."

"What's there in this that you can't tell me?" asked Cuilu, "But I know all about it, so there's no need for you to keep me on pins and needles."

"Xiangyun blurted out laughing. "What do you know?" she said.

"That you, Miss, are Yang, and that I'm Yin," answered Cuilu.

Xiangyun produced her handkerchief, and, while screening her mouth with it, burst out into a loud fit of laughter.

"What I say must be right for you to laugh in this way," Cuilu observed.

"Perfectly right, perfectly right!" acquiesced Xiangyun.

"People say," continued Cuilu, "that masters are Yang, and that servant-girls are Yin; don't I even apprehend this primary principle?"

"You apprehend it thoroughly," responded Xiangyun laughingly. But while she was speaking, she espied, under the trellis with the cinnamon roses, something glistening like gold. "Do you see that? What is it?" Xiangyun asked pointing at it.

Hearing this, Cuilu hastily went over and picked up the object. While scrutinising it, she observed with a smile, "Let us find out whether it's Yin or Yang!"

So saying, she first laid hold of the unicorn, belonging to Shi Xiangyun, and passed it under inspection.

Shi Xiangyun longed to be shown what she had picked up, but Cuilu would not open her hand.

"It's a precious gem," she smiled. "You mayn't see it, Miss. Where can it be from? How very strange it is! I've never seen anyone in here with anything of the kind."

"Give it to me and let me look at it," retorted Xiangyun.

Cuilu stretched out her hand with a dash. "Yes, Miss, please look at it!" she laughed.

Xiangyun raised her eyes. She perceived, at a glance, that it was a golden unicorn, so beautiful and so bright; and so much larger and handsomer than the one she had on. Xiangyun put out her arm and, taking the gem in the palm of her hand, she fell into a silent reverie and uttered not a word. She was quite absent-minded when suddenly Baoyu appeared in the opposite direction.

"What are you two," he asked smiling, "doing here in the sun? How is it you don't go and find Xiren?"

Shi Xiangyun precipitately concealed the unicorn. "We were just going," she replied, "so let us all go together."

Conversing, they, in a company, wended their steps into the Yihong court. Xiren was leaning on the balustrade at the bottom of the steps, her face turned to the breeze. Upon unexpectedly seeing Xiangyun arrive she with alacrity rushed down to greet her; and taking her hand in hers, they cheerfully canvassed the events that had transpired during their separation, while they entered the room and took a seat.

"You should have come earlier," Baoyu said. "I've got something nice and was only waiting for you."

Saying this, he searched and searched about his person. After a long interval, "Ai-ya!" he ejaculated. "Have you perchance put that thing away?" he eagerly asked Xiren.

"What thing?" inquired Xiren.

"The unicorn," explained Baoyu, "I got the other day."

"You've daily worn it about you, and how is it you ask me?" remarked Xiren.

As soon as her answer fell on his ear, Baoyu clapped his hands. "I've lost it!" he cried. "Where can I go and look for it!" There and then, he meant to go and search in person; but Shi Xiangyun heard his inquiries, and concluded that it must be he who had lost the gem. "When did you too," she promptly smiled, "get a unicorn?"

"I got it the other day, after ever so much trouble;" rejoined Baoyu, "but I can't make out when I can have lost it! I've also become quite addle-headed."

"Fortunately," smiled Shi Xiangyun, "it's only a sort of a toy! Still, are you so careless?" While speaking, she flung open her hand. "Just see," she laughed, "is it this or not?"

As soon as he saw it, Baoyu was seized with unwonted delight. But, reader, if you care to know the cause of his delight, peruse the explanation contained in the next chapter.

CHAPTER 32

Xiren and Xiangyun tell their secret thoughts. Daiyu is infatuated with the living Baoyu. While trying to conceal her sense of shame and injury Jinchuan is driven by her impetuous feelings to seek death.

But to resume our narrative, at the sight of the unicorn, Baoyu was filled with intense delight. So much so, that he forthwith put out his hand and made a grab for it. "Lucky enough it was you who picked it up!" he said, with a face beaming with smiles. "But when did you find it?"

"Fortunately it was only this!" rejoined Shi Xiangyun laughing. "If you by and bye also lose your seal, will you likely banish it at once from your mind, and never make an effort to discover it?"

"After all," smiled Baoyu, "the loss of a seal is an ordinary occurrence. But had I lost this, I would have deserved to die."

Xiren then poured a cup of tea and handed it to Shi Xiangyun. "Miss Senior," she remarked smilingly, "I heard that you had occasion the other day to be highly pleased."

Shi Xiangyun flushed crimson. She went on drinking her tea and did not utter a single word.

"Here you are again full of shame!" Xiren smiled. "But do you remember when we were living, about ten years back, in those warm rooms on the west side and you confided in me one evening, you didn't feel any shame then; and how is it you blush like this now?"

"Do you still speak about that!" exclaimed Shi Xiangyun laughingly. "You and I were then great friends. But when our mother subsequently died and I went home for a while, how is it you were at once sent to be with my cousin Secundus, and that now that I've come back you don't treat me as you did once?"

"Are you yet harping on this!" retorted Xiren, putting on a smile. "Why, at first, you used to coax me with a lot of endearing terms to comb your hair and to wash your face, to do this and that for you. But now that you've become a big girl, you assume the manner of a young mistress towards me, and as you put on these airs of a young mistress, how can I ever presume to be on a familiar footing with you?"

"Amituo Fo," cried Shi Xiangyun. "What a false accusation! If I be guilty of anything of the kind, may I at once die! Just see what a broiling hot day this is, and yet as soon as I arrived I felt bound to come and look you up first. If you don't believe me, well, ask Lu'er! And while at home, when did I not at every instant say something about you?"

Scarcely had she concluded than Xiren and Baoyu tried to soothe her. "We were only joking," they said, "but you've taken everything again as gospel. What! are you still so impetuous in your temperament!"

"You don't say," argued Shi Xiangyun, "that your words are hard things to swallow, but contrariwise, call people's temperaments impetuous!"

As she spoke, she unfolded her handkerchief and, producing a ring, she gave it to Xiren.

Xiren did not know how to thank her enough. "When," she consequently smiled, "you sent those to your cousin the other day, I got one also; and here you yourself bring me another today! It's clear enough therefore that you haven't forgotten me. This alone has been quite enough to test you. As for the ring itself, what is its worth? but it's a token of the sincerity of your heart!"

"Who gave it to you?" inquired Shi Xiangyun.

"Miss Bao let me have it," replied Xiren.

"I was under the impression," remarked Xiangyun with a sigh, "that it was a present from cousin Lin. But is it really cousin Bao, that gave it to you! When I was at home, I day after day found myself reflecting that among all these cousins of mine, there wasn't one able to compare with cousin Bao, so excellent is she. How I do regret that we are not the offspring of one mother! For could I boast of such a sister of the same flesh and blood as myself, it wouldn't matter though I had lost both father and mother!"

While indulging in these regrets, her eyes got quite red.

"Never mind! never mind!" interposed Baoyu. "Why need you speak of these things!"

"If I do allude to this," answered Shi Xiangyun, "what does it matter? I know that weak point of yours. You're in fear and trembling lest your cousin Lin should come to hear what I say, and get angry with me again for eulogizing cousin Bao! Now isn't it this, eh!"

"Chi!" laughed Xiren, who was standing by her. "Miss Yun," she said, "now that you've grown up to be a big girl you've become more than ever openhearted and outspoken."

"When I contend," smiled Baoyu, "that it is difficult to say a word to any one of you I'm indeed perfectly correct!"

"My dear cousin," observed Shi Xiangyun laughingly, "don't go on in that strain! You'll provoke me to displeasure. When you are with me all you are good for is to talk and talk away; but were you to catch a glimpse of cousin Lin, you would once more be quite at a loss to know what best to do!"

"Now, enough of your jokes!" urged Xiren. "I have a favor to crave of you."

"What is it?" vehemently inquired Shi Xiangyun.

"I've got a pair of shoes," answered Xiren, "for which I've stuck the padding together; but I'm not feeling up to the mark these last few days, so I haven't been able to work at them. If you have any leisure, do finish them for me."

"This is indeed strange!" exclaimed Shi Xiangyun. "Putting aside all the skilful workers engaged in your household, you have besides some people for doing needlework and others for tailoring and cutting; and how is it you appeal to me to take your shoes in hand? Were you to ask any one of those men to execute your work, who could very well refuse to do it?"

"Here you are in another stupid mood!" laughed Xiren. "Can it be that you don't know that our sewing in these quarters mayn't be done by these needleworkers."

At this reply, it at once dawned upon Shi Xiangyun that the shoes must be intended for Baoyu. "Since that be the case," she in consequence smiled; "I'll work them for you. There's however one thing. I'll readily attend to any of yours, but I will have nothing to do with any for other people."

"There you are again!" laughed Xiren. "Who am I to venture to trouble you to make shoes for me? I'll tell you plainly, however, that they are not mine. But no matter whose they are, it is anyhow I who'll be the recipient of your favor; that is sufficient."

"To speak the truth," rejoined Shi Xiangyun, "you've put me to the trouble of working, I don't know how many things for you. The reason why I refuse on this occasion should be quite evident to you!"

"I can't nevertheless make it out!" answered Xiren.

"I heard the other day," continued Shi Xiangyun, a sardonic smile on her lip, "that while the fan-case, I had worked, was being held and compared with that of someone else, it too was slashed away in a fit of high dudgeon. This reached my ears long ago, and do you still try to dupe me by asking me again now to make something more for you? Have I really become a slave to you people?

"As to what occurred the other day," hastily explained Baoyu smiling, "I positively had no idea that that thing was your handiwork."

"He never knew that you'd done it," Xiren also laughed. "I deceived him by telling him that there had been of late some capital hands at needlework outside, who could execute any embroidery with surpassing beauty, and that I had asked them to bring a fan-case so as to try them and to see whether they could actually work well or not. He at once believed what I said. But as he produced the case and gave it to this one and that one to look at, he somehow or other, I don't know how, managed again to put someone's back up, and she cut it into two. On his return, however, he bade me hurry the men to make another; and when at length I explained to him that it had been worked by you, he felt, I can't tell you, what keen regret!"

"This is getting stranger and stranger!" said Shi Xiangyun. "It wasn't worth the while for Miss Lin to lose her temper about it. But as she plies the scissors so admirably, why, you might as well tell her to finish the shoes for you."

"She couldn't," replied Xiren, "for besides other things our venerable lady is still in fear and trembling lest she should tire herself in any way. The doctor likewise says that she will continue to enjoy good health, so long as she is carefully looked after; so who would wish to ask her to take them in hand? Last year she managed to just get through a scented bag, after a whole year's work. But here we've already reached the middle of the present year, and she hasn't yet taken up any needle or thread!"

In the course of their conversation, a servant came and announced that the gentleman who lived in the Xing Lung Street had come. "Our master," he added, "bids you, Mr. Secundus, come out and greet him."

As soon as Baoyu heard this announcement, he knew that Jia Yucun must have arrived. But he felt very unhappy at heart. Xiren hurried to go and bring his clothes. Baoyu, meanwhile, put on his boots, but as he did so, he gave way to resentment. "Why there's father," he soliloquized, "to sit with him; that should be enough; and must he, on every visit he pays, insist upon seeing me!"

"It is, of course, because you have such a knack for receiving and entertaining visitors that Mr. Jia Zheng will have you go out," laughingly interposed Shi Xiangyun from one side, as she waved her fan.

"Is it father's doing?" Baoyu rejoined. "Why, it's he himself who asks that I should be sent for to see him."

"'When a host is courteous, visitors come often,'" smiled Xiangyun, "so it's surely because you possess certain qualities, which have won his regard, that he insists upon seeing you."

"But I am not what one would call courteous," demurred Baoyu. "I am, of all coarse people, the coarsest. Besides, I do not choose to have any relations with such people as himself."

"Here's again that unchangeable temperament of yours!" laughed Xiangyun. "But you're a big fellow now, and you should at least, if you be loath to study and go and pass your examinations for a provincial graduate or a metropolitan graduate, have frequent intercourse with officers and ministers of state and discuss those varied attainments, which one acquires in an official career, so that you also may be able in time to have some idea about matters in general; and that when by and bye you've made friends, they may not see you spending the whole day long in doing nothing than loafing in our midst, up to every imaginable mischief."

"Miss," exclaimed Baoyu, after this harangue, "pray go and sit in some other girl's room, for mind one like myself may contaminate a person who knows so much of attainments and experience as you do."

"Miss," ventured Xiren, "drop this at once! Last time Miss Bao too tendered him this advice, but without troubling himself as to whether people would feel uneasy or not, he simply came out with an ejaculation of 'hai,' and rushed out of the place. Miss Bao hadn't meanwhile concluded her say, so when she saw him fly, she got so full of shame that, flushing scarlet, she could neither open her lips, nor hold her own counsel. But lucky for him it was only Miss Bao. Had it been Miss Lin, there's no saying what row there may not have been again, and what tears may not have been shed! Yet the very mention of all she had to tell him is enough to make people look up to Miss Bao with respect. But after a time, she also betook herself away. I then felt very unhappy as I imagined that she was angry; but contrary to all my expectations, she was by and bye just the same as ever. She is, in very truth, long-suffering and indulgent! This other party contrariwise became quite distant to her, little though one would have thought it of him; and as Miss Bao perceived that he had lost his temper, and didn't choose to heed her, she subsequently made I don't know how many apologies to him."

"Did Miss Lin ever talk such trash!" exclaimed Baoyu. "Had she ever talked such stuff and nonsense, I would have long ago become chilled towards her."

"What you say is all trash!" Xiren and Xiangyun remarked with one voice, while they shook their heads to and fro and smiled.

Lin Daiyu, the fact is, was well aware that now that Shi Xiangyun was staying in the mansion, Baoyu too was certain to hasten to come and tell her all about the unicorn he had got, so she thought to herself: "In the foreign traditions and wild stories, introduced here of late by Baoyu, literary persons and pretty girls are, for the most part, brought together in marriage, through the agency of some trifling but ingenious nick-nack. These people either have miniature ducks, or phoenixes, jade necklets, or gold pendants, fine handkerchiefs or elegant sashes; and they have, through the instrumentality of such trivial objects, invariably succeeded in accomplishing the wishes they entertained throughout their lives." When she recently discovered, by some unforeseen way, that Baoyu had likewise a unicorn she began to apprehend lest he should make this circumstance a pretext to create an estrangement with her, and indulge with Shi Xiangyun as well in various free and easy flirtations and fine doings. She therefore quietly crossed over to watch her opportunity and take such action as would enable her to get an insight into his and her sentiments. Contrary, however, to all her calculations, no sooner did she reach her destination, than she overheard Shi Xiangyun dilate on the topic of experience, and Baoyu go on to observe: "Cousin Lin has never indulged in such stuff and nonsense. Had she ever uttered any such trash, I would have become chilled even towards her!" This language suddenly produced, in Lin Daiyu's mind, both surprise as well as delight; sadness as well as regret. Delight, at having indeed been so correct in her perception that he whom she had ever considered in the light of a true friend had actually turned out to be a true friend. Surprise, "because," she said to herself: "he has, in the presence of so many witnesses, displayed such partiality as to speak in my praise, and has shown such affection and friendliness for me as to make no attempt whatever to shirk suspicion." Regret, "for since," (she pondered), "you are my intimate friend, you could certainly well look upon me too as your intimate friend; and if you and I be real friends, why need there be any more talk about gold and jade? But since there be that question of gold and jade, you and I should have such things in our possession. Yet, why should this Baochai step in again between us?" Sad, "because," (she reflected), "my father and mother departed life at an early period; and because I have, in spite of the secret engraven on my heart and imprinted on my bones, not a soul to act as a mentor to me. Besides, of late, I continuously feel confusion creep over my mind, so my disease must already have gradually developed itself. The doctors further state that my breath is weak and my blood poor, and that they dread lest consumption should declare itself, so despite that sincere friendship I foster for you, I cannot, I fear, last for very long. You are, I admit, a true friend to me, but what can you do for my unfortunate destiny!"

Upon reaching this point in her reflections, she could not control her tears, and they rolled freely down her cheeks. So much so, that when about to enter and meet her cousins, she experienced such utter lack of zest, that, while drying her tears she turned round, and wended her steps back in the direction of her apartments.

Baoyu, meanwhile, had hurriedly got into his new costume. Upon coming out of doors, he caught sight of Lin Daiyu, walking quietly ahead of him engaged, to all appearances, in wiping tears from her eyes. With rapid stride, he overtook her.

"Cousin Lin," be smiled, "where are you off to? How is it that you're crying again? Who has once more hurt your feelings?"

Lin Daiyu turned her head round to look; and seeing that it was Baoyu, she at once forced a smile. "Why should I be crying," she replied, "when there is no reason to do so?"

"Look here!" observed Baoyu smilingly. "The tears in your eyes are not dry yet and do you still tell me a fib?"

Saying this, he could not check an impulse to raise his arm and wipe her eyes, but Lin Daiyu speedily withdrew several steps backwards. "Are you again bent," she said, "upon compassing your own death! Then why do you knock your hands and kick your feet about in this wise?"

"While intent upon speaking, I forgot," smiled Baoyu, "all about propriety and gesticulated, yet quite inadvertently. But what care I whether I die or live!"

"To die would, after all" added Lin Daiyu, "be for you of no matter; but you'll leave behind some gold or other, and a unicorn too or other; and what would they do?"

This insinuation was enough to plunge Baoyu into a fresh fit of exasperation. Hastening up to her: "Do you still give vent to such language?" he asked. "Why, it's really tantamount to invoking imprecations on me! What, are you yet angry with me!"

This question recalled to Lin Daiyu's mind the incidents of a few days back, and a pang of remorse immediately gnawed her heart for having been again so indiscreet in her speech. "Now don't you distress your mind!" she observed hastily, smiling. "I verily said what I shouldn't! Yet what is there in this to make your veins protrude, and to so provoke you as to bedew your whole face with perspiration?"

While reasoning with him, she felt unable to repress herself, and, approaching him, she extended her hand, and wiped the perspiration from his face.

Baoyu gazed intently at her for a long time. "Do set your mind at ease!" he at length observed.

At this remark, Lin Daiyu felt quite nervous. "What's there to make my mind uneasy?" she asked after a protracted interval. "I can't make out what you're driving at; tell me what's this about making me easy or uneasy?"

Baoyu heaved a sigh. "Don't you truly fathom the depth of my words?" he inquired. "Why, do you mean to say that I've throughout made such poor use of my love for you as not to be able to even divine your feel-ings? Well, if so, it's no wonder that you daily lose your temper on my account!"

"I actually don't understand what you mean by easy or uneasy," Lin Daiyu replied.

"My dear girl," urged Baoyu, nodding and sighing. "Don't be mak-ing a fool of me! For if you can't make out these words, not only have I ever uselessly lavished affection upon you, but the regard, with which you have always treated me, has likewise been entirely of no avail! And it's mostly because you won't set your mind at ease that your whole frame is riddled with disease. Had you taken things easier a bit, this ailment of yours too wouldn't have grown worse from day to day!"

These words made Lin Daiyu feel as if she had been blasted by thun-der, or struck by lightning. But after carefully weighing them within herself, they seemed to her far more fervent than any that might have emanated from the depths of her own heart, and thousands of senti-ments, in fact, thronged together in her mind; but though she had every wish to frame them into language, she found it a hard task to pronounce so much as half a word. All she therefore did was to gaze at him with vacant stare.

Baoyu fostered innumerable thoughts within himself, but unable in a moment to resolve from which particular one to begin, he too ab-sently looked at Daiyu. Thus it was that the two cousins remained for a long time under the spell of a deep reverie.

An ejaculation of "Hai!" was the only sound that issued from Lin Daiyu's lips; and while tears streamed suddenly from her eyes, she turned herself round and started on her way homeward.

Baoyu jumped forward, with alacrity, and dragged her back. "My dear cousin," he pleaded, "do stop a bit! Let me tell you just one thing; after that, you may go."

"What can you have to tell me?" exclaimed Lin Daiyu, who while wiping her tears, extricated her hand from his grasp. "I know," she cried, "all you have to say."

As she spoke, she went away, without even turning her head to cast a glance behind her.

As Baoyu gazed at her receding figure, he fell into abstraction.

He had, in fact, quitted his apartments a few moments back in such precipitate hurry that he had omitted to take a fan with him and Xi-ren, fearing lest he might suffer from the heat, promptly seized one and ran to find him and give it to him. But upon casually raising her head, she espied Lin Daiyui standing with him. After a time, Daiyu walked away; and as he still remained where he was without budging, she approached him.

"You left," she said, "without even taking a fan with you. Happily I noticed it, and so hurried to catch you up and bring it to you."

But Baoyu was so lost in thought that as soon as he caught Xiren's voice, he made a dash and clasped her in his embrace, without so much as trying to make sure who she was.

"My dear cousin," he cried, "I couldn't hitherto muster enough courage to disclose the secrets of my heart; but on this occasion I shall make bold and give utterance to them. For you I'm quite ready to even pay the penalty of death. I have too for your sake brought ailments upon my whole frame. It's in here! But I haven't ventured to breathe it to any one. My only alternative has been to bear it patiently, in the hope that when you got all right, I might then perchance also recover. But whether I sleep, or whether I dream, I never, never forget you."

These declarations quite dumfoundered Xiren. She gave way to incessant apprehensions. All she could do was to shout out: "Oh spirits, oh heaven, oh Buddha, he's compassing my death!" Then pushing him away from her, "what is it you're saying?" she asked. "May it be that you are possessed by some evil spirit! Don't you quick get yourself off?"

This brought Baoyu to his senses at once. He then became aware that it was Xiren, and that she had come to bring him a fan. Baoyu was overpowered with shame; his whole face was suffused with scarlet; and, snatching the fan out of her hands, he bolted away with rapid stride.

When Xiren meanwhile saw Baoyu effect his escape, "Lin Daiyu," she pondered, "must surely be at the bottom of all he said just now. But from what one can see, it will be difficult, in the future, to obviate the occurrence of some unpleasant mishap. It's sufficient to fill one with fear and trembling!"

At this point in her cogitations, she involuntarily melted into tears, so agitated was she; while she secretly exercised her mind how best to act so as to prevent this dreadful calamity.

But while she was lost in this maze of surmises and doubts, Baochai unexpectedly appeared from the off side. "What!" she smilingly exclaimed, "are you dreaming away in a hot broiling sun like this?"

Xiren, at this question, hastily returned her smiles. "Those two birds," she answered, "were having a fight, and such fun was it that I stopped to watch them."

"Where is cousin Bao off to now in such a hurry, got up in that fine attire?" asked Baochai, "I just caught sight of him, as he went by. I meant to have called out and stopped him, but as he, of late, talks greater rubbish than ever, I didn't challenge him, but let him go past."

"Our master," rejoined Xiren, "sent for him to go out."

"Ai-ya!" hastily exclaimed Baochai, as soon as this remark reached her ears. "What does he want him for, on a scalding day like this? Might he not have thought of something and got so angry about it as to send for him to give him a lecture!"

"If it isn't this," added Xiren laughing, "some visitor must, I presume, have come and he wishes him to meet him."

"With weather like this," smiled Baochai, "even visitors afford no amusement! Why don't they, while this fiery temperature lasts, stay at home, where it's much cooler, instead of gadding about all over the place?"

"Could you tell them so?" smiled Xiren.

"What was that girl Xiangyun doing in your quarters?" Baochai then asked.

"She only came to chat with us on irrelevant matters." Xiren replied smiling. "But did you see the pair of shoes I was pasting the other day? Well, I meant to ask her tomorrow to finish them for me."

Baochai, at these words, turned her head round, first on this side, and then on the other. Seeing that there was no one coming or going: "How is it," she smiled, "that you, who have so much gumption, don't ever show any respect for people's feelings? I've been of late keeping an eye on Miss Yun's manner, and, from what I can glean from the various rumors afloat, she can't be, in the slightest degree, her own mistress at home! In that family of theirs, so little can they stand the burden of any heavy expenses that they don't employ any needlework-people, and ordinary everyday things are mostly attended to by their ladies themselves. (If not), why is it that every time she has come to us on a visit, and she and I have had a chat, she at once broached the subject of their being in great difficulties at home, the moment she perceived that there was no one present? Yet, whenever I went on to ask her a few questions about their usual way of living, her very eyes grew red, while she made some indistinct reply; but as for speaking out, she wouldn't. But when I consider the circumstances in which she is placed, for she has certainly had the misfortune of being left, from her very infancy, without father and mother, the very sight of her is too much for me, and my heart begins to bleed within me."

"Quite so! Quite so!" observed Xiren, clapping her hands, after listening to her throughout. "It isn't strange then if she let me have the ten butterfly knots I asked her to tie for me only after ever so many days, and if she said that they were coarsely done, but that I should make the best of them and use them elsewhere, and that if I wanted any nice ones, I should wait until by and bye when she came to stay here, when she would work some neatly for me. What you've told me now reminds me that, as she had found it difficult to find an excuse when we appealed to her, she must have had to slave away, who knows how much, till the third watch in the middle of the night. What a stupid thing I was! Had I known this sooner, I would never have told her a word about it."

"Last time," continued Baochai, "she told me that when she was at home she had ample to do, that she kept busy as late as the third watch, and that, if she did the slightest stitch of work for any other people, the various ladies belonging to her family, did not like it."

"But as it happens," explained Xiren, "that mulish-minded and perverse-tempered young master of ours won't allow the least bit of needlework, no matter whether small or large, to be made by those persons employed to do sewing in the household. And as for me, I have no time to turn my attention to all these things."

Why mind him?" laughed Baochai. "Simply ask someone to do the work and finish."

How could one bamboozle him?" resumed Xiren. "Why, he'll promptly find out everything. Such a thing can't even be suggested. The only thing I can do is to quietly slave away, that's all."

"You shouldn't work so hard," smiled Baochai. "What do you say to my doing a few things for you?"

"Are you in real earnest!" ventured Xiren smiling. "Well, in that case, it is indeed a piece of good fortune for me! I'll come over myself in the evening."

But before she could conclude her reply, she of a sudden noticed an old matron come up to her with precipitate step. "Where does the report come from," she interposed, "that Miss Jinchuan'er has gone, for no rhyme or reason, and committed suicide by jumping into the well?"

This bit of news startled Xiren. "Which Jinchuan'er is it," she speedily inquired.

"Where are two Jinchuan'ers to be found!" rejoined the old matron. "It's the one in our Mistress' Madame Wang's, apartments, who was the other day sent away for something or other, I don't know what. On her return home, she raised her groans to the skies and shed profuse tears, but none of them worried their minds about her, until, who'd have thought it, they could see nothing of her. A servant, however, went just now to draw water and he says that while he was getting it from the well in the southeast corner, he caught sight of a dead body, that he hurriedly called men to his help, and that when they fished it out, they unexpectedly found that it was she, but that though they bustled about trying to bring her round, everything proved of no avail."

"This is odd!" Baochai exclaimed.

The moment Xiren heard the tidings, she shook her head and moaned. At the remembrance of the friendship, which had ever existed between them, tears suddenly trickled down her cheeks. And as for Baochai, she listened to the account of the accident and then hastened to Madame Wang's quarters to try and afford her consolation.

Xiren, during this interval, returned to her room. But we will leave her without further notice, and explain that when Baochai reached the interior of Madame Wang's home, she found everything plunged in perfect stillness. Madame Wang was seated all alone in the inner chamber indulging her sorrow. But such difficulties did Baochai experience to allude to the occurrence, that her only alternative was to take a seat next to her.

"Where do you come from?" asked Madame Wang.

"I come from inside the garden," answered Baochai.

"As you come from the garden," Madame Wang inquired, "did you see anything of your cousin Baoyu?"

"I saw him just now," Baochai replied, "go out, dressed up in his fineries. But where he is gone to, I don't know."

"Have you perchance heard of any strange occurrence?" asked Madame Wang, while she nodded her head and sighed. "Why, Jinchuan'er jumped into the well and committed suicide."

"How is it that she jumped into the well when there was nothing to make her do so?" Baochai inquired. "This is indeed a remarkable thing!"

"The fact is," proceeded Madame Wang, "that she spoilt something the other day, and in a sudden fit of temper, I gave her a slap and sent her away, simply meaning to be angry with her for a few days and then bring her in again. But, who could have ever imagined that she had such a resentful temperament as to go and drown herself in a well! And is not this all my fault?"

"It's because you are such a kind-hearted person, aunt," smiled Baochai, "that such ideas cross your mind! But she didn't jump into the well when she was in a tantrum; so what must have made her do so was that she had to go and live in the lower quarters. Or, she might have been standing in front of the well, and her foot slipped, and she fell into it. While in the upper rooms, she used to be kept under restraint, so when this time she found herself outside, she must, of course, have felt the wish to go strolling all over the place in search of fun. How could she have ever had such a fiery disposition? But even admitting that she had such a temper, she was, after all, a stupid girl to do as she did; and she doesn't deserve any pity."

"In spite of what you say," sighed Madame Wang, shaking her head to and fro, "I really feel unhappy at heart."

"You shouldn't, aunt, distress your mind about it!" Baochai smiled. "Yet, if you feel very much exercised, just give her a few more taels than you would otherwise have done, and let her be buried. You'll thus carry out to the full the feelings of a mistress towards her servant."

"I just now gave them fifty taels for her," pursued Madame Wang. "I also meant to let them have some of your cousin's new clothes to enshroud her in. But, who'd have thought it, none of the girls had, strange coincidence, any newly-made articles of clothing; and there were only that couple of birthday suits of your cousin Lin's. But as your cousin Lin has ever been such a sensitive child and has always too suffered and ailed, I thought it would be unpropitious for her, if her clothes were also now handed to people to wrap their dead in, after she had been told that they were given her for her birthday. So I ordered a tailor to get a suit for her as soon as possible. Had it been any other servant-girl, I could have given her a few taels and have finished. But Jinchuan'er was, albeit a servant-maid, nearly as dear to me as if she had been a daughter of mine."

Saying this, tears unwittingly ran down from her eyes.

"Aunt!" vehemently exclaimed Baochai. "What earthly use is it of hurrying a tailor just now to prepare clothes for her? I have a couple of suits I made the other day and won't it save trouble were I to go and bring them for her? Besides, when she was alive, she used to wear my old clothes. And what's more our figures are much alike."

"What you say is all very well," rejoined Madame Wang; "but can it be that it isn't distasteful to you?"

"Compose your mind," urged Baochai with a smile. "I have never paid any heed to such things."

As she spoke, she rose to her feet and walked away.

Madame Wang then promptly called two servants. "Go and accompany Miss Bao!" she said.

In a brief space of time, Baochai came back with the clothes, and discovered Baoyu seated next to Madame Wang, all melted in tears. Madame Wang was reasoning with him. At the sight of Baochai, she, at once, desisted. When Baochai saw them go on in this way, and came to weigh their conversation and to scan the expression on their countenances, she immediately got a pretty correct insight into their feelings. But presently she handed over the clothes, and Madame Wang sent for Jinchuan'er's mother, to take them away.

But, reader, you will have to peruse the next chapter for further details.

CHAPTER 33

A brother is prompted by ill-feeling to wag his tongue a bit. A depraved son receives heavy blows with a rattan cane.

Madame Wang, for we shall now continue our story, sent for Jin-chuan'er's mother. On her arrival, she gave her several hair-pins and rings, and then told her that she could invite several Buddhist priests as well to read the prayers necessary to release the spirit from purgatory. The mother prostrated herself and expressed her gratitude; after which, she took her leave.

Indeed, Baoyu, on his return from entertaining Yucun, heard the tidings that Jinchuan'er had been instigated by a sense of shame to take her own life and he at once fell a prey to grief. So much so, that, when he came inside, and was again spoken to and admonished by Madame Wang, he could not utter a single word in his justification. But as soon as he perceived Baochai make her appearance in the room, he seized the opportunity to scamper out in precipitate haste. Whither he was trudging, he himself had not the least idea. But throwing his hands behind his back and drooping his head against his chest, he gave way to sighs, while with slow and listless step he turned towards the hall. Scarcely, however, had he rounded the screen-wall, which stood in front of the doorway, when, by a strange coincidence, he ran straight into the arms of someone, who was unawares approaching from the opposite direction, and was just about to go towards the inner portion of the compound.

"Hallo!" that person was heard to cry out, as he stood still.

Baoyu sustained a dreadful start. Raising his face to see, he discovered that it was no other than his father. At once, he unconsciously drew a long breath and adopted the only safe course of dropping his arms against his body and standing on one side.

"Why are you," exclaimed Jia Zheng, "drooping your head in such a melancholy mood, and indulging in all these moans? When Yucun came just now and he asked to see you, you only put in your appearance after a long while. But though you did come, you were not in the least disposed to chat with anything like cheerfulness and animation;

you behaved, as you ever do, like a regular fool. I detected then in your countenance a certain expression of some hidden hankering and sadness; and now again here you are groaning and sighing! Does all you have not suffice to please you? Are you still dissatisfied? You've no reason to be like this, so why is it that you go on in this way?"

Baoyu had ever, it is true, shown a glib tongue, but on the present occasion he was so deeply affected by Jinchuan'er's fate, and vexed at not being able to die that very instant and follow in her footsteps that although he was now fully conscious that his father was speaking to him he could not, in fact, lend him an ear, but simply stood in a timid and nervous mood. Jia Zheng noticed that he was in a state of trembling and fear, not as ready with an answer as he usually was, and his sorry plight somewhat incensed him, much though he had not at first borne him any ill-feeling. But just as he was about to chide him, a messenger approached and announced to him: "Someone has come from the mansion of the imperial Prince Zhongshun, and wishes to see you, Sir." At this announcement, surmises sprung up in Jia Zheng's mind. "Hitherto," he secretly mused, "I've never had any dealings with the Zhongshun mansion, and why is it that someone is despatched here today?" As he gave way to these reflections. "Be quick," he shouted, "and ask him to take a seat in the pavilion," while he himself precipitately entered the inner room and changed his costume. When he came out to greet the visitor, he discovered that it was the senior officer of the Zhongshun mansion. After the exchange of the salutations prescribed by the rites, they sat down and tea was presented. But before (Jia Zheng) had time to start a topic of conversation, the senior officer anticipated him, and speedily observed: "Your humble servant does not pay this visit today to your worthy mansion on his own authority, but entirely in compliance with instructions received, as there is a favor that I have to beg of you. I make bold to trouble you, esteemed Sir, on behalf of his highness, to take any steps you might deem suitable, and if you do, not only will his highness remember your kindness, but even I, your humble servant, and my colleagues will feel extremely grateful to you."

Jia Zheng listened to him, but he could not nevertheless get a clue of what he was driving at. Promptly returning his smile, he rose to his feet. "You come, Sir," he inquired, "at the instance of his royal highness, but what, I wonder, are the commands you have to give me? I hope you will explain them to your humble servant, worthy Sir, in order to enable him to carry them out effectively."

The senior officer gave a sardonic smile.

"There's nothing to carry out," he said. "All you, venerable Sir, have to do is to utter one single word and the whole thing will be effected. There is in our mansion a certain Qiguan, who plays the part of young ladies. He hitherto stayed quietly in the mansion; but for the last three or five days or so no one has seen him return home. Search has been instituted in every locality, yet his whereabouts cannot be discovered. But throughout these various inquiries, eight out of the ten-tenths of the inhabitants of the city have, with one consent, asserted that he has of late been on very friendly terms with that honorable son of yours, who was born with the jade in his mouth. This report was told your servant and his colleagues, but as your worthy mansion is unlike such residences as we can take upon ourselves to enter and search with impunity, we felt under the necessity of laying the matter before our imperial master. 'Had it been any of the other actors,' his highness also says, 'I wouldn't have minded if even one hundred of them had disappeared; but this Qiguan has always been so ready with pat repartee, so respectful and trustworthy that he has thoroughly won my aged heart, and I could never do without him.' He entreats you, therefore, worthy Sir, to, in your turn, plead with your illustrious scion, and request him to let Qiguan go back, in order that the feelings, which prompt the Prince to make such earnest supplications, may, in the first place, be satisfied: and that, in the next, your mean servant and his associates may be spared the fatigue of toiling and searching."

At the conclusion of this appeal, he promptly made a low bow. As soon as Jia Zheng found out the object of his errand, he felt both astonishment and displeasure. With all promptitude, he issued directions that Baoyu should be told to come out of the garden. Baoyu had no notion whatever why he was wanted. So speedily he hurried to appear before his father.

"What a regular scoundrel you are!" Jia Zheng exclaimed. "It is enough that you won't read your books at home; but will you also go in for all these lawless and wrongful acts? That Qiguan is a person whose present honorable duties are to act as an attendant on his highness the Prince of Zhongshun, and how extremely heedless of propriety must you be to have enticed him, without good cause, to come away, and thus have now brought calamity upon me?"

These reproaches plunged Baoyu in a dreadful state of consternation. With alacrity he said by way of reply: "I really don't know anything about the matter! To what do, after all, the two words Qiguan refer, I wonder! Still less, besides, am I aware what entice can imply!"

As he spoke, he started crying.

But before Jia Zheng could open his month to pass any further remarks, "Young gentleman," he heard the senior officer interpose with a sardonic smile: "you shouldn't conceal anything! if he be either hidden in your home, or if you know his whereabouts, divulge the truth at once; so that less trouble should fall to our lot than otherwise would. And will we not then bear in mind your virtue, worthy scion!"

"I positively don't know. " Baoyu time after time maintained. "There must, I fear, be some false rumor abroad; for I haven't so much as seen anything of him."

The senior officer gave two loud smiles, full of derision. "There's evidence at hand," he rejoined, "so if you compel me to speak out before your venerable father, won't you, young man, have to suffer the consequences? But as you assert that you don't know who this person is, how is it that that red sash has come to be attached to your waist?"

When Baoyu caught this allusion, he suddenly felt quite out of his senses. He stared and gaped; while within himself, he argued: "How has he come to hear anything about this! But since he knows all these secret particulars, I cannot, I expect, put him off in other points; so wouldn't it be better for me to pack him off, in order to obviate his blubbering anything more?" "Sir," he consequently remarked aloud, "how is it that despite your acquaintance with all these minute details, you have no inkling of his having purchased a house? Are you ignorant of an essential point like this? I've heard people say that he's, at present, staying in the eastern suburbs at a distance of twenty li from the city walls; at some place or other called Zitan Bao, and that he has bought there several acres of land and a few houses. So I presume he's to be found in that locality; but of course there's no saying."

"According to your version," smiled the senior officer, as soon as he heard his explanation, "he must for a certainty be there. I shall therefore go and look for him. If he's there, well and good; but if not, I shall come again and request you to give me further directions."

These words were still on his lips, when he took his leave and walked off with hurried step.

Jia Zheng was by this time stirred up to such a pitch of indignation that his eyes stared aghast, and his mouth opened in bewilderment; and as he escorted the officer out, he turned his head and bade Baoyu not budge. "I have," (he said,) "to ask you something on my return." Straightway he then went to see the officer off. But just as he was turning back, he casually came across Jia Huan and several servant-boys running wildly about in a body. "Quick, bring him here to me!" shouted Jia Zheng to the young boys. "I want to beat him."

Jia Huan, at the sight of his father, was so terrified that his bones mollified and his tendons grew weak, and, promptly lowering his head, he stood still.

"What are you running about for?" Jia Zheng asked. "These menials of yours do not mind you, but go who knows where, and let you roam about like a wild horse! Where are the attendants who wait on you at school?" he cried.

When Jia Huan saw his father in such a dreadful rage, he availed himself of the first opportunity to try and clear himself. "I wasn't running about just now" he said. "But as I was passing by the side of that well, I caught sight, for in that well a servant-girl was drowned, of a human head that large, a body that swollen, floating about in really a frightful way and I therefore hastily rushed past."

Jia Zheng was thunderstruck by this disclosure. "There's been nothing up, so who has gone and jumped into the well?" he inquired. "Never has there been anything of the kind in my house before! Ever since the time of our ancestors, servants have invariably been treated with clemency and consideration. But I expect that I must of late have become remiss in my domestic affairs, and that the managers must have arrogated to themselves the right of domineering and so been the cause of bringing about such calamities as violent deaths and disregard of life. Were these things to reach the ears of people outside, what will become of the reputation of our seniors? Call Jia Lian and Lai Da here!" he shouted.

The servant-lads signified their obedience with one voice. They were about to go and summon them, when Jia Huan hastened to press forward. Grasping the lapel of Jia Zheng's coat, and clinging to his knees, he knelt down. "Father, why need you be angry?" he said. "Excluding the people in Madame Wang's rooms, this occurrence is entirely unknown to any of the rest; and I have heard my mother mention…" At this point, he turned his head, and cast a glance in all four quarters.

Jia Zheng guessed his meaning, and made a sign with his eyes. The young boys grasped his purpose and drew far back on either side.

Jia Huan resumed his confidences in a low tone of voice. "My mother," he resumed, "told me that when brother Baoyu was, the other day, in Madame Wang's apartments, he seized her servant-maid Jinchuan'er with the intent of dishonoring her. That as he failed to carry out his design, he gave her a thrashing, which so exasperated Jinchuan'er that she threw herself into the well and committed suicide…"

Before however he could conclude his account, Jia Zheng had been incensed to such a degree that his face assumed the color of silver paper. "Bring Baoyu here," he cried. While uttering these orders, he walked into the study. "If anyone does again today come to dissuade me," he vociferated, "I shall take this official hat and sash, my home and private property, and surrender everything at once to him to go and bestow them upon Baoyu; for if I cannot escape blame (with a son like the one I have), I mean to shave this scanty trouble-laden hair about my temples and go in search of some unsullied place where I can spend the rest of my days alone! I shall thus also avoid the crime of heaping, above, insult upon my predecessors, and, below, of having given birth to such a rebellious son."

At the sight of Jia Zheng in this exasperation, the family companions and attendants speedily realised that Baoyu must once more be the cause of it, and the whole posse hastened to withdraw from the study, biting their fingers and putting their tongues out.

Jia Zheng panted with excitement. He stretched his chest out and sat bolt upright on a chair. His whole face was covered with the traces of tears. "Bring Baoyu! Bring Baoyu!" he shouted consecutively. "Fetch a big stick; bring a rope and tie him up; close all the doors! If anyone does communicate anything about it in the inner rooms, why, I'll immediately beat him to death."

The servant-boys felt compelled to express their obedience with one consent, and some of them came to look after Baoyu.

As for Baoyu, when he heard Jia Zheng enjoin him not to move, he forthwith became aware that the chances of an unpropitious issue outnumbered those of a propitious one, but how could he have had any idea that Jia Huan as well had put in his word? There he still stood in the pavilion, revolving in his mind how he could get someone to speed inside and deliver a message for him. But, as it happened, not a soul appeared. He was quite at a loss to know where even Beiming could be. His longing was at its height, when he perceived an old nurse come on the scene. The sight of her exulted Baoyu, just as much as if he had obtained pearls or gems; and hurriedly approaching her, he dragged her and forced her to halt. "Go in," he urged, "at once and tell them that my father wishes to beat me to death. Be quick, be quick, for it's urgent, there's no time to be lost."

But, first and foremost, Baoyu's excitement was so intense that he spoke with indistinctness. In the second place, the old nurse was, as luck would have it, dull of hearing, so that she did not catch the drift of what he said, and she misconstrued the two words: "it's urgent," for the two representing jumped into the well. Readily smiling therefore: "If she wants to jump into the well, let her do so," she said. "What's there to make you fear, Master Secundus?"

"Go out," pursued Baoyu, in despair, on discovering that she was deaf, "and tell my page to come."

"What's there left unsettled?" rejoined the old nurse. "Everything has been finished long ago! A tip has also been given them; so how is it things are not settled?"

Baoyu fidgetted with his hands and feet. He was just at his wits' ends, when he espied Jia Zheng's servant-boys come up and press him to go out.

As soon as Jia Zheng caught sight of him, his eyes got quite red. Without even allowing himself any time to question him about his gadding about with actors, and the presents he gave them on the sly, during his absence from home; or about his playing the truant from school and lewdly importuning his mother's maid, during his stay at home, he simply shouted: "Gag his mouth and positively beat him till he dies!"

The servant-boys did not have the boldness to disobey him. They were under the necessity of seizing Baoyu, of stretching him on a bench, and of taking a heavy rattan and giving him about ten blows.

Baoyu knew well enough that he could not plead for mercy, and all he could do was to whimper and cry.

Jia Zheng however found fault with the light blows they administered to him. With one kick he shoved the castigator aside, and snatching the rattan into his own hands, he spitefully let (Baoyu) have ten blows and more.

Baoyu had not, from his very birth, experienced such anguish. From the outset, he found the pain unbearable; yet he could shout and weep as boisterously as ever he pleased; but so weak subsequently did his breath, little by little, become, so hoarse his voice, and so choked his throat that he could not bring out any sound.

The family companions noticed that he was beaten in a way that might lead to an unpropitious end, and they drew near with all despatch and made earnest entreaties and exhortations. But would Jia Zheng listen to them?

"You people," he answered, "had better ask him whether the tricks he has been up to deserve to be overlooked or not! It's you who have all along so thoroughly spoilt him as to make him reach this degree of depravity! And do you yet come to advise me to spare him? When by and bye you've incited him to commit parricide or regicide, you will at length, then, give up trying to dissuade me, eh?"

This language jarred on the ears of the whole party; and knowing only too well that he was in an exasperated mood, they fussed about endeavoring to find someone to go in and convey the news.

But Madame Wang did not presume to be the first to inform dowager lady Jia about it. Seeing no other course open to her, she hastily dressed herself and issued out of the garden. Without so much as worrying her mind as to whether there were any male inmates about or not, she straightway leant on a waiting-maid and hurriedly betook herself into the library, to the intense consternation of the companions, pages, and all the men present, who could not manage to clear out of the way in time.

Jia Zheng was on the point of further belaboring his son, when at the sight of Madame Wang walking in, his temper flared up with such increased violence, just as fire on which oil is poured, that the rod fell with greater spite and celerity. The two servant-boys, who held Baoyu down, precipitately loosened their grip and beat a retreat. Baoyu had long ago lost all power of movement. Jia Zheng, however, was again preparing to assail him, when the rattan was immediately locked tightly by Madame Wang, in both her arms.

"Of course, of course," Jia Zheng exclaimed, "what you want to do today is to make me succumb to anger!"

"Baoyu does, I admit, merit to be beaten," sobbed Madame Wang; "but you should also, my lord, take good care of yourself! The weather, besides, is extremely hot, and our old lady is not feeling quite up to the mark. Were you to knock Baoyu about and kill him, it would not matter much; but were perchance our venerable senior to suddenly fall ill, wouldn't it be a grave thing?"

"Better not talk about such things!" observed Jia Zheng with a listless smile. "By my bringing up such a degenerate child of retribution I have myself become unfilial! Whenever I've had to call him to account, there has always been a whole crowd of you to screen him; so isn't it as well for me to avail myself of today to put an end to his cur-like existence and thus prevent future misfortune?"

As he spoke, he asked for a rope to strangle him; but Madame Wang lost no time in clasping him in her embrace, and reasoning with him as she wept. "My lord and master," she said, "it is your duty, of course, to keep your son in proper order, but you should also regard the relationship of husband and wife. I'm already a woman of fifty and I've only got this scapegrace. Was there any need for you to give him such a bitter lesson? I wouldn't presume to use any strong dissuasion; but having, on this occasion, gone so far as to harbor the design of killing him, isn't this a fixed purpose on your part to cut short my own existence? But as you are bent upon strangling him, be quick and first strangle me before you strangle him! It will be as well that we, mother and son, should die together, so that if even we go to hell, we may be able to rely upon each other!"

At the conclusion of these words, she enfolded Baoyu in her embrace and raised her voice in loud sobs.

After listening to her appeal, Jia Zheng could not restrain a deep sigh; and taking a seat on one of the chairs, the tears ran down his cheeks like drops of rain.

But while Madame Wang held Baoyu in her arms, she noticed that his face was sallow and his breath faint, and that his green gauze nether garments were all speckled with stains of blood, so she could not check her fingers from unloosening his girdle. And realising that from the thighs to the buttocks, his person was here green, there purple, here whole, there broken, and that there was, in fact, not the least bit, which had not sustained some injury, she of a sudden burst out in bitter lamentations for her offspring's wretched lot in life. But while bemoaning her unfortunate son, she again recalled to mind the memory of Jia Zhu, and vehemently calling out "Jia Zhu," she sobbed: "if but you were alive, I would not care if even one hundred died!"

But by this time, the inmates of the inner rooms discovered that Madame Wang had gone out, and Li Gongcai, Wang Xifeng, and Yingchun and her sisters promptly rushed out of the garden and came to join her.

While Madame Wang mentioned, with eyes bathed in tears, the name of Jia Zhu, everyone listened with composure, with the exception of Li Gongcai, who unable to curb her feelings also raised her voice in sobs. As soon as Jia Zheng heard her plaints, his tears trickled down with greater profusion, like pearls scattered about. But just as there seemed no prospect of their being consoled, a servant-girl was unawares heard to announce: "Our dowager lady has come!" Before this announcement was ended, her tremulous accents reached their ears from outside the window. "If you were to beat me to death and then despatch him," she cried, "won't you be clear of us!"

Jia Zheng, upon seeing that his mother was coming, felt distressed and pained. With all promptitude, he went out to meet her. He perceived his old parent, toddling along, leaning on the arm of a servant-girl, wagging her head and gasping for breath.

Jia Zheng drew forward and made a curtsey. "On a hot broiling day like this," he ventured, forcing a smile, "what made you, mother, get so angry as to rush over in person? Had you anything to enjoin me, you could have sent for me, your son, and given me your orders."

Old lady Jia, at these words, halted and panted. "Are you really chiding me?" she at the same time said in a stern tone. "It's I who should call you to task! But as the son, I've brought up, isn't worth a straw, to whom can I go and address a word?"

When Jia Zheng heard language so unlike that generally used by her, he immediately fell on his knees. While doing all in his power to contain his tears: "The reason why," he explained, "your son corrects his offspring is a desire to reflect luster on his ancestors and splendor on his seniors; so how can I, your son, deserve the rebuke with which you greet me, mother?"

At this reply, old lady Jia spurted contemptuously. "I made just one remark," she added, "and you couldn't stand it, and can Baoyu likely put up with that death-working cane? You say that your object in correcting your son is to reflect luster on your ancestors and splendor on your seniors, but in what manner did your father correct you in days gone by?"

Saying this, tears suddenly rolled down from her eyes also.

Jia Zheng forced another smile. "Mother;" he proceeded, "you shouldn't distress yourself! Your son did it in a sudden fit of rage, but from this time forth I won't touch him again."

Dowager lady Jia smiled several loud sneering smiles. "But you shouldn't get into a huff with me!" she urged. "He's your son, so if you choose to flog him, you can naturally do so, but I cannot help thinking that you're sick and tired of me, your mother, of your wife, and of your son, so wouldn't it be as well that we should get out of your way, the sooner the better, as we shall then be able to enjoy peace and quiet?"

So speaking, "Go and look after the chairs," she speedily cried to a servant. "I and your lady as well as Baoyu will, without delay, return to Nanjing."

The servant had no help but to assent.

Old lady Jia thereupon called Madame Wang over to her. "You needn't indulge in sorrow!" she exhorted her. "Baoyu is now young, and you cherish him fondly; but does it follow that when in years to come he becomes an official, he'll remember that you are his mother? You mustn't therefore at present lavish too much of your affection upon him, so that you may by and bye, spare yourself, at least, some displeasure."

When these exhortations fell on Jia Zheng's ear, he instantly prostrated himself before her. "Your remarks mother," he observed, "cut the ground under your son's very feet."

"You distinctly act in a way," cynically smiled old lady Jia, "sufficient to deprive me of any ground to stand upon, and then you, on the contrary, go and speak about yourself! But when we shall have gone back, your mind will be free of all trouble. We'll see then who'll interfere and dissuade you from beating people!"

After this reply, she went on to give orders to directly get ready the baggage, carriages, chairs, and horses necessary for their return.

Jia Zheng stiffly and rigidly fell on his knees, and knocked his head before her, and pleaded guilty. Dowager lady Jia then addressed him some words, and as she did so, she came to have a look at Baoyu. Upon perceiving that the thrashing he had got this time was unlike those of past occasions, she experienced both pain and resentment. So clasping him in her arms, she wept and wept incessantly. It was only after Madame Wang, lady Feng, and the other ladies had reasoned with her for a time that they at length gradually succeeded in consoling her.

But waiting-maids, married women, and other attendants soon came to support Baoyu and take him away. Lady Feng however at once expostulated with them. "You stupid things," she exclaimed, won't you open your eyes and see! How ever could he be raised and made to walk in the state he's in! Don't you yet instantly run inside and fetch some rattan slings and a bench to carry him out of this on?

At this suggestion, the servants rushed hurry-scurry inside and actually brought a bench; and, lifting Baoyu, they placed him on it. Then following dowager lady Jia, Madame Wang, and the other inmates into the inner part of the building, they carried him into his grandmother's apartments. But Jia Zheng did not fail to notice that his old mother's passion had not by this time yet abated, so without presuming to consult his own convenience, he too came inside after them. Here he discovered how heavily he had in reality castigated Baoyu. Upon perceiving Madame Wang also crying, with one breath, "My flesh;" and, with another, saying with tears: "My son, if you had died sooner, instead of Zhu'er, and left Zhu'er behind you, you would have saved your father these fits of anger, and even I would not have had to fruitlessly worry and fret for half of my existence! Were anything to happen now to make you forsake me, upon whom will you have me depend?" And then after heaping reproaches upon herself for a time, break out afresh in lamentations for her unavailing offspring, Jia Zheng was much cut up and felt conscious that he should not with his own hand have struck his son so ruthlessly as to bring him to this state, and he first and foremost directed his attention to consoling dowager lady Jia.

"If your son isn't good," rejoined the old lady, repressing her tears, "it is naturally for you to exercise control over him. But you shouldn't beat him to such a pitch! Don't you yet bundle yourself away? What are you dallying in here for? Is it likely, pray, that your heart is not yet satisfied, and that you wish to feast your eyes by seeing him die before you go?"

These taunts induced Jia Zheng to eventually withdraw out of the room. By this time, Mrs. Xue together with Baochai, Xiangling, Xiren, Shi Xiangyun, and his other cousins had also congregated in the apartments. Xiren's heart was overflowing with grief; but she could not very well give expression to it. When she saw that a whole company of people shut him in, some pouring water over him, others fanning him; and that she herself could not lend a hand in any way, she availed herself of a favorable moment to make her exit. Proceeding then as far as the second gate, she bade the servant-boys go and fetch Beiming. On his arrival, she submitted him to a searching inquiry. "Why is it," she asked, "that he was beaten just now without the least provocation; and that you didn't run over soon to tell me a word about it?"

"It happened," answered Beiming in great perplexity, "that I wasn't present. It was only after he had given him half the flogging that I heard what was going on, and lost no time in ascertaining what it was all about. It's on account of those affairs connected with Qiguan and that girl Jinchuan."

"How did these things come to master's knowledge?" inquired Xiren.

"As for that affair with Qiguan," continued Beiming, "it is very likely Mr. Xue Pan who has let it out; for as he has ever been jealous, he may, in the absence of any other way of quenching his resentment, have instigated someone or other outside, who knows, to come and see master and add fuel to his anger. As for Jinchuan'er's affair it has presumably been told him by Master Tertius. This I heard from the lips of some person, who was in attendance upon master."

Xiren saw how much his two versions tallied with the true circumstances, so she readily credited the greater portion of what was told her. Subsequently, she returned inside. Here she found a whole crowd of people trying to do the best to benefit Baoyu. But after they had completed every arrangement, dowager lady Jia impressed on their minds that it would be better were they to carefully move him into his own quarters. With one voice they all signified their approval, and with a good deal of bustling and fussing, they speedily transferred Baoyu into the Yihong court, where they stretched him out comfortably on his own bed. Then after some further excitement, the members of the family began gradually to disperse. Xiren at last entered his room, and waited upon him with singleness of heart.

But, reader, if you feel any curiosity to hear what follows, listen to what you will find divulged in the next chapter.

CHAPTER 34

Daiyu loves Baoyu with extreme affection;
but, on account of this affection, her female
cousin gets indignant. Xue Pan commits a
grave mistake; but Baochai makes this mistake
a pretext to tender advice to her brother.

When Xiren saw dowager lady Jia, Madame Wang, and the other members of the family take their leave, our narrative says, she entered the room, and, taking a seat next to Baoyu, she asked him, while she did all she could to hide her tears: "How was it that he beat you to such extremes?"

Baoyu heaved a sigh. "It was simply," he replied, "about those trifles. But what's the use of your asking me about them? The lower part of my body is so very sore! Do look and see where I'm bruised!"

At these words, Xiren put out her hand, and inserting it gently under his clothes, she began to pull down the middle garments. She had but slightly moved them, however, when Baoyu ground his teeth and groaned "ai-ya." Xiren at once stayed her hand. It was after three or four similar attempts that she, at length, succeeded in drawing them down. Then looking closely, Xiren discovered that the upper part of his legs was all green and purple, one mass of scars four fingers wide, and covered with huge blisters.

Xiren gnashed her teeth. "My mother!" she ejaculated, "how is it that he struck you with such a ruthless hand! Had you minded the least bit of my advice to you, things wouldn't have come to such a pass! Luckily, no harm was done to any tendon or bone; for had you been crippled by the thrashing you got, what could we do?"

In the middle of these remarks, she saw the servant-girls come, and they told her that Miss Baochai had arrived. Hearing this, Xiren saw well enough that she had no time to put him on his middle garments, so forthwith snatching a double gauze coverlet, she threw it over Baoyu. This done, she perceived Baochai walk in, her hands laden with pills and medicines.

"At night," she said to Xiren, "take these medicines and dissolve them in wine and then apply them on him, and, when the fiery virus from that stagnant blood has been dispelled, he'll be all right again."

After these directions, she handed the medicines to Xiren. "Is he feeling any better now?" she proceeded to inquired.

"Thanks!" rejoined Baoyu. "I'm feeling better," he at the same time went on to say; after which, he pressed her to take a seat.

Baochai noticed that he could open his eyes wide, that he could speak and that he was not as bad as he had been, and she felt considerable inward relief. But nodding her head, she sighed. "If you had long ago listened to the least bit of the advice tendered to you by people things would not have reached this climax today," she said. "Not to speak of the pain experienced by our dear ancestor and aunt Wang, the sight of you in this state makes even us feel at heart..."

Just as she had uttered half of the remark she meant to pass, she quickly suppressed the rest; and smitten by remorse for having spoken too hastily, she could not help getting red in the face and lowering her head.

Baoyu was realizing how affectionate, how friendly, and how replete with deep meaning were the sentiments that dropped from her month, when, of a sudden, he saw her seal her lips and, flashing crimson, droop her head, and simply fumble with her girdle. Yet so fascinating was she in those timid blushes, which completely baffle description, that his feelings were roused within him to such a degree, that all sense of pain flew at once beyond the empyrean. "I've only had to bear a few blows," he reflected, "and yet everyone of them puts on those pitiful looks sufficient to evoke love and regard; so were, after all, any mishap or untimely end to unexpectedly befall me, who can tell how much more afflicted they won't be! And as they go on in this way, I shall have them, were I even to die in a moment, to feel so much for me; so there will indeed be no reason for regret, albeit the concerns of a whole lifetime will be thus flung entirely to the winds!"

While indulging in these meditations, he overheard Baochai ask Xiren: "How is it that he got angry, without rhyme or reason, and started beating him?" and Xiren tell her, in reply, the version given to her by Beiming.

Baoyu had, in fact, no idea as yet of what had been said by Jia Huan, and, when he heard Xiren's disclosures, he eventually got to know what it was; but as it also criminated Xue Pan, he feared lest Baochai might feel unhappy, so he lost no time in interrupting Xiren.

"Cousin Xue," he interposed, "has never been like that; you people mustn't therefore give way to idle surmises!"

These words were enough to make Baochai see that Baoyu had thought it expedient to say something to stop Xiren's mouth, apprehending that her suspicions might get roused; and she consequently secretly mused within herself: "He has been beaten to such a pitch, and yet, heedless of his own pains and aches, he's still so careful not to hurt people's feelings. But since you can be so considerate, why don't you take a little more care in greater concerns outside, so that your father should feel a little happier, and that you also should not have to suffer such bitter ordeals! But notwithstanding that the dread of my feeling hurt has prompted you to interrupt Xiren in what she had to tell me, is it likely that I am blind to the fact that my brother has ever followed his fancies, allowed his passions to run riot, and never done a thing to exercise any check over himself? His temperament is such that he some time back created, all on account of that fellow Qin Zhong, a rumpus that turned heaven and earth topsy-turvy; and, as a matter of course, he's now far worse than he was ever before!

"You people," she then observed aloud, at the close of these cogitations, "shouldn't bear this one or that one a grudge. I can't help thinking that it's, after all, because of your usual readiness, cousin Baoyu, to hobnob with that set that your father recently lost control over his temper. But assuming that my brother did speak in a careless manner and did casually allude to you cousin Baoyu, it was with no design to instigate any one! In the first place, the remarks he made were really founded on actual facts; and secondly, he's not one to ever trouble himself about such petty trifles as trying to guard against animosities. Ever since your youth up, Miss Xi, you've simply had before your eyes a person so punctilious as cousin Baoyu, but have you ever had any experience of one like that brother of mine, who neither fears the powers in heaven or in earth, and who readily blurts out all he thinks?"

Xiren, seeing Baoyu interrupt her, at the bare mention of Xue Pan, understood at once that she must have spoken recklessly and gave way to misgivings lest Baochai might not have been placed in a false position, but when she heard the language used by Baochai, she was filled with a keener sense of shame and could not utter a word. Baoyu too, after listening to the sentiments, which Baochai expressed, felt, partly because they were so magnanimous and noble, and partly because they banished all misconception from his mind, his heart and soul throb with greater emotion then ever before. When, however, about to put in his word, he noticed Baochai rise to her feet.

"I'll come again to see you tomorrow," she said, "but take good care of yourself! I gave the medicines I brought just now to Xiren; let her rub you with them at night and I feel sure you'll get all right."

With these recommendations, she walked out of the door.

Xiren hastened to catch her up and escorted her beyond the court. "Miss," she remarked, "we've really put you to the trouble of coming. Some other day, when Mr. Secundus is well, I shall come in person to thank you."

"What's there to thank me for?" replied Baochai, turning her head round and smiling. "But mind, you advise him to carefully tend his health, and not to give way to idle thoughts and reckless ideas, and he'll recover. If there's anything he fancies to eat or to amuse himself with, come quietly over to me and fetch it for him. There will be no use to disturb either our old lady, or Madame Wang, or any of the others; for in the event of its reaching Mr. Jia Zheng's ear, nothing may, at the time, come of it; but if by and bye he finds it to be true, we'll, doubtless, suffer for it!"

While tendering this advice, she went on her way.

Xiren retraced her steps and returned into the room, fostering genuine feelings of gratitude for Baochai. But on entering, she espied Baoyu silently lost in deep thought, and looking as if he were asleep, and yet not quite asleep, so she withdrew into the outer quarters to comb her hair and wash.

Baoyu meanwhile lay motionless in bed. His buttocks tingled with pain, as if they were pricked with needles, or dug with knives; giving him to boot a fiery sensation just as if fire were eating into them. He tried to change his position a bit, but unable to bear the anguish, he burst into groans. The shades of evening were by this time falling. Perceiving that though Xiren had left his side there remained still two or three waiting-maids in attendance, he said to them, as he could find nothing for them to do just then, "You might as well go and comb your hair and perform your ablutions; come in, when I call you."

Hearing this, they likewise retired. During this while, Baoyu fell into a drowsy state. Qiguan then rose before his vision and told him all about his capture by men from the Zhongshun mansion. Presently, Jinchuan'er too appeared in his room bathed in tears, and explained to him the circumstances which drove her to leap into the well. But Baoyu, who was half dreaming and half awake, was not able to give his mind to anything that was told him. Unawares, he became conscious of someone having given him a push; and faintly fell on his ear the plaintive tones of some person in distress. Baoyu was startled out of his dreams. On opening his eyes, he found it to be no other than Lin Daiyu. But still fearing that it was only a dream, he promptly raised himself, and drawing near her face he passed her features under a minute scrutiny. Seeing her two eyes so swollen, as to look as big as peaches, and her face glistening all over with tears: "If it is not Daiyu," (he thought,) "who else can it be?"

Baoyu meant to continue his scrutiny, but the lower part of his person gave him such unbearable sharp twitches that finding it a hard task to keep up, he, with a shout of "Ai-yo," lay himself down again, as he heaved a sigh. "What do you once more come here for?" he asked. "The sun, it is true, has set; but the heat remaining on the ground hasn't yet gone, so you may, by coming over, get another sunstroke. Of course, I've had a thrashing but I don't feel any pains or aches. If I behave in this fashion, it's all put on to work upon their credulity, so that they may go and spread the reports outside in such a way as to reach my father's ear. Really it's all sham; so you mustn't treat it as a fact!"

Though Lin Daiyu was not giving way at the time to any wails or loud sobs, yet the more she indulged in those suppressed plaints of hers, the worse she felt her breath get choked and her throat obstructed; so that when Baoyu's assurances fell on her ear, she could not express a single sentiment, though she treasured thousands in her mind. It was only after a long pause that she at last could observe, with agitated voice: "You must after this turn over a new leaf."

At these words, Baoyu heaved a deep sigh. "Compose your mind," he urged. "Don't speak to me like this; for I am quite prepared to even lay down my life for all those persons!"

But scarcely had he concluded this remark than someone outside the court was heard to say: "Our lady Secunda has arrived."

Lin Daiyu readily concluded that it was lady Feng coming, so springing to her feet at once, "I'm off," she said; "out by the back-court. I'll look you up again by and bye."

"This is indeed strange!" exclaimed Baoyu as he laid hold of her and tried to detain her. "How is it that you've deliberately started living in fear and trembling of her!"

Lin Daiyu grew impatient and stamped her feet. "Look at my eyes!" she added in an undertone. "Must those people amuse themselves again by poking fun at me?"

After this response, Baoyu speedily let her go.

Lin Daiyu with hurried step withdrew behind the bed; and no sooner had she issued into the back-court, than lady Feng made her appearance in the room by the front entrance.

"Are you better?" she asked Baoyu. "If you fancy anything to eat, mind you send someone over to my place to fetch it for you."

Thereupon Mrs. Xue also came to pay him a visit. Shortly after, a messenger likewise arrived from old lady Jia (to inquire after him).

When the time came to prepare the lights, Baoyu had a couple of mouthfuls of soup to eat, but he felt so drowsy and heavy that he fell asleep.

Presently, Zhou Rui's wife, Wu Xindeng's wife, and Zheng Haoshi's wife, all of whom were old dames who frequently went to and fro, heard that Baoyu had been flogged and they too hurried into his quarters.

Xiren promptly went out to greet them. "Aunts," she whispered, smiling, "you've come a little too late; Master Secundus is sleeping."

Saying this, she led them into the room on the opposite side, and, pressing then to sit down, she poured them some tea.

After sitting perfectly still for a time, "When Master Secundus awakes" the dames observed, "do send us word!"

Xiren assured them that she would, and escorted them out. Just, however, as she was about to retrace her footsteps, she met an old matron, sent over by Madame Wang, who said to her: "Our mistress wants one of Master Secundus attendants to go and see her."

Upon hearing this message, Xiren communed with her own thoughts. Then turning round, she whispered to Qingwen, Sheyue, Qiuwen, and the other maids: "Our lady wishes to see one of us, so be careful and remain in the room while I go. I'll be back soon."

At the close of her injunctions, she and the matron made their exit out of the garden by a short cut, and repaired into the drawingroom.

Madame Wang was seated on the cool couch, waving a banana-leaf fan. When she became conscious of her arrival: "It didn't matter whom you sent," she remarked, "anyone would have done. But have you left him again? Who's there to wait on him?"

At this question, Xiren lost no time in forcing a smile. "Master Secundus," she replied, "just now fell into a sound sleep. Those four or five girls are all right now, they are well able to attend to their master, so please, Madame, dispel all anxious thoughts! I was afraid that your ladyship might have some orders to give, and that if I sent any of them, they might probably not hear distinctly, and thus occasion delay in what there was to be done."

"There's nothing much to tell you," added Madame Wang. "I only wish to ask how his pains and aches are getting on now?"

"I applied on Mr. Secundus," answered Xiren, "the medicine, which Miss Baochai brought over; and he's better than he was. He was so sore at one time that he couldn't lie comfortably; but the deep sleep, in which he is plunged now, is a clear sign of his having improved."

"Has he had anything to eat?" further inquired Madame Wang.

"Our dowager mistress sent him a bowl of soup," Xiren continued, "and of this he has had a few mouthfuls. He shouted and shouted that his mouth was parched and fancied a decoction of sour plums, but remembering that sour plums are astringent things, that he had been thrashed only a short time before, and that not having been allowed to groan, he must, of course, have been so hard pressed that fiery virus and heated blood must unavoidably have accumulated in the heart, and that were he to put anything of the kind within his lips, it might be driven into the cardiac regions and give rise to some serious illness; and what then would we do? I therefore reasoned with him for ever so long and at last succeeded in deterring him from touching any. So simply taking that syrup of roses, prepared with sugar, I mixed some with water and he had half a small cup of it. But he drank it with distaste; for, being surfeited with it, he found it neither scented nor sweet."

"Ai-ya!" ejaculated Madame Wang. "Why didn't you come earlier and tell me? Someone sent me the other day several bottles of scented water. I meant at one time to have given him some, but as I feared that it would be mere waste, I didn't let him have any. But since he is so sick and tired of that preparation of roses, that he turns up his nose at it, take those two bottles with you. If you just mix a teaspoonful of it in a cup of water, it will impart to it a very strong perfume."

So saying, she hastened to tell Caiyun to fetch the bottles of scented water, which she had received as a present a few days before.

"Let her only bring a couple of them, they'll be enough!" Xiren chimed in. "If you give us more, it will be a useless waste! If it isn't enough, I can come and fetch a fresh supply. It will come to the same thing!"

Having listened to all they had to say, Caiyun left the room. After some considerable time, she, in point of fact, returned with only a couple of bottles, which she delivered to Xiren.

On examination, Xiren saw two small glass bottles, no more than three inches in size, with screwing silver stoppers at the top. On the gosling-yellow labels was written, on one: "Pure extract of *Olea fragrans*," on the other, "Pure extract of roses."

"What fine things these are!" Xiren smiled. "How many small bottles the like of this can there be?"

"They are of the kind sent to the palace," rejoined Madame Wang. "Didn't you notice that gosling-yellow slip? But mind, take good care of them for him; don't fritter them away!"

Xiren assented. She was about to depart when Madame Wang called her back. "I've thought of something," she said, "that I want to ask you."

Xiren hastily came back.

Madame Wang made sure that there was no one in the room. "I've heard a faint rumor," she then inquired, "to the effect that Baoyu got a thrashing on this occasion on account of something or other which

Huan'er told my husband. Have you perchance heard what it was that he said? If you happen to learn anything about it, do confide in me, and I won't make any fuss and let people know that it was you who told me."

"I haven't heard anything of the kind," answered Xiren. "It was because Mr. Secundus forcibly detained an actor, and that people came and asked master to restore him to them that he got flogged."

"It was also for this," continued Madame Wang as she nodded her head, "but there's another reason besides."

"As for the other reason, I honestly haven't the least idea about it," explained Xiren. "But I'll make bold today, and say something in your presence, Madame, about which I don't know whether I am right or wrong in speaking. According to what's proper…"

She had only spoken half a sentence, when hastily she closed her mouth again.

"You are at liberty to proceed," urged Madame Wang.

"If your ladyship will not get angry, I'll speak out," remarked Xiren.

"Why should I get angry?" observed Madame Wang. "Proceed!"

"According to what's proper," resumed Xiren, "our Mr. Secundus should receive our master's admonition, for if master doesn't hold him in check, there's no saying what he mightn't do in the future."

As soon as Madame Wang heard this, she clasped her hands and uttered the invocation, "Amituo Fo!" Unable to resist the impulse, she drew near Xiren. "My dear child," she added, "you have also luckily understood the real state of things. What you told me is in perfect harmony with my own views! Is it likely that I don't know how to look after a son? In former days, when your elder master, Zhu, was alive, how did I succeed in keeping him in order? And can it be that I don't, after all, now understand how to manage a son? But there's a why and a wherefore in it. The thought is ever present in my mind now, that I'm already a woman past fifty, that of my children there only remains this single one, that he too is developing a delicate physique, and that, what's more, our dear senior prizes him as much as she would a jewel, that were he kept under strict control, and anything perchance to happen to him, she might, an old lady as she is, sustain some harm from resentment, and that as the high as well as the low will then have no peace or quiet, won't things get in a bad way? So I feel prompted to spoil him by overindulgence.

Time and again I reason with him. Sometimes, I talk to him; sometimes, I advise him; sometimes, I cry with him. But though, for the time being, he's all right, he doesn't, later on, worry his mind in any way about what I say, until he positively gets into some other mess, when he settles down again. But should any harm befall him, through these floggings, upon whom will I depend by and bye?"

As she spoke, she could not help melting into tears.

At the sight of Madame Wang in this disconsolate mood, Xiren herself unconsciously grew wounded at heart, and as she wept along with her, "Mr. Secundus," she ventured, "is your ladyship's own child, so how could you not love him? Even we, who are mere servants, think it a piece of good fortune when we can wait on him for a time, and all parties can enjoy peace and quiet. But if he begins to behave in this manner, even peace and quiet will be completely out of the question for us. On what day, and at what hour, don't I advise Mr. Secundus; yet I can't manage to stir him up by any advice! But it happens that all that crew are ever ready to court his friendship, so it isn't to be wondered that he is what he is! The truth is that he thinks the advice we give him is not right and proper! As you have today, Madame, alluded to this subject, I've got something to tell you which has weighed heavy on my mind. I've been anxious to come and confide it to your ladyship and to solicit your guidance, but I've been in fear and dread lest you should give way to suspicion. For not only would then all my disclosures have been in vain, but I would have deprived myself of even a piece of ground wherein my remains could be laid."

Madame Wang perceived that her remarks were prompted by some purpose. "My dear child," she eagerly urged; "go on, speak out! When I recently heard one and all praise you secretly behind your back, I simply fancied that it was because you were careful in your attendance on Baoyu; or possibly because you got on well with everyone; all on account of minor considerations like these (but I never thought it was on account of your good qualities). As it happens, what you told me just now concerns, in all its bearings, a great principle, and is in perfect accord with my ideas, so speak out freely, if you have aught to say! Only let no one else know anything about it, that is all that is needed."

"I've got nothing more to say," proceeded Xiren. "My sole idea was to solicit your advice, Madame, as to how to devise a plan to induce Mr. Secundus to move his quarters out of the garden by and bye, as things will get all right then."

This allusion much alarmed Madame Wang. Speedily taking Xiren's hand in hers: "Is it likely," she inquired, "that Baoyu has been up to any mischief with anyone?"

"Don't be too suspicious!" precipitately replied Xiren. "It wasn't at anything of the kind that I was hinting. I merely expressed my humble opinion. Mr. Secundus is a young man now, and the young ladies inside are no more children. More than that, Miss Lin and Miss Bao may be two female maternal first cousins of his, but albeit his cousins, there is nevertheless the distinction of male and female between them; and day and night, as they are together, it isn't always convenient, when they have to rise and when they have to sit; so this cannot help making one give way to misgivings. Were, in fact, any outsider to see what's going on, it would not look like the propriety, which should exist in great families. The proverb appositely says that: 'when there's no trouble, one should make provision for the time of trouble.' How many concerns there are in the world, of which there's no making head or tail, mostly because what persons do without any design is construed by such designing people, as chance to have their notice attracted to it, as having been designedly accomplished, and go on talking and talking till, instead of mending matters, they make them worse! But if precautions be not taken beforehand, something improper will surely happen, for your ladyship is well aware of the temperament Mr. Secundus has shown all along! Besides, his great weakness is to fuss in our midst, so if no caution be exercised, and the slightest mistake be sooner or later committed, there'll be then no question of true or false: for when people are many one says one thing and another, and what is there that the mouths of that mean lot will shun with any sign of respect? Why, if their hearts be well disposed, they will maintain that he is far superior to Buddha himself. But if their hearts be badly disposed, they will at once knit a tissue of lies to show that he cannot even reach the standard of a beast! Now, if people by and bye speak well of Mr. Secundus, we'll all go on smoothly with our lives. But should he perchance give reason to anyone to breathe the slightest disparaging remark, won't his body, needless for us to say, be smashed to pieces, his bones ground to powder, and the blame, which he might incur, be made ten thousand times more serious than it is? These things are all commonplace trifles; but won't Mr. Secundus' name and reputation be subsequently done for for life? Secondly, it's no easy thing for your ladyship to see anything of our master. A proverb also says: 'The perfect man makes provision beforehand;' so wouldn't it be better that we should, this very minute, adopt such steps as will enable us to guard against such things? Your ladyship has much to attend to, and you couldn't, of course, think of these things in a moment. And as for us, it would have been well and good, had they never suggested themselves to our minds; but since they have, we should be the more to blame did we not tell you anything about them, Madame. Of late, I have racked my mind, both day and night on this score; and though I couldn't very well confide to anyone, my lamp alone knows everything!"

After listening to these words, Madame Wang felt as if she had been blasted by thunder and struck by lightning; and, as they fitted so appositely with the incident connected with Jinchuan'er, her heart was more than ever fired with boundless affection for Xiren. "My dear girl," she promptly smiled, "it's you, who are gifted with enough foresight to be able to think of these things so thoroughly. Yet, did I not also think of them? But so busy have I been these several times that they slipped from my memory. What you've told me today, however, has brought me to my senses! It's, thanks to you, that the reputation of me, his mother, and of him, my son, is preserved intact! I really never had the faintest idea that you were so excellent! But you had better go now; I know of a way. Yet, just another word. After your remarks to me, I'll hand him over to your charge; please be careful of him. If you preserve him from harm, it will be tantamount to preserving me from harm, and I shall certainly not be ungrateful to you for it."

Xiren said several consecutive yes's, and went on her way. She got back just in time to see Baoyu awake. Xiren explained all about the scented water; and, so intensely delighted was Baoyu, that he at once asked that some should be mixed and brought to him to taste. In very deed, he found it unusually fragrant and good. But as his heart was a prey to anxiety on Daiyu's behalf, he was full of longings to despatch someone to look her up. He was, however, afraid of Xiren. Readily therefore he devised a plan to first get Xiren out of the way, by despatching her to Baochai's, to borrow a book. After Xiren's departure, he forthwith called Qingwen. "Go," he said, "over to Miss Lin's and see what she's up to. Should she inquire about me, all you need tell her is that I'm all right."

"What shall I go empty-handed for?" rejoined Qingwen. "If I were, at least, to give her a message, it would look as if I had gone for something."

"I have no message that you can give her," added Baoyu.

"If it can't be that," suggested Qingwen; "I might either take something over or fetch something. Otherwise, when I get there, what excuse will I be able to find?"

After some cogitation, Baoyu stretched out his hand and, laying hold of a couple of handkerchiefs, he threw them to Qingwen. "These will do," he smiled. "Just tell her that I bade you take them to her."

"This is strange!" exclaimed Qingwen. "Will she accept these two half worn-out handkerchiefs! She'll besides get angry and say that you were making fun of her."

"Don't worry yourself about that;" laughed Baoyu. "She will certainly know what I mean."

Qingwen, at this rejoinder, had no help but to take the handkerchiefs and to go to the Xiaoxiang lodge, where she discovered Chunxian in the act of hanging out handkerchiefs on the railings to dry. As soon as she saw her walk in, she vehemently waved her hand. "She's gone to sleep!" she said. Qingwen, however, entered the room. It was in perfect darkness. There was not even so much as a lantern burning, and Daiyu was already ensconced in bed. "Who is there?" she shouted.

"It's Qingwen!" promptly replied Qingwen.

"What are you up to?" Daiyu inquired.

"Mr. Secundus," explained Qingwen, "sends you some handkerchiefs, Miss."

Daiyu's spirits sunk as soon as she caught her reply. "What can he have sent me handkerchiefs for?" she secretly reasoned within herself. "Who gave him these handkerchiefs?" she then asked aloud. "They must be fine ones, so tell him to keep them and give them to someone else; for I don't need such things at present."

"They're not new," smiled Qingwen. "They are of an ordinary kind, and old."

Hearing this, Lin Daiyu felt downcast. But after minutely searching her heart, she at last suddenly grasped his meaning and she hastily observed: "Leave them and go your way."

Qingwen was compelled to put them down; and turning round, she betook herself back again. But much though she turned things over in her mind during the whole of her way homewards, she did not succeed in solving their import.

When Daiyu guessed the object of the handkerchief, her very soul unawares flitted from her. "As Baoyu has gone to such pains," she pondered, "to try and probe this dejection of mine, I have, on one hand, sufficient cause to feel gratified; but as there's no knowing what my dejection will come to in the future there is, on the other, enough to make me sad. Here he abruptly and deliberately sends me a couple of handkerchiefs; and, were it not that he has divined my inmost feelings, the mere sight of these handkerchiefs would be enough to make me treat the whole thing as ridiculous. The secret exchange of presents between us," she went on to muse, "fills me also with fears; and the thought that those tears, which I am ever so fond of shedding to myself, are of no avail, drives me likewise to blush with shame."

And by dint of musing and reflecting, her heart began, in a moment, to bubble over with such excitement that, much against her will, her thoughts in their superabundance rolled on incessantly. So speedily directing that a lamp should be lighted, she little concerned herself about avoiding suspicion, shunning the use of names, or any other such things, and set to work and rubbed the ink, soaked the brush, and then wrote the following stanzas on the two old handkerchiefs:

Vain in my eyes the tears collect; those tears in vain they flow,
Which I in secret shed; they slowly drop; but for whom though?
The silk kerchiefs, which he so kindly troubled to give me,
How ever could they not with anguish and distress fill me?

The second ran thus:

Like falling pearls or rolling gems, they trickle on the sly.
Daily I have no heart for aught; listless all day am I.
As on my pillow or sleeves' edge I may not wipe them dry,
I let them dot by dot, and drop by drop to run freely.

And the third:

The colored thread cannot contain the pearls cov'ring my face.
Tears were of old at Xiangjiang shed, but faint has waxed each trace.
Outside my window thousands of bamboos, lo, also grow,
But whether they be stained with tears or not, I do not know.

Lin Daiyu was still bent upon going on writing, but feeling her whole body burn like fire, and her face scalding hot, she advanced towards the cheval-glass, and, raising the embroidered cover, she looked in. She saw at a glance that her cheeks wore so red that they, in very truth, put even the peach blossom to the shade. Yet little did she dream that from this date her illness would assume a more serious phase. Shortly, she threw herself on the bed, and, with the handkerchiefs still grasped in her hand, she was tost in a reverie.

Putting her aside, we will now take up our story with Xiren. She went to pay a visit to Baochai, but as it happened, Baochai was not in the garden, but had gone to look up her mother. Xiren, however, could not very well come back with empty hands so she waited until the second watch, when Baochai eventually returned to her quarters.

Indeed, so correct an estimate of Xue Pan's natural disposition did Baochai ever have, that from an early moment she entertained within herself some faint suspicion that it must have been Xue Pan, who had instigated some person or other to come and lodge a complaint against Baoyu. And when she also unexpectedly heard Xiren's disclosures on the subject she became more positive in her surmises. The one, who had, in fact, told Xiren was Beiming. But Beiming too had arrived at the conjecture in his own mind, and could not adduce any definite proof, so that everyone treated his statements as founded partly on mere suppositions, and partly on actual facts; but, despite this, they felt quite certain that it was (Xue Pan) who had intrigued.

Xue Pan had always enjoyed this reputation; but on this particular instance the harm was not, actually, his own doing; yet as everyone, with one consent, tenaciously affirmed that it was he, it was no easy matter for him, much though he might argue, to clear himself of blame.

Soon after his return, on this day, from a drinking bout out of doors, he came to see his mother; but finding Baochai in her rooms, they exchanged a few irrelevant remarks. "I hear," he consequently asked, "that cousin Baoyu has got into trouble; why is it?"

Mrs. Xue was at the time much distressed on this score. As soon therefore as she caught this question, she gnashed her teeth with rage, and shouted: "You good-for-nothing spiteful fellow! It's all you who are at the bottom of this trouble; and do you still have the face to come and ply me with questions?"

These words made Xue Pan wince. "When did I stir up any trouble?" he quickly asked.

"Do you still go on shamming!" cried Mrs. Xue. "Everyone knows full well that it was you, who said those things, and do you yet prevaricate?"

"Were everyone," insinuated Xue Pan, "to assert that I had committed murder, would you believe even that?"

"Your very sister is well aware that they were said by you." Mrs. Xue continued, "and is it likely that she would accuse you falsely, pray?"

"Mother," promptly interposed Baochai, "you shouldn't be brawling with brother just now! If you wait quietly, we'll find out the plain and honest truth." Then turning towards Xue Pan: "Whether it's you, who said those things or not," she added, "it's of no consequence. The whole affair, besides, is a matter of the past, so what need is there for any arguments; they will only be making a mountain of a mole-hill! I have just one word of advice to give you; don't, from henceforward, be up to so much reckless mischief outside; and concern yourself a little less with other people's affairs! All you do is day after day to associate with your friends and foolishly gad about! You are a happy-go-lucky sort of creature! If nothing happens well and good; but should by and bye anything turn up, everyone will, though it be none of your doing, imagine again that you are at the bottom of it! Not to speak of others, why I myself will be the first to suspect you!"

Xue Pan was naturally open-hearted and plain-spoken, and could not brook anything in the way of innuendoes, so, when on the one side, Baochai advised him not to foolishly gad about, and his mother, on the other, hinted that he had a foul tongue, and that he was the cause that Baoyu had been flogged, he at once got so exasperated that he jumped about in an erratic manner and did all in his power, by vowing and swearing, to explain matters. "Who has," he ejaculated, heaping abuse upon everyone, "laid such a tissue of lies to my charge! I'd like to take the teeth of that felon and pull them out! It's clear as day that they shove me forward as a target; for now that Baoyu has been flogged they find no means of making a display of their zeal. But, is Baoyu forsooth the lord of the heavens that because he has had a thrashing from his father, the whole household should be fussing for days? The other time, he behaved improperly, and my uncle gave him two whacks. But our venerable ancestor came, after a time, somehow or other, I don't know how, to hear about it, and, maintaining that it was all due to Mr. Jia Zhen, she called him before her, and gave him a good blowing up. And here today, they have gone further, and involved me. They may drag me in as much as they like, I don't fear a rap! But won't it be better for me to go into the garden, and take Baoyu and give him a bit of my mind and kill him? I can then pay the penalty by laying down my life for his, and one and all will enjoy peace and quiet!"

While he clamored and shouted, he looked about him for the bar of the door, and, snatching it up, he there and then was running off, to the consternation of Mrs. Xue, who clutched him in her arms. "You murderous child of retribution!" she cried. "Whom would you go and beat? come first and assail me?"

From excitement Xue Pan's eyes protruded like copper bells. "What are you up to," he vociferated, "that you won't let me go where I please, and that you deliberately go on calumniating me? But every day that Baoyu lives, the longer by that day I have to bear a false charge, so it's as well that we should both die that things be cleared up?"

Baochai too hurriedly rushed forward. "Be patient a bit!" she exhorted him. "Here's mamma in an awful state of despair. Not to mention that it should be for you to come and pacify her, you contrariwise kick up all this rumpus! Why, saying nothing about her who is your parent, were even a perfect stranger to advise you, it would be meant for your good! But the good counsel she gave you has stirred up your monkey instead."

"From the way you're now speaking," Xue Pan rejoined, "it must be you, who said that it was I; no one else but you!"

"You simply know how to feel displeased with me for speaking," argued Baochai, "but you don't feel displeased with yourself for that reckless way of yours of looking ahead and not minding what is behind."

"You now bear me a grudge," Xue Pan added, "for looking to what is ahead and not to what is behind; but how is it you don't feel indignant with Baoyu for stirring up strife and provoking trouble outside? Leaving aside everything else, I'll merely take that affair of Qiguan'er's, which occurred the other day, and recount it to you as an instance. My friends and I came across this Qiguan'er, ten times at least, but never has he made a single intimate remark to me, and how is it that, as soon as he met Baoyu the other day, he at once produced his sash, and gave it to him, though he did not so much as know what his surname and name were? Now is it likely, forsooth, that this too was something that I started?"

"Do you still refer to this?" exclaimed Mrs. Xue and Baochai, out of patience. "Wasn't it about this that he was beaten? This makes it clear enough that it's you who gave the thing out."

"Really, you're enough to exasperate one to death!" Xue Pan exclaimed. "Had you confined yourselves to saying that I had started the yarn, I wouldn't have lost my temper; but what irritates me is that such a fuss should be made for a single Baoyu, as to subvert heaven and earth!"

"Who fusses?" shouted Baochai. "You are the first to arm yourself to the teeth and start a row, and then you say that it's others who are up to mischief!"

Xue Pan, seeing that every remark made by Baochai, contained so much reasonableness that he could with difficulty refute it, and that her words were even harder for him to reply to than were those uttered by his mother, he was consequently bent upon contriving a plan to make use of such language as could silence her and compel her to return to her room, so as to have no one bold enough to interfere with his speaking; but, his temper being up, he was not in a position to weigh his speech. "Dear Sister!" he readily therefore said, "you needn't be flying into a huff with me! I've long ago divined your feelings. Mother told me some time back that for you with that gold trinket, must be selected some suitor provided with a jade one; as such a one will be a suitable match for you. And having treasured this in your mind, and seen that Baoyu has that rubbishy thing of his, you naturally now seize every occasion to screen him…"

However, before he could finish, Baochai trembled with anger, and clinging to Mrs. Xue, she melted into tears. "Mother," she observed, "have you heard what brother says, what is it all about?"

Xue Pan, at the sight of his sister bathed in tears, became alive to the fact that he had spoken inconsiderately, and, flying into a rage, he walked away to his own quarters and retired to rest. But we can well dispense with any further comment on the subject.

Baochai was, at heart, full of vexation and displeasure. She meant to give vent to her feelings in some way, but the fear again of upsetting her mother compelled her to conceal her tears. She therefore took leave of her parent, and went back all alone. On her return to her chamber, she sobbed and sobbed throughout the whole night. The next day, she got out of bed, as soon as it dawned; but feeling even no inclination to comb her chevelure or perform her ablutions, she carelessly adjusted her clothes and came out of the garden to see her mother.

As luck would have it, she encountered Daiyu standing alone under the shade of the trees, who inquired of her where she was off to?

"I'm going home," Xue Baochai replied. And as she uttered these words, she kept on her way.

But Daiyu perceived that she was going off in a disconsolate mood; and, noticing that her eyes betrayed signs of crying, and that her manner was unlike that of other days, she smilingly called out to her from behind: "Sister, you should take care of yourself a bit. Were you even to cry so much as to fill two water jars with tears, you wouldn't heal the wounds inflicted by the cane."

But as what reply Xue Baochai gave is not yet known to you, reader, lend an ear to the explanation contained in the next chapter.

CHAPTER 35

Bai Yuchuan tastes too the lotus-leaf soup.
Huang Jinying skilfully plaits the
plum-blossom-knotted nets.

Baochai had, our story goes, distinctly heard Lin Daiyu's sneer, but in her eagerness to see her mother and brother, she did not so much as turn her head round, but continued straight on her way.

During this time, Lin Daiyu halted under the shadow of the trees. Upon casting a glance, in the distance towards the Yihong Yuan, she observed Li Gongcai, Yingchun, Tanchun, Xichun, and various inmates wending their steps in a body in the direction of the Yihong court; but after they had gone past, and company after company of them had dispersed, she only failed to see lady Feng come. "How is it," she cogitated within herself, "that she doesn't come to see Baoyu? Even supposing that there was some business to detain her, she should also have put in an appearance, so as to curry favor with our venerable senior and Madame Wang. But if she hasn't shown herself at this hour of the day, there must certainly be some cause or other."

While preoccupied with conjectures, she raised her head. At a second glance, she discerned a crowd of people, as thick as flowers in a bouquet, pursuing their way also into the Yihong court. On looking fixedly, she recognised dowager lady Jia, leaning on lady Feng's arm, followed by Mesdames Xing and Wang, Mrs. Zhou, and servant-girls, married women, and other domestics. In a body they walked into the court. At the sight of them, Daiyu unwittingly nodded her head, and reflected on the benefit of having a father and mother; and tears forthwith again bedewed her face. In a while, she beheld Baochai, Mrs. Xue, and the rest likewise go in.

But at quite an unexpected moment she became aware that Zichuan was approaching her from behind. "Miss," she said, "you had better go and take your medicine! The hot water too has got cold."

"What do you, after all, mean by keeping on pressing me so?" inquired Daiyu. "Whether I have it or not, what's that to you?"

"Your cough," smiled Zijuan, "has recently got a trifle better, and won't you again take your medicine? This is, it's true, the fifth moon, and the weather is hot, but you should, nevertheless, take good care of yourself a bit! Here you've been at this early hour of the morning standing for ever so long in this damp place; so you should go back and have some rest!"

This single hint recalled Daiyu to her senses. She at length realized that her legs felt rather tired. After lingering about abstractedly for a long while, she quietly returned into the Xiaoxiang lodge, supporting herself on Zijuan. As soon as they stepped inside the entrance of the court, her gaze was attracted by the confused shadows of the bamboos, which covered the ground, and the traces of moss, here thick, there thin, and she could not help recalling to mind those two lines of the passage in the "Xixiang Ji":

> "In that lone nook someone saunters about,
> White dew coldly bespecks the verdant moss."

"Shuangwen," she consequently secretly communed within herself, as she sighed, "had of course a poor fate; but she nevertheless had a widowed mother and a young brother; but in the unhappy destiny, to which I, Daiyu, am at present doomed, I have neither a widowed mother nor a young brother."

At this point in her reflections, she was about to melt into another fit of crying, when of a sudden, the parrot under the verandah caught sight of Daiyu approaching, and, with a shriek, he jumped down from his perch, and made her start with fright.

"Are you bent upon compassing your own death!" she exclaimed. "You've covered my head all over with dust again!"

The parrot flew back to his perch. "Xue Yan," he kept on shouting, "quick, raise the portiere! Miss is come!"

Daiyu stopped short and rapped on the frame with her hand. "Have his food and water been replenished?" she asked.

The parrot forthwith heaved a deep sigh, closely resembling, in sound, the groans usually indulged in by Daiyu, and then went on to recite:

> "Here I am fain these flowers to inter, but humankind will laugh
> me as a fool.
> Who knows who will in years to come commit me to my grave."

As soon as these lines fell on the ear of Daiyu and Zijuan, they blurted out laughing.

"This is what you were repeating some time back, Miss." Zijuan laughed, "How did he ever manage to commit it to memory?"

Daiyu then directed someone to take down the frame and suspend it instead on a hook, outside the circular window, and presently entering her room, she seated herself inside the circular window. She had just done drinking her medicine, when she perceived that the shade cast by the cluster of bamboos, planted outside the window, was reflected so far on the gauze lattice as to fill the room with a faint light, so green and mellow, and to impart a certain coolness to the teapoys and mats. But Daiyu had no means at hand to dispel her ennui, so from inside the gauze lattice, she instigated the parrot to perform his pranks; and selecting some verses, which had ever found favor with her, she tried to teach them to him.

But without descending to particulars, let us now advert to Xue Baochai. On her return home, she found her mother alone combing her hair and having a wash. "Why do you run over at this early hour of the morning?" she speedily inquired when she saw her enter.

"To see," replied Baochai, "whether you were all right or not, mother. Did he come again, I wonder, after I left yesterday and make any more trouble or not?"

As she spoke, she sat by her mother's side, but unable to curb her tears, she began to weep.

Seeing her sobbing, Mrs. Xue herself could not check her feelings, and she, too, burst out into a fit of crying. "My child," she simultaneously exhorted her, "don't feel aggrieved! Wait, and I'll call that child of wrath to order; for were anything to happen to you, from whom will I have anything to hope?"

Xue Pan was outside and happened to overhear their conversation, so with alacrity he ran over, and facing Baochai he made a bow, now to the left and now to the right, observing the while: "My dear sister, forgive me this time. The fact is that I took some wine yesterday; I came back late, as I met a few friends on the way. On my return home, I hadn't as yet got over the fumes, so I unintentionally talked a lot of nonsense. But I don't so much as remember anything about all I said. It isn't worth your while, however, losing your temper over such a thing.'"

Baochai was, in fact, weeping, as she covered her face, but the moment this language fell on her ear, she could scarcely again refrain from laughing. Forthwith raising her head, she sputtered contemptuously on the ground. "You can well dispense with all this sham!" she exclaimed, "I'm well aware that you so dislike us both, that you're anxious to devise some way of inducing us to part company with you, so that you may be at liberty."

Xue Pan, at these words, hastened to smile. "Sister," he argued, "what makes you say so? once upon a time, you weren't so suspicious and given to uttering anything so perverse!"

Mrs. Xue hurriedly took up the thread of the conversation. "All you know," she interposed, "is to find fault with your sister's remarks as being perverse; but can it be that what you said last night was the proper thing to say? In very truth, you were drunk!"

"There's no need for you to get angry, mother!" Xue Pan rejoined, "nor for you sister either; for from this day, I shan't any more make common cause with them nor drink wine or gad about. What do you say to that?"

"That's equal to an acknowledgment of your failings," Baochai laughed.

"Could you exercise such strength of will," added Mrs. Xue, "why, the dragon too would lay eggs."

"If I again go and gad about with them," Xue Pan replied, "and you, sister, come to hear of it, you can freely spit in my face and call me a beast and no human being. Do you agree to that? But why should you two be daily worried; and all through me alone? For you, mother, to be angry on my account is anyhow excusable; but for me to keep on worrying you, sister, makes me less then ever worthy of the name of a human being! If now that father is no more, I manage, instead of showing you plenty of filial piety, mamma, and you, sister, plenty of love, to provoke my mother to anger, and annoy my sister, why I can't compare myself to even a four-footed creature!"

While from his mouth issued these words, tears rolled down from his eyes; for he too found it hard to contain them.

Mrs. Xue had not at first been overcome by her feelings; but the moment his utterances reached her ear, she once more began to experience the anguish, which they stirred in her heart.

Baochai made an effort to force a smile. "You've already," she said, "been the cause of quite enough trouble, and do you now provoke mother to have another cry?"

Hearing this, Xue Pan promptly checked his tears. As he put on a smiling expression, "When did I," he asked, "make mother cry? But never mind; enough of this! let's drop the matter, and not allude to it any more! Call Xiangling to come and give you a cup of tea, sister!"

"I don't want any tea. " Baochai answered. "I'll wait until mother has finished washing her hands and then go with her into the garden."

"Let me see your necklet, sister," Xue Pan continued. "I think it requires cleaning."

"It is so yellow and bright," rejoined Baochai, "and what's the use of cleaning it again?"

"Sister," proceeded Xue Pan, "you must now add a few more clothes to your wardrobe, so tell me what color and what design you like best."

"I haven't yet worn out all the clothes I have," Baochai explained, "and why should I have more made?"

But, in a little time, Mrs. Xue effected the change in her costume, and hand in hand with Baochai, she started on her way to the garden.

Xue Pan thereupon took his departure. During this while, Mrs. Xue and Baochai trudged in the direction of the garden to look up Baoyu. As soon as they reached the interior of the Yihong court, they saw a large concourse of waiting-maids and matrons standing inside as well as outside the antechambers and they readily concluded that old lady Jia and the other ladies were assembled in his rooms. Mrs. Xue and her daughter stepped in. After exchanging salutations with everyone present, they noticed that Baoyu was reclining on the couch and Mrs. Xue inquired of him whether he felt any better.

Baoyu hastily attempted to bow. "I'm considerably better," he said. "All I do," he went on, "is to disturb you, aunt, and you, my cousin, but I don't deserve such attentions."

Mrs. Xue lost no time in supporting and laying him down. "Mind you tell me whatever may take your fancy!" she proceeded.

"If I do fancy anything," retorted Baoyu smilingly, "I shall certainly send to you, aunt, for it."

"What would you like to eat," likewise inquired Madame Wang, "so that I may, on my return, send it round to you?"

"There's nothing that I care for," smiled Baoyu, "though the soup made for me the other day, with young lotus leaves, and small lotus cores was, I thought, somewhat nice."

"From what I hear, its flavor is nothing very grand," lady Feng chimed in laughingly, from where she stood on one side. "It involves, however, a good deal of trouble to concoct; and here you deliberately go and fancy this very thing."

"Go and get it ready!" cried dowager lady Jia several successive times.

"Venerable ancestor," urged lady Feng with a smile, "don't you bother yourself about it! Let me try and remember who can have put the moulds away." Then turning her head round, "Go and bid," she enjoined an old matron, "the chief in the cook-house go and apply for them!"

After a considerable lapse of time, the matron returned. "The chief in the cook-house," she explained, "says that the four sets of moulds for soups have all been handed up.

Upon hearing this, lady Feng thought again for a while. "Yes, I remember," she afterwards remarked, they were handed up, but I can't recollect to whom they were given. Possibly they're in the tearoom."

Thereupon, she also despatched a servant to go and inquire of the keeper of the tearoom about them; but he too had not got them; and it was subsequently the butler, entrusted with the care of the gold and silver articles, who brought them round.

Mrs. Xue was the first to take them and examine them. What, in fact, struck her gaze was a small box, the contents of which were four sets of silver moulds. Each of these was over a foot long, and one square inch (in breadth). On the top, holes were bored of the size of beans. Some resembled chrysanthemums, others plum blossom. Some were in the shape of lotus seed-cases, others like water chestnuts. They numbered in all thirty or forty kinds, and were ingeniously executed.

"In your mansion," she felt impelled to observe smilingly to old lady Jia and Madame Wang, "everything has been amply provided for! Have you got all these things to prepare a plate of soup with! Hadn't you told me, and I happened to see them, I wouldn't have been able to make out what they were intended for!"

Lady Feng did not allow time to anyone to put in her word. "Aunt," she said, "how could you ever have divined that these were used last year for the Imperial viands! They thought of a way by which they devised, somehow or other, I can't tell how, some dough shapes, which borrow a little of the pure fragrance of the new lotus leaves. But as all mainly depends upon the quality of the soup, they're not, after all, of much use! Yet who often goes in for such soup! It was made once only, and that at the time when the moulds were brought; and how is it that he has come to think of it today?"

So speaking, she took (the moulds), and handed them to a married woman, to go and issue directions to the people in the cook-house to procure at once several fowls, and to add other ingredients besides and prepare ten bowls of soup.

"What do you want all that lot for?" observed Madame Wang.

"There's good reason for it," answered lady Feng. "A dish of this kind isn't, at ordinary times, very often made, and were, now that brother Baoyu has alluded to it, only sufficient prepared for him, and none for you, dear senior, you, aunt, and you, Madame Wang, it won't be quite the thing! So isn't it better that this opportunity should be availed of to get ready a whole supply so that everyone should partake of some, and that even I should, through my reliance on your kind favor, taste this novel kind of relish."

"You are sharper than a monkey!" Dowager lady Jia laughingly exclaimed in reply to her proposal. "You make use of public money to confer boons upon people."

This remark evoked general laughter.

"This is a mere bagatelle!" eagerly laughed lady Feng. "Even I can afford to stand you such a small treat!" Then turning her head round, "Tell them in the cook-house," she said to a married woman, "to please make an extra supply, and that they'll get the money from me."

The matron assented and went out of the room.

Baochai, who was standing near, thereupon interposed with a smile. "During the few years that have gone by since I've come here, I've carefully noticed that sister-in-law Secunda, cannot, with all her acumen, outwit our venerable ancestor."

"My dear child!" forthwith replied old lady Jia at these words. "I'm now quite an old woman, and how can there still remain any wit in me! When I was, long ago, of your manlike cousin Feng's age, I had far more wits about me than she has! Albeit she now avers that she can't reach our standard, she's good enough; and compared with your aunt Wang, why, she's infinitely superior. Your aunt, poor thing, won't speak much! She's like a block of wood; and when with her father and mother-in-law, she won't show herself off to advantage. But that girl Feng has a sharp tongue, so is it a wonder if people take to her."

"From what you say," insinuated Baoyu with a smile, "those who don't talk much are not loved."

"Those who don't speak much," resumed dowager lady Jia, "possess the endearing quality of reserve. But among those with glib tongues, there's also a certain despicable lot; thus it's better, in a word, not to have too much to say for one's self."

"Quite so," smiled Baoyu, "yet though senior sister-in-law Jia Zhu doesn't, I must confess, talk much, you, venerable ancestor, treat her just as you do cousin Feng. But if you maintain that those alone, who can talk, are worthy of love, then among all these young ladies, sister Feng and cousin Lin are the only ones good enough to be loved."

"With regard to the young ladies," remarked dowager lady Jia, "it isn't that I have any wish to flatter your aunt Xue in her presence, but it is a positive and incontestable fact that there isn't, beginning from the four girls in our household, a single one able to hold a candle to that girl Baochai."

At these words, Mrs. Xue promptly smiled. "Dear venerable senior!" she said, "you're rather partial in your verdict."

"Our dear senior," vehemently put in Madame Wang, also smiling, "has often told me in private how nice your daughter Baochai is; so this is no lie."

Baoyu had tried to lead old lady Jia on, originally with the idea of inducing her to speak highly of Lin Daiyu, but when unawares she began to eulogize Baochai instead the result exceeded all his thoughts and went far beyond his expectations. Forthwith he cast a glance at Baochai, and gave her a smile, but Baochai at once twisted her head round and went and chatted with Xiren. But of a sudden, someone came to ask them to go and have their meal. Dowager lady Jia rose to her feet, and enjoined Baoyu to be careful of himself. She then gave a few directions to the waiting-maids, and resting her weight on lady Feng's arm, and pressing Mrs. Xue to go out first, she, and all with her, left the apartment in a body. But still she kept on inquiring whether the soup was ready or not. "If there's anything you might fancy to eat," she also said to Mrs. Xue and the others, "mind you, come and tell me, and I know how to coax that hussey Feng to get it for you as well as me."

"My venerable senior!" rejoined Mrs. Xue, "you do have the happy knack of putting her on her mettle; but though she has often got things ready for you, you've, after all, not eaten very much of them."

"Aunt," smiled lady Feng, "don't make such statements! If our worthy senior hasn't eaten me up it's purely and simply because she dislikes human flesh as being sour. Did she not look down upon it as sour, why, she would long ago have gobbled me up!"

This joke was scarcely ended, when it so tickled the fancy of old lady Jia and all the inmates that they broke out with one voice in a boisterous fit of laughter. Even Baoyu, who was inside the room, could not keep quiet.

"Really," Xiren laughed, "the mouth of our mistress Secunda is enough to terrify people to death!"

Baoyu put out his arm and pulled Xiren. "You've been standing for so long," he smiled, "that you must be feeling tired."

Saying this, he dragged her down and made her take a seat next to him.

"Here you've again forgotten!" laughingly exclaimed Xiren. "Avail yourself now that Miss Baochai is in the court to tell her to kindly bid their Ying'er come and plait a few girdles with twisted cords."

"How lucky it is you've reminded me?" Baoyu observed with a smile. And putting, while he spoke, his head out of the window: "Cousin Baochai," he cried, "when you've had your repast, do tell Ying'er to come over. I would like to ask her to plait a few girdles for me. Has she got the time to spare?"

Baochai heard him speak; and turning round: "How about no time?" she answered. "I'll tell her by and bye to come; it will be all right."

Dowager lady Jia and the others, however, failed to catch distinctly the drift of their talk; and they halted and made inquiries of Baochai what it was about. Baochai gave them the necessary explanations.

"My dear child," remarked old lady Jia, "do let her come and twist a few girdles for your cousin! And should you be in need of anyone for anything, I have over at my place a whole number of servant-girls doing nothing! Out of them, you are at liberty to send for any you like to wait on you!"

"We'll send her to plait them!" Mrs. Xue and Baochai observed smilingly with one consent. "What can we want her for? she also daily idles her time away and is up to every mischief!"

But chatting the while, they were about to proceed on their way when they unexpectedly caught sight of Xiangyun, Ping'er, Xiangling, and other girls picking balsam flowers near the rocks; who, as soon as they saw the company approaching, advanced to welcome them.

Shortly, they all sallied out of the garden. Madame Wang was worrying lest dowager lady Jia's strength might be exhausted, and she did her utmost to induce her to enter the drawing room and sit down. Old lady Jia herself was feeling her legs quite tired out, so she at once nodded her head and expressed her assent. Madame Wang then directed a waiting-maid to hurriedly precede them, and get ready the seats. But as Mrs. Zhao had, about this time, pleaded indisposition, there was only therefore Mrs. Zhou, with the matrons and servant-girls at hand, so they had ample to do to raise the portières, to put the back-cushions in their places, and to spread out the rugs.

Dowager lady Jia stepped into the room, leaning on lady Feng's arm. She and Mrs. Xue took their places, with due regard to the distinction between hostess and visitors; and Xue Baochai and Shi Xiangyun seated themselves below. Madame Wang then came forward, and presented with her own hands tea to old lady Jia, while Li Gongcai handed a cup to Mrs. Xue.

"You'd better let those young sisters-in law do the honors," remonstrated old lady Jia, "and sit over there so that we may be able to have a chat."

Madame Wang at length sat on a small bench. "Let our worthy senior's viands," she cried, addressing herself to lady Feng, "be served here. And let a few more things be brought!"

Lady Feng acquiesced without delay, and she told a servant to cross over to their old mistress' quarters and to bid the matrons, employed in that part of the household, promptly go out and summon the waiting-girls. The various waiting-maids arrived with all despatch. Madame Wang directed them to ask their young ladies round. But after a protracted absence on the errand, only two of the girls turned up: Tanchun and Xichun. Yingchun, was not, in her state of health, equal to the fatigue, or able to put anything in her mouth, and Lin Daiyu, superfluous to add, could only safely partake of five out of ten meals, so no one thought anything of their nonappearance.

Presently the eatables were brought, and the servants arranged them in their proper places on the table.

Lady Feng took a napkin and wrapped a bundle of chopsticks in it. "Venerable ancestor and you, Mrs. Xue," she smiled, standing the while below, "there's no need of any yielding! Just you listen to me and I'll make things all right."

"Let's do as she wills!" old lady Jia remarked to Mrs. Xue laughingly.

Mrs. Xue signified her approval with a smile; so lady Feng placed, in due course, four pairs of chopsticks on the table; the two pairs on the upper end for dowager lady Jia and Mrs. Xue; those on the two sides for Xue Baochai and Shi Xiangyun. Madame Wang, Li Gongcai, and a few others, stood together below and watched the attendants serve the viands. Lady Feng first and foremost hastily asked for clean utensils, and drew near the table to select some eatables for Baoyu. Presently, the soup â la lotus leaves arrived. After old lady Jia had well scrutinized it, Madame Wang turned her head, and catching sight of Yuchuan'er, she immediately commissioned her to take some over to Baoyu.

"She can't carry it single-handed," demurred lady Feng.

But by a strange coincidence, Ying'er then walked into the room along with Xi'er, and Baochai knowing very well that they had already had their meal forthwith said to Ying'er: "Your Master Secundus, Mr. Baoyu, just asked that you should go and twist a few girdles for him; so you two might as well proceed together!"

Ying'er expressed her readiness and left the apartment, in company with Yuchuan'er.

"How can you carry it, so very hot as it is, the whole way there?" observed Ying'er.

"Don't distress yourself!" rejoined Yuchuan smiling. "I know how to do it."

Saying this, she directed a matron to come and place the soup, rice, and the rest of the eatables in a present box; and bidding her lay hold of it and follow them, the two girls sped on their way with empty hands, and made straight for the entrance of the Yihong court. Here Yuchuan'er at length took the things herself, and entered the room in company with Ying'er. The trio, Xiren, Sheyue, and Qiuwen were at the time chatting and laughing with Baoyu; but the moment they saw their two friends arrive they speedily jumped to their feet. "How is it," they exclaimed laughingly, "that you two drop in just the nick of time? Have you come together?"

With these words on their lips, they descended to greet them. Yu-chuan took at once a seat on a small stool. Ying'er, however, did not presume to seat herself; and though Xiren was quick enough in moving a foot-stool for her, Ying'er did not still venture to sit down.

Ying'er's arrival filled Baoyu with intense delight. But as soon as he noticed Yuchuan, he recalled to memory her sister Jinchuan'er, and he felt wounded to the very heart, and overpowered with shame. And, without troubling his mind about Ying'er, he addressed his remarks to Yuchuan'er.

Xiren saw very well that Ying'er failed to attract his attention and she began to fear lest she felt uncomfortable; and when she further realised that Ying'er herself would not take a seat, she drew her out of the room and repaired with her into the outer apartment, where they had a chat over their tea.

Sheyue and her companions had, in the meantime, got the bowls and chopsticks ready and came to wait upon (Baoyu) during his meal. But Baoyu would not have anything to eat. "Is your mother all right," he forthwith inquired of Yuchuan'er.

An angry scowl crept over Yuchuan'er's face. She did not even look straight at Baoyu. And only after a long pause was it that she at last uttered merely the words, "all right," by way of reply. Baoyu, therefore, found talking to her of little zest. But after a protracted silence he felt impelled to again force a smile, and to ask: "Who told you to bring these things over to me?"

"The ladies," answered Yuchuan'er.

Baoyu discerned the mournful expression, which still beclouded her countenance and he readily jumped at the conclusion that it must be entirely occasioned by the fate which had befallen Jinchuan'er, but when fain to put on a meek and unassuming manner, and endeavor to cheer her, he saw how little he could demean himself in the presence of so many people, and consequently he did his best and discovered the means of getting everyone out of the way. Afterwards, straining another smile, he plied her with all sorts of questions.

Yuchuan'er, it is true, did not at first choose to heed his advances, yet when she observed that Baoyu did not put on any airs, and, that in spite of all her querulous reproaches, he still continued pleasant and agreeable, she felt disconcerted and her features at last assumed a certain expression of cheerfulness. Baoyu thereupon smiled. "My dear girl," he said, as he gave way to entreaties, "bring that soup and let me taste it!"

"I've never been in the habit of feeding people," Yuchuan'er replied. "You'd better wait till the others return; you can have some then."

"I don't want you to feed me," laughed Baoyu. "It's because I can't move about that I appeal to you. Do let me have it! You'll then get back early and be able, when you've handed over the things, to have your meal. But were I to go on wasting your time, won't you feel upset from hunger? Should you be lazy to budge, well then, I'll endure the pain and get down and fetch it myself."

As he spoke, he tried to alight from bed. He strained every nerve, and raised himself, but unable to stand the exertion, he burst out into groans. At the sight of his anguish, Yuchuan'er had not the heart to refuse her help. Springing up, "Lie down!" she cried. "In what former existence did you commit such evil that your retribution in the present one is so apparent? Which of my eyes however can brook looking at you going on in that way?"

While taunting him, she again blurted out laughing, and brought the soup over to him.

"My dear girl;" smiled Baoyu, "if you want to show temper, better do so here! When you see our venerable senior and madame, my mother, you should be a little more even-tempered, for if you still behave like this, you'll at once get a scolding!"

"Eat away, eat away!" urged Yuchuan'er. "There's no need for you to be so sweet-mouthed and honey-tongued with me. I don't put any faith in such talk!"

So speaking, she pressed Baoyu until he had two mouthfuls of soup.

"It isn't nice, it isn't nice!" Baoyu purposely exclaimed.

"Amituo Fo!" ejaculated Yuchuan'er. "If this isn't nice, what's nice?"

"There's no flavor about it at all," resumed Baoyu. "If you don't believe me taste it, and you'll find out for yourself."

Yuchuan'er in a tantrum actually put some of it to her lips.

"Well," laughed Baoyu, "it is nice!"

This exclamation eventually enabled Yuchuan to see what Baoyu was driving at, for Baoyu had in fact been trying to beguile her to have a mouthful.

"As, at one moment, you say you don't want any," she forthwith observed, "and now you say it is nice, I won't give you any."

While Baoyu returned her smiles, he kept on earnestly entreating her to let him have some.

Yuchuan'er however would still not give him any; and she, at the same time, called to the servants to fetch what there was for him to eat.

But the instant the waiting-maid put her foot into the room, servants came quite unexpectedly to deliver a message.

"Two nurses," they said, "have arrived from the household of Mr. Fu, Secundus, to present his compliments. They have now come to see you, Mr. Secundus." As soon as Baoyu heard this report, he felt sure that they must be nurses sent over from the household of Deputy Sub-Prefect, Fu Shi.

This Fu Shi had originally been a pupil of Jia Zheng, and had, indeed, had to rely entirely upon the reputation enjoyed by the Jia family for the realization of his wishes. Jia Zheng had, likewise, treated him with such genuine regard, and so unlike any of his other pupils, that he (Fu Shi) ever and anon despatched inmates from his mansion to come and see him so as to keep up friendly relations.

Baoyu had at all times entertained an aversion for bold-faced men and unsophisticated women, so why did he once more, on this occasion, issue directions that the two matrons should be introduced into his presence? There was, in fact, a reason for his action. It was simply that Baoyu had come to learn that Fu Shi had a sister, Qiufang by name, a girl as comely as a magnificent gem, and perfection itself, the report of outside people went, as much in intellect as in beauty. He had, it is true, not yet seen anything of her with his own eyes, but the sentiments, which made him think of her and cherish her, from a distance, were characterized by such extreme sincerity, that dreading lest he should, by refusing to admit the matrons, reflect discredit upon Fu Qiufang, he was prompted to lose no time in expressing a wish that they should be ushered in.

This Fu Shi had really risen from the vulgar herd, so seeing that Qiufang possessed several traits of beauty and exceptional intellectual talents, Fu Shi arrived at the resolution of making his sister the means of joining relationship with the influential family of some honorable clan. And so unwilling was he to promise her lightly to any suitor that things were delayed up to this time. Therefore Fu Qiufang, though at present past her twentieth birthday, was not as yet engaged. But the various well-to-do families, belonging to honorable clans, looked down, on the other hand, on her poor and mean extraction, holding her in such light esteem, as not to relish the idea of making any offer for her hand. So if Fu Shi cultivated intimate terms with the Jia household, he, needless to add, did so with an interested motive.

The two matrons, deputed on the present errand, completely lacked, as it happened, all knowledge of the world, and the moment they heard that Baoyu wished to see them, they wended their steps inside. But no sooner had they inquired how he was, and passed a few remarks than

Yuchuan'er, becoming conscious of the arrival of strangers, did not bandy words with Baoyu, but stood with the plate of soup in her hands, engrossed in listening to the conversation. Baoyu, again, was absorbed in speaking to the matrons; and, while eating some rice, he stretched out his arm to get at the soup; but both his and her (Yuchuan'er's) eyes were rivetted on the women, and as he thoughtlessly jerked out his hand with some violence, he struck the bowl and turned it clean over. The soup fell over Baoyu's hand. But it did not hurt Yuchuan'er. She sustained, however, such a fright that she gave a start.

"How did this happen!" she smilingly shouted with vehemence to the intense consternation of the waiting-maids, who rushed up and clasped the bowl. But notwithstanding that Baoyu had scalded his own hand, he was quite unconscious of the accident; so much so, that he assailed Yuchuan'er with a heap of questions, as to where she had been burnt, and whether it was sore or not.

Yuchuan'er and everyone present were highly amused.

"You yourself," observed Yuchuan'er, "have been scalded, and do you keep on asking about myself?"

At these words, Baoyu became at last aware of the injury he had received. The servants rushed with all promptitude and cleared the mess. But Baoyu was not inclined to touch any more food. He washed his hands, drank a cup of tea, and then exchanged a few further sentences with the two matrons. But subsequently, the two women said good-bye and quitted the room. Qingwen and some other girls saw them as far as the bridge, after which, they retraced their steps.

The two matrons perceived, that there was no one about, and while proceeding on their way, they started a conversation.

"It isn't strange," smiled the one, "if people say that this Baoyu of theirs is handsome in appearance, but stupid as far as brains go. Nice enough a thing to look at but not to put to one's lips; rather idiotic in fact; for he burns his own hand, and then he asks someone else whether she's sore or not. Now, isn't this being a regular fool?"

"The last time I came," the other remarked, also smiling, "I heard that many inmates of his family feel ill-will against him. In real truth he is a fool! For there he drips in the heavy downpour like a water fowl, and instead of running to shelter himself, he reminds other people of the rain, and urges them to get quick out of the wet. Now, tell me, isn't this ridiculous, eh? Time and again, when no one is present, he cries to himself, then laughs to himself. When he sees a swallow, he instantly talks to it; when he espies a fish, in the river, he forthwith speaks to it. At the sight of stars or the moon, if he doesn't groan and sigh, he mutters and mutters. Indeed, he hasn't the least bit of character; so much so, that he even puts up with the temper shown by those low-bred maids. If he takes a fancy to a thing, it's nice enough even though it be a bit of thread. But as for waste, what does he mind? A thing may be worth a thousand or ten thousand pieces of money, he doesn't worry his mind in the least about it."

While they talked, they reached the exterior of the garden, and they betook themselves back to their home; where we will leave them.

As soon as Xiren, for we will return to her, saw the women leave the room, she took Ying'er by the hand and led her in, and they asked Baoyu what kind of girdle he wanted made.

"I was just now so bent upon talking," Baoyu smiled to Ying'er, "that I forgot all about you. I put you to the trouble of coming, not for anything else, but that you should also make me a few nets."

"Nets! To put what in?" Ying'er inquired.

Baoyu, at this question, put on a smile. "Don't concern yourself about what they are for!" he replied. "Just make me a few of each kind!"

Ying'er clapped her hand and laughed. "Could this ever be done!" she cried, "If you want all that lot, why, they couldn't be finished in ten years time."

"My dear girl," smiled Baoyu, "work at them for me then whenever you are at leisure, and have nothing better to do."

"How could you get through them all in a little time?" Xiren interposed smilingly. "First choose now therefore such as are most urgently needed and make a couple of them."

"What about urgently needed?" Ying'er exclaimed, "They are merely used for fans, scented pendants, and handkerchiefs."

"Nets for handkerchiefs will do all right." Baoyu answered.

"What's the color of your handkerchief?" inquired Ying'er.

"It's a deep red one." Baoyu rejoined.

"For a deep red one," continued Ying'er, "a black net will do very nicely, or one of dark green. Both these agree with the color."

"What goes well with brown?" Baoyu asked.

"Peach-red goes well with brown." Ying'er added.

"That will make them look gaudy!" Baoyu observed. "Yet with all their plainness, they should be somewhat gaudy."

"Leek-green and willow-yellow are what are most to my taste," Ying'er pursued.

"Yes, they'll also do!" Baoyu retorted. "But make one of peach-red too and then one of leek-green."

"Of what design?" Ying'er remarked.

"How many kinds of designs are there?" Baoyu said.

"There are 'the stick of incense,' 'stools upset towards heaven,' 'part of elephant's eyes,' 'squares,' 'chains,' 'plum blossom,' and 'willow leaves.'" Ying'er answered.

"What was the kind of design you made for Miss Tertia the other day?" Baoyu inquired.

"It was the 'plum blossom with piled cores,'" Ying'er explained in reply.

"Yes, that's nice." Baoyu rejoined.

As he uttered this remark, Xiren arrived with the cords. But no sooner were they brought than a matron cried, from outside the window: "Girls, your viands are ready!"

"Go and have your meal," urged Baoyu, "and come back quick after you've had it."

"There are visitors here," Xiren smiled, "and how can I very well go?"

"What makes you say so?" Ying'er laughed, while adjusting the cords. "If's only right and proper that you should go and have your food at once and then return."

Hearing this, Xiren and her companions went off, leaving behind only two youthful servant-girls to answer the calls.

Baoyu watched Ying'er make the nets. But, while keeping his eyes intent on her, he talked at the same time of one thing and then another, and next went on to ask her how far she was in her teens.

Ying'er continued plaiting. "I'm sixteen," she simultaneously rejoined.

"What was your original surname?" Baoyu added.

"It was Huang," answered Ying'er.

"That's just the thing," Baoyu smiled; "for in real truth there's the 'Huang Ying'er' (oriole)."

"My name, at one time, consisted of two characters," continued Ying'er. "I was called Jinying; but Miss Baochai didn't like it, as it was difficult to pronounce, and only called me Ying'er; so now I've come to be known under that name."

"One can very well say that cousin Baochai is fond of you!" Baoyu pursued. "By and bye, when she gets married, she's sure to take you along with her."

Ying'er puckered up her lips, and gave a significant smile.

"I've often told Xiren," Baoyu smiled, "that I can't help wondering who'll shortly be the lucky ones to win your mistress and yourself."

"You aren't aware," laughed Ying'er, "that our young mistress possesses several qualities not to be found in a single person in this world; her face is a second consideration."

Baoyu noticed how captivating Ying'er's tone of voice was, how complaisant she was, and how simpleton-like unaffected in her language and smiles, and he soon felt the warmest affection for her; and particularly so, when he started the conversation about Baochai.

"Where do her qualities lie?" he readily inquired. "My dear girl, please tell me!"

"If I tell you," said Ying'er, "you must, on no account, let her know anything about it again."

"This goes without saying," smiled Baoyu.

But this answer was still on his lips, when they overheard someone outside remark: "How is it that everything is so quiet?"

Both gazed round to see who possibly it could be. They discovered, strange enough, no one else than Baochai herself.

Baoyu hastily offered her a seat. Baochai seated herself, and then wanted to know what Ying'er was busy plaiting. Inquiring the while, she approached her and scrutinised what she held in her hands, half of which had by this time been done. "What's the fun of a thing like this?" she said. "Wouldn't it be preferable to plait a net, and put the jade in it?"

This allusion suggested the idea to Baoyu. Speedily clapping his hands, he smiled and exclaimed: "Your idea is splendid, cousin. I'd forgotten all about it! The only thing is what color will suit it best?"

"It will never do to use mixed colors," Baochai rejoined. "Deep red will, on one hand, clash with the color; while yellow is not pleasing to the eye; and black, on the other hand, is too somber. But wait, I'll try and devise something. Bring that gold cord and use it with the black beaded cord; and if you twist one of each together, and make a net with them, it will look very pretty!"

Upon hearing this, Baoyu was immeasurably delighted, and time after time he shouted to the servants to fetch the gold cord. But just at that moment Xiren stepped in, with two bowls of eatables. "How very strange this is today!" she said to Baoyu. "Why, a few minutes back, my mistress, your mother, sent someone to bring me two bowls of viands."

"The supply," replied Baoyu smiling, "must have been so plentiful today, that they've sent some to everyone of you."

"It isn't that," continued Xiren, "for they were distinctly given to me by name. What's more, I wasn't bidden go and knock my head; so this is indeed remarkable!"

"If they're given to you," Baoyu smiled, "why, you had better go and eat them. What's there in this to fill you with conjectures?"

"There's never been anything like this before," Xiren added, "so, it makes me feel uneasy."

Baochai compressed her lips. "If this," she laughed, "makes you fell uneasy, there will be by and bye other things to make you far more uneasy."

Xiren realised that she implied something by her insinuations, as she knew from past experience that Baochai was not one given to lightly and contemptuously poking fun at people; and, remembering the notions entertained by Madame Wang on the last occasion she had seen her, she dropped at once any further allusions to the subject and brought the eatables up to Baoyu for his inspection. "I shall come and hold the cords," she observed, "as soon as I've rinsed my hands."

This said, she immediately quitted the apartment. After her meal, she washed her hands and came inside to hold the gold cords for Ying'er to plait the net with.

By this time, Baochai had been called away by a servant, despatched by Xue Pan. But while Baoyu was watching the net that was being made he caught sight, at a moment least expected, of two servant-girls, who came from the part of Madame Xing of the other mansion, to bring him a few kinds of fruits, and to inquire whether he was able to walk. "If you can go about," they told him, "(our mistress) desires you, Mr. Baoyu, to cross over tomorrow and have a little distraction. Her ladyship really longs to see you."

"Were I able to walk," Baoyu answered with alacrity, "I would feel it my duty to go and pay my respects to your mistress! Anyhow, the pain is better than before, so request your lady to allay her solicitude."

As he bade them both sit down, he, at the same time, called Qiuwen. "Take," he said to her, "half of the fruits, just received, to Miss Lin as a present."

Qiuwen signified her obedience, and was about to start on her errand, when she heard Daiyu talking in he court, and Baoyu eagerly shout out: "Request her to walk in at once!"

But should there be any further particulars, which you, reader might feel disposed to know, peruse the details given in the following chapter.

CHAPTER 36

While Xiren is busy embroidering mandarin ducks, Baoyu receives, in the Jiangyun Pavilion, an omen from a dream. Baoyu apprehends that there is a destiny in affections, when his feelings are aroused to a sense of the situation in the Pear Fragrance court.

Ever since dowager lady Jia's return from Madame Wang's quarters, for we will now take up the string of our narrative, she naturally felt happier in her mind as she saw that Baoyu improved from day to day; but nervous lest Jia Zheng should again in the future send for him, she lost no time in bidding a servant summon a head-page, a constant attendant upon Jia Zheng, to come to her, and in impressing upon him various orders. "Should," she enjoined him, "anything turn up henceforward connected with meeting guests, entertaining visitors, and other such matters, and your master mean to send for Baoyu, you can dispense with going to deliver the message. Just you tell him that I say that after the severe thrashing he has had, great care must be first taken of him during several months before he can be allowed to walk; and that, secondly, his constellation is unpropitious and that he could not see any outsider, while sacrifices are being offered to the stars; that I won't have him therefore put his foot beyond the second gate before the expiry of the eighth moon."

The head-page listened patiently to her instructions, and, assenting to all she had to say, he took his leave.

Old lady Jia thereupon also sent for nurse Li, Xiren, and the other waiting-maids and recommended them to tell Baoyu about her injunctions so that he might be able to quiet his mind.

Baoyu had always had a repugnance for entertaining high officials and men in general, and the greatest horror of going in official hat and ceremonial dress, to offer congratulations, or express condolences, to pay calls, return visits, or perform other similar conventionalities, but upon receipt on the present occasion of this message, he became so much the more confirmed in his dislikes that not only did he suspend all intercourse with every single relative and friend, but even went so far as to study more than he had ever done before, his own caprices in the fulfilment of those morning and evening salutations due to the senior members of his family. Day after day he spent in the garden, doing nothing else than loafing about, sitting down here, or reclining there. Of a morning, he would, as soon as it was day, stroll as far as the quarters of dowager lady Jia and Madame Wang, to repair back, however, in no time. Yet ever ready was he every day that went by to perform menial services for any of the waiting-maids. He, in fact, wasted away in the most complete dolce far niente days as well as months. If perchance Baochai or any other girl of the same age as herself found at any time an opportunity to give him advice, he would, instead of taking it in good part, fly into a huff. "A pure and spotless maiden," he would say, "has likewise gone and deliberately imitated those persons, whose aim is to fish for reputation and to seek praise; that set of government thieves and salaried devils. This result entirely arises from the fact that there have been people in former times, who have uselessly stirred up trouble and purposely fabricated stories with the primary object of enticing the filthy male creatures, who would spring up in future ages, to follow in their steps! And who would have thought it, I have had the misfortune of being born a masculine being! But, even those beautiful girls, in the female apartments, have been so contaminated by this practice that verily they show themselves ungrateful for the virtue of Heaven and Earth, in endowing them with perception, and in rearing them with so much comeliness."

Seeing therefore what an insane mania possessed him, not one of his cousins came forward to tender him one proper word of counsel. Lin Daiyu was the only one of them, who, from his very infancy, had never once admonished him to strive and make a position and attain fame, so thus it was that he entertained for Daiyu profound consideration. But enough of minor details.

We will now turn our attention to lady Feng. Soon after the news of Jinchuan'er's death reached her, she saw that domestics from various branches of the family paid her frequent visits at most unexpected hours, and presented her a lot of things, and that they courted her presence at most unseasonable moments, to pay their compliments and adulate her, and she begun to harbor suspicions, in her own mind, as she little knew what their object could possibly be. On this date, she again noticed that some of them had brought their gifts, so, when evening arrived, and no one was present, she felt compelled to inquire jocosely of Ping'er what their aim could be.

"Can't your ladyship fathom even this?" Ping'er answered with a sardonic smile. "Why, their daughters must, I fancy, be servant-girls in Madame Wang's apartments! For her ladyship's rooms four elderly girls are at present allotted with a monthly allowance of one tael; the rest simply receiving several hundreds of cash each month; so now that Jinchuan'er is dead and gone, these people must, of course, be anxious to try their tricks and get this one-tael job!"

Hearing this, lady Feng smiled a significant smile. "That's it. Yes, that's it!" she exclaimed. "You've really suggested the idea to my mind! From all appearances, these people are a most insatiable lot; for they make quite enough in the way of money! And as for any business that requires a little exertion, why they are never ready to bear a share of it! They make use of their girls as so many tools to shove their own duties upon. Yet one overlooks that. But must they too have designs upon this job? Never mind! These people cannot easily afford to spend upon me the money they do. But they bring this upon their own selves, so I'll keep every bit of thing they send. I've, after all, resolved how to act in the matter!"

Having arrived at this decision, lady Feng purely and simply protracted the delay until all the women had sent her enough to satisfy her, when she at last suited her own convenience and spoke to Madame Wang (on the subject of the vacant post).

Mrs. Xue and her daughter were sitting one day, at noon, in Madame Wang's quarters, together with Lin Daiyu and the other girls, when lady Feng found an opportunity and broached the topic with Madame Wang. "Ever since," she said, "sister Jinchuan'er's death, there has been one servant less in your ladyship's service. But you may possibly have set your choice upon some girl; if so, do let me know who it is, so that I may be able to pay her her monthly wages."

This reminder made Madame Wang commune with her own self. "I fancy," she remarked; "that the custom is that there should be four or five of them; but as long as there are enough to wait upon me, I don't mind, so we can really dispense with another."

"What you say is, properly speaking, perfectly correct," smiled lady Feng; "but it's an old established custom. There are still a couple to be found in other people's rooms and won't you, Madame, conform with the rule? Besides, the saving of a tael is a small matter."

After this argument, Madame Wang indulged in further thought. "Never mind," she then observed, "just you bring over this allowance and pay it to me. And there will be no need to supply another girl. I'll hand over this tael to her younger sister, Yuchuan'er, and finish with it. Her elder sister came to an unpleasant end, after a long term of service with me; so if the younger sister, she leaves behind in my employ, receives a double share, it won't be any too excessive."

Lady Feng expressed her approval and turning round she said smilingly to Yuchuan'er: "I congratulate you, I congratulate you!"

Yuchuan'er thereupon crossed over and prostrated herself.

"I just want to ask you," Madame Wang went on to inquire, "how much Mrs. Zhao and Mrs. Zhou are allowed monthly?"

"They have a fixed allowance," answered lady Feng, "each of them draws two taels. But Mrs. Zhao gets two taels for cousin Jia Huan, so hers amounts in all to four taels; besides these, four strings of cash."

"Are they paid in full month after month?" Madame Wang inquired.

Lady Feng thought the question so very strange that she hastened to exclaim by way of reply: "How are they not paid in full?"

"The other day," Madame Wang proceeded, "I heard a faint rumor that there was someone, who complained in an aggrieved way that she had got a string short. How and why is this?"

"The monthly allowances of the servant-girls, attached to the secondary wives," lady Feng hurriedly added with a smile, "amounted originally to a diao each, but ever since last year, it was decided, by those people outside, that the shares of each of those ladies' girls should be reduced by half, that is, each to five hundred cash; and, as each lady has a couple of servant-girls, they receive therefore a tiao short. But for this, they can't bear me a grudge. As far as I'm concerned, I would only be too glad to let them have it; but our people outside will again disallow it; so is it likely that I can authorize any increase, pray? In this matter of payments I merely receive the money, and I've nothing to do with how it comes and how it goes. I nevertheless recommended, on two or three occasions, that it would be better if these two shares were again raised to the old amount; but they said that there's only that much money, so that I can't very well volunteer any further suggestions! Now that the funds are paid into my hands, I give them to them every month, without any irregularity of even so much as a day. When payments hitherto were effected outside, what month were they not short of money? And did they ever, on any single instance, obtain their pay at the proper time and date?"

Having heard this explanation, Madame Wang kept silent for a while. Next she proceeded to ask how many girls there were with dowager lady Jia drawing one tael.

"Eight of them," rejoined lady Feng, "but there are at present only seven; the other one is Xiren."

"Quite right," assented Madame Wang. "But your cousin Baoyu hasn't any maid at one tael; for Xiren is still a servant belonging to old lady Jia's household."

"Xiren," lady Feng smiled, "is still our dear ancestor's servant; she's only lent to cousin Baoyu; so that she still receives this tael in her capacity of maid to our worthy senior. Any proposal, therefore, that might now be made, that this tael should, as Xiren is Baoyu's servant, be curtailed, can, on no account, be entertained. Yet, were it suggested that another servant should be added to our senior's staff, then in this way one could reduce the tael she gets. But if this be not curtailed, it will be necessary to also add a servant in cousin Jia Huan's rooms, in order that there should be a fair apportionment. In fact, Qingwen, Sheyue and the others, numbering seven senior maids, receive each a tiao a month; and Jiahui and the rest of the junior maids, eight in all, get each five hundred cash per mensem; and this was recommended by our venerable ancestor herself; so how can anyone be angry and feel displeasure?"

"Just listen," laughed Mrs. Xue, "to that girl Feng's mouth! It rattles and rattles like a cart laden with walnuts, which has turned topsy-turvy! Yet, her accounts are, from what one can gather, clear enough, and her arguments full of reason."

'Aunt," rejoined lady Feng smiling, "was I likely, pray, wrong in what I said?"

"Who ever said you were wrong?" Mrs. Xue smiled. "But were you to talk a little slower, wouldn't it be a saving of exertion for you?"

Lady Feng was about to laugh, but hastily checking herself, she lent an ear to what Madame Wang might have to tell her.

Madame Wang indulged in thought for a considerable time. Afterwards, facing lady Feng, "You'd better," she said, "select a waiting-maid tomorrow and send her over to our worthy senior to fill up Xiren's place. Then, discontinue that allowance, which Xiren draws, and keep out of the sum of twenty taels, allotted to me monthly, two taels and a tiao, and give them to Xiren. So henceforward what Mrs. Zhao and Mrs. Zhou will get, Xiren will likewise get, with the only difference that the share granted to Xiren, will be entirely apportioned out of my own allowance. Mind, therefore, there will be no necessity to touch the public funds!"

Lady Feng acquiesced to each one of her recommendations, and, pushing Mrs. Xue, "Aunt," she inquired, "have you heard her proposal? What have I all along maintained? Well, my words have actually come out true today!"

"This should have been accomplished long ago," Mrs. Xue answered. "For without, of course, making any allusion to her looks, her way of doing business is liberal; her speech and her relations with people are always prompted by an even temper, while inwardly she has plenty of singleness of heart and eagerness to hold her own. Indeed, such a girl is not easy to come across!"

Madame Wang made every effort to conceal her tears. "How could you people ever rightly estimate Xiren's qualities?" she observed. "Why, she's a hundred times better than my own Baoyu. How fortunate, in reality, Baoyu is! Well would it be if he could have her wait upon him for the whole length of his life!"

"In that case," lady Feng suggested, "why, have her face shaved at once, and openly place her in his room as a secondary wife. Won't this be a good plan?"

"This won't do!" Madame Wang retorted. "For first and foremost he's of tender years. In the second place, my husband won't countenance any such thing! In the third, so long as Baoyu sees that Xiren is his waiting-maid, he may, in the event of anything occurring from his having been allowed to run wild, listen to any good counsel she might give him. But were she now to be made his secondary wife, Xiren would not venture to tender him any extreme advice, even when it's necessary to do so. It's better, therefore, to let things stand as they are for the present, and talk about them again, after the lapse of another two or three years."

At the close of these arguments, lady Feng could not put in a word, by way of reply, to refute them, so turning round, she left the room. She had no sooner, however, got under the verandah, than she discerned the wives of a number of butlers, waiting for her to report various matters to her. Seeing her issue out of the room, they with one consent smiled. "What has your ladyship had to lay before Madame Wang," they remarked, "that you've been talking away this length of time? Didn't you find it hot work?"

Lady Feng tucked up her sleeves several times. Then resting her foot on the step of the side door, she laughed and rejoined: "The draft in this passage is so cool, that I'll stop, and let it play on me a bit before I go on. You people," she proceeded to tell them, "say that I've been talking to her all this while, but Madame Wang conjured up all that has occurred for the last two hundred years and questioned me about it; so could I very well not have anything to say in reply? But from this day forth," she added with a sarcastic smile, "I shall do several mean things, and should even (Mrs. Zhao and Mrs. Zhou) go, out of any ill-will, and tell Madame Wang, I won't know what fear is for such stupid, glib-tongued, foul-mouthed creatures as they, who are bound not to see a good end! It isn't for them to indulge in those fanciful dreams of becoming primary wives, for there will come soon a day when the whole lump sum of their allowance will be cut off! They grumble against us for having now reduced the perquisites of the servant-maids, but they don't consider whether they deserve to have so many as three girls to dance attendance on them!"

While heaping abuse on their heads, she started homewards, and went all alone in search of some domestic to go and deliver a message to old lady Jia.

But without any further reference to her, we will take up the thread of our narrative with Mrs. Xue, and the others along with her. During this interval they finished feasting on melons. After some more gossip, each went her own way; and Baochai, Daiyu, and the rest of the cousins returned into the garden. Baochai then asked Daiyu to repair with her to the Ouxiang Arbor. But Daiyu said that she was just going to have her bath, so they parted company, and Baochai walked back all by herself. On her way, she stepped into the Yihong court, to look up Baoyu and have a friendly hobnob with him, with the idea of dispelling her mid-day lassitude; but, contrary to her expectations, the moment she put her foot into the court, she did not so much as catch the caw of a crow. Even the two storks stood under the banana trees, plunged in sleep. Baochai proceeded along the covered passage and entered the rooms. Here she discovered the servant-girls sleeping soundly on the bed of the outer apartment; some lying one way, some another; so turning round the decorated screen, she wended her steps into Baoyu's chamber. Baoyu was asleep in bed. Xiren was seated by his side, busy plying her needle. Next to her, lay a yak tail. Baochai advanced up to her. "You're really far too scrupulous," she said smilingly in an undertone. "Are there still flies or mosquitos in here? and why do yet use that fly-flap for, to drive what away?"

Xiren was quite taken by surprise. But hastily raising her head, and realising that it was Baochai, she hurriedly put down her needlework. "Miss," she whispered with a smile, "you came upon me so unawares that you gave me quite a start! You don't know, Miss, that though there be no flies or mosquitoes there is, no one would believe it, a kind of small insect, which penetrates through the holes of this gauze; it is scarcely to be detected, but when one is asleep, it bites just like ants do!"

"It isn't to be wondered at," Baochai suggested, "for the back of these rooms adjoins the water; the whole place is also one mass of fragrant flowers, and the interior of this room is, too, full of their aroma. These insects grow mostly in the core of flowers, so no sooner do they scent the smell of any than they at once rush in."

Saying this, she cast a look on the needlework she (Xiren) held in her hands. It consisted, in fact, of a belt of white silk, lined with red, and embroidered on the upper part with designs representing mandarin ducks, disporting themselves among some lotus. The lotus flowers were red, the leaves green, the ducks of variegated colors.

"Ai-ya!" ejaculated Baochai, "what very beautiful work! For whom is this, that it's worth your while wasting so much labor on it?"

Xiren pouted her lips towards the bed.

"Does a big strapping fellow like this," Baochai laughed, "still wear such things?"

"He would never wear any before," Xiren smiled, "that's why such a nice one was specially worked for him, in order that when he was allowed to see it, he should not be able to do otherwise than use it. With the present hot weather, he goes to sleep anyhow, but as he has been coaxed to wear it, it doesn't matter if even he doesn't cover himself well at night. You say that I bestow much labor upon this, but you haven't yet seen the one he has on!"

"It is a lucky thing," Baochai observed, smiling, "that you're gifted with such patience."

"I've done so much of it today," remarked Xiren, "that my neck is quite sore from bending over it. My dear Miss," she then urged with a beaming countenance, "do sit here a little. I'll go out for a turn. I'll be back shortly."

With these words, she sallied out of the room.

Baochai was intent upon examining the embroidery, so in her absentmindedness, she, with one bend of her body, settled herself on the very same spot, which Xiren had recently occupied. But she found, on second scrutiny, the work so really admirable, that impulsively picking up the needle, she continued it for her. At quite an unforeseen moment—for Lin Daiyu had met Shi Xiangyun and asked her to come along with her and present her congratulations to Xiren—these two girls made their appearance in the court. Finding the whole place plunged in silence, Xiangyun turned round and betook herself first into the side-rooms in search of Xiren. Lin Daiyu, meanwhile, walked up to the window from outside, and peeped in through the gauze frame. At a glance, she espied Baoyu, clad in a silvery-red coat, lying carelessly on the bed, and Baochai, seated by his side, busy at some needlework, with a fly-brush resting by her side.

As soon as Lin Daiyu became conscious of the situation, she immediately slipped out of sight, and stopping her mouth with one hand, as she did not venture to laugh aloud, she waved her other hand and beckoned to Xiangyun. The moment Xiangyun saw the way she went on, she concluded that she must have something new to impart to her, and she approached her with all promptitude. At the sight, which opened itself before her eyes, she also felt inclined to laugh. Yet the sudden recollection of the kindness, with which Baochai had always dealt towards her, induced her to quickly seal her lips. And knowing well enough that Daiyu never spared anyone with her mouth, she was seized with such fear lest she should jeer at them, that she immediately dragged her past the window. "Come along!" she observed. "Xiren, I remember, said that she would be going at noon to wash some clothes at the pond. I presume she's there already so let's go and join her."

Daiyu inwardly grasped her meaning, but, after indulging in a couple of sardonic smiles, she had no alternative but to follow in her footsteps.

Baochai had, during this while, managed to embroider two or three petals, when she heard Baoyu begin to shout abusively in his dreams. "How can," he cried, "one ever believe what bonzes and Daoist priests say? What about a match between gold and jade? My impression is that it's to be a union between a shrub and a stone!"

Xue Baochai caught every single word uttered by him and fell unconsciously in a state of excitement. Of a sudden, however, Xiren appeared on the scene. "Hasn't he yet woke up?" she inquired.

Baochai nodded her head by way of reply.

"I just came across," Xiren smiled, "Miss Lin and Miss Shi. Did they happen to come in?"

"I didn't see them come in," Baochai answered. "Did they tell you anything?" she next smilingly asked of Xiren.

Xiren blushed and laughed significantly. "They simply came out with some of those jokes of theirs," she explained. "What decent things could such as they have had to tell me?"

"They made insinuations today," Baochai laughed, "which are anything but a joke! I was on the point of telling you them, when you rushed away in an awful hurry."

But no sooner had she concluded, than she perceived a servant, come over from lady Feng's part to fetch Xiren. "It must be on account of what they hinted," Baochai smilingly added.

Xiren could not therefore do otherwise than arouse two servant-maids and go. She proceeded, with Baochai, out of the Yihong court, and then repaired all alone to lady Feng's on this side. It was indeed to communicate to her what had been decided about her, and to explain to her, as well, that though she could go and prostrate herself before Madame Wang, she could dispense with seeing dowager lady Jia. This news made Xiren feel very awkward; to such an extent, that no sooner had she got through her visit to Madame Wang, than she returned in a hurry to her rooms.

Baoyu had already awoke. He asked the reason why she had been called away, but Xiren temporized by giving him an evasive answer. And only at night, when everyone was quiet, did Xiren at length give him a full account of the whole matter. Baoyu was delighted beyond measure. "I'll see now," he said, with a face beaming with smiles, "whether you'll go back home or not. On your return, after your last visit to your people, you stated that your brother wished to redeem you, adding that this place was no home for you, and that you didn't know what would become of you in the long run. You freely uttered all that language devoid of feeling and reason, and enough too to produce an estrangement between us, in order to frighten me; but I'd like to see who'll henceforward have the audacity to come and ask you to leave!"

Xiren, upon hearing this, smiled a smile full of irony. "You shouldn't say such things!" she replied. "From henceforward I shall be our Madame Wang's servant, so that, if I choose to go I needn't even breathe a word to you. All I'll have to do will be to tell her and then I shall be free to do as I like."

"But supposing that I behaved improperly," demurred Baoyu laughingly, "and that you took your leave after letting mother know, you yourself will be placed in no nice fix, when people get wind that you left on account of my having been improper."

"What no nice fix!" smiled Xiren. "Is it likely that I am bound to serve even highway robbers? Well, failing anything else, I can die; for human beings may live a hundred years, but they're bound, in the long run, to fall a victim to death! And when this breath shall have departed, and I shall have lost the sense of hearing and of seeing, all will then be well!"

When her rejoinder fell on his ear, Baoyu promptly stopped her mouth with both his hands. "Enough! enough! that will do," he shouted. "There's no necessity for you to utter language of this kind."

Xiren was well aware that Baoyu was gifted with such a peculiar temperament, that he even looked upon flattering or auspicious phrases with utter aversion, treating them as meaningless and consequently insincere, so when, after listening to those truths, she had spoken with such pathos, he, lapsed into another of his melancholy moods, she blamed herself for the want of consideration she had betrayed. Hastily therefore putting on a smile, she tried to hit upon some suitable remarks, with which to interrupt the conversation. Her choice fell upon those licentious and immodest topics, which had ever been a relish to the taste of Baoyu; and from these the conversation drifted to the subject of womankind. But when, subsequently, reference was made to the excellency of the weak sex, they somehow or other also came to touch upon the mortal nature of women, and Xiren promptly closed her lips in silence.

Noticing however that now that the conversation had reached a point so full of zest for him, she had nothing to say for herself, Baoyu smilingly remarked: "What human being is there that can escape death? But the main thing is to come to a proper end! All that those abject male creatures excel in is, the civil officers, to sacrifice their lives by remonstrating with the Emperor; and, the military, to leave their bones on the battlefield. Both these deaths do confer, after life is extinct, the fame of great men upon them; but isn't it, in fact, better for them not to die? For as it is absolutely necessary that there should be a disorderly Emperor before they can afford any admonition, to what future fate do they thus expose their sovereign, if they rashly throw away their lives, with the sole aim of reaping a fair name for themselves? War too must supervene before they can fight; but if they go and recklessly lay down their lives, with the exclusive idea of gaining the reputation of intrepid warriors, to what destiny will they abandon their country by and bye? Hence it is that neither of these deaths can be looked upon as a legitimate death."

"Loyal ministers," Xiren argued, "and excellent generals simply die because it isn't in their power to do otherwise."

"Military officers," Baoyu explained, "place such entire reliance upon brute force that they become lax in their stratagems and faulty in their plans. It's because they don't possess any inherent abilities that they lose their lives. Could one therefore, pray, say that they had no other alternative? Civil officials, on the other hand, can still less compare with military officers. They read a few passages from books, and commit them to memory; and, on the slightest mistake made by the Emperor, they're at once rash enough to remonstrate with him, prompted by the sole idea of attaining the fame of loyalty and devotion. But, as soon as their stupid notions have bubbled over, they forfeit their lives, and is it likely that it doesn't lie within their power to do otherwise? Why, they should also bear in mind that the Emperor receives his decrees from Heaven; and, that were he not a perfect man, Heaven itself would, on no account whatever, confer upon him a charge so extremely onerous. This makes it evident therefore that the whole pack and parcel of those officers, who are dead and gone, have invariably fallen victims to their endeavors to attain a high reputation, and that they had no knowledge whatever of the import of the great principle of right! Take me as an instance now. Were really mine the good fortune of departing life at a fit time, I'd avail myself of the present when all you girls are alive, to pass away. And could I get you to shed such profuse tears for me as to swell out into a stream large enough to raise my corpse and carry it to some secluded place, whither no bird even has ever wended its flight, and could I become invisible like the wind, and nevermore from this time, come into existence as a human being, I shall then have died at a proper season."

Xiren suddenly awoke to the fact that he was beginning to give vent to a lot of twaddle, and speedily, pleading fatigue, she paid no further notice to him. This compelled Baoyu to at last be quiet and go to sleep. By the morrow, all recollection of the discussion had vanished from his mind.

One day, Baoyu was feeling weary at heart, after strolling all over the place, when remembering the song of the "Peony Pavilion," he read it over twice to himself; but still his spirits continued anything but joyous. Having heard, however, that among the twelve girls in the Pear Fragrance Court there was one called Lingguan, who excelled in singing, he purposely issued forth by a side gate and came in search of her. But the moment he got there, he discovered Baoguan, and Yuguan in the court. As soon as they caught sight of Baoyu, they, with one consent, smiled and urged him to take a seat. Baoyu then inquired where Lingguan was. Both girls explained that she was in her room, so Baoyu hastened in. Here he found Lingguan alone, reclining against a pillow. Though perfectly conscious of his arrival, she did not move a muscle. Baoyu ensconced himself next to her. He had always been in the habit of playing with the rest of the girls, so thinking that Lingguan was like the others, he felt impelled to draw near her and to entreat her, with a forced smile, to get up and sing part of the "Niao Qing Si." But his hopes were baffled; for as soon as Lingguan perceived him sit down, she impetuously raised herself and withdrew from his side. "I'm hoarse," she rejoined with a stern expression on her face. "The Empress the other day called us into the palace; but I couldn't sing even then."

Seeing her sit bolt upright, Baoyu went on to pass her under a minute survey. He discovered that it was the girl, whom he had, some time ago beheld under the cinnamon roses, drawing the character "Qiang." But seeing the reception she accorded him, who had never so far known what it was to be treated contemptuously by anyone, he blushed crimson, while muttering some abuse to himself, and felt constrained to quit the room.

Baoguan and her companion could not fathom why he was so red and inquired of him the reason. Baoyu told them. "Wait a while," Baoguan said, "until Mr. Qiang Secundus comes; and when he asks her to sing, she is bound to sing."

Baoyu at these words felt very sad within himself. "Where's brother Qiang gone to?" he asked.

"He's just gone out," Baoguan answered. "Of course, Lingguan must have wanted something or other, and he's gone to devise ways and means to bring it to her."

Baoyu thought this remark very extraordinary. But after standing about for a while, he actually saw Jia Qiang arrive from outside, carrying a cage, with a tiny stage inserted at the top, and a bird as well; and wend his steps, in a gleeful mood, towards the interior to join Lingguan. The moment, however, he noticed Baoyu, he felt under the necessity of halting.

"What kind of bird is that?" Baoyu asked. "Can it hold a flag in its beak, or do any tricks?"

"It's the 'jade-crested and gold-headed bird,'" smiled Jia Qiang.

"How much did you give for it?" Baoyu continued.

"A tael and eight mace," replied Jia Qiang.

But while replying to his inquiries, he motioned to Baoyu to take a seat, and then went himself into Lingguan's apartment.

Baoyu had, by this time, lost every wish of hearing a song. His sole desire was to find what relations existed between his cousin and Lingguan, when he perceived Jia Qiang walk in and laughingly say to her, "Come and see this thing."

"What' s it?" Lingguan asked, rising.

"I've bought a bird for you to amuse yourself with," Jia Qiang added, "so that you mayn't daily feel dull and have nothing to distract yourself with. But I'll first play with it and let you see."

With this prelude, he took a few seeds and began to coax the bird, until it, in point of fact, performed various tricks, on the stage, clasping in its beak a mask and a flag.

All the girls shouted out: "How nice," with the sole exception of Lingguan, who gave a couple of apathetic smirks, and went in a huff to lie down. Again Jia Qiang, however, kept on forcing smiles, and inquiring of her whether she liked it or not.

"Isn't it enough," Lingguan observed, "that your family entraps a fine lot of human beings like us and coops us up in this hole to study this stuff and nonsense, but do you also now go and get a bird, which likewise is, as it happens, up to this sort of thing? You distinctly fetch it to make fun of us, and mimick us, and do you still ask me whether I like it or not?"

Hearing this reproach, Jia Qiang of a sudden sprang to his feet with alacrity and vehemently endeavored by vowing and swearing to establish his innocence. "How ever could I have been such a fool today," he proceeded, "as to go and throw away a tael or two to purchase this bird? I really did it in the hope that it would afford you amusement. I never for a moment entertained such thoughts as those you credit me with. But never mind; I'll let it go, and save you all this misery!"

So saying, he verily gave the bird its liberty; and, with one blow, he smashed the cage to atoms.

"This bird," still argued Lingguan, "differs, it's true, from a human being; but it too has a mother and father in its nest, and could you have had the heart to bring it here to perform these silly pranks? In coughing today, I expectorated two mouthfuls of blood, and Madame Wang sent someone here to find you so as to tell you to ask the doctor round to minutely diagnose my complaint, and have you instead brought this to mock me with? But it so happens that I, who have not a soul to look after me, or to care for me, also have the fate to fall ill!"

Jia Qiang listened to her. "Yesterday evening," he eagerly explained, "I asked the doctor about it. He said that it was nothing at all, that you should take a few doses of medicine, and that he would be coming again in a day or two to see how you were getting on. But who'd have thought it, you have again today expectorated blood. I'll go at once and invite him to come round."

Speaking the while, he was about to go immediately when Lingguan cried out and stopped him. "Do you go off in a tantrum in this hot broiling sun?" she said. "You may ask him to come, but I won't see him."

When he heard her resolution, Jia Qiang had perforce to stand still.

Baoyu, perceiving what transpired between them, fell unwittingly in a dull reverie. He then at length got an insight into the deep import of the tracing of the character "Qiang." But unable to bear the ordeal any longer, he forthwith took himself out of the way. So absorbed, however, was Jia Qiang's whole mind with Lingguan that he could not even give a thought to escorting anyone; and it was, in fact, the rest of the singing-girls who saw (Baoyu) out.

Baoyu's heart was gnawed with doubts and conjectures. In an imbecile frame of mind, he came to the Yihong court. Lin Daiyu was, at the moment, sitting with Xiren, and chatting with her. As soon as Baoyu entered his quarters, he addressed himself to Xiren, with a long sigh. "I was very wrong in what I said yesterday evening," he remarked. "It's no matter of surprise that father says that I am so narrow-minded that I look at things through a tube and measure them with a clam-shell. I mentioned something last night about having nothing but tears, shed by all of you girls, to be buried in. But this was a mere delusion! So as I can't get the tears of the whole lot of you, each one of you can henceforward keep her own for herself, and have done."

Xiren had flattered herself that the words he had uttered the previous evening amounted to idle talk, and she had long ago dispelled all thought of them from her mind, but when Baoyu unawares made further allusion to them, she smilingly rejoined: "You are verily somewhat cracked!"

Baoyu kept silent, and attempted to make no reply. Yet from this time he fully apprehended that the lot of human affections is, in every instance, subject to predestination, and time and again he was wont to secretly muse, with much anguish: "Who, I wonder, will shed tears for me, at my burial?"

Lin Daiyu, for we will now allude to her, noticed Baoyu's behavior, but readily concluding that he must have been, somewhere or other, once more possessed by some malignant spirit, she did not feel it advisable to ask many questions. "I just saw," she consequently observed, "my maternal aunt, who hearing that tomorrow is Miss Xue's birthday, bade me come at my convenience to ask you whether you'll go or not, (and to tell you) to send someone ahead to let them know what you mean to do."

I didn't go the other day, when it was Mr. Jia She's birthday, so I won't go now." Baoyu answered. "If it is a matter of meeting anyone, I won't go anywhere. On a hot day like this to again don my ceremonial dress! No, I won't go. Aunt is not likely to feel displeased with me!"

"What are you driving at?" Xiren speedily ventured. "She couldn't be put on the same footing as our senior master! She lives close by here. Besides she's a relative. Why, if you don't go, won't you make her imagine things? Well, if you dread the heat, just get up at an early hour and go over and prostrate yourself before her, and come back again, after you've had a cup of tea. Won't this look well?"

Before Baoyu had time to say anything by way of response, Daiyu anticipated him. "You should," she smiled, "go as far as there for the sake of her, who drives the mosquitoes away from you."

Baoyu could not make out the drift of her insinuation. "What about driving mosquitoes away?" he vehemently inquired.

Xiren then explained to him how while he was fast asleep the previous day and no one was about to keep him company, Miss Baochai had sat with him for a while.

"It shouldn't have been done!" Baoyu promptly exclaimed, after hearing her explanations. "But how did I manage to go to sleep and show such utter discourtesy to her? I must go tomorrow!" he then went on to add. But while these words were still on his lips, he un-expectedly caught sight of Shi Xiangyun walk in in full dress, to bid them adieu, as she said that someone had been sent from her home to fetch her away.

The moment Baoyu and Daiyu heard what was the object of her visit, they quickly rose to their feet and pressed her to take a seat. But Shi Xiangyun would not sit down, so Baoyu and Daiyu were compelled to escort her as far as the front part of the mansion.

Shi Xiangyun's eyes were brimming with tears; but realizing that several people from her home were present, she did not have the courage to give full vent to her feelings. But when shortly Baochai ran over to find her, she felt so much the more drawn towards them, that she could not brook to part from them. Baochai, however, inwardly understood that if her people told her aunt anything on their return, there would again be every fear of her being blown up, as soon as she got back home, and she therefore urged her to start on her way. One and all then walked with her up to the second gate, and Baoyu wished to accompany her still further outside, but Shi Xiangyun deterred him. Presently, they turned to go back. But once more, she called Baoyu to her, and whispered to him in a soft tone of voice: "Should our vener-able senior not think of me do often allude to me, so that she should depute someone to fetch me."

Baoyu time after time assured her that he would comply with her wishes. And having followed her with their eyes, while she got into her curricle and started, they eventually retraced their steps towards the inner compound. But, reader, if you like to follow up the story, peruse the details contained in the chapter below.

CHAPTER 37

In the Study of Autumnal Cheerfulness is accidentally formed the Cydonia Japonica Society. In the Hengwu Court, the chrysanthemum is, on a certain night, proposed as a subject for verses.

But to continue, after Shi Xiangyun's return home, Baoyu and the other inmates spent their time, as of old, in rambling about in the garden in search of pleasure, and in humming poetical compositions. But without further reference to their doings, let us take up our narrative with Jia Zheng.

Ever since the visit paid to her home by the Imperial consort, he fulfilled his official duties with additional zeal, for the purpose of reverently making requital for the grace shown him by the Emperor. His correct bearing and his spotless reputation did not escape His Majesty's notice, and he conferred upon him the special appointment of Literary Chancellor, with the sole object of singling out his true merit; for though he had not commenced his career through the arena of public examinations, he belonged nevertheless to a family addicted to letters during successive generations. Jia Zheng had, therefore, on the receipt of the imperial decree, to select the twentieth day of the eighth moon to set out on his journey. When the appointed day came, he worshipped at the shrines of his ancestors, took leave of them and of dowager lady Jia, and started for his post. It would be a needless task, however, to recount with any full particulars how Baoyu and all the inmates saw him off, how Jia Zheng went to take up his official duties, and what occurred abroad, suffice it for us to notice that Baoyu, ever since Jia Zheng's departure, indulged his caprices, allowed his feelings to run riot, and gadded wildly about. In fact, he wasted his time, and added fruitless days and months to his age.

On this special occasion, he experienced more than ever a sense of his lack of resources, and came to look up his grandmother Jia and Madame Wang. With them, he whiled away some of his time, after which he returned into the garden. As soon as he changed his costume, he perceived Cuimo enter, with a couple of sheets of fancy notepaper, in her hand, which she delivered to him.

"It quite slipped from my mind," Baoyu remarked. "I meant to have gone and seen my cousin Tertia; is she better that you come?"

"Miss is all right," Cuimo answered. "She hasn't even had any medicine today. It's only a slight chill."

When Baoyu heard this reply, he unfolded the fancy notepaper. On perusal, he found the contents to be: "Your cousin, Tanchun, respectfully lays this on her cousin Secundus' study-table. When the other night the blue sky newly opened out to view, the moon shone as if it had been washed clean! Such admiration did this pure and rare panorama evoke in me that I could not reconcile myself to the idea of going to bed. The clepsydra had already accomplished three turns, and yet I roamed by the railing under the dryandra trees. But such poor treatment did I receive from wind and dew (that I caught a chill), which brought about an ailment as severe (as that which prevented the man of old from) picking up sticks. You took the trouble yesterday to come in person and cheer me up. Time after time also did you send your attendants round to make affectionate inquiries about me. You likewise presented me with fresh lichees and relics of writings of Zhen Qing. How deep is really your gracious love! As I leant today on my table plunged in silence, I suddenly remembered that the ancients of successive ages were placed in circumstances, in which they had to struggle for reputation and to fight for gain, but that they nevertheless acquired spots with hills and dripping streams, and, inviting people to come from far and near, they did all they could to detain them, by throwing the linch-pins of their chariots into wells or by holding on to their shafts; and that they invariably joined friendship with two or three of the same mind as themselves, with whom they strolled about in these grounds, either erecting altars for song, or establishing societies for writing poetical works. Their meetings were, it is true, prompted on the spur of the moment, by a sudden fit of good cheer, but these have again and again proved, during many years, a pleasant topic of conversation. I, your cousin, may, I admit, be devoid of talent yet I have been fortunate enough to enjoy your company amidst streams and rockeries, and to furthermore admire the elegant verses composed by Xue Baochai and Lin Daiyu. When we were in the breezy hall and the moonlit pavilion, what a pity we never talked about poets! But near the almond tree with the sign and the peach tree by the stream, we may perhaps, when under the fumes of wine, able to fling round the cups, used for humming verses! Who is it who opines that societies with any claim to excellent abilities can only be formed by men? May it not be that the pleasant meetings on the Dong Shan might yield in merit to those, such as ourselves, of the weaker sex? Should you not think it too much to walk on the snow, I shall make bold to ask you round, and sweep the way clean of flowers and wait for you. Respectfully written."

The perusal of this note filled Baoyu unawares with exultation. Clapping his hands; "My third cousin," he laughed, "is the one eminently polished; I'll go at once today and talk matters over with her."

As he spoke, he started immediately, followed by Cuimo. As soon as they reached the Qinfang pavilion, they espied the matron, on duty that day at the back door of the garden, advancing towards them with a note in her hand. The moment she perceived Baoyu she forthwith came up to meet him. "Mr. Yun," she said, "presents his compliments to you. He is waiting for you at the back gate. This is a note he bade me bring you."

Upon opening the note, Baoyu found it to read as follows: "An unfilial son, Yun, reverently inquires about his worthy father's boundless happiness and precious health. Remembering the honor conferred upon me by your recognising me, in your heavenly bounty, as your son, I tried both day as well as night to do something in evidence of my pious obedience, but no opportunity could I find to perform anything filial. When I had, some time back, to purchase flowers and plants, I succeeded, thanks to your vast influence, venerable senior, in finally making friends with several gardeners and in seeing a good number of gardens. As the other day I unexpectedly came across a white Begonia, of a rare species, I exhausted every possible means to get some and managed to obtain just two pots. If you, worthy senior, regard your son as your own very son, do keep them to feast your eyes upon! But with this hot weather today, the young ladies in the garden will, I fear, not be at their ease. I do not consequently presume to come and see you in person, so I present you this letter, written with due respect, while knocking my head before your table. Your son, Yun, on his knees, lays this epistle at your feet. A joke!"

After reading this note, Baoyu laughed. "Has he come alone?" he asked. "Or has he anyone else with him?"

"He's got two flower pots as well," rejoined the matron.

"You go and tell him," Baoyu urged, "that I've informed myself of the contents of his note, and that there are few who think of me as he does! If you also take the flowers and, put them in my room, it will be all right."

So saying, he came with Cuimo into the Qiushuang study, where he discovered Baochai, Daiyu, Yingchun, and Xichun already assembled.

When they saw him drop in upon them, they all burst out laughing. "Here comes still another!" they exclaimed.

"I'm not a boor," smiled Tanchun, "so when the idea casually crossed my mind, I wrote a few notes to try and see who would come. But who'd have thought that, as soon as I asked you, you would all come."

"It's unfortunately late," Baoyu smilingly observed. "We should have started this society long ago."

"You can't call this late!" Daiyu interposed, "so why give way to regret! The only thing is, you must form your society, without including me in the number; for I daren't be one of you."

"If you daren't," Yingchun smiled, "who can presume to do so?"

"This is," suggested Baoyu, "a legitimate and great purpose; and we should all exert our energies. You shouldn't be modest, and I yielding; but everyone of us, who thinks of anything, should freely express it for general discussion. So senior cousin Baochai do make some suggestion; and you junior cousin Lin Daiyu say something."

"What are you in this hurry for?" Baochai exclaimed. "We are not all here yet."

This remark was barely concluded, when Li Wan also arrived. As soon as she crossed the threshold, "It's an excellent proposal," she laughingly cried, "this of starting a poetical society. I recommend myself as controller. Some time ago in spring, I thought of this, 'but,' I mused, 'I am unable to compose verses, so what's the use of making a mess of things?' This is why I dispelled the idea from my mind, and made no mention about it. But since it's your good pleasure, cousin Tertia, to start it, I'll help you to set it on foot."

"As you've made up your minds," Daiyu put in, "to initiate a poetical society, everyone of us will be poets, so we should, as a first step, do away with those various appellations of cousin and uncle and aunt, and thus avoid everything that bears a semblance of vulgarity."

"First rate," exclaimed Li Wan, "and why should we not fix upon some new designations by which to address ourselves? This will be a far more refined way! As for my own, I've selected that of the 'Old farmer of Daoxiang;' so let none of you encroach on it."

"I'll then call myself the 'resident-scholar of the Qiushuang,' and have done," Tanchun observed with a smile.

"'Resident-scholar or master' is, in fact, not to the point. It's clumsy, besides," Baoyu interposed. "The place here is full of dryandra and banana trees, and if one could possibly hit upon some name bearing upon the dryandra and banana, it would be preferable."

"I've got one," shouted Tanchun smilingly. "I'll style myself 'the guest under the banana trees.'"

"How uncommon!" they unanimously cried. "It's a nice one!"

"You had better," laughed Daiyu, "be quick and drag her away and stew some slices of her flesh, for people to eat with their wine."

No one grasped her meaning, "Zhuangzi," Daiyu proceeded to explain, smiling, "says: 'The banana leaves shelter the deer,' and as she styles herself the guest under the banana tree, is she not a deer? So be quick and make pieces of dried venison of her."

At these words, the whole company laughed.

"Don't be in a hurry!" Tanchun remarked, as she laughed. "You make use of specious language to abuse people; but I've thought of a fine and most apposite name for you!" Whereupon addressing herself to the party, "In days gone by," she added, "an imperial concubine, Xiang, sprinkled her tears on the bamboo, and they became spots, so from olden times to the present spotted bamboos have been known as the 'Xiang Imperial concubine bamboo.' Now she lives in the Xiaoxiang lodge, and has a weakness too for tears, so the bamboos over there will by and bye, I presume, likewise become transformed into speckled bamboos; everyone therefore must henceforward call her the 'Xiaoxiang imperial concubine' and finish with it."

After listening to her, they one and all clapped their hands, and cried out: "Capital!" Lin Daiyu however drooped her head and did not so much as utter a single word.

"I've also," Li Wan smiled, "devised a suitable name for senior cousin, Xue Baochai. It too is one of three characters."

"What's it?" eagerly inquired the party.

"I'll raise her to the rank of 'Princess of Hengwu,'" Li Wan rejoined. "I wonder what you all think about this."

"This title of honor," Tanchun observed, "is most apposite."

"What about mine?" Baoyu asked. "You should try and think of one for me also!"

"Your style has long ago been decided upon," Baochai smiled. "It consists of three words: 'fussing for nothing!' It's most pat!"

"You should, after all, retain your old name of 'master of the flowers in the purple cave,'" Li Wan suggested. "That will do very well."

"Those were some of the doings of my youth; why rake them up again?" Baoyu laughed.

"Your styles are very many," Tanchun observed, "and what do you want to choose another for? All you've got to do is to make suitable reply when we call you whatever takes our fancy."

"I must however give you a name," Baochai remarked. "There's a very vulgar name, but it's just the very thing for you. What is difficult to obtain in the world are riches and honors; what is not easy to combine with them is leisure. These two blessings cannot be enjoyed together, but, as it happens, you hold one along with the other, so that we might as well dub you the 'rich and honorable idler.'"

"It won't do; it isn't suitable," Baoyu laughed. "It's better that you should call me, at random, whatever you like."

"What names are to be chosen for Miss Secunda and Miss Quarta?" Li Wan inquired.

"We also don't excel in versifying; what's the use consequently of giving us names, all for no avail?" Yingchun said.

"In spite of this," argued Tanchun, "it would be well to likewise find something for you!"

"She lives in the Zilingzhou, (purple caltrop Isle), so let us call her 'Lingzhou,'" Baochai suggested. "As for that girl Quarta, she lives in the Ouxiang Xie, (lotus fragrance pavilion); she should thus be called Ouxie and have done!"

"These will do very well!" Li Wan cried. "But as far as age goes, I am the senior, and you should all defer to my wishes; but I feel certain that when I've told you what they are, you will unanimously agree to them. We are seven here to form the society, but neither I, nor Miss Secunda, nor Miss Quarta can write verses; so if you will exclude us three, we'll each share some special duties."

"Their names have already been chosen," Tanchun smilingly demurred; "and do you still keep on addressing them like this? Well, in that case, won't it be as well for them to have no names? But we must also decide upon some scale of fines, for future guidance, in the event of any mistakes."

"There will be ample time to fix upon a scale of fines after the society has been definitely established." Li Wan replied. "There's plenty of room over in my place so let's hold our meetings there. I'm not, it is true, a good hand at verses, but if you poets won't treat me disdainfully as a rustic boor, and if you will allow me to play the hostess, I may certainly also gradually become more and more refined. As for conceding to me the presidentship of the society, it won't be enough, of course, for me alone to preside; it will be necessary to invite two others to serve as vice-presidents; you might then enlist Lingzhou and Ouxie, both of whom are cultured persons. The one to choose the themes and assign the meter, the other to act as copyist and supervisor. We three cannot, however, definitely say that we won't write verses, for, if we come across any comparatively easy subject and meter, we too will indite a stanza if we feel so disposed. But you four will positively have to do so. If you agree to this, well, we can proceed with the society; but, if you don't fall in with my wishes, I can't presume to join you."

Yingchun and Xichun had a natural aversion for verses. What is more, Xue Baochai and Lin Daiyu were present. As soon therefore as they heard these proposals, which harmonized so thoroughly with their own views, they both, with one voice, approved them as excellent. Tanchun and the others were likewise well aware of their object, but they could not, when they saw with what willingness they accepted the charge insist, with any propriety, upon their writing verses, and they felt obliged to say yes.

"Your proposals," she consequently said, "may be right enough; but in my views they are ridiculous. For here I've had the trouble of initiating this idea of a society, and, instead of my having anything to say in the matter, I've been the means of making you three come and exercise control over me."

"Well then," Baoyu suggested, "let's go to the Daoxiang village."

"You're always in a hurry!" Li Wan remarked. "We're here today to simply deliberate. So wait until I've sent for you again."

"It would be well," Baochai interposed, "that we should also decide every how many days we are to meet."

"If we meet too often," argued Tanchun, "there won't be fun in it. We should simply come together two or three times in a month."

"It will be ample if we meet twice or thrice a month," Baochai added. "But when the dates have been settled neither wind nor rain should prevent us. Exclusive, however, of these two days, anyone in high spirits and disposed to have an extra meeting can either ask us to go over to her place, or you can all come to us; either will do well enough! But won't it be more pleasant if no hard-and-fast dates were laid down?"

"This suggestion is excellent," they all exclaimed.

"This idea was primarily originated by me," Tanchun observed, "and I should be the first to play the hostess, so that these good spirits of mine shouldn't all go for nothing."

"Well, after this remark," Li Wan proceeded, "what do you say to your being the first to convene a meeting tomorrow?"

"Tomorrow," Tanchun demurred, "is not as good as today; the best thing is to have it at once! You'd better therefore choose the subjects, while Lingzhou can fix the meter, and Ouxie act as supervisor."

"According to my ideas," Yingchun chimed in, "we shouldn't yield to the wishes of any single person in the choice of themes and the settlement of the rhythm. What would really be fair and right would be to draw lots."

"When I came just now," Li Wan pursued, "I noticed them bring in two pots of white Begonias, which were simply beautiful; and why should you not write some verses on them?"

"Can we write verses," Yingchun retorted, "before we have as yet seen anything of the flowers?"

"They're purely and simply white Begonias," Baochai answered, "and is there again any need to see them before you put together your verses? Men of old merely indited poetical compositions to express their good cheer and conceal their sentiments; had they waited to write on things they had seen, why, the whole number of their works would not be in existence at present!"

"In that case," Yingchun said, "let me fix the meter."

With these words, she walked up to the bookcase, and, extracting a volume, she opened it, at random, at some verses which turned out to be a heptameter stanza. Then handing it round for general perusal, everybody had to compose lines with seven words in each. Yingchun next closed the book of verses and addressed herself to a young waiting-maid. "Just utter," she bade her, "the first character that comes to your mouth."

The waiting-maid was standing, leaning against the door, so readily she suggested the word "door."

"The rhyme then will be the word 'door,'" Yingchun smiled, "under the thirteenth character 'Yuan.' The final word of the first line is therefore 'door.'"

Saying this, she asked for the box with the rhyme slips, and, pulling out the thirteenth drawer with the character "Yuan," she directed a young waiting-maid to take four words as they came under her hand. The waiting-maid complied with her directions, and picked out four slips, on which were written "p'en, hun, hen, and hun," pot, spirit, traces, and dusk.

"The two characters pot and door," observed Baoyu, "are not very easy to rhyme with."

But Shishu then got ready four lots of paper and brushes, share and share alike, and one and all quietly set to work, racking their brains to perform their task, with the exception of Daiyu, who either kept on rubbing the dryandra flowers, or looking at the autumnal weather, or bandying jokes as well with the servant-girls; while Yingchun ordered a waiting-maid to light a "dream-sweet" incense stick.

This "dream-sweet" stick was, it must be explained, made only about three inches long and about the thickness of a lamp-wick, in order to easily burn down. Setting therefore her choice upon one of these as a limit of time, anyone who failed to accomplish the allotted task, by the time the stick was consumed, had to pay a penalty.

Presently, Tanchun was the first to think of some verses, and, taking up her brush, she wrote them down; and, after submitting them to several alterations, she handed them up to Yingchun.

"Princess of Hengwu," she then inquired of Baochai, "have you finished?"

As for finishing, I have finished," Baochai rejoined; "but they're worth nothing."

Baoyu paced up and down the verandah with his hands behind his back. "Have you heard?" he thereupon said to Daiyu, "they've all done!"

"Don't concern yourself about me!" Daiyu returned for answer.

Baoyu also perceived that Baochai had already copied hers out. "Dreadful!" he exclaimed. "There only remains an inch of the stick and I've only just composed four lines. The incense stick is nearly burnt out," he continued, speaking to Daiyu, "and what do you keep squatting on that damp ground like that for?"

But Daiyu did not again worry her mind about what he said.

"Well," Baoyu added, "I can't be looking after you! Whether good or bad, I'll write mine out too and have done."

As he spoke, he likewise drew up to the table and began putting his lines down.

"We'll now peruse the verses," Li Wan interposed, "and if by the time we've done, you haven't as yet handed up your papers, you'll have to be fined."

"Old farmer of Daoxiang," Baoyu remarked, "you're not, it is true, a good hand at writing verses, but you can read well, and, what's more, you're the fairest of the lot; so you'd better adjudge the good and bad, and we'll submit to your judgment."

"Of course!" responded the party with one voice.

In due course, therefore, she first read Tanchun's draft. It ran as follows:

Verses on the Begonia.

What time the sun's rays slant, and the grass waxeth cold, close the double doors.
After a shower of rain, green moss plenteously covers the whole pot.
Beauteous is jade, but yet with thee in purity it cannot ever vie.
Thy frame, spotless as snow, from admiration easy robs me of my wits
Thy fragrant core is like unto a dot, so full of grace, so delicate!
When the moon reacheth the third watch, thy comely shade begins to show itself.

> Do not tell me that a chaste fairy like thee can take wings and pass
> away.
> How lovely are thy charms, when in thy company at dusk I sing
> my play!

After she had read them aloud, one and all sang their praise for a time. She then took up Baochai's, which consisted of:

> If thou would'st careful tend those fragrant lovely flowers, close of
> a day the doors,
> And with thine own hands take the can and sprinkle water o'er
> the mossy pots.
> Red, as if with cosmetic washed, are the shadows in autumn on
> the steps.
> Their crystal snowy bloom invites the dew on their spirits to heap
> itself.
> Their extreme whiteness mostly shows that they're more comely
> than all other flowers.
> When much they grieve, how can their jade-like form lack the traces
> of tears?
> Would'st thou the god of those white flowers repay? then purity
> need'st thou observe.
> In silence plunges their fine bloom, now that once more day yields
> to dusk.

"After all," observed Li Wan, "it's the Princess of Hengwu, who expresses herself to the point."

Next they bestowed their attention on the following lines, composed by Baoyu:

> Thy form in autumn faint reflects against the double doors.
> So heaps the snow in the seventh feast that it filleth thy pots.
> Thy shade is spotless as Tai Zhen, when from her bath she hails.
> Like Xizi's, whose hand ever pressed her heart, jade-like thy soul.
> When the morn-ushering breeze falls not, thy thousand blossoms
> grieve.
> To all thy tears the evening shower addeth another trace.
> Alone thou lean'st against the colored rails as if with sense imbued.
> As heavy-hearted as the fond wife, beating clothes, or her that sadly
> listens to the flute, thou mark'st the fall of dusk.

When they had perused his verses, Baoyu opined that Tanchun's carried the palm. Li Wan was, however, inclined to concede to the stanza, indited by Baochai, the credit of possessing much merit. But she then went on to tell Daiyu to look sharp.

"Have you all done?" Daiyu asked.

So saying, she picked up a brush and completing her task, with a few dashes, she threw it to them to look over. On perusal, Li Wan and her companions found her verses to run in this strain:

> Half rolled the speckled portiere hangs, half closed the door.
> Thy mould like broken ice it looks, jade-like thy pot.

This couplet over, Baoyu took the initiative and shouted: "Capital." But he had just had time to inquire where she had recalled them to mind from, when they turned their mind to the succeeding lines:

> Three points of whiteness from the pear petals thou steal'st;
> And from the plum bloom its spirit thou borrowest.

"Splendid!" everyone (who heard) them read, felt impelled to cry. "It is a positive fact," they said, "that her imagination is, compared with that of others, quite unique."

But the rest of the composition was next considered. Its text was:

> The fairy in Selene's cavity donneth a plain attire.
> The maiden, plunged in autumn grief, dries in her room the prints of tears.
> Winsome she blushes, in silence she's plunged, with none a word she breathes;
> But wearily she leans against the eastern breeze, though dusk has long since fall'n.

"This stanza ranks above all!" they unanimously remarked, after it had been read for their benefit.

"As regards beauty of thought and originality, this stanza certainly deserves credit," Li Wan asserted; "but as regards pregnancy and simplicity of language, it, after all, yields to that of Hengwu."

"This criticism is right." Tanchun put in. "That of the Xiaoxiang consort must take second place."

"Yours, gentleman of Yihong," Li Wan pursued, "is the last of the lot. Do you agreeably submit to this verdict?"

"My stanza," Baoyu ventured, "isn't really worth a straw. Your criticism is exceedingly fair. But," he smilingly added, "the two poems, written by Hengwu and Xiaoxiang, have still to be discussed."

"You should," argued Li Wan, "fall in with my judgment; this is no business of any of you, so whoever says anything more will have to pay a penalty."

Baoyu at this reply found that he had no alternative but to drop the subject.

"I decide that from henceforward," Li Wan proceeded, "we should hold meetings twice every month, on the second and sixteenth. In the selection of themes and the settlement of the rhymes, you'll all have then to do as I wish. But any person who may, during the intervals, feel so disposed, will be at perfect liberty to choose another day for an extra meeting. What will I care if there's a meeting every day of the moon? It will be no concern of mine, so long as when the second and sixteenth arrive, you do, as you're bound to, and come over to my place."

"We should, as is but right," Baoyu suggested, "choose some name or other for our society."

"Were an ordinary one chosen, it wouldn't be nice," Tanchun explained, "and anything too new-fangled, eccentric, or strange won't also be quite the thing! As luck would have it, we've just started with the poems on the Begonia, so let us call it the 'Begonia Poetical Society.' This title is, it's true, somewhat commonplace; but as it's positively based on fact, it shouldn't matter."

After this proposal of hers, they held further consultation; and partaking of some slight refreshments, each of them eventually retired. Some repaired to their quarters. Others went to dowager lady Jia's or Madame Wang's apartments. But we will leave them without further comment.

When Xiren, for we will now come to her, perceived Baoyu peruse the note and walk off in a great flurry, along with Cuimo, she was quite at a loss what to make of it. Subsequently, she also saw the matrons, on duty at the back gate, bring two pots of Begonias. Xiren inquired of them where they came from. The women explained to her all about them. As soon as Xiren heard their reply, she at once desired them to put the flowers in their proper places, and asked them to sit down in the lower rooms. She then entered the house, and, weighing six mace of silver, she wrapped it up properly, and fetching besides three hundred cash, she came over and handed both the amounts to the two matrons. "This silver," she said, "is a present for the boys, who carried the flowers; and these cash are for you to buy yourselves a cup of tea with."

The women rose to their feet in such high glee that their eyebrows dilated and their eyes smiled; but, though they waxed eloquent in the expression of their deep gratitude, they would not accept the money. It was only after they had perceived how obstinate Xiren was in not taking it back that they at last volunteered to keep it.

"Are there," Xiren then inquired, "any servant-boys on duty outside the back gate?"

"There are four of them every day," answered one of the matrons. "They're put there with the sole idea of attending to any orders that might be given them from inside. But, Miss, if you've anything to order them to do, we'll go and deliver your message."

"What orders can I have to give them?" Xiren laughed. "Mr. Bao, our master Secundus, was purposing to send someone today to the young marquis' house to take something over to Miss Shi. But you come at an opportune moment so you might, on your way out, tell the servant-boys at the back gate to hire a carriage; and on its return you can come here and get the money. But don't let them rush recklessly against people in the front part of the compound!"

The matrons signified their obedience and took their leave. Xiren retraced her steps into the house to fetch a tray in which to place the presents intended for Shi Xiangyun, but she discovered the shelf for trays empty. Upon turning round, however, she caught sight of Qingwen, Qiuwen, Sheyue, and the other girls, seated together, busy with their needlework. "Where is the white cornelian tray with twisted threads gone to?" Xiren asked.

At this question, one looked at the one, and the other stared at the other, but none of them could remember anything about it. After a protracted lapse of time, Qingwen smiled. "It was taken to Miss Tertia's with a present of lichees," she rejoined, "and it hasn't as yet been returned."

"There are plenty of articles," Xiren remarked, "for sending over things on ordinary occasions; and do you deliberately go and carry this off?"

"Didn't I maintain the same thing?" Qingwen retorted. "But so well did this tray match with the fresh lichees it contained, that when I took it over, Miss Tanchun herself noticed the fact. 'How splendid,' she said, and lo, putting even the tray by, she never had it brought over. But, look! hasn't the pair of beaded vases, which stood on the very top of that shelf, been fetched as yet?"

"The mention of these vases," Qiuwen laughed, "reminds me again of a funny incident. Whenever our Mr. Baoyu's filial piety is aroused, he shows himself filial over and above the highest degree! The other day, he espied the olea flowers in the park, and he plucked two twigs. His original idea was to place them in a vase for himself, but a sudden thought struck him. 'These are flowers,' he mused, 'which have newly opened in our garden, so how can I presume to be the first to enjoy them?' And actually taking down that pair of vases, he filled them with water with his own hands, put the flowers in, and, calling a servant to carry them, he in person took one of the vases into dowager lady Jia's, and then took the other to Madame Wang's. But, as it happens, even his attendants reap some benefit, when once his filial feelings are stirred up! As luck would have it, the one who carried the vases over on that day was myself. The sight of these flowers so enchanted our venerable lady that there was nothing that she wouldn't do. 'Baoyu,' she said to everyone she met, 'is the one, after all, who shows me much attention. So much so, that he has even thought of bringing me a twig of flowers! And yet, the others bear me a grudge on account of the love that I lavish on him!' Our venerable mistress, you all know very well, has never had much to say to me. I have all along not been much of a favorite in the old lady's eyes. But on that occasion she verily directed someone to give me several hundreds of cash. 'I was to be pitied,' she observed, 'for being born with a weak physique.' This was, indeed, an unforeseen piece of good luck! The several hundreds cash are a mere trifle; but what's not easy to get is this sort of honor! After that, we went over into Madame Wang's. Madame Wang was, at the time, with our lady Secunda, Mrs. Zhao, and a whole lot of people; turning the boxes topsy-turvy, trying to find some colored clothes her ladyship had worn long ago in her youth, so as to give them to someone or other. Who it was, I don't know. But the moment she saw us, she did not even think of searching for any clothes, but got lost in admiration for the flowers. Our lady Secunda was also standing by, and she made sport of the matter. She extolled our master Bao, for his filial piety and for his knowledge of right and wrong; and what with what was true and what wasn't, she came out with two cart-loads of compliments. These things spoken in the presence of the whole company so added to Madame Wang's luster and sealed everyone's mouth, that her ladyship was more and more filled with gratification, and she gave me two ready-made clothes as a present. These too are of no consequence; one way or another, we get some every year; but nothing can come up to this sort of lucky chance!"

"Psha!" Qingwen ejaculated with a significant smile, "you are indeed a mean thing, who has seen nothing of the world! She gave the good ones to others and the refuse to you; and do you still pat on all this side?"

"No matter whether what she gave me was refuse or not," Qiuwen protested, "it's, after all, an act of bounty on the part of her ladyship."

"Had it been myself," Qingwen pursued, "I would at once have refused them! It wouldn't have mattered if she had given me what had been left by someone else; but we all stand on an equal footing in these rooms, and is there any one, forsooth, so much the more exalted or honorable than the other as to justify her taking what is good and bestowing it upon her and giving me what is left? I had rather not take them! I might have had to give offence to Madame Wang, but I wouldn't have put up with such a slight!"

"To whom did she give any in these rooms?" Qiuwen vehemently inquired. "I was unwell and went home for several days, so that I am not aware to whom any were given. Dear sister, do tell me who it is so that I may know."

"Were I to tell you," Qingwen rejoined, "is it likely that you would return them at this hour to Madame Wang?"

"What nonsense," Qiuwen laughed. "Ever since I've heard about it, I've been delighted and happy. No matter if she even bestowed upon me what remained from anything given to a dog in these rooms, I would have been thankful for her ladyship's kindness. I wouldn't have worried my mind with anything else!"

After listening to her, everybody laughed. "Doesn't she know how to jeer in fine style!" they ejaculated unanimously; "for weren't they given to that foreign spotted pug dog?"

"You lot of filthy-tongued creatures!" Xiren laughed, "when you've got nothing to do, you make me the scapegoat to crack your jokes, and poke your fun at! But what kind of death will, I wonder, each of you have!"

"Was it verily you, sister, who got them?" Qiuwen asked with a smile. "I assure you I had no idea about it! I tender you my apologies."

"You might be a little less domineering!" Xiren remarked smilingly. "The thing now is, who of you will go and fetch the tray."

"The vases too," Sheyue suggested, "must be got back when there's any time to spare; for there's nothing to say about our venerable mistress' quarters, but Madame Wang's apartments teem with people and many hands. The rest are all right; but Mrs. Zhao and all that company will, when they see that the vase hails from these rooms, surely again foster evil designs, and they won't feel happy until they've done all they can to spoil it! Besides, Madame Wang doesn't trouble herself about such things. So had we not as well bring it over a moment sooner?"

Hearing this, Qingwen threw down her needlework. "What you say is perfectly right," she assented, "so you'd better let me go and fetch it."

"I'll, after all, go for it." Qiuwen cried. "You can go and get that tray of yours!"

"You should let me once go for something!" Qingwen pleaded. "Whenever any lucky chance has turned up, you've invariably grabbed it; and can it be that you won't let me have a single turn?"

"Altogether," Sheyue said laughingly, "that girl Qiuwen got a few clothes just once; can such a lucky coincidence present itself again today that you too should find them engaged in searching for clothes?"

"Albeit I mayn't come across any clothes," Qingwen rejoined with a sardonic smile, "our Madame Wang may notice how diligent I am, and apportion me a couple of taels out of her public expenses; there's no saying." Continuing, "Don't you people," she laughed, "try and play your pranks with me; for is there anything that I don't do?"

As she spoke, she ran outside. Qiuwen too left the room in her company; but she repaired to Tanchun's quarters and fetched the tray.

Xiren then got everything ready. Calling an old nurse attached to the same place as herself, Song by name, "Just go first and wash, comb your hair and put on your out-of-door clothes," she said to her, "and then come back as I want to send you at once with a present to Miss Shi."

"Miss," urged the nurse Song, "just give me what you have; and, if you have any message, tell it me; so that when I've tidied myself I may go straightway."

Xiren, at this proposal, brought two small twisted wire boxes; and, opening first the one in which were two kinds of fresh fruits, consisting of caltrops and "chicken head" fruit, and afterwards uncovering the other, containing a tray with new cakes, made of chestnut powder, and steamed in sugar, scented with the olea, "All these fresh fruits are newly plucked this year from our own garden," she observed; "our Mr. Secundus sends them to Miss Shi to taste. The other day, too, she was quite taken with this cornelian tray so let her keep it for her use. In this silk bag she'll find the work, which she asked me some time ago to do for her. (Tell her) that she mustn't despise it for its coarseness, but make the best of it and turn it to some account. Present respects to her from our part and inquire after her health on behalf of Mr. Baoyu; that will be all there's to say."

"Has Mr. Bao, I wonder, anything more for me to tell her?" the nurse Song added, "Miss, do go and inquire, so that on my return, he mayn't again say that I forgot."

"He was just now," Xiren consequently asked Qiuwen, "over there in Miss Tertia's rooms, wasn't he?"

"They were all assembled there, deliberating about starting some poetical society or other," Qiuwen explained, "and they all wrote verses too. But I fancy he's got no message to give you; so you might as well start."

After this assurance, nurse Song forthwith took the things, and quitted the apartment. When she had changed her clothes and arranged her hair, Xiren further enjoined them to go by the back door, where there was a servant-boy, waiting with a curricle. Nurse Song thereupon set out on her errand. But we will leave her for the present.

In a little time Baoyu came back. After first cursorily glancing at the begonias for a time, he walked into his rooms, and explained to Xiren all about the poetical society they had managed to establish. Xiren then told him that she had sent the nurse Song along with some things to Shi Xiangyun. As soon as Baoyu heard this, he clapped his hands. "I forgot all about her!" he cried. "I knew very well that I had something to attend to; but I couldn't remember what it was! Luckily, you've alluded to her! I was just meaning to ask her to come, for what fun will there be in this poetical society without her?"

"Is this of any serious import?" Xiren reasoned with him. "It's all, for the mere sake of recreation! She's not however able to go about at her own free will as you people do. Nor can she at home have her own way. When you therefore let her know, it won't again rest with her, however willing she may be to avail herself of your invitation. And if she can't come, she will long and crave to be with you all, so isn't it better that you shouldn't be the means of making her unhappy?"

"Never mind!" responded Baoyu. "I'll tell our venerable senior to despatch someone to bring her over."

But in the middle of their conversation, nurse Song returned already from her mission, and expressed to him, (Xiangyun's) acknowledgment; and to Xiren her thanks for the trouble. "She also inquired," the nurse proceeded, "what you, master Secundus, were up to, and I told her that you had started some poetical club or other with the young ladies and that you were engaged in writing verses. Miss Shi wondered why it was, if you were writing verses, that you didn't even mention anything to her; and she was extremely distressed about it."

Baoyu, at these words, turned himself round and betook himself immediately into his grandmother's apartments, where he did all that lay in his power to urge her to depute servants to go and fetch her.

"It's too late today," dowager lady Jia answered; "they'll go tomorrow, as soon as it's daylight."

Baoyu had no other course but to accede to her wishes. He, however, retraced his steps back to his room with a heavy heart. On the morrow, at early dawn, he paid another visit to old lady Jia and brought pressure to bear on her until she sent someone for her. Soon after midday, Shi Xiangyun arrived. Baoyu felt at length much relieved in his mind. Upon meeting her, he recounted to her all that had taken place from beginning to end. His purpose was likewise to let her see the poetical composition, but Li Wan and the others remonstrated. "Don't," they said, "allow her to see them! First tell her the rhymes and number of feet; and, as she comes late, she should, as a first step, pay a penalty by conforming to the task we had to do. Should what she writes be good, then she can readily be admitted as a member of the society; but if not good, she should be further punished by being made to stand a treat; after which, we can decide what's to be done."

"You've forgotten to ask me round," Xiangyun laughed, "and I should, after all, fine you people! But produce the meter; for though I don't excel in versifying, I shall exert myself to do the best I can, so as to get rid of every slur. If you will admit me into the club, I shall be even willing to sweep the floors and burn the incense."

When they all saw how full of fun she was, they felt more than ever delighted with her and they reproached themselves, for having somehow or other managed to forget her on the previous day. But they lost no time in telling her the meter of the verses.

Shi Xiangyun was inwardly in ecstasies. So much so, that she could not wait to beat the tattoo and effect any alterations. But having succeeded, while conversing with her cousins, in devising a stanza in her mind, she promptly inscribed it on the first piece of paper that came to hand. "I have," she remarked, with a precursory smile, "stuck to the meter and written two stanzas. Whether they be good or bad, I cannot say; all I've kept in view was to simply comply with your wishes."

So speaking, she handed her paper to the company.

"We thought our four stanzas," they observed, "had so thoroughly exhausted everything that could be imagined on the subject that another stanza was out of the question, and there you've devised a couple more! How could there be so much to say? These must be mere repetitions of our own sentiments."

While bandying words, they perused her two stanzas. They found this to be their burden:

No. 1.

The fairies yesterday came down within the city gates.
And like those gems, sown in the grassy field, planted one pot.
How clear it is that the goddess of frost is fond of cold!
It is no question of a pretty girl bent upon death!
Where does the snow, which comes in gloomy weather, issue from?
The drops of rain increase the prints, left from the previous night.
How the flowers rejoice that bards are not weary of song.
But are they ever left to spend in peace a day or night?

No. 2.

> The "heng zhi" covered steps lead to the creeper-laden door.
> How fit to plant by the corner of walls; how fit for pots?
> The flowers so relish purity that they can't find a mate.
> Easy in autumn snaps the soul of sorrow-wasted man.
> The tears, which from the jade-like candle drip, dry in the wind.
> The crystal-like portiere asunder rends Selene's rays.
> Their private feelings to the moon goddess they longed to tell,
> But gone, alas! is the luster she shed on the empty court!

Every line filled them with wonder and admiration. What they read, they praised. "This," they exclaimed, with one consent, "is not writing verses on the begonia for no purpose! We must really start a Begonia Society!"

"Tomorrow," Shi Xiangyun proposed, "first fine me by making me stand a treat, and letting me be the first to convene a meeting; may I?"

"This would be far better!" they all assented. So producing also the verses, composed the previous day, they submitted them to her for criticism.

In the evening, Xiangyun came at the invitation of Baochai, to put up with her for the night. By lamplight, Xiangyun consulted with her how she was to play the hostess and fix upon the themes; but, after lending a patient ear to all her proposals for a long time, Baochai thought them so unsuitable for the occasion, that turning towards her, she raised objections. "If you want," she said, "to hold a meeting, you have to pay the piper. And albeit it's for mere fun, you have to make every possible provision; for while consulting your own interests, you must guard against giving umbrage to people. In that case everyone will afterwards be happy and contented. You count for nothing too in your own home; and the whole lump sum of those few tiaos you draw each month, are not sufficient for your own wants, and do you now also wish to burden yourself with this useless sort of thing? Why, if your aunt gets wind of it, won't she be more incensed with you than ever! What's more, even though you might fork out all the money you can call your own to bear the outlay of this entertainment with, it won't be anything like enough, and can it possibly be, pray, that you would go home for the express purpose of requisitioning the necessary funds? Or will you perchance ask for some from in here?"

This long tirade had the effect of bringing the true facts of the case to Xiangyun's notice, and she began to waver in a state of uncertainty.

"I have already fixed upon a plan in my mind," Baochai resumed. "There's an assistant in our pawnshop from whose family farm come some splendid crabs. Some time back, he sent us a few as a present, and now, starting from our venerable senior and including the inmates of the upper quarters, most of them are quite in love with crabs. It was only the other day that my mother mentioned that she intended inviting our worthy ancestor into the garden to look at the olea flowers and partake of crabs, but she has had her hands so full that she hasn't as yet asked her round. So just you now drop the poetical meeting, and invite the whole crowd to a show; and if we wait until they go, won't we be able to indite as many poems as we like? But let me speak to my brother and ask him to let us have several baskets of the fattest and largest crabs he can get, and to also go to some shop and fetch several jars of luscious wine. And if we then lay out four or five tables with plates full of refreshments, won't we save trouble and all have a jolly time as well?"

As soon as Xiangyun heard (the alternative proposed by Baochai,) she felt her heart throb with gratitude and in most profuse terms she praised her for her forethought.

"The proposal I've made," Baochai pursued smilingly; "is prompted entirely by my sincere feelings for you; so whatever you do don't be touchy and imagine that I look down upon you; for in that case we two will have been good friends all in vain. But if you won't give way to suspicion, I'll be able to tell them at once to go and get things ready."

"My dear cousin," eagerly rejoined Xiangyun, a smile on her lips, "if you say these things it's you who treat me with suspicion; for no matter how foolish a person I may be, as not to even know what's good and bad, I'm still a human being! Did I not regard you, cousin, in the same light as my own very sister, I wouldn't last time have had any wish or inclination to disclose to you every bit of those troubles, which ordinarily fall to my share at home."

After listening to these assurances, Baochai summoned a matron and bade her go out and tell her master, Xue Pan, to procure a few hampers of crabs of the same kind as those which were sent on the previous occasion. "Our venerable senior," (she said,) "and aunt Wang are asked to come tomorrow after their meal and admire the olea flowers, so mind, impress upon your master to please not forget, as I've already today issued the invitations."

The matron walked out of the garden and distinctly delivered the message. But, on her return, she brought no reply.

During this while, Baochai continued her conversation with Xiangyun. "The themes for the verses," she advised her, "mustn't also be too out-of-the-way. Just search the works of old writers, and where will

you find any eccentric and peculiar subjects, or any extra difficult meter! If the subject be too much out-of-the-way and the meter too difficult, one cannot get good verses. In a word, we are a mean lot and
our verses are certain, I fear, to consist of mere repetitions. Nor is it
advisable for us to aim at excessive originality. The first thing for us
to do is to have our ideas clear, as our language will then not be commonplace. In fact, this sort of thing is no vital matter; spinning and
needlework are, in a word, the legitimate duties of you and me. Yet, if
we can at any time afford the leisure, it's only right and proper that we
should take some book, that will benefit both body and mind, and read
a few chapters out of it."

Xiangyun simply signified her assent. "I'm now cogitating in my
mind," she then laughingly remarked, "that as the verses we wrote yesterday treated of begonias, we should, I think, compose on this occasion some on chrysanthemums, eh? What do you say?"

"Chrysanthemums are in season," Baochai replied. "The only objection to them is that too many writers of old have made them the subject of their poems."

"I also think so," Xiangyun added, "so that, I fear, we shall only be
following in their footsteps."

After some reflection, Baochai exclaimed, "I've hit upon something!
If we take, for the present instance, the chrysanthemums as a secondary
term, and man as the primary, we can, after all, select several themes.
But they must all consist of two characters: the one, an empty word; the
other, a full one. The full word might be chrysanthemums; while for the
empty one, we might employ some word in general use. In this manner, we shall, on one hand, sing the chrysanthemum; and, on the other,
compose verses on the theme. And as old writers have not written much
in this style, it will be impossible for us to drift into the groove of their
ideas. Thus in versifying on the scenery and in singing the objects, we
will, in both respects, combine originality with liberality of thought."

"This is all very well," smiled Xiangyun. "The only thing is what
kind of empty words will, I wonder, be best to use? Just you first think
of one and let me see."

Baochai plunged in thought for a time, after which she laughingly
remarked: "Dream of chrysanthemums is good."

"It's positively good." Xiangyun smiled. "I've also got one: 'the Chrysanthemum shadow,' will that do?"

"Well enough," Baochai answered, "the only objection is that people
have written on it; yet if the themes are to be many, we might throw
this in. I've got another one too!"

"Be quick, and tell it!" Xiangyun urged.

"What do you say to 'ask the Chrysanthemums?'" Baochai observed.

Xiangyun clapped her hand on the table. "Capital," she cried. "I've thought of one also." She then quickly continued, "It is, search for chrysanthemums; what's your idea about it?"

Baochai thought that too would do very well. "Let's choose ten of them first," she next proposed; "and afterwards note them down!"

While talking, they rubbed the ink and moistened the brushes. These preparations over, Xiangyun began to write, while Baochai enumerated the themes. In a short time, they got ten of them.

"Ten don't form a set," Xiangyun went on to smilingly suggest, after reading them over. "We'd better complete them by raising their number to twelve; they'll then also be on the same footing as people's pictures and books."

Hearing this proposal, Baochai devised another couple of themes, thus bringing them to a dozen. "Well, since we've got so far," she pursued, "let's go one step further and copy them out in their proper order, putting those that are first, first; and those that come last, last."

"It would be still better like that," Xiangyun acquiesced, "as we'll be able to make up a 'chrysanthemum book.'"

"The first stanza should be: 'Longing for chrysanthemums,'" Baochai said, "and as one cannot get them by wishing, and has, in consequence, to search for them, the second should be 'searching for chrysanthemums.' After due search, one finds them, and plants them, so the third must be: 'planting chrysanthemums.' After they've been planted, they blossom, and one faces them and enjoys them, so the fourth should be 'facing the chrysanthemums.' By facing them, one derives such excessive delight that one plucks them and brings them in and puts them in vases for one's own delectation, so the fifth must be 'placing chrysanthemums in vases.' If no verses are sung in their praise, after they've been placed in vases, it's tantamount to seeing no point of beauty in chrysanthemums, so the sixth must be 'sing about chrysanthemums.' After making them the burden of one's song, one can't help representing them in pictures. The seventh place should therefore be conceded to 'drawing chrysanthemums.' Seeing that in spite of all the labor bestowed on the drawing of chrysanthemums, the fine traits there may be about them are not yet, in fact, apparent, one impulsively tries to find them out by inquiries, so the eighth should be 'asking the chrysanthemums.' As any perception, which the chrysanthemums might display in fathoming the questions set would help to make the inquirer immoderately happy, the ninth must be 'pinning the chrysanthemums in the hair.' And as after everything has been accomplished, that comes within the sphere of man, there will remain still some chrysanthemums about which something could be written, two stanzas on the 'shadow of the chrysanthemums,' and the 'dream about chrysanthemums' must be tagged on as numbers ten and eleven. While the last section should be 'the withering of the chrysanthemums' so as to bring to a close the sentiments expressed in the foregoing subjects. In this wise the fine scenery and fine doings of the third part of autumn, will both alike be included in our themes."

Xiangyun signified her approval, and taking the list she copied it out clean. But after once more passing her eye over it, she went on to inquire what rhymes should be determined upon.

"I do not, as a rule, like hard-and-fast rhymes," Baochai retorted. "It's evident enough that we can have good verses without them, so what's the use of any rhymes to shackle us? Don't let us imitate that mean lot of people. Let's simply choose our subject and pay no notice to rhymes. Our main object is to see whether we cannot by chance hit upon some well-written lines for the sake of fun. It isn't to make this the means of subjecting people to perplexities."

"What you say is perfectly right," Xiangyun observed. "In this manner our poetical composition will improve one step higher. But we only muster five members, and there are here twelve themes. Is it likely that each one of us will have to indite verses on all twelve?"

"That would be far too hard on the members!" Baochai rejoined. "But let's copy out the themes clean, for lines with seven words will have to be written on everyone, and stick them tomorrow on the wall for general perusal. Each member can write on the subject which may be most in his or her line. Those with any ability, may choose all twelve. While those with none, may only limit themselves to one stanza. Both will do. Those, however, who will show high mental capacity, combined with quickness, will be held the best. But anyone who shall have completed all twelve themes won't be permitted to hasten and begin over again; we'll have to fine such a one, and finish."

"Yes, that will do," assented Xiangyun. After settling everything satisfactorily, they extinguished the lamp and went to bed.

Reader, do you want to know what subsequently took place? If you do, then listen to what is contained in the way of explanation in the following chapter.

CHAPTER 38

Lin Xiaoxiang carries the first prize in the poems on chrysanthemums. Xue Hengwu chaffs Baoyu by composing verses in the same style as his on the crabs.

After Baochai and Xiangyun, we will now explain, settled everything in their deliberations, nothing memorable occurred, the whole night, which deserves to be put on record.

The next day, Xiangyun invited dowager lady Jia and her other relatives to come and look at the olea flowers. Old lady Jia and everyone else answered that as she had had the kind attention to ask them, they felt it their duty to avail themselves of her gracious invitation, much though they would be putting her to trouble and inconvenience. At twelve o'clock, therefore, old lady Jia actually took with her Madame Wang and lady Feng, as well as Mrs. Xue and other members of her family whom she had asked to join them, and repaired into the garden.

"Which is the best spot?" old lady Jia inquired.

"We are ready to go wherever you may like, dear senior," Madame Wang ventured in response.

"A collation has already been spread in the Lotus Fragrance Arbor," lady Feng interposed. "Besides, the two olea plants, on that hill, yonder, are now lovely in their full blossom, and the water of that stream is jade-like and pellucid, so if we sit in the pavilion in the middle of it, won't we enjoy an open and bright view? It will be refreshing too to our eyes to watch the pool."

"Quite right!" assented dowager lady Jia at this suggestion; and while expressing her approbation, she ushered her train of followers into the Arbor of Lotus Fragrance.

This Arbor of Lotus Fragrance had, in fact, been erected in the center of the pool. It had windows on all four sides. On the left and on the right, stood covered passages, which spanned the stream and connected with the hills. At the back, figured a winding bridge.

As the party ascended the bamboo bridge, lady Feng promptly advanced and supported dowager lady Jia. "Venerable ancestor," she said, "just walk boldly and with confident step; there's nothing to fear; it's the way of these bamboo bridges to go on creaking like this."

Presently, they entered the arbor. Here they saw two additional bamboo tables, placed beyond the balustrade. On the one, were arranged cups, chopsticks, and every article necessary for drinking wine. On the other, were laid bamboo utensils for tea, a tea-service, and various cups and saucers. On the off side, two or three waiting-maids were engaged in fanning the stove to boil the water for tea. On the near side were visible several other girls, who were trying with their fans to get a fire to light in the stove so as to warm the wines.

"It was a capital idea," dowager lady Jia hastily exclaimed laughingly with vehemence, "to bring tea here. What's more, the spot and the appurtenances are alike so spick and span!"

"These things were brought by cousin Baochai," Xiangyun smilingly explained, "so I got them ready."

"This child is, I say, so scrupulously particular," old lady Jia observed, "that everything she does is thoroughly devised."

As she gave utterance to her feelings, her attention was attracted by a pair of scrolls of black lacquer, inlaid with mother-of-pearl, suspended on the pillars, and she asked Xiangyun to tell her what the mottoes were.

The text she read was:

> Snapped is the shade of the hibiscus by the fragrant oar of a boat homeward bound.
> Deep flows the perfume of the lily and the lotus underneath the bamboo bridge.

After listening to the motto, old lady Jia raised her head and cast a glance upon the tablet; then turning round: "Long ago, when I was young," she observed, addressing herself to Mrs. Xue, "we likewise had at home a pavilion like this called 'the Hall reclining on the russet clouds,' or some other such name. At that time, I was of the same age as the girls, and my wont was to go day after day and play with my sisters there. One day, I, unexpectedly, slipped and fell into the water, and I had a narrow escape from being drowned; for it was after great difficulty, that they managed to drag me out safe and sound. But my head was, after all, bumped about against the wooden nails; so much so, that this hole of the length of a finger, which you can see up to this day on my temple, comes from the bruises I sustained. All my people were in a funk that I'd be the worse for this ducking and continued in fear and trembling lest I should catch a chill. 'It was dreadful, dreadful!' they opined, but I managed, little though everyone thought it, to keep in splendid health."

Lady Feng allowed no time to anyone else to put in a word; but anticipating them: "Had you then not survived, who would now be enjoying these immense blessings!" she smiled. "This makes it evident that no small amount of happiness and long life were in store for you, venerable ancestor, from your very youth up! It was by the agency of the spirits that this hole was knocked open so that they might fill it up with happiness and longevity! The old man Shouxing had, in fact, a hole in his head, which was so full of every kind of blessing conducive to happiness and long life that it bulged up ever so high!"

Before, however, she could conclude, dowager lady Jia and the rest were convulsed with such laughter that their bodies doubled in two.

"This monkey is given to dreadful tricks!" laughed old lady Jia. "She's always ready to make a scapegoat of me to evoke amusement. But would that I could take that glib mouth of yours and rend it in pieces."

"It's because I feared that the cold might, when you by and bye have some crabs to eat, accumulate in your intestines," lady Feng pleaded, "that I tried to induce you, dear senior, to have a laugh, so as to make you gay and merry. For one can, when in high spirits, indulge in a couple of them more with impunity."

"By and bye," smiled old lady Jia, "I'll make you follow me day and night, so that I may constantly be amused and feel my mind diverted; I won't let you go back to your home."

"It's that weakness of yours for her, venerable senior," Madame Wang observed with a smile, "that has got her into the way of behaving in this manner, and, if you go on speaking to her as you do, she'll soon become ever so much the more unreasonable."

"I like her such as she is," dowager lady Jia laughed. "Besides, she's truly no child, ignorant of the distinction between high and low. When we are at home, with no strangers present, we ladies should be on terms like these, and as long, in fact, as we don't overstep propriety, it's all right. If not, what would be the earthly use of making them behave like so many saints?"

While bandying words, they entered the pavilion in a body. After tea, lady Feng hastened to lay out the cups and chopsticks. At the upper table then seated herself old lady Jia, Mrs. Xue, Baochai, Daiyu, and Baoyu. Round the table, on the east, sat Shi Xiangyun, Madame Wang, Yingchun, Tanchun, and Xichun. At the small table, leaning against the door on the west side, Li Wan and lady Feng assigned themselves places. But it was for the mere sake of appearances, as neither of them ventured to sit down, but remained in attendance at the two tables, occupied by old lady Jia and Madame Wang.

"You'd better," lady Feng said, "not bring in too many crabs at a time. Throw these again into the steaming-basket! Only serve ten; and when they're eaten, a fresh supply can be fetched!"

Asking, at the same time, for water, she washed her hands, and, taking her position near dowager lady Jia, she scooped out the meat from a crab, and offered the first help to Mrs. Xue.

"They'll be sweeter were I to open them with my own hands," Mrs. Xue remarked, "there's no need for anyone to serve me."

Lady Feng, therefore, presented it to old lady Jia and handed a second portion to Baoyu.

"Make the wine as warm as possible and bring it in!" she then went on to cry. "Go," she added, directing the servant-girls, "and fetch the powder, made of green beans, and scented with the leaves of chrysanthemums and the stamens of the olea fragrans; and keep it ready to rinse our hands with."

Shi Xiangyun had a crab, but no sooner had she done than she retired to a lower seat, from where she helped her guests. When she, however, walked out a second time to give orders to fill two dishes and send them over to Mrs. Zhao, she perceived lady Feng come up to her again. "You're not accustomed to entertaining," she said, "so go and have your share to eat. I'll attend to the people for you first, and, when they've gone, I'll have all I want."

Xiangyun would not agree to her proposal. But giving further directions to the servants to spread two tables under the verandah on the off-side, she pressed Yuanyang, Hupo, Caixia, Caiyun, and Ping'er to go and seat themselves.

"Lady Secunda," consequently ventured Yuanyang, "you're in here doing the honors, so may I go and have something to eat?"

"You can all go," replied lady Feng; "leave everything in my charge, and it will be all right."

While these words were being spoken, Shi Xiangyun resumed her place at the banquet. Lady Feng and Li Wan then took hurryscurry something to eat as a matter of form; but lady Feng came down once more to look after things. After a time, she stepped out on the verandah where Yuanyang and the other girls were having their refreshments in high glee. As soon as they caught sight of her, Yuanyang and her companions stood up. "What has your ladyship come out again for?" they inquired. "Do let us also enjoy a little peace and quiet!"

"This chit Yuanyang is worse than ever!" lady Feng laughed. "Here I'm slaving away for you, and, instead of feeling grateful to me, you bear me a grudge! But don't you yet quick pour me a cup of wine?"

Yuanyang immediately smiled, and filling a cup, she applied it to lady Feng's lips. Lady Feng stretched out her neck and emptied it. But Hupo and Caixia thereupon likewise replenished a cup and put it to lady Feng's mouth. Lady Feng swallowed the contents of that as well. Ping'er had, by this time, brought her some yellow meat which she had picked out from the shell. "Pour plenty of ginger and vinegar!" shouted lady Feng, and, in a moment, she made short work of that too. "You people," she smiled, "had better sit down and have something to eat, for I'm off now."

"You brazen-faced thing," exclaimed Yuanyang laughingly, "to eat what was intended for us!"

"Don't be so captious with me!" smiled lady Feng. "Are you aware that your master Secundus, Mr. Lian, has taken such a violent fancy to you that he means to speak to our old lady to let you be his secondary wife!"

Yuanyang blushed crimson. "Cui!" she shouted. "Are these really words to issue from the mouth of a lady! But if I don't daub your face all over with my filthy hands, I won't feel happy!"

Saying this, she rushed up to her. She was about to besmear her face, when lady Feng pleaded: "My dear child, do let me off this time!"

"Lo, that girl Yuan," laughed Hupo, "wishes to smear her, and that hussey Ping still spares her! Look here, she has scarcely had two crabs, and she has drunk a whole saucerful of vinegar!"

Ping'er was holding a crab full of yellow meat, which she was in the act of cleaning. As soon therefore as she heard this taunt, she came, crab in hand, to spatter Hupo's face, as she laughingly reviled her. "I'll take you, minx, with that cajoling tongue of yours" she cried, "and…"

But, Hupo, while also indulging in laughter, drew aside; so Ping'er beat the air, and fell forward, daubing, by a strange coincidence, the cheek of lady Feng. Lady Feng was at the moment having a little good-humored raillery with Yuanyang, and was taken so much off her guard, that she was quite startled out of her senses. "Ai-ya!" she ejaculated. The bystanders found it difficult to keep their countenance, and, with one voice, they exploded into a boisterous fit of laughter. Lady Feng as well could not help feeling amused, and smilingly she upbraided her. "You stupid wench!" she said; "Have you by gorging lost your eyesight that you recklessly smudge your mistress' face?"

Ping'er hastily crossed over and wiped her face for her, and then went in person to fetch some water.

"Amituo Fo," ejaculated Yuanyang, "this is a distinct retribution!"

Dowager lady Jia, though seated on the other side, overheard their shouts, and she consecutively made inquiries as to what they had seen to tickled their fancy so. "Tell us," (she urged), "what it is so that we too should have a laugh."

"Our lady Secunda," Yuanyang and the other maids forthwith laughingly cried, "came to steal our crabs and eat them, and Ping'er got angry and daubed her mistress' face all over with yellow meat. So our mistress and that slave-girl are now having a scuffle over it."

This report filled dowager lady Jia, Madame Wang, and the other inmates with them with much merriment. "Do have pity on her," dowager lady Jia laughed, "and let her have some of those small legs and entrails to eat, and have done!"

Yuanyang and her companions assented, much amused. "Mistress Secunda," they shouted in a loud tone of voice, "you're at liberty to eat this whole tableful of legs!"

But having washed her face clean, lady Feng approached old lady Jia and the other guests and waited upon them for a time, while they partook of refreshments.

Daiyu did not, with her weak physique, venture to overload her stomach, so partaking of a little meat from the claws, she left the table. Presently, however, dowager lady Jia too abandoned all idea of having anything more to eat. The company therefore quitted the banquet; and, when they had rinsed their hands, some admired the flowers, some played with the water, others looked at the fish.

After a short stroll, Madame Wang turned round and remarked to old lady Jia: "There's plenty of wind here. Besides, you've just had crabs; so it would be prudent for you, venerable senior, to return home and rest. And if you feel in the humor, we can come again for a turn tomorrow."

"Quite true!" acquiesced dowager lady Jia, in reply to this suggestion. "I was afraid that if I left, now that you're all in exuberant spirits, I mightn't again be spoiling your fun, (so I didn't budge). But as the idea originates from yourselves do go as you please, (while I retire). But," she said to Xiangyun, "don't allow your cousin Secundus Baoyu, and your cousin Lin to have too much to eat." Then when Xiangyun had signified her obedience, "You two girls," continuing, she recommended Xiangyun and Baochai, "must not also have more than is good for you. Those things are, it's true, luscious, but they're not very wholesome; and if you eat immoderately of them, why, you'll get stomachaches."

Both girls promised with alacrity to be careful; and, having escorted her beyond the confines of the garden, they retraced their steps and ordered the servants to clear the remnants of the banquet and to lay out a new supply of refreshments.

"There's no use of any regular spread out!" Baoyu interposed. "When you are about to write verses, that big round table can be put in the center and the wines and eatables laid on it. Neither will there be any need to ceremoniously have any fixed seats. Let those who may want anything to eat, go up to it and take what they like; and if we seat ourselves, scattered all over the place, won't it be far more convenient for us?"

"Your idea is excellent!" Baochai answered.

"This is all very well," Xiangyun observed, "but there are others to be studied besides ourselves!"

Issuing consequently further directions for another table to be laid, and picking out some hot crabs, she asked Xiren, Zijuan, Siqi, Shishu, Ruhua, Ying'er, Cuimo and the other girls to sit together and form a party. Then having a couple of flowered rugs spread under the olea trees on the hills, she bade the matrons on duty, the waiting-maids and other servants to likewise make themselves comfortable and to eat and drink at their pleasure until they were wanted, when they could come and answer the calls.

Xiangyun next fetched the themes for the verses and pinned them with a needle on the wall. "They're full of originality," one and all exclaimed after perusal, "we fear we couldn't write anything on them."

Xiangyun then went onto explain to them the reasons that had prompted her not to determine upon any particular rhymes.

"Yes, quite right!" put in Baoyu. "I myself don't fancy hard and fast rhymes!"

But Lin Daiyu, being unable to stand much wine and to take any crabs, told, on her own account, a servant to fetch an embroidered cushion; and, seating herself in such a way as to lean against the railing, she took up a fishing-rod and began to fish. Baochai played for a time with a twig of olea she held in her hand, then resting on the window-sill, she plucked the petals, and threw them into the water, attracting the fish, which went by, to rise to the surface and nibble at them. Xiangyun, after a few moments of abstraction, urged Xiren and the other girls to help themselves to anything they wanted, and beckoned to the servants, seated at the foot of the hill, to eat to their heart's content. Tanchun, in company with Li Wan and Xichun, stood meanwhile under the shade of the weeping willows, and looked at the widgeons and egrets. Yingchun, on the other hand, was all alone under the shade of some trees, threading double jasmine flowers, with a needle specially adapted for the purpose. Baoyu too watched Daiyu fishing for a while. At one time he leant next to Baochai and cracked a few jokes with her. And at another, he drank, when he noticed Xiren feasting on crabs with her companions, a few mouthfuls of wine to keep her company. At this, Xiren cleaned the meat out of a shell, and gave it to him to eat.

Daiyu then put down the fishing-rod, and, approaching the seats, she laid hold of a small black tankard, ornamented with silver plum flowers, and selected a tiny cup, made of transparent stone, red like a Begonia, and in the shape of a banana leaf. A servant-girl observed her movements, and, concluding that she felt inclined to have a drink, she drew near with hurried step to pour some wine for her.

"You girls had better go on eating," Daiyu remonstrated, "and let me help myself; there'll be some fun in it then!"

So speaking, she filled for herself a cup half full; but discovering that it was yellow wine, "I've eaten only a little bit of crab," she said, "and yet I feel my mouth slightly sore; so what would do for me now is a mouthful of very hot distilled spirit."

Baoyu hastened to take up her remark. "There's some distilled spirit," he chimed in. "Take some of that wine," he there and then shouted out to a servant, "scented with acacia flowers, and warm a tankard of it."

When however it was brought Daiyu simply took a sip and put it down again. Baochai too then came forward, and picked up a double cup; but, after drinking a mouthful of it, she lay it aside, and, moistening her brush, she walked up to the wall, and marked off the first theme: "longing for chrysanthemums," below which she appended a character "Heng."

"My dear cousin," promptly remarked Baoyu. "I've already got four lines of the second theme so let me write on it!"

"I managed, after ever so much difficulty, to put a stanza together," Baochai smiled, "and are you now in such a hurry to deprive me of it?"

Without so much as a word, Daiyu took a brush and put a distinctive sign opposite the eighth, consisting of: "ask the chrysanthemums;" and, singling out, in quick succession, the eleventh: "dream of chrysanthemums," as well, she too affixed for herself the word "xiao" below. But Baoyu likewise got a brush, and marked his choice, the twelfth on the list: "seek for chrysanthemums," by the side of which he wrote the character "jiang."

Tanchun thereupon rose to her feet. "If there's no one to write on 'pinning the chrysanthemums'" she observed, while scrutinising the themes, "do let me have it! It has just been ruled," she continued, pointing at Baoyu with a significant smile, "that it is on no account permissible to introduce any expressions, bearing reference to the inner chambers, so you'd better be on your guard!"

But as she spoke, she perceived Xiangyun come forward, and jointly mark the fourth and fifth, that is: "facing the chrysanthemums," and "putting chrysanthemums in vases," to which she, like the others, appended a word, "Hsiang."

"You too should get a style or other!" Tanchun suggested.

"In our home," smiled Xiangyun, "there exist, it is true, at present several halls and structures, but as I don't live in either, there'll be no-run in it were I to borrow the name of any one of them!"

"Our venerable senior just said," Baochai observed laughingly, that there was also in your home a water-pavilion called 'leaning on russet clouds hall,' and is it likely that it wasn't yours? But albeit it doesn't exist now-a-days, you were anyhow its mistress of old."

"She's right!" one and all exclaimed.

Baoyu therefore allowed Xiangyun no time to make a move, but forthwith rubbed off the character "xiang," for her and substituted that of "xia" (russet).

A short time only elapsed before the compositions on the twelve themes had all been completed. After they had each copied out their respective verses, they handed them to Yingchun, who took a separate sheet of snow-white fancy paper, and transcribed them together, affixing distinctly under each stanza the style of the composer. Li Wan and her assistants then began to read, starting from the first on the list, the verses which follow:

"Longing for chrysanthemums," by the "Princess of Hengwu."

> With anguish sore I face the western breeze, and wrapt in grief, I
> pine for you!
> What time the smart weed russet turns, and the reeds white, my
> heart is rent in two.
> When in autumn the hedges thin, and gardens waste, all trace of
> you is gone.
> When the moon waxeth cold, and the dew pure, my dreams then
> know something of you.
> With constant yearnings my heart follows you as far as wild geese
> homeward fly.
> Lonesome I sit and lend an ear, till a late hour to the sound of the
> block!
> For you, ye yellow flowers, I've grown haggard and worn, but who
> doth pity me,
> And breathe one word of cheer that in the ninth moon I will soon
> meet you again?

"Search for chrysanthemums," by the "Gentleman of Yihong."

When I have naught to do, I'll seize the first fine day to try and
    stroll about.
Neither wine-cups nor cups of medicine will then deter me from
    my wish.
Who plants the flowers in all those spots, facing the dew and under
    the moon's rays?
Outside the rails they grow and by the hedge; but in autumn where
    do they go?
With sandals waxed I come from distant shores; my feelings all
    exuberant;
But as on this cold day I can't exhaust my song, my spirits get de-
    pressed.
The yellow flowers, if they but knew how comfort to a poet to af-
    ford,
Would not let me this early morn trudge out in vain with my cash
    laden staff.

"Planting chrysanthemums," by the "Gentleman of Yihong."

When autumn breaks, I take my hoe, and moving them myself out
    of the park,
I plant them everywhere near the hedges and in the foreground of
    the halls.
Last night, when least expected, they got a good shower, which
    made them all revive.
This morn my spirits still rise high, as the buds burst in bloom be-
    decked with frost.
Now that it's cool, a thousand stanzas on the autumn scenery I sing.
In ecstasies from drink, I toast their blossom in a cup of cold, and
    fragrant wine.
With spring water, I sprinkle them, cover the roots with mould
    and well tend them,
So that they may, like the path near the well, be free of every grain
    of dirt.

"Facing the chrysanthemums," by the "Old friend of the Hall reclining on the russet clouds."

From other gardens I transplant them, and I treasure them like gold.
One cluster bears light-colored bloom; another bears dark shades.

I sit with head uncovered by the sparse-leaved artemesia hedge,
And in their pure and cool fragrance, clasping my knees, I hum
   my lays.
In the whole world, methinks, none see the light as peerless as
   these flowers.
From all I see you have no other friend more intimate than me.
Such autumn splendor, I must not misuse, as steadily it fleets.
My gaze I fix on you as I am fain each moment to enjoy!

"Putting chrysanthemums in vases," by the "Old Friend of the hall
reclining on the russet clouds."

The lute I thrum, and quaff my wine, joyful at heart that ye are
   meet to be my mates.
The various tables, on which ye are laid, adorn with beauteous
   grace this quiet nook.
The fragrant dew, next to the spot I sit, is far apart from that by
   the three paths.
I fling my book aside and turn my gaze upon a twig full of your
   autumn (bloom).
What time the frost is pure, a new dream steals o'er me, as by the
   paper screen I rest.
When cold holdeth the park, and the sun's rays do slant, I long
   and yearn for you, old friends.
I too differ from others in this world, for my own tastes resemble
   those of yours.
The vernal winds do not hinder the peach tree and the pear from
   bursting forth in bloom.

"Singing chrysanthemums," by the "Xiaoxiang consort."

Eating the bread of idleness, the frenzy of poetry creeps over me
   both night and day.
Round past the hedge I wend, and, leaning on the rock, I intone
   verses gently to myself.
From the point of my brush emanate lines of recondite grace, so
   near the frost I write.
Some scent I hold by the side of my mouth, and, turning to the
   moon, I sing my sentiments.
With self-pitying lines pages I fill, so as utterance to give to all my
   cares and woes.

From these few scanty words, who could fathom the secrets of my heart about the autumntide?

Beginning from the time when T'ao, the magistrate, did criticize the beauty of your bloom,

Yea, from that date remote up to this very day, your high renown has ever been extolled.

"Drawing chrysanthemums," by the "Princess of Hengwu."

Verses I've had enough, so with my brushes I play; with no idea that I am mad.

Do I make use of pigments red or green as to involve a task of toilsome work?

To form clusters of leaves, I sprinkle simply here and there a thousand specks of ink. And when I've drawn the semblance of the flowers, some spots I make to represent the frost.

The light and dark so life-like harmonize with the figure of those there in the wind,

That when I've done tracing their autumn growth, a fragrant smell issues under my wrist.

Do you not mark how they resemble those, by the east hedge, which you leisurely pluck?

Upon the screens their image I affix to solace me for those of the ninth moon.

"Asking the chrysanthemums," by the "Xiaoxiang consort."

Your heart, in autumn, I would like to read, but know it no one could!

While humming with my arms behind my back, on the east hedge I rap.

So peerless and unique are ye that who is meet with you to stay?

Why are you of all flowers the only ones to burst the last in bloom?

Why in such silence plunge the garden dew and the frost in the hall?

When wild geese homeward fly and crickets sicken, do you think of me?

Do not tell me that in the world none of you grow with power of speech?

But if ye fathom what I say, why not converse with me a while?

"Pinning the chrysanthemums in the hair," by the "Visitor under the banana trees."

I put some in a vase, and plant some by the hedge, so day by day
I have ample to do.

I pluck them, yet don't fancy they are meant for girls to pin before
the glass in their coiffure.

My mania for these flowers is just as keen as was that of the squire,
who once lived in Chang'an.

I rave as much for them as raved Mr. Peng Ze, when he was under
the effects of wine.

Cold is the short hair on his temples and moistened with dew,
which on it dripped from the three paths.

His flaxen turban is suffused with the sweet fragrance of the autumn frost in the ninth moon.

That strong weakness of mine to pin them in my hair is viewed
with sneers by my contemporaries.

They clap their hands, but they are free to laugh at me by the roadside as much us e'er they list.

"The shadow of the chrysanthemums," by the "Old Friend of the
hall reclining on the russet clouds."

In layers upon layers their autumn splendor grows and e'er thick
and thicker.

I make off furtively, and stealthily transplant them from the three
crossways.

The distant lamp, inside the window-frame, depicts their shade
both far and near.

The hedge riddles the moon's rays, like unto a sieve, but the flowers stop the holes.

As their reflection cold and fragrant tarries here, their soul must
too abide.

The dew-dry spot beneath the flowers is so like them that what is
said of dreams is trash.

Their precious shadows, full of subtle scent, are trodden down to
pieces here and there.

Could any one with eyes half closed from drinking, not mistake
the shadow for the flowers.

"Dreaming of chrysanthemums," by the "Xiaoxiang consort."

What vivid dreams arise as I dose by the hedge amidst those autumn scenes!

Whether clouds bear me company or the moon be my mate, I can't discern.

In fairyland I soar, not that I would become a butterfly like Zhuang.
So long I for my old friend Tao, the magistrate, that I again seek him.

In a sound sleep I fell; but so soon as the wild geese cried, they broke my rest.

The chirp of the cicadas gave me such a start that I bear them a grudge.

My secret wrongs to whom can I go and divulge, when I wake up from sleep?

The faded flowers and the cold mist make my feelings of anguish know no bounds.

"Fading of the chrysanthemums," by the "Visitor under the banana trees."

The dew congeals; the frost waxes in weight; and gradually dwindles their bloom.

After the feast, with the flower show, follows the season of the 'little snow.'

The stalks retain still some redundant smell, but the flowers' golden tinge is faint.

The stems do not bear sign of even one whole leaf; their verdure is all past.

Naught but the chirp of crickets strikes my ear, while the moon shines on half my bed.

Near the cold clouds, distant a thousand li, a flock of wild geese slowly fly.

When autumn breaks again next year, I feel certain that we will meet once more.

We part but only for a time, so don't let us indulge in anxious thoughts.

Each stanza they read they praised; and they heaped upon each other incessant eulogiums.

"Let me now criticise them; I'll do so with all fairness!" Li Wan smiled. "As I glance over the page," she said, "I find that each of you has some distinct admirable sentiments; but in order to be impartial in my criticism today, I must concede the first place to: 'Singing the chrysanthemums;' the second to: 'Asking the chrysanthemums;' and the third to: 'Dreaming of chrysanthemums.' The original nature of the themes makes the verses full of originality, and their conception still more original. But we must allow to the 'Xiaoxiang consort' the credit of being the best; next in order following: 'Pinning chrysanthemums in the hair,' 'Facing the chrysanthemums,' 'Putting the chrysanthemums in vases,' 'Drawing the chrysanthemums,' and 'Longing for chrysanthemums' as second best."

This decision filled Baoyu with intense gratification. Clapping his hands, "Quite right! it's most just," he shouted.

"My verses are worth nothing!" Daiyu remarked. "Their fault, after all, is that they are a little too minutely subtle."

"They are subtle but good," Li Wan rejoined; "for there's no artificialness or stiffness about them."

"According to my views," Daiyu observed, "the best line is:

"'When cold holdeth the park and the sun's rays do slant, I long and yearn for you, old friends.'

"The metonomy:

"'I fling my book aside and turn my gaze upon a twig of autumn.'

is already admirable! She has dealt so exhaustively with 'putting chrysanthemums in a vase' that she has left nothing unsaid that could be said, and has had in consequence to turn her thought back and consider the time anterior to their being plucked and placed in vases. Her sentiments are profound!"

"What you say is certainly so," explained Li Wan smiling; "but that line of yours:

"'Some scent I hold by the side of my mouth,...'

"beats that."

"After all," said Tanchun, "we must admit that there's depth of thought in those of the 'Princess of Hengwu' with:

"'...in autumn all trace of you is gone;'

"and

"'...my dreams then know something of you!'

"They really make the meaning implied by the words 'long for' stand out clearly."

"Those passages of yours:

"'Cold is the short hair on his temples and moistened...'

"and

"'His flaxen turban is suffused with the sweet fragrance...;'"

laughingly observed Baochai, "likewise bring out the idea of 'pinning the chrysanthemums in the hair' so thoroughly that one couldn't get a loop hole for fault-finding."

Xiangyun then smiled.

"'...who is meet with you to stay'"

she said, "and

"'....burst the last in bloom.'

"are questions so straight to the point set to the chrysanthemums, that they are quite at a loss what answer to give."

"Were what you say:

"'I sit with head uncovered...'

"and

"'...clasping my knees, I hum my lays...'

"as if you couldn't, in fact, tear yourself away for even a moment from them," Li Wan laughed, "to come to the knowledge of the chrysanthemums, why, they would certainly be sick and tired of you."

This joke made everyone laugh.

"I'm last again!" smiled Baoyu. "Is it likely that:

"'Who plants the flowers?...
...in autumn where do they go?
With sandals waxed I come from distant shores...
...and as on this cold day I can't exhaust my song...'

"do not all forsooth amount to searching for chrysanthemums? And that

"'Last night they got a shower....
And this morn ... bedecked with frost,'

"don't both bear on planting them? But unfortunately they can't come up to these lines:

"'Some scent I hold by the side of my mouth and turning to the moon I sing my sentiments.'
'In their pure and cool fragrance, clasping my knees I hum my lays.' '...short hair on his temples...'
'His flaxen turban...
...golden tinge is faint.
...verdure is all past.
...in autumn ... all trace of you is gone.
...my dreams then know something of you.'

"But tomorrow," he proceeded, "if I have got nothing to do, I'll write twelve stanzas myself."

"Yours are also good," Li Wan pursued, "the only thing is that they aren't as full of original conception as those other lines, that's all."

But after a few further criticisms, they asked for some more warm crabs; and, helping themselves, as soon as they were brought, from the large circular table, they regaled themselves for a time.

"With the crabs today in one's hand and the olea before one's eyes, one cannot help inditing verses," Baoyu smiled. "I've already thought of a few; but will any of you again have the pluck to devise any?"

With this challenge, he there and then hastily washed his hands and picking up a brush he wrote out what, his companions found on perusal, to run in this strain:

When in my hands I clasp a crab what most enchants my heart is the cassia's cool shade.
While I pour vinegar and ground ginger, I feel from joy as if I would go mad.
With so much gluttony the prince's grandson eats his crabs that he should have some wine.
The side-walking young gentleman has no intestines in his frame at all.
I lose sight in my greediness that in my stomach cold accumulates.

> To my fingers a strong smell doth adhere and though I wash them
> yet the smell clings fast.
> The main secret of this is that men in this world make much of
> food.
> The P'o Spirit has laughed at them that all their lives they only seek
> to eat.

"I could readily compose a hundred stanzas with such verses in no time," Daiyu observed with a sarcastic smile.

"Your mental energies are now long ago exhausted," Baoyu rejoined laughingly, "and instead of confessing your inability to devise any, you still go on heaping invective upon people!"

Daiyu, upon catching this insinuation, made no reply of any kind; but slightly raising her head she hummed something to herself for a while, and then taking up a brush she completed a whole stanza with a few dashes.

The company then read her lines. They consisted of:

> E'en after death, their armor and their lengthy spears are never
> cast away.
> So nice they look, piled in the plate, that first to taste them I'd fain
> be.
> In every pair of legs they have, the crabs are full of tender jade-like
> meat.
> Each piece of ruddy fat, which in their shell bumps up, emits a fra-
> grant smell.
> Besides much meat, they have a greater relish for me still, eight feet
> as well.
> Who bids me drink a thousand cups of wine in order to enhance
> my joy?
> What time I can behold their luscious food, with the fine season
> doth accord
> When cassias wave with fragrance pure, and the chrysanthemums
> are decked with frost.

Baoyu had just finished reading it over and was beginning to sing its praise, when Daiyu, with one snatch, tore it to pieces and bade a servant go and burn it.

"As my compositions can't come up to yours," she then observed, "I'll burn it. Yours is capital, much better than the lines you wrote a little time back on the chrysanthemums, so keep it for the benefit of others."

"I've likewise succeeded, after much effort, in putting together a stanza," Baochai laughingly remarked. "It cannot, of course, be worth much, but I'll put it down for fun's sake."

As she spoke, she too wrote down her lines. When they came to look at them, they read:

> On this bright beauteous day, I bask in the dryandra shade, with a cup in my hand.
> When I was at Chang'an, with driveling mouth, I longed for the ninth day of the ninth moon.
> The road stretches before their very eyes, but they can't tell between straight and transverse.
> Under their shells in spring and autumn only reigns a vacuum, yellow and black.

At this point, they felt unable to refrain from shouting: "Excellent!" "She abuses in fine style!" Baoyu shouted. "But my lines should also be committed to the flames."

The company thereupon scanned the remainder of the stanza, which was couched in this wise:

> When all the stock of wine is gone, chrysanthemums then use to scour away the smell.
> So as to counteract their properties of gath'ring cold, fresh ginger you should take.
> Alas! now that they have been dropped into the boiling pot, what good do they derive?
> About the moonlit river banks there but remains the fragrant aroma of corn.

At the close of their perusal, they with one voice, explained that this was a first-rate song on crab-eating; that minor themes of this kind should really conceal lofty thoughts, before they could be held to be of any great merit, and that the only thing was that it chaffed people rather too virulently.

But while they were engaged in conversation, Ping'er was again seen coming into the garden. What she wanted is not, however, yet known; so, reader, peruse the details given in the subsequent chapter.

CHAPTER 39

The tongue of the village old dame finds as free vent as a river that has broken its banks. The affectionate cousin makes up his mind to sift to the very bottom the story told by old goody Liu.

Upon seeing, the story explains, Ping'er arrive, they unanimously inquired, "What is your mistress up to? How is it she hasn't come?"

"How ever could she spare the time to get as far as here?" Ping'er smiled and replied. "But, she said, she hasn't anything good to eat, so she bade me, as she couldn't possibly run over, come and find out whether there be any more crabs or not; (if there be), she enjoined me to ask for a few to take to her to eat at home."

"There are plenty!" Xiangyun rejoined; and directing, with alacrity, a servant to fetch a present box, she put in it ten of the largest crabs.

"I'll take a few more of the female ones," Ping'er remarked.

One and all then laid hands upon Ping'er and tried to drag her into a seat, but Ping'er would not accede to their importunities.

"I insist upon your sitting down," Li Wan laughingly exclaimed, and as she kept pulling her about, and forcing her to sit next to her, she filled a cup of wine and put it to her lips. Ping'er hastily swallowed a sip and endeavored immediately to beat a retreat.

"I won't let you go," shouted Li Wan. "It's so evident that you've only got that woman Feng in your thoughts as you don't listen to any of my words!"

Saying this, she went on to bid the nurses go ahead, and take the box over. "Tell her," she added, "that I've kept Ping'er here."

A matron presently returned with a box. "Lady Secunda," she reported, "says that you, lady Zhu, and our young mistresses must not make fun of her for having asked for something to eat; and that in this box you'll find cakes made of water-lily powder, and rolls prepared with chicken fat, which your maternal aunt, on the other side, just sent for your ladyship and for you, young ladies, to taste. That she bids you," (the matron) continued, turning towards Ping'er, "come over on duty, but your mind is so set upon pleasure that you loiter behind and don't go back. She advises you, however, not to have too many cups of wine."

"Were I even to have too much," Ping'er smiled, "what could she do to me?"

Uttering these words, she went on with her drink; after which she partook of some more crab.

"What a pity it is," interposed Li Wan, caressing her, "that a girl with such good looks as you should have so ordinary a fortune as to simply fall into that room as a menial! But wouldn't anyone, who is not acquainted with actual facts, take you for a lady and a mistress?"

While she went on eating and drinking with Baochai, Xiangyun, and the other girls, Ping'er turned her head round. "Don't rub me like that!" she laughed, "It makes me feel quite ticklish."

"Ai-yo!" shouted Li Wan. "What's this hard thing?"

"It's a key," Ping'er answered.

"What fine things have you got that the fear lest people should take it away, prompts you to carry this about you? I keep on, just for a laugh, telling people the whole day long that when the bonze Tang was fetching the canons, a white horse came and carried him! That when Liu Zhiyuan was attacking the empire, a melon-spirit appeared and brought him a coat of mail, and that in the same way, where our vixen Feng is, there you are to be found! You are your mistress' general key; and what do you want this other key for?"

"You've primed yourself with wine, my lady," Ping'er smiled, and here you once more chaff me and make a laughing-stock of me."

"This is really quite true," Baochai laughed. "Whenever we've got nothing to do, and we talk matters over, (we're quite unanimous) that not one in a hundred could be picked out to equal you girls in here. The beauty is that each one of you possesses her own good qualities!"

"In everything, whether large or small, a heavenly principle rules alike," Li Wan explained. "Were there, for instance, no Yuanyang in our venerable senior's apartments, how would it ever do? Commencing with Madame Wang herself, who is it who could muster sufficient courage to expostulate with the old lady? Yet she plainly has the pluck to put in her remonstrances with her; and, as it happens, our worthy ancestor lends a patient ear to only what she says and no one else. None of the others can remember what our old senior has in the way of clothes and head-ornaments, but she can remember everything; and, were she not there to look after things, there is no knowing how many would not be swindled away. That child besides is so straightforward at heart, that, despite all this, she often puts in a good word for others, and doesn't rely upon her influence to look down disdainfully upon anyone!"

"It was only yesterday," Xichun observed with a smile, "that our dear ancestor said that she was ever so much better than the whole lot of us!"

"She's certainly splendid!" Ping'er ventured. "How could we rise up to her standard?"

"Caixia," Baoyu put in, "who is in mother's rooms, is a good sort of girl!"

"Of course she is!" Tanchun assented. "But she's good enough as far as external appearances go, but inwardly she's a sly one! Madame Wang is just like a joss; she does not give her mind to any sort of business; but this girl is up to everything; and it is she who in all manner of things reminds her mistress what there is to be done. She even knows everything, whether large or small, connected with Mr. Jia Zheng's staying at home or going out of doors; and when at any time Madame Wang forgets, she, from behind the scenes, prompts her how to act."

"Well, never mind about her!" Li Wan suggested. "But were," she pursued, pointing at Baoyu, "no Xiren in this young gentleman's quarters, just you imagine what a pitch things would reach! That vixen Feng may truly resemble the prince Pa of the Chu kingdom; and she may have two arms strong enough to raise a tripod weighing a thousand catties, but had she not this maid (Ping'er), would she be able to accomplish everything so thoroughly?"

"In days gone by," Ping'er interposed, "four servant-girls came along with her, but what with those who've died and those who've gone, only I remain like a solitary spirit."

"You're, after all, the fortunate one!" Li Wan retorted, "but our hussey Feng too is lucky in having you! Had I not also once, just remember, two girls, when your senior master Zhu was alive? Am I not, you've seen for yourselves, a person to bear with people? But in such a surly frame of mind did I find them both day after day that, as soon as your senior master departed this life, I availed myself of their youth (to give them in marriage) and to pack both of them out of my place. But had either of them been good for anything and worthy to be kept, I would, in fact, have now had someone to give me a helping hand!"

As she spoke, the very balls of her eyes suddenly became quite red.

"Why need you again distress your mind?" they with one voice, exclaimed. "Isn't it better that we should break up?"

While conversing, they rinsed their hands; and, when they had agreed to go in a company to dowager lady Jia's and Madame Wang's and inquire after their health, the matrons and servant-maids swept the pavilion and collected and washed the cups and saucers.

Xiren proceeded on her way along with Ping'er. "Come into my room," said Xiren to Ping'er, "and sit down and have another cup of tea."

"I won't have any tea just now," Ping'er answered. "I'll come some other time."

So saying, she was about to go off when Xiren called out to her and stopped her.

"This month's allowances," she asked, "haven't yet been issued, not even to our old mistress and Madame Wang; why is it?"

Upon catching this inquiry, Ping'er hastily retraced her steps and drew near Xiren. After looking about to see that no one was in the neighborhood, she rejoined in a low tone of voice, "Drop these questions at once! They're sure, anyhow, to be issued in a couple of days."

"Why is it," smiled Xiren, "that this gives you such a start?"

"This month's allowances," Ping'er explained to her in a whisper, "have long ago been obtained in advance by our mistress Secunda and given to people for their own purposes; and it's when the interest has been brought from here and there that the various sums will be lumped together and payment be effected. I confide this to you, but, mind, you mustn't go and tell any other person about it."

"Is it likely that she hasn't yet enough money for her own requirements?" Xiren smiled. "Or is it that she's still not satisfied? And what's the use of her still going on bothering herself in this way?"

"Isn't it so!" laughed Ping'er. "From just handling the funds for this particular item, she has, during these few years, so manipulated them as to turn up several hundreds of taels profit out of them. Nor does she spend that monthly allowance of hers for public expenses. But the moment she accumulates anything like eight or ten taels odd, she gives them out too. Thus the interest on her own money alone comes up to nearly a thousand taels a year."

"You and your mistress take our money," Xiren observed laughingly, "and get interest on it; fooling us as if we were no better than idiots."

"Here you are again with your uncharitable words!" Ping'er remonstrated. "Can it be that you haven't yet enough to meet your own expenses with?"

"I am, it's true, not short of money," Xiren replied, "as I have nowhere to go and spend it; but the thing is that I'm making provision for that fellow of ours (Baoyu)."

"If you ever find yourself in any great straits and need money," Ping'er resumed, "you're at liberty to take first those few taels I've got over there to suit your own convenience with, and by and bye I can reduce them from what is due to you and we'll be square."

"I'm not in need of any just now," retorted Xiren. "But should I not have enough, when I want some, I'll send someone to fetch them, and finish."

Ping'er promised that she would let her have the money at any time she sent for it, and, and taking the shortest cut, she issued out of the garden gate. Here she encountered a servant despatched from the other side by lady Feng. She came in search of Ping'er. "Our lady," she said, "has something for you to do, and is waiting for you."

"What's up that it's so pressing?" Ping'er inquired. "Our senior mistress detained me by force to have a chat, so I couldn't manage to get away. But here she time after time sends people after me in this manner!"

"Whether you go or not is your own look out," the maid replied. "It isn't worth your while getting angry with me! If you dare, go and tell these things to our mistress!"

Ping'er spat at her contemptuously, and rushed back in anxious haste. She discovered, however, that lady Feng was not at home. But unexpectedly she perceived that the old goody Liu, who had paid them a visit on a previous occasion for the purpose of obtaining pecuniary assistance, had come again with Ban'er, and was seated in the opposite room, along with Zhang Cai's wife and Zhou Rui's wife, who kept her company. But two or three servant-maids were inside as well, emptying on the floor bags containing dates, squash, and various wild greens.

As soon as they saw her appear in the room, they promptly stood up in a body. Old goody Liu had, on her last visit, learnt what Ping'er's status in the establishment was, so vehemently jumping down, she enquired, "Miss, how do you do? All at home," she pursued, "send you their compliments. I meant to have come earlier and paid my respects to my lady and to look you up, miss; but we've been very busy on the farm. We managed this year to reap, after great labor, a few more piculs of grain than usual. But melons, fruits, and vegetables have also been plentiful. These things, you see here, are what we picked during the first crop; and as we didn't presume to sell them, we kept the best to present to our lady and the young ladies to taste. The young ladies must, of course, be surfeited with all the delicacies and fine things they daily get, but by having some of our wild greens to eat, they will show some regard for our poor attention."

"Many thanks for all the trouble you have taken!" Ping'er eagerly rejoined. Then pressing her to resume her place, she sat down herself; and, urging Mrs. Zhang and Mrs. Zhou to take their seats, she bade a young waiting-maid go and serve the tea.

"There's a joyous air about your face today, Miss, and your eyeballs are all red," the wife of Zhou Rui and the wife of Zhang Cai thereupon smilingly ventured.

"Naturally!" Ping'er laughed. "I generally don't take any wine, but our senior mistress, and our young ladies caught hold of me and insisted upon pouring it down my throat. I had no alternative therefore but to swallow two cups full; so my face at once flushed crimson."

"I have a longing for wine," Zhang Cai's wife smiled; "but there's no one to offer me any. But when anyone by and by invites you, Miss, do take me along with you!"

At these words, one and all burst out laughing.

"Early this morning," Zhou Rui's wife interposed, "I caught a glimpse of those crabs. Only two or three of them would weigh a catty; so in those two or three huge hampers, there must have been, I presume, seventy to eighty catties!"

"If some were intended for those above as well as for those below," Zhou Rui's wife added, "they couldn't, nevertheless, I fear, have been enough."

"How could everyone have had any?" Ping'er observed. "Those simply with any name may have tasted a couple of them; but, as for the rest, some may have touched them with the tips of their hands, but many may even not have done as much."

"Crabs of this kind!" put in old goody Liu, "cost this year five candareens a catty; ten catties for five mace; five times five make two taels five, and three times five make fifteen; and adding what was wanted for wines and eatables, the total must have come to something over twenty taels. Amituo Fo! why, this heap of money is ample for us country-people to live on through a whole year!"

"I expect you have seen our lady?" Ping'er then asked.

"Yes, I have seen her," assented old goody Liu. "She bade us wait."

As she spoke, she again looked out of the window to see what the time of the day could be. "It's getting quite late," she afterwards proceeded. "We must be going, or else we mayn't be in time to get out of the city gates; and then we'll be in a nice fix."

"Quite right," Zhou Rui's wife observed. "I'll go and see what she's up to for you."

With these words, she straightway left the room. After a long absence, she returned. "Good fortune has, indeed, descended upon you, old dame!" she smiled. "Why, you've won the consideration of those two ladies!"

"What about it?" laughingly inquired Ping'er and the others.

"Lady Secunda," Zhou Rui's wife explained with a smile, "was with our venerable lady, so I gently whispered to her: 'old goody Liu wishes to go home; it's getting late and she fears she mightn't be in time to go out of the gates!' 'It's such a long way off!' Our lady Secunda rejoined, 'and she had all the trouble and fatigue of carrying that load of things; so if it's too late, why, let her spend the night here and start on the morrow!' Now isn't this having enlisted our mistress' sympathies? But not to speak of this! Our old lady also happened to overhear what we said, and she inquired: 'who is old goody Liu?' Our lady Secunda forthwith told her all. 'I was just longing,' her venerable ladyship pursued, 'for someone well up in years to have a chat with; ask her in, and let me see her!' So isn't this coming in for consideration, when least unexpected?"

So speaking, she went on to urge old goody Liu to get down and betake herself to the front.

"With a figure like this of mine," old goody Liu demurred, "how could I very well appear before her? My dear sister-in-law, do tell her that I've gone!"

"Get on! Be quick!" Ping'er speedily cried. "What does it matter? Our old lady has the highest regard for old people and the greatest pity for the needy! She's not one you could compare with those haughty and overbearing people! But I fancy you're a little too timid, so I'll accompany you as far as there, along with Mrs. Zhou."

While tendering her services, she and Zhou Rui's wife led off old goody Liu and crossed over to dowager lady Jia's apartments on this side of the mansion. The boy-servants on duty at the second gate stood up when they saw Ping'er approach. But two of them also ran up to her, and, keeping close to her heels: "Miss!" they shouted out. "Miss!"

"What have you again got to say?" Ping'er asked.

"It's pretty late just now," one of the boys smilingly remarked; "and mother is ill and wants me to go and call the doctor, so I would, dear Miss, like to have half a day's leave; may I?"

"Your doings are really fine!" Ping'er exclaimed. "You've agreed among yourselves that each day one of you should apply for furlough; but instead of speaking to your lady, you come and bother me! The other day that Zhu'er went, Mr. Secundus happened not to want him, so I assented, though I also added that I was doing it as a favor; but here you too come today!"

"It's quite true that his mother is sick," Zhou Rui's wife interceded; "so, Miss, do say yes to him also, and let him go!"

"Be back as soon as it dawns tomorrow!" Ping'er enjoined. "Wait, I've got something for you to do, for you'll again sleep away, and only turn up after the sun has blazed away on your buttocks. As you go now, give a message to Wang'er! Tell him that our lady bade you warn him that if he does not hand over the balance of the interest due by tomorrow, she won't have anything to do with him. So he'd better let her have it to meet her requirements and finish."

The servant-lad felt in high glee and exuberant spirits. Expressing his obedience, he walked off.

Ping'er and her companions repaired then to old lady Jia's apartments. Here the various young ladies from the Garden of Broad Vista were at the time assembled paying their respects to their grandmother. As soon as old goody Liu put her foot inside, she saw the room thronged with girls (as seductive) as twigs of flowers waving to and fro, and so richly dressed, as to look enveloped in pearls, and encircled with king-fisher ornaments. But she could not make out who they all were. Her gaze was, however, attracted by an old dame, reclining alone on a divan. Behind her sat a girl, a regular beauty, clothed in gauze, engaged in patting her legs. Lady Feng was on her feet in the act of cracking some joke.

Old goody Liu readily concluded that it must be dowager lady Jia, so promptly pressing forward, she put on a forced smile and made several curtseys. "My obeisance to you, star of longevity!" she said.

Old lady Jia hastened, on her part, to bow and to inquire after her health. Then she asked Zhou Rui's wife to bring a chair over for her to take a seat. But Ban'er was still so very shy that he did not know how to make his obeisance.

"Venerable relative," dowager lady Jia asked, "how old are you this year?"

Old goody Liu immediately rose to her feet. "I'm seventy-five this year," she rejoined.

"So old and yet so hardy!" Old lady Jia remarked, addressing herself to the party. "Why she's older than myself by several years! When I reach that age, I wonder whether I shall be able to move!"

"We people have," old goody Liu smilingly resumed, "to put up, from the moment we come into the world, with ever so many hardships; while your venerable ladyship enjoys, from your birth, every kind of blessing! Were we also like this, there'd be no one to carry on that farming work."

"Are your eyes and teeth still good?" Dowager lady Jia went on to inquire.

"They're both still all right," old goody Liu replied. "The left molars, however, have got rather shaky this year."

"As for me, I'm quite an old fossil," dowager lady Jia observed. "I'm no good whatever. My eyesight is dim; my ears are deaf, my memory is gone. I can't even recollect any of you old family connections. When therefore any of our relations come on a visit, I don't see them for fear lest I should be ridiculed. All I can manage to eat are a few mouthfuls of anything tender enough for my teeth; and I can just doze a bit or, when I feel in low spirits, I distract myself a little with these grandsons and grand-daughters of mine; that's all I'm good for."

"This is indeed your venerable ladyship's good fortune!" old goody Liu smiled. "We couldn't enjoy anything of the kind, much though we may long for it."

"What good fortune!" dowager lady Jia exclaimed. "I'm a useless old thing, no more."

This remark made everyone explode into laughter.

Dowager lady Jia also laughed. "I heard our lady Feng say a little while back," she added, "that you had brought a lot of squash and vegetables, and I told her to put them by at once. I had just been craving to have newly-grown melons and vegetables; but those one buys outside are not as luscious as those produced in your farms."

"This is the rustic notion," old goody Liu laughed, "to entirely subsist on fresh things! Yet, we long to have fish and meat for our fare, but we can't afford it."

"I've found a relative in you today," dowager lady Jia said, "so you shouldn't go empty-handed! If you don't despise this place as too mean, do stay a day or two before you start! We've also got a garden here; and this garden produces fruits too; you can taste some of them tomorrow and take a few along with you home, in order to make it look like a visit to relatives."

When lady Feng saw how delighted old lady Jia was with the prospects of the old dame's stay, she too lost no time in doing all she could to induce her to remain. "Our place here," she urged, "isn't, it's true, as spacious as your threshing-floor; but as we've got two vacant rooms, you'd better put up in them for a couple of days, and choose some of your village news and old stories and recount them to our worthy senior."

"Now you, vixen Feng," smiled dowager lady Jia, "don't raise a laugh at her expense! She's only a country woman; and will an old dame like her stand any chaff from you?"

While remonstrating with her, she bade a servant go before attending to anything else, and pluck a few fruits. These she handed to Ban'er to eat. But Ban'er did not venture to touch them, conscious as he was of the presence of such a number of bystanders. So old lady Jia gave orders that a few cash should be given him, and then directed the pages to take him outside to play.

After sipping a cup of tea, old goody Liu began to relate, for the benefit of dowager lady Jia, a few of the occurrences she had seen or heard of in the country. These had the effect of putting old lady Jia in a more exuberant frame of mind. But in the midst of her narration, a servant, at lady Feng's instance, asked goody Liu to go and have her evening meal. Dowager lady Jia then picked out, as well, several kinds of eatables from her own repast, and charged someone to take them to goody Liu to feast on.

But the consciousness that the old dame had taken her senior's fancy induced lady Feng to send her back again as soon as she had taken some refreshments. On her arrival, Yuanyang hastily deputed a matron to take goody Liu to have a bath. She herself then went and selected two pieces of ordinary clothes, and these she entrusted to a servant to hand to the old dame to change. Goody Liu had hitherto not set eyes upon any such grand things, so with eagerness she effected the necessary alterations in her costume. This over, she made her appearance outside, and, sitting in front of the divan occupied by dowager lady Jia, she went on to narrate as many stories as she could recall to mind. Baoyu and his cousins too were, at the time, assembled in the room, and as they had never before heard anything the like of what she said, they, of course, thought her tales more full of zest than those related by itinerant blind storytellers.

Old goody Liu was, albeit a rustic person, gifted by nature with a good deal of discrimination. She was besides advanced in years; and had gone through many experiences in her lifetime, so when she, in the first place, saw how extremely delighted old lady Jia was with her, and, in the second, how eager the whole crowd of young lads and lasses were to listen to what fell from her mouth, she even invented, when she found her own stock exhausted, a good many yarns to recount to them.

"What with all the sowing we have to do in our fields and the vegetables we have to plant," she consequently proceeded, "have we ever in our village any leisure to sit with lazy hands from year to year and day to day; no matter whether it's spring, summer, autumn, or winter, whether it blows or whether it rains? Yea, day after day all that we can do is to turn the bare road into a kind of pavilion to rest and cool ourselves on! But what strange things don't we see! Last winter, for instance, snow fell for several consecutive days, and it piled up on the ground three or four feet deep. One day, I got up early, but I hadn't as yet gone out of the door of our house when I heard outside the noise of firewood (being moved). I fancied that someone must have come to steal it, so I crept up to a hole in the window; but, lo, I discovered that it was no one from our own village."

"It must have been," interposed dowager lady Jia, "some wayfarers, who being smitten with the cold, took some of the firewood, they saw ready at hand, to go and make a fire and warm themselves with! That's highly probable!"

"It was no wayfarers at all," old goody Liu retorted smiling, "and that's what makes the story so strange. Who do you think it was, venerable star of longevity? It was really a most handsome girl of seventeen or eighteen, whose hair was combed as smooth as if oil had been poured over it. She was dressed in a deep red jacket, a white silk petticoat..."

When she reached this part of her narrative, suddenly became audible the voices of people bawling outside. "It's nothing much," they shouted, "don't frighten our old mistress!" Dowager lady Jia and the other inmates caught, however, their cries and hurriedly inquired what had happened. A servant-maid explained in reply that a fire had broken out in the stables in the southern court, but that there was no danger, as the flames had been suppressed.

Their old grandmother was a person with very little nerve. The moment, therefore, the report fell on her ear, she jumped up with all despatch, and leaning on one of the family, she rushed on to the verandah to ascertain the state of things. At the sight of the still brilliant light, shed by the flames, on the southeast part of the compound, old lady Jia was plunged in consternation, and invoking Buddha, she went on to shout to the servants to go and burn incense before the god of fire.

Madame Wang and the rest of the members of the household lost no time in crossing over in a body to see how she was getting on. "The fire has been already extinguished," they too assured her, "please, dear ancestor, repair into your rooms!"

But it was only after old lady Jia had seen the light of the flames entirely subside that she at length led the whole company indoors. "What was that girl up to, taking the firewood in that heavy fall of snow?" Baoyu thereupon vehemently inquired of goody Liu. "What, if she had got frostbitten and fallen ill?"

"It was the reference made recently to the firewood that was being abstracted," his grandmother Jia said, "that brought about this fire; and do you still go on asking more about it? Leave this story alone, and tell us something else!"

Hearing this reminder, Baoyu felt constrained to drop the subject, much against his wishes, and old goody Liu forthwith thought of something else to tell them.

"In our village," she resumed, "and on the eastern side of our farm-stead, there lives an old dame, whose age is this year, over ninety. She goes in daily for fasting, and worshipping Buddha. Who'd have thought it, she so moved the pity of the goddess of mercy that she gave her this message in a dream: 'It was at one time ordained that you should have no posterity, but as you have proved so devout, I have now memo-rialized the Pearly Emperor to grant you a grandson!' The fact is, this old dame had one son. This son had had too an only son; but he died after they had with great difficulty managed to rear him to the age of seventeen or eighteen. And what tears didn't they shed for him? But, in course of time, another son was actually born to him. He is this year just thirteen or fourteen, resembles a very ball of flower, (so plump is he), and is clever and sharp to an exceptional degree! So this is indeed a clear proof that those spirits and gods do exist!"

This long tirade proved to be in harmony with dowager lady Jia's and Madame Wang's secret convictions on the subject. Even Madame Wang therefore listened to every word with all profound attention. Baoyu, however, was so preoccupied with the story about the stolen firewood that he fell in a brown study and gave way to conjectures.

"Yesterday," Tanchun at this point remarked, "We put cousin Shi to a lot of trouble and inconvenience, so, when we get back, we must con-sult about convening a meeting, and, while returning her entertain-ment, we can also invite our venerable ancestor to come and admire the chrysanthemums; what do you think of this?"

"Our worthy senior," smiled Baoyu, "has intimated that she means to give a banquet to return cousin Shi's hospitality, and to ask us to do the honors. Let's wait therefore until we partake of grandmother's col-lation, before we issue our own invitations; there will be ample time then to do so."

"The later it gets, the cooler the weather becomes," Tanchun ob-served, "and our dear senior is not likely to enjoy herself."

"Grandmother," added Baoyu, "is also fond of rain and snow, so wouldn't it be as well to wait until the first fall, and then ask her to come and look at the snow. This will be better, won't it? And were we to recite our verses with snow about us, it will be ever so much more fun!"

"To hum verses in the snow," Lin Daiyu speedily demurred with a smile, "won't, in my idea, be half as nice as building up a heap of fire-wood and then stealing it, with the flakes playing about us. This will be by far more enjoyable!"

This proposal made Baochai and the others laugh. Baoyu cast a glance at her but made no reply.

But, in a short time, the company broke up. Baoyu eventually gave old goody Liu a tug on the sly and plied her with minute questions as to who the girl was. The old dame was placed under the necessity of fabricating something for his benefit. "The truth is," she said, "that there stands on the north bank of the ditch in our village a small ancestral hall, in which offerings are made, but not to spirits or gods. There was in former days some official or other..."

While speaking, she went on to try and recollect his name and surname.

"No matter about names or surnames!" Baoyu expostulated. "There's no need for you to recall them to memory! Just mention the facts; they'll be enough."

"This official," old goody Liu resumed, "had no son. His offspring consisted of one young daughter, who went under the name of Mingyu, (like Jade). She could read and write, and was doated upon by this official and his consort, just as if she were a precious jewel. But, unfortunately, when this young lady, Mingyu, grew up to be seventeen, she contracted some disease and died."

When these words fell on Baoyu's ears, he stamped his foot and heaved a sigh. "What happened after that?" he then asked.

Old goody Liu pursued her story.

"So incessantly," she continued, "did this official and his consort think of their child that they raised this ancestral hall, erected a clay image of their young daughter Mingyu in it, and appointed someone to burn incense and trim the fires. But so many days and years have now elapsed that the people themselves are no more alive, the temple is in decay, and the image itself is become a spirit."

"It hasn't become a spirit," remonstrated Baoyu with vehemence. "Human beings of this kind may, the rule is, die, yet they are not dead."

"Amituo Fo!" ejaculated old goody Liu; "is it really so! Had you, sir, not enlightened us, we would have remained under the impression that she had become a spirit! But she repeatedly transforms herself into a human being, and there she roams about in every village, farmstead, inn, and roadside. And the one I mentioned just now as having taken the firewood is that very girl! The villagers in our place are still consulting with the idea of breaking this clay image and razing the temple to the ground."

"Be quick and dissuade them!" eagerly exclaimed Baoyu. "Were they to raze the temple to the ground, their crime won't be small."

"It's lucky that you told me, Sir," old goody Liu added. "When I get back tomorrow, I'll make them relinquish the idea and finish!"

"Our venerable senior and my mother," Baoyu pursued, "are both charitable persons. In fact, all the inmates of our family, whether old or young, do, in like manner, delight in good deeds, and take pleasure in distributing alms. Their greatest relish is to repair temples, and to put up images to the spirits; so tomorrow, I'll make a subscription and collect a few donations for you, and you can then act as incense-burner. When sufficient money has been raised, this fane can be repaired, and another clay image put up; and month by month I'll give you incense and fire money to enable you to burn joss-sticks; won't this be a good thing for you?"

"In that case," old goody Liu rejoined, "I shall, thanks to that young lady's good fortune, have also a few cash to spend."

Baoyu thereupon likewise wanted to know what the name of the place was, the name of the village, how far it was there and back, and whereabout the temple was situated.

Old goody Liu replied to his questions, by telling him every idle thought that came first to her lips. Baoyu, however, credited the information she gave him and, on his return to his rooms, he exercised, the whole night, his mind with building castles in the air.

On the morrow, as soon as daylight dawned, he speedily stepped out of his room, and, handing Beiming several hundreds of cash, he bade him proceed first in the direction and to the place specified by old goody Liu, and clearly ascertain every detail, so as to enable him, on his return from his errand, to arrive at a suitable decision to carry out his purpose. After Beiming's departure, Baoyu continued on pins on needles and on the tiptoe of expectation. Into such a pitch of excitement did he work himself, that he felt like an ant in a burning pan. With suppressed impatience, he waited and waited until sunset. At last then he perceived Beiming walk in, in high glee.

"Have you discovered the place?" hastily inquired Baoyu.

"Master," Beiming laughed, "you didn't catch distinctly the directions given you, and you made me search in a nice way! The name of the place and the bearings can't be those you gave me, Sir; that is why I've had to hunt about the whole day long! I prosecuted my inquiries up to the very ditch on the northeast side, before I eventually found a ruined temple."

Upon hearing the result of his researches, Baoyu was much gratified. His very eyebrows distended. His eyes laughed. "Old goody Liu," he said with eagerness, "is a person well up in years, and she may at the moment have remembered wrong; it's very likely she did. But recount to me what you saw."

"The door of that temple," Beiming explained, "really faces south, and is all in a tumble-down condition. I searched and searched till I was driven to utter despair. As soon, however, as I caught sight of it, 'that's right,' I shouted, and promptly walked in. But I at once discovered a clay figure, which gave me such a fearful start, that I scampered out again; for it looked as much alive as if it were a real living being."

Baoyu smiled full of joy. "It can metamorphose itself into a human being," he observed, "so, of course, it has more or less a life-like appearance."

"Was it ever a girl?" Beiming rejoined clapping his hands. "Why it was, in fact, no more than a green-faced and red-haired god of plagues."

Baoyu, at this answer, spat at him contemptuously. "You are, in very truth, a useless fool!" he cried. "Haven't you even enough gumption for such a trifling job as this?"

"What book, I wonder, have you again been reading, master?" Beiming continued. "Or you may, perhaps, have heard someone prattle a lot of trash and believed it as true! You send me on this sort of wild goose chase and make me go and knock my head about, and how can you ever say that I'm good for nothing?"

Baoyu did not fail to notice that he was in a state of exasperation so he lost no time in trying to calm him. "Don't be impatient!" he urged. "You can go again some other day, when you've got nothing to attend to, and institute further inquiries! If it turns out that she has hoodwinked us, why, there will, naturally, be no such thing. But if, verily, there is, won't you also lay up for yourself a store of good deeds? I shall feel it my duty to reward you in a most handsome manner."

As he spoke, he espied a servant-lad, on service at the second gate, approach and report to him: "The young ladies in our venerable ladyship's apartments are standing at the threshold of the second gate and looking out for you, Mr. Secundus."

But as, reader, you are not aware what they were on the look-out to tell him, the subsequent chapter will explain it for you.

CHAPTER 40

The venerable lady Shi attends a second banquet in the garden of Broad Vista. Jin Yangyuan three times promulgates, by means of dominoes, the order to quote passages from old writers.

As soon as Baoyu, we will now explain, heard what the lad told him, he rushed with eagerness inside. When he came to look about him, he discovered Hupo standing in front of the screen. "Be quick and go," she urged. "They're waiting to speak to you."

Baoyu wended his way into the drawing rooms. Here he found dowager lady Jia, consulting with Madame Wang and the whole body of young ladies, about the return feast to be given to Shi Xiangyun.

"I've got a plan to suggest," he consequently interposed. "As there are to be no outside guests, the eatables too should not be limited to any kind or number. A few of such dishes, as have ever been to the liking of any of us, should be fixed upon and prepared for the occasion. Neither should any banquet be spread, but a high teapoy can be placed in front of each, with one or two things to suit our particular tastes. Besides, a painted box with partitions and a decanter. Won't this be an original way?"

"Capital!" shouted old lady Jia. "Go and tell the people in the cookhouse," she forthwith ordered a servant, "to get ready tomorrow such dishes as we relish, and to put them in as many boxes as there will be people, and bring them over. We can have breakfast too in the garden."

But while they were deliberating, the time came to light the lamps. Nothing of any note transpired the whole night. The next day, they got up at early dawn. The weather, fortunately, was beautifully clear. Li Wan turned out of bed at daybreak. She was engaged in watching the old matrons and servant-girls sweeping the fallen leaves, rubbing the tables and chairs, and preparing the tea and wine vessels, when she perceived Feng'er usher in old goody Liu and Ban'er. "You're very busy, our senior lady!" they said.

"I told you that you wouldn't manage to start yesterday," Li Wan smiled, "but you were in a hurry to get away."

"Your worthy old lady," goody Liu replied laughingly, "wouldn't let me go. She wanted me to enjoy myself too for a day before I went."

Feng'er then produced several large and small keys. "Our mistress Lian says," she remarked, "that she fears that the high teapoys which are out are not enough, and she thinks it would be as well to open the loft and take out those that are put away and use them for a day. Our lady should really have come and seen to it in person, but as she has something to tell Madame Wang, she begs your ladyship to open the place, and get a few servants to bring them out."

Li Wan there and then told Suyun to take the keys. She also bade a matron go out and call a few servant-boys from those on duty at the second gate. When they came, Li Wan remained in the lower story of the Daguan loft, and looking up, she ordered the servants to go and open the Chuojin hall and to bring the teapoys one by one. The young servant-lads, matrons, and servant-maids then set to work, in a body, and carried down over twenty of them.

"Be careful with them," shouted Li Wan. "Don't be bustling about just as if you were being pursued by ghosts! Mind you don't break the tenons!" Turning her head round, "old dame," she observed, addressing herself smilingly to goody Liu, "go upstairs too and have a look!"

Old goody Liu was longing to satisfy her curiosity, so at the bare mention of the permission, she uttered just one word ("come") and, dragging Ban'er along, she trudged up the stairs. On her arrival inside, she espied, pile upon pile, a whole heap of screens, tables, and chairs, painted lanterns of different sizes, and other similar articles. She could not, it is true, make out the use of the various things, but, at the sight of so many colors, of such finery and of the unusual beauty of each article, she muttered time after time the name of Buddha, and then forthwith wended her way downstairs. Subsequently (the servants) locked the doors and everyone of them came down.

"I fancy," cried Li Wan, "that our dowager lady will feel disposed (to go on the water), so you'd better also get the poles, oars, and awnings for the boats and keep them in readiness."

The servants expressed their obedience. Once more they unlocked the doors, and carried down everything required. She then bade a lad notify the boatwomen go to the dock and punt out two boats. But while all this bustle was going on, they discovered that dowager lady Jia had already arrived at the head of a whole company of people. Li Wan promptly went up to greet them.

"Dear venerable senior," she smiled, "you must be in good spirits to have come in here! Imagining that you hadn't as yet combed your hair, I just plucked a few chrysanthemums, meaning to send them to you."

While she spoke, Biyue at once presented to her a jadite tray, of the size of a lotus leaf, containing twigs cut from every species of chrysanthemum. Old lady Jia selected a cluster of deep red and pinned it in her hair about her temples. But turning round, she noticed old goody Liu. "Come over here," she vehemently cried with a smile; "and put on a few flowers."

Scarcely was this remark concluded, than lady Feng dragged goody Liu forward. "Let me deck you up!" she laughed. With these words, she seized a whole plateful of flowers and stuck them three this way, four that way, all over her head. Old lady Jia, and the whole party were greatly amused; so much so, that they could not check themselves.

"I wonder," shouted goody Liu smiling, "what blessings I have brought upon my head that such honors are conferred upon it today!"

"Don't you yet pull them away," they all laughed, "and chuck them in her face! She has got you up in such a way as to make a regular old elf of you!"

"I'm an old hag, I admit," goody Liu pursued with a laugh; "but when I was young, I too was pretty and fond of flowers and powder! But the best thing I can do now is to keep to such fineries as befit my advanced age!"

While they bandied words, they reached the Qinfang pavilion. The waiting maids brought a large embroidered rug and spread it over the planks of the divan near the balustrade. On this rug dowager lady Jia sat, with her back leaning against the railing; and, inviting goody Liu to also take a seat next to her, "Is this garden nice or not?" she asked her.

Old goody Liu invoked Buddha several times. "We country-people," she rejoined, "do invariably come, at the close of each year, into the city and buy pictures and stick them about. And frequently do we find ourselves in our leisure moments wondering how we too could manage to get into the pictures, and walk about the scenes they represent. I presumed that those pictures were purely and simply fictitious, for how could there be any such places in reality? But, contrary to my expectations, I found, as soon as I entered this garden today and had a look about it, that it was, after all, a hundred times better than these very pictures. But if only I could get someone to make me a sketch of this garden, to take home with me and let them see it, so that when we die we may have reaped some benefit!"

Upon catching the wish she expressed, dowager lady Jia pointed at Xichun. "Look at that young granddaughter of mine!" she smiled. "She's got the knack of drawing. So what do you say to my asking her tomorrow to make a picture for you?"

This suggestion filled goody Liu with enthusiasm and speedily crossing over, she clasped Xichun in her arms. "My dear Miss!" she cried, "so young in years, and yet so pretty, and so accomplished too! Mightn't you be a spirit come to life!"

After old lady Jia had had a little rest, she in person took goody Liu and showed her everything there was to be seen. First, they visited the Xiaoxiang lodge. The moment they stepped into the entrance, a narrow avenue, flanked on either side with kingfisher-like green bamboos, met their gaze. The earth below was turfed all over with moss. In the center, extended a tortuous road, paved with pebbles. Goody Liu left dowager lady Jia and the party walk on the raised road, while she herself stepped on the earth. But Hupo tugged at her. "Come up, old dame, and walk here!" she exclaimed. "Mind the fresh moss is slippery and you might fall."

"I don't mind it!" answered goody Liu. "We people are accustomed to walking (on such slippery things)! So, young ladies, please proceed. And do look after your embroidered shoes! Don't splash them with mud."

But while bent upon talking with those who kept on the raised road, she unawares reached a spot, which was actually slippery, and with a sound of "gu dong" she tumbled over.

The whole company clapped their hands and laughed boisterously.

"You young wenches," shouted out dowager lady Jia, "don't you yet raise her up, but stand by giggling?"

This reprimand was still being uttered when goody Liu had already crawled up. She too was highly amused. "Just as my mouth was bragging," she observed, "I got a whack on the lips!"

"Have you perchance twisted your waist?" inquired old lady Jia. "Tell the servant-girls to pat it for you!"

"What an idea!" retorted goody Liu, "am I so delicate? What day ever goes by without my tumbling down a couple of times? And if I had to be patted every time wouldn't it be dreadful!"

Zijuan had at an early period raised the speckled bamboo portiere. Dowager lady Jia and her companions entered and seated themselves. Lin Daiyu with her own hands took a small tray and came to present a covered cup of tea to her grandmother.

"We won't have any tea!" Madame Wang interposed, "so, miss, you needn't pour any."

Lin Daiyu, hearing this, bade a waiting-maid fetch the chair from under the window where she herself often sat, and moving it to the lower side, she pressed Madame Wang into it. But goody Liu caught sight of the brushes and inkslabs, lying on the table placed next to the window, and espied the bookcase piled up to the utmost with books. "This must surely," the old dame ejaculated, "be some young gentleman's study!"

"This is the room of this granddaughter-in-law of mine," dowager lady Jia explained, smilingly pointing to Daiyu.

Goody Liu scrutinised Lin Daiyu with intentness for a while. "Is this anything like a young lady's private room?" she then observed with a smile. "Why, in very deed, it's superior to any first class library!"

"How is it I don't see Baoyu?" his grandmother Jia went on to inquire.

"He's in the boat, on the pond," the waiting-maids, with one voice, returned for answer.

"Who also got the boats ready?" old lady Jia asked.

"The loft was open just now so they were taken out," Li Wan said, "and as I thought that you might, venerable senior, feel inclined to have a row, I got everything ready."

After listening to this explanation, dowager lady Jia was about to pass some remark, but someone came and reported to her that Mrs. Xue had arrived. No sooner had old lady Jia and the others sprung to their feet than they noticed that Mrs. Xue had already made her appearance. While taking a seat: "Your venerable ladyship," she smiled, "must be in capital spirits today to have come at this early hour!"

"It's only this very minute that I proposed that anyone who came late, should be fined," dowager lady Jia laughed, "and, who'd have thought it, here you, Mrs. Xue, arrive late!"

After they had indulged in good-humored raillery for a time, old lady Jia's attention was attracted by the faded color of the gauze on the windows, and she addressed herself to Madame Wang. "This gauze," she said, "may have been nice enough when it was newly pasted, but after a time nothing remained of kingfisher green. In this court too there are no peach or apricot trees and these bamboos already are green in themselves, so were this shade of green gauze to be put up again, it would, instead of improving matters, not harmonize with the surroundings. I remember that we had at one time four or five kinds of colored gauzes for sticking on windows, so give her some tomorrow to change that on there."

"When I opened the store yesterday," hastily put in Lady Feng, "I noticed that there were still in those boxes, made of large planks, several rolls of 'cicada wing' gauze of silvery red color. There were also several rolls with designs of twigs of flowers of every kind, several with 'the rolling clouds and bats' pattern, and several with figures representing hundreds of butterflies, interspersed among flowers. The colors of all these were fresh, and the gauze supple. But I failed to see anything of the kind you speak of. Were two rolls taken (from those I referred to), and a couple of bed-covers of embroidered gauze made out of them, they would, I fancy, be a pretty sight!"

"Pshaw!" laughed old lady Jia, "everyone says that there's nothing you haven't gone through and nothing you haven't seen, and don't you even know what this gauze is? Will you again brag by and bye, after this?"

Mrs. Xue and all the others smiled. "She may have gone through a good deal," they remarked, "but how can she ever presume to pit herself against an old lady like you? So why don't you, venerable senior, tell her what it is so that we too may be edified."

Lady Feng too gave a smile. "My dear ancestor," she pleaded, "do tell me what it is like."

Dowager lady Jia thereupon proceeded to enlighten Mrs. Xue and the whole company. "That gauze is older in years than any one of you," she said. "It isn't therefore to be wondered, if you make a mistake and take it for 'cicada wing' gauze. But it really bears some resemblance to it; so much so, indeed, that any one, not knowing the difference, would imagine it to be the 'cicada wing' gauze. Its true name, however, is 'soft smoke' silk."

"This is also a nice sounding name," lady Feng agreed. "But up to the age I've reached, I have never heard of any such designation, in spite of the many hundreds of specimens of gauzes and silks, I've seen."

"How long can you have lived?" old lady Jia added smilingly, "and how many kinds of things can you have met, that you indulge in this tall talk? Of this 'soft smoke' silk, there only exist four kinds of colors. The one is red-blue; the other is russet; the other pine green; the other silvery-red; and it's because, when made into curtains or stuck on window-frames, it looks from far like smoke or mist, that it is called 'soft smoke' silk. The silvery-red is also called 'russet shadow' gauze. Among the gauzes used in the present day, in the palace above, there are none so supple and rich, light and closely-woven as this!"

"Not to speak of that girl Feng not having seen it," Mrs. Xue laughed, "why, even I have never so much as heard anything of it."

While the conversation proceeded in this strain, lady Feng soon directed a servant to fetch a roll. "Now isn't this the kind!" dowager lady Jia exclaimed. "At first, we simply had it stuck on the window frames, but we subsequently used it for covers and curtains, just for a trial, and really they were splendid! So you had better tomorrow try and find several rolls, and take some of the silvery-red one and have it fixed on the windows for her."

While lady Feng promised to attend to her commission, the party scrutinized it, and unanimously extolled it with effusion. Old goody Liu too strained her eyes and examined it, and her lips incessantly muttered Buddha's name. "We couldn't," she ventured, "afford to make clothes of such stuff, much though we may long to do so; and won't it be a pity to use it for sticking on windows?"

"But it doesn't, after all, look well, when made into clothes," old lady Jia explained.

Lady Feng hastily pulled out the lapel of the deep-red brocaded gauze jacket she had on, and, facing dowager lady Jia and Mrs. Xue, "Look at this jacket of mine," she remarked.

"This is also of first-rate quality!" old lady Jia and Mrs. Xue rejoined. "This is nowadays made in the palace for Imperial use, but it can't possibly come up to this!"

"It's such thin stuff," lady Feng observed, "and do you still say that it was made in the palace for Imperial use? Why, it doesn't, in fact, compare favorably with even this, which is worn by officials!"

"You'd better search again!" old lady Jia urged; "I believe there must be more of it! If there be, bring it all out, and give this old relative Liu a couple of rolls! Should there be any red-blue, I'll make a curtain to hang up. What remains can be matched with some lining, and cut into a few double waistcoats for the waiting-maids to wear. It would be sheer waste to keep these things, as they will be spoilt by the damp."

Lady Feng vehemently acquiesced; after which, she told a servant to take the gauze away.

"These rooms are so small," dowager lady Jia then observed, smiling. "We had better go elsewhere for a stroll."

"Everyone says," old goody Liu put in, "that big people live in big houses! When I saw yesterday your main apartments, dowager lady, with all those large boxes, immense presses, big tables, and spacious beds to match, they did, indeed, present an imposing sight! Those presses are larger than our whole house; yea loftier too! But strange to say there were ladders in the back court. 'They don't also,' I thought, 'go up to the house tops to sun things, so what can they keep those ladders in readiness for?' Well, after that, I remembered that they must be required for opening the presses to take out or put in things. And that without those ladders, how could one ever reach that height? But now that I've also seen these small rooms, more luxuriously got up than the large ones, and full of various articles, all so fascinating and hardly even known to me by name, I feel, the more I feast my eyes on them, the more unable to tear myself away from them."

"There are other things still better than this," lady Feng added. "I'll take you to see them all!"

Saying this, they straightway left the Xiaoxiang lodge. From a distance, they spied a whole crowd of people punting the boats in the lake.

"As they've got the boats ready," old lady Jia proposed, "we may as well go and have a row in them!"

As she uttered this suggestion, they wended their steps along the persicary-covered bank of the Purple Lily Isle. But before reaching the lake, they perceived several matrons advancing that way with large multi-colored boxes in their hands, made all alike of twisted wire and inlaid with gold. Lady Feng hastened to inquire of Madame Wang where breakfast was to be served.

"Ask our venerable senior," Madame Wang replied, "and let them lay it wherever she pleases."

Old lady Jia overheard her answer, and turning her head round: "Miss Tertia," she said, "take the servants, and make them lay breakfast wherever you think best! We'll get into the boats from here."

Upon catching her senior's wishes, lady Feng retraced her footsteps, and accompanied by Li Wan, Tanchun, Yuanyang, and Hupo, she led off the servants, carrying the eatables, and other domestics, and came by the nearest way, to the Qiushuang library, where they arranged the tables in the Xiaocui hall.

"We daily say that whenever the gentlemen outside have anything to drink or eat, they invariably have someone who can raise a laugh and whom they can chaff for fun's sake," Yuanyang smiled, "so let's also today get a female family-companion."

Li Wan, being a person full of kindly feelings, did not fathom the insinuation, though it did not escape her ear. Lady Feng, however, thoroughly understood that she alluded to old goody Liu. "Let us too today," she smilingly remarked, "chaff her for a bit of fun!"

These two then began to mature their plans.

Li Wan chided them with a smile. "You people," she said, "don't know even how to perform the least good act! But you're not small children any more, and are you still up to these pranks? Mind, our venerable ancestor might call you to task!"

"That has nothing whatever to do with you, senior lady," Yuanyang laughed, "it's my own look out!"

These words were still on her lips, when she saw dowager lady Jia and the rest of the company arrive. They each sat where and how they pleased. First and foremost, a waiting-maid brought two trays of tea. After tea, lady Feng laid hold of a napkin, made of foreign cloth, in which were wrapped a handful of blackwood chopsticks, encircled with three rings, of inlaid silver, and distributed them on the tables, in the order in which they were placed.

"Bring that small hardwood table over," old lady Jia then exclaimed; "and let our relative Liu sit next to me here!"

No sooner did the servants hear her order than they hurried to move the table to where she wanted it. Lady Feng, during this interval, made a sign with her eye to Yuanyang. Yuanyang there and then dragged goody Liu out of the hall and began to impress in a low tone of voice various things on her mind. "This is the custom which prevails in our household," she proceeded, "and if you disregard it we'll have a laugh at your expense!"

Having arranged everything she had in view, they at length returned to their places. Mrs. Xue had come over, after her meal, so she simply seated herself on one side and sipped her tea. Dowager lady Jia with Baoyu, Xiangyun, Daiyu, and Baochai sat at one table. Madame Wang took the girls, Yingchun, and her sisters, and occupied one table. Old goody Liu took a seat at a table next to dowager lady Jia. Heretofore, while their old mistress had her repast, a young servant-maid usually stood by her to hold the finger bowl, yak-brush, napkin, and other such necessaries, but Yuanyang did not of late fulfil any of these duties, so when, on this occasion, she deliberately seized the yak-brush and came over and flapped it about, the servant-girls concluded that she was bent upon playing some tricks upon goody Liu, and they readily withdrew and let her have her way.

While Yuanyang attended to her self-imposed duties, she winked at the old dame.

"Miss," goody Liu exclaimed, "set your mind at ease!" Goody Liu sat down at the table and took up the chopsticks, but so heavy and clumsy did she find them that she could not handle them conveniently. The fact is that lady Feng and Yuanyang had put their heads together and decided to only assign to goody Liu a pair of antiquated four-cornered ivory chopsticks, inlaid with gold.

"These forks," shouted goody Liu, after scrutinizing them, "are heavier than the very iron-lever over at my place. How ever can I move them about?"

This remark had the effect of making everyone explode into a fit of laughter. But a married woman standing in the center of the room, with a box in her hands, attracted their gaze. A waiting-maid went up to her and removed the cover of the box. Its contents were two bowls of eatables. Li Wan took one of these and placed it on dowager lady Jia's table, while lady Feng chose the bowl with pigeon's eggs and put it on goody Liu's table.

"Please (commence)," dowager lady Jia uttered from the near side, where she sat.

Goody Liu at this speedily sprung to her feet. "Old Liu, old Liu," she roared with a loud voice, "your eating capacity is as big as that of a buffalo! You've gorged like an old sow and can't raise your head up!" Then puffing out her cheeks, she added not a word.

The whole party was at first taken quite aback. But, as soon as they heard the drift of her remarks, everyone, both high as well as low, began to laugh boisterously. Xiangyun found it so difficult to restrain herself that she spurted out the tea she had in her mouth. Lin Daiyu indulged in such laughter that she was quite out of breath, and propping herself up on the table, she kept on ejaculating "Ai-yo." Baoyu rolled into his grandmother's lap. The old lady herself was so amused that she clasped Baoyu in her embrace, and gave way to endearing epithets. Madame Wang laughed, and pointed at lady Feng with her finger; but as for saying a word, she could not. Mrs. Xue had much difficulty in curbing her mirth, and she sputtered the tea, with which her mouth was full, all over Tanchun's petticoat. Tanchun threw the contents of the teacup, she held in her hand, over Yingchun; while Xichun quitted her seat, and, pulling her nurse away, bade her rub her stomach for her.

Below, among the lower seats, there was not one who was not with bent waist and doubled-up back. Some retired to a corner and, squatting down, laughed away. Others suppressed their laughter and came up and changed the clothes of their young mistresses. Lady Feng and Yuanyang were the only ones, who kept their countenance. Still they continued helping old goody Liu to food.

Old goody Liu took up the chopsticks. "Even the chickens in this place are fine," she went on to add, pretending, she did not hear what was going on; "the eggs they lay are small, but so dainty! How very pretty they are! Let me help myself to one!"

The company had just managed to check themselves, but, the moment these words fell on their ears, they started again with their laughter. Old lady Jia laughed to such an extent that tears streamed from her eyes. And so little could she bear the strain any longer that Hupo stood behind her and patted her.

"This must be the work of that vixen Feng!" old lady Jia laughed. "She has ever been up to tricks like a very imp, so be quick and disbelieve all her yarns!"

Goody Liu was in the act of praising the eggs as small yet dainty, when lady Feng interposed with a smile. "They're one tael each, be quick, and taste them;" she said; "they're not nice when they get cold!"

Goody Liu forthwith stretched out the chopsticks with the intent of catching one; but how could she manage to do so? They rolled and

rolled in the bowl for ever so long; and, it was only after extreme difficulty that she succeeded in shoving one up. Extending her neck forward, she was about to put it in her mouth, when it slipped down
again, and rolled onto the floor. She hastily banged down the chopsticks, and was going herself to pick it up, when a servant, who stood
below, got hold of it and took it out of the room.

Old goody Liu heaved a sigh. "A tael!" she soliloquized, "and here it
goes without a sound!"

Everyone had long ago abandoned all idea of eating, and, gazing at
her, they enjoyed the fun.

"Who has now brought out these chopsticks again?" old lady Jia
went on to ask. "We haven't invited any strangers or spread any large
banquet! It must be that vixen Feng who gave them out! But don't you
yet change them!"

The servants, standing on the floor below, had indeed had no hand
in getting those ivory chopsticks; they had, in fact, been brought by
lady Feng and Yuanyang; but when they heard these remarks, they hurried to put them away and to change them for a pair similar to those
used by the others, made of blackwood inlaid with silver.

"They've taken away the gold ones," old goody Liu shouted, "and here
come silver ones! But, after all, they're not as handy as those we use!"

"Should there be any poison in the viands," lady Feng observed,
"you can detect it, as soon as this silver is dipped into them!"

"If there's poison in such viands as these," old goody Liu added,
"why those of ours must be all arsenic! But though it be the death of
me, I'll swallow every morsel!"

Seeing how amusing the old woman was and with what relish she
devoured her food, dowager lady Jia took her own dishes and passed
them over to her.

She then likewise bade an old matron take various viands and put
them in a bowl for Ban'er. But presently, the repast was concluded, and
old lady Jia and all the other inmates adjoined into Tanchun's bedroom for a chat.

The remnants were, meanwhile, cleared away, and fresh tables were
laid.

Old goody Liu watched Li Wan and lady Feng sit opposite each
other and eat. "Putting everything else aside," she sighed, "what most
takes my fancy is the way things are done in your mansion. It isn't to
be wondered at that the adage has it that: 'propriety originates from
great families.'"

"Don't be too touchy," lady Feng hastily smiled, "we all made fun
of you just now."

But barely had she done speaking, when Yuanyang too walked in. "Old goody Liu," she said laughingly, "don't be angry! I tender you my apologies, venerable dame!"

"What are you saying, Miss?" old goody Liu rejoined smiling. "We've coaxed our dowager lady to get a little distraction; and what reason is there to be angry? From the very first moment you spoke to me, I knew at once that it was intended to afford merriment to you all! Had I been angry at heart, I wouldn't have gone so far as to say what I did!"

Yuanyang then blew up the servants. "Why," she shouted, "don't you pour a cup of tea for the old dame?"

"That sister-in-law," promptly explained old goody Liu, "gave me a cup a little while back. I've had it already. But you, Miss, must also have something to eat."

Lady Feng dragged Yuanyang into a seat. "Have your meal with us!" she said. "You'll thus save another fuss by and bye."

Yuanyang readily seated herself. The matrons came up and added to the number of bowls and chopsticks, and the trio went through their meal.

"From all I see," smiled goody Liu, "you people eat just a little and finish. It's lucky you don't feel the pangs of hunger! But it isn't astonishing if a whiff of wind can puff you over!"

"A good many eatables remained over today. Where are they all gone to?" Yuanyang inquired.

"They haven't as yet been apportioned!" the matrons responded. "They're kept in here until they can be given in a lump to them to eat!"

"They can't get through so many things!" Yuanyang resumed. "You had as well therefore choose two bowls and send them over to that girl Ping, in your mistress Secundus' rooms."

"She has had her repast long ago." lady Feng put in. "There's no need to give her any!"

"With what she can't eat, herself," Yuanyang continued, "she can feed the cats."

At these words, a matron lost no time in selecting two sorts of eatables, and, taking the box, she went to take them over.

"Where's Su Yun gone to?" Yuanyang asked.

"They're all in here having their meal together." Li Wan replied. "What do you want her for again?"

"Well, in that case, never mind," Yuanyang answered.

"Xiren isn't here," lady Feng observed, "so tell someone to take her a few things!"

Yuanyang, hearing this, directed a servant to send her also a few eatables. "Have the partition boxes been filled with wine for by and bye?" Yuanyang went on to ask the matrons.

"They'll be ready, I think, in a little while," a matron explained.

"Hurry them up a bit!" Yuanyang added.

The matron signified her assent.

Lady Feng and her friends then came into Tanchun's apartments, where they found the ladies chatting and laughing.

Tanchun had ever shown an inclination for plenty of room. Hence that suite of three apartments had never been partitioned. In the center was placed a large table of rosewood and Ta li marble. On this table, were laid in a heap every kind of copyslips written by persons of note. Several tens of valuable inkslabs and various specimens of rubes and receptacles for brushes figured also about; the brushes in which were as thickly packed as trees in a forest. On the off side, stood a flower bowl from the "Ru" kiln, as large as a bushel measure. In it was placed, till it was quite full, a bunch of white chrysanthemums, in appearance like crystal balls. In the middle of the west wall, was suspended a large picture representing vapor and rain; the handiwork of Mi Xiangyang. On the left and right of this picture was hung a pair of antithetical scrolls—the autograph of Yan Lu. The lines on these scrolls were:

> Wild scenes are to the taste of those who leisure love,
> And springs and rookeries are their rustic resort.

On the table, figured a large tripod. On the left, stood on a blackwood cabinet, a huge bowl from a renowned government kiln. This bowl contained about ten "Buddha's hands" of beautiful yellow and fine proportions. On the right, was suspended, on a Japanese lacquered frame, a white jade sonorous plate. Its shape resembled two eyes, one by the side of the other. Next to it hung a small hammer.

Ban'er had become a little more confident and was about to seize the hammer and beat the plate, when the waiting-maids hastened to prevent him. Next, he wanted a "Buddha's hand" to eat. Tanchun chose one and let him have it. "You may play with it," she said, "but you can't eat it."

On the east side stood a sleeping divan. On a movable bed was hung a leek-green gauze curtain, ornamented with double embroideries, representing flowers, plants, and insects. Ban'er ran up to have a look. "This is a green-cicada," he shouted; "this a grasshopper!"

But old goody Liu promptly gave him a slap. "You mean scamp!" she cried. "What an awful rumpus you're kicking up! I simply brought you along with me to look at things; and lo, you put on airs;" and she beat Ban'er until he burst out crying. It was only after everyone quickly combined in using their efforts to solace him that he at length desisted.

Old lady Jia then looked through the gauze casement into the back court for some time. "The dryandra trees by the eaves of the covered passage are growing all right," she remarked. "The only thing is that their foliage is rather sparse."

But while she passed this remark, a sudden gust of wind swept by, and faintly on her ear fell the strains of music. "In whose house is there a wedding?" old lady Jia inquired. "This place must be very near the street!"

"How could one hear what's going on in the street?" Madame Wang and the others smiled. "It's our twelve girls practicing on their wind and string instruments!"

"As they're practicing," dowager lady Jia eagerly cried, smilingly, "why not ask them to come in here and practice? They'll be able to have a stroll also, while we, on our part, will derive some enjoyment."

Upon hearing this suggestion, lady Feng immediately directed a servant to go out and call them in. She further issued orders to bring a table and spread a red cover over it.

"Let it be put," old lady Jia chimed in, "in the water-pavilion of the Lotus Fragrance Arbor, for (the music) will borrow the ripple of the stream and sound ever so much more pleasant to the ear. We can by and bye drink our wine in the Chuojin Hall; we'll thus have ample room, and be able to listen from close!"

Everyone admitted that the spot was well adapted. Dowager lady Jia turned herself towards Mrs. Xue. "Let's get ahead!" she laughed. "The young ladies don't like anyone to come in here, for fear lest their quarters should get contaminated; so don't let us show ourselves disregardful of their wishes! The right thing would be to go and have our wine aboard one of those boats!"

As she spoke, one and all rose to their feet. They were making their way out when Tanchun interposed. "What's this that you're saying?" she smiled. "Please do seat yourselves, venerable senior, and you, Mrs. Xue, and Madame Wang! You can't be going yet?"

"These three girls of mine are really nice! There are only two mistresses that are simply dreadful." Dowager lady Jia said smilingly. "When we get drunk shortly, we'll go and sit in their rooms and have a lark!"

These words evoked laughter from everyone. In a body they quitted the place. But they had not proceeded far before they reached the bank covered with aquatic plants, to which place the boat-women, who had been brought from Gusu, had already punted two crab-wood boats. Into one of these boats, they helped old lady Jia, Madame Wang, Mrs. Xue, old goody Liu, Yuanyang, and Yuchuan'er. Last in order Li Wan followed on board. But lady Feng too stepped in, and standing up on the bow, she insisted upon punting.

Dowager lady Jia, however, remonstrated from her seat in the bottom of the boat. "This isn't a joke," she cried, "we're not on the river, it's true, but there are some very deep places about, so be quick and come in. Do it for my sake."

"What's there to be afraid of?" lady Feng laughed. "Compose your mind, worthy ancestor."

Saying this, the boat was pushed off with one shove. When it reached the middle of the lake, lady Feng became nervous, for the craft was small and the occupants many, and hastily handing the pole to a boatwoman, she squatted down at last.

Yingchun, her sisters, their cousins, as well as Baoyu subsequently got on board the second boat, and followed in their track; while the rest of the company, consisting of old nurses and a bevy of waiting-maids, kept pace with them along the bank of the stream.

"All these broken lotus leaves are dreadful!" Baoyu shouted. "Why don't you yet tell the servants to pull them off?"

"When was this garden left quiet during all the days of this year?" Baochai smiled. "Why, people have come, day after day, to visit it, so was there ever any time to tell the servants to come and clean it?"

"I have the greatest abhorrence," Lin Daiyu chimed in, "for Li Yi's poetical works, but there's only this line in them which I like:

"'Leave the dry lotus leaves so as to hear the patter of the rain.'

"and here you people deliberately mean again not to leave the dry lotus stay where they are."

"This is indeed a fine line!" Baoyu exclaimed. "We mustn't hereafter let them pull them away!"

While this conversation continued, they reached the shoaly inlet under the flower-laden beech. They felt a coolness from the shady overgrowth penetrate their very bones. The decaying vegetation and the withered aquatic chestnut plants on the sand-bank enhanced, to a greater degree, the beauty of the autumn scenery.

Dowager lady Jia at this point observed some spotless rooms on the bank, so spick and so span. "Are not these Miss Xue's quarters," she asked. "Eh?"

"Yes, they are!" everybody answered.

Old lady Jia promptly bade them go alongside, and wending their way up the marble steps, which seemed to lead to the clouds, they in a body entered the Hengwu court. Here they felt a peculiar perfume come wafting into their nostrils, for the colder the season got the greener grew that strange vegetation, and those fairy-like creepers. The various plants were laden with seeds, which closely resembled red coral beans, as they drooped in lovely clusters.

The house, as soon as they put their foot into it, presented the aspect of a snow cave. There was a total absence of every object of ornament. On the table figured merely an earthenware vase, in which were placed several chrysanthemums. A few books and teacups were also conspicuous, but no further knick-nacks. On the bed was suspended a green gauze curtain, and of equally extreme plainness were the coverlets and mattresses belonging to it.

"This child," dowager lady Jia sighed, "is too simple! If you've got nothing to lay about, why not ask your aunt for a few articles? I would never raise any objection. I never thought about them. Your things, of course, have been left at home, and have not been brought over."

So saying, she told Yuanyang to go and fetch several bric-a-brac. She next went on to call lady Feng to task.

"She herself wouldn't have them," (lady Feng) rejoined. "We really sent over a few, but she refused everyone of them and returned them."

"In her home also," smiled Mrs. Xue, "she does not go in very much for such sort of things."

Old lady Jia nodded her head. "It will never do!" she added. "It does, it's true, save trouble; but were some relative to come on a visit, she'll find things in an impossible way. In the second place, such simplicity in the apartments of young ladies of tender age is quite unpropitious! Why, if you young people go on in this way, we old fogies should go further and live in stables! You've all heard what is said in those books and plays about the dreadful luxury, with which young ladies' quarters are got up. And though these girls of ours could not presume to place themselves on the same footing as those young ladies, they shouldn't nevertheless exceed too much the bounds of what constitutes the right thing. If they have any objects ready at hand, why shouldn't they lay them out? And if they have any strong predilection for simplicity, a few things less will do quite as well. I've always had the greatest knack for decorating a room, but being an old woman now I haven't the ease and inclination to attend to such things! These girls are, however, learning how to do things very nicely. I was afraid that there would be an appearance of vulgarity in what they did, and that, even had they anything worth having, they'd so place them about as to spoil them; but from what I can see there's nothing vulgar about them. But let me now put things right for you, and I'll wager that everything will look grand as well as plain. I've got a couple of my own knick-nacks, which I've managed to keep to this day, by not allowing Baoyu to get a glimpse of them; for had he ever seen them, they too would have long ago disappeared!" Continuing, she called Yuanyang. "Fetch that marble pot with scenery on it," she said to her; "that gauze screen, and that tripod of transparent stone with black streaks, which you'll find in there, and lay out all three on this table. They'll be ample! Bring likewise those ink pictures and white silk curtains, and change these curtains."

Yuanyang expressed her obedience. "All these articles have been put away in the eastern loft," she smiled. "In what boxes they've been put, I couldn't tell; I must therefore go and find them quietly and if I bring them over tomorrow, it will be time enough."

"Tomorrow or the day after will do very well; but don't forget, that's all," dowager lady Jia urged.

While conversing, they sat for a while. Presently, they left the rooms and repaired straightway into the Chuojin hall. Wenguan and the other girls came up and paid their obeisance. They next inquired what songs they were to practise.

"You'd better choose a few pieces to rehearse out of those you know best," old lady Jia rejoined.

Wenguan and her companions then withdrew and betook themselves to the Lotus Fragrance Pavilion. But we will leave them there without further allusion to them.

During this while, lady Feng had already, with the help of servants, got everything in perfect order. On the left and right of the side of honor were placed two divans. These divans were completely covered with embroidered covers and fine variegated mats. In front of each divan stood two lacquer teapoys, inlaid, some with designs of crab-apple flowers; others of plum blossom, some of lotus leaves, others of sunflowers. Some of these teapoys were square, others round. Their shapes were all different. On each was placed a set consisting of a stove and a bottle, also a box with partitions. The two divans and four teapoys, in the place of honor, were used by dowager lady Jia and Mrs. Xue. The chair and two teapoys in the next best place, by Madame Wang. The rest of the inmates had, all alike, a chair and a teapoy. On the east side sat old goody Liu. Below old goody Liu came Madame Wang. On the west was seated Shi Xiangyun. The second place was occupied by Baochai; the third by Daiyu; the fourth by Yingchun. Tanchun and Xichun filled the lower seats, in their proper order; Baoyu sat in the last place. The two teapoys assigned to Li Wan and lady Feng stood within the third line of railings, and beyond the second row of gauze frames. The pattern of the partition-boxes corresponded likewise with the pattern on the teapoys. Each inmate had a black decanter, with silver, inlaid in foreign designs; as well as an ornamented, enamelled cup.

After they had all occupied the seats assigned to them, dowager lady Jia took the initiative and smilingly suggested: "Let's begin by drinking a couple of cups of wine. But we should also have a game of forfeits today, we'll have plenty of fun then."

"You, venerable senior, must certainly have a good wine order to impose," Mrs. Xue laughingly observed, "but how could we ever comply with it? But if your aim be to intoxicate us, why, we'll all straightway drink one or two cups more than is good for us and finish!"

"Here's Mrs. Xue beginning to be modest again today!" old lady Jia smiled. "But I expect it's because she looks down upon me as being an old hag!"

"It isn't modesty!" Mrs. Xue replied smiling. "It's all a dread lest I shouldn't be able to observe the order and thus incur ridicule."

"If you don't give the right answer," Madame Wang promptly interposed with a smile, "you'll only have to drink a cup or two more of wine, and should we get drunk, we can go to sleep; and who'll, pray, laugh at us?"

Mrs. Xue nodded her head. "I'll agree to the order," she laughed, "but, dear senior, you must, after all, do the right thing and have a cup of wine to start it."

"This is quite natural!" old lady Jia answered laughingly; and with these words, she forthwith emptied a cup.

Lady Feng with hurried steps advanced to the center of the room. "If we are to play at forfeits," she smilingly proposed, "we'd better invite sister Yuanyang to come and join us."

The whole company was perfectly aware that if dowager lady Jia had to give out the rule of forfeits. Yuanyang would necessarily have to suggest it, so the moment they heard the proposal they, with common consent, approved it as excellent. Lady Feng therefore there and then dragged Yuanyang over.

"As you're to take a part in the game of forfeits," Madame Wang smilingly observed, "there's no reason why you should stand up." And turning her head round, "Bring over," she bade a young waiting-maid, "a chair and place it at your Mistress Secunda's table."

Yuanyang, half refusing and half assenting, expressed her thanks, and took the seat. After partaking also of a cup of wine, "Drinking rules," she smiled, "resemble very much martial law; so irrespective of high or low, I alone will preside. Anyone therefore who disobeys my words will have to suffer a penalty."

"Of course, it should be so!" Madame Wang and the others laughed, "so be quick and give out the rule!"

But before Yuanyang had as yet opened her lips to speak, old goody

Liu left the table, and waving her hand: "Don't," she said, "make fun of people in this way, for I'll go home."

"This will never do!" One and all smilingly protested.

Yuanyang shouted to the young waiting-maids to drag her back to her table; and the maids, while also indulging in laughter, actually pulled her and compelled her to rejoin the banquet.

"Spare me!" old goody Liu kept on crying, "spare me!"

"Anyone who says one word more," Yuanyang exclaimed, "will be fined a whole decanter full."

Old goody Liu then at length observed silence.

"I'll now give out the set of dominoes." Yuanyang proceeded. "I'll begin from our venerable mistress and follow down in proper order until I come to old goody Liu, when I shall stop. So as to illustrate what I meant just now by giving out a set, I'll take these three dominoes and place them apart; you have to begin by saying something on the first, next, to allude to the second, and, after finishing with all three, to take the name of the whole set and match it with a line, no matter whether it be from some stanza or roundelay, song or idyl, set phrases or proverbs. But they must rhyme. And anyone making a mistake will be mulcted in one cup."

"This rule is splendid; begin at once!" they all exclaimed.

"I've got a set," Yuanyang pursued; "on the left, is the piece 'heaven,' (twelve dots)."

"Above head stretches the blue heaven," dowager lady Jia said.

"Good!" shouted everyone.

"In the center is a five and six," Yuanyang resumed.

"Six,"

"The fragrance of the plum blossom pierces the bones on the bridge"

old lady Jia added.

"There now remains," Yuanyang explained, "one piece, the six and one."

"From among the fleecy clouds issues the wheel-like russet sun."

dowager lady Jia continued.

"The whole combined," Yuanyang observed "forms 'the devil with dishevelled hair.'"

"This devil clasps the leg of the Zhongqiu devil,"

old lady Jia observed.

At the conclusion of her recitation, they all burst out laughing. "Capital!" they shouted. Old lady Jia drained a cup. Yuanyang then went on to remark, "I've got another set; the one on the left is a double five."

"Bud after bud of the plum bloom dances in the wind,"

Mrs. Xue replied.

"The one on the right is a ten spot," Yuanyang pursued.

"In the tenth moon the plum bloom on the hills emits its fragrant smell,"

Mrs. Xue added.

"The middle piece is the two and five, making the 'unlike seven;'" Yuanyang observed.

"The 'spinning damsel' star meets the 'cow-herd' on the eve of the seventh day of the seventh moon,"

Miss Xue said.

"Together they form: 'Er Niang strolls on the five mounds,'" Yuanyang continued.

"Mortals cannot be happy as immortals,"

Mrs. Xue rejoined.

Her answers over, the whole company extolled them and had a drink. "I've got another set!" Yuanyang once more exclaimed. "On the left, are distinctly the distant dots of the double ace."

"Both sun and moon are so suspended as to shine on heaven and earth,"

Xiangyun ventured.

"On the right, are a couple of spots, far apart, which clearly form a one and one." Yuanyang pursued.

"What time a lonesome flower falls to the ground, no sound is audible,"

Xiangyun rejoined.

"In the middle, there is the one and four," Yuanyang added.

> "The red apricot tree is planted by the sun, and leans against the clouds,"

Xiangyun answered.

"Together they form the 'cherry fruit ripens for the ninth time,'" Yuanyang said.

> "In the imperial garden it is pecked by birds,"

Xiangyun replied.

When she had done with her part, she drank a cup of wine. "I've got another set," Yuanyang began, "the one on the left is a double three."

> "The swallows, pair by pair, chatter on the beams,"

Baochai remarked.

"The right piece is a six," Yuanyang added.

> "The marsh flower is stretched by the breeze e'en to the length of a green sash,"

Baochai returned.

"The center piece is a three and six, making a nine spot," Yuanyang pursued.

> "The three hills tower half beyond the azure skies,"

Baochai rejoined.

"Lumped together they form a 'chain-bound solitary boat,'" Yuanyang resumed.

> "Where there are wind and waves, there I feel sad,"

Baochai answered.

When she had finished her turn and drained her cup, Yuanyang went on again. "On the left," she said, "there's a 'heaven.'"

> "A morning fine and beauteous scenery, but, alas, what a day for me!"

Daiyu replied.

When this line fell on Baochai's ear, she turned her head round and cast a glance at her, but Daiyu was so nervous lest she should have to pay a forfeit that she did not so much as notice her.

"In the middle there's the 'color of the embroidered screen, (ten spots, four and six), is beautiful,'" Yuanyang proceeded.

"Not e'en Hong Niang to the gauze window comes, any message to bring."

Daiyu responded.

"There now remains a two and six, eight in all," Yuanyang resumed.

"Twice see the jady throne when led in to perform the court ritual,"

Daiyu replied.

"Together they form 'a basket suitable for putting plucked flowers in,'" Yuanyang continued.

"The fairy wand smells nice as on it hangs a peony,"

Daiyu retorted.

At the close of her replies, she took a sip of wine. Yuanyang then resumed. "On the left," she said, "there's a four and five, making a 'different-combined nine.'"

"The peach blossoms bear heavy drops of rain,"

Yingchun remarked.

The company laughed. "She must be fined!" they exclaimed. "She has made a mistake in the rhyme. Besides, it isn't right!"

Yingchun smiled and drank a sip. The fact is that both lady Feng and Yuanyang were so eager to hear the funny things that would be uttered by old goody Liu, that they with one voice purposely ruled that everyone answered wrong and fined them. When it came to Madame Wang's turn, Yuanyang recited something for her. Next followed old goody Liu.

"When we country-people have got nothing to do," old goody Liu said, "a few of us too often come together and play this sort of game; but the answers we give are not so high-flown; yet, as I can't get out of it, I'll likewise make a try!"

"It's easy enough to say what there is," one and all laughed, "so just you go on and don't mind!"

"On the left," Yuanyang smiled, "there's a double four, i.e. 'man.'"

Goody Liu listened intently. After considerable reflection,

"It's a peasant!"

she cried.

One and all in the room blurted out laughing.

"Well-said!" dowager lady Jia observed with a laugh, "that's the way."

"All we country-people know," old goody Liu proceeded, also laughing, "is just what comes within our own rough-and-ready wits, so young ladies and ladies pray don't poke fun at me!"

"In the center there's the three and four, green matched with red," Yuanyang pursued.

"The large fire burnt the hairy caterpillar,"

old goody Liu ventured.

"This will do very well!", the party laughed, "go on with what is in your line."

"On the right," Yuanyang smilingly continued, "there's a one and four, and is really pretty."

"A turnip and a head of garlic."

old goody Liu answered.

This reply evoked further laughter from the whole company.

"Altogether, it's a twig of flowers," Yuanyang added laughing.

"The flower dropped, and a huge melon formed."

old goody Liu observed, while gesticulating with both her hands by way of illustration.

The party once more exploded in loud merriment.

But, reader, if you entertain any curiosity to hear what else was said during the banquet, listen to the explanation given in the next chapter.

CHAPTER 41

Jia Baoyu tastes tea in the Longcui monastery. Old goody Liu gets drunk and falls asleep in the Yihong court.

Old goody Liu, so the story goes, exclaimed, while making signs with both hands,

"The flower dropped and a huge melon formed,"

to the intense amusement of all the inmates, who burst into a boisterous fit of laughter. In due course, however, she drank the closing cup. Then she made another effort to evoke merriment. "To speak the truth today," she smilingly observed, "my hands and my feet are so rough, and I've had so much wine that I must be careful; or else I might, by a slip of the hand, break the porcelain cups. If you have got any wooden cups, you'd better produce them. It wouldn't matter then if even they were to slip out of my hands and drop on the ground!"

This joke excited some more mirth. But lady Feng, upon hearing this speedily put on a smile. "Well," she said, "if you really want a wooden one, I'll fetch you one at once! But there's just one word I'd like to tell you beforehand. Wooden cups are not like porcelain ones. They go in sets; so you'll have to do the right thing and drink from every cup of the set."

"I just now simply spoke in jest about those cups in order to induce them to laugh," old goody Liu at these words, mused within herself, "but, who would have thought that she actually has some of the kind. I've often been to the large households of village gentry on a visit, and even been to banquets there and seen both gold cups and silver cups; but never have I beheld any wooden ones about! Ah, of course! They must, I expect, be the wooden bowls used by the young children. Their object must be to inveigle me to have a couple of bowlfuls more than is good for me! But I don't mind it. This wine is, verily, like honey, so if I drink a little more, it won't do me any harm.

Bringing this train of thought to a close, "Fetch them!" she said aloud. "We'll talk about them by and bye."

Lady Feng then directed Feng'er to go and bring the set of ten cups, made of bamboo roots, from the bookcase in the front inner room. Upon hearing her orders, Feng'er was about to go and execute them, when Yuanyang smilingly interposed. "I know those ten cups of yours," she remarked, "they're small. What's more, a while back you mentioned wooden ones, and if you have bamboo ones brought now, it won't look well; so we'd better get from our place that set of ten large cups, scooped out of whole blocks of aspen roots, and pour the contents of all ten of them down her throat?"

"Yes, that would be much better," lady Feng smiled.

The cups were then actually brought by a servant, at the direction of Yuanyang. At the sight of them, old goody Liu was filled with surprise as well as with admiration. Surprise, as the ten formed one set going in gradation from large to small; the largest being amply of the size of a small basin, the smallest even measuring two of those she held in her hand. Admiration, as they were all alike, engraved, in perfect style, with scenery, trees, and human beings, and bore inscriptions in the "grass" character as well as the seal of the writer.

"It will be enough," she consequently shouted with alacrity, "if you give me that small one."

"There's no one," lady Feng laughingly insinuated, "with the capacity to tackle these! Hence it is that not a soul can pluck up courage enough to use them! But as you, old dame, asked for them, and they were fished out, after ever so much trouble, you're bound to do the proper thing and drink out of each, one after the other."

Old goody Liu was quite taken aback. "I daren't!" she promptly demurred. "My dear lady, do let me off!"

Dowager lady Jia, Mrs. Xue, and Madame Wang were quite alive to the fact that a person advanced in years as she was could not be gifted with such powers of endurance, and they hastened to smilingly expostulate. "To speak is to speak, and a joke is a joke, but she mayn't take too much," they said; "let her just empty this first cup, and have done."

"Amituo Fo!" ejaculated old goody Liu. "I'll only have a small cupful, and put this huge fellow away, and take it home and drink at my leisure."

At this remark, the whole company once more gave way to laughter. Yuanyang had no alternative but to give in and she had to bid a servant fill a large cup full of wine. Old goody Liu laid hold of it with both hands and raised it to her mouth.

"Gently a bit!" old lady Jia and Mrs. Xue shouted. "Mind you don't choke!"

Mrs. Xue then told lady Feng to put some viands before her. "Goody Liu!" smiled lady Feng, "tell me the name of anything you fancy, and I'll bring it and feed you."

"What names can I know?" old goody Liu rejoined. "Everything is good!"

"Bring some eggplant and salt-fish for her!" dowager lady Jia suggested with a smile.

Lady Feng, upon hearing this suggestion, complied with it by catching some eggplant and salt-fish with two chopsticks and putting them into old goody Liu's mouth. "You people," she smiled, "daily feed on eggplants; so taste these of ours and see whether they've been nicely prepared or not."

"Don't be making a fool of me!" old goody Liu answered smilingly. "If eggplants can have such flavor, we ourselves needn't sow any cereals, but confine ourselves to growing nothing but eggplants!"

"They're really eggplants!" one and all protested. "She's not pulling your leg!"

Old goody Liu was amazed. "If these be actually eggplants," she said, "I've uselessly eaten them so long! But, my lady, do give me a few more; I'd like to taste the next mouthful carefully!"

Lady Feng brought her, in very deed, another lot, and put it in her mouth. Old goody Liu munched for long with particular care. "There is, it's true, something about them of the flavor of eggplant," she laughingly remarked, "yet they don't quite taste like eggplants. But tell me how they're cooked, so that I may prepare them in the same way for myself."

"There's nothing hard about it!" lady Feng answered smiling. "You take the newly cut eggplants and pare the skin off. All you want then is some fresh meat. You hash it into fine mince, and fry it in chicken fat. Then you take some dry chicken meat, and mix it with mushrooms, new bamboo shoots, sweet mushrooms, dry beancurd paste, flavored with five spices, and every kind of dry fruits, and you chop the whole lot into fine pieces. You then bake all these things in chicken broth, until it's absorbed, when you fry them, to finish, in sweet oil, and adding some oil, made of the grains of wine, you place them in a porcelain jar, and close it hermetically. At any time that you want any to eat, all you have to do is to take out some, and mix it with some roasted chicken, and there it is all ready."

Old goody Liu a shook her head and put out her tongue. "My Buddha's ancestor!" she shouted. "One wants about ten chickens to prepare this dish! It isn't strange then that it has this flavor!"

Saying this, she quietly finished her wine. But still she kept on minutely scrutinizing the cup.

"Haven't you yet had enough to satisfy you?" lady Feng smiled. "If you haven't, well, then drink another cup."

"Dreadful!" eagerly exclaimed old goody Liu. "I shall be soon getting so drunk that it will be the very death of me. I was only looking at it as I admire pretty things like this! But what a trouble it must have cost to turn out!"

"Have you done with your wine?" Yuanyang laughingly inquired. "But, after all, what kind of wood is this cup made of?"

"It isn't to be wondered at," old goody Liu smiled, "that you can't make it out Miss! How ever could you people, who live inside golden doors and embroidered apartments, know anything of wood! We have the whole day long the trees in the woods as our neighbors. When weary, we use them as our pillows and go to sleep on them. When exhausted, we sit with our backs leaning against them. When, in years of dearth, we feel the pangs of hunger, we also feed on them. Day after day, we see them with our eyes; day after day we listen to them with our ears; day after day, we talk of them with our mouths. I am therefore well able to tell whether any wood be good or bad, genuine or false. Do let me then see what it is!

As she spoke, she intently scanned the cup for a considerable length of time. "Such a family as yours," she then said, "could on no account own mean things! Any wood that is easily procured, wouldn't even find a place in here. This feels so heavy, as I weigh it in my hands, that if it isn't aspen, it must, for a certainty, be yellow cedar."

Her rejoinder amused everyone in the room. But they then perceived an old matron come up. After asking permission of dowager lady Jia to speak: "The young ladies," she said, "have got to the Lotus Fragrance pavilion, and they request your commands, as to whether they should start with the rehearsal at once or tarry a while."

"I forgot all about them!" old lady Jia promptly cried with a smile. "Tell them to begin rehearsing at once!"

The matron expressed her obedience and walked away. Presently, became audible the notes of the pan-pipe and double flute, now soft, now loud, and the blended accents of the pipe and fife. So balmy did the breeze happen to be and the weather so fine that the strains of music came wafted across the arbors and over the stream, and, needless to say, conduced to exhilarate their spirits and to cheer their hearts. Unable to resist the temptation, Baoyu was the first to snatch a decanter and to fill a cup for himself. He quaffed it with one breath. Then pouring another cup, he was about to drain it, when he noticed that Madame Wang too was anxious for a drink, and that she bade a servant bring a warm supply of wine. "With alacrity, Baoyu crossed over to her, and, presenting his own cup, he applied it to Madame Wang's lips. His mother drank two sips while he held it in his hands, but on the arrival of the warm wine, Baoyu resumed his seat. Madame Wang laid hold of the warm decanter, and left the table, while the whole party quitted their places at the banquet; and Mrs. Xue too rose to her feet.

"Take over that decanter from her," dowager lady Jia promptly shouted to Li Wan and lady Feng, "and press your aunt into a seat. We shall all then feel at ease!"

Hearing this, Madame Wang surrendered the decanter to lady Feng and returned to her seat.

"Let's all have a couple of cups of wine!" old lady Jia laughingly cried. "It's capital fun today!"

With this proposal, she laid hold of a cup and offered it to Mrs. Xue. Turning also towards Xiangyun and Baochai: "You two cousins!" she added, "must also have a cup. Your cousin Lin can't take much wine, but even she mustn't be let off."

While pressing them, she drained her cup. Xiangyun, Baochai, and Daiyu then had their drink. But about this time old goody Liu caught the strains of music, and, being already under the influence of liquor, her spirits became more and more exuberant, and she began to gesticulate and skip about. Her pranks amused Baoyu to such a degree that leaving the table, he crossed over to where Daiyu was seated and observed laughingly: "Just you look at the way old goody Liu is going on!"

"In days of yore," Daiyu smiled, "every species of animal commenced to dance the moment the sounds of music broke forth. She's like a buffalo now."

This simile made her cousins laugh. But shortly the music ceased. "We've all had our wine," Mrs. Xue smilingly proposed, "so let's go and stroll about for a time; we can after that sit down again!"

Dowager lady Jia herself was at the moment feeling a strong inclination to have a ramble. In due course, therefore, they all left the banquet and went with their old senior, for a walk. Dowager lady Jia, however, longed to take goody Liu along with her to help her dispel her ennui, so promptly seizing the old dame's hand in hers, they threaded their way as far as the trees, which stood facing the hill. After lolling about with her for a few minutes, "What kind of tree is this?" she went on to inquire of her. "What kind of stone is this? What species of flower is that?"

Old goody Liu gave suitable reply to each of her questions. "Who'd ever have imagined it," she proceeded to tell dowager lady Jia; "not only are the human beings in the city grand, but even the birds are grand.

Why, the moment these birds fly into your mansion, they also become beautiful things, and acquire the gift of speech as well!"

The company could not make out the drift of her observations. "What birds get transformed into beautiful things and become able to speak?" they felt impelled to ask.

"Those perched on those gold stands, under the verandah, with green plumage and red beaks are parrots. I know them well enough!" Goody Liu replied. "But those old black crows in the cages there have crests like phoenixes! They can talk too!"

One and all laughed. But not long elapsed before they caught sight of several waiting-maids, who came to invite them to a collation.

"After the number of cups of wine I've had," old lady Jia said, "I don't feel hungry. But never mind, bring the things here. We can nibble something at our leisure."

The maids speedily went off and fetched two teapoys; but they also brought a couple of small boxes with partitions. When they came to be opened and to be examined, the contents of each were found to consist of two kinds of viands. In the one, were two sorts of steamed eatables. One of these was a sweet cake, made of lotus powder, scented with sun-flower. The other being rolls with goose fat and fir cone seeds. The second box contained two kinds of fried eatables; one of which was small dumplings, about an inch in size.

"What stuffing have they put in them?" dowager lady Jia asked.

"They're with crabs inside," hastily rejoined the matrons.

Their old mistress, at this reply, knitted her eyebrows. "These fat, greasy viands for such a time!" she observed. "Who'll ever eat these things?"

But finding, when she came to inspect the other kind, that it consisted of small fruits of flour, fashioned in every shape, and fried in butter, she did not fancy these either. She then however pressed Mrs. Xue to have something to eat, but Mrs. Xue merely took a piece of cake, while dowager lady Jia helped herself to a roll; but after tasting a bit, she gave the remaining half to a servant girl.

Goody Liu saw how beautifully worked those small flour fruits were, made as they were in various colors and designs, and she took, after picking and choosing, one which looked like a peony.

"The most ingenious girls in our village could not, even with a pair of scissors, cut out anything like this in paper!" she exclaimed. "I would like to eat it, but I can't make up my mind to! I had better pack up a few and take them home and give them to them as specimens!"

Her remarks amused everyone.

"When you start for home," dowager lady Jia said, "I'll give you a whole porcelain jar full of them; so you may as well eat these first, while they are hot!"

The rest of the inmates selected such of the fruits as took their fancy, but after they had helped themselves to one or two, they felt satisfied. Goody Liu, however, had never before touched such delicacies. These were, in addition, made small, dainty, and without the least semblance of clumsiness, so when she and Ban'er had served themselves to a few of each sort, half the contents of the dish vanished. But what remained of them were then, at the instance of lady Feng, put into two plates, and sent, together with a partition-box, to Wenguan and the other singing girls as their share.

At an unexpected moment, they perceived the nurse come in with Da Jie'er in her arms, and they all induced her to have a romp with them for a time. But while Da Jie'er was holding a large pumelo and amusing herself with it, she casually caught sight of Ban'er with a 'Buddha's hand.' Da Jie would have it. A servant-girl endeavored to coax (Ban'er) to surrender it to her, but Da Jie'er, unable to curb her impatience, burst out crying. It was only after the pumelo had been given to Ban'er, and that the 'Buddha's hand' had, by dint of much humoring, been got from Ban'er and given to her, that she stopped crying.

Ban'er had played quite long enough with the 'Buddha's hand,' and had, at the moment, his two hands laden with fruits, which he was in the course of eating. When he suddenly besides saw how scented and round the pumelo was, the idea dawned on him that it was more handy for play, and, using it as a ball, he kicked it along and went off to have some fun, relinquishing at once every thought of the 'Buddha's hand.'

By this time dowager lady Jia and the other members had had tea, so leading off again goody Liu, they threaded their way to the Longcui monastery. Miaoyu hastened to usher them in. On their arrival in the interior of the court, they saw the flowers and trees in luxuriant blossom.

"Really," smiled old lady Jia, "it's those people, who devote themselves to an ascetic life and have nothing to do, who manage, by constant repairs, to make their places much nicer than those of others!"

As she spoke, she wended her steps towards the Eastern hall. Miaoyu, with a face beaming with smiles, made way for her to walk in. "We've just been filling ourselves with wines and meats," dowager lady Jia observed, "and with the josses you've got in here, we shall be guilty of profanity. We'd better therefore sit here! But give us some of that good tea of yours; and we'll get off so soon as we have had a cup of it."

Baoyu watched Miaoyu's movements intently, when he noticed her lay hold of a small tea-tray, fashioned in the shape of a peony, made of red carved lacquer, and inlaid with designs in gold representing a drag-on ensconced in the clouds with the character "longevity" clasped in its jaws, a tray, which contained a small multi-colored cup with cover, fabricated at the "Cheng" Kiln, and present it to his grandmother.

"I don't care for 'Liuan' tea!" old lady Jia exclaimed.

"I know it; but this is old 'Junmei,'" Miaoyu answered with a smile.

Dowager lady Jia received the cup. "What water is this?" she went on to inquire.

"It's rain water collected last year," Miaoyu added by way of reply.

Old lady Jia readily drank half a cup of the tea; and smiling, she prof-fered it to goody Liu. "Just you taste this tea!" she said.

Goody Liu drained the remainder with one draught. "It's good, of course," she remarked laughingly, "but it's rather weak! It would be far better were it brewed a little stronger!"

Dowager lady Jia and all the inmates laughed. But subsequently, each of them was handed a thin, pure white covered cup, all of the same make, originating from the "Guan" kiln. Miaoyu, however, soon gave a tug at Baochai's and Daiyu's lapels, and both quitted the apartment along with her. But Baoyu too quietly followed at their heels. Spying Miaoyu show his two cousins into a side-room, Baochai take a seat in the court, Daiyu seat herself on Miaoyu's rush mat, and Miaoyu her-self approach a stove, fan the fire, and boil some water, with which she brewed another pot of tea, Baoyu walked in. "Are you bent upon drink-ing your own private tea?" he smiled.

"Here you rush again to steal our tea," the two girls laughed with one accord. "There's none for you!"

But just as Miaoyu was going to fetch a cup, she perceived an old Daoist matron bring away the tea things, which had been used in the upper rooms. "Don't put that 'Cheng' kiln tea-cup by!" Miaoyu hastily shouted. "Go and put it outside!"

Baoyu understood that it must be because old goody Liu had drunk out of it that she considered it too dirty to keep. He then saw Miaoyu produce two other cups. The one had an ear on the side. On the bowl itself were engraved in three characters: "calabash cup," in the plain "square" writing. After these, followed a row of small characters in the "true" style, to the effect that the cup had been an article much trea-sured by Wang Kai. Next came a second row of small characters stating: that in the course of the fourth moon of the fifth year of Yuan Feng, of the Song dynasty, Sushi of Mei Shan had seen it in the "Secret" palace.

This cup, Miaoyu filled, and handed to Baochai.

The other cup was, in appearance, as clumsy as it was small; yet on it figured an engraved inscription, consisting of "spotted rhinoceros cup," in three "seal" characters, which bore the semblance of pendent pearls. Miaoyu replenished this cup and gave it to Daiyu; and taking the green jade cup, which she had, on previous occasions, often used for her own tea, she filled it and presented it to Baoyu.

"'The rules observed in the world,' the adage says, 'must be impartial,'" Baoyu smiled. "But while my two cousins are handling those antique and rare gems, here am I with this coarse object!"

"Is this a coarse thing?" Miaoyu exclaimed. "Why, I'm making no outrageous statement when I say that I'm inclined to think that it is by no means certain that you could lay your hand upon any such coarse thing as this in your home!"

"'Do in the country as country people do,' the proverb says," Baoyu laughingly rejoined. "So when one gets in a place like this of yours, one must naturally look down upon everything in the way of gold, pearls, jade, and precious stones as coarse rubbish!"

This sentiment highly delighted Miaoyu. So much so, that producing another capacious cup, carved out of a whole bamboo root, which with its nine curves and ten rings, with twenty knots in each ring, resembled a coiled dragon, "Here," she said with a face beaming with smiles, "there only remains this one! Can you manage this large cup?"

"I can!" Baoyu vehemently replied, with high glee.

"Albeit you have the stomach to tackle all it holds," Miaoyu laughed, "I haven't got so much tea for you to waste! Have you not heard how that the first cup is the 'taste'-cup; the second 'the stupid thing-for-quenching-one's-thirst,' and the third 'the drink-mule' cup? But were you now to go in for this huge cup, why what more wouldn't that be?"

At these words, Baochai, Daiyu, and Baoyu simultaneously indulged in laughter. But Miaoyu seized the teapot, and poured well-nigh a whole cupful of tea into the big cup. Baoyu tasted some carefully, and found it, in real truth, so exceptionally soft and pure that he extolled it with incessant praise.

"If you've had any tea this time," Miaoyu pursued with a serious expression about her face, "it's thanks to these two young ladies; for had you come alone, I wouldn't have given you any."

"I'm well aware of this," Baoyu laughingly rejoined, "so I too will receive no favor from your hands, but simply express my thanks to these two cousins of mine, and have done!"

"What you say makes your meaning clear enough!" Miaoyu said, when she heard his reply.

"Is this rain water from last year?" Daiyu then inquired.

"How is it," smiled Miaoyu sardonically, "that a person like you can be such a boor as not to be able to discriminate water, when you taste it? This is snow collected from the plum blossom, five years back, when I was in the Panxiang temple at Xuanmu. All I got was that flower jar, green as the devil's face, full, and as I couldn't make up my mind to part with it and drink it, I interred it in the ground, and only opened it this summer. I've had some of it once before, and this is the second time. But how is it you didn't detect it, when you put it to your lips? Has rain water, obtained a year back, ever got such a soft and pure flavor? and how possibly could it be drunk at all?"

Daiyu knew perfectly what a curious disposition she naturally had, and she did not think it advisable to start any lengthy discussion with her. Nor did she feel justified to protract her stay, so after sipping her tea, she intimated to Baochai her intention to go, and they quitted the apartment.

Baoyu gave a forced smile to Miaoyu. "That cup," he said, "is, of course, dirty; but is it not a pity to put it away for no valid reason? To my idea it would be preferable, wouldn't it? to give it to that poor old woman; for were she to sell it, she could have the means of subsistence! What do you say, will it do?"

Miaoyu listened to his suggestion, and then nodded her head, after some reflection. "Yes, that will be all right!" she answered. "Lucky for her I've never drunk a drop out of that cup, for had I, I would rather have smashed it to atoms than have let her have it! If you want to give it to her, I don't mind a bit about it; but you yourself must hand it to her! Now, be quick and clear it away at once!"

"Of course; quite so!" Baoyu continued. "How could you ever go and speak to her? Things would then come to a worse pass. You too would be contaminated! If you give it to me, it will be all right."

Miaoyu there and then directed someone to fetch it and to give it to Baoyu. When it was brought, Baoyu took charge of it. "Wait until we've gone out," he proceeded, "and I'll call a few servant-boys and bid them carry several buckets of water from the stream and wash the floors; eh, shall I?"

"Yes, that would be better!" Miaoyu smiled. "The only thing is that you must tell them to bring the water, and place it outside the entrance door by the foot of the wall; for they mustn't come in."

"This goes without saying!" Baoyu said; and, while replying, he produced the cup from inside his sleeve, and handed it to a young waiting-maid from dowager lady Jia's apartments to hold. "Tomorrow," he told her, "give this to goody Liu to take with her, when she starts on her way homewards!"

By the time he made (the girl) understand the charge he entrusted her with, his old grandmother issued out and was anxious to return home. Miaoyu did not exert herself very much to induce her to prolong her visit; but seeing her as far the main gate, she turned round and bolted the doors. But without devoting any further attention to her, we will now allude to dowager lady Jia.

She felt thoroughly tired and exhausted. To such a degree, that she desired Madame Wang, Yingchun, and her sisters to see that Mrs. Xue had some wine, while she herself retired to the Daoxiang village to rest. Lady Feng immediately bade some servants fetch a bamboo chair. On its arrival, dowager lady Jia seated herself in it, and two matrons carried her off hemmed in by lady Feng, Li Wan, and a bevy of servant-girls, and matrons. But let us now leave her to herself, without any additional explanations.

During this while, Mrs. Xue too said good bye and departed. Madame Wang then dismissed Wenguan and the other girls, and, distributing the eatables, that had been collected in the partition-boxes, to the servant-maids to go and feast on, she availed herself of the leisure moments to lie off; so reclining as she was, on the couch, which had been occupied by her old relative a few minutes back, she bade a young maid lower the portiere; after which, she asked her to massage her legs.

"Should our old lady yonder send any message, mind you call me at once," she proceeded to impress on her mind, and, laying herself down, she went to sleep.

Baoyu, Xiangyun, and the rest watched the servant-girls take the partition-boxes and place them among the rocks, and seat themselves some on boulders, others on the turf-covered ground, some lean against the trees, others squat down besides the pool, and thoroughly enjoy themselves. But in a little time, they also perceived Yuanyang arrive. Her object in coming was to carry off goody Liu for a stroll, so in a body they followed in their track, with a view of deriving some fun. Shortly, they got under the honorary gateway put up in the additional grounds, reserved for the Imperial consort's visits to her parents, and old goody Liu shouted aloud: "Ai-yo! What! Is there another big temple here!"

While speaking, she prostrated herself and knocked her head, to the intense amusement of the company, who were quite doubled up with laughter.

"What are you laughing at?" goody Liu inquired. "I can decipher the characters on this honorary gateway. Over at our place temples of this kind are exceedingly plentiful; and they've all got archways like this! These characters give the name of the temple."

"Can you make out from those characters what temple this is?" they laughingly asked.

Goody Liu quickly raised her head, and, pointing at the inscription, "Aren't these," she said, "the four characters 'Pearly Emperor's Precious Hall?'"

Everybody laughed. They clapped their hands and applauded. But when about to chaff her again, goody Liu experienced a rumbling noise in her stomach, and vehemently pulling a young servant-girl, and asking her for a couple of sheets of paper, she began immediately to loosen her garments. "It won't do in here!" one and all laughingly shouted out to her, and quickly they directed a matron to lead her away. When they got at the northeast corner, the matron pointed the proper place out to her, and in high spirits she walked off and went to have some rest.

Goody Liu had taken plenty of wine; she could not too touch yellow wine; she had, what is more, drunk and eaten so many fat things that in the thirst, which supervened, she had emptied several cups of tea; the result was that she unavoidably got looseness of the bowels. She therefore squatted for ever so long before she felt any relief. But on her exit from the private chamber, the wind blew the wine to her head. Besides, being a woman well up in years, she felt, upon suddenly rising from a long squatting position, her eyes grow so dim and her head so giddy that she could not make out the way. She gazed on all four quarters, but the whole place being covered with trees, rockeries, towers, terraces, and houses, she was quite at a loss how to determine her whereabouts, and where each road led to. She had no alternative but to follow a stone road, and to toddle on her way with leisurely step. But when she drew near a building, she could not make out where the door could be. After searching and searching, she accidentally caught sight of a bamboo fence. "Here's another trellis with flat bean plants creeping on it!" Goody Liu communed within herself. While giving way to reflection, she skirted the flower-laden hedge, and discovering a moon-like, cave-like, entrance, she stepped in. Here she discerned, stretching before her eyes a sheet of water, forming a pond, which measured no more than seven or eight feet in breadth. Its banks were paved with slabs of stone. Its jade-like waves flowed in a limpid stream towards the opposite direction. At the upper end, figured a slab of white marble, laid horizontally over the surface. Goody Liu wended her steps over the slab and followed the raised stone-road; then turning two bends, in the lake, an entrance into a house struck her gaze. Forthwith, she crossed the doorway, but her eyes were soon attracted by a young girl, who advanced to greet her with a smile playing upon her lips.

"The young ladies," goody Liu speedily remarked laughing, "have cast me adrift; they made me knock about, until I found my way in here."

But seeing, after addressing her, that the girl said nothing by way of reply, goody Liu approached her and seized her by the hand, when, with a crash, she fell against the wooden partition wall and bumped her head so that it felt quite sore. Upon close examination, she discovered that it was a picture. "Do pictures really so bulge out!" Goody Liu mused within herself, and, as she exercised her mind with these cogitations, she scanned it and rubbed her hand over it. It was perfectly even all over. She nodded her head, and heaved a couple of sighs. But the moment she turned round, she espied a small door over which hung a soft portiere, of leek-green color, bestrewn with embroidered flowers. Goody Liu lifted the portiere and walked in. Upon raising her head, and casting a glance round, she saw the walls, artistically carved in fretwork. On all four sides, lutes, double-edged swords, vases, and censers were stuck everywhere over the walls; and embroidered covers and gauze nets, glistened as brightly as gold, and shed a luster vying with that of pearls. Even the bricks, on the ground on which she trod, were jade-like green, inlaid with designs, so that her eyes got more and more dazzled. She tried to discover an exit, but where could she find a doorway? On the left, was a bookcase. On the right, a screen. As soon as she repaired behind the screen, she faced a door; but, she then caught sight of another old dame stepping in from outside, and advancing towards her, goody Liu was wonderstruck. Her mind was full of uncertainty as to whether it might not be her son-in-law's mother. "I expect," she felt prompted to ask with vehemence, "you went to the trouble of coming to hunt for me, as you didn't see me turn up at home for several days, eh? But what young lady introduced you in here?" Then noticing that her whole head was bedecked with flowers, old goody Liu laughed. "How ignorant of the ways of the world you are!" she said. "Seeing the nice flowers in this garden, you at once set to work, forgetful of all consequences, and loaded your pate with them!"

However, while she derided her, the other old dame simply laughed, without making any rejoinder. But the recollection suddenly flashed to her memory that she had often heard of some kind of chevalglasses, found in wealthy and well-to-do families, and, "May it not be," (she wondered), "my own self reflected in this glass!" After concluding this train of thoughts, she put out her hands, and feeling it and then minutely scrutinizing it, she realised that the four wooden partition walls were made of carved blackwood, into which mirrors had been inserted. "These have so far impeded my progress," she consequently exclaimed, "and how am I to manage to get out?

As she soliloquized, she kept on rubbing the mirror. This mirror was, in fact, provided with some western mechanism, which enabled it to open and shut, so while goody Liu inadvertently passed her hands, quite at random over its surface, the pressure happily fell on the right spot, and opening the contrivance, the mirror flung round, exposing a door to view. Old goody Liu was full of amazement as well as of admiration. With hasty step, she egressed. Her eyes unexpectedly fell on a most handsome set of bed-curtains. But being at the time still seven or eight tenths in the wind, and quite tired out from her tramp, she with one jump squatted down on the bed, saying to herself: "I'll just have a little rest." So little, however, did she, contrary to her expectations, have any control over herself, that, as she reeled backwards and forwards, her eyes got quite drowsy, and then the moment she threw herself in a recumbent position, she dropped into a sound sleep.

But let us now see what the others were up to. They waited for her and waited; but they saw nothing of her. Ban'er got, in the absence of his grandmother, so distressed that he melted into tears. "May she not have fallen into the place?" one and all laughingly observed. "Be quick and tell someone to go and have a look!"

Two matrons were directed to go in search of her; but they returned and reported that she was not to be found. The whole party instituted a search in every nook and corner, but nothing could be seen of her.

"She was so drunk," Xiren suggested, "that she's sure to have lost her way, and following this road, got into our back-rooms. Should she have crossed to the inner side of the hedge, she must have come to the door of the backhouse and got in. Nevertheless, the young maids she must have come across, must know something about her. If she did not get inside the hedge, but continued in a south westerly direction, she's all right, if she made a detour and walked out. But if she hasn't done so, why, she'll have enough of roaming for a good long while! I had better therefore go and see what she's up to."

With these words still on her lips, she retraced her footsteps and repaired into the Yihong court. She called out to the servants, but, who would have thought it, the whole bevy of young maids, attached to those rooms, had seized the opportunity to go and have a romp, so Xiren straightway entered the door of the house. As soon as she turned the multi-colored embroidered screen, the sound of snoring as loud as peals of thunder, fell on her ear. Hastily she betook herself inside, but her nostrils were overpowered by the foul air of wine and wind, which infected the apartment. At a glance, she discovered old goody Liu lying on the bed, face downwards, with hands sprawled out and feet knocking about all over the place. Xiren sustained no small shock. With precipitate hurry, she rushed up to her, and, laying hold of her, lying as she was more dead than alive, she pushed her about until she succeeded in rousing her to her senses. Old goody Liu was startled out of her sleep. She opened wide her eyes, and, realising that Xiren stood before her, she speedily crawled up. "Miss!" she pleaded. "I do deserve death! I have done what I shouldn't; but I haven't in any way soiled the bed."

So saying, she swept her hands over it. But Xiren was in fear and trembling lest the suspicions of any inmate should be aroused, and lest Baoyu should come to know of it, so all she did was to wave her hand towards her, bidding her not utter a word. Then with alacrity grasping three or four handfuls of "Baihe" incense, she heaped it on the large tripod, which stood in the centre of the room, and put the lid back again; delighted at the idea that she had not been so upset as to be sick.

"It doesn't matter!" she quickly rejoined in a low tone of voice with a smile, "I'm here to answer for this. Come along with me!"

While old goody Liu expressed her readiness to comply with her wishes, she followed Xiren out into the quarters occupied by the young maids. Here (Xiren) desired her to take a seat. "Mind you say," she enjoined her, "that you were so drunk that you stretched on a boulder and had a snooze!"

"All right! I will!" old goody Liu promised.

Xiren afterwards helped her to two cups of tea, when she, at length, got over the effects of the wine. "What young lady's room is this that it is so beautiful?" she then inquired. "It seemed to me just as if I had gone to the very heavenly palace."

Xiren gave a faint smile. "This one?" she asked. "Why, it's our master Secundus, Mr. Bao's bedroom."

Old goody Liu was quite taken aback, and could not even presume to utter a sound. But Xiren led her out across the front compound; and, when they met the inmates of the family, she simply explained to them that she had found her fast asleep on the grass, and brought her along. No one paid any heed to the excuse she gave, and the subject was dropped.

Presently, dowager lady Jia awoke, and the evening meal was at once served in the Daoxiang village. Dowager lady Jia was however quite listless, and felt so little inclined to eat anything that she forthwith got into a small open chair, with bamboo seat, and returned to her suite of rooms to rest. But she insisted that lady Feng and her companions should go and have their repast, so the young ladies eventually adjourned once more into the garden.

But, reader, you do not know the sequel, so peruse the circumstances given in detail in the next chapter.

CHAPTER 42

The Princess of Hengwu dispels, with sweet words, some insane suspicions. The inmate of Xiaoxiang puts, with excellent repartee, the final touch to the jokes made about goody Liu.

We will now resume our story by adding that, on the return of the young ladies into the garden, they had their meal. This over, they parted company, and nothing more need be said about them. We will notice, however, that old goody Liu took Ban'er along with her, and came first and paid a visit to lady Feng. "We must certainly start for home tomorrow, as soon as it is daylight," she said. "I've stayed here, it's true, only two or three days, but in these few days I have reaped experience in everything that I had not seen from old till now. It would be difficult to find anyone as compassionate of the poor and considerate to the old as your venerable dame, your Madame Wang, your young ladies, and the girls too attached to the various rooms, have all shown themselves in their treatment of me! When I get home now, I shall have no other means of showing how grateful I am to you than by purchasing a lot of huge joss-sticks and saying daily prayers to Buddha on your behalf; and if he spares you all to enjoy a long life of a hundred years my wishes will be accomplished."

"Don't be so exultant!" lady Feng smilingly replied. "It's all on account of you that our old ancestor has fallen ill, by exposing herself to draughts and that she suffers from disturbed sleep; also that our Da Jie'er has caught a chill and is laid up at home with fever."

Goody Liu, at these words, speedily heaved a sigh. "Her venerable ladyship," she said, "is a person advanced in years and not accustomed to any intense fatigue!"

"She has never before been in such high spirits as yesterday!" lady Feng observed. "As you were here, so anxious was she to let you see everything, that she trudged over the greater part of the garden. And Da Jie'er was given a piece of cake by Madame Wang, when I came to hunt you up, and she ate it, who knows in what windy place, and began at once to get feverish."

"Da Jie'er," goody Liu remarked, "hasn't, I fancy, often put her foot into the garden; and young people like her mustn't really go into strange places, for she's not like our children, who are able to use their legs! In what graveyards don't they ramble about! A puff of wind may, on the one hand, have struck her, it's not at all unlikely; or being, on the other, so chaste in body, and her eyes also so pure she may, it is to be feared, have come across some spirit or other. I can't help thinking therefore that you should consult some book of exorcisms on her behalf; for mind she may have run up against some evil influence."

This remark suggested the idea to lady Feng. There and then she called Ping'er to fetch the "Jade Box Record." When brought, she desired Caiming to look over it for her. Caiming turned over the pages for a time, and then read: 'Those who fall ill on the 25th day of the 8th moon have come across, in a due westerly quarter, of some flower spirit; they feel heavy, with no inclination for drink or food. Take seven sheets of white paper money, and, advancing forty steps due west, burn them and exorcise the spirit; recovery will follow at once!'"

"There's really no mistake about that!" lady Feng smiled. "Are there not flower spirits in the garden? But what I dread is that our old lady mayn't have come across one too."

Saying this, she bade a servant purchase two lots of paper money. On their arrival, she sent for two proper persons, the one to exorcise the spirits for dowager lady Jia and the other to expel them from Da Jie'er; and these observances over, Da Jie'er did, in effect, drop quietly to sleep.

"It's verily people advanced in years like you," lady Feng smilingly exclaimed; "who've gone through many experiences! This Da Jie'er of mine has often been inclined to ail, and it has quite puzzled me to make out how and why it was."

"This isn't anything out of the way!" goody Liu said. "Affluent and honorable people bring up their offspring to be delicate. So naturally, they are not able to endure the least hardship! Moreover, that young child of yours is so excessively cuddled that she can't stand it. Were you, therefore, my lady, to pamper her less from henceforth, she'll steadily improve."

"There's plenty of reason in that too!" lady Feng observed. "But it strikes me that she hasn't as yet got a name, so do give her one in order that she may borrow your long life! In the next place, you are country-people, and are, after all—I don't expect you'll get angry when I mention it—somewhat in poor circumstances. Were a person then as poor as you are to suggest a name for her, you may, I trust, have the effect of counteracting this influence for her."

When old goody Liu heard this proposal, she immediately gave herself up to reflection. "I've no idea of the date of her birth!" she smiled after a time.

"She really was born on no propitious date!" lady Feng replied. "By a remarkable coincidence she came into the world on the seventh day of the seventh moon!"

"This is certainly splendid!" old goody Liu laughed with alacrity. "You had better name her at once Qiao Ge'er (seventh moon and ingenuity). This is what's generally called: combating poison by poison and attacking fire by fire. If therefore your ladyship fixes upon this name of mine, she will, for a surety, attain a long life of a hundred years; and when she by and bye grows up to be a big girl, everyone of you will be able to have a home and get a patrimony! Or if, at any time, there occur anything inauspicious and she has to face adversity, why it will inevitably change into prosperity; and if she comes across any evil fortune, it will turn into good fortune. And this will all arise from this one word, 'Qiao' (ingenuity)."

Lady Feng was, needless to say, delighted by what she heard, and she lost no time in expressing her gratitude. "If she be preserved," she exclaimed, "to accomplish your good wishes, it will be such a good thing!" Saying this, she called Ping'er. "As you and I are bound to be busy tomorrow," she said, "and won't, I fear, be able to spare any leisure moments, you'd better, if you have nothing to do now, get ready the presents for old goody Liu, so as to enable her to conveniently start at early dawn tomorrow."

"How could I presume to be the cause of such reckless waste?" goody Liu interposed. "I've already disturbed your peace and quiet for several days, and were I to also take your things away, I'd feel still less at ease in my heart!"

"There's nothing much!" lady Feng protested. "They consist simply of a few ordinary things. But, whether good or bad, do take them along, so that the people in the same street as yourselves and your next-door neighbors may have some little excitement, and that it may look as if you had been on a visit to the city!"

But while she endeavoured to induce the old dame to accept the presents, she noticed Ping'er approach. "Goody Liu," she remarked, "come over here and see!"

Old goody Liu precipitately followed Ping'er into the room on the off side. Here she saw the stove-couch half-full with piles of things. Ping'er took these up one by one and let her have a look at them. "This," she explained, "is a roll of that green gauze you asked for yesterday. Besides this, our lady Feng gives you a piece of thick bluish-white gauze to use as lining. These are two pieces of pongee, which will do for wadded coats and jupes as well. In this bundle are two pieces of silk, for you to make clothes with, for the end of the year. This is a box containing various home-made cakes. Among them are some you've already tasted and some you haven't; so take them along, and put them in plates and invite your friends; they'll be ever so much better than any that you could buy! These two bags are those in which the melons and fruit were packed up yesterday. This one has been filled with two bushels of fine rice, grown in the Imperial fields, the like of which for congee, it would not be easy to get. This one contains fruits from our garden and all kinds of dry fruits. In this packet, you'll find eight taels of silver. These various things are presents for you from our Mistress Secunda. Each of these packets contains fifty taels so that there are in all a hundred taels; they're the gift of Madame Wang. She bids you accept them so as to either carry on any trade, for which no big capital is required, or to purchase several acres of land, in order that you mayn't henceforward have any more to beg favors of relatives, or to depend upon friends." Continuing, she added smilingly, in a low tone of voice, "These two jackets, two jupes, four head bands, and a bundle of velvet and thread are what I give you, worthy dame, as my share. These clothes are, it is true, the worse for use, yet I haven't worn them very much. But if you disdain them, I won't be so presuming as to say anything."

After mention of each article by Ping'er, goody Liu muttered the name of Buddha, so already she had repeated Buddha's name several thousands of times. But when she saw the heap of presents which Ping'er too bestowed on her, and the little ostentation with which she did it, she promptly smiled. "Miss!" she said, "what are you saying? Could I ever disdain such nice gifts as these! Had I even the money, I couldn't buy them anywhere. The only thing is that I feel overpowered with shame. If I keep them, it won't be nice, and if I don't accept them, I shall be showing myself ungrateful for your kind attention."

"Don't utter all this irrelevant talk!" Ping'er laughed. "You and I are friends; so compose your mind and take the things I gave you just now! Besides, I have, on my part, something to ask of you. When the close of the year comes, select a few of your cabbages, dipped in lime, and dried in the sun, as well as some lentils, flat beans, tomatoes, and pumpkin strips, and various sorts of dry vegetables and bring them over. We're all, both high or low, fond of such things. These will be quite enough! We don't want anything else, so don't go to any useless trouble!"

Goody Liu gave utterance to profuse expressions of gratitude and signified her readiness to comply with her wishes.

"Just you go to sleep," Ping'er urged, "and I'll get the things ready for you and put them in here. As soon as the day breaks tomorrow, I'll send the servant-lads to hire a cart and pack them in; don't you therefore worry yourself in the least on that score!"

Goody Liu felt more and more ineffably grateful. So crossing over, she again said, with warm protestations of thankfulness, good bye to lady Feng; after which, she repaired to dowager lady Jia's quarters on this side, where she slept, with one sleep, during the whole night. Early the next day, as soon as she had combed her hair and performed her ablutions, she asked to go and pay her adieus to lady Jia. But as old lady Jia was unwell, the various members of the family came to see how she was getting on. On their reappearance outside, they transmitted orders that the doctor should be sent for. In a little time, a matron reported that the doctor had arrived, and an old nurse invited dowager lady Jia to ensconce herself under the curtain.

"I'm an old woman!" lady Jia remonstrated. "Am I not aged enough to be a mother to that fellow? and am I, pray, to still stand on any ceremonies with him? There's no need to drop the curtain; I'll see him as I am, and have done."

Hearing her objections, the matrons fetched a small table, and, laying a small pillow on it, they directed a servant to ask the doctor in.

Presently, they perceived the trio Jia Zhen, Jia Lian, and Jia Rong, bringing Dr. Wang. Dr. Wang did not presume to use the raised road, but confining himself to the side steps, he kept pace with Jia Zhen until they reached the platform. Two matrons, who had been standing, one on either side from an early hour, raised the portiere. A couple of old women servants then took the lead and showed the way in. But Baoyu too appeared on the scene to meet them.

They found old lady Jia seated bolt upright on the couch, dressed in a blue crape jacket, lined with sheep skin, every curl of which resembled a pearl. On the right and left stood four young maids, whose hair had not as yet been allowed to grow, with fly-brushes, finger-bowls, and other such articles in their hands. Five or six old nurses were also drawn up on both sides like wings. At the back of the jade-green gauze mosquito-house were faintly visible several persons in red and green habiliments, with gems on their heads, and gold trinkets in their coiffures.

Dr. Wang could not muster the courage to raise his head. With speedy step, he advanced and paid his obeisance. Dowager lady Jia noticed that he wore the official dress of the sixth grade, and she accordingly concluded that he must be an Imperial physician. "How are you noble doctor?" she inquired, forcing a smile. "What is the worthy surname of this noble doctor?" she then asked Jia Zhen.

Jia Zhen and his companions made prompt reply. "His surname is Wang," they said.

"There was once a certain Wang Junxiao who filled the chair of President of the College of Imperial Physicians," dowager lady smilingly proceeded. "He excelled in feeling the pulse."

Dr. Wang bent his body, and with alacrity he lowered his head and returned her smile. "That was," he explained, "my grand-uncle."

"Is it really so!" laughingly pursued dowager lady Jia, upon catching this reply. "We can then call ourselves old friends!"

So speaking, she quietly put out her hand and rested it on the small pillow. A nurse laid hold of a small stool and placed it before the small table, slightly to the side of it. Dr. Wang bent one knee and took a seat on the stool. Drooping his head, he felt the pulse of the one hand for a long while; next, he examined that of the other; after which, hastily making a curtsey, he bent his head and started on his way out of the apartment.

"Excuse me for the trouble I've put you to!" dowager lady Jia smiled. "Zhen'er, escort him outside, and do see that he has a cup of tea."

Jia Zhen, Jia Lian, and the rest of their companions immediately acquiesced by uttering several yes's, and once more they led Dr. Wang into the outer study.

"Your worthy senior," Dr. Wang explained, "has nothing else the matter with her than a slight chill, which she must have inadvertently contracted. She needn't, after all, take any medicines; all she need do is to diet herself and keep warm a little; and she'll get all right. But I'll now write a prescription, in here. Should her venerable ladyship care to take any of the medicine, then prepare a dose, according to the prescription, and let her have it. But should she be loath to have any, well, never mind, it won't be of any consequence."

Saying this, he wrote the prescription, as he sipped his tea. But when about to take his leave, he saw a nurse bring Da Jie'er into the room. "Mr. Wang," she said, "do also have a look at our Jie'er!

Upon hearing her appeal, Dr. Wang immediately rose to his feet. While she was clasped in her nurse's arms, he rested Da Jie'er's hand on his left hand and felt her pulse with his right, and rubbing her forehead, he asked her to put out her tongue and let him see it. "Were I to express my views about Jie'er, you would again abuse me! If she's, however, kept quiet and allowed to go hungry for a couple of meals, she'll get over this. There's no necessity for her to take any decocted medicines. I'll just send her some pills, which you'll have to dissolve in a preparation of ginger, and give them to her before she goes to sleep; when she has had these, there will be nothing more the matter with her."

At the conclusion of these recommendations, he bade them good-bye and took his departure. Jia Zhen and his companions then took the prescription and came and explained to old lady Jia the nature of her indisposition, and, depositing on the table, the paper given to them by the doctor, they quitted her presence. But nothing more need be said about them.

Madame Wang and Li Wan, lady Feng, Baochai, and the other young ladies noticed, meanwhile, that the doctor had gone, and they eventually egressed from the back of the mosquito-house. After a short stay, Madame Wang returned to her quarters. Goody Liu repaired, when she perceived everything quiet again, into the upper rooms and made her adieus to dowager lady Jia.

"When you've got any leisure, do pay us another visit," old lady Jia urged, and bidding Yuanyang come to her, "Do be careful," she added, "and see dame Liu safely on her way out; for not being well I can't escort you myself."

Goody Liu expressed her thanks, and saying good bye a second time, she betook herself, along with Yuanyang, into the servants' quarters. Here Yuanyang pointed at a bundle on the stove-couch. "These are," she said, "several articles of clothing, belonging to our old mistress; they were presented to her in years gone by, by members of our family on her birthdays and various festivals; her ladyship never wears any-thing made by people outside; yet to hoard these would be a downright pity! Indeed, she hasn't worn them even once. It was yesterday that she told me to get out two costumes and hand them to you to take along with you, either to give as presents, or to be worn by someone in your home; but don't make fun of us! In the box you'll find the flour-fruits, for which you asked. This bundle contains the medicines to which you alluded the other day. There are 'plum-blossom-spotted-tongue pills,' and 'purple-gold ingot-pills,' also 'vivifying-blood-vessels-pills,' as well as 'driving offspring and preserving-life pills;' each kind being rolled up in a sheet bearing the prescription; and the whole lot of them are packed up in here. While these two are purses for you to wear in the way of ornaments." So saying, she forthwith loosened the cord, and, producing two ingots representing brushes, and with "ru yi" on them, implying "your wishes will surely be fulfilled," she drew near and showed them to her, "Take the purses," she pursued smiling, "but do leave these behind and give them to me."

Goody Liu was so overjoyed that she had, from an early period, come out afresh with several thousands of invocations of Buddha's names.

When she therefore heard Yuanyang's suggestion, "Miss," she quickly rejoined, "you're at perfect liberty to keep them!"

Yuanyang perceived that her words were believed by her; so smiling she once more dropped the ingots into the purse. "I was only joking with you for fun!" she observed. "I've got a good many like these; keep them therefore and give them, at the close of the year, to your young children."

Speaking the while, she espied a young maid walk in with a cup from the "Cheng" kiln, and hand it to old goody Liu. "This," (she said,) "our master Secundus, Mr. Bao, gives you."

"Whence could I begin enumerating the things I got!" Goody Liu exclaimed. "In what previous existence did I accomplish anything so meritorious as to bring today this heap of blessings upon me!"

With these words, she eagerly took possession of the cup.

"The clothes I gave you the other day, when I asked you to have a bath, were my own," Yuanyang resumed, "and if you don't think them too mean, I've got a few more, which I would also like to let you have."

Goody Liu thanked her with vehemence, so Yuanyang, in point of fact, produced several more articles of clothing, and these she packed up for her. Goody Liu thereupon expressed a desire to also go into the garden and take leave of Baoyu and the young ladies, Madame Wang, and the other inmates and to thank them for all they did for her, but Yuanyang raised objections. "You can dispense with going!" she remarked. "They don't see anyone just now! But I'll deliver the message for you by and bye! When you've got any leisure, do come again. Go to the second gate," she went on to direct an old matron, "and call two servant-lads to come here, and help this old dame to take her things away!"

After the matron had signified her obedience, Yuanyang returned with goody Liu to lady Feng's quarters, on the off part of the mansion, and, taking the presents as far as the side gate, she bade the servant-lads carry them out. She herself then saw goody Liu into her curricle and start on her journey homewards.

But without commenting further on this topic, let us revert to Baochai and the other girls. After breakfast, they recrossed into their grandmother's rooms and made inquiries about her health. On their way back to the garden, they reached a point where they had to take different roads. Baochai then called out to Daiyu. "Pin'er!" she observed, "come with me; I've got a question to ask you."

Daiyu wended her steps therefore with Baochai into the Hengwu court. As soon as they entered the house, Baochai threw herself into a seat. "Kneel down!" she smiled. "I want to examine you about something!"

Daiyu could not fathom her object, and consequently laughed. "Look here." she cried, "this chit Bao has gone clean off her senses! What do you want to examine me about?"

Baochai gave a sardonic smile. "My dear, precious girl, my dear maiden," she exclaimed, "what utter trash fills your mouth! Just speak the honest and candid truth, and finish!"

Daiyu could so little guess her meaning that her sole resource was to smile. Inwardly, however, she could not help beginning to experience certain misgivings. "What did I say?" she remarked. "You're bent upon picking out my faults! Speak out and let me hear what it's all about!"

"Do you still pretend to be a fool?" Baochai laughed. "When we played yesterday that game of wine-forfeits, what did you say? I really couldn't make out any head or tail."

Daiyu, after a moment's reflection, remembered eventually that she had the previous day been guilty of a slip of the tongue and come out with a couple of passages from the "Peony Pavilion," and the "Record of the West Side-house," and, of a sudden, her face got scarlet with blushes. Drawing near Baochai she threw her arms round her. "My dear cousin!" she smiled, "I really wasn't conscious of what I was saying! It just blurted out of my mouth! But now that you've called me to task, I won't say such things again."

"I've no idea of what you were driving at," Baochai laughingly rejoined. "What I heard you recite sounds so thoroughly unfamiliar to me, that I beg you to enlighten me!"

"Dear cousin," pleaded Daiyu, "don't tell anyone else! I won't, in the future, breathe such things again."

Baochai noticed how from shame the blood rushed to her face, and how vehement she was in her entreaties, and she felt loath to press her with questions; so pulling her into a seat to make her have a cup of tea, she said to her in a gentle tone, "Whom do you take me for? I too am wayward; from my youth up, yea ever since I was seven or eight, I've been enough trouble to people! Our family was also what one would term literary. My grandfather's extreme delight was to be ever with a book in his hand. At one time, we numbered many members, and sisters and brothers all lived together; but we had a distaste for wholesome books. Among my brothers, some were partial to verses; others had a weakness for blank poetical compositions; and there were none of such works as the 'Western side-House,' and 'the Guitar,' even up to the hundred and one books of the 'Yüan' authors, which they hadn't managed to get. These books they stealthily read behind our backs; but we, on our part, devoured them, on the sly, without their knowing it. Subsequently, our father came to get wind of it; and some of us he beat, while others he scolded; burning some of the books, and throwing away others. It is therefore as well that we girls shouldn't know anything of letters. Men, who study books and don't understand the right principle, can't, moreover, reach the standard of those, who don't go in for books; so how much more such as ourselves? Even versifying, writing, and the like pursuits aren't in the line of such as you and me. Indeed, neither are they within the portion of men. Men, who go in for study and fathom the right principles, should cooperate in the government of the empire, and should rule the nation; this would be a nobler purpose; but one doesn't now-a-days hear of the very existence of such persons! Hence, the study of books makes them worse than they ever were before. But it isn't the books that ruin them; the misfortune is that they make improper use of books! That is why study doesn't come up to ploughing and sowing and trading; as these pursuits exercise no serious pernicious influences. As far, however, as you and I go, we should devote our minds simply to matters connected with needlework and spinning; for we will then be fulfilling our legitimate duties. Yet, it so happens that we too know a few characters. But, as we can read, it behoves us to choose no other than wholesome works; for these will do us no harm! What are most to be shirked are those low books, as, when once they pervert the disposition, there remains no remedy whatever!"

While she indulged in this long rigmarole, Daiyu lowered her head and sipped her tea. And though she secretly shared the same views on the subject, all the answer she gave her in assent was limited to one single word "yes." But at an unexpected moment, Suyun appeared in the room. "Our lady Lian," she said, "requests the presence of both of you, young ladies, to consult with you in an important matter. Miss Secunda, Miss Tertia, Miss Quarta, Miss Shi and Mr. Bao, our master Secundus, are there waiting for you."

"What's up again?" Baochai inquired.

"You and I will know what it is when we get there," Daiyu explained.

So saying, she came, with Baochai, into the Daoxiang village. Here they, in fact, discovered everyone assembled. As soon as Li Wan caught sight of the two cousins, she smiled. "The society has barely been started," she observed, "and here's one who wants to give us the slip; that girl Quarta wishes to apply for a whole year's leave."

"It's that single remark of our worthy senior's yesterday that is at the bottom of it!" Daiyu laughed. "For by bidding her execute some painting or other of the garden, she has put her in such high feather that she applies for leave!"

"Don't be so hard upon our dear ancestor!" Baochai rejoined, a smile playing on her lips. "It's entirely due to that allusion of grandmother Liu's."

Daiyu speedily took up the thread of the conversation. "Quite so!" she smiled. "It's all through that remark of hers! But of what branch of the family is she a grandmother? We should merely address her as the 'female locust,' that's all."

As she spoke, one and all were highly amused.

"When any mortal language finds its way into that girl Feng's mouth," Baochai laughed, "she knows how to turn it to the best account! What a fortunate thing it is that that vixen Feng has no idea of letters and can't boast of much culture! Her forte is simply such vulgar things as suffice to raise a laugh! Worse than her is that Pin'er with that coarse tongue! She has recourse to the devices of the 'Chun Qiu!' By selecting, from the vulgar expressions used in low slang, the most noteworthy points, she eliminates what's commonplace, and makes, with the addition of a little elegance and finish, her style so much like that of the text that each sentence has a peculiar character of its own! The three words representing 'female locust' bring out clearly the various circumstances connected with yesterday! The wonder is that she has been so quick in devising them!"

After lending an ear to her arguments, they all laughed. "Those explanations of yours," they cried, "show well enough that you are not below those two!"

"Pray, let's consult as to how many days' leave to grant her!" Li Wan proposed. "I gave her a month, but she thinks it too little. What do you say about it?"

"Properly speaking," Daiyu put in, "one year isn't much! The laying out of this garden occupied a whole year; and to paint a picture of it now will certainly need two years' time. She'll have to rub the ink, to moisten the brushes, to stretch the paper, to mix the pigments, and to…"

When she had reached this point, even Daiyu could not restrain herself from laughing. "If she goes on so leisurely to work," she exclaimed, "won't she require two years' time?"

Those, who caught this insinuation, clapped their hands and indulged in incessant merriment.

"Her innuendoes are full of zest!" Baochai ventured laughingly. "But what takes the cake is that last remark about leisurely going to work, for if she weren't to paint at all, how could she ever finish her task? Hence those jokes cracked yesterday were, sufficient, of course, to evoke laughter, but, on second thought, they're devoid of any fun! Just you carefully ponder over Pin'er's words! Albeit they don't amount to much, you'll nevertheless find, when you come to reflect on them, that there's plenty of gusto about them. I've really had such a laugh over them that I can scarcely move!

"It's the way that cousin Baochai puffs her up," Xichun observed "that makes her so much the more arrogant that she turns me also into a laughing-stock now!"

Daiyu hastily smiled and pulled her towards her. "Let me ask you," she said, "are you only going to paint the garden, or will you insert us in it as well?"

"My original idea was to have simply painted the garden," Xichun explained; "but our worthy senior told me again yesterday that a mere picture of the grounds would resemble the plan of a house, and recommended that I should introduce some inmates too so as to make it look like what a painting should. I've neither the knack for the fine work necessary for towers and terraces, nor have I the skill to draw representations of human beings; but as I couldn't very well raise any objections, I find myself at present on the horns of a dilemma about it!"

"Human beings are an easy matter!" Daiyu said. "What beats you are insects."

"Here you are again with your trash!" Li Wan exclaimed. "Will there be any need to also introduce insects in it? As far, however, as birds go, it may probably be advisable to introduce one or two kinds!"

"If any other insects are not put in the picture," Daiyu smiled, "it won't matter; but without yesterday's female locust in it, it will fall short of the original!"

This retort evoked further general amusement. While Daiyu laughed, she beat her chest with both hands. "Begin painting at once!" she cried. "I've even got the title all ready. The name I've chosen is, 'Picture of a locust brought in to have a good feed.'"

At these words, they laughed so much the more heartily that at a time they bent forward, and at another they leant back. But a sound of "gu dong" then fell on their ears, and unable to make out what could have dropped, they anxiously and precipitately looked about. It was, they found, Shi Xiangyun, who had been reclining on the back of the chair. The chair had, from the very outset, not been put in a sure place, and while indulging in hearty merriment she threw her whole weight on the back. She did not, besides, notice that the dovetails on each side had come out, so with a tilt towards the east, she as well as the chair toppled over in a heap. Luckily, the wooden partition-wall was close enough to arrest her fall, and she did not sprawl on the ground. The sight of her created more amusement than ever among all her relatives; so much so, that they could scarcely regain their equilibrium. It was only after

Baoyu had rushed up to her, and given her a hand and raised her to her feet again that they at last managed to gradually stop laughing.

Baoyu then winked at Daiyu. Daiyu grasped his meaning, and, forthwith withdrawing into the inner room, she lifted the cover of the mirror, and looked at her face. She found the hair about her temples slightly dishevelled, so, promptly opening Li Wan's toiletcase, and extracting a narrow brush, she stood in front of the mirror, and smoothed it down with a few touches. Afterwards, laying the brush in its place she stepped into the outer suite. "Is this," she said pointing at Li Wan, "doing what you're told and showing us how to do needlework and teaching us manners? Why, instead of that, you press us to come here and have a good romp and a hearty laugh!"

"Just you listen to her perverse talk," Li Wan laughed. "She takes the lead and kicks up a rumpus, and incites people to laugh, and then she throws the blame upon me! In real truth, she's a despicable thing! What I wish is that you should soon get some dreadful mother-in-law, and several crotchety and abominable older and younger sisters-in-law, and we'll see then whether you'll still be as perverse or not!"

Daiyu at once became quite scarlet in the face, and pulling Baochai, "Let us," she added, "give her a whole year's leave!"

"I've got an impartial remark to make. Listen to me all of you!" Baochai chimed in. "Albeit the girl, Ou, may have some idea about painting, all she can manage are just a few outline sketches, so that unless, now that she has to accomplish the picture of this garden, she can lay a claim to some ingenuity, will she ever be able to succeed in effecting a painting? This garden resembles a regular picture. The rockeries and trees, towers and pavilions, halls and houses are, as far as distances and density go, neither too numerous, nor too few. Such as it is, it is fitly laid out; but were you to put it on paper in strict compliance with the original, why, it will surely not elicit admiration. In a thing like this, it's necessary to pay due care to the various positions and distances on paper, whether they should be large or whether small; and to discriminate between main and secondary; adding what is needful to add, concealing and reducing what should be concealed and reduced, and exposing to view what should remain visible. As soon as a rough copy is executed, it should again be considered in all its details, for then alone will it assume the semblance of a picture. In the second place, all these towers, terraces and structures must be distinctly delineated; for with just a trifle of inattention, the railings will slant, the pillars will be topsy-turvy, doors and windows will recline in a horizontal position, steps will separate, leaving clefts between them, and even tables will be crowded into the walls, and flower-pots piled on portieres; and won't it, instead of turning out into a picture, be a mere caricature? Thirdly, proper care must also be devoted, in the insertion of human beings, to density and height, to the creases of clothing, to jupes and sashes, to fingers, hands, and feet, as these are most important details; for if even one stroke be not thoroughly executed, then, if the hands be not swollen, the feet will be made to look as if they were lame. The coloring of faces and the drawing of the hair are minor points; but, in my own estimation, they really involve intense difficulty. Now a year's leave is, on one hand, too excessive, and a month's is, on the other, too little; so just give her half a year's leave. Depute, besides, cousin Baoyu to lend her a hand in her task. Not that cousin Bao knows how to give any hints about painting; that in itself would be more of a drawback; but in order that, in the event of there being anything that she doesn't comprehend, or of anything perplexing her as to how best to insert it, cousin Bao may take the picture outside and make the necessary inquiries of those gentlemen who excel in painting. Matters will thus be facilitated for her."

At this suggestion Baoyu was the first to feel quite enchanted. "This proposal is first-rate!" he exclaimed. "The towers and terraces minutely executed by Zhan Ziliang are so perfect, and the beauties painted by Cheng Rixing so extremely fine that I'll go at once and ask them of them!"

"I've always said that you fuss for nothing!" Baochai interposed. "I merely passed a cursory remark, and there you want to go immediately and ask for things. Do wait until we arrive at some decision in our deliberations, and then you can go! But let's consider now what would be best to use to paint the picture on?"

"I've got, in my quarters," Baoyu answered, "some snow-white, wavy paper, which is both large in size, and proof against ink as well."

Baochai gave a sarcastic smile. "I do maintain," she cried, "that you are a perfectly useless creature! That snow-white, wavy paper is good for pictures consisting of characters and for outline drawings. Or else, those who have the knack of making landscapes, use it for depicting scenery of the southern Sung era, as it resists ink and is strong enough to bear coarse painting. But were you to employ this sort of paper to make a picture of this garden on, it will neither stand the colors, nor will it be easy to dry the painting by the fire. So not only won't it be suitable, but it will be a pity too to waste the paper. I'll tell you a way how to get out of this. When this garden was first laid out, some detailed plan was used, which although executed by a mere house-decorator, was perfect with regard to sites and bearings. You'd better therefore ask for it of your worthy mother, and apply as well to lady Feng for a piece of thick glazed lustring of the size of that paper, and hand them to the gentlemen outside, and request them to prepare a rough copy for you, with any alterations or additions as might be necessary to make so as to accord with the style of these grounds. All that will remain to be done will be to introduce a few human beings; no more. Then when you have to match the azure and green pigments as well as the ground gold and ground silver, you can get those people again to do so for you. But you'll also have to bring an extra portable stove, so as to have it handy for melting the glue, and for washing your brushes, after you've taken the glue off. You further require a large table, painted white and covered with a cloth. That lot of small dishes you have aren't sufficient; your brushes too are not enough. It will be well consequently for you to purchase a new set of each."

"Do I own such a lot of painting materials!" Xichun exclaimed. "Why, I simply use any brush that first comes under my hand to paint with; that's all. And as for pigments, I've only got four kinds, ochrey stone, 'Guang' flower paint, rattan yellow, and rouge. Besides these, all I have amount to a couple of brushes for applying colors; no more."

"Why didn't you say so earlier?" Baochai remarked. "I've still got some of these things remaining. But you don't need them, so were I to give you any, they'd lie uselessly about. I'll put them away for you now for a time, and, when you want them, I'll let you have some. You should, however, keep them for the exclusive purpose of painting fans; for were you to paint such big things with them it would be a pity! I'll draw out a list for you today to enable you to go and apply to our worthy senior for the items; as it isn't likely that you people can possibly know all that's required. I'll dictate them, and cousin Bao can write them down!"

Baoyu had already got a brush and inkslab ready, for, fearing lest he might not remember clearly the various necessaries, he had made up his mind to write a memorandum of them; so the moment he heard Baochai's suggestion, he cheerfully took up his brush, and listened quietly.

"Four brushes of the largest size," Baochai commenced, "four of the third size; four of the second size; four brushes for applying colors on big ground; four on medium ground; four for small ground; ten claws of large southern crabs; ten claws of small crabs; ten brushes for painting side-hair and eyebrows; twenty for laying heavy colors; twenty for light colors; ten for painting faces; twenty willow-twigs; four ounces of 'arrow head' pearls; four ounces of southern ochre; four ounces of stone yellow; four ounces of dark green; four ounces of malachite; four ounces of tube-yellow; eight ounces of 'Guang' flower; four boxes of lead powder; ten sheets of rouge; two hundred sheets of thin red-gold leaves; two hundred sheets of lead; four ounces of smooth glue, from the two Guang; and four ounces of pure alum. The glue and alum for sizing the lustring are not included, so don't bother yourselves about them, but just take the lustring and give it to them outside to size it with alum for you. You and I can scour and clarify all these pigments, and thus amuse ourselves, and prepare them for use as well. I feel sure you'll have an ample supply to last you a whole lifetime. But you must also get ready four sieves of fine lustring; a pair of coarse ones; four brush-brushes; four bowls, some large, some small; twenty large, coarse saucers; ten five-inch plates; twenty three-inch coarse, white plates; two stoves; four large and small earthenware pans; two new porcelain jars; four new water buckets; four one-foot-long bags, made of white cloth; two catties of light charcoal; one or two catties of willow-wood charcoal; a wooden box with three drawers; a yard of thick gauze, two ounces of fresh ginger; half a catty of soy..."

"An iron kettle and an iron shovel," hastily chimed in Daiyu with a smile full of irony.

"To do what with them?" Baochai inquired.

"You ask for fresh ginger, soy, and all these condiments, so I indent for an iron kettle for you to cook the paints and eat them." Daiyu answered, to the intense merriment of one and all, who gave way to laughter.

"What do you, Pin'er, know about these things?" Baochai laughed. "I am not certain in my mind that you won't put those coarse colored plates straightway on the fire. But unless you take the precaution beforehand of rubbing the bottom with ginger juice, mixed with soy, and of warming them dry, they're bound to crack, the moment they experience the least heat."

"It's really so," they exclaimed with one voice, after this explanation.

Daiyu perused the list for a while. She then smiled and gave Tanchun a tug. "Just see," she whispered, "we want to paint a picture, and she goes on indenting for a number of water jars and boxes! But, I presume, she's got so muddled, that she inserts a list of articles needed for her trousseau."

Tanchun, at her remark, laughed with such heartiness, that it was all she could do to check herself. "Cousin Bao," she observed, "don't you wring her mouth? Just ask her what disparaging things she said about you."

"Why need I ask?" Baochai smiled. "Is it likely, pray, that you can get ivory out of a cur's mouth?"

Speaking the while, she drew near, and, seizing Daiyu, she pressed her down on the stove-couch with the intention of pinching her face. Daiyu smilingly hastened to implore for grace. "My dear cousin," she cried, "spare me! Pin'er is young in years; all she knows is to talk at random; she has no idea of what's proper and what's improper. But you are my elder cousin, so teach me how to behave. If you, cousin, don't let me off, to whom can I go and address my entreaties?"

Little did, however, all who heard her apprehend that there lurked some hidden purpose in her insinuations. "She's right there," they consequently pleaded smilingly. "So much is she to be pitied that even we have been mollified; do spare her and finish!"

Baochai had, at first, meant to play with her, but when she unawares heard her drag in again the advice she had tendered her the other day, with regard to the reckless perusal of unwholesome books, she at once felt as if she could not have any farther fuss with her, and she let her rise to her feet.

"It's you, after all, elder cousin," Daiyu laughed. "Had it been I, I wouldn't have let anyone off."

Baochai smiled and pointed at her. "It is no wonder," she said, "that our dear ancestor doats on you and that everyone loves you. Even I have today felt my heart warm towards you! But come here and let me put your hair up for you!"

Daiyu then, in very deed, swung herself round and crossed over to her. Baochai arranged her coiffure with her hands. Baoyu, who stood by and looked on, thought the style, in which her hair was being made up, better than it was before. But, of a sudden, he felt sorry at what had happened, as he fancied that she should not have let her brush her side hair, but left it alone for the time being and asked him to do it for her. While, however, he gave way to these erratic thoughts, he heard Baochai speak. "We've done with what there was to write," she said, "so you'd better tomorrow go and tell grandmother about the things. If there be any at home, well and good; but if not, get some money to buy them with. I'll then help you both in your preparations."

Baoyu vehemently put the list away; after which, they all joined in a further chat on irrelevant matters; and, their evening meal over, they once more repaired into old lady Jia's apartments to wish her goodnight. Their grandmother had, indeed, had nothing serious the matter with her. Her ailment had amounted mainly to fatigue, to which a slight chill had been super-added, so that having kept in the warm room for the day and taken a dose or two of medicine, she entirely got over the effects, and felt, in the evening, quite like own self again.

But, reader, the occurrences of the next day are as yet a mystery to you, but the nest chapter will divulge them.

CHAPTER 43

Having time to amuse themselves,
the Jia inmates raise, when least expected,
funds to celebrate lady Feng's birthday.
In his ceaseless affection for Jinchuan,
Baoyu uses, for the occasion, a pinch
of earth as incense and burns it.

When Madame Wang saw, for we will now proceed with our narrative, that the extent of dowager lady Jia's indisposition, contracted on the day she had been into the garden of Broad Vista, amounted to a simple chill, that no serious ailment had supervened, and that her health had improved soon after the doctor had been sent for and she had taken a couple of doses of medicine, she called lady Feng to her and asked her to get ready a present of some kind for her to take to her husband, Jia Zheng. But while they were engaged in deliberation, they perceived a waiting-maid arrive. She came from their old senior's part to invite them to go to her. So, with speedy step, Madame Wang led the way for lady Feng, and they came over into her quarters.

"Pray, may I ask," Madame Wang then inquired, "whether you're feeling nearly well again now?"

"I'm quite all right today," old lady Jia replied. "I've tasted the young-pheasant soup you sent me a little time back and find it full of relish. I've also had two pieces of meat, so I feel quite comfortable within me."

"These dainties were presented to you, dear ancestor, by that girl Feng," Madame Wang smiled. "It only shows how sincere her filial piety is. She does not render futile the love, which you, venerable senior, ever lavish on her."

Dowager lady Jia nodded her head assentingly. "She's too kind to think of me!" she answered smiling. "But should there be any more uncooked, let them fry a couple of pieces; and, if these be thoroughly immersed in wine, the congee will taste well with them. The soup is, it's true, good, but it shouldn't, properly speaking, be prepared with fine rice."

After listening to her wishes, lady Feng expressed with alacrity her readiness to see them executed, and directed a servant to go and deliver the message in the cook-house.

"I sent the servant for you," dowager lady Jia meanwhile said to Madame Wang with a smile, "not for anything else, but for the birthday of that girl Feng, which falls on the second. I had made up my mind two years ago to celebrate her birthday in proper style, but when the time came, there happened to be again something important to attend to, and it went by without anything being done. But this year, the inmates are, on one hand, all here, and there won't, I fancy, be, on the other, anything to prevent us, so we should all do our best to enjoy ourselves thoroughly for a day."

"I was thinking the same thing," Madame Wang rejoined, laughingly, "and, since it's your good pleasure, venerable senior, why shouldn't we deliberate at once and decide upon something?"

"To the best of my recollection," dowager lady Jia resumed smiling, "whenever in past years I've had any birthday celebrations for anyone of us, no matter who it was, we have ever individually sent our respective presents; but this method is common and is also apt, I think, to look very much as if there were some disunion. But I'll now devise a new way; a way, which won't have the effect of creating any discord, and will be productive of good cheer."

"Let whatever way you may think best, dear ancestor, be adopted." Madame Wang eagerly rejoined.

"My idea is," old lady Jia laughingly continued, "that we too should follow the example of those poor families and raise a subscription among ourselves, and devote the whole of whatever we may collect to meet the outlay for the necessary preparations. What do you say, will this do or not?"

"This is a splendid idea!" Madame Wang acquiesced. "But what will, I wonder, be the way adopted for raising contributions?"

Old lady Jia was the more inspirited by her reply. There and then she despatched servants to go and invite Mrs. Xue, Madame Xing and the rest of the ladies, and bade others summon the young ladies and Baoyu. But from the other mansion, Jia Zhen's spouse, Lai Da's wife, even up to the wives of such stewards as enjoyed a certain amount of respectability, were likewise to be asked to come round.

The sight of their old mistress' delight filled the waiting-maids and married women with high glee as well; and each hurried with vehemence to execute her respective errand. Those that were to be invited were invited, and those that had to be sent for were sent for; and, before the lapse of such time as could suffice to have a meal in, the old as well as young, the high as well as low, crammed, in a black mass, every bit of the available space in the rooms.

Only Mrs. Xue and dowager lady Jia sat opposite to each other. Mesdames Xing and Wang simply seated themselves on two chairs, which faced the door of the apartment. Baochai and her five or six cousins occupied the stove-couch. Baoyu sat on his grandmother's lap. Below, the whole extent of the floor was crowded with inmates on their feet. But old lady Jia forthwith desired that a few small stools should be fetched. When brought, these were proffered to Lai Da's mother and some other nurses, who were advanced in years and held in respect; for it was the custom in the Jia mansion that the family servants, who had waited upon any of the fathers or mothers, should enjoy a higher status than even young masters and mistresses. Hence it was that while Mrs. You, lady Feng, and other ladies remained standing below, Lai Da's mother and three or four other old nurses had, after excusing themselves for their rudeness, seated themselves on small stools.

Dowager lady Jia recounted, with a face beaming with smiles, the suggestions she had shortly made, for the benefit of the various inmates present; and one and all, of course, were only too ready to contribute for the entertainment. More, some of them, were on friendly terms with lady Feng, so they, of their own free will, adopted the proposal; others lived in fear and trembling of lady Feng, and these were only too anxious to make up to her. Everyone, besides, could well afford the means, so that, as soon as they heard of the proposed subscriptions, they, with one consent, signified their acquiescence.

"I'll give twenty taels!" old lady Jia was the first to say with a smile playing round her lips.

"I'll follow your lead, dear senior," Mrs. Xue smiled, "and also subscribe twenty taels."

"We don't presume to place ourselves on an equal footing with your ladyship," Mesdames Xing and Wang pleaded. "We, of course, come one degree lower; each of us therefore will contribute sixteen taels."

"We too naturally rank one step lower," Mrs. You and Li Wan also smiled, "so we'll each give twelve taels."

"You're a widow," dowager lady Jia eagerly demurred, addressing herself to Li Wan, "and have lost all your estate, so how could we drag you into all this outlay! I'll contribute for you!"

"Don't be in such high feather, dear senior," lady Feng hastily observed laughing, "but just look to your accounts before you saddle yourself with this burden! You've already taken upon yourself two portions; and do you now also volunteer sixteen taels on behalf of my elder sister-in-law? You may willingly do so, while you speak in the abundance of your spirits, but when you, by and bye, come to ponder over what you've done, you'll feel sore at heart again! 'It's all that girl Feng that's driven me to spend the money,' you'll say in a little time; and you'll devise some ingenious way to inveigle me to fork out three or four times as much as your share and thus make up your deficit in an underhand way; while I will still be as much in the clouds as if I were in a dream!"

These words made everyone laugh.

"According to you, what should be done?" dowager lady Jia laughingly inquired.

"My birthday hasn't yet come," lady Feng smiled; "and already now I've been the recipient of so much more than I deserve that I am quite unhappy. But if I don't contribute a single cash, I shall feel really ill at ease for the trouble I shall be giving such a lot of people. It would be as well, therefore, that I should bear this share of my senior sister-in-law; and, when the day comes, I can eat a few more things, and thus be able to enjoy some happiness."

"Quite right!" cried Madame Xing and the others at this suggestion. So old lady Jia then signified her approval.

There's something more I'd like to add," lady Feng pursued smiling. "I think that it's fair enough that you, worthy ancestor, should, besides your own twenty taels, have to stand two shares as well, the one for cousin Liu, the other for cousin Baoyu, and that Mrs. Xue should, beyond her own twenty taels, likewise bear cousin Baochai's portion. But it's somewhat unfair that the two ladies Mesdames Xing and Wang should each only give sixteen taels, when their share is small, and when they don't subscribe anything for anyone else. It's you, venerable senior, who'll be the sufferer by this arrangement."

Dowager lady Jia, at these words, burst out into a boisterous fit of laughter. "It's this hussey Feng," she observed, "who, after all, takes my side! What you say is quite right. Hadn't it been for you, I would again have been duped by them!"

"Dear senior!" lady Feng smiled. Just hand over our two cousins to those two ladies and let each take one under her charge and finish. If you make each contribute one share, it will be square enough."

"This is perfectly fair," eagerly rejoined old lady Jia. "Let this suggestion be carried out!"

Lai Da's mother hastily stood up. "This is such a subversion of right," she smiled, "that I'll put my back up on account of the two ladies. She's a son's wife, on the other side, and, in here, only a wife's brother's child; and yet she doesn't incline towards her mother-inlaw and her aunt, but takes other people's part. This son's wife has therefore become a perfect stranger; and a close niece has, in fact, become a distant niece!"

As she said this, dowager lady Jia and everyone present began to laugh. "If the junior ladies subscribe twelve taels each," Lai Da's mother went on to ask, "we must, as a matter of course, also come one degree lower, eh?"

Upon hearing this, old lady Jia remonstrated. "This won't do!" she observed. "You naturally should rank one degree lower, but you're all, I am well aware, wealthy people; and, in spite of your status being somewhat lower, your funds are more flourishing than theirs. It's only just then that you should be placed on the same standing as those people!"

The posse of nurses expressed with promptness their acceptance of the proposal their old mistress made.

"The young ladies," dowager lady Jia resumed, "should merely give something for the sake of appearances! If each one contributes a sum proportionate to her monthly allowance, it will be ample!" Turning her head, "Yuanyang!" she cried, "a few of you should assemble in like manner, and consult as to what share you should take in the matter. So bring them along!"

Yuanyang assured her that her desires would be duly attended to and walked away. But she had not been absent for any length of time, when she appeared on the scene along with Ping'er, Xiren, Caixia, and other girls, and a number of waiting-maids as well. Of these, some subscribed two taels; others contributed one tael.

"Can it be," dowager lady Jia then said to Ping'er, "that you don't want any birthday celebrated for your mistress, that you don't range yourself also among them?"

"The other money I gave," Ping'er smiled, "I gave privately, and is extra. This is what I am publicly bound to contribute along with the lot."

"That's a good child!" lady Jia laughingly rejoined.

"Those above as well as those below have all alike given their share," lady Feng went on to observe with a smile. "But there are still those two secondary wives; are they to give anything or not? Do go and ask them! It's but right that we should go to the extreme length and include them. Otherwise, they'll imagine that we've looked down upon them!"

"Just so!" eagerly answered lady Jia, at these words. "How is it that we forgot all about them? The only thing is, I fear, they've got no time to spare; yet, tell a servant-girl to go and ask them what they'll do!"

While she spoke, a servant-girl went off. After a long absence, she returned. "Each of them," she reported, "will likewise contribute two taels."

Dowager lady Jia was delighted with the result. "Fetch a brush and inkslab," she cried, "and let's calculate how much they amount to, all together."

Mrs. You abused lady Feng in a low tone of voice. "I'll take you, you mean covetous creature, and ...! All these mothers-in-law and sisters-in-law have come forward and raised money to celebrate your birthday, and are you yet not satisfied that you must also drag in those two miserable beings! But what do you do it for?"

"Try and talk less trash!" lady Feng smiled; also in an undertone. "We'll be leaving this place in a little time and then I'll square up accounts with you! But why ever are those two miserable? When they have money, they uselessly give it to other people; and isn't it better that we should get hold of it, and enjoy ourselves with it?"

While she uttered these taunts, they computed that the collections would reach a sum over and above one hundred and fifty taels.

"We couldn't possibly run through all this for a day's theatricals and banquet!" old lady Jia exclaimed.

"As no outside guests are to be invited," Mrs. You interposed, "and the number of tables won't also be many, there will be enough to cover two or three days' outlay! First of all, there won't be anything to spend for theatricals, so we'll effect a saving on that item."

"Just call whatever troupe that girl Feng may say she likes best," dowager lady Jia suggested.

"We've heard quite enough of the performances of that company of ours," lady Feng said; "let's therefore spend a little money and send for another, and see what they can do."

"I leave that to you, brother Zhen's wife," old lady Jia pursued, "in order that our girl Feng should have occasion to trouble her mind with as little as possible, and be able to enjoy a day's peace and quiet. It's only right that she should."

Mrs. You replied that she would be only too glad to do what she could. They then prolonged their chat for a little longer, until one and all realised that their old senior must be quite fagged out, and they gradually dispersed.

After seeing Mesdames Xing and Wang off, Mrs. You and the other ladies adjourned into lady Feng's rooms to consult with her about the birthday festivities.

"Don't ask me!" lady Feng urged. "Do whatever will please our worthy ancestor."

"What a fine thing you are to come across such a mighty piece of luck!" Mrs. You smiled. "I was wondering what had happened that she summoned us all! Why, was it simply on this account? Not to breathe a word about the money that I'll have to contribute, must I have trouble and annoyance to bear as well? How will you show me any thanks?"

"Don't bring shame upon yourself!" lady Feng laughed. "I didn't send for you; so why should I be thankful to you! If you funk the exertion, go at once and let our venerable senior know, and she'll depute someone else and have done."

"You go on like this as you see her in such excellent spirits, that's why!" Mrs. You smilingly answered. "It would be well, I advise you, to pull in a bit; for if you be too full of yourself, you'll get your due reward!"

After some further colloquy, these two ladies eventually parted company.

On the next day, the money was sent over to the Ning Guo Mansion at the very moment that Mrs. You had got up, and was performing her toilette and ablutions. "Who brought it?" she asked.

"Nurse Lin," the servant-girl said by way of response.

"Call her in," Mrs. You said.

The servant-girls walked as far as the lower rooms and called Lin Zixiao's wife to come in. Mrs. You bade her seat herself on the footstool. While she hurriedly combed her hair and washed her face and hands, she wanted to know how much the bundle contained in all.

"This is what's subscribed by us servants. " Lin Zixiao's wife replied, "and so I collected it and brought it over first. As for the contributions of our venerable mistress, and those of the ladies, they aren't ready yet."

But simultaneously with this reply, the waiting-maids announced: "Our lady of the other mansion and Mrs. Xue have sent over someone with their portions."

"You mean wenches!" Mrs. You cried, scolding them with a smile. "All the gumption you've got is to simply bear in mind this sort of nonsense! In a fit of good cheer, your old mistress yesterday purposely expressed a wish to imitate those poor people, and raise a subscription. But you at once treasured it up in your memory, and, when the thing came to be canvassed by you, you treated it in real earnest! Don't you yet quick bundle yourselves out, and bring the money in! Be careful and give them some tea before you see them off."

The waiting-maids smilingly hastened to go and take delivery of the money and bring it in. It consisted, in all, of two bundles, and contained Baochai's and Daiyu's shares as well.

"Whose shares are wanting?" Mrs. You asked.

"Those of our old lady, of Madame Wang, the young ladies, and of our girls below are still missing," Lin Zixiao's wife explained.

"There's also that of your senior lady," Mrs. You proceeded.

"You'd better hurry over, my lady," Lin Zixiao's wife said; "for as this money will be issued through our mistress Secunda, she'll nobble the whole of it."

While conversing, Mrs. You finished arranging her coiffure and performing her ablutions; and, giving orders to see that the carriage was got ready, she shortly arrived at the Rong mansion. First and foremost she called on lady Feng. Lady Feng, she discovered, had already put the money into a packet, and was on the point of sending it over.

"Is it all there?" Mrs. You asked.

"Yes, it is," lady Feng smiled, "so you might as well take it away at once; for if it gets mislaid, I've nothing to do with it."

"I'm somewhat distrustful," Mrs. You laughed, "so I'd like to check it in your presence."

These words over, she verily checked sum after sum. She found Li Wan's share alone wanting. "I said that you were up to tricks!" laughingly observed Mrs. You. "How is it that your elder sister-in-law's isn't here?"

"There's all that money; and isn't it yet enough?" lady Feng smiled. "If there's merely a portion short it shouldn't matter! Should the money prove insufficient, I can then look you up, and give it to you."

"When the others were present yesterday," Mrs. You pursued, "you were ready enough to act as any human being would; but here you're again today prevaricating with me! I won't, by any manner of means, agree to this proposal of yours! I'll simply go and ask for the money of our venerable senior."

"I see how dreadful you are!" lady Feng laughed. "But when something turns up by and bye, I'll also be very punctilious; so don't you then bear me a grudge!"

"Well, never mind if you don't give your quota!" Mrs. You smilingly rejoined. "Were it not that I consider the dutiful attentions you've all along shown me would I ever be ready to humor you?"

So rejoining, she produced Ping'er's share. "Ping'er, come here," she cried, "take this share of yours and put it away! Should the money collected turn out to be below what's absolutely required, I'll make up the sum for you."

Ping'er apprehended her meaning. "My lady," she answered, with a cheerful countenance, "it would come to the same thing if you were to first spend what you want and to give me afterwards any balance that may remain of it."

"Is your mistress alone to be allowed to do dishonest acts," Mrs. You laughed, "and am I not to be free to bestow a favor?"

Ping'er had no option, but to retain her portion.

"I want to see," Mrs. You added, "where your mistress, who is so extremely careful, will run through all the money, we've raised! If she can't spend it, why she'll take it along with her in her coffin, and make use of it there."

While still speaking, she started on her way to dowager lady Jia's suite of rooms. After first paying her respects to her, she made a few general remarks, and then betook herself into Yuanyang's quarters where she held a consultation with Yuanyang. Lending a patient ear to all that Yuanyang had to recommend in the way of a programme, and as to how best to give pleasure to old lady Jia, she deliberated with her until they arrived at a satisfactory decision. When the time came for Mrs. You to go, she took the two taels, contributed by Yuanyang, and gave them back to her. "There's no use for these!" she said, and with these words still on her lips, she straightway quitted her presence and went in search of Madame Wang. After a short chat, Madame Wang stepped into the family shrine reserved for the worship of Buddha, so she likewise restored Caiyun's share to her; and, availing herself of lady Feng's absence, she presently reimbursed to Mrs. Zhu and Mrs. Zhao the amount of their respective contributions.

These two dames would not however presume to take their money back. "Your lot, ladies, is a pitiful one!" Mrs. You then expostulated. "How can you afford all this spare money! That hussey Feng is well aware of the fact. I'm here to answer for you!"

At these assurances, both put the money away, with profuse expressions of gratitude.

In a twinkle, the second day of the ninth moon arrived. The inmates of the garden came to find out that Mrs. You was making preparations on an extremely grand scale; for not only was there to be a theatrical performance, but jugglers and women storytellers as well; and they combined in getting everything ready that could conduce to afford amusement and enjoyment.

"This is," Li Wan went on to say to the young ladies, "the proper day for our literary gathering, so don't forget it. If Baoyu hasn't appeared, it must, I presume, be that his mind is so preoccupied with the fuss that's going on that he has lost sight of all pure and refined things."

Speaking, "Go and see what he is up to!" she enjoined a waiting-maid; "and be quick and tell him to come."

The waiting-maid returned after a long absence. "Sister Hua says," she reported, "that he went out of doors, soon after daylight this morning."

The result of the inquiries filled everyone with surprise. "He can't have gone out!" they said. "This girl is stupid, and doesn't know how to speak." They consequently also directed Cuimo to go and ascertain the truth. In a little time, Cuimo returned. "It's really true," she explained, "that he has gone out of doors. He gave out that a friend of his was dead, and that he was going to pay a visit of condolence."

"There's certainly nothing of the kind," Tanchun interposed. "But whatever there might have been to call him away, it wasn't right of him to go out on an occasion like the present one! Just call Xiren here, and let me ask her!"

But just as she was issuing these directions, she perceived Xiren appear on the scene. "No matter what he may have had to attend to today," Li Wan and the rest remarked, "he shouldn't have gone out! In the first place, it's your mistress Secunda's birthday, and our dowager lady is in such buoyant spirits that the various inmates, whether high or low, are coming from either mansion to join in the fun; and lo, he goes off! Secondly, this is the proper day as well for holding our first literary gathering, and he doesn't so as apply for leave, but stealthily sneaks away."

Xiren heaved it sigh. "He said last night," she explained, "that he had something very important to do this morning; that he was going as far as Prince Beijing's mansion, but that he would hurry back. I advised him not to go; but, of course, he wouldn't listen to me. When he got out of bed, at daybreak this morning, he asked for his plain clothes and put them on, so, I suppose, some lady of note belonging to the household of Prince Beijing must have departed this life; but who can tell?"

"If such be truly the case," Li Wan and her companions exclaimed, it's quite right that he should have gone over for a while; but he should have taken care to be back in time!"

This remark over, they resumed their deliberations. "Let's write our verses," they said, "and we can fine him on his return."

As these words were being spoken, they espied a messenger despatched by dowager lady Jia to ask them over, so they at once adjourned to the front part of the compound.

Xiren then reported to his grandmother what Baoyu had done. Old lady Jia was upset by the news; so much so, that she issued immediate orders to a few servants to go and fetch him.

Baoyu had, in fact, been brooding over some affair of the heart. A day in advance he therefore gave proper injunctions to Beiming. "As I shall be going out of doors tomorrow at daybreak," he said, "you'd better get ready two horses and wait at the back door! No one else need follow as an escort! Tell Li Gui that I've gone to the Bei mansion. In the event of anyone wishing to start in search of me, bid him place every obstacle in the way, as all inquiries can well be dispensed with! Let him simply explain that I've been detained in the Bei mansion, but that I shall surely be back shortly."

Beiming could not make out head or tail of what he was driving at; but he had no alternative than to deliver his message word for word. At the first blush of morning of the day appointed, he actually got ready two horses and remained in waiting at the back gate. When daylight set in, he perceived Baoyu make his appearance from the side door; got up, from head to foot, in a plain suit of clothes. Without uttering a word, he mounted his steed; and stooping his body forward, he proceeded at a quick step on his way down the road. Beiming had no help but to follow suit; and, springing on his horse, he smacked it with his whip, and overtook his master. "Where are we off to?" he eagerly inquired, from behind.

"Where does this road lead to?" Baoyu asked.

"This is the main road leading out of the northern gate." Beiming replied. "Once out of it, everything is so dull and dreary that there's nothing worth seeing!"

Baoyu caught this answer and nodded his head. "I was just thinking that a dull and dreary place would be just the thing!" he observed. While speaking, he administered his steed two more whacks. The horse quickly turned a couple of corners, and trotted out of the city gate. Beiming was more and more at a loss what to think of the whole affair; yet his only course was to keep pace closely in his master's track. With one gallop, they covered a distance of over seven or eight lis. But it was only when human habitations became gradually few and far between that Baoyu ultimately drew up his horse. Turning his head round: "Is there any place here," he asked, "where incense is sold?"

"Incense!" Beiming shouted, "yes, there is; but what kind of incense it is I don't know."

"All other incense is worth nothing," Baoyu resumed, after a moment's reflection. "We should get sandalwood, conifer, and cedar, these three."

"These three sorts are very difficult to get," Beiming smiled.

Baoyu was driven to his wits' ends. But Beiming noticing his dilemma, "What do you want incense for?" he felt impelled to ask. "Master Secundus, I've often seen you wear a small purse, about your person, full of tiny pieces of incense; and why don't you see whether you've got it with you?"

This allusion was sufficient to suggest the idea to Baoyu's mind. Forthwith, he drew back his hand and felt the purse suspended on the lapel of his coat. It really contained two bits of "Chen Su." At this discovery, his heart expanded with delight. The only thing that (damped his spirits) was the notion that there was a certain want of reverence in his proceedings; but, on second consideration, he concluded that what he had about him was, after all, considerably superior to any he could purchase, and, with alacrity, he went on to inquire about a censer and charcoal.

"Don't think of such things!" Beiming urged. "Where could they be procured in a deserted and lonely place like this? If you needed them, why didn't you speak somewhat sooner, and we could have brought them along with us? Would not this have been more convenient?"

"You stupid thing!" exclaimed Baoyu. "Had we been able to bring them along, we wouldn't have had to run in this way as if for life!"

Beiming indulged in a protracted reverie, after which, he gave a smile. "I've thought of something," he cried, "but I wonder what you'll think about it, Master Secundus! You don't, I expect, only require these things; you'll need others too, I presume. But this isn't the place for them; so let's move on at once another couple of lis, when we'll get to the 'Water Spirit' monastery."

"Is the 'Water Spirit' monastery in this neighborhood?" Baoyu eagerly inquired, upon hearing his proposal. "Yes, that would be better; let's press forward."

With this reply, he touched his horse with his whip. While advancing on their way, he turned round. "The nun in this 'Water Spirit' monastery," he shouted to Beiming, "frequently comes on a visit to our house, so that when we now get there and ask her for the loan of a censer, she's certain to let us have it."

"Not to mention that that's a place where our family burns incense," Beiming answered, "she could not dare to raise any objections, to any appeal from us for a loan, were she even in a temple quite unknown to us. There's only one thing, I've often been struck with the strong dislike you have for this 'Water Spirit' monastery, master, and how is that you're now so delighted with the idea of going to it?

"I've all along had the keenest contempt for those low-bred persons," Baoyu rejoined, "who, without knowing why or wherefore, foolishly offer sacrifices to the spirits, and needlessly have temples erected. The reason of it all is that those rich old gentlemen and unsophisticated wealthy women, who lived in past days, were only too ready, the moment they heard of the presence of a spirit anywhere, to take in hand the erection of temples to offer their sacrifices in, without even having the faintest notion whose spirits they were. This was because they readily credited as gospel-truth such rustic stories and idle tales as chanced to reach their ears. Take this place as an example. Offerings are presented in this 'Water Spirit' nunnery to the spirit of the 'Luo' stream; hence the name of 'Water Spirit' monastery has been given to it. But people really don't know that in past days, there was no such thing as a 'Luo' spirit! These are, indeed, no better than legendary yarns invented by Cao Zijian, and who would have thought it, this sort of stupid people have put up images of it, to which they offer oblations. It serves, however, my purpose today, so I'll borrow of her whatever I need to use."

While engaged in talking, they reached the entrance. The old nun saw Baoyu arrive, and was thoroughly taken aback. So far was this visit beyond her expectations, that well did it seem to her as if a live dragon had dropped from the heavens. With alacrity, she rushed up to him; and making inquiries after his health, she gave orders to an old Daoist to come and take his horse.

Baoyu stepped into the temple. But without paying the least homage to the image of the "Luo" spirit, he simply kept his eyes fixed intently on it; for albeit made of clay, it actually seemed, nevertheless, to flutter as does a terror-stricken swan, and to wriggle as a dragon in motion. It looked like a lotus, peeping its head out of the green stream, or like the sun, pouring its rays upon the russet clouds in the early morn. Baoyu's tears unwittingly trickled down his cheeks.

The old nun presented tea. Baoyu then asked her for the loan of a censer to burn incense in. After a protracted absence, the old nun returned with some incense as well as several paper horses, which she had got ready for him to offer. But Baoyu would not use any of the things she brought. "Take the censer," he said to Beiming, "and go out into the back garden and find a clean spot!"

But having been unable to discover one, "What about, the platform round that well?" Beiming inquired.

Baoyu nodded his head assentingly. Then along with him, he repaired to the platform of the well. He deposited the censer on the ground, while Beiming stood on one side. Baoyu produced the incense, and threw it on the fire. With suppressed tears, he performed half of the ceremony, and, turning himself round, he bade Beiming clear the things away. Beiming acquiesced; but, instead of removing the things, he speedily fell on his face, and made several prostrations, as his lips uttered this prayer: "I, Beiming, have been in the service of Master Secundus for several years. Of the secrets of Mr. Secundus' heart there are none, which I have not known, save that with regard to this sacrifice today; the object of which, he has neither told me; nor have I had the presumption to ask. But thou, oh spirit! who art the recipient of these sacrificial offerings, must, I expect, unknown though thy surname and name be to me, be a most intelligent and supremely beautiful elder or younger sister, unique among mankind, without a peer

even in heaven! As my Master Secundus cannot give vent to the sentiments, which fill his heart, allow me to pray on his behalf! Should
thou possess spirituality, and holiness be thy share, do thou often come
and look up our Mr.Secundus, for persistently do his thoughts dwell
with thee! And there is no reason why thou should'st not come! But
should'st thou be in the abode of the dead, grant that our Mr. Secundus too may, in his coming existence, be transformed into a girl, so that
he may be able to amuse himself with you all! And will not this prove
a source of pleasure to both sides?"

At the close of his invocation, he again knocked his head several times
on the ground, and, eventually, rose to his feet.

Baoyu lent an ear to his utterances, but, before they had been brought
to an end, he felt it difficult to repress himself from laughing. Giving
him a kick, "Don't talk such stuff and nonsense!" he shouted. "Were
any looker-on to overhear what you say, he'd jeer at you!"

Beiming got up and put the censer away. While he walked along
with Baoyu, "I've already," he said, "told the nun that you hadn't as yet
had anything to eat, Master Secundus, and I bade her get a few things
ready for you, so you must force yourself to take something. I know
very well that a grand banquet will be spread in our mansion today,
that exceptional bustle will prevail, and that you have, on account of
this, Sir, come here to get out of the way. But as you're, after all, going
to spend a whole day in peace and quiet in here, you should try and
divert yourself as best you can. It won't, therefore, by any manner of
means do for you to have nothing to eat."

"I won't be at the theatrical performance to have any wine," Baoyu
remarked, "so what harm will there be in my having a drink here, as the
fancy takes me?"

"Quite so!" rejoined Beiming. "But there's another consideration.
You and I have run over here; but there must be some whose minds are
ill at ease. Were there no one uneasy about us, well, what would it matter if we got back into town as late as we possibly could? But if there
be any solicitous on your account, it's but right, Master Secundus, that
you should enter the city and return home. In the first place, our worthy old mistress and Madame Wang, will thus compose their minds;
and secondly, you'll observe the proper formalities, if you succeed in
doing nothing else. But even supposing that, when once you get home,
you feel no inclination to look at the plays and have anything to drink,
you can merely wait upon your father and mother, and acquit yourself
of your filial piety! Well, if it's only a matter of fulfilling this obligation, and you don't care whether our old mistress and our lady, your
mother, experience concern or not, why, the spirit itself, which has just

been the recipient of your oblations, won't feel in a happy frame of mind! You'd better therefore, master, ponder and see what you think of my words!"

"I see what you're driving at!" Baoyu smiled. "You keep before your mind the thought that you're the only servant, who has followed me as an attendant out of town, and you give way to fear that you will, on your return, have to bear the consequences. You hence have recourse to these grandiloquent arguments to shove words of counsel down my throat! I've come here now with the sole object of satisfying certain rites, and then going to partake of the banquet and be a spectator of the plays; and I never mentioned one single word about any intention on my part not to go back to town for a whole day! I've, however, already accomplished the wish I fostered in my heart, so if we hurry back to town, so as to enable everyone to set their solicitude at rest, won't the right principle be carried out to the full in one respect as well as another?"

"Yes, that would be better!" exclaimed Beiming.

Conversing the while, they wended their way into the Buddhistic hall. Here the nun had, in point of fact, got ready a table with lenten viands. Baoyu hurriedly swallowed some refreshment and so did Beiming; after which, they mounted their steeds and retraced their steps homewards, by the road they had come.

Beiming followed behind. "Master Secundus!" he kept on shouting, "be careful how you ride! That horse hasn't been ridden very much, so hold him in tight a bit."

As he urged him to be careful, they reached the interior of the city walls, and, making their entrance once more into the mansion by the back gate, they betook themselves, with all possible despatch, into the Yihong court. Xiren and the other maids were not at home. Only a few old women were there to look after the rooms. As soon as they saw him arrive, they were so filled with gratification that their eyebrows dilated and their eyes smiled. "Amituo Fo!" they said laughingly, "you've come! You've all but driven Miss Hua mad from despair! In the upper quarters, they're just seated at the feast, so be quick, Mr. Secundus, and go and join them."

At these words, Baoyu speedily divested himself of his plain clothes and put on a colored costume, reserved for festive occasions, which he hunted up with his own hands. This done, "Where are they holding the banquet?" he inquired.

"They're in the newly erected large reception pavilion," the old women responded.

Upon catching their reply, Baoyu straightway started for the reception-pavilion. From an early moment, the strains of flageolets and pipes, of song and of wind-instruments faintly fell on his ear. The moment he reached the passage on the opposite side, he discerned Yuchuan'er seated all alone under the eaves of the verandah giving way to tears. As soon as she became conscious of Baoyu's arrival, she drew a long, long breath. Smacking her lips, "Ai!" she cried, "the phoenix has alighted! go in at once! Hadn't you come for another minute, everyone would have been quite upset!"

Baoyu forced a smile. "Just try and guess where I've been?" he observed.

Yuchuan'er twisted herself round, and, paying no notice to him, she continued drying her tears. Baoyu had, therefore, no option but to enter with hasty step. On his arrival in the reception-hall, he paid his greetings to his grandmother Jia, to Madame Wang, and the other inmates, and one and all felt, in fact, as happy to see him back as if they had come into the possession of a phoenix.

"Where have you been," dowager lady Jia was the first to ask, "that you come back at this hour? Don't you yet go and pay your congratulations to your cousin?" And smiling she proceeded, addressing herself to lady Feng, "Your cousin has no idea of what's right and what's wrong. Even though he may have had something pressing to do, why didn't he utter just one word, but stealthily bolted away on his own hook? Will this sort of thing ever do? But should you behave again in this fashion by and bye, I shall, when your father comes home, feel compelled to tell him to chastise you."

Lady Feng smiled. "Congratulations are a small matter?" she observed. "But, cousin Bao, you must, on no account, sneak away any more without breathing a word to anyone, and not sending for some people to escort you, for carriages and horses throng the streets. First and foremost, you're the means of making people uneasy at heart; and, what's more, that isn't the way in which members of a family such as ours should go out of doors!"

Dowager lady Jia meanwhile went on reprimanding the servants, who waited on him. "Why," she said, "do you all listen to him and readily go wherever he pleases without even reporting a single word? But where did you really go?" Continuing, she asked, "Did you have anything to eat? Or did you get any sort of fright, eh?"

"A beloved wife of the duke of Beijing departed this life," Baoyu merely returned for answer, "and I went today to express my condolences to him. I found him in such bitter anguish that I couldn't very well leave him and come back immediately. That's the reason why I tarried with him a little longer."

"If hereafter you do again go out of doors slyly and on your own hook," dowager lady Jia impressed on his mind, "without first telling me, I shall certainly bid your father give you a caning!"

Baoyu signified his obedience with all promptitude. His grandmother Jia was then bent upon having the servants, who were on attendance on him, beaten, but the various inmates did their best to dissuade her. "Venerable senior!" they said, "you can well dispense with flying into a rage! He has already promised that he won't venture to go out again. Besides, he has come back without any misadventure, so we should all compose our minds and enjoy ourselves a bit!"

Old lady Jia had, at first, been full of solicitude. She had, as a matter of course, been in a state of despair and displeasure; but, seeing Baoyu return in safety, she felt immoderately delighted, to such a degree, that she could not reconcile herself to visit her resentment upon him. She therefore dropped all mention of his escapade at once. And as she entertained fears lest he may have been unhappy or have had, when he was away, nothing to eat, or got a start on the road, she did not punish him, but had, contrariwise, recourse to every sort of inducement to coax him to feel at ease. But Xiren soon came over and attended to his wants, so the company once more turned their attention to the theatricals. The play acted on that occasion was, "The record of the boxwood hair-pin." Dowager lady Jia, Mrs. Xue, and the others were deeply impressed by what they saw and gave way to tears. Some, however, of the inmates were amused; others were provoked to anger; others gave vent to abuse.

But, reader, do you wish to know the sequel? If so, the next chapter will explain it.

CHAPTER 44

By some inscrutable turn of affairs, lady
Feng begins to feel the pangs of jealousy.
Baoyu experiences joy, beyond all his
expectations, when Ping'er (receives a slap
from lady Feng and) has to adjust her hair.

But to resume our narrative, at the performance of the "Record of the
boxwood hair-pin," at which all the inmates of the household were
present, Baoyu and his female cousins sat together. When Lin Daiyu noticed that the act called, "The man offers a sacrifice" had been
reached, "This Wang Shipeng," she said to Baochai, "is very stupid! It
would be quite immaterial where he offered his sacrifices, and why
must he repair to the riverside? 'At the sight of an object,' the proverb
has it, 'one thinks of a person. All waters under the heavens revert but
to one source.' So had he baled a bowlful from any stream, and given
way to his lamentations, while gazing on it, he could very well have
satisfied his feelings."

Baochai however made no reply.

Baoyu then turned his head round and asked for some warm wine
to drink to lady Feng's health. The fact is, that dowager lady Jia had
enjoined on them that this occasion was unlike others, and that it was
absolutely necessary for them to do the best to induce lady Feng to
heartily enjoy herself for the day. She herself, nevertheless, felt too listless to join the banquet, so simply reclining on a sofa of the inner
room, she looked at the plays in company with Mrs. Xue; and choosing several kinds of such eatables as were to her taste, she placed them
on a small teapoy, and now helped herself to some, and now talked,
as the fancy took her. Then allotting what viands were served on the
two tables assigned to her to the elder and younger waiting-maids, for
whom no covers were laid, and to those female servants and other domestics who were on duty and had to answer calls, she urged them not
to mind but to seat themselves outside the windows, under the eaves of
the verandahs, and to eat and drink at their pleasure, without any regard to conventionalities. Madame Wang and Madame Xing occupied

places at the high table below; while round several tables outside sat the posse of young ladies.

"Do let that girl Feng have the seat of honor," old lady Jia shortly told Mrs. You and her contemporaries, "and mind be careful in doing the honors for me, for she is subjected to endless trouble from one year's end to another!"

"Very well," said Mrs. You. "I fancy," she went on to smile, "that little used as she is to filling the place of honor, she's bound, if she takes the high seat, to be so much at a loss how to behave, as to be loath even to have any wine!"

Dowager lady Jia was much amused by her reply. "Well, if you can't succeed," she said, "wait and I'll come and offer it to her."

Lady Feng with hasty step walked into the inner room. "Venerable ancestor!" she smiled, "don't believe all they tell you! I've already had several cups!"

"Quick, pull her out," old lady Jia laughingly cried to Mrs. You, "and shove her into a chair, and let all of you drink by turns to her health! If she then doesn't drink, I'll come myself in real earnest and make her have some!"

At these words, Mrs. You speedily dragged her out, laughing the while, and forced her into a seat, and, directing a servant to fetch a cup, she filled it with wine. "You've got from one year's end to another," she smiled, "the trouble and annoyance of conferring dutiful attentions upon our venerable senior, upon Madame Wang, and upon myself, so, as I've nothing today, with which to prove my affection for you, have a sip, from my hand, my own dear, of this cup of wine I poured for you myself!"

"If you deliberately wish to present me a glass," lady Feng laughed, "fall on your knees and I'll drink at once!"

"What's this you say?" Mrs. You replied with a laugh. "And who are you, I wonder? But let me tell you this once for all and finish that though we've succeeded, after ever so many difficulties, in getting up this entertainment today, there's no saying whether we shall in the future be able to have anything more the like of this or not. Let's avail ourselves then of the present to put our capacity to the strain and drink a couple of cups!"

Lady Feng saw very well that she could not advance any excuses, and necessity obliged her to swallow the contents of two cups. In quick succession, however, the various young ladies also drew near her, and lady Feng was constrained again to take a sip from the cup each held. But nurse Lai Da too felt compelled, at the sight of dowager lady Jia still in buoyant spirits, to come forward and join in the merriment, so putting herself at the head of a number of nurses, she approached and proffered wine to lady Feng who found it once more so difficult to refuse that she had to swallow a few mouthfuls. But Yuanyang and her companions next appeared, likewise, on the scene to hand her their share of wine; but lady Feng felt, in fact, so little able to comply with their wishes, that she promptly appealed to them entreatingly. "Dear sisters," she pleaded, "do spare me! I'll drink some more tomorrow!"

"Quite so! we're a mean lot," Yuanyang laughed. "But now that we stand in the presence of your ladyship, do condescend to look upon us favorably! We've always enjoyed some little consideration, and do you put on the airs of a mistress on an occasion like the present, when there's such a crowd of people standing by? Really, I shouldn't have come. But, as you won't touch our wine, we might as well be quick and retire!"

While she spoke, she was actually walking away, when lady Feng hastened to lay hold of her and to detain her. "Dear sister," she cried, "I'll drink some and have done!"

So saying, she took the wine and filled a cup to the very brim, and drained it. Yuanyang then at length gave her a smile, (and she and her friends) dispersed.

Subsequently, the company resumed their places at the banquet. But lady Feng was conscious that the wine she had primed herself with was mounting to her head, so abruptly staggering to the upper end, she meant to betake herself home to lie down, when seeing the jugglers arrive, "Get the tips ready!" she shouted to Mrs. You. "I'm off to wash my face a bit."

Mrs. You nodded her head assentingly; and lady Feng, noticing that the inmates were off their guard, left the banquet, and wended her steps beneath the eaves towards the back entrance of the house. Ping'er had, however, been keeping her eye on her, so hastily she followed in her footsteps. Lady Feng at once propped herself on her arm. But no sooner did they reach the covered passage than she discerned a young maid, attached to her quarters, standing under it. (The girl), the moment she perceived them, twisted herself round and beat a retreat. Lady Feng forthwith began to give way to suspicion; and she immediately shouted out to her to halt. The maid pretended at first not to hear, but, as, while following her they called out to her time after time, she found herself compelled to turn round. Lady Feng was seized with greater doubts than ever. Quickly therefore entering the covered passage with Ping'er, she bade the maid go along with them. Then opening a folding screen, lady Feng seated herself on the steps leading to the small courtyard, and made the girl fall on her knees. "Call two boy-servants from among those on duty at the second gate," she cried out to Ping'er, "to bring a whip of twisted cords, and to take this young wench, who has no regard for her mistress, and beat her to shreds."

The servant-maid fell into a state of consternation, and was scared out of her very wits. Sobbing the while, she kept on bumping her head on the ground and soliciting for grace.

"I'm really no ghost! So you must have seen me! Don't you know what good manners mean and stand still?" lady Feng asked. "Why did you instead persist in running on?"

"I truly did not see your ladyship coming," the maid replied with tears in her eyes. "I was, besides, much concerned as there was no one in the rooms; that's why I was running on."

"If there's no one in the rooms, who told you to come out again?" lady Feng inquired. "And didn't you see me, together with Ping'er, at your heels, stretching out our necks and calling out to you about ten times? But the more we shouted, the faster you ran! You weren't far off from us either, so is it likely that you got deaf? And are you still bent upon bandying words with me?"

So speaking, she raised her hand and administered her a slap on the face. But, while the girl staggered from the blow, she gave her a second slap on the other side of the face, so both cheeks of the maid quickly began to get purple and to swell.

Ping'er hastened to reason with her mistress. "My lady!" she said, "be careful you'll be hurting your hand!"

"Go on, pommel her," urged lady Feng, "and ask her what made her run! and, if she doesn't tell you, just you take her mouth and tear it to pieces for her!"

At the outset, the girl obstinately prevaricated, but when she eventually heard that lady Feng intended to take a red-hot branding-iron and burn her mouth with, she at last sobbingly spoke out. "Our Master Secundus, Mr. Lian, is at home," she remarked, "and he sent me here to watch your movements, my lady; bidding me go ahead, when I saw you leave the banquet, and convey the message to him. But, contrary to his hopes, your ladyship came back just now!"

Lady Feng saw very well that there lurked something behind all she said. "What did he ask you to watch me for?" she therefore eagerly asked. "Can it be, pray, that he dreaded to see me return home? There must be some other reason; so be quick and tell it to me and I shall henceforward treat you with regard. If you don't minutely confess all to me, I shall this very moment take a knife and pare off your flesh!"

Threatening her the while, she turned her head round, and, extracting a hair-pin from her coiffure, she stuck it promiscuously about the maid's mouth. This so frightened the girl that, as she made every effort to get out of her way, she burst out into tears and entreaties. "I'll tell your ladyship everything," she cried, "but you mustn't say that it was I who told you."

Ping'er, who stood by, exhorted her to obey; but she at the same time impressed on her mind to speak out without delay.

"Mr. Secundus himself arrived only a few minutes back," the maid began. "The moment, however, he came, he opened a bag, and, taking two pieces of silver, two hair-pins, and a couple of rolls of silk, he bade me stealthily take them to Bao'er's wife and tell her to come in. As soon as she put the things away, she hurried to our house, and Master Secundus ordered me to keep an eye on your ladyship; but of what happened after that, I've no idea whatever."

When these disclosures fell on lady Feng's ears, she flew into such a rage that her whole person felt quite weak; and, rising immediately, she straightway repaired home. The instant she reached the gate of the courtyard, she espied a waiting-maid peep out of the entrance. Seeing lady Feng, she too drew in her head, and tried at once to effect her escape. But lady Feng called her by name, and made her stand still. This girl had ever been very sharp, so when she realized that she could not manage to beat a retreat, she went so far as to run out to her. "I was just going to tell your ladyship," she smiled, "and here you come! What a strange coincidence!"

"Tell me what?" lady Feng exclaimed.

"That Mr. Secundus is at home," the girl replied, "and has done so and so." She then recounted to her all the incidents recorded a few minutes back.

"Cui!" ejaculated lady Feng. "What were you up to before? Now, that I've seen you, you come and try to clear yourself!"

As she spoke, she raised her arm and administered the maid a slap, which upset her equilibrium. So with hurried step, she betook herself away. Lady Feng then drew near the window. Lending an ear to what was going on inside, she heard someone in the room laughingly observe: "When that queen-of-hell sort of wife of yours dies, it will be a good riddance!"

"When she's gone," Jia Lian rejoined, "and I marry another, the like of her, what will I again do?"

"When she's dead and gone," the woman resumed, "just raise Ping'er to the rank of primary wife. I think she'll turn out considerably better than she has."

"At present," Jia Lian put in, "she won't even let me enjoy Ping'er's society! Ping'er herself is full of displeasure; yet she dares not speak.

How is it that it has been my fate to bring upon myself the influence of this evil star?"

Lady Feng overheard these criticisms and flew into a fit of anger, which made her tremble violently. When she, however, also caught the praise heaped by both of them upon Ping'er, she harbored the suspicion that Ping'er too must, as a matter of course, have all along employed the sly resentful language against her. And, as the wine bubbled up more and more into her head, she did not so much as give the matter a second thought, but, twisting round, she first and foremost gave Ping'er a couple of whacks, and, with one kick, she banged the door open, and walked in. Then, without allowing her any time to give any explanation in her own defence, she clutched Bao'er's wife, and, tearing her about, she belabored her with blows. But the dread lest Jia Lian should slip out of the room, induced her to post herself in such a way as to obstruct the doorway. "What a fine wench!" she shouted out abusingly. "You make a paramour of your mistress' husband, and then you wish to compass your master's wife's death, for Ping'er to transfer her quarters in here! You base hirelings! You're all of the same stamp, thoroughly jealous of me; you try to cajole me by your outward display!"

While abusing them, she once more laid hold of Ping'er and beat her several times. Ping'er was pummelled away till her heart thrilled with a sense of injury, but she had nowhere to go, and breathe her woes. Such resentment overpowered her feelings that she sobbed without a sign of a tear. "You people," she railingly shouted, "go and do a lot of shameful things, and then you also deliberately involve me; but why?"

So shouting, she too clutched Bao'er's wife and began to assail her. Jia Lian had freely primed himself with wine, so, on his return home, he was in such exuberance of spirits that he observed no secrecy in his doings. The moment, however, he perceived lady Feng appear on the scene, he got to his wits' end. Yet when he saw Ping'er also start a rumpus, the liquor he had had aroused his ire. The sight of the assault committed by lady Feng on Bao'er's wife had already incensed him and put him to shame, but he had not been able with any consistency to interfere; but the instant he espied Ping'er herself lay hands on her, he vehemently jumped forward and gave her a kick. "What a vixen!" he cried. "Are you likewise going to start knocking people about?"

Ping'er was of a timid disposition. At once, therefore, she withheld her hands, and melted into tears. "Why do you implicate me," she said, "in things you say behind my back?"

When lady Feng descried in what fear and dread Ping'er was of Jia Lian, she lost more than ever control over her temper, and, starting again in pursuit of her, she struck Ping'er, while urging her to go for Bao'er's wife.

Ping'er was driven to exasperation; and forthwith rushing out of the apartment, she went in search of a knife to commit suicide with. But the company of old matrons, who stood outside, hastened to place impediments in her way, and to argue with her.

Lady Feng, meanwhile, realized that Ping'er had gone to take her life, and rolling head foremost, into Jia Lian's embrace, "You put your heads together to do me harm," she said, "and, when I overhear your designs, you people conspire to frighten me! But strangle me and have done."

Jia Lian was driven to despair; to such a degree that unsheathing a sword suspended on the wall, "There's no need for anyone of you to commit suicide!" he screamed. "I too am thoroughly exasperated, so I'll kill the whole lot of you and pay the penalty with my own life! We'll all then be free from further trouble!"

The bustle had just reached a climax beyond the chance of a settlement, when they perceived Mrs. You and a crowd of inmates make their appearance in the room. "What's the matter?" they asked. "There was nothing up just now, so why is all this row for?"

At the sight of the new arrivals, Jia Lian more than ever made the three parts of intoxication, under which he labored, an excuse to assume an air calculated to intimidate them, and to pretend, in order to further his own ends, that he was bent upon despatching lady Feng.

But lady Feng, upon seeing her relatives appear, got into a mood less perverse than the one she had been in previous to their arrival; and, leaving the whole company of them, she scampered, all in tears, over to the off side, into dowager lady Jia's quarters.

By this time, the play was over. Lady Feng rushed consequently into the old lady's presence and fell into her lap. "Venerable ancestor! help me!" she exclaimed. "Mr. Jia Lian wishes to kill me."

"What's up?" precipitately inquired dowager lady Jia, Mesdames Xing and Wang, and the rest.

"I was just going to my rooms to change my dress," lady Feng wept, "when I unexpectedly found Mr. Jia Lian at home, talking with someone. Fancying that visitors had come, I was quite taken aback, and not presuming to enter, I remained outside the window and listened. It turned out, in fact, to be Bao'er's wife holding council with him. She said that I was dreadful, and that she meant to poison me so as to get me out of the way and enable Ping'er to be promoted to be first wife. At this, I lost my temper. But not venturing, none the less, to have a row with him, I simply gave Ping'er two slaps; and then I asked him why he wished to do me harm. But so stricken did he get with shame that he tried there and then to despatch me."

Dowager lady Jia treated every word that fell on her ear as truth. "Dreadful!" she ejaculated. "Bring here at once that low-bred offspring!"

Barely was, however, this exclamation out of her lips, than they perceived Jia Lian, a sword in hand, enter in pursuit of his wife, followed closely by a bevy of inmates. Jia Lian evidently placed such thorough reliance upon the love which old lady Jia had all along lavished upon them, that he entertained little regard even for his mother or his aunt, so he came, with perfect effrontery, to stir up a disturbance in their presence. When Mesdames Xing and Wang saw him, they got into a passion, and, with all despatch, they endeavored to deter him from his purpose. "You mean thing!" they shouted, abusing him. "Your crime is more heinous, for our venerable senior is in here!"

"It's all because our worthy ancestor spoils her," cried Jia Lian, with eyes awry, "that she behaved as she did and took upon herself to rate even me!"

Madame Xing was full of resentment. Snatching the sword from his grasp, she kept on telling him to quit the room at once. But Jia Lian continued to prattle foolish nonsense in a driveling and maudlin way. His manner exasperated dowager lady Jia. "I'm well aware," she observed, "that you haven't the least consideration for any one of us. Tell someone to go and call his father here and we'll see whether he doesn't clear out."

When Jia Lian caught these words, he eventually tottered out of the apartment. But in such a state of frenzy was he that he did not return to his quarters, but betook himself into the outer study.

During this while, Mesdames Xing and Wang also called lady Feng to task. "Why, what serious matter could it ever have been?" old lady Jia remarked. "But children of tender years are like greedy kittens, and how can one say for certain that they won't do such things? Human beings have, from their very infancy, to go through experiences of this kind! It's all my fault, however, for pressing you to have a little more wine than was good for you. But you've also gone and drunk the vinegar of jealousy!"

This insinuation made everyone laugh.

"Compose your mind!" proceeded dowager lady Jia. "Tomorrow I'll send for him to apologize to you; but, you'd better today not go over, as you might put him to shame!" Continuing, she also went on to abuse Ping'er. "I've always thought highly of that wench," she said, "and how is it that she's turned out to be secretly so bad?"

"Ping'er isn't to blame!" Mrs. You and the others smiled. "It's lady Feng who makes people her tools to give vent to her spite! Husband and wife could not very well come to blows face to face, so they combined in using Ping'er as their scapegoat! What injuries haven't fallen to Ping'er's lot! And do you, venerable senior, still go on blowing her up?"

"Is it really so!" exclaimed old lady Jia. "I always said that that girl wasn't anything like that artful shrew! Well, in that case, she is to be pitied, for she has had to bear the brunt of her anger, and all through no fault of hers!" Calling Hupo to her, "Go," she added, "and tell Ping'er all I enjoin you, 'that I know that she has been insulted and that tomorrow I'll send for her mistress to make amends, but that being her mistress' birthday today, I won't have her give rise to any reckless fuss!'"

Ping'er had, we may explain, from an early hour, been dragged by Li Wan into the garden of Broad Vista. Here Ping'er gave way to bitter tears. So much so, that her throat choked with sobs, and could not give utterance to speech.

"You are an intelligent person," exhorted Baochai, "and how considerately has your lady treated you all along! It was simply because she has had a little too much wine that she behaved as she did today! But had she not made you the means of giving vent to her spite, is it likely that she could very well have aired her grievances upon anyone else? Besides, anyone else would have laughed at her for acting in a sham way!"

While she reasoned with her, she saw Hupo approach, and deliver dowager lady Jia's message. Ping'er then felt in herself that she had come out of the whole affair with some credit, and she, little by little, resumed her equilibrium. She did not, nevertheless, put her foot anywhere near the front part of the compound.

After a little rest, Baochai and her companions came and paid a visit to old lady Jia and lady Feng, while Baoyu pressed Ping'er to come to the Yihong court. Xiren received her with alacrity. "I meant," she said, "to be the first to ask you, but as our senior lady, Jia Zhu, and the young ladies invited you, I couldn't very well do so myself."

Ping'er returned her smile. "Many thanks!" she rejoined. "How words ever commenced between us," she then went on, "when there was no provocation, I can't tell! But without rhyme or reason, I came in for a spell of resentment."

"Our lady Secunda has always been very good to you," laughingly remarked Xiren, "so she must have done this in a sudden fit of exasperation!"

"Our lady Secunda did not, after all, say anything to me," Ping'er explained. "It was that wench that blew me up. And she deliberately made a laughing-stock of me. But that fool also of a master of ours struck me!"

While recounting her experiences, she felt a keener sense of injustice than before, and she found it hard to restrain her tears from trickling down her cheeks.

"My dear sister," Baoyu hastily advised her, "don't wound your heart! I'm quite ready to express my apologies on behalf of that pair!"

"What business is that of yours?" Ping'er smiled.

"We cousins, whether male or female, are all alike." Baoyu smilingly argued. "So when they hurt anyone's feelings, I apologize for them; it's only right that I should do so. What a pity;" he continued, "these new clothes too have been stained! But you'll find your sister Hua's costumes in here, and why don't you put one on, and take some hot wine and spurt it over yours and iron them out? You might also remake your coiffure."

Speaking, he directed the young maids to draw some water for washing the face and to heat an iron and bring it.

Ping'er had ever heard people maintain that all that Baoyu excelled in was in knitting friendships with girls. But Baoyu had so far been loath, seeing that Ping'er was Jia Lian's beloved secondary wife, and lady Feng's confidante, to indulge in any familiarities with her. And being precluded from accomplishing the desire upon which his heart was set, he time and again gave way to vexation. When Ping'er, however, remarked his conduct towards her on this occasion, she secretly resolved within herself that what was said of him was indeed no idle rumor. But as he had anticipated everyone of her wants, and she saw moreover that Xiren had, for her special benefit, opened a box and produced two articles of clothing, not much worn by her, she speedily drew near and washed her face.

Baoyu stood by her side. "You must, dear girl, also apply a little cosmetic and powder," she smiled; "otherwise you'll look as if you were angry with lady Feng. It's her birthday, besides; and our old ancestor has sent someone again to come and cheer you up."

Hearing how reasonable his suggestions were, Ping'er readily went in search of powder; but she failed to notice any about, so Baoyu hurriedly drew up to the toilet-table, and, removing the lid of a porcelain box made at the "Xuan" kiln, which contained a set of ten small ladles, tuberose-like in shape, (for helping one's self to powder with), he drew out one of them and handed it to Ping'er. "This isn't lead powder," he smiled. "This is made of the seeds of red jasmine, well triturated, and compounded with suitable first class ingredients."

Ping'er emptied some on the palm of her hand. On examination, she really found that it was light, clear, red, and scented; perfect in all four properties; that it was easy to apply evenly to the face, that it kept moist, and that it differed from other kinds of powder, ordinarily so rough. She subsequently noticed that the cosmetic too was not spread on a sheet, but that it was contained in a tiny box of white jade, the contents of which bore the semblance of rose-paste.

"The cosmetic one buys in the market isn't clean," Baoyu remarked smilingly. "Its color is faint as well. But this is cosmetic of superior quality. The juice was squeezed out, strained clear, mixed with perfume of flowers and decocted. All you need do is to take some with that hair-pin and rub it on your lips, that will be enough; and if you dissolve some in a little water, and rub it on the palm of your hand, it will be ample for you to cover your whole face with."

Ping'er followed his directions and performed her toilette. She looked exceptionally fresh and beautiful. A sweet fragrance pervaded her cheeks. Baoyu then cut, with a pair of bamboo scissors, a stalk, with two autumn orchids, which had blossomed in a flower pot, and he pinned it in her side-hair. But a maid was unexpectedly seen to enter the room, sent by Li Wan to come and call her, so she quitted his quarters with all possible despatch.

Baoyu had not so far been able to have his wishes to revel in Ping'er's society gratified. Ping'er was furthermore a girl of a high grade, most intelligent, most winsome, and unlike that sort of vulgar and dull-minded beings, so that he cherished intense disgust against his fate.

The present occasion had been the anniversary of Jinchuan'er's birth, and he had remained, in consequence, plunged in a disconsolate frame of mind throughout the whole day. But, contrary to his expectations, the incident eventually occurred, which afforded him, after all, an opportunity to dangle in Ping'er's society and to gratify to some small degree a particle of his wish. This had been a piece of good fortune he so little expected would fall to his share during the course of his present existence, that as he reclined on his bed, his heart swelled with happiness and contentment. Suddenly, he reflected that Jia Lian's sole thought was to make licentious pleasures the means of gratifying his passions, and that he had no idea how to show the least regard to the fair sex; and he mused that Ping'er was without father or mother, brothers or sisters, a solitary being destined to dance attendance upon a couple such as Jia Lian and his wife; that Jia Lian was vulgar, and lady Feng haughty, but that she was gifted nevertheless with the knack of splendidly managing things; and that (Ping'er) had again today come across bitter sorrow, and that her destiny was extremely unfortunate.

At this stage of his reverie, he began to feel wounded and distressed. When he rose once more to his feet, he noticed that the wine, which she had spurted on the clothes, she had a few minutes back divested herself of, had already half dried, and, taking up the iron, he smoothed them and folded them nicely for her. He then discovered that she had left her handkerchief behind, and that it still bore traces of tears, so throwing it into the basin, he rinsed it and hung it up to dry, with feelings bordering on joy as well as sadness. But after a short time spent in a brown study, he too betook himself to the Daoxiang village for a chat; and it was only when the lamps had been lit that he got up to take his leave.

Ping'er put up in Li Wan's quarters for the night. Lady Feng slept with dowager lady Jia, while Jia Lian returned at a late hour to his home. He found it however very lonely. Yet unable to go and call his wife over, he had no alternative but to sleep as best he could for that night. On the morrow, he remembered, as soon as he opened his eyes, the occurrence of the previous day, and he fell a prey to such extreme unhappiness that he could not be conscience-stricken enough.

Madame Xing pondered with solicitude on Jia Lian's drunken fit the day before. The moment therefore it was light, she hastily crossed over, and sent for Jia Lian to repair to dowager lady Jia's apartments. Jia Lian was thus compelled to suppress all timidity and to repair to the front part of the mansion and fall on his knees at the feet of his old senior.

"What was the matter?" inquired old lady Jia.

"I really had too much wine yesterday," Jia Lian promptly answered with a forced smile. "I must have given you a fright, worthy ancestor, so I come today to receive condign punishment."

"You mean fellow!" shouted dowager lady Jia, spitting at him disdainfully. "You go and glut yourself with spirits, and, not to speak of your not going to stretch yourself like a corpse and sleep it off, you contrariwise start beating your wife! But that vixen Feng brags away the whole day long, as if she were a human being as valiant as any tyrant, and yet yesterday she got into such a funk that she presented a woeful sight! Had it not been for me, you would have done her bodily harm; and what would you feel like now?"

Jia Lian was at heart full of a sense of injury, but he could not master sufficient courage to say anything in his own defence. The only course open to him was therefore to make a confession of fault.

"Don't lady Feng and Ping'er possess the charms of handsome women?" dowager lady Jia resumed. "And aren't you yet satisfied with them that you must, of a day, go slyly prowling and gallavanting about, dragging indiscriminately into your rooms frowsy and filthy people? Is it for the sake of this sort of wenches that you beat your wife and belabor the inmates of your quarters? You've nevertheless had the good fortune of starting in life as the scion of a great family; and do you, with eyes wide open, bring disgrace upon your own head? If you have any regard for me, well, then get up and I'll spare you! And if you make your apologies in a proper manner to your wife and take her home, I'll be satisfied. But if you don't, just you clear out of this, for I won't even presume to have any of your genuflexions!"

Jia Lian took to heart the injunctions that fell on his ear. Espying besides lady Feng standing opposite to him in undress, her eyes swollen from crying, and her face quite sallow, without cosmetic or powder, he thought her more lovable and charming than ever. "Wouldn't it be well," he therefore mused, "that I should make amends, so that she and I may be on friendly terms again and that I should win the good pleasure of my old ancestor?"

At the conclusion of his reflections, he forthwith put on a smile. "After your advice, venerable senior," he said, "I couldn't be so bold as not to accede to your wishes! But this is shewing her more indulgence than ever!"

"What nonsense!" exclaimed dowager lady Jia laughingly. "I am well aware that with her extreme decorum she couldn't hurt anyone's susceptibilities. But should she, in the future, wrong you in any way, I shall, of course, take the law into my own hands and bid you make her submit to your authority and finish."

Jia Lian, at this assurance, crawled up and made a bow to lady Feng. "It was really my fault, so don't be angry, lady Secunda," he said.

Everyone in the room laughed.

"Now, my girl Feng," lady Jia laughingly observed, "you are not to lose your temper; for if you do, I'll lose mine too!"

Continuing, she directed a servant to go and call Ping'er; and, on her arrival, she advised lady Feng and Jia Lian to do all they could to reconcile her. At the sight of Ping'er, Jia Lian showed less regard than ever for the saying that 'a primary wife differs from a secondary wife,' and the instant he heard old lady Jia's exhortation he drew near her. "The injuries," he remarked, "to which you were subjected yesterday, Miss, were entirely due to my shortcoming. If your lady hurt your feelings, it was likewise all through me that the thing began. So I express my regret; but, besides this, I tender my apologies as well on behalf of your mistress."

Saying this, he made another bow. This evoked a smile from dowager lady Jia. Lady Feng, however, also laughed. Their old ancestor then desired lady Feng to come and console Ping'er, but Ping'er hastily advanced and knocked her head before lady Feng. "I do deserve death," she urged, "for provoking your ladyship to wrath on the day of your birthday!"

Lady Feng was at the moment pricked by shame and remorse for having so freely indulged in wine the previous day as to completely have lost sight of longstanding friendships, and for allowing her temper to so thoroughly flare up as to lend a patient ear to the gossip of outsiders, and unjustly put Ping'er out of countenance, so when she contrariwise now saw her make advances, she felt both abashed and grieved, and, promptly extending her arms, she dragged her up and gave way to tears.

"I've waited upon your ladyship for all these years," Ping'er pleaded, "and you've never so much as given me a single fillip; and yet, you beat me yesterday. But I don't bear you any grudge, my lady, for it was that wench, who was at the bottom of it all. Nor do I wonder that your ladyship lost control over your temper."

As she spoke, tears trickled down her cheeks too.

"Escort those three home!" dowager lady Jia shouted to the servants. "If any one of them makes the least allusion to the subject, come at once and tell me of it; for without any regard as to who it may be, I shall take my staff and give him or her a sound flogging."

The trio then prostrated themselves before dowager lady Jia and the two ladies, Mesdames Xing and Wang. And assenting to her old mistress' injunctions, an old nurse accompanied the three inmates to their quarters.

When they got home, lady Feng assured herself that there was no one about. "How is it," she next asked, "that I'm like a queen of hell, or like a 'Yecha' demon? That courtesan swore at me and wished me dead; and did you too help her to curse me? If I'm not nice a thousand days, why, I must be nice on someone day! But if, poor me, I'm so bad as not even to compare with a disorderly woman, how can I have the face to come and spend my life with you here?"

So speaking, she melted into tears.

"Aren't you yet gratified?" cried Jia Lian. "Just reflect carefully who was most to blame yesterday! And yet, in the presence of so many people, it was I who, after all, fell today on my knees and made apologies as well. You came in for plenty of credit, and do you now go on jabber, jabber? Can it be that you'd like to make me kneel at your feet before you let matters rest? If you try and play the bully beyond bounds, it won't be a good thing for you!"

To these arguments, lady Feng could find no suitable response.

Ping'er then blurted out laughing.

"She's all right again!" Jia Lian smiled. "But I'm really quite at a loss what to do with this one."

These words were still on his lips, when they saw a married woman walk in. "Bao'er's wife has committed suicide by hanging herself," she said.

This announcement plunged both Jia Lian and lady Feng into great consternation. Lady Feng, however, lost no time in putting away every sign of excitement. "Dead, eh? What a riddance!" she shouted instead. "What's the use of making such a fuss about a mere trifle?"

But not long elapsed before she perceived Lin Zixiao's wife make her appearance in the room. "Bao'er's wife has hung herself," she whispered to lady Feng in a low tone of voice, "and her mother's relatives want to take legal proceedings."

Lady Feng gave a sardonic smile. "That's all right!" she observed. "I myself was just thinking about lodging a complaint!"

"I and the others tried to dissuade them," Lin Zixiao's wife continued. "And by having recourse to intimidation as well as to promises of money, they, at last, agreed to our terms."

"I haven't got a cash," lady Feng replied. "Had I even any money, I wouldn't let them have it; so just let them go and lodge any charge they fancy. You needn't either dissuade them or intimidate them. Let them go and complain as much as they like. But if they fail to establish a case against me, they'll, after all, be punished for trying to make the corpse the means of extorting money out of me!"

Lin Zixiao's wife was in a dilemma, when she espied Jia Lian wink at her. Comprehending his purpose, she readily quitted the apartment and waited for him outside.

"I'll go out and see what they're up to!" Jia Lian remarked.

"Mind, I won't have you give them any money!" shouted lady Feng.

Jia Lian straightway made his exit. He came and held consultation with Lin Zixiao, and then directed the servants to go and use some fair means, others harsh. The matter was, however, not brought to any satisfactory arrangement until he engaged to pay two hundred taels for burial expenses. But so apprehensive was Jia Lian lest something might occur to make the relatives change their ideas, that he also despatched a messenger to lay the affair before Wang Ziteng, who bade a few constables, coroners, and other official servants come and help him to effect the necessary preparations for the funeral. The parties concerned did not venture, when they saw the precautions he had adopted, to raise any objections, disposed though they may have been to try and bring forward other arguments. Their sole alternative therefore was to suppress their resentment, to refrain from further importunities and let the matter drop into oblivion.

Jia Lian then impressed upon Lin Zixiao to insert the two hundred taels in the accounts for the current year, by making such additions to various items here and there as would suffice to clear them off, and presented Bao'er with money out of his own pocket as a crumb of comfort, adding, "By and bye, I'll choose a nice wife for you." When Bao'er, therefore, came in for a share of credit as well as of hard cash, he could not possibly do otherwise than practice contentment; and forthwith, needless to dilate on this topic, he began to pay court to Jia Lian as much as ever.

In the inner rooms, lady Feng was, it is true, much cut up at heart; but she strained every nerve to preserve an exterior of total indifference. Noticing that there was no one present in the apartment, she drew Ping'er to her. "I drank yesterday," she smiled, "a little more wine than was good for me, so don't bear me a grudge. Where did I strike you, let me see?"

"You didn't really strike me hard!" Ping'er said by way of reply.

But at this stage they heard someone remark that the ladies and young ladies had come in.

If you desire, reader, to know any of the subsequent circumstances, peruse the account given in the following chapter.

CHAPTER 45

Friends interchange words of friendship. Daiyu feels dull on a windy and rainy evening, and indites verses on wind and rain.

Lady Feng, we will now go on to explain, was engaged in comforting Ping'er, when upon unawares perceiving the young ladies enter the room, she hastened to make them sit down while Ping'er poured the tea.

"So many of you come today," lady Feng smiled, "that it looks as if you'd been asked to come by invitation."

Tanchun was the first to speak. "We have," she smilingly rejoined, "two objects in view, the one concerns me; the other cousin Quarta; but among these are, besides, certain things said by our venerable senior."

"What's up?" inquired lady Feng with a laugh. "Is it so urgent?"

"Some time ago," Tanchun proceeded laughingly, "we started a rhyming club; but the first meeting was not quite a success. Everyone of us proved so soft-hearted! The rules therefore were set at naught. So I can't help thinking that we must enlist your services as president of the society and superintendent; for what is needed to make the thing turn out well is firmness and no favor. The next matter is: cousin Quarta explained to our worthy ancestor that the requisites for painting the picture of the garden were short of one thing and another, and she said: that there must still be, she fancied, in the lower story of the back loft some articles, remaining over from previous years, and that we should go and look for them. That if there be any, they should be taken out, but that in the event of their being none, someone should be commissioned to go and purchase a supply of them."

"I'm not up to doing anything wet or dry, (play on word 'shi,' verses)," lady Feng laughed, "and would you have me, pray, come and gorge?"

"You may, it's possible, not be up to any of these things," Tanchun replied, "but we don't expect you to do anything! All we want you for is to see whether there be among us any remiss or lazy, and to decide how they should be punished, that's all."

"You shouldn't try and play your tricks upon me!" lady Feng smiled, "I can see through your little game! Is it that you wish me to act as president and superintendent? No! it's as clear as day that your object is that I should play the part of that copper merchant, who put in contributions in hard cash. You have, at every meeting you hold, to each take turn and pay the piper; but, as your funds are not sufficient, you've invented this plan to come and inveigle me into your club, in order to wheedle money out of me! This must be your little conspiracy!"

These words evoked general laughter. "You've guessed right!" they exclaimed.

"In very truth," Li Wan smiled, "you're a creature with an intellect as transparent as crystal, and with wits as clear as glass!"

"You've got the good fortune of being their elder sister-in-law," lady Feng smilingly remarked, "so the young ladies asked you to take them in hand, and teach them how to read, and make them learn good manners and needlework; and it's for you to guide and direct them in everything! But here they start a rhyming society, for which not much can be needed, and don't you concern yourself about them? We'll leave our worthy ancestor and our Madame Wang aside; they are old people, but you receive each moon an allowance of ten taels, which is twice as much as what any one of us gets. More, our worthy ancestor and Madame Wang maintain that being a widow, and having lost your home, you haven't, poor thing, enough to live upon, and that you have a young child as well to bring up; so they added with extreme liberality another ten taels to your original share. Your allowance therefore is on a par with that of our dear senior. But they likewise gave you a piece of land in the garden, and you also come in for the lion's share of rents, collected from various quarters, and of the annual allowances, apportioned at the close of each year. Yet, you and your son don't muster, masters and servants, ten persons in all. What you eat and what you wear comes, just as ever, out of the general public fund, so that, computing everything together, you get as much as four to five hundred taels. Were you then to contribute each year a hundred or two hundred taels, to help them to have some fun, how many years could this outlay continue? They'll very soon be getting married, and, are they likely then to still expect you to make any contributions? So loath are you, however, at present to fork out any cash that you've egged them on to come and worry me! I'm quite prepared to spend away until we've drained our chest dry! Don't I know that the money isn't mine?"

"Just you listen to her," Li Wan laughed. "I simply made one single remark, and out she came with two cartloads of nonsensical trash! You're as rough a diamond as a leg made of clay! All you're good for is to work the small abacus, to divide a catty and to fraction an ounce, so finicking are you! A nice thing you are, and yet, you've been lucky enough to come to life as the child of a family of learned and high officials. You've also made such a splendid match; and do you still behave in the way you do? Had you been a son or daughter born in some poverty-stricken, humble and low household, there's no saying what a mean thing you wouldn't have been! Everyone in this world has been gulled by you; and yesterday you went so far as to strike Ping'er! But it wasn't the proper thing for you to stretch out your hand on her! Was all that liquor, forsooth, poured down a cur's stomach? My monkey was up, and I meant to have taken upon myself to avenge Ping'er's grievance; but, after mature consideration, I thought to myself, 'her birthday is as slow to come round as a dog's tail grows to a point.' I also feared lest our venerable senior might be made to feel unhappy; so I did not come forward. Anyhow, my resentment isn't yet spent; and do you come today to try and irritate me? You aren't fit to even pick up shoes for Ping'er! You two should therefore change your respective places!"

These taunts created merriment among the whole party.

"Oh!" hastily exclaimed lady Feng, laughingly, "I know everything! You don't at all come to look me up on account of verses or paintings, but simply to take revenge on Ping'er's behalf! I never had any idea that Ping'er had such a backer as yourself to bolster her up! Had I known it, I wouldn't have ventured to strike her, even though a spirit had been tugging my arm! Miss Ping come over and let me tender my apologies to you, in the presence of your senior lady and the young ladies. Do bear with me for having proved so utterly wanting in virtue, after I had had a few drinks!"

Everyone felt amused by her insinuations.

"What do you say?" Li Wan asked Ping'er smiling. "As for me, I think it my bounden duty to vindicate your wrongs, before we let the matter drop!"

"Your remarks, ladies, may be spoken in jest," Ping'er smiled, "but I am not worthy of such a fuss!"

"What about worthy and unworthy?" Li Wan observed. "I'm here for you! Quick, get the key, and let your mistress go and open the doors and hunt up the things!"

"Dear sister-in-law," lady Feng said with a smile, "you'd better go along with them into the garden. I'm about to take the rice accounts in hand and square them up with them. Our senior lady, Madame Xing, has also sent someone to call me; what she wants to tell me again, I can't make out; but I must need go over for a turn. There are, besides, all those extra clothes for you people to wear at the end of the year, and I must get them ready and give them to be made!"

"These matters are none of my business!" Li Wan laughingly answered. "First settle my concerns so as to enable me to retire to rest, and escape the bother of having all these girls at me!"

"Dear sister-in-law," vehemently smiled lady Feng, "be good enough to give me a little time! You've ever been the one to love me best, and how is it that you have, on Ping'er's account, ceased to care for me? Time and again have you impressed on my mind that I should, despite my manifold duties, take good care of my health, and manage things in such a way as to find a little leisure for rest, and do you now contrariwise come to press the very life out of me? There's another thing besides. Should such clothes as will be required at the end of the year by any other persons be delayed, it won't matter; but, should those of the young ladies be behind time, let the responsibility rest upon your shoulders! And won't our old lady bear you a grudge, if you don't mind these small things? But as for me, I won't utter a single word against you, for, as I had rather bear the blame myself, I won't venture, to involve you!"

"Listen to her!" Li Wan smiled. "Hasn't she got the gift of the gab? But let me ask you. Will you, after all, assume the control of this rhyming society or not?"

"What's this nonsense you're talking?" lady Feng laughed. "Were I not to enter the society, and spend a little money, won't I be treated as a rebel in this garden of Broad Vista? And will I then still think of tarrying here to eat my head off? So soon as the day dawns tomorrow, I'll arrive at my post, dismount from my horse, and, after kneeling before the seals, my first act will be to give fifty taels for you to quietly cover the expenses of your meetings. Yet after a few days, I shall neither indite any verses, nor write any compositions, as I am simply a rustic boor, nothing more! But it will be just the same whether I assume the direction or not; for after you pocket my money, there's no fear of your not driving me out of the place!"

As these words dropped from her lips, one and all laughed again.

"I'll now open the loft," proceeded lady Feng. "Should there be any of the articles you want, you can tell the servants to bring them out for you to look at them! If any will serve your purpose, keep them and use them. If any be short, I'll bid a servant go and purchase them according to your list. I'll go at once and cut the satin for the painting. As for the plan, it isn't with Madame Wang; it's still over there, at Mr. Jia Zhen's. I tell you all this so that you should avoid going over to Madame Wang's and getting into trouble! But I'll go and depute someone to fetch it. I'll direct also a servant to take the satin and give it to the gentlemen to size with alum; will this be all right?"

Li Wan nodded her head by way of assent and smiled. "This will be putting you to much trouble and inconvenience," she said. "But we must really act as you suggest. Well in that case, go home all of you, and, if after a time, she doesn't send the thing round, you can come again and bully her."

So saying, she there and then led off the young ladies, and was making her way out, when lady Feng exclaimed: "It's Baoyu and he alone, who has given rise to all this fuss."

Li Wan overheard her remark and hastily turned herself round. "We did, in fact, come over," she smiled, "on account of Baoyu, and we forgot, instead, all about him! The first meeting was deferred through him; but we are too soft-hearted, so tell us what penalty to inflict on him!"

Lady Feng gave herself to reflection. "There's only one thing to do," she then remarked. "Just punish him by making him sweep the floor of each of your rooms. This will do!"

"Your verdict is faultless!" they laughed with one accord.

While they conversed they were on the point of starting on their way back, when they caught sight of a young maid walk in, supporting nurse Lai. Lady Feng and her companions immediately rose to their feet, their faces beaming with smiles. "Venerable mother!" they said, "do take a seat!" They then in a body presented their congratulations to her.

Nurse Lai seated herself on the edge of the stove-couch and returned their smiles. "I'm to be congratulated," she rejoined, "but you, mistresses, are to be congratulated as well; for had it had not been for the bountiful grace displaced by you, mistresses, whence would this joy of mine have come? Your ladyship sent Cai Ge again yesterday to bring me presents, but my grandson kotowed at the door, with his face turned towards the upper quarters."

"When is he going to his post?" Li Wan inquired, with a smile.

Nurse Lai heaved a sigh. "How can I interfere with them?" she answered. "Why, I let them have their own way and start when they like! The other day, they were at my house, and they prostrated themselves before me; but I could find no complimentary remark to make to him, so, 'Sir!' I said, 'putting aside that you're an official, you've lived in a reckless and dissolute way, for now thirty years. You should, it's true, have been people's bond-servant, but from the moment you came out of your mother's womb, your master graciously accorded you your liberty. Thanks, above, to the boundless blessings showered upon you by your lord, and, below, to the favor of your father and mother, you're like a noble scion and a gentleman, able to read and to write; and you have been carried about by maids, old matrons, and nurses, just as if you had been a very phoenix! But now that you've grown up and reached this age, do you have the faintest notion of what the two words 'bond-servant' imply? All you think of is to enjoy your benefits. But what hardships your grandfather and father had to bear, in slaving away for two or three generations, before they succeeded, after ever so many ups and downs, in raising up a thing like you, you don't at all know! From your very infancy, you ever ailed from this, or sickened for that, so that the money that was expended on your behalf, would suffice to fuse into a lifelike silver image of you! At the age of twenty, you again received the bounty of your master in the shape of a promise to purchase official status for you. But just mark, how many inmates of the principal branch and main offspring have to endure privation, and suffer the pangs of hunger! So beware you, who are the offshoot of a bond-servant, lest you snap your happiness! After enjoying so many good things for a decade, by the help of what spirits, and the agency of what devils have you, I wonder, managed to so successfully entreat your master as to induce him to bring you to the fore again and select you for office? Magistrates may be minor officials, but their functions are none the less onerous. In whatever district they obtain a post, they become the father and mother of that particular locality. If you therefore don't mind your business, and look after your duties in such a way as to acquit yourself of your loyal obligations, to prove your gratitude to the state and to show obedience and reverence to your lord, heaven, I fear, will not even bear with you!'"

Li Wan and lady Feng laughed. "You're too full of misgivings!" they observed. "From what we can see of him, he's all right! Some years back, he paid us a visit or two; but it's many years now that he hasn't put his foot here. At the close of each year, and on birthdays, we've simply seen his name brought in, that's all. The other day, that he came to knock his head before our venerable senior and Madame Wang, we caught sight of him in her courtyard yonder; and, got up in the uniform of his new office, he looked so dignified, and stouter too than before. Now that he has got this post, you should be quite happy; instead of that you worry and fret about this and that! If he does get bad, why, he has his father and mother yet to take care of him, so all you need do is to be cheerful and content! When you've got time to spare, do get into a chair and come in and have a game of cards and a chat with our worthy senior; and who ever will have the face to hurt your feelings? Why, were you go to your home, you'd also have there houses and halls, and who is there who would not hold you in high respect? You're certainly, what one would call, a venerable old dame!"

Ping'er poured a cup of tea and brought it to her. Nurse Lai speedily stood up. "You could have asked any girl to do this for me; it wouldn't have mattered! But here I'm troubling you again!"

Apologizing, she resumed, sipping her tea the while: "My lady you're not aware that young girls of this age must be in everything kept strictly in hand. In the event of any license, they're sure to find time to kick up trouble, and annoy their elders. Those, who know (how well they are supervised), will then say that children are always up to mischief. But those, who don't, will maintain that they take advantage of their wealthy position to despise people; to the detriment as well of their mistresses' reputation. How I regret that there's nothing that I can do with him. Time after time, have I had to send for his father; and he has been the better, after a scolding from him." Pointing at Baoyu, "I don't mind whether you feel angry with me for what I'm going to say," she proceeded, "but if your father were to attempt now to exercise ever so little control over you, your venerable grandmother is sure to try and screen you. Yet, when in days gone by your worthy father was young, he used to be beaten by your grandfather. Who hasn't seen him do it? But did your father, in his youth resemble you, who have neither fear for God or man? There was also our senior master, on the other side, Mr. Jia She. He was, I admit, wild; but never such a crossgrained fellow as yourself; and yet he too had his daily dose of the whip. There was besides the father of your elder cousin Zhen, of the eastern mansion. He had a disposition that flared up like a fire over which oil is poured. If anything was said, and he flew into a rage, why, talk about a son, it was really as if he tortured a robber. From all I can now see and hear, Mr. Zhen keeps his son in check just as much as was the custom in old days among his ancestors; the only thing is that he abides by it in some respects, but not in others. Besides, he doesn't exercise the least restraint over his own self, so is it to be wondered at if all his cousins and nieces don't respect him? If you've got any sense about you, you'll only be too glad that I speak to you in this wise; but if you haven't, you mayn't be very well able to say anything openly to me, but you'll inwardly abuse me, who knows to what extent!"

As she reproved him, they saw Lai Da's wife arrive. In close succession came Zhou Rui's wife along with Zhang Cai's wife to report various matters.

"A wife," laughed lady Feng, "has come to fetch her mother-in-law!"

I haven't come to fetch our old dame," Lai Da's wife smilingly rejoined, "but to inquire whether you, my lady and the young ladies, will confer upon us the honor of your company?"

When nurse Lai caught this remark, she smiled. "I've really grown quite idiotic! What," she exclaimed, "was right and proper for me to say, I didn't say, but I went on talking instead a lot of rot and rubbish! As our relatives and friends are presenting their congratulations to our grandson for having been selected to fill up that office of his, we find ourselves under the necessity of giving a banquet at home. But I was thinking that it wouldn't do, if we kept a feast going the whole day, and we invited this one, and not that one. Reflecting also that it was thanks to our master's vast bounty that we've come in for this unforeseen glory and splendor, I felt quite agreeable to do anything, even though it may entail the collapse of our household. I therefore advised his father to give banquets on three consecutive days. That he should, on the first, put up several tables, and a stage in our mean garden, and invite your venerable dowager lady, the senior ladies, junior ladies, and young ladies to come and have some distraction during the day, and that he should have several tables laid on the stage in the main pavilion outside, and request the senior and junior gentlemen to confer upon us the luster of their presence. That for the second day, we should ask our relatives and friends; and that for the third, we should invite our companions from the two mansions. In this way, we'll have three days' excitement, and, by the boundless favor of our master, we'll have the benefit of enjoying the honor of your society."

"When is it to be?" Li Wan and lady Feng inquired, smilingly. "As far as we are concerned, we'll feel it our duty to come. And we hope that our worthy senior may feel in the humor to go. But there's no saying for certain!"

"The day chosen is the fourteenth," Lai Da's wife eagerly replied. "Just come for the sake of our old mother-in-law!"

"I can't tell about the others," lady Feng explained with a laugh, "but as for me I shall positively come. I must however tell you beforehand that I've no congratulatory presents to give you. Nor do I know anything about tips to players or others. As soon as I shall have done eating, I shall bolt, so don't laugh at me."

"Fiddlesticks!" Lai Da's wife laughed. "Were your ladyship disposed, you could well afford to give us twenty and thirty thousand taels."

"I'm off now to invite our venerable mistress," nurse Lai smilingly remarked. "And if her ladyship also agrees to come, I shall deem it a greater honor than ever conferred upon me."

Having said this, she went on to issue some injunctions; after which, she got up to go, when the sight of Zhou Rui's wife reminded her of something.

"Of course!" she consequently observed. "I've got one more question to ask you, my lady. What did sister-in-law Zhou's son do to incur blame, that he was packed off, and his services dispensed with?"

"I was just about to tell your daughter-in-law," lady Feng answered smilingly, after listening to her question, "but with so many things to preoccupy me, it slipped from my memory! When you get home, sister-in-law Lai, explain to that old husband of yours that we won't have his, (Zhou Rui's,) son kept in either of the mansions; and that he can tell him to go about his own business!"

Lai Da's wife had no option but to express her acquiescence. Zhou Rui's wife however speedily fell on her knees and gave way to urgent entreaties.

"What is it all about?" nurse Lai shouted. "Tell me and let me determine the right and wrong of the question."

"The other day," lady Feng observed, "that my birthday was celebrated, that young fellow of his got drunk, before the wine ever went round; and when the old dame, over there, sent presents, he didn't go outside to give a helping hand, but squatted down, instead, and upbraided people. Even the presents he wouldn't carry inside. And it was only after the two girls had come indoors that he eventually got the servant-lads and brought them in. Those lads were however careful enough in what they did, but as for him, he let the box he held slip from his hands, and bestrewed the whole courtyard with cakes. When everyone had left, I deputed Caiming to go and talk to him; but he then turned round and gave Caiming a regular scolding. So what's the use of not bundling off a disorderly rascal like him, who neither shows any regard for discipline or heaven?"

"I was wondering what it could be!" nurse Lai ventured. "Was it really about this? My lady, listen to me! If he has done anything wrong, thrash him and scold him, until you make him mend his ways, and finish with it! But to drive him out of the place, will never, by any manner of means, do. He isn't, besides, to be treated like a child born in our household. He is at present employed as Madame Wang's attendant, so if you carry out your purpose of expelling him, her ladyship's face will be put to the blush. My idea is that you should, my lady, give him a lesson by letting him have several whacks with a cane so as to induce him to abstain from wine in the future. If you then retain him in your service as hitherto he'll be all right! If you don't do it for his mother's sake, do it at least for that of Madame Wang!"

After lending an ear to her arguments, lady Feng addressed herself to Lai Da's wife. "Well, in that case," she said, "call him over tomorrow and give him forty blows; and don't let him after this touch any more wine!"

Lai Da's wife promised to execute her directions. Zhou Rui's wife then kotowed and rose to her feet. But she also persisted upon prostrating herself before nurse Lai; and only desisted when Lai Da's wife pulled her up. But presently the trio took their departure, and Li Wan and her companions sped back into the garden.

When evening came, lady Feng actually bade the servants go and look (into the loft), and when they discovered a lot of painting materials, which had been put away long ago, they brought them into the garden. Baochai and her friends then selected such as they deemed suitable. But as they only had as yet half the necessaries they required, they drew out a list of the other half and sent it to lady Feng, who, needless for us to particularize, had the different articles purchased, according to the specimens supplied.

By a certain day, the silk had been sized outside, a rough sketch drawn, and both returned into the garden. Baoyu therefore was day after day to be found over at Xichun's, doing his best to help her in her hard work. But Tanchun, Li Wan, Yingchun, Baochai, and the other girls likewise congregated in her quarters, and sat with her when they were at leisure, as they could, in the first place, watch the progress of the painting, and as secondly they were able to conveniently see something of each other.

When Baochai perceived how cool and pleasant the weather was getting, and how the nights were beginning again to gradually draw out, she came and found her mother, and consulted with her, until they got some needlework ready. Of a day, she would cross over to the quarters of dowager lady Jia and Madame Wang, and twice pay her salutations, but she could not help as well amusing them and sitting with them to keep them company. When free, she would come and see her cousins in the garden, and have, at odd times, a chat with them, so having, during daylight no leisure to speak of, she was wont, of a night, to ply her needle by lamplight, and only retire to sleep after the third watch had come and gone.

As for Daiyu, she had, as a matter of course, a relapse of her complaint regularly every year, soon after the spring equinox and autumn solstice. But she had, during the last autumn, also found her grandmother Jia in such buoyant spirits, that she had walked a little too much on two distinct occasions, and naturally fatigued herself more than was good for her. Recently, too, she had begun to cough and to feel heavier than she had done at ordinary times, so she never by any chance put her foot out of doors, but remained at home and looked after her health. When at times, dullness crept over her, she longed for her cousins to come and chat with her and dispel her despondent feelings. But whenever Baochai or any of her cousins paid her a visit, she barely uttered half a dozen words, before she felt quite averse to any society. Yet one and all made every allowance for her illness. And as she had ever been in poor health and not strong enough to resist any annoyance, they did not find the least fault with her, despite even any lack of propriety she showed in playing the hostess with them, or any remissness on her part in observing the prescribed rules of etiquette.

Baochai came, on this occasion to call on her. The conversation started on the symptoms of her ailment. "The various doctors, who visit this place," Baochai consequently remarked, "may, it's true, be all very able practitioners, but you take their medicines and don't reap the least benefit! Wouldn't it be as well therefore to ask some other person of note to come and see you? And could he succeed in getting you all right, wouldn't it be nice? Here you year by year ail away throughout the whole length of spring and summer; but you're neither so old nor so young, so what will be the end of it? Besides, it can't go on forever."

"It's no use," Daiyu rejoined. "I know well enough that there's no cure for this complaint of mine! Not to speak of when I'm unwell, why even when I'm not, my state is such that one can see very well that there's no hope!"

Baochai shook her head. "Quite so!" she ventured. "An old writer says: 'Those who eat, live.' But what you've all along eaten hasn't been enough to strengthen your energies and physique. This isn't a good thing!"

Daiyu heaved a sigh. "Whether I'm to live or die is all destiny!" she said. "Riches and honors are in the hands of heaven; and human strength cannot suffice to forcibly get even them! But my complaint this year seems to be far worse than in past years, instead of any better."

While deploring her lot, she coughed two or three times. "It struck me," Baochai said, "that in that prescription of yours I saw yesterday there was far too much ginseng and cinnamon. They are splendid tonics, of course, but too many heating things are not good. I think that the first urgent thing to do is to ease the liver and give tone to the stomach. When once the fire in the liver is reduced, it will not be able to overcome the stomach; and, when once the digestive organs are free of ailment, drink, and food will be able to give nutriment to the human frame. As soon as you get out of bed, every morning, take one ounce of birds' nests, of superior quality, and five mace of sugar candy and prepare congee with them in a silver kettle. When once you get into the way of taking this decoction, you'll find it far more efficacious than medicines; for it possesses the highest virtue for invigorating the vagina and bracing up the physique."

"You've certainly always treated people with extreme consideration," sighed Daiyu, "but such a supremely suspicious person am I that I imagined that you inwardly concealed some evil design! Yet ever since the day on which you represented to me how unwholesome it was to read obscene books, and you gave me all that good advice, I've felt most grateful to you! I've hitherto, in fact, been mistaken in my opinion; and the truth of the matter is that I remained under this misconception up to the very present. But you must carefully consider that when my mother died, I hadn't even any sisters or brothers; and that up to this my fifteenth year there has never been a single person to admonish me as you did the other day. Little wonder is it if that girl Yün speaks well of you! Whenever, in former days, I heard her heap praise upon you, I felt uneasy in my mind, but, after my experiences of yesterday, I see how right she was. When you, for instance, began to tell me all those things, I didn't forgive you at the time, but, without worrying yourself in the least about it you went on, contrariwise, to tender me the advice you did. This makes it evident that I have labored under a mistaken idea! Had I not made this discovery the other day, I wouldn't be speaking like this to your very face today. You told me a few minutes back to take bird's nest congee; but birds' nests are, I admit, easily procured; yet all on account of my sickly constitution and of the relapses I have every year of this complaint of mine, which amounts to nothing, doctors have had to be sent for, medicines, with ginseng and cinnamon, have had to be concocted, and I've given already such trouble as to turn heaven and earth topsy-turvey; so were I now to start again a new fad, by having some birds' nests congee or other prepared, our worthy senior, Madame Wang, and lady Feng, will, all three of them, have no objection to raise; but that posse of matrons and maids below will unavoidably despise me for my excessive fussiness! Just notice how everyone in here ogles wildly like tigers their prey; and stealthily says one thing and another, simply because they see how fond our worthy ancestor is of both Baoyu and lady Feng, and how much more won't they do these things with me? What's more, I'm not a mistress. I've really come here as a mere refugee, for I had no one to sustain me and no one to depend upon. They already bear me considerable dislike; so much so, that I'm still quite at a loss whether I should stay or go; and why should I make them heap execrations upon me?"

"Well, in that case," Baochai observed, "I'm too in the same plight as yourself!"

"How can you compare yourself with me?" Daiyu exclaimed. "You have a mother; and a brother as well! You've also got some business and land in here, and, at home, you can call houses and fields your own. It's only therefore the ties of relationship, which make you stay here at all. Neither are you in anything whether large or small, in their debt for one single cash or even half a one; and when you want to go, you're at liberty to go. But I have nothing whatever that I can call my own. Yet, in what I eat, wear, and use, I am, in every trifle, entirely on the same footing as the young ladies in their household, so how ever can that mean lot not despise me out and out?"

"The only extra expense they'll have to go to by and bye," Baochai laughed, "will be to get one more trousseau, that's all. And for the present, it's too soon yet to worry yourself about that!"

At this insinuation, Daiyu unconsciously blushed scarlet. "One treats you," she smiled, "as a decent sort of person, and confides in you the woes of one's heart, and, instead of sympathizing with me, you make me the means of raising a laugh!"

"Albeit I raise a laugh at your expense," Baochai rejoined, a smile curling her lips, "what I say is none the less true! But compose your mind! I'll try every day that I'm here to cheer you up; so come to me with every grievance or trouble, for I shall, needless to say, dispel those that are within my power. Notwithstanding that I have a brother, you yourself know well enough what he's like! All I have is a mother, so I'm just a trifle better off than you! We can therefore well look upon ourselves as being in the same boat, and sympathize with each other. You have, besides, plenty of wits about you, so why need you give way to groans, as did Sima Niu? What you said just now is quite right; but, you should worry and fret about as little and not as much as you can. On my return home, tomorrow, I'll tell my mother; and, as I think there must be still some birds' nests in our house, we'll send you several ounces of them. You can then tell the servant-maids to prepare some for you at whatever time you want every day; and you'll thus be suiting your own convenience and be giving no trouble or annoyance to anyone."

"The things are, of themselves, of little account," eagerly responded Daiyu laughingly. "What's difficult to find is one with as much feeling as yourself."

"What's there in this worth speaking about?" Baochai said. "What grieves me is that I fail to be as nice as I should be with those I come across. But, I presume, you feel quite done up now, so I'll be off!"

"Come in the evening again," Daiyu pressed her, "and have a chat with me."

While assuring her that she would come, Baochai walked out, so let us leave her alone for the present.

Daiyu, meanwhile, drank a few sips of thin congee, and then once more lay herself down on her bed. But before the sun set, the weather unexpectedly changed, and a fine drizzling rain set in. So gently come the autumn showers that dull and fine are subject to uncertain alternations. The shades of twilight gradually fell on this occasion. The heavens too got so overcast as to look deep black. Besides the effect of this change on her mind, the patter of the rain on the bamboo tops intensified her despondency, and, concluding that Baochai would be deterred from coming, she took up, in the lamp light, the first book within her reach, which turned out to be the "Treasury of Miscellaneous Lyrics." Finding among these "the Pinings of a maiden in autumn," "the Anguish of Separation," and other similar poems, Daiyu felt unawares much affected; and, unable to restrain herself from giving vent to her feelings in writing, she, there and then, improvised the following stanza, in the same strain as the one on separation; complying with the rules observed in the "Spring River-Flower" and "Moonlight Night." These verses, she then entitled "the Poem on the Autumn evening, when wind and rain raged outside the window." Their burden was:

> In autumn, flowers decay; herbage, when autumn comes, doth yellow turn.
> On long autumnal nights, the autumn lanterns with bright radiance burn.
> As from my window autumn scenes I scan, autumn endless doth seem.
> This mood how can I bear, when wind and rain despondency enhance?
> How sudden break forth wind and rain, and help to make the autumntide!
> Fright snaps my autumn dreams, those dreams which under my lattice I dreamt.
> A sad autumnal gloom enclasps my heart, and drives all sleep away!
> In person I approach the autumn screen to snuff the weeping wick.
> The tearful candles with a flickering flame consume on their short stands.
> They stir up grief, dazzle my eyes, and a sense of parting arouse.
> In what family's courts do not the blasts of autumn winds intrude?
> And where in autumn does not rain patter against the windowframes?
> The silken quilt cannot ward off the nipping force of autumn winds.

The drip of the half drained water-clock impels the autumn rains.
A lull for few nights reigned, but the wind has again risen in
   strength.
By the lantern I weep, as if I sat with someone who must go.
The small courtyard, full of bleak mist, is now become quite deso-
   late.
With quick drip drops the rain on the distant bamboos and vacant
   sills.
What time, I wonder, will the wind and rain their howl and patter
   cease?
The tears already I have shed have soaked through the window
   gauze.

After scanning her verses, she flung the brush aside, and was just
on the point of retiring to rest, when a waiting-maid announced that
"master Secundus, Mr. Baoyu, has come." Barely was the announcement out of her lips, than Baoyu appeared on the scene with a large
bamboo hat on his head, and a wrapper thrown over his shoulders.
Of a sudden, a smile betrayed itself on Daiyu's lips. "Where does this
fisherman come from?" she exclaimed.

"Are you better today?" Baoyu inquired with alacrity. "Have you had
any medicines? How much rice have you had to eat today?"

While plying her with questions, he took off the hat and divested
himself of the wrapper; and, promptly raising the lamp with one hand,
he screened it with the other and threw its rays upon Daiyu's face.
Then straining his eyes, he scrutinized her for a while. "You look better
today," he smiled.

As soon as he threw off his wrapper, Daiyu noticed that he was clad in
a short red silk jacket, the worse for wear; that he was girded with a green
sash, and that, about his knees, his nether garments were visible, made
of green thin silk, brocaded with flowers. Below these, he wore embroidered gauze socks, worked all over with twisted gold thread, and a pair
of shoes ornamented with butterflies and clusters of fallen flowers.

"Above, you fight shy of the rain," Daiyu remarked, "but aren't these
shoes and socks below afraid of rain? Yet they're quite clean!"

"This suit is complete!" Baoyu smiled. "I've got a pair of crab-wood
clogs, I put on to come over; but I took them off under the eaves of
the verandah."

Daiyu's attention was then attracted by the extreme fineness and
lightness of the texture of his wrapper and hat, which were unlike those
sold in the market places. "With what grass are they plaited?" she con-

sequently asked. "It would be strange if you didn't, with these sort of things on, look like a very hedgehog!"

"These three articles are a gift from the Prince of Beijing," Baoyu answered. "Ordinarily, when it rains, he too wears this kind of outfit at home. But if it has taken your fancy, I'll have a suit made for you. There's nothing peculiar about the other things, but this hat is funny! The crown at the top is movable; so if you want to wear a hat, during snowy weather in wintertime, you pull off the bamboo pegs, and remove the crown, and there you only have the circular brim. This is worn, when it snows, by men and women alike. I'll give you one therefore to wear in the wintry snowy months."

"I don't want it!" laughed Daiyu. "Were I to wear this sort of thing, I'd look like one of those fisherwomen, one sees depicted in pictures or represented on the stage!"

Upon reaching this point, she remembered that there was some connection between her present remarks and the comparison she had some time back made with regard to Baoyu, and, before she had time to indulge in regrets, a sense of shame so intense overpowered her that the color rushed to her face, and, leaning her head on the table, she coughed and coughed till she could not stop. Baoyu, however, did not detect her embarrassment; but catching sight of some verses lying on the table, he eagerly snatched them up and read them from beginning to end. "Splendid!" he could not help crying. But the moment Daiyu heard his exclamation, she speedily jumped to her feet, and clutched the verses and burnt them over the lamp.

"I've already committed them sufficiently to memory!" Baoyu laughed.

"I want to have a little rest," Daiyu said, "so please get away; come back again tomorrow."

At these words, Baoyu drew back his hand, and producing from his breast a gold watch about the size of a walnut, he looked at the time. The hand pointed between eight and nine P.M.; so hastily putting it away, "You should certainly retire to rest!" he replied. "My visit has upset you. I've quite tired you out this long while." With these apologies, he threw the wrapper over him, put on the rain-hat, and quitted the room. But turning round, he retraced his steps inside. "Is there anything you fancy to eat?" he asked. "If there be, tell me, and I'll let our venerable ancestor know of it tomorrow as soon as it's day. Won't I explain things clearer than any of the old matrons could?"

"Let me," rejoined Daiyu smiling, "think in the night. I'll let you know early tomorrow. But harken, it's raining harder than it did; so be off at once! Have you got any attendants, or no?"

"Yes!" interposed the two matrons. "There are servants to wait on him. They're outside holding his umbrella and lighting the lanterns."

"Are they lighting lanterns with this weather?" laughed Daiyu.

"It won't hurt them!" Baoyu answered. "They're made of sheep's horn, so they don't mind the rain."

Hearing this, Daiyu put back her hand, and, taking down an ornamented glass lantern in the shape of a ball from the bookcase, she asked the servants to light a small candle and bring it to her; after which, she handed the lantern to Baoyu. "This," she said, "gives out more light than the others; and is just the thing for rainy weather."

"I've also got one like it." Baoyu replied. "But fearing lest they might slip, fall down, and break it, I did not have it lighted and brought round."

"What's of more account," Daiyu inquired, "harm to a lantern or to a human being? You're not besides accustomed to wearing clogs, so tell them to walk ahead with those lanterns. This one is as light and handy as it is light-giving; and is really adapted for rainy weather, so wouldn't it be well if you carried it yourself? You can send it over to me tomorrow! But, were it even to slip from your hand, it wouldn't matter much. How is it that you've also suddenly developed this money-grabbing sort of temperament? It's as bad as if you ripped your intestines to secrete pearls in."

After these words, Baoyu approached her and took the lantern from her. Ahead then advanced two matrons, with umbrellas and sheep horn lanterns, and behind followed a couple of waiting-maids also with umbrellas. Baoyu handed the glass lantern to a young maid to carry, and, supporting himself on her shoulder, he straightway wended his steps on his way back.

But presently arrived an old servant from the Hengwu court, provided as well with an umbrella and a lantern, to bring over a large bundle of birds' nests, and a packet of foreign sugar, pure as powder, and white as petals of plum-blossom and flakes of snow. "These," she said, "are much better than what you can buy. Our young lady sends you word, miss, to first go on with these. When you've done with them, she'll let you have some more."

"Many thanks for the trouble you've taken!" Daiyu returned for answer; and then asked her to go and sit outside and have a cup of tea.

"I won't have any tea," the old servant smiled. "I've got something else to attend to."

"I'm well aware that you've all got plenty in hand," Daiyu resumed with a smiling countenance. "But the weather being cool now and the nights long, it's more expedient than ever to establish two things: a nightclub and a gambling place."

"I won't disguise the fact from you, miss," the old servant laughingly observed, "that I've managed this year to win plenty of money. Several servants have, under any circumstances, to do night duty; and, as any neglect in keeping watch wouldn't be the right thing, isn't it as well to have a nightclub, as one can sit on the lookout and dispel dullness as well? But it's again my turn to play the croupier today, so I must be getting along to the place, as the garden gate, will, by this time, be nearly closing!"

This rejoinder evoked a laugh from Daiyu. "I've given you all this bother," she remarked, "and made you lose your chances of getting money, just to bring these things in the rain." And calling a servant she bade her present her with several hundreds of cash to buy some wine with, to drive the damp away.

"I've uselessly put you again, miss, to the expense of giving me a tip for wine," the old servant smiled. But saying this she knocked her forehead before her; and issuing outside, she received the money, after which, she opened her umbrella, and trudged back.

Zijuan meanwhile put the birds' nests away; and removing afterwards the lamps, she lowered the portières and waited upon Daiyu until she lay herself down to sleep.

While she reclined all alone on her pillow, Daiyu thought gratefully of Baochai. At one moment, she envied her for having a mother and a brother; and at another, she mused that with the friendliness Baoyu had ever shown her they were bound to be the victims of suspicion. But the pitter-patter of the rain, dripping on the bamboo tops and banana leaves, fell on her ear; and, as a fresh coolness penetrated the curtain, tears once more unconsciously trickled down her cheeks. In this frame of mind, she continued straight up to the fourth watch, when she at last gradually dropped into a sound sleep.

For the time, however, there is nothing that we can add. So should you, reader, desire to know any subsequent details, peruse what is written in the next chapter.

CHAPTER 46

An improper man with difficulty keeps from improprieties. The maid, Yuanyang, vows to break off the marriage match.

Lin Daiyu, to resume our story, dropped off gradually to sleep about the close of the fourth watch. As there is therefore nothing more that we can for the present say about her, let us take up the thread of our narrative with lady Feng.

Upon hearing that Madame Xing wanted to see her, she could not make out what it could be about, so hurriedly putting on some extra things on her person and head, she got into a carriage and crossed over.

Madame Xing at once dismissed every attendant from her suite of apartments. "I sent for you," she began, addressing herself to lady Feng, in a confidential tone, "not for anything else, but on account of something which places me on the horns of a dilemma. My husband has entrusted me with a job; and being quite at my wits' ends how to act, I'd like first to consult with you. My husband has taken quite a fancy to Yuanyang, who is in our worthy senior's rooms; so much so that he's desirous to get her into his quarters as a secondary wife. He has deputed me therefore to ask her of our venerable ancestor. I know that this is quite an ordinary matter. Yet I can't help fearing that our worthy senior may refuse to give her. But do you perchance see your way to bring this concern about?"

Lady Feng listened to her. "You shouldn't, I say, go and bang your head against a nail!" she then vehemently exclaimed. "Were our old ancestor separated from Yuanyang, she wouldn't even touch her rice! How ever could she reconcile herself to part from her? Besides, our worthy senior has time and again said, in the course of a chat, that she can't see the earthly use of a man well up in years, as your lord and master is, having here one concubine, and there another? That cooping them up in his rooms, is a mere waste of human beings. That he neglects his constitution and doesn't husband it; and that he doesn't either attend diligently to his official duties, but spends his whole days in boozing with his young concubines. When your ladyship hears these nice doings of his, don't you feel enamored with that fine gentleman of ours? Were he even to try, at this juncture, to beat a retreat, he couldn't, I fear, effectively do so.

"Yet, instead of (making an effort to turn tail), he wants to go and dig the tiger's nostrils with a blade of straw. Don't, my lady, be angry with me; but I daren't undertake the errand. It's clear as day that it will be a wild goose chase. What's more, it will do him no good; but will, contrariwise, heap disgrace upon his own head! Our Mr. Jia She is now so stricken in years, that in all his actions he unavoidably behaves somewhat as a dotard. It would be well therefore for your ladyship to advise him what to do. It isn't as if he were in the prime of life to be able to do all these things with impunity! He's got at present a whole array of brothers, nieces, sons, and grandsons; and should he still go on in this wild sort of way, how will he be able to face any of them?"

Madame Xing gave a sardonic smile. "There are endless wealthy families with three and four concubines," she said, "and is it in ours that such a thing won't do? But were I even to tender him as much advice as I can, it isn't at all likely that he'll abide by it! Even though that maid be one beloved by our venerable senior, it doesn't follow that she'll very well be able to give a rebuff to a hoary-bearded elderly son, and, erewhile, an official, were he to express a wish to have her as an inmate of his household! I sent for you for no other purpose than to deliberate with you, and here you take the initiative and enumerate a whole array of shortcomings. But is there any reason why I should commission you to go? Of course I'll go and speak to her! You make a bold statement that I don't give him any good counsel; but don't you yet know that with a disposition, such as his, he rushes, before I can very well open my lips to advise him, into a tantrum with me?"

Lady Feng was well alive to the fact that Madame Xing was, by nature, simple and weak-minded, and that all she knew was to adulate Jia She so as to ensure her own safety. That she was, in the next place, ever ready, so greedy was she, to grasp as much hard cash and as many effects, as she could lay hold of, for her own private gain. That she left all family matters, irrespective of important or unimportant, under the sole control of Jia She; but that, whenever anything turned up, involving any receipts or payments, she extorted an unusual percentage, the moment the money passed through her clutches, giving out as a pretence: "Well Jia She is so extravagant that I have to interfere and effect sufficient economies to enable us to make up our deficits." And that she would not trust anyone, whether son, daughter, or servant, nor lend an ear to a single word of remonstrance. When she therefore now heard Madame Xing speak as she did, she concluded that she must be in another of her perverse moods, and that any admonitions would be of no avail. So hastily forcing a smile: "My lady," she observed, "you're perfectly right in your remarks! But how long can I have lived, and what discrimination can I boast of? It seems to me that if a father and mother do not bestow, not a mere servant-girl like she is, but a living jewel of the size of her, on one like Mr. Jia She, to whom are they likely to give her? How can one give faith to words spoken behind one's back? So what a fool I was (in cramming what I heard down my throat)! Just take our Mr. Secundus, (my husband), as an instance. If ever he does anything to incur blame, Mr. Jia She and you, my lady, feel so wrath with him as to only wish you could lay hands upon him there and then and give him such a blow as would kill him downright, but the moment you set eyes on his face, your whole resentment vanishes, and lo, you again let him have, as of old, everything, and anything, much though both of you might relish it in your hearts! Our worthy ancestor will certainly therefore behave in the present instance, with equal liberality, towards Mr. Jia She! So if her ladyship feels in the humor today, she'll let him have her, I fancy, at once this very day, if he makes the proper advances. But I'll go ahead and coax our venerable senior; and, when your ladyship comes over, I'll find some pretence to get out of the way, and take along with me those too who may be present in her rooms, so as to make it convenient for you to broach the subject. If she gives her, so much the better. But if even she doesn't, it won't matter; for none of the inmates will have any idea what the object of your mission could have been."

After listening to her suggestion, Madame Xing began again to feel in a happier frame of mind. "My idea is," she observed, "that I shouldn't start by mentioning anything to our venerable senior, for were she to say that she wouldn't give her, the matter would be simply quashed on the head. I can't help thinking that I should first and foremost quietly approach Yuanyang on the subject. She will, of course, feel extremely ashamed, but when I explain everything minutely to her, she'll certainly have nothing to say against the proposal, and everything will be all right. I can then speak to our old senior; and, despite any desire on her part not to accede to our wishes, she won't be able to put the girl off, provided she herself be willing; for as the adage says: 'If a person wishes to go, it's no use trying to keep him.' Thus needless to say, the whole thing will be satisfactorily settled!"

"You're really shrewd in your devices, my lady!" lady Feng smilingly ejaculated. "This is perfect in every respect! For without taking Yuan-yang into account, what girl does not long to rise high, or hope to exalt herself, or think of pushing herself forward above the rest as to cast away the chances of becoming half a mistress, and prefer instead being a maid, and merely becoming by and bye the mate of some servant-lad?"

"Quite so!" Madame Xing smiled. "But let's put Yuanyang aside. Who is there, even among the various elderly waiting-maids, who look after the house, who wouldn't be only too willing to step into these shoes? You'd better then go ahead. But, mind, don't let the cat out of the bag! I'll join you as soon as I can finish my evening meal."

"Yuanyang," thereupon secretly reflected lady Feng, "has always been an extremely shrewd-minded girl; to such a degree, that there is notwithstanding all our arguments, no saying positively whether she'll accept or refuse. So were I to go ahead, and Madame Xing to follow me by and bye, there won't be any occasion for her to grumble or complain, so long as she assents; but, if she doesn't, why, Madame Xing, who is so suspicious a creature, will possibly imagine that I've been gassing with her, and been the means of making her put on side and assume high airs. When Madame Xing finds then that my conjectures have turned out true again, her shame will be converted into anger, and she'll so vent her spite upon me that I shall, after all, be put in a false position. Would it not be better then that she and I should go together; for, if she says 'yes,' I'll be all right; and, if she replies 'no,' I'll be on the safe side; and no suspicion, of any kind, will fall upon me!"

At the close of her reflections, "As I was about to cross over here," she remarked laughingly, "our aunt yonder sent us two baskets of quails, and I gave orders that they should be fried, with the idea that they should be brought to your ladyship, in time for you to have some at your evening repast. Just as I was stepping inside the main entrance, I saw the servant-boys carrying your curricle; they said that it was your ladyship's vehicle, that it had cracked, and that they were taking it to be repaired. Wouldn't it be as well then that you should now come in my carriage, for it will be better for you and me to get there together?"

At this suggestion, Madame Xing directed her servants to come and change her costume. Lady Feng quickly waited upon her, and in a while the two ladies got into one and the same curricle and drove over.

"My lady," lady Feng went on to say, "it would be well for you to look up our worthy senior, for were I to accompany you, and her ladyship to ask me what was the object of my visit, it would be rather awkward. The best way is for your ladyship to go first, and I'll join you, as soon as I divest myself of my fine clothes."

Madame Xing noticed how reasonable her proposal was, and she readily betook herself to old lady Jia's quarters. But after a chat with her senior, she quitted the apartment, under the pretence that she was going to Madame Wang's rooms. Then making her exit by the back door, she passed in front of Yuanyang's bedroom. Here she saw Yuanyang sitting, hard at work at some needlework. The moment she caught sight of Madame Xing, she rose to her feet.

"What are you up to?" Madame Xing laughingly inquired. "Let me see! How much nicer you embroider artificial flowers now!"

So speaking, she entered, and, taking the needlework from her hands, she scrutinized it, while extolling its beauty. Then laying down the work, and scanning her again from head to foot, she observed that her costume consisted of a half-new, gray thin silk jacket, and a bluish satin waistcoat with scollops; that below this came a water-green jupe; that her waist was slim as that of a wasp; that her shoulders sloped as if pared; that her face resembled a duck's egg; that her hair was black and shiny; that her nose was very high, and that on both her cheeks were slightly visible several small flat moles.

Yuanyang realised how intently she was being passed under scrutiny, and began to feel inwardly uneasy; while utter astonishment prevailed in her mind. "Madame," she felt impelled to ask, "what do you come for at this impossible hour?"

At a wink from Madame Xing, her attendants withdrew from the room. Madame Xing forthwith seated herself, and grasped Yuanyang's hand in hers. "I've come," she smiled, "with the special purpose of presenting you my congratulations."

This reply enabled Yuanyang at once to form within herself some surmise more or less correct of the object of her errand, and suddenly blushing crimson, she lowered her head, and uttered not a word.

"You know well enough," she next heard Madame Xing resume, "that there's not a single reliable person with my husband; but much though we'd like to purchase some other girl we fear that such as might come out of a broker's household wouldn't be quite spotless and taintless. Nor would one be able to get any idea what her failings are, until after she has been purchased and brought home; when she too will be sure, in two or three days, to behave like an imp and play some monkey tricks! That's why we thought of choosing some home-born girl out of those which throng in our mansion, but then again we could find none decent enough; for if her looks were not at fault, her disposition was not proper; and if she possessed this quality, she lacked that one. Hence it is that after repeatedly choosing with dispassionate eye, during half a year, (he finds) that there's only you among that whole bevy of girls, who's worth anything; that in looks, behavior, and deportment, you're gentle, trustworthy, and perfection itself in every respect. His intention therefore is to ask your hand of our old lady and take you over and attach you to his quarters. You won't be treated as one newly-purchased, or newly-sought for outside; for the moment you put your foot into our house, you'll at once have your face shaved and be promoted to a secondary wife; so you'll thus attain as much dignity as honor. More, you're one who is anxious to excel; and, as the proverb says, 'gold will still be exchanged for gold.' My husband has, who'd have thought it, taken a fancy to you, so when you now enter our threshold, you'll fulfill the wish you've cherished all along with such high purpose and lofty aim, and stop the mouths of those persons, who are envious of your lot. Follow me therefore and let's go and lay the matter before our venerable ancestor."

Arguing the while, she dragged her by the hand with the idea of hurrying her off there and then. Yuanyang, however, blushed to her very ears, and, snatching her hand out of her grip she refused to budge.

Madame Xing was conscious that she was under the spell of intense shame. "What's there in this to be ashamed?" she continued, "You needn't besides breathe a word! All you have to do is to follow me, that's all."

Yuanyang continued to droop her head and to decline to go with her. Madame Xing, perceiving her behavior, went on to exhort her. "Is it likely, pray," she said, "that you still hesitate? If you actually don't feel inclined to accept the offer, you're, in real truth, a foolish girl; for here you let go the chances of becoming the secondary consort of a master, and choose instead to continue a servant-girl. You'll be united, in two or three years, to no one higher than some young domestic, and remain as much a bond-servant as ever! If you come along with us, you know that my disposition too is gentle; that I'm not one of those persons, who don't show any regard for anyone; that my husband will also treat you as well as he does everyone else, and that when, in the course of a year or so, you give birth to a son or daughter, you'll be placed on the same footing as myself. And of all the servants at home, will any you may wish to employ not deign to move to execute your orders? If now that you have a chance of becoming a mistress, you don't choose to, why, you'll miss the opportunity, and then you may repent it, but it will be too late!"

Yuanyang still kept her head bent against her chest and spake not a syllable by way of reply.

"How is it," added Madame Xing, "that you, who've ever been so quick have now too begun to be so infirm of purpose? What is there that doesn't fall in with your wishes? Just tell me; and I can safely assure you that you'll have everything done to satisfy you." Yuanyang observed, as hitherto, perfect silence.

"I suppose," laughed Madame Xing, "that having a father and mother, you yourself don't wish to speak, for fear of being put to the blush, and that you want to wait until such time as they consult you about it, eh? This is quite right! But you'd better let me go and make the proposal to them and tell them to come and ascertain your wishes; and whatever your answer then may be just entrust it to them."

This said, she sped into lady Feng's suite of rooms.

Lady Feng had long ago changed her attire, and availed herself of the absence of any bystander in her apartments to confide the whole matter to Ping'er.

Ping'er nodded her head and smiled. "According to my views, success is not so certain," she observed. "She and I have often secretly talked this matter over, and the arguments I heard her propound don't make it the least probable that she'll consent. But all we can say now is: 'We'll see!'"

"Madame Xing," lady Feng remarked, "is sure to come over here to consult with me. If she has assented, well and good; but, if she hasn't, she'll bring displeasure upon her own self, and won't she feel out of countenance, if all of you are present? So tell the others to fry several quails, and get anything nice that goes well with them, and prepare it for our repast, while you can go and stroll about in some other spot, and return when you fancy she has gone."

Hearing this, Ping'er transmitted her wishes word for word to the matrons; after which, she sauntered leisurely all alone, into the garden.

When Yuanyang saw Madame Xing depart, she concluded that she was bound to go into lady Feng's rooms to consult with her, and that someone was sure to come and ask her about the proposal, so thinking it advisable to cross over to this side of the mansion to get out of the way, she consequently repaired in quest of Hupo.

"Should our old mistress," she said to her, "ask for me, just say that I was so unwell that I couldn't even have any breakfast; that I've gone into the garden for a stroll, but that I will be back at once."

Hupo undertook to tell her so, and Yuanyang then betook herself too into the garden. While lolling all over the place, she, contrary to her expectations, encountered Ping'er. Ping'er looked round to see that there was no one about. "Here comes the new secondary wife!" she smilingly exclaimed.

Yuanyang caught this greeting, and promptly the color rose to her face. "How strange it is," she rejoined, "that you've all colluded together to come, with one accord, and scheme against me! But wait until I've had it out with your mistress, and then I'll set things all right."

When Ping'er observed the angry look on Yuanyang's countenance, her conscience was so stricken with remorse, on account of the inconsiderate remark she had passed, that drawing her under the maple tree, she made her sit on the same boulder as herself, and then went so far as to recount to her, from beginning to end, all that transpired, and everything that was said on lady Feng's return, a short while back, from the off mansion.

Blushes flew to Yuanyang's cheeks. Facing Ping'er, she gave a sardonic smile. "We've all ever been friends," she said, "that is: Xiren, Hupo, Suyun, Zijuan, Caixia, Yuchuan, Sheyue, Cuimo, Cuilu, who was in Miss Shi's service and is now gone, Keren, and Jinchuan, now deceased, Xixue, who left, and you, and I. Ever since our youth up, how many chats have the ten or dozen of us not had, and what have we not been up to together? But now that we've grown up, each of us has gone her own way! Yet, my heart is just what it was in days gone by. Whenever there's anything for me to say or do, I don't try to impose upon any of you; so just first treasure in your heart the secret I'm going to tell you, and don't mention it to our lady Secunda! Not to speak of our senior master wishing to make me his concubine, were even our lady to die this very moment, and he to send endless go-betweens, and countless betrothal presents, with the idea of wedding me and taking me over as his lawful primary wife, I wouldn't also go."

Ping'er was at this point desirous to put in some observation, when from behind the boulder became audible the loud tones of laughter. "You most barefaced girl!" a voice cried. "It's well you're not afraid of your teeth falling when you utter such things!"

These words reached the ears of both girls, and, so unawares were they taken, that they got a regular start, and jumping up with all haste they went to see behind the boulder. They found no one else than Xiren, who presented herself before them, with a smiling countenance, and asked: "What's up? Do tell me!"

As she spoke, the trio seated themselves on a rock. Ping'er then imparted to Xiren as well the drift of their recent conversation.

"Properly speaking, we shouldn't pass such judgments," Xiren remarked, after listening to her confidences, "but this senior master of ours is really a most licentious libertine. So much so, that whenever he comes across a girl with any good looks about her, he won't let her out of his grasp."

"Since you don't like to entertain his offer," Ping'er suggested, "I'll put you up to a plan."

"What plan is it?" Yuanyang inquired.

"Just simply tell our old mistress," Ping'er laughed, "this answer: that you've already been promised to our master Secundus, Mr. Lien. Our senior master then won't very well be able to be importunate."

"Ts'ui!" ejaculated Yuanyang. "What a thing you are! Do you still make such suggestions? Didn't your mistress the other day utter this silly nonsense! Who'd have thought it, her words have now come true!"

"If you won't have either of them," Xiren smiled, "my idea is that you should tell our old lady point blank and ask her to give out that she promised you long ago to our master, number two. Our senior master will then banish this fad from his mind."

Yuanyang was overcome with anger, shame, and exasperation. "What dreadful vixens both of you are!" she shouted. "You don't deserve a natural death! I find myself in a fix, and treat you as decent sort of persons and confide in you so that you should arrange matters for me; and not to say that you don't bother yourselves a rap about me, you take turn and turn about to poke fun at me! You're under the impression, in your own minds, that your fates are sealed, and that both of you are bound by and bye to become secondary wives; but I can't help thinking that affairs under the heavens don't so certainly fall in always with one's wishes and expectations! So you'd better now pull up a bit, and not be cheeky to such an excessive degree!"

Both her companions then realized in what state of despair she was, and promptly forcing a smile, "Dear sister," they said, "don't be so touchy! We've been, ever since we were little mites, like very sisters! All we've done is to spontaneously indulge in a little fun in a spot where there's no one present. But tell us what you've decided to do, so that we too should know, and set our minds at ease."

"Decided what?" Yuanyang cried. "All I know is that I won't go; that's finished."

Ping'er shook her head. "You mightn't go," she interposed, "but it isn't likely that the matter will drop. You're well aware what sort of temperament that of our senior master's is. It's true that you're attached to our old mistress' rooms, and that he can't, just at present, presume to do the least thing to you; but can it be, forsooth, that you'll be with the old dame for your whole lifetime? You'll also have to leave to get married, and if you then fall into his hands, it won't go well with you."

Yuanyang smiled ironically. "I won't leave this place so long as my old lady lives!" Yuanyang protested. "In the event of her ladyship departing this life, he'll have, under any circumstances, to also go into mourning for three years; for there's no such thing as starting by marrying a concubine, soon after a mother's death! And while he waits for three years to expire, can one say what may not happen? It will be time enough to talk about it when that date comes. But should I be driven to despair from being hard pressed, I'll cut my hair off and become a nun. If not, there's yet another thing: death! And as for a whole life time I shall not join myself to a man, what joy will not then be mine, for having managed to preserve my purity?"

"In very truth," Ping'er and Xiren laughed, "this vixen has no sense of shame! She has now more than ever spoken whatever came foremost to her lips!"

"What matters a moment's shame," Yuanyang rejoined, "when things have reached this juncture? But if you don't believe my words, well, you'll be able to see by and bye; then you'll feel convinced. Madame Hsing said a short while back that she was going to look up my father and mother, but I'd like to see whether she'll proceed to Nanking to find them."

"Your parents are in Nanking looking after the houses," Ping'er said, "and they can't come up; yet, in the long run, they can be found out. Your elder brother and your sister-in-law are besides in here at present. You, poor thing, are a child born in this establishment. You're not like us two, who are solitary creatures here."

"What does it matter whether I be born here or not?" Yuanyang exclaimed. "'You can lead a horse to a fountain, but you can't make him drink!' So if I don't listen to any proposals, is it likely, may I ask, that they'll kill my father and mother?" While the words were still on her lips, they caught sight of her sister-in-law, advancing from the opposite side. "As they couldn't at once get at your parents," Xiren remarked, "they've, for a certainty, told your sister-in-law."

"All this wench is good for," Yuanyang shouted, "is 'to rush about as if selling camels in the six states!' If she heard what I said, she won't feel flattered."

But while she spoke, her sister-in-law approached them. "Where didn't I look for you?" her sister-in-law smilingly observed. "Have you, miss, run over here? Come along with me; I've got something to tell you!"

Ping'er and Xiren speedily motioned to her to sit down, but (Yuanyang's) sister-in-law demurred. "Young ladies, pray be seated; I've come in search of our girl to tell her something."

Xiren and Ping'er feigned perfect ignorance. "What can it be that it's so pressing?" they said with a smile. "We were engaged in guessing puns here, so let's find out this, before you go."

"What do you want to tell me?" Yuanyang inquired. "Speak out!"

"Follow me!" her sister-in-law laughed. "When we get over there, I'll tell you. It's really some good tidings!"

"Is it perchance what Madame Xing has told you?" Yuanyang asked.

"Since you, miss, know what it's all about," her sister-in-law added smilingly, "what else remains for me to do? Be quick and come with me and I'll explain everything. Verily, it's a piece of happiness as large as the heavens!"

Yuanyang, at these words, rose to her feet and spat contemptuously with all her might in her sister-in-law's face. Pointing at her: "Be quick," she cried abusively, "and stop that filthy tongue of yours! It would be ever so much better, were you to bundle yourself away from this! What good tidings and what piece of happiness! Little wonder is it that you long and crave the whole day long to see other people's daughter turned into a secondary wife as one and all of your family would rely upon her to act contrary to reason and right! A whole household has been converted into secondary wives! But the sight fills you with such keen jealousy that you would like to also lay hold of me and throw me into the pit-fire! If any honors fall to my share, all of you outside will do everything disorderly and improper, and raise yourselves, in your own estimations, to the status of uncles (and aunts). But if I don't get any, and come to grief, you'll draw in your foul necks, and let me live or die as I please!"

While indulging in this raillery, she gave vent to tears. Ping'er and Xiren did all they could to reason with her so as to prevent her from crying.

Her sister-in-law felt quite out of countenance. "Whether you mean to accept the proposal, or not," she consequently said, "you can anyhow speak nicely. It isn't worth the while dragging this one in and involving that one! The proverb adequately says: 'In the presence of a dwarf one mustn't speak of dwarfish things!' Here you've been heaping insult upon me, but I didn't presume to retaliate. These two young ladies have however given you no provocation whatever; and yet by referring, as you've done, in this way and that way to secondary wives how can people stand it peacefully?"

"You shouldn't speak so!" Xiren and Ping'er quickly remonstrated. "She didn't allude to us; so don't be implicating others! Have you heard of any ladies or gentlemen who'd like to raise us to the rank of secondary wives? What's more, we two have neither father nor mother, nor brothers, within these doors, to avail themselves of our positions to act in a way contrary to right and reason! If she abuses people, let her do so; it isn't worth our while to be touchy!"

"Seeing," Yuanyang resumed, "that the abuse I've heaped upon her head has put her to such shame that she doesn't know where to go and screen her face, she tries to egg you two on! But you two have, fortunately, your wits about you! Though quite impatient, I never started arguing the question; she it was who chose to speak just now."

Her sister-in-law felt inwardly much disconcerted, and beat a retreat in high dudgeon. But Yuanyang so lost her temper that she still went on to abuse her; and it was only after Ping'er and Xiren had admonished her for ever so long that she let the matter drop.

"What were you hiding there for?" Ping'er then asked Xiren. "We couldn't see anything of you."

"I went," Xiren explained, "into Miss Quarta's rooms to see our Mr. Baoyu, but, who'd have thought it, I got there a little too late, and they told me that he had gone home. But my suspicions were, however, aroused as I couldn't make out how it was that I hadn't come across him, and I was about to go and hunt him up in Miss Lin's apartments, when I met one of her servants who said that he hadn't been there either. Then just as I was surmising that he must have gone out of the garden, behold, you came, as luck would have it, from the opposite direction. But I dodged you, so you didn't see anything of me. Subsequently, she too appeared on the scene; but I got behind the boulder, from the back of these trees. I, however, saw that you two had come to have a chat. Strange to say, though you have four eyes between you, you never caught a glimpse of me."

Scarcely had she concluded this remark, than they heard someone else from behind, laughingly exclaim, "Four eyes never saw you, but your six eyes haven't as yet found me out!"

The three girls received quite a shock from fright; but turning round, they perceived that it was no other person than Baoyu.

Xiren smiled, and was the first to speak. "You've made me have a good search," she said. "Where do you hail from?"

"I was just leaving cousin Quarta's," Baoyu laughed, "when I noticed you coming along, just in front of me; and knowing well enough that you were bent upon finding me, I concealed myself to have a lark with you. I saw you then go by, with uplifted head, enter the court, walk out again, and ask everyone you met on your way; but there I stood convulsed with laughter. I was only waiting to rush up to you and frighten you, when I afterwards realized that you too were prowling stealthily about, so I readily inferred that you also were playing a trick upon someone. Then when I put out my head and looked before me, I saw that it was these two girls, so I came behind you, by a circuitous way; and as soon as you left, I forthwith sneaked into your hiding place."

"Let's go and look behind there," Ping'er suggested laughingly; "we may possibly discover another couple; there's no saying."

"There's no one else!" Baoyu laughed.

Yuanyang had long ago concluded that every word of their conversation had been overheard by Baoyu; but leaning against the rock, she pretended to be fast asleep.

Baoyu gave her a push. "This stone is cold!" he smiled. "Let's go and sleep in our rooms. Won't it be better there?"

Saying this, he made an attempt to pull Yuanyang to her feet. Then hastily pressing Ping'er to repair to his quarters and have some tea, he united his efforts with those of Xiren, and tried to induce Yuanyang to come away. Yuanyang, at length, got up, and the quartet betook themselves, after all, into the Yihong court.

Baoyu had caught every word that had fallen from their lips a few minutes back, and felt, indeed, at heart so much distressed on Yuanyang's behalf, that throwing himself silently on his bed, he left the three girls in the outer rooms to prosecute their chat and laugh.

On the other side of the compound, Madame Xing about this time inquired of lady Feng who Yuanyang's father was.

"Her father," lady Feng replied, "is called Jin Cai. He and his wife are in Nanjing; they have to look after our houses there, so they can't pay frequent visits to the capital. Her brother is Wenxiang, who acts at present as our senior's accountant; but her sister-in-law too is employed in our worthy ancestor's yonder as head washerwoman."

Madame Xing thereupon despatched a servant to go and call Yuanyang's sister-in-law. On Mrs. Jin Wenxiang's arrival, she told her all. Mrs. Jin was naturally pleased and left in capital spirits to find Yuanyang, in the hope that the moment she communicated the offer to her, the whole thing would be satisfactorily arranged. But contrary to all her anticipations, she had to bear a good blowing up from Yuanyang, and to be told several unpleasant things by Xiren and Ping'er, so that she was filled with as much shame as indignation. She then came and reported the result to Madame Xing. "It's no use," she said, "she gave me a scolding." But as lady Feng was standing by, she could not summon up courage enough to allude to Ping'er, so she added: "Xiren too helped her to rate me, and they told me a whole lot of improper words, which could not be breathed in a mistress' ears. It would thus be better to arrange with our master to purchase a girl and have done; for from all I see, neither can that mean vixen enjoy such great good fortune, nor we such vast propitious luck!"

"What's that again to do with Xiren? How came they to know anything about it?" Madame Xing exclaimed upon learning the issue. "Who else was present?" she proceeded to inquire.

"There was Miss Ping!" was Jin's wife's reply.

"Shouldn't you have given her a slap on the mouth?" lady Feng precipitately shouted. "As soon as I ever put my foot outside the door, she starts gadding about; and I never see so much as her shadow, when I get home. She too is bound to have had a hand in telling you something or other!"

"Miss Ping wasn't present," Jin's wife protested. "Looking from a distance it seemed to me like her; but I couldn't see distinctly. It was a mere surmise on my part that it was she at all."

"Go and fetch her at once!" lady Feng shouted to a servant. "Tell her that I've come home, and that Madame Xing is also here and wants her to help her in her hurry."

Feng'er quickly came up to her. "Miss Lin," she observed, "despatched a messenger for her, and asked her in writing three and four times before she at last went. I advised her to get back so soon as your ladyship stepped inside the gate, but 'tell your mistress,' Miss Lin said, 'that I've put her to the inconvenience of coming round, as I've got something for her to do for me.'"

This explanation satisfied lady Feng and she let the matter drop. "What has she got to do," she purposely went on to ask, "that she will trouble her day after day?"

Madame Xing was driven to her wits' ends. As soon as the meal was over, she returned home; and, in the evening, she communicated to Jia She the result of her errand. After some reflection, Jia She promptly summoned Jia Lian.

"There are other people in Nanjing to look after our property," he told him on his arrival; "there's not only one family, so be quick and depute someone to go and summon Jin Cai to come up to the capital."

"Last night a letter arrived from Nanjing," Jia Lian rejoined, "to the effect that Jin Cai had been suffering from some phlegm-obstruction in the channels of the heart. So a coffin and money were allowed from the other mansion. Whether he be dead or alive now, I don't know. But even if alive, he must have lost all consciousness. It would therefore be a fruitless errand to send for him. His wife, on the other hand, is quite deaf."

Hearing this, Jia She gave vent to an exclamation of reproof, and next launched into abuse. "You stupid and unreasonable rascal!" he shouted. "Is it you of all people, who are up to those things? Don't you yet bundle yourself off from my presence?"

Jia Lian withdrew out of the room in a state of trepidation. But in a short while, (Jia She) gave orders to call Jin Wenxiang. Jia Lian (meanwhile) remained in the outer study, for as he neither ventured to go home, nor presumed to face his father, his only alternative was to tarry behind. Presently, Jin Wenxiang arrived. The servant-lads led him straightway past the second gate; and he only came out again and took his departure after sufficient time had elapsed to enable one to have four or five meals in.

Jia Lian could not for long summon up courage enough to ask what was up, but when he found out, after a time, that Jia She had gone to sleep, he eventually crossed over to his quarters. In the course of the evening lady Feng told him the whole story. Then, at last, he understood the meaning of the excitement.

But to revert to Yuanyang. She did not get, the whole night, a wink of sleep. On the morrow, her brother reported to dowager lady Jia that he would like to take her home on a visit. Dowager lady Jia accorded her consent and told her she could go and see her people. Yuanyang, however, would have rather preferred to stay where she was, but the fear lest her old mistress should give way to suspicion, placed her under the necessity of going, much against her own inclinations though it was. Her brother then had no course but to lay before her Jia She's proposal, and all his promises that she would occupy an honorable position, and that she would be a secondary wife, with control in the house; but Yuanyang was so persistent in her refusal that her brother was quite nonplussed and he was compelled to return, and inform Jia She.

Jia She flew into a dreadful passion. "I'll tell you what," he shouted; "bid your wife go and tell her that I say: that she must, like the goddess Chang'e herself who has from olden times shown a predilection for young people, only despise me for being advanced in years; that, as far as I can see, she must be hankering after some young men; that it must, most likely, be Baoyu; but probably Lian'er too! If she fosters these affections, warn her to at once set them at rest; for should she not come, when I'm ready to have her, who will by and bye venture to take her? This is the first thing. Should she imagine, in the next place, that because our venerable senior is fond of her, she may, in the future, be engaged to be married in the orthodox way, tell her to consider carefully that she won't very well be able to escape my grip, no matter in what family she may marry. That it's only in case of her dying or of her not wedding anyone throughout her life that I shall submit to her decision. Under other circumstances, urge her to seize the first opportunity and change her mind, as she'll come in for many benefits."

To every remark that Jia She uttered, Jin Wenxiang acquiesced. "Yes!" he said.

"Mind you don't humbug me!" Jia She observed. "I shall tomorrow send again your mistress round to ask Yuanyang. If you two have spoken to her, and she hasn't given a favorable answer, well, then, no blame will fall on you. But if she does assent, when she broaches the subject with her, look out for your heads!"

Jin Wenxiang eagerly expressed his obedience over and over again, and withdrawing out of the room, he retraced his footsteps homeward. Nor did he have the patience to wait until he could commission his womankind to speak to her. Indeed he went in person and told her face to face the injunctions entrusted to him. Yuanyang was incensed to such a degree that she was at a loss what reply to make. "I'm quite ready to go," she rejoined, after some cogitation, "but you people must take me before my old mistress first and let me tell her something about it."

Her brother and sister-in-law flattered themselves that reflection had induced her to alter her previous decision, and they were both immeasurably delighted. Her sister-in-law there and then led her into the upper quarters and ushered her into the presence of old lady Jia. As luck would have it, Madame Wang, Mrs. Xue, Li Wan, lady Feng, Baochai, and the other girls were, together with several respectable outside married women who acted as housekeepers, having some fun with old lady Jia. Yuanyang observed where her mistress was seated, and hastily dragging her sister-in-law before her, she fell on her knees, and explained to her, with tears in her eyes, what proposal Madame Xing had made to her, what her sister-in-law, who lived in the garden, had told her, and what message her brother had recently conveyed to her. "As I would not accept his advances," (she continued), "our senior master has just now gone so far as to insinuate that I was violently attached to Baoyu; or if that wasn't the case, my object was to gain time so as to espouse someone outside. That were I even to go up to the very heavens, I couldn't, during my lifetime, escape his clutches, and that he would, in the long run, wreak his vengeance on me. I have obstinately made up my mind, so I may state in the presence of all of you here, that I'll, under no circumstances, marry, as long as I live, any man whatsoever, not to speak of his being a Baoyu, (precious jade); but even a Bao Jin, (precious gold,) a Bao Yin, (precious silver,) a Bao Tian Wang, (precious lord of heaven,) or a Bao Huangdi, (precious Emperor,) and have done! Were even your venerable ladyship to press me to take such a step, I couldn't comply with your commands, though you may threaten to cut my throat with a sword. I'm quite prepared to wait upon your ladyship, till you depart this life; but go with my father, mother, or brother, I won't! I'll either commit suicide, or cut my hair off, and go and become a nun. If you fancy that I'm not in earnest, and that I'm temporarily using this language to put you off, may, as surely as heaven, earth, the spirits, the sun, and moon look upon me, my throat be covered with boils!"

Yuanyang had, in fact, upon entering the room, brought along a pair of scissors, concealed in her sleeve, and, while she spoke, she drew her hand back, and, dishevelling her tresses, she began to clip them. When the matrons and waiting-maids saw what she was up to, they hurriedly did everything they could to induce her to desist from her purpose; but already half of her locks had gone. And when they found on close inspection, that with the thick crop of hair she happily had, she had not succeeded in cutting it all, they immediately dressed it up for her.

Upon hearing of Jia She's designs, dowager lady Jia was provoked to displeasure. Her whole body trembled and shook. "Of all the attendants I've had," she cried, "there only remains this single one, upon whom I can depend, and now they want to conspire and carry her off!" Noticing then Madame Wang standing close to her, she turned herself towards her. "All you people really know is to impose upon me!" she resumed. "Outwardly, you display filial devotion; but, secretly, you plot and scheme against me. If I have aught that's worth having, you come and dun me for it. If I have anyone who's nice, you come and ask for her. What's left to me is this low waiting-maid, but as you see that she serves me faithfully, you naturally can't stand it, and you're doing your utmost to estrange her from me so as to be the better able to play your tricks upon me."

Madame Wang quickly rose to her feet. She did not, however, dare to return a single syllable in self-defence.

Mrs. Xue noticed that Madame Wang herself came in for her share of blame, and she did not feel as if she could any longer make an attempt to tender words of advice. Li Wan, the moment she heard Yuanyang speak in the strain she did, seized an early opportunity to lead the young ladies out of the room. Tanchun was a girl with plenty of common sense, so reflecting within herself that Madame Wang could not, in spite of the insult heaped upon her, very well presume to say anything to exculpate herself, that Mrs. Xue could not, of course, in her position of sister, bring forward any arguments, that Baochai was unable to explain things on behalf of her maternal aunt, and that Li Wan, lady Feng, or Baoyu could, still less, take upon themselves the right of censorship, she thought the opportunity rendered necessary the services of a daughter; but, as Yingchun was so quiet, and Xichun so young, she consequently walked in, no sooner did she overhear from outside the window what was said inside, and forcing a smile, she addressed herself to her grandmother. "How does this matter concern Madame Wang, my mother?" she interposed. "Venerable senior, just consider! This is a matter affecting her husband's eldest brother; and how could she, a junior sister-in-law, know anything about it?..."

But before she had exhausted all her arguments, dowager lady Jia's countenance thawed into a smile. "I've really grown stupid from old age!" she exclaimed. "Mrs. Xue, don't make fun of me! This eldest sister of yours is most reverent to me; and so unlike that senior lady of mine, who only knows how to regard her lord and master and to simply do things for the mere sake of appearances when she deals with her mother-in-law. I've therefore done her a wrong!"

Mrs. Xue confined her reply to a "yes." Dear senior, you're so full of prejudices," she afterwards observed, "that you love your youngest son's wife more than any one of the others; but it's quite natural."

"I have no prejudices," old lady Jia protested. "Baoyu," she then proceeded, "I unjustly found fault with your mother; but, how was it that even you didn't tell me anything, but that you looked on, while she was having her feelings trampled upon?"

"Could I," smiled Baoyu, "have taken my mother's part, and run down my senior uncle and aunt? If my mother did not bear the whole blame, upon whom could she throw it? And had I admitted that it was I who was entirely at fault, you, venerable ancestor, wouldn't have believed me."

"What you say is quite reasonable," his grandmother laughed. "So be quick and fall on your knees before your mother and tell her: 'mother, don't feel aggrieved! Our old lady is so advanced in years. Do it for Baoyu's sake!'"

At this suggestion, Baoyu hastily crossed over, and dropping on his knees, he was about to open his lips, when Madame Wang laughingly pulled him up. "Get up," she cried, "at once! This won't do at all! Is it likely, pray, that you would tender apologies to me on behalf of our venerable ancestor?" Hearing this, Baoyu promptly stood up.

"Even that girl Feng didn't call me to my senses," dowager lady Jia smiled again.

"I don't lay a word to your charge, worthy senior," lady Feng remarked smilingly, "and yet you brand me with reproach!"

This rejoinder amused dowager lady Jia. "This is indeed strange!" she said to all around. "But I'd like to listen to these charges."

"Who told you, dear senior," lady Feng resumed, "to look after your attendants so well, and lavish such care on them as to make them plump and fine as water onions? How ever can you therefore bear people a grudge, if they ask for her hand? I'm, lucky for you, your grandson's wife; for were I your grandson, I would long ere this have proposed to her. Would I have ever waited up to the present?"

"Is this any fault of mine?" dowager lady Jia laughed.

"Of course, it's your fault, venerable senior!" lady Feng retorted with a smile.

"Well, in that case, I too don't want her," old lady Jia proceeded laughing. "Take her away, and have done!"

"Wait until I go through this existence," lady Feng responded, "and, in the life to come, I'll assume the form of a man and apply for her hand."

"Take her along," dowager lady Jia laughed, "and give her to Lian'er to attach to his apartments; and we'll see whether that barefaced father-in-law of yours will still wish to have her or not."

"Lian'er is not a match for her!" lady Feng added. "He's only a fit mate for such as myself and Ping'er. A pair of loutish bumpkins like us to have anything to do with such a one as herself!"

At this rejoinder, they all exploded into a hearty fit of laughter. But a waiting-maid thereupon announced: "Our senior lady has come." So Madame Wang immediately quitted the room to go and meet her.

But any further particulars, which you, reader may like to know, will be given in the following chapter; so listen to it.

CHAPTER 47

An idiotic bully tries to be lewd and comes in for a sound thrashing. A cold-hearted fellow is prompted by a dread of trouble to betake himself to a strange place.

As soon as Madame Wang, so runs our narrative, heard of Madame Xing's arrival, she quickly went out to welcome her. Madame Xing was not yet aware that dowager lady Jia had learnt everything connected with Yuanyang's affair, and she was coming again to see which way the wind blew. The moment, however, she stepped inside the courtyard-entrance, several matrons promptly explained to her, quite confidentially, that their old mistress had been told all only a few minutes back, and she meant to retrace her steps, (but she saw that) every inmate in the suite of rooms was already conscious of her presence. When she caught sight, besides, of Madame Wang walking out to meet her she had no option but to enter. First and foremost, she paid her respects to dowager lady Jia, but old lady Jia did not address her a single remark, so she felt within herself smitten with shame and remorse.

Lady Feng soon gave something or other as an excuse and withdrew. Yuanyang then returned also quite alone to her chamber to give vent to her resentment; and Mrs. Xue, Madame Wang, and the other inmates, one by one, retired in like manner, for fear of putting Madame Xing out of countenance. Madame Xing, however, could not muster courage to beat a retreat. Dowager lady Jia noticed that there was no one but themselves in her apartments. "I hear," she remarked, "that you had come to play the part of a go-between for your lord and master! You can very well observe the three obediences and four virtues, but this softness of yours is a work of supererogation! You people have also got now a whole lot of grandchildren and sons. Do you still live in fear and trembling lest he should put his monkey up? Rumor has it that you yet let that disposition of your husband's run riot!"

Madame Xing's whole face got suffused with blushes. "I advised him time and again," she explained, "but he wouldn't listen to me. How is it, venerable senior, that you don't yet know that he turns a deaf ear to me? That's why I had no choice in the matter!"

"Would you go and kill anyone," dowager lady Jia asked, "that he might instigate you to? But consider now. Your brother's wife is naturally a quiet sort of person, and is born with many ailments; but is there anything, whether large or small, that she doesn't go to the trouble of looking after? And notwithstanding that that daughter-in-law of yours lends her a helping hand, she is daily so busy that she 'no sooner puts down the pick than she has to take up the broom.' So busy, that I have myself now curtailed a hundred and one things. But whenever there's anything those two can't manage, there's Yuanyang to come to their assistance. She is, it's true, a mere child, but nevertheless very careful; and knows how to concern herself about my affairs a bit; indenting for anything that need be indented, and availing herself of an opportunity to tell them to supply every requisite. Were Yuanyang not the kind of girl she is, how could those two ladies not neglect a whole or part of those matters, both important as well as unimportant, connected with the inner and outer quarters? Would I not at present have to worry my own mind, instead of leaving things to others? Why, I'd daily have to rack my brain and go and ask them to give me whatever I might need! Of those girls, who've come to my quarters and those who've gone, there only remains this single one. She's, besides other respects, somewhat older in years, and has as well a slight conception of my ways of doing things, and of my tastes. In the second place, she has managed to win her mistresses' hearts, for she never tries to extort aught from me, or to dun this lady for clothes or that one for money. Hence it is that beginning from your sister-in-law and daughter-in-law down to the servants in the house, irrespective of old or young, there isn't a soul, who doesn't readily believe every single word she says in anything, no matter what it is! Not only do I thus have someone upon whom I can rely, but your young sister-in-law and your daughter-in-law are both as well spared much trouble. With a person such as this by me, should even my daughter-in-law and granddaughter-in-law not have the time to think of anything, I am not left without it; nor am I given occasion to get my temper ruffled. But were she now to go, what kind of creature would they hunt up again to press into my service? Were you even to bring me a person made of real pearls, she'd be of no use; if she doesn't know how to speak! I was just about to send someone to go and explain to your husband that 'I've got money in here enough to buy any girl he fancies,' and to tell him that 'he's at liberty to give for her purchase from eight to ten thousand taels; that, if he has set his heart upon this girl, he can't however have her; and that by leaving her behind to attend to me, during the few years to come, it will be just the same as if he tried to acquit himself of his filial duties by waiting upon me day and night,' so you come at a very opportune moment. Were you therefore to go yourself at once and deliver him my message, it will answer the purpose far better!"

These words over, she called the servants. "Go," she said, "and ask Mrs. Xue, and your young mistresses to come! We were in the middle of a chat full of zest, and how is it they've all dispersed?"

The waiting-maids immediately assented and left to go in search of their mistresses, one and all of whom promptly re-entered her apartments, with the sole exception of Mrs. Xue.

"I've only now returned," she observed to the waiting-maid, "and what shall I go again for? Just tell her that I'm fast asleep!"

"Dearest Mrs. Xue!" the waiting-maid pleaded, "my worthy senior! our old mistress will get angry. If you, venerable lady, don't appear nothing will appease her; so do it for the love of us! Should you object to walking, why I'm quite ready to carry you on my back."

"You little imp!" Mrs. Xue laughed. "What are you afraid of? All she'll do will be to scold you a little; and it will all be over soon!"

While replying, she felt that she had no course but to retrace her footsteps, in company with the waiting-maid.

Dowager lady Jia at once motioned her into a seat. "Let's have a game of cards!" she then smilingly proposed. "You, Mrs. Xue, are not a good hand at them; so let's sit together, and see that lady Feng doesn't cheat us!"

"Quite so," laughed Mrs. Xue. "But it will be well if your venerable ladyship would look over my hand a bit! Are we four ladies to play, or are we to add one or two more persons to our number?"

"Naturally only four!" Madame Wang smiled.

"Were one more player let in," lady Feng interposed, "it would be merrier!"

"Call Yuanyang here," old lady Jia suggested, "and make her take this lower seat; for as Mrs. Xue's eyesight is rather dim, we'll charge her to look over our two hands a bit."

"You girls know how to read and write," lady Feng remarked with a smile, addressing herself to Tanchun, "and why don't you learn fortune-telling?"

"This is again strange!" Tanchun exclaimed. "Instead of bracing up your energies now to rook some money out of our venerable senior, you turn your thoughts to fortune-telling!"

"I was just wishing to consult the fates," lady Feng proceeded, "as to how much I shall lose today. Can I ever dream of winning? Why, look here. We haven't commenced playing, and they have placed themselves in ambush on the left and right."

This remark amused dowager lady Jia and Mrs. Xue. But presently Yuanyang arrived, and seated herself below her old mistress. After Yuanyang sat lady Feng. The red cloth was then spread; the cards were shuffled; the dealer was decided upon and the quintet began to play. After the game had gone on for a time, Yuanyang noticed that dowager lady Jia had a full hand and was only waiting for one two-spotted card, and she made a secret sign to lady Feng. Lady Feng was about to lead, but purposely lingered for a few moments. "This card will, for a certainty, be snatched by Mrs. Xue," she smiled, "yet if I don't play this one, I won't be able later to come out with what I want."

"I haven't got any cards you want in my hand," Mrs. Xue remarked.

"I mean to see by and bye," lady Feng resumed.

"You're at liberty to see," Mrs. Xue said. "But go on, play now! Let me look what card it is."

Lady Feng threw the card in front of Mrs. Xue. At a glance, Mrs. Xue perceived that it was the two spot. "I don't fancy this card," she smiled. "What I fear is that our dear senior will get a full hand."

"I've played wrong!" lady Feng laughingly exclaimed at these words.

Dowager lady Jia laughed, and throwing down her cards, "If you dare," she shouted, "take it back! Who told you to play the wrong card?"

"Didn't I want to have my fortune told?" lady Feng observed. "I played this card of my own accord, so there's no one with whom I can find fault."

"You should then beat your own lips and punish your own self; it's only fair;" old lady Jia remarked. Then facing Mrs. Xue, "I'm not a niggard, fond of winning money," she went on to say, "but it was my good luck!"

"Don't we too think as much?" Mrs. Xue smiled. "Who's there stupid enough to say that your venerable ladyship's heart is set upon money?"

Lady Feng was busy counting the cash, but catching what was said, she restrung them without delay. "I've got my share," she said, laughingly to the company. "It isn't at all that you wish to win. It's your good luck that made you come out a winner! But as for me, I am really a mean creature; and, as I managed to lose, I count the money and put it away at once."

Dowager lady Jia usually made Yuanyang shuffle the cards for her, but being engaged in chatting and joking with Mrs. Xue, she did not notice Yuanyang take them in hand. "Why is it you're so huffed," old lady Jia asked, "that you don't even shuffle for me?"

"Lady Feng won't let me have the money!" Yuanyang replied, picking up the cards.

"If she doesn't give the money," dowager lady Jia observed, "it will be a turning-point in her luck. Take that string of a thousand cash of hers," she accordingly directed a servant, "and bring it bodily over here!"

A young waiting-maid actually fetched the string of cash and deposited it by the side of her old mistress.

"Let me have them," lady Feng eagerly cried smiling, "and I'll square all that's due, and finish."

"In very truth, lady Feng, you're a miserly creature!" Mrs. Xue laughed. "It's simply for mere fun, nothing more!"

Lady Feng, at this insinuation, speedily stood up, and, laying her hand on Mrs. Xue, she turned her head round, and pointed at a large wooden box, in which old lady Jia usually deposited her money. "Aunt," she said, a smile curling her lips, "look here! I couldn't tell you how much there is in that box that was won from me! This tiao will be wheedled by the cash in it, before we've played for half an hour! All we've got to do is to give them sufficient time to lure this string in as well; we needn't trouble to touch the cards. Your temper, worthy ancestor, will thus calm down. If you've also got any legitimate thing for me to do, you might bid me go and attend to it!"

This joke had scarcely been concluded than it evoked incessant laughter from dowager lady Jia and everyone else. But while she was bandying words, Ping'er happened to bring her another string of cash prompted by the apprehension that her capital might not suffice to meet her wants.

"It's useless putting them in front of me!" lady Feng cried. "Place these too over there by our old lady and let them be wheedled in along with the others! It will thus save trouble, as there won't be any need to make two jobs of them, to the inconvenience of the cash already in the box."

Dowager lady Jia had a hearty laugh, so much so, that the cards, she held in her hand, flew all over the table; but pushing Yuanyang. "Be quick," she shouted, "and wrench that mouth of hers!"

Ping'er placed the cash according to her mistress' directions. But after indulging too in laughter for a time, she retraced her footsteps. On reaching the entrance into the court, she met Jia Lian. "Where's your Madame Xing?" he inquired. "Mr. Jia She told me to ask her to go round."

"She's been standing in there with our old mistress," Ping'er hastily laughed, "for ever so long, and yet she isn't inclined to budge! Seize the earliest opportunity you can get to wash your hands clean of this business! Our old lady has had a good long fit of fuming and raging.

Luckily, our lady Secunda cracked an endless stock of jokes, so she, at length, got a bit calmer!"

"I'll go over," Jia Lian said. "All I have to do is to find out our venerable senior's wishes, as to whether she means to go to Lai Da's house on the fourteenth, so that I might have time to get the chairs ready. As I'll be able to tell Madame Xing to return, and have a share of the fun, won't it be well for me to go?"

"My idea is," Ping'er suggested laughingly, "that you shouldn't put your foot in there! Everyone, even up to Madame Wang, and Baoyu, have alike received a rap on the knuckles, and are you also going now to fill up the gap?"

"Everything is over long ago," Jia Lian observed, "and can it be that she'll cap the whole thing by blowing me up too? What's more, it's no concern of mine. In the next place, Mr. Jia She enjoined me that I was to go in person, and ask his wife round, so, if I at present depute someone else, and he comes to know about it, he really won't feel in a pleasant mood, and he'll take advantage of this pretext to give vent to his spite on me."

These words over, he quickly marched off. And Ping'er was so impressed with the reasonableness of his arguments, that she followed in his track.

As soon as Jia Lian reached the reception hall, he trod with a light step. Then peeping in he saw Madame Xing standing inside. Lady Feng, with her eagle eye, was the first to espy him. But she winked at him and dissuaded him from coming in, and next gave a wink to Madame Xing. Madame Xing could not conveniently get away at once, and she had to pour a cup of tea, and place it in front of dowager lady Jia. But old lady Jia jerked suddenly round, and took Jia Lian at such a disadvantage that he found it difficult to beat a retreat. "Who is outside?" exclaimed old lady Jia. "It seemed to me as if some servant-boy had poked his head in."

Lady Feng sprung to her feet without delay. "I also," she interposed, "indistinctly noticed the shadow of someone."

Saying this, she walked away and quitted the room. Jia Lian entered with hasty step. Forcing a smile, "I wanted to ask," he remarked, "whether you, venerable senior, are going out on the fourteenth, so that the chairs may be got ready."

"In that case," dowager lady Jia rejoined, "why didn't you come straight in; but behaved again in that mysterious way?"

"I saw that you were playing at cards, dear ancestor," Jia Lian explained with a strained laugh, "and I didn't venture to come and disturb you. I therefore simply meant to call my wife out to find out from her."

"Is it anything so very urgent that you had to say it this very moment?" old lady Jia continued. "Had you waited until she had gone home, couldn't you have asked her any amount of questions you may have liked? When have you been so full of zeal before? I'm puzzled to know whether it isn't as an eavesdropping spirit that you appear on the scene; nor can I say whether you don't come as a spy. But that impish way of yours gave me quite a start! What a low-bred fellow you are! Your wife will play at cards with me for a good long while more, so you'd better bundle yourself home, and conspire again with Zhao'er's wife how to do away with your better half."

Her remarks evoked general merriment.

"It's Bao'er's wife," Yuanyang put in laughingly, "and you, worthy senior, have dragged in again Zhao'er's wife."

"Yes!" assented old lady Jia, likewise with a laugh. "How could I remember whether he wasn't (bao) embracing her, or (bei) carrying her on his back. The bare mention of these things makes me lose all self-control and provokes me to anger! Ever since I crossed these doors as a great-grandson's wife, I have never, during the whole of these fifty-four years, seen anything like these affairs, albeit it has been my share to go through great frights, great dangers, thousands of strange things, and a hundred and one remarkable occurrences! Don't you yet pack yourself off from my presence?"

Jia Lian could not muster courage to utter a single word to vindicate himself, but retired out of the room with all promptitude. Ping'er was standing outside the window. "I gave you due warning in a gentle tone, but you wouldn't hear; you've, after all, rushed into the very meshes of the net!"

These reproaches were still being heaped on him when he caught sight of Madame Xing, as she likewise made her appearance outside. "My father," Jia Lian ventured, "is at the bottom of all this trouble; and the whole blame now is shoved upon your shoulders as well as mine, mother."

"I'll take you, you unfilial thing and..." Madame Xing shouted. "People lay down their lives for their fathers; and you are prompted by a few harmless remarks to murmur against heaven and grumble against earth! Won't you behave in a proper manner? He's in high dudgeon these last few days, so mind he doesn't give you a pounding!"

"Mother, cross over at once," Jia Lian urged; "for he told me to come and ask you to go a long time ago."

Pressing his mother, he escorted her outside as far as the other part of the mansion. Madame Xing gave (her husband) nothing beyond a general outline of all that had been recently said; but Jia She found himself deprived of the means of furthering his ends. Indeed, so stricken was he with shame that from that date he pleaded illness. And so little able was he to rally sufficient pluck to face old lady Jia, that he merely commissioned Madame Xing and Jia Lian to go daily and pay their respects to her on his behalf. He had no help too but to despatch servants all over the place to make every possible search and inquiry for a suitable concubine for him. After a long time they succeeded in purchasing, for the sum of eighty taels, a girl of seventeen years of age, Yen Hung by name, whom he introduced as secondary wife into his household.

But enough of this subject. In the rooms on the near side, they protracted for a long time their noisy game of cards, and only broke up after they had something to eat. Nothing worthy of note, however, occurred during the course of the following day or two. In a twinkle, the fourteenth drew near. At an early hour before daybreak, Lai Da's wife came again into the mansion to invite her guests. Dowager lady Jia was in buoyant spirits, so taking along Madame Wang, Mrs. Xue, Baoyu, and the various young ladies, she betook herself into Lai Da's garden, where she sat for a considerable time.

This garden was not, it is true, to be compared with the garden of Broad Vista; but it also was most beautifully laid out, and consisted of spacious grounds. In the way of springs, rockeries, arbors, and woods, towers and terraces, pavilions and halls, it likewise contained a good many sufficient to excite admiration. In the main hall outside, were assembled Xue Pan, Jia Zhen, Jia Lian, Jia Rong, and several close relatives. But Lai Da had invited as well a number of officials, still in active service, and numerous young men of wealthy families, to keep them company. Among that party figured one Liu Xianglian, whom Xue Pan had met on a previous occasion and kept ever since in constant remembrance. Having besides discovered that he had a passionate liking for theatricals, and that the parts he generally filled were those of a young man or lady, in fast plays, he had unavoidably misunderstood the object with which he indulged in these amusements, to such a degree as to misjudge him for a young rake. About this time, he had been entertaining a wish to cultivate intimate relations with him, but he had, much to his disgust, found no one to introduce him, so when he, by a strange coincidence, came to be thrown in his way, on the present occasion, he revelled in intense delight. But Jia Zhen and the other guests had heard of his reputation, so as soon as wine had blinded their sense of shame, they entreated him to sing two short plays; and when subsequently they got up from the banquet, they ensconced themselves near him, and, pressing him with questions, they carried on a conversation on one thing and then another.

This Liu Xianglian was, in fact, a young man of an old family; but he had been unsuccessful in his studies, and had lost his father and mother. He was naturally light-hearted and magnanimous; not particular in minor matters; immoderately fond of spear-exercise and fencing, of gambling and boozing; even going to such excesses as spending his nights in houses of easy virtue; playing the fife, thrumming the harp, and going in for everything and anything. Being besides young in years, and of handsome appearance, those who did not know what his standing was, invariably mistook him for an actor. But Lai Da's son had all along been on such friendly terms with him, that he consequently invited him for the nonce to help him do the honors.

Of a sudden, while everyone was, after the wines had gone round, still on his good behaviour, Xue Pan alone got another fit of his old mania. From an early stage, his spirits sunk within him and he would fain have seized the first convenient moment to withdraw and consummate his designs but for Lai Shangrong, who then said: "Our Mr. Baoyu told me again just now that although he saw you, as he walked in, he couldn't speak to you with so many people present, so he bade me ask you not to go when the party breaks up, as he has something more to tell you. But as you insist upon taking your leave, you'd better wait until I call him out, and when you've seen each other, you can get away; I'll have nothing to say then."

While delivering the message, "Go inside," he directed the servant-boys, "and get hold of some old matron and tell her quietly to invite Mr. Baoyu to come out."

A servant-lad went on the errand, and scarcely had time enough elapsed to enable one to have a cup of tea in, than Baoyu, actually, made his appearance outside.

"My dear sir," Lai Shangrong smilingly observed to Baoyu, "I hand him over to you. I'm going to entertain the guests!"

With these words, he was off.

Baoyu pulled Liu Xianglian into a side study in the hall, where they sat down.

"Have you been recently to Qin Zhong's grave?" he inquired of him.

"How could I not go?" Xianglian answered. "The other day a few of us went out to give our falcons a fly; and we were yet at a distance of two li from his tomb, when remembering the heavy rains we've had this summer, I gave way to fears lest his grave may not have been proof against them; so evading the notice of the party I went over and had a look. I found it again slightly damaged; but when I got back home, I speedily raised a few hundreds of cash, and issued early on the third day, and hired two men, who put it right."

"It isn't strange then!" exclaimed Baoyu, "When the lotus blossomed last month in the pond of our garden of Broad Vista, I plucked ten of them and bade Caiming go out of town and lay them as my offering on his grave. On his return, I also inquired of him whether it had been damaged by the water or not; and he explained that not only had it not sustained any harm, but that it looked better than when last he'd seen it. Several of his friends, I argued, must have had it put in proper repair; and I felt it irksome that I should, day after day, be so caged at home as to be unable to be my own master in the least thing, and that if even I move, and anyone comes to know of it, this one is sure to exhort me, if that one does not restrain me. I can thus afford to brag, but can't manage to act! And though I've got plenty of money, I'm not at liberty to spend any of it!"

"There's no use your worrying in a matter like this!" Liu Xianglian said. "I am outside, so all you need do is to inwardly foster the wish; that's all. But as the first of the tenth moon will shortly be upon us, I've already prepared the money necessary for going to the graves. You know well enough that I'm as poor as a rat; I've no hoardings at home; and when a few cash find their way into my pocket, I soon remain again quite empty-handed. But I'd better make the best of this opportunity, and keep the amount I have, in order that, when the time comes, I mayn't find myself without a cash."

"It's exactly about this that I meant to send Beiming to see you," Baoyu added. "But it isn't often that one can manage to find you at home. I'm well aware how uncertain your movements are; one day you are here, and another there; you've got no fixed resort."

"There's no need sending anyone to hunt me up!" Liu Xianglian replied. "All that each of us need do in this matter is to acquit ourselves of what's right. But in a little while, I again purpose going away on a tour abroad, to return in three to five years' time."

When Baoyu heard his intention, "Why is this?" he at once inquired.

Liu Xianglian gave a sardonic smile. "When my wish is on a fair way to be accomplished," he said, "you'll certainly hear everything. I must now leave you."

"After all the difficulty we've had in meeting," Baoyu remarked, "wouldn't it be better were you and I to go away together in the evening?"

"That worthy cousin of yours," Xianglian rejoined, "is as bad as ever, and were I to stay any longer, trouble would inevitably arise. So it's as well that I should clear out of his way."

Baoyu communed with himself for a time. "In that case," he then observed, "it's only right, that you should retire. But if you really be bent upon going on a distant tour, you must absolutely tell me something beforehand. Don't, on any account, sneak away quietly!"

As he spoke, the tears trickled down his cheeks.

"I shall, of course, say good-bye to you," Liu Xianglian rejoined. "But you must not let any one know anything about it!"

While uttering these words, he stood up to get away. "Go in at once," he urged, "there's no need to see me off!"

Saying this, he quitted the study. As soon as he reached the main entrance, he came across Xue Pan, bawling out boisterously, "Who let young Liu'er go?"

The moment these shouts fell on Liu Xianglian's ear, his anger flared up as if it had been sparks spurting wildly about, and he only wished he could strike him dead with one blow. But on second consideration, he pondered that a fight after the present festive occasion would be an insult to Lai Shangrong, and he perforce felt bound to stifle his indignation.

When Xue Pan suddenly espied him walking out, he looked as delighted as if he had come in for some precious gem. With staggering step he drew near him. Clutching him with one grip, "My dear brother," he smirked, "where are you off to?"

"I'm going somewhere, but will be back soon," Xianglian said by way of response.

"As soon as you left," Xue Pan smiled, "all the fun went. But pray sit a while! If you do so, it will be a proof of your regard for me! Don't flurry yourself. With such a senior brother as myself to stand by you, it will be as easy a job for you to become an official as to reap a fortune."

The sight of his repulsive manner filled the heart of Xianglian with disgust and shame. But speedily devising a plan, he drew him to a secluded spot. "Is your friendship real," he smiled, "or is it only a sham?"

This question sent Xue Pan into such raptures that he found it difficult to check himself from gratifying his longings. But glancing at him with the corner of his eye, "My dear brother," he smiled, "what makes you ask me such a thing? If my friendship for you is a sham, may I die this moment, before your very eyes."

"Well, if that be so," Xianglian proceeded, "it isn't convenient in here, so sit down and wait a bit. I'll go ahead, but come out of this yourself by and bye, and follow me to my place, where we can drink the whole night long. I've also got there two first-rate young fellows who never go out of doors. But don't bring so much as a single follower with you, as you'll find, when you get there, plenty of people ready at hand to wait on you."

So high did this assignation raise Xue Pan's spirits that he recovered, to a certain extent, from the effects of wine. "Is it really so?" he asked.

"How is it," Xianglian laughed, "that when people treat you with a sincere heart, you don't, after all, believe them?"

"I'm no fool," eagerly exclaimed Xue Pan, "and how could I not believe you? But since this be the case, how am I, who don't even know the way, to find your whereabouts if you are to go ahead of me?"

"My place is outside the northern gate." Xianglian explained. "But can you tear yourself away from your home to spend the night outside the city walls?"

"As long as you're there," Xue Pan said, "what will I want my home for?"

"If that be so," Xianglian resumed, "I'll wait for you on the bridge outside the northern gate. But let us meanwhile rejoin the banquet and have some wine. Come along after you've seen me go; they won't notice us then."

"Yes!" shouted Xue Pan with alacrity as he acquiesced to the proposal.

The two young fellows thereupon returned to the feast, and drank for a time. Xue Pan, however, could with difficulty endure the suspense. He kept his gaze intent upon Xianglian; and the more he pondered within himself upon what was coming, the more exuberance swelled in his heart. Now he emptied one wine-kettle; now another; and, without waiting for anyone to press him, he, of his own accord, gulped down one drink after another, with the result that he unconsciously made himself nearly quite tipsy. Xianglian then got up and quitted the room, and perceiving everyone off his guard, he egressed out of the main entrance. "Go home ahead," he directed his page Xingnu. "I'm going out of town, but I'll be back at once."

By the time he had finished giving him these directions, he had already mounted his horse, and straightway he proceeded to the bridge beyond the northern gate, and waited for Xue Pan. A long while elapsed, however, before he espied Xue Pan in the distance, hurrying along astride of a high steed, with gaping mouth, staring eyes, and his head, banging from side to side like a pedlar's drum. Without intermission, he glanced confusedly about, sometimes to the left, and sometimes to the right; but, as soon as he got where he had to pass in front of Xianglian's horse, he kept his gaze fixed far away, and never troubled his mind with the immediate vicinity.

Xianglian felt amused and angry with him, but forthwith giving his horse also the rein, he followed in his track, while Xue Pan continued to stare ahead.

Little by little the habitations got scantier and scantier, so pulling his horse round, (Xue Pan) retraced his steps. The moment he turned back, he unawares caught sight of Xianglian, and his spirits rose within him, as if he had got hold of some precious thing of an extraordinary value. "I knew well enough," he eagerly smiled, "that you weren't one to break faith."

"Quick, let's go ahead!" Xianglian smilingly urged. "Mind people might notice us and follow us. It won't then be nice!"

While instigating him, he took the lead, and letting his horse have the rein, he wended his way onwards, followed closely by Xue Pan. But when Xianglian perceived that the country ahead of them was already thinly settled and saw besides a stretch of water covered with a growth of weeds, he speedily dismounted, and tied his horse to a tree. Turning then round; "Get down!" he said, laughingly, to Xue Pan. "You must first take an oath, so that in the event of your changing your mind in the future, and telling anything to anyone, the oath might be accomplished."

"You're quite right!" Xue Pan smiled; and jumping down with all despatch, he too made his horse fast to a tree and then crouched on his knees.

"If I ever in days to come," he exclaimed, "know any change in my feelings and breathe a word to any living soul, may heaven blast me and earth annihilate me!"

Scarcely had he ended this oath, when a crash fell on his ear, and lo, he felt as if an iron hammer had been brought down to bear upon him from behind. A black mist shrouded his eyes, golden stars flew wildly about before his gaze and losing all control over himself, he sprawled on the ground.

Xianglian approached and had a look at him; and, knowing how little he was accustomed to thrashings, he only exerted but little of his strength, and struck him a few blows on the face. But about this time a fruit shop happened to open, and Xue Pan strained at first every nerve to rise to his feet, when another slight kick from Xianglian tumbled him over again.

"Both parties should really be agreeable," he shouted. "But if you were not disposed to accept my advances, you should have simply told me in a proper way. And why did you beguile me here to give me a beating?"

So speaking, he went on boisterously to heap invective upon his head.

"I'll take you, you blind fellow, and show you who Mr. Liu is," Xianglian cried. "You don't appeal to me with solicitous entreaties, but go on abusing me! To kill you would be of no use, so I'll merely give you a good lesson!"

With these words, he fetched his whip, and administered him, thirty or forty blows from his back down to his shins.

Xue Pan had sobered down considerably from the effects of wine, and found the stings of pain so intolerable, that little able to restrain himself, he gave way to groans.

"Do you go on in this way?" Xianglian said, with an ironical smile. "Why, I thought you were not afraid of beatings."

While uttering this taunt, he seized Xue Pan by the left leg, and dragging him several steps into a miry spot among the reeds, he rolled him about till he was covered with one mass of mud. "Do you now know what stuff I'm made of?" he proceeded to ask. Xue Pan made no reply but simply lay prostrate, and moaned. Then throwing away his whip Xianglian gave him with his fist several thumps all over the body.

Xue Pan began to wriggle violently and vociferate wildly. "Oh, my ribs are broken!" he shouted. "I know you're a proper sort of person! It's all because I made the mistake of listening to other people's gossip!"

"There's no need for you to drag in other people!" Xianglian went on. "Just confine yourself to those present!"

"There's nothing up at present!" Xue Pan cried. "From what you say, you're a person full of propriety. So it's I who am at fault."

"You'll have to speak a little milder," Xianglian added, "before I let you off."

"My dear younger brother," Xue Pan pleaded, with a groan.

Xianglian at this struck him another blow with his fist.

"Ai!" ejaculated Xue Pan. "My dear senior brother!" he exclaimed.

Xianglian then gave him two more whacks, one after the other.

"Ai Yo!" Xue Pan precipitately screamed. "My dear Sir, do spare me, an eyeless beggar; and henceforth I'll look up to you with veneration; I'll fear you!"

"Drink two mouthfuls of that water!" shouted Xianglian.

"That water is really too foul," Xue Pan argued, in reply to this suggestion, wrinkling his eyebrows the while; "and how could I put any of it in my mouth?"

Xianglian raised his fist and struck him.

"I'll drink it, I'll drink it!" quickly bawled Xue Pan.

So saying, he felt obliged to lower his head to the very roots of the reeds and drink a mouthful. Before he had had time to swallow it, a sound of "ai" became audible, and up came all the stuff he had put into his mouth only a few seconds back.

"You filthy thing!" exclaimed Xianglian. "Be quick and finish drinking and I'll let you off."

Upon hearing this, Xue Pan bumped his head repeatedly on the ground. "Do please," he cried, "lay up a store of meritorious acts for yourself and let me off! I couldn't take that were I even on the verge of death!"

"This kind of stench will suffocate me!" Xianglian observed, and, with this remark, he abandoned Xue Pan to his own devices; and, pulling his horse, he put his foot to the stirrup, and rode away.

Xue Pan, meanwhile, became aware of his departure, and felt at last relieved in his mind. Yet his conscience pricked him for he saw that he should not misjudge people. He then made an effort to raise himself, but the racking torture he experienced all over his limbs was so sharp that he could with difficulty bear it.

Jia Zhen and the other guests present at the banquet became, as it happened, suddenly alive to the fact that the two young fellows had disappeared; but though they extended their search everywhere, they saw nothing of them. Someone insinuated, in an uncertain way, that they had gone outside the northern gate; but as Xue Pan's pages had ever lived in dread of him, who of them had the audacity to go and hunt him up after the injunctions he had given them that they were not to follow him? But waxing solicitous on his account, Jia Zhen subsequently bade Jia Rong take a few servant-boys and go and discover some clue of him, or institute inquiries as to his whereabouts. Straightway therefore they prosecuted their search beyond the northern gate, to a distance of two li below the bridge, and it was quite by accident that they discerned Xue Pan's horse made fast by the side of a pit full of reeds.

"That's a good sign!" they with one voice exclaimed; "for if the horse is there, the master must be there too!"

In a body, they thronged round the horse, when, from among the reeds, they caught the sound of human groans, so hurriedly rushing forward to ascertain for themselves, they, at a glance, perceived Xue Pan, his costume all in tatters, his countenance and eyes so swollen and bruised that it was hard to make out the head and face, and his whole person, inside as well as outside his clothes, rolled like a sow in a heap of mud.

Jia Rong surmised pretty nearly the truth. Speedily dismounting, he told the servants to prop him up. "Uncle Xue," he laughed, "you daily go in for lewd dalliance; but have you today come to dissipate in a reed-covered pit? The King of the dragons in this pit must have also fallen in love with your charms, and enticed you to become his son-in-law that you've come and gored yourself on his horns like this!"

Xue Pan was such a prey to intense shame that he would fain have grovelled into some fissure in the earth had he been able to detect any. But so little able was he to get on his horse that Jia Rong directed a servant to run to the suburbs and fetch a chair. Ensconced in this, Xue

Pan entered town along with the search party.

Jia Rong still insisted upon carrying him to Lai Da's house to join the feast, so Xue Pan had to make a hundred and one urgent appeals to him to tell no one, before Jia Rong eventually yielded to his solicitations and allowed him to have his own way and return home.

Jia Rong betook himself again to Lai Da's house, and narrated to Jia Zhen their recent experiences. When Jia Zhen also learnt of the flogging (Xue Pan) had received from Xianglian, he laughed. "It's only through scrapes," he cried, "that he'll get all right!"

In the evening, after the party broke up, he came to inquire after him. But Xue Pan, who was lying all alone in his bedroom, nursing himself, refused to see him, on the plea of indisposition.

When dowager lady Jia and the other inmates had returned home, and everyone had retired into their respective apartments, Mrs. Xue and Baochai observed that Xiangling's eyes were quite swollen from crying, and they questioned her as to the reason of her distress. (On being told), they hastily rushed to look up Xue Pan; but, though they saw his body covered with scars, they could discover no ribs broken, or bones dislocated.

Mrs. Xue fell a prey to anguish and displeasure. At one time, she scolded Xue Pan; at another, she abused Liu Xianglian. Her wish was to lay the matter before Madame Wang in order that someone should be despatched to trace Liu Xianglian and bring him back, but Baochai speedily dissuaded her. "It's nothing to make a fuss about," she represented. "They were simply drinking together; and quarrels after a wine bout are ordinary things. And for one who's drunk to get a few whacks more or less is nothing uncommon! Besides, there's in our home neither regard for God nor discipline. Everyone knows it. If it's purely out of love, mother, that you desire to give vent to your spite, it's an easy matter enough. Have a little patience for three or five days, until brother is all right and can go out. Mr. Jia Zhen and Mr. Jia Lian over there are not people likely to let the affair drop without doing anything! They'll, for a certainty, stand a treat, and ask that fellow, and make him apologize and admit his wrong in the presence of the whole company, so that everything will be properly settled. But were you now, ma, to begin making much of this occurrence, and telling everyone, it would, on the contrary, look as if you had, in your motherly partiality and fond love for him, indulged him to stir up a row and provoke people! He has, on this occasion, had unawares to eat humble pie, but will you, ma, put people to all this trouble and inconvenience and make use of the prestige enjoyed by your relatives to oppress an ordinary person?"

"My dear child," Mrs. Xue rejoined, "after listening to the advice proffered by her, you've, after all, been able to foresee all these things! As for me, that sudden fit of anger quite dazed me!"

"All will thus be square," Baochai smiled, "for, as he's neither afraid of you, mother, nor gives an ear to people's exhortations, but gets wilder and wilder every day that goes by, he may, if he gets two or three lessons, turn over a new leaf."

While Xue Pan lay on the stove-couch, he reviled Xianglian with all his might. Next, he instigated the servant-boys to go and demolish his house, kill him, and bring a charge against him. But Mrs. Xue hindered the lads from carrying out his purpose, and explained to her son "that Liu Xianglian had casually, after drinking, behaved in a disorderly way, that now that he was over the effects of wine, he was exceedingly filled with remorse, and that, prompted by the fear of punishment, he had effected his escape."

But, reader, if you feel any interest to know what happened when Xue Pan heard the version his mother gave him, listen to what you will find in the next chapter.

CHAPTER 48

A sensual-minded man gets into such trouble through his sensuality that he entertains the idea of going abroad. An estimable and refined girl manages, after great exertion, to compose verses at a refined meeting.

But to resume our story, after hearing his mother's arguments, Xue Pan's indignation gradually abated. But notwithstanding that his pains and aches completely disappeared, in three or five days' time, the scars of his wounds were not yet healed and shamming illness, he remained at home, so ashamed was he to meet any of his relations or friends.

In a twinkle, the tenth moon drew near; and as several among the partners in the various shops, with which he was connected, wanted to go home, after the settlement of the annual accounts, he had to give them a farewell spread at home. In their number was one Zhang Dehui, who from his early years filled the post of manager in Xue Pan's pawnshop; and who enjoyed in his home a living of two or three thousand taels. His purpose too was to visit his native place this year, and to return the following spring.

"Stationery and perfumery have been so scarce this year," he consequently represented, "that prices will next year inevitably be high; so when next year comes, what I'll do will be to send up my elder and younger sons ahead of me to look after the pawnshop, and when I start on my way back, before the dragon festival, I'll purchase a stock of paper, scents, and fans and bring them for sale. And though we'll have to reduce the duties, payable at the barriers, and other expenses, there will still remain for us a considerable percentage of profit."

This proposal set Xue Pan musing, "With the dressing I've recently had," he pondered, "I cannot very well, at present, appear before anyone. Were the fancy to take me to get out of the way for half a year or even a year, there isn't a place where I can safely retire. And to sham illness, day after day, isn't again quite the right thing! In addition to this, here I've reached this grown-up age, and yet I'm neither a civilian nor a soldier. It's true I call myself a merchant, but I've never in point of fact handled the scales or the abacus. Nor do I know anything about our territories, customs and manners, distances and routes. So wouldn't it be advisable that I should also get ready some of my capital, and go on a tour with Zhang Dehui for a year or so? Whether I earn any money or not, will be equally immaterial to me. More, I shall escape from all disgrace. It will, secondly, be a good thing for me to see a bit of country."

This resolution once arrived at in his mind, he waited until they rose from the banquet, when he, with calmness and equanimity, brought his plans to Zhang Dehui's cognizance, and asked him to postpone his departure for a day or two so that they should proceed on the journey together.

In the evening, he imparted the tidings to his mother. Mrs. Xue, upon hearing his intention, was, albeit delighted, tormented with fresh misgivings lest he should stir up trouble abroad—for as far as the expense was concerned she deemed it a mere bagatelle—and she consequently would not permit him to go. "You have," she reasoned with him, "to take proper care of me, so that I may be able to live in peace. Another thing is, that you can well dispense with all this buying and selling, for you are in no need of the few hundreds of taels you may make."

Xue Pan had long ago thoroughly resolved in his mind what to do and he did not therefore feel disposed to listen to her remonstrances. "You daily tax me," he pleaded, "with being ignorant of the world, with not knowing this, and not learning that, and now that I stir up my good resolution, with the idea of putting an end to all trifling, and that I wish to become a man, to do something for myself, and learn how to carry on business, you won't let me! But what would you have me do? Besides I'm not a girl that you should coop me up at home! And when is this likely to come to an end? Zhang Dehui is, moreover, a man well up in years; and he is an old friend of our family, so if I go with him, how ever will I be able to do anything that's wrong? Should I at any time be guilty of any impropriety, he will be sure to speak to me, and to exhort me. He even knows the prices of things and customs of trade; and as I shall, as a matter of course, consult him in everything, what advantage won't I enjoy? But if you refuse to let me go, I'll wait for a couple of days, and, without breathing a word to anyone at home, I'll furtively make my preparations and start, and, when by next year I shall have made my fortune and come back, you'll at length know what stuff I'm made off!"

When he had done speaking, he flew into a huff and went off to sleep.

Mrs. Xue felt impelled, after the arguments she heard him propound, to deliberate with Baochai.

"If brother," Baochai smilingly rejoined, "were in real earnest about gaining experience in some legitimate concerns, it would be well and good. But though he speaks, now that he is at home, in a plausible manner, the moment he gets abroad, his old mania will break out again, and it will be hard to exercise any check over him. Yet, it isn't worth the while distressing yourself too much about him! If he does actually mend his ways, it will be the happiness of our whole lives. But if he doesn't change, you won't, mother, be able to do anything more; for though, in part, it depends on human exertion, it, in part, depends upon the will of heaven! If you keep on giving way to fears that, with his lack of worldly experience, he can't be fit to go abroad and can't be up to any business, and you lock him up at home this year, why next year he'll be just the same! Such being the case, you'd better, ma—since his arguments are right and specious enough—make up your mind to sacrifice from eight hundred to a thousand taels and let him have them for a try. He'll, at all events, have one of his partners to lend him a helping hand, one who won't either think it a nice thing to play any of his tricks upon him. In the second place, there will be, when he's gone, no one to the left of him or to the right of him, to stand by him, and no one upon whom to rely, for when one goes abroad, who cares for any one else? Those who have, eat; and those who haven't starve. When he therefore casts his eyes about him and realizes that there's no one to depend upon, he may, upon seeing this, be up to less mischief than were he to stay at home; but of course, there's no saying."

Mrs. Xue listened to her, and communed within herself for a moment. "What you say is, indeed, right and proper!" she remarked. "And could one, by spending a small sum, make him learn something profitable, it will be well worth!"

They then matured their plans; and nothing further of any note transpired during the rest of the night.

The next day, Mrs. Xue sent a messenger to invite Zhang Dehui to come round. On his arrival, she charged Xue Pan to regale him in the library. Then appearing, in person, outside the window of the covered back passage, she made thousands of appeals to Zhang Dehui to look after her son and take good care of him.

Zhang Dehui assented to her solicitations with profuse assurances, and took his leave after the collation.

"The fourteenth," he went on to explain to Xue Pan. "is a propitious day to start. So, worthy friend, you'd better be quick and pack up your baggage, and hire a mule, for us to begin our long journey as soon as the day dawns on the fourteenth."

Xue Pan was intensely gratified, and he communicated their plans to Mrs. Xue. Mrs. Xue then set to, and worked away, with the assistance of Baochai, Xiangling, and two old nurses, for several consecutive days, before she got his luggage ready. She fixed upon the husband of Xue Pan's nurse an old man with hoary head, two old servants with ample experience and long services, and two young pages, who acted as Xue Pan's constant attendants, to go with him as his companions, so the party mustered, inclusive of master and followers, six persons in all. Three large carts were hired for the sole purpose of carrying the baggage and requisites; and four mules, suitable for long journeys, were likewise engaged. A tall, dark brown, home-bred mule was selected for Xue Pan's use; but a saddle horse, as well, was provided for him.

After the various preparations had been effected, Mrs. Xue, Baochai and the other inmates tendered him, night after night, words of advice. But we can well dispense with dilating on this topic. On the arrival of the thirteenth, Xue Pan went and bade good-bye to his maternal uncles. After which, he came and paid his farewell visit to the members of the Jia household. Jia Zhen and the other male relatives unavoidably prepared an entertainment to speed him off. But to these festivities, there is likewise little need to allude with any minuteness.

On the fourteenth, at break of day, Mrs. Xue, Baochai, and the other members of the family accompanied Xue Pan beyond the ceremonial gate. Here his mother and her daughter stood and watched him, their four eyes fixed intently on him, until he got out of sight, when they, at length, retraced their footsteps into the house.

Mrs. Xue had, in coming up to the capital, only brought four or five family domestics and two or three old matrons and waiting-maids with her, so, after the departure on the recent occasion, of those who followed Xue Pan, no more than one or two men-servants remained in the outer quarters. Mrs. Xue repaired therefore on the very same day into the study, and had the various ornaments, bric-à-brac, curtains, and other articles removed into the inner compound and put away. Then bidding the wives of the two male attendants, who had gone with Xue Pan, likewise move their quarters inside, along with the other women, she went on to impress upon Xiangling to put everything carefully away in her own room as well, and to lock the doors; "for," (she said,) "you must come at night and sleep with me."

"Since you've got all these people to keep you company, ma," Baochai remarked, "wouldn't it be as well to tell sister Ling to come and be my companion? Our garden is besides quite empty and the nights are so long! And as I work away every night, won't it be better for me to have an extra person with me?"

"Quite so!" smiled Mrs. Xue, "I forgot that! I should have told her to go with you; it's but right. It was only the other day that I mentioned to your brother that: 'Wenxing too was young, and not fit to attend to everything that turns up, that Ying'er could not alone do all the waiting, and that it was necessary to purchase another girl for your service.'"

"If we buy one, we won't know what she's really like!" Baochai demurred. "If she gives us the slip, the money we may have spent on her will be a mere trifle, so long as she hasn't been up to any pranks! So let's quietly make inquiries, and, when we find one with well-known antecedents, we can purchase her, and we'll be on the safe side then!"

While speaking, she told Xiangling to collect her bedding and clothes; and desiring an old matron and Zhen'er to take them over to the Heng-wu Yuan, Baochai returned at last into the garden in company with Xiangling.

"I meant to have proposed to my lady," Xiangling said to Baochai, "that, when master left, I should be your companion, miss; but I feared lest her ladyship should, with that suspicious mind of hers, have maintained that I was longing to come into the garden to romp. But who'd have thought it, it was you, after all, who spoke to her about it!"

"I am well aware," Baochai smiled, "that you've been inwardly yearning for this garden, and that not for a day or two, but with the little time you can call your own, you would find it no fun, were you even able to run over once in a day, so long as you have to do it in a hurry-scurry! Seize therefore this opportunity of staying, better still, for a year; as I, on my side, will then have an extra companion; and you, on yours, will be able to accomplish your wishes."

"My dear miss!" laughingly observed Xiangling, "do let's make the best of this time, and teach me how to write verses!"

"I say," Baochai laughed, "'you no sooner, get the Long state than you long for the Shu'! I advise you to wait a bit. This is the first day that you spend in here, and you should, first and foremost, go out of the garden by the eastern side gate and look up and salute everyone in her respective quarters commencing from our old lady. But you needn't make it a point of telling them that you've moved into the garden. If anyone does allude to the reason why you've shifted your quarters, you can simply explain cursorily that I've brought you in as a companion, and then drop the subject. On your return by and bye into the garden, you can pay a visit to the apartments of each of the young ladies."

Xiangling signified her acquiescence, and was about to start when she saw Ping'er rush in with hurried step. Xiangling hastened to ask after her health, and Ping'er felt compelled to return her smile, and reciprocate her inquiry.

"I've brought her in today," Baochai thereupon smilingly said to Ping'er, "to make a companion of her. She was just on the point of going to tell your lady about it!"

"What is this that you're saying, Miss?" Ping'er rejoined, with a smile. "I really am at a loss what reply to make to you!"

"It's the right thing!" Baochai answered. "'In a house, there's the master, and in a temple there's the chief priest.' It's true, it's no important concern, but something must, in fact, be mentioned, so that those who sit up on night duty in the garden may be aware that these two have been added to my rooms, and know when to close the gates and when to wait. When you get back therefore do mention it, so that I mayn't have to send someone to tell them."

Ping'er promised to carry out her wishes. "As you're moved in here," she said to Xiangling, "won't you go and pay your respects to your neighbors?"

"I had just this very moment," Baochai smiled, "told her to go and do so."

"You needn't however go to our house," Ping'er remarked, "our Mr. Secundus is laid up at home."

Xiangling assented and went off, passing first and foremost by dowager lady Jia's apartments. But without devoting any of our attention to her, we will revert to Ping'er.

Seeing Xiangling walk out of the room, she drew Baochai near her. "Miss! have you heard our news?" she inquired in a low tone of voice.

"I haven't heard any news," Baochai responded. "We've been daily so busy in getting my brother's things ready for his voyage abroad, that we know nothing whatever of any of your affairs in here. I haven't even seen anything of my female cousins these last two days."

"Our master, Mr. Jia She, has beaten our Mr. Secundus to such a degree that he can't budge," Ping'er smiled. "But is it likely, miss, that you've heard nothing about it?"

"This morning," Baochai said by way of reply, "I heard a vague report on the subject, but I didn't believe it could be true. I was just about to go and look up your mistress when you unexpectedly arrived. But why did he beat him again?"

Ping'er set her teeth to and gave way to abuse. "It's all on account of some Jia Yuncun or other; a starved and half-dead boorish bastard, who went yonder quite unexpectedly. It isn't yet ten years since we've known him, and he has been the cause of ever so much trouble! In the spring of this year, Mr. Jia She saw somewhere or other, I can't tell where, a lot of antique fans; so, when on his return home, he noticed that the fine fans stored away in the house were all of no use, he at once directed servants to go everywhere and hunt up some like those he had seen. Who'd have anticipated it, they came across a reckless creature of retribution, dubbed by common consent the 'stone fool,' who though so poor as to not even have any rice to put to his mouth, happened to have at home twenty antique fans. But these he utterly refused to take out of his main door. Our Mr. Secundus had thus a precious lot of bother to ask ever so many favors of people. But when he got to see the man, he made endless appeals to him before he could get him to invite him to go and sit in his house; when producing the fans, he allowed him to have a short inspection of them. From what our Mr. Secundus says, it would be really difficult to get any the like of them. They're made entirely of spotted black bamboo, and the stags and jadelike clusters of bamboo on them are the genuine pictures, drawn by men of olden times. When he got back, he explained these things to Mr. Jia She, who readily asked him to buy them, and give the man his own price for them. The 'stone fool,' however, refused. 'Were I even to be dying from hunger,' he said, 'or perishing from frostbites, and so much as a thousand taels were offered me for each single fan, I wouldn't part with them.' Mr. Jia She could do nothing, but day after day he abused our Mr. Secundus as a good-for-nothing. Yet he had long ago promised the man five hundred taels, payable cash down in advance, before delivery of the fans, but he would not sell them. 'If you want the fans,' he had answered, 'you must first of all take my life.' Now, miss, do consider what was to be done? But, Yuncun is, as it happens, a man with no regard for divine justice. Well, when he came to hear of it, he at once devised a plan to lay hold of these fans, so fabricating the charge against him of letting a government debt drag on without payment, he had him arrested and brought before him in the Yamen; when he adjudicated that his family property should be converted into money to make up the amount due to the public chest; and, confiscating the fans in question, he set an official value on them and sent them over here. And as for that 'stone fool,' no one now has the faintest idea whether he be dead or alive. Mr. Jia She, however, taunted Mr. Secundus. 'How is it,' he said, 'that other people can manage to get them?' Our master simply rejoined 'that to bring ruin upon a person in such a trivial matter could not be accounted ability.' But, at these words, his father suddenly rushed into a fury, and averred that Mr. Secundus had said things to gag his mouth. This was the main cause. But several minor matters, which I can't even recollect, also occurred during these last few days. So, when all these things accumulated, he set to work and gave him a sound thrashing. He didn't, however, drag him down and strike him with a rattan or cane, but recklessly assaulted him, while he stood before him, with something or other, which he laid hold of, and broke his face open in two places. We understand that Mrs. Xue has in here some medicine or other for applying on wounds, so do try, miss, and find a ball of it and let me have it!"

Hearing this, Baochai speedily directed Ying'er to go and look for some, and, on discovering two balls of it, she brought them over and handed them to Ping'er.

"Such being the case," Baochai said, "do make, on your return, the usual inquiries for me, and I won't then need to go."

Ping'er turned towards Baochai, and expressed her readiness to execute her commission, after which she betook herself home, where we will leave her without further notice.

After Xiangling, for we will take up the thread of our narrative with her, completed her visits to the various inmates, she had her evening meal. Then when Baochai and everyone else went to dowager lady Jia's quarters, she came into the Xiaoxiang lodge. By this time Daiyu had got considerably better. Upon hearing that Xiangling had also moved into the garden, she, needless to say, was filled with delight.

"Now, that I've come in here," Xiangling then smiled and said, "do please teach me, at your leisure, how to write verses. It will be a bit of good luck for me if you do."

"Since you're anxious to learn how to versify," Daiyu answered with a smile, "you'd better acknowledge me as your tutor; for though I'm not a good hand at poetry, yet I know, after all, enough to be able to teach you."

"Of course you do!" Xiangling laughingly remarked. "I'll readily treat you as my tutor. But you mustn't put yourself to any trouble!"

"Is there anything so difficult about this," Daiyu pursued, "as to make it necessary to go in for any study? Why, it's purely and simply a matter of openings, elucidations, embellishments, and conclusions. The elucidations and embellishments, which come in the center, should form two antithetical sentences, the even tones must pair with the uneven. Empty words must correspond with full words; and full words with empty words. In the event of any out-of-the-way lines, it won't matter if the even and uneven tones, and the empty and full words do not pair."

"Strange though it may appear," smiled Xiangling, "I often handle books with old poems, and read one or two stanzas, whenever I can steal the time; and some among these I find pair most skilfully, while others don't. I have also heard that the first, third, and fifth lines are of no consequence; and that the second, fourth, and sixth must be clearly distinguished. But I notice that there are in the poetical works of ancient writers both those which accord with the rules, as well as those whose second, fourth, and sixth lines are not in compliance with any rule. Hence it is that my mind has daily been full of doubts. But after the hints you've given me, I really see that all these formulas are of no account, and that the main requirement is originality of diction."

"Yes, that's just the principle that holds good," Daiyu answered. "But diction is, after all, a last consideration. The first and foremost thing is the choice of proper sentiments; for when the sentiments are correct, there'll even be no need to polish the diction; it's certain to be elegant. This is called versifying without letting the diction affect the sentiments."

"What I admire," Xiangling proceeded with a smile, "are the lines by old Lu Fang;

"The double portière, when not raised, retains the fragrance long. An old inkslab, with a slight hole, collects plenty of ink.

"Their language is so clear that it's charming."

"You must on no account," Daiyu observed, "read poetry of the kind. It's because you people don't know what verses mean that you, no sooner read any shallow lines like these, than they take your fancy. But when once you get into this sort of style, it's impossible to get out of it. Mark my words! If you are in earnest about learning, I've got here Wang Mojie's complete collection; so you'd better take his one hundred stanzas, written in the pentameter rule of versification, and carefully study them, until you apprehend them thoroughly. Afterwards, look over the one hundred and twenty stanzas of Lao Du, in the heptameter rule; and next read a hundred or two hundred of the heptameter four-lined stanzas by Li Qinglian. When you have, as a first step, digested these three authors, and made them your foundation, you can take Tao Yuanming, Ying, Liu, Xie, Yuan, Yu, Bao, and other writers and go through them once. And with those sharp and quick wits of yours, I've no doubt but that you will become a regular poet before a year's time."

"Well, in that case," Xiangling smiled, after listening to her, "bring me the book, my dear miss, so that I may take it along. It will be a good thing if I can manage to read several stanzas at night."

At these words, Daiyu bade Zijuan fetch Wang Youcheng's pentameter stanzas. When brought, she handed them to Xiangling. "Only peruse those marked with red circles," she said. "They've all been selected by me. Read each one of them; and should there be any you can't fathom, ask your miss about them. Or when you come across me, I can explain them to you."

Xiangling took the poems and repaired back to the Hengwu Yuan. And without worrying her mind about anything she approached the lamp and began to con stanza after stanza. Baochai pressed her, several consecutive times, to go to bed; but as even rest was far from her thoughts, Baochai let her, when she perceived what trouble she was taking over her task, have her own way in the matter.

Daiyu had one day just finished combing her hair and performing her ablutions, when she espied Xiangling come with smiles playing about her lips, to return her the book and to ask her to let her have Du's poetical compositions in exchange.

"Of all these, how many stanzas can you recollect?" Daiyu asked, smiling.

"I've read everyone of those marked with a red circle," Xiangling laughingly rejoined.

"Have you caught the ideas of any of them, yes or no?" Daiyu inquired.

"Yes, I've caught some!" Xiangling smiled. "But whether rightly or not I don't know. Let me tell you."

"You must really," Daiyu laughingly remarked, "minutely solicit people's opinions if you want to make any progress. But go on and let me hear you."

"From all I can see," Xiangling smiled, "the beauty of poetry lies in certain ideas, which though not quite expressible in words are, nevertheless, found, on reflection, to be absolutely correct. Some may have the semblance of being totally devoid of sense, but, on second thought, they'll truly be seen to be full of sense and feeling."

"There's a good deal of right in what you say," Daiyu observed. "But I wonder how you arrived at this conclusion?"

"I notice in that stanza on 'the borderland,' the antithetical couplet:

"In the vast desert reigns but upright mist.
In the long river setteth the round sun.

"Consider now how ever can mist be upright? The sun is, of course, round. But the word 'upright' would seem to be devoid of common sense; and 'round' appears far too commonplace a word. But upon throwing the whole passage together, and pondering over it, one fancies having seen the scenery alluded to. Now were anyone to suggest that two other characters should be substituted for these two, one would verily be hard pressed to find any other two as suitable. Besides this, there's also the couplet:

"When the sun sets, rivers and lakes are white;
When the mist falls, the heavens and earth azure.

"Both 'white' and 'azure', apparently too lack any sense; but reflection will show that these two words are absolutely necessary to bring out thoroughly the aspect of the scenery. And in conning them over, one feels just as if one had an olive, weighing several thousands of catties, in one's mouth, so much relish does one derive from them. But there's this too:

"At the ferry stays the setting sun,
O'er the mart hangs the lonesome mist.

"And how much trouble must these words 'stay,' and 'over,' have caused the author in their conception! When the boats made fast, in the evening of a certain day of that year in which we came up to the capital, the banks were without a trace of human beings; and there were only just a few trees about; in the distance loomed the houses of several families engaged in preparing their evening meal, and the mist was, in fact, azure like jade, and connected like clouds. So, when I, as it happened, read this couplet last night, it actually seemed to me as if I had come again to that spot!"

But in the course of their colloquy, Baoyu and Tanchun arrived; and entering the room, they seated themselves, and lent an ear to her arguments on the verses.

"Seeing that you know so much," Baoyu remarked with a smiling face, "you can dispense with reading poetical works, for you're not far off from proficiency. To hear you expatiate on these two lines, makes it evident to my mind that you've even got at their secret meaning."

"You say," argued Daiyu with a significant smile, "that the line:

"'O'er (the mart) hangs the lonesome mist,'

"is good; but aren't you yet aware that this is only plagiarized from an ancient writer? But I'll show you the line I'm telling you of. You'll find it far plainer and clearer than this."

While uttering these words, she turned up Dao Yuanming's:

Dim in the distance lies a country place;
Faint in the hamlet-market hangs the mist;

and handed it to Xiangling.

Xiangling perused it, and, nodding her head, she eulogized it. "Really," she smiled, "the word 'over' is educed from the two characters implying 'faint.'"

Baoyu burst out into a loud fit of exultant laughter. "You've already got it!" he cried. "There's no need of explaining anything more to you! Any further explanations will, in lieu of benefiting you, make you unlearn what you've learnt. Were you therefore to, at once, set to work, and versify, your lines are bound to be good."

"Tomorrow," observed Tanchun with a smile, "I'll stand an extra treat and invite you to join the society."

"Why make a fool of me, miss?" Xiangling laughingly ejaculated. "It's merely that mania of mine that made me apply my mind to this subject at all; just for fun and no other reason."

Tanchun and Daiyu both smiled. "Who doesn't go in for these things for fun?" they asked. "Is it likely that we improvise verses in real earnest? Why, if anyone treated our verses as genuine verses, and took them outside this garden, people would have such a hearty laugh at our expense that their very teeth would drop."

"This is again self-violence and self-abasement!" Baoyu interposed. "The other day, I was outside the garden, consulting with the gentlemen about paintings, and, when they came to hear that we had started a poetical society, they begged of me to let them have the rough copies to read. So I wrote out several stanzas, and gave them to them to look over, and who did not praise them with all sincerity? They even copied them and took them to have the blocks cut."

"Are you speaking the truth?" Tanchun and Daiyu eagerly inquired.

"If I'm telling a lie," Baoyu laughed, "I'm like that cockatoo on that frame!"

"You verily do foolish things!" Daiyu and Tanchun exclaimed with one voice, at these words. "But not to mention that they were doggerel lines, had they even been anything like what verses should be, our writings shouldn't have been hawked about outside."

"What's there to fear?" Baoyu smiled. "Hadn't the writings of women of old been handed outside the limits of the inner chambers, why, there would, at present, be no one with any idea of their very existence."

While he passed this remark, they saw Ruhua arrive from Xichun's quarters to ask Baoyu to go over; and Baoyu eventually took his departure.

Xiangling then pressed (Daiyu) to give her Du's poems. "Do choose some theme," she also asked Daiyu and Tanchun, "and let me go and write on it. When I've done, I'll bring it for you to correct."

"Last night," Daiyu observed, "the moon was so magnificent, that I meant to improvise a stanza on it; but as I haven't done yet, go at once and write one using the fourteenth rhyme, 'han' (cool). You're at liberty to make use of whatever words you fancy."

Hearing this, Xiangling was simply delighted, and taking the poems, she went back. After considerable exertion, she succeeded in devising a couplet, but so little able was she to tear herself away from the "Du" poems, that she perused another couple of stanzas, until she had no inclination for either tea or food, and she felt in an unsettled mood, try though she did to sit or recline.

"Why," Baochai remonstrated, "do you bring such trouble upon yourself? It's that Pin'er, who has led you on to it! But I'll settle accounts with her! You've all along been a thick-headed fool; but now that you've burdened yourself with all this, you've become a greater fool."

"Miss," smiled Xiangling, "don't confuse me."

So saying, she set to work and put together a stanza, which she first and foremost handed to Baochai to look over.

"This isn't good!" Baochai smilingly said. "This isn't the way to do it! Don't fear of losing face, but take it and give it to her to peruse. We'll see what she says."

At this suggestion, Xiangling forthwith went with her verses in search of Daiyu. When Daiyu came to read them, she found their text to be:

The night grows cool, what time Selene reacheth the mid-heavens.
Her radiance pure shineth around with such a spotless sheen.
Bards oft for inspiration raise on her their thoughts and eyes.
The rustic daren't see her, so fears he to enhance his grief.
Jade mirrors are suspended near the tower of malachite.
An icelike plate dangles outside the gem-laden portière.
The eve is fine, so why need any silvery candles burn?
A clear light shines with dazzling luster on the painted rails.

"There's a good deal of spirit in them," Daiyu smiled, "but the language is not elegant. It's because you've only read a few poetical works that you labor under restraint. Now put this stanza aside and write another. Pluck up your courage and go and work away."

After listening to her advice, Xiangling quietly wended her way back, but so much the more (preoccupied) was she in her mind that she did not even enter the house, but remaining under the trees, planted by the side of the pond, she either seated herself on a rock and plunged in a reverie, or squatted down and dug the ground, to the astonishment of all those who went backwards and forwards. Li Wan, Baochai, Tanchun, Baoyu, and some others heard about her; and, taking their position some way off on the mound, they watched her, much amused. At one time, they saw her pucker up her eyebrows; and at another smile to herself.

"That girl must certainly be cracked!" Baochai laughed. "Last night she kept on muttering away straight up to the fifth watch, when she at last turned in. But shortly, daylight broke, and I heard her get up and comb her hair, all in a hurry, and rush after Pin'er. In a while, however, she returned; and, after acting like an idiot the whole day, she managed to put together a stanza. But it wasn't after all, good, so she's, of course, now trying to devise another."

"This indeed shows," Baoyu laughingly remarked, "that the earth is spiritual, that man is intelligent, and that heaven does not in the creation of human beings bestow on them natural gifts to no purpose. We've been sighing and lamenting that it was a pity that such a one as she, should, really, be so unpolished; but who could ever have anticipated that things would, in the long run, reach the present pass? This is a clear sign that heaven and earth are most equitable!"

"If only," smiled Baochai, at these words, "you could be as painstaking as she is, what a good thing it would be. And would you fail to attain success in anything you might take up?"

Baoyu made no reply. But realising that Xiangling had crossed over in high spirits to find Daiyu again, Tanchun laughed and suggested, "Let's follow her there, and see whether her composition is any good."

At this proposal, they came in a body to the Xiaoxiang lodge. Here they discovered Daiyu holding the verses and explaining various things to her.

"What are they like?" they all thereupon inquired of Daiyu.

"This is naturally a hard job for her!" Daiyu rejoined. "They're not yet as good as they should be. This stanza is far too forced; you must write another."

One and all however expressed a desire to look over the verses. On perusal, they read:

'Tis not silver, neither water that on the windows shines so cold.
Selene, mark! covers, like a jade platter, the clear vault of heaven.
What time the fragrance faint of the plum bloom is fain to tinge the air,
The dew-bedecked silken willow trees begin to lose their leaves.
'Tis the remains of powder which methinks besmear the golden steps.
Her lustrous rays enshroud like light hoar-frost the jade-like balustrade.
When from my dreams I wake, in the west tower, all human trace is gone.
Her slanting orb can yet clearly be seen across the bamboo screen.

"It doesn't sound like a song on the moon," Baochai smilingly observed. "Yet were, after the word 'moon', that of 'light' supplied, it would be better; for, just see, if each of these lines treated of the moonlight, they would be all right. But poetry primarily springs from nonsensical language. In a few days longer, you'll be able to do well."

Xiangling had flattered herself that this last stanza was perfect, and the criticisms that fell on her ear, damped her spirits again. She was not however disposed to relax in her endeavors, but felt eager to commune with her own thoughts, so when she perceived the young ladies chatting and laughing, she betook herself all alone to the bamboo-grove at the foot of the steps; where she racked her brain, and ransacked her mind with such intentness that her ears were deaf to everything around her and her eyes blind to everything beyond her task.

"Miss Ling," Tanchun presently cried, smiling from inside the window, "do have a rest!"

"The character 'rest'," Xiangling nervously replied, "comes from lot number 15, under 'shan', (to correct), so it's the wrong rhyme."

This rambling talk made them involuntarily burst out laughing.

"In very fact," Baochai laughed, "she's under a poetical frenzy, and it's all Pin'er who has incited her."

"The holy man says," Daiyu smilingly rejoined, "that 'one must not be weary of exhorting people' and if she comes, time and again, to ask me this and that how can I possibly not tell her?"

"Let's take her to Miss Quarta's rooms," Li Wan smiled, "and if we could coax her to look at the painting, and bring her to her senses, it will be well."

Speaking the while, she actually walked out of the room, and laying hold of her, she brought her through the Lotus Fragrance arbor to the bank of Warm Fragrance. Xichun was tired and languid, and was lying on the window, having a midday siesta. The painting was resting against the partition-wall, and was screened with a gauze cover. With one voice, they roused Xichun, and raising the gauze cover to contemplate her work, they saw that three-tenths of it had already been accomplished. But their attention was attracted by the representation of several beautiful girls, inserted in the picture, so pointing at Xiangling: "Everyone who can write verses is to be put here," they said, "so be quick and learn."

But while conversing, they played and laughed for a time, after which, each went her own way.

Xiangling was meanwhile preoccupied about her verses, so, when evening came, she sat facing the lamp absorbed in thought. And the third watch struck before she got to bed. But her eyes were so wide awake, that it was only after the fifth watch had come and gone, that she, at length, felt drowsy and fell fast asleep.

Presently, the day dawned, and Baochai woke up; but, when she lent an ear, she discovered (Xiangling) in a sound sleep. "She has racked her brains the whole night long," she pondered. "I wonder, however, whether she has succeeded in finishing her task. She must be tired now, so I won't disturb her."

But in the midst of her cogitations, she heard Xiangling laugh and exclaim in her sleep: "I've got it. It cannot be that this stanza too won't be worth anything."

"How sad and ridiculous!" Baochai soliloquized with a smile. And, calling her by name, she woke her up. "What have you got?" she asked. "With that firmness of purpose of yours, you could even become a spirit! But before you can learn how to write poetry, you'll be getting some illness."

Chiding her the while, she combed her hair and washed; and, this done, she repaired, along with her cousins, into dowager lady Jia's quarters.

Xiangling made, in fact, such desperate efforts to learn all about poetry that her system got quite out of order. But although she did not in the course of the day hit upon anything, she quite casually succeeded in her dreams in devising eight lines; so concluding her toilette and her ablutions, she hastily jotted them down, and betook herself into the Qinfang pavilion. Here she saw Li Wan and the whole bevy of young ladies, returning from Madame Wang's suite of apartments.

Baochai was in the act of telling them of the verses composed by Xiangling, while asleep, and of the nonsense she had been talking, and everyone of them was convulsed with laughter. But upon raising their heads, and perceiving that she was approaching, they vied with each other in pressing her to let them see her composition.

But, reader, do you wish to know any further particulars? If you do, read those given in the next chapter.

CHAPTER 49

White snow and red plum blossom in the crystal world. The pretty girl, fragrant with powder, cuts some meat and eats it.

Xiangling, we will now proceed, perceived the young ladies engaged in chatting and laughing, and went up to them with a smiling countenance. "Just you look at this stanza!" she said. "If it's all right, then I'll continue my studies; but if it isn't worth any thing, I'll banish at once from my mind all idea of going in for versification."

With these words, she handed the verses to Daiyu and her companions. When they came to look at them, they found this to be their burden:

> If thou would'st screen Selene's beauteous sheen, thou'lt find it hard.
> Her shadows are by nature full of grace, frigid her form.
> A row of clothes-stones batter, while she lights a thousand li.
> When her disc's half, and the cock crows at the fifth watch, 'tis cold.
> Wrapped in my green cloak in autumn, I hear flutes on the stream.
> While in the tower the red-sleeved maid leans on the rails at night.
> She feels also constrained to ask of the goddess Chang'e:
> Why it is that she does not let the moon e'er remain round?

"This stanza is not only good," they with one voice exclaimed, after perusing it, "but it's original, it's charming. It bears out the proverb: 'In the world, there's nothing difficult; the only thing hard to get at is a human being with a will.' We'll certainly ask you to join our club."

Xiangling caught this remark; but so little did she credit it that fancying that they were making fun of her, she still went on to press Daiyu, Baochai, and the other girls to give her their opinions. But while engaged in speaking, she spied a number of young waiting-maids, and old matrons come with hurried step. "Several young ladies and ladies have come," they announced smilingly, "but we don't know any of them. So your ladyship and you, young ladies, had better come at once and see what relatives they are."

"What are you driving at?" Li Wan laughed. "You might, after all, state distinctly whose relatives they are."

"Your ladyship's two young sisters have come," the matrons and maids rejoined smiling. "There's also another young lady, who says she's miss Xue's cousin, and a gentleman who pretends to be Mr. Xue Pan's junior cousin. We are now off to ask Mrs. Xue to meet them. But your ladyship and the young ladies might go in advance and greet them." As they spoke, they straightway took their leave.

"Has our Xue Ke come along with his sisters?" Baochai inquired, with a smile.

"My aunt has probably also come to the capital," Li Wan laughed. "How is it they've all arrived together? This is indeed a strange thing!" Then adjourning in a body into Madame Wang's drawing rooms, they saw the floor covered with a black mass of people.

Madame Xing's sister-in-law was there as well. She had entered the capital with her daughter, Xiuyan, to look up madame Xing. But lady Feng's brother, Wang Ren, had, as luck would have it, just been preparing to start for the capital, so the two family connexions set out in company for their common destination. After accomplishing half their journey, they encountered, while their boats were lying at anchor, Li Wan's widowed sister-in-law, who also was on her way to the metropolis, with her two girls, the elder of whom was Li Wen and the younger Li Qi. They all them talked matters over, and, induced by the ties of relationship, the three families prosecuted their voyage together. But subsequently, Xue Pan's cousin Xue Ke—whose father had, when on a visit years ago to the capital, engaged his uterine sister to the son of the Mei Hanlin, whose residence was in the metropolis—came while planning to go and consummate the marriage, to learn of Wang Ren's departure, so taking his sister with him, he kept in his track till he managed to catch him up. Hence it happened that they all now arrived in a body to look up their respective relatives. In due course, they exchanged the conventional salutations; and these over, they had a chat.

Dowager lady Jia and madame Wang were both filled with ineffable delight.

"Little wonder is it," smiled old lady Jia, "if the snuff of the lamp crackled time and again; and if it formed and reformed into a head! It was, indeed, sure to come to this today!"

While she conversed on everyday topics, the presents had to be put away; and, as she, at the same time, expressed a wish to keep the new arrivals to partake of some wine and eatables, lady Feng had, needless to say, much extra work added to her ordinary duties.

Li Wan and Baochai descanted, of course, with their aunts and cousins on the events that had transpired since their separation. But Daiyu, though when they first met, continued in cheerful spirits, could not again, when the recollection afterwards flashed through her mind that one and all had their relatives, and that she alone had not a soul to rely upon, avoid withdrawing out of the way, and giving vent to tears.

Baoyu, however, read her feelings, and he had to do all that lay in his power to exhort her and to console her for a time before she cheered up. Baoyu then hurried into the Yihong court. Going up to Xiren, Sheyue, and Qingwen: "Don't you yet hasten to go and see them?" he smiled. "Who'd ever have fancied that cousin Baochai's own cousin would be what he is? That cousin of hers is so unique in appearance and in deportment. He looks as if he were cousin Baochai's uterine younger brother. But what's still more odd is that you should have kept on saying the whole day long that cousin Baochai is a very beautiful creature. You should now see her cousin, as well as the two girls of her senior sister-in-law. I couldn't adequately tell you what they're like. Good heavens! Good heavens! What subtle splendor and spiritual beauty must you possess to produce beings like them, so superior to other human creatures! How plain it is that I'm like a frog wallowing at the bottom of a well! I've throughout every hour of the day said to myself that nowhere could any girls be found to equal those at present in our home; but, as it happens, I haven't had far to look! Even in our own native sphere, one would appear to eclipse the other! Here I have now managed to add one more stratum to my store of learning! But can it possibly be that outside these few, there can be any more like them?

As he uttered these sentiments, he smiled to himself. But Xiren noticed how much under the influence of his insane fits he once more was, and she promptly abandoned all idea of going over to pay her respects to the visitors.

Qingwen and the other girls had already gone and seen them and come back. Putting on a smile, "You'd better," they urged Xiren, "be off at once and have a look at them. Our elder mistress' niece, Miss Bao's cousin, and our senior lady's two sisters resemble a bunch of four leeks so pretty are they!"

But scarcely were these words out of their lips, than they perceived Tanchun too enter the room, beaming with smiles. She came in quest of Baoyu.

"Our poetical society is in a flourishing way," she remarked.

"It is," smiled Baoyu. "Here no sooner do we, in the exuberance of our spirits, start a poetical society, than the devils and gods bring through their agency, all these people in our midst! There's only one thing however. Have they, I wonder, ever learnt how to write poetry or not?"

"I just now asked everyone of them," Tanchun replied. "Their ideas of themselves are modest, it's true, yet from all I can gather there's not one who can't versify. But should there even be any who can't, there's nothing hard about it. Just look at Xiangling. Her case will show you the truth of what I say."

"Of the whole lot," smiled Qingwen, "Miss Xue's cousin carries the palm. What do you think about her, Miss Tertia?"

"It's really so!" Tanchun responded. "In my own estimation, even her elder cousin and all this bevy of girls are not fit to hold a candle to her!"

Xiren felt much surprise at what she heard. "This is indeed odd!" she smiled. "Whence could one hunt up any better? We'd like to go and have a peep at her."

"Our venerable senior," Tanchun observed, "was at the very first sight of her so charmed with her that there's nothing she wouldn't do. She has already compelled our Madame Xing to adopt her as a godchild. Our dear ancestor wishes to bring her up herself; this point was settled a little while back."

Baoyu went into ecstasies. "Is this a fact?" he eagerly inquired.

"How often have I gone in for yarns?" Tanchun said. "Now that our worthy senior," continuing, she laughed, "has got this nice granddaughter, she has banished from her mind all thought of a grandson like you!"

"Never mind," answered Baoyu smiling. "It's only right that girls should be more doated upon. But tomorrow is the sixteenth, so we should have a meeting."

"That girl Lin Daiyu is no sooner out of bed," Tanchun remarked, "than cousin Secunda falls ill again. Everything is, in fact, up and down!"

"Our cousin Secunda," Baoyu explained, "doesn't also go in very much for verses, so, what would it matter if she were left out?"

"It would be well to wait a few days," Tanchun urged, "until the newcomers have had time to see enough of us to become intimate. We can then invite them to join us. Won't this be better? Our senior sister-in-law and cousin Bao have now no mind for poetry. Besides, Xiangyun has not arrived. Pin'er is just over her sickness. The members are not all therefore in a fit state, so wouldn't it be preferable if we waited until that girl Yun came? The new arrivals will also have a chance of becoming friendly. Pin'er will likewise recover entirely. Our senior sister-in-law and cousin Bao will have time to compose their minds; and Xiangling to improve in her verses. We shall then be able to convene a full meeting and won't it be better? You and I must now go over to our worthy ancestor's, on the other side, and hear what's up. But, barring cousin Baochai's cousin—for we needn't take her into account, as it's sure to have been decided that she should live in our home—if the other three are not to stay here with us, we should entreat our grandmother to let them as well take up their quarters in the garden. And if we succeed in adding a few more to our number, won't it be more fun for us?"

Baoyu at these words was so much the more gratified that his very eyebrows distended, and his eyes laughed. "You've got your wits about you!" he speedily exclaimed. "My mind is ever so dull! I've vainly given way to a fit of joy. But to think of these contingencies was beyond me!"

So saying the two cousins repaired together to their grandmother's suite of apartments; where, in point of fact, Madame Wang had already gone through the ceremony of recognizing Xue Baoqin as her godchild. Dowager lady Jia's fascination for her, however, was so much out of the common run that she did not tell her to take up her quarters in the garden. Of a night, she therefore slept with old lady Jia in the same rooms; while Xue Ke put up in Xue Pan's study.

"Your niece needn't either return home," dowager lady Jia observed to Madame Xing. "Let her spend a few days in the garden and see the place before she goes."

Madame Xing's brother and sister-in-law were, indeed, in straitened circumstances at home. So much so that they had, on their present visit to the capital, actually to rely upon such accommodation as Madame Xing could procure for them and upon such help towards their traveling expenses as she could afford to give them. When she consequently heard her proposal, Madame Xing was, of course, only too glad to comply with her wishes, and readily she handed Xing Xiuyan to the charge of lady Feng. But lady Feng, bethinking herself of the number of young ladies already in the garden, of their divergent dispositions and, above all things, of the inconvenience of starting a separate household, deemed it advisable to send her to live along with Yingchun; for in the event, (she thought,) of Xing Xiuyan meeting afterwards with any contrarieties, she herself would be clear of all responsibility, even though Madame Xing came to hear about them. Deducting, therefore any period, spent by Xing Xiuyan on a visit home, lady Feng allowed Xing Xiuyan as well, if she extended her stay in the garden of Broad Vista for any time over a month, an amount equal to that allotted to Yingchun.

Lady Feng weighed with unprejudiced eye Xing Xiuyan's temperament and deportment. She found in her not the least resemblance to

Madame Xing, or even to her father and mother; but thought her a most genial and love-inspiring girl. This consideration actuated lady Feng (not to deal harshly with her), but to pity her instead for the poverty in which they were placed at home, and for the hard lot she had to bear, and to treat her with far more regard than she did any of the other young ladies. Madame Xing, however, did not lavish much attention on her.

Dowager lady Jia, Madame Wang and the rest had all along been fond of Li Wan for her virtuous and benevolent character. Besides, her continence in remaining a widow at her tender age commanded general esteem. When they therefore now saw her husbandless sister-in-law come to pay her a visit, they would not allow her to go and live outside the mansion. Her sister-in-law was, it is true, extremely opposed to the proposal, but as dowager lady Jia was firm in her determination, she had no other course but to settle down, along with Li Wen and Li Qi, in the Daoxiang village.

They had by this time assigned quarters to all the newcomers, when, who would have thought it, Shi Nai, Marquis of Baoling, was once again appointed to a high office in another province, and he had shortly to take his family and proceed to his post. But so little could old lady Jia brook the separation from Xiangyun that she kept her behind and received her in her own home. Her original idea was to have asked lady Feng to have separate rooms arranged for her, but Shi Xiangyun was so obstinate in her refusal, her sole wish being to put up with Baochai, that the idea had, in consequence, to be abandoned.

At this period, the garden of Broad Vista was again much more full of life than it had ever been before. Li Wan was the chief inmate. The rest consisted of Yingchun, Tanchun, Xichun, Baochai, Daiyu, Xiangyun, Li Wen, Li Qi, Baoqin, and Xing Xiuyan. In addition to these, there were lady Feng and Baoyu, so that they mustered thirteen in all. As regards age, irrespective of Li Wan, who was by far the eldest, and lady Feng, who came next, the other inmates did not exceed fourteen, sixteen, or seventeen. But the majority of them had come into the world in the same year, though in different months, so they themselves could not remember distinctly who was senior, and who junior. Even dowager lady Jia, Madame Wang, and the matrons and maids in the household were unable to tell the differences between them with any accuracy, given as they were to the simple observance of addressing themselves promiscuously and quite at random by the four words representing "female cousin" and "male cousin."

Xiangling was gratifying her wishes to her heart's content and devoting her mind exclusively to the composition of verses, not presuming however to make herself too much of a nuisance to Baochai, when, by a lucky coincidence, Shi Xiangyun came on the scene. But how was it possible for one so loquacious as Xiangyun to avoid the subject of verses, when Xiangling repeatedly begged her for explanations? This inspirited her so much the more, that not a day went by, yea not a single night, on which she did not start some loud argument and lengthy discussion.

"You really," Baochai felt impelled to laugh, "kick up such a din, that it's quite unbearable! Fancy a girl doing nothing else than turning poetry into a legitimate thing for raising an argument! Why, were some literary persons to hear you, they would, instead of praising you, have a laugh at your expense, and say that you don't mind your own business. We hadn't yet got rid of Xiangling with all her rubbish, and here we have a chatterbox like you thrown on us! But what is it that that mouth of yours keeps on jabbering? What about the bathos of Du Gongbu; and the unadorned refinement of Wei Suzhou? What also about Wen Bacha's elegant diction; and Li Yishan's abstruseness? A pack of silly fools that you are! Do you in any way behave like girls should?"

These sneers evoked laughter from both Xiangling and Xiangyun.

But in the course of their conversation, they perceived Baoqin drop in, with a waterproof wrapper thrown over her, so dazzling with its gold and purplish colors, that they were at a loss to make out what sort of article it could be.

"Where did you get this?" Baochai eagerly inquired.

"It was snowing," Baoqin smilingly replied, "so her venerable ladyship turned up this piece of clothing and gave it to me."

Xiangling drew near and passed it under inspection. "No wonder," she exclaimed, "it looks so handsome! It's verily woven with peacock's feathers."

"What about peacock's feathers?" Xiangyun laughed. "It's made of the feathers plucked from the heads of wild ducks. This is a clear sign that our worthy ancestor is fond of you, for with all her love for Baoyu, she hasn't given it to him to wear."

"Truly does the proverb say: 'that every human being has his respective lot.'" Baochai smiled. "Nothing ever was further from my thoughts than that she would, at this juncture, drop on the scene! Come she may, but here she also gets our dear ancestor to lavish such love on her!"

"Unless you stay with our worthy senior," Xiangyun said, "do come into the garden. You may romp and laugh and eat and drink as much as you like in these two places. But when you get over to Madame Xing's rooms, talk and joke with her, if she be at home, to your heart's content; it won't matter if you tarry ever so long. But should she not be in, don't put your foot inside; for the inmates are many in those rooms and their hearts are evil. All they're up to is to do us harm."

These words much amused Baochai, Baoqin, Xiangling, Ying'er, and the others present.

"Were one to say," Baochai smiled, "that you're heartless, (it wouldn't do); for you've got a heart. But despite your having a heart, your tongue is, in fact, a little too outspoken! You should really today acknowledge this Qin'er of ours as your own sister!"

"This article of clothing," Xiangyun laughed, casting another glance at Baoqin, "is only meet for her to wear. It wouldn't verily look well on anyone else."

Saying this, she espied Hupo enter the room. "Our old mistress," she put in smiling, "bade me tell you, Miss Baochai, not to keep too strict a check over Miss Qin, for she's yet young; that you should let her do as she pleases, and that whatever she wants you should ask for, and not be afraid."

Baochai hastily jumped to her feet and signified her obedience. Pushing Baoqin, she laughed. "Even you couldn't tell whence this piece of good fortune hails from," she said. "Be off now; for mind, we might hurt your feelings. I can never believe myself so inferior to you!"

As she spoke, Baoyu and Daiyu walked in. But as Baochai continued to indulge in raillery to herself, "Cousin Bao," Xiangyun smilingly remonstrated, "you may, it's true, be jesting, but what if there were anyone to entertain such ideas in real earnest?"

"If anyone took things in earnest," Hupo interposed laughing, "why, she'd give offence to no one else but to him." Pointing, as she uttered this remark, at Baoyu.

"He's not that sort of person!" Baochai and Xiangyun simultaneously ventured, with a significant smile.

"If it isn't he," Hupo proceeded still laughing, "it's she." Turning again her finger towards Daiyu.

Xiangyun expressed not a word by way of rejoinder.

"That's still less likely," Baochai smiled, "for my cousin is like her own sister; and she's far fonder of her than of me. How could she therefore take offence? Do you credit that nonsensical trash uttered by Yun'er! Why what good ever comes out of that mouth of hers?"

Baoyu was ever well aware that Daiyu was gifted with a somewhat mean disposition. He had not however as yet come to learn anything of what had recently transpired between Daiyu and Baochai. He was therefore just giving way to fears lest his grandmother's fondness for Baoqin should be the cause of her feeling dejected. But when he now heard the remarks passed by Xiangyun, and the rejoinders made, on the other hand, by Baochai, and, when he noticed how different Daiyu's voice and manner were from former occasions, and how they actually bore out Baochai's insinuation, he was at a great loss how to solve the mystery. "These two," he consequently pondered, "were never like this before! From all I can now see, they're, really, a hundred times far more friendly than any others are!" But presently he also observed Lin Daiyu rush after Baoqin, and call out "Sister," and, without even making any allusion to her name or any mention to her surname, treat her in every respect, just as if she were her own sister.

This Baoqin was young and warm-hearted. She was naturally besides of an intelligent disposition. She had, from her very youth up, learnt how to read and how to write. After a stay, on the present occasion, of a couple of days in the Jia mansion, she became acquainted with nearly every inmate. And as she saw that the whole bevy of young ladies were not of a haughty nature, and that they kept on friendly terms with her own cousin, she did not feel disposed to treat them with any discourtesy. But she had likewise found out for herself that Lin Daiyu was the best among the whole lot, so she started with Daiyu, more than with anyone else, a friendship of unusual fervor. This did not escape Baoyu's notice; but all he could do was to secretly give way to amazement.

Shortly, however, Baochai and her cousin repaired to Mrs. Xue's quarters. Xiangyun then betook herself to dowager lady Jia's apartments, while Lin Daiyu returned to her room and lay down to rest. Baoyu thereupon came to look up Daiyu.

"Albeit I've read the 'Record of the Western Side-Room,'" he smiled, "and understood a few passages of it, yet when I quoted some in order to make you laugh, you flew into a huff! But I now remember that there is, indeed, a passage, which is not intelligible to me; so let me quote it for you to explain it for me!"

Hearing this, Daiyu immediately concluded that his words harbored some secret meaning, so putting on a smile, "Recite it and let me hear it," she said.

"In the 'Confusion' chapter," Baoyu laughingly began, "there's a line couched in most beautiful language. It's this: 'What time did Meng Guang receive Liang Hong's candlestick?' (When did you and Baochai get to be such friends?) These five characters simply bear on a stock story; but to the credit of the writer be it, the question contained in the three empty words representing, 'What time' is set so charmingly! When did she receive it? Do tell me!"

At this inquiry, Daiyu too could not help laughing. "The question was originally nicely put," she felt urged to rejoin with a laugh. "But though the writer sets it gracefully, you ask it likewise with equal grace!"

"At one time," Baoyu observed, "all you knew was to suspect that I (was in love with Baochai); and have you now no faults to find?"

"Who ever could have imagined her such a really nice girl!" Daiyu smiled. "I've all along thought her full of guile!" And seizing the occasion, she told Baoyu with full particulars how she had, in the game of forfeits, made an improper quotation, and what advice Baochai had given her on the subject; how she had even sent her some birds' nests, and what they had said in the course of the chat they had had during her illness.

Baoyu then at length came to see why it was that such a warm friendship had sprung up between them. "To tell you the truth," he consequently remarked smilingly, "I was just wondering when Meng Guang had received Liang Hong's candlestick; and, lo, you, indeed, got it, when a mere child and through some reckless talk (and your friendship was sealed)."

As the conversation again turned on Baoqin, Daiyu recalled to mind that she had no sister, and she could not help melting once more into tears.

Baoyu hastened to reason with her. "This is again bringing trouble upon yourself!" he argued. "Just see how much thinner you are this year than you were last; and don't you yet look after your health? You deliberately worry yourself every day of your life. And when you've had a good cry, you feel at last that you've acquitted yourself of the duties of the day."

"Of late," Daiyu observed, drying her tears, "I feel sore at heart. But my tears are scantier by far than they were in years gone by. With all the grief and anguish, which gnaw my heart, my tears won't fall plentifully."

"This is because weeping has become a habit with you," Baoyu added. "But though you fancy to yourself that it is so, how can your tears have become scantier than they were?"

While arguing with her, he perceived a young waiting-maid, attached to his room, bring him a red felt wrapper. "Our senior mistress, lady Jia Zhu," she went on, "has just sent a servant to say that, as it snows, arrangements should be made for inviting people tomorrow to write verses."

But hardly was this message delivered, than they saw Li Wan's maid enter, and invite Daiyu to go over. Baoyu then proposed to Daiyu to accompany him, and together they came to the Daoxiang village. Daiyu changed her shoes for a pair of low shoes made of red scented sheep skin, ornamented with gold, and hollowed clouds. She put on a deep red crape cloak, lined with white fox fur; girdled herself with a lapis-lazuli colored sash, decorated with bright green double rings and four scepters; and covered her head with a hat suitable for rainy weather. After which, the two cousins trudged in the snow, and repaired to this side of the mansion. Here they discovered the young ladies assembled, dressed all alike in deep red felt or camlet capes, with the exception of Li Wan, who was clad in a woollen jacket, buttoning in the middle.

Xue Baochai wore a pinkish-purple twilled pelisse, lined with foreign "pa" fur, worked with threads from abroad, and ornamented with double embroidery. Xing Xiuyan was still attired in an old costume, she ordinarily used at home, without any garment for protection against the rain. Shortly, Shi Xiangyun arrived. She wore the long pelisse, given her by dowager lady Jia, which gave warmth both from the inside and outside, as the top consisted of martin-head fur, and the lining of the long-haired coat of the dark grey squirrel. On her head, she had a deep red woollen hood, made by Zhao Jun, with designs of clouds scooped out on it. This was lined with gosling-yellow, gold-streaked silk. Round her neck, she had a collar of sable fur.

"Just see here!" Daiyu was the first to shout with a laugh. "Here comes Sun Xingzhe the 'monkey-walker!' Lo, like him, she holds a snow cloak, and purposely puts on the air of a young bewitching ape!"

"Look here, all of you!" Xiangyun laughed. "See what I wear inside!"

So saying, she threw off her cloak. This enabled them to notice that she wore underneath a half-new garment with three different colored borders on the collar and cuffs, consisting of a short pelisse of russet material lined with ermine and ornamented with dragons embroidered in variegated silks whose coils were worked with golden threads. The lapel was narrow. The sleeves were short. The folds buttoned on the side. Under this, she had a very short light-red brocaded satin bodkin, lined with fur from foxes' ribs. Round her waist was lightly attached a many-hued palace sash, with butterfly knots and long tassels. On her feet, she too wore a pair of low shoes made of deer leather. Her waist looked more than ever like that of a wasp, her back like that of the gibbon. Her bearing resembled that of a crane, her figure that of a mantis.

"Her weak point," they laughed unanimously, "is to get herself up to look like a young masher. But she does, there's no denying, cut a much handsomer figure like this, than when she's dressed up like a girl!"

On his arrival in the Luxue pavilion, Baoyu found the maids and matrons engaged in sweeping away the snow and opening a passage.

This Luxue (Water-rush snow) pavilion was, we might explain, situated on a side hill, in the vicinity of a stream and spanned the rapids formed by it. The whole place consisted of several thatched roofs, mud walls, side fences, bamboo lattice windows and pushing windows, out of which fishing-lines could be conveniently dropped. On all four sides flourished one mass of reeds, which concealed the single path out of the pavilion. Turning and twisting, he penetrated on his way through the growth of reeds until he reached the spot where stretched the bamboo bridge leading to the Lotus Fragrance Arbor.

The moment the maids and matrons saw him approach with his waterproof-wrapper thrown over his person and his rain-hat on his head, they with one voice laughed, "We were just remarking that what was lacking was a fisherman, and lo, now we've got everything that was wanted! The young ladies are coming after their breakfast; you're in too impatient a mood!"

At these words, Baoyu had no help but to retrace his footsteps. As soon as he reached the Qinfang pavilion, he perceived Tanchun, issuing from the Qiushuang Study, wrapped in a deep red woollen waterproof, and a "Guanyin" hood on her head, supporting herself on the arm of a young maid. Behind her, followed a married woman, holding a glazed umbrella made of green satin.

Baoyu knew very well that she was on her way to his grandmother's, so speedily halting by the side of the pavilion, he waited for her to come up. The two cousins then left the garden together, and betook themselves to the front part of the mansion. Baoqin was at the time in the inner apartments, combing her hair, washing her hands and face, and changing her apparel. Shortly, the whole number of girls arrived. "I feel peckish!" Baoyu shouted; and again and again he tried to hurry the meal. It was with great impatience that he waited until the eatables could be laid on the table.

One of the dishes consisted of kid, boiled in cow's milk. "This is medicine for us, who are advanced in years," old lady Jia observed. "They're things that haven't seen the light! The pity is that you young people can't have any. There's some fresh venison today as an extra course, so you'd better wait and eat some of that!"

One and all expressed their readiness to wait. Baoyu however could not delay having something to eat. Seizing a cup of tea, he soaked a bowlful of rice, to which he added some meat from a pheasant's leg, and gobbled it down in a scramble.

"I'm well aware," dowager lady Jia said, "that as you're up to something again today, you people have no mind even for your meal. Let them keep," she therefore cried, "that venison for their evening repast!"

"What an idea!" lady Feng promptly put in. "We'll have enough with what remains of it."

Shi Xiangyun thereupon consulted with Baoyu. "As there's fresh venison," she said, "wouldn't it be nice to ask for a haunch and take it into the garden and prepare it ourselves? We'll thus be able to sate our hunger, and have some fun as well."

At this proposal, Baoyu actually asked lady Feng to let them have a haunch, and he bade a matron carry it into the garden.

Presently, they all got up from table. After a time, they entered the garden and came in a body to the Lu Xue pavilion to hear Li Wan give out the themes, and fix upon the rhymes. But Xiangyun and Baoyu were the only two of whom nothing was seen.

"Those two," Daiyu observed, "can't get together! The moment they meet, how much trouble doesn't arise! They must surely have now gone to hatch their plans over that haunch of venison."

These words were still on her lips when she saw "sister-in-law" Li coming also to see what the noise was all about. "How is it," she then inquired of Li Wan, "that that young fellow, with the jade, and that girl, with the golden unicorn round her neck, both of whom are so cleanly and tidy, and have besides ample to eat, are over there conferring about eating raw meat? There they are chatting, saying this and saying that; but I can't see how meat can be eaten raw!"

This remark much amused the party. "How dreadful!" they exclaimed, "Be quick and bring them both here!"

"All this fuss," Daiyu smiled, "is the work of that girl Yun. I'm not far off again in my surmises."

Li Wan went out with precipitate step in search of the cousins. "If you two are bent upon eating raw meat," she cried, "I'll send you over to our old senior's; you can do so there. What will I care then if you have a whole deer raw and make yourselves ill over it? It won't be any business of mine. But it's snowing hard and it's bitterly cold, so be quick and go and write some verses for me and be off!"

"We're doing nothing of the kind," Baoyu hastily rejoined. "We're going to eat some roasted meat."

"Well, that won't matter!" Li Wan observed. And seeing the old matrons bring an iron stove, prongs, and a gridiron of iron wire, "Mind you don't cut your hands," Li Wan resumed, "for we won't have any crying!"

This remark concluded, she walked in.

Lady Feng had sent Ping'er from her quarters to announce that she was unable to come, as the issue of the customary annual money gave her just at present, plenty to keep her busy.

Xiangyun caught sight of Ping'er and would not let her go on her errand. But Ping'er too was fond of amusement, and had ever followed lady Feng everywhere she went, so, when she perceived what fun was to be got, and how merrily they joked and laughed, she felt impelled to take off her bracelets (and to join them). The trio then pressed round the fire; and Ping'er wanted to be the first to roast three pieces of venison to regale themselves with.

On the other side, Baochai and Daiyu had, even in ordinary times, seen enough of occasions like the present. They did not therefore think it anything out of the way; but Baoqin and the other visitors, inclusive of "sister-in-law" Li, were filled with intense wonder.

Tanchun had, with the help of Li Wan, and her companions, succeeded by this time in choosing the subjects and rhymes. "Just smell that sweet fragrance," Tanchun remarked. "One can smell it even here! I'm also going to taste some."

So speaking, she too went to look them up. But Li Wan likewise followed her out. "The guests are all assembled," she observed. "Haven't you people had enough as yet?"

While Xiangyun munched what she had in her month, she replied to her question. "Whenever," she said, "I eat this sort of thing, I feel a craving for wine. It's only after I've had some that I shall be able to rhyme. Were it not for this venison, I would today have positively been quite unfit for any poetry." As she spoke, she discerned Baoqin, standing and laughing opposite to her, in her duck-down garment.

"You idiot," Xiangyun laughingly cried, "come and have a mouthful to taste."

"It's too filthy!" Baoqin replied smiling.

"You go and try it." Baochai added with a laugh. "It's capital! Your cousin Lin is so very weak that she couldn't digest it, if she had any. Otherwise she too is very fond of this."

Upon hearing this, Baoqin readily crossed over and put a piece in her mouth; and so good did she find it that she likewise started eating some of it.

In a little time, however, lady Feng sent a young maid to call Ping'er.

"Miss Shi," Ping'er explained, "won't let me go. So just return ahead of me."

The maid thereupon took her leave; but shortly after they saw lady Feng arrive; she too with a wrapper over her shoulders.

"You're having," she smiled; "such dainties to eat, and don't you tell me?"

Saying this, she also drew near and began to eat.

"Where has this crowd of beggars turned up from?" Daiyu put in with a laugh. "But never mind, never mind! Here's the Luxue pavilion come in for this calamity today, and, as it happens, it's that chit Yun by whom it has been polluted! But I'll have a good cry for the Luxue pavilion."

Xiangyun gave an ironical smile. "What do you know?" she exclaimed. "A genuine man of letters is naturally refined. But as for the whole lot of you, your poor and lofty notions are all a sham! You are most loathsome! We may now be frowzy and smelly, as we munch away lustily with our voracious appetites, but by and bye we'll prove as refined as scholars, as if we had cultured minds and polished tongues."

"If by and bye," Baochai laughingly interposed, "the verses you compose are not worth anything, I'll tug out that meat you've eaten, and take some of these snow-buried weeds and stuff you up with. I'll thus put an end to this evil fortune!"

While bandying words, they finished eating. For a time, they busied themselves with washing their hands. But when Ping'er came to put on her bracelets, she found one missing. She looked in a confused manner, at one time to the left, at another to the right; now in front of her, and then behind her for ever so long, but not a single vestige of it was visible. One and all were therefore filled with utter astonishment.

"I know where this bracelet has gone to," lady Feng suggested smilingly. "But just you all go and attend to your poetry. We too can well dispense with searching for it, and repair to the front. Before three days are out, I'll wager that it turns up. What verses are you writing today?" continuing, she went on to inquire. "Our worthy senior says that the end of the year is again nigh at hand, and that in the first moon some more conundrums will have to be devised to be affixed on lanterns, for the recreation of the whole family."

"Of course we'll have to write a few," they laughingly rejoined, upon hearing her remarks. "We forgot all about it. Let's hurry up now, and compose a few fine ones, so as to have them ready to enjoy some good fun in the first moon."

Speaking the while, they came in a body into the room with the earthen couches, where they found the cups, dishes, and eatables already laid out in readiness. On the walls had been put up the themes, meter, and specimen verses. Baoyu and Xiangyun hastened to examine what was written. They saw that they had to take for a theme something on the present scenery and indite a stanza with antithetical pentameter lines; that the word "hsiao," second (in the book of meter), had been fixed upon as a rhyme; but that there was, below that, no mention, as yet, made of any precedence.

"I can't write verses very well," Li Wan pleaded, "so all I'll do will be to devise three lines, and the one, who'll finish the task first, we'll have afterwards to pair them."

"We should, after all," Baochai urged, "make some distinction with regard to order."

But, reader, if you entertain any desire to know the sequel, peruse the particulars recorded in the chapter that follows.

CHAPTER 50

In the Luxue pavilion, they vie with each other in pairing verses on the scenery. In the Nuanxiang village, they compose, in beautiful style, riddles for the spring lanterns.

But to continue, "We should, after all," Baochai suggested, "make some distinction as to order. Let me write out what's needful."

After uttering this proposal, she urged everyone to draw lots and determine the precedence. The first one to draw was Li Wan. After her, a list of the respective names was made in the order in which they came out.

"Well, in that case," lady Feng rejoined, "I'll also give a top line."

The whole party laughed in chorus. "It will be ever so much better like this," they said.

Baochai supplied above "the old laborer of Daoxiang" the word "Feng," whereupon Li Wan went on to explain the theme to her.

"You musn't poke fun at me!" lady Feng smiled, after considerable reflection. "I've only managed to get a coarse line. It consists of five words. As for the rest, I have no idea how to manage them."

"The coarser the language, the better it is," one and all laughed. "Out with it! You can then go and attend to your legitimate business!"

"I fancy," lady Feng observed, "that when it snows there's bound to be northerly wind, for last night I heard the wind blow from the north the whole night long. I've got a line, it's:

"'The whole night long the northern wind was high;'

"but whether it will do or not, I am not going to worry my mind about it."

One and all, upon hearing this, exchanged looks. "This line is, it's true, coarse," they smiled, "and gives no insight into what comes below, but it's just the kind of opening that would be used by such as understand versification. It's not only good, but it will afford to those, who come after you, inexhaustible scope for writing. In fact, this line will take the lead, so 'old laborer of Daoxiang' be quick and indite some more to tag on below."

Lady Feng, "sister-in-law" Li, and Ping'er had then another couple of glasses, after which each went her own way. During this while Li Wan wrote down:

The whole night long the northern wind was high;

and then she herself subjoined the antithetical couplet:

The door I ope, and lo the flakes of snow are still toss'd by the
    wind,
And drop into the slush. Oh, what a pity they're so purely white!

Xiangling recited:

All o'er the ground is spread, alas, this bright, refulgent gem;
But with an aim; for it is meant dry herbage to revive.

Tanchun said:

Without design the dying sprouts of grain it nutrifies.
But in the villages the price of mellow wine doth rise.

Li Qi added:

In a good year, grain in the house is plentiful.
The bulrush moves and the ash issues from the tube.

Li Wen continued:

What time spring comes the handle of the Dipper turns.
The bleaky hills have long ago their verdure lost.

Xiuyan proceeded:

On a frost-covered stream, no tide can ever rise.
Easy the snow hangs on the sparse-leaved willow twigs.

Xiangyun pursued:

Hard 'tis for snow to pile on broken plantain leaves.
The coal, musk-scented, burns in the precious tripod.

Baoqin recited:

Th' embroidered sleeve enwraps the golden sable in its folds.
The snow transcends the mirror by the window in luster.

Baoyu suggested:

The fragrant pepper clings unto the wall.
The side wind still in whistling gusts doth blow.

Daiyu added:

A quiet dream becomes a cheerless thing.
Where is the fife with plum bloom painted on?

Baochai continued:

In whose household is there a flute made of green jade?
The fish fears lest the earth from its axis might drop.

"I'll go and see that the wine is warm for you people," Li Wan smiled.

But when Baochai told Baoqin to connect some lines, she caught sight of Xiangyun rise to her feet and put in:

What time the dragon wages war, the clouds dispel.
Back to the wild shore turns the man with single scull.

Baoqin thereupon again appended the couplet:

The old man hums his lines, and with his whip he points at the "Pa" bridge.
Fur coats are, out of pity, on the troops at the frontiers bestowed.

But would Xiangyun allow anyone to have a say? The others could not besides come up to her in quickness of wits so that, while their eyes were fixed on her, she with eyebrows uplifted and figure outstretched proceeded to say:

More cotton coats confer, for bear in memory th' imperial serfs!
The rugged barbarous lands are (on account of snow) with dangers fraught.

Baochai praised the verses again and again, and next contributed the distich:

> The twigs and branches live in fear of being tossed about.
> With what whiteness and feath'ry step the flakes of snow descend!

Daiyu eagerly subjoined the lines:

> The snow as nimbly falls as moves the waist of the "Sui" man when brandishing the sword.
> The tender leaves of tea, so acrid to the taste, have just been newly brewed and tried.

As she recited this couplet, she gave Baoyu a shove and urged him to go on. Baoyu was, at the moment, enjoying the intense pleasure of watching the three girls Baochai, Baoqin, and Daiyu make a joint onslaught on Xiangyun, so that he had of course not given his mind to tagging any antithetical verses. But when he now felt Daiyu push him he at length chimed in with:

> The fir is the sole tree which is decreed forever to subsist.
> The wild goose follows in the mud the prints and traces of its steps.

Baoqin took up the clue, adding:

> In the forest, the axe of the woodcutter may betimes be heard.
> With (snow) covered contours, a thousand peaks their heads jut in the air.

Xiangyun with alacrity annexed the verses:

> The whole way tortuous winds like a coiled snake.
> The flowers have felt the cold and ceased to bud.

Baochai and her companions again with one voice eulogized their fine diction.
Tanchun then continued:

> Could e'er the beauteous snow dread the nipping of frost?
> In the deep court the shivering birds are startled by its fall.

Xiangyun happened to be feeling thirsty and was hurriedly swallowing a cup of tea, when her turn was at once snatched by Xiuyan, who gave out the lines,

On the bare mountain wails the old man Xiao.
The snow covers the steps, both high and low.

Xiangyun immediately put away the tea-cup and added:

On the pond's surface, it allows itself to float.
At the first blush of dawn with effulgence it shines.

Daiyu recited with alacrity the couplet:

In confused flakes, it ceaseless falls the whole night long.
Troth one forgets that it implies three feet of cold.

Xiangyun hastened to smilingly interpose with the distich:

Its auspicious descent dispels the Emperor's grief.
There lies one frozen-stiff, but who asks him a word?

Baoqin too speedily put on a smile and added:

Glad is the proud wayfarer when he's pressed to drink.
Snapped is the weaving belt in the heavenly machine.

Xiangyun once again eagerly quoted the line:

In the seaside market is lost a silk kerchief.

But Lin Daiyu would not let her continue, and taking up the thread, she forthwith said:

With quiet silence, it enshrouds the raised kiosk.

Xiangyun vehemently gave the antithetical verse:

The utter poor clings to his pannier and his bowl.

Baoqin too would not give in as a favor to anyone, so hastily she exclaimed:

The water meant to brew the tea with gently bubbles up.

Xiangyun saw how excited they were getting and she thought it naturally great fun. Laughing, she eagerly gave out:

When wine is boiled with leaves 'tis not easy to burn.

Daiyu also smiled while suggesting:

The broom, with which the bonze sweepeth the hill, is sunk in snow.

Baoqin too smilingly cried:

The young lad takes away the lute interred in snow.

Xiangyun laughed to such a degree that she was bent in two; and she muttered a line with such rapidity that one and all inquired of her: "What are you, after all, saying?"

In the stone tower leisurely sleeps the stork.

Xiangyun repeated.

Daiyu clasped her breast so convulsed was she with laughter. With loud voice she bawled out:

Th' embroidered carpet warms the affectionate cat.

Baoqin quickly, again laughingly, exclaimed:

Inside Selene's cave lo, roll the silvery waves.

Xiangyun added, with eager haste:

Within the city walls at eve was hid a purple flag.

Daiyu with alacrity continued with a smile:

The fragrance sweet, which penetrates into the plums, is good to eat.

Baochai smiled. "What a fine line!" she ejaculated; after which, she hastened to complete the couplet by saying:

> The drops from the bamboo are meet, when one is drunk, to mix with wine.

Baoqin likewise made haste to add:

> Betimes, the hymeneal girdle it moistens.

Xiangyun eagerly paired it with:

> Oft, it freezeth on the kingfisher shoes.

Daiyu once more exclaimed with vehemence:

> No wind doth blow, but yet there is a rush.

Baoqin promptly also smiled, and strung on:

> No rain lo falls, but still a patter's heard.

Xiangyun was leaning over, indulging in such merriment that she was quite doubled up in two. But everybody else had realized that the trio was struggling for mastery, so without attempting to versify they kept their gaze fixed on them and gave way to laughter.

Daiyu gave her another push to try and induce her to go on. "Do you also sometimes come to your wits' ends and run to the end of your tether?" she went on to say. "I'd like to see what other stuff and nonsense you can come out with!"

Xiangyun however simply fell forward on Baochai's lap and laughed incessantly.

"If you've got any gumption about you," Baochai exclaimed, shoving her up, "take the second rhymes under 'Xiao' and exhaust them all, and I'll then bend the knee to you."

"It isn't as if I were writing verses," Xiangyun laughed rising to her feet; "it's really as if I were fighting for very life."

"It's for you to come out with something," they all cried with a laugh.

Tanchun had long ago determined in her mind that there could be no other antithetical sentences that she herself could possibly propose, and she forthwith set to work to copy out the verses. But as she passed the remark: "They haven't as yet been brought to a proper close,"

Li Wen took up the clue, as soon as she caught her words, and added the sentiment:

My wish is to record this morning's fun.

Li Qi then suggested as a finale the line:
By these verses, I'd fain sing th' Emperor's praise.

"That's enough, that will do!" Li Wan cried. "The rhymes haven't, I admit, been exhausted, but any outside words you might introduce, will, if used in a forced sense, be worth nothing at all."

While continuing their arguments, the various inmates drew near and kept up a searching criticism for a time.

Xiangyun was found to be the one among them, who had devised the largest number of lines.

"This is mainly due," they unanimously laughed, "to the virtue of that piece of venison!"

"Let's review them line by line as they come," Li Wan smilingly proposed, "but yet as if they formed one continuous poem. Here's Baoyu last again!"

I haven't, the fact is, the knack of pairing sentences," Baoyu rejoined with a smile. "You'd better therefore make some allowance for me!"

There's no such thing as making allowances for you in meeting after meeting," Li Wan demurred laughing, "that you should again after that give out the rhymes in a reckless manner, waste your time and not show yourself able to put two lines together. You must absolutely bear a penalty today. I just caught a glimpse of the red plum in the Longcui monastery; and how charming it is! I meant to have plucked a twig to put in a vase, but so loathsome is the way in which Miaoyu goes on, that I won't have anything to do with her! But we'll punish him by making him, for the sake of fun, fetch a twig for us to put in water."

"This penalty," they shouted with one accord, "is both excellent as well as pleasant."

Baoyu himself was no less delighted to carry it into execution, so signifying his readiness to comply with their wishes, he felt desirous to be off at once.

"It's exceedingly cold outside," Xiangyun and Daiyu simultaneously remarked, "so have a glass of warm wine before you go."

Xiangyun speedily took up the kettle, and Daiyu handed him a large cup, filled to the very brim.

"Now swallow the wine we give you," Xiangyun smiled. "And if you don't bring any plum blossom, we'll inflict a double penalty."

Baoyu gulped down hurry-scurry the whole contents of the cup and started on his errand in the face of the snow.

"Follow him carefully." Li Wan enjoined the servants.

Daiyu, however, hastened to interfere and make her desist. "There's no such need," she cried. "Were anyone to go with him, he'll contrariwise not get the flowers."

Li Wan nodded her head. "Yes!" she assented, and then went on to direct a waiting-maid to bring a vase, in the shape of a beautiful girl with high shoulders, to fill it with water, and get it ready to put the plum blossom in. "And when he comes back," she felt induced to add, "we must recite verses on the red plum."

"I'll indite a stanza in advance," eagerly exclaimed Xiangyun.

"We'll on no account let you indite any more today," Baochai laughed. "You beat everyone of us hollow; so if we sit with idle hands, there won't be any fun. But by and bye we'll fine Baoyu; and, as he says that he can't pair antithetical lines, we'll now make him compose a stanza himself."

"This is a capital idea!" Daiyu smiled. "But I've got another proposal. As the lines just paired are not sufficient, won't it be well to pick out those who've put together the fewest distiches, and make them versify on the red plum blossom?"

"An excellent proposal!" Baochai ventured laughing. "The three girls Xing Xiuyan, Li Wen, and Li Qi, failed just now to do justice to their talents; besides they are visitors; and as Qin'er, Pin'er, and Yun'er got the best of us by a good deal, it's only right that none of us should compose any more, and that that trio should only do so."

"Qin'er," Li Wan thereupon retorted, "is also not a very good hand at verses, let therefore cousin Qin have a try!"

Baochai had no alternative but to express her acquiescence.

"Let the three words 'red plum blossom,'" she then suggested, "be used for rhymes; and let each person compose an heptameter stanza. Cousin Xing to indite on the word 'red;' your elder cousin Li on 'plum;' and Qin'er on 'blossom.'"

"If you let Baoyu off," Li Wan interposed, "I won't have it!"

"I've got a capital theme," Xiangyun eagerly remarked, "so let's make him write some!"

"What theme is it?" one and all inquired.

"If we made him," Xiangyun resumed, "versify on: 'In search of Miaoyu to beg for red plum blossom,' won't it be full of fun?"

"That will be full of zest," the party exclaimed, upon hearing the theme propounded by her. But hardly had they given expression to their approval than they perceived Baoyu come in, beaming with smiles and glee, and holding with both hands a branch of red plum blossom.

The maids hurriedly relieved him of his burden and put the branch in the vase, and the inmates present came over in a body to feast their eyes on it.

"Well, may you look at it now," Baoyu smiled. "You've no idea what an amount of trouble it has cost me!"

As he uttered these words, Tanchun handed him at once another cup of warm wine; and the maids approached, and took his wrapper and hat, and shook off the snow.

But the servant-girls attached to their respective quarters then brought them over extra articles of clothing. Xiren, in like manner, despatched a domestic with a pelisse, the worse for wear, lined with fur from foxes' ribs, so Li Wan, having directed a servant to fill a plate with steamed large taros, and to make up two dishes with red-skinned oranges, yellow coolie oranges, olives, and other like things, bade someone take them over to Xiren.

Xiangyun also communicated to Baoyu the subject for verses they had decided upon a short while back. But she likewise urged Baoyu to be quick and accomplish his task.

"Dear senior cousin, dear junior cousin," pleaded Baoyu, "let me use my own rhymes. Don't bind me down to any."

"Go on as you like," they replied with one consent.

But conversing the while, they passed the plum blossom under inspection.

This bough of plum blossom was, in fact, only two feet in height; but from the side projected a branch, crosswise, about two or three feet in length the small twigs and stalks on which resembled coiled dragons, or crouching earthworms; and were either single and trimmed brush-like, or thick and bushy grove-like. Indeed, their appearance was as if the blossom spurted cosmetic. This fragrance put orchids to the blush. So everyone present contributed her quota of praise.

Xiuyan, Li Wen, and Baoqin had, little though it was expected, all three already finished their lines and each copied them out for herself, so the company began to peruse their compositions, subjoined below, in the order of the three words: "red plum blossom."

Verses to the red plum blossom by Xing Xiuyan.

The peach tree has not donned its fragrance yet, the almond is not red.

What time it strikes the cold, it's first joyful to smile at the east wind.

When its spirit to the Yuling hath flown, 'tis hard to say 'tis spring.

The russet clouds across the "Luo Fu" lie, so e'en to dreams it's
  closed.
The green petals add grace to a coiffure, when painted candles burn.
The simple elf when primed with wine doth the waning rainbow
  bestride.
Does its appearance speak of a color of ordinary run? Both dark
  and light fall of their own free will into the ice and snow.

The next was the production of Li Wen, and its burden was:

To write on the white plum I'm not disposed, but I'll write on the
  red.
Proud of its beauteous charms, 'tis first to meet the opening drunk-
  en eye.
On its frost-nipped face are marks; and these consist wholly of
  blood.
Its heart is sore, but no anger it knows; to ashes too it turns.
By some mistake a pill (a fairy) takes and quits her real frame.
From the fairyland pool she secret drops, and casts off her old form.
In spring, both north and south of the river, with splendor it doth
  bloom.
Send word to bees and butterflies that they need not give way to
  fears!

This stanza came next from the brush of Xue Baoqin:

Far distant do the branches grow; but how beauteous the blossom
  blooms!
The maidens try with profuse show to compete in their spring head-
  dress.
No snow remains on the vacant pavilion and the tortuous rails.
Upon the running stream and desolate hills descend the russet
  clouds.
When cold prevails one can in a still dream follow the lass-blown
  fife.
The wandering elf roweth in fragrant spring, the boat in the red
  stream.
In a previous existence, it must sure have been of fairy form.
No doubt need 'gain arise as to its beauty differing from then.

The perusal over, they spent some time in heaping, smiling the while,
eulogiums upon the compositions. And they pointed at the last stanza

as the best of the lot; which made it evident to Baoyu that Baoqin, albeit the youngest in years, was, on the other hand, the quickest in wits.

Daiyu and Xiangyun then filled up a small cup with wine and simultaneously offered their congratulations to Baoqin.

"Each of the three stanzas has its beauty," Baochai remarked, a smile playing round her lips. "You two have daily made a fool of me, and are you now going to fool her also?"

"Have you got yours ready?" Li Wan went on to inquire of Baoyu.

"I'd got them," Baoyu promptly answered, "but the moment I read their three stanzas, I once more became so nervous that they quite slipped from my mind. But let me think again."

Xiangyun, at this reply, fetched a copper poker, and, while beating on the hand-stove, she laughingly said: "I shall go on tattooing. Now mind if when the drumming ceases, you haven't accomplished your task, you'll have to bear another fine."

"I've already got them!" Baoyu rejoined, smilingly.

Daiyu then picked up a brush. "Recite them," she smiled, "and I'll write them down."

Xiangyun beat one stroke (on the stove). "The first tattoo is over," she laughed.

"I'm ready," Baoyu smiled. "Go on writing."

At this, they heard him recite:

> The wine bottle is not opened, the line is not put into shape.

Daiyu noted it down, and shaking her head, "They begin very smoothly," she said, as she smiled.

"Be quick!" Xiangyun again urged.

Baoyu laughingly continued:

> To fairyland I speed to seek for spring, and the twelfth moon to find.

Daiyu and Xiangyun both nodded. "It's rather good," they smiled. Baoyu resumed, saying:

> I will not beg the high god for a bottle of the (healing) dew,
> But pray Chang'e to give me some plum bloom beyond the rails.

Daiyu jotted the lines down and wagged her head to and fro. "They're ingenious, that's all," she observed.

Xiangyun gave another rap with her hand.

Baoyu thereupon smilingly added:

I come into the world and, in the cold, I pick out some red snow.
I leave the dusty sphere and speed to pluck the fragrant purple
   clouds.
I bring a jagged branch, but who in pity sings my shoulders thin?
On my clothes still sticketh the moss from yon Buddhistic court.

As soon as Daiyu had done writing, Xiangyun and the rest of the
company began to discuss the merits of the verses; but they then saw
several servant-maids rush in, shouting: "Our venerable mistress has
come."

One and all hurried out with all despatch to meet her. "How comes
it that she is in such good cheer?" everyone also laughed.

Speaking the while, they discerned, at a great distance, their grandmother Jia seated, enveloped in a capacious wrapper, and rolled up in
a warm hood lined with squirrel fur, in a small bamboo sedan-chair
with an open green silk glazed umbrella in her hand, Yuanyang, Hupo,
and some other girls, mustering in all five or six, held each an umbrella
and pressed round the chair, as they advanced.

Li Wan and her companions went up to them with hasty step; but
dowager lady Jia directed the servants to make them stop; explaining
that it would be quite enough if they stood where they were.

On her approach, old lady Jia smiled. "I've given," she observed, "your
Madame Wang and that girl Feng the slip and come. What deep snow
covers the ground! For me, I'm seated in this, so it doesn't matter; but
you mustn't let those ladies trudge in the snow."

The various followers rushed forward to take her wrapper and to
support her, and as they did so, they expressed their acquiescence.

As soon as she got indoors old lady Jia was the first to exclaim with
a beaming face: "What beautiful plum blossom! You well know how to
make merry; but I too won't let you off!"

But in the course of her remarks, Li Wan quickly gave orders to a
domestic to fetch a large wolf skin rug, and to spread it in the center, so
dowager lady Jia made herself comfortable on it. "Just go on as before
with your romping and joking, drinking and eating," she then laughed.
"As the days are so short, I did not venture to have a midday siesta.
After therefore playing at dominoes for a time, I bethought myself of
you people, and likewise came to join the fun."

Li Wan soon also presented her a hand-stove, while Tanchun brought
an extra set of cups and chopsticks, and filling with her own hands a

cup with warm wine, she handed it to her grandmother Jia. Old lady Jia swallowed a sip. "What's there in that dish?" she afterwards inquired.

The various inmates hurriedly carried it over to her, and explained that they were pickled quails.

"These won't hurt me," dowager lady Jia said, "so cut off a piece of the leg and give it to me."

"Yes!" promptly acquiesced Li Wan, and asking for water, she washed her hands, and then came in person to carve the quail.

"Sit down again," dowager lady Jia said, pressing them, "and go on with your chatting and laughing. Let me hear you, and feel happy. Just you also seat yourself," continuing, she remarked to Li Wan, "and behave as if I were not here. If you do so, well and good. Otherwise, I shall take myself off at once."

But it was only when they heard how persistent she was in her solicitations that they all resumed the seats, which accorded with their age, with the exception of Li Wan, who moved to the furthest side.

"What were you playing at?" old lady Jia thereupon asked.

"We were writing verses," answered the whole party.

"Wouldn't it be well for those who are up to poetry," dowager lady Jia suggested, "to devise a few puns for lanterns so that the whole lot of us should be able to have some fun in the first moon?"

With one voice, they expressed their approval. But after they had jested for a little time: "It's damp in here," old lady Jia said, "so don't you sit long, for mind you might be catching cold. Where it's nice and warm is in your cousin Quarta's over there, so let's all go and see how she is getting on with her painting, and whether it will be ready or not by the end of the year."

"How could it be completed by the close of the year?" they smiled. "She could only, we fancy, get it ready by the dragon boat festival next year."

"This is dreadful!" old lady Jia exclaimed. "Why, she has really wasted more labor on it than would have been actually required to lay out this garden!"

With these words still on her lips, she ensconced herself again in the bamboo sedan, and closed in or followed by the whole company, she repaired to the Lotus Fragrance Arbor, where they got into a narrow passage, flanked on the east as well as the west, with doors from which they could cross the street. Over these doorways on the inside as well as outside were inserted alike tablets made of stone. The door they went in by, on this occasion, lay on the west. On the tablet facing outwards, were cut out the two words representing: "Penetrating into the clouds." On that inside, were engraved the two characters meaning:

"crossing to the moon." On their arrival at the hall, they walked in by the main entrance, which looked towards the south. Dowager lady Jia then alighted from her chair. Xichun had already made her appearance out of doors to welcome her, so taking the inner covered passage, they passed over to the other side and reached Xichun's bedroom; on the door posts of which figured the three words: "Warm fragrance isle." Several servants were at once at hand; and no sooner had they raised the red woollen portiere, than a soft fragrance wafted itself into their faces. The various inmates stepped into the room. Old lady Jia, however, did not take a seat, but simply inquired where the painting was.

"The weather is so bitterly cold," Xichun consequently explained smiling, "that the glue, whose property is mainly to coagulate, cannot be moistened, so I feared that, were I to have gone on with the painting, it wouldn't be worth looking at; and I therefore put it away."

"I must have it by the close of the year," dowager lady Jia laughed, "so don't idle your time away. Produce it at once and go on painting for me, as quick as you can."

But scarcely had she concluded her remark, than she unexpectedly perceived lady Feng arrive, smirking and laughing, with a purple pelisse, lined with deer fur, thrown over her shoulders. "Venerable senior!" she shouted, "You don't even so much as let anyone know today, but sneak over stealthily. I've had a good hunt for you!"

When old lady Jia saw her join them, she felt filled with delight. "I was afraid," she rejoined, "that you'd be feeling cold. That's why, I didn't allow anyone to tell you. You're really as sharp as a spirit to have, at last, been able to trace my whereabouts! But according to strict etiquette, you shouldn't show filial piety to such a degree!"

"Is it out of any idea of filial piety that I came after you? Not at all!" lady Feng added with a laugh. "But when I got to your place, worthy senior, I found everything so quiet that not even the caw of a crow could be heard, and when I asked the young maids where you'd gone, they wouldn't let me come and search in the garden. So I began to give way to surmises. Suddenly also arrived two or three nuns; and then, at length, I jumped at the conclusion that these women must have come to bring their yearly prayers, or to ask for their annual or incense allowance, and that, with the amount of things you also, venerable ancestor, have to do for the end of the year, you had for certain got out of the way of your debts. Speedily therefore I inquired of the nuns what it was that brought them there, and, for a fact, there was no mistake in my surmises. So promptly issuing the annual allowances to them, I now come to report to you, worthy senior, that your creditors have gone, and that there's no need for you to skulk away. But I've had some tender pheasant prepared; so please come, and have your evening meal; for if you delay any longer, it will get quite stale."

As she spoke, everybody burst out laughing. But lady Feng did not allow any time to dowager lady Jia to pass any observations, but forthwith directed the servants to bring the chair over. Old lady Jia then smilingly laid hold of lady Feng's hand and got again into her chair; but she took along with her the whole company of relatives for a chat and a laugh.

Upon issuing out of the gate on the east side of the narrow passage, the four quarters presented to their gaze the appearance of being adorned with powder, and inlaid with silver. Unawares, they caught sight of Baoqin, in a duck down cloak, waiting at a distance at the back of the hill slope; while behind her stood a maid, holding a vase full of red plum blossoms.

"Strange enough," they all exclaimed laughingly, "two of us were missing! But she's waiting over there. She's also been after some plumblossom."

"Just look," dowager lady Jia eagerly cried out joyfully, "that human creature has been put there to match with the snow-covered hill! But with that costume, and the plum-blossom at the back of her, to what does she bear a resemblance?"

"She resembles," one and all smiled, "Chou Shizhou's beautiful snow picture, suspended in your apartments, venerable ancestor."

"Is there in that picture any such costume?" Old lady Jia demurred, nodding her head and smiling. "What's more the persons represented in it could never be so pretty!"

Hardly had this remark dropped from her mouth, than she discerned someone else, clad in a deep red woollen cloak, appear to view at the back of Baoqin. "What other girl is that?" dowager lady Jia asked.

"We girls are all here." they laughingly answered. "That's Baoyu."

"My eyes," old lady Jia smiled, "are getting dimmer and dimmer!"

So saying, they drew near, and of course, they turned out to be Baoyu and Baoqin.

"I've just been again to the Longcui monastery," Baoyu smiled to Baochai, Daiyu, and his other cousins, "and Miaoyu gave me for each of you a twig of plum blossom. I've already sent a servant to take them over."

"Many thanks for the trouble you've been put to," they, with one voice, replied.

But speaking the while, they sallied out of the garden gate, and repaired to their grandmother Jia's suite of apartments. Their meal over, they joined in a further chat and laugh, when unexpectedly they saw Mrs. Xue also arrive.

"With all this snow," she observed, "I haven't been over the whole day to see how you, venerable senior, were getting on. Your ladyship couldn't have been in a good sort of mood today, for you should have gone and seen the snow."

"How not in a good mood?" old lady Jia exclaimed. "I went and looked up these young ladies and had a romp with them for a time."

"Last night," Mrs. Xue smiled, "I was thinking of getting from our Madame Wang today the loan of the garden for the nonce and spreading two tables with our mean wine, and inviting you, worthy senior, to enjoy the snow; but as I saw that you were having a rest and I heard, at an early hour, that Baoyu had said that you were not in a joyful frame of mind, I did not, in consequence, presume to come and disturb you today. But had I known sooner the real state of affairs, I would have felt it my bounden duty to have asked you round."

"This is," rejoined dowager lady Jia with a smile, "only the first fall of snow in the tenth moon. We'll have, after this, plenty of snowy days so there will be ample time to put your ladyship to wasteful expense."

"Verily in that case," Mrs. Xue laughingly added, "my filial intentions may well be looked upon as having been accomplished."

"Mrs. Xue," interposed lady Feng smiling, "mind you don't forget it! But you might as well weigh fifty taels this very moment, and hand them over to me to keep, until the first fall of snow, when I can get everything ready for the banquet. In this way, you will neither have anything to bother you, aunt, nor will you have a chance of forgetting."

"Well, since that be so," old lady Jia remarked with a laugh, "your ladyship had better give her fifty taels, and I'll share it with her; each one of us taking twenty-five taels; and on any day it might snow, I'll pretend I don't feel in proper trim and let it slip by. You'll have thus still less occasion to trouble yourself, and I and lady Feng will reap a substantial benefit."

Lady Feng clapped her hands. "An excellent idea," she laughed. "This quite falls in with my views."

The whole company were much amused.

"Pshaw!" dowager lady Jia laughingly ejaculated. "You barefaced thing! (You're like a snake, which) avails itself of the rod, with which it is being beaten, to crawl up (and do harm)! You don't try to convince us that it properly devolves upon us, as Mrs. Xue is our guest and receives such poor treatment in our household, to invite her; for with what right could we subject her ladyship to any reckless outlay? but you have the impudence, of impressing upon our minds to insist upon the payment, in advance, of fifty taels! Are you really not thoroughly ashamed of yourself?"

"Oh, worthy senior," lady Feng laughed, "you're most sharpsighted! You try to see whether Mrs. Xue will be soft enough to produce fifty taels for you to share with me, but fancying now that it's of no avail, you turn round and begin to rate me by coming out with all these grand words! I won't however take any money from you, Mrs. Xue. I'll, in fact, contribute some on your ladyship's account, and when I get the banquet ready and invite you, venerable ancestor, to come and partake of it, I'll also wrap fifty taels in a piece of paper, and dutifully present them to you, as a penalty for my officious interference in matters that don't concern me. Will this be all right or not?"

Before these words were brought to a close, the various inmates were so convulsed with hearty laughter that they reeled over on the stove-couch.

Dowager lady Jia then went on to explain how much nicer Baoqin was, plucking plum blossom in the snow, than the very picture itself; and she next minutely inquired what the year, moon, day and hour of her birth were, and how things were getting on in her home.

Mrs. Xue conjectured that the object she had in mind was, in all probability, to seek a partner for her. In the secret recesses of her heart, Mrs. Xue on this account fell in also with her views. (Baoqin) had, however, already been promised in marriage to the Mei family. But as dowager lady Jia had made, as yet, no open allusion to her intentions, (Mrs. Xue) did not think it nice on her part to come out with any definite statement, and she accordingly observed to old lady Jia in a vague sort of way: "What a pity it is that this girl should have had so little good fortune as to lose her father the year before last. But ever since her youth up, she has seen much of the world, for she has been with her parent to every place of note. Her father was a man fond of pleasure; and as he had business in every direction, he took his family along with him. After tarrying in this province for a whole year, he would next year again go to that province, and spend half a year roaming about it everywhere. Hence it is that he had visited five-or six-tenths of the whole empire. The other year, when they were here, he engaged her to the son of the Hanlin Mei. But, as it happened, her father died the year after, and here is her mother too now ailing from a superfluity of phlegm."

Lady Feng gave her no time to complete what she meant to say. "Hai!" she exclaimed, stamping her foot. "What you say isn't opportune! I was about to act as a go-between. But is she too already engaged?"

"For whom did you mean to act as go-between?" old lady Jia smiled.

"My dear ancestor," lady Feng remarked, "don't concern yourself about it! I had determined in my mind that those two would make a suitable match. But as she has now long ago been promised to someone, it would be of no use, were I even to speak out. Isn't it better that I should hold my peace, and drop the whole thing?"

Dowager lady Jia herself was cognizant of lady Feng's purpose, so upon hearing that she already had a suitor, she at once desisted from making any further reference to the subject. The whole company then continued another chat on irrelevant matters for a time, after which, they broke up.

Nothing of any interest transpired the whole night. The next day, the snowy weather had cleared up. After breakfast, her grandmother Jia again pressed Xichun. "You should go on," she said, "with your painting, irrespective of cold or heat. If you can't absolutely finish it by the end of the year, it won't much matter! The main thing is that you must at once introduce in it Qin'er and the maid with the plum blossom, as we saw them yesterday, in strict accordance with the original and without the least discrepancy of so much as a stroke."

Xichun listened to her and felt it her duty to signify her assent, in spite of the task being no easy one for her to execute.

After a time, a number of her relatives came, in a body, to watch the progress of the painting. But they discovered Xichun plunged in a reverie. "Let's leave her alone," Li Wan smilingly observed to them all, "to proceed with her meditations; we can meanwhile have a chat among ourselves. Yesterday our worthy senior bade us devise a few lantern-conundrums, so when we got home, I and Qi'er and Wen'er did not turn in (but set to work). I composed a couple on the Four Books; but those two girls also managed to put together another pair of them."

"We should hear what they're like," they laughingly exclaimed in chorus, when they heard what they had done. "Tell them to us first, and let's have a guess!"

> "The goddess of mercy has not been handed down by any ancestors."

Li Qi smiled. "This refers to a passage in the Four Books."

> "In one's conduct, one must press towards the highest benevolence."

Xiangyun quickly interposed; taking up the thread of the conversation.

"You should ponder over the meaning of the three words implying: 'handed down by ancestors,'" Baochai smiled, "before you venture a guess."

"Think again!" Li Wan urged with a smile.

"I've guessed it!" Daiyu smiled. "It's:

"If, notwithstanding all that benevolence, there be no outward visible sign...'"

"That's the line," one and all unanimously exclaimed with a laugh.

"'The whole pond is covered with rush.'"

"Now find the name of the rush?" Li Wan proceeded.

"This must certainly be the cat-tail rush!" hastily again replied Xiangyun. "Can this not be right?"

"You've succeeded in guessing it," Li Wan smiled. "Li Wen's is:

"'Cold runs the stream along the stones;'
"bearing on the name of a man of old."

"Can it be Shan Tao?" Tanchun smilingly asked.

"It is!" answered Li Wan.

"Qi'er's is the character 'Ying' (glow-worm). It refers to a single word," Li Wan resumed.

The party endeavored for a long time to hit upon the solution.

"The meaning of this is certainly deep," Baoqin put in. "I wonder whether it's the character, 'hua,' (flower) in the combination, 'hua cao, (vegetation).'"

"That's just it!" Li Qi smiled.

"What has a glow-worm to do with flowers?" one and all observed.

"It's capital!" Daiyu ventured with a smile. "Isn't a glow-worm transformed from plants?"

The company grasped the sense; and, laughing the while, they, with one consent, shouted out, "splendid!"

"All these are, I admit, good," Baochai remarked, "but they won't suit our venerable senior's taste. Won't it be better therefore to compose a few on some simple objects; some which all of us, whether polished or unpolished, may be able to enjoy?"

"Yes," they all replied, "we should also think of some simple ones on ordinary objects."

"I've devised one on the 'Dian Jiang Chun' meter," Xiangyun pursued, after some reflection. "But it's really on an ordinary object. So try and guess it."

Saying this, she forthwith went on to recite:

The creeks and valleys it leaves;
Traveling the world, it performs.
In truth how funny it is!
But renown and gain are still vain;
Ever hard behind it is its fate.

None of those present could fathom what it could be. After protracted thought, some made a guess, by saying it was a bonze. Others maintained that it was a Daoist priest. Others again divined that it was a marionette.

"All your guesses are wrong," Baoyu chimed in, after considerable reflection. "I've got it! It must for a certainty be a performing monkey."

"That's really it!" Xiangyun laughed.

"The first part is all right," the party observed, "but how do you explain the last line?"

"What performing monkey," Xiangyun asked, "has not had its tail cut off?"

Hearing this, they exploded into a fit of merriment. "Even," they argued, "the very riddles she improvises are perverse and strange!"

"Mrs. Xue mentioned yesterday that you, cousin Qin, had seen much of the world," Li Wan put in, "and that you had also gone about a good deal. It's for you therefore to try your hand at a few conundrums. What's more your poetry too is good. So why shouldn't you indite a few for us to guess?"

Baoqin, at this proposal, nodded her head, and while repressing a smile, she went off by herself to give way to thought.

Baochai then also gave out this riddle:

Carved sandal and cut cedar rise layer upon layer.
Have they been piled and fashioned by workmen of skill!
In the mid-heavens it's true, both wind and rain fleet by;
But can one hear the tingling of the Buddhists' bell?

While they were giving their mind to guessing what it could be, Baoyu too recited:

Both from the heavens and from the earth, it's indistinct to view.
What time the "Lang Gan" feast goes past, then mind you take great
    care.

When the "luan's" notes you catch and the crane's message thou'lt
  look up:
It is a splendid thing to turn and breathe towards the vault of heav-
  en, (a kite)

Daiyu next added:

Why need a famous steed be a with bridle e'er restrained?
Through the city it speeds; the moat it skirts; how fierce it looks.
The master gives the word and wind and clouds begin to move.
On the "fish backs" and the "three isles" it only makes a name, (a
  rotating lantern).

Tanchun had also one that she felt disposed to tell them, but just
as she was about to open her lips, Baoqin walked up to them. "The
relics of various places I've seen since my youth," she smiled, "are not
few, so I've now selected ten places of historic interest, on which I've
composed ten odes, treating of antiquities. The verses may possibly be
coarse, but they bear upon things of the past, and secretly refer as well
to ten commonplace articles. So, cousins, please try and guess them!"

"This is ingenious!" they exclaimed in chorus, when they heard the
result of her labor. "Why not write them out, and let us have a look at
them?"

But, reader, peruse the next chapter, if you want to learn what follows.

CHAPTER 51

The young maiden Xue Baoqin devises, in novel style, odes bearing on antiquities. A stupid doctor employs, in reckless manner, drugs of great strength.

When the party heard, the story goes, that Baoqin had made the old places of interest she had, in days gone by, visited in the various provinces, the theme of her verses, and that she had composed ten stanzas with four lines in each, which though referring to relics of antiquity, bore covertly on ten common objects, they all opined that they must be novel and ingenious, and they vied with each other in examining the text. On perusal, they read:

On the relics of Chibi:

Deep in Chibi doth water lie concealed which does not onward flow.
There but remains a name and surname contained in an empty boat.
When with a clamorous din the fire breaks out, the sad wind waxes cold.
An endless host of eminent spirits wander about inside.

On the ancient remains in Jiaozhi:

Posts of copper and walls of gold protect the capital.
Its fame is spread beyond the seas, scattered in foreign lands.
How true it is that Ma Yuan's achievements have been great.
The flute of iron need not trouble to sing of Zifang.

On the vestiges of former times in Zhongshan:

Renown and gain do they, at any time, fall to a woman's share?
For no reason have I been bidden come into the mortal world.

How hard a task, in point of fact, it is to stop solicitude!
Don't bear a rudge against such people as may oft times jeer at you!

O things of historic interest in Huai Yin:

The sturdy man must ever mind the insults of the vicious dog.
Th' official's rank in San Qi was but fixed when his coffin was
    closed
Tell all people that upon earth do dwell to look down upon none.
The bounty of one single bowl of rice should be treasured till death.

On events of old in Guangling:

Cicadas chirp; crows roost; but, in a twinkle, they are gone.
How fares these latter days the scenery in Sui Ti?
It's all because he has so long enjoyed so fine a fame,
That he has given rise around to so many disputes.

On the ancient remains of the Taoye ferry:

Dry grass and parched plants their reflex cast upon the shallow
    pond.
The peach tree branches and peach leaves will bid farewell at last.
What a large number of structures in Liuchao raise their heads.
A small picture with a motto hangs on the hollow wall.

On the antique vestiges of Qingzhong:

The black stream stretches far and wide, but hindered is its course.
What time were no more thrummed the frozen cords, the songs
    waxed sad.
The policy of the Han dynasty was in truth strange!
A worthless officer must for a thousand years feel shame.

On things of historic renown in Mawei:

Quiet the spots of rouge with sweat pile up and shine.
Gentleness in a moment vanishes and goes.
It is because traces remain of his fine looks,
That to this day his clothes a fragrance still emit.

On events of the past connected with the Pu Tung temple:

> The small red lamp is wholly made of thin bone, and is light.
> Furtively was it brought along but by force was it stol'n.
> Oft was it, it is true, hung by the mistress' own hands,
> But long ere this has she allured it to speed off with her.

On the scenery about the Mei Hua (Plum Bloom) monastery:

> If not by the plum trees, then by the willows it must be.
> Has anyone picked up in there the likeness of a girl?
> Don't fret about meeting again; in spring its scent returns.
> Soon as it's gone, and west winds blow, another year has flown.

When the party had done reading the verses, they with perfect unanimity extolled their extraordinary excellence. Baochai was, however,
the first to raise any objections. "The first eight stanzas," she said, "are
founded upon the testimony of the historical works. But as for the last
two stanzas, there's no knowing where they come from. Besides, we
don't quite fathom their meaning. Wouldn't it be better then if two
other stanzas were written?"

Daiyu hastened to interrupt her. "The lines composed by cousin Baoqin are indeed devised in a too pigheaded and fast-and-loose sort of
way," she observed. "The two stanzas are, I admit, not to be traced in
the historical works, but though we've never read such outside traditions, and haven't any idea what lies at the bottom of them, have we
not likely seen a couple of plays? What child of three years old hasn't
some notion about them, and how much more such as we?"

"What she says is perfectly correct," Tanchun chimed in.

"She has besides," Li Wan then remarked, "been to these places herself. But though there be no mention anywhere of these two references, falsehoods have from old till now been propagated, and busy-
bodies have, in fact, intentionally invented such relics of ancient times
with a view of bamboozling people. That year, for instance, in which
we traveled up here to the capital, we came across graves raised to
Guan, the sage, in three or four distinct places. Now the circumstances of the whole existence of Guan the sage are established by actual
proof, so how could there again in his case exist a lot of graves? This
must arise from the esteem in which he is held by posterity for the way
he acquitted himself of his duties during his lifetime. And it is presumably to this esteem that this fiction owes its origin. This is quite
possible enough. Even in the 'Guang Yu Ji', you will see that not only

are numerous tombs of the sage Guan spoken of, but that bygone persons of note are assigned tombs not few in number. But there are many more relics of antiquity, about which no testimony can be gathered. The matter treated in the two stanzas, now in point, is, of course, not borne out by any actual record; yet in every story, that is told, in every play, that is sung, and on the various slips as well used for fortune telling, it is invariably to be found. Old and young, men and women, do all understand it and speak of it, whether in proverbs or in their everyday talk. They don't resemble, besides, the ballads encountered in the 'Xixiang Ji,' and 'Moudan,' to justify us to fear that we might be setting eyes upon some corrupt text. They are quite harmless; so we'd better keep them!"

Baochai, after these arguments, dropped at length all discussion. They thereupon tried for a time to guess the stanzas. None, however, of their solutions turned out to be correct. But as the days in winter are short, and they saw that it was time for their evening meal, they adjourned to the front part of the compound for their supper.

The servants at this stage announced to Madame Wang that Xiren's elder brother, Hua Zifang, was outside, and reported to her that he had entered the city to say that his mother was lying in bed dangerously ill, and that she was so longing to see her daughter that he had come to beg for the favor of taking Xiren home on a visit. As soon as Madame Wang heard the news, she dilated for a while upon people's mothers and daughters, and of course she did not withhold her consent. Sending therefore at the same time for lady Feng, she communicated the tidings to her, and enjoined her to deliberate, and take suitable action.

Lady Feng signified her willingness to do what was necessary, and, returning to her quarters, she there and then commissioned Zhou Rui's wife to go and break the news to Xiren. "Send also," she went on to direct Mrs. Zhou, "for one of the married women, who are in attendance when we go out-of-doors, and let you two, together with a couple of young maids, follow Xiren home. But despatch four cart attendants, well up in years, to look everywhere for a spacious curricle for you as well as her, and a small carriage for the maids."

"All right!" acquiesced Zhou Rui's wife. But just as she was about to start, lady Feng continued her injunctions. "Xiren," she added, "is a person not fond of any fuss, so tell her that it's I who have given the orders; and impress upon her that she must put on several nice, colored clothes, and pack up a large valise full of wearing apparel. Her valise, must be a handsome one; and she must take a decent hand-stove. Bid her too first come and look me up here when she's about to start."

Mrs. Zhou promised to execute her directions and went on her way.

After a long interval, (lady Feng) actually saw Xiren arrive, got up in full costume and head-gear, and with her two waiting-maids and Zhou Rui's wife, who carried the hand-stove and the valise packed up with clothes. Lady Feng's eye was attracted by several golden hairpins and pearl ornaments of great brilliancy and beauty, which Xiren wore in her coiffure. Her gaze was further struck by the peach-red stiff silk jacket she had on, brocaded with all sorts of flowers and lined with ermine, by her leek-green wadded jupe, artistically ornamented with coils of gold thread, and by the bluish satin and grey squirrel pelisse she was wrapped in.

"These three articles of clothing, given to you by our dowager lady," lady Feng smiled, "are all very nice; but this pelisse is somewhat too plain. If you wear this, you'll besides feel cold, so put on one with long fur."

"Our Madame Wang," Xiren laughingly rejoined, "gave me this one with the grey squirrel. I've also got one with ermine. She says that when the end of the year draws nigh, she'll let me have one with long fur."

"I've got one with long fur," lady Feng proceeded with a smile. "I don't fancy it much as the fringe does not hang with grace. I was on the point of having it changed; but, never mind, I'll let you first use it; and, when at the close of the year, Madame Wang has one made for you, I can then have mine altered, and it will come to the same thing as if you were returning it like that to me."

One and all laughed. "That's the way of talking into which her ladyship has got!" they observed. "There she is the whole year round recklessly, carelessly, and secretly making good, on Madame Wang's account, ever so many things; how many there is no saying; for really the things for which compensation is made, cannot be so much as enumerated; and does she ever go, and settle scores with Madame Wang? and here she comes, on this occasion, and gives vent again to this mean language, in order to poke fun at people!"

"How could Madame Wang," lady Feng laughed, "ever give a thought to such trifles as these? They are, in fact, matters of no consequence. Yet were I not to look after them, it would be a disgrace to all of us, and needless to say, I would myself get into some scrape. It's far better that I should dress you all properly, and so get a fair name and finish; for were each of you to cut the figure of a burnt cake, people would first and foremost ridicule me, by saying that in looking after the household I have, instead of doing good, been the means of making beggars of you!"

After hearing her out, the whole party heaved a sigh. "Who could ever be," they exclaimed, "so intuitively wise as you, to show, above, such regard for Madame Wang, and below, such consideration for her subordinates?"

In the course of these remarks, they noticed lady Feng bid Ping'er find the dark green stiff silk cloak with white fox she had worn the day before, and give it to Xiren. But perceiving, also, that in the way of a valise, she only had a double one made of black spotted, figured sarcenet, with a lining of light red pongee silk, and that its contents consisted merely of two wadded jackets, the worse for wear, and a pelisse, lady Feng went on to tell Ping'er to fetch a woollen wrapper, lined with jade-green pongee. But she ordered her besides to pack up a snow-cloak for her.

Ping'er walked away and produced the articles. The one was made of deep-red felt, and was old. The other was of deep-red soft satin, neither old nor new.

"I don't deserve so much as a single one of these," Xiren said.

"Keep this felt one for yourself," Ping'er smiled, "and take this one along with you and tell someone to send it to that elderly girl, who while everyone, in that heavy fall of snow yesterday, was rolled up in soft satin, if not in felt, and while about ten dark red dresses were reflected in the deep snow and presented such a fine sight, was the only one attired in those shabby old clothes. She seems more than ever to raise her shoulders and double her back. She is really to be pitied; so take this now and give it to her!"

"She surreptitiously wishes to give my things away!" lady Feng laughed. "I haven't got enough to spend upon myself and here I have you, better still, to instigate me to be more open-handed!"

"This comes from the filial piety your ladyship has ever displayed towards Madame Wang," everyone laughingly remarked, "and the fond love for those below you. For had you been mean and only thought of making much of things and not cared a rap for your subordinates, would that girl have presumed to behave in this manner?"

"If anyone therefore has read my heart, it's she," lady Feng rejoined with a laugh, "but yet she only knows it in part."

At the close of this rejoinder, she again spoke to Xiren. "If your mother gets well, all right," she said; "but if anything happens to her, just stay over, and send someone to let me know so that I may specially despatch a servant to bring you your bedding. But whatever you do, don't use their bedding, nor any of their things to comb your hair with. As for you people," continuing, she observed to Mrs. Zhou Rui, "you no doubt are aware of the customs, prevailing in this establishment, so that I can dispense with giving you any injunctions."

"Yes, we know them all," Mrs. Zhou Rui assented. "As soon as we get there, we'll, of course, request their male inmates to retire out of the way. And in the event of our having to stay over, we'll naturally apply for one or two extra inner rooms."

With these words still on her lips, she followed Xiren out of the apartment. Then directing the servant-boys to prepare the lanterns, they, in due course, got into their curricle, and came to Hua Zifang's quarters, where we will leave them without any further comment.

Lady Feng, meanwhile, sent also for two nurses from the Yihong court. "I am afraid," she said to them, "that Xiren won't come back, so if there be any elderly girl, who has to your knowledge, so far, had her wits about her, depute her to come and keep night watch in Baoyu's rooms. But you nurses must likewise take care and exercise some control, for you mustn't let Baoyu recklessly kick up any trouble!"

"Quite so," answered the two nurses, agreeing to her directions, after which, they quitted her presence. But not a long interval expired before they came to report the result of their search. "We've set our choice upon Qingwen and Sheyue to put up in his rooms," they reported. "We four will take our turn and look after things during the night."

When lady Feng heard these arrangements, she nodded her head. "At night," she observed, "urge him to retire to bed soon; and in the morning press him to get up at an early hour."

The nurses replied that they would readily carry out her orders and returned alone into the garden.

In a little time Zhou Rui's wife actually brought the news, which she imparted to lady Feng, that: "as her mother was already beyond hope, Xiren could not come back."

Lady Feng then explained things to Madame Wang, and sent, at the same time, servants to the garden of Broad Vista to fetch (Xiren's) bedding and toilet effects.

Baoyu watched Qingwen and Sheyue get all her belongings in proper order. After the things had been despatched, Qingwen and Sheyue divested themselves of their remaining fineries and changed their jupes and jackets. Qingwen seated herself round a warming-frame.

"Now," Sheyue smiled, "you're not to put on the airs of a young lady! I advise you to also move about a bit."

"When you're all clean gone," Qingwen returned for answer, "I shall have ample time to budge. But every day that you people are here, I shall try and enjoy peace and quiet."

"My dear girl," Sheyue laughed, "I'll make the bed, but drop the cover over that cheval-glass and put the catches right; you are so much taller than I."

So saying, she at once set to work to arrange the bed for Baoyu.

"Hai!" ejaculated Qingwen smiling, "one just sits down to warm one's self, and here you come and disturb one!"

Baoyu had at this time been sitting, plunged in a despondent mood. The thought of Xiren's mother had crossed through his mind and he was wondering whether she could be dead or alive, when unexpectedly overhearing Qingwen pass the remarks she did, he speedily sprung up, and came out himself and dropped the cover of the glass, and fastened the contrivance, after which he walked into the room. "Warm yourselves," he smiled, "I've done all there was to be done."

"I can't manage," Qingwen rejoined smiling, "to get warm at all. It just also strikes me that the warming-pan hasn't yet been brought."

"You've had the trouble to think of it!" Sheyue observed. "But you've never wanted a chafing-dish before. It's so warm besides on that warming-frame of ours; not like the stove-couch in that room, which is so cold; so we can very well do without it today."

"If both of you are to sleep on that," Baoyu smiled, "there won't be a soul with me outside, and I shall be in an awful funk. Even you won't be able to have a wink of sleep during the whole night!"

"As far as I'm concerned," Qingwen put in, "I'm going to sleep in here. There's Sheyue, so you'd better induce her to come and sleep outside."

But while they kept up this conversation, the first watch drew near, and Sheyue at once lowered the mosquito-curtain, removed the lamp, burnt the joss-sticks, and waited upon Baoyu until he got into bed. The two maids then retired to rest. Qingwen reclined all alone on the warming-frame, while Sheyue lay down outside the winter apartments.

The third watch had come and gone, when Baoyu, in the midst of a dream, started calling Xiren. He uttered her name twice, but no one was about to answer him. And it was after he had stirred himself out of sleep that he eventually recalled to mind that Xiren was not at home, and he had a hearty fit of laughter to himself.

Qingwen however had been roused out of her sleep, and she called Sheyue. "Even I," she said, "have been disturbed, fast asleep though I was; and, lo, she keeps a look-out by his very side and doesn't as yet know anything about his cries! In very deed she is like a stiff corpse!"

Sheyue twisted herself round and yawned. "He calls Xiren," she smilingly rejoined, "so what's that to do with me? What do you want?" proceeding, she then inquired of him.

"I want some tea," Baoyu replied.

Sheyue hastily jumped out of bed, with nothing on but a short wadded coat of red silk.

"Throw my pelisse over you;" Baoyu cried; "for mind it's cold!"

Sheyue at these words put back her hands, and, taking the warm pelisse, lined even up to the lapel, with fur from the neck of the sable, which Baoyu had put on on getting up, she threw it over her shoulders and went below and washed her hands in the basin. Then filling first a cup with tepid water, she brought a large cuspidor for Baoyu to wash his mouth. Afterwards, she drew near the tea-case, and getting a cup, she first rinsed it with lukewarm water, and pouring half a cup of tea from the warm teapot, she handed it to Baoyu. After he had done, she herself rinsed her mouth, and swallowed half a cupful of tea.

"My dear girl," Qingwen interposed smiling, "do give me also a sip."

"You put on more airs than ever," Sheyue laughed.

"My dear girl," Qingwen added, "tomorrow night, you needn't budge; I'll wait on you the whole night long. What do you say to that?"

Hearing this, Sheyue had no help but to attend to her as well, while she washed her mouth, and to pour a cup of tea and give it to her to drink.

"Won't you two go to sleep," Sheyue laughed, "but keep on chatting? I'll go out for a time; I'll be back soon."

"Are there any evil spirits waiting for you outside?" Qingwen smiled.

"It's sure to be bright moonlight out of doors," Baoyu observed, "so go, while we continue our chat."

So speaking, he coughed twice.

Sheyue opened the back-door, and raising the woollen portière and looking out, she saw what a beautiful moonlight there really was.

Qingwen allowed her just time enough to leave the room, when she felt a wish to frighten her for the sake of fun. But such reliance did she have in her physique, which had so far proved better than that of others, that little worrying her mind about the cold, she did not even throw a cloak over her, but putting on a short jacket, she descended, with gentle tread and light step, from the warming-frame and was making her way out to follow in her wake, when "Hallo!" cried Baoyu warning her. "It's freezing; it's no joke!"

Qingwen merely responded with a wave of the hand and sallied out of the door to go in pursuit of her companion. The brilliancy of the moon, which met her eye, was as limpid as water. But suddenly came a slight gust of wind. She felt it penetrate her very flesh and bore through her bones. So much so, that she could not help shuddering all over. "Little wonder is it," she argued within herself, "if people say 'that one mustn't, when one's body is warm, expose one's self to the wind.' This cold is really dreadful!" She was at the same time just on the point of giving (Sheyue) a start, when she heard Baoyu shout from inside, "Qingwen has come out."

Qingwen promptly turned back and entered the room. "How could I ever frighten her to death?" she laughed. "It's just your way; you're as great a coward as an old woman!"

"It isn't at all that you might do her harm by frightening her," Baoyu smiled, "but, in the first place, it wouldn't be good for you to get frost-bitten; and, in the second, you would take her so much off her guard that she won't be able to prevent herself from uttering a shout. So, in the event of rousing any of the others out of their sleep, they won't say that we are up to jokes, but maintain instead that just as Xiren is gone, you two behave as if you'd come across ghosts or seen evil spirits. Come and tuck in the coverlets on this side!"

When Qingwen heard what he wanted done she came accordingly and tucked in the covers, and, putting out her hands, she inserted them under them, and set to work to warm the bedding.

"How cold your hand is!" Baoyu laughingly exclaimed. "I told you to look out or you'd freeze!"

Noticing at the same time that Qingwen's cheeks were as red as rouge, he rubbed them with his hands. But as they felt icy cold to his touch, "Come at once under the cover and warm yourself!" Baoyu urged.

Hardly, however, had he concluded these words, than a sound of "lo teng" reached their ears from the door, and Sheyue rushed in all in a tremor, laughing the while.

"I've had such a fright," she smiled, as she went on speaking. "Goodness me! I saw in the black shade, at the back of the boulders on that hill, someone squatting, and was about to scream, when it turned out to be nothing else than that big golden pheasant. As soon as it caught sight of a human being, it flew away. But it was only when it reached a moonlit place that I at last found out what it was. Had I been so heedless as to scream, I would have been the means of getting people out of their beds!"

Recounting her experiences, she washed her hands.

"Qingwen, you say, has gone out," she proceeded laughing, "but how is it I never caught a glimpse of her? She must certainly have gone to frighten me!"

"Isn't this she?" Baoyu inquired with a smile. "Is she not here warming herself? Had I not been quick in shouting, she would verily have given you a fright."

"There was no need for me to go and frighten her," Qingwen laughingly observed. "This hussy has frightened her own self."

With these words she ensconced herself again under her own coverlet. "Did you forsooth go out," Sheyue remarked, "in this smart dress of a circus-performer?"

"Why, of course, she went out like this!" Baoyu smiled.

"You wouldn't know, for the life of you, how to choose a felicitous day!" Sheyue added. "There you go and stand about on a fruitless errand. Won't your skin get chapped from the frost?"

Saying this, she again raised the copper cover from the brasier, and, picking up the shovel, she buried the live charcoal deep with ashes, and taking two bits of incense of Cambodia fragrant wood, she threw them over them. She then re-covered the brasier, and repairing to the back of the screen, she gave the lamp a thorough trimming to make it throw out more light; after which, she once more laid herself down.

As Qingwen had some time before felt cold, and now began to get warm again, she unexpectedly sneezed a couple of times.

"How about that?" sighed Baoyu. "There you are; you've after all caught a chill!"

"Early this morning," Sheyue smiled, "she shouted that she wasn't feeling quite herself. Neither did she have the whole day a proper bowl of food. And now, not to speak of her taking so little care of herself, she is still bent upon playing larks upon people! But if she falls ill by and bye, we'll let her suffer what she will have brought upon herself."

"Is your head hot?" Baoyu asked.

"It's nothing at all!" Qingwen rejoined, after coughing twice. "When did I get so delicate?"

But while she spoke, they heard the striking clock, suspended on the partition wall in the outer rooms, give two sounds of "tang, tang," and the matron, on the night watch outside, say: "Now, young girls, go to sleep. Tomorrow will be time enough for you to chat and laugh!"

"Don't let's talk!" Baoyu then whispered, "for, mind, we'll also induce them to start chattering." After this, they at last went to sleep.

The next day, they got up at an early hour. Qingwen's nose was indeed considerably stopped. Her voice was hoarse; and she felt no inclination to move.

"Be quick," urged Baoyu, "and don't make a fuss, for your mistress, my mother, may come to know of it, and bid you also shift to your house and nurse yourself. Your home might, of course, be all very nice, but it's in fact somewhat cold. So isn't it better here? Go and lie down in the inner rooms, and I'll give orders to someone to send for the doctor to come quietly by the back door and have a look at you. You'll then get all right again."

"In spite of what you say," Qingwen demurred, "you must really say something about it to our senior lady, Mrs. Jia Zhu; otherwise the doctor will be coming unawares, and people will begin to ask questions; and what answer could one give them?"

Baoyu found what she said so full of reason that he called an old nurse. "Go and deliver this message to your senior mistress," he enjoined her. "Tell her that Qingwen got a slight chill yesterday. That as it's nothing to speak of, and Xiren is besides away, there would be, more than ever, no one here to look after things, were she to go home and attend to herself, so let her send for a doctor to come quietly by the back entrance and see what's the matter with her; but don't let her breathe a word about it to Madame Wang, my mother."

The old nurse was away a considerable time on the errand. On her return, "Our senior mistress," she reported, "has been told everything. She says that: 'if she gets all right, after taking a couple of doses of medicine, it will be well and good. But that in the event of not recovering, it would, really, be the right thing for her to go to her own home. That the season isn't healthy at present, and that if the other girls caught her complaint it would be a small thing; but that the good health of the young ladies is a vital matter.'"

Qingwen was lying in the winter apartment, coughing and coughing, when overhearing (Li Wan's) answer, she lost control over her temper. "Have I got such a dreadful epidemic," she said, "that she fears that I shall bring it upon others? I'll clear off at once from this place; for mind you don't get any headaches and hot heads during the course of your lives."

"While uttering her grievances, she was bent upon getting up immediately, when Baoyu hastened to smile and to press her down.

"Don't lose your temper," he advised her. "This is a responsibility which falls upon her shoulders, so she is afraid lest Madame Wang might come to hear of it, and call her to task. She only made a harmless remark. But you've always been prone to anger, and now, as a matter of course your spleen is larger than ever."

But in the middle of his advice to her, a servant came and told him that the doctor had arrived. Baoyu accordingly crossed over to the off side, and retired behind the bookcase; from whence he perceived two or three matrons, whose duty it was to keep watch at the back door, usher the doctor in.

The waiting-maids, meanwhile, withdrew out of the way. Three or four old nurses dropped the deep-red embroidered curtain, suspended in the winter apartment. Qingwen then simply stretched out her hand from among the folds of the curtain. But the doctor noticed that on two of the fingers of her hand, the nails, which measured fully two or three inches in length, still bore marks of the pure red dye from the China balsam, and forthwith he turned his head away. An old nurse speedily fetched a towel and wiped them for her, when the doctor set to work and felt her pulse for a while, after which he rose and walked into the outer chamber.

"Your young lady's illness," he said to the old nurses, "arises from external sources, and internal obstructive influences, caused by the unhealthiness of the season of late. Yet it's only a slight chill, after all. Fortunately, the young lady has ever been moderate in her drinking and eating. The cold she has is nothing much. It's mainly because she has a weak constitution that she has unawares got a bit of a chill. But if she takes a couple of doses of medicine to dispel it with, she'll be quite right."

So saying, he followed once more the matron out of the house.

Li Wan had, by this time, sent word to the various female domestics at the back entrance, as well as to the young maids in the different parts of the establishment to keep in retirement. All therefore that the doctor perceived as he went along was the scenery in the garden. But not a single girl did he see.

Shortly, he made his exit out of the garden gate, and taking a seat in the duty-lodge of the servant-lads, who looked after the garden-entrance, he wrote a prescription.

"Sir," urged an old nurse, "don't go yet. Our young master is fretful and there may be, I fancy, something more to ask you."

"Wasn't the one I saw just now a young lady," the doctor exclaimed with eagerness, "but a young man, eh? Yet the rooms were such as are occupied by ladies. The curtains were besides let down. So how could the patient I saw have ever been a young man?"

"My dear sir," laughed the old nurse, "it isn't strange that a servant-girl said just now that a new doctor had been sent for on this occasion, for you really know nothing about our family matters. That room is that of our young master, and that is a girl attached to the apartments; but she's really a servant-maid. How ever were those a young lady's rooms? Had a young lady fallen ill, would you ever have penetrated inside with such ease?"

With these words, she took the prescription and wended her way into the garden.

When Baoyu came to peruse it, he found, above, such medicines mentioned as sweet basil, platycodon, carraway seeds, *Mosla dianthera*, and the like; and, below, *Citrus fusca* and sida as well.

"He deserves to be hanged! He deserves death!" Baoyu shouted. "Here he treats girls in the very same way as he would us men! How could this ever do? No matter what internal obstruction there may be, how could she ever stand citrus and sida? Who asked him to come? Bundle him off at once; and send for another, who knows what he's about."

"Whether he uses the right medicines or not," the old nurse pleaded, "we are not in a position to know. But we'll now tell a servant-lad to go and ask Dr. Wang round. It's easy enough! The only thing is that as this doctor wasn't sent for through the head manager's office his fee must be paid to him."

"How much must one give him?" Baoyu inquired.

"Were one to give him too little, it wouldn't look nice," a matron ventured. "He should be given a tael. This would be quite the thing with such a household as ours."

"When Dr. Wang comes," Baoyu asked, "how much is he given?"

"Whenever Dr. Wang and Dr. Zhang come," a matron smilingly explained, "no money is ever given them. At the four seasons of each year however presents are simply sent to them in a lump. This is a fixed annual custom. But this new doctor has come only this once so he should be given a tael."

After this explanation, Baoyu readily bade Sheyue go and fetch the money.

"I can't make out where sister Hua put it," Sheyue rejoined.

"I've often seen her take money out of that lacquered press, ornamented with designs made with shells;" Baoyu added; "so come along with me, and let's go and search."

As he spoke, he and Sheyue came together into what was used as a storeroom by Xiren. Upon opening the shell-covered press, they found the top shelf full of brushes, pieces of ink, fans, scented cakes, various kinds of purses, handkerchiefs, and other like articles, while on the lower shelf were piled several strings of cash. But, presently they pulled out the drawer, when they saw, in a small wicker basket, several pieces of silver, and a steelyard.

Sheyue quickly snatched a piece of silver. Then raising the steelyard, "Which is the one tael mark?" she asked.

Baoyu laughed. "It's amusing that you should appeal to me!" he said. "You really behave as if you had only just come!"

Sheyue also laughed, and was about to go and make inquiries of someone else, when Baoyu interfered. "Choose a piece out of those big ones and give it to him, and have done," he said. "We don't go in for buying and selling, so what's the use of minding such trifles!"

Sheyue, upon hearing this, dropped the steelyard, and selected a piece, which she weighed in her hand. "This piece," she smiled, "must, I fancy, be a tael. But it would be better to let him have a little more. Don't let's give too little as those poor brats will have a laugh at our expense. They won't say that we know nothing about the steelyard; but that we are designedly mean."

A matron who stood at the threshold of the door, smilingly chimed in. "This ingot," she said, "weighs five taels. Even if you cut half of it off, it will weigh a couple of taels, at least. But there are no sycee shears at hand, so, miss, put this piece aside and choose a smaller one."

Sheyue had already closed the press and walked out. "Who'll go and fumble about again?" she laughed. "If there's a little more, well, you take it and finish."

"Be quick," Baoyu remarked, "and tell Beiming to go for another doctor. It will be all right."

The matron received the money and marched off to go and settle matters.

Presently, Dr. Wang actually arrived, at the invitation of Beiming. First and foremost he felt the pulse and then gave the same diagnosis of the complaint (as the other doctor did) in the first instance. The only difference being that there was, in fact, no citrus or sida or other similar drugs, included in the prescription. It contained, however, false sarsaparilla roots, dried orange peel, *Peonia albifora*, and other similar medicines. But the quantities were, on the other hand, considerably smaller, as compared with those of the drugs mentioned in the former prescription.

"These are the medicines," Baoyu ejaculated exultingly, "suitable for girls! They should, it's true, be of a laxative nature, but never over and above what's needful. When I fell ill last year, I suffered from a chill, but I got such an obstruction in the viscera that I could neither take anything liquid or substantial, yet though he saw the state I was in, he said that I couldn't stand sida, ground gypsum, citrus, and other such violent drugs. You and I resemble the newly-opened white Begonia, Yun'er sent me in autumn. And how could you resist medicines which are too much for me? We're like the lofty aspen trees, which grow in people's burial grounds. To look at, the branches and leaves are of luxuriant growth, but they are hollow at the core."

"Do only aspen trees grow in waste burial grounds?" Sheyue smiled. "Is it likely, pray, that there are no fir and cypress trees? What's more loathsome than any other is the aspen. For though a lofty tree, it only has a few leaves; and it makes quite a confused noise with the slightest puff of wind! If you therefore deliberately compare yourself to it, you'll also be ranging yourself too much among the common herd!"

"I daren't liken myself to fir or cypress," Baoyu laughingly retorted. "Even Confucius says: 'after the season waxes cold, one finds that the fir and cypress are the last to lose their foliage,' which makes it evident that these two things are of high excellence. Thus it's those only, who are devoid of every sense of shame, who foolishly liken themselves to trees of the kind!"

While engaged in this colloquy, they perceived the old matron bring the drugs, so Baoyu bade her fetch the silver pot, used for boiling medicines in, and then he directed her to prepare the decoction on the brasier.

"The right thing would be," Qingwen suggested, "that you should let them go and get it ready in the tearoom; for will it ever do to fill this room with the smell of medicines?"

"The smell of medicines," Baoyu rejoined, "is far nicer than that emitted by the whole lot of flowers. Fairies pick medicines and prepare medicines. Besides this, eminent men and cultured scholars gather medicines and concoct medicines; so that it constitutes a most excellent thing. I was just thinking that there's everything and anything in these rooms and that the only thing that we lack is the smell of medicines; but as luck would have it, everything is now complete."

Speaking, he lost no time in giving orders to a servant to put the medicines on the fire. Next, he advised Sheyue to get ready a few presents and bid a nurse take them and go and look up Xiren, and exhort her not to give way to excessive grief. And when he had settled everything that had to be seen to, he repaired to the front to dowager lady Jia's and Madame Wang's quarters, and paid his respects and had his meal.

Lady Feng, as it happened, was just engaged in consulting with old lady Jia and Madame Wang. "The days are now short as well as cold," she argued, "so wouldn't it be advisable that my senior sister-in-law, Mrs. Jia Zhu, should henceforward have her repasts in the garden, along with the young ladies? When the weather gets milder, it won't at all matter, if they have to run backward and forward."

"This is really a capital idea!" Madame Wang smiled. "It will be so convenient during windy and rainy weather. To inhale the chilly air after eating isn't good. And to come quite empty, and begin piling up a lot of things in a stomach full of cold air isn't quite safe. It would be as well therefore to select two cooks from among the women, who have, anyhow, to keep night duty in the large five-roomed house, inside the garden back entrance, and station them there for the special purpose of preparing the necessary viands for the girls. Fresh vegetables are subject to some rule of distribution, so they can be issued to them from the general manager's office. Or they might possibly require money or be in need of some things or other. And it will be all right if a few of those pheasants, deer, and every kind of game, be apportioned to them."

"I too was just thinking about this," dowager lady Jia observed. "The only thing I feared was that with the extra work that would again be thrown upon the cook-house, they mightn't have too much to do."

"There'll be nothing much to do," lady Feng replied. "The same apportionment will continue as ever. In here, something may be added; but in there something will be reduced. Should it even involve a little trouble, it will be a small matter. If the girls were exposed to the cold wind, everyone else might stand it with impunity; but how could cousin Lin, first and foremost above all others, resist anything of the kind? In fact, brother Bao himself wouldn't be proof against it. What's more, none of the various young ladies can boast of a strong constitution."

What rejoinder old lady Jia made to lady Feng, at the close of her representations, is not yet ascertained; so, reader, listen to the explanations you will find given in the next chapter.

CHAPTER 52

The beautiful Ping'er endeavors to conceal the loss of the bracelet, made of work as fine as the feelers of a shrimp. The brave Qingwen mends the down-cloak during her indisposition.

But let us return to our story, "Quite so!" was the reply with which dowager lady Jia (greeted lady Feng's proposal). "I meant the other day to have suggested this arrangement, but I saw that everyone of you had so many urgent matters to attend to, (and I thought) that although you would not presume to bear me a grudge, were several duties now again superadded, you would unavoidably imagine that I only regarded those young grandsons and granddaughters of mine, and had no consideration for any of you, who have to look after the house. But since you make this suggestion yourself, it's all right."

And seeing that Mrs. Xue, and "sister-in-law" Li were sitting with her, and that Madame Xing, and Mrs. You, and the other ladies, who had also crossed over to pay their respects, had not as yet gone to their quarters, old lady Jia broached the subject with Madame Wang, and the rest of the company. "I've never before ventured to give utterance to the remarks that just fell from my lips," she said, "as first of all I was in fear and trembling lest I should have made that girl Feng more presumptuous than ever, and next, lest I should have incurred the displeasure of one and all of you. But since you're all here today, and everyone of you knows what brothers' wives and husbands' sisters mean, is there (I ask) any one besides her as full of forethought?"

Mrs. Xue, "sister-in-law" Li and Mrs. You smiled with one consent. "There are indeed but few like her!" they cried. "That of others is simply a conventional 'face' affection, but she is really fond of her husband's sisters and his young brother. In fact, she's as genuinely filial with you, venerable senior."

Dowager lady Jia nodded her head. "Albeit I'm fond of her," she sighed, "I can't, on the other hand, help distrusting that excessive shrewdness of hers, for it isn't a good thing."

"You're wrong there, worthy ancestor," lady Feng laughed with alacrity. "People in the world as a rule maintain that 'too shrewd and clever a person can't, it is feared, live long.' Now what people of the world invariably say people of the world invariably believe. But of you alone, my dear senior, can no such thing be averred or believed. For there you are, ancestor mine, a hundred times sharper and cleverer than I; and how is it that you now enjoy both perfect happiness and longevity? But I presume that I shall by and bye excel you by a hundredfold, and die at length, after a life of a thousand years, when you venerable senior shall have departed from these mortal scenes!"

"After everyone is dead and gone," dowager lady Jia laughingly observed, "what pleasure will there be, if two antiquated elves, like you and I will be, remain behind?"

This joke excited general mirth.

But so concerned was Baoyu about Qingwen and other matters that he was the first to make a move and return into the garden. On his arrival at his quarters, he found the rooms full of the fragrance emitted by the medicines. Not a soul did he, however, see about. Qingwen was reclining all alone on the stove-couch. Her face was feverish and red. When he came to touch it, his hand experienced a scorching sensation. Retracing his steps therefore towards the stove, he warmed his hands and inserted them under the coverlet and felt her. Her body as well was as hot as fire.

"If the others have left," he then remarked, "there's nothing strange about it, but are Sheyue and Qiuwen too so utterly devoid of feeling as to have each gone after her own business?"

"As regards Qiuwen," Qingwen explained, "I told her to go and have her meal. And as for Sheyue, Ping'er came just now and called her out of doors and there they are outside confabbing in a mysterious way! What the drift of their conversation can be I don't know. But they must be talking about my having fallen ill, and my not leaving this place to go home."

"Ping'er isn't that sort of person," Baoyu pleaded. "Besides, she had no idea whatever about your illness, so that she couldn't have come specially to see how you were getting on. I fancy her object was to look up Sheyue to hobnob with her, but finding unexpectedly that you were not up to the mark, she readily said that she had come on purpose to find what progress you were making. This was quite a natural thing for a person with so wily a disposition to say, for the sake of preserving harmony. But if you don't go home, it's none of her business. You two have all along been, irrespective of other things, on such good terms that she could by no means entertain any desire to injure the friendly relations which exist between you, all on account of something that doesn't concern her."

"Your remarks are right enough," Qingwen rejoined, "but I do suspect her, as why did she too start, all of a sudden, imposing upon me?"

"Wait, I'll walk out by the back door," Baoyu smiled, "and go to the foot of the window, and listen to what she's saying. I'll then come and tell you."

Speaking the while, he, in point of fact, sauntered out of the back door; and getting below the window, he lent an ear to their confidences.

"How did you manage to get it?" Sheyue inquired with gentle voice.

"When I lost sight of it on that day that I washed my hands," Ping'er answered, "our lady Secunda wouldn't let us make a fuss. But the moment she left the garden, she there and then sent word to the nurses, stationed in the various places, to institute careful search. Our suspicions, however, fell upon Miss Xing's maid, who has ever also been poverty-stricken; surmising that a young girl of her age, who had never set eyes upon anything of the kind, may possibly have picked it up and taken it. But never did we positively believe that it could be someone from this place of yours! Happily, our lady Secunda wasn't in the room, when that nurse Song who is with you here went over, and said, producing the bracelet, that the young maid, Zhui'er, had stolen it, and that she had detected her, and come to lay the matter before our lady Secunda. I promptly took over the bracelet from her; and recollecting how imperious and exacting Baoyu is inclined to be, fond and devoted as he is to each and all of you; how the jade which was prigged the other year by a certain Liang'er, is still, just as the matter has cooled down for the last couple of years, canvassed at times by some people eager to serve their own ends; how someone has now again turned up to purloin this gold trinket; how it was filched, to make matters worse, from a neighbor's house; how as luck would have it, she took this of all things; and how it happened to be his own servant to give him a slap on his mouth, I hastened to enjoin nurse Song to, on no account whatever, let Baoyu know anything about it, but simply pretend that nothing of the kind had transpired, and to make no mention of it to any single soul. 'In the second place,' (I said), 'our dowager lady and Madame Wang would get angry, if they came to hear anything. Thirdly, Xiren as well as yourselves would not also cut a very good figure.' Hence it was that in telling our lady Secunda, I merely explained 'that on my way to our senior mistress, the bracelet got unclasped, without my knowing it; that it fell among the roots of the grass; that there was no chance of seeing it while the snow was deep, but that when the snow completely disappeared today there it glistened, so yellow and bright, in the rays of the sun, in precisely the very place where it had dropped, and that I then picked it up.' Our lady Secunda at once credited my version. So here I come to let you all know so as to be henceforward a little on your guard with her, and not get her a job anywhere else. Wait until Xiren's return, and then devise means to pack her off, and finish with her."

"This young vixen has seen things of this kind before," Sheyue ejaculated, "and how is it that she was so shallow-eyed?"

"What could, after all, be the weight of this bracelet?" Ping'er observed. "It was once our lady Secunda's. She says that this is called the 'shrimp-feeler'-bracelet. But it's the pearl, which increases its weight. That minx Qingwen is as fiery as a piece of crackling charcoal, so were anything to be told her, she may, so little able is she to curb her temper, flare up suddenly into a huff, and beat or scold her, and kick up as much fuss as she ever has done before. That's why I simply tell you. Exercise due care, and it will be all right."

With this warning, she bid her farewell and went on her way.

Her words delighted, vexed, and grieved Baoyu. He felt delighted, on account of the consideration shown by Ping'er for his own feelings. Vexed, because Zhui'er had turned out a petty thief. Grieved, that Zhui'er, who was otherwise such a smart girl, should have gone in for this disgraceful affair. Returning consequently into the house, he told Qingwen every word that Ping'er had uttered. "She says," he went on to add, "that you're so fond of having things all your own way that were you to hear anything of this business, now that you are ill, you would get worse, and that she only means to broach the subject with you, when you get quite yourself again."

Upon hearing this, Qingwen's ire was actually stirred up, and her beautiful moth-like eyebrows contracted, and her lovely phoenix eyes stared wide like two balls. So she immediately shouted out for Zhui'er.

"If you go on bawling like that," Baoyu hastily remonstrated with her, "won't you show yourself ungrateful for the regard with which Ping'er has dealt with you and me? Better for us to show ourselves sensible of her kindness and by and bye pack the girl off, and finish."

"Your suggestion is all very good," Qingwen demurred, "but how could I suppress this resentment?"

"What's there to feel resentment about?" Baoyu asked. "Just you take good care of yourself; it's the best thing you can do."

Qingwen then took her medicine. When evening came, she had another couple of doses. But though in the course of the night, she broke out into a slight perspiration, she did not see any change for the better in her state. Still she felt feverish, her head sore, her nose stopped, her voice hoarse. The next day, Dr. Wang came again to examine her pulse and see how she was getting on. Besides other things, he increased the proportions of certain medicines in the decoction and reduced others; but in spite of her fever having been somewhat brought down, her head continued to ache as much as ever.

"Go and fetch the snuff," Baoyu said to Sheyue, "and give it to her to sniff. She'll feel more at ease after she has had several strong sneezes."

Sheyue went, in fact, and brought a flat crystal bottle, inlaid with a couple of golden stars, and handed it to Baoyu.

Baoyu speedily raised the cover of the bottle. Inside it, he discovered, represented on western enamel, a fair-haired young girl, in a state of nature, on whose two sides figured wings of flesh. This bottle contained some really first-rate foreign snuff.

Qingwen's attention was fixedly concentrated on the representation.

"Sniff a little!" Baoyu urged. "If the smell evaporates, it won't be worth anything."

Qingwen, at his advice, promptly dug out a little with her nail, and applied it to her nose. But with no effect. So digging out again a good quantity of it, she pressed it into her nostrils. Then suddenly she experienced a sensation in her nose as if some pungent matter had penetrated into the very duct leading into the head, and she sneezed five or six consecutive times, until tears rolled down from her eyes and mucus trickled from her nostrils.

Qingwen hastily put the bottle away. "It's dreadfully pungent!" she laughed. "Bring me some paper, quick!"

A servant-girl at once handed her a pile of fine paper.

Qingwen extracted sheet after sheet, and blew her nose.

"Well," said Baoyu smiling, "how are you feeling now?"

"I'm really considerably relieved." Qingwen rejoined laughing. "The only thing is that my temples still hurt me."

"Were you to treat yourself exclusively with western medicines, I'm sure you'd get all right," Baoyu added smilingly. Saying this, "Go," he accordingly desired Sheyue, "to our lady Secunda, and ask her for some. Tell her that I spoke to you about them. My cousin over there often uses some western plaster, which she applies to her temples when she's got a headache. It's called 'Yi-fo-na.' So try and get some of it!"

Sheyue expressed her readiness. After a protracted absence, she, in very deed, came back with a small bit of the medicine; and going quickly for a piece of red silk cutting, she got the scissors and slit two round slips off as big as the tip of a finger. After which, she took the medicine, and softening it by the fire, she spread it on them with a hairpin.

Qingwen herself laid hold of a looking-glass with a handle and stuck the bits on both her temples.

"While you were lying sick," Sheyue laughed, "you looked like a mangy-headed devil! But with this stuff on now you present a fine sight! As for our lady Secunda she has been so much in the habit of sticking these things about her that they don't very much show off with her!"

This joke over, "Our lady Secunda said," she resumed, addressing herself to Baoyu, "'that tomorrow is your maternal uncle's birthday, and that our mistress, your mother, asked her to tell you to go over. That whatever clothes you will put on tomorrow should be got ready tonight, so as to avoid any trouble in the morning.'"

"Anything that comes first to hand," Baoyu observed, "will do well enough! There's no getting, the whole year round, at the end of all the fuss of birthdays!"

Speaking the while, he rose to his feet and left the room with the idea of repairing to Xichun's quarters to have a look at the painting. As soon as he got outside the door of the courtyard, he unexpectedly spied Baoqin's young maid, Xiao Luo by name, crossing over from the opposite direction. Baoyu, with rapid step, strode up to her, and inquired of her whither she was going.

"Our two young ladies," Xiao Luo answered with a smile, "are in Miss Lin's rooms; so I'm also now on my way thither."

Catching this answer, Baoyu wheeled round and came at once with her to the Xiaoxiang Lodge. Here not only did he find Baochai and her cousin, but Xing Xiuyan as well. The quartet was seated in a circle on the warming-frame; carrying on a friendly chat on everyday domestic matters; while Zijuan was sitting in the winter apartment, working at some needlework by the side of the window.

The moment they caught a glimpse of him, their faces beamed with smiles. "There comes someone else!" they cried. "There's no room for you to sit!"

"What a fine picture of beautiful girls, in the winter chamber!" Baoyu smiled. "It's a pity I come a trifle too late! This room is, at all events, so much warmer than any other, that I won't feel cold if I plant myself on this chair."

So saying, he made himself comfortable on a favorite chair of Daiyu's over which was thrown a grey squirrel cover. But noticing in the winter apartment a jadestone bowl, full of single narcissi, in clusters of three or five, Baoyu began praising their beauty with all the language he could command. "What lovely flowers!" he exclaimed. "The warmer the room gets, the stronger is the fragrance emitted by these flowers! How is it I never saw them yesterday?"

"These are," Daiyu laughingly explained, "from the two pots of narcissi, and two pots of allspice, sent to Miss Xue Secunda by the wife of

Lai Da, the head butler in your household. Of these, she gave me a pot of narcissi; and to that girl Yun, a pot of allspice. I didn't at first mean to keep them, but I was afraid of showing no consideration for her kind attention. But if you want them, I'll, in my turn, present them to you. Will you have them, eh?"

"I've got two pots of them in my rooms," Baoyu replied, "but they're not up to these. How is it you're ready to let others have what cousin Qin has given you? This can on no account do!"

"With me here," Daiyu added, "the medicine pot never leaves the fire the whole day long. I'm only kept together by medicines. So how could I ever stand the smell of flowers bunging my nose? It makes me weaker than ever. Besides, if there's the least whiff of medicines in this room, it will, contrariwise, spoil the fragrance of these flowers. So isn't it better that you should have them carried away? These flowers will then breathe a purer atmosphere, and won't have any mixture of smells to annoy them."

"I've also got now someone ill in my place," Baoyu retorted with a smile, "and medicines are being decocted. How comes it you happen to know nothing about it?"

"This is strange!" Daiyu laughed. "I was really speaking quite thoughtlessly; for who ever knows what's going on in your apartments? But why do you, instead of getting here a little earlier to listen to old stories, come at this moment to bring trouble and vexation upon your own self?"

Baoyu gave a laugh. "Let's have a meeting tomorrow," he proposed, "for we've also got the themes. Let's sing the narcissus and allspice."

"Never mind, drop that!" Daiyu rejoined, upon hearing his proposal. "I can't venture to write any more verses. Whenever I indite any, I'm mulcted. So I'd rather not be put to any great shame."

While uttering these words she screened her face with both hands.

"What's the matter?" Baoyu smiled. "Why are you again making fun of me? I'm not afraid of any shame, but, lo, you screen your face."

"The next time," Baochai felt impelled to interpose laughingly, "I convene a meeting, we'll have four themes for odes and four for songs; and each one of us will have to write four odes and four roundelays. The theme of the first ode will treat of the plan of the great extreme; the rhyme fixed being 'xian' (first), and the meter consisting of five words in each line. We'll have to exhaust everyone of the rhymes under 'xian,' and mind, not a single one may be left out."

"From what you say," Baoqin smilingly observed, "it's evident that you're not in earnest, cousin, in setting the club on foot. It's clear enough that your object is to embarrass people. But as far as the verses go, we could forcibly turn out a few, just by higgledy-piggledy taking several passages from the 'Canon of Changes,' and inserting them in our own; but, after all, what fun will there be in that sort of thing? When I was eight years of age, I went with my father to the western seaboard to purchase foreign goods. Who'd have thought it, we came across a girl from the 'Zhen Zhen' kingdom. She was in her eighteenth year, and her features were just like those of the beauties one sees represented in foreign pictures. She had also yellow hair, hanging down, and arranged in endless plaits. Her whole head was ornamented with one mass of cornelian beads, amber, cats' eyes, and 'grandmother-greenstone.' On her person, she wore a chain armor plaited with gold, and a coat, which was up to the very sleeves, embroidered in foreign style. In a belt, she carried a Japanese sword, also inlaid with gold and studded with precious gems. In very truth, even in pictures, there is no one as beautiful as she. Some people said that she was thoroughly conversant with Chinese literature, and could explain the 'Five Classics,' that she was able to write odes and devise roundelays, and so my father requested an interpreter to ask her to write something. She thereupon wrote an original stanza, which all, with one voice, praised for its remarkable beauty, and extolled for its extraordinary merits."

"My dear cousin," eagerly smiled Baoyu, "produce what she wrote, and let's have a look at it."

"It's put away in Nanjing," Baoqin replied with a smile. "So how could I at present go and fetch it?"

Great was Baoyu's disappointment at this rejoinder. "I've no luck," he cried, "to see anything like this in the world."

Daiyu laughingly laid hold of Baoqin. "Don't be humbugging us!" she remarked. "I know well enough that you are not likely, on a visit like this, to have left any such things of yours at home. You must have brought them along. Yet here you are now again palming off a fib on us by saying that you haven't got them with you. You people may believe what she says, but I, for my part, don't."

Baoqin got red in the face. Drooping her head against her chest, she gave a faint smile; but she uttered not a word by way of response.

"Really Pin'er you've got into the habit of talking like this!" Baochai laughed. "You're too shrewd by far."

"Bring them along," Daiyu urged with a smile, "and give us a chance of seeing something and learning something; it won't hurt them."

"There's a whole heap of trunks and baskets," Baochai put in laughing, "which haven't been yet cleared away. And how could one tell in which particular one they're packed up? Wait a few days, and when things will have been put straight a bit, we'll try and find them: and everyone of us can then have a look at them; that will be all right. But if you happen to remember the lines," she pursued, speaking to Baoqin, "why not recite them for our benefit?"

"I remember so far that her lines consisted of a stanza with five characters in each line," Baoqin returned for answer. "For a foreign girl, they're verily very well done."

"Don't begin for a while," Baochai exclaimed. "Let me send for Yun'er, so that she too might hear them."

After this remark, she called Xiao Luo to her. "Go to my place," she observed, "and tell her that a foreign beauty has come over, who's a splendid hand at poetry. 'You, who have poetry on the brain,' (say to her), 'are invited to come and see her,' and then lay hold of this versemaniac of ours and bring her along."

Xiao Luo gave a smile, and went away. After a long time, they heard Xiangyun laughingly inquire, "What foreign beauty has come?" But while asking this question, she made her appearance in company with Xiangling.

"We heard your voices long before we caught a glimpse of your persons!" the party laughed.

Baoqin and her companions motioned to her to sit down, and, in due course, she reiterated what she had told them a short while back.

"Be quick, out with it! Let's hear what it is!" Xiangyun smilingly cried.

Baoqin thereupon recited:

Last night in the Purple Chamber I dreamt.
This evening on the "Shui Guo" Isle I sing.
The clouds by the isle cover the broad sea.
The zephyr from the peaks reaches the woods.
The moon has never known present or past.
From shallow and deep causes springs love's fate.
When I recall my springs south of the Han,
Can I not feel disconsolate at heart?

After listening to her, "She does deserve credit," they unanimously shouted, "for she really is far superior to us, Chinese though we be."

But scarcely was this remark out of their lips, when they perceived Sheyue walk in. "Madame Wang," she said, "has sent a servant to inform you, Master Secundus, that you are to go at an early hour tomorrow morning to your maternal uncle's, and that you are to explain to him that her ladyship isn't feeling quite up to the mark, and that she cannot pay him a visit in person."

Baoyu precipitately jumped to his feet (out of deference to his mother), and signified his assent, by answering "Yes." He then went on to inquire of Baochai and Baoqin, "Are you two going?"

"We're not going," Baochai rejoined. "We simply went there yesterday to take our presents over but we left after a short chat."

Baoyu thereupon pressed his female cousins to go ahead and he then followed them. But Daiyu called out to him again and stopped him. "When is Xiren, after all, coming back?" she asked.

"She'll naturally come back after she has accompanied the funeral," Baoyu retorted.

Daiyu had something more she would have liked to tell him, but she found it difficult to shape it into words. After some moments spent in abstraction, "Off with you!" she cried.

Baoyu too felt that he treasured in his heart many things he would fain confide to her, but he did not know what to bring to his lips, so after cogitating within himself for a time, he likewise observed smilingly: "We'll have another chat tomorrow," and, as he said so, he wended his way down the stairs. Lowering his head, he was just about to take a step forward, when he twisted himself round again with alacrity. "Now that the nights are longer than they were, you're sure to cough often and wake several times in the night, eh?" he asked.

"Last night," Daiyu answered, "I was all right; I coughed only twice. But I only slept at the fourth watch for a couple of hours and then I couldn't close my eyes again."

"I really have something very important to tell you," Baoyu proceeded with another smile. "It only now crossed my mind." Saying this, he approached her and added in a confidential tone: "I think that the birds' nests sent to you by cousin Baochai…"

Barely, however, had he had time to conclude than he spied dame Zhao enter the room to pay Daiyu a visit. "Miss, have you been all right these last few days?" she inquired.

Daiyu readily guessed that this was an attention extended to her merely as she had, on her way back from Tanchun's quarters, to pass by her door, so speedily smiling a forced smile, she offered her a seat.

"Many thanks, dame Zhao," she said, "for the trouble of thinking of me, and for coming in person in this intense cold."

Hastily also bidding a servant pour the tea, she simultaneously winked at Baoyu.

Baoyu grasped her meaning, and forthwith quitted the apartment. As this happened to be about dinner time, and he had been enjoined as well by Madame Wang to be back at an early hour, Baoyu returned to his quarters, and looked on while Qingwen took her medicine. Baoyu did not desire Qingwen this evening to move into the winter apartment, but stayed with Qingwen outside; and, giving orders to bring the warming-frame near the winter apartment, Sheyue slept on it.

Nothing of any interest worth putting on record transpired during the night. On the morrow, before the break of day, Qingwen aroused Sheyue.

"You should awake," she said. "The only thing is that you haven't had enough sleep. If you go out and tell them to get the water for tea ready for him, while I wake him, it will be all right."

Sheyue immediately jumped up and threw something over her. "Let's call him to get up and dress in his fine clothes," she said. "We can summon them in, after this fire-box has been removed. The old nurses told us not to allow him to stay in this room for fear the virus of the disease should pass on to him; so now if they see us bundled up together in one place, they're bound to kick up another row."

"That's my idea too," Qingwen replied.

The two girls were then about to call him, when Baoyu woke up of his own accord, and speedily leaping out of bed, he threw his clothes over him.

Sheyue first called a young maid into the room and put things shipshape before she told Qingwen and the other servant-girls to enter; and along with them, she remained in waiting upon Baoyu while he combed his hair, and washed his face and hands. This part of his toilet over, Sheyue remarked: "It's cloudy again, so I suppose it's going to snow. You'd better therefore wear a woollen overcoat!"

Baoyu nodded his head approvingly; and set to work at once to effect the necessary change in his costume. A young waiting-maid then presented him a covered bowl, in a small tea tray, containing a decoction made of Fujian lotus and red dates. After Baoyu had had a couple of mouthfuls, Sheyue also brought him a small plateful of brown ginger, prepared according to some prescription. Baoyu put a piece into his mouth, and, impressing some advice on Qingwen, he crossed over to dowager lady Jia's suite of rooms.

His grandmother had not yet got out of bed. But she was well aware that Baoyu was going out of doors so having the entrance leading into her bedroom opened she asked Baoyu to walk in. Baoyu espied behind the old lady, Baoqin lying with her face turned towards the inside, and not awake yet from her sleep.

Dowager lady Jia observed that Baoyu was clad in a deep-red felt fringed overcoat, with woollen lichee-colored archery-sleeves and with an edging of dark green glossy satin, embroidered with gold rings. "What!" old lady Jia inquired, "is it snowing?"

"The weather is dull," Baoyu replied, "but it isn't snowing yet."

Dowager lady Jia thereupon sent for Yuanyang and told her to fetch the peacock down pelisse, finished the day before, and give it to him. Yuanyang signified her obedience and went off, and actually returned with what was wanted.

When Baoyu came to survey it, he found that the green and golden hues glistened with bright luster, that the jade-like variegated colors on it shone with splendor, and that it bore no resemblance to the duck-down coat, which Baoqin had been wearing.

"This," he heard his grandmother smilingly remark, "is called 'bird gold'. This is woven of the down of peacocks, caught in Russia, twisted into thread. The other day, I presented that one with the wild duck down to your young female cousin, so I now give you this one."

Baoyu prostrated himself before her, after which he threw the coat over his shoulders.

"Go and let your mother see it before you start," his grandmother laughingly added.

Baoyu assented, and quitted her apartments, when he caught sight of Yuanyang standing below rubbing her eyes. Ever since the day on which Yuanyang had sworn to have done with the match, she had not exchanged a single word with Baoyu. Baoyu was therefore day and night a prey to dejection. So when he now observed her shirk his presence again, Baoyu at once advanced up to her, and, putting on a smile, "My dear girl," he said, "do look at the coat I've got on. Is it nice or not?"

Yuanyang shoved his hand away, and promptly walked into dowager lady Jia's quarters.

Baoyu was thus compelled to repair to Madame Wang's room, and let her see his coat. Retracing afterwards his footsteps into the garden, he let Qingwen and Sheyue also have a look at it, and then came and told his grandmother that he had attended to her wishes.

"My mother," he added, "has seen what I've got on. But all she said was: 'what a pity!' and then she went on to enjoin me to be 'careful with it and not to spoil it.'"

"There only remains this single one," old lady Jia observed, "so if you spoil it you can't have another. Even did I want to have one made for you like it now, it would be out of the question."

At the close of these words, she went on to advise him. "Don't," she said, "have too much wine and come back early." Baoyu acquiesced by uttering several yes's.

An old nurse then followed him out into the pavilion. Here they discovered six attendants, (that is), Baoyu's milk-brother Li Gui, and Wang Rong, Zhang Ruojin, Zhao Yihua, Qian Qi, and Zhou Rui, as well as four young servant-lads: Beiming, Banhe, Chuyao, and Sao Hong; some carrying bundles of clothes on their backs, some holding cushions in their hands, others leading a white horse with engraved saddle and variegated bridles. They had already been waiting for a good long while. The old nurse went on to issue some directions, and the six servants, hastily expressing their obedience by numerous yes's, quickly caught hold of the saddle and weighed the stirrup down while Baoyu mounted leisurely. Li Gui and Wang Rong then led the horse by the bit. Two of them, Qian Qi and Zhou Rui, walked ahead and showed the way; Zhang Ruojin and Zhao Yihua followed Baoyu closely on each side.

"Brother Zhou and brother Qian," Baoyu smiled, from his seat on his horse, "let's go by this side-gate. It will save my having again to dismount, when we reach the entrance to my father's study."

"Mr. Jia Zheng is not in his study," Zhou Rui laughed, with a curtsey. "It has been daily under lock and key, so there will be no need for you, master, to get down from your horse."

"Though it be locked up," Baoyu smiled, "I shall have to dismount all the same."

"You're quite right in what you say, master," both Qian Qi and Li Gui chimed in laughingly; "but pretend you're lazy and don't get down. In the event of our coming across Mr. Lai Da and our number two Mr. Lin, they're sure, rather awkward though it be for them to say anything to their master, to tender you one or two words of advice, but throw the whole of the blame upon us. You can also tell them that we had not explained to you what was the right thing to do."

Zhou Rui and Qian Qi accordingly wended their steps straight for the side-gate. But while they were keeping up some sort of conversation, they came face to face with Lai Da on his way in.

Baoyu speedily pulled in his horse, with the idea of dismounting. But Lai Da hastened to draw near and to clasp his leg. Baoyu stood up on his stirrup, and, putting on a smile, he took his hand in his, and made several remarks to him.

In quick succession, he also perceived a young servant-lad make his appearance inside, leading the way for twenty or thirty servants, laden with brooms and dust-baskets. The moment they espied Baoyu, they, one and all, stood along the wall, and dropped their arms against their sides, with the exception of the head lad, who bending one knee, said: "My obeisance to you, sir."

Baoyu could not recall to mind his name or surname, but forcing a faint smile, he nodded his head to and fro. It was only when the horse had well gone past, that the lad eventually led the bevy of servants off, and that they went after their business.

Presently, they egressed from the side-gate. Outside, stood the servant-lads of the six domestics, Li Gui and his companions, as well as several grooms, who had, from an early hour, got ready about ten horses and been standing, on special duty, waiting for their arrival. As soon as they reached the further end of the side-gate, Li Gui and each of the other attendants mounted their horses, and pressed ahead to lead the way. Like a streak of smoke, they got out of sight, without any occurrence worth noticing.

Qingwen, meanwhile, continued to take her medicines. But still she experienced no relief in her ailment. Such was the state of exasperation into which she worked herself that she abused the doctor right and left. "All he's good for," she cried, "is to squeeze people's money. But he doesn't know how to prescribe a single dose of efficacious medicine for his patients."

"You have far too impatient a disposition!" Sheyue said, as she advised her, with a smile. "'A disease,' the proverb has it, 'comes like a crumbling mountain, and goes like silk that is reeled.' Besides, they're not the divine pills of 'Lao Jun'. How ever could there be such efficacious medicines? The only thing for you to do is to quietly look after yourself for several days, and you're sure to get all right. But the more you work yourself into such a frenzy, the worse you get!"

Qingwen went on to heap abuse on the head of the young-maids.

"Where have they gone? Have they bored into the sand?" she ejaculated. "They see well enough that I'm ill, so they make bold and run away. But by and bye when I recover, I shall take one by one of you and flay your skin off for you."

Zhuan'er, a young maid, was struck with dismay, and ran up to her with hasty step. "Miss," she inquired, "what's up with you?"

"Is it likely that the rest are all dead and gone, and that there only remains but you?" Qingwen exclaimed.

But while she spoke, she saw Zhui'er also slowly enter the room. "Look at this vixen!" Qingwen shouted. "If I don't ask for her, she won't come. Had there been any monthly allowances issued and fruits distributed here, you would have been the first to run in! But approach a bit! Am I tigress to gobble you up?"

Zhui'er was under the necessity of advancing a few steps nearer to her. But, all of a sudden, Qingwen stooped forward, and with a dash clutching her hand, she took a long pin from the side of her pillow, and pricked it at random all over.

"What's the use of such paws?" she railed at her. "They don't ply a needle, and they don't touch any thread! All you're good for is to prig things to stuff that mouth of yours with! The skin of your phiz is shallow and those paws of yours are light! But with the shame you bring upon yourself before the world, isn't it right that I should prick you, and make mincemeat of you?"

Zhui'er shouted so wildly from pain that Sheyue stepped forward and immediately drew them apart. She then pressed Qingwen, until she induced her to lie down.

"You're just perspiring," she remarked, "and here you are once more bent upon killing yourself. Wait until you are yourself again! Won't you then be able to give her as many blows as you may like? What's the use of kicking up all this fuss just now?"

Qingwen bade a servant tell nurse Song to come in. "Our master Secundus, Mr. Baoyu, recently asked me to tell you," she remarked on her arrival, "that Zhui'er is very lazy. He himself gives her orders to her very face, but she is ever ready to raise objections and not to budge. Even when Xiren bids her do things, she vilifies her behind her back. She must absolutely therefore be packed off today. And if Mr. Bao himself lays the matter tomorrow before Madame Wang, things will be square."

After listening to her grievances, nurse Song readily concluded in her mind that the affair of the bracelet had come to be known. "What you suggest is well and good, it's true," she consequently smiled, "but it's as well to wait until Miss Hua (flower) returns and hears about the things. We can then give her the sack."

"Mr. Baoyu urgently enjoined this today," Qingwen pursued, "so what about Miss Hua (flower) and Miss Cao (grass)? We've, of course, got rules of propriety here, so you just do as I tell you; and be quick and send for someone from her house to come and fetch her away!"

"Well, now let's drop this!" Sheyue interposed. "Whether she goes soon or whether she goes late is one and the same thing; so let them take her away soon; we'll then be the sooner clear of her."

At these words, nurse Song had no alternative but to step out, and to send for her mother. When she came, she got ready all her effects, and then came to see Qingwen and the other girls. "Young ladies," she said, "what's up? If your niece doesn't behave as she ought to, why, call her to account. But why banish her from this place? You should, indeed, leave us a little face!"

"As regards what you say," Qingwen put in, "wait until Baoyu comes, and then we can ask him. It's nothing to do with us."

The woman gave a sardonic smile. "Have I got the courage to ask him?" she answered. "In what matter doesn't he lend an ear to any settlement you, young ladies, may propose? He invariably agrees to all you say! But if you, young ladies, aren't agreeable, it's really of no avail. When you, for example, spoke just now—it's true it was on the sly—you called him straightway by his name, miss. This thing does very well with you, young ladies, but were we to do anything of the kind, we'd be looked upon as very savages!"

Qingwen, upon hearing her remark, became more than ever exasperated, and got crimson in the face. "Yes, I called him by his name," she rejoined, "so you'd better go and report me to our old lady and Madame Wang. Tell them I'm a rustic and let them send me too off."

"Sister-in-law," urged Sheyue, "just you take her away; and if you've got aught to say, you can say it by and bye. Is this a place for you to bawl in and to try and explain what is right? Whom have you seen discourse upon the rules of propriety with us? Not to speak of you, sister-in-law, even Mrs. Lai Da and Mrs. Lin treat us fairly well. And as for calling him by name, why, from days of yore to the very present, our dowager mistress has invariably bidden us do so. You yourselves are well aware of it. So much did she fear that it would be a difficult job to rear him that she deliberately wrote his infant name on slips of paper and had them stuck everywhere and anywhere with the design that one and all should call him by it. And this in order that it might exercise a good influence upon his bringing up. Even water-coolies and scavenger-coolies indiscriminately address him by his name; and how much more such as we? So late, in fact, as yesterday Mrs. Lin gave him but once the title of 'Sir,' and our old mistress called even her to task. This is one side of the question. In the next place, we all have to go and make frequent reports to our venerable dowager lady and Madame Wang, and don't we with them allude to him by name in what we have to say? Is it likely we'd also style him 'Sir?' What day is there that we don't utter the two words 'Baoyu' two hundred times? And is it for you, sister-in-law, to come and pick out this fault? But in a day or so, when you've leisure to go to our old mistress' and Madame Wang's, you'll hear us call him by name in their very presence, and then you'll feel convinced. You've never, sister-in-law, had occasion to fulfill any honorable duties by our old lady and our lady. From one year's end to the other, all you do is to simply loaf outside the third door. So it's no matter of surprise, if you don't happen to know anything of the customs which prevail with us inside. But this isn't a place where you, sister-in-law, can linger for long. In another moment, there won't be any need for us to say anything; for someone will be coming to ask you what you want, and what excuse will you be able to plead? So take her away and let Mrs. Lin know about it; and commission her to come and find our Mr. Secundus and tell him all. There are in this establishment over a thousand inmates; one comes and another comes, so that though we know people and inquire their names, we can't nevertheless imprint them clearly on our minds."

At the close of this long rigmarole, she at once told a young maid to take the mop and wash the floors.

The woman listened patiently to her arguments, but she could find no words to say anything to her by way of reply. Nor did she have the audacity to protract her stay. So flying into a huff, she took Zhui'er along with her, and there and then made her way out.

"Is it likely," nurse Song hastily observed, "that a dame like you doesn't know what manners mean? Your daughter has been in these rooms for some time, so she should, when she is about to go, knock her head before the young ladies. She has no other means of showing her gratitude. Not that they care much about such things. Yet were she to simply knock her head, she would acquit herself of a duty, if nothing more. But how is it that she says I'm going, and off she forthwith rushes?"

Zhui'er overheard these words, and felt under the necessity of turning back. Entering therefore the apartment, she prostrated herself before the two girls, and then she went in quest of Qiuwen and her companions, but neither did they pay any notice whatever to her.

"Hai!" ejaculated the woman, and heaving a sigh—for she did not venture to utter a word—she walked off, fostering a grudge in her heart.

Qingwen had, while suffering from a cold, got into a fit of anger into the bargain, so instead of being better, she was worse, and she tossed and rolled until the time came for lighting the lamps. But the moment she felt more at ease, she saw Baoyu come back. As soon as he put his foot inside the door, he gave way to an exclamation, and stamped his foot.

"What's the reason of such behavior?" Sheyue promptly asked him.

"My old grandmother," Baoyu explained, "was in such capital spirits that she gave me this coat today; but, who'd have thought it, I inadvertently burnt part of the back lapel. Fortunately however the evening was advanced so that neither she nor my mother noticed what had happened."

Speaking the while, he took it off. Sheyue, on inspection, found indeed a hole burnt in it of the size of a finger. "This," she said, "must have been done by some spark from the hand-stove. It's of no consequence."

Immediately she called a servant to her. "Take this out on the sly," she bade her, "and let an experienced weaver patch it. It will be all right then."

So saying, she packed it up in a wrapper, and a nurse carried it outside.

"It should be ready by daybreak," she urged. "And by no means let our old lady or Madame Wang know anything about it." The matron brought it back again, after a protracted absence. "Not only," she explained; "have weavers, first-class tailors, and embroiderers, but even those, who do women's work, been asked about it, and they all have no idea what this is made of. None of them therefore will venture to undertake the job."

"What's to be done?" Sheyue inquired. "But it won't matter if you don't wear it tomorrow."

"Tomorrow is the very day of the anniversary," Baoyu rejoined. "Grandmother and my mother bade me put this on and go and pay my visit; and here I go and burn it, on the first day I wear it. Now isn't this enough to throw a damper over my good cheer?"

Qingwen lent an ear to their conversation for a long time, until unable to restrain herself, she twisted herself round. "Bring it here," she chimed in, "and let me see it! You haven't been lucky in wearing this; but never mind!"

These words were still on Qingwen's lips, when the coat was handed to her. The lamp was likewise moved nearer to her. With minute care she surveyed it. "This is made," Qingwen observed, "of gold thread, spun from peacock's feathers. So were we now to also take gold thread, twisted from the feathers of the peacock, and darn it closely, by imitating the woof, I think it will pass without detection."

"The peacock-feather-thread is ready at hand," Sheyue remarked smilingly. "But who's there, exclusive of you, able to join the threads?"

"I'll, needless to say, do my level best to the very cost of my life and finish," Qingwen added.

"How ever could this do?" Baoyu eagerly interposed. "You're just slightly better, and how could you take up any needlework?"

"You needn't go on in this chicken-hearted way!" Qingwen cried. "I know my own self well enough."

With this reply, she sat up, and, putting her hair up, she threw something over her shoulders. Her head felt heavy; her body light. Before her eyes, confusedly flitted golden stars. In real deed, she could not stand the strain. But when inclined to give up the work, she again dreaded that Baoyu would be driven to despair. She therefore had perforce to make a supreme effort and, setting her teeth to, she bore the exertion. All the help she asked of Sheyue was to lend her a hand in reeling the thread.

Qingwen first took hold of a thread, and put it side by side (with those in the pelisse) to compare the two together. "This," she remarked, "isn't quite like them; but when it's patched up with it, it won't show very much."

"It will do very well," Baoyu said. "Could one also go and hunt up a Russian tailor?"

Qingwen commenced by unstitching the lining, and, inserting under it, a bamboo bow, of the size of the mouth of a tea cup, she bound it tight at the back. She then turned her mind to the four sides of the aperture, and these she loosened by scratching them with a golden knife. Making next two stitches across with her needle, she marked out the warp and woof; and, following the way the threads were joined, she first and foremost connected the foundation, and then keeping to the original lines, she went backwards and forwards mending the hole; passing her work, after every second stitch, under further review. But she did not ply her needle three to five times, before she lay herself down on her pillow, and indulged in a little rest.

Baoyu was standing by her side. Now he inquired of her whether she would like a little hot water to drink. Later on, he asked her to repose herself. Now he seized a grey-squirrel wrapper and threw it over her shoulders. Shortly after, he took a pillow and propped her up. (The way he fussed) so exasperated Qingwen that she begged and entreated him to leave off.

"My junior ancestor!" she exclaimed, "do go to bed and sleep! If you sit up for the other half of the night, your eyes will tomorrow look as if they had been scooped out, and what good will possibly come out of that?"

Baoyu realised her state of exasperation and felt compelled to come and lie down anyhow. But he could not again close his eyes.

In a little while, she heard the clock strike four, and just managing to finish she took a small toothbrush, and rubbed up the pile.

"That will do!" Sheyue put in. "One couldn't detect it, unless one examined it carefully."

Baoyu asked with alacrity to be allowed to have a look at it. "Really," he smiled, "it's quite the same thing."

Qingwen coughed and coughed time after time, so it was only after extreme difficulty that she succeeded in completing what she had to patch. "It's mended, it's true," she remarked, "but it does not, after all, look anything like it. Yet, I cannot stand the effort any more!"

As she shouted "Ai-ya," she lost control over herself, and dropped down upon the bed.

But, reader, if you choose to know anything more of her state, peruse the next chapter.

CHAPTER 53

In the Ning Guo, mansion sacrifices are offered to their ancestors on the last night of the year. In the Rong Guo mansion, a banquet is given on the evening of the 15th of the first moon.

But to resume our story, when Baoyu saw that Qingwen had in her attempt to finish mending the peacock-down cloak exhausted her strength and fatigued herself, he hastily bade a young maid help him massage her; and setting to work they tapped her for a while, after which, they retired to rest. But not much time elapsed before broad daylight set in. He did not however go out of doors, but simply called out that they should go at once and ask the doctor round.

Presently, Dr. Wang arrived. After feeling her pulse, his suspicions were aroused. "Yesterday," he said, "she was much better, so how is it that today she is instead weaker, and has fallen off so much? She must surely have had too much in the way of drinking or eating! Or she must have fatigued herself. A complaint arising from outside sources is, indeed, a light thing. But it's no small matter if one doesn't take proper care of one's self, as she has done after perspiring."

As he passed these remarks, he walked out of the apartment, and, writing a prescription, he entered again.

When Baoyu came to examine it, he perceived that he had eliminated the laxatives, and all the drugs, whose properties were to expel noxious influences, but added pachyma cocos, rhubarb, *Arolia edulis*, and other such medicines, which could stimulate the system and strengthen her physique.

Baoyu, on one hand, hastened to direct a servant to go and decoct them, and, on the other, he heaved a sigh. "What's to be done?" he exclaimed. "Should anything happen to her, it will all be through the evil consequences of my shortcomings!"

"Hai!" cried Qingwen, from where she was reclining on her pillow. "Dear Mr. Secundus, go and mind your own business! Have I got such a dreadful disease?"

Baoyu had no alternative but to get out of the way. But in the afternoon, he gave out that he was not feeling up to the mark, and hurried back to her side again.

The symptoms of Qingwen's illness were, it is true, grave; yet fortunately for her she had ever had to strain her physical strength, and not to tax the energies of her mind. Furthermore, she had always been frugal in her diet, so that she had never sustained any harm from under or over-eating. The custom in the Jia mansion was that as soon as any one, irrespective of masters or servants, contracted the slightest chill or cough, quiet and starving should invariably be the main things observed, the treatment by medicines occupying only a secondary place. Hence it was that when the other day she unawares felt unwell, she at once abstained from food during two or three days, while she carefully also nursed herself by taking proper medicines. And although she recently taxed her strength a little too much, she gradually succeeded, by attending with extra care to her health for another few days, in bringing about her complete recovery.

Of late, his female cousins, who lived in the garden, had been having their meals in their rooms, so with the extreme convenience of having a fire to prepare drinks and eatables, Baoyu himself was able, needless for us to go into details, to ask for soups and order broths for (Qingwen), with which to recoup her health.

Xiren returned soon after she had followed the funeral of her mother. Sheyue then minutely told Xiren all about Zhui'er's affair, about Qingwen having sent her off, and about Baoyu having been already informed of the fact, and so forth, yet to all this Xiren made no further comment than: "what a very hasty disposition (that girl Qingwen has)."

But consequent upon Li Wan being likewise laid up with a cold, she got through the inclemency of the weather; Madame Xing suffering so much from sore eyes that Yingchun and Xiuyan had to go morning and evening and wait on her, while she used such medicines as she had; Li Wan's brother, having also taken her sister-in-law Li, together with Li Wen and Li Qi, to spend a few days at his home, and Baoyu seeing, on one hand, Xiren brood without intermission over the memory of her mother, and give way to secret grief, and Qingwen, on the other, continue not quite convalescent, there was no one to turn any attention to such things as poetical meetings, with the result that several occasions, on which they were to have assembled, were passed over without anything being done. By this time, the twelfth moon arrived. The end of the year was nigh at hand, so Madame Wang and lady Feng were engaged in making the necessary annual preparations. But, without alluding to Wang Ziteng, who was promoted to be Lord High

Commissioner of the Nine Provinces; Jia Yuncun, who filled up the post of Chief Inspector of Cavalry, Assistant Grand Councillor, and Commissioner of Affairs of State, we will resume our narrative with Jia Zhen, in the other part of the establishment. After having the Ancestral Hall thrown open, he gave orders to the domestics to sweep the place, to get ready the various articles, and bring over the ancestral tablets. Then he had the upper rooms cleaned, so as to be ready to receive the various images that were to be hung about. In the two mansions of Ning and Rong, inside as well as outside, above as well as below, everything was, therefore, bustle and confusion. As soon as Mrs. You, of the Ning mansion, put her foot out of bed on this day, she set to work, with the assistance of Jia Rong's wife, to prepare such needlework and presents as had to be sent over to dowager lady Jia's portion of the establishment, when it so happened that a servant-girl broke in upon them with a tea-tray in hand, containing ingots of silver of the kind given the evening before new year.

"Xing'er," she said, "informs your ladyship that the pieces of gold in that bundle of the other day amount in all to one hundred and fifty-three taels, one mace, and seven candareens; and that the ingots of pure metal and those not, contained in here, number all together two hundred and twenty."

With these words, she presented the tray. Mrs. You passed the ingots under survey. She found some resembling plum-blossom; others peonies. Among them were some with brushes and "as you like, (your wishes are bound to be fulfilled);" and others representing the eight precious things linked together, for use in spring-time.

Mrs. You directed that the silver ingots should be made up into a parcel, and then she bade Xing'er take them and deliver them immediately inside.

The servant-girl signified her obedience, and went away. But shortly Jia Zhen arrived for his meal, and Jia Rong's wife withdrew.

"Have we received," thereupon inquired Jia Zhen, "the bounty conferred (by His Majesty) for our spring sacrifices or not?"

"I've sent Rong'er today to go and receive it," Mrs. You rejoined.

"Albeit," continued Jia Zhen, "our family can well do without those paltry taels, yet they are, whatever their amount may be, an Imperial gift to us so take them over as soon as you can, and send them to our old lady, on the other side, to get ready the sacrifices to our ancestors. Above, we shall then receive the Emperor's bounty; below, we shall enjoy the goodwill of our progenitors. For no matter if we went so far as to spend ten thousand ounces of silver to present offerings to our forefathers with, they could not, in the long run, come up this gift in high repute. Added to this, we shall be the participators of grace and the recipients of blessings. Putting one or two households such as our own aside, what resources would those poverty-stricken families of hereditary officials have at their command wherewith to offer their sacrifices and celebrate the new year, if they could not rely upon this money? In very truth, therefore, the Imperial favor is vast, and all-providing!"

"Your arguments are quite correct!" Mrs. You ventured.

But while these two were indulging in this colloquy, they caught sight of a messenger, who came and announced: "Our young master has arrived."

Jia Zhen accordingly enjoined that he should be told to enter; whereupon they saw Jia Rong step into the room and present with both hands a small bag made of yellow cloth.

"How is it you've been away the whole day?" Jia Zhen asked.

Jia Rong strained a smile. "I didn't receive the money today from the Board of Rites," he replied. "The issue was again made at the treasury of the Guanglu temple; so I had once more to trudge away to the Guanglu temple before I could get it. The various officials in the Guanglu temple bade me present their compliments to you, father. (They asked me to tell you) that they had not seen you for many days, and that they are really longing for your company."

"What an idea! Do they care to see me?" Jia Zhen laughed. "Why, here's the end of the year drawing nigh again; so if they don't hanker after my presents, they must long and crave for my entertainments."

While he spoke his eye espied a slip of paper affixed to the yellow cloth bag, bearing the four large characters, "the Imperial favor is everlasting." On the other side figured also a row of small characters with the seal of the Director of Ancestral Worship in the Board of Rites. These testified that the enclosed consisted of two shares, conferred upon the Ning Guo duke, Jia Yan, and the Rong Guo duke, Jia Yuan, as a bounty (from the Emperor), for sacrifices to them every spring in perpetuity, (and gave) the number of taels, computed in pure silver, and the year, moon, and day, on which they were received in open hall by Jia Rong, Controller in the Imperial Prohibited City and Expectant Officer of the Guards. The signature of the official in charge of the temple for that year was appended below in purple ink.

After Jia Zhen had perused the inscription, he finished his meal, rinsed his mouth, and washed his hands. This over, he changed his shoes and hat, and bidding Jia Rong follow him along with the money, he went and informed dowager lady Jia and Madame Wang (of the receipt of the Imperial bounty), and repairing back to the near side, he communicated the fact to Jia She and Madame Xing; after which, he, at length, betook himself to his quarters. He then emptied the money and gave orders that the bag should be taken and burnt in the large censer in the Ancestral Hall.

"Go and ask your aunt Tertia, yonder," he further enjoined Jia Rong, "whether the day on which the new year wine is to be drunk has been fixed or not? If it has been determined upon, timely notice should be given in the library to draw out a proper list in order that when we again issue our invitations, there should be no chance of two entertainments coming off on the same day. Last year, not sufficient care was exercised, and several persons were invited to both mansions on the very same occasion. And people didn't say that we hadn't been careful enough, but that, as far as appearances went, the two households had made up their minds among themselves to show an empty attention, prompted by the fear of trouble."

Jia Rong immediately replied that he would attend to his injunctions, and not much time elapsed before he brought a list mentioning the days on which the inmates were to be invited to partake of the new year wine.

Jia Zhen examined it. "Go," he then said, "and give it to Lai Sheng so that he may see its contents and invite the guests. But mind he doesn't fix anything else for the dates specified in here."

But while watching from the pavilion the servant-boys carrying the enclosing screens and rubbing the tables and the gold and silver sacrificial utensils, he perceived a lad appear on the scene holding a petition and a list, and report that "Wu, the head-farmer in the Hei Shan village, has arrived." "What does this old executioner come for today?" Jia Zhen exclaimed.

Jia Rong took the petition and the list, and, unfolding them with all despatch, he held them up (to his father). Jia Zhen however glanced at the papers, as they were held by Jia Rong, keeping the while both hands behind his back. The petition on red paper ran as follows: "Your servant, the head farmer, Wu Jinxiao, prostrates himself before his master and mistress and wishes them every kind of happiness and good health, as well as good health to their worthy scion and daughter. May great joy, great blessings, brilliant honors, and peace be their share in this spring, which is about to dawn! May official promotion and increase of emoluments be their lot! May they see in everything the accomplishment of their wishes."

Jia Zhen smiled. "For a farmer," he remarked, "it has several good points!"

"Pay no heed to the style," urged Jia Rong, also smiling; "but to the good wishes."

Saying this, he speedily opened the list. The articles mentioned were, on examination, found to consist of: "Thirty big deer; five thousand musk deer; fifty roebuck deer; twenty Siamese pigs; twenty boiled pigs; twenty 'dragon' pigs; twenty wild pigs; twenty home-salted pigs; twenty wild sheep; twenty gray sheep; twenty home-boiled sheep; twenty home-dried sheep; two hundred sturgeon; two hundred catties of mixed fish; live chickens, ducks, and geese, two hundred of each; two hundred dried chickens, ducks, and geese; two hundred pair of pheasants and hares; two hundred pair of bears' paws; twenty catties of deer tendons; fifty catties of beche-de-mer; fifty deer tongues; fifty ox tongues; twenty catties of dried clams; filberts, fir-cones, peaches, apricots, and squash, two hundred bags of each; fifty pair of salt prawns; two hundred catties of dried shrimps; a thousand catties of superfine, picked charcoal; two thousand catties of medium charcoal; twenty thousand catties of common charcoal; two piculs of red rice, grown in the Imperial grounds; fifty bushels of greenish, glutinous rice; fifty bushels of white glutinous rice; fifty bushels of pounded non-glutinous rice; fifty bushels of various kinds of corn and millet; a thousand piculs of ordinary common rice. Exclusive of a cartload of every sort of vegetables, and irrespective of two thousand five hundred taels, derived from the sale of corn and millet and every kind of domestic animals, your servant respectfully presents, for your honor's delectation, two pair of live deer, four pair of white rabbits, four pair of black rabbits, two pair of live variegated fowls, and two pair of duck, from western countries."

When Jia Zhen had exhausted the list, "Bring him in!" he cried. In a little time, he perceived Wu Jinxiao make his appearance inside. But simply halting in the court, he bumped his head on the ground and paid his respects.

Jia Zhen desired a servant to raise him up. "You're still so hale!" he smiled.

"I don't deceive you, Sir," Wu Jinxiao observed, "when I say that yours servants are so accustomed to walking, that had we not come, we wouldn't have felt exceedingly dull. Isn't the whole crowd of them keen upon coming to see what the world is like at the feet of the son of heaven? Yet they're, after all, so young in years, that there's the fear of their going astray on the way. But, in a few more years, I shall be able to appease my solicitude on their account."

"How many days have you been on the way?" Jia Zhen inquired.

"To reply to your question, Sir," Wu Jinxiao ventured, "so much snow has fallen this year that it's everywhere out of town four and five feet in depth. The other day, the weather suddenly turned mild, and with the thaw that set in, it became so very hard to make any progress that we wasted several days. Yet albeit we've been a month and two days in accomplishing the journey; it isn't anything excessive. But as I feared lest you, Sir, would be giving way to anxiety, didn't I hurry along to arrive in good time?"

"How is it, I said, that he's come only today!" Jia Zhen observed.

"But upon looking over the list just now it seemed to me that you, old fossil, had come again to make as much as fun of me, as if you were putting up a stage for a boxing-match."

Wu Jinxiao hastily drew near a couple of steps. "I must tell you, Sir," he remarked, "that the harvest this year hasn't really been good. Rain set in ever since the third moon, and there it went on incessantly straight up to the eighth moon. Indeed, the weather hasn't kept fine for five or six consecutive days. In the ninth moon, there came a storm of hail, each stone of which was about the size of a saucer. And over an area of the neighboring two or three hundred li, the men and houses, animals and crops, which sustained injury, numbered over thousands and ten thousands. Hence it is that the things we've brought now are what they are. Your servant would not have the audacity to tell a lie."

Jia Zhen knitted his eyebrows. "I had computed," he said, "that the very least you would have brought would have been five thousand taels. What's this enough for? There are only now eight or nine of you farmers, and from two localities reports have contrariwise reached us during the course of this very year of the occurrence of droughts; and do you people come again to try your larks with us? Why, verily these aren't sufficient to see the new year in with."

"And yet," Wu Jinxiao argued, "your place can be looked upon as having fared well; for my brother, who's only over a hundred li away from where I am, has actually fallen in with a vastly different lot! He has at present eight farms of that mansion under his control, and these considerably larger than those of yours, Sir; and yet this year they too have only produced but a few things. So nothing beyond two or three thousand taels has been realized. What's more, they've had to borrow money."

"Quite so!" Jia Zhen exclaimed. "The state of things in my place here is passable. I've got no outside outlay. The main thing I have to mind is to make provision for a year's necessary expenses. If I launch out into luxuries, I have to suffer hardships, so I must try a little self-denial and manage to save something. It's the custom, besides, at the end of the year to send presents to people and invite others; but I'll thicken the skin of my face a bit, (and dispense with both,) and have done. I'm not like the inmates in that mansion, who have, during the last few years, added so many items of expenditure, that it's, of course, a matter of impossibility for them to avoid loosening their purse strings. But they haven't, on the other hand, made any addition to their funds and landed property. During the course of the past year or two, they've had to make up many deficits. And if they don't appeal to you, to whom can they go?"

Wu Jinxiao laughed. "It's true," he said, "that in that mansion many items have been added, but money goes out and money comes in. And won't the Empress and His Majesty the Emperor bestow their favor?"

At these words, Jia Zhen smilingly faced Jia Rong and the other inmates. "Just you listen to his arguments!" he exclaimed. "Aren't they ridiculous, eh?"

Jia Rong and the rest promptly smiled. "Among your hills and seaboard can anything," they observed, "be known with regard to this principle? Is it likely, pray, that the Empress will ever make over to us the Emperor's treasury? Why, even supposing she may at heart entertain any such wish, she herself cannot possibly adopt independent action. Of course, she does confer her benefits on them, but this is at stated times and fixed periods, and they merely consist of a few colored satins, antiquities, and bric-a-brac. In fact, when she does bestow hard cash on them, it doesn't exceed a hundred ounces of silver. But did she even give them so much as a thousand and more taels, what would these suffice for? During which of the two last years have they not had to fork out several thousands of taels? In the first year, the Imperial consort paid a visit to her parents; and just calculate how much they must have run through in laying out that park, and you'll then know how they stand! Why, if in another couple of years, the Empress comes and pays them a second visit, they'll be, I'm inclined to fancy, regular paupers."

"That's why," urged Jia Zhen smiling, "country people are such unsophisticated creatures, that though they behold what lies on the surface, they have no idea of what is inside hidden from view. They're just like a piece of yellow cedar made into a mallet for beating the sonorous stones with. The exterior looks well enough; but it's all bitter inside."

"In very truth," Jia Rong added, laughing also the while, as he addressed himself to Jia Zhen, "that mansion is impoverished. The other day, I heard a consultation held on the sly between aunt Secunda and Yuanyang. What they wanted was to filch our worthy senior's things and go and pawn them in order to raise money."

"This is just another devilish trick of that minx Feng!" Jia Zhen smiled. "How ever could they have reached such straits? She's certain to have seen that expenses were great, and that heavy deficits had to be squared, so wishing again to curtail some item or other, who knows which, she devised this plan as a preparatory step, in order that when it came to be generally known, people should say that they had been reduced to such poverty. But from the result of the calculations I have arrived at in my mind, things haven't as yet attained this climax."

Continuing, he issued orders to a servant to take Wu Jinxiao outside, and to treat him with every consideration. But no further mention need be made of him.

During this while, Jia Zhen gave directions to keep from the various perquisites just received such as would prove serviceable for the sacrifices to their ancestors, and, selecting a few things of each kind, he told Jia Rong to have them taken to the Rong mansion. After this, he himself kept what was required for his own use at home; and then allotting the rest, with due compliance to gradation, he had share after share piled up at the foot of the moon-shaped platform, and sending servants to summon the young men of the clan, he distributed them among them.

In quick succession, numerous contributions for the ancestral sacrifices were likewise sent from the Rong mansion; also presents for Jia Zhen. Jia Zhen inspected the things, and having them removed, he completed preparing the sacrificial utensils. Then putting on a pair of slipshod shoes and throwing over his shoulders a long pelisse with "Sheli-sun" fur, he bade the servants spread a large wolf-skin rug in a sunny place on the stone steps below the pillars of the pavilion; and with his back to the warm sun, he leisurely watched the young people come and receive the new year gifts. Perceiving that Jia Qin had also come to fetch his share, Jia Zhen called him over. "How is it that you've come too?" he asked. "Who told you to come?"

Jia Qin respectfully dropped his arms against his sides. "I heard," he replied, "that you, senior Sir, had sent for us to appear before you here and receive our presents; so I didn't wait for the servants to go and tell me, but came straightway."

"These things," Jia Zhen added, "are intended for distribution among all those uncles and cousins who have nothing to do and who enjoy no source of income. Those two years you had no work, I gave you plenty of things too. But you're entrusted at present with some charge in the other mansion, and you exercise in the family temples control over the bonzes and taoist priests, so that you as well derive every month your share of an allowance. Irrespective of that, the allowances and money of the Buddhist priests pass through your hands. And do you still come to fetch things of this kind? You're far too greedy. Just you look at the fineries you wear. Why, they look like the habiliments of one who has money to spend, of a regular man of business. You said some time back that you had nothing which could bring you in any money, but how is it that you've got none again now? You really don't look as if you were in the same plight that you were in once upon a time."

"I have in my home a goodly number of inmates," Jia Qin explained, "so my expenses are great."

Jia Zhen gave a saturnine laugh. "Are you trying again to excuse yourself with me?" he cried. "Do you flatter yourself that I have no idea of your doings in the family temples? When you get there, you, of course, play the grand personnage and no one has the courage to run counter to your wishes. Then you've also got the handling of money. Besides you're far away from us, so you're arrogant and audacious. Night after night, you get bad characters together; you gamble for money; and you keep women and young boys. And though you now fling away money with such a high hand, do you still presume to come and receive gifts? But as you can't manage to filch anything to take along with you, it will do you good to get beans, with the pole used for carrying water. Wait until the new year is over, and then I'll certainly report you to your uncle Secundus."

Jia Qin got crimson in the face, and did not venture to utter a single word by way of extenuation. A servant, however, then announced that the Prince from the Bei mansion had sent a pair of scrolls and a purse.

At this announcement, Jia Zhen immediately told Jia Rong to go out and entertain the messengers. "And just say," he added, "that I'm not at home."

Jia Rong went on his way. Jia Zhen, meanwhile, dismissed Jia Qin; and, seeing the things taken away, he returned to his quarters and finished his evening meal with Mrs. You. But nothing of any note occurred during that night.

The next day, he had, needless to say, still more things to give his mind to. Soon arrived the twenty-ninth day of the twelfth moon, and everything was in perfect readiness. In the two mansions alike, the gate guardian gods and scrolls were renovated. The hanging tablets were newly varnished. The peach charms glistened like new. In the Ning Guo mansion, every principal door, starting from the main entrance, the ceremonial gates, the doors of the large pavilions, of the winter apartments, and inner pavilions, the inner three gates, the inner ceremonial gates, and the inner boundary gates, straight up to the doors of the main halls, was flung wide open. At the bottom of the steps, were placed on either side large and lofty vermilion candles, of uniform color; which when lit presented the appearance of a pair of golden dragons.

On the morrow, dowager lady Jia and those with any official status, donned the court dress consistent with their grade, and taking first and foremost a retinue of inmates with them, they entered the palace in eight bearer state chairs, and presented their congratulations. After acquitting themselves of the ceremonial rites, and partaking of a banquet, they betook themselves back, and alighted from their chairs on their arrival at the winter hall of the Ning mansion. The young men, who had not followed the party to court, waited, arranged in their proper order, in front of the entrance the Ning mansion, and subsequently led the way into the ancestral temple.

But to return to Baoqin. This was the first occasion on which she put her foot inside to look at the inner precincts of the Jia ancestral temple, and as she did so, she scrutinized with minute attention all the details that met her gaze in the halls dedicated to their forefathers. These consisted, in fact, of a distinct courtyard on the west side of the Ning mansion. Within the balustrade, painted black, stood five apartments. Over the main entrance to these was suspended a flat tablet with the inscription in four characters: "Ancestral hall of the Jia family." On the side of these was recorded the fact that it had been the handiwork of Wang Xifeng, specially promoted to the rank of Grand Tutor of the Heir Apparent, and formerly Chancellor of the Imperial Academy. On either side, was one of a pair of scrolls, bearing the motto:

Besmear the earth with your liver and brains, all ye people, out of gratitude for the bounty of (the Emperor's) protection!
The reputation (of the Jia family) reaches the very skies. Hundred generations rejoice in the splendor of the sacrifices accorded them.

This too had been executed by Wang, the Grand Tutor.

As soon as the court was entered, a raised road was reached, paved with white marble, on both sides of which were planted deep green fir trees and kingfisher-green cypress trees. On the moon-shaped platform were laid out antiquities, tripods, libation-vases, and other similar articles. In front of the antechamber was hung a gold-colored flat tablet, with nine dragons, and the device:

Like a dazzling star is the statesman, who assists the Emperor.

This was the autograph of a former Emperor.

On both sides figured a pair of antithetical scrolls, with the motto:

Their honors equal the sun and moon in luster.
Their fame is without bounds. It descends to their sons and grandsons.

These lines were likewise from the Imperial brush. Over the five-roomed main hall was suspended a tablet, inlaid with green, representing wriggling dragons. The sentiments consisted of:

Mindful of the remotest and heedful of the most distant ancestors.

A pair of antithetical scrolls was hung on the sides; on which was written:

After their death, their sons and grandsons enjoy their beneficent
   virtues.
Up to the very present the masses think of the Rong and Ning
   families.

Both these mottoes owed their origin to the Imperial brush.

Inside, lanterns and candles burnt with resplendent brightness. Embroidered curtains and decorated screens were hung in such profusion that though a large number of ancestral tablets were placed about they could not be clearly discerned. The main thing that struck the eye was the inmates of the Jia mansion standing about, on the left and right, disposed in their proper order. Jia Jing was overseer of the sacrifices. Jia She played the part of assistant. Jia Zhen presented the cups for libations. Jia Lian and Jia Cong offered up the strips of paper. Baoyu held the incense. Jia Chang and Jia Ling distributed the hassocks and looked after the receptacles for the ashes of joss-sticks. The black clad musicians discoursed music. The libation-cups were offered thrice in sacrifice. These devotions over, paper money was burnt; and libations of wine were poured. After the observance of the prescribed rites, the band stopped, and withdrew. The whole company then pressed round dowager lady Jia, and repaired to the main hall, where the images were placed. The embroidered curtains were hung high up. The variegated screens shut in the place from view. The fragrant candles burnt with splendor. In the place of honor, of the main apartment, were suspended the portraits of two progenitors of the Ning and Rong, both of whom were attired in costumes, ornamented with dragons, and clasped with belts of jade. On the right and left of them, were also arrayed the likenesses of a number of eminent ancestors.

Jia Xing, Jia Zhi, and the others of the same status stood according to their proper grades in a row extending from the inner ceremonial gate straight up to the verandah of the main hall. Outside the balustrade came at last Jia Jing and Jia She. Inside the balustrade figured the various female members of the family. The domestics and pages were arrayed beyond the ceremonial gate. As each set of eatables arrived, they transmitted them as far as the ceremonial gate, where Jia Xing, Jia Zhi, and his companions were ready to receive them. From one to another, they afterwards reached the bottom of the steps and found their way into Jia Jing's hands.

Jia Rong, being the eldest grandson of the senior branch, was the only person who penetrated within the precincts of the balustrade reserved for the female inmates. So whenever Jia Jing had any offerings to pass on, he delivered them to Jia Rong, and Jia Rong gave them to his wife; who again handed them to lady Feng, Mrs. You, and the several ladies. And when these offerings reached the sacrificial altar, they were at length surrendered to Madame Wang. Madame Wang thereupon placed them in dowager lady Jia's hands, and old lady Jia deposited them on the altar.

Madame Xing stood on the west-east side of the sacrificial altar, and along with old lady Jia, she offered the oblations and laid them in their proper places. After the vegetables, rice, soup, sweets, wine, and tea had been handed up, Jia Rong eventually retired outside and resumed his position above Jia Qin.

Of the male inmates, whose names were composed with the radical "wen," "literature," Jia Jing was at the time the head. Below followed those with the radical "Yu," "gem," led by Jia Zhen. Next to these, came the inmates with the radical "cao," "grass," headed by Jia Rong. These were arranged in proper order, with due regard to left and right. The men figured on the east; the women on the west.

When dowager lady Jia picked up a joss-stick and prostrated herself to perform her devotions, one and all fell simultaneously on their knees, packing up the five-roomed principal pavilion, the inside as well as outside of the three antechambers, the verandahs, the top and bottom of the stairs, the interior of the two vermilion avenues so closely with all their fineries and embroideries that not the slightest space remained vacant among them. Not so much as the caw of a crow struck the ear. All that was audible was the report of jingling and tinkling, and the sound of the gold bells and jade ornaments slightly rocked to and fro. Besides these, the creaking noise made by the shoes of the inmates, while getting up and kneeling down.

In a little time, the ceremonies were brought to a close. Jia Jing, Jia She, and the rest hastily retired and adjourned to the Rong mansion, where they waited with the special purpose of paying their obeisance to dowager lady Jia.

Mrs. You's drawing rooms were entirely covered with red carpets. In the center stood a large gold cloisonne brasier, with three legs, in imitation of rhinoceros tusks, washed with gold. On the stove-couch in the upper part was laid a new small red hair rug. On it were placed deep red back-cushions with embroidered representations of dragons, which were embedded among clouds and clasped the character longevity, as well as reclining-pillows and sitting-rugs. Covers made of black fox skin were moreover thrown over the couch, along with skins of pure white fox for sitting-cushions.

Dowager lady Jia was invited to place herself on the couch; and on the skin-rugs spread, on either side, two or three of the sisters-in-law, of the same standing as old lady Jia, were urged to sit down.

After the necessary arrangements had been concluded, skin rugs were also put on the small couch, erected in a horizontal position on the near portion of the apartments, and Madame Xing and the other ladies of her age were motioned to seat themselves. On the two sides stood, face to face on the floor, twelve chairs carved and lacquered, over which were thrown antimacassars and small gray squirrel rugs, of uniform color. At the foot of each chair was a large copper foot-stove.

On these chairs, Baoqin and the other young ladies were asked to sit down.

Mrs. You took a tray and with her own hands she presented tea to old lady Jia. Jia Rong's wife served the rest of their seniors. Subsequently, Mrs. You helped Madame Xing too and her contemporaries; and Jia Rong's wife then gave tea to the various young ladies; while lady Feng, Li Wan, and a few others simply remained below, ready to minister to their wants. After their tea, Madame Xing and her compeers were the first to rise and come and wait on dowager lady Jia, while she had hers. Dowager lady Jia chatted for a time with her old sisters-in-law and then desired the servants to look to her chair.

Lady Feng thereupon speedily walked up and supported her to rise to her feet.

"The evening meal has long ago been got ready for you, venerable ancestor," Mrs. You smiled. "You've year by year shown no desire to honor us with your presence, but tarry a bit on this occasion and partake of some refreshment before you cross over. Is it likely, in fact, that we can't come up to that girl Feng?"

"Go on, worthy senior!" laughed lady Feng, as she propped old lady Jia. "Let's go home and eat our own. Don't heed what she says!"

"In what bustle and confusion aren't you in over here," smiled dowager lady Jia, "with all the sacrifices to our ancestors, and how could you stand all the trouble I'm putting you to? I've never, furthermore, had every year anything to eat with you; but you've always been in the way of sending me things. So isn't it as well that you should again let me have a few? And as I'll keep for the next day what I shan't be able to get through, won't I thus have a good deal more?"

This remark evoked general laughter.

"Whatever you do," she went on to enjoin her, "mind you depute some reliable persons to sit up at night and look after the incense fires; but they mustn't let their wits go wool-gathering."

Mrs. You gave her to understand that she would see to it, and they sallied out, at the same time, into the fore part of the winter-apartments.

And when Mrs. You and her friends went past the screen, the pages introduced the bearers, who shouldered the sedan and walked out by the main entrance. Then following too in the track of Madame Xing and the other ladies, Mrs. You repaired in their company into the Rong mansion.

(Dowager lady Jia's) chair had, meanwhile, got beyond the principal gateway. Here again were deployed, on the east side of the street, the bearers of insignia, the retinue and musicians of the duke of Ning Guo. They crammed the whole extent of the street. Comers and goers were alike kept back. No thoroughfare was allowed. Shortly, the Rong mansion was reached. The large gates and main entrances were also thrown open straight up to the very interior of the compound. On the present occasion, however, the bearers did not put the chair down by the winter quarters, but passing the main hall, and turning to the west, they rested it on their arrival at the near side of dowager lady Jia's principal pavilion. The various attendants pressed round old lady Jia and followed her into her main apartment, where decorated mats and embroidered screens had also been placed about, and everything looked as if brand-new.

In the brasier, deposited in the center of the room, burnt fir and cedar incense, and a hundred mixed herbs. The moment dowager lady Jia ensconced herself into a seat, an old nurse entered and announced that: "the senior ladies have come to pay their respects."

Old lady Jia rose with alacrity to her feet to go and greet them, when she perceived that two or three of her old sisters-in-law had already stepped inside, so clasping each other's hands, they now laughed, and now they pressed each other to sit down. After tea, they took their departure; but dowager lady Jia only escorted them as far as the inner ceremonial gate, and retracing her footsteps, she came and resumed the place of honor. Jia Jing, Jia She, and the other seniors then ushered the various junior male members of the household into her apartments.

"I put you," smiled old lady Jia, "to ever so much trouble and inconvenience from one year's end to another; so don't pay any obeisance."

But while she spoke, the men formed themselves into one company, and the women into another, and performed their homage, group by group. This over, armchairs were arranged on the left and on the right; and on these chairs they too subsequently seated themselves, according to their seniority and gradation, to receive salutations. The men and women servants, and the pages and maids employed in the two mansions then paid, in like manner, the obeisance consonant with their positions, whether high, middle, or low; and this ceremony observed, the new year money was distributed, together with purses, gold and silver ingots, and other presents of the same description. A "rejoicing together" banquet was spread. The men sat on the east; the women on the west. "T'u Su," new year's day, wine was served; also "rejoicing together" soup, "propitious" fruits, and "as you like" cakes. At the close of the banquet, dowager lady Jia rose and penetrated into the inner chamber with the purpose of effecting a change in her costume, so the several inmates present could at last disperse and go their own way.

That night, incense was burnt and offerings presented at the various altars to Buddha and the kitchen god. In the courtyard of Madame Wang's main quarters paper horses and incense for sacrifices to heaven and earth were all ready. At the principal entrance of the garden of Broad Vista were suspended horn lanterns, which from their lofty places cast their bright rays on either side. Every place was hung with street lanterns. Every inmate, whether high or low, was got up in gala dress. Throughout the whole night, human voices resounded confusedly. The din of talking and laughing filled the air. Strings of crackers and rockets were let off incessantly.

The morrow came. At the fifth watch, dowager lady Jia and the other senior members of the family donned the grand costumes, which accorded with their status, and with a complete retinue they entered the palace to present their court congratulations; for that day was, in addition, the anniversary of Yuanchun's birth. After they had regaled themselves at a collation, they wended their way back, and betaking themselves also into the Ning mansion, they offered their oblations to their ancestors, and then returned home and received the conventional salutations, after which they put off their fineries and retired to rest.

None of the relatives and friends, who came to wish their compliments of the season, were admitted into (old lady Jia's) presence, but simply had a friendly chat with Mrs. Xue and "sister-in-law" Li, and studied their own convenience. Or along with Baoyu, Baochai, and the other young ladies, they amused themselves by playing the game of war or dominoes.

Madame Wang and lady Feng had one day after another their hands full with the invitations they had to issue for the new year wine. In the halls and courts of the other side theatricals and banquets succeeded each other and relations and friends dropped in in an incessant string. Bustle reigned for seven or eight consecutive days, before things settled down again.

But presently the festival of the full moon of the first month drew near, and both mansions, the Ning as well as the Rong, were everywhere ornamented with lanterns and decorations. On the eleventh, Jia She invited dowager lady Jia and the other inmates. On the next day, Jia Zhen also entertained his old senior and Madame Wang and lady Feng. But for us to record on how many consecutive days invitations were extended to them to go and drink the new year wine would be an impossible task.

The fifteenth came. On this evening dowager lady Jia gave orders to have several banqueting tables laid in the main reception hall, to engage a company of young actors, to have every place illuminated with flowered lanterns of various colors, and to assemble at a family entertainment all the sons, nephews, nieces, grandchildren and grandchildren's wives and other members of the two mansions of Ning and Rong. As however Jia Jing did not habitually have any wine or take any ordinary food, no one went to press him to come.

On the seventeenth, he hastened, at the close of the ancestral sacrifices, out of town to chasten himself. In fact, even during the few days he spent at home, he merely frequented retired rooms and lonely places, and did not take the least interest in any single concern. But he need not detain us any further.

As for Jia She, after he had received dowager lady Jia's presents, he said good-bye and went away. But old lady Jia herself was perfectly aware that she could not conveniently tarry any longer on this side so she too followed his example and took her departure.

When Jia She got home, he along with all the guests feasted his eyes on the illuminations and drank wine with them. Music and singing deafened the ear. Embroidered fineries were everywhere visible. For his way of seeking amusement was unlike that customary in this portion of the establishment.

In dowager lady Jia's reception hall, ten tables were meanwhile arranged. By each table was placed a teapoy. On these teapoys stood censers and bottles; three things in all. (In the censers) was burnt "Baihe" palace incense, a gift from his Majesty the Emperor. But small pots, about eight inches long, four to five inches broad and two or three inches high, adorned with scenery in the shape of rockeries, were also placed about. All of which contained fresh flowers. Small foreign lacquer trays were likewise to be seen, laden with diminutive painted teacups of antique ware. Transparent gauze screens with frames of carved blackwood, ornamented with a fringe representing flowers and giving the text of verses, figured too here and there. In different kinds of small old vases were combined together the three friends of winter (pine, bamboo, and plum,) as well as "jade-hall," "happiness and honor," and other fresh flowers.

At the upper two tables sat "sister-in-law" Li and Mrs. Xue. On the east was only laid a single table. But there as well were placed carved screens, covered with dragons, and a short low-footed couch, with a full assortment of back-cushions, reclining-cushions, and skin-rugs. On the couch stood a small teapoy, light and handy, of foreign lacquer, inlaid with gold. On the teapoy were arrayed cups, bowls, foreign cloth napkins, and such things.

Dowager lady Jia was reposing on the couch. At one time, she chatted and laughed with the whole company; at another, she took up her spectacles and looked at what was going on on the stage.

"Make allowances," she said, "for my old age. My bones are quite sore; so if I be a little out of order in my conduct bear with me, and let us entertain each other while I remain in a recumbent position." Continuing, she desired Hupo to make herself comfortable on the couch, and take a small club and tap her legs. No table stood below the couch, but only a high teapoy. On it were a high stand with tassels, flowervases, incense-burners and other similar articles. But, a small, high table, laden with cups and chopsticks, had besides been got ready. At the table next to this, the four cousins, Baoqin, Xiangyun, Daiyu, and Baoyu were told to seat themselves. The various viands and fruits that were brought in were first presented to dowager lady Jia for inspection. If they took her fancy, she kept them at the small table. But once tasted by her, they were again removed and placed on their table. We could therefore safely say that none but the four cousins sat along with their old grandmother.

The seats occupied by Madame Xing and Madame Wang were below. Lower down came Mrs. You, Li Wan, lady Feng, and Jia Rong's wife. On the west sat Baochai, Li Wen, Li Qi, Xiuyan, Yingchun, and the other cousins. On the large pillars, on either side, were suspended, in groups of three and five, glass lanterns ornamented with fringes. In front of each table stood a candlestick in the shape of drooping lotus leaves. The candlesticks contained colored candles. These lotus leaves were provided with enamelled springs, of foreign make, so they could be twisted outward, thus screening the rays of the lights and throwing them (on the stage), enabling one to watch the plays with exceptional distinctness. The window-frames and doors had all been removed. In every place figured colored fringes, and various kinds of court lanterns. Inside and outside the verandahs, and under the roofs of the covered passages, which stretched on either side, were hung lanterns of sheep-horn, glass, embroidered gauze, or silk, decorated or painted, of satin or of paper.

Round different tables sat Jia Zhen, Jia Lian, Jia Huan, Jia Cong, Jia Rong, Jia Yun, Jia Qin, Jia Chang, Jia Ling, and other male inmates of the family.

Dowager lady Jia had at an early hour likewise sent servants to invite the male and female members of the whole clan. But those advanced in years were not disposed to take part in any excitement. Some had no one at the time to look after things; others too were detained by ill-health; and much though these had every wish to be present, they were not, after all, in a fit state to come. Some were so envious of riches, and so ashamed of their poverty, that they entertained no desire to avail themselves of the invitation. Others, what is more, fostered such a dis-like for, and stood in such awe of, lady Feng that they felt bitter towards her and would not accept. Others again were timid and shy, and so little accustomed to seeing people, that they could not muster sufficient courage to come. Hence it was that despite the large number of female relatives in the clan, none came but Jia Lan's mother, nee Lou, who brought Jia Lan with her. In the way of men, there were only Jia Qin, Jia Yun, Jia Chang, and Jia Ling; the four of them and no others. The managers, at present under lady Feng's control, were however among those who accepted. But albeit there was not a complete gathering of the inmates on this occasion, yet, for a small family entertainment, sufficient animation characterized the proceedings.

About this time, Lin Zixiao's wife also made her appearance, with half a dozen married women who carried three divan tables between them. Each table was covered with a red woollen cloth, on which lay a lot of cash, picked out clean and of equal size, and recently issued from the mint. These were strung together with a deep-red cord. Each couple carried a table, so there were in all three tables.

Lin Zixiao's wife directed that two tables should be placed below the festive board, round which were seated Mrs. Xue and "sister-in-law" Li, and that one should be put at the foot of dowager lady Jia's couch.

"Place it in the middle!" old lady Jia exclaimed. "These women have never known what good manners mean. Put the table down." Saying this, she picked up the cash, and loosening the knots, she unstrung them and piled them on the table.

"The reunion in the western chamber" was just being sung. The play was drawing to a close. They had reached a part where Yu Shu runs off at night in high dudgeon, and Wen Bao jokingly cried out: "You go off with your monkey up; but, as luck would have it, this is the very day of the fifteenth of the first moon, and a family banquet is being given by the old lady in the Rong Guo mansion, so wait and I'll jump on this horse and hurry in and ask for something to eat. I must look sharp!" The joke made old lady Jia, and the rest of the company laugh.

"What a dreadful, impish child!" Mrs. Xue and the others exclaimed. "Yet poor thing!"

"This child is only just nine years of age," lady Feng interposed.

"He has really made a clever hit!" dowager lady Jia laughed. "Tip him!" she shouted.

This shout over, three married women, who has previously got ready several small wicker baskets, came up, as soon as they heard the word "tip", and, taking the heaps of loose cash piled on the table, they each filled a basket full, and, issuing outside, they approached the stage. "Dowager lady Jia, Mrs. Xue, and the family relative, Mrs. Li, present Wen Bao this money to purchase something to eat with," they said.

At the end of these words, they flung the contents of the baskets upon the stage. So all then that fell on the ear was the rattle of the cash flying in every direction over the boards.

Jia Zhen and Jia Lian had, by this time, enjoined the pages to fetch big baskets full of cash and have them in readiness. But as, reader, you do not know as yet in what way these presents were given, listen to the circumstances detailed in the subsequent chapter.

CHAPTER 54

Dowager lady Jia does away with rotten old customs. Wang Xifeng imitates in jest (the dutiful son), by getting herself up in gaudy theatrical clothes.

Jia Zhen and Jia Lian had, we will now explain, secretly got ready large baskets of cash, so the moment they heard old lady Jia utter the word "tip," they promptly bade the pages be quick and fling the money. The noise of the cash, running on every side of the stage, was all that fell on the ear. Dowager lady Jia thoroughly enjoyed it.

The two men then rose to their feet. The pages hastened to lay hold of a silver kettle, newly brought in with fresh wine, and to deposit it in Jia Lian's hands, who followed Jia Zhen with quick step into the inner rooms. Jia Zhen advanced first up to "sister-in-law" Li's table, and curtseying, he raised her cup, and turned round, whereupon Jia Lian quickly filled it to the brim. Next they approached Mrs. Xue's table and they also replenished her cup.

These two ladies lost no time in standing up, and smilingly expostulating. "Gentlemen," they said, "please take your seats. What's the use of standing on such ceremonies?"

But presently everyone, with the exception of the two ladies Mesdames Xing and Wang, quitted the banquet and dropping their arms against their bodies they stood on one side. Jia Zhen and his companion then drew near dowager lady Jia's couch. But the couch was so low that they had to stoop on their knees. Jia Zhen was in front, and presented the cup. Jia Lian was behind, and held the kettle up to her. But notwithstanding that only these two offered her wine, Jia Cong and the other young men followed them closely in the order of their age and grade; so the moment they saw them kneel, they immediately threw themselves on their knees. Baoyu too prostrated himself at once.

Xiangyun stealthily gave him a push. "What's the use of your now following their lead again and falling on your knees?" she said. "But since you behave like this, wouldn't it be well if you also went and poured wine all round?"

Baoyu laughed. "Hold on a bit," he rejoined in a low tone, "and I'll go and do so."

So speaking, he waited until his two relatives had finished pouring the wine and risen to their feet, when he also went and replenished the cups of Mesdames Wang and Xing.

"What about the young ladies?" Jia Zhen smilingly asked.

"You people had better be going," old lady Jia and the other ladies unanimously observed. "They'll, then, be more at their ease."

At this hint Jia Zhen and his companions eventually withdrew. The second watch had not, at the time, yet gone. The play that was being sung was: "The eight worthies look at the lanterns," consisting of eight acts; and had now reached a sensational part.

Baoyu at this stage left the feast and was going out. "Where are you off to?" inquired his grandmother Jia. "The crackers outside are dreadful. Mind, the lighted pieces of paper falling from above might burn you."

Baoyu smiled. "I'm not going far," he answered. "I'm merely going out of the room, and will be back at once."

Dowager lady Jia directed the matrons to "be careful and escort him."

Baoyu forthwith sallied out; with no other attendants however than Sheyue, Qiuwen, and several youthful maids.

"How is it," his grandmother Jia felt obliged so ask, "that I don't see anything of Xiren? Is she too now putting on high and mighty airs that she only sends these juvenile girls here?"

Madame Wang rose to her feet with all haste. "Her mother," she explained, "died the other day; so being in deep mourning, she couldn't very well present herself."

Dowager lady Jia nodded her head assentingly. "When one is in service," she smilingly remarked, "there should be no question of mourning or no mourning. Is it likely that, if she were still in my pay, she wouldn't at present be here? All these practices have quite become precedents!"

Lady Feng crossed over to her. "Had she even not been in mourning tonight," she chimed in with a laugh, "she would have had to be in the garden and keep an eye over that pile of lanterns, candles, and fireworks, as they're most dangerous things. For as soon as any theatricals are set on foot in here, who doesn't surreptitiously sneak out from the garden to have a look? But as far as she goes, she's diligent, and careful of every place. Moreover, when the company disperses and brother Baoyu retires to sleep, everything will be in perfect readiness. But, had she also come, that bevy of servants wouldn't again have cared a straw for anything; and on his return, after the party, the bedding would have been cold, the tea-water wouldn't have been ready, and he would have had to put up with every sort of discomfort. That's why I told her that there was no need for her to come. But should you, dear senior, wish her here, I'll send for her straightway and have done."

Old lady Jia lent an ear to her arguments. "What you say," she promptly put in, "is perfectly right. You've made better arrangements than I could. Quick, don't send for her! But when did her mother die? How is it I know nothing about it?"

"Some time ago," lady Feng laughed, "Xiren came in person and told you, worthy ancestor, and how is it you've forgotten it?"

"Yes," resumed dowager lady Jia smiling, after some reflection, "I remember now. My memory is really not of the best."

At this, everybody gave way to laughter. "How could your venerable ladyship," they said, "recollect so many matters?"

Dowager lady Jia thereupon heaved a sigh. "How I remember," she added, "the way she served me ever since her youth up; and how she waited upon Yun'er also; how at last she was given to that prince of devils, and how she has slaved away with that imp for the last few years. She is, besides, not a slave-girl, born or bred in the place. Nor has she ever received any great benefits from our hands. When her mother died, I meant to have given her several taels for her burial; but it quite slipped from my mind."

"The other day," lady Feng remarked, "Madame Wang presented her with forty taels; so that was all right."

At these words, old lady Jia nodded assent. "Yes, never mind about that," she observed. "Yuanyang's mother also died, as it happens, the other day; but taking into consideration that both her parents lived in the south, I didn't let her return home to observe a period of mourning. But as both these girls are now in mourning, why not allow them to live together? They'll thus be able to keep each other company. Take a few fruits, eatables, and other such things," continuing she bade a matron, "and give them to those two girls to eat."

"Would she likely wait until now?" Hupo laughingly interposed. "Why, she joined (Xiren) long ago."

In the course of this conversation, the various inmates partook of some more wine, and watched the theatricals.

But we will now turn our attention to Baoyu. He made his way straight into the garden. The matrons saw well enough that he was returning to his rooms, but instead of following him in, they ensconced themselves near the fire in the tearoom situated by the garden-gate, and made the best of the time by drinking and playing cards with the girls in charge of the tea. Baoyu entered the court. The lanterns burnt brightly, yet not a human voice was audible. "Have they all, forsooth, gone to sleep?" Sheyue ventured. "Let's walk in gently, and give them a fright!"

Presently, they stepped, on tiptoe, past the mirrored partition-wall. At a glance, they discerned Xiren lying on the stove-couch, face to face with some other girl. On the opposite side sat two or three old nurses nodding, half asleep. Baoyu conjectured that both the girls were plunged in sleep, and was just about to enter, when of a sudden someone was heard to heave a sigh and to say: "How evident it is that worldly matters are very uncertain! Here you lived all alone in here, while your father and mother tarried abroad, and roamed year after year from east to west, without any fixed place of abode. I ever thought that you wouldn't have been able to be with them at their last moments; but, as it happened, (your mother) died in this place this year, and you could, after all, stand by her to the end."

"Quite so!" rejoined Xiren. "Even I little expected to be able to see any of my parents' funeral. When I broke the news to our Madame Wang, she also gave me forty taels. This was really a kind attention on her part. I hadn't nevertheless presumed to indulge in any vain hopes."

Baoyu overheard what was said. Hastily twisting himself round, he remarked in a low voice, addressing himself to Sheyue and her companions: "Who would have fancied her also in here? But were I to enter, she'll bolt away in another tantrum! Better then that we should retrace our steps, and let them quietly have a chat together, eh? Xiren was alone, and down in the mouth, so if s a fortunate thing that she joined her in such good time."

As he spoke, they once more walked out of the court with gentle tread. Baoyu went to the back of the rockery, and stopping short, he raised his clothes. Sheyue and Qiuwen stood still, and turned their faces away. "Stoop," they smiled, "and then loosen your clothes! Be careful that the wind doesn't blow on your stomach!"

The two young maids, who followed behind, surmised that he was bent upon satisfying a natural want, and they hurried ahead to the tearoom to prepare the water.

Just, however, as Baoyu was crossing over, two married women came in sight, advancing from the opposite direction. "Who's there?" they inquired.

"Baoyu is here," Qiuwen answered. "But mind, if you bawl and shout like that, you'll give him a start."

The women promptly laughed. "We had no idea," they said, "that we were coming, at a great festive time like this, to bring trouble upon ourselves! What a lot of hard work must day after day fall to your share, young ladies."

Speaking the while, they drew near. Sheyue and her friends then asked them what they were holding in their hands.

We're taking over," they replied, "some things to the two girls: Miss Jin and Miss Hua."

"They're still singing the 'Eight Worthies' outside," Sheyue went on to observe laughingly, "and how is it you're running again to Miss Jin's and Miss Hua's before the 'Trouble-first moon-box' has been gone through?"

"Take the lid off," Baoyu cried, "and let me see what there's inside."

Qiuwen and Sheyue at once approached and uncovered the boxes. The two women promptly stooped, which enabled Baoyu to see that the contents of the two boxes consisted alike of some of the finest fruits and tea-cakes, which had figured at the banquet, and, nodding his head, he walked off, while Sheyue and her friend speedily threw the lids down anyhow, and followed in his track.

"Those two dames are pleasant enough," Baoyu smiled, "and they know how to speak decently; but it's they who get quite worn out every day, and they contrariwise say that you've got ample to do daily. Now, doesn't this amount to bragging and boasting?"

"Those two women," Sheyue chimed in, "are not bad. But such of them as don't know what good manners mean are ignorant to a degree of all propriety."

"You, who know what's what," Baoyu added, "should make allowances for that kind of rustic people. You should pity them; that's all."

Speaking, he made his exit out of the garden gate. The matrons had, though engaged in drinking and gambling, kept incessantly stepping out of doors to furtively keep an eye on his movements, so that the moment they perceived Baoyu appear, they followed him in a body. On their arrival in the covered passage of the reception-hall, they espied two young waiting-maids; the one with a small basin in her hand; the other with a towel thrown over her arm. They also held a bowl and small kettle, and had been waiting in that passage for ever so long.

Qiuwen was the first to hastily stretch out her hand and test the water. "The older you grow," she cried, "the denser you get! How could one ever use this icy-cold water?"

"Miss, look at the weather!" the young maid replied. "I was afraid the water would get cold. It was really scalding; is it cold now?"

While she made this rejoinder, an old matron was, by a strange coincidence, seen coming along, carrying a jug of hot water. "Dear dame," shouted the young maid, "come over and pour some for me in here!"

"My dear girl," the matron responded, "this is for our old mistress to brew tea with. I'll tell you what; you'd better go and fetch some yourself. Are you perchance afraid lest your feet might grow bigger by walking?"

"I don't care whose it is," Qiuwen put in. "If you don't give me any, I shall certainly empty our old lady's teapot and wash my hands."

The old matron turned her head; and, catching sight of Qiuwen, she there and then raised the jug and poured some of the water. "That will do!" exclaimed Qiuwen. "With all your years, don't you yet know what's what? Who isn't aware that it's for our old mistress? But would one presume to ask for what shouldn't be asked for?"

"My eyes are so dim," the matron rejoined with a smile, "that I didn't recognise this young lady."

When Baoyu had washed his hands, the young maid took the small jug and filled the bowl; and, as she held it in her hand, Baoyu rinsed his mouth. But Qiuwen and Sheyue availed themselves likewise of the warm water to have a wash; after which, they followed Baoyu in.

Baoyu at once asked for a kettle of warm wine, and, starting from sister-in-law Li, he began to replenish their cups. (Sister-in-law Li and his aunt Xue) pressed him, however, with smiling faces, to take a seat; but his grandmother Jia remonstrated. "He's only a youngster," she said, "so let him pour the wine! We must all drain this cup!"

With these words, she quaffed her own cup, leaving no heel-taps. Mesdames Xing and Wang also lost no time in emptying theirs; so Mrs. Xue and "sister-in-law" Li had no alternative but to drain their share.

"They're still singing the 'Eight Worthies' outside," Sheyue went on to observe laughingly, "and how is it you're running again to Miss Jin's and Miss Hua's before the 'Trouble-first moon-box' has been gone through?"

"Take the lid off," Baoyu cried, "and let me see what there's inside."

Qiuwen and Sheyue at once approached and uncovered the boxes. The two women promptly stooped, which enabled Baoyu to see that the contents of the two boxes consisted alike of some of the finest fruits and tea-cakes, which had figured at the banquet, and, nodding his head, he walked off, while Sheyue and her friend speedily threw the lids down anyhow, and followed in his track.

"Fill the cups too of your female cousins, senior or junior," dowager lady Jia went on to tell Baoyu. "And you mayn't pour the wine anyhow. Each of you must swallow every drop of your drinks."

Baoyu upon hearing her wishes, set to work, while signifying his assent, to replenish the cups of the several young ladies in their proper gradation. But when he got to Daiyu, she raised the cup, for she would not drink any wine herself, and applied it to Baoyu's lips. Baoyu drained the contents with one breath; upon which Daiyu gave him a smile, and said to him: "I am much obliged to you."

Baoyu next poured a cup for her. But lady Feng immediately laughed and expostulated. "Baoyu!" she cried, "you mustn't take any cold wine. Mind, your hand will tremble, and you won't be able tomorrow to write your characters or to draw the bow."

"I'm not having any cold wine," Baoyu replied.

"I know you're not," lady Feng smiled, "but I simply warn you."

After this, Baoyu finished helping the rest of the inmates inside, with the exception of Jia Rong's wife, for whom he bade a maid fill a cup. Then emerging again into the covered passage, he replenished the cups of Jia Zhen and his companions; after which, he tarried with them for a while, and at last walked in and resumed his former seat.

Presently, the soup was brought, and soon after that the "feast of lanterns" cakes were handed round.

Dowager lady Jia gave orders that the play should be interrupted for a time. "Those young people," (she said) "are be to pitied! Let them too have some hot soup and warm viands. They then can go on again. Take of every kind of fruit," she continued, "'feast of lanterns' cakes, and other such dainties and give them a few."

The play was shortly stopped. The matrons ushered in a couple of blind singing-girls, who often came to the house, and put two benches, on the opposite side, for them. Old lady Jia desired them to take a seat, and banjos and guitars were then handed to them.

"What stories would you like to hear?" old lady Jia inquired of "sister-in-law" Li and Mrs. Xue.

"We don't care what they are," both of them rejoined with one voice. "Any will do!"

"Have you of late added any new stories to your stock?" old lady Jia asked.

"We've got a new story," the two girls explained. "It's about an old affair of the time of the Five Dynasties, which trod down the Tang dynasty."

"What's its title?" old lady Jia inquired.

"It's called: 'A Feng seeks a Luan in marriage' (the male phoenix asks the female phoenix in marriage)," one of the girls answered.

"The title is all very well," dowager lady Jia proceeded, "but why I wonder was it ever given to it. First tell us its general purport, and if it's interesting, you can continue."

"This story," the girl explained, "treats of the time when the Tang dynasty was extinguished. There lived then one of the gentry, who had originally been a denizen of Jin Ling. His name was Wang Zhong. He had been minister under two reigns. He had, about this time, pleaded old age and returned to his home. He had about his knees only one son, called Wang Xifeng."

When the company heard so far, they began to laugh.

"Now isn't this a duplicate of our girl Feng's name?" old lady Jia laughingly exclaimed.

A married woman hurried up and pushed (the girl). "That's the name of your lady Secunda," she said, "so don't use it quite so heedlessly!"

"Go on with your story!" dowager lady Jia shouted.

The girl speedily stood up, smiling the while. "We do deserve death!" she observed. "We weren't aware that it was our lady's worthy name."

"Why should you be in such fear and trembling?" lady Feng laughed. "Go on! There are many duplicate names and duplicate surnames."

The girl then proceeded with her story. "In a certain year," she resumed, "his honor old Mr. Wang saw his son Mr. Wang off for the capital to be in time for the examinations. One day, he was overtaken by a heavy shower of rain and he betook himself into a village for shelter. Who'd have thought it, there lived in this village, one of the gentry, of the name of Li, who had been an old friend of his honor old Mr. Wang, and he kept Mr. Wang junior to put up in his library. This Mr. Li had no son, but only a daughter. This young daughter's worthy name was Chuluan. She could perform on the lute; she could play chess; and she had a knowledge of books and of painting. There was nothing that she did not understand."

Old lady Jia eagerly chimed in. "It's no wonder," she said, "that the story has been called: 'A Feng seeks a Luan in marriage,' (a male phoenix seeks a female phoenix in marriage). But you needn't proceed. I've already guessed the denouement. There's no doubt that Wang Xifeng asks for the hand of this Miss Chuluan."

"Your venerable ladyship must really have heard the story before," the singing-girl smiled.

"What hasn't our worthy senior heard?" they all exclaimed. "But she's quick enough in guessing even unheard of things."

"All these stories run invariably in one line," old lady Jia laughingly rejoined. "They're all about pretty girls and scholars. There's no fun in them. They abuse people's daughters in every possible way, and then they still term them nice pretty girls. They're so concocted that there's not even a semblance of truth in them. From the very first, they canvass the families of the gentry. If the paterfamilias isn't a president of a board; then he's made a minister. The heroine is bound to be as lovable as a gem. This young lady is sure to understand all about letters, and propriety. She knows everything and is, in a word, a peerless beauty. At the sight of a handsome young man, she pays no heed as to whether he be relation or friend, but begins to entertain thoughts of the primary affair of her life, and forgets her parents and sets her books on one side. She behaves as neither devil nor thief would: so in what respect does she resemble a nice pretty girl? Were even her brain full of learning, she couldn't be accounted a nice pretty girl, after behaving in this manner!

Just like a young fellow, whose mind is well stored with book-lore, and who goes and plays the robber! Now is it likely that the Imperial laws would look upon him as a man of parts, and that they wouldn't bring against him some charge of robbery? From this it's evident that those who fabricate these stories contradict themselves. Besides, they may, it's true, say that the heroines belong to great families of official and literary status, that they're conversant with propriety and learning and that their honorable mothers too understand books and good manners, but great households like theirs must, in spite of the parents having pleaded old age and returned to their natives places, contain a great number of inmates; and the nurses, maids, and attendants on these young ladies must also be many; and how is it then that, whenever these stories make reference to such matters, one only hears of young ladies with but a single close attendant? What can, think for yourselves, all the other people be up to? Indeed, what is said before doesn't accord with what comes afterwards. Isn't it so, eh?"

The party listened to her with much glee. "These criticisms of yours, venerable ancestor," they said, "have laid bare every single discrepancy."

"They have however their reasons," old lady Jia smilingly resumed. "Among the writers of these stories, there are some, who begrudge people's wealth and honors, or possibly those, who having solicited a favor (of the wealthy and honorable), and not obtained the object, upon which their wishes were set, have fabricated lies in order to disparage people. There is moreover a certain class of persons, who become so corrupted by the perusal of such tales that they are not satisfied until they themselves pounce upon some nice pretty girl. Hence is it that, for fun's sake, they devise all these yarns. But how could such as they ever know the principle which prevails in official and literary families? Not to speak of the various official and literary families spoken about in these anecdotes, take now our own immediate case as an instance. We're only such a middle class household, and yet we've got none of those occurrences; so don't let her go on spinning these endless yarns. We must on no account have any of these stories told us! Why, even the maids themselves don't understand any of this sort of language. I've been getting so old the last few years, that I felt unawares quite melancholy whenever the girls went to live far off, so my wont has been to have a few passages recounted to me; but as soon as they got back, I at once put a stop to these things."

"Sister-in-law" Li and Mrs. Xue both laughed. "This is just the rule," they said, "which should exist in great families. Not even in our homes is any of this confused talk allowed to reach the ears of the young people."

Lady Feng came forward and poured some wine. "Enough, that will do!" she laughed. "The wine has got quite cold. My dear ancestor, do take a sip and moisten your throat with, before you begin again to dilate on falsehoods. What we've been having now can well be termed 'Record of a discussion on falsehoods.' It has had its origin in this reign, in this place, in this year, in this moon, on this day and at this very season. But, venerable senior, you've only got one mouth, so you couldn't very well simultaneously speak of two families. 'When two flowers open together,' the proverb says, 'one person can only speak of one.' But whether the stones be true or fictitious, don't let us say anything more about them. Let's have the footlights put in order, and look at the players. Dear senior, do let these two relatives have a glass of wine and see a couple of plays; and you can then start arguing about one dynasty after another. Eh, what do you say?"

Saying this, she poured the wine, laughing the while. But she had scarcely done speaking before the whole company were convulsed with laughter. The two singing girls were themselves unable to keep their countenance.

"Lady Secunda," they both exclaimed, "what a sharp tongue you have! Were your ladyship to take to storytelling, we really would have nowhere to earn our rice."

"Don't be in such overflowing spirits," Mrs. Xue laughed. "There are people outside; this isn't like any ordinary occasion."

"There's only my senior brother-in-law Zhen outside," lady Feng smiled. "And we've been like brother and sister from our youth up. We've romped and been up to every mischief to this age together. But all on account of my marriage, I've had of late years to stand on ever so many ceremonies. Why besides being like brother and sister from the time we were small kids, he's anyhow my senior brother-in-law, and I his junior sister-in-law. (One among) those twenty-four dutiful sons, travestied himself in theatrical costume (to amuse his parents), but those fellows haven't sufficient spirit to come in some stage togs and try and make you have a laugh, dear ancestor. I've however succeeded, after ever so much exertion, in so diverting you as to induce you to eat a little more than you would, and in putting everybody in good humor; and I should be thanked by one and all of you; it's only right that I should. But can it be that you will, on the contrary, poke fun at me?"

"I've truly not had a hearty laugh the last few days," old lady Jia smiled, "but thanks to the funny things she recounted just now, I've managed to get in somewhat better spirits in here. So I'll have another cup of wine." Then having drunk her wine, "Baoyu," she went on to say, "come and present a cup to your sister-in-law!"

Lady Feng gave a smile. "There's no use for him to give me any wine," she ventured. "(I'll drink out of your cup,) so as to bring upon myself your longevity, venerable ancestor."

While uttering this response, she raised dowager lady Jia's cup to her lips, and drained the remaining half of the contents; after which, she handed the cup to a waiting-maid, who took one from those which had been rinsed with tepid water, and brought it to her. But in due course, the cups from the various tables were cleared, and clean ones, washed in warm water, were substituted; and when fresh wine had been served round, (lady Feng and the maid) resumed their seats.

"Venerable lady," a singing-girl put in, "you don't like the stories we tell; but may we thrum a song for you?"

"You two," remarked old lady Jia, "had better play a duet of the 'Jiang Jun Ling' song: 'The General's Command.'"

Hearing her wishes, the two girls promptly tuned their cords to suit the pitch of the song and struck up on their guitars.

"What watch of the night is it?" old lady Jia at this point inquired.

"It's the third watch," the matrons replied with alacrity.

"No wonder it has got so chilly and damp!" old lady Jia added.

Extra clothes were accordingly soon fetched by the servants and maids.

Madame Wang speedily rose to her feet and forced a smile. "Venerable senior," she said, "wouldn't it be prudent for you to move on to the stove-couch in the winter apartments? It would be as well. These two relatives are no strangers. And if we entertain them, it will be all right."

"Well, in that case," dowager lady Jia smilingly rejoined, "why shouldn't the whole company adjourn inside? Wouldn't it be warmer for us all?"

"I'm afraid there isn't enough sitting room for everyone of us," Madame Wang explained.

"I've got a plan," old lady Jia added. "We can now dispense with these tables. All we need are two or three, placed side by side; we can then sit in a group, and by bundling together it will be both sociable as well as warm."

"Yes, this will be nice!" one and all cried.

Assenting, they forthwith rose from table. The married women hastened to remove the debandade of the banquet. Then placing three large tables lengthways side by side in the inner rooms, they went on to properly arrange the fruits and viands, some of which had been replenished, others changed.

"You must none of you stand on any ceremonies!" dowager lady Jia observed. "If you just listen while I allot you your places, and sit down accordingly, it will be all right!"

Continuing, she motioned to Mrs. Xue and "sister-in-law" Li to take the upper seats on the side of honor, and, making herself comfortable on the west, she bade the three cousins Baoqin, Daiyu, and Xiangyun sit close to her on the left and on the right. "Baoyu," she proceeded "you must go next to your mother." So presently she put Baoyu, and Baochai, and the rest of the young ladies between Mesdames Xing and Wang. On the west, she placed, in proper gradation, dame Lou, along with Jia Jun, and Mrs. You and Li Wan, with Jia Lan, between them. While she assigned a chair to Jia Rong's wife among the lower seats, put crosswise.

"Brother Zhen," old lady Jia cried, "take your cousins and be off! I'm also going to sleep in a little time."

Jia Zhen and his associates speedily expressed their obedience, and made, in a body, their appearance inside again to listen to any injunctions she might have to give them.

"Bundle yourself away at once!" shouted dowager lady Jia. "You needn't come in. We've just sat down, and you'll make us get up again. Go and rest; be quick! Tomorrow, there are to be some more grand doings!" Jia Zhen assented with alacrity. "But Rong'er should remain to replenish the cups," he smiled; "it's only fair that he should."

"Quite so!" answered old lady Jia laughingly. "I forgot all about him."

"Yes!" acquiesced Jia Zhen. Then twisting himself round, he led Jia Lian and his companions out of the apartment.

(Jia Zhen and Jia Lian) were, of course, both pleased at being able to get away. So bidding the servants see Jia Cong and Jia Huang to their respective homes, (Jia Zhen) arranged with Jia Lian to go in pursuit of pleasure and in quest of fun. But we will now leave them to their own devices without another word.

"I was just thinking," meanwhile dowager lady Jia laughed, "that it would be well, although you people are numerous enough to enjoy yourselves, to have a couple of great-grandchildren present at this banquet, so Rong'er now makes the full complement. But Rong'er sit near your wife, for she and you will then make the pair complete."

The wife of a domestic thereupon presented a playbill.

"We, ladies," old lady Jia demurred, "are now chatting in high glee, and are about to start a romp. Those young folks have, also, been sitting up so far into the night that they must be quite cold, so let the plays alone. Tell them then to have a rest. Yet call our own girls to come and sing a couple of plays on this stage. They too will thus have a chance of watching us a bit."

After lending an ear to her, the married women assented and quitted the room. And immediately finding some servant to go to the garden of

Broad Vista and summon the girls, they betook themselves, at the same time, as far as the second gate and called a few pages to wait on them.

The pages went with hurried step to the rooms reserved for the players, and taking with them the various grown-up members of the company, they only left the more youthful behind. Then fetching, in a little time, Wenguan and a few other girls, twelve in all, from among the novices in the Pear Fragrance court, they egressed by the corner gate leading out of the covered passage. The matrons took soft bundles in their arms, as their strength was not equal to carrying boxes. And under the conviction that their old mistress would prefer plays of three or five acts, they had put together the necessary theatrical costumes.

After Wenguan and the rest of the girls had been introduced into the room by the matrons, they paid their obeisance, and, dropping their arms against their sides, they stood reverentially.

"In this propitious first moon," old lady Jia smiled, "won't your teacher let you come out for a stroll? What are you singing now? The eight acts of the 'Eight worthies' recently sung here were so noisy, that they made my head ache; so you'd better let us have something more quiet. You must however bear in mind that Mrs. Xue and Mrs. Li are both people who give theatricals, and have heard I don't know how many fine plays. The young ladies here have seen better plays than our own girls; and they have heard more beautiful songs than they. These actresses, you see here now, formed once, despite their youth, part of a company belonging to renowned families, fond of plays; and though mere children, they excel any troupe composed of grown-up persons. So whatever we do, don't let us say anything disparaging about them. But we must now have something new. Tell Fangguan to sing us the 'Xun Meng' ballad; and let only flutes and Pandean pipes be used. The other instruments can be dispensed with."

"Your venerable ladyship is quite right," Wenguan smiled. "Our acting couldn't, certainly, suit the taste of such people as Mrs. Xue, Mrs. Li, and the young ladies. Nevertheless, let them merely heed our enunciation, and listen to our voices; that's all."

"Well said!" dowager lady Jia laughed.

"Sister-in-law" Li and Mrs. Xue were filled with delight. "What a sharp girl!" they remarked smilingly. "But do you also try to imitate our old lady by pulling our leg?"

"They're intended to afford us some ready-at-hand recreation," old lady Jia smiled. "Besides, they don't go out to earn money. That's how it is they are not so much up to the times." At the close of this remark, she also desired Kuiguan to sing the play: "Hui Ming sends a letter." "You needn't," she added, "make your face up. Just sing this couple of plays so as to merely let both those ladies hear a kind of parody of them. But if you spare yourselves the least exertion, I shall be unhappy."

When they heard this, Wenguan and her companions left the apartment and promptly apparelled themselves and mounted the stage. First in order, was sung the "Xun Meng;" next, "(Hui Ming) sends a letter;" during which, everybody observed such perfect silence that not so much as the caw of a crow fell on the ear.

"I've verily seen several hundreds of companies," Mrs. Xue smiled, "but never have I come across any that confined themselves to flutes."

"There are some," dowager lady Jia answered. "In fact, in that play acted just now called: 'Love in the western tower at Chu Jiang,' there's a good deal sung by young actors in unison with the flutes. But lengthy unison pieces of this description are indeed few. This too, however, is purely a matter of taste; there's nothing out of the way about it. When I was of her age," resuming, she pointed at Xiangyun, "her grandfather kept a troupe of young actresses. There was among them one, who played the lute so efficiently that she performed the part when the lute is heard in the 'Xixiang Ji,' the piece on the lute in the 'Yu Zan Ji,' and that in the supplementary 'Pi Pa Chi,' on the Mongol flageolet with the eighteen notes, in every way as if she had been placed in the real circumstances herself. Yea, far better than this!"

"This is still rarer a thing!" the inmates exclaimed.

Old lady Jia then shortly called the married women, and bade them tell Wenguan and the other girls to use both wind and string instruments and render the piece: "At the feast of lanterns, the moon is round."

The women servants received her orders and went to execute them. Jia Rong and his wife meanwhile passed the wine round.

When lady Feng saw dowager lady Jia in most exuberant spirits, she smiled. "Won't it be nice," she said, "to avail ourselves of the presence of the singing girls to pass plum blossom round and have the game of forfeits: 'Spring-happy eyebrow-corners-go-up,' eh?"

"That's a fine game of forfeits!" Old lady Jia cried, with a smile. "It just suits the time of the year."

Orders were therefore given at once to fetch a forfeit drum, varnished black, and ornamented with designs executed with copper tacks. When brought, it was handed to the singing girls to put on the table and rap on it. A twig of red plum blossom was then obtained. "The one in whose hand it is when the drum stops," dowager lady Jia laughingly proposed, "will have to drink a cup of wine, and to say something or other as well."

"I'll tell you what," lady Feng interposed with a smile. "Who of us can pit herself against you, dear ancestor, who have ever ready at hand whatever you want to say? With the little use we are in this line, won't there be an absolute lack of fun in our contributions? My idea is that it would be nicer were something said that could be appreciated both by the refined as well as the unrefined. So won't it be preferable that the person, in whose hands the twig remains, when the drum stops, should crack some joke or other?"

Everyone who heard her was fully aware what a good hand she had always been at witty things, and how she, more than any other, had an inexhaustible supply of novel and amusing rules of forfeits, ever stocked in her mind, so her suggestion not only gratified the various inmates of the family seated at the banquet, but even filled the whole posse of servants, both old and young, who stood in attendance below, with intense delight. The young waiting-maids rushed with eagerness in search of the young ladies and told them to come and listen to their lady Secunda, who was on the point again of saying funny things. A whole crowd of servant-girls anxiously pressed inside and crammed the room. In a little time, the theatricals were brought to a close, and the music was stopped. Dowager lady Jia had some soup, fine cakes, and fruits handed to Wenguan and her companions to regale themselves with, and then gave orders to sound the drum. The singing-girls were both experts, so now they beat fast; and now slow. Either slow like the dripping of the remnants of water in a clepsydra. Or quick, as when beans are being sown. Or with the velocity of the pace of a scared horse, or that of the flash of a swift lightning. The sound of the drum came to a standstill abruptly. The twig of plum blossom had just reached old lady Jia, when by a strange coincidence, the rattle ceased. Everyone blurted out into a boisterous fit of laughter. Jia Rong hastily approached and filled a cup. "It's only natural," they laughingly cried, "that you venerable senior, should be the first to get exhilarated; for then, thanks to you, we shall also come in for some measure of good cheer."

"To gulp down this wine is an easy job," dowager lady smiled, "but to crack jokes is somewhat difficult."

"Your jokes, dear ancestor, are even wittier than those of lady Feng," the party shouted, "so favor us with one, and let's have a laugh!"

"I've nothing out of the way to evoke laughter with," old lady Jia smilingly answered. "Yet all that remains for me to do is to thicken the skin of my antiquated phiz and come out with some joke. In a certain family," she consequently went on to narrate, "there were ten sons; these married ten wives. The tenth of these wives was, however, so intelligent, sharp, quick of mind, and glib of tongue, that her father and mother-in-law loved her best of all, and maintained from morning to night that the other nine were not filial. These nine felt much aggrieved and they accordingly took counsel together. 'We nine,' they said, 'are filial enough at heart; the only thing is that that shrew has the gift of the gab. That's why our father and mother-in-law think her so perfect. But to whom can we go and confide our grievance?' One of them was struck with an idea. 'Let's go tomorrow,' she proposed, 'to the temple of the King of Hell and burn incense. We can then tell the King our grudge and ask him how it was that, when he bade us receive life and become human beings, he only conferred a glib tongue on that vixen and that we were only allotted such blunt mouths?' The eight listened to her plan, and were quite enraptured with it. 'This proposal is faultless!' they assented. On the next day, they sped in a body to the temple of the God of Hell, and after burning incense, the nine sisters-in-law slept under the altar, on which their offerings were laid. Their nine spirits waited with the special purpose of seeing the carriage of the King of Hell arrive; but they waited and waited, and yet he did not come. They were just giving way to despair when they espied Sun Xingzhe, (the god of monkeys,) advancing on a rolling cloud. He espied the nine spirits, and felt inclined to take a golden rod and beat them. The nine spirits were plunged in terror. Hastily they fell on their knees, and pleaded for mercy.

"'What are you up to?' Sun Xingzhe inquired.

"The nine women, with alacrity, told him all.

"After Sun Xingzhe had listened to their confidences, he stamped his foot and heaved a sigh. 'Is that the case?' he asked. 'Well, it's lucky enough you came across me, for had you waited for the God of Hell, he wouldn't have known anything about it.'

"At these assurances, the nine women gave way to entreaties. 'Great saint,' they pleaded, 'if you were to display some commiseration, we would be all right.'

"Sun Xingzhe smiled. 'There's no difficulty in the way,' he observed. 'On the day on which you ten sisters-in-law came to life, I was, as luck would have it, on a visit to the King of Hell's place. So I (saw) him do something on the ground, and the junior sister-of-law of yours lap it up. But if you now wish to become smart and sharp-tongued, the remedy lies in water. If I too were therefore to do something, and you to drink it, the desired effect will be attained.'"

At the close of her story, the company roared with laughter.

"Splendid!" shouted lady Feng. "But luckily we're all slow of tongue and dull of intellect, otherwise, we too must have had the water of monkeys to drink."

"Who among us here," Mrs. You and dame Lou smilingly remarked, addressing themselves to Li Wan, "has tasted any monkey's water. So don't sham ignorance of things!"

"A joke must hit the point to be amusing," Mrs. Xue ventured.

But while she spoke, (the girls) began again to beat the drum. The young maids were keen to hear lady Feng's jokes. They therefore explained to the singing girls, in a confidential tone, that a cough would be the given signal (for them to desist). In no time (the blossom) was handed round on both sides. As soon as it came to lady Feng, the young maids purposely gave a cough. The singing-girl at once stopped short. "Now we've caught her!" shouted the party laughingly; "drink your wine, be quick! And mind you tell something nice! But don't make us laugh so heartily as to get stomachaches."

Lady Feng was lost in thought. Presently, she began with a smile. "A certain household," she said, "was celebrating the first moon festival. The entire family was enjoying the sight of the lanterns, and drinking their wine. In real truth unusual excitement prevailed. There were great-grandmothers, grandmothers, daughters-in-law, grandsons' wives, great-grandsons, granddaughters, granddaughters-in-law, aunts' granddaughters, cousins' granddaughters; and ai-yo-yo, there was verily such a bustle and confusion!"

While minding her story, they laughed. "Listen to all this mean mouth says!" they cried. "We wonder what other ramifications she won't introduce!"

"If you want to bully me," Mrs. You smiled, "I'll tear that mouth of yours to pieces."

Lady Feng rose to her feet and clapped her hands.

"One does all one can to rack one's brain," she smiled, "and here you combine to do your utmost to confuse me! Well, if it is so, I won't go on."

"Proceed with your story," old lady Jia exclaimed with a smile. "What comes afterwards?"

Lady Feng thought for a while. "Well, after that," she continued laughingly, "they all sat together and crammed the whole room. They primed themselves with wine throughout the hours of night and then they broke up."

The various inmates noticed in what a serious and sedate manner she narrated her story, and none ventured to pass any further remarks, but waited anxiously for her to go on, when they became aware that she coldly and drily came to a stop.

Shi Xiangyun stared at her for ever so long.

"I'll tell you another," lady Feng laughingly remarked. "At the first moon festival, several persons carried a cracker as large as a room and went out of town to let it off. Over and above ten thousand persons were attracted, and they followed to see the sight. One among them was of an impatient disposition. He could not reconcile himself to wait; so stealthily he snatched a joss-stick and set fire to it. A sound of 'pu chi' was heard. The whole number of spectators laughed boisterously and withdrew. The persons, who carried the cracker, felt a grudge against the cracker-seller for not having made it tight, (and wondered) how it was that everyone had left without hearing it go off."

Is it likely that the men themselves didn't hear the report?" Xiang-yun insinuated.

"Why, the men themselves were deaf," lady Feng rejoined.

After listening to her, they pondered for a while, and then suddenly they laughed aloud in chorus. But remembering that her first story had been left unfinished, they inquired of her: "What was, after all, the issue of the first story? You should conclude that too."

Lady Feng gave a rap on the table with her hand. "How vexatious you are!" she exclaimed. "Well, the next day was the sixteenth; so the festivities of the year were over, and the feast itself was past and gone. I see people busy putting things away, and fussing about still, so how can I make out what will be the end of it all?"

At this, one and all indulged in renewed merriment.

"The fourth watch has long ago been struck outside," lady Feng smilingly said. "From what I can see, our worthy senior is also tired out; and we should, like when the cracker was let off in that story of the deaf people, be bundling ourselves off and finish!"

Mrs. You and the rest covered their mouths with their handkerchiefs and laughed. Now they stooped forward; and now they bent backward. And pointing at her, "This thing," they cried, "has really a mean tongue."

Old lady Jia laughed. "Yes," she said, "this vixen Feng has, in real truth, developed a meaner tongue than ever! But she alluded to crackers," she added, "so let's also let off a few fireworks so as to counteract the fumes of the wine."

Jia Rong overheard the suggestion. Hurriedly leaving the room, he took the pages with him, and having a scaffolding erected in the court, they hung up the fireworks, and got everything in perfect readiness. These fireworks were articles of tribute, sent from different states, and were, albeit not large in size, contrived with extreme ingenuity. The representations of various kinds of events of antiquity were perfect, and in them were inserted all sorts of crackers.

Lin Daiyu was naturally of a weak disposition, so she could not stand the report of any loud intonation. Her grandmother Jia therefore clasped her immediately in her embrace. Mrs. Xue, meanwhile, took Xiangyun in her arms.

"I'm not afraid," smiled Xiangyun.

"Nothing she likes so much as letting off huge crackers," Baochai smilingly interposed, "and could she fear this sort of thing?"

Madame Wang, thereupon, laid hold of Baoyu, and pulled him in her lap.

"We've got no one to care a rap for us," lady Feng laughed.

"I'm here for you," Mrs. You rejoined with a laugh. "I'll embrace you. There you're again behaving like a spoilt child. You've heard about crackers, and you comport yourself as if you'd had honey to eat! You're quite frivolous again today!"

"Wait till we break up," lady Feng answered laughing, "and we'll go and let some off in our garden. I can fire them far better than any of the young lads!"

While they bandied words, one kind of firework after another was lighted outside, and then later on some more again. Among these figured "fill-heaven-stars;" "nine dragons-enter-clouds;" "over-whole-land-a-crack-of-thunder;" "fly-up-heavens;" "sound-ten shots," and other such small crackers.

The fireworks over, the young actresses were again asked to render the "Lotus-flowers-fall,'" and cash were strewn upon the stage. The young girls bustled all over the boards, snatching cash and capering about.

The soup was next brought. "The night is long," old lady Jia said, "and somehow or other I feel peckish."

"There's some congee," lady Feng promptly remarked, "prepared with duck's meat."

"I'd rather have plain things," dowager lady Jia answered.

"There's also some congee made with non-glutinous rice and powder of dates. It's been cooked for the ladies who fast."

"If there's any of this, it will do very well," old lady Jia replied.

While she spoke, orders were given to remove the remnants of the banquet, and inside as well as outside were served every kind of recherché small dishes. One and all then partook of some of these refreshments, at their pleasure, and rinsing their mouths with tea, they afterwards parted.

On the seventeenth, they also repaired, at an early hour, to the Ning mansion to present their compliments; and remaining in attendance, while the doors of the ancestral hall were closed and the images put away, they, at length, returned to their quarters.

Invitations had been issued on this occasion to drink the new year wine at Mrs. Xue's residence. But dowager lady Jia had been out on several consecutive days, and so tired out did she feel that she withdrew to her rooms, after only a short stay.

After the eighteenth, relatives and friends arrived and made their formal invitations; or else they came as guests to the banquets given. But so little was old lady Jia in a fit state to turn her mind to anything that the two ladies, Madame Xing and lady Feng, had to attend between them to everything that cropped up. But Baoyu as well did not go anywhere else than to Wang Ziteng's, and the excuse he gave out was that his grandmother kept him at home to dispel her ennui.

We need not, however, dilate on irrelevant details. In due course, the festival of the fifteenth of the first moon passed. But, reader, if you have any curiosity to learn any subsequent events, listen to those given in the chapter below.

CHAPTER 55

The stupid secondary wife, dame Zhao, needlessly loses her temper and insults her own daughter, Tanchun. The perverse servant-girls are so full of malice that they look down contemptuously on their youthful mistresses.

We will now resume our narration with the Rong Mansion. Soon after the bustle of the new year festivities, lady Feng who, with the most arduous duties she had had to fulfil both before and after the new year, had found little time to take proper care of herself, got a miscarriage and could not attend to the management of domestic affairs. Day after day two and three doctors came and prescribed for her. But lady Feng had ever accustomed herself to be hardy, so although unable to go out of doors, she nevertheless devised the ways and means for everything, and made the various arrangements she deemed necessary, and whatever concern suggested itself to her mind, she entrusted to Ping'er to lay before Madame Wang. But however much people advised her to be careful, she would not lend an ear to them. Madame Wang felt as if she had been deprived of her right arm. And as she alone had not sufficient energy to see to everything, she bestowed her own attention upon such important affairs, as turned up, and entrusted, for the time being, all miscellaneous domestic matters to the co-operation of Li Wan.

Li Wan had at all times held virtue at a high price, and set but little value on talents of any kind, so that she, as a matter of course, displayed leniency to those who were placed under her. Madame Wang accordingly bade Tanchun combine with Li Wan in the management of the household. "In a month," she argued, "lady Feng will be getting all right again, and then you can once more hand over charge to her."

Little, however, though one would think it, lady Feng was endowed with a poor physique. From her youth up, moreover, she had not known how to husband her health; and emulation and contentiousness had, more than anything else, combined to undermine her vital energies. Hence it was that although her complaint was a simple miscarriage, it had really, after all, been the outcome of loss of vigor. After a month symptoms of emissions of blood began also to show themselves. And notwithstanding her reluctance to utter what she felt everyone, at the sight of her sallow and emaciated face, readily concluded that she was not nursing herself as well as she should.

Madame Wang therefore enjoined her merely to take her medicines and look to herself with due care; and she would not allow her to disquiet her mind about the least thing. But (lady Feng) herself also gave way to misgivings lest her illness should assume some grave phase, and much though she laughed with one and all, she was ever mindful to steal time to attend to her health, feeling inwardly vexed at not being able to soon get back her old strength again. But she had, as it happened, to dose herself with medicines and to nurse herself for three whole months, before she gradually began to rally and before the discharges stopped by degrees. But we will abstain from any reference to these details which pertain to the future, suffice it now to add that though Madame Wang noticed her improved state, (she thought it) impossible for the time being for Tanchun and Li Wan to resign their charge. But so fidgetty was she lest with the large number of inmates in the garden proper control should not be exercised that she specially sent for Baochai and begged of her to keep an eye over every place, explaining to her that the old matrons were of no earthly use, for whenever they could obtain any leisure, they drank and gambled; and slept during broad daylight, while they played at cards during the hours of night. "I know all about their doings" (she said). "When that girl Feng is well enough to go out, they have some little fear. But they're bound at present to consult again their own convenience. Yet you, dear child, are one in whom I can repose complete trust. Your brother and your female cousins are, on the one hand, young; and I can, on the other, afford no spare time; so do exert yourself on my behalf for a couple of days, and exercise proper supervision. And should anything unexpected turn up, just come and tell it to me. Don't wait until our old lady inquires about it, as I shall then find myself in a corner with nothing to say in my defence. If those servants aren't on their good behavior, mind you blow them up; and if they don't listen to you, come and lay your complaint before me; for it will be best not to let anything assume a serious aspect."

Baochai listened to her appeal and felt under the necessity of volunteering to undertake the charge.

The season was about the close of spring, so Daiyu got her cough back again. But Xiangyun was likewise laid up in the Hengwu Yuan, as she too was affected by the weather, and day after day she saw numberless doctors and took endless medicines.

Tanchun and Li Wan lived apart, but as they had of late assumed joint management of affairs, it was, unlike former years, extremely inconvenient even for the servants to go backwards and forwards to make their reports. They consequently resolved that they should meet early every day in the small three-roomed reception-hall, at the south side of the garden gate, to transact what business there was, and that their morning meal over, they should after noon return again to their quarters.

This three-roomed hall had originally been got ready at the time of the visit of the Imperial consort to her parents, to accommodate the attendants and eunuchs. This visit over, it proved, therefore, no longer of use, and the old matrons simply came to it every night to keep watch. But mild weather had now set in, and any complete fittings were quite superfluous. All that could be seen about amounted to a few small pieces of furniture just sufficient for them to make themselves comfortable with. Over this hall was likewise affixed a placard, with the inscription in four characters: "Perfected philanthropy, published virtue!"

Yet the place was generally known among the domestics as "the discuss-matters-hall." To this hall, (Li Wan and Tanchun) would daily adjourn at six in the morning, and leave it at noon, and the wives of the managers and other servants, who had any matters to lay before them, came and went in incessant strings.

When the domestics heard that Li Wan would assume sole control, each and all felt secretly elated; for as Li Wan had always been considerate, forbearing, and loath to inflict penalties, she would be, of course, they thought, easier to put off than lady Feng. Even when Tanchun was added, they again remembered that she was only a youthful unmarried girl and that she too had ever shown herself goodnatured and kindly to a degree, so none of them worried their minds about her, and they became considerably more indolent than when they had to deal with lady Feng. But after the expiry of three or four days several concerns passed through her hands, which gave them an opportunity to gradually find out that Tanchun did not, in smartness and thoroughness, yield to lady Feng, and that the only difference between them was that she was soft in speech and gentle in disposition. By a remarkable coincidence, princes, dukes, marquises, earls, and hereditary officials arrived for consecutive days from various parts; all of whom were, if not the relatives of the Rong and Ning mansions, at least their old friends. There were either those who had obtained transfers on promotion, or others who had been degraded; either those, who had married, or those who had gone into mourning, and Madame Wang had so much congratulating and condoling, receiving and escorting to do that she had no time to attend to any entertaining. There was therefore less than ever anyone in the front part to look after things. So while (Tanchun and Li Wan) spent their whole days in the hall, Baochai tarried all day in the drawing-rooms, to keep an eye over what was going on; and they only betook themselves back to their quarters after Madame Wang's return. Of a night, they whiled away their leisure hours by doing needlework; but they would, previous to retiring to sleep, get into their chairs, and, taking along with them the servants, whose duty it was to be on night watch in the garden, and other domestics as well, they visited each place on their round. Such was the control exercised by these three inmates that signs were not wanting to prove that greater severity was observed than in the days when the management devolved on lady Feng. To this reason must be assigned the fact that all the servants attached inside as well as outside cherished a secret grudge against them. "No sooner," they insinuated, "has one patrolling ogre come than they add three more cerberean sort of spring josses so that even at night we've got less time than ever to sip a cup of wine and indulge in a romp!"

On the day that Madame Wang was going to a banquet at the mansion of the Marquis of Jinxiang, Li Wan and Tanchun arranged their coiffure and performed their ablutions at an early hour; and after waiting upon her until she went out of doors, they repaired into the hall and installed themselves in their seats. But just as they were sipping their tea, they espied Wu Xindeng's wife walk in. "Mrs. Zhao's brother, Zhao Guoji," she observed, "departed this life yesterday; the tidings have already been reported to our old mistress and our lady, who said that it was all right, and bade me tell you, Miss."

At the close of this announcement, she respectfully dropped her arms against her body, and stood aloof without adding another word. The servants, who came at this season to lay their reports before (Tanchun and Li Wan), mustered no small number. But they all endeavored to find out how their two new mistresses ran the household; for as long they managed things properly, one and all willingly resolved to respect them, but in the event of the least disagreement or improper step, not only did they not submit to them, but they also spread, the moment they put their foot outside the second gate, numberless jokes on their account and made fun of them. Wu Xindeng's wife had thus devised an experiment in her own mind. Had she had to deal with lady Feng, she would have long ago made an attempt to show off her zeal by proposing numerous alternatives and discovering various bygone precedents, and then allowed lady Feng to make her own choice and take action; but, in this instance, she looked with such disdain on Li

Wan, on account of her simplicity, and on Tanchun, on account of her youthfulness, that she volunteered only a single sentence, in order to put both these ladies to the test, and see what course they would be likely to adopt.

"What shall we do?" Tanchun asked Li Wan.

Li Wan reflected for a while. "The other day," she rejoined, "that Xiren's mother died, I heard that she was given forty taels. So now give her forty taels as well and have done!"

Upon hearing this proposal, Wu Xindeng's wife eagerly expressed her acquiescence, by uttering a yes; and taking over the permit she was going on her way at once.

"Come back," shouted Tanchun.

"Wu Xingdeng's wife had perforce to retrace her footsteps.

"Wait, don't get the money yet," Tanchun remarked. "I want to ask you something. Some of the old secondary wives, attached years back to our venerable senior's rooms, lived inside the establishment; others outside; there were these two distinctions between them. Now if any of them died at home, how much was allowed them? And how much was allotted to such as died outside? Tell us what was given in either case for our guidance."

As soon as Wu Xindeng's wife was asked this question, every detail bearing on the subject slipped from her memory. Hastily forcing a smile, "This is," she replied, "nothing of any such great consequence. Whether much or little be allowed, who'll ever venture to raise a quarrel about it?"

Tanchun then smiled. "This is all stuff and nonsense!" she exclaimed. "My idea is that it would be better to give a hundred taels. For if we don't comply with what's right, we shall, not to speak of your ridiculing us, find it also a hard job by and bye to face your mistress Secunda."

"Well, in that case," laughed Wu Xindeng's wife, "I'll go and look up the old accounts. I can't recollect anything about them just at this moment."

"You're quite an old hand in the management of affairs," Tanchun observed with a significant smile, "and can't you remember, but come instead to perplex us? Whenever you've had anything of the kind to lay before your lady Secunda, have you also had to go first and look it up? But if this has been the practice, lady Feng can't be looked upon as being such a dreadful creature. One could very well call her lenient and kind. Yet don't you yet hurry to go and hunt them up and bring them to me to see? If we dilly-dally another day, they won't run you people down for your coarse-mindedness, but we will seem to have been driven to our wits' ends!"

Wu Xindeng's wife got quite scarlet in the face. Promptly twisting herself round, she quitted the hall; while the whole bevy of married women stretched out their tongues significantly.

During her absence, other matters were reported. But in a little while, Wu Xindeng's wife returned with the old accounts. On inspection, Tanchun found that for a couple of secondary wives, who had lived in the establishment, twenty-four taels had been granted, and that for two, whose quarters had been outside, forty taels had in each case been allowed. Besides these two, others were mentioned, who had lived outside the mansion; to one of whom a hundred taels had been given, and to the other, sixty taels. Under these two records, the reasons were assigned. In the one case, the coffins of father and mother had had to be removed from another province, and sixty taels extra had consequently been granted. In the other, an additional twenty taels had been allowed, as a burial-place had to be purchased at the time.

Tanchun handed the accounts to Li Wan for her perusal.

"Give her twenty taels," readily suggested Tanchun. "Leave these accounts here for us to examine minutely."

Wu Xindeng's wife then walked away. But unexpectedly Mrs. Zhao entered the hall. Li Wan and Tanchun speedily pressed her to take a seat.

Mrs. Zhao then broke the silence. "All the inmates of these rooms have trampled me under heel," she said, "but never mind! Yet, my child, just ponder, it is only fair that you should take my part."

While ventilating her grievances, her eyes got moist, her nose watered, and she began to sob.

"To whom are you alluding Mrs. Zhao?" Tanchun hastily inquired. "I can't really make out what you're driving at. Who tramples you under foot? Speak out and I'll take up your cudgels."

"You're now trampling me down yourself, young lady," Mrs. Zhao observed. "And to whom can I go and tell my grievance?"

Tanchun, at these words, jumped up with alacrity. "I never would presume to do any such thing," she protested.

Li Wan too vehemently sprung to her feet to proffer her some good counsel.

"Pray seat yourselves, both of you," Mrs. Zhao cried, "and listen to what I have to say. I've had, like simmering oil, to consume away in these rooms to this advanced age. There's also your brother besides. Yet I can't compare myself now even to Xiren, and what credit do I enjoy? But you haven't as well any face, so don't let's speak of myself."

"It was really on account of this," Tanchun smiled, "that I said that I didn't presume to disregard right and to violate propriety."

While she spoke, she resumed her seat, and taking up the accounts, she turned them over for Mrs. Zhao to glance at, after which she read them out to her for her edification. "These are old customs," she proceeded, "enforced by the seniors of the family, and everyone complies with them, and could I ever, pray, have changed them? These will hold good not only with Xiren; but even when by and bye Huan'er takes a concubine, the same course will naturally be adopted as in the case of Xiren. This is no question for any large quarrels or small disputes, and no mention should be made about face or no face. She's our Madame Wang's servant-girl, and I've dealt with her according to a long-standing precedent. Those who say that I've taken suitable action will come in for our ancestors' bounty and our lady's bounty as well. But should anyone uphold that I've adopted an unfair course, that person is devoid of all common sense and totally ignorant of what a blessing means. The only thing she can do is to foster as much resentment as she chooses. Our lady, Madame Wang, may even give a present of a house to anyone; what credit is that to me? Again, she may not give a single cash, but even that won't imply any loss of face, as far as I am concerned. What I have to say is that as Madame Wang is away from home, you should quietly look after yourself a bit. What's the good of worrying and fretting? Our lady is extremely fond of me; and, if, at different times, a chilliness has sprung up on her part, it's because you, Mrs. Zhao, have again and again been officious. Had I been a man and able to have gone abroad, I would long ago have run away and started some business. I would then have had something of my own to attend to. But, as it happens, I am a girl, so that I can't even recklessly utter so much as a single remark. Madame Wang is well aware of it in her heart. And it's now because she entertains a high opinion of me that she recently bade me assume the charge of domestic affairs. But before I've had time enough to do a single good act, here you come, Mrs. Zhao, to lay down the law. If this reaches Madame Wang's ear, I fear I shall get into trouble. She won't let me exercise any control, and then I shall, in real earnest, come in for no face. But even you, Mrs. Zhao, will then actually lose countenance."

Reasoning with her, she so little could repress her tears that they rolled down her cheeks.

Mrs. Zhao had not a word more to say to refute her arguments with. "If Madame Wang loves you," she simply responded, "there's still more reason why you should have drawn us into her favor. (Instead of that), all you think about is to try and win Madame Wang's affections, and you forget all about us."

"How ever did I forget you?" Tanchun exclaimed. "How would you have me drag you into favor? Go and ask everyone of them, and you'll see what mistress is indifferent to anyone, who exerts her energies and makes herself useful, and what worthy person requires being drawn into favor?"

Li Wan, who stood by, did her best to pacify them with her advice. "Mrs. Zhao," she argued, "don't lose your temper! Neither should you feel any ill-will against this young lady of yours. Had she even at heart every good intention to lend you a hand, how could she put it into words?"

"This worthy senior dame," Tanchun impatiently interposed, "has also grown quite dense! Whom could I drag into favor? Why, in what family, do the young ladies give a lift to slave-girls? Their qualities as well as defects should all alike be well known to you people. And what have they got to do with me?"

Mrs. Zhao was much incensed. "Who tells you," she asked, "to give a lift to anyone? Were it not that you looked after the house, I wouldn't have come to inquire anything of you. But anything you may suggest is right; so had you, now that your maternal uncle is dead, granted twenty or thirty taels in excess, is it likely that Madame Wang would not have given you her consent? It's evident that our Madame Wang is a good woman and that it's you people who are mean and stingy. Unfortunately, however, her ladyship has with all her bounty no opportunity of exercising it. You could, my dear girl, well set your mind at ease. You wouldn't, in this instance, have had to spend any of your own money; and at your marriage by and bye, I would still have borne in mind the exceptional regard you had shown the Zhao family. But now that you've got your full plumage, you've forgotten your extraction, and chosen a lofty branch to fly to."

Before Tanchun had heard her to the end, she flew into such a rage that her face blanched; and choking for breath, she gasped and panted. Sobbing, she asked the while: "Who's my maternal uncle? My maternal uncle was at the end of the year promoted to be High Commissioner of the Nine Provinces! How can another maternal uncle have cropped up? It's because I've ever shown that reverence enjoined by the rites that other relatives have now more than ever turned up. If what you say be the case, how is it that every day that Huan'er goes out, Zhao Guoji too stands up, and follows him to school? Why doesn't he put on the airs of an uncle? What's the reason that he doesn't? Who isn't aware of the fact that I'm born of a concubine? Would it require two or three months' time to trace my extraction? But the fact is you've come to kick up all this hullaballoo for fear lest people shouldn't be alive to the truth; and with the express design of making it public all over the place! But I wonder who of us two will make the other lose face? Luckily, I've got my wits about me; for had I been a stupid creature ignorant of good manners, I would long ago have lost all patience."

Li Wan was much concerned, but she had to continue to exhort them to desist. But Mrs. Zhao proceeded with a long rigmarole until a servant was unexpectedly heard to report that lady Secunda had sent Miss Ping to deliver a message. Mrs. Zhao caught the announcement, and eventually held her peace, when they espied Ping'er making her appearance. Mrs. Zhao hastily forced a saturnine smile, and motioned to her to take a seat. "Is your lady any better?" she went on to inquire with vehemence. "I was just thinking of going to look her up; but I could find no leisure!"

Upon seeing Ping'er enter, Li Wan felt prompted to ask her the object of her visit.

"My lady says," Ping'er smilingly responded, "that she apprehends, now that Mrs. Zhao's brother is dead, that your ladyship and you, miss, are not aware of the existence of an old precedent. According to the ordinary practice no more need be given than twenty taels; but she now requests you, miss, to consider what would be best to do; if even you add a good deal more, it will do well enough."

Tanchun at once wiped away all traces of tears. "What's the use of another addition, when there's no valid reason for it?" she promptly demurred. "Who has again been twenty months in the womb? Or is it forsooth anyone who's gone to the wars, and managed to escape with his life, carrying his master on his back? Your mistress is certainly very ingenious! She tells me to disregard the precedent, in order that she should pose as a benefactress! She wishes to take the money, which Madame Wang spurns, so as to reap the pleasure of conferring favors! Just you tell her that I could not presume to add or reduce anything, or even to adopt any reckless decision. Let her add what she wants and make a display of bounty. When she gets better and is able to come out, she can effect whatever additions she fancies."

The moment Ping'er arrived, she obtained a fair insight (into lady Feng's designs), so when she heard the present remarks, she grasped a still more correct idea of things. But perceiving an angry look about Tanchun's face, she did not have the temerity to behave towards her as she would, had she found her in the high spirits of past days. All she did therefore was to stand aloof with her arms against her sides and to wait in rigid silence. Just at that moment, however, Baochai dropped in, on her return from the upper rooms. Tanchun quickly rose to her feet, and offered her a seat. But before they had had time to exchange any words, a married woman likewise came to report some business.

But as Tanchun had been having a good cry, three or four young maids brought her a basin, towel, and hand-glass and other articles of toilette. Tanchun was at the moment seated cross-legged, on a low wooden couch, so the maid with the basin had, when she drew near, to drop on both her knees and lift it high enough to bring it within reach. The other two girls prostrated themselves next to her and handed the towels and the rest of the toilet things, which consisted of a looking-glass, rouge, and powder. But Ping'er noticed that Shishu was not in the room, and approaching Tanchun with hasty step, she tucked up her sleeves for her and unclasped her bracelets. Seizing also a large towel from the hands of one of the maids, she covered the lapel on the front part of Tanchun's dress; whereupon Tanchun put out her hands, and washed herself in the basin.

"My lady and miss," the married woman observed, "may it please you to pay what has been spent in the family school for Mr. Jia Huan and Mr. Jia Lan during the year."

Ping'er was the first to speak. "What are you in such a hurry for?" she cried. "You've got your eyes wide open, and must be able to see our young lady washing her face; instead of coming forward to wait on her, you start talking! Do you also behave in this blind sort of way in the presence of your lady Secunda? This young lady is, it's true, generous and lenient, but I'll go and report you to your mistress. I'll simply tell her that you people have no eye for Miss Tanchun. But when you find yourselves in a mess, don't bear me any malice."

At this hint the woman took alarm, and hastily forcing a smile, she pleaded guilty. "I've been rude," she exclaimed. With these words, she rushed with all despatch out of the room.

Tanchun smoothed her face. While doing so, she turned herself towards Ping'er and gave her a cynical smile. "You've come just one step too late," she remarked. "You weren't in time to see something laughable! Even sister Wu, an old hand at business though she be, failed to look up clearly an old custom and came to play her tricks on us. But when we plied her with questions, she luckily had the face to admit that it had slipped from her memory. 'Do you,' I insinuated, 'also forget, when you've got anything to report to lady Secunda? and have you subsequently to go and hunt up all about it?' Your mistress can't, I fancy, be so patient as to wait while she goes and institutes proper search."

Ping'er laughed. "Were she to have behaved but once in this wise," she observed, "I feel positive that a couple of the tendons of her legs would have long ago been snapped. But, Miss, don't credit all they say. It's because they see that our senior mistress is as sweet tempered as a 'Pusa,' and that you, miss, are a modest young lady, that they, naturally, shirk their duties and come and take liberties with you. Your mind is set upon playing the giddy dogs," continuing, she added, speaking towards those beyond the doorway; "but when your mistress gets quite well again, we'll tell her all."

"You're gifted with the greatest perspicacity, miss," the married women, standing outside the door, smiled in chorus. "The proverb says: 'the person who commits a fault must be the one to suffer.' We don't in any way presume to treat any mistress with disdain. Our mistress at present is in delicate health, and if we intentionally provoke her, may we, when we die, have no place to have our corpses interred in."

Ping'er laughed a laugh full irony. "So long as you're aware of this, it's well and good," she said. And smiling a saturnine smile, she resumed, addressing herself to Tanchun: "Miss, you know very well how busy our lady has been and how little she could afford the time to keep this tribe of people in order. Of course, they couldn't therefore, be prevented from becoming remiss. The adage has it: 'Lookers-on are clear of sight!' During all these years that you have looked on dispassionately, there have possibly been instances on which, though additions or reductions should have been made, our lady Secunda has not been able to effect them, so, miss, do add or curtail whatever you may deem necessary, in order that, first, Madame Wang may be benefited, and that, secondly, you mayn't too render nugatory the kindness with which you ever deal towards our mistress."

But scarcely had she finished, than Baochai and Li Wan smilingly interposed. "What a dear girl!" they ejaculated. "One really can't feel angry with that hussy Feng for being partial to her and fond of her. We didn't, at first, see how we could very well alter anything by any increase or reduction, but after what you've told us, we must hit upon one or two things and try and devise means to do something, with a view of not showing ourselves ungrateful of the advice you've tendered us."

"My heart was swelling with indignation," Tanchun observed laughing, "and I was about to go and give vent to my temper with her mistress, but now that she (Ping'er) has happened to come, she has, with a few words, quite dissuaded me from my purpose."

While she spoke, she called the woman, who had been with them a few minutes back, to return into the room. "For what things for Mr. Jia Huan and Mr. Jia Lan was the money expended during the year in the family school?" she inquired of her.

"For cakes," replied the woman, "they ate during the year at school; or for the purchase of paper and brushes. Each one of them is allowed eight taels."

"The various expenses on behalf of the young men," Tanchun added, "are invariably paid in monthly instalments to the respective households. For cousin Jia Huan's, Mrs. Zhao receives two taels. For Baoyu's, Xiren draws two taels from our venerable senior's suite of apartments. For cousin Jia Lan's, someone, in our senior lady's rooms, gets the proper allowance. So how is it that these extra eight taels have to be disbursed at school for each of these young fellows? Is it really for these eight taels that they go to school? But from this day forth I shall put a stop to this outlay. So Ping'er, when you get back, tell your mistress that I say that this item must absolutely be done away with."

"This should have been done away with long ago," Ping'er smiled. "Last year our lady expressed her intention to eliminate it, but with the endless things that claimed her attention about the fall of the year, she forgot all about it."

The woman had no other course than to concur with her views and to walk away. But the married women thereupon arrived from the garden of Broad Vista with the boxes of eatables. So Shishu and Suyun at once brought a small dining-table, and Ping'er began to fuss about laying the viands on it.

"If you've said all you had," Tanchun laughed, "you'd better be off and attend to your business. What's the use of your bustling about here?"

"I've really got nothing to do," Ping'er answered smiling. "Our lady Secunda sent me first, to deliver a message; and next, because she feared that the servants in here weren't handy enough. The fact is, she bade me come and help the girls wait on you, my lady, and on you, miss."

"Why don't you bring Mrs. Bao's meal so that she should have it along with us?" Tanchun then inquired.

As soon as the waiting-maids heard her inquiry, they speedily rushed out and went under the eaves. "Go," they cried, directing the married women, "and say that Miss Baochai would like to have her repast just now in the hall along with the others, and tell them to send the eatables here."

Tanchun caught their directions. "Don't be deputing people to go on reckless errands!" she vociferated. "Those are dames, who manage important matters and look after the house, and do you send them to ask for eatables and inquire about tea? You haven't even the least notion about gradation. Ping'er is standing here, so tell her to go and give the message."

Ping'er immediately assented, and issued from the room, bent upon going on the errand. But the married women stealthily pulled her back. "How could you, miss, be made to go and tell them?" they smiled. "We've got someone here who can do so!"

So saying, they dusted one of the stone steps with their handker-chiefs. "You've been standing so long," they observed, "that you must feel quite tired. Do sit in this sunny place and have a little rest."

Ping'er took a seat on the step. Two matrons attached to the tea-room then fetched a rug and spread it out for her. "It's cold on those stones," they ventured; "this is, as clean as it can be. So, miss, do make the best of it, and use it!"

Ping'er hastily forced a smile. "Many thanks," she replied.

Another matron next brought her a cup of fine new tea. "This isn't the tea we ordinarily drink," she quietly smiled. "This is really for en-tertaining the young ladies with. Miss, pray moisten your mouth with some."

Ping'er lost no time in bending her body forward and taking the cup. Then pointing at the company of married women, she observed in a low voice: "You're all too fond of trouble! The way you're going on won't do at all! She (Tanchun) is only a young girl, so she is loath to show any severity, or display any temper. This is because she's full of respect. Yet you people look down on her and insult her. Should she, however, be actually provoked into any violent fit of anger, people will simply say that her behavior was rather rough, and all will be over. But as for you, you'll get at once into endless trouble. Even though she might show herself somewhat willful, Madame Wang treats her with considerable forbearance, and lady Secunda too hasn't the courage to meddle with her; and do you people have such arrogance as to look down on her? This is certainly just as if an egg were to go and bang itself against a stone!"

"When were we ever so audacious?" the servants exclaimed with one voice. "This fuss is all the work of Mrs. Zhao!"

"Never mind about that!" Ping'er urged again in an undertone. "My dear ladies, 'when a wall falls, everyone gives it a shove.' That Mrs. Zhao has always been rather topsy-turvy in her ways, and done things by halves; so whenever there has been any rumpus, you've invariably shoved the blame on to her shoulders. Never have you had any regard for any single person. Your designs are simply awful! Is it likely that all these years that I've been here, I haven't come to know of them? Had our lady Secunda mismanaged things just a little bit, she would have long ago been run down by everyone of you, ladies! Even such as she is, you would, could you only get the least opportunity, be ready to place her in a fix! And how many, many times hasn't she been abused by you?"

"She's dreadful," one and all of them rejoined. "You all live in fear and trembling of her. But we know well enough that no one could say that she too does not in the depths of her heart entertain some little dread for the lot of you. The other day, we said, in talking matters over, that things could not go on smoothly from beginning to end, and that some unpleasantness was bound to happen. Miss Tertia is, it's true, a mere girl, and you've always treated her with little consideration, but out of that company of senior and junior young ladies, she is the only soul whom our lady Secunda funks to some certain extent. And yet you people now won't look up to her."

So speaking Qiuwen appeared to view. The married women ran up to her and inquired after her health. "Miss," they said, "do rest a little. They've had their meal served in there, so wait until things have been cleared away, before you go and deliver your message."

"I'm not like you people," Qiuwen smiled. "How can I afford to wait?"

With these words on her lips, she was about to go into the hall, when Ping'er quickly called her back. Qiuwen, upon turning her head round, caught sight of Ping'er. "Have you too," she remarked with a smile, "come here to become something like those guardians posted outside the enclosing walls?"

Retracing, at the same time, her footsteps, she took a seat on the rug, occupied by Ping'er.

"What message have you got to deliver?" Ping'er gently asked.

"I've got to ask when we can get Baoyu's monthly allowance and our own too," she responded.

"Is this any such pressing matter?" Ping'er answered. "Go back quick, and tell Xiren that my advice is that no concern whatever should be brought to their notice today. That every single matter reported is bound to be objected to; and that even a hundred will just as surely be vetoed."

"Why is it?" vehemently inquired Qiuwen, upon hearing this explanation.

Ping'er and the other servants then promptly told her the various reasons. "She's just bent," they proceeded, "upon finding a few weighty concerns in order to establish, at the expense of any decent person who might chance to present herself, a precedent of some kind or other so as to fix upon a mode of action, which might help to put down expenses to their proper level, and afford a lesson to the whole household; and why are you people the first to come and bump your heads against the nails? If you went now and told them your errand, it would also reflect discredit upon our venerable old mistress and Madame Wang, were they to pounce upon one or two matters to make an example of you. But if they complied with one or two of your applications, others will again maintain 'that they are inclined to favor this one and show partiality to that one; that as you had your old mistress' and Madame Wang's authority to fall back upon, they were afraid and did not presume to provoke their displeasure; that they only avail themselves of soft-natured persons to make scapegoats of.' Just mark my words! She even means to raise objections in one or two matters connected with our lady Secunda, in order to be the better able to shut up people's mouths."

Qiuwen listened to her with patient ear; and then stretching out her tongue, "It's lucky enough you were here, sister Ping," she smiled; "otherwise, I would have had my nose well rubbed on the ground. I shall seize the earliest opportunity and give the lot of them a hint."

While replying, she immediately rose to her feet and took leave of them. Soon after her departure, Baochai's eatables arrived, and Ping'er hastened to enter and wait on her. By that time Mrs. Zhao had left, so the three girls seated themselves on the wooden bed, and went through their repast. Baochai faced the south. Tanchun the west. Li Wan the east. The company of married women stood quietly under the verandah ready to answer any calls. Within the precincts of the chamber, only such maids remained in waiting as had ever been their closest attendants. None of the other servants ventured, of their own accord, to put their foot anywhere inside.

The married women (meanwhile) discussed matters in a confidential whisper. "Let's do our downright best to save trouble," they argued. "Don't let us therefore harbor any evil design, for even dame Wu will, in that case, be placed in an awkward fix. And can we boast of any grand honors to expect to fare any better?"

While they stood on one side, and held counsel together, waiting for the meal to be over to make their several reports, they could not catch so much as the caw of a crow inside the rooms. Neither did the clatter of bowls and chopsticks reach their ears. But presently, they discerned a maid raise the frame of the portiere as high as she could, and two other girls bring the table out. In the tearoom, three maids waited with three basins in hand. The moment they saw the dining-table brought out, all three walked in. But after a brief interval, they egressed with the basins and rinsing cups. Shishu, Suyun, and Ying'er thereupon entered with three covered cups of tea, placed in trays. Shortly however these three girls also made their exit. Shishu then recommended a young maid to be careful and attend to the wants (of their mistresses). "When we've had our rice," she added, "we'll come and relieve you. But don't go stealthily again and sit down!"

The married women at length delivered their reports in a quiet and orderly manner; and as they did not presume to be as contemptuous and offhandish as they had been before, Tanchun eventually cooled down.

"I've got something of moment," she then observed to Ping'er, "about which I would like to consult your mistress. Happily, I remembered it just now, so come back as soon as you've had your meal. Miss Bao-chai is also here at present, so, after we four have deliberated together, you can carefully ask your lady whether action is to be taken accordingly or not."

Ping'er acquiesced and returned to her quarters. "How is it," inquired lady Feng, "that you've been away such an age?"

Ping'er smiled and gave her a full account of what had recently transpired.

"What a fine, splendid girl Miss Tertia is.'" she laughingly ejaculated. "What I said was quite right! The only pity is that she should have had such a miserable lot as not to have been born of a primary wife."

"My lady, you're also talking a lot of trash!" Ping'er smiled. "She, mayn't be Madame Wang's child, but is it likely that anyone would be so bold as to point the finger of scorn at her, and not treat her like the others?"

Lady Feng sighed. "How could you know everything?" she remarked. "She is, of course, the offspring of a concubine, but as a mere girl, she can't be placed on the same footing as a man! By and bye, when any one aspires to her hand, the sort of supercilious parties, who now tread the world, will, as a first step, ask whether this young lady is the child of a No. 1 or No. 2 wife. And many of these won't have anything to say to her, as she is the child of a No. 2. But really people haven't any idea that, not to speak of her as the offspring of a secondary wife, she would be, even as a mere servant-girl of ours, far superior than the very legitimate daughter of any family. Who, I wonder, will in the future be so devoid of good fortune as to break off the match; just because he may be inclined to pick and choose between a wife's child and a concubine's child? And who, I would like to know, will be that lucky fellow, who'll snatch her off without any regard to No. 1 and No. 2?"

Continuing, she resumed, turning smilingly towards Ping'er, "You know well enough how many ways and means I've had all these years to devise in order to effect retrenchment, and how there isn't, I may safely aver, a single soul in the whole household, who doesn't detest me behind my back. But now that I'm astride on the tiger's back (I must go on; for if I put my foot on the ground, I shall be devoured). It's true, my tactics have been more or less seen through, but there's no help for it; I can't very well become more open-handed in a moment! In the second place, much goes out at home, and little comes in; and the hundred and one, large and small things, which turn up, are still managed with that munificence so characteristic of our old ancestors. But the funds, that come in throughout the year, fall short of the immense sums of past days. And if I try again to effect any savings people will laugh at me, our venerable senior and Madame Wang suffer wrongs, and the servants abhor me for my stinginess. Yet, if we don't seize the first opportunity to think of some plan for enforcing retrenchment, our means will, in the course of a few more years, be completely exhausted."

"Quite so!" assented Ping'er. "By and bye, there will be three or four daughters and two or three more sons added; and our old mistress won't be able, singlehanded, to meet all this heavy outlay."

"I myself entertain fears on the same score," lady Feng smiled. "But, after all, there will be ample. For when Baoyu and cousin Lin get married, there won't be any need to touch a cent of public money, as our old lady has her own private means, and she can well fork out some. Miss Secunda is the child of your senior master yonder, and she too needn't be taken into account. So there only remain three or four, for each of whom one need only spend, at the utmost, ten thousand taels. Cousin Huan will marry in the near future; and if an outlay of three thousand taels prove insufficient, we will be able, by curtailing the bandoline, used in those rooms for smoothing the hair with, make both ends meet. And should our worthy senior's end come about, provision for everything is already made. All that we'll have to do will be to spend some small sum for a few miscellaneous trifles; and three to five thousand taels will more than suffice. So with further economies at present, there will be plenty for all our successive needs. The only fear is lest anything occur at an unforeseen juncture; for then it will be dreadful! But don't let us give way to apprehensions with regard to the future! You'd better have your rice; and when you've done, be quick and go and hear what they mean to treat about in their deliberations. I must now turn this opportunity to the best account. I was only this very minute lamenting that I had no help at my disposal. There's Baoyu, it's true, but he too is made of the same stuff as the rest of them in here. Were I even to get him under my thumb, it would be of no earthly use whatever. Senior lady is as good-natured as a joss; and she likewise is no good. Miss Secunda is worse than useless. Besides, she doesn't belong to this place. Miss Quarta is only a child. That young fellow Lan and Huan'er are, more than any of the others, like frozen kittens with frizzled coats. They only wait to find some warm hole in a stove into which they may poke themselves! Really from one and the same womb have been created two human beings (Tanchun and Jia Huan) so totally unlike each other as the heavens are distant from the earth. But when I think of all this, I feel quite angry! Again, that girl Lin and Miss Bao are both deserving enough, but as they also happen to be our connexions, they couldn't very well be put in charge of our family affairs. What's more, the one resembles a lantern, decorated with nice girls, apt to spoil so soon as it is blown by a puff of wind. The other has made up her mind not to open her month in anything that doesn't concern her. When she's questioned about anything, she simply shakes her head, and repeats thrice: 'I don't know,' so that it would be an extremely difficult job to go and ask her to lend a helping hand. There's only therefore Miss Tertia, who is as sharp of mind as of tongue. She's besides a straightforward creature in this household of ours and Madame Wang is attached to her as well. It's true that she outwardly makes no display of her feelings for her, but it's all that old thing Mrs. Zhao, who has done the mischief, for, in her heart, she actually holds her as dear as she does Baoyu. She's such a contrast to Huan'er! He truly makes it hard for anyone to care a rap for him. Could I have had my own way, I would long ere this have packed him out of the place. But since she (Tanchun) has now got this idea into her mind, we must cooperate with her. For if we can afford each other a helping hand, I too won't be single-handed and alone. And as far as every right principle, eternal principle, and honesty of purpose go, we shall with such a person as a helpmate, be able to save ourselves considerable anxiety, and Madame Wang's interests will, on the other hand, derive every advantage. But, as far as unfairness and bad faith go, I've run the show with too malicious a hand, and I must turn tail and draw back from my old ways. When I review what I've done, I find that if I still push my tyrannical rule to the bitter end, people will hate me most relentlessly; so much so, that under their smiles they'll harbor daggers, and much though we two may then be able to boast of having four eyes and two heads between us, they'll compass our ruin, when they can at any moment find us off our guard. We should therefore make the best of this crisis, so that as soon as she takes the initiative and sets things in order, all that tribe of people may for a time lose sight of the bitter feelings they cherish against us for the way we've dealt with them in the past. But there's another thing besides. I naturally know the great talents you possess, but I feel mistrust lest you should, by your own wits, not be able to bring things round. I enjoin these things then on you, now, for although a mere girl she has everything at her fingers' ends. The only thing is that she must try and be wary in speech. She's besides so much better read than I am that she's a harder nut to crack. Now the proverb says: 'in order to be able to catch the rebels, you must first catch their chief.' So if she's at present disposed to mature some plan and set to work to put it into practice, she'll certainly have to first and foremost make a start with me. In the event consequently of her raising objections to anything I've done, mind you don't begin any dispute with her. The more virulent she is in her censure of me, the more deferential you should be towards her. That's your best plan. And whatever you do, don't imagine that I'm afraid of any loss of face. But the moment you flare up with her, things won't go well."

Ping'er did not allow her time to conclude her argument. "You're too much disposed to treat us as simpletons!" she smiled. "I've already carried out your wishes, and do you now enjoin all these things on me?"

Lady Feng smiled. "It's because," she resumed, "I feared lest you, who have your eyes and mouth so full of me, and only me, might be inclined to show no regard whatever for her, that's why. I couldn't, therefore, but tender you the advice I did. But since you've already done what I wanted you to do, you've shown yourself far sharper than I am. There's nothing in this to drive you into another tantrum, and to make that mouth of yours begin to chatter away so much about 'you and I,' 'you and I!'"

"I've actually addressed you as 'you,'" Ping'er rejoined; "but if you be displeased at it, isn't this a case of a slap on the mouth? You can very well give me another one, for is it likely that this phiz of mine hasn't as yet tasted any, pray?"

"What a vixen you are!" lady Feng said smilingly. "How many faults will you go on picking out, before you shut up? You see how ill I am, and yet you come to rub me the wrong way. Come and sit down; for you and I can at all events have our meal together when there is no one to break in upon us. It's only right that we should."

While these remarks dropped from her lips, Feng'er and some three or four other maids entered the room and laid the small stove-couch table. Lady Feng only ate some birds' nests' soup and emptied two small plates of some recherche light viands; for she had long ago temporarily reduced her customary diet.

Feng'er placed the four kinds of eatables allotted to Ping'er on the table. After which, she filled a bowl of rice for her. Then with one leg bent on the edge of the stove-couch, while the other rested on the ground, Ping'er kept lady Feng company during her repast; and waiting on her, afterwards, until she finished rinsing her mouth, she issued certain directions to Feng'er, and crossed over at length to Tanchun's quarters. Here she found the courtyard plunged in perfect stillness, for the various inmates, who had been assembled there, had already taken their leave.

But, reader, do you wish to follow up the story? If so, listen to the circumstances detailed in the next chapter.

CHAPTER 56

The clever Tanchun increases their income and removes long standing abuses. The worthy Baochai preserves intact, by the display of a little intelligence, the great reputation enjoyed by the Jia family.

But let us pick up the clue of our story. Ping'er bore lady Feng company during her meal; then attending to her, while she rinsed her mouth and washed her hands, she betook herself eventually to Tanchun's quarters, where she discovered the courtyard in perfect stillness. Not a soul was about beyond several maids, matrons, and close attendants of the inner rooms, who stood outside the windows on the alert to obey any calls. Ping'er stepped into the hall. The two cousins and their sister-in-law were all three engaged in discussing some domestic affairs. They were talking about the feast, to which they had been invited during the new year festivities by Lai Da's wife, and various details in connection with the garden she had in her place. But as soon as she (Ping'er) appeared on the scene, Tanchun desired her to seat herself on her footstool.

"What was exercising my mind," she thereupon observed, "confines itself to this. I was computing that the head-oil, and rouge, and powder, we use during the course of a month, are also a matter of a couple of taels; and I was thinking that what with the sum of two taels, already allotted us every month, and the extra monthly amount given as well to the maids, allowances are, with the addition again of that of eight taels for school expenses, we recently spoke about, piled to be sure one upon another. The thing is, it's true, a mere trifle, and the amount only a bagatelle, but it doesn't seem to be quite proper. But how is it that your mistress didn't take this into account?"

Ping'er smiled. "There's a why and a wherefore," she answered. "All the things required by you, young ladies, must absolutely be subject to a fixed rule; for the different compradores have to lay in a stock of each every month; and to send them to us by the maids to take charge of; but purely and simply to keep in readiness for you to use. No such thing could ever be tolerated as that each of us should have to get money every day and try and hunt up someone to go and buy these articles for us! That's how it is that the compradores outside receive a lump sum, and that they send us, month by month, by the female servants the supplies allotted for the different rooms. As regards the two taels monthly allowed you, young ladies, they were not originally intended that you should purchase any such articles with, but that you should, if at any time the ladies in charge of the household affairs happened to be away from home or to have no leisure, be saved the trouble of having to go in search of the proper persons, in the event of your suddenly finding yourselves in need of money. This was done simply because it was feared that you would be subjected to inconvenience. But an unprejudiced glance about me now shows me that at least half of our young mistresses in the various quarters invariably purchase these things with ready money of their own; so I can't help suspecting that, if it isn't a question of the compradores shirking their duties, it must be that what they buy is all mere rubbish."

Tanchun and Li Wan laughed. "You must have kept a sharp lookout to have managed to detect these things!" they said. "But as for shirking the purchases, they don't actually do so. It's simply that they're behind time by a good number of days. Yet when one puts on the screw with them, they get some articles from somewhere or other, who knows where? These are however only a sham; for, in reality, they aren't fit for use. But as they're now as ever obtained with cash down, a couple of taels could very well be given to the brothers or sons of some of the other people's nurses to purchase them with. They'll then be good for something! Were we however to employ any of the public domestics in the establishment, the things will be just as bad as ever. I wonder how they do manage to get such utter rot as they do?"

"The purchases of the compradores may be what they are," Ping'er smiled; "but were anyone else to buy any better articles, the compradores themselves won't ever forgive them. Besides other things, they'll aver that they harbor evil designs, and that they wish to deprive them of their post. That's how it comes about that the servants would much rather give offence to you all inside, (by getting inferior things,) and that they have no desire to hurt the feelings of the managers outside (by purchasing anything of superior quality). But if you, young ladies, requisition the services of the nurses, these men won't have the arrogance to make any nonsensical remarks."

"This accounts for the unhappy state my heart is in," Tanchun observed. "But as we're called upon to squander money right and left, and as the things purchased are half of them uselessly thrown away, wouldn't it, after all, be better for us to eliminate this monthly allowance to the compradores? This is the first thing. The next I'd like to ask you is this. When they went, during the new year festivities, to Lai Da's house, you also went with them; and what do think of that small garden as compared with this of ours?"

"It isn't half as big as ours," Ping'er laughingly explained. "The trees and plants are likewise fewer by a good deal."

"When I was having a chat with their daughter," Tanchun proceeded, "she said that, besides the flowers they wear, and the bamboo shoots, vegetables, fish, and shrimps they eat from this garden of theirs, there's still enough every year for people to take over under contract, and that at the close of each year there's a surplus in full of two hundred taels. Ever since that day is it that I've become alive to the fact that even a broken lotus leaf, and a blade of withered grass are alike worth money."

"This is, in very truth, the way wealthy and well-to-do people talk!" Baochai laughed. "But notwithstanding your honorable position, young ladies, you really understand nothing about these concerns. Yet, haven't you, with all your book-lore, seen anything of the passage in the writing of Zhu Fuzi: 'Throw not they self away?'"

"I've read it, it's true," Tanchun smiled, "but its object is simply to urge people to exert themselves; it's as much empty talk as any random arguments, and how could it be bodily treated as gospel?"

"Zhuzi's work all as much empty talk as any random arguments?" Baochai exclaimed. "Why every sentence in it is founded on fact. You've only had the management of affairs in your hands for a couple of days, and already greed and ambition have so beclouded your mind that you've come to look upon Zhuzi as full of fraud and falsehood. But when you by and bye go out into the world and see all those mighty concerns reeking with greed and corruption, you'll even go so far as to treat Confucius himself as a fraud!"

"Haven't you with all your culture read a book like that of Jizi's?" Tanchun laughed. "Jizi said in bygone days 'that when one descends into the arena where gain and emoluments are to be got, and enters the world of planning and plotting, one makes light of the injunctions of Yao and Shun, and disregards the principles inculcated by Confucius and Mencius.'"

"What about the next line?" Baochai insinuated with a significant smile.

"I now cut the text short," Tanchun smilingly rejoined, "in order to adapt the sense to what I want to say. Would I recite the following sentence, and heap abuse upon my own self; is it likely I would, eh?"

"There's nothing under the heavens that can't be turned to some use," Baochai added. "And since everything can be utilized, everything must be worth money. But can it be that a person gifted with such intelligence as yours can have had no experience in such great matters and legitimate concerns as these?"

"You send for a person," Li Wan laughingly interposed, "and you don't speak about what's right and proper, but you start an argument on learning."

"Learning is right and proper," Baochai answered. "If we made no allusion to learning, we'd all soon enough drift among the rustic herd!"

The trio bandied words for a while, after which they turned their attention again to pertinent affairs.

Tanchun took up once more the thread of the conversation. "This garden of ours," she argued, "is only half as big as theirs, so if you double the income they derive, you will see that we ought to reap a net profit of four hundred taels a year. But were we also now to secure a contract for our surplus products, the money we'd earn, would, of course, be a mere trifle and not one that a family like ours should hanker after. And were we to depute two special persons (to attend to the garden), the least permission given by them to anyone to turn anything to improper uses, would, since there be so many things of intrinsic value, be tantamount to a reckless destruction of the gifts of heaven. So would it not be preferable to select several quiet, steady and experienced old matrons, out of those stationed in the grounds, and appoint them to put them in order and look after things? Neither will there be any need then to make them pay any rent, or give any taxes in kind. All we can ask them is to supply the household with whatever they can afford during the year. In the first place, the garden will, with special persons to look after the plants and trees, naturally so improve from year to year that there won't be any bustle or confusion, whenever the time draws nigh to utilize the grounds. Secondly, people won't venture to injure or uselessly waste anything. In the third place, the old matrons themselves will, by availing themselves of these small perquisites, not labor in the gardens year after year and day after day all for no good. Fourthly, it will in like manner be possible to effect a saving in the expenditure for gardeners, rockery-layers, sweepers, and other necessary servants. And this excess can be utilized for making up other deficiencies. I don't see any reason why this shouldn't be practicable!"

Baochai was standing below contemplating the pictures with characters suspended on the walls. Upon hearing these suggestions, she readily nodded her head assentingly and smiled. "Excellent!" she cried. "'Within three years, there will be no more famines and dearths.'"

"What a first-rate plan!" Li Wan chimed in. "This, if actually adopted, will delight the heart of Madame Wang. Pecuniary economies are of themselves a paltry matter; but there will be then in the garden those to sweep the grounds, and those whose special charge will be to look after them. Besides, were the persons selected allowed to turn up an honest cash by selling part of the products, they will be so impelled by a sense of their responsibilities, and prompted by a desire of gain that there won't any longer be any who won't acquit themselves of their duties to the fullest measure."

"It remained for you, miss, to put these suggestions in words," Ping'er remarked. "Our mistress may have entertained the idea, but it is by no means certain that she thought it nice on her part to give utterance to it. For as you, young ladies, live at present in the garden, she could not possibly, unable as she is to supply such additional ornaments as will make it more showy, contrariwise depute people to exercise authority in it, and to keep it in order, with a view of effecting a reduction in expenses. Such a proposal could never have dropped from her lips."

Baochai advanced up to her with alacrity. Rubbing her face: "Open that mouth of yours wide," she laughed, "and let me see of what stuff your teeth and tongue are made! Ever since you put your foot out of bed this morning you've jabbered away up to this very moment! And your song has all been in one strain. For neither have you been very complimentary to Miss Tertia, nor have you admitted that your mistress is, as far as wits go, so much below the mark as to be unable to effect suitable provision. Yet whenever Miss Tertia advanced any arguments, you've at once made use of endless words to join issue with her. This is because the plan devised by Miss Tertia was also hit upon by your lady Feng. But there must surely have been a reason why she couldn't carry it into execution. Again, as the young ladies have now their quarters in the garden, she couldn't, with any decency, direct any one to go and rule over it, for the mere sake of saving a few cash. Just consider this. If the garden is actually handed to people to make profit out of it, the parties interested will, of course, not even permit a single spray of flowers to be plucked, and not a single fruit to be taken away. With such as come within the category of senior young ladies, they won't naturally have the audacity to be particular; but they'll daily have endless rows with the junior girls. (Lady Feng) has, with her fears about the future and her misgivings about the present, shown herself neither too overbearing nor too servile. This mistress of theirs is not friendly disposed towards us, but when she hears of her various proposals, shame might induce her to turn over a new leaf."

"Early this morning," Tanchun laughingly observed, "I was very cross, but as soon as I heard of her (Ping'er's) arrival, I casually remembered that her mistress employed, during her time, such domestics as were up to all kinds of larks, and at the sight of her, I got more cross than ever. But, little though one would have thought it, she behaved from the moment she came, like a rat that tries to get out of the way of a cat. And as she had had to stand for ever so long, I pitied her very much; but she took up the thread of the conversation, and went on to spin that long yarn of hers. Yet, instead of mentioning that her mistress treats me with every consideration, she, on the contrary, observed: 'The kindness with which you have all along dealt with our lady miss, has not been to no purpose.' This remark therefore not only dispelled my anger, but filled me with so much shame that I began to feel sore at heart. And, when I came to think carefully over the matter, I failed to see how I, a mere girl, who had personally done so much mischief that not a soul cared a straw for me and not a soul took any interest in me, could possess any such good qualities as to treat anyone kindly..."

When she reached this point, she could not check her tears from brimming over. Li Wan and her associates perceived how pathetically she spoke; and, recalling to mind how Mrs. Zhao had always run her down, and how she had ever been involved in some mess or other with Madame Wang, on account of this Mrs. Zhao, they too found it difficult to refrain from melting into sobs. But they then used their joint efforts to console her.

"Let's avail ourselves of this quiet day," they suggested, "to try and find out how we could increase our revenue and remove abuses, so as not to render futile the charge laid on us by Madame Wang. What use or purpose is it to allude to such trivial matters?"

"I've already grasped your object," Ping'er hastily ventured. "Miss, speak out; who do you consider fit? And as soon as the proper persons have been fixed upon, everything will be square enough."

"What you say is all very well," Tanchun rejoined, "but it will be necessary to let your lady know something about it. It has never been the proper thing for us in here to scrape together any small profits. But as your mistress is full of gumption, I adopted the course I did. Had she been at all narrowminded, with many prejudices and many jealousies, I wouldn't have shown the least willingness in the matter. But, as it will look as if I were bent upon pulling her to pieces, how can I take action without consulting her?"

"In that case," Ping'er smiled, "I'll go and tell her something about it."

With this response, she went on the errand; and only returned after a long lapse of time. "I said," she laughed, "that it would be perfectly useless for me to go. How ever could our lady not readily accede to an excellent proposal like this?"

Hearing this, Tanchun forthwith joined Li Wan in directing a servant to ask for the roll, containing the names of the matrons in the garden, and bring it to them. When produced, they all held council together, and fixing cursorily upon several persons, they summoned them to appear before them. Li Wan then explained to them the general outline of their duties; and not one was there among the whole company, who listened to her, who would not undertake the charge. One said: "If you confide that bamboo tree for twelve months to my care, it will again next year be a single tree, but besides the shoots, which will have been eaten at home, I shall be able, in the course of the year, to also pay in some money." "Hand me over," another one remarked, "that portion of paddy field, and there will, during the year, be no need to touch any public funds on account of the various birds, large and small, which are kept for mere fun. Besides that, I shall be in a position to give in something more."

Tanchun was about to pass a remark when a servant reported that the doctor had come; and that he had entered the garden to see Miss Shi. So the matrons were obliged to go and usher the doctor in.

"Were there a hundred of you here," promptly expostulated Ping'er, "you wouldn't know what propriety means! Are there perchance no couple of housekeepers about to push themselves forward and see the doctor in?"

"There's dame Wu and dame Tan," the servant, who brought the message, replied. "The two are on duty at the southwest corner at the 'accumulated splendor' gate."

At this answer, Ping'er allowed the subject to drop.

After the departure of the matrons, Tanchun inquired of Baochai what she thought of them.

"Such as are diligent at the outset," Baochai answered smiling, "become remiss in the end; and those who have a glib tongue have an eye to gain."

Tanchun listened to her reply; and nodding her head, she extolled its wisdom. Then showing them with her finger several names on the list, she submitted them for the perusal of the trio. Ping'er speedily went and fetched a brush and inkslab.

"This old mother Zhu," the trio observed, "is a trustworthy woman. What's more, this old dame and her sons have generation after generation done the sweeping of the bamboo groves. So let's now place the various bamboo trees under her control. This old mother Tian was originally a farmer, and everything in the way of vegetables and rice, in and about the Daoxiang village, should, albeit they couldn't, planted as they are as a mere pastime, be treated in such earnest as to call for large works and extensive plantations, be entrusted to her care; for won't they fare better if she can be on the spot and tend them with extra diligence at the proper times and seasons?"

"What a pity it is," Tanchun proceeded smilingly, "that two places so spacious as the Hengwu garden and the Yihong court bring no grit to the mill."

"Things in the Hengwu garden are in a worse state," Li Wan hastily interposed. "Aren't the scented wares and scented herbs sold at present everywhere in perfumery shops, large fairs, and great temples the very counterpart of these things here? So if you reckon up, you will find how much greater a return these articles will give than any other kind of product. As for the Yihong court, we needn't mention other things, but only take into account the roses that bud during the two seasons of spring and summer; to how many don't they amount in all? Besides these, we've got along the whole hedge, cinnamon roses and monthly roses, stock roses, honey-suckle and westeria. Were these various flowers dried and sold to the tea and medicine shops, they'd also fetch a good deal of money."

"Quite so!" Tanchun acquiesced with a smile. "The thing is that there's no one with any notion how to deal with scented herbs."

"There's Ying'er who waits on Miss Baochai," Ping'er promptly smiled. "Her mother is well-versed in these things. It was only the other day that she plucked a few, and plaited them, after drying them well in the sun, into a flower-basket and a gourd, and gave them to me to play with. But miss can you have forgotten all about it?"

"I was this very minute speaking in your praise," Baochai observed smiling, "and do you come to chaff me?"

"What makes you say so?" exclaimed the trio, in utter astonishment.

"It will on no account do," Baochai added. "You employ such a lot of people in here that they all lead a lazy life and have nothing to put a hand to, and were I also now to introduce some more, that tribe will look even upon me with utter contempt. But let me think of someone for you. There's in the Yihong court, an old dame Ye; she's Beiming's mother. That woman is an honest old lady; and is furthermore on the best of terms with our Ying'er's mother. So wouldn't it be well were this charge given to this dame Ye? Should there even be anything that she doesn't know, there'll be no necessity for us to tell her. She can go straightway and consult with Ying'er's mother. And if she can't attend to everything herself, it won't matter to whom she relegates some of her duties. These will be purely private favors. In the event too of any one making any mean insinuations, the blame won't fall on our shoulders. By adopting this course, you'll be managing things in such a way as to do extreme justice to all; and the trust itself will also be placed on a most satisfactory footing."

"Excellent!" ejaculated Li Wan and Ping'er simultaneously.

"This may be well and good," Tanchun laughed, "but the fear is that at the sight of gain, they'll forget all about propriety."

"That's nothing to do with us!" Ping'er rejoined, a smile playing about her lips. "It was only the other day that Ying'er recognised dame Ye as her adopted mother, and invited her to eat and drink with them, so that the two families are on the most intimate terms."

At this assurance, Tanchun relinquished the topic of conversation, and, holding council together, they selected several persons, all of whom the four had ever viewed with impartial favor and they marked off their names, by dotting them with a brush.

In a little while, the matrons came to report that the doctor had gone and they handed the prescription. Their three mistresses then perused its contents. On the one hand, they despatched domestics to take it outside, so that the drugs should be got, and to superintend their decoction. On the other, Tanchun and Li Wan explicitly explained to the various servants chosen what particular place each had to look after. "Exclusive," they added, "of what fixed custom requires for home consumption during the four seasons, you are still at liberty to pluck whatever remains and have it taken away. As for the profits, we'll settle accounts at the close of the year."

"I've also bethought myself of something," Tanchun smiled. "If the settlement of accounts takes place at the end of the year, the money will, at the time of delivery, be naturally paid into the accountancy. Those high up will then as usual add a whole lot of controllers; and these will, on their part, fleece their own share as soon as the money gets into the palms of their hand. But as by this system, we've now initiated, you've been singled out for appointment, you've already ridden so far above their heads, that they foster all sorts of animosity against you. They don't, however, give vent to their feelings; but if they don't seize the close of the year, when you have to deliver your accounts, to play their tricks on you, for what other chances will they wait? Moreover, they obtain, in everything that comes under their control during the year, half of every share their masters get. This is an old custom. Everyone is aware of its existence. But this is a new regime I now introduce in this

garden, so don't let the money find its way into their hands! Whenever
the annual settling of accounts arrives, bring them in to us."

"My idea is," Baochai smilingly suggested, "that no accounts need
be handed even inside. This one will have a surplus, that one a deficit,
so that it will involve no end of trouble; wouldn't it be better therefore
if we were to find out who of them would take over this or that particular kind and let them purvey the various things? These are for the
exclusive use of the inmates of the garden; and I've already made an
estimate of them for you. They amount to just a few sorts, and simply
consist of head-oil, rouge, powder, and scented paper; in all of which,
the young ladies and maids are subject to a fixed rule. Then, besides
these, there are the brooms, dust-baskets, and poles, wanted in different localities, and the food for the large and small animals and birds,
and the deer and rabbits. These are the only kinds of things required.
And if they contract for them, there'll be little need for anyone to go to
the accountancy for money. But just calculate what a saving will thus
be effected!"

"All these items are, I admit, mere trifles," Ping'er smiled, "but if you
lump together what's used during a year, you will find that a saving of
four hundred taels will be effected."

"Again!" smilingly remarked Baochai, "it would be four hundred
taels in one year; but eight hundred taels in two years; and with these,
we could purchase a few more houses and let them; and in the way
of poor, sandy land we could also add several acres to those we've already got. There will, of course, still remain a surplus; but as they will
have ample trouble and inconvenience to put up with during the year,
they should also be allowed some balance in hand so as to make up
what's wanted for themselves. The main object is, of course, to increase
profits and curtail expenses, yet we couldn't be stingy to any excessive
degree. In fact, were we even able to make any further economy of
over two or three hundred taels, it would never be the proper thing;
should this involve a breach of the main principles of decorum. With
this course duly put into practice, outside, the accountancy will issue
in one year four or five hundred taels less, without even the semblance
of any parsimony; while, inside, the matrons will obtain, on the other
hand, some little thing to supply their wants with; the nurses, who have
no means of subsistence, will likewise be placed in easy circumstances; and the plants and trees in the garden will year by year increase in
strength and grow more abundantly. In this wise, you too will have
such articles as will be fit for use. So that this plan will, to some extent, not constitute a breach of the high principles of propriety. And
if ever we want to retrench a little more from there won't we be able

to get money? But if the whole balance, if any, be put to the credit of the public fund, everyone, inside as well as outside, will fill the streets with the din of murmurings! And won't this be then a slur upon the code of honor of a household such as yours? So were any charge to be entrusted to this one, out of the several tens of old nurses at present employed in the garden, and not to that one, the remainder will naturally resent such injustice. As I said a while back all that these women will have to provide among themselves amounts to a few articles, so they will unavoidably have ample means. Hence each should be told to contribute, beyond the articles that fall to her share during the year, a certain number of diaos, whether she may or may not realize any balance, and then jointly lump these sums together, and distribute them among those nurses only on service in the garden. For although they may not have anything to do with the control of these things, they themselves will have to stay in the grounds, to keep an eye over the servants on duty, to shut the doors, to close the windows, and to get up early and retire late. Whenever it rains in torrents or it snows hard and chairs have to be carried, for you, young ladies, to go out and come in; or boats have to be punted, and sledges drawn, these rough and arduous duties come alike within their sphere of work. They have to labor in the garden from one year's end to the other, and though, they earn something in those grounds, it's only right that they should able to get some small benefits in the discharge of their legitimate duties. But there's another most trivial point that I would broach with less reserve. If you only think of your ease, and don't share the profits with them, they will, of course, never presume to show their displeasure, but in their hearts they won't cherish you any good feeling. What they'll do will be to make public business a pretext to serve their own private ends with; they'll pluck more of your fruits than they should; and cut greater quantities of your flowers than they ought. And you people will have a grievance, but you won't have anywhere to go and confide it. But should they too reap some gain, they'll readily look after such things on your behalf as you won't have the time to attend to."

The matrons listened to her explanations; (and finding that) they would be removed from the control of the accountancy, that they would not be compelled to go and settle accounts with lady Feng, and that all that they would be called upon to do every year would be to supply a few more tiaos, were each and all delighted to an exceptional degree. So much so, that everyone of them exclaimed in a chorus that they were quite prepared to agree to the terms. "It is better," they said, "than to be obliged to go out and be squeezed by them; and to have to fork out our own money as well."

Those too not entrusted with the care of any portion of land were also highly elated, when they heard that at the close of each year they would, though they had no valid claim, come in for some share of hard cash.

"They'll have to bear the trouble," they however argued, "to keep things in order, so it's only right that they should be left with a few cash to meet their various wants with; and how could we very well gobble our three meals without doing a stroke of work?"

"Worthy dames," Baochai smiled, "you mustn't decline. These duties are within your province and you should fulfil them. All you need do is to exert yourselves a bit by day and night, and not be so remiss and careless as to suffer any of the servants to drink and gamble; that's all. Otherwise, I myself must have nothing to do with the control. But you, yourselves, know well enough that it's my aunt who appealed to me with her own lips three and five times to do it as a favor to her. 'Your eldest sister-in-law,' she represented, 'has at present no leisure, and the other girls are young,' and then she asked me to look after things. So if I now don't accede, it's as clear as day that I shall be the cause of much worry to my aunt. Our lady Feng herself is seriously ill, and our domestic affairs can't hang fire. I'm really with nothing to do, so were even a mere neighbor to solicit my help, I would also feel bound to lend her a hand in her pressure of work. How much more therefore when it's my own aunt, who invokes my aid? Setting aside the way I'm execrated by one and all, how would I ever be able to stare my aunt in the face, if, while I gave my sole mind to winning fame and fishing for praise, any one got so intoxicated and lost so much in gambling as to stir up trouble? At such a juncture remorse on your part will be too late! Even the old reputation you have ever enjoyed will entirely be lost and gone. Those young ladies and girls and this vast garden are alike placed under your supervision, purely and simply because one takes into account that you have been nurses to three or four generations and that you have most scrupulously observed the rules of etiquette and propriety. It's but fair that you should try, with one mind, and show some little regard for what's right and proper. But if you contrariwise behave with such laxity as to let people gratify their wishes by guzzling and gambling, and my aunt comes to hear of these nice doings, a little scolding from her will be of little consequence. But if the various women, who attend to the household, get scent of the state of affairs, they will haul you over the coals, without even so much as breathing one single word beforehand to my aunt. And venerable people, though you are, you will then, instead of tendering advice to young people, be called to account by them. As housekeepers, they exercise, it's true, authority over you; but why shouldn't you yourselves observe a certain amount of decorum? And if you do so, will they have any occasion to bully you? The reason why I've now bethought myself of this special boon for you is that you should unanimously strain every nerve to diligently attend to the garden, in order that the powers that be may, at the sight of your unrelenting care and zeal, have no cause to give way to solicitude. And won't they inwardly look up to you with regard? Neither will you render of no effect the various benefits devised for them. But go now and minutely ponder over all my advice!"

All the women received her words with gratification. "What you say is quite right," they replied. "From this time forth you, miss, and you, our lady, can well compose your minds. With the interest both of you feel on our behalf, may heaven and earth not spare us, if we do not display a full amount of gratitude for all your kindnesses."

These assurances were still being uttered when they saw Lin Zixiao's wife walk in. "The family of the Zhen mansion of Jiangnan," she explained, "arrived in the capital yesterday. Today, they're going into the palace to offer their congratulations. But they've now sent messengers ahead to come and bring presents and pay their respects."

While she spoke, she produced the list of presents and handed it up. Tanchun took it over from her. "They consist," she said, perusing it, "of twelve rolls of brocades and satins embroidered with dragons, such as are for Imperial use; twelve rolls of satins of various colors, of the kind worn by the Emperor; twelve rolls of every sort of Imperial gauze; twelve rolls of palace silks of the quality used by his majesty; and twenty rolls of satins, gauzes, silks, and thin silks of different colors, generally worn by officials."

After glancing over the list, Li Wan and Tanchun suggested that a first-class tip should be given to the messengers who brought them, after which, they went on to direct a servant to convey the tidings to dowager lady Jia.

Old lady Jia gave orders to call Li Wan, Tanchun, Baochai, and the other girls. On their arrival, the presents were passed under review; and this over, Li Wan put them aside. "You must wait," she said to the servants of the inner storeroom, "until Madame Wang comes back and sees them; you can then lock them up."

"This Zhen family too," old lady Jia thereupon added, "isn't like any other family; the highest tips should therefore be conferred upon the men. But as in a twinkle, they may also send some of their womankind to come and make their obeisance, silks should be got ready in anticipation."

Scarcely was this remark concluded before a domestic actually announced that four ladies of the Zhen mansion had come to pay their respects.

Upon hearing this, dowager lady Jia hastily directed that they should be introduced into her presence. The four women ranged from forty years and over. Their clothing and head-gear were not, in any material degree, different from those of mistresses. As soon as they presented their compliments and inquired about their healths, old lady Jia desired that four footstools should be moved forward. But though the four women thanked her for bidding them sit down, they only occupied the stools after Baochai had seated herself.

"When did you enter the capital?" old lady Jia inquired.

The four women jumped to their feet with alacrity. "We entered the capital yesterday," they answered. "Our lady has taken our young lady today into the palace to pay their homage. That's why she bade us come and give you their compliments, and see how the young ladies are getting on."

"You hadn't paid a visit to the capital for ever so many years," dowager lady Jia smilingly observed, "and here you appear now quite unexpectedly!"

The four women simultaneously smiled again. "Quite so!" they said. "We received this year Imperial orders, summoning us to the capital!"

"Has the whole family come?" old lady Jia asked.

"Our old mistress, our young master, the two young ladies, and the other ladies haven't come up," the four women explained. "Only our lady has come, together with Miss Tertia."

"Is she engaged to anyone?" old lady Jia asked.

"Not yet," rejoined the quartet.

"The two families, that of your senior married lady and that of your lady Secunda are both on most intimate terms with ours," dowager lady Jia smilingly added.

"Yes, they are," replied the four women with a smile. "The letters received each year from our young ladies, assure us that they're entirely dependent upon the kindness bestowed upon them, in your worthy mansion, for their well-being."

"What kindness?" old lady Jia exclaimed laughingly. "These two families are really friends of long standing. In addition to this, they're old relatives. So what we do is our simple bounden duty. What's more in the favor of your two young ladies is, that they're not full of their own importance. That's how it is that we've come to be on such close terms."

The four women smiled. "This is mainly due to your venerable ladyship's excessive humility," they answered.

"Is that young gentleman of yours too with your old mistress?" old lady Jia went on to inquire.

"Yes, he has also come with our old mistress," the four women retorted.

"How old is he?" old lady Jia then asked. "Does he go to school?" she afterwards inquired.

"He's thirteen this year," the four women said by way of response. "But all through those good looks of his, our old mistress cherishes him so fondly that from his youth up, he has been wayward to the extreme, and that he now daily plays the truant. But our master and mistress as well don't keep any great check over him."

"Yet, he can't resemble that young fellow of ours," old lady Jia laughed. "What's the name of your young gentleman?"

"As our old mistress treats him just like a real precious gem," the quartet explained, "and as his complexion is naturally so white, her ladyship calls him Baoyu."

"Here's another one with the name of Baoyu!" old lady Jia laughingly said to Li Wan.

Li Wan and her companions hastily made a curtsey. "There have been, from old times to the present," they smiled, "very many among contemporaries and persons of different generations as well, who have borne duplicate names."

The four women also smiled. "After the selection of this infant name," they proceeded, "we all, both high or low, began to give way to surmises, as we could not make out in what relative's or friend's family there was a lad also called by the same name. But as we hadn't come to the capital for ten years or so, we couldn't remember."

"That young fellow is my grandson," dowager lady Jia remarked. "Hallo! someone come here!"

The married women and maids assented and approached several steps.

"Go into the garden," old lady Jia smilingly said, "and call our Baoyu here, so that these four housekeeping dames should see how he compares with their own Baoyu."

The married women, upon hearing her orders, promptly went off. After a while, they entered the room pressing round Baoyu. The moment the four dames caught sight of him, they speedily rose to their feet. "He has given us such a start!" they exclaimed smilingly. "Had we not come into your worthy mansion, and perchance, met him elsewhere, we would have taken him for our own Baoyu, and followed him as far as the capital."

While speaking they came forward and took hold of his hands and assailed him with questions.

Baoyu however also put on a smile and inquired after their healths.

"How do his looks compare with those of your young gentleman?" dowager lady Jia asked as she smiled.

"The way the four dames ejaculated just now," Li Wan and her companions explained, "was sufficient to show how much they resemble in looks."

"How could there ever be such a coincidence?" old lady Jia laughed. "Yet, the children of wealthy families are so delicately nurtured that unless their faces are so deformed as to make them downright ugly, they're all equally handsome, as far as general appearances go. So there's nothing strange in this!"

"As we gaze at his features," the quartet added, with smiling faces, "we find him the very image of him; and from what we gather from your venerable ladyship, he's also like him in waywardness. But, as far as we can judge, this young gentleman's disposition is ever so much better than that of ours."

"What makes you think so?" old lady Jia precipitately inquired.

"We saw it as soon as we took hold of the young gentleman's hands," the four women laughingly rejoined, "and when he spoke to us. Had it been that fellow of ours, he would have simply called us fools. Not to speak of taking his hand in ours, why we daren't even slightly move any of his things. That's why, those who wait on him are invariably young girls."

Before the four dames had time to conclude what they had to say, Li Wan and the rest found it so hard to check themselves that with one voice they burst into loud laughter.

Old lady Jia also laughed. "Let's also send someone now," she said, "to have a look at your Baoyu. When his hand is taken, he too is sure to make an effort to put up with it. But don't you know that children of families such as yours and mine are bound, notwithstanding their numerous perverse and strange defects, to return the orthodox civilities, when they come across any strangers. But should they not return the proper civilities, they should, by no manner of means, be suffered to behave with such perverseness. It's the way that grown-up people doat on them that makes them what they are. And as they can, first and foremost, boast of bewitching good looks and they comport themselves, secondly, towards visitors with all propriety, in fact, with less faulty deportment than their very seniors, they manage to win the love and admiration of such as only get a glimpse of them. Hence it is that they're secretly indulged to a certain degree. But if they don't show the least regard to anyone inside or outside, and so reflect no credit upon their parents, they deserve, with all their handsome looks, to be flogged to death."

These sentiments evoked a smile from the four dames. "Your words venerable lady," they exclaimed, "are quite correct. But though our Baoyu be willful and strange in his ways, yet, whenever he meets any visitors, he behaves with courteousness and good manners; so much so, that he's more pleasing to watch than even grown-up persons. There is no one, therefore, who sees him without falling in love with him. But you'll say: 'why is he then beaten?' You really aren't aware that at home he has no regard either for precept or for leave; that he comes out with things that never suggest themselves to the imagination of grown-up people, and that he does everything that takes one by surprise. The result is that his father and mother are driven to their wits' ends. But wilfulness is natural to young children. Reckless expenditure is a common characteristic of young men. Antipathy to school is a common feeling with young people. Yet there are ways and means to bring him round. The worse with him is that his disposition is so crotchety and whimsical. Can this ever do?…"

This reply was barely ended when a servant informed them that their mistress had returned. Madame Wang entered the room and saluted the women. The four dames paid their obeisance to her. But they had just had sufficient time to pass a few general observations, when dowager lady Jia bade them go and rest. Madame Wang then handed the tea in person and withdrew from the apartment. But when the four dames got up to say good-bye, old lady Jia adjourned to Madame Wang's quarters. After a chat with her on domestic affairs, she however told the women to go back; so let us put them by without any further allusion to them.

During this while, old lady Jia's spirits waxed so high, that she told everyone and anyone she came across that there was another Baoyu, and that he was, in every respect, the very image of her grandson.

But as each and all bore in mind that there were many inmates among the large households of those officials with official ancestors, called by the same names, that it was an ordinary occurrence for a grandmother to be passionately fond of her grandson, and that there was nothing out-of-the-way about it, they treated the matter as of no significance. Baoyu alone however was such a hair-brained simpleton that he conjectured that the statements made by the four dames had been intended to flatter his grandmother Jia.

But subsequently he betook himself into the garden to see how Shi Xiangyun was getting on.

"Compose your mind now," Shi Xiangyun then said to him, "and go on with your larks! Once, you were as lonely as a single fiber, which can't be woven into thread, and like a single bamboo, which can't form a grove, but now you've found your pair. When you exasperate your parents, and they give you beans, you'll be able to bolt to Nanjing in quest of the other Baoyu."

"What utter rubbish!" Baoyu exclaimed. "Do you too believe that there's another Baoyu?"

"How is it," Xiangyun asked, "that there was someone in the Lie state called Lin Xiangru, and that during the Han dynasty there lived again another person, whose name was Sima Xiangru?"

"This matter of names is all well enough," Baoyu rejoined with a smile. "But as it happens, his very appearance is the counterpart of mine. Such a thing could never be!"

"How is it," Xiangyun inquired, "that when the Kuang people saw Confucius, they fancied it was Yang Hu?"

"Confucius and Yang Hu," Baoyu smilingly argued, "may have been alike in looks, but they hadn't the same names. Lin and Sima were again, notwithstanding their identical names, nothing like each other in appearances. But can it ever be possible that he and I should resemble each other in both respects?"

Xiangyun was at a loss what reply to make to his arguments. "You may," she consequently remarked smiling, "propound any rubbish you like, I'm not in the humor to enter into any discussion with you. Whether there be one or not is quite immaterial to me. It doesn't concern me at all."

Saying this, she lay herself down.

Baoyu however began again to exercise his mind with further surmises. "If I say," he cogitated, "that there can't be one, there seems from all appearances to be one. And if I say that there is one, I haven't, on the other hand, seen him with my own eyes."

Sad and dejected he returned therefore to his quarters, and reclining on his couch, he silently communed with his own thoughts until he unconsciously became drowsy and fell fast asleep.

Finding himself (in his dream) in some garden or other, Baoyu was seized with astonishment. "Besides our own garden of Broad Vista," he reflected, "is there another such garden?" But while indulging in these speculations, several girls, all of whom were waiting-maids, suddenly made their appearance from the opposite direction. Baoyu was again filled with surprise. "Besides Yuanyang, Xiren, and Ping'er," he pondered, "are there verily such maidens as these?"

"Baoyu!" he heard that company of maids observe, with faces beaming with smiles, "how is it you find yourself in here?"

Baoyu labored under the impression that they were addressing him. With hasty step, he consequently drew near them, and returned their smiles. "I got here," he answered, "quite listlessly. What old family friend's garden is this, I wonder? But sisters, pray, take me for a stroll."

The maids smiled with one consent. "Really!" they exclaimed, "this isn't our Baoyu. But his looks too are spruce and nice; and he is as precocious too with his tongue."

Baoyu caught their remarks. "Sisters!" he eagerly cried, "is there actually a second Baoyu in here?"

"As for the two characters 'Baoyu,'" the maids speedily explained, "everyone in our house has received our old mistress' and our mistress' injunctions to use them as a spell to protract his life for many years and remove misfortune from his path, and when we call him by that name, he simply goes into ecstasies at the very mention of it. But you, young brat, from what distant parts of the world do you hail that you've recklessly been also dubbed by the same name? But beware lest we pound that frowzy flesh of yours into mincemeat."

"Let's be off at once!" urged another maid, as she smiled. "Don't let our Baoyu see us here and say again that by hobnobbing with this stinking young fellow, we've been contaminated by all his pollution."

With these words on her lips, they straightway walked off.

Baoyu fell into a brown study. "There's never been," he mused, "anyone to treat me with such disdain before! But what is it, in fact, that induces them to behave towards me in this manner? May it not be true that there lives another human being the very image of myself?"

While lost in reverie, he advanced with heedless step, until he reached a courtyard. Baoyu was struck with wonder. "Is there actually," he cried, "besides the Yihong court another court like it?" Spontaneously then ascending the steps, he entered an apartment, in which he discerned someone reclining on a couch. On the off side sat several girls, busy at needlework; now laughing joyfully; now practicing their jokes; when he overheard the young person on the couch heave a sigh.

"Baoyu," smilingly inquired a maid, "what, aren't you asleep? What are you once more sighing for? I presume it's because your sister is ill that you abandon yourself again to idle fears and immoderate anguish!"

These words fell on Baoyu's ears and took him quite aback.

"I've heard grandmother say," he overheard the young person on the couch observe, "that there lives at Chang'an, the capital, another Baoyu endowed with the same disposition as myself. I never believed what she told me; but I just had a dream, and in this dream I found myself in a garden of the metropolis where I came across several maidens; all of whom called me a 'stinking young brat,' and would have nothing whatever to do with me. But after much difficulty, I succeeded in penetrating into his room. He happened to be fast asleep. There he lay like a mere bag of bones. His real faculties had flown somewhere or other; whither it was hard for me to say."

Hearing this, "I've come here," Baoyu said with alacrity, "in search of Baoyu; and are you, indeed, that Baoyu?"

The young man on the couch jumped down with all haste and enfolded him in his arms. "Are you verily Baoyu?" he laughingly asked. "This isn't by any means such stuff as dreams are made of!"

"How can you call this a dream?" Baoyu rejoined. "It's reality, yea, nothing but reality!"

But scarcely was this rejoinder over, than he heard someone come, and say: "our master, your father, wishes to see you, Baoyu."

The two lads started with fear. One Baoyu rushed off with all despatch. The other promptly began to shout, "Baoyu! come back at once! Baoyu, be quick and return!"

Xiren, who stood by (Baoyu), heard him call out his own name, in his dreams, and immediately gave him a push and woke him up. "Where is Baoyu gone to?" she laughed.

Although Baoyu was by this time aroused from sleep, his senses were as yet dull, so pointing towards the door, "He's just gone out," he replied, "he's not far off."

Xiren laughed. "You're under the delusion of a dream," she said. "Rub your eyes and look carefully! It's your reflection in the mirror."

Baoyu cast a glance in front of him, and actually caught sight of the large inlaid mirror, facing him quite opposite, so he himself burst out laughing. But, presently, a maid handed him a rince-bouche and tea and salt, and he washed his mouth.

"Little wonder is it," Sheyue ventured, "if our old mistress has repeatedly enjoined that it isn't good to have too many mirrors about in young people's rooms, for as the spirit of young persons is not fully developed there is every fear, with mirrors casting their reflections all over the place, of their having wild dreams in their sleep. And is a bed now placed before that huge mirror there? When the covers of the mirrors are let down, no harm can befall; but as the season advances, and the weather gets hot, one feels so languid and tired, that is one likely to think of dropping them? Just as it happened a little time back; it slipped entirely from your memory. Of course, when he first got into bed, he must have played with his face towards the glass; but upon shortly closing his eyes, he must naturally have fallen into such confused dreams, that they thoroughly upset his rest. Otherwise, how is it possible that he should have started shouting his own name? Would it not be as well if the bed were moved inside tomorrow? That's the proper place for it."

Hardly had she, however, done, before they perceived a servant, sent by Madame Wang to call Baoyu. But what she wanted to tell him is not yet known, so, reader, listen to the circumstances recorded in the subsequent chapter.